WILBUR SMITH

The novels of Wilbur Smith

THE COURTNEY NOVELS:
When the Lion Feeds
The Sound of Thunder
A Sparrow Falls
The Burning Shore
Power of the Sword
Rage
A Time to Die

THE BALLANTYNE NOVELS:
A Falcon Flies
Men of Men
The Angels Weep
The Leopard Hunts in Darkness

ALSO:
The Dark of the Sun
Shout at the Devil
Gold Mine
The Diamond Hunters
The Sunbird
Eagle in the Sky
The Eye of the Tiger
Cry Wolf
Hungry as the Sea
Wild Justice
Golden Fox
Elephant Song
River God

WILBUR SMITH

MEN OF MEN
SHOUT AT THE DEVIL
THE DIAMOND HUNTERS

CHANCELLOR
⚜ PRESS ⚜

Men of Men first published in Great Britain in 1981 by William
Heinemann Ltd
Shout at the Devil first published in Great Britain in 1968 by William
Heinemann Ltd
The Diamond Hunters first published in Great Britain in 1971 by
William Heinemann Ltd

This collected volume first published in Great Britain in 1994 by
Chancellor Press an imprint of
Reed Consumer Books Ltd
Michelin House, 81 Fulham Road, London SW3 6RB
and Auckland, Melbourne, Singapore and Toronto

ISBN 1 85152 707 9

A CIP catalogue record for this book is available from the British Library

Printed and bound in Great Britain by
William Clowes Limited, Beccles and London

Contents

Men of Men

This book is for my wife, Danielle

with all my love forever

I t had never been exposed to the light of day, not once in the 200 million years since it assumed its present form, and yet it seemed in itself to be a drop of distilled sunlight.

It had been conceived in heat as vast as that of the sun's surface, in those unholy depths below the earth's crust, in the molten magma that welled up from the earth's very core.

In those terrible temperatures all impurity had been burned from it, leaving only the unadulterated carbon atoms, and under pressures that would have crushed mountains these had been reduced in volume and packed to a density beyond that of any other substance in nature.

This tiny bubble of liquid carbon had been carried up in the slow subterranean river of molten lava through one of the weak spots in the earth's crust, and it had almost, but not quite, reached the surface before the laval flow faltered and finally stopped.

The lava cooled over the ensuing millennium, and it altered its form and became a mottled bluish rock, composed of gravelly fragments loosely cemented in a solid matrix. This formation was naturally unassociated with the country rock which surrounded it, and filled only a deep circular well whose mouth was shaped like a funnel almost a mile in diameter and whose tail descended sheer into the uncounted depths of the earth.

While the lava was cooling, the purged bubble of carbon was undergoing an even more marvellous transformation. It solidified into an eight-faced crystal of geometrical symmetry the size of a green fig, and so thoroughly had it been purged of impurity in the hellish furnace of the earth's core that it was transparent and clear as the sun's own rays. So fierce and constant had been the pressures to which the single crystal had been subjected and so evenly had it cooled that there was no cracking or shearing within its body.

It was perfect, a thing of cold fire so white that it would appear electric blue in good light – but that fire had never been awakened, for it had been trapped in total darkness across the ages, and no single glimmer of light had ever probed its lucid depths. Yet for all those millions of years the sunlight had been no great distance away, a matter only of two hundred feet or less, a thin skin of earth when compared to the immense depths from whence its journey to the surface had begun.

Now, in the last wink of time, a mere few years out of all those millions, the intervening ground had steadily been chipped and whittled and hacked away by the puny, inefficient but persistent efforts of an antlike colony of living creatures.

The forebears of these creatures had not even existed upon this earth when that single pure crystal achieved its present form, but now with each day the disturbance caused by their metal tools set up faint vibrations within the rock that had been dormant so long; and each day those vibrations were stronger, as the layer between it and the surface shrank from two hundred feet to a hundred and then to fifty, from ten feet to two, until now only inches separated the crystal from the brilliant sunlight which would at last bring to life its slumbering fires.

Major Morris Zouga Ballantyne stood on the lip of the aerial rope-way high above the deep circular chasm where once a small hillock had risen above the flat and dreary landscape of the African continental shield.

Even in the fierce heat he wore a silk scarf at his throat, the tail of which was tucked into the buttoned front of his flannel shirt. Though recently washed and pressed with a heated stroking-iron, his shirt was indelibly stained to a dull reddish ochre colour.

It was the pigment of the African earth, red earth, almost like raw meat, where the iron-shod wheels of the wagons had cut it or the shovels of the diggers had turned the surface. Earth that rose in dense red dust clouds when the hot dry winds scoured it, or turned to bleeding glutinous red mud when the thunderstorms thrashed its surface.

Red was the colour of the diggings. It stained the hair of dogs and beasts of burden, it stained the clothing of the men and their beards and the skin of their arms, it stained their canvas tents and coated the corrugated iron shanties of the settlement.

Only in the gaping hole below where Zouga stood was the colour altered to the soft yellow of a thrush's breast.

The hole was almost a mile across, the rim of it nearly a perfect circle, and its bottom already two hundred feet deep in places. The men working down there were tiny insect-like figures, spiders perhaps, for only spiders could have spun the vast web that glittered in a silvery cloud over the entire excavation.

Zouga paused a moment to lift the wide-brimmed hat, its pointed peak stained by his own sweat and the blown red dust. Carefully he mopped the beads of sweat from the smooth paler skin along his hairline, and then inspected the damp red stain on the silk bandanna and grimaced with distaste.

His dense curling hair had been protected by the hat from the fierce African sunlight and was still the colour of smoked wild honey, but his beard had been bleached to pale gold and the years had laced it with silver strands. His skin was dark also, baked like a crust of new bread, only the scar on his cheek was porcelain white where the elephant gun had burst so many years before.

There were little creases below his eyes from squinting in the sunlight at far horizons, and harsh lines cut his cheeks from the corner of his nose and ran down into the beard – lines of hardship and heartbreak. He looked down into the gaping pit below him and the green of his eyes clouded as he remembered the high hopes and bounding expectation that had brought him here – was it ten years before? It seemed like a day and an eternity.

He had first heard the name, Colesberg kopje, when he had stepped out of the bumboat onto the beach at Rogger Bay below the vast square monolithic bulk of Table Mountain, and the sound of it had made his skin tingle and raised the hair at the nape of his neck.

'They have struck diamonds at Colesberg kopje, diamonds big as grapeshot and so thick they'll wear out the soles of your boots just walking across them!'

In a clairvoyant flash he had known that this was where his destiny would lead him. He knew that the two years he had just spent in old England, trying desperately to raise backing for his grand venture in the north, had been marking time for this moment.

The road to the north began in the diamond gravels of Colesberg kopje. He knew it with certainty as he heard the name.

He had one single wagon left, and a depleted span of draught oxen. Within forty-eight hours they were plodding through the deep sands that clogged the track across the Cape Flats, northwards six hundred miles to that kopje below the Vaal river.

The wagon carried all his possessions, and there were precious few of these. Twelve years following a grandiose dream had wasted his substance all away. The considerable royalties from the book that he had written after his travels to the unexplored lands below the Zambezi river, the gold and ivory that he had brought back from that remote interior, the ivory from four more hunting expeditions to that same haunting and yet sadly flawed paradise – all of it was gone. Thousands of pounds and twelve years of heartbreak and frustration, until the splendid dream had become clouded and soured and all he had to show for it was a tattered scrap of parchment on which the ink was beginning to yellow and the folds were almost worn through so that it had to be glued to a backing sheet to hold it together.

That parchment was 'The Ballantyne Concession' title for one thousand years to all the mineral wealth of a huge tract of the wild African interior, a tract the size of France which he had cajoled from a savage black king. In that vast territory Zouga had panned red native gold from the outcropping quartz reef.

It was a rich land and all of it was his, but it needed capital, huge amounts of capital, to take possession of it and to win the treasures that lay below it. Half his adult life had been spent in struggle to raise that capital – a fruitless struggle, for he had not yet found a single man of substance to share his vision and his dream with him. Finally, he had in desperation appealed to the British public. He had journeyed to London once more to promote the formation of the 'Central African Lands and Mining Co.' to exploit his concession.

He had designed and had printed a handsome brochure, extolling the riches of the land he had named Zambezia. He had illustrated the pages with his own drawings of fine forests and grassy plains abounding with elephant and other game. He had included a facsimile of the original concession, with the great elephant seal of Mzilikazi, King of the Matabele, at its foot. And he had distributed the brochure throughout the British Isles.

He had travelled from Edinburgh to Bristol lecturing and holding public meetings, and he had backed up this campaign with full-page advertisements in *The Times* and other reputable newspapers.

However, the same newspapers that had accepted his advertising fees had ridiculed his claims, while the attention of the investing public was seduced by the flotations of the South American railway companies which unhappily coincided with Zouga's promotion. He had been left with the bill for printing and distribution of the brochure, the fees for advertising and for the lawyers and the expenses of his own travelling, and when he had paid them and his passage back to Africa there remained only a few hundred sovereigns from what had once been considerable wealth.

The wealth was gone, but the responsibilities remained. Zouga looked back from the head of the span of dappled black oxen.

Aletta sat on the wagon box. Her hair was still pale gold and silky in the sunlight, but her eyes were grave and the line of her lips no longer sweet and soft, as though she had set herself against the hardships that she knew lay ahead.

Looking at her now it seemed impossible that she had once been a pretty carefree butterfly of a girl, the pampered darling of a rich father, with no thought in her head beyond London fashion newly arrived on the mailship and the preparations for the next ball in the glittering social whirl of Cape society.

She had been attracted by the romance surrounding young Major Zouga Ballantyne. He was the traveller and adventurer in far places of the African continent. There was the legend of the great elephant hunter that surrounded him, the glamour of the book that he had recently published in London. All Cape Town society was agog with this young man and envied her his suit.

That had been many years ago, and the legend had tarnished.

Aletta's delicate breeding had not been equal to the rigours of the savage interior beyond the gentle and temperate airs of the Cape littoral – and the rough country and rougher peoples had appalled her. She had succumbed swiftly to the fevers and pestilences which had weakened her so that she suffered repeated miscarriages.

All her married life she seemed to be in childbed, or lost in the mists of malarial fever, or waiting interminably for the golden-bearded, godlike figure whom she worshipped to return from across an ocean or from the hot and unhealthy hinterland to which she could no longer follow him.

On this journey to the diamond fields, Zouga had taken it for granted that she would once again remain at her father's home at the Cape, to guard her failing health and to care for their two boys, fruit of the only pregnancies which she had succeeded in bringing to full term. However, she had suddenly shown an uncharacteristic determination, and none of his arguments to make her remain behind had prevailed. Perhaps she had some premonition of what was to follow – 'I have been alone too long,' she answered him, softly but stubbornly.

Ralph, the eldest boy, was old enough by then to ride ahead of the wagon with his father and take his shot at the springbuck herds which drifted like thin pale brown smoke across the scrubby plains of the wide Karroo. Already he sat his rugged little Basuto pony with the panache of a hussar and he shot like a man.

Jordan, the younger boy, would sometimes take his turn at leading the fore oxen of the span, or wander away from the wagons to chase a butterfly or pick a wild flower; but mostly he was content to sit beside his mother on the wagon box while she read aloud from a small leather-bound book of romantic poetry, his green eyes sparkling with the thrilling sound of the words that he was still too young properly to understand and the brilliant Karroo sunlight turning his golden curls into an angel's halo.

It was six hundred miles from Good Hope to the fields, a journey that took the family eight weeks. They camped each night on the open veld and the night sky was clear and cold and brilliant with white stars that shone like the diamonds that they were certain awaited them at the end of the journey.

Sitting beside the watch-fire with his two sons flanking him, Zouga would talk in that magnetic compelling tone that had the two small boys rigid with attention. He spun descriptions of great elephant hunts and ancient ruined cities, of graven idols and red native gold in the land to the north, the land to which he would one day take them.

Listening quietly from across the fire, wrapped in a shawl against the night chill,

Aletta would find herself enchanted with the romantic dream, as she had been as a girl, and she wondered again at herself and the strange attraction of this intense golden-bearded man who was her husband of so many years and still so often seemed a stranger to her.

She listened as he told the boys how he would fill their caps with diamonds, fat glistening diamonds, and then at last they would set out on the final journey northwards.

She found herself believing it all again, though she had long ago experienced the first disillusion. He was so persuasive, so vital and strong and convincing, that the failures and the frustrations seemed of no account, only a temporary check on the destiny he had set for all of them.

The days rolled by at the leisurely pace of the wagon wheels and became weeks, weeks in which they travelled across a great sun-washed plain that was furrowed by steep dry watercourses and studded with the dense dark-green camel-thorn trees in whose branches hung the enormous communal nests of thousands of dry-land weaver birds, each nest the size of a haystack, growing until it snapped off the sturdy branch that supported it.

The monotonous line of the horizon was relieved by the occasional low hillock, the kopje of the African continent, and the track led them directly towards one of these.

Colesberg kopje. It was only weeks after they had arrived at it that Zouga heard the story of how the diamond hillock had been discovered.

A few miles north of Colesberg kopje the plain was broken by the bed of a wide shallow river, along whose banks the trees were taller and greener. The trek Boers had called it the Vaal river, which in the African Dutch taal means 'the grey river', the colour of its sluggish waters. From its bed and from the alluvial gravels of the flood plains along its course, a small colony of diamond diggers had for years been gleaning the odd sparkling stone.

It was dreary, back-breaking work and after the first rush of hopeful diggers only the hardiest had remained. These doughty souls had known for years that it was possible to pick up an occasional small diamond of inferior quality on the dry ground thirty miles south of the river, in fact the surly old Boer named De Beer who owned the ground in that area was selling licences to diamond claims on his property – although he favoured diggers of his own people and was notoriously prejudiced against granting 'briefies' to Englishmen.

For these reasons, and also for the more pleasant living conditions along the river, the diggers had not taken too much interest in the 'dry diggings' to the south.

Then one day a Hottentot servant of one of the river diggers rendered himself blind falling-down drunk with Cape Smoke, the fierce Cape brandy, and while in that state accidentally set fire to his master's tent and burned it to the ground.

When he was once again sober, his master beat him with a sjambok whip of cured rhinoceros-hide until he was once more unable to stand. When he recovered from his treatment, his master ordered him, still in disgrace, to go into the dry country 'and dig until you find a diamond'.

Chastened and still wobbly on his feet, the Hottentot had shouldered his shovel and pack and limped away. His master promptly forgot him, until he returned unannounced two weeks later and placed in his master's hand half a dozen fine white stones – the largest the size of the first joint of a lady's little finger.

'Where?' demanded Fleetwood Rawstorne, the single word all that he could choke through a throat suddenly parched and closed with excitement.

Minutes later, Fleetwood galloped furiously out of camp, a cartload of scrapings from the river bed left untreated and his diamond 'cradle' abandoned halfway through the process of concentrating the heavier diamondiferous gravel. Daniel, the Hottentot servant, hung from his stirrup leather, his bare feet kicking up little puffs of dust as they skimmed the dry earth, and the red woollen cap that was the insignia of Fleetwood's party blowing back from his bald head to flap like a flag beckoning others to follow.

Such behaviour instantly precipitated a wild panic amongst the fiercely competitive little community of diggers along the river. Within an hour a tall column of red dust rose above the flat dry land; a headlong column of horsemen flogged their mounts while behind them the Scotch carts rumbled and the less fortunate stumbled and slipped in the sandy footing as they ran the miles back southwards to old man De Beer's barren hard-scrabble little farm on which rose another bald stony little kopje, just like ten thousand others, that studded the plains.

The kopje was that same day in the bleak, dry winter of 1871 named 'Colesberg' kopje, for Colesberg was Fleetwood Rawstorne's birthplace, and De Beer's New Rush came swarming out of the dusty sun-bleached distances towards it.

It was almost dark when Fleetwood reached the kopje, only just ahead of his followers. His horse was blown, lathered with sweat and white froth, but the Hottentot servant clung to the stirrup leather still.

Master and servant flung themselves from the heaving staggering animal and ran at the slope. Their scarlet caps bobbing above the scrub thorn could be seen from a half mile distance, and a hoarse excited cheer went up from the ragged column that pursued them.

On the crest of the hill, the Hottentot servant had burrowed a shaft ten feet into the hard earth, a tiny scratch when compared to what was to follow. Frantic with haste, casting fearful glances down the hillside at the horde that raced up towards him, Fleetwood drove the centre line of his claim pegs across the narrow mouth of the shallow prospect shaft.

Night fell over a battlefield on which brawny diggers cursed each other and swung punches and pick-handles to clear the ground and drive their own claim pegs. By noon the next day, when farmer De Beer rode across from his primitive two-roomed dwelling to begin writing out the 'briefies', which was taal for 'letters', the entire kopje was covered with claim pegs; even the flat plain for a quarter of a mile below the slopes was bristling with pegs.

Each claim was thirty feet square, its centre and corners marked with a sharpened wood stake cut from a camel-thorn branch. On payment of an annual fee of ten shillings to farmer De Beer, the digger received his written 'briefie' which entitled him to hold and work the claim in perpetuity.

Before nightfall that first day the lucky diggers who had pegged the centre of the new rush had merely scratched the stony earth, but had turned up over forty stones of the first water; and already horsemen were away southwards carrying the word to the world that Colesberg kopje was a mountain of diamonds.

When Zouga Ballantyne's single wagon creaked the last few miles down the rutted red earth track towards Colesberg kopje, it was already half demolished, eaten away as though by the maggots in a rotten cheese, and men still swarmed over what remained. On the dusty plain below it were encamped almost ten thousand souls, black and brown and white. The smoke from their cooking fires blurred the high china-blue sky with dirty grey, and for miles in each direction the diggers had almost denuded the plain of the beautiful camel-thorn trees to feed those fires.

The settlement was strewn about under dirty weather-worn canvas, although already some sheets of the ubiquitous corrugated iron had been laboriously transported from the coast and knocked up into boxlike shanties. Some of these, with a fine sense of order, had been arranged in an approximation of a straight line, forming the first rudimentary streets.

These belonged to the 'kopje-wallopers', the previously nomadic diamond buyers who had until recently roamed the diggings, but who had now found it worth their while to set up permanent shop below the crumbling remains of Colesberg kopje. According to the infant diamond laws of the Boer Free State, each licensed buyer was obliged to display his name prominently. This they did in crudely lettered signs upon the little iron sweat-box offices, but most of them went further and flew a disproportionately large gaudy and fancifully designed flag from a mast on the roof to announce to the diggers that the incumbent was in office and ready to do business. The flags lent a carnival air to the settlement.

Zouga Ballantyne walked beside the offside lead ox of his team, following one of the narrow meandering rutted tracks that ran through the settlement. Occasionally the team had to be swung to avoid the tailings that had spilled into the track from one of the recovery stations, or to avoid a deep morass formed by spilled sewerage and washings from the sorting-tables.

The settlement was densely crowded upon itself – that was the first impression that struck Zouga. He was a man of the plains and savannah forests, accustomed to long uninterrupted horizons, and the crowding jarred upon his senses. The diggers lived within touching distance of each other, every man attempting to get as close to his claim as he could so that the gravel that he won from it would not have to be carried too far to the place where he would process it.

Zouga had hoped to find an open space upon which to outspan his wagon and erect the big bell tent, but there was no open space within a quarter of a mile of the kopje.

He glanced back at Aletta on the box. She was sitting very still, moving only as the wagon jolted, looking straight ahead as though oblivious of the almost naked men, many wearing merely a scrap of trade cloth about the loins, who milled the crunchy lumps of yellow gravel and then shovelled it into the waiting cradles. Swearing or singing as they worked, all of them oiled with their own sweat in the cruel white sunlight.

The filth appalled even Zouga, who had known the kraals of the Mashona in the north and had lived in a bushman settlement with the little creatures who never bathed in their entire lifetimes.

Civilized man generates particularly loathsome wastes, and it seemed that every square inch of the dusty red earth between the tents and the shanties of the settlement was covered with a litter of rusty bully beef tins, broken fragments of bottles and porcelain that glittered in the sunlight, a snowstorm of paper scraps, the decomposing corpses of stray kittens and unwanted dogs, the scrapings from the cooking pots, the excrement of those too lazy to dig a latrine in the hard earth and screen it with a thatch of the silvery Karroo grass, and all the other unidentifiable offal and castings with which ten thousand human beings without control or sanitary regulations had surrounded themselves.

Zouga caught Aletta's eyes and smiled at her reassuringly, but she did not return the smile. Her lips were set bravely, but her eyes were huge and brimming with tears that lapped at her lower lids.

They squeezed past a transport rider who had brought up a wagonload of goods from the coast, six hundred miles, and had set up shop from the tailboard of his wagon, displaying a sign on which he had chalked up a price list:

Candles – £1 a pkt
Whisky – £12 a case
Soap – 5/- a piece

Zouga did not look back again at Aletta, the prices were twenty times higher than those prevailing at the coast. De Beer's New Rush was probably at that moment the most expensive spot on the surface of the globe. The remaining sovereigns in the wide leather money-belt around Zouga's waist seemed suddenly feather light.

By noon that day they had found space to outspan the wagon on the periphery of the huge circular encampment. While Jan Cheroot, Zouga's Hottentot retainer, drove the cattle away to find grazing and water, Zouga hurriedly erected the heavy canvas tent, Aletta and the boys holding the guy ropes while he drove the pegs.

'You must eat,' Aletta mumbled, still not looking at him as she squatted over the smouldering cooking fire and stirred the cast iron stew pot that contained the remains of a springbuck that Ralph had shot three days before.

Zouga went to her, stooped and with his hands on her shoulders lifted her to her feet. She moved stiffly as an old woman, the long hard journey had taken a heavy toll of her frail body.

'It will be all right,' he told her, and still she would not look at him, perhaps she had heard that assurance too often. He cupped her chin and lifted her face, and the tears broke at last and slid down her cheeks, leaving little runnels through the red dust that powdered her skin. The tears angered Zouga unreasonably, as though they were an accusation. He dropped his hands and stepped back from her.

'I will be back before dark,' he told her harshly and, turning from her, he strode away towards the ruined silhouette of the Colesberg kopje which stood out starkly, even through the stinking miasma of smoke and dust that hovered over the camp.

Zouga might have been a wraith, a thing of air, invisible to human eyes. They hurried by him on the narrow track, or remained stooped over mill and cradle while he passed, without an inclination of head or even a casual glance, an entire community living for one thing only, completely absorbed and obsessed.

From experience Zouga knew there was one place where he might be able to establish human contact, and through it glean the information he so desperately needed. He was looking for a canteen that sold hard liquor.

Below the kopje there was an open space, the only one in the camp. It was roughly square in shape, bordered by shacks of canvas and iron, cluttered with the wagons of the transport riders.

Zouga selected one of the shacks that grandly announced itself as 'The London Hotel' and on the same board advertised:

Whisky 7/6. Best English Beer 5/- a schooner.

He was picking his way across the littered, rutted market square towards it when ragged cheers and a bellowed chorus of 'For he's a jolly good fellow' from the direction of the kopje checked him. A motley band of diggers came stamping through the dust carrying one of their number upon their shoulders, singing and yelling, their faces brick red with dust and excitement. They shouldered their way into the rickety bar ahead of Zouga, while from the other canteens and from the parked wagons men came running to find the cause of the excitement.

'What happened?' the question was yelled.

'Black Thomas pulled a monkey,' the reply was hurled back.

It was only later that Zouga learned the diggers' parlance. A 'monkey' was a diamond of fifty carats or more, while a 'pony' was that impossible diggers' dream, a stone of one hundred carats.

'Black Thomas pulled a *monkey*.' The reply was picked up and called across the square and through the encampment, and soon the crowd overflowed the rickety canteen so that the frothing schooners of beer had to be passed overhead to the men on the fringes.

The fortunate Black Thomas was hidden from Zouga's view in the crowd that pressed about him, everybody trying to draw close as though some of the man's luck might rub off onto them.

The kopje-wallopers heard the excitement, hastily lowered their flags and hurried across the square, gathering like carrion birds to the lion's kill. The first of them arrived breathless on the fringe of the revellers, hopping up and down for a glimpse of the man.

'Tell Black Thomas that Lion-heart Werner will make an open offer – pass it on to him.'

'Hey, Blackie, Lion-arse will go open.' The offer changed shape as it was yelled through the packed doorway. An 'open offer' was firm and the digger was free to tout the other buyers. If he received no higher bid for his diamond, he was entitled to return and close with the open offer.

Once again Black Thomas was raised by his fellows until he could see over their heads. He was a little gypsy-dark Welshman and his moustache was rimed with beer froth. His voice had the sweet Welsh lilt as he sang his defiance:

'Hear me, then, Lion-arse the robber, I would sooner—' what he proposed to do with his diamond made even the rough men about him blink and then guffaw with surprise '—rather than let you get your thieving paws on it.'

His voice rang with the memory of a hundred humiliations and unfair bargains that had been forced upon him. Today Black Thomas with his 'monkey' was king of the diggings, and though his reign might be short, he was determined to reap all the sweets that it promised.

Zouga never laid eyes on that stone; he never saw Black Thomas again; for by noon the following day the little Welshman had sold his diamond, and sold too his 'briefies', and taken the long road south on the beginning of his journey home to a fairer, greener land.

Zouga waited in the press of hot sweat-stinking bodies that filled the canteen, choosing a man with care while he listened to the voices grow louder and the chaff coarser as the schooners went down.

He selected one who by his comportment and speech was a gentleman, and home-bred rather than colonial born. The man was drinking whisky, and when his glass was empty Zouga moved closer and ordered it refilled.

'Very decent of you, old man,' the man thanked him. He was in his twenties still and remarkably good-looking, with fair English skin and silky sideburns. 'The name is Pickering, Neville Pickering,' he said.

'Ballantyne – Zouga Ballantyne.' Zouga took the proffered hand and the man's expression altered.

'Good Lord, you are the elephant hunter.' Pickering raised his voice. 'I say, fellows, this is Zouga Ballantyne. You know, the one who wrote *Hunter's Odyssey*.'

Zouga doubted half of them could read, but the fact that he had written a book made him an object of wonder. He found the centre of interest had shifted from Black Thomas to himself.

It was after dark when he started back to the wagon. He had always had a strong head for liquor and there was a good moon, so he could pick his way through the ordure that littered the track.

He had spent a few sovereigns on liquor, but in return he had learned a great deal about the diggings. He had learned of the diggers' expectations and fears. He knew now the going price for 'briefies', the politics and economics of diamond pricing, the geological composition of the strike and a hundred other related facts. He had also made a friendship that would alter his whole life.

Although Aletta and the boys were already asleep in the wagon tent, Jan Cheroot, the little Hottentot, was waiting for him, squatting beside the watch-fire, a small gnome-like figure in the silver moonlight.

'There is no free water,' he told Zouga morosely. 'The river is a full day's trek away, and the thieving Boer who owns the wells sells water at the same price as they sell brandy in this hell-hole.' Jan Cheroot could be relied upon to know the going price of liquor ten minutes after arriving in a new town.

Zouga climbed into the wagon body, careful not to jolt the boys awake; but Aletta was lying rigidly in the narrow riempie bed. He lay down beside her and neither of them spoke for many minutes.

Then she whispered. 'You are determined to stay in this,' her voice checked, then went on with quiet vehemence, 'in this awful place.'

He did not reply, and in the cot behind the canvas screen across the body of the wagon Jordan whimpered and then was silent. Zouga waited until he had settled before he replied.

'Today a Welshman named Black Thomas found a diamond. They say he has been offered twelve thousand pounds by one of the buyers.'

'A woman came to sell me a little goat's milk while you were away.' Aletta might not have heard him. 'She says there is camp fever here. A woman and two children have died already and others are sick.'

'A man can buy a good claim on the kopje for one thousand pounds.'

'I fear for the boys, Zouga,' Aletta whispered. 'Let us go back. We could give up this wandering gypsy life for ever. Daddy has always wanted you to come into the business–'

Aletta's father was a rich Cape merchant, but Zouga shuddered in the darkness at the thought of a high desk in the dingy counting-room of Cartwright and Company.

'It is time the boys went to a good school, else they will grow up as savages. Please let us go back now, Zouga.'

'A week,' he said. 'Give me a week – we have come so far.'

'I do not think I can bear the flies and filth for another week.' She sighed and turned her back to him, careful not to touch him in the narrow cot.

The family doctor in Cape Town, who had attended Aletta's own birth, the birth of both boys and her numerous miscarriages, had warned them ominously.

'Another pregnancy could be your last, Aletta. I cannot be responsible for what may happen.' For the three years since then she had lain with her back to him, on those occasions when they had been able to share a bed.

Before dawn Zouga slipped out of the wagon while Aletta and the boys still slept. In the darkness before first light he stirred the ashes and drank a cup of coffee crouching over them. Then in the first rosy glow of dawn he joined the stream of carts and hurrying men that moved up for the day's assault on the hill.

In the strengthening light and rising heat and whirls of dust he moved from claim to claim, looking and assessing. He had long ago trained himself as an amateur geologist. He had read every book that he could find on the subject, often by candle-light on the lonely hunting veld; and on his infrequent returns home he had passed days and weeks in the Natural History Museum in London, much of the time in the Geological Section. He had trained his eye and sharpened his instinct for the lie of the rock formations and for the grain and weight and colour of a sample of reef.

At most of the claims his overtures were met with a shrug and a turned back, but one or two of the diggers remembered him as the 'elephant hunter' or the 'writer fellow' and used his visit as an excuse to lean on their shovels and talk for a few minutes.

'I've got two briefies,' a digger who introduced himself as Jock Danby told Zouga, 'but I call them The Devil's Own. With these two hands,' he held up his huge paws, the palms studded with raised calluses, the nails chipped away and black with dirt, 'with my own hands I've shifted fifteen thousand tons of stuff, and the biggest stone I've pulled is a two. That there,' he pointed to the adjoining claim, 'was Black Thomas's claim. Yesterday he pulled a monkey, a bloody fat stinking monkey, only two feet from my side peg. Christ! It's enough to break your heart.'

'Buy you a beer.' Zouga jerked his head towards the nearest canteen, and the man licked his lips then shook his head regretfully.

'My kid is hungry – you can see the ribs sticking out of the little bugger and I have to pay wages by noon tomorrow.' He indicated the dozen half-naked black tribesmen labouring with pick and bucket in the bottom of the neatly squared off excavation with him. 'These bastards cost me a fortune every day.'

Jock Danby spat on his callused palms and hefted the shovel, but Zouga cut in smoothly.

'They do say the strike will pinch out at the level of the plain.' At this point the kopje had been reduced to a mere twenty feet above the surrounding plain. 'What do you think?'

'Mister, it's bad luck to even talk like that.' Jock checked the swing of his shovel and scowled heavily up at Zouga on the roadway above him, but there was fear in his eyes.

'You ever thought of selling out?' Zouga asked him, and immediately Jock's fear faded to be replaced by a sly expression.

'Why, mister? You thinking of buying?' Jock straightened. 'Let me give you a little tip for free. Don't even think about it, not unless you got six thousand pounds to do the talking for you.'

He peered up at Zouga hopefully, and Zouga stared back at him without expression.

'Thank you for your time, sir, and for your sake I hope the gravel lasts.'

Zouga touched the wide brim of his hat and sauntered away. Jock Danby watched him go, then spat viciously on the yellow ground at his feet and swung the shovel at it as though it were a mortal enemy.

As he walked away Zouga felt a strange sense of elation. There was a time when he had lived by the turn of a card and the fall of a die, and he felt the gambler's instinct now. He knew the gravel would not pinch out. He knew it sank down, pure and rich into the depths. He knew it with a deep unshakable certainty, and he knew something else with equal certainty.

'The road to the north begins here.' He spoke aloud, and felt his blood thrill in his veins. 'This is where it begins.'

He felt the need to make an act of faith, of total affirmation, and he knew what it must be. The price of livestock on the diggings was vastly inflated, and his oxen were costing him a guinea a day to water. He knew how to close the road back.

By mid-afternoon he had sold the oxen: a hundred pounds a head, and five hundred for his wagon. Now he was committed, and he felt the currents of excitement coursing through his body as he paid the gold coin over the raw wooden counter of the tin shack that housed the branch of the Standard Bank.

The road back was cut. He was chancing it all on the yellow gravel and the road northwards.

'Zouga, you promised,' Aletta whispered when the buyer came to Zouga's camp to collect the oxen. 'You promised that in one week –' Then she fell silent when she saw his face. She knew that expression. She drew the two boys to her and held them close.

Jan Cheroot went to each of the animals in turn and whispered to them as tenderly as a lover, and his stare was reproachful as he turned to Zouga while the span was led away.

Neither man spoke, and at last Jan Cheroot dropped his gaze and walked away, a slight, bare-footed, bow-legged little gnome.

Zouga thought he had lost him, and he felt a rush of distress, for the little man was a friend, a teacher and a companion of twelve years. It was Jan Cheroot who had tracked his first elephant, and stood shoulder to shoulder with him as he shot it down. Together they had marched and ridden the breadth of a savage continent. They had drunk from the same bottle and eaten from the same pot at a thousand camp fires. Yet he could not bring himself to call him back. He knew that Jan Cheroot must make his own decision.

He need not have worried. When 'dop' time came that evening, Jan Cheroot was there to hold out his chipped enamel mug. Zouga smiled and, ignoring the line that measured his daily ration of brandy, he filled the mug to the brim.

'It was necessary, old friend,' he said, and Jan Cheroot nodded gravely. 'They were good beasts,' he said. 'But then I have had many fine beasts go from my life, four-legged and two-legged ones.' He tasted the raw spirit. 'After a little time and a dram or two, it does not matter so much.'

Aletta did not speak again until the boys were asleep in the tent.

'Selling the oxen and the wagon was your answer,' she said.

'It cost a guinea a day to water them, and the grazing has been eaten flat for miles about.'

'There have been three more deaths in the camp. I counted thirty wagons leaving today. It's a plague camp.'

'Yes.' Zouga nodded. 'Some of the claim holders are getting nervous. A claim that I was offered for eleven hundred pounds yesterday was sold for nine hundred today.'

'Zouga, it's not fair to me or the children,' she began, but he interrupted her.

'I can arrange a passage for you and the boys with a transport rider. He has sold his stock and he leaves in the next few days. He will take you back to Cape Town.'

They undressed in darkness and silence, and when Aletta followed him into the hard narrow cot the silence continued until he thought she had fallen asleep. Then he felt her hand, smooth and soft, touch his cheek lightly.

'I am sorry, my darling.' Her voice was as light as her touch, and her breath stirred his beard. 'I was so tired and depressed.'

He took her hand and held the tips of her fingers to his lips.

'I have been such a poor wife to you, always too sick and weak when you needed someone strong.' Timidly she let her body touch his. 'And now when I should be a comfort to you, I do nothing but snivel.'

'No,' he said. 'That's not true.' And yet over the years he had resented her often enough for just those reasons. He had felt like a man trying to run with shackles on his ankles.

'And yet I love you, Zouga. I loved you the first day I laid eyes on you, and I have never ceased to love you.'

'I love you too, Aletta,' he assured her, yet the words came automatically; and to make up for the lack of spontaneity, he placed his arm around her shoulders and she drew closer still and laid her cheek against his chest.

'I hate myself for being so weak and sickly,' she hesitated, 'for not being able to be a real wife any more.'

'Shh! Aletta, do not upset yourself.'

'I will be strong now – you will see.'

'You have always been strong, deep inside.'

'No, but I will be now. We shall find that capful of diamonds together, and afterwards we shall go north.' He did not reply, and it was she who spoke again. 'Zouga, I want you to make love to me – now.'

'Aletta, you know that is dangerous.'

'Now,' she repeated. 'Now, please.' And she took his hand down and placed it under the hem of her nightdress against the smooth warm skin of her inner thigh. She had never done that before, and Zouga found himself shocked but strangely aroused, and afterwards he was filled with a deep tenderness and compassion for her that he had not felt for many years.

When her breathing had become regular once more, she pulled his hands away gently and slipped out of the cot.

Leaning on one elbow he watched her light the candle and then kneel by the trunk that was lashed to the foot of the cot. She had plaited her hair with a ribbon in it, and her body was slim as a young girl's. The candlelight flattered her, smoothing out the lines of sickness and worry. He remembered how lovely she had been.

She lifted the lid of the trunk, took something from the interior and brought it to him. It was a small cask with an ornate brass lock. The key was in the lock.

'Open it,' she said.

In the candlelight he saw that the cask contained two thick rolls of five-pound notes, each bound up with a scrap of ribbon, and a draw-string pouch of dark green velvet. He lifted out the pouch and it was heavy with gold coin.

'I was keeping it,' she whispered, 'for the day it was really needed. There is almost a thousand pounds there.'

'Where did you get this?'

'My father, on our wedding day. Take it, Zouga. Buy that claim with it. This time we will make it all right. This time is going to be all right.'

In the morning the purchaser came to claim the wagon. He waited impatiently while the family moved their meagre possessions into the bell tent.

Once Zouga had removed the cots from the tented half of the wagon body he was able to lift the planking from the narrow compartment over the rear wheel truck. Here the heavier goods were stored to keep the vehicle's centre of gravity low. The spare trek chain, the lead for moulding into bullet, axe heads, a small anvil – and then Zouga's household god which he and Jan Cheroot strained to lift from its padded bed and lower to the ground beside the wagon.

Between them they carried it to the tent and set it upright against the far screen of the bell tent.

'I've lugged this rubbish from Matabeleland to Cape Town and back,' complained Jan Cheroot disgustedly as he stood back from the graven birdlike figure on its stone plinth.

Zouga smiled indulgently. The Hottentot had hated that ancient idol from the very first day they uncovered it together in the overgrown ruins of an ancient walled city, a city they had stumbled on while hunting elephant in that wild untamed land so far to the north.

'It's my good-luck charm,' Zouga smiled.

'What luck?' Jan Cheroot demanded bitterly. 'Is it luck to have to sell the oxen? Is it luck to live in a tent full of flies amongst a tribe of white savages?' Muttering and mumbling bitterly, Jan Cheroot stamped out of the tent and snatched up the halters of the two remaining horses to take them down to water.

Zouga paused for a moment in front of the statue. It stood almost as high as his head on its slim column of polished green soapstone. Atop the column crouched a stylized bird figure on the edge of flight. The cruel curve of the falcon beak fascinated Zouga, and in a habitual gesture he stroked the smooth stone and the blank eyes stared back at him inscrutably.

Zouga opened his lips to whisper to the bird, and at that moment Aletta stooped into the triangular opening of the tent and saw what he was doing.

Quickly, almost guiltily, Zouga dropped his hand and turned to face her. Aletta hated that stone image even more bitterly than did Jan Cheroot. Now she stood very still. Her arms were filled with a pile of neatly folded linen and clothing – but her eyes were troubled.

'Zouga, must we have that thing in here?'

'It takes up no room,' he told her lightly, and came to take her burden from her, place it on the truckle bed, and then turn back to take her in his arms.

'I will never forget what you did last night,' he told her, and felt the rigidity go out of her body. She swayed against him and lifted her face to his. Once again he felt his chest squeezed with compassion as he saw the lines of sickness and worry at the corners of her eyes and mouth, saw the grey patina of fatigue on her skin.

He bowed his head to kiss her lips, feeling awkward at such unaccustomed demonstration of affection; but at that moment the two boys burst into the tent, raucous with laughter and excitement and dragging between them a stray puppy on a string, and Aletta broke hurriedly from Zouga's embrace and, flushing with embarrassment, adjusted her apron, beginning to scold her offspring fondly.

'Out with it! It's covered in fleas.'

'Oh please, Mama!'

'Out, I say!'

She watched Zouga set off into the sprawling settlement, striding down the dusty track with his shoulders squared and the old jaunty spring in his step, then she turned back to the cone of soiled canvas set on a bleak dry plain under the cruel blue African sky, and she sighed. The weariness came upon her again in waves.

In her girlhood there had been servants to perform the menial tasks of cooking and cleaning. She still had not mastered the smoky fluttering open flames of the camp fire, and already a fine red coating of dust had settled upon everything, even the surface of the goat's milk in its earthenware jug. With an enormous effort of will, she gathered her resolve and stooped determinedly into the tent.

Ralph had followed Jan Cheroot down to the wells to help with the horses. She knew that the two of them would not return until the next mealtime. They made an incongruous pair, the wizened little old man and the handsome reckless child already taller and more sturdy than his inseparable protector and tutor.

Jordan stayed with her. He was not yet ten years of age, but without his companionship she doubted that she could have borne the terrible journey across those bone-breaking miles, the burning dusty days and the frosty nights of aching cold.

Already the child could cook the simple camp dishes, and his unleavened bread and griddle scones were family favourites at every meal. She had taught him to read and write, and given to him her love of poetry and fine and beautiful things. He could already darn a torn shirt and wield the heavy coal-filled stroking-iron to smooth a shirt. His sweet piping tones and angelic beauty were constant sources of intense joy to her. She had grown his golden curls long for once, resisting her husband when he wanted to scissor them short as he had done Ralph's.

Jordan stood below her now, helping her to string a canvas-screen across the tent that would divide the sleeping and living areas. She was suddenly compelled to lean down and touch those soft fine curls.

At the touch he smiled sweetly up at her, and abruptly her senses spun dizzily. She swayed wildly on the rickety cot, trying to keep her balance and, as she fell, Jordan struggled to hold and steady her. He did not have the strength and her weight bore them both to the ground.

Jordan's eyes were huge and swimming with horror. He helped her half crawl, half stagger back to the cot and collapse upon it.

Waves of heat and nausea and giddiness broke over her.

*

15

Zouga was the first customer at the office of the Standard Bank when the clerk opened the door onto Market Square. Once he had deposited the contents of Aletta's casket and the clerk had locked it in the big green iron safe against the far wall, Zouga had a balance of almost £2,500 to his credit.

That knowledge armed his resolve. He felt tall and powerful as he strode up the ramp of the central causeway.

The roadways were seven feet wide. The mining commissioner, after the lesson of the diggings at Bultfontein and Dutoitspan, had insisted that these access roads be left open to service the claims in the centre of the growing pit. The workings were a mosaic of square platforms, each precisely thirty feet square. Some of the diggers, with more capital and better organization, were sinking their claims faster than others, so that the slower workers were isolated on towers of golden yellow earth, high above their neighbouring claims, while the fastest miners had sunk deep square shafts at the bottom of which toiled the naked black labourers.

For a man to move from one claim to another was already a laborious and often downright dangerous journey: crossing rickety board walks above the dizzying shaft of a deep claim, scrambling up high swaying rope ladders or down the steps of a pole ladder, lengths of native timber lashed together with cross-steps that creaked and gave with a man's weight.

Standing on the crumbling roadway with the workings gaping below him, Zouga wondered what would be the outcome if the strike continued to great depth. It already required a level head and strong stomach to chance the uneven pit, and he wondered again at man's determination to accumulate wealth against any odds, in the face of any danger.

He watched while from the bottom of the workings a leather bucket, brimming with broken lumps of the compacted yellow gravel, was hauled up, swinging at the end of a long rope, two sweating black men dipping and swinging over the windlass, their muscles swelling and subsiding in the bright sunlight.

The bucket reached the lip of the roadway, and they seized it, lugged it to the waiting cart with its patient pair of mules, and dumped the contents into the half-full body. Then one of them dropped the empty bucket over the side of the roadway to the waiting men fifty feet below. At hundreds of points along the fourteen causeways the same operation was being repeated, endlessly the loaded buckets came swinging up and were dropped back empty.

Occasionally, breaking the monotonous rhythm, the seam of a leather bucket would burst, showering the men below with jagged chunks of rock, or a worn rope would snap and, with warning shouts, the toilers at the bottom of the pit would hurl themselves aside to avoid the plunging missile.

There was an impatient humming excitement that seemed to embrace the entire workings. The urgent shouted commands between pit and roadway, the squeal of rope sheaves, the thudding jar of pick and swinging shovel, the rich lilting chorus of a gang of Basuto tribesmen singing as they worked, small wiry little mountaineers from the Dragon Range.

The white diggers, bullying and bustling, scrambled down the swaying ladder-works or stood over their gangs on the pit floor, hawk-eyed to forestall a 'pick-up': the possibility of a valuable diamond being exposed by a spade and swiftly palmed by one of the black workers, to be slipped into the mouth or other body opening at the first opportunity.

Illegal diamond selling and buying was already the plague of the diggers. In their eyes, every black man was a suspect. Only men with less than one quarter black blood were allowed to hold and work claims. This law made it easier to apportion blame, for a black face with a diamond in his possession was guilty without appeal. However, this law could not control the shady white men that hung around the diggings, ostensibly travelling salesmen, actors or proprietors of infamous drinking canteens but in reality all I.D.B., Illegal Diamond Buyers. The diggers hated them with a ferocity that sometimes boiled over in a night of rioting and beating and burning in which innocent merchants, as well as the guilty, lost all their possessions in the flames, while the mob of diggers danced about the burning shacks chanting: 'I.D.B.! I.D.B.!'

Zouga moved cautiously out along the crest of the roadway, at times pushed perilously close to the edge by a passing cart laden with diamondiferous earth.

He reached the point above Jock Danby's claims from which he had spoken to the friendly digger the previous day.

The two claims were deserted, the leather bucket and rope coils abandoned, a pick handle standing upright with its point driven into the earth far below the level of the roadway.

There was a big bearded digger working the adjoining claim, and he scowled up in response to Zouga's hail.

'What you want?'

'I'm looking for Jock Danby.'

'Well, you are looking in the wrong place.'

The man turned and aimed a kick at the nearest labourer. 'Sebenza, you black monkey!'

'Where will I find him?'

'Other side of Market Square, behind the Lord Nelson.' The man answered off-handedly without turning his head.

The dusty pitted open square was as littered with filth as the rest of the settlement, and crowded with the wagons of the transport riders and the carts of farmers who had come in to sell milk or produce and of the water sellers, peddling the precious stuff by the bucket.

The Lord Nelson was stained red dusty canvas over a wooden frame. Three of the previous night's drinkers were laid out like embalmed corpses in the narrow alley beside the canteen, while the single bar-room was already filling with the early morning customers.

A pariah-dog sniffed the breath of one of the unconscious drunks, and recoiled with shock before slinking away to raid the open drum that served as a rubbish bin behind the shack.

Zouga stepped over the sprawling bodies and gingerly made his way into the noisome slum beyond. He had to make half a dozen further enquiries until he found Jock Danby's hut. So obsessed were the diggers with their own race for the hidden glitter of wealth, and so transient the population of the diggings, that a man seemed to know only the names of his immediate neighbours. It was a community of strangers, every man caring only for himself, completely uninterested in the other human beings about him, except in as much as they could either hinder or help him in his quest for the bright stones.

Jock Danby's hut was hardly distinguishable from a thousand others. Two rooms built of adobe bricks and covered with thatch and tattered canvas. There was a lean-to at one end, with a smoking cooking fire on which stood a sooty black three-legged pot.

In the cluttered dusty yard stood the inevitable diamond sorting-table, a low structure with sturdy wooden legs, the top covered with a sheet of flat iron which was scoured shiny bright by the diamondiferous pebbles that had brushed over the surface. The wooden scrapers lay abandoned on the table top, and a heap of sieved and washed gravel formed a glittering pyramid in the centre of the table.

A two-wheeled cart stood in front of the main door of the hut, two somnolent donkeys still in the traces, flicking their ears at the swarming black cloud of flies. The cart was piled with lumps of yellow earth, but the yard was deserted.

Incongruously there were a few straggling scarlet geraniums growing in galvanized one-gallon syrup cans on each side of the doorway. There were also dainty lace curtains in the single window, so freshly washed that they had not yet turned ochre red with dust, nor become speckled with the excrement of the swarming flies.

The touch of a woman was unmistakable, and to confirm Zouga's guess there was the faint but harrowing sound of a woman weeping from the open doorway.

As Zouga hesitated in the yard, disconcerted by the sounds of grief, a brawny figure filled the doorway and stood blinking in the sunlight, shading his eyes with a gnarled and dirt-ingrained hand.

'Who are you?' Jock Danby demanded, with unnecessary roughness.

'I spoke to you yesterday,' Zouga explained, 'up at the pit.'

'What do you want?' the digger demanded, showing no sign of recognition, his features screwed up in an expression of truculence and something else, some other emotion which Zouga did not immediately recognize.

'You spoke of selling your briefies,' Zouga reminded him.

Jock Danby's face seemed to swell and turn dark ugly red; the veins and cords stood out in his throat as he ducked his head down on the thickly muscled shoulders.

'You filthy bloody vulture,' he choked, and he came out into the sunlight with the heavy irresistible crabbing rush of a gut-shot buffalo bull.

He was taller than Zouga by a head, ten years younger and fifty pounds heavier. Taken completely by surprise, Zouga was a hundredth part of a second late in ducking and spinning away from the man's charge. A fist like a cannon ball smashed into his shoulder, a glancing blow but with the force to send Zouga reeling to sprawl on his back across the sorting-table, scattering diamondiferous gravel across the dusty yard.

Jock Danby charged again, his swollen face working, his eyes mad, his thick stained fingers hooked as they reached for Zouga's throat. Zouga jack-knifed his legs, drawing himself into a ball, tense as the arch in an adder's neck at the moment before it strikes, and he drove the heels of his boots into the man's chest.

The breath whistled out of Jock Danby's throat, and he stopped in mid-charge as though hit in the chest with a double charge of buck-shot. His head and arms snapped forward, nerveless as a straw-man, and he flew backwards, crashing into the unbaked brick wall of the hut and beginning to slide down onto his knees.

Zouga bounded off the tabletop. His left arm was numb to the fingertips from the unexpected blow, but he was light on his feet as a dancer, and the quick rush of cold anger armed and strengthened him. He closed the gap between them with two swift strides and hooked Jock Danby, high in the side of his head just above and in front of his ear; the shock of the punch jarred his own teeth but sent the man spinning along the wall to slump on his knees in the red dust.

Jock Danby was stunned and his eyes were glazing over, but Zouga jerked him to his feet and propped him against the side of the cart, setting him up carefully for the next punch. His anger and outrage driving him on to revenge that unprovoked and senseless attack, Zouga shifted his weight, holding Jock Danby steady with his left hand and pulling back the right fist for a full-blooded swing.

Then he froze. He never threw the punch. Instead he stared incredulously. Jock Danby was blubbering like a child, his heavy shoulders shaking uncontrollably, tears greasing down the sunraddled cheeks into the dusty beard.

It was somehow shocking and embarrassing to see a man like this weep, and Zouga felt his anger swiftly extinguished. He dropped his fist and unclenched it at his side.

'Christ –' Jock Danby choked hoarsely. 'What kind of man are you to try and make a profit of another man's grief?'

Zouga stared at him, unable to answer the accusation.

'You must have smelt it, like a hyena or a fat bloody vulture.'

'I came to make you a fair offer – that's all,' Zouga replied stiffly. He took the handkerchief from his jacket pocket and handed it to Jock Danby. 'Wipe your face, man,' he ordered gruffly.

Jock smeared his tears and then studied the stained linen. 'You didn't know then?' he whispered. 'You didn't know about the boy?' He looked up and studied Zouga's face sharply and, seeing his answer, he handed back the handkerchief and shook his head like a spaniel shaking off the water from its ears, trying to steady his reeling senses. 'I'm sorry,' he grunted. 'I thought somehow you had learned about the boy – and come to buy me out.'

'I don't understand,' Zouga told him, and Jock Danby started for the door of the shack.

'Come,' he said, and led Zouga through the hot stuffy little front room. The chairs covered with dark green velvet were too bulky for the size of the room, and the family treasures – Bible and faded ancestral photographs, cheap cutlery and a porcelain dish commemorating the Queen's wedding to Prince Albert – were on display upon the central table.

In the door of the back room Zouga paused, and felt a sickening little lurch in the pit of his stomach. A woman knelt beside the bed. She had a shawl spread over head and shoulders. Her hands clasped before her face were roughened and reddened by the drudgery of labour over the diamond sorting-table.

She lifted her head and looked at Zouga in the doorway. She might once have been a pretty girl, but the sun had coarsened her skin and her eyes were swollen and reddened with grief. The wisps of hair that hung lankly from under the shawl were greasy and prematurely greyed.

After that one glance she lowered her head again and her lips moved silently as she prayed.

A child lay upon the bed, a boy no older than Jordan. His eyes were closed, his features very pale, bloodless as candlewax, but infinitely peaceful. He was dressed in a clean nightshirt, his limbs neatly arranged, the hands folded on his chest.

It took Zouga a full minute to realize that he was dead. 'The fever,' whispered Jock at Zouga's side. He broke off and stood dumb and massive as an ox awaiting the butcher's stroke.

*

19

Zouga took Jock Danby's cart down to Market Square and purchased a dozen rough-sawn planks of lumber, paying the transport rider's price without haggling.

In the dusty yard in front of Danby's shack he stripped to his shirtsleeves and planed the raw planks, while Jock sawed and shaped them. They worked in silence except for the whicker of plane and saw.

The rough coffin was ready before noon, but as Jock lifted his son's body into it Zouga caught the first whiff of corruption; it happens very swiftly in the African heat.

Jock's wife rode on the battered cart with the coffin and Zouga walked beside Jock Danby.

The fever was ravaging the camp. There were two other carts already at the burial ground, a mile beyond the last tents on the Transvaal road, each surrounded with a silent knot of mourners; and there were graves ready dug, and a grave-digger to demand his guinea.

On the way back from the burial ground Zouga stopped the cart in front of one of the canteens that fronted the market square, and with the remaining coins in his pocket he bought three bottles of Cape brandy.

He and Jock sat facing each other on the over-stuffed green velvet chairs, with an open bottle and two tumblers on the table between them. The tumblers were embossed with cheery gold letters:

'The Queen, God Bless Her.'

Zouga half-filled the tumblers and pushed one across to Jock.

The big man studied the contents of the tumbler, holding it in his huge fists between his knees, hunching his shoulders and drooping his head.

'It was so quick,' he muttered. 'Yesterday evening he ran to meet the cart, and rode home on my shoulder.' He took a swallow of the dark liquor and shuddered. His voice was husky as he went on. 'He was so light. No meat on his little bones.'

They drank in unison.

'There was a jinx on me from the moment I drove my first peg on these bloody claims.' Jock shook his great shaggy head. 'I should have stayed on the river-diggings, like Alice told me.'

Outside the single lace-covered window the sun was already setting, a lurid red show through the dust clouds; and as the gloom gathered in the room, Alice Danby came through and placed a smoky hurricane lantern on the table between them and followed it with two bowls of Boer-meal porridge swimming in a thin and oily mutton stew. Then she disappeared silently into the back room and, from time to time during the long night, Zouga heard her gentle sobs through the thin dividing wall.

In the dawn Jock Danby lolled in the green velvet armchair, his shirt open to the navel and his hairy stomach bulging out of it. The third bottle was half empty.

'You are a gentleman,' Jock slurred unevenly. 'I don't mean a swell or a toff but a bloody gentleman, that's what you are.'

Zouga sat upright, grave and attentive; except for a slight reddening of his eyes he seemed totally unaffected by the night's drinking.

'I wouldn't want to wish the Devil's Own on a gentleman like you.'

Zouga said quietly, 'If you're going, you have to sell to someone.'

'They're jinxed, those two claims,' mumbled Jock. 'They've killed five men already, they've broken me, they've given me the worst year of my life. I've seen men on each side of me pull big stones; I've seen them become rich – while me –' he made a drunken gesture that encompassed the sordid little shack, 'look at me.'

The canvas that screened the connecting doorway was jerked aside and Alice Danby stood bareheaded beside her husband. It was evident by her drawn grey features that she had not slept either.

'Sell them,' she said. 'I cannot stay here another day. Sell them, sell everything – let's go, Jock, let's get away from this dreadful place. I cannot bear to spend another night here.'

The mining commissioner was a dour little magistrate appointed by President Brand of the fledgling Boer Free State, who laid claim to the diggings.

Brand was not the only one to have done so. Old Waterboer, the chief of the Griqua Bastaards, made cross claim to the arid plains where his people had lived for fifty years and more. In London, Lord Kimberley, Secretary of State for the Colonies, had only just awakened to the potential wealth of the diamond diggings, and for the first time was listening attentively to the pleas of the Imperialists to support old Nicholaas Waterboer's claim and take Griqualand into the sphere of British influence.

In the meantime the Free State mining commissioner was trying, with only qualified success, to maintain some order over the unruly diggers. Just as his roadways were crumbling into the surrounding pits on Colesberg kopje, so his authority was eroding before the onrush of events with the gathering of national interests and the emergence from obscurity of the first powerful figures as the financial aristocracy of the fields.

Zouga and Jock Danby found the commissioner bewailing his task over a liquid breakfast in the bar of the London Hotel and, supporting him by each elbow, they escorted him back across Market Square to his office.

By mid-morning that day, the commissioner had copied the details of the Devil's Own, claims Nos 141 and 142 held under perpetual quit-rent letter, from J. A. Danby, Esq. to Major M. Z. Ballantyne, and noted payment in full in the sum of £2,000 by cheque drawn on the Standard Bank.

An hour after noon, Zouga stood at the corner of Market Square, and watched the cart piled high with the green velvet armchairs and the brass bedstead pull away towards the northern corner of the square. Jock Danby led the team, and his wife sat thin and erect upon the load. Neither of them looked back at Zouga, and the moment they disappeared into the maze of narrow alleys and shanties Zouga turned towards the kopje.

Despite the night of sleep that he had missed, he felt no fatigue, and his step was so light that he almost ran out along the narrow causeway that intersected the jumble of claims and workings.

The Devil's Own were deserted, two forlorn patches of raw yellow earth, neatly squared off and littered with abandoned equipment. Jock Danby's black workers had gone, for there was always a desperate shortage of labourers on the diggings. When

Jock had not mustered them the previous dawn they had simply wandered away to take daily hire with one of the other diggers.

Most of the mining gear left on the claims seemed worn out, the buckets on the point of bursting and the ropes furry as fat yellow caterpillars. Zouga would not trust them with his own weight.

Gingerly he climbed down the swaying ladder, his cautious movements alerting the diggers on the neighbouring claims that he was an outsider.

'Those are Jock Danby's briefies, man,' one of them shouted a challenge. 'You breaking the diggers' law. That's private ground. You better clear out – and bloody quick, at that.'

'I bought Jock out,' Zouga shouted back. 'He left town an hour ago.'

'How do I know that?'

'Why don't you go up to the commissioner's office?' Zouga asked. The challenger scowled up at him uncertainly, the level of his claim twenty feet below the Devil's Own.

Men had stopped work along the length of the irregular pit, others had lined the causeway high above, and there was an ugly mood on all of them – that was broken by a clear young voice speaking in the cadence and intonation of a refined English gentleman.

'Major Ballantyne – that is you, is it not?' And, peering up at the causeway, Zouga recognized Neville Pickering, his drinking companion from the first day in the London Hotel.

'It is indeed, Mr Pickering.'

'That's all right, fellows. I'll vouch for Major Ballantyne. He is the famous elephant hunter, don't you know?'

Almost immediately they lost interest and turned away to become absorbed once more in their own race to get the buckets of gravelly yellow stuff to the surface.

'Thank you,' Zouga called up to the man on the causeway above him.

'My pleasure, sir.' Pickering flashed a brilliant smile, touched the brim of his hat and sauntered away, a slim and elegant figure in the press of bearded dust-caked diggers.

Zouga was left alone, as alone in spirit as he had ever been in any of his wanderings across the vast African continent. He had spent almost the last penny he owned on these few square feet of yellow earth at the bottom of this hot and dusty pit. He had no men to help him work it, no experience, no capital – and he doubted that he would recognize an uncut diamond if he held one in the palm of his hand.

As suddenly as it had descended upon him, the gambler's elation, the premonition of good fortune that awaited him here evaporated. He was instantly overwhelmed by his own presumption and by the enormity of the gamble he was taking.

He had risked it all on claims that so far had not yielded a single good stone, the price of diamonds was plummeting, the 'pool goods', small splints of half a carat or less which formed the vast bulk of stones recovered, were fetching only five shillings each.

It was a wild chance, and his stomach slid sickeningly as he faced the consequences of failure.

The sun was almost directly overhead, burning down into the bottom of the workings; the air around him wavered with the heat and it came up through the leather of his boots to scorch the soles of his feet. He felt as though he were suffocating, as though he could not bear it another moment, as though he must scramble up out of this loathsome pit to where the air was cooler and sweeter.

He knew then he was afraid. It was an emotion to which he was not accustomed. He had stood down the charge of a wounded bull elephant, and taken his chance – man to man, steel to steel – on the frontiers of India and in the wild border wars of the Cape.

He was not accustomed to feeling fear, but the waves of panic rose up out of some dark place in his soul and he fought to control them. The sense of impending disaster crushed down upon him. Under his feet he could almost feel the sterility of the baking earth, the barren earth which would cripple him at last, and destroy the dream which had been the fuel on which his life had run for all these years.

Was it all to end here in this hot and hellish pit?

He took a deep breath, and held it for a moment, fighting off the waves of blind panic, and slowly they receded, leaving him feeling weak and shaken as though from a heavy dose of malarial fever.

He went down on one knee and took a handful of the yellow stuff, sifting it through his fingers, and then examined the residue of dull and worthless pebbles. He let them drop and dusted his hand against his thigh.

He had beaten back the engulfing panic, but he was left with a terrible sense of despondency, and a weariness that ached in his bones so that he hardly had strength enough to climb the swaying rope ladder and his feet dragged and scuffed the ochre-red earth of the track, while around him the encampment swam and wavered in the heat and dust as he started back towards the outspan.

Above the hubbub of the camp a clear childish voice rang, and Zouga lifted the golden beard from his chest, his mood lightening as he recognized his son's sweet piping tones.

'Papa! Oh Papa!'

Jordan was racing towards him, wild abandon in every frantic pace, his arms pumping and his feet flying over the rutted track, while the mass of silken curls flew about his lovely face.

'Oh Papa, we have searched for you – all night, all day.'

'What is it, Jordan?' The child's distress alarmed Zouga afresh, and he started forward.

Jordan reached him and threw both arms about Zouga's waist, he pressed his face to Zouga's coat front so that his voice was muffled and he trembled like a frightened little wild animal.

'It's Mama! Something has happened to Mama! Something terrible has happened.'

The delirium of typhoid fever came upon Aletta in hot grey fog banks that blotted out reality and filled her head with phantoms and fantasies which cleared abruptly, leaving her too weak to sit upright, but with her senses enhanced so that her hot skin was hypersensitive to the touch of the clammy flannel against her face and the oppressive weight of her clothing threatened to smother her.

Her vision was sharp and the images enlarged as though seen through a fine reading glass. She could study each long curved eyelash that made up the dense fringe about Jordan's beautiful green eyes. She could see each individual pore in the satiny skin of his cheeks, could delight in the texture of his perfectly bowed lips that trembled now with his agitation and fear as he stooped over her.

She was lost in wonder at her son's beauty, and then the roaring started in her ears again and the beloved child's face receded, until she was looking at it down a long narrow tunnel through the roaring darkness.

She clung desperately to the image, but it began to turn, slowly at first like the wheel of a carriage, then faster still until Jordan's face blurred dizzily and she felt herself tumbling down into the humid darkness again like a leaf upon the roaring wind.

Again the darkness opened, a veil drawn aside in some deep place in her head, and with joy she sought the boy's face again – but instead she saw the falcon high above her.

It was the bird figure of the graven idol that had always been a part of her life since Zouga had come into it. At every cottage, at every outspan or room that they had called home for a day or a week or a month, that stone idol seemed to have been there with them, silent, implacable, heavy with a brooding and ancient malevolence. She had always hated that idol, had always sensed the aura of evil that surrounded it – but now her hatred and her fear could focus fully upon the stone bird that stood tall above the cot on which she lay.

She cursed it weakly, silently, lying on her back on the narrow cot, the robe she wore clinging damply to her skin with the fever-sweat; and she mouthed her hatred at the stone image that towered above her on its polished green soapstone column. Again her vision narrowed, became concentrated so that the falcon head was her whole existence.

Then miraculously the blank stone eyes began to glow with a strange golden light; they revolved slowly in the sockets of the polished stone skull, and suddenly they were looking down at her. The pupils were black and glossy, alive and seeing – but cruel and so truly evil that she quailed in terror, staring up at the bird.

The curved stone beak opened, the tongue was sharp as an arrow-head, and from its tip was suspended a single perfect ruby drop of blood in which a star of light glowed – and Aletta knew it was the blood of the sacrifice. The darkness about the bird was filled with moving shadows, the wraiths of the sacrificial victims, the shades of the falcon-priests dead these thousand years, gathering again to reinforce the powers, gathering again to welcome her –

She screamed, again and again, her terror ringing insanely in her own ears – and then firm hands were shaking her gently, tenderly. Her vision cleared again, but not completely. Everything was dim and blurred, so she screwed up her eyes, still panting wildly from her screams.

'Ralph, is that you?' The strong dark features, already taking on the set of manhood, so different from the sweet angel face of his brother, were close above her.

'Don't take on so, Mama.'

'Ralphie, why is it so dark?' she mumbled.

'It's night time.'

'Where is Jordie?'

'He is asleep, Mama; he could not keep awake. I sent him to sleep.'

'Call Papa,' she whispered.

'Jan Cheroot is searching for him – he will come soon.'

'I'm cold.' She was trembling violently, and felt him draw the rough blanket up beneath her chin before she sank back into the darkness.

In the darkness she saw the shapes of men hurrying forward, pressing about her; she caught their urgency, the passion of their terrible purpose, and she saw their arms glint in the shadows, the flash of white steel, bared and honed for war. She heard the snick of breech-block, the rattle of bayonet in the scabbard, and here and there in the press she recognized a face, faces she had never seen before but which she recognized instantly with a clairvoyant flash of intuition. One was a man full grown, bearded, strong, who was her son – riding into war – and others, so many others, her blood, her flesh, her bones going forward in that awful expectant throng. She was consumed with terrible grief for them, but she could not weep. Instead, she lifted her eyes and saw the falcon on high, clear in the single brilliant shaft of sunshine that pierced the sombre and ominous clouds that rolled from horizon to horizon, the dun and terrible clouds of war.

The falcon hovered on outstretched pinions against the belly of the clouds, twisting the cruelly beautiful head to peer down, then the long pointed wings folded and the bird dropped in a stoop like the lightning bolt, the great talons reaching forward in the strike. She saw them hook into living flesh, saw the grimace on the face that she had never seen before but knew as deeply as she did her own.

And she screamed again. Then strong arms held her, the familiar beloved arms for which she had waited so long. She looked up at him. The clear emerald eyes so close to hers, the powerful jut of his jaw-line half-masked by the full golden-streaked beard.

'Zouga,' she breathed.

'I am here, my love.'

The phantoms receded, the terrible nightmare world of her delirium was gone, and she found herself in a tent upon a dusty plain beneath a half-ruined hillock, and the bright African sunlight through the tent opening cut a stark slash of white light across the powdered red dust floor. She was mildly amazed by the swift transition from night to noonday, from fantasy to reality, and her mouth and throat were filled with the dry chalk of terrible thirst.

'I am thirsty,' she whispered huskily.

He held the pitcher to her cracked lips, and the coolness and the sweetness of the liquid in her throat made her vision swim with delight.

But immediately afterwards, the memory of the nightmares assailed her and she darted a fearful glance across the tent at the silent statue. It seemed suddenly harmless, insignificant, the image blind and dumb, but a flicker of the night's terror remained.

'Beware the falcon,' she whispered, and she saw in his green eyes that he thought her words were still fever ravings. She wanted to convince him but she was terribly, deadly tired, and she closed her eyes and slept in his arms.

When she awoke, the sun's rays had mellowed to a glorious orange light that filled the whole tent and lit little stars in Zouga's beard and curls. She was filled with a deep sense of peace. His arms were so strong, so all-encompassing.

'Look after my babies,' she said softly, but very clearly, and then she died.

*

Aletta's grave was just another mound of red dirt in the long, neat row of freshly turned mounds.

After he had buried her, Zouga sent the boys back to the outspan with Jan Cheroot. Jordan was weeping inconsolably, his lovely face smudged with grief. Ralph sat behind his brother on the back of the gaunt bay gelding, holding the smaller child with both arms clasped about his waist. Ralph was silent, stoic, but his body was rigid with controlled emotion, and his eyes, the same clear deep green of his father's, smouldered with unexpressed grief.

Jan Cheroot led the bay, and the two boys seemed as frail and forlorn as swallows left on a fence rail long after the others had flown the oncoming winter.

Zouga stood beside the grave with military bearing, as expressionless as his elder son had been, but behind the handsome mask he was stunned by his own sorrow and pervading sense of guilt.

He wanted to speak aloud, to tell Aletta that he was sorry, that he knew that he was responsible for this lonely grave so far from her loving family and the beautiful forested mountains of Good Hope which he had loved so dearly. He wanted to ask for forgiveness for sacrificing her to a dream, an impossible grandiose dream. Yet he knew that words were futile and the red earth stopped Aletta's ears.

He stooped and with his bare hand dressed the mound where the earth had collapsed at one corner.

With the first diamond I will buy the headstone, he promised himself silently. The red earth had stained under his fingernails, little half-moons the colour of blood.

With a supreme effort he overcame his sense of futility, overcame the self-consciousness sufficiently to speak aloud to someone who could not hear.

'I will look after them, my dear,' he said. 'That is my last promise to you.'

'Jordie will not eat, Papa.' Ralph greeted him as he stooped into the tent, and Zouga felt the leap of alarm swamp his sorrow and his guilt. He strode to the cot on which the child lay, facing the canvas wall of the tent with his knees drawn up to his chest.

Jordan's skin was burning hot as the sun-scorched rocks that littered the plain outside the tent, and his silken cheeks smeared with tears were flushed a furious fever red.

By morning Ralph was feverish also, both boys tossing and muttering in delirium, their bodies hot as two little furnaces, the blankets sodden with their sweat and the tent reeking with the carrion stench of fever.

Ralph fought the fever.

'Ja, just look at him.' Jan Cheroot paused fondly in the act of sponging down the robust strong-boned body. 'He takes the sickness like an enemy, and struggles with it.'

Helping him, kneeling on the opposite side of the cot, Zouga felt the familiar glow of pride surface through his concern as he looked down at him. Already there were little smoky wisps of hair under Ralph's arms, and a darker explosion of curls at the base of his belly; and his penis was no longer the little wormlike appendage with a childish cap of wrinkled loose skin. His shoulders were squaring and filling with muscle, and his legs were straight and sturdy.

'He will be all right,' Jan Cheroot repeated, and Ralph thrashed out angrily in his delirium, his features scowling and dark with determination.

The two men drew the blanket up over him and turned to the other cot.

Jordan's long thick lashes fluttered like the wings of a beautiful butterfly, and he whimpered pitifully, unresisting as they stripped and sponged him. His little body was as sweetly formed as his features, but clad still in its puppy-fat so that his buttocks were round as apples and plump as a girl's; but his limbs were delicately boned and shapely, his feet and hands long and narrow and graceful.

'Mama,' he whimpered. 'I want my Mama.'

The two men nursed the boys, taking turns day and night, everything else neglected or forgotten, an hour snatched here to water and tend the horses, another hour for a hurried journey into the camp to purchase patent medicine from a transport rider or scramble for the few vegetables offered for sale on the farmers' carts. But diamonds were forgotten, never mentioned in the hot little tent where the struggle for life went on, and the Devil's Own claims were abandoned and deserted.

In forty-eight hours Ralph had regained consciousness, in three days he was sitting up unaided and wolfing his food, in six days they could no longer keep him in his cot.

Jordan rallied briefly on the second day, becoming lucid and demanding his mother fretfully, and then remembered that she was gone, began weeping again and immediately began to sink. His life teetered, the pendulum swinging erratically back and forth, but each time he fell back the presence of death grew stronger in the baking canvas tent, until its stench overpowered the odour of fever.

The flesh melted from his body, burned away by the fever, and his skin took on a pearly translucent sheen, so that it seemed in that uncertain light of dusk and early dawn that the very outline of the delicate bone-structure showed through.

Jan Cheroot and Zouga nursed him in turns, one sleeping while the other watched – or, when neither could sleep, sitting together, seeking comfort and companionship from each other, trying to discount their helplessness in the face of onrushing death.

'He's young and strong,' they told each other. 'He will be all right also.'

And day after day Jordan sank lower, his cheekbones rising up out of his flesh, and his eyes receding into deep cavities the colour of old bruises.

Exhausted with guilt and sorrow, with helpless worry, Zouga left the tent each dawn before sunrise to be the first at Market Square – perhaps there was a transport rider freshly arrived with medicines in his chests, and certainly there would be Boer farmers with cabbages and onions and, if he was lucky, a few wizened and half-green tomatoes, all of which would be sold half an hour after dawn.

On the tenth morning, as Zouga hurried back to the tent, he paused for a moment at the entrance, frowning angrily. The falcon statue had been dragged from the tent, and there was a long furrow scraped by its base in the loose dust. It stood now at a careless angle, leaning against the trunk of the scraggy camel-thorn tree that gave meagre shade to the camp.

The branches of the tree were festooned with black ribbons of dried springbuck meat, with saddlery and trek gear – so that the statue seemed to be part of this litter. There was one of the camp's brown hens perched on the falcon's head, and it had dropped a long chalky smear of liquid excrement down the stone figure.

Still frowning, Zouga ducked into the tent. Jan Cheroot squatted beside Ralph's cot, and the two of them were deeply involved in a game of five stones, using polished pebbles of agate and quartz for the counters.

Jordan lay very still and pale, so that Zouga felt a lurch of dismay under his ribs. It was only when he stooped over the cot that he saw the rise and fall of Jordan's chest and caught the faint whisper of his breathing.

'Did you move the stone falcon?'

Jan Cheroot grunted without looking up from the shiny stones. 'It seemed to trouble Jordie. He wóke up crying again – and kept calling to it.'

Zouga would have taken it further, but suddenly it did not seem worth the effort. He was so tired and dispirited. He would bring the statue back into the tent later, he decided.

'There are a few sweet potatoes – nothing else,' he grunted as he took up the vigil beside Jordan's cot.

Jan Cheroot made a stew of dried beans and mutton, and mashed this with the boiled potatoes. It was an unappetizing mess, but that evening, for the first time, Jordan did not roll his head away from the proffered spoon, and after that his recovery was startlingly swift.

He asked only once more after Aletta, when he and Zouga were alone in the tent.

'Has she gone to heaven, Papa?'

'Yes.' The certainty in Zouga's tone seemed to reassure him.

'Will she be one of God's angels?'

'Yes, Jordie, and from now on she will always be there – watching over you.'

The child thought about that seriously and then nodded contentedly, and the next day he seemed strong enough for Zouga to leave him in Ralph's charge while he and Jan Cheroot went up to the kopje and walked out along No. 6 Roadway to look down on the Devil's Own claims.

All the mining equipment, shovels and picks, buckets and ropes, sheave wheels and ladders had been stolen. At the prices the transport riders were charging it would cost a hundred guineas to replace them.

'We will need men,' Zouga said.

'What will you do when you have them?' Jan Cheroot asked.

'Dig the stuff out.'

'And then?' the little Hottentot demanded with a malicious gleam in his dark eyes, his features wrinkled as a sour windfallen apple. 'What do you then?' he insisted.

'I intend to find out,' Zouga replied grimly. 'We have wasted enough time here already.'

'My dear fellow,' Neville Pickering gave him that charming smile. 'I'm delighted that you asked. Had you not, then I should have offered. It's always a little problematic for a new chum to find his feet,' he coughed deferentially, and went on quickly, 'not that you are a new chum, by any means –'

That was a term usually reserved for the fresh-faced hopefuls newly arrived on the boat from 'home'. 'Home' was England, even those who were colonial-born referred to it as 'home'.

'I'd bet a fiver to a pinch of giraffe dung that you know more about this country than any of us here.'

'African born,' Zouga admitted, 'on the Zouga river up north in Khama's land; accounts for the odd name – Zouga.'

'By jove, didn't realize that, I must say!'

'Don't hold it against me.' Zouga smiled lightly, but he knew that there were many who would. Home-born was vastly superior to colonial born. It was for that reason that he had insisted that Aletta should make the long sea voyage with him when it seemed that her pregnancies would reach full term. Both Ralph and Jordan had been born in the same house in south London, and both had arrived back at Good Hope before they were weaned. They were home-born: that was his first gift to them.

Pickering glossed over the remark tactfully. He did not have to declare his own birth. He was an English gentleman, and nobody would ever mistake that.

'There are many parts of your book that fascinated me. I'll teach you what I know about sparklers if you'll answer my questions. Bargain?'

Over the days that followed they bombarded each other with questions, Zouga demanding every detail of the process of raising and sorting the yellow gravel from the deepening pit, while Pickering kept turning the conversation back to the land to the north, asking about the tribes and the gold reefs, about the rivers and mountains and the wild animals that swarmed upon the plains and in the lonely forests that Zouga had conjured up so vividly in *Hunter's Odyssey*.

Each morning an hour before the first light, Zouga would meet Pickering at the edge of the roadway above the workings. There would be an enamelled kettle bubbling on the brazier and they drank black coffee that was strong enough to stain the teeth, while around them in the gloom the black mine-workers gathered sleepily, still hugging their fur karosses over their shoulders, their voices muted but musical, their movements stiff and slow with sleepiness and the dawn chill.

At a hundred other points around the growing pit the gangs assembled, waiting for the light; and when it glimmered on the eastern horizon the men went swarming down into the workings, like columns of ants along the board walks and down the swaying ladders, spreading out on the chequer board of claims, the hubbub rising, the chant of tribesmen, the squeal of ropes, the hectoring shouts of the white overseers, and then the rattle of bucket loads of yellow gravel into the waiting carts upon the roadway.

Pickering was working four claims, which be owned in partnership.

'My partner is down in Cape Town. Heaven knows when he will be back.'

Neville Pickering shrugged with that deceptively indolent air which he cultivated. 'You'll meet him one of these fine days, and it will be an experience – memorable but not necessarily enjoyable.'

It amused Zouga to see how Neville contrived to maintain his foppish elegance of dress, how he could walk the length of the No. 6 Roadway without the dust hazing the shine of his boots; how he could scramble across the ladderworks without dampening his shirt with sweat, or exchange a flurry of blows with a brawny digger who was encroaching on his claims without it seeming to affect the drape of his Norfolk jacket. His casual sauntering gait carried him from one end of the diggings to the other, at a pace which had Zouga stretching his own legs.

The four claims were not in a single block, but each separated from the others by a dozen or so intervening claims, and Pickering moved from one to the other co-ordinating the work, pulling a gang of half-naked black men from one claim and leading them across to another where the work had fallen behind.

Abruptly he was on the roadway, checking the loading of the carts, and then again, just as abruptly, at the fenced-off plot beyond Market Square where his black workers were rocking the cradles of gravel.

The diamond cradles were like giant versions of the old-fashioned baby cradles from which they took their name. Standing on their half-moon-shaped feet, a man on each side kept them swinging easily from side to side while a third worker shovelled the yellow gravel into the top deck of the cradle from the mound that the cart had dumped. The top deck was a coarse steel sieve, with inch and a half openings in the mesh.

As the cradle rocked rhythmically, the gravel tumbled and bounced across the sloping sieve, the finer stuff under one and a half inches in diameter dropping through onto the second deck of the cradle while the coarse pebbles and waste rolled over under the surveillance of the two cradle men, who watched for the highly unlikely flash of a diamond too big to fall through onto the second deck.

A diamond more than one and a half inches across would be the fortune-maker, the finder's passport to great wealth, the almost impossible 'pony' of the diggers' dreams, a stone heavier than one hundred carats.

On the second deck the mesh was much finer, half-inch square, and a yellow dust blew away like smoke as the cradle agitated it, while on the third deck the mesh was finer still, allowing only the worthless tailings to drop to waste, stuff smaller than the crystals of refined sugar.

From the third deck the gravel was gathered with reverential care, and this was washed in a tub of precious water, every drop of which had been transported thirty miles from the Vaal river.

The gravel was washed in a circular sieve of the No. 3 mesh, the finest of all. The worker agitating and dipping over the tub, muddy to the elbows. Finally the contents of the sieve, cleansed of mud, were dumped onto the flat metal surface of the sorting-table, and the sorters began picking over it with the flat wooden blades of their scrapers.

Women were far away the best sorters, they had the patience, the manual dexterity and the fine eye for colour and texture that was needed. The married diggers kept their wives and daughters at the sorting-table from the minute the mellow morning light was strong enough until the dusk faded each evening.

Pickering was not lucky enough to have women working his tables, but the Africans he had were carefully trained, although never trusted.

'You would never credit what they do with a good stone to try and get away with it. I smile sometimes at what the Duchess would think if she knew that the shiner hanging around her neck had been up the tail end of a big black Basuto,' Pickering chuckled. 'Come, I'll show you what to look for.'

The wiry little black sorter at the head of the table advertised his superior status by his European finery, embroidered waistcoat and Derby hat, but his feet were bare and he carried his snuff-horn in the pierced lobe of his ear. He vacated his seat at the table cheerfully, and Neville Pickering took up the scraper and began to sift through the gravel, a few pebbles at a time.

'There!' he grunted suddenly. 'Your first wild diamond, old man! Take a good look at it, and let's hope it isn't your last.'

Zouga was surprised. It was not what he had expected, and then his surprise was replaced immediately by disappointment. It was a drab little chip of stone, barely the size of one of the sand fleas which swarmed in the red dust of the camp.

It lacked the fire and flash that Zouga had expected, and its colour was a dingy yellow: the colour of champagne perhaps, but without that wine's sparkle.

'Are you sure?' Zouga asked. 'It doesn't look like a diamond to me. How can you tell?'

'It's a splint-chip, probably a piece of a larger stone. It will go ten points, that's a tenth part of a carat, and we will be lucky to get five shillings for it, but it will pay the wages of one of my men for a week.'

'How do you tell the difference between that – and those?' Zouga indicated the mound of gravel in the centre of the table, still wet from the washing-tub, glistening in a thousand different shades of red and gold, anthracite black and flesh pinks, the gaudy show of diamondiferous gravel.

'It's the soapiness,' Pickering explained, 'the soap texture. You will train your eye to it soon, don't bother about the colour – look for the soap.' He took the stone in the teeth of a pair of wooden tweezers and turned it in the sunlight. 'A diamond is unwettable, it repels water; so in the wet gravel it stands out, and the difference is that soapy look.'

Neville proffered the stone. 'There, I tell you what, you keep it as a gift, your first diamond.'

They had been hunting for nearly ten days now, and had gradually moved farther and farther north.

Twice they had sighted quarry, small groups, but each time the quarry had scattered at the first approach.

Zouga was getting desperate. His claims were lying abandoned in the New Rush workings, the level of the surrounding claims would be sinking swiftly, making his more difficult to work and every day increasing the danger of rock slide. Those claims had already killed five men. Jock Danby had warned him.

He was lying now, belly down, on a tiny rocky kopje fifty miles north of the Vaal river, eighty miles from New Rush, and he was still not certain when he could finish this business and turn southwards again.

Jan Cheroot and the two boys were farther down the slope with the horses, holding them in a shallow ravine that was choked with scrub thorn. Jordan's girlish tones carried to where Zouga sat, blending with the cries of circling birds, and Zouga lowered the binoculars to rest his eyes and to listen to his son's voice.

He had worried about taking the boy on this rough journey, especially so soon after that bout of camp fever, but there had been no alternative, no safe place to leave him. Once again Jordan's stamina had belied his delicate looks. He had ridden hard and kept up well with his brother, at the same time recovering the flesh that the fever had burned from his body; and in the last days the deathly pallor of his skin had been gilded to velvety peach.

Thinking about Jordan led directly to memories of Aletta, memories still so filled with sorrow and raw guilt that he could not bear them and he lifted the binoculars again and raked the plain, seeking distraction. He found it with relief.

31

There was unusual movement far out on the wide plain. Through the lens Zouga picked up a herd of a hundred wildebeest, the 'wild cattle' of the Boers. These ungainly animals, with their mournful Roman noses and scraggly beards, were the clowns of the veld. They chased each other in aimless circles, nose to earth and heels kicking at the sky, then abruptly they ceased this lunatic cavorting and stood snorting at one another with wild-eyed expressions of amazement.

Beyond them Zouga caught a flicker of other movement: until that moment it had been hidden by the dust kicked up by the splayed wildebeest hooves. Carefully he adjusted the bevelled focus ring of his binoculars, and the heat mirage trembled and melted before his gaze, turning the movement into a serpentine wriggle that seemed to float above the plain on a lake of silver shimmering water.

'Ostriches!' he thought disgustedly. The distant shapes seemed to wriggle like long black tadpoles in the watery wavering mirage of distance. The long-legged birds seemed to float free of the earth, blooming miraculously in the tortured air above the plain. Zouga tried to count them, but they changed shape and coagulated into a dark wavering mass, their plumed backs bobbing.

Suddenly Zouga sat up. He dropped the binoculars and polished the lens with the tail of the silk bandanna around his throat, then quickly lifted them to his eyes again. The grotesque dark shapes had separated, the lumpy wriggling bodies fined down, the elongated legs had assumed normal proportions.

'Men!' whispered Zouga, and counted them eagerly, as eagerly as he had ever made a first sighting of the huge ivory-carrying grey bull elephants in the hunting veld. He reached eleven before another layer of heated air intervened and altered the distant man-shapes to grotesque unsteady monsters once again.

Zouga slung the binoculars over his shoulder and went down the slope with the loose scree rolling under his boots. Jan Cheroot and the boys lay in the bottom of the ravine on their saddle blankets, their saddles propped behind them as bolsters.

Zouga slid down the bank and landed between them before they had returned from the fairyland that Jan Cheroot had been spinning for them.

'A good bunch,' he told Jan Cheroot.

Zouga reached down and withdrew the short Martini-Henry carbine from the leather bucket of Ralph's saddle. He levered the breech-block down and checked the weapon was empty.

'We aren't after springbuck. Don't you load until either Jan Cheroot or I tell you,' he ordered sternly.

Jordan was still too little to handle the heavy rifle, but he rode well enough to make the encircling sweep with which they would try to close the net.

'Remember, Jordie, that you stay close enough to Jan Cheroot to hear what he tells you,' Zouga told him, glancing up at the sun as he did so.

It was well past noon; he would have to move fairly soon – for if they could not surround the little band of black men at the first attempt, if they did not achieve surprise, then it would be the old time-consuming business of spooring them down individually. So far attempts at doing so had always been interrupted by the sudden African nightfall.

'Saddle up,' Zouga ordered, and they scrambled to their horses.

Zouga swung up onto the bay gelding and glared sternly at Ralph.

'Now you do what you are told – or I'll warm your tail feathers for you, young man.'

He swung the horse's head and pointed it down the ravine, while behind his back Ralph grinned at Jan Cheroot conspiratorially, his face flushed with excitement, and the little Hottentot closed one eyelid briefly but kept his flat wrinkled oriental features expressionless.

Zouga had chosen the kopje with care; from it a ravine meandered out across the plain in an approximate east to west direction – and he followed it now, slouching in the saddle to keep his head below the level of the banks and keeping the gelding down to a walk so as not to raise dust.

After half a mile he removed the wide-brimmed hat from his head and raised himself cautiously in the stirrups until his eyes were just above the bank, and he darted a quick glance into the north and then immediately ducked down again.

'Station here,' he told Ralph. 'And don't move until I do.'

They moved on down the ravine, while Zouga placed Jan Cheroot and Jordan side by side in a bend of the ravine where the bank had collapsed and formed an easy ramp up which they could launch their charge.

'Keep Jordie close,' Zouga cautioned Jan Cheroot, and swung the gelding around with the saddlery creaking as the animal turned in the narrow gut of the ravine; then Zouga trotted back until he was in the centre of the waiting line, and there he halted and contained his impatience, glancing up repeatedly at the lowering sun.

There would probably not be another chance for many days, and each day was vital for those untended claims. Zouga jerked the rifle from the leather bucket at his knee, selected a cartridge from the bandolier around his waist and slipped it into the breech. Then he returned the weapon uncocked to the bucket. It was merely a precaution, but he had no means of knowing what manner of men those approaching figures were.

Even if their intentions were peaceable, and their ultimate object identical to Zouga's own, yet they would be armed and nervous, so nervous that they had avoided the road from the north and were travelling over the open veld. They were in company for defence, and Zouga knew they would have been harassed often along the way, by black men and white: the black men trying to rob and cheat them of their meagre possessions, the white men of something infinitely more valuable, their right to contract their labour to the highest bidder.

On the day that Zouga thanked Neville Pickering for his tuition and began preparing to work the Devil's Own claims for his personal account, he had faced the problem that was already wracking the entire sub-continent.

Only black men could stand the conditions of physical labour in the diggings. Only black men would work for a wage that made the diggings profitable, and even that beggarly wage was many times more than the Boer farmers of the surrounding backveld republics could afford to pay.

The diamond diggings had denuded the countryside of labourers for five hundred miles around; and the Boers resented that as fiercely as they resented the nest of adventurers and fortune seekers that the diggings supported.

The diamonds had caused an upheaval in the Boers' traditional way of life; not only were the miners threatening the supply of cheap labour, which only just allowed a diligent and frugal farmer to eke out a living for himself and his family from the savage land, but the diggers were doing something else that from the Boer point of view was unforgivable, that went against all their deeply held beliefs and threatened not just their livelihood but their very physical existence.

The diamond diggers were paying the black tribesmen with *guns*. The Boers had fought the tribes at Blood River and Mosega, they had stood to the laager in ten thousand threatening dawns, the favourite hour of attack. They had seen the smoke rising from their burning homesteads and crops, they had ridden out on commando on the spoor of their stolen herds, and they had buried the pale corpses of their children, the blood drained from the frail bodies through the gaping and terrible wounds of the assegai. They had buried them at Weenen – the Place of Weeping – and at other accursed and abandoned grave sites across the land.

The payment of black men with guns went against every one of their instincts; it flew full in the face of their laws and offended the memories of their dead heroes.

For these reasons Boer commandos from the little backveld republics were sweeping the land and patrolling the lonely roads from the north to try and prevent the tribesmen reaching the diggings and instead press them to work upon the land.

However, five shillings a week and a musket at the end of a three years' contract were a lure that brought the tribesmen, on foot, against a hundred hazards, on a journey of hundreds of miles, daring the commandos and all else, to reach the diggings.

They came in their hundreds, but still not enough of them arrived to fill those hungry diamond pits. In vain Zouga and Jan Cheroot had ridden the workings. Every black man was signed on contract, and jealously guarded by his employer.

Zouga had told Jan Cheroot, 'We'll offer seven shillings and sixpence a week.'

They signed five men that same day at the higher wage, and the next day there were a dozen deserters waiting outside Zouga's camp, eager for the new coin.

Before Zouga could sign them, Neville Pickering sauntered up. 'Official visit, old man,' he murmured apologetically. 'As a member of the jolly old Diggers' Committee, I have to tell you the rate is five shillings not seven and six.'

When Zouga opened his mouth to protest, Pickering smiled easily and held up his hand.

'No, Major. I'm sorry. It's five shillings, and not a penny more.'

Zouga was already in no doubt about the sweeping powers of the Diggers' Committee. An edict from the elected body was enforced firstly by a warning, then a beating, and finally by the full aggression of the entire community of diggers which could end in a burning or even a lynching.

'What do I do for a gang, then?' Zouga demanded.

'You do what we all do; you go out and find a gang, before another digger or a Boer commando grabs them.'

'I might have to go as far north as the Shashi river,' Zouga snapped sarcastically, and Pickering nodded in agreement.

'Yes, you might.'

Zouga smiled thinly at the memory of his first lesson in digger labour relations, and now he settled his hat firmly and gathered up his reins.

'All right,' he muttered, 'let's go recruiting!' And he put his heels into the gelding's flanks and went lunging up the bank of the ravine onto the open plain.

The tribesmen were five hundred yards dead ahead, and he counted swiftly: sixteen of them. If he could take them all he could start back for New Rush in tomorrow's dawn. Sixteen men were sufficient to work the Devil's Own, and at that moment they had, for Zouga, the same value as a fifty-carat diamond. They were in single file, moving swiftly, the trotting gait of the fighting impis of Zulu, no women or children with them.

'Good,' grunted Zouga as the gelding stretched out under him, and he held him back in an easy canter as he glanced right.

Jan Cheroot was tearing across the plain, Jordan plugging along in his dust fifty strides behind. At this distance Jordan did not look like a child; they might have been a pair of armed riders, and Jan Cheroot was swinging wide, trying to get behind the little group of men, pinning them before they scattered, pinning them long enough for Zouga to get within hail.

Zouga glanced left and scowled as he saw that Ralph was at full gallop, leaning low over his horse's neck, brandishing the Martini-Henry rifle – and Zouga hoped it was still unloaded, wished that he had specially ordered Ralph not to show the rifle, and yet even in that moment of anger he experienced a little prickle of pride as he watched his son ride; the boy was born to the saddle.

Zouga checked the gelding again, bringing him down to a trot, giving his flank men time to complete the circle, and at the same time trying to reduce the dramatic effect of his approach. He knew that they would appear to the tribesmen to be an armed commando, their intentions warlike, and he tried to soften this by lifting his hat and waving it over his head.

Then suddenly Jan Cheroot was reining in, gesturing to Jordan to do the same. They had got behind the band, and opposite them, facing them across the wide circle, Ralph was wheeling his filly and bringing her up sharply on her hind legs, rearing and shaking out her mane theatrically.

In the centre the tribesmen had moved swiftly, and with the concerted action of trained fighting men.

They had dropped the rolled bundles of sleeping-mat, cooking-pot and leather grain bag that they had been carrying on their heads, and they had bunched into a defensive circle shoulder to shoulder, war shield overlapping war shield, while above them the steel of their assegais flicked little pinpricks of sunlight.

They did not wear the full regalia of their fighting regiments, the kilts of monkey tails, the cloaks of desert fox furs, the tall headdress of ostrich and widow-bird feathers, they were travelling with weapons only; but the shields they presented to the approaching horseman and the glint of steel told Zouga all he wanted to know. The shields gave the tribe its name, the Matabele – the people of the long shields.

The little group of men who stood impassively in the sunlight and watched Zouga ride up were the finest warriors that Africa had ever spawned. Yet they were almost five hundred miles south of the borders of Matabeleland.

'I set for a covey of partridge,' Zouga smiled to himself, 'and I have trapped a brood of eagles.'

A hundred yards from the ring of shields, Zouga reined in; but the gelding, infected by the tension, fidgeted under him.

The long shields were made of dappled black and white oxhide, every regiment of the Matabele carried a distinctive shield.

Zouga knew that black dappled with white was the regimental colour of the Inyati, the Buffaloes Regiment, and again he felt a twist of nostalgia.

Once the induna who commanded the Inyati had been a friend; they had travelled together across the mimosa-clad plains of Matabeleland; they had hunted together and shared the comfort of the same camp fires. It was all so long ago, on his first visit to the land below the Zambezi river, but Zouga was carried back so vividly that it required an effort of will to shake off the memory.

He lifted his right hand, fingers spread in the universal gesture of goodwill.

'Warriors of Matabele, I see you,' he called to them, speaking their language as fluently as one of them, the words returning to his tongue readily.

He saw the small stir behind the war-shields, the shift of heads with which they greeted his words.

'Jordan!' Zouga called, and the child circled out and reined in his pony at Zouga's side. Now the difference in size between man and boy was apparent.

'See, warriors of King Lobengula, my son rides with me.' No man took his children to war. The ring of shields sank a few inches so Zouga could see the dark and watchful eyes of the men behind them; but as Zouga pushed the gelding a few paces forward, the shields were immediately lifted again defensively.

'What news of Gandang, induna of the Inyati Regiment, Gandang who is as my brother?' Zouga called again persuasively.

At the mention of the name one of the warriors could no longer contain himself, swept aside his shield and stepped from the ring of spears.

'Who calls Gandang brother?' he demanded in a clear firm voice, a young voice, yet with the timbre and inflection of one used to authority.

'I am Bakela, the Fist,' Zouga gave his Matabele name, and he realized that the warrior facing him was still a youth, barely older than Ralph. But he was lean and straight, narrow in the hips and with muscle in the shoulder and arms built up in the games of war. Zouga guessed he had probably already killed his man, washed his spear in blood.

Now he crossed the open ground towards Zouga, his stride lithe, his legs long and shapely beneath the short leather kilt.

'Bakela,' he said, as he stopped a dozen paces from the gelding's head. 'Bakela.' He smiled, a brilliant show of white even teeth in the broad and handsome Nguni face. 'That is a name I took with the first draught of my mother's milk, for I am Bazo, the Axe, son of the same Gandang whom you call brother, and who remembers you as an old and trusted friend. I know you by the scar on your cheek and the gold in your beard. I greet you, Bakela.'

Zouga swung down off the gelding, leaving the rifle in the saddle scabbard, and, grinning broadly, went to clasp the youth's upper arms in an affectionate salute.

Then, turning with his fists on his hips, still smiling, Zouga shouted to Ralph. 'Go and see if you can shoot a springbuck, or better even, a wildebeest; we'll need plenty of meat for tonight.'

Ralph let out a whoop at the command, and provoked the filly with his heels, forcing her to rear again and then come down in full run, mane flying, hooves pounding as she bore away. Without being ordered, Jan Cheroot shook his bony mare into a canter and followed the flying filly.

The two riders returned in the dusk, and the hunt had gone well. They had found rare quarry, a bull eland so old that his neck and shoulders had turned blue with age and the swinging dewlap almost swept the dusty earth between his stubby forelegs.

He was as big as a prize stud bull, with a chest round as a brandy cask of Limousine oak, and Zouga guessed he would weigh not much under a ton, for he was fat and sleek; there would be a tubful of rich white lard in the chest cavity, and thick layers of yellow fat beneath the glossy hide. He was a prize indeed, and the little band of Matabele drummed their assegai against the hide shields and shouted with delight when they saw him.

The bull snorted at the hubbub and broke into a lumbering gallop, trying to break away, but Ralph swung the filly to head him off and within a hundred yards the bull changed the gallop for a short winded trot and allowed himself to be turned back towards the group of waiting men.

Ralph reined in the filly, kicked his feet from the stirrups and jumped easily to the earth, throwing up the carbine as he landed cat-like on his toes and seeming to fire in the same instant.

The bull's head flinched at the shot, blinking the huge shining eyes convulsively as the bullet slammed into his skull between them, and he collapsed with a meaty thud that seemed to tremble in the earth.

The Matabele streamed out like a pack of wild dogs, swarming over the mountainous carcass, using the razor edge of their war-assegai as butchers' knives, going for the tidbits, the tripes and the liver, the heart and the sweet white fat.

The Matabele gorged on fat eland meat, grilling the tripes over the coals, threading garlands of liver and fat and succulent heart onto wet white mimosa twigs from which they had peeled the bark, so that the melting fat sizzled and bubbled over the layers of meat.

'We have killed no game since we left the forests,' Bazo explained their ravenous appetites. Though the desert teemed with springbuck herds, they were not the type of game that a man on foot, armed only with a stabbing spear, could run down easily.

'Without meat a man's belly is like a war drum, full of nothing except noise and wind.'

'You are far from the land of the Matabele,' Zouga agreed. 'No Matabele has been this far south since the old king took the tribe north across the Limpopo, and in that time even Gandang, your father, was a child.'

'We are the first to make this journey,' Bazo agreed proudly. 'We are the point of the spear.'

In the firelight the warriors about him looked up and their expressions echoed his pride in their achievement. They were all youths, the eldest only a few years older than Bazo, not one of them over nineteen years of age.

'Where does this long journey take you?' Zouga asked.

'To a wonderful place in the south from which a man returns with great treasures.'

'What manner of treasures?' Zouga asked again.

'These.' Bazo reached across the circle to where Ralph leaned against his saddle, using it as a pillow, and Bazo touched the polished wooden butt of the Martini-Henry that protruded from the gun bucket.

'*Isibamu* – guns!' said Bazo.

'Guns?' Zouga asked. 'A Matabele *indoda* with a gun?' His voice mildly derisive. 'Is not the assegai the weapon of the true warrior?'

Bazo looked uncomfortable for a moment and then recovered his aplomb.

'The old ways are not always the best,' he said. 'The old men tell us that they are, so that young men will consider them wise.' And the Matabele in the circle about the fire nodded and made little sounds of agreement.

Although he was certainly the youngest of the group, Bazo was clearly their leader. Son of Gandang, he was therefore the nephew of King Lobengula, grandson of old King Mzilikazi himself. His noble birth assured him preference, but it was clear that he was quick and clever also.

'To earn the guns you covet a man must work hard, in a deep pit in the earth,' Zouga said. 'He must milk himself of his sweat by the calabash full every day for three years, before he is paid with a gun.'

'We have heard these things,' Bazo nodded.

'Then you shall have your guns, each of you a fine gun, at the end of three years. I, Bakela, the Fist, give you my word on it.'

It was a custom of the diggings, a ceremony of initiation, that when a gang of raw tribesmen arrived at New Rush the established black labourers would rush to line each side of the track, most of them dressed in cast-off European finery as a badge of their sophistication.

They would jeer their newly arrived brethren:

'Behold, the baboons have come down from the hills.'

'Nay! Baboons are cunning; these cannot be baboons.' And they pelted the newcomers with pieces of filth as well as insults.

Bazo's group were the first Matabele to reach the diggings. The Matabele language is almost identical to that of Zululand, and very closely associated to the Southern Xhosa. Bazo understood every word of the banter, and he gave a quiet but grim order to his little group.

His men dropped their sleeping-mats and the long shields rattled one against the other, the broad bright assegais whispered in the sunlight as they were bared, and the taunts and derisive laughter dried on the instant, to be replaced with expressions of astonishment and real dismay.

'*Manje*! Now!' hissed Bazo. The ring of shields exploded outwards, and the crowd fled before it in disordered panic.

From the back of the gelding, Zouga had a grandstand view of the charge, and he had no illusions as to the danger of the moment. Even such a tiny war party of Matabele *amadoda* on the rampage through the camp could cause chaos and frightful slaughter amongst the unarmed black labourers.

'Bazo! Kawulisa! Stop them!' he roared, spurring across the front of the murderous rank of rawhide shields and steel.

The erstwhile tormentors ran with their heads twisted backwards, yelling with terror and eyes popping. They knocked each other down and the fallen grovelled in the dust. A portly black man, dressed in grubby duck breeches many sizes too small and a frock coat many sizes too large, ran into the side of one of the shacks lining the track, the home of one of the less affluent diggers, and the canvas wall burst open before the power of his run, the thatch roof collapsed on top of the fugitive, covering him completely with a haystack of dried grass and probably saving his life – for the point of a Matabele assegai had been inches from the straining seam of his bulging breeches at the moment the shack collapsed.

Bazo gave a single blast on the buckhorn whistle that hung on a thong at his throat, and the spearsmen froze. The charge stopped dead on the instant, and the Matabele trotted back to where they had dropped their baggage, all of them grinning with delight; as they formed up again, Bazo sang the first line of the Inyati regimental war chant in a high ringing voice:

> 'See the war shields black as midnight,
> white as the high storm clouds at noon –'

And the men behind him came crashing in with the chorus:

> 'Black as the Inyati bull, white as the egrets
> that he carries upon his back –'

The entry of the little band of warriors to the New Rush diggings became a triumphal procession. Riding at their head Zouga felt like a Roman emperor.

Yet not one of the young warriors had ever swung a pick or hefted a shovel. Jan Cheroot had to place the tools in their hands, positioning their fingers correctly on the handles, all the while muttering his disdain of such ignorance. However, they had the knack of it within minutes, and the velvety black muscles, forged in war and the training for war, changed the mundane tools into lethal weapons; they attacked the yellow earth as though it were a mortal adversary.

Confronted with a wheelbarrow for the first time, two of them lifted it bodily and walked away with it and its contents. When Ralph demonstrated the correct use of the vehicle, their wonder and delight was childlike, and Bazo told them smugly: 'I promised you many wonders, did I not?'

They were a highly disciplined group of young men, accustomed since childhood firstly to the strict structure of family life in the kraals and then from puberty to the communal training and teamwork of the fighting regiments.

They were also fiercely competitive, delighting in any challenge to pit their strength or skill against one another.

Zouga, knowing all these things, organized them in four teams of four men, each named after a bird – the Cranes, the Hawks, the Shrikes and the Khorhaans – and each week the team with the best performance in lashing the gravel was entitled to wear the feathers of their adopted bird in their hair and to a double ration of meat and mealie-meal and *twala*, the African beer fermented from millet grain. They turned the work into a game.

There were some small adjustments to be made. The Matabele were cattle-men, their whole lives devoted to raising, protecting and enlarging their herds, even if these expansions were often at the expense of their less warlike neighbours. Their staple diet was beef and *maas*, the calabash-soured milk of the Nguni.

Beef was an expensive item on the diggings, and it was with patent distaste that they sampled the greasy stringy mutton that Zouga provided. However, hard physical labour builds appetites, and within days they were eating this new diet if not with relish at least without complaint.

Within those same few days the labour was apportioned and each man learned his task.

Jan Cheroot could not be inveigled down into the workings.

'*Ek is nie 'n meerkat nie,*' he told Zouga loftily, reverting to the bastard Dutch of Cape Colony. 'I am not a mongoose; I do not live in a hole in the ground.'

Zouga needed a trusted man on the sorting-tables, and that was where Jan Cheroot presided. Squatting like a yellow idol over the glittering piles of washed gravel, the triangular shape of his face was emphasized by the scraggy little beard on the point of his chin – by the high oriental cheekbones and slanted eyes, each in their spider-web of wrinkles.

He was quick to pick out the soapy sheen of the noble stones in the piles of dross, but there was another pair of eyes sharper and quicker. Traditionally the women made the best sorters, but little Jordan proved immediately to have an uncanny talent at picking out diamonds, no matter what their size or colour.

The child picked the very first stone from the very first sieveful. It was a minute stone, twenty points, a fifth part of a carat, and the colour was a dark cognac brown, so that Zouga doubted its integrity. But when be showed it to one of the kopje-wallopers, it was a veritable diamond and the buyer offered him three shillings for it.

After that nobody questioned Jordan, instead a doubtful stone was passed to him for judgement. Within a week he was the Devil's Own chief sorter.

He sat opposite Jan Cheroot at the low metal table, almost the same size as the Hottentot. He wore a huge sombrero of platted maize stalks to protect his delicate peachlike skin from the sun, and he sorted the gravel as though it were a game of which he never tired. Competing with Jan Cheroot avidly, a high-pitched shriek of excitement signalled each discovery, and his neat little hands flew over the gravel like those of a pianist over the ivory keyboard.

Zouga had found a woman to give both Ralph and Jordan their lessons. The wife of a Lutheran preacher, she was a plump-breasted, sweet-faced woman with iron-grey hair swept up into an enormous bun at the back of her head. Mrs Gander was the only schoolmistress within five hundred miles, and for a few hours each morning she gave a small group of diggers' children their reading, writing and arithmetic in the little galvanized-iron church at the back of Market Square.

It was a daily ritual to which Ralph had to be driven by his father's threats, and to which Jordan hurried with the same enthusiasm as he did to the sorting-table after school was out. With his angelic looks, and the intense interest in the written word that Aletta had germinated in him, Jordan was instantly Mrs Gander's darling.

She made no effort to conceal her preference. She called him 'Jordie-dear' and gave to him the task of wiping clean the blackboard, which immediately made it an honour for which the dozen other children in the class would have scratched out his lovely densely-lashed angel eyes.

There was a pair of twins in Mrs Gander's class. The tough sons of a tough out-of-luck digger from the Australian opal fields, they were a matched pair, with shaven heads to inhibit the breeding of lice, bare-footed, for their father was working a poor claim on the eastern edge of the diggings, their braces supporting patched canvas breeches over faded and frayed shirts. Henry and Douglas Stewart made a formidable pair, acting in complete concert, quick with a cruel jibe too soft for Mrs Gander to hear or a crafty jab with the elbow or a tug of the hair too quick for her to see.

Jordan was natural prey. 'Jordie-girl' they christened him, and his soft curls felt good between their fingers, and his tears were enormously satisfying – especially when they realized that Jordan for some strange reason of pride would not appeal to his big brother for protection.

'You tell Goosie-Gander that I've a belly ache,' Ralph instructed Jordan. 'And that Papa says I am too sick to come to class.'

'Where are you going?' Jordan demanded. 'What are you going to do?'

'I'm going to the nest – I think the chicks may be ready.' Ralph had discovered a lanner falcon's nest on the top ledge of a rocky kopje five miles out on the Cape road. He was planning to take the chicks and train them as hunting falcons. Ralph always had exciting plans; it was one of the many reasons why Jordan adored him.

'Oh, let me come with you. Please, Ralph.'

'You're still just a baby, Jordie.'

'I'm nearly eleven.'

'You're only just ten,' Ralph corrected him loftily, and from experience Jordan knew there was no profit in arguing.

Jordan delivered Ralph's lie for him in such sweet piping tones and with such a guileless flutter of the long lashes, that it never occurred to Mrs Gander to doubt it, and the Stewart twins exchanged a quick glance of complete accord.

There was a latrine at the back of the church, a sentry box of corrugated iron, a boxwood seat with an oval cut from it suspended over a galvanized steel bucket. The heat in the tiny room was ovenlike and the contents of the bucket ripened swiftly. The twins trapped Jordan there in the mid-morning break.

They had hold of an ankle each and were standing on the wooden seat, the hole between them, and Jordan was dangling upside down, clinging desperately to the boxwood seat as they tried to force his head and shoulders through the opening and into the brimming bucket.

'Stamp on his fingers,' Douglas panted. Jordan had offered unexpected opposition. Douglas had a red scratch down his neck, and they had had to pry Jordan's jaws open to release their grip on Henry's thumb. The injuries had changed the mood of the twins. They had started out with laughter, spiteful laughter, but laughter all the same; now they were angry and vicious, their self-esteem smarting as much as their injuries.

'Shut up, you little sissy,' blurted Henry, as he obeyed his brother and brought down his horny heel on Jordan's white knuckles. Jordan's shrieks of agony and horror and terror reverberated in the tiny iron shed as he kicked and fought.

Against their combined strength, Jordan's wildest efforts were ineffectual. His fingernails scratched white splinters from the wooden seat, and his shrieks mounted hysterically, but his head was forced down. The stench was suffocating, the disgust choked his throat and strangled his cries.

At the moment that he felt the cold wet filth soaking into his golden curls the door of the shed was wrenched open and Mrs Gander's motherly bulk filled the opening.

For a moment she stared incredulously, and then she began to swell with outrage. Her right arm, muscled from kneading bread and pounding wet washing, flew out in a round open-handed blow that knocked both twins flying into a corner of the latrine – and she gathered Jordan up, holding him at arms' length. With her flushed face wrinkling at the smell of his soaked curls, she rushed out with him, shouting to her husband to bring a bucket of precious water and a bar of the yellow and blue mottled soap.

Half an hour later Jordan reeked of carbolic soap and his curls were fluffing out again as the sun dried them into a shining halo, and from behind the closed doors of the vestry the yells of pain emitted by the twins were punctuated by the clap of the Reverend Gander's Malacca cane walkingstick as his wife urged him on to greater endeavour.

Around the whittled remains of Colesberg kopje had grown up a miniature range of man-made hillocks. These were the tailings from the diamond cradles, dumped haphazardly on the open ground beyond the settlement. Some of these artificial hills were already twenty feet high, and they formed a wasteland where no tree nor blade of grass grew. A maze of narrow footpaths laced the area, made by the daily pilgrimage of hundreds of black workers to the pit.

The shortcut between the Lutheran church and Zouga's camp followed one of these footpaths, and in the heat-hushed hour of noon, the labourers were still in the workings and the hills were deserted. The sun directly overhead threw only narrow black strips of shade below the mounds of loose gravel as Jordan hurried along the dusty path, his eyes still red-rimmed with weeping the tears of humiliation and stinging from the foam of carbolic soap.

'Hello Jordie-girl.' Jordan recognized the voice instantly, and it stopped him dead, blinking his swimming eyes in the sunlight, peering up at the summit of one of the gravel mounds beside the path.

One of the twins stood silhouetted against the pale blue noon sky. His thumbs hooked into his braces, his shaven head thrust forward, his eyes with their thin colourless lashes as vicious as those of a ferret.

'You told, Jordie-girlie,' the twin accused flatly.

'I never told,' Jordan denied, his voice squeaking uncertainly.

'You screamed. That's the same as telling – and now you are going to scream again, but this time there isn't going to be anyone to hear you, Jordie-girl.'

Jordan spun around, and in the same movement he was running with all the desperation and speed of a gazelle pursued by a hunting cheetah; but he had not gone a dozen frantic paces when the second twin slid down the sloping bank, the gravel hissing around his bare feet, full into the narrow pathway ahead of Jordan, his arms spread in welcome, his mouth twisted into a grin of anticipation.

They had laid the trap with care. They had caught him in a narrow place, where the gravel banks were highest, and behind him the first twin slid adroitly down to block the path, keeping his balance on the little avalanche of rolling gravel under his bare feet until he hit the level pathway.

'Jordie-dear,' called one twin.

'Jordie-girl,' echoed the other, and they closed from each side, slowly, tantalizing themselves, so that Henry giggled almost breathlessly.

'Little girls shouldn't tell tales.'

'I'm not a girl,' whispered Jordan, backing away from him.

'Then you shouldn't have curls; only girls have curls.' Douglas groped in his pocket and brought out a bone-handled clasp knife. He opened the blade with his teeth. 'We are going to turn you into a boy, Jordie-girl.'

'Then we are going to teach you not to tell tales.' Henry brought out his hand from behind his back. He had cut a camel-thorn branch, and stripped the bunches of lacy leaves, but not the thorns. 'We are going to do the same to you as old Goosey-Gander did to us. Fifteen cuts each. That's thirty for you, Jordie-girl.'

Jordan's gaze fastened on the branch with sickened fascination. It was twice as thick as a man's thumb, more a club than a cane, and the thorns were half an inch long, each on a little raised knob of rough black bark. Henry swung it in an experimental cut and it hissed like an adder.

The sound galvanized Jordan, he whirled and flew at the high bank of gravel beside him; it slid treacherously under his feet so that he had to use his hands to claw his way towards the summit.

Behind him the twins yipped with excitement, like the hunting call of a pack of wild dogs, and they raced after him, scrambling up the soft collapsing bank.

Their weight buried them at each pace above the ankles, so that Jordan, lighter and buoyant with terror, reached the top of the bank ahead of them, and he raced silent and white-faced across the flattened table of the summit, opening the gap further.

Henry snatched up a stone as he ran, a lump of quartz as big as his own fist, and he used his own momentum to hurl it. It flew an inch past Jordan's ear, and he flinched and whimpered, losing his balance, stumbled at the far edge of the dump, and went tumbling down the steep slope.

'Stop him,' yipped Douglas, and launched himself over the edge.

At the bottom Jordan rolled to his feet, dusty and wildly dishevelled, his curls bushed out and dangling in his eyes. He wasted a second, glancing about desperately, and then darted away along the narrow footpath through the gut of the pass between the gravel dumps.

'Catch him. Don't let him get away.' The twins yelled at each other, panting with laughter, like two cats with a mouse, and here on the flat their longer legs quickly narrowed Jordan's lead.

He heard their bare feet slapping on hard earth in a broken rhythm close behind him, and he twisted his head back over his shoulder, almost blinded with his own sweat and dancing curls, his breath sobbing, his skin white as bone-china and his huge brimming eyes seeming to fill his whole face.

Henry steadied himself, poised with his right arm held back at full stretch and then he threw the thorn stick, cartwheeling it low over the ground so that it slammed into the back of Jordan's knees, the thorns ripping the soft bare skin, raising deep parallel scratches as though from the slash of a cat's claws.

Jordan's legs folded under him and be went down, sliding on his belly, the wind driven from his lungs as he hit the baked earth of the pathway. Before he could raise himself, Douglas landed with all his weight between Jordan's shoulder blades and shoved his face, cheek down, against the ground, while Henry snatched up the thorn branch and danced about them, looking for an opening, the branch held in both hands above his head.

'His hair first,' gasped Douglas, choking with laughter and his own excitement. 'Hold his head.'

Henry dropped the cane and stooped over Jordan, grabbing a double handful of the fine curls and leaning back against it with all his weight so that Jordan's neck was stretched out. Douglas was still perched between Jordan's shoulder blades. Pinning him against the earth and brandishing the open clasp knife, he told his twin, 'Hold him still.' The fine golden hair was stretched like the strings of a violin and Douglas hacked at it.

It came away in tufts in Henry's fists, some of it cut through, some of it torn out at the roots, like feathers from the carcass of a slaughtered chicken, and he threw it high in the air, shouting with laughter as it sparkled in the sunlight.

'Now you will be a boy!'

All the resistance went out of Jordan. He lay crushed against the earth, shaken only by his own sobs, and Henry grabbed another handful of his curls.

'Cut closer,' he ordered his twin, and then shrieked with shock and pain.

The thin tapered end of a rhinoceros-hide riding whip curled with a snap around the seat of Henry's breeches, over the fresh bruises raised by the Reverend Gander's Malacca cane, and Henry shot erect clutching at his own buttocks with both hands and hopping up and down on the same spot.

A hand closed on the collar of his shirt and he was yanked into the air and held suspended, kicking, a foot above the ground, still clutching the seat of his breeches that felt as though they were filled with live coals.

His brother looked up from his seat on Jordan's back. In the excitement of tormenting the smaller boy, neither of the twins had heard or seen the horseman. He had walked his horse around the bend in the footpath between the gravel heaps and come across the squirming yelling knot of small bodies in the middle of the path. He recognized the twins immediately; they had earned quick notoriety on the diggings, and it had taken only another second to guess the cause of the commotion, to understand who were the attackers and who the victim.

Douglas was quick to realize the changed circumstances as he looked up at his twin, dangling like a man on the gallows from the horseman's fist. He scrambled to his feet and darted away, but the horseman turned his mount with his heels and, like a polo player, cut back-handed with the long rhino-hide sjambok, and the agony of it paralysed Douglas. But for the thick canvas breeches it would have opened his skin.

Before he could begin to run again the horseman stooped in the saddle, seized his upper arm and lifted him easily. On each side of the horse, the twins wriggled and whimpered with the sting of the lash and the rider looked down at them thoughtfully.

'I know you two,' he told them quietly. 'You are the Stewart brats, the ones who drove old Jacob's mule into the barbed wire.'

'Please, sir, please,' blubbered Douglas.

'Keep quiet, boy,' said the rider evenly. 'You are the ones that cut the reins on De Kock's wagon. That cost your daddy a penny, and the Diggers' Committee would like to know who set fire to Carlo's tent then–'

'It weren't us, Mister,' Henry pleaded. It was clear they both knew who their captor was, and that they were truly afraid of him.

Jordan crawled to his knees and peered up at his rescuer. He must be somebody very important – perhaps even a member of the committee he had mentioned. Even in his distress Jordan was awed by that possibility. Ralph had explained to him that a committee member was something between a policeman, a prince and the ogre of the fairy tales which their mother used to read to them.

Now this fabulous being looked down at Jordan as he knelt in the pathway, with his cheek smeared with dust and tears, his shirt torn and the buttons dangling on their threads, while the backs of his knees were criss-crossed with bloody welts.

'This little one is half your size,' the horseman said. His eyes were blue, a strange electric blue – the eyes of a poet – or of a fanatic.

'It was just a game, sir,' mumbled Henry; the collar of his shirt was twisted up under his ear.

'We didn't mean nothing, Mister.'

The horseman transferred that glowing blue gaze from Jordan to the two wriggling bodies in his hands.

'A game, was it?' he asked. 'Well, next time I catch you playing your games, you and your father had better have a story for the committee, do you hear me?'

He shook them roughly. 'Do you understand me clearly?'

'Yes, sir –'

'So you enjoy games, do you? Well then, here is a new one, and we shall play it every time you so much as lay a finger on a child smaller than you are.'

He dropped them unexpectedly to earth, and before the twins could recover their balance had cut left and right with the sjambok, starting them away at a run, and then he cantered easily along behind them for a hundred yards or so, leaning from the saddle to flick the whip at the back of their legs to keep them at their best speed. Then abruptly he let them go and wheeled the horse, cantering back to where Jordan stood trembling and pale in the pathway.

'If you are going to fight, then one at a time is the best policy, young man,' said the rider and stepped down easily from the stirrup and threw the reins over his shoulder as he squatted on his haunches facing Jordan.

'Now where does it hurt most?' he asked.

It was suddenly terribly important to Jordan that he did not appear a baby. He gulped noisily as he fought his tears, and the man seemed to understand.

'Good fellow,' he nodded. 'That's the spirit.' And he drew a cotton handkerchief from his pocket and wiped away the muddy tears.

'What's your name?'

'Jordie – Jordan,' he corrected himself and sniffed noisily.

How old are you, Jordan?'

'Almost eleven, sir.'

The sting of his injuries and of his humiliation began to recede, to be replaced by a warm flood of gratitude towards his rescuer.

'Spit!' ordered the horseman, proffering the handkerchief, and Jordan obeyed, dampening a corner of the cloth with his saliva.

The man turned him with a hand on his shoulder, and with the handkerchief cleaned the bloody lines on his legs. It was perfunctory treatment, and the man's touch was masculine and ungentle, but Jordan was powerfully reminded of his mother by the attention, and that empty place inside him ached so that he almost began weeping again. He held back the tears, and twisted his neck to watch the man work on his injured legs.

The fingers were square and powerful, but a little uncoordinated. The nails were big and strong and even, cut short, with a pearly translucent lustre. The back of his hands were covered with fine golden hairs that caught the sun.

The man glanced up from his task at Jordan. His face was fair, the skin was smooth-shaven and unblemished except for the small fine moustache. His lips were full, high-coloured, sensual. His nose was large, but not too large for the big round head and the thick waves of light-brown hair.

He was young, probably ten years older than Jordan, though he had such a powerful presence, such a sense of maturity and of power seemed to invest him, that he appeared much older.

Yet there was something else about him that seemed to contradict the first appearance. The high colour in his lips and cheeks was not the flush of health and the open air life. It was a shade hectic, and though the skin was unlined, there were the subtle marks of suffering and pain at the corners of his eyes and mouth, while behind that penetrating gaze, that compelling intensity, there was a tragic shadow, a sense of sadness that was perhaps only readily apparent to the uncomplicated view of a child.

For a moment the man and the boy looked into each other's eyes, and something twisted almost painfully deep in Jordan's soul, a sweet pang – gratitude, puppy love, compassion, hero-worship – it was all of those and something else for which he would never have words.

Then the man stood; he was tall and big built, over six foot in his riding boots, and Jordan only reached as high as his ribs.

'Who is your father, Jordan?' And Jordan was grateful that he did not use the diminutive . The rider nodded at his reply.

'Yes,' he said. 'I have heard of him. The elephant hunter. Well, then, we had best get you home.'

He stepped up into the stirrup and from the saddle reached down, took Jordan by the arm and swung him up onto the horse's rump. Jordan sat sideways, and as the horse started forward, he put both arms round the rider's waist to balance himself.

Jan Cheroot came hurrying from the sorting-table as they trotted into Zouga's camp, and when the rider reined in, he reached up and lifted Jordan down.

'He has been in a fight,' the rider told Jan Cheroot. 'Put a little iodine on his cuts, and he'll be all right. The boy has spirit.'

Jan Cheroot was obsequious, almost cringing, far from his usual acerbic and cynical self. He seemed to be rendered speechless by the direct and startling gaze of the big man on the rangy horse. He held Jordan with one hand and with the other lifted the old regimental cap from his head and held it against his chest, nodding in servile agreement with the orders the man gave him.

The rider transferred his steady gaze back to Jordan, and for the first time he smiled.

'Next time pick on somebody your own size, Jordan,' he advised, took up the reins and trotted out of the camp without looking back.

'You know who that was, Jordie?' Jan Cheroot asked portentously, staring after the rider and not waiting for Jordan's reply. 'That's the big boss of the Diggers' Committee, that's the most important man on New Rush, Jordie –' he paused theatrically, and then announced, 'That's Mr Rhodes.'

'Mr Rhodes.' Jordan repeated the name to himself, 'Mr Rhodes.' It had a heroic sound to it, like some of the poetry that his mother had read to him. He knew that something important had just happened in his life.

Every member of Zouga's family and following quickly found his place in the work, almost as though a special niche had been reserved for each of them: Jan Cheroot and Jordan at the sorting-table, the Matabele *amadoda* in the open diggings, and, naturally there was only one place for Ralph – in the diggings with them.

So they found the stones; they won them from the tiny squares of ground in the depths of the growing pit, and carried them to the surface in the swinging buckets, and carted them out along the rotten crumbling roadways which each day became more dangerous and they washed and sieved them, until at last Jan Cheroot or Jordie could pounce upon them on the sorting-table.

Then in the evening there might be three or four of Zouga's Matabele workmen waiting under the camel-thorn tree beside Zouga's tent.

'Let me see,' Zouga would grunt, and with a deal of showmanship the man would unknot a scrap of grubby cloth to display a chip of stone or a small transparent crystal.

These were the 'pick-ups' from the claims. As the Matabele handled the stuff, shovelling it and emptying the leather buckets, a glitter or shine of a pebble may catch their eye – and there was a reward for a diamond 'picked-up' and handed in.

Most of these 'pick-ups' were not veritable diamonds, for they took anything that sparkled, or anything pretty and unusually coloured. They brought in agate and quartz, feldspar and rock crystal, jasper and zircons – and once in a while a diamond; and then for each diamond, large or small, clear or discoloured, Zouga would hand over a golden sovereign from his dwindling hoard and add the diamond to the contents of the little chamois leather drawstring bag that he carried buttoned into his breast pocket, and which was under his pillow when he slept at night.

Then each Saturday morning, while Jan Cheroot and the two boys gathered around the camp table under the camel-thorn tree beside the tent, Zouga would carefully tip the contents of the leather bag onto a sheet of clean white paper, and they examined and discussed the week's recovery; and always Zouga tried to cover his disappointment, tried to ignore the nauseating bite of worry in his guts as he looked at the tiny, discoloured and flawed diamonds which the Devil's Own so reluctantly yielded up.

Then with the chamois bag buttoned into his pocket once again, his riding boots freshly waxed and polished by Ralph, his frayed shirt collar neatly darned and the buttons replaced by Jordan, and the gelding curried to a gloss by Jan Cheroot, Zouga would ride into the settlement, putting on the best face he could muster, smoking a cigar to show how little he really needed the money, and he would hitch the gelding at the door of the first diamond-buyer's galvanized iron shack.

'The Devil's Own.' The first kopje-walloper was a Hollander, and his accent was difficult to understand, but Zouga's brave show did not deceive him, and he sucked his teeth and shook his head dismally over Zouga's offering. 'The Devil's Own,' he repeated. 'It killed five men, and broke three others. Jocky Danby was lucky to get out at the price you paid him.'

'What's your offer?' Zouga asked quietly, and the buyer prodded the scattering of tiny stones.

'You want to see a real diamond?' he asked, and without waiting for Zouga's reply, swivelled his chair and opened the iron safe on the wall behind his desk.

Reverently he unfolded a square of white paper and displayed the beautiful flashing crystal, almost the size of a ripe acorn.

'Fifty-eight carats,' he whispered, and Zouga stared at it with the sour acid of envy in the back of his throat. 'I bought it yesterday.'

'How much?' he asked, hating himself for the weakness.

'Six thousand pounds!' said the buyer and carefully refolded the paper, placed the diamond back in the safe, locked the thick iron door, hung the key on his watch chain and glanced at Zouga's stones.

'Forty pounds,' he said off-handedly.

'The lot?' Zouga asked quietly. He had sixteen men to pay and feed and he needed new rope, and he would have to pay the piratical prices of the transport riders for it.

'The price of pool goods is right down.' The buyer shrugged. 'Every digger south of the Vaal is bringing in rubbish like this.'

Zouga refilled the bag and stood up.

'I made you that price as a favour,' warned the buyer. 'If you come back later, it will be thirty pounds.'

'I'll take that chance.' Zouga touched the brim of his hat and strode out into the sunlight.

The second buyer he visited poured the diamonds into the bowl of the diamond balance and then carefully added weights to the other arm until the scale was in balance.

'You should have stuck to elephant hunting,' he said, as he wrote down the weights and made his calculations in a leather notebook. 'The diamond market is flooded. There is a limit to the number of rich ladies who want to hang baubles round their necks, and here on the Vaal diggings we have mined more stones in a few years than were found in the six thousand years before that.'

'They are using them in watch movements, and tools for cutting glass and steel,' Zouga said quietly.

'A fad,' the buyer waved his hands in dismissal. 'Diamonds are finished. I'll give you fifty-five pounds for this lot and that's generous.'

One morning Zouga found Ralph working side by side with Bazo in the bottom of the pit, swinging the pick in rhythm with the Matabele chant. He stood there watching for a few minutes, saw the shape of mature muscle emerging from the soft flesh of childhood, saw the breadth of shoulder. Ralph's belly was greyhound slim and the cloth of his breeches, that were suddenly many sizes too small, strained over neat round buttocks as he stooped to break the point of the pick from the compacted yellow earth.

'Ralph,' he called him at last.

'Yes, Papa.' His throat was greasy with sweat, and it had cut little runnels down through the dust that coated his upper body, fat glistening drops clung in the little nest of fine dark curls that had abruptly appeared in the centre of his chest.

'Put your shirt on,' Zouga ordered.

'Why?' Ralph looked surprised.

'Because you are an Englishman. By God's grace and, if necessary, the strength of my right arm you are going to be a gentleman as well.'

So Ralph worked booted and buttoned to the throat beside the naked Matabele, and he earned firstly their respect and then their affection and friendship.

From the first day when they had met in the open veld, the Matabele had been impressed with his horsemanship, and with the marksmanship which had brought down the old eland bull. Now they began to accept him amongst them, first in the patronizing manner of elder brothers, then gradually on more and more equal terms, until Ralph was competing with them in all they did, their work and their sport. He was not yet as tall or strong as the Matabele, so he won very seldom; and when he failed or was beaten, he scowled until his face darkened and the heavy brows met above the big nose.

'A good sportsman knows how to lose graciously,' Zouga told him.

'I don't want to be a sportsman, I don't want to learn how to lose,' Ralph replied. 'I want to learn how to win.' And he threw himself back at the task with fiercely renewed determination.

It seemed that his strength grew with each day in the diggings, the puppy fat was burned away, and he made that final spurt to his full height without outstripping his strength. And he learned how to win.

He began to win the contests with Bazo at lashing gravel, frenziedly filling bucket after huge leather bucket so that the yellow dust flew in choking clouds. He won one of the dangerous races down the ladderworks from the roadway to the bottom of the pit, scorching his palms on the ropes and swinging out over the drop to pass another man on the reverse side of the ladder, using the pole of a gantry to cross a deep void between two claims, running across it upright, like a tight-rope walker, without looking at his feet or the hundred-foot drop beneath him. Even Bazo shook his head and said 'Hau!' which is an exclamation of deep amazement, and Ralph stood panting in the bottom of the pit, looking up at Bazo, and shouted with triumphant laughter.

Then Ralph learned to use the fighting sticks the hard way – for this was the game the Matabele had played since their first day as herd boys in the veld. Before he mastered the art of the sticks he had, perforce, to learn how to staunch a bleeding cut in his own scalp inflicted by Bazo's stick by plugging it with a handful of dust snatched in the midst of the contest.

A week short of his sixteenth birthday, Ralph beat Bazo for the first time. They fought behind the thatched beehive huts that the Matabele had built on the open veld beyond Zouga's camp.

It started light-heartedly, Bazo the instructor, hectoring his pupil, executing the weaving steps of the traditional combat with indolent grace like a sleepy black panther, a fighting stick held in each hand and flourished with studied artistry of movement to form a fluid screen from which a vicious cutting attack could be launched with either hand.

Ralph turned to face him so that they revolved smoothly as a balanced wheel, like a pair of trained dancers, and when they taunted each other Ralph's repartee was in fluent and colloquial Matabele. He was stripped to the waistband of his riding breeches, and his torso, which had at Zouga's orders been so long protected from the sun, was creamy pale; only his arms and the deep V at his throat were sun dark.

'I once had a pet baboon,' Bazo told him. 'It was an albino baboon, white as the moon, and so stupid it never learned even a simple trick. That baboon reminds me of somebody, though I cannot think who.'

Ralph smiled with his lips only, exposing square white teeth, but the black brows were joined above his nose. 'I am only surprised that a Matabele thought he could teach a baboon – surely it should be the other way around.'

Bazo jumped back and hooted, beginning the *giya* – the challenge dance of the warrior – leaping high and making the kerries sing in the air until they blurred like the wings of a sunbird in flight.

'Let us see if your sticks are as quick as your tongue,' he shouted; and then suddenly he was attacking, the song of the fighting sticks rising to a shriek as he cut for Ralph's knee, the shriek ending with a crack like a rifle shot as Ralph caught it on his guard; and instantly Bazo cut with the other hand, for the elbow and – crack – again as Ralph warded off the blow with his own kerrie.

The sticks clattered against each other in a rising tempo, and the circle of Matabele watchers encouraged them with the deep drawn-out 'Jee!' as a stroke was skilfully countered and turned into a hissing riposte to be countered in its turn.

Bazo broke first, jumping back with a light sheen of sweat turning his muscles to black velvet, his chest swelling and subsiding, his chuckle only slightly hoarse.

There should be a pause now, as the combatants circled each other again, in that stylized shuffling dance, trading light insults, catching breath, stooping to dry their hands in the dust to improve their grip on the sticks – but, not this time, for as Bazo broke and jumped back and for an instant dropped his right hand, so Ralph went in.

Even the pretence of a smile was gone from Ralph's mouth. His jaw was clenched, lumps of muscles knotted with determination beneath his ears. Bazo's right guard had dropped, and his attention had switched to the audience of Matabele faces, for whose benefit he was already composing the next jibe.

'Jee!' They shouted encouragement and warning, and Bazo tried desperately to raise his guard and swivel to face the unexpected attack. He managed a touch of stick against stick, just enough to cushion the blow, otherwise it would have broken bone. Ralph's kerrie smashed into the point of his shoulder, and abruptly it was no longer a game.

The blow to Bazo's shoulder raised a welt as thick as a finger across the muscle, and almost paralysed the arm to the fingertips. So as he caught Ralph's next cut he felt the kerrie jerk and turn in his numb fingers, almost breaking his grip, and the shock of it was transferred into the abused muscle so that he grunted involuntarily, a little grunt of agony that seemed only to goad Ralph.

His sun-dark features were a mask of fighting fury, his eyes cold and green, and little droplets of sweat flew from his long black hair with the force of every blow that he swung.

The Matabele had never seen him like this, but they recognized the killing madness, for they had themselves all been in battle and killed, and it infected them so that they danced and stamped with excitement and spurred Ralph with their voices.

'Jee!' they sang, and Bazo fell back, giving ground to Ralph's attack as the sticks cracked and rattled. His mouth was wide open now as he gasped for air and his throat was a deep pink cavern. Blood ran in a thin shining slick down behind his ear, spreading over his straining throat and then onto his right shoulder like a mantle. A glancing blow above his eye had not opened the flesh, but had formed a blister of black blood as large as a walnut under the skin. It hung from Bazo's forehead like some bizarre bloodsucking leech, and still the blows hissed and cracked about him, thick as tropical rain, falling on his guard so that the shock was carried through arm and shoulder and jarred his head upon the thick black column of his neck.

Then another blow went through and the ivory flash of Bazo's teeth was dulled with a film of blood that snaked down from one nostril into his mouth, and another blow went through, on the line of his thigh, the swelling rising instantaneously, the skin stretched glossy and black, and almost crippled Bazo who was pinned by the injured leg – and Ralph was still attacking, instinctively swinging him against the bad leg so that Bazo was slow and clumsy in the turn, and again one of Ralph's sticks fluted and thumped into rubbery muscle and Bazo reeled and almost went down, recovering with an immense effort, his counter-stroke loose and lacking power, so that Ralph spurned it aside and used his point.

He drove the end of his right-hand kerrie through Bazo's guard, using it as though it were a sword rather than a club, and Bazo was not ready for it. With all Ralph's weight behind it, the kerrie tore into Bazo's belly muscles, up under the heavy ribcage, and the Matabele doubled over the blow, one kerrie flying from his hand the other dropping to dangle uselessly at his side.

He dropped on his knees, head bowed to expose the back of his neck, the knuckles of his spine standing out between the ridges of hard black muscle.

Ralph's eyes were fastened on the unprotected neck, and they were glazed over with the same soapy sheen as an uncut diamond, his movements too swift to be anything but instinctive. He threw the kerrie on high and shifted his weight from the back foot to the leading foot, and all his strength flowed into his back and shoulders as he went into the killing stroke.

'Jee!' roared the watchers, themselves carried beyond the frontiers of sanity on the hot wave of fighting madness, crowding forward for the death.

Ralph froze like that, right arm high, his entire body arched like a drawn bow, the fallen Matabele at his feet – and then slowly the tension went out of his limbs and he shook his head with the fumbling uncertainty of a man awaking from a nightmare. He looked about him with stunned disbelief, blinking his eyes as though to clear them of that opaque glittering madness, and suddenly his legs were trembling, unable to hold his weight. He sank down in front of Bazo, knelt facing him and put out one arm and wrapped it around the Matabele's neck, and laid his cheek against Bazo's.

'God,' he whispered. 'Oh God – I nearly killed you.'

Their blood and their sweat mingled, and both of them were pumping for air, their chests heaving, their bodies racked for the precious stuff.

'Never teach an albino baboon a trick,' Bazo spoke at last, his voice was husky and unsteady. 'He might learn it a little too well.'

Then they were dragged to their feet by the laughing, hooting Matabele and carried to the nearest hut.

Ralph drank first from the calabash of gruel – thick bubbling millet beer – and then handed it across to Bazo.

Bazo washed the blood from his mouth and spat it on the ground, then he drank with his head tilted back, a dozen deep swallows before he lowered the gourd and looked at Ralph.

For a moment they were grave, green eyes holding the gaze of smouldering black, and then suddenly they were both laughing, great gusts of shaking uncontrolled laughter, so that the men that squatted in the circle about them began to chuckle also, and then to laugh with them.

Still laughing, Bazo leaned across and gripped Ralph's right forearm briefly. 'I am your man,' he said, through his laughter, and through the blood in his mouth.

When Zouga stepped off the ladder in the bottom level of the Devil's Own, the heat was already enough to bring out a dark patch of sweat between the shoulder blades of his blue flannel shirt. He lifted his hat to mop the dewdrops along his hairline and then paused and frowned quickly.

'Ralph!' he snapped, and his son sank the pickhead into the yellow gravel, let it stand like that and then straightened with his hands on his hips.

'Just what do you think you are doing?' Zouga demanded.

'I've worked out a new way of doing it,' Ralph told him. 'First Bazo's gang breaks rock, then Wengi comes along behind and–'

'You know what I'm talking about.' Zouga cut in impatiently. 'It's Monday; you are supposed to be at school.'

'I'm sixteen now,' Ralph told him. 'And besides, I know how to read and to write.'

'Don't you think you might have mentioned your decision,' Zouga asked with deceptive mildness, 'if only in passing?'

'You were busy, Papa, I didn't want to worry you with something so unimportant. You've got enough to worry about without that.'

Zouga hesitated. Was that just his usual clever twisting, or did Ralph truly realize how finely stretched they were, just how much Zouga truly did have to worry about?

Ralph sensed his advantage. 'We need every pair of hands we can get, and these are free.' He held them up, and Zouga noticed for the first time that they were powerful and broad with yellow callouses on the palms.

'Just what is this new idea of yours?' Zouga's scowl smoothed away, and Ralph grinned as he realized that he was no longer a schoolboy; and he began to explain, gesturing with spread hands while Zouga nodded.

'All right,' he said at last. 'It makes sense. We'll try it.'

Zouga turned and walked away, and Ralph spat on his hands and shouted in Matabele.

'Come on, you are not a bunch of women hoeing for yams; let's break ground.'

*

On Claim No. 183 an American digger named Calvin Hine hit an enrichment, a tiny pocket, and in a single bucket he took out two hundred and sixteen diamonds, the biggest over twenty carats. In a stroke he was transformed from a ragged, bearded sun-blackened beggar grovelling in the yellow dust into a rich man.

Calvin was there that night when Diamond Lil climbed up onto the wooden counter of her grog-shop, with her ostrich feathers swirling and her sequins aglitter in the lamplight. She asked in Cockney that chimed like Bow Bells:

'Will some sporting gent name me a price for these fancy goods?' and squeezed out her own big round breasts between painted red fingertips, so that they bulged over the top of her crimson velvet bodice, the skin smoother than the velvet and the big pink coin of a nipple coming up like the dawn over the horizon of her neckline.

'Come on, dearies, one night of paradise, one little glimpse of heaven, me loves.'

'Tenner, Lil darling. Ten iron men,' shouted a digger at the back of the bar, and Lil turned and flipped up the back of her skirts at him.

'Shame on you, for a mean little man,' she chided him over her white shoulder; and the laced and beribboned pantaloons beneath her rustling skirts had no crotch to them, so for a fleeting part of a second they saw what she was selling, and bellowed like trek-oxen five days in the desert when they smell the waterhole.

'Lil, my beauty.' Calvin climbed unsteadily onto the packing case that acted as a table. He had been drinking since noon when he left the kopje-walloper's office. 'Lily, the moon of my soul,' he crooned, 'every night for a year and more I dreamed of this moment.'

He dug into the back pocket of his coat and held up a fistful of crumpled five-pound notes.

'I don't know how much that is,' he blurted, 'but it's yours.'

For a moment Lily's plucked and pencilled eyebrows contracted as she made a rapid calculation of the proffered wad of banknotes; and then she smiled so that the tiny diamond set in her front tooth sparkled like the evening star.

'You beautiful boy,' she sang. 'Tonight I am your bride. Take me in your arms, my lover.'

The next day someone took a thirty carat stone on the eastern section, a lovely white stone of the first water, and the day after that a huge champagne-coloured diamond came from Neville Pickering's block.

'You'll be leaving now?' Zouga asked him when they met on the roadway above the Devil's Own, and he hoped that the envy did not show in his smile.

'No.' Pickering shook his head, and answered with his own charming sunny smile. 'I always bet on a winning streak. My partner and I are staying in the game.'

It seemed that the diamond god was intent on showering sudden largesse on the New Rush, and a fever of expectation and excitement gripped them all so that the great pit at noon sounded like a hive of wild bees when the acacia forests are in yellow bloom. Three great finds in three days; nobody had seen it happen before.

At night around the camp fires, and in the lantern-lit grog-shops and canteens, the wild theories were aired by dusty diggers drunk on bad liquor and reborn hope.

'It's a stratal enrichment,' pontificated one. 'It's a layer of fat babies right across the kopje. You mark my words, somebody will take a pony before the week is out.'

'Hell no,' argued another. 'The stones are lying in pot-holes. Some lucky bastard is going to scoop the pot again, like Calvin's two one six or Pickering's monkey.'

Thursday night of the crazy week it rained. Here on the fringes of the Kalahari desert the rainfall was less than twenty inches a year. They had almost half of that on that single night.

The rain was a slanting curtain of silver arrow shafts in the brilliant crackling blue flare of the lighting. The clouds piled to the heavens banged against one another like fighting bulls, mountainous in the lightning bursts, and the thunder jarred the earth while the rain hissed down.

In the dawn it was still raining, and at another time the diggers might have stayed out of the pit and waited for it to dry out. But not on this day, not with the fierce excitement that gripped the entire settlement. That day nothing would keep them out of the pit.

The diggings were greasy with yellow mud. The lowest claims were knee deep with the insidious clinging stuff. It coated the bare legs of the black workmen to the thigh; it built up in mud bricks on the boots of the white overseers, weighing them down like convicts shackled to a ball and chain.

The thick red mud on the roadways clogged the wheels of the gravel carts and had to be prised clear with the point of a crowbar. They shovelled the slush into the buckets and as they were hoisted the thin watery mud cascaded down on the men below, so that it was no longer possible to tell black man from white behind their slick and glistening yellow masks.

What none of the men in the workings realized was that, apart from the discomfort and filth that the downpour of the night's thunderstorms had brought to the pit, they had created a less obvious but infinitely graver change in the riddled remains of Colesberg kopje.

The rushing rivulets had found a fissure at the neck of No. 6 Roadway and had poured into it, carving and cutting and weakening; and the slimy yellow mud had hidden the deep vertical cracks in the hundred-foot high earthen embankment.

There were sixteen mule carts crowded onto the causeway, most of them fully laden with the first load of the morning, the drivers swearing at each other, the long trek whips firing explosively as they tried to clear a path to get their load out to the waiting cradles.

Down on the Devil's Own the Matabele teams were working side by side, but the icy sting of the rain on bare shoulders and backs slowed the swing of the picks, and at each forward pace they slithered and slipped in the treacherous footing. The work chant sounded like a dirge; Zouga snarled at them to keep them moving, and the mood was ugly.

Up on the roadway an overladen gravel cart began to slide sideways in the mud, and the wheeler mule was pulled down on his knees, unable to hold it. The off wheel dropped over the edge, and the cart sagged drunkenly and then hung out over the pit. The team slewed across the narrow causeway in tangled traces while the unequal weight of gravel snapped the outer axle of the cart. Zouga's cart was directly behind the stranded team, facing in the same direction, and Ralph jumped down off the driver's seat and shouted furiously.

'You damned fool – you've jammed us in.'

'You cheeky puppy,' the driver of the bogged-down vehicle yelled back. 'You need a lick of the whip across your backside.'

Immediately half a dozen diggers were joining in, taking sides, shouting advice or abuse.

'Cut the traces, get those bloody animals off the roadway.'

'Dump the gravel out, you're overloaded.'

'You don't touch my rig,' yelled the driver of the stricken cart. Ralph had drawn the sheath knife from his belt and run forward.

'That's the ticket, Ralph.'

'That little blighter needs a lesson.'

Men and vehicles and mud-smeared beasts formed an angry, unstable knot at the top of the high earthen wall. In the bottom of the diggings, Zouga threw his head back and cupped his hands to his mouth.

'Ralph!' he bellowed. He could see how dangerous the tangle had become. Tempers were flaring; he could sense how close they were to mortal danger as fighting men lost control of panicking animals.

In the uproar Zouga's voice was almost drowned, and if Ralph heard him, he gave no sign of doing so. He was kneeling beside the downed wheel mule, hacking at the thongs of the traces with his sheath knife.

'Get away from there,' howled the driver, and reared back, the long trek whip flying out high above his shoulders and then snaking forward, twenty feet long, whispering like the wing of a wild duck in flight.

Ralph saw it, and ducked behind the mule's heavy barrel-like body; the lash exploded in the air like a bursting grenade, and the mule lunged wildly, swinging the disselboom of the cart across the causeway so that the broken axle collapsed before the snapping of the half-severed leather thongs allowed the mule to regain its feet and then gallop away down the muddy track to firmer ground.

Ralph leaned out and ran to his own team. He called to his wheeler mule, 'Pull, Bishop!' The wheels sucked and farted in the mud as Ralph drove them at the narrow gap, the stranded cart on one side, sprawled half across the track, on the other the sheer unguarded drop into the open workings.

'Ha, Rosie!' Ralph grabbed the bridle of the lead mule and, running at her head, guided her into the gap.

'Ralph, damn you!' Zouga roared. 'Stop! Do you hear me, stop!'

But he was a helpless spectator. It would take five minutes or longer to reach the causeway across the complicated system of ladderworks and board walks. There was nothing he could do to prevent the developing tragedy.

The infuriated owner of the stranded cart was still on the body of the vehicle, brandishing his long whip and howling with anger and frustration. He was not a big man, an inch or so shorter than Ralph – but heavy in the shoulder and the belly, not flabby fat but work-braided muscle, and his hands on the stock of the whip were rough as oak bark, baked by the sun and scoured by gravel and the haft of pick and shovel.

'I'll settle your account, you little bugger,' he shouted, and again threw back the whip; again Ralph ducked under the flailing lash, but it caught the sleeve of his faded and patched shirt, splitting the rotted material and opening the skin of Ralph's upper arm in a thin red razor cut from which the bright blood bloomed instantly.

Rising from his crouch in the mud, Ralph placed one hand on the wheel mule's withers and used his own impetus and the leverage of his arm to leap high in the air. It was a trick that Jan Cheroot had taught him, the way a good teamsman crosses from one side of the span to another. In mid-air Ralph tucked his legs and swung his body, vaulting cleanly over the mules' backs and landing on the far side of the team alongside the leading wheel. His next jump carried him onto the truck of the cart, and with the same movement he had snatched his own long trek whip from its slot beside the brake handle.

The handle was ten feet long, and the tapered lash another twenty. A skilled teamsman could cut a fly off the tip of the lead mule's ear with the lash, and Jan Cheroot had trained Ralph: he was good with the whip, very good.

Ralph's lips were a thin chalky white line, his eyes green and furious. The sting of the whip had driven him into murderous, unthinking rage.

'Ralph!' Zouga shouted vainly. He had seen his son like this before. It frightened him. 'Ralph! Stop!'

Standing high on the cart bed Ralph shot the lash out to full stretch behind him. It was an easy graceful movement like a salmon fisherman putting up the fly, and in the same action he brought the tip of the whip stock forward, all wrist and shoulders, and the lash whined and reached out to the other driver.

It cut him like a sword stroke, from breast to belt buckle, and only the heavy wet oilskin he wore protected him from serious injury. The torn fabric flapped about his body, and the rain diluted the dribble of blood from the shallow wound.

Ralph's mules swung from the crack of the whip, and the off wheel hooked that of the stranded cart, locking both vehicles hopelessly in the soft mud.

Ralph was too close now to the other driver to stretch the lash, and he reversed the whip stock, using it like a club, and swung it at the man's head.

Below them in the diggings, the Matabele were encouraging their favourite with the fighting 'Jee!' and it goaded Ralph. He was quicker than the other driver, nimble to avoid his swinging stock, using his own like the fighting sticks with which he had trained so assiduously.

The mules were panicked by the uproar, the crack of whips, the Matabele war chant, the shrieked insults and the bellow of the watchers.

Rosie reared and cut with her fore-hooves, whinnying hysterically, and her team mate lunged and struggled against the jammed off wheel.

Bishop shirked the yoke, turned from it; his hind legs scrabbled on the crumbling edge of the causeway and he went over, hanging in the tangle of reins and chains, kicking and pawing at the air and shrieking wildly.

Then quite gently, like a sleeper awaking from deep slumber, the yellow earthen causeway shook itself.

The movement started below the wheels of the locked carts and the trampling hooves of the terrified mules – and then it rippled along the embankment to the neck where it joined the rim of the pit – and at that point a deep vertical crack opened miraculously in the muddy yellow wall. It opened with only a soft wet sound like an infant suckling at the breast, but it silenced the shouting, chanting men who watched.

Suddenly the only sound in the open diggings was the rustle of the falling rain and the shrieks of the dangling mule. On the cart Ralph stood poised like a Greek statue of an athlete, the whip stock thrown back, the cords in his throat relaxing, the insane rage in his green eyes clearing to leave a bemused expression of disbelief; for beneath his feet the earth was moving.

'Ralph!' This time Zouga's voice reached him clearly, and he looked down into the pit, saw their faces, the shock, the terror upon them.

'Run!' shouted Zouga, and the urgency galvanized Ralph. 'Get off the roadway.'

Ralph threw the whip aside and jumped down off the cart. The sheath knife in his hand again.

The rein that held Bishop, the big grey mule, was stretched tight as an iron bar. It parted cleanly to the touch of the blade and the mule dropped free, twisting in the air so that the men below scattered away, and the heavy body smacked into the mud. Then the beast scrambled to its feet and stood trembling miserably, belly deep in the yellow mud that had saved it.

The earth trembled like jelly under Ralph's feet as he hacked at the traces that held the other three mules and the moment they were free of the trapped cart he drove them ahead of him along the causeway, yelling them into a gallop. The yellow mud shook and tilted as the cracks yawned open, and the entire causeway began to sag.

'Run, you bloody fool,' Ralph panted at the man he had been fighting, as he stood in the rain and looked about him, the tattered oilskins dangling about his legs, his expression bewildered.

'Come on, run,' and Ralph grabbed his arm and dragged him after the galloping mule team.

One after another the gantries that lined the roadway, some of them with the huge buckets still hanging from the sheaves, began to topple over into the pit, the timber crackling and twisting, the ropes tangling and snapping like strands of cotton.

Ahead of Ralph the three yoked mules reached firm ground and galloped away, whisking their tails and kicking out skittishly at relief from their burden.

The causeway tilted and sagged, so that suddenly Ralph seemed to be running up a steep hill. The driver beside him missed his footing and went down on his knees, and then as he started to slide backwards he threw himself face down and spread his arm as though to hug the earth.

'Get up.' Ralph checked his own run, and stood over him.

Behind them the earth growled like a voracious animal, moving gravel grinding upon itself; and there were still fourteen carts out on the collapsing causeway. Half a dozen of the drivers had abandoned their teams and were running back along the trembling, sagging roadway, but they had left it too late. They stopped in a little group. Some of them fell flat and clung to the earth. One turned and leapt boldly from the edge into the gaping pit.

He plugged into the mud, and three black workers seized him and dragged him to safety, a broken leg twisting and slithering over the mud behind him.

One of the laden carts, with four mules in the traces, toppled over and, as it hit the bottom of the diggings, the weight of gravel shattered it to ragged splinters of raw white wood, and a shaggy black mule impaled on the disselboom screamed with shockingly human agony and kicked wildly, tearing out its own entrails from the gaping wound in its flank.

Ralph stooped and dragged the driver to his feet, pulling him up the steepening incline, but the man was semi-paralysed by terror and hampered by the flapping tails of his heavy oilskins.

The centre of the roadway cracked through abruptly and a hundred feet of it collapsed sideways with a swift rumbling rush, hurling carts and animals into the pit as though from some gigantic catapult.

Ralph glanced once over his shoulder at the terrifying carnage and saw that the whole roadway was going, starting from that centre point and running swiftly towards him, a breaking wave of soft yellow earth seeming to be of some thick and viscid fluid, breaking with that grinding whisper.

'Come on,' Ralph grunted at the man on his arm, and suddenly the earth beneath their feet lunged the other way, throwing them forward towards the rim of the pit – and safety.

They went forward with a rush, the driver clutching at Ralph's shoulder for support. A dozen paces to go to firm ground, and Ralph did not look back again. The hideous sounds from the pit were unnerving, and he sensed that another glimpse of that onrushing wave of collapsing earth might paralyse his own legs.

'Come on,' he gasped. 'We'll make it – almost there. Come on!' And as he said it the earth opened in front of their feet as though from a giant's axe stroke. It opened with a smacking sound, as of kissing lips, and the mouth of it was sheer, eighty feet deep and three feet across, but in the brief seconds that they tottered on the edge it gaped wider, six feet, eight feet, and the causeway tilted sideways – the final convulsion.

'Jump!' said Ralph. 'Jump for it, man.' And he shoved the driver at it, forcing him at that frightful crack that seemed to split the earth to its very core.

The man stumbled off balance, his arms waving wildly for control, and then he made a clumsy scrambling leap out over the drop. The torn oilskins tangled with his limbs and fluttered about his head. He hit the far lip of the crack with his chest, his legs hanging into the drop and kicking hopelessly, and clawed at the muddy lip. But there was no purchase and inexorably he began to slide backwards.

Ralph knew there was no chance of making a run-up to the jump. He had to take it from a standstill, and it was gaping wider with every second, ten feet or more now – and the quivering bank of collapsing earth was an unstable platform.

He sank on one knee, steadied himself with a clenched fist against the earth, and then straightened his legs and body in a sudden burst of energy like a released coil-spring, jumping high because the causeway had already sagged below the level of the rim.

The power of that leap surprised even Ralph; he cleared the driver's wriggling body and landed deep, on firm and rock-steady ground, stumbled with his own forward impetus and then ran on half a dozen paces.

Behind him the driver wailed and slid back a few inches, and around his spread fingers opened a mesh of smaller cracks, running parallel to the gaping sheer line. Ralph spun and ran back. He threw himself flat and reached for the driver's wrist. It was greasy with mud, slippery as a freshly netted trout, and he knew he could not hold him for long.

Over the driver's head Ralph stared down into the diggings. He watched the final collapse of the causeway, a massive rush of earth, some of it liquid mud, mixed with huge chunks of compacted gravel that ground together like the jaws of some mindless monster, crushing and smothering men and animals between them.

The entire No. 6 Roadway was gone, and across the floor of the pit, deep dark cracks spread out like a grotesque spider's web.

In the bottom of the diggings the figures of men seemed frail and insectlike, their cries feeble and without consequence, their pathetic scurrying without purpose.

Ralph suddenly recognized his father. He alone was standing firm, his head thrown back, and even across that dizzy space Ralph could feel the strength of his gaze.

'Hold on, boy!' Zouga's voice carried faintly above the pandemonium. 'They're coming. Hold on!'

But under Ralph's belly the earth whispered and shrugged impatiently and the driver's weight pulled him another inch towards the drop.

'Hold on, Ralph!'

Across that aching breathless space Zouga was reaching out with both hands, a gesture that was more eloquent than *any words* – a gesture of suffering and helpless love.

Then suddenly Ralph felt rough hands seize the ankles of his muddy boots, the shouts of many men behind him, the rasp of a hairy manila rope against his cheek, the noose dangling in front of his face – and with a huge surge of relief he saw the dangling driver thrust his free arm through the noose and saw it drawn tight.

Ralph could let the muddy wrist slip from his grip, and he crawled back from the edge.

He looked down at his father. It was too far for either of them to see the expression on each other's face.

For a moment longer Zouga stared up at him. Then he turned away abruptly, his stride businesslike, his gestures imperative as he ordered his Matabele forward to the rescue work.

The rescue went on all that day. For once every digger on New Rush was united by a common purpose.

The Diggers' Committee closed the workings and ordered every man out of the unaffected areas. The five other roadways that had not collapsed were declared out of bounds to all traffic and they stood high and menacing in the silver clouds of drifting rain.

On the churned and collapsed remnants of No. 6 Roadway the rescuers swarmed. These were the men who had been trapped on the floor by the severed ladderworks and the fallen system of gantries.

There were no members of the Committee in the No. 6 area, and Zouga Ballantyne with his natural air of authority was quickly accepted as the leader. He had marked the position of the gravel carts and drivers on the roadway at the moment of the cave-in, and he split the available men into gangs and set them to digging where he guessed men and vehicles were buried. They attacked the treacherous shapeless mass of earth with a passion which was a mixture of hatred and stale fear, an expression of their own relief at having escaped that smothering, entombing yellow cascade.

For the first hour they dug men out alive, some miraculously protected by an overturned cart or the body of a dead mule. One of these survivors rose shakily to his feet unaided when the earth was shovelled away, and the rescuers cheered him with a kind of wild hysteria.

Three mules had survived the drop (one of these was Zouga's old grey Bishop) but others were fearfully mutilated by the wrecked carts. Someone lowered a pistol and a packet of cartridges from the ground level and Zouga slipped and slid from one team to the other and shot the unfortunate beasts as they lay screaming and kicking in the mud.

While this was going on there were teams of men busy above them at ground level. Under the direction of the Diggers' Committee they were rigging rope ladders and a makeshift gantry to bring up the dead and the injured. By noon that day they could begin taking the injured out, strapped to six-by-three timber boards and hoisted on the new gantry, swaying up the high wall of the pit.

Then they began to find the dead men.

The last of the missing men was locked like a foetus into the cold muddy womb of the earth. Zouga and Bazo stooped shoulder to shoulder into the mouth of the excavation, seized the limp wrist that protruded from the bank and, straining together, freed the corpse. It came out in a rush of slippery mud, like the moment of birth, but the man's limbs were convulsed in *rigor mortis* and his eye sockets packed with mud. Other hands lifted the corpse and carried it away, and Zouga flexed his back and groaned. Cold and weariness had tied knots in his muscles.

'We are not finished yet,' he said, and the young Matabele nodded.

'What is there still to do?' he asked simply, and Zouga felt a rush of gratitude and affection towards him. He placed his hand on Bazo's shoulder and for a moment they considered each other gravely, then Bazo asked again, 'What must be done?'

'The roadway is gone. There will be no work on these claims – not for a long time,' Zouga explained, his voice dulled and his hand dropping wearily from Bazo's shoulder. 'If we leave any tools or equipment down here, they will be stolen.'

They had lost the gravel cart, the hoist with its iron sheave wheels and valuable rope, and the gravel buckets.

Zouga sighed, and the fatigue swept over him like a cold dark wave. There was no money to replace those essentials. 'We must save what we can from the vultures.'

Bazo called to his men in their own language and led them along the shapeless bank of broken earth from which protruded shattered pieces of equipment and tangles of sodden rope, to the deserted Devil's Own claims.

The fallen roadway had buried the eastern corner of No. 142, but the rest of the claims were clear. However, a pressure crack had opened in a deep zigzag across the floor and some of Zouga's equipment had fallen into it and lay half submerged in muddy water.

Bazo clambered down into the fissure and groped for the mess of rope and tools, passing it up to the Matabele on the bank above his head. Here Zouga supervised them as they tied the tools into bundles and then staggered away with them to the high eastern bank, there to wait their turn for the single functioning gantry to hoist the bundles out to ground level.

As they worked the last pale rays of the sun pierced the mass of low cloud and struck down into the huge man-made pit.

In the bottom of the fissure Bazo found the last missing pick, passed it up, and then leaned against the bank to rest for a few moments. He felt that he no longer had the strength to climb out of the deep crack. The cold had numbed his legs and softened his skin until it was wrinkled and water-logged like that of a drowned man. He shivered and laid his forehead on his arm, bracing himself against the bank of yellow earth. He felt that if he closed his eyes he would fall asleep on his feet.

He kept them open with an effort, and stared at the earth in front of his face. A trickle of rainwater was still running down from the level above his head; it had cut a narrow runnel a few inches wide and deep. Most of the mud had settled out of this little streamlet, and it was almost clear, only slightly milked with colour.

At one point in its trickle down the mud wall it had encountered an obstacle, and was pouring over it, forming a little plume of running water.

Suddenly Bazo was thirsty. His throat was rough and dry. He leaned forward, and let the trickle flow over his lips and tongue, and then slurped a mouthful.

The watery sun touched the bank, and a strange brilliant light flared inches from Bazo's face. It came pouring up, powerful and pure and dancing white, from the tiny freshet from which he was drinking.

He stared at it dully, and slowly it dawned upon him that the obstruction over which the water was pouring was something embedded in the gravel bank, something that glowed and flickered as the random beam of sunlight played upon it, something that seemed to change shape and substance through the trickling yellow-tinged waters.

He touched it with his forefinger, and the cold water ran down his forearm and dripped from his elbow. He tried to work it loose, but it was firmly implanted, and soapy feeling in his raw numb fingers so that he could not get a fair grip upon it.

He took the buckhorn whistle from around his neck and used the point to prise the pretty fiery object loose, and it dropped heavily into the raw pink palm of his hand, almost filling it.

It was a stone, but a stone such as he had never seen before. He held it under the trickle of rainwater, and with his thumb rubbed off the clinging mud until it was clean. Then he looked at it again, turning it curiously in the weak sunlight.

Until Bazo had arrived at New Rush he had never thought about rocks and stones as being different from one another, any more than one drop of water differed from another or one cloud in the sky was more valuable or useful than the others. The Matabele language did not differentiate between a granite pebble and a diamond, they were both simply 'imitshe'. Only the white men's maniacal obsession with stones had made him look at them afresh.

In all these months he had spent toiling in the diggings, he had seen many strange things and learned much of the white men and their ways. At first he had not been able to believe the extraordinary value they placed on the most trivial items. That a single pebble could be exchanged for six hundred head of prime cattle seemed some grotesque madman's dream, but at last he had seen that it was true and he and his little band of amadoda had become fanatical gatherers of pebbles. Every sparkling or coloured stone they had pounced upon like magpies and carried proudly to Bakela for their reward.

This initial enthusiasm had swiftly waned, for there was neither logic nor system in the white man's mind. The showiest stones were discarded contemptuously. Lovely shiny red and blue pebbles, some of them shot through with different colours like ceramic beads, Bakela handed back to them with a grunt and a shake of the head. While occasionally, very occasionally, he would select some dull and uninteresting little chip and hand the delighted finder a gold coin.

At first, payment in coin had confused the Matabele, but they learned fast. Those little metal discs could be exchanged in their turn for anything a man desired, as long as he had enough of them he could have a gun, or a horse, a woman or a fine ox.

Bakela had tried to explain to Bazo and his Matabele how to recognize the stones for which he would pay a red gold coin. Firstly, they were small, never much bigger than the seed of the camel-thorn tree.

Bazo considered the stone in his palm. It was huge; he could barely close his fingers over it. The stones that Bakela wanted were usually of a certain shape, a regular shape with eight sides, one for every finger less the thumbs. This huge stone was not so shaped. It had one clean side, as though cut through with a knife blade, and the rest of it was rounded and polished to a strange soapy sheen.

Bazo held it under the trickle of rainwater again, and when he brought it out the film of water that covered the surface instantly coagulated into little droplets and shrank away, leaving the stone dry and glittering.

That was strange, Bazo decided, but the stone was the wrong colour. Bakela had explained that they must look for pale lemon, or glossy grey, even brown colour. This stone was like looking into a clear pool in the mountains. He could see the shape of his own hand through it, and it was full of stars of moving light that hurled little darts of sunlight into his eyes as he turned it curiously. No, it was too big and much too pretty to be of value, Bazo decided.

'Bazo! *Checha*!' Bakela was calling him. 'Come on, let's go where we can eat and sleep.'

Bazo dropped the stone into the leather pouch at his waist and scrambled up out of the open fissure. Already the file of Matabele workers led by Zouga were plodding away through the mud, each of them bowed under a bundle of spades or picks, one of the big leather buckets or a coil of sodden muddy rope.

'He has the lives of six men on his hands. I was there, I saw it all happen. He drove his team into Mark Sanderson's gravel bucky.' The accuser was a tall digger with a huge shaggy head of greying hair, heavy shoulders and heavier paunch. He was working himself up into a boil of righteous indignation, and Zouga saw that it was infectious, the crowd was beginning to growl and surge restlessly around the wagon body.

The New Rush Diggers' Committee was in public session. Ten minutes previously they had formed themselves into a Board of Enquiry into the cave-in of No. 6 Roadway.

A wagon had been dragged into the centre of Market Square to provide a platform for their deliberations, and around it was a solid packed crowd of diggers from the No. 6 Section. Since the cave-in, they had not been able to get back into the diggings to work their claims and they had just come from the mass funeral of the six men that had been crushed to death by the treacherous yellow gravel. Most of them had begun the wake for their mates and were carrying uncorked green bottles.

Mixed with the diggers were all the loafers of New Rush, the transport riders and merchants; even the kopje-wallopers had closed their offices for the meeting. This was something that affected all their futures directly.

'Let's have a look at the little blighter,' somebody yelled out at the back of the crowd, and there was a menacing growl of agreement.

'Right, let's see him.'

Zouga stood beside the tall back wheel of the wagon, hemmed in by the press of bodies, and he glanced at Ralph who stood at his shoulder. He no longer had to look down at his son, their eyes were on a level.

'I'll go up and face them,' Ralph whispered huskily. Under the dark tan, his skin was grey and his eyes dark green and worried. He knew as well as Zouga did how grave was his position: he was to be tried by a mob that was angry and vindictive and mostly filled with cheap liquor.

The collapse of the roadway had destroyed the value of their claims. They could no longer get the gravel out; their claims were isolated, cut off from ground level, and they were spoiling to place the blame and extract vengeance. That vengeance would be brutal.

Ralph put one hand on the spokes of the wagon wheel, ready to climb up onto the wagon body where the dozen members of the Committee were already waiting.

'Ralph.' Zouga stopped him with a hand on his arm. 'Wait here.'

'Papa–' Ralph began to protest quietly, the fear still dark in his eyes.

'Stay,' Zouga repeated softly, and vaulted up onto the wagon body lightly.

He nodded briefly to the members of the Committee and then turned to face the mob. He was bare-headed, his beard catching the sunlight and jutting aggressively as he placed his clenched fists on his hips and set his feet easily apart.

'Gentlemen,' he said, and his voice carried clearly to the last row of the crowd, 'my son is only sixteen years old. I am here to answer for him.'

'If he's old enough to kill six men, then he's old enough to face the music himself.'

'He killed nobody,' Zouga answered coldly. 'If you look to place the blame, then put it on the rain. Go down to the pit, and you will see where it undercut the bank.'

'He started fighting,' the shaggy-headed accuser bellowed. 'I saw him use his whip on Mark Sanderson.'

'There is a fight on one of the causeways every hour of every day,' Zouga shot at him. 'I've seen you throwing punches out there, and getting your arse whipped at that.'

There was a ripple of laughter, a lightening of the mood, and Zouga took his advantage.

'In the name of all that's holy, gentlemen, there is not one of us here who does not protect his rights. My son was doing that, against a man older and stronger than himself, and if he's guilty for that, then so are all of you.'

They liked that, liked being told they were tough and independent, proud of being hard fighters and hard livers.

'Are you telling me that one boy with a trek whip brought down the No. 6 causeway all on his own? If so, then I'm proud that boy is my son.'

They laughed again, and on the wagon behind Zouga the tall blond untidily dressed man with the cleft chin and pale blue eyes smiled thoughtfully and murmured to the Committee member beside him.

'He's good, Pickling,' using Neville Pickering's familiar nickname. 'He talks as well as he writes, and that's well enough.'

'No, gentlemen,' Zouga changed pace. 'That causeway was a death-trap, ready to go off before the first gravel bucky went out on it Friday morning. The collapse was nobody's fault; we had just dug too deep, and there was too much rain.'

Heads were nodding now, their expressions concerned and grave as Zouga went on.

'We are too deep on the New Rush, and unless we work out a new system of getting the stuff out of our claims, then there are going to be a lot more dead men for us to bury.'

Zouga glanced down as one of the diggers shouldered his way through the crowd and climbed up onto the disselboom of the wagon.

'Now you pay attention, you bunch of dirt-hounds,' he yelled.

'The chair acknowledges Mister Sanderson,' Neville Pickering murmured sarcastically.

'Thanking you, Guv.' The digger lifted his battered Derby hat, finery that he had donned especially for this meeting, then turned and scowled at the crowd. 'This nipper of Zouga Ballantyne's is going to be a bad one to mess with, and a good one to have at your side when things get hard.' Still scowling, he turned and called to Ralph. 'You come up here, young Ballantyne.'

Still pale and worried, Ralph hung back, but rough hands pushed him forward and hoisted him onto the wagon.

The digger had to reach up to put his arm around Ralph's shoulder.

'This boy could have let me drop into the pit like a rotten tomato, and squash the same way when I hit the bottom.' He made a vaguely obscene squelching sound with his lips to illustrate his own demise. 'He could have run and left me, but he didn't.'

'That's 'cause he's young and stupid,' someone called. 'If he had any sense he'd have given you a shove, you miserable bastard.'

There was a hubbub of cheers and hooted derision.

'I'm going to buy this boy a drink,' announced Sanderson belligerently.

'That will be some sort of record. You ain't never bought nobody a drink yet.'

Sanderson ignored them haughtily. 'Just as soon as he turns eighteen, I'm going to buy him a drink.'

The meeting started to break up in a storm of friendly catcalls and laughter, the diggers streaming away across the square to the canteens.

It was obvious to even the most bloody-minded of them that there wasn't going to be a lynching, and hardly any of them bothered to wait for the Committee's verdict. It was more important to get a good place at the bar.

'Which doesn't mean we approve of your behaviour, young man,' Pickering told Ralph severely. 'This isn't Bultfontein or Dutoitspan. Here on New Rush we try to set an example to the other diggings. In future, do try and behave like a gentleman. I mean fists are one thing, but whips–' He raised one eyebrow disdainfully and turned to Zouga. 'If you have any ideas about how we are going to work the No. 6 area now that the causeway has gone, we'd like to hear them, Major Ballantyne.'

Hendrick Naaiman would have called himself a 'Bastaard', and would have used the term with a deep sense of pride. However, the British Foreign Office had found the word awkward, possibly the double 'A' in the spelling offended the proper order of official correspondence and treaties, especially if one of those treaties should ever be laid for signature before Queen Victoria. So the nation was now referred to as Griqua, and the land on which New Rush stood was renamed Griqualand West, a definition which made it easier for Whitehall to champion old Nicholaas Waterboer, the Bastaard captain's claim to the area, over that of the Boer presidents of the backveld republics which also claimed the area as part of their dominions.

It was remarkable how before the discovery of the bright stones nobody, and especially not Great Britain, had shown the slightest interest in this desolate and arid plain, no matter what it was called.

In Hendrick Naaiman's veins flowed the rich intermingled blood of numerous peoples.

Its basis was that of the Hottentot, the sturdy golden-skinned, dark-eyed people who had met the first Portuguese circumnavigators of the globe when they stepped onto the gleaming white beach sands of Good Hope.

Added to the Hottentot was the blood of the captured yellow bushman girls. Tiny doll-like creatures whose buttery yellow skins and dainty triangular faces with orientally slanted eyes and flattened pug features were only part of their attraction. To a people who regarded a large female posterior as a mark of beauty, the buttocks of the bushmen girls were irresistible, a bountiful double bulge that stood out behind them like the hump of a camel – and in the arid deserts of the Kalahari served the same purpose.

To this blood mixture was added the contribution of outcast Fingo and Pondo tribesmen, fugitives from the wiles of their own cruel chiefs and merciless witchdoctors, and Malayan slaves, escaped from their Dutch burgher masters, who had found their way through the secret passes of the mountains that defended the Cape of Good Hope like the turreted walls of a great castle. They also joined the bands of wandering Griquas on the vast plains of the interior.

This blood mixture was compounded with that of little English girls, orphaned survivors of shipwrecked East India men that had perished on the treacherous rocks scoured by the Agulhas current, and taken to wife at puberty by their darker-skinned rescuers. And there was other northern blood, that of British seamen, pressed into the Royal Navy's service in the time of Napoleon's wars and desperate to exchange that harsh duty even for the life of deserter in such a wild and desert land as Southern Africa. Others had fled into the same wilderness, escaped convicts from the transport ships that had called at Good Hope to reprovision for the long eastern leg of the voyage to Australia and penal settlement of Botany Bay.

Then came travelling Jewish pedlars, Scottish missionaries taking God's injunction 'Be fruitful' as their text for the day – riders on commando, collecting slaves and taking others of the traditional spoils of war in a dusty donga or behind a thorn bush under the inscrutable African sky. The old hunters had passed this way at the century's turn, and had paused in their pursuit of the great elephant herds to take on more tender game at closer range.

These were Hendrick Naaiman's ancestors. He was a Bastaard and proud of it. He had dark gypsy ringlets that dangled to the collar of his tanned buckskin jacket. His teeth were square and strong and starred with tiny white specks from drinking the lime-rich waters of the Karroo wells since childhood.

His eyes were black as tarpits, and his toffee-coloured skin thickly sown with the darker coin-like scars of smallpox, for his white ancestors had bestowed upon the tribe many of the other virtues of civilization: gunpowder, alcohol and more than one variety of the pox.

Despite the scarring, Hendrick was a handsome man, tall, broadshouldered, with long powerful legs, flashing black eyes and a sunny smile. He squatted across the fire from Bazo now, with his wide-brimmed hat still on his head; the ostrich feathers nodded and swirled above the flat crown as he gestured widely, laughing and talking persuasively.

'Only the ant-bear and the meercat dig in the earth for no reward more than a mouthful of insects.' Naaiman spoke in fluent Zulu, which was close enough to their own tongue for the Matabele to follow him readily. 'Do these hairy white-faced creatures own all the earth and everything upon and beneath it? Are they then some kind of magical creature, some god from the heavens that they can say to you "I own every stone in the earth, every drop of water in the—" ' Hendrick paused, for he was about to say oceans, but he knew that his audience had never seen the sea, " ' – every drop of water in the rivers and lakes." '

Hendrick shook his head so that the ringlets danced on his cheeks. 'I tell you then to see how, when the sun burns away their skin, the red meat that shows through is the same coloured meat as yours or mine. If you think them gods, then smell their breath in the morning or watch them squatting over the latrine pit. They do it the same way as you or me, my friends.'

The circle of black men listened fascinated, for they had never heard ideas like these expressed aloud.

'They have guns,' Bazo pointed out, and Hendrick laughed derisively.

'Guns,' he repeated, and patted the Enfield in his own lap. 'I have a gun, and when you finish your contract you also will have a gun. Then we are gods also, you and me. Then we own the stones and the rivers also.'

Cunningly Hendrick used 'we' and 'ours', not 'me' and 'mine', although he despised these naked black savages as heartily as did any of the other bigots on New Rush.

Bazo took the stopper from his snuff-horn and poured a little of the fine red powder onto the pink palm of his hand, a palm still riven and scabbed from the rescue in No. 6 Section, and he closed one nostril with his thumb and with the other sniffed the powder deep, left and right, and then sat back blinking deliciously at the ecstatic tears before passing the snuff-horn on to Kamuza, his cousin, who sat beside him.

Hendrick Naaiman waited with the patience of a man of old Africa, waited for the snuff-horn to complete the circle and come into his own hands. He took a pinch in each nostril and threw back his head to sneeze into the fire, then settled into silence again, waiting for Bazo to speak.

The Matabele frowned into the living coals, watching the devils form and fade, the figures and faces of strange men and beasts, the spirits of the flames – and he wished they had counsel for him.

At last he lifted his gaze to the man across the fire, once again studying the laced velskoen on his feet, the breeches of fine corduroy, the Sheffield-steel knife on his brass-studded belt, the embroidered waistcoat of beautiful thread and velvet and the flaming silk at his throat.

He was without doubt an important man, and a rogue. Bazo did not trust him. He could almost smell the deceit and cunning upon him.

'Why does a great chief, a man of worth, like yourself, come to tell us these things?'

'Bazo, son of Gandang,' Hendrick intoned, his voice becoming deep and laden with portent, 'I dreamed a dream last night. I dreamed that under the floor of your hut lie buried certain stones.'

For a moment the eyes of every Matabele warrior swivelled from Hendrick's face to the mud-plastered floor at the back of the low, smoky thatched hut, the darkest area of the circular room, and Hendrick suppressed the smile that crowded his lips.

Treasure was always buried under the floor of the hut, where a man could spread his sleeping-mat over it at night and guard it even in his sleep. It had not been difficult to guess where, the only question had been whether or not the gang of Matabele had yet learned the value of diamonds and begun gathering their own, as every other gang on the diggings was doing. Those furtive, guilty glances were his answer, but he let no trace of satisfaction show as he went on quietly.

'In my dream I saw that you were cheated, that when you took the stones to the white man, Bakela, he gave you a single gold coin with the head of the white queen upon it.' Hendrick's broad handsome face darkened with melancholy. 'My friend, I come to warn you. To save you from being cheated. To tell you that there is a man who will pay you the true value of your stones, and that you will have a fine new gun, a horse with a saddle, a bag of gold coins; whatever you desire will be yours.'

'Who is this man?' Bazo asked cautiously, and Hendrick spread his arms and for the first time smiled.

'It is me, Hendrick Naaiman, your friend.'

'How much will you give? How many white queens for these stones?'

Hendrick shrugged. 'I must see these stones. But one thing I promise, it will be many, many times more than the single coin that Bakela will give you.'

Again Bazo was silent.

'I have a stone,' he admitted at last. 'But I do not know if it has the spirit you seek, for it is a strange stone, like none other we have ever seen.'

'Let me see it, my old friend,' Hendrick whispered encouragingly. 'I will give you the advice of a father to his favourite son.'

Bazo took the snuff-horn and turned it over and over between his fingers, the muscles in his shoulders and arms bulged and subsided and his smooth regular features, knitted now in thought, seemed to be carved from the wood of the wild ebony.

'Go,' he said at last. 'Return when the moon sets. Come alone, without a gun, without a knife. And know you that one of my brothers will stand always at your back ready to drive the blade of his assegai out of your breastbone if you so much as think a treacherous thought.'

When Hendrick Naaiman crawled through the low doorway again it was past midnight; the fire had sunk to a puddle of ruddy ash, the smoke swirled like grey phantoms in the light of the bull's-eye lantern he carried, and the naked blades of the short broad stabbing spears flickered blue and deadly in the shadows.

He could smell the nervous sweat of the men that wielded those dreadful weapons, and the vulture wings of death seemed to rustle in the dark recesses of the hut. Hendrick knew how close that dark presence could crowd about him, for frightened men are dangerous men. It was part of his trade, this ever-present threat of death, but he could never accustom himself to it, and he heard the quaver in his own voice as he greeted Bazo.

The young Matabele sat as he had last seen him, facing the single door of the hut, his back protected by the thick mud wall and his assegai at his side, the shaft ready to his hand.

'Sit,' he instructed the Griqua, and Hendrick squatted opposite him.

Bazo nodded to two of his men and they slipped away as silently as hunting leopards to stand guard in the starlight, while two others knelt at Hendrick's back, their assegais in their right hand, the points merely inches from his cringing spine.

There was the weird 'woo woo' call of a nightjar out in the starlight, clearly the signal for which Bazo waited; one of his Matabele assuring him that they were unobserved. Hendrick Naaiman nodded in approval, the young Matabele was clever and careful.

Now Bazo lifted into his lap a small cloth-wrapped package on which fresh earth still clung in little yellow balls. He unwrapped it swiftly and, leaning forward across the smouldering fire, placed the contents in Hendrick's cupped hands.

The big Griqua sat paralysed like that, his cupped hands before his face, his dark pock-marked features frozen in an expression of disbelief, of utter astonishment. Then his hands began to tremble slightly, and quickly he placed the huge glittering stone on the hard-packed mud floor as though it had burned his fingers, but his tar-dark eyes seemed to bulge from their deep sockets as he stared at it still.

Nobody spoke or moved for almost a minute, and then Hendrick shook himself as though he were waking from deep sleep, but his eyes never left that stone.

'It is too big,' he whispered in English. 'It cannot be.'

Then suddenly he was hasty; he snatched up the stone and dipped it and his hand wrist-deep into the calabash of drinking water which stood beside the fire; then, holding it up in the lantern light, he watched the great stone shed water as though it had been greased, as though it were the feather of a wild goose.

'By my daughter's virgin blood,' he whispered again, and the men watching him stirred darkly into the shadows. His emotions had infected them with restless excitement.

Hendrick reached for the side pocket of his buckskin coat, and immediately the point of the assegai pricked the soft skin behind his ear.

'Tell him!' Hendrick blurted, and Bazo shook his head. The prick of steel ceased and Hendrick took from his pocket a shard of curved dark green glass, part of a shattered champagne bottle discarded in the veld behind one of the grog-shops.

Hendrick set it firmly on the floor of the hut, pressing the sharp points of glass into the clay. Then he closely examined the stone for a moment. One plane of the crystal had sheared through cleanly, leaving a sharp ridge around the rim, and the curved upper surface fitted neatly into Hendrick's cupped hand.

He placed the sharp ridge of the stone against the polished dark green curve of the broken bottle, then pressed down with the full strength of his right forearm and began to draw the edge across the glass. There was a thin abrasive screech that set his big white-starred teeth on edge, and behind the moving edge of the glittering stone a deep white groove appeared in the green glass, the stone had cut it as a hot knife cuts cheese.

Reverently the Griqua placed the stone in front of him, on the bare floor, and it seemed to be moving as the light played within its limpid depths, turned to magical stars of mauve and green and flaming crimson.

His voice had dried, his throat cleaved closed, he could barely breathe for iron bands of avarice had bound his chest, but his eyes glittered like a wolf in the firelight.

Hendrick Naaiman knew diamonds as a jockey knows fine horse flesh or a tailor the feel of good tweed cloth between his fingers. Diamonds were his salt, his bread, his very breath, and he knew that before him on the swept mud floor of this smoky little thatched hut lay something that would one day repose in the treasure house of the palace of some great king.

It was a living legend already: something that only a king could buy, something whose value, when converted to gold pounds or dollars, would stun even a rich man.

'Has this stone the spirit you seek?' Bazo asked quietly, and Hendrick swallowed before he could talk.

'I will give you five hundred gold queens for this stone,' he answered, and his voice was hoarse, ragged as though he were in pain.

His words struck the dark group of Matabele the way the east wind off the sea strikes the forests of Tzikhama, so that they swayed and rustled with the shock.

'Five hundred,' repeated Hendrick Naaiman. 'Which will buy you fifty guns or many fine cattle.'

'Give the stone to me,' Bazo ordered, and when Hendrick hesitated, the assegai pricked him again so that he started violently.

Bazo took the stone and stared at it broodingly, then he sighed.

'This is a heavy matter,' he said. 'I must think on it. Go now and return tomorrow at the same time. I will have an answer for you then.'

Long after the Griqua left, the silence persisted in the darkened hut, broken at last by Kamuza.

'Five hundred gold pieces,' he said. 'I long to see the hills of Matopos again; I long for the sweet milk of my father's herds again. With five hundred gold queens we could leave this place.'

'Do you know what the white men do to people who steal these stones?' Bazo asked softly.

'Not their stones. The Bastaard told us –'

'No matter what the yellow Bastaard told you, you will be a very dead Matabele if the white men catch you.'

'One man they burned alive in his hut. They say he smelled like a roasting joint of warthog meat,' one of the others murmured.

'Another they tied by his heels and dragged behind a galloping horse as far as the river. When they were finished, he no longer looked like a man at all.'

They thought about these atrocities a while, not shocked by them for they had seen men burned alive before. On one of the cattle raids to the east of Matabeleland their own regiment had chased two hundred Mashona men and women and children into the maze of caves that honeycombed the kopjes above their village.

It would have been a tedious task to hunt them out of the dark belly of the hills, so they had packed every entrance to the underground passages with branches of mopani trees and then put in fire. At the end some of the Mashona had run out through the flames, living torches of shrieking flame.

'Fire is a bad way to die,' said Kamuza, and uncorked his own snuff-horn.

'And five hundred pieces is a great deal of gold,' one of his friends answered him across the fire.

'Does a son steal the calves from his father's herd?' Bazo asked them, and now they were shocked indeed. To the Matabele the great herds of cattle were the nation's wealth, and the harsh laws and penalties that governed the management of the herds they had learned as part of their existence as *'mujiba'*, the apprenticeship as herd boys which every Matabele boy must serve.

'It is death even to squirt the milk of another man's cow into your mouth,' Bazo reminded them; and they all remembered how they had taken that chance at least once in the solitude of the bush, spurting it directly from the teat so that it dribbled down their chins onto their naked chests – risking their lives for a mouthful of warm sweet milk and the respect of their peers.

'It is not a calf,' Kamuza reminded, 'but a single little stone.'

'Gandang, who is my father, looks upon the white man Bakela as a brother. If I take anything from Bakela, then it is as taking from my own father.'

'If you take this stone to Bakela he will give you a single coin. If you take it to the Bastaard he will give you five hundred.'

'It is a heavy matter,' Bazo agreed. 'I will think on it.' And long after all the others had curled on their reed sleeping-mats under the karosses of fur, he sat alone over the dying fire with the great diamond burning coldly in his right hand.

Three men rode into Zouga's camp that Monday morning, and Zouga stooped out of his tent to meet them, standing bareheaded in the sunlight.

Neville Pickering led the party, and as he stepped down from the stirrup, he said, 'I hope we do not disturb you, Major, but I'd like you to meet some friends of mine.'

'I know Mr Hayes.' Zouga shook the hand of the lanky Texan engineer and then turned to the third man.

'And of course I know Mr Rhodes by sight and reputation.'

Rhodes' hand was cool, the skin dry and the knuckles large and bony. It had the feel of strength, although his grip was quick and light. Zouga found the pale blue eyes on a level with his. The man was tall, and startlingly young, he could be very little older than twenty, young to have earned such a formidable reputation.

'Mr Rhodes.' Nobody, not even Pickering, used his Christian name. It was said he even signed his letters to his own mother 'Your affectionate son, C. J. Rhodes'.

'Major Ballantyne.' Zouga was startled again, for Rhodes had a slight voice, pitched high and with a breathless quality. 'I am delighted to meet you at last. Of course, I have read your book, and there are many questions I should like to ask you.'

'Jordan, take the horses,' Zouga called, and began to lead his guests towards the scant shade of the camel-thorn tree. But Rhodes paused as Jordan scurried from the tent, obedient to his father's order.

'Good morning, young Jordan,' he said, and the child stopped abruptly and stared up at him speechlessly, beginning to blush a deep pink with transparent hero-worship, overcome at being recognized and addressed by name.

'I see you have taken to reading rather than fisticuffs now.'

In his haste Jordan still carried a book in his hand. Rhodes stooped and took it from him.

'Good Lord –' he said. 'Plutarch! You have cultivated taste for one so young.'

'It's a fascinating book, sir.'

'Indeed it is, one of my favourites. Have you yet read Gibbon?'

'No, sir,' Jordan whispered shyly, the blush subsiding to leave him only faintly pink. 'I do not know where I could find a copy.'

'I will lend you one, when you have finished this.' He handed the battered dog-eared copy of Plutarch's *Lives* back to Jordan. 'Do you know where my camp is?'

'Oh, yes, Mr Rhodes.'

Every day of his life Jordan made a detour on his way back from his lessons in the church, a detour that passed the tented and thatched camp where Pickering and Rhodes kept a bachelor mess, and Jordan passed with dragging footsteps. Twice he had glimpsed his idol at a distance and each time overcome with shyness had scampered away.

'Good. Call in when you are ready for it.' For a moment longer he studied the angelic child, and then turned and followed the other men to the shade of the tree.

There were empty packing cases and logs to sit on, and the four men arranged themselves in a casual circle. Zouga was relieved that it was too early to offer his guests liquor. He had barely sufficient money to buy food for his family, let alone to afford whisky, and he guessed that a bottle would not last long in this company; all three guests were drinking men.

They sipped coffee and swapped the news of the settlement for a few minutes before Pickering brought up the real business of their visit.

'There are only two schemes we have come up with to get the No. 6 area back to work,' he said. 'The first is the ramp –'

'I'm against that,' Rhodes said brusquely, impatiently. 'Within months we'll be back at the same problem – just too damned deep!'

'I would agree with Mr Rhodes,' said Hayes, the engineer. 'At best it would be only a temporary measure. Then the ramp itself would start collapsing.'

'Major Ballantyne's idea is the only one worth considering,' Rhodes cut in, and Zouga was struck forcibly by the man's manner of cutting through unnecessary discussion and getting to the core of a problem. 'The idea of building stagings on the rim of the workings, and running wires to the floor of the diggings is the only one that will beat the problem of depth. Hayes, here, has done some drawings.'

The engineer unrolled the plans he carried, spread them on the dusty earth at his feet and anchored the corners with diamondiferous pebbles from Zouga's tailing dump which had spilled into and was threatening to engulf the entire camp.

'I have considered a cantilever design.' Hayes began to explain the drawings in crisp technical terms, and the others moved their seats closer and bowed over the plans. 'We will have to use hand winches, and perhaps horse whims, until we can get a steam engine to do the haulage.'

They discussed it quietly, asking penetrating questions and, when the answers were obscure, cutting down for them with sharp minds and quick words. There was no waste of words, no repetitions, no drawn-out discussion and the work went swiftly.

The stagings would be tall scaffoldings built on the edge of the pit, and they would house the haulage winches.

'We will have to use steel hawsers. Manila will never do the job,' Hayes told them. 'There will have to be a single wire to each individual claim. A lot of wire.'

'How long to get it out?'

'Two months to Cape Town.'

'How much is this going to cost?' Zouga asked the question which had been burning his lips all morning.

'More than any of us can afford,' smiled Pickering. A man with a thousand guineas in his pocket was a rich man on New Rush in these days.

'What we cannot afford is not to do it,' Rhodes answered him without a smile.

'What about those diggers who cannot afford their share of the stagings?' Zouga persisted, and Rhodes shrugged.

'Either they find the money, or they will not have a wire down to their claims. From now on it's going to take capital to work a claim on New Rush.'

'Those who haven't got it, will have to sell out – it's as easy as that.'

'Since the cave-in the price of claims in the No. 6 has dropped to £100,' Zouga said. 'Anybody who sells now is going to take a hell of a knock.'

'And anybody who buys at £100 is going to make a killing,' Rhodes answered him, and lifted his pale blue eyes from Hayes' plans, and for a moment held Zouga's gaze significantly. He was giving advice, Zouga realized, but what impressed Zouga was the strength and determination behind that level gaze. He no longer wondered why somebody so young commanded such widespread respect on the diggings.

'Are we all agreed, then?' he asked.

With less than twenty pounds cash in the world and his claims cut off eighty feet below ground level and partially covered by the earth fall of the roadway, Zouga hesitated.

'Major Ballantyne.' They were all looking at him. 'Are you in?'

'Yes,' he nodded firmly. 'Count me in.' He would find the money, somewhere, somehow.

They all relaxed, and Pickering chuckled. 'It's never easy to play it all on one card.' He understood.

'Pickling, didn't I hear your saddle-bag clink when you dismounted?' Rhodes asked, and Pickering laughed again and went to fetch the bottle.

'Cordon Argent,' he said as he pulled the cork. 'The right juice for such an occasion, gentlemen.'

They swished the coffee grounds from their mugs and held them out for a dram of the cognac.

'The No. 6 stagings – fast may they rise and long may they stand!' Pickering gave them the toast, and they drank together.

Hayes wiped his whiskers with the back of his hand and stood up. 'I'll have the quantities ready to send off on the noon coach tomorrow,' he said, and hurried to his mount. Men who worked for Rhodes were always in a hurry. But neither Pickering or Rhodes moved to follow him.

Instead, Rhodes stretched out his long legs in the stained white cricket flannels and crossed his dusty riding boots at the ankles, at the same time offering his coffee mug to Pickering.

'I'll be damned if we don't have something else to celebrate this day,' he said as Pickering glugged cognac into their mugs.

'The Imperial Factor,' Pickering suggested.

'The Imperial Factor,' Rhodes agreed, and when he smiled the cleft in his smooth chin deepened and the melancholy line of his full lips under the fair moustache relaxed. 'Even this awful creature Gladstone has not been able to halt the march of Empire northwards through Africa. The Foreign Office has moved at last. The

Griquas are to be recognized as British subjects, and Waterboer's request has been granted. Griqualand West is to become part of Cape Colony, and of the Empire. We have lord Kimberley's assurance on it.'

'That's wonderful news,' Zouga interrupted.

'You think so?' The pale blue eyes sought and held Zouga's.

'I know it to be so,' Zouga told him. 'There is only one way to bring peace and civilization to Africa and that is under the Union Jack.'

Immediately there was a relaxation of the relationship between the three men, an unspoken accord, so that even without moving they seemed to have drawn closer, and their talk was easier, more intimate.

'We are the first nation in the world and anything less than our total duty is unworthy of us,' Zouga went on, and Rhodes nodded. 'We destroyed the slave trade on this continent; that was only a beginning. When you have seen the conditions that still exist, the savagery and barbarism, to the north of us, only then can you appreciate how deep that duty still is.'

'Tell me about the hinterland,' Rhodes demanded in that thin, almost querulous voice that so ill-suited his big loose-knit frame.

'The hinterland.' It was an unusual term, but it stuck like a burr, and Zouga heard himself use it as he described that wilderness through which he had travelled and hunted and prospected.

Rhodes sat on a log of firewood, the shaggy leonine head sunk forward, brooding and silent, only his eyes quick and attentive, listening with an almost religious fervour, rousing himself every few minutes, lifting his head to ask a question and then letting it sink again to the answer.

Zouga spoke of the wide slow rivers that ran in their deep valleys where the cream of tartar trees grew upon the banks and in the green shallows herds of hippopotamus challenged the traveller with gaping pink mouths and curved white tusks.

He described the deadly malarial swamps, vast stands of papyrus reeds swaying like dancers from horizon to horizon, where the sky pressed down, smothering the world under a heavy blue blanket sodden with steamy vapours, and he told of the relief of climbing the steep rocky escarpments to the cool high plateau of golden grasslands.

With words he showed them the vast and empty spaces, the plains dotted with moving herds of wild game, the cool green forests of standing timber, the streams of sweet water, crystal cold, from which a man could water his herds or his homestead.

He talked of vanished kingdoms of long dead kings, the Mambo and the Monomatapa, who had built cities of massive grey stone and left them to the smothering vines – their idols thrown down and shattered, the foundations of the walls menaced by the twisted grey python roots of the wild fig trees which found the joints in the stonework and forced them inexorably apart.

He told them of the square mine shafts that these vanished people had driven into the matrix and then abandoned, leaving the gold-bearing quartz where they had piled it before they fled.

'Visible gold,' he told them, 'thick as butter in the reef. Lying out there in the bush.'

He spoke of the people, the remnants of the subjects of the Monomatapa, their glories long past, decimated by war. He told them of the conquerors, the Matabele, the cruel legions from the south, calling the subservient tribes 'cattle' and, contemptuously, 'Mashona – eaters of dirt', taking them as slaves, killing them as sport, to prove their manhood, or merely on the king's whim.

He described the wealth of the Matabele, their uncountable herds of cattle, thousands upon tens of thousands of fine beasts, glossy hump-backed bulls whose blood lines ran back to Egypt and the land between the Tigris and Euphrates, big rangy animals with widespread horns and hides of every colour from unrelieved black to purest white.

He told them of deep and secret caverns in the hills where the priests of the vanished kings still conducted their mysteries and sustained the oracle, weaving a gossamer net of witchcraft and magic which enfolded even their proud and arrogant Matabele overlords.

Then, as the day wasted away and the sun began to set behind a flaming curtain of red dust, Zouga told them of the kraals of the Matabele, the impis trained into the most merciless killing machine Africa had ever brought forth, racing barefoot into battle behind their tall rawhide shields, the plumes nodding and streaming from their dark heads and the dazzle of their assegais lighting the plains as the stars light the night sky.

'How would you fight them, Ballantyne?' Rhodes fired the question harshly, and it checked Zouga in full lyrical flow. They stared at each other for a moment, but a moment that was fraught with portent, a moment in which the lives of many thousands – black men and white teetered in the balance. Then slowly the arm of the balance came down on one side, and the destiny of a continent moved, like a fiery planet shifting its orbit through the universe.

'I would thrust for the heart,' Zouga said, suddenly his eyes cold and green, 'a small mobile force of mounted men –'

'How many men?'

And suddenly they were talking war as the sun fell below the dusty mauve and purple plain, leaving the sinister shadows to draw in around the little group under the camel-thorn tree.

Jan Cheroot threw logs on the fire and they sat on in the ruddy wavering light and the talk was of gold and of war, diamonds and gold and war, Empire and war, and their words conjured columns of armed and mounted men from the night, dark phantoms riding into the future.

Suddenly Zouga checked in the middle of a sentence, his expression changed as though he had seen a ghost or recognized an old implacable enemy in the shadows under the camel-thorn tree.

'What is it, Ballantyne?' Rhodes asked sharply, swivelling the big untidy head to follow the direction of Zouga's gaze.

Against the bole of the thorn tree stood the tall green soapstone bird-statue. Unnoticed until now, hidden by the welter of harness and loose equipment that festooned the branches around it, some trick of the flames, the fall and flare of one of the burning logs, had illuminated it with sudden and dramatic firelight.

It stood taller than the seated men, seeming to preside over their counsels, listening to and directing the talk of gold and of blood. The falcon head, timeless as evil itself, as ancient as the hills of the far land from which it had been hewn, stared back at Zouga with sightless, yet somehow all-seeing, blank eyes, the cruel curve of the beak seemed on the point of opening to emit the falcon's hunting cry – or to bury itself in living flesh. To Zouga it seemed that in the darkness above the statue the

74

words of the prophecy, spoken so long ago in that deep cavern of the Matopos hills by the beautiful naked witch who was the *Umlimo* of Monomatapa, still persisted, hovering in the shadows like living things:

> The stone falcons will fly afar. . . . There shall be no peace in the kingdoms of the Mambos or the Monomatapas until they return. For the white eagle will war with the black bull until the stone falcons return to roost.

In his memory Zouga heard the words again, spoken by that silken voice, and they seemed to echo against the dome of his skull and fill the drums of his ears.

'What is it, my dear fellow?' Pickering repeated the question and something slithered along Zouga's spine and crawled upon the skin of his forearms so that the hair came erect and he had to shudder to free himself of it.

'Nothing,' he answered, huskily. 'It's nothing; a grey goose walked over my grave.' But he stared still at the statue and Rhodes followed his gaze.

'By Jove. Isn't that the bird you wrote about in the book?' Rhodes sprang to his feet.

Eagerly he strode to where it stood and paused before it for a long silent moment before he reached out and touched the head.

'What an extraordinary piece of work,' he said softly, and went down on one knee to examine the shark-tooth pattern that was carved into the plinth. In that attitude he seemed like a worshipper, a priest conducting some weird rite before the idol.

Again Zouga felt that superstitious flutter of nerves crawl like insects upon his skin, and to break the mood he called loudly for Jan Cheroot to bring a lantern.

In the lantern's beam they scrutinized the polished greenish stone, and as Rhodes ran his big large-knuckled hand over it his expression was rapt, the gaze of those strange pale eyes remote, like a poet hearing words in his head.

Long after Pickering and Zouga had returned to their seats by the log fire, Rhodes stood alone under the camel-thorn tree with the falcon – and when at last he left it to join them once more, his tone was brittle with accusation.

'That thing is a treasure, Ballantyne. It is unforgivable to leave it lying out under a tree.'

'It's lain in worse conditions for hundreds, perhaps thousands of years,' Zouga replied drily.

'You are right.' Rhodes sighed, his attention straying back to the bird. 'It's yours to do with as you wish.' And then, impulsively, 'I wish to purchase it from you. Name a price.'

'It's not for sale,' Zouga told him.

'Five hundred pounds,' said Rhodes.

The sum startled Zouga, but his reply was immediate.

'No.'

'A thousand.'

'I say,' Pickering intervened. 'You can pick up ten claims in No. 6 Section for that.'

Rhodes did not glance at him, but he nodded. 'Yes, you could, or Major Ballantyne could pay for his share of the new stagings with a thousand pounds.'

A thousand pounds. Zouga felt himself tempted. A thousand pounds would see him clear.

'No.' He shook his head. 'I'm sorry.' He felt he had to explain. 'It has become the household god, my personal good-luck symbol.'

'Good luck!' snorted Jan Cheroot from across the fire, and all three of them turned their heads in his direction. None of them noticed him sitting on the edge of the shadows like a wizened little yellow gnome.

'Good luck!' the Hottentot repeated scornfully. 'Since we picked up that verdamned bird we haven't seen a day's good luck.' He spat into the fire, and his phlegm sizzled and exploded in a little puff of steam. 'That bird has put blisters on our feet and rubbed the skin from our backs, it has broken the axles of our wagons and lamed our horses. It has brought us fever, and sickness and death. Miss Aletta died looking at that bird, and Jordie would have followed her if I hadn't thrown the verdamned thing out.'

'That's nonsense,' Zouga snapped sharply. 'That's an old Hottentot maid's superstition.'

'Ja,' Jan Cheroot challenged him hotly. 'Is it an old Hottentot superstition that we are sitting in the dust of this hell-hole, swatting flies and rubbing empty bellies? Is it superstition that all around us they are pulling fat diamonds and we find only the droppings and manure? Is it superstition that the earth has fallen on our claims, and that it nearly swallowed Ralph? Is that your good luck that you boast the bird brings you, Master Zouga? If it is, then hear the words of old Jan Cheroot and take the thousand pounds that Mr Rhodes offers you; take it with both hands, and thank him for getting rid of that – that –' Jan Cheroot ran out of words and glared across the fire at the birdshape under the thorn tree.

'Damn me,' Pickering smiled. 'But you nag like a wife.'

None of them were surprised at the familiar address between servant and master. In Africa relationships like this were common; the servant considering himself to be part of the family with a voice in the affairs of the family, and his claim was accepted by all.

'Jan Cheroot has hated the idol since the day we discovered it.'

'Tell me about that day, Jan Cheroot,' ordered Rhodes brusquely; and Jan Cheroot puffed up visibly with self-importance. There were few things he enjoyed more than an important and attentive audience and a good story to tell them. While he made a show of packing his clay pipe with black Magaliesberg shag tobacco and lighting it with an ember from the fire, the two boys crept out of the tent drawn by the prospect of a story. They glanced cautiously at Zouga and, when he made no move to send them back, they were emboldened.

Jordie sat next to Jan Cheroot and leaned his curly golden head against the Hottentot's shoulder, while Ralph came diffidently to sit with the men beside the fire.

'We had been one year in the bush,' Jan Cheroot began, 'one year without seeing a civilized man, one year trekking and hunting—' And the boys settled down with delicious anticipation. They had heard the story a hundred times before and enjoyed each telling more than the last.

'We had killed two hundred great elephant since leaving the Zambezi river, and we had fought bad men and savages. Our porters had mostly deserted or died of disease and wild animals, our provisions were long finished, no salt, no tea, no medicine and little gunpowder. Our clothes were rags, our boots worn through and repaired with the wet hide of buffalo.

'It had been a killing journey, over mountains with no passes and rivers with no names, and ordinary men would long ago have fallen and the birds would have picked their bones white. Even we were tired and sick and we were lost. Around us, as far as our eyes could see, there was nothing but wild hills and bad bush through which only the buffalo could pass.'

'And you needed honey for your strength,' Jordie burst out, unable to contain himself, and knowing the story word perfect. 'Otherwise you would have died in the bush.'

'And we needed honey for our strength or we would have died in the bush,' Jan Cheroot agreed solemnly.

'Out of the bush came a little brown honey guide, and he sang thus – ' Jan Cheroot imitated the high-pitched burring call and fluttered his fingers in an uncanny imitation of the bird. ' "Come!" he called to us. "Come, follow me, and I will lead you to the hive." '

'But he wasn't a real honey-bird, was he, Jan Cheroot?' Jordie cried excitedly.

'No, Jordie, he wasn't a real honey-bird.'

'And you followed him!'

'And we followed him for many days through bad country. Even when Master Zouga, your father, would have turned back, old Jan Cheroot was firm. We must go on, I told him, for by this time I, who have a deep knowledge and understanding of ghosts and spirits, realized that this was not a real honey-bird but a hobgoblin in the guise of a bird.'

Zouga smiled softly. He remembered the incident differently. They had followed the bird for some hours, and it was Jan Cheroot who had lost interest in the hunt and had to be prodded and cajoled to continue.

'Then suddenly –' Jan Cheroot paused and flung out both hands theatrically, ' – before our eyes, a wall of grey stone rose out of the bush. A wall so high it was like a mountain. With my axe I chopped away the vines and found a great gateway, guarded by fierce spirits –'

'Spirits?' Zouga smiled.

'They were invisible to ordinary eyes,' Jan Cheroot explained loftily. 'And I put them to flight with a magical sign.'

Zouga winked at Pickering, but Jan Cheroot ignored their smiles.

'Beyond the gateway was a temple yard, in which lay the falcon statues, cast down, some of them shattered, but all of them covered with heaps of gold, mountains of gold.'

Zouga sighed. 'Fifty pounds weight to be exact. Fragments and tiny pieces which we had to sift from the soil. How I wish it had been a mountain.'

'We gathered the gold from where it lay, and we took up that statue on our shoulders and carried it one thousand miles–'

'Complaining every step of the way,' Zouga pointed out.

' – until we reached Cape Town again.'

It was after midnight when Jan Cheroot brought the saddled horses to the camp fire, and as Rhodes took the reins he paused in the act of mounting.

'Tell me, Major, this land to the north, this Zambezia as you call it in your book – what is it that keeps you from it? What are you doing here?'

'I need money,' Zouga told him simply. 'And somehow I know that the road to the north begins here. The money to take and hold Zambezia will come from the workings of New Rush.'

'I like a man who thinks big, a man who counts not in ones and twos but in tens of thousands,' Rhodes nodded approval.

'At this moment I count my fortune in ones and twos.'

'We could change that.' Rhodes shot a pale piercing glance towards the bird carving, but Zouga chuckled and shook his head.

'I would like first refusal,' Rhodes persisted.

'If I sell, it will be to you,' Zouga agreed, and Rhodes stepped up in the stirrup, swung a leg over the horse's rump, settled in the saddle and rode out of the camp.

Pickering edged his mount closer to Zouga and leaned down from the saddle to tell him seriously:

'He will have it from you – in the end he will have it.'

'I think not.' Zouga shook his head.

But Pickering smiled. 'He always gets what he sets his heart on. Always.'

He saluted Zouga with the hand that held the reins and then started his horse into a canter and followed Rhodes out onto the dusty starlit track.

'Give the stone to the yellow man,' Kamuza urged quietly. 'Five hundred gold queens, and we will return to our own people with treasures. Your father, the induna of Inyati, will be pleased, even the king will call us to the great kraal at Thabas Indunas for audience. We will become important men.'

'I do not trust the Bastaard.'

'Do not trust him. Trust only the yellow coins he brings.'

'I do not like his eyes. They are cold and he hisses like a yellow cobra when he speaks.'

They were silent then, a circle of dark figures in the smoky hut, squatting around the diamond as it lay on the clay floor and flickered with weird lights in the reflection of the fire.

They had argued since the sunset had released them from their labours. They had argued over the meal of stringy mutton with its rind of greasy fat and maize porridge baked until it was stiff as cake.

They had argued over the snuff-horn and beer pot, and now it was late. Soon, very soon, there would be a scratching at the door of the hut as the Bastaard came for his answer.

'The stone is not ours to sell. It belongs to Bakela. Does a son sell the calves from his father's herds?'

Kamuza made a clucking sound of exasperation. 'Surely it is against law and custom to steal from the tribe, from the elders of the tribe, but Bakela is not Matabele. He is *buni*, white man, it is not wrong doing to take from him any more than it is against law and custom to send the assegai through the heart of a Mashona dog, or to mount his wife in sport, or to take the cattle of a Tswana and put fire into his kraal to hear his children squeal. Those are natural and right things for a man to do.'

'Bakela is my father, the stone is his calf, given into my care.'

'He will give you a single coin,' Kamuza lamented, and Bazo seemed not to hear him.

He picked up the diamond again and turned it in his hand.

'It is a large stone,' he mused aloud, 'a very large stone.' He held it to his eye and looked into the stone as though it were a mountain pool, and he watched with awe the fires and shapes move within it.

Still holding it to his eye, he said, 'If I bring my father a newborn calf, he will be happy and give me a reward. But if I bring him one hundred calves how much greater will be his joy, and one hundred times greater the reward that he will give me.'

He lowered the stone and gave a series of orders that sent his men hurrying out into the night, to return immediately with the tools Bazo had sent them to fetch.

Then in silence they watched him make his preparations.

Firstly he spread a kaross of silver jackal pelts on the earth floor and then in the centre of the fur he placed a small steel anvil at which he had watched Zouga shaping horse-shoes and working the iron hoops to repair the wagon wheels.

On the anvil Bazo placed the diamond, and then he threw aside his cloak so that he stood stark naked in the firelight, tall and lean and hard, his belly muscles standing up in concentric ridges under the dark satiny skin and the wide rangy shoulders overdeveloped by practice with shield and spear.

With his legs braced wide, he stood over the anvil, and hefted the sweat-polished handle of the pick, feeling the balance and weight of the steel head that had become so familiar.

Bazo narrowed his eyes, measuring his stroke, and then he reared back with the pick almost touching the thatched roof. He drove his body weight into the stroke, and the steel pick head came hissing down from on high.

The point caught the diamond exactly on the high centre of its curved upper surface, and the great stone exploded as though a bucketful of mountain water had been dashed to the earth. The sparkling drops, the shattered fragments, the glowing chips of priceless crystal, seemed to fill the whole hut with a burst of sunlight.

They pattered against the thatched walls, stung the naked skins of the watching Matabele, kicked little puffs of grey ash as they fell into the fire, and scattered on the lustrous fur of the silver jackal kaross, shining there like live fish in the net.

'Son of the Great Snake,' hooted Kamuza joyously. 'We are rich men.' And the laughing Matabele flung themselves into the task of gathering up the fragments.

They picked them from the ashes, swept them up from the earthen floor, shook them out of the jackal skin kaross – and piled them into Bazo's cupped hand until it was filled to overflowing. Even then they missed some of the tiny chips that had fallen into the dust or the fire and were lost for ever.

'You are a wise man,' Kamuza told Bazo with unaffected admiration. 'Bakela has his stones – a hundred calves – and we will have more coins than the yellow Bastaard would give us.'

There was no work in the collapsed No. 6 Section, no need to rise before dawn, so the sun was clear of the horizon when Zouga strode out of the tent, clinching his belt as he joined Jan Cheroot and the two boys under the camel-thorn tree.

The table was a packing-case, the lid stained with candle grease and spilled coffee, and breakfast was maize-meal porridge in chipped enamel bowls, unsweetened, for the price of sugar had recently risen to a pound a pound on the diamond fields.

Zouga's eyes were red-rimmed, for he had slept little the previous night, but had lain awake worrying and scheming, going over and over in his mind every detail of the plans for the new staging – and coming back each time to the most important detail, the one for which there seemed to be no solution: the cost, the enormous cost of it all.

The two boys saw his face, recognized his mood, and were immediately silent, applying themselves with complete absorption to the unappetizing grey gruel in their bowls.

A shadow fell across the group, and Zouga looked up irritably, squinting into the early sunlight with the spoon half raised to his lips. 'What is it, Bazo?'

'Pick-ups, Bakela.' The tall young Matabele used the English words. 'Pick-ups.' Zouga grunted.

'Let me see it.' Zouga was immediately uninterested. Almost certainly it would be a worthless chip of quartz or rock crystal. But Bazo placed a small bundle wrapped in a dirty scrap of cloth beside Zouga's bowl.

'Well, open it,' Zouga ordered; and Bazo picked the knot, and spread the cloth.

'Glass!' thought Zouga disgustedly. There was almost a handful of it, chips and pieces, the biggest not much bigger than the head of a wax Vesta.

'Glass!' and he made the gesture of sweeping it away, and then stayed his hand as the sunlight fell on the pile and a shaft of it pricked his eyes in a rainbow burst of colours.

Slowly, disbelievingly, he changed the gesture of dismissal and reached hesitantly, almost reverently for the glittering heap, but Jordan forestalled him.

With a shriek of joy the child's small graceful fingers danced over the pile.

'Diamonds, Papa,' he screamed. 'They are diamonds, real diamonds.'

'Are you sure, Jordie?' Zouga asked the question unnecessarily, his voice hoarse, realizing it was too good to be true. There must be many hundreds of precious stones in the pile, small, very small, but of what superb colour, white, ice-white, seeming to crackle like lightning they were so bright.

Still hesitantly Zouga took one of the largest stones from Jordan's fingers.

'Are you sure, Jordie?' he repeated.

'They are diamonds, Papa. All of them.'

Zouga's last doubts faded, to be replaced immediately by a deeper uncertainty.

'Bazo,' he said. 'There are so many–' And then something else puzzled him. Quickly he picked out twenty of the largest stones and stood them in a row across the top of the packing case.

'The same colour, they are all the same colour, exactly!'

Zouga shook his head, frowning, confused; and then suddenly the shadows in his eyes cleared.

'Oh my God,' he whispered, and slowly all blood drained from his face, leaving the skin dirty yellow like a man ten days gone in malaria fever.

'The same; they are all the same. The breaks are clean and fresh.'

Slowly he lifted his eyes to Bazo's face.

'Bazo, how big –' his voice roughened and dried, so that he had to clear his throat, 'how big was the stone before – before you cracked it?'

'This big.' Bazo clenched and showed his fist. 'With my pick I made it into many stones, for you, Bakela, knowing how you value many stones.'

Zouga's voice was still a husky whisper. 'I will kill you,' he said in English. 'For this, I will kill you.'

The scar across his cheek turned slowly into an ugly inflamed weal, the stigmata of his rage, and now he was shaking, his lips trembling as he rose slowly to his feet.

'I will kill you.' His voice rose to a bellow, and Jordan shrieked again, this time with terror. He had never seen his father like this before; there was a terrifying maniacal quality about him.

'That was the stone I was waiting for, you bastard, you black bastard, that was it. That was the key to the north.'

Zouga snatched the Martini-Henry rifle from where it leaned against the bole of the camel-thorn tree beside the falcon carving. The steel clashed and snickered as he pumped a cartridge into the chamber and in the same moment swung up the barrel.

'I'm going to kill you,' be roared, and then checked.

Ralph had jumped to his feet, and now he faced his father, stepping forward until the muzzle of the loaded and fully cocked rifle almost touched the entwined brass snakes of his belt buckle.

'You will have to kill me first, Papa,' he said. He was as pale as Zouga, his eyes the same deep haunted green.

'Get out of the way.' Zouga's voice sank into that croaking, husky whisper and Ralph could not answer him, but he shook his head, his heavy jaw clenched so determinedly that his teeth grated audibly.

'I warn you, stand aside,' Zouga choked, and they stood confronting each other, both trembling with tension and outrage.

Then the muzzle of the heavy rifle wavered in Zouga's hands, lowered slowly until it pointed to the dusty red earth between the toes of Ralph's boots.

The silence went on for many seconds; then Zouga took a full breath and the barrel of his chest swelled under the faded blue flannel shirt.

With a gesture of utter frustration he hurled the rifle against the treetrunk and the butt snapped through. Then he sank back into his seat at the packing-case table and his golden head sank slowly into his hands.

'Get out.' All the fire and fury had gone from his voice; it was quiet and hopeless. 'Get out, all of you.'

Zouga sat on alone under the thorn tree. He felt burned out with emotion and anger, empty and blackened and devastated within, like the veld after fire has swept through it.

When at last he lifted his head the first thing he saw was the falcon squatting opposite him on its greenstone plinth. It seemed to be smiling, a cruel and sardonic twist to the predator's beak, but when he stared at it Zouga saw that it was merely a trick of shadow and sunlight through the thorn branches.

The kopje-walloper was a small man, with legs so short that his polished high-heeled boots did not touch the floor when he sat on the swivel piano stool behind his desk.

The desk filled most of the tiny galvanized-iron hut, and it was furnace-hot in the room; the heat quivered and danced down from the roof. On the raw deal planks of the desk stood the accoutrements of the kopje-walloper's trade. The whisky bottle and shot-glasses to mellow the man with stones to sell; the sheet of white paper on which to examine the goods for colour; the wooden tweezers, the jeweller's eyeglass, the balance and scales, and the cheque book.

The cheque book was the size of a family Bible, each cheque form embossed in gold leaf and printed in multi-colours, the border depicting choirs of heavenly angels, sea nymphs riding in half clam shells drawn by teams of leaping dolphins, the Queen as Britannia with helmet, shield and trident, twisting cornucopia from which poured the treasures of Empire and a dozen other patriotic symbols of Victorian might.

The cheque book was by far the most impressive item in the hut, not excepting the buyer's flowing silk Ascot tie and the yellow spats that covered his boots. It was unlikely that a digger would be able to refuse payment offered in such flamboyant style.

'How much, Mr Werner?' Zouga asked.

Werner had swiftly sorted the glittering heap of diamond chips into separate piles, grading them by size alone for each stone was of the same fine white colour.

The smallest stones were three points, three hundredth parts of a carat, barely bigger than a grain of beach sand, the largest was almost a carat.

Now Werner laid aside his tweezers and ran his hand through his dark locks.

'Have another whisky,' he murmured, and when Zouga refused, 'Well, me, I'm having one now.'

He poured both glasses full to the brim, and despite Zouga's frown pushed one across to him.

'How much?' Zouga persisted.

'The weight?' Werner sipped the whisky and smacked his thick liver-coloured lips. 'Ninety-six carats, all told. What a diamond it must have been. We will never see the likes again—'

'How much in cash?'

'Major, I would have offered you fifty thousand pounds, if that had been a single stone.'

Zouga winced and blinked his eyes closed for an instant, as though he had been slapped across the face with an open hand.

With fifty thousand pounds he could have taken Zambezia – money for men, horses and guns, money for wagons and bullock teams, machinery to mine the reef and mill the gold, money for the farms, the seed and implements. He opened his eyes again.

'Damn you, I'm not interested in what might have been,' he whispered. 'Just tell me how much you will pay for that.'

'Two thousand pounds; that's my top price, and it's not an "open" offer.'

The stone had splintered into almost two hundred chips. That meant a 'pick-up' payment to Bazo of that many sovereigns. Zouga would intensely resent having to make that payment, but he owed it and he would make it. Of what remained after paying Bazo, at least a thousand would go for his share of the new stagings on the No. 6 Section.

Eight hundred left, and it cost him a hundred a week to work his claims, so he had won himself two months. Sixty days, instead of a land. Sixty days instead of a hundred thousand square miles of rich land.

'I'll take it,' he said quietly, picked up the whisky glass and drained it. It burned away the bitter taste at the back of his throat.

*

Ralph's bird was a lanner, one of the true members of the family *Falco*, long-winged and perfect for hunting the open plains of Griqualand. At last, after many attempts, he had found her and taken her for his own, a falcon and therefore bigger than the male bird, which was not a falcon but a tercel or, in the case of a lanner, a 'lanneret'.

She was 'eyas', the falconers' term for a wild bird taken at the nest when almost full-fledged. Ralph had climbed to the nest high on the top branches of a giant acacia and brought the bird down in his shirt, bleeding where she had raked him with her talons across his belly.

Bazo had helped him fashion the hood and jesses of soft glove leather for the proud head, but it was Ralph who walked her on his hand, hour after hour, day after day, stroking and gentling her, calling her 'darling' and 'beauty' and 'lovely' until she would eat from his fist and greet him with a soft 'Kweet! Kweet!' of recognition when she saw him. Then he introduced her to the lure of stuffed pigeon feathers, teaching her to hit it as he swung it on its long cord.

Finally, in the traditional ritual of the falconer, he sat up all night with the bird on his fist and a candle burning beside him. He sat with her in the trial of wills which would prove his domination over her, staring into her fierce yellow eyes, in the candlelight, hour after hour, outlasting her until the lids closed over her eyes and she slept perched upon his fist and Ralph had won. Then at last he could hunt her.

Jordan loved the bird for her beauty, and once she was trained Ralph occasionally let him carry her and stroke the hot sleek plumage under his gentle fingers. It was Jordan who found her name. He took it from Plutarch's *Lives*, which he was re-reading, and so the falcon was named Scipio, but Jordan accompanied the hunt only once, disgracing himself irretrievably by bursting into tears at the moment of the kill. Ralph never invited him again.

The same rains that had undermined the No. 6 causeway had flooded every depression and vlei for a hundred miles around the New Rush diggings. Slowly, in the hot dry months since that deluge, the shallower pools and swamps had dried out; but five miles south on the Cape Road, halfway to the low line of blue Magersfontein hills, there was still a wide body of open water, and already reed-beds had grown up around its perimeter and colonies of scarlet and ebony bishop birds had woven their hanging basket nests on the nodding reed staffs. Amongst the reeds Ralph and Bazo built their blind.

They drew the long, leafy fronds down over their own heads, careful not to slice their hands on the razor-edged leaves; the fluffy white silks snowed down on them from the laden seed heads of the reeds, and they plaited the roof of stems in place, concealing themselves from the open sky.

Ralph scooped a handful of black mud and smeared it over his face. He knew that his white face turned upwards would shine like a mirror, catching the eye of even a high-flighted bird.

'You should have been born Matabele, then you would not need mud.' Bazo chuckled as he watched him, and Ralph made an obscene sign at him with his fingers before they settled down to wait.

It was fascinating to see how Scipio, blind under the leather hood, could still pick up the beat of approaching wings long before the men could see or hear them, and they were alerted by the set of her head and the anticipatory stretch of her talons.

'Not yet, darling,' Ralph whispered. 'Soon now, darling.'

Then Bazo whistled sharply and pointed with his chin.

Across the swamp, still two miles out, very high against the empty sky, Ralph saw them. There were three of them, big black wings curving on the downbeat in that characteristic unhurried, weighty action.

'Here they come, my love,' Ralph murmured to Scipio, and touched the russet-dappled breast with his lips and felt the beat of the fierce heart against his face.

'God, but they are big,' Ralph murmured, and the tiny shapely body on his arm was feather light. He had never flown her against geese before, and he was torn with doubts.

The V-shaped flight of geese went far out across the swamp in a leisurely descending circle and then they were coming back, low, flying into the sun. It was perfect. Scipio would have the sun behind her when she towered, and Ralph thrust his doubts aside.

He slipped the soft leather hood off Scipio's beautiful dove-grey head, and the yellow eyes opened like full moons, focusing swiftly. She shook out her feathers, swelling in size for a moment, puffing out her breast – until she saw the thick black skein of geese against the sky, and her plumage flattened, going sleek and polished, steely in the early sunlight, and she crouched forward on Ralph's wrist.

Turning with her to follow the flight of the geese, Ralph could feel the rapier points of her talons through the cuff of his leather gauntlet and sense the tension of the small neat body. She seemed to vibrate like a violin's strings as the bow is drawn lightly across them.

With his free hand he broke the quick-release knot that secured the jesses to Scipio's leg.

'Hunt!' he cried, and launched her, throwing her clear of the reed; and she went on high like a javelin, towering swiftly for the sun on wings shaped like the wicked blades of a pair of fighting knives.

The geese saw her instantly, and stalled back on great wings that were suddenly ungainly with shock. Their tight V-formation broke up as each bird turned away – two of them rising, driving hard for height while the third bird swung north again towards the river, dropped height steeply to pick up the speed he had lost in the initial stall of shock, and then levelled out low and winged hard, neck outstretched, webbed feet tucked up under his tail.

Scipio was still towering, going up on wings that blurred with speed and turned to golden discs in the early slanting sunlight.

Her tactics were those of the instinctive killer. She needed every inch of height that she could achieve. She needed it to exchange for speed when she began her stoop, her body weight was many times lighter than the huge birds she was hunting, and she had to kill with shock and speed.

Even as she went up her head was twisted to the side, watching, judging, as the game scattered away below her.

'Don't duck, my sweeting,' Ralph called to her.

There was very real danger of it, for though Scipio was hungry to hunt, she had never been flown against birds such as these. Geese were not her natural prey; nature had not equipped her for the shock of binding to something so massive.

As she climbed so the difference in size of hunter and hunted was emphasized; and then abruptly Scipio was at the height she judged sufficient and she hovered, ten beats of Ralph's own heart as he watched her standing in the air.

She was daunted, the game was too big, she was going to duck.

84

'Hunt, darling, hunt!' he called to her and she seemed to have heard him. She screamed that terrible death cry of the falcon, high and shrill and fierce, and then she folded her wings and dropped into her stoop.

'She's taking the low bird,' Ralph shouted his triumph; she was not going to duck, she had selected the goose that had dropped close to earth and was now crossing her front at an acute angle.

'There is the liver of a lion in that small body.' Bazo's voice was full of wonder as he stared upwards at the tiny deadly dart that fell against the blue.

They could hear the wind hissing through her half-cocked wings, see the infinitesimal movements of her tip feathers with which she controlled that terrible headlong plunge.

The goose flogged at the air, heavy, massive, black flashed with frosty white, its panic evident in every beat of its frantic wings.

The speed with which Scipio closed was chilling. Ralph felt the hair on the nape of his neck come erect as though an icy wind had touched him as Scipio reached forward with her steely talons.

This was the moment for which he and the bird had worked and trained so long. The supreme moment of the kill – an involuntary cry burst from his throat, a primeval and animal sound, as Scipio bound to the great goose and the sound of the hit was like a single beat of a bass drum that seemed to shake the very air about Ralph's head.

The goose's spread wings spun like the spokes of a wheel, and a burst of black feathers filled the air as though a shrapnel shell had been fired from a heavy cannon; and then the goose's body collapsed under the shock, one wing snapped and trailed down the sky as it fell, the long serpentine goose neck was arched back in the convulsion of death, and Scipio was bound to the gigantic black body, her talons locked deep into the still frantically beating heart. The impetus of Scipio's stoop had shattered bone in the big body and burst the pulsing blood vessels around the goose's heart.

Ralph started to run, whooping with excitement, and Bazo was at his shoulder, laughing, head thrown back, watching the birds fall, leaving a tracery of feathers like the plume of a comet in the sky behind them.

A hawk binds to its prey, from the moment of strike unto the earth. A falcon does not. Scipio should break, and let the goose fall, but she had not; she was still locked in, and Ralph felt the first frost of worry cool his excitement. Had his bird broken bone, or otherwise injured herself in that frightful impact?

'Beauty!' he called to her. 'Unbind! Unbind!' She could be caught under the heavy goose and crushed against the earth. It was not her way to hold on all the way in.

'Unbind!' he screamed again, and saw her flutter, stabbing at the air with those sharp-bladed wings. She was stunned, and the earth rushed up at her.

Then suddenly she lunged, unbinding, breaking loose from her kill, hovering, letting the goose go on to thud into the rocky earth beyond the swamp, only then sinking, dainty and poised, and settling again upon the humped black carcass. Ralph felt his chest choked with pride and love for her courage and her beauty.

'Kweet,' Scipio called, when she saw Ralph. 'Kweet,' the recognition call, and she left the prize that she had risked her life to take and came readily to Ralph's hand.

He stooped over her, his eyes burning with pride, and kissed her lovely head.

'I won't make you do it again,' he whispered. 'I just had to see if you could do it – but I won't ever make you do it again.'

Ralph fed the goose's head to Scipio, and she tore it to pieces with her curved beak, between each morsel pausing to stare at Ralph.

'The bird loves you,' Bazo looked up from the fire over which he was roasting chunks of fat goose, the grease dripping onto the coals and frizzling sharply. Ralph smiled, lifted the bird and kissed its bloody beak.

'And I love her.'

'You and the bird have the same spirit. Kamuza and I have spoken of it often.'

'Nothing is as brave as my Scipio.'

Bazo shook his head. 'Do you remember the day that Bakela would have killed me? In the moment that he took the gun to me he was mad, mad to the point of killing.'

Ralph's expression changed. It was many months since he had intervened to save the young Matabele from the wrath of his father.

'I have not spoken of it before.' Bazo held Ralph's eyes steadily. 'It is not the kind of matter about which a man chatters like a woman at the water hole. We will probably never speak of it again, you and I, but know you that it will never be forgotten –' Bazo paused, and then he said it solemnly. 'I shall remember, Henshaw.'

Ralph understood immediately. 'Henshaw, the hawk.' The Matabele had given him a praise name, a thing not lightly done, a mark of enormous respect. His father was Bakela, the Fist, and now he was Henshaw, the Hawk, named for the brave and beautiful bird upon his wrist.

'I shall remember, Henshaw, my brother,' repeated Bazo, the Axe. 'I shall remember.'

Zouga was never entirely sure why he kept the rendezvous; certainly it was not merely because Jan Cheroot urged him to do so, nor the fact that the payment of £2,000 for the shattered chips of the great Ballantyne diamond had not lasted him as long as he had hoped, nor that the cost of the new stagings was rising all the time. His share looked to be more like two thousand than a thousand pounds. Sometimes in his least charitable moods Zouga suspected that Pickering and Rhodes and some other members of the committee were content to see the costs of the stagings rise and the pressure begin to squeeze out the smaller diggers. The going price of claims in the collapsed No. 6 Section continued to drop as the cost of the stagings rose; and somebody was buying, if not Rhodes and his partners, then it must be Beit or Werner, or even the newcomer, Barnato.

Perhaps Zouga kept the rendezvous to distract himself from these grave problems, perhaps he was merely intrigued by the mystery that surrounded it all, but when he looked at himself honestly it was more likely the prospect of profit. The whole affair reeked of profit, and Zouga was a desperate man. He had very little left to sell apart from the claims themselves. To sell the claims was to abandon his dream. He was ready to explore any other path, to take any risks, rather than that.

'There is a man who wishes to speak with you.' Jan Cheroot's words had started it, and something in his tone made Zouga look up sharply. They had been together many years and there was little they did not know of each other's moods and meanings.

'That is simple enough,' Zouga had told him. 'Send him to the camp.'

'He wishes to speak secretly, at a place where no other eyes will be watching.'

'That sounds like the way of a rogue,' Zouga frowned. 'What is the man's name?'

'I do not know his name,' Jan Cheroot admitted, and then when he saw Zouga's expression, he explained. 'He sent a child with a message.'

'Then send the child back to him, whoever he is. Tell him he will find me here every evening, and anything he has to discuss I will be pleased to listen to in the privacy of my tent.'

'As you wish,' Jan Cheroot grunted, and the wrinkles on his face deepened so that he looked like a pickled walnut. 'Then we will continue to eat maize porridge.' And they did not discuss it again, not for many weeks, but the worm was planted and it gnawed away at Zouga until he was the one who asked.

'Jan Cheroot, what of your nameless friend. What was his reply?'

'He sent word that it was not possible to help a man who refused to help himself,' Jan Cheroot told him airily. 'And it is clear to all the world that we have no need of help. Look at your fine clothes, it is the fashion now to have the buttocks hanging out of the pants.'

Zouga smiled at the hyperbole, for his breeches were neatly patched. Jordan had seen to that.

'And look at me,' Jan Cheroot went on. 'What reason do I have for complaint? I was paid a year ago, wasn't I?'

'Six months ago,' Zouga corrected him.

'I cannot remember,' Jan Cheroot sulked. 'The same way I have forgotten what beef tastes like.'

'When the stagings are completed –' Zouga began, and Jan Cheroot snorted.

'They are more likely to fall on our heads. At least then we won't have to worry about being hungry.'

Serious defects had shown up in the design of the stagings. They had been unable to support the weight of cable. The cables between them weighed over three hundred tons and they had to be stretched to sufficient tension to carry the gravel buckies without sagging excessively.

The very first day of operation the stagings at the north end of the section gave under the strain. Two winches tore loose and the wires fell twanging and snaking into the diggings. There had been a gravel bucky on the rope, carrying five black workmen down to the floor of the workings to begin re-opening the long deserted claims. They screamed the whole way down as the bucky spun and twisted, throwing them clear, and the tangle of snapping silver cables caught them up like the tentacles of some voracious sea-monster.

It took the rest of the day to bring out the fearfully mutilated bodies, and the Diggers' Committee closed the No. 6 Section again while modifications were made to reinforce the stagings.

The No. 6 Section was still closed.

Zouga had one bottle of Cape brandy left which he had been saving, but now he fetched it from his locker, pulled the cork with his teeth and poured into their two mugs.

He and Jan Cheroot drank in moody silence for a while, and then Zouga sighed.

'Tell your friend I will meet him,' he said.

Pale dust chalked the sky above the plain, so that the distances drifted away, dream-like and insubstantial, to an indefinite horizon.

There was no living thing, no bird nor vulture in the milky blue sky, no ripple of flocks nor smoky drift of springbuck herds through the low scrub.

In this loneliness the little cluster of buildings stood forlorn, long deserted, roofs sagging and the adobe plaster falling from the walls in chunks exposing the unsawn timber frames beneath.

Zouga touched the reins and brought the gelding down to a walk, while he slouched in the saddle, riding with long stirrups and the disinterested mien of a man on a long and boring journey – but his eyes under the brim of the wide hat were quick and restless.

He was uncomfortably aware of the empty rifle scabbard under his right knee.

'Unarmed.' The invitation had been unequivocal. 'You will be watched.'

The man had chosen an ideal rendezvous. There was no approach to this deserted farmhouse except across miles of bare veld, no cover higher than a man's knee – and it was good shooting light, with the sun in the west. Zouga shifted his weight restlessly in the saddle, and the big ungainly Colt revolver under his coat dug into his side, a pain he did not resent – although the comfort it gave him was illusory. A man with a rifle could pick his shot and take his time as Zouga rode in.

The sheep kraal was part of the homestead, unplastered stone walls, and there was a well in front of the house, again with a stone coping. Beside the well lay the remains of a wagon, three wheels and the disselboom missing, the paint dried and cracked away, the weed growing up through the wagon bed.

Zouga touched the gelding's neck and he stopped beside the wagon. He dismounted swiftly, dropping off on the side farthest from the building, using the horse as cover, and while he made a show of adjusting the girth, he studied the empty building again.

The windows were dark empty holes, like missing teeth, and there could be an unseen marksman standing well back in the gloomy interior. The front door was blanched by the sun; Zouga could see the light through the cracks. It banged aimlessly and unrhythmically in the wind, and the wind hooted and moaned in the eaves and through the empty windows.

Behind the gelding's body Zouga loosened the revolver in his belt, making certain that it was ready to hand. He tied the gelding's reins to the wagon body with a slippery knot that would come undone at a tug, and then he consciously steeled himself, drew breath and squared his shoulders and stepped out from behind the horse.

He began to walk towards the front door, but his right hand was on his hip, under the tail of his jacket, almost touching the checkered grip of the revolver.

He reached the doorway, keeping clear of the entrance, and then flattened his back against the wall.

With faint surprise he realized that his breathing was rough, as though he had been running. Then another surprise – he was enjoying his own fear, the feeling of heightened sensitivity of his skin, the enhanced clarity of vision, the singing of the adrenalin in his blood, the nervous tension of his sinew and muscle, the awareness of being alive in the threat of death. He had been too long without this stimulant.

He placed one hand on the sill of the window and vaulted through it lightly, dropping to the earthen floor as he landed and rolling swiftly to his feet again in the corner, facing the room. It was small and empty, bunches of dusty cobwebs hung from the rafters, and the floor was scattered with the white-flecked droppings of gecko lizards.

Zouga moved down the wall, keeping his back covered, and stepped through into the second room. The kagel fireplace was blackened with soot, and the smell of dead ash caught in his throat. He looked through the open doorway into the sunlit sheep kraal beyond. There was a riderless horse tethered in the angle of the wall. A grey, dappled quarters, uncropped dark mane and full tail almost sweeping the ground. The rifle scabbard on the saddle was empty, and Zouga's nerves fizzed. The unknown rider must have the gun with him.

Zouga loosed the long barrel of the Colt revolver in his belt, peering out into the sunlight.

'Keep your hand away from that gun.' The voice came from behind him, from the empty front room through which Zouga had just passed. 'Don't draw it, and don't turn around.'

The voice was quiet, controlled and very close. Zouga obeyed it, standing awkwardly with his right hand under his coat, and he felt the touch of steel between his shoulder blades. It had been well done; the man had been lying outside, had let him walk through the house and then had come in behind him.

'Now very slowly bring out the gun and put it on the floor between your feet. Very slowly, please, Major Ballantyne. I don't want to have to kill you, but if I hear the hammer cocked I will – believe me, I will.'

Slowly Zouga freed the heavy pistol and stooped to place it on the littered kitchen floor. He glanced back between his own legs and saw the man's feet. He was wearing velskoen of tanned kudu hide and leather leggings, big feet, big man, strong legs.

Zouga straightened up, holding his hands well away from his body.

'You should not have brought a gun, Major. That is very distrustful of you, and dangerous for both of us.' He could hear the relief in the man's tone, and the voice was familiar, he searched his memory. That strange accent, where had he heard it? The footsteps retreated across the kitchen.

'Slowly now, Major, very slowly, you may turn around.'

The man stood in the gloom of the soot-darkened walls, but the shaft of sunlight from the high window fell on his hands and the weapon they held.

It was a shotgun. Both big fancy hammers were at full cock, and the man's fingers were hooked around the triggers.

'You!' said Zouga.

'Yes, Major, me!' The pockmarked Griqua Bastaard smiled at him, white teeth in the darkly handsome face and the gypsy ringlets dangling to his collar. 'Hendrick Naaiman, at your service, once again.'

'If you are buying cattle, it's a hell of a way to do business.' The Griqua was the one who had bought Zouga's bullock team, the money he had used to buy the Devil's Own.

'No, Major, this time I am selling.' And then sharply, 'No, Major, do not move, and keep your hands there, where I can see them. I have loaded with Big Loopers – lion-shot, Major. At this range it will cut you in half.'

Zouga lifted his hands away from his sides.

'What are you selling?'

'Wealth, Major, a new way of life for you, and for me.'

Zouga smiled bleakly, sarcastically.

'I am truly grateful for your kindness, Naaiman.'

'Please call me Hendrick, Major – if we are to be partners.'

'We are?' Zouga inclined his head gravely. 'I am honoured.'

'You see, you have something I need and I have something you need.'

'Go on.'

'You have two excellent claims, they are truly excellent claims in all except they yield very few diamonds.'

Zouga felt the scar on his cheek heating up, but he kept his expression neutral.

'And as you know, Major, my ancestry, the touch of the tarbrush, I think is the polite term, or more succinctly my kaffir blood, precludes me from owning claims.'

They were silent then, regarding each other warily across the darkened kitchen. Zouga had abandoned any idea of going for the shotgun. He was starting to become intrigued by the articulate and persuasive voice of the tall Griqua.

'For that reason I cannot sell you my claims, not even at gunpoint,' Zouga said quietly.

'No, no, you do not understand. You have the claims but no diamonds, while I have no claims but –'

Hendrick drew a drawstring tobacco bag from his inner pocket and dangled it by its string from his forefinger.

'—But I have diamonds.' He finished the sentence and tossed the bag across the room.

Instinctively Zouga reached out one hand and caught it. The bag crunched in his hands like a bag of humbugs, bringing back childhood memories. He held it, staring still at Hendrick Naaiman.

'Open it, please, Major.'

Slowly Zouga obeyed, pulling open the mouth of the cloth bag, and then peered into it.

The light was bad, but in the bag something gleamed like the coils of a sleeping serpent.

Zouga felt the diamond thrill close its fist upon his chest. It never failed, he thought, always that choking feeling when the stones shine.

He tipped the bag and spilled a small rush of uncut diamonds into his hand. He counted them quickly; there were eight of them altogether.

One was a canary bright stone, twenty carats if it was a point. Two thousand pounds' worth, Zouga estimated.

'These are just samples of my wares, Major, a week's takings.'

There was another perfect eight-sided crystal, slick and soapy silver-grey, bigger than the yellow diamond, at least three thousand pounds' worth.

Another of the stones was a symmetrical triangular shape, like those throat loz-enges that tasted of liquorice, more childhood memories. A clear silver stone, limpid and lovely. Zouga picked it up between thumb and forefinger and held it to the light of the high window.

'These are I.D.B?' he asked.

'Dirty words, Major; they offend my delicate breeding. Do not concern yourself further with where they come from, or how I get them. Just be certain that there will be more, many more, every week there will be a parcel of first water stones.'

'Every week?' Zouga asked, and heard the greed in his own voice.

'Every week,' Hendrick agreed, watching Zouga's expression, and he knew the fly had touched the sticky strands of his web. He let the barrel of the shotgun sag towards the mud floor, and he smiled that flashing flamboyant smile. 'Every week you will have a parcel like this to seed into your own cradle, to throw out on your own sorting-table.'

There was another stone in his palm. At first Zouga had thought it to be black boart, the almost worthless industrial diamond; but his heart bounced suddenly as the poor light caught it and he saw the deep emerald colour flash from its heart. His fingers trembled slightly as he lifted it.

'Yes, Major.' Hendrick Naaiman nodded approval. 'You have a good eye; that's a green dragon.'

A freak stone, a green diamond, a 'fancy' in the parlance of the kopje-wallopers. There were fancy diamonds the colour of rubies, or sapphires or topaz, and fancies commanded whatever the trade would bear. It was not impossible that this green dragon would fetch ten thousand pounds, and end up in the crown jewels of an emperor.

'You said partners?' Zouga asked softly.

'Yes, partners,' Hendrick nodded. 'I will find the stones. Let me give you an example. I paid three hundred to one of my men for that green dragon. You put it across your table and register it from the Devil's Own –'

Zouga was staring at him fixedly, hungrily, his hands still trembling, and Hendrick stepped towards him confidently.

' – You should get four thousand pounds for a stone like that, a profit of three thousand seven hundred; and we share that fiftyfifty, because I am not a greedy man. Equal partners, Major, eighteen fifty for you and eighteen fifty for me.'

Zouga poured the glittering stones into his left hand. His eyes had not left Hendrick Naaiman's lips.

'What do you say, Major? Equal partners.' Hendrick transferred the shotgun to his left hand and reached out with his right.

'Equal partners,' he repeated. 'Let's shake hands on it.'

Slowly Zouga stretched out his own right hand, fingers open, palm upwards. And then, as their fingers touched, he hurled the handful of diamonds into Hendrick Naaiman's face. All Zouga's strength was behind the throw, all his anger at being so sorely tempted, all his outrage at this devilish assault upon his own self-esteem.

The diamonds tore into Hendrick Naaiman's flesh, one sharp-sided crystal ripped open his smooth olive-skinned forehead above the right eye, another sliced his lip.

Involuntarily Hendrick threw up his hands, lifting the shotgun muzzle high before his face as he staggered back from this unexpected assault, but at the same instant his right hand closed over the pistol grip and his forefinger hooked for the triggers. The gun was still at full cock, each barrel loaded with lion-shot. Hendrick started to drop the muzzles, pointing for Zouga's belly.

Zouga grabbed the barrel six inches below the gaping muzzles and forced the gun upwards, grasping with his left hand for Hendrick's right wrist. The big Griqua jerked backwards with both arms, and Zouga made no effort to resist him; instead he lunged forward, thrusting the gun into Hendrick's own face. The blue steel barrels cracked against his cheekbone, and Hendrick gasped at the blow and reeled backwards. Zouga drove at him again, forcing him into the soot-blackened wall so that he grunted with pain, pinned there for a moment with the shotgun pointing at the roof. In these seconds Zouga reached with his left hand, hooked his thumb through the trigger guard and jerked back against the triggers.

Both barrels fired simultaneously.

The burst of gunfire in the tiny confined kitchen was deafening. The bright orange muzzle flashes lit the gloom like a lightning strike, and the charges of shot crashed through the rotten roof, blowing gaping holes through which the sun shot long bright shafts of light.

The massive recoil of the double-shotted gun drove the butt back into Hendrick's own belly, and he doubled over with a gasp of shock and agony.

The gun was empty, harmless. Zouga let it go and dived full length across the dusty floor. At full stretch his fingers touched the cool checkered grip of the ugly black Colt revolver. As he fumbled for it desperately, he heard the light crunch of footsteps across the earthen floor behind him, and rolled right, flicking over on his back without raising his head.

Hendrick was over him, the empty shotgun raised above his head with both hands like an executioner's axe, and he had already launched the stroke. The gun swung down in a wide arc, the blue steel glittering sullenly in the gloom and the hiss of it like the sound of a goose's wing. Zouga rolled again flipping his body aside. But the butt of the shotgun caught him.

It was only a touch, high in the shoulder, but it jerked his head so that his teeth clashed in his skull, and his right arm was instantly nerveless, numb from his shoulder to fingertips. The Colt revolver went flying from his grip, spinning away across the kitchen floor until it hit the far wall.

Instantly Hendrick turned to chase the pistol, and Zouga kicked out at the back of his knee, landing solidly with the heel of his boot. Hendrick's leg folded under the blow, and he would have gone down but the wall was there to hold him. He fell against it, pinned for a moment by his crippled leg, and Zouga rolled to his feet.

He stabbed with his good left hand, feeling the solid shock of the Griqua's jawbone under his fist. Then again Zouga caught him with the left and heard the gristle in the beaky nose give with a crunch like chewing on a ripe apple, and the fresh blood from Hendrick's nostrils gave him a fierce joy.

He was going to beat this man to a bleeding pulp.

'Wait!' Hendrick shouted. 'Please! Don't hit me again.'

The appeal was so frantic, the terror on the Griqua's bloody face so pitiful, that even in his own cold killing anger, Zouga checked.

He stepped back and lowered his hands, and the Griqua hurled the empty shotgun at Zouga's face. It was completely unexpected, Zouga was off-guard, and even as he started to duck, Zouga knew it was too late, and he hated himself for a fool.

It felt as though somebody had slammed a door behind Zouga's eyes, and his vision was suddenly narrowed and dimmed with blood. He hurled himself forward, and dived again for the revolver. He got a hand on the barrel, and as he touched it the full weight of Hendrick's charging body crashed into his back, driving him into a heap against the doorjamb. But he still had a grip on the pistol barrel, and he struck out blindly using it like a club.

He felt the steel butt sock into flesh, and he hit again and again, some of the blows dying in the air, others thudding into the floor, but others cracking against bone.

He was sobbing and panting, blinded by his own blood, and for seconds he did not realize that Hendrick no longer clutched and tore at him.

Zouga shrank back against the wall and wiped the blood from his eyes. Then he peered like an old man through the red film. Hendrick was beside him. He was on his back, his arms flung wide as a crucifix and the blood snored and bubbled from his nostrils. He lay very still, his breathing the only sign of life.

Zouga lowered the pistol, and used the wall to hoist himself to his feet. He stood there swaying, his head hanging, the pistol dangling from his hand that was suddenly so weak that he could barely support its weight.

'Master Zouga!' Jan Cheroot dashed into the yard, panting from his run, carrying the Lee-Enfield rifle at high port across his chest, sweat streaking down from under his brimless pillbox infantry cap and his face crumpling with dismay as he saw Zouga's bloody torn face.

'You took your time,' Zouga accused him huskily, still clinging to the door for support. He had left Jan Cheroot with the rifle hidden in a ravine half a mile out across the dusty plain.

'I started running as soon as I heard the shots.'

Zouga realized that the fight had lasted only a few minutes, as long as it takes a man to run half a mile. Jan Cheroot unslung the water bottle from his shoulder and tried to wash a little of the blood from Zouga's face.

'Leave that.' Zouga pulled away brusquely. 'See if there is a rope in the Bastaard's saddle bags, something to tie him, a knee halter, anything.'

There was a coil of braided rawhide rope on the pommel of the grey mare's saddle. Jan Cheroot hurried back with it and then paused in the door of the derelict shanty.

'I know him.' He stared at Hendrick Naaiman's bloody snoring face. 'I think I know him, but you made such a mess of him.'

'Tie him,' Zouga whispered, and drank from the water bottle. Then he unwound the silk scarf from around his throat and wetted it from the bottle before tenderly wiping away the blood and dust from his cuts and scratches.

The worst injury was in his hairline, where the breech of the broken shotgun had caught him; by the feel of it, it needed to be stitched.

Jan Cheroot was muttering insults and abuse at Hendrick Naaiman as he worked.

'You yellow snake.' He rolled the Griqua onto his back. 'You got shoes on your feet and pants covering your black arse, and you think you are a gentleman.'

He pulled Hendrick's arms up behind him and trussed them, quickly and expertly, at wrist and elbow.

'You'd give a vulture a bad name.' Jan Cheroot looped the rawhide around his ankles and pulled it up tight. 'Even the hyenas wouldn't eat dung alongside of you, my beauty.'

Zouga capped the water bottle and picked up the empty tobacco bag. Then he hunted for the diamonds. They had been kicked and scattered about the kitchen. The eighth and last was the green dragon, dark and inconspicuous in one gloomy corner.

Zouga tossed the bag to Jan Cheroot, and he whistled as he peered into it.

'I.D.B.,' he muttered, his wrinkled brown face puckering into a sculpture of pure avarice. 'The yellow snake was I.D.B.'

'He wanted us to run those stones across our sorting-tables.'

'What shares?' Jan Cheroot demanded, playing with the stones.

'Half shares.'

'That's a good deal. We could be rich in six months and get out of this god-damned and blasted desert for ever.'

Abruptly Zouga snatched the bag back again. He had been through the temptation once already.

'Get his horse,' he ordered angrily.

They hoisted the Griqua's inert body and threw it over the grey's saddle. As Jan Cheroot was tying the Griqua to the horse, Hendrick kicked his legs weakly and tried to raise his head, twisting his neck to peer blearily at Zouga.

'Major,' he croaked, only half conscious. 'Major, let me explain. You don't understand.'

'Shut your mouth,' Zouga growled at him.

'Major. I am not a thief, let me explain about those diamonds.'

'I told you to hold your mouth,' Zouga warned, and wrenched the Griqua's jaw open, roughly digging his thumbs into the sallow bloody cheeks; then he thrust the bag of diamonds into his slack mouth.

'Choke on your bloody diamonds, you thieving, treacherous bastard,' he told him grimly as he bound the man's mouth closed with his scarf, jamming the bag in place, while Hendrick squawked and rolled his eyes, jerking his head from side to side, his cries muffled and his spittle soaking the gay band of silk.

'That will keep you quiet until we get you in front of the Committee.'

Jan Cheroot sat up behind the trussed Griqua on the grey's back and followed Zouga on the gelding.

He sucked his teeth mournfully, sighed and shook his head.

'What a waste!' he grumbled just loud enough for Zouga to hear. 'That bag would take us back to the north.'

He rolled his eyes sideways at Zouga, but there was no reaction.

'The Committee is going to see this yellow bastard lynched anyway. He is as good as vulture breakfast already –'

Hendrick wriggled helplessly and snuffled through his swollen nose.

' – If we just did the job for them, nice and quietly, a bullet in the head, and leave him for his brothers and sisters, the jackals and the hyena, man, nobody will ever know.'

He glanced hopefully at Zouga again. 'What's in that bag will take us north again, as far as we want to go.'

Zouga kicked the gelding into a canter, and ahead of them the iron roofs and dusty tent cones of New Rush glowed ruddily in the slanting rays of the sunset. Jan Cheroot sighed, swatted the double-laden grey across the quarters and followed Zouga into the camp.

Pickering and Rhodes messed with a few other bachelor diggers directly beyond Market Square, at the edge of the main tailing dumps. There were two good spreading acacias to give them shade, and they had planted a hedge of milkbush around the cluster of iron huts and walled shanties.

Every member of the mess owned good claims and was recovering stones; he had to do so to afford the mess bills for champagne and old cognac that seemed to form the group's staple diet. One of them was the younger son of a belted earl, another was a baronet in his own right, although merely of the Irish aristocracy. Most of them were members of the Diggers' Committee, and their style had earned the group the title of 'The Swells'.

When Zouga rode into their camp, half a dozen of the Swells were lounging under the acacia trees, dining on Veuve Cliquot champagne, although the sun was still above the horizon, and wrangling amiably over the heavy wagers that they were placing against how many flies would settle on the sugar lumps that each had on the camp table in front of him.

Pickering looked up, his fair open features for once puckered in astonishment, as Zouga rode into the camp.

'Gentlemen,' Zouga announced grimly. 'I have something for you.'

He leaned out of his saddle and cut the thongs that secured Hendrick Naaiman's heels to the saddle girth of the grey mare, and then tipped him off the horse, letting him fall head-first into the dust in front of the seated group of Diggers' Committee members.

'I.D.B.,' Zouga told them, as they stared at him.

Pickering moved first. He jumped to his feet.

'Where are the diamonds, Major?' he asked.

'In his mouth.'

Pickering went down on one knee next to the Griqua, and he undid the scarf.

He worked the saliva-drenched bag out of Hendrick's broken mouth, and poured the contents onto the camp table amongst the flies and sugar lumps and champagne bottles.

'Eight,' Rhodes counted them swiftly, and looked immensely relieved. 'They are all there.'

'I told you not to worry. I bet fifty guineas on them all being there. Don't forget it.'

Pickering smiled at Rhodes and turned back to the Griqua, who was flapping around in the dust like a trussed chicken.

Pickering helped him solicitously to his feet.

'My dear fellow,' he asked. 'Are you all right?'

'He nearly killed me,' Hendrick bleated bitterly. 'He's a madman!'

'I told you to be careful,' Pickering agreed. 'He's not a man to trifle with.' He patted the Griqua's back. 'Well done, Hendrick; you did a good job.'

Then Pickering turned to Zouga. 'We owe you a little apology, Major.' He spread his hands and smiled winningly.

Zouga had been staring at him, unable to speak, his face so pale that his scratches and gouges stood out lividly. But now the scar under his eyes began to glow and he found his voice.

'A trap!' he whispered. 'You set a trap for me.'

'We had to be sure of you,' Rhodes explained reasonably. 'We had to know what kind of man you really were before we got you onto the Diggers' Committee.'

'You swine,' Zouga husked. 'You arrogant swine.'

'You came out of it with flying colours, sir,' Rhodes told him stiffly. He was not accustomed to being addressed in those terms.

'If I had fallen for your trap, what would you have done?'

Rhodes shrugged his heavy shoulders. 'The question doesn't arise. You acted like a true English gentleman.'

'You will never know how close it was,' Zouga told him.

'Oh yes, I do. Most of us here have been tested.'

Zouga turned to Pickering. 'What would have happened, a lynching party?'

'Oh, my dear fellow, probably nothing so theatrical. You just might have slipped on the roadway and taken a tumble into the diggings, or had the misfortune to be standing under a gravel bucky when the rope parted.' He laughed merrily, and the men at the table laughed with him.

'You need a glass of Charlie Champers, Major, or something stronger perhaps.'

'Do join us, sir,' cried another, making room for him at the table. 'An honour to drink with a gentleman.'

'Come along, Major.' Pickering smiled. 'I'll send for the quack to see to that cut on your head.'

Then Pickering stopped and his expression changed.

Zouga had kicked his feet loose from the stirrups and jumped down to face him. They were of an even height, both big men, and the group at the camp table was instantly enchanted. This would be more diverting than watching bluebottles settling on sugar lumps.

'By gad, he's going to bang Pickling's head.'

'Or Pickling his.'

'Ten guineas the elephant hunter to win.'

'I don't approve of brawling,' murmured Rhodes, 'but I'll take Pickling for ten.'

'I say, the other horse has run a fair chase already. I do think you might offer some odds.'

Pickering's smile had turned frosty, and he was on his toes, his fists clenched, and his guard half raised.

Zouga dropped his own guard and turned disgustedly to the group under the acacia.

'I've provided you with enough amusement for one day,' he told them coldly. 'You can take your bloody diamonds, and your damned Committee and you can –'

There was a burst of clapping and laughing cheers to cover Zouga's outburst. Zouga swung back onto the gelding's back and kicked him into a gallop, and the ironical applause followed him out of the camp.

'I hope we haven't lost him.' Pickering lowered his fists and stared after Zouga. 'God knows, we need honest men.'

'Oh, don't worry,' Rhodes told him. 'Give him time to simmer down and then we'll square him.'

'Henshaw.' Bazo held the woven reed basket on his lap and peered into it mournfully.

'Henshaw, she is not ready to fight again so soon.'

They sat in a circle about the cooking fire in the centre of the thatched beehive. Ralph felt more at home here than in the tent under the camel-thorn tree. Here he was with friends, the closest friends he had ever known in his nomadic life, and here also he was beyond the severe and unrelenting surveillance of his father.

Ralph dipped into the communal three-legged black pot with his left hand and scooped up a little of the stiff fluffy white maize porridge. While he rolled it into a ball between his fingers he argued with the Matabele princeling opposite him.

'If it were you to decide, she would never fight again,' Ralph told him, and dipped the maize ball into the flavouring of mutton gravy and wild herbs.

'Her new leg is not strong enough yet,' Bazo shook his head.

Ralph popped the morsel and chewed as he talked. 'The leg is hard and bright as a knife.'

Bazo puffed out his cheeks and looked even more lugubrious, and on her perch in the shadows behind him Scipio, the falcon, shook out her feathers and 'kweeted' softly as though in sympathy with him.

Bazo's decision, although heavily influenced by Ralph's arguments and by the urgings of the other young Matabele, would be final. For it was Bazo who had made the original capture of the animal under discussion.

'Every night that she does not fight, we, your brothers, are the poorer,' Kamuza came in to support Ralph. 'Henshaw is right. She is fierce as a lioness and ready to earn us all many gold queens.'

'Already you speak and think like a white man,' Bazo replied loftily. 'The yellow coins fill your head day and night.'

'What other reason for that,' Kamuza shuddered slightly as he pointed at the basket, 'that thing. If it stings you, the spear of your manhood will shrivel like a rotten fruit until it is no bigger than the finger of a new born baby.'

'What a shrivelling that would be,' Ralph chuckled. 'Like a bull hippopotamus shrivelling into a striped field mouse.'

Bazo grinned and made the gesture of placing the tiny basket on Kamuza's lap. 'Come, let her suckle a little to give her strength for the conflict,' he suggested, and the circle exploded with a roar of delighted laughter at Kamuza's patent horror as he yelled and leapt violently away.

The noisy jeers covered their own uneasiness at the close proximity of the basket, and they were immediately silent as Bazo cautiously lifted the lid.

They craned forward with sickly fascination, and in the bottom of the basket something dark and furry and big as a rat stirred.

'Hau! Inkosikazi!' Bazo greeted it, and the creature reared up on its multiple legs, raising the front pair defensively, and the rows of eyes glittered in the softly wavering firelight. Bazo lifted his own right hand to return the salute of long hairy legs.

'I see you also, Inkosikazi.'

Bazo had named her Inkosikazi, the queen, for, as he explained to Ralph, 'She is right royal in her rage, and as thirsty for blood as a Matabele queen.'

He and Ralph had been unloading timber baulks at the eastern end of the new stagings, and as one load had swung upwards in the slings the great spider had come out from its nest between the sawn planks, and, raising its swollen velvety abdomen, had scampered over Ralph's arm and leapt ten feet to the ground.

The spider was the size of a dinner plate when its legs were extended. Its hirsute appearance and its extraordinary jumping prowess had given the species the common name of baboon spider.

'Get him, Bazo!' Ralph yelled from the top of the loaded wagon.

For now that Griqualand West and the New Rush diggings were part of Cape Colony and the British Empire there had been changes.

New Rush had been re-named Kimberley, after Lord Kimberley, the Colonial Secretary in London, and the town of Kimberley was starting to enjoy the benefits of British civilization and Victorian morality, amongst which was the total ban on cock fighting which was strictly enforced by the new administrator. The diggers, always eager for distraction, had not taken long to find an alternative sport. Spider fighting was the rage of the diggings.

'Don't let him get away!' Ralph vaulted down from the wagon, ripping off his shirt, but Bazo was quicker. He whipped the loincloth from his waist and flared it at the spider like a matador caping the bull, bringing the huge arachnid to bay on its hind legs, threatening him with its waving arms, then, naked and triumphant, Bazo had flipped the cloth over it and swiftly bundled it into a bag.

Now he slowly but deliberately extended his own hand into the basket, and the spider raised itself higher, the wolflike mandibles chewing menacingly, and between them the single curved red fang rising from its shallow sheath, a pale droplet of venom shining upon the needlesharp tip.

There was not even the sound of breathing in the dark hut, and the soft tick and rustle of the ashes sounded deafening in the silence as they watched Bazo's open hand draw closer and closer to the creature.

Then he touched it with his fingertips and began to stroke the soft furry carapace. Slowly the spider subsided from her threatening posture, and the watchers sighed and began to breathe again.

Inkosikazi had fought five times, and five times she had killed, although in the last conflict against another huge and ferocious female she had lost one of her legs, chewed through at the elbow joint. That had been almost three months previously; but the severed limb had now regenerated itself, and the new leg was lighter coloured than the others like the fresh shoots on a rose bush.

Slowly Bazo turned his hand palm upwards and the spider scuttled up into it and crouched there, filling it completely without extending her many jointed legs.

'A queen,' he said, 'a veritable queen.' And then, frowning, he told her, 'Henshaw would like to see you fight again.' He glanced up at Ralph, and there was a mischievous twist to his full lips.

'Go to Henshaw and tell him if you will fight or no.' And he offered the spider to Ralph.

Ralph felt the crawling of the tiny feet of horror across his skin as he stared at the spider crouching like a hairy toad before his face.

'Come, Henshaw,' Bazo smiled. 'Talk to her.'

It was a challenge, and the watchers stirred with anticipation. If the challenge was not taken up, then their mockery would be merciless. Ralph tried to force himself to move, but his loathing was a cold nauseating lump under his ribs, and the sheen of sweat on his forehead was suddenly glacially cold.

Bazo was still smiling, but the challenge in his direct gaze was slowly changing to taunting disdain. With an enormous effort Ralph raised his hand, and at the movement the spider lifted itself and the soft bloated abdomen seemed to pulse softly, obscenely.

Only one person had ever handled Inkosikazi, and her reaction to a strange touch was totally unpredictable; but Ralph forced himself to reach out towards her.

Slowly his fingertips drew closer, six inches, two inches from the hairy body, and then the spider sprang. It launched itself in a high parabola, and landed on Ralph's shoulder.

The circle of watchers broke up in comic panic, yelling with terror and falling over one another to reach the single low doorway. Only Bazo and Ralph had not moved. Ralph sat with his hand still extended and the spider squatted massively on his shoulder. Infinitely slowly Ralph cocked his head and peered down at it, and it began to move; lifting the long bristled legs with a chilling daintiness, it crept sideways into the hollow of Ralph's neck – so that he could no longer see it but suddenly he felt the sharp points of its feet scratching the soft of his throat.

There was a horrified yell locked in the back of Ralph's throat, but he kept it there with a total effort of will. The spider climbed his chin and hung upside down for a moment like a huge hairy bat, and Ralph did not move.

Instead he lifted his gaze and held that of the Matabele opposite him. The mockery was gone from Bazo's eyes, and behind him the other watchers drew closer, fascinated and fearful. Perhaps for a minute they sat like that, and then Ralph lifted his hand. The gesture was so calm, so controlled, that the spider showed only perfunctory symptoms of alarm, and then quite willingly scuttled onto the inviting fingers and Ralph transferred her gently back into her basket.

Ralph wanted to leap up and run out into the darkness, to be alone while he vomited up his horror, but he forced himself to sit and stare impassively at Bazo until the Matabele lowered his eyes.

'She will fight,' he said softly. 'As you wish, Henshaw, she will fight again tomorrow.' And he closed the lid of the basket.

Inkosikazi had not fought for almost three months, and the punters, always fickle, had forgotten her. Other champions had emerged in her absence and commanded the fanatic loyalty of their followers. They gathered four deep around the handlers, trying to peer into the baskets and assess the fighting metal of the caged creatures, as they waited for the first bout of the afternoon.

Although lantern-lit contests were held each evening behind Diamond Lil's canteen, Sunday afternoon was the main event of the week when every digger in Kimberley was free to crowd the western corner of Market Square and pick his fancy.

The arena was a square wooden structure, six feet by six and three deep, covered by a sheet of clear glass. This sheet of glass was the largest in Griqualand; originally intended as a display window for a ladies' dress shop on Main Street, it had miraculously survived the long wagon journey from the coast – and was now probably one of the most cherished items in Kimberley. Without it the sport would die, and Sunday afternoons would be tedium indeed.

The sheet of glass and the wooden arena were owned by a onetime kopje-walloper who had found there was more money in spiders than in diamonds. Ownership of the glass gave him a monopoly of the game and allowed him to charge a cruel entrance fee, and take a lion's share of the winnings.

Half a dozen wagons had been drawn up in a square around the arena to make grandstand accommodation for the crowds. The canteens around the square provided *al fresco* service, their waiters staggering under trays laden with foaming schooners of beer to quench the raging thirsts that men had built up during a week in the pit.

The female population had doubled and re-doubled since Kimberley had become part of the Empire, and the ladies used the occasion to show off a pretty hat and a nicely sculptured ankle. Their delighted squeals of horror when the fighting spiders were released into the arena added to the feverish air of excitement.

In one of the alleys that led into the square, Ralph and his Matabele were huddled in solemn discussion.

'I do not know what that name means,' Bazo was protesting to Ralph.

'It is the name of a dangerous woman, who danced so beautifully that when she asked for it the king cut off a man's head and gave it to her.'

They all looked impressed. It was the kind of story which appealed to a Matabele.

'What is the name again?' Bazo asked thoughtfully.

'Salome –'

'But why cannot she fight under her real name?' Bazo glanced down at the basket under his arm. 'Why must we change Inkosikazi's name for this fight? It is not a good omen.'

Ralph looked exasperated. 'If we use that name they will know it is the same Inkosikazi who has already killed five times. If we call her Salome, why, one spider looks like another. They will not recognize her. They will believe her to be unblooded, and we shall win more money.'

'That is a good reason,' Kamuza cut in, and Bazo ignored him.

'Who found this name?' Bazo insisted.

'Jordie. He found it in the big book.' That decided it. Bazo had vast respect for the lovely gentle boy and his knowledge of books.

'Salome.' He nodded. 'It is agreed, but only for today.'

'Good.' Ralph rubbed his palms together briskly. 'Now where is the money?' And they all looked to Kamuza. He was the treasurer of the group. In their years of unbroken labour the gang of young Matabele had accumulated a hoard of gold and silver coin, for to their wages they had added the bounty on 'pick-ups'. Then of course there were the considerable winnings from Inkosikazi's previous bouts.

Kamuza kept this treasure buried under the floor of the communal hut, but he had reluctantly exhumed part of it the evening before, and now he produced a soft furry white bag, made from tanned scrotal skin of a springbuck ram, and reluctantly counted out coins into Ralph's hand. No white bookmaker would accept a wager from a black man, so Ralph was frontman for the Matabele syndicate.

'Make a book,' Kamuza said, and Ralph scribbled a receipt for sixteen sovereigns on a page of his notebook, tore it out and handed it to Kamuza, who examined it minutely. He trusted Ralph without question. He could not read, but the rituals of European commerce fascinated Kamuza and he had seen white men passing slips of paper whenever they exchanged coin.

'Good.' He tucked the receipt into the springbuck-skin wallet.

'I have four gold queens of my own.' Ralph displayed his life savings. 'I will pay my share of the entrance fee and bet the rest of it.'

'May the gods go with us all, Henshaw,' said Bazo, and handed Ralph the precious little basket.

Ralph adjusted his cap to an angle that would hide as much of his face as possible. It was unlikely that his father would be amongst the crowd, and if he was, the cap would hardly disguise his firstborn sufficiently for him not to be recognized – so the gesture was instinctive, as was his fear of his father's wrath.

'I will wait here for the money,' Kamuza told him.

'If she wins,' Ralph agreed.

'She will win,' said Bazo darkly. 'Would that I could serve her with my own hands.'

There was no law to prevent a black man entering a fancy in the lists, but none of them had ever done so. The niceties of this complex society were unwritten but understood by all.

Ralph slipped out of the alley and mingled with the crowd, working his way through the press until he was on the outskirts of the group of handlers, each of them with his woven basket, as they waited to enter their fancy.

'Ah, young Ballantyne.' Chaim Cohen looked up from his register, the wire-rimmed spectacles on the end of his nose, sweating jovially in the dust and blazing sun. 'Haven't seen you in some time.'

'Didn't have a fancy, Mr Cohen. Caught a new one now,' Ralph lied glibly.

'What happened to – what did you call her, some kaffir name?'

'She died. Lost a leg and died after her last fight.'

'What is your new lady's name?'

'Salome, sir.'

'Salome it is, then. That will be two pounds, young Ballantyne.' The coins disappeared with uncanny speed into the enlarged pocket that Cohen had sewn into the inside of his long frock coat, and with relief Ralph sidled into the crowd, trying to lose himself until the draw was announced.

He found a place near the tailboard of one of the wagons, where he was partly concealed and from where he could watch the ladies in the crowd. Some of them were young and pretty, and they knew it. Every few minutes one would pass close enough to Ralph for him to hear the frou-frou of her petticoats and to smell her, for the heat brought out the subtle musk of womankind that was emphasized and not concealed by the sweet reek of French perfume. It seemed to catch in Ralph's throat, too poignant to breathe, and there was a hollow aching place at the base of his belly and weird thoughts in his head.

The fruity smell of cognac suddenly blotted out that French perfume and a hoarse voice close to his ear put the imaginings to flight.

'You are fighting a new fancy, I see, young Ballantyne.'

'Yes, sir. That's right, sir, Mr Lennox.'

Mr Barry Lennox was a big man, a brawler with a reputation for quick fists that was respected as far as the river workings. He was a plunger, who had bet a thousand guineas on a single cock fight, and won. That was in the days before civilization had reached the diggings, but now he chanced as much on the spider fights. He was a rich man by the standards of New Rush, for he owned eighteen claims in the No. 4 Roadway block. He had the red-veined cheeks and husky voice of the heavy drinker, but what intrigued Ralph most about this man was that he employed three young women, not one but three women to keep house for him. One was a pretty pug-faced daffodil-yellow Griqua girl, another a bold-eyed Portuguese mulatto from Mozambique, and the third a mulberry black Basuto with haunches on her like a brood mare. Whenever Ralph thought about this dusky trio, which was often, his imagination conjured up a garden of forbidden delights.

Of course, neither Ralph's father nor any other member of the Committee would acknowledge Lennox's existence and cut him elaborately on the street. Lennox's application to join the Kimberley Club had been met with a record-breaking fifty-six black balls. But Ralph removed his cap respectfully now, as Lennox asked throatily:

'What happened to Inkosikazi? I made a bundle on her.'

'She died, Mr Lennox. Old age, I suppose.'

'Baboon spiders live nearly twenty years and more,' Lennox grunted. 'Let's have a look at your new lady.'

'I don't like to unsettle her – not just before a bout, sir.'

'Does your daddy know where you spend your Sunday afternoons, young Ballantyne?'

'All right, sir.' Ralph capitulated swiftly and lifted the lid of the basket a crack. Lennox cocked a bloodshot but knowledgeable eye at it.

'That looks like a strong left front – new grown.'

'No, sir. Well, it might be. Caught her just the other day. Don't know her history, Mr Lennox.'

'Boy, you wouldn't be running a ringer, would you! 'Fess up now.' Lennox looked sternly into Ralph's eyes, and Ralph dropped them.

'You don't want to go up before the Diggers' Committee, do you? The shame you would bring on your daddy. It might break his heart.'

It might not break Zouga Ballantyne's heart, but it would certainly break Ralph's head.

Miserably Ralph shook his head. 'Very well then, Mr Lennox. It's Inkosikazi, she grew a new leg. I thought I'd get better odds – but, I'll withdraw her now. I'll go tell Mr Cohen I lied.'

Barry Lennox leaned so close that his lips touched Ralph's ear and the smell of fine old cognac on his breath almost overpowered him.

'You don't do anything so stupid, Ralph, my lad. You fight your fancy, and if she wins there will be a special treat for you. That's a promise. Barry Lennox will see you right – and then some. Now, if you will excuse me, I've got some business to attend to.' Lennox twirled his cane and drove a wedge into the crowd with his bow-fronted belly.

Chaim Cohen climbed up onto the disselboom of the nearest wagon to the arena and began chalking up the draw on a greenruled board, and the bookmakers craned for the matchings and then began calling their odds for each bout.

'Threes on Mr Gladstone in the first.'

'Dreadnought even money. Buttercup fives in the second.'

Ralph waited as bout after bout was drawn, and each time that Inkosikazi's name was omitted his nerves stretched tighter. There were only ten bouts, and Mr Cohen had finished chalking the ninth already.

'Bout No. 10,' he called as he wrote. 'This is a biblical match, gentlemen and ladies, a diamondiferous bout straight out of the Old Testament.' Chaim Cohen used the adjective 'diamondiferous' to describe anything from a thoroughbred horse to a fifteen-year-old whisky. 'A pure diamondiferous match, the one and only, the great and deadly, Goliath!' There was a burst of applause and whistles of approval. Goliath was the champion spider of the diamond fields, with twelve straight kills to her credit. 'Matched against your favourite is a pretty little newcomer, Salome!'

The name was greeted with indifference as the punters scrambled to get money onto the champion.

'I'm giving tens on Salome,' called one desperate bookie as he tried to stem the flow of wagers. They were taking Goliath at odds on, and Ralph shared his distress.

Leaden-footed he traipsed back to the alleyway. Kamuza had heard the draw announced.

'Give us back the sixteen queens,' he greeted Ralph; but the demand stung Bazo: 'Inkosikazi will drink her blood –'

'The other is a giant –'

'Inkosikazi is quick, fast as a mamba, brave as a honey badger.' Bazo chose the most fearless and indomitable fighters of the veld as comparisons for his fancy.

They argued while the sudden roar of voices from the square signalled the beginning of the first bout, and the squeals of the ladies told that the kill had been swiftly made.

They argued fiercely, Bazo becoming so agitated that he could no longer sit still. He leapt up and began to *giya*, the challenge dance of the Matabele warrior preparing for battle.

'Thus Inkosikazi sprang, and thus she drove her assegai into the chest of Nelo,' Bazo shouted, as he imitated the death stroke of his fancy; but the Matabele always found difficulty in pronouncing the letter 'R', and the Roman Emperor's was mutilated in the recounting of the battle.

'You must decide,' Ralph broke in on his heroics, and Bazo abruptly ended his *giya* and looked at Kamuza.

In matters of money Kamuza was without question the leader of the group, just as Bazo was in all else.

'Henshaw,' Kamuza asked gravely. 'Are you risking your four queens against this monster?'

'Inkosikazi is risking her life,' Ralph replied, without hesitation. 'And I am risking my money for her.'

'So be it, then. We will follow you.'

There were only minutes left before the tenth bout of the afternoon. Already Chaim Cohen was upending his schooner of beer and, considerably refreshed, wiping the froth from his whiskers. At any moment he would climb back onto the wagon and call for the handlers to bring their fighters to the arena for the final bout.

Ralph still had five sovereigns to place.

'You said twelves,' he argued desperately with the ferret-eyed bookmaker in the flowing Ascot tie.

'If you are betting your own fancy, then it's tens.'

'That's welshing.'

'Life is all a welsh,' the bookie shrugged. 'Take it or leave it.'

'All right, I'll take it.' Ralph snatched the slip and pushed towards the circle of wagons, and once again found his way blocked by the grand belly of Barry Lennox.

'Are you betting her yourself?'

'With everything I've got, sir.'

'That's all I wanted to know, Ralph me boy.' And he strode to the nearest book-maker, pulling his purse from his hip pocket just as Chaim Cohen crowed from his perch on the wagon.

'Lovely ladies and sporting gentlemen! The tenth and final bout of the day! The mighty Goliath meets the dancing lady Salome!'

Goliath crabbed into the glass-topped arena. Her four pairs of legs undulated sinu-ously so that her progress was stately and deliberate.

She was a huge beast, newly moulted, for her chintyl armoured covering was a lustrous coppery colour and the long hairs that covered her abdomen and legs were burnished like newly spun gold wire. She left a double necklace of tiny stippled footprints in the swept sand of the arena floor, and the crowd cheered her. Their inhibitions had long been lost in the primeval conflicts in the little arena, and most of them had been drinking since noon: there was a peculiar ring of ferocity and cruelty in their voices.

'Kill her!' screamed a pretty blond girl with gold ringlets and flowers in her hat. 'Rip her to pieces!' Her face flushed feverishly and her eyes were glittering.

'All right, Mr Ballantyne. Put your fancy in,' Chaim Cohen commanded, raising his voice to be heard above the uproar. But Ralph delayed a few seconds longer, letting the other spider complete its circuit and face away from his side of the cage. Then he lifted the sliding door and tapped the basket to rouse Inkosikazi.

She crawled forward cautiously, lifting her abdomen clear of the sand, stepping on the spiked toes of her ranked legs, and then freezing as she saw her adversary across the cage. Her multiple jewelled eyes were sparkling like chips of black diamond.

Goliath sensed her presence and leaped high, turned in the air and landed facing her. The two spiders confronted each other across the smoothly swept floor of white river sand – and only now was the difference in their sizes apparent. Goliath was enormous, swelling in rage, the long silken mane of burnished hair rising like the quills of a porcupine to enhance her size as she began to dance her challenge to her smaller adversary.

Immediately Inkosikazi replied to the challenge, raising and lowering her abdo-men in time to the rhythmic swaying of her carapace, lifting her legs in pairs and weaving them with an awful grace, like the many-armed Hindu god, Shiva.

An utter silence had fallen on the watchers as they strained to catch every nuance of this stylized dance of death – and then a lust-choked roar burst from them as Goliath sprang.

She exploded into flight, soaring with her talons fully extended, clearing the length of the arena without effort and landing precisely where Inkosikazi had stood a thousandth part of a second before. Inkosikazi had evaded that flashing leap with a bouncing side jump of her own, and now she faced the huge enraged creature and danced her defiance.

The dazzling agility of these great spiders was the essential attraction that drew such a following of eager spectators. There was no preliminary bracing or crouching to herald one of those swallowlight bounds. The spiders fired themselves like bullets, suddenly and unerringly at their rival, and reacted as swiftly to the counter-attack. Then between each onslaught that mesmeric and chilling dance resumed.

'Jee! Jee!' The tightly drawn silence was interrupted by the chilling, killing cry of a Matabele warrior.

'Jee! Jee!' The deep hissing chorus that had carried a black wave of naked bodies across a continent, a wave crested by the plumes of the war bonnets and lit by the glitter of the bright silver assegais.

Bazo had not been able to skulk in the alley beyond the square. He had edged forward into the crowd until he reached the wagons, but as the conflict mounted, so had his warrior passions. He thrust forward through the packed ranks and now he was in the forefront, and he could not contain himself further.

'Jee! Jee!' He hissed his battle cry, and Ralph found himself echoing it.

Inkosikazi was fighting instinctively, reacting mindlessly to the presence of another female in deadly sexual rivalry. It was the waving arms of the gigantic female across the cage which infuriated her, and it was mere coincidence that her first attacking leap was synchronized with the war chant.

Twice she launched herself, and twice Goliath gave her ground. and then on her third leap Inkosikazi vaulted too high and touched the glass roof of the arena. The impact broke the perfect parabola of her flight, and she fell short and out of balance, scrabbling frantically in the fine white sand as Goliath saw her chance and flew in for the kill.

The men howled with cruel glee, the women trilled with delicious horror as the two huge furry bodies came together chest to chest and entangled each other's limbs in a hideous octopus embrace.

The impetus of Goliath's leap sent them rolling across the arena like an india-rubber ball, until they struck the far wall and wrestled in a flurry of serpentine limbs. Both their long hooked fangs were fully erect, and they slashed at each other with their hairy wolf mouths, the needle points of the fangs striking the impenetrable shiny armour of carapace and jointed legs, glancing off the polished surface and leaving minute dribbles of colourless honey-thick venom on each other's chests.

Instinctively they were holding their vulnerable abdomens clear, while straining to tear from the embrace for a chance to strike into the soft skin of the other. They came up on their hind legs and wrestled together, and immediately Goliath's weight began to take effect.

With a sharp crackling sound, like a walnut in the jaw of a silver nutcracker, one of Inkosikazi's legs was torn bodily from the joint of her carapace, and she jerked convulsively, contracting her soft belly in a dreadful spasm.

'Kill her! Rip her to pieces!' screamed the pretty blond girl, and tore at her perfumed silk handkerchief, shredding it between her fingers. Her face was swollen and inflamed and her eyes wild.

Goliath shifted the grip of her many legs, groping for a soft spot into which to plunge the jerking red fang.

'Jee! Jee!' sang Bazo, his eyes bloodshot with passion, and Inkosikazi strained with all her remaining legs to break the grip that was slowly smothering her under the huge hairy body. Again there was that grisly crackling, one of her front legs broke off in a little spurt of body juices, and instinctively Goliath lifted the severed limb to her mouth.

The distraction was sufficient, and Inkosikazi tore herself free and bounded half-way across the arena, landing in an unbalanced sprawl, her body fluids oozing from the leg stumps, but gathering herself swiftly. Goliath was still worrying the severed legs, the smell of her opponent's blood enrapturing her so that she mouthed the twitching limbs, striking at them with her fang, her full attention upon them – and Inkosikazi rebounded like a rubber ball thrown against a brick wall.

She dropped lightly onto Goliath's broad furry back, locked in with her remaining legs, and then plunged the long blood-red fang into Goliath's abdomen, her head pumping as she forced a steady gush of poison into the bloated body.

Goliath's body arched, her long jointed legs straightened into an agonized rictus, and the balloon of her belly spasmed and convulsed as the venom pulsed into her. Crouched upon her back like some grotesque incubus, Inkosikazi squirted in the fatal fluid until the bigger creature's limbs wilted and crumpled under her and her belly sagged gradually to the white sand of the arena.

In the roaring consternation of disappointed punters and squeaks of women, both loathing and gloating at the same time, Ralph and Bazo rushed together and embraced with whoops of triumph. In the glassed arena Inkosikazi slowly withdrew the long curved hypodermic fang. Her venom not only paralysed and killed but also liquefied the body tissue of her prey. Her jaws opened and then locked into the jelly-soft passive body beneath her, and her own abdomen began to swell and subside as she sucked her vanquished adversary's fluids from her – while she still lived.

Ralph broke from the embrace of Bazo's thickly muscled arms.

'Get her out of the cage,' he told him. 'I'll go and get the money.'

Bazo bore the basket high on the return from the conflict. His bare-chested Matab-ele ran behind him, in that floating stylized gait, half dance, half trot, and they brandished their fighting sticks and sang the praise song which Kamuza had com-posed in Inkosikazi's honour:

> 'See with your thousand eyes,
> Hold hard with many arms of steel,
> Kiss with your long red assegai,
> Taste the blood, is it not richer
> than the milk of Mzilikazi's herds?
> Taste the blood, is it not sweeter
> than the wild honey in the comb?
> Bayete! Bayete!
> Royal greetings, Black Queen,
> Loyal greetings, Great Queen.'

Ralph dearly wanted to run with them in that triumphant procession, but he knew what his father would say if he heard that his son had joined such a barbaric display through the dusty streets, past the very portals of the Kimberley Club where Zouga Ballantyne was almost certainly passing his Sunday afternoon.

Ralph followed them in a fashion that better suited Zouga's idea of how a young English gentleman should comport himself, but his cap was on the back of his head, his hands were thrust deeply into pockets jingling the gold coin, and there was a beatific grin on his face. The smile broadened further as a familiar big-gutted figure rolled out through the doors of Diamond Lil's canteen.

'Mr Ballantyne,' bellowed Barry Lennox across the street. 'Mr Ballantyne, will you do me the very great honour of taking a glass with me?'

'Enchanted indeed, sir.' Ralph felt cocky enough to reply facetiously, and Lennox guffawed and flung an arm around Ralph's shoulders and led him into the canteen.

Ralph looked about him quickly; it was the first time he had ever entered a place such as this. He hoped to see naked women dancing on the tables and gamblers in flowered waistcoats fanning open hands full of aces and kings and sweeping up pots of gold sovereigns.

The only partially nude figure was that of Charlie, the undertaker, snoring on the sawdust floor with his shirt open to his hairy belly button; and the gamblers were all familiar faces, men beside whom Ralph worked every day on the stagings or in the pit. They were dressed in their work clothes and the cards were dog-eared and greasy and the pot was a small pile of copper and worn silver.

'Ralph,' said one of them, looking up. 'Your daddy know where you are?'

'Does yours?' Ralph shot back, the cockiness unabated. 'And do you know *who* he is?'

There was a hoot of laughter from the others, and the man grinned good-naturedly. 'Damn me, but the boy has a sharp enough tongue.'

'Give my sporting friend a beer,' Lennox told the barman, and he looked dubious. 'How old is your sporting friend?'

'He will be forty years old on one of his future birthdays. However, sir, I consider that question to be a direct slur on my sporting friend's honour. I have broken jaws that asked less impertinent questions.'

'Two beers coming up, Mr Lennox.'

Barry Lennox and Ralph saluted each other with the schooners, and Lennox gave them a toast.

'To a lady of our mutual acquaintance, bless her bright eyes and all her lovely legs.'

The beer was faintly warm and tasted like soap and quinine, but Ralph forced down a mouthful and smacked his lips appreciatively. He would have much preferred a cool green bottle of ginger beer with a pop up marble in the neck.

'Cigar?' Lennox opened his silver case, and Ralph hesitated only a moment, then selected one of the thick Havanas and bit off the end in a faithful imitation of Zouga Ballantyne.

He sucked from the Vesta that Lennox held for him, and cautiously held the smoke in his mouth. That was the last draw he took, and after that he used the cigar like a conductor's baton, waving it airily and creating about himself a cloud of perfumed blue without actually touching it to his lips again. Somehow he was able to impart the impression of swagger while standing at the rough-sawn bar counter.

' – I mean, anybody knows the classic Zulu battle tactics. They wait for bad ground and thick bush, there are few soldiers who use cover and defilade the way they do.' Ralph sipped his beer and waved his cigar as he discussed Lord Chelmsford's current campaign against the Zulu King Cetewayo. The views he was expressing were those of Zouga Ballantyne, learned by heart and unadulterated; so though his listeners winked and nudged at his pretensions, they could not fault his logic. 'The device of decoying Chelmsford's flying column out of the camp and then doubling back to destroy the base with its depleted defences is as old as Chaka Zulu himself. Chelmsford was at fault, there, no doubt on it.'

There was a gloomy shaking of heads, as there always was when anyone mentioned the catastrophic reversal of British arms that Chelmsford had been manoeuvred into at the Hill of the Little Hand, Isandhlwana, across the Buffalo river in Zululand.

The corpses of seven hundred British dead, militia and regular regiments, had already lain for six months on the bleak grassland below the little hill. Lord Chelmsford had abandoned the field, and his dead lay where they had fallen, their bellies ripped open by Zulu assegais to allow their souls to escape, the litter of wagons and broken equipment scattered about them, their flesh taken off the bone by vulture and jackal and hyena.

The thought of leaving British soldiers unburied on the battlefield seemed to threaten the very foundation of the greatest empire the world had ever known.

'Chelmsford must retake the field,' said one of the men at the bar.

'No, sir,' Ralph shook his head firmly. 'That will be inviting another disaster for a sentimental gesture.'

'What do you propose, Mr Ballantyne?' the man asked sarcastically.

'A page from the Boer book.' Ralph had an audience of grown men listening to him – perhaps not with respect, but at least with attention. This was heady stuff, even though the ideas were his father's, and Ralph threw in an oath. 'By God, those fellows know how to fight the tribes. Mounted men as a screen around a column of wagons that can be thrown into laager within minutes. Go for the heart of the Zulu nation – their cattle herds – pull the impis into the open, make them come in across good shooting ground against the laagered wagons –' Ralph did not finish his plan of battle; abruptly he lost his sequence of ideas and began to stutter like an idiot, a blush darkening his tanned, handsome young face.

Barry Lennox followed the direction of Ralph's gaze, and then he grinned delightedly.

Diamond Lil had entered the canteen through the rear door. It was six o'clock in the evening and an hour before she had risen, stretching and yawning like a sleepy leopard, from the brass bed in the darkened room behind the canteen.

A servant had filled the enamelled hip bath with buckets of steaming water, and Lil had poured in a vial of perfume before stepping into the bath and settling luxuriously into the fragrant water, shouting for her canteen manager.

She listened attentively, a small frown cracking the perfect pale skin of her forehead, as he recited the figures of the previous night's take, his eyes averted from the white skin of her shoulders and the tight pink-tipped bosom that peeked through the hot suds. Then she had dismissed him with a wave of her hand and stepped naked from the bath, glowing pinkly from the hot water, her steam-damp hair dangling down the sleek white body. She poured a little gin into a coloured Venetian glass and sipped it neat as she started the powdering and the painting, rolling her eyes at herself in the mirror, practising her professional smile with the tiny diamond twinkling in the centre of the wide display of white teeth, then, at last, considering herself levelly and appraisingly.

She was twenty-three years old, and she had come a long hard way from the house in Mayfair where Madame Hortense had sold her maidenhood to an elderly

Whig minister of state for one hundred guineas. She had been thirteen years old then, only ten years ago, but it seemed like a dozen lifetimes.

The house in Mayfair was truly the only home she had ever known, and she often thought back with nostalgia to those days. Madame Hortense had treated her more like a daughter than a house girl. There was always a pretty bonnet or a new dress on her birthday and at Christmas, and she had had special privileges. Lil would ever be grateful for what she learned about men and money and power from Hortense.

Then one Saturday evening a half dozen young officers from a famous cavalry regiment, celebrating their orders for foreign service, had visited the house in Mayfair. Amongst them was a young captain, dashing, rich and beautiful; he saw Lil across the salon the moment he entered. Ten days later Lil had sailed with him for India on the Peninsular and Orient mailship, while Madame Hortense wept on the quay and waved until the ship cleared the pool of London and disappeared beyond the first bend of the river. Forty days later Lil found herself abandoned by her protector.

From an upper window of the Mount Nelson Hotel in Cape Town she watched her cavalry captain's ship clear Table Bay for Calcutta, her sorrow at parting alleviated by the luxurious surroundings in which her protector had left her. Lil shrugged off her grief, drank a glass of gin, bathed and re-painted her face, then sent for the manager.

'I cannot pay my bill,' she told him and, taking his hand, led him unprotestingly into the bedroom of her suite.

'Madame, may I give you some advice?' he asked a little later as he retied his Ascot and shrugged into his waistcoat.

'Good advice is always welcome, sir.'

'There is a place called New Rush five hundred miles north of here and there are five thousand diggers there, each with a pocket full of diamonds.'

Now Lil entered her canteen. It was still early for a Sunday. It was one of the things she had learned from Madame Hortense, always be there long before you are expected. It keeps clients satisfied and employees honest.

Quickly she checked her clientele. It was the usual Sunday afternoon crowd. It would be better soon. She stooped and counted the bottles under the bar counter, examining the wax seals to make certain they had not been tampered with.

'Never be greedy, darling,' Hortense had taught her. 'Water the beer, they expect that, but keep good whisky.'

She straightened and opened the huge ornate cash register with a chime of bells, making certain that it flagged the correct price, and then touched the line of gold sovereigns in their special slotted drawer. The metal had a marvellous feel under her fingertips, and she picked up a coin as though merely to feel the weight and take pleasure from it. Gold was the only thing in all the world she trusted. Her barman was watching her in the mirror as he swabbed the counter top; she pretended to replace the sovereign in its slot, letting it clink and then palmed it smoothly and closed the drawer of the register. The barman was new. It would be interesting to see if he covered the shortage or reported it, little things like that had made her rich at the age of twenty-three.

She glanced up into the mirror, once again appraising her own face and shoulders in the less flattering sunlight that streamed into the canteen. Her eyes were sharp as a stropped razor, but the skin around them was clear and fresh as rose petals without the first sign of wrinkling.

'You will wear well, my dear,' Hortense had told her, 'if you use the gin and don't let it use you.' She had been right, Lil decided. She looked as she had when she was sixteen years old.

She shifted her gaze from her own face, and swept the canteen. The mirror was imperfect, and the silvering was beginning to go in dark spots, slightly distorting the young face that was watching her intently. Her gaze flicked over it, and then came back.

The boy was blushing as he studied her avidly, that was the only thing that had caught her attention. Now when she looked at him again she realized he was probably under-age, and she already had trouble with the Committee. He wore a boy's cloth cap on the back of his head and he was very obviously still growing, his Norfolk jacket straining around the sturdy arms and across the shoulders.

Too young and certainly penniless. She had to get him out fast, and she turned quickly, her fists on her hips, her blond head cocked aggressively.

'Good afternoon, Miss Lil.' Ralph was stunned by his own audacity at addressing this heavenly presence directly. 'I was about to buy my friends a round of drinks. We should be honoured if you would take a glass with us, ma'am.' Ralph slapped the counter with a sovereign, and Lil uncocked her head and raised one hand from her hip to touch her hair.

'I like a big spending gent.' She flashed the little diamond in her front tooth at him and nodded to the barman. He would pour from her special bottle labelled Booth's Gin but filled with rain water from the galvanized tank beside the backdoor.

Suddenly she realized that the boy was bonny, with a strong jaw and good white teeth. Now that his blush had subsided, his skin was clear and smooth as her own, and his eyes a penetrating emerald green. And the eagerness and freshness that he exuded was so different from that of the hairy diggers, caked with red dirt and smelling like goats, that formed her usual clientele.

Let the boy pay for his round of drinks, and there would be time to get rid of him after that. In the meantime his transparent adoration was amusing and flattering.

'Lil, me darling.' Barry Lennox leaned across the counter and she did not flinch from his breath. 'Give me your pearl-like little ear.'

Smiling her bright smile she held her ear to his lips, and cupped her hand in an exaggerated pantomime of secrecy.

'Are you working tonight, Lil?'

'I'm always ready for a quick rattle of the dice with you, my sweet. You want to go right now or finish your drink?'

'No, darling, not me. How would you like to be first to put the saddle on an unbroken colt?'

Her eyes flicked to Ralph's face again, and her hard bright smile softened thoughtfully. He was a lovely boy, and for the first time since her cavalryman had left her in Cape Town she felt the prickle of her loins and bitter sweet catch in her throat, so that she did not trust her voice entirely.

'It's still early, Lil, and business isn't good this time on Sunday, Lil dearie.' Barry Lennox wheedled and chuckled beerily at the same time. 'He is a pretty boy, and I should charge you for the pleasure, but I'll just let you make me a special price instead.'

Lil's throat cleared instantly and the languid expression disappeared. Her reply was crisp.

'I'll not charge you school fees, Barry Lennox, just the usual ten guineas.'

Lennox shook his head. 'You are a hard one, Lil. I'll send him to you, love. But just one thing, make it good, make it something that he will remember if he lives a hundred years.'

'I don't teach you to dig diamonds, Barry Lennox,' she said, and without looking back swept from the canteen. They heard the door of her bedroom bang, and Ralph stared after her in dismay – but Barry Lennox put an arm around his shoulders and as he talked quietly, punctuating each sentence with a throaty lewd chuckle, all the colour fled from Ralph's face.

'Come in.' Her voice reminded Ralph of the gentle contented cooing that the plump wild pigeons made at sunset in the top branch of the camel-thorn tree above Zouga's camp.

With his hand on the brass doorknob, he lifted his feet one at a time and polished the toe-cap of his boots against the back of his trouser leg. He had doused his head under the tap of the rainwater tank and combed his hair while it was still wet, sleeking it away from his forehead, and the droplets had run down his neck, turning the dust on his darned shirt collar into damp red mud.

He glanced down at his hand on the doorknob, saw the black rinds under his finger nails and lifted it quickly to his mouth, trying desperately to pick out the dirt with his eye tooth.

'Come in!' The command was repeated; but this time there was no cooing of pigeons, but a sharp imperious command, and Ralph lunged for the door handle. There was no resistance, the door flew open, and Ralph went with it. He entered Diamond Lil's boudoir like a cavalry charge, tripped on the frayed edge of a cheap oriental carpet and sprawled headlong across the brass bed.

There was a Chinese lacquer screen across one corner of the small violently furnished room, and over the top of it rose Diamond Lil's magnificently sculptured blond coiffure.

'Oh,' she said sweetly, the sharp slanted eyes widening with amusement. 'Are you going to start without me then, darling?'

Ralph scrambled untidily to his feet like a puppy with oversized paws and stood to attention in the middle of the floor, holding his cloth cap to his stomach with both hands.

From behind the screen came the most evocative sounds he had ever heard. The rustle of lace and cloth, the clink of china and the gurgle of water poured from a jug. The lacquer screen was ornamented with oriental figures, women bathing in a willow-screened pool with a waterfall in the background. The women were all naked, and the artist had lingered on their physical charms. Ralph felt his ears and neck heating again – and hated himself for it.

He wished he had kept the cigar, as a proof of his manhood. He wished that he had worn a fresh shirt, he wished – but then there was no further time for wishing.

Lil stepped out from behind the screen. She was barefooted, and her toes were chubby and rosy pink like those of a little girl.

'I have seen you on the street, Mr Ballantyne,' Lil told him quietly. 'And I have admired your manly disposition. I am so glad we have had an opportunity to meet.'

The words worked a miracle. Ralph felt himself growing in stature, the trembling in his legs stilled and they felt strong and sure under him.

'Do you like my robe?' Lil asked, and took the long skirts in her hands, turning to make them flare.

Ralph nodded dumbly, his new-found strength had not yet reached his tongue, but his eyes were wide and feverish.

She came to him and without her heels she stood only as high as his shoulder. 'Let me help you with your coat.' And when he was in his shirtsleeves, she said, 'Come and sit on the sofa.' She took his hand and led him across the room.

'Do you like me, Mr Ballantyne?'

At last he could speak, 'Oh yes. Oh yes!'

'May I call you Ralph? I feel I know you so well.'

Very early one January morning long ago she had left the Mayfair house, and reached the deserted park where it had snowed during the night. The snow lay white and smooth and unmarked. She left the gravelled path, and the snow crumbled like sugar under her feet. When she looked back her tiny footprints were strung out across the unblemished snow, as though she were the first and only woman in the world. It gave her an extraordinary feeling of her own importance. Now as she lay on the wide bedstead beside the lad, she experienced that same feeling.

He was not a lad, but she thought of him as that. His body was fully matured, but his innocence made him as vulnerable as an unweaned infant, and his body was like the snow which no other feet had trodden.

The sun had stained his throat in a deep V down onto his chest, but the skin of his chest and flat belly were the lustrous white of watered marble or of freshly fallen snow. She touched it with her lips and when his little dusty rose nipples puckered and started her own skin crawling deliciously, she took his hands. His palms were rough and calloused from work on the stagings and in the pit. The fingernails were torn and cracked, with ingrained dirt beneath them. But it was honest dirt, and the hands were shapely, long and graceful. She had learned to judge men by the shape of their hands, and now she lifted Ralph's to her lips and kissed them lightly, watching his eyes as she did so.

Then slowly she took his hands down and cupped them over her own soft breasts. She felt the rough skin rasp her own nipples, and they popped out like full moons, pale pink and tense.

'You like that, Ralph?'

She asked that same question five times, and the last time was when the room was almost dark and he was convulsed and shaking within the circle of her arms and her pliant thighs, drenched with his own sweet young sweat, and breathing in little choking sobs.

'You like that, Ralph?' And his reply was broken and ragged:

'Oh yes. Oh yes, Miss Lil.'

Suddenly she was sad. The snow was trodden, the magic was passing, just as the power she had wielded was transitory.

She had not cried in ten long hard years, not since that first evening in the Mayfair house, but now she was shocked to find the constriction in her throat and the burning behind her eyes.

112

'What is there to cry for?' she wondered desolately. 'It's far too late for tears.'

She rolled Ralph expertly onto his back, his body limp and unresisting – and for a moment she stared at him hatefully. He had touched something in her which had hurt unbearably. Then the hating passed and there was only the sadness.

She kissed him once more, softly and regretfully.

'You must go now, Ralph,' she said.

He lingered at the door, with his jacket over his arm and his cap in his hand.

'I will come and see you again, Lilly.'

She formed a bow with her lips and painted them with quick deft strokes before she replied, but while she worked she was watching him in the mirror.

He was altered already, she saw. He stood four-square, his shoulders wide and his neat young head proud on the column of his sun-tanned neck. The sweet diffidence was gone, the appealing shyness evaporated. An hour before he would have said:

'Please can I come and see you again, Miss Lil.'

She smiled at him in the mirror, that bright burnished smile, and the diamond in her tooth winked sardonically.

'You come any time, dearie – any time you have saved ten guineas.'

It was only surprising that the full report of Ralph's foray into the lilac fields of Venus took so long to reach Zouga, for Barry Lennox had repeated the story with zest and embroidery to anyone who would listen, and the chaff and banter had flown like a Kalahari dust-storm every evening in Diamond Lil's canteen.

'Gentlemen, you are speaking about the eldest son of one of the pillars of Kimberley Society,' Lil admonished them saucily. 'Remember that Major Ballantyne is not only a member of the Kimberley Club, but a respected ornament of the Diggers' Committee.' She knew that one of them would soon succumb to the temptation to take the story to Zouga Ballantyne. 'I would love to hear what that cold-bellied, stuck-up prig will say when he hears,' she told herself secretly. 'Even the iced water in his veins will boil.'

'Whores and whore masters,' said Zouga. He stood on the wide verandah, in the shade of the thatched roof which had replaced the original tent of the first camp.

Ralph stood below him in the sunlight, blinking up at his father.

'Perhaps you have no respect for your family, for the name of Ballantyne – but do you have none for yourself and for your own body?'

Zouga was barring the front door to the cottage of raw unbaked brick. He was bare-headed, so that his thick dark gold hair shone like a war helmet and his neatly-cropped beard emphasized the jut of his heavy jaw, and the long black tapered hippohide kurbash whip hung from his right hand, touching the floor at the toe of his riding boot.

'Do you have an answer?' Zouga's tone was quiet, and deadly cold.

Ralph was still dusty as a miller from the pit. The dust was thick and red in his hair, and outlined the curl of his nostrils and ran like tears from the corners of his eyes. He wiped his forehead on his shirtsleeve, an excuse to break the gaze of his father's eyes, and then examined the muddy smear with attention.

'Answer me,' Zouga's voice did not alter. 'Give me a reason – just one reason why I should not throw you out of this home – for ever.'

Jordan could bear it no longer, the thought of losing Ralph overcame his terror of his father's wrath.

He ran down the length of the verandah, and seized the arm that held the whip.

'Papa! Please, Papa – don't send him away.'

Without glancing at Jordan, Zouga lashed out and the blow caught Jordan across the chest and hurled him back against the verandah wall.

'Jordie did nothing,' said Ralph, as quietly as his father had spoken.

'Oh, you do have a tongue?' Zouga asked.

'Get out of it, Jordie,' Ralph ordered. 'This is not your business.'

'Stay where you are, Jordan.' Zouga still did not look at him, his gaze was riveted on Ralph's face. 'Stay here and learn about whores and the kind of men who lust after them.'

Jordan was stricken, his face like last night's camp-fire ashes, his lips dry and white as bone. He knew what they were talking about – for he had listened while Bazo and Ralph wove their fantasies aloud, and with his interest piqued, he had questioned Jan Cheroot furtively – and the replies had disgusted and terrified him.

'Not like animals, Jan Cheroot, surely not like dogs or goats.'

Jordan's questions to Jan Cheroot had been generalized – men and women, not any person he knew or loved or respected. It had taken him days fully to appreciate Jan Cheroot's reply, and then the terrible realization had struck – all men and women, his father who epitomized for him all that was noble and strong and right, his mother, that sweet and gentle being who was already a fading wraithlike memory – not them, surely not them.

He had been physically sickened, vomiting and wracked by excruciating bowel cramps so that Zouga had dosed him with sulphur and treacle molasses.

Now they were talking about that thing, that thing so dreadful that he had tried to purge his memory of it. Now the two most important people in his world were talking about it openly, using words he had only seen in print and which had even then shamed him. They were mouthing those words and the air was full of shame and hatred and revulsion.

'You have wallowed like a pig where a thousand other pigs have wallowed before you, in the foetid cesspool between that scarlet whore's thighs.'

Jordan crept away along the wall, and reached the corner of the stoep. He could go no further.

'If you were not ashamed to muck in that trough, did you not give a thought to what those other rutting boars had left there for you?'

His father's words conjured up vivid images in Jordan's mind. His stomach heaved, and he covered his mouth with his hand.

'The sickness a harlot carries there is the curse of God upon venery and lust. If you could only see them in the pox hospital at Greenwich, raving idiots with their brains eaten half away by the disease, drooling from empty mouths, their teeth rotted out, their noses fallen into black festering holes, blind eyes rolling in their crazed skulls –'

Jordan doubled over, and sicked up on his own rawhide boots.

'Stop it,' said Ralph. 'You have made Jordie sick.'

'I have made him sick?' Zouga asked quietly. 'It is you who would make any decent person sick.'

Zouga came down the steps into the dusty yard, and he swung the whip, cutting the air with it, across and back and the lash fluted sharply.

Ralph stood his ground, and now his chin was up defiantly.

'If you take that whip to me, Papa – I shall defend myself.'

'You challenge me,' Zouga stopped.

'You only use a whip on an animal.'

'Yes,' Zouga nodded. 'An animal – that's why I take it to you.'

'Papa, I warn you.'

Gravely Zouga inclined his head and considered the young man before him. 'Very well. You claim to be a man, make good that claim.' Zouga tossed the hippohide whip casually onto the verandah, and then turned back to his son.

Ralph was prepared, his weight balanced on the balls of his feet, although his hands were held low before him, they were balled into fists.

He never saw it. For a moment he thought that someone else had used a club on him from behind. The crack of it seemed to explode under the dome of his skull. He reeled backwards, his nose felt numb and at the same time swollen horribly. There was a tickling warmth on his upper lip and dumbly he licked it. It tasted of coppery salt, and he wiped at it with the back of his hand and then stared at the smear of blood on the back of his wrist.

His rage came on him with startling ferocity, as though a beast had pounced upon his back, a black beast that goaded him with its claws. He heard the beast growl in his ears, not recognizing his own voice, and then he rushed forward.

His father's face was in front of him, handsome, grave and cold, and he swung his fist at it with all his strength, wanting to feel the flesh crush under his knuckles, the gristle of that arrogant beaked nose break and crackle, the teeth snap out of that unforgiving mouth.

His fist spun through air, meeting no check, swinging high about the level of his own head, and the blow died there, the sinews of his shoulder wrenched by the unexpected travel of his arm.

Again that burst of sound in his skull, his teeth jarring, his head snapping back, his vision starring momentarily into pinpoints of light and areas of deep echoing black, and then clearing again so that his father's face floated back towards him.

Until that instant the only feelings he had ever had for Zouga were respect and fear and a weighty monumental love, but suddenly from some deep place in his soul rose a raging unholy hatred.

He hated him for a hundred humiliations and punishments, he hated him for the checks and frustrations with which be filled each precious day of Ralph's life, he hated him for the reverence and deep respect in which other men held him, for the example that he knew he would be expected to follow faithfully all his life and doubted that he could. He hated him for the enormous load of duty and devotion he owed him and which he knew he could never discharge. He hated him for the love he had stolen from him, the love his mother had given unstintingly to his father and which he wanted all for himself. He hated him because his mother was dead, and his father had not prevented her going.

But most of all he hated him because he had taken something which had been wonderful and made it filthy, had taken a magical moment and made him ashamed of it, sick and dirty ashamed.

He rushed back at Zouga, swinging wildly with both fists meeting only air, and the blows that landed on his own head and face sounded as though somebody far away was chopping down a tree with a steel axe.

Zouga fell away neatly before each charge, swaying his head back or to the side, deflecting a blow with his arms, ducking carefully under a flying fist, and counter-punching only with his left hand, flicking it in with deceptive lightness, for at each shot Ralph's head snapped backwards sharply and the blood from his nose and his swollen lips slowly turned his face into a running red mess.

'Stop it, oh please stop it!' Jordan crouched against the verandah wall with the yellow vomit staining his shirt front. 'Please stop it!'

He wanted to cover his face with his hands, to blot out the violence and the blood and the terrible black hatred – but he could not. He was locked in an awful fascination, watching every stinging cruel blow, every droplet of flung blood from his brother's face.

Like a corrida bull Ralph came up short at last, and stood with his feet wide apart, his knees giving like reeds overweighted with dew, trying feebly to shake the blackness from his head and the blood from his eyes, his fists bunched up still but too heavy and weak to lift above his waist, his chest heaving for air, swaying and catching his balance every few seconds with an uncontrolled stagger, peering blindly about him for his tormentor.

'Here,' said Zouga quietly, and Ralph lurched towards the voice and Zouga used his right hand for the first time. He chopped him cleanly under the ear, a short measured blow, and Ralph flopped face forward into the dust and snored into it, blowing little red puffs with each breath.

Jordan flew down the steps and dropped to his knees beside his brother, turning his head to one side so he could breathe freely and dabbing ineffectually at the blood with his fingers.

'Jan Cheroot,' Zouga called. He was breathing deeply but slowly; there was colour in his cheeks above his beard, and he touched a few beads of perspiration on his forehead with the kerchief from around his throat.

'Jan Cheroot!' he called again irritably, and this time the little Hottentot roused himself and hurried down the steps.

'Get a bucket of water,' Zouga told him.

Jan Cheroot dashed the contents of a gallon bucket into Ralph's face, washing away the bloody mask, and Ralph gasped and snorted and tried to crawl to his knees.

Jan Cheroot dropped the bucket and grabbed his arm; Jordan stooped and got his head under Ralph's other armpit and between them they lifted him to his feet.

They were both much smaller than Ralph and he hung between them like a dirty blanket on a washline, with the mixture of water and blood dripping to form pale pink rosettes on his shirt front.

Zouga lit a cheroot, studied the ash to be sure it was drawing evenly, then replaced it between his teeth.

He stepped up to his eldest son. With his thumb he pulled down each lower eyelid in turn and peered into his pupils, then grunted with satisfaction. He studied the cut in Ralph's eyebrow, then took his nose between his fingers and moved it gently from side to side to check it for damage, then finally he pulled back Ralph's lip and inspected his teeth for chips or breakage and stepped back.

'Jan Cheroot, take him down to Jameson's surgery. Ask Doc to stitch that eye and give him a handful of mercury pills for the pox.'

Jan Cheroot started to lead Ralph away but Zouga went on, 'Then on your way back stop at Barnato's Gymnasium and sign him up for a course of boxing lessons. He'll have to learn to fight a bit better than that or he's going to get his head beaten in even before he dies of the clap.'

On the way back from Market Square Jan Cheroot and Ralph walked with their heads together, talking seriously.

'Why do you think they call him Bakela, the Fist?' Jan Cheroot asked, and Ralph grimaced painfully.

His face was lumpy and the colour was coming up in his bruises, deep plum and cloudy blue like summer thunderclouds. The horsehair stitches stuck up stiffly out of his eyebrow and lip, and the cuts were soft-scabbed like cranberry jam.

Jan Cheroot grinned and clucked with sympathy, and then asked the question that had burned his tongue since first he had learned the cause of Zouga's wrath.

'So how did you like your first taste of pink sugar?'

The question stopped Ralph in his tracks while he considered it seriously, then he answered without moving his damaged lip.

'It was bloody marvellous,' he said.

Jan Cheroot giggled and hugged himself with delight. 'Now you listen to me, boy, and you listen good. I love your daddy, we been together so many years I can't count, and when he tells you something you can believe it – nearly every time. But me, I have never in my life passed up a chance for a slice of that warm stuff – never once, old or young or in between, ugly as a monkey or so pretty it would break your heart, whenever it was offered and lots of times when it wasn't, old Jan Cheroot grabbed it, boy.'

'And it never killed you.' Ralph supplied the summation.

'I guess I would have died without it.'

Ralph started walking again. 'I hope Bazo will fight his fancy again next Sunday. I'm going to need ten guineas pretty badly by then.'

The moon was lipping the horizon, putting the stars to pale shame. It was still a few days short of full, but on the stoep of Zouga's cottage it was light enough to read the headlines of a crumpled copy of the *Diamond Fields Advertiser* that lay beside Zouga's empty riempie chair.

The only sounds were the distant baying of a moon-crazy hound, and the flirt of bats' wings as they spun high parabolas in the moonlight or came fluttering in under the overhang of the verandah roof to pick a moth from the air. The front door was stopped wide open to allow the night's cool to penetrate the inner rooms of the cottage. Jordan crept through it timidly.

He was bare-footed, and the old flannel shirt he wore as a nightdress was one of Zouga's cast-offs. The tails flapped around his bare knees as he moved down the verandah and stopped before the tall falcon-headed carving that stood on its pedestal at the end of the covered stoep.

The slanting moonlight lit the graven bird image from the side, leaving half of it in black mysterious shadow.

Jordan stopped before the image. The clay floor was cold on his bare soles, and he shivered not entirely from the cold, and looked about him surreptitiously.

Zouga's camp slept, that deep pre-dawn sleep.

Jordan's curls, bushed wildly from the pillow, sparkled like a halo in the moonlight, and his eyes were in shadow, dark holes like those of a skull. All night he had lain rigid in his narrow bed and listened to his brother's heavy breathing through his swollen nose.

Lack of sleep made Jordan feel light-headed and fey. He opened the little twist of newspaper which he had hidden under his pillow when he went to bed.

It contained half a handful of rice and a thin slice of cold roasted lamb. He laid it at the foot of the soapstone column, and stepped back.

Once more he looked about him to make sure that he was alone and unobserved. Then he sank down to his bare knees with the book held against his chest, and bowed his head.

The book was bound in blue leather with gold leaf titling on its spine: *Religions of the American Indians*.

'I greet you, Panes,' Jordan whispered, his swollen eyelids tightly closed.

'The Indians of California, the Acagchemem tribe adore the great buzzard Panes.' The book Jordan held to his breast had become far and away the most precious of all his possessions. He did not like to remember how he had obtained it. It was the only thing he had ever stolen in his life, but he had been forgiven for that sin. He had prayed to the goddess and been forgiven.

'The Panes was a woman, a young and beautiful woman, who had run off into the mountains and been changed into a bird by the god Chinigchinich.'

Jordan knew with all his being whom this description depicted. His mother had been young and beautiful, and she had run away to the black mountain of Death without him.

Now he opened the book and bowed his head over it. It was not light enough to read the fine print of the text, but Jordan knew the invocation to the goddess by heart.

'Why did you run away?' he whispered. 'You would have been better with us. Are we not the ones who love you? It was better that you stayed, for now you are Panes. If we make you a sacrifice of rice and meat, will you not come back to us? See the sacrifice we set for you, great Panes.'

The morning wind stirred, and Jordan heard the branch of the camel-thorn scrape upon the roof before the wind touched him. It was a warm, soft wind, and it ruffled his hair.

Jordan clenched his eyes even tighter, and the little insects of awe crawled upon his skin. The goddess had many ways of showing her presence. This was the first time she had come as a soft warm wind.

'Oh great Panes, I don't want to wallow in filth like Ralph. I don't ever want to smell the trough where a thousand pigs have wallowed. I don't want to go mad, and have my teeth rot out of my mouth.' He whispered softly but ardently, and then the tears began to squeeze out from between his lids.

'Please save me, great Panes.' He poured out all his horror and disgust to the sacred bird-woman. 'They were hitting each other. They were hating each other, and the blood, oh the blood –'

At last he was silent, head bowed, shivering, and then he rose to his bare feet, and for the first time looked at the image.

The bird stared back at him stonily, but Jordan cocked his lovely golden head as though he were listening, and the moonlight silvered his skin.

He turned, still clutching the book, and crept back along the verandah. As he turned the far corner there was a furry rush of dark bodies out of the shadows, and the soft squeals of the bush rats as they squabbled over the sacrifice.

Jordan pushed open the door of the kitchen and it smelled of woodsmoke and curry powder and carbolic soap.

He stooped to the ashbox of the black iron stove, and when he blew lightly through the grating the ashes glowed.

He pushed a long wax taper through the bars and blew again and a little blue flame popped into life. He carried it carefully across the kitchen, sheltering it with his cupped hand, and transferred the flame to the stump of candle in the neck of the dark green champagne bottle. Then he blew out the taper and placed the bottle on the scrubbed yellow deal table and stepped back.

For a few seconds longer he hesitated, then he took the skirts of the faded and patched nightshirt, lifted them as high as his shoulders and looked down at his body.

The puppy fat had disappeared from his belly and hips. His navel was a dark eye in the flat clean plain of his trunk, and his legs were gracefully shaped. His buttocks lean and tight, like immature fruit.

His body was smooth and hairless except for the golden wisps at the juncture of his legs. It was not yet thick enough to curl, and was sparse and fine as silk thread freshly spun upon the cocoon.

From the centre of this cloudy web his penis hung down limply. It had grown alarmingly in the last few months, and in Jordan's horrified imagination, he foresaw the day when it would be thick and heavy as his arm, a huge shameful burden to carry through life.

At this moment it looked so soft and white and innocent, but when he woke in the mornings it was hard as bone, hot and throbbing with a sinfully pleasurable ache.

That was bad, but in these last weeks that terrible swelling and stiffening had come upon him at the most unexpected times: at the dinner table with his father seated opposite him, in the schoolroom when the new schoolmistress had leaned over him to correct his spelling, seated at the sorting-table beside Jan Cheroot, on the gelding's back when the friction of the saddle had triggered it, and that awful stiff thing had thrust out the front of his breeches.

He took it in his hand now and it seemed helpless and soft as a newborn kitten, but he was not deceived. He stroked it softly back and forth and instantly he felt it change shape between his fingers. He released it quickly.

The joint of mutton that the family had dined off the previous evening stood on the deal table, under a steel mesh fly-cover. Jordan lifted the cover, and the leg was hacked down to the bone.

His father's hunting knife lay beside the cold joint. The handle was stag-horn and the blade was nine inches long, sweeping up to a dagger point, and the white mutton fat had congealed upon the blade.

Jordan picked up the knife in his right hand.

The previous evening he had watched his father flicking the edge of the blade across the long steel. It always fascinated him, because Zouga held the razor edge towards his own fingers as he worked.

The proof of his father's expertise with the steel was the way in which the heavy knife seemed to glide effortlessly through the meat of the joint. It was wickedly sharp.

Jordan looked down again at that long white thing that stuck out of his body. The loose skin at the tip was half retracted so that the pink acorn pushed out from beneath it.

He tucked the tail of his shirt under his chin to free both hands and seized himself at the root, enclosing within the circle of his fingers the wrinkled bag with its tender marbles of flesh, and he pulled it out, stretching it out like the neck of the condemned man upon the headsman's block, while with the other hand he brought the knife down and laid the blade against his own belly, just above the fine golden fluff of pubic hair.

The blade was so cold that he gasped, and the mutton fat left a little greasy smear on his belly. He took a long breath to steel himself, and then slowly began to draw the blade downwards, to free himself for ever of that shameful wormlike growth.

'Jordie, what are you doing?' The voice from the doorway behind him startled him so that he cried out aloud. He threw the knife onto the table and at the same time dropped the shirt to cover himself.

'Jordie!'

He turned swiftly, breathing in sharp little gasps, and Ralph came towards him from the kitchen door. He wore only a pair of baggy shorts, and there were goosebumps on the smooth bare skin of his chest from the pre-dawn chill.

'What were you doing?' he repeated.

'Nothing. I wasn't doing anything.' Jordan shook his head wildly.

'You were whacking your old winker, weren't you?' Ralph accused and grinned. 'You dirty little bugger.'

Jordan let out a choking sob and fled past him to the door, and Ralph chuckled and shook his head.

Then he picked up the stag-handled knife and cut a thick slab of mutton off the joint, dipped the blade into the stone pot and smeared a gob of yellow mustard over the meat, and munched it as he went about building up the fire in the stove and setting the coffee water to boil.

The following Sunday afternoon on the white sand of the fighting arena, Inkosikazi, the spider, died an agonizing death in the ghastly embrace of a smaller more agile adversary.

Bazo mourned her as he would a lover, and Kamuza sang the dirge with him just as sadly, for the Matabele syndicate had lost twenty sovereigns with her passing.

The return from Market Square to Zouga's camp resembled Napoleon's retreat from Moscow, headed by Ralph and Bazo bearing between them the basket and its sorry contents.

Opposite Diamond Lil's canteen, Ralph halted the cortege for a moment and wistfully contemplated the painted windows across the street, and listened for a moment to the sounds of laughter from beyond the green door – imagining that he could distinguish Lil's tinkling chimes.

When they reached the thatched beehive communal hut, Kamuza passed Ralph the clay pot of bubbling millet beer.

'How much did you lose, Henshaw?'

'Everything,' Ralph replied tragically. 'The very reason for living.' He took a long swallow of the thick gruel-like beer.

'That is bad; only a foolish man keeps all his cows in the same kraal.'

'Kamuza, your words are always a great solace,' Ralph told him bitterly. 'But I am unworthy of such wisdom. Keep those treasures for yourself alone.'

Kamuza looked smug and turned to Bazo. 'Now you know why I would not lay fifty gold queens, as you bid me.'

Bazo shot a glance at Ralph, and they acted together.

Ralph draped a seemingly brotherly arm over Kamuza's shoulders, but it was a steely yoke that held him helpless, and with the other hand he pulled open the front of Kamuza's loincloth – and Bazo scooped the soft furry carcass of the great spider out of the basket and dropped it into the opening.

As Ralph released him, Kamuza went up into the air, rearing like an unbroken stallion feeling the saddle and spur for the first time, whinnying wildly with horror, beating at his own loins with both hands.

If Ralph had not caught him, Bazo, in a shaking paralysis of mirth, might have fallen into the fire in the centre of the hut.

Kamuza had been gone almost three years.

When Bazo and the other Matabele had signed their contracts for a third period, Kamuza alone had asked Bakela to '*Bala Isitupa*', to write off the contract as complete, and he had taken the road north back to Matabeleland.

Bazo had missed him deeply. He had missed the spiked tongue and shrewd acerbic counsel. He had missed Kamuza's intuitive understanding of the white man's ways of thinking, ways which Bazo still found unfathomable.

Even though Henshaw was his friend, had worked at Bazo's shoulder for all those long years, though they had hawked and hunted together, dipped into the same baking of maize porridge and drunk from the lip of the same beer pot – though Henshaw spoke his language so easily that sitting in the darkness when the fire had burned down to embers it might have been a young Matabele buck talking, so faithfully did Henshaw echo the deep cadence of the north, so complete was his command of the colloquial, so poetic the imagery he used – yet Henshaw would never be Matabele as Kamuza was Matabele, could never be brother as Kamuza was, had never shared the initiation rites with Bazo as Kamuza had, had never formed the 'horns of the bull' with him as the impi closed for the kill, and had never driven the assegai deep and seen the bright blood fly as Kamuza had.

Thus Bazo was filled with joy when he heard the word.

'Kamuza is amongst us again.'

Bazo heard it first whispered by another Matabele as they formed a line at the gate of the security compound.

'Kamuza comes as the king's man,' they whispered around the watch-fires, and there was respect, even fear, in their voices. 'Kamuza wears the headring now.'

Many young Matabele had come to work at *Umgodi Kakulu*, 'The Big Hole', these last few years, and each month more came down the long and weary road from the north, small bands of ten or twenty, sometimes only in pairs, or threes and occasionally even a man travelling alone.

How many had reached Kimberley? There was nobody to keep a tally, a thousand certainly, two thousand perhaps, and each of them had been given the road southwards by the great black elephant, each of them had the king's permission to journey beyond the borders of Matabeleland, for without it they would have been speared to death by the bright assegais of the impis that guarded every road to and from the king's great kraal at Thabas Indunas – the Hills of the Chiefs.

Even in exile these young Matabele formed a closeknit tribal association. Each newcomer from the north carried tidings, long messages from fathers and indunas, repeated verbatim with every nuance of the original. Just as every Matabele who left the diamond fields, whether he had worked out his three-year contract or was bored and homesick or had fallen foul of the white man's complicated and senseless laws and was deserting, carried back with him messages and instructions that he had committed to the phenomenal memory of a people who did not have the written word.

Now the word passed swiftly from Matabele to Matabele.

'Kamuza is here.'

Kamuza had never warranted such attention before. He had been one amongst a thousand; but now he had returned as the king's man, and they lowered their voices when they spoke his name.

Bazo looked for him each day, searching the faces on the high stagings and on the running skips. He lay sleepless on his mat beside the cooling watch-fire, listening for Kamuza's whisper in the darkness.

He waited for many days and many nights, and then suddenly Kamuza was there, stooping through the low entrance and greeting Bazo.

'I see you, Bazo, son of Gandang.'

Bazo stifled his joy and replied calmly.

'I see you also, Kamuza.'

And they made a place for Kamuza in the circle, not pressing him too closely, giving him space, for now Kamuza wore the simple black tiara upon his close-cropped pate, the badge of the Councillor, the induna of the king of Matabeleland.

They called him 'Baba', a term of great respect, and even Bazo clapped his hands softly in greeting and passed him the beer pot.

Only after Kamuza had refreshed himself could Bazo begin to ask the questions of home, disguising his eagerness behind measured tones and an expression of calm dignity.

Kamuza was no longer a youth, neither of them were; the years had sped away and they were both in the full flowering of their manhood. Kamuza's features were sharper than the true Matabele of Zanzi blood, the old blood from Zululand, for his was mixed with Tswana, the less warlike but shrewd and cunning peoples of King Khama. Kamuza's grandmother had been captured as a maiden, still short of puberty, by one of King Mzilikazi's raiding impis, and taken to wife by the induna who commanded her captors. From her Kamuza had inherited his mulberry black skin and the Egyptian slant of his eyes, the narrow nostrils and the thin and knowing twist of his lips.

There were very few Matabele who could still trace their bloodline back to the pure Zanzi, to the line of Chaka and Dingaan, the Zulus, the Sons of Heaven, and Bazo was one of those. Yet it was Kamuza who wore the ring of the induna on his head now.

In the time of Mzilikazi, a man would have the hoar frost of wisdom and age powdering his hair, and the cowtails bound about his elbows and knees would proclaim his deeds in battle to the world before the king ordered him to take the *isicoco*. Then his wives would plait and twist the headring into his own hair and cement it permanently into place with gum and clay and ox blood, a permanent halo of honour that entitled the wearer to his seat on the Council of the Matabele nation.

However, the old times were changing. More cunning than fierce, Lobengula, son of Mzilikazi, looked for cunning in those about him. Mzilikazi had been a warrior and lived by the white flash of the assegai. Lobengula, though he had blooded his spear, had never been a warrior, and he scorned the warriors' simpleness of thought and directness of action. As his father's greybeards faltered, he replaced them with men who thought as swiftly as the old ones had stabbed.

He had no patience with the old men's preoccupation with a world that was passing, and he sought out the young ones with clear fresh eyes, men who could see with him the dark clouds gathering on the southern borders like the soaring thunderheads of high summer.

Men who could sense the change and terrible events which his wizards and his own divinations warned him would soon rush down upon him like the fires that sweep the papyrus beds of the Zambezi swamps at the end of the dry season.

Lobengula, the great Black Elephant, whose very tread shakes the earth's foundations, and whose voice splits the skies, was choosing young men with eyes to see and ears to hear.

Thus Kamuza now wore the *isicoco* of the induna and, as he spoke over the fire in his dry whisper, his slanted eyes black and bright as those of a mamba in the firelight, men listened – and listened with great attention.

It was a measure of the gravity of the news he carried from the north that Kamuza began the council – the *indaba* – with a recital of the history of the Matabele nation. Each of them had heard it first with their mother's breast in their mouths, had drunk it in with her milk, but they listened now as avidly as then, reinforcing their memories so that when the time came they would be able to repeat it perfectly in each detail to their own children, that the story might never be lost.

The history began with Mzilikazi, war chief of the impis of Zulu, warrior without peer, beloved comrade and trusted intimate of King Chaka himself. It told of the black sickness of King Chaka, driven mad with grief at the death of his mother Nandi, the Sweet One. Chaka ordering the year of mourning in which no man might sow seed, on pain of death; in which the milk from the cows must be thrown upon the earth, on pain of death; in which no man might lie with his woman, on pain of death.

Mad Chaka brooded in his great hut and looked for cause to strike down all around him, even the most trusted, even the most beloved.

So it was that Chaka's messengers came to Mzilikazi, the young war chieftain. They found him in the field with his impis about him, five thousand of Zululand's bravest and finest, all of them still hot from battle, driving before them the spoils they had taken – the captured herds, the young and comely girls roped neck to neck.

The king's messengers wore the long tail feathers of the stately blue cranes in their headdress, token of their solemn mission.

'The king accuses the induna Mzilikazi,' began the first messenger, and looking into his arrogant face Mzilikazi knew that he looked upon the face of death. 'The king accuses Mzilikazi of stealing the king's share of the spoils of war.'

Then the second messenger spoke, and his words were an echo of the king's black madness, so that the words of King Chaka stood in the air above Mzilikazi's impis the way that the vultures circle above the battlefields on wide and motionless pinions.

If the sentence of death had been upon him alone, Mzilikazi might have gone to his king and met it with courage and dignity. But his five thousand fighting men were doomed also, and Mzilikazi called them his children.

So Mzilikazi reached out and seized the king's messengers, and for a moment the earth seemed to lurch in its courses, for to touch these who wore the blue crane feathers was to touch the person of the king himself. With the razor edge of his assegai, Mzilikazi slashed the blue feathers from their heads, and threw them into the faces of the grovelling messengers.

'That is my reply to Chaka – who is no longer my king.'

Thus began the great exodus towards the north and, seated over the watch-fire, Kamuza, the king's man, related it all again.

He told the battle honours of Mzilikazi, the renegade. He told how Chaka sent his most famous impis after the fleeing five thousand, and how Mzilikazi met them in the classic battle tactics of the Nguni, how he waited for them in the bad ground.

Kamuza told how Mzilikazi threw the 'horns of the bull' around the impis of Chaka, and how his young men shouted '*Ngi dhla!* I have eaten!' as they drove in the steel; and the listeners in the dark hut murmured and moved restlessly, and their eyes shone and their spear hands twitched.

When it was over, the survivors of Chaka's shattered impi came to Mzilikazi and, on their knees, swore allegiance to him, to Mzilikazi who was no longer a renegade, but a little king.

Kamuza told how the little king marched north with his swollen impi, and how he defeated other little kings and became a great king.

Kamuza told how after Chaka was murdered by his brothers, Dingaan, the new leader of the Zulu nation, did not dare to send out more impis to pursue Mzilikazi. So Mzilikazi flourished, and like a ravaging lion he ate up the tribes. Their warriors swelled his fighting impis, and his Zanzi, the pure-blooded Zulu, bred upon the bellies of the captured maidens and the Matabele became a nation and Mzilikazi became a black emperor whose domain overshadowed even that of Chaka.

The men about the fire listened and felt their hearts swell with pride.

Then Kamuza told how the *buni*, the strange white men, crossed the river in their little wagons and outspanned upon the land that Mzilikazi had won with the assegai. Then Mzilikazi paraded his impis, and they danced with their war plumes aflutter, and their long shields clashing as they passed before him.

After he had reviewed the might of his nation, Mzilikazi took the little ceremonial spear of his kingship, and he poised before his impis and then hurled the toy-like weapon towards the banks of the Gariep river on which the white men had outspanned their wagons.

They took them in the hour before dawn, at the time of the horns, when the horns of the cattle can first be seen against the lightening sky. The front ranks of racing black warriors received the first volley of the long muzzle-loading guns, absorbing it as though it were a handful of pebbles thrown into a stormy black sea.

Then they stabbed the bearded men as they worked frantically with powderhorn and ramrod. They stabbed the white women as they ran from the wagons in their nightdresses, trying to carry the second gun to their men. They snatched the infants from their cradles on the wagonbed, and dashed out their brains against the tall steel-shod wheels of the wagons.

Oh, it was a rare feast that they set for Mzilikazi's chickens, the grotesque naked-headed vultures. They believed it was an ending – but it was only a beginning, for the Matabele were about to learn of the persistence and the dour courage of these strange pale people.

The next wave of white men came out of the south, and when they found the abandoned wagons and the jackal-chewed bones on the banks of the Gariep, theirs was a fury such as the Matabele had never encountered in all their wars.

So the *buni* met the impis on the open ground, refusing to be drawn into the ravines and thorn scrub. They came in pitifully small squadrons on shaggy ponies to dismount and discharge their volleys in a thunder of blue powder smoke. Then they went up into the saddle to wheel away from under the wall of charging rawhide shields, and reload and circle back to let loose the thunder again into the mass of half-naked bodies glistening with oil and sweat.

The *buni* built fortresses on the open plain, fortresses with their wagons' bodies which they lashed wheel to wheel; and they let the impis come to die upon the wooden walls of the fortress, while their womenfolk stood close behind them to take the gun while the barrel was still hot and pass up the second gun, charged and primed.

Then when the impis drew back, mauled and shaken, the wagons uncoiled from their circle, like a slow but deadly puffadder, and crawled forward towards the kraal of Mzilikazi. And the dreadful horsemen galloped ahead of them, firing and circling, firing and circling.

Sadly Mzilikazi counted his dead and the price was too high, the red mud through which the iron-shod wheels churned was puddled with the blood of Zanzi, the blood of Heaven.

So he called his nation, and the herd boys brought in the herds, and the women rolled the sleeping-mats, and the little girls balanced the clay cooking-pots upon their heads, and Mzilikazi put fire into his kraals and led the Matabele nation away. A vast throng of people and animals were guarded by the depleted impis, while the white men on their sturdy ponies drove them and pointed them the way the sheepdog works the flock. Mzilikazi led them northwards until they crossed the great river into a new land.

'Now the white birds are gathering again,' Kamuza told the young men about the watch-fire. 'Each day they come up the road to Thabas Indunas, and they bring their tawdry gifts and the little green bottles of madness. Their words are sweet as honey on the tongue, but they catch in the throat of those who try to swallow them as though they were the green bile of the crocodile.'

'What is it they seek from the king?' Bazo asked the question for all those who listened, and Kamuza shrugged.

'This one asks for the right to hunt elephant and take the teeth, this one asks for the young girls to be sent to his wagon, another wants to tell the nation of a strange white god that has three heads, another wishes to dig a hole and look for the yellow iron, yet another wishes to buy cattle. One says he wants only this, and another only that, but they want it all. These people are consumed by a hunger that can never be appeased, they burn with a thirst that can never be assuaged. They want everything they see, and even that is never enough for them. They take the very earth, but that is not enough, so they tear it open like a man tearing a child from the mother's womb. They take the rivers, and that is not enough, so they build walls across them and turn them into lakes. They ride after the elephant herds and shoot them down, not just one or two, not just the big bulls, but all of them – the breeding cows and the calves with ivory no longer than your finger. Everything they see they take; and they see everything, for they are always moving and searching and looking.'

'Lobengula must eat them up,' Bazo said. 'He must eat them up as Mzilikazi his father would have eaten them.'

'Hau!'Kamuza smiled his thin twisted smile. 'Such wisdom from my brother. He recalls how Mzilikazi ate the white men on the banks of the Gariep, and lost a land. Listen to Bazo, my children. He counsels the King Lobengula to throw the war spear and loose his impis as Cetewayo the King of Zulu did at the Hill of the Little Hand. How many Englishmen did Cetewayo slay? There was no counting, for their red jackets lay one upon the other like the snows of the Dragon Mountains when the sunset turns them to fire, and their blood fed the land so that the grass still grows greener and thicker and sweeter upon the slopes of the Little Hand to this day. Oh a fine killing, my children, a great and beautiful stabbing – and afterwards Cetewayo paid for it with the spear of his kingship. He paid for it with his royal herds, he paid for it with the liver and heart of his young men, with the grassy hills of Zululand. For after the avengers had made the great slaughter at Ulundi they took it all, and they placed chains of iron upon Cetewayo's wrists and ankles and they chained his indunas and his war captains and led them away. Now Bazo, the wise, would have you know what a good bargain King Cetewayo made, and he urges Lobengula to make the same bargain with these white men.'

Bazo's expression remained grave and dignified while Kamuza chided and mocked him but he twisted the snuff-horn between his fingers and once he glanced to the dark corner of the thatched hut where the long war shields and the broad assegai were stacked.

But when Kamuza finished, Bazo shook his head. 'No one here dares counsel the king; we are his dogs only. No one here doubts the might and resolve of the white men, we who live each day with their strange and wonderful ways. All we ask is this: what is the king's word? Tell us what Lobengula wishes – for to hear is to obey.'

Kamuza nodded. 'Hear then the king's voice, for the king has travelled with all his senior indunas – Babiaan and Somabula and Gandang – all the indunas of the house of Kumalo – they have gone into the hills of Matopos to the place of the Umlimo –'

A superstitious tremor shook the group, a little shiver as though the name of the wizard of the Matopos had crawled upon their skins like the sickle-winged tsetse fly.

'The Umlimo has given the oracle,' Kamuza told them, and then was silent, the pause theatrical, to pique their attention, to dramatize the effect of his next words.

'On the first day the Umlimo repeated the ancient prophecy, the words that have come down from the time of Monomatapa. On the first day the Umlimo spoke thus:

"The stone falcons will fly afar. There shall be no peace in the kingdoms of the Mambos or the Monomatapas until they return. For the white eagle will war with the black bull until the stone falcons return to roost."

They had all of them heard the prophecy before, but now it had a new and sinister impact.

'The king has pondered the ancient prophecy, and he says thus: "The white birds are gathering. Eagle and vulture – all of them white, they roost already upon the roof of my kraal." '

'What is the meaning of the stone falcons?' one of his listeners asked.

'The stone falcons are the bird gods that the ancient ones left at the burial place of the old kings, Zimbabwe.'

'How will stone birds fly?'

'One has flown already,' Bazo answered this time. 'One of the stone falcons stands close by us now. It stands under the roof of Bakela, the Fist. It was he who took the falcon, and carried it away.'

'When the other birds fly, then war will sweep over Matabeleland,' Kamuza affirmed. 'But listen now to the oracle of the Umlimo.' And their questions were stilled.

'On the second day the Umlimo prophesied thus:

"When the midnight sky turns to noon, and the stars shine on the hills – then the fist will hold the blade to the throat of the black bull."

'This was the prophecy of the second day.'

Again they were silent as they pondered the words then, mystified, they looked to Kamuza for the meaning of the prophecy.

'Lobengula, the Black Elephant, alone understands the meaning of the prophecy of the second day. Is he not versed in the mysteries of the wizards? Did he not pass his childhood in the caves and secret places of the wizards? Thus says Lobengula. "This is not yet the time to explain the words of the Umlimo to my children, for they are momentous words indeed, and there will be a time for the nation to understand." '

Bazo nodded and passed his snuff-horn. Kamuza took it and drew the red powder up into his nostrils with two sharp inhalations of breath and, watching him, Bazo did not dare to voice his own suspicion that perhaps Lobengula, the mighty thunder of the skies, was as mystified by the prophecy of the second day as was the little group around the fire.

'Was this all the oracle?' Bazo asked instead, and Kamuza shook his head.

'On the third day the Umlimo prophesied for the last time:

"Sting the mamba with his own venom, pull down the lion with his own claws, deceive the clever chacma baboon with his own trickery."

'This was the prophecy of the third and final day.'

'Does the king intend that we, his humble cattle, should know the meaning of the prophecy of the third day?'

'Thus spoke Lobengula: "We the Matabele cannot prevail until we arm ourselves as our adversary is armed, until we gather to ourselves the strength that is found only in the yellow coins and shining stones. For it is these things which have made the white man strong." '

Nobody interrupted the silence that followed, for they all sensed that there was more to come.

'Thus the king summoned me to the royal kraal and bid me carry his word to all the Matabele who live beyond the borders of the king's domains. For thus spoke the king: "Bring me guns to answer the smoke of the white man's guns. Bring me diamonds and bring me the yellow coins that I may grow as strong as the white Queen who lives beyond the sea. For then her soldiers will not dare to come against me." '

Bazo replied for them all. 'Let Lobengula know that what he requires of us he shall have. Guns he shall have, for it is part of our contract with the white man. Each of us will carry a gun when we return to Matabeleland, some of us who have worked out two *Isitupa* will carry two guns when we return. Some of us will bring three guns.'

'That is known,' Kamuza nodded.

'Lobengula will have gold coins, for we are paid in coin, and what we bring home to Thabas Indunas belongs to the king.'

'That is right and proper.'

'But diamonds?' Bazo asked. 'The diamonds belong to the white man. They are fierce for them as a lioness is fierce for her cubs. How are we to bring diamonds to the king?'

'Listen to me,' whispered Kamuza. 'There will be no more "pick-ups". When one of you turns up the shine of a diamond in the yellow gravel, then that diamond belongs to Lobengula.'

'It is against the law.'

'Against the white man's law only, not against the law of Lobengula, who is your king.'

'To hear is to obey,' Bazo grunted, but he thought of Bakela, the Fist, who was his father, and Henshaw, the Hawk, who was his brother, and he did not relish stealing the stones for which they laboured as hard as Bazo did himself.

'Not only in the pit,' Kamuza went on. 'Each of you will watch for the chance on the sorting-tables, you, Donsela –' He picked out a Matabele across the fire from him, a young man with a deep intelligent brow and strong jaw. 'You have been chosen to work in the new grease house.'

'The tables are guarded,' Donsela replied. 'They are covered with a steel screen.'

They had all of them heard Donsela speak of the marvel of the new grease house.

Once again the ingenuity of the white men had put the diamond's unique qualities to his own advantage. The diamond was unwetable, shedding moisture like the body feathers of a goose. So while wet gravel would roll across a steel table smeared with thick yellow grease, the dry diamond would stick fast.

The pipeline from the Vaal river had at last reached Kimberley, and this water supply was augmented by the subterranean water pumped up from the depths of the vast excavation. There was water enough now to wash the gravel, instead of laboriously dry-sorting it, water enough to wash the sieved gravel over the slanting grease tables. The diamonds stuck like fat little blisters, half embedded in the grease, ready to be scraped off with a steel spatula at the end of each shift.

'There is a steel screen over the tables,' Donsela repeated, and Kamuza smiled and passed him a thin reed, cut from the riverbank. On the tip of the reed was a little lump of beeswax.

'The reed will pass through the mesh of the screen,' Kamuza told him. 'The diamond will stick more firmly to the wax than to the grease.'

Donsela examined the reed cautiously. 'Last week a Basuto was found with a stone. That same day he fell from the skip as they were bringing him out of the pit. Men who steal stones have accidents. Those accidents always kill them.'

'A warrior's duty is to die for his king,' Kamuza told him drily. 'Do not let the overseer catch you, and pick out only the biggest and brightest stones.'

In the three years between Kamuza's departure from Kimberley and his abrupt return, Ralph had reached his full growth. Only months short of his twenty-first birthday, he stood as tall as Zouga; but unlike his father, he was cleanshaven except for the thick dark moustache which he allowed to curl down at the corners of his mouth.

At rare intervals he was still able to gather together the ten gold sovereigns necessary to keep his surreptitious friendship with Diamond Lil alive. Then suddenly that was no longer relevant, for Ralph fell in love.

It happened in the street outside that exclusive institution, already the most famous in Africa south of the equator, membership of which conferred enormous prestige and a semi-mystical entrée to the elite band of men who wielded the growing wealth and burgeoning power of the diamond fields.

Yet the Kimberley Club was merely a single-storeyed wood-and-iron building as drab as any on the diggings. True it boasted a billiard room with a full-sized table, a picket fence of ornate cast iron and a stained-glass front door – but it was situated in the noisiest street just off Market Square, and it enjoyed its fair share of the flies and the all-pervading red dust.

It was mid-morning and Ralph was bringing one of the gravel carts back from the blacksmith who had replaced the iron tyres on the wooden-spoked wheels.

There was a stir in the street ahead of him. He saw men run from the canteens and kopje-wallopers' offices, most of them bareheaded and in shirtsleeves.

A vehicle came bowling out of the square – an extraordinary vehicle, light and fast, with high narrow wheels, so cunningly sprung that it seemed to float behind the pair that drew it. They were matched, a strange pale brazen colour, softer than the colour of honey, and their manes were white blond.

Both horses were martingaled to force them to arch their necks, and the long-combed platinum manes flew like the battle colours of a famous regiment.

The driver, either by chance, but more probably by skill, had them leading with their off fores in perfect unison, and their gait was an exaggerated trot in which they threw their forehooves so high that they seemed almost to touch the shining heads as they nodded to the rhythm of their run.

Ralph was stabbed by such a pang of envy that it was a physical pain. He had never seen anything so beautiful as those pale glistening animals and the vehicle that they drew – until he raised his eyes to the driver.

She wore a tricorn hat of midnight blue, set at a jaunty angle over one eyebrow.

Her eyebrows were jet black, narrow and exquisitely arched over huge drop-shaped eyes.

As she came up to the plodding gravel cart she barely lifted the gloved hand that held the reins, and the plunging pair of pale horses swerved neatly and the elegant vehicle flashed past so close that, had he dared, Ralph might have reached up and touched one of those slim ankles in its high-buttoned patent leather boot which just showed under the tailored skirt of moire taffeta.

Then she dropped her hand again, and the matched pair swung the carriage in neatly before the wrought-iron gate of the Kimberley Club and stopped, shaking out their manes fretfully and stamping their forefeet.

'Bazo, take them,' Ralph called urgently. 'Go on to the stagings. I'll follow you.'

Then he darted across the street and reached up to seize the head of the nearest thoroughbred.

He was only just in time, for half a dozen other loiterers had raced him to it. Ralph removed his cap and looked up at the woman on the buttoned leather seat of the carriage. She glanced down at him and fleetingly smiled her thanks, and Ralph saw that her eyes were the same midnight blue as the hat on her head. Those eyes touched him for only an instant and then went back to the stained-glass front door of the club, but Ralph felt a physical shock from her gaze like a blow in the chest, so that he could not catch his breath.

Ralph was aware of voices, men's voices, from the direction of the club, but he could not tear his eyes from that lovely face. He was absorbing each fine detail, the braid of her hair, the colour of freshly-washed coal, thick as the tail of a lioness, which dropped from under the hat over her shoulder and hung to her waist. The fine peppering of dark freckles high on her cheekbones seemed to emphasize the purity of the rest of her skin. Her small pointed ears were set at an alert listening angle which gave a peculiar vivacity to her face. The dark V of the widow's peak below the brim of her hat pointed up the depth of forehead. Her nose was narrow and straight with elegantly flared nostrils that gave her expression an hauteur that was instantly belied when she smiled, as she was smiling now, but not at Ralph.

She was smiling at the group of men who came out onto the porch of the club, chatting animatedly as they adjusted their hats.

'A splendid lunch, sir.' The only stranger to Ralph in the group thanked his host and then led them down the short walk to the street.

He was a tall, well-proportioned man. His dress was sober. The cut was not English but he wore it with a dash that made the dark colours appear flamboyant.

He wore a dark patch over one eye, and it gave him a piratical air. His beard was trimmed to a point, and touched with silver.

'He is at least forty years old,' Ralph thought, bitterly, as he realized that the woman was smiling directly at this man.

At his right hand was a small neat figure, a man with an unremarkable face and thin receding hair, a small moustache of indeterminate colour – but eyes so intelligent and humorous that they altered the man's appearance – made it striking and interesting.

'Ah, Ralph,' this man murmured, as he noticed the young man standing at the horse's head; but Ralph could not meet his eyes.

Doctor Leander Starr Jameson was an intimate friend of his father's, and privy to Ralph's shame and disgrace. It was he who had administered the mercury tablets, and washed them down with a stern admonition to avoid in future the snares of harlotry. For a moment Ralph wondered if the doctor would impart his vile secret to the lovely lady on the seat of the carriage – and the thought burned his soul like hoar frost.

On the bearded man's other hand was Mr Rhodes, big and serious, his dress untidy, the knot of his tie slipping and his breeches baggy, but with that sense of determination and certainty about him that always awed Ralph.

Behind them all followed the stooped scholarly figure of Alfred Beit, like Mr Rhodes' shadow.

The four men paused in a group beside the carriage, and the tall stranger reached up and took the woman's hand.

He touched her fingers to his lips.

'Gentlemen, may I present my wife, Mrs St John.' The big man's accent was unmistakable, even Ralph recognized the soft drawl that emanated from the Southern States of America.

However, it was the title the man used and not the accent which struck like a fiery dart into Ralph's breast.

' – Mrs St John, my wife – Mrs St John.'

While Ralph stood rigid at the horse's head, destroyed by his adoration which he now knew was hopeless, the group ignored him and the men made their bows.

'Louise, my dear, this is Mr Rhodes of whom you have heard so much – '

The formal phrases might have been spoken in a foreign language as far as Ralph was affected by them. Her name was Louise, and she was married. That is all that he understood.

General St John climbed up beside his wife. He moved lithely for such a big man, and one so old, Ralph conceded reluctantly, and hated him anew for that. St John took the reins from Louise's gloved hand, lifted his hat to the three men and started the horses. Ralph had to jump back to avoid being knocked down, and Louise was talking animatedly to the General. Neither of them glanced at Ralph again, and the carriage whirled away, down the street.

Ralph stared after it wistfully.

Jordan decorated the borders of the menus with romanticized scenes of the diggings: the stagings soaring above the gaping pit, heroic figures working on the walls of yellow earth, a sorter at his table – and at the head of the sheet a man's cupped hands overflowing with uncut diamonds – and he coloured the illustrations with water paints.

'What's Velouté de la Nouvelle Ruée?' Ralph asked.

'Soup New Rush,' Jordie told him without looking up from his artistic labours.

'What's going to be in it?'

'Marrow bones and pearl barley.'

' – And what's Quartier de Chevreuil Diamant Bleu?'

'Haunch of springbuck in the style of a blue diamond.'

'I don't know why we can't just speak English,' Ralph complained. 'What's the style of a blue diamond, anyway?'

'Lard the haunch with bacon fat, marinade it in olive oil and cognac with wild garlic, and then bake it in a pie crust.'

Ralph swallowed his saliva. Jordan's culinary skills were always a source of delight to him.

'All right – I'll eat it.'

Jordan licked his brush, leaving a streak of Prussian blue on his tongue, and then looked up at his brother.

'You are going to serve it, not eat it –' Jordan paused portentously, 'Mr Rhodes is coming to lunch,' as though that explained it all.

'Well, if I'm not good enough to sit at the same table as your famous Mr Rhodes – I'll be damned if I'll play waiter. You can get Donsela. For a shilling Donsela will spill soup on Mr Rhodes, for a shilling Donsela would throw soup on King Lobengula himself. I'm going to bribe him.'

However, in the end curiosity and Jordan's promise of the leftovers prevailed and Ralph dressed himself in the ridiculous monkey-jacket that Jordan had designed and tailored for him and carried the tray of Velouté out on the wide verandah of Zouga's camp – and there nearly dropped it.

'Madame, you remind me of the heroine from Mr Longfellow's poem,' Neville Pickering complimented Louise St John, and she smiled back at him from her seat at the centre of the luncheon table.

'Thank you, sir.'

Her jacket was in pale creamy buckskin with tasselled sleeves, and the bodice was crusted with bright-coloured beads in bold geometrical patterns. Louise had parted her thick black hair in the centre, braided a blue ribbon into each of the thick tresses, bound them with a band about her forehead, and then let them hang onto her bosom. The soft tanned buckskin was divided into ankle-length culottes, and her boots were also of soft beaded leather.

Louise was the only woman at the long trestle table on the open verandah of Zouga's camp. The men seated on each side of her were already emerging as the most influential subjects on this continent of an omnipotent queen. Like the men that another English queen had sent out to the corners of the earth, these were the new Elizabethans, most of them already rich – all of them restless and consumed with their lust for power, for wealth, for land. Each with a separate dream that he would follow relentlessly all his life, every one of them driving, ruthless men.

Ballantyne. Beit. Jameson. Rhodes. Robinson. The list of names read like a roll-call for a regiment of filibusters, and yet here they were listening to a discourse on women's fashion as though it were a company report on tonnage treated and cartage recovered.

Only Zouga Ballantyne was not smiling. The woman offended Zouga. Her beauty was too flamboyant, her colouring too vivid. Zouga preferred the pale gold blond hair and the complexion of sugared cream and strawberries. An Englishman's idea of beauty.

This woman's dress was outrageous, the styling of her hair pretentious. Her gaze was too direct, her eyes too blue, her conversation too easy and her style of address too familiar. Of course American women had the reputation of affecting masculine manners, but Zouga found himself wishing that Louise St John had kept those manners on the other side of the Atlantic Ocean where they belonged.

It was enough that she had galloped into his camp ahead of her husband, riding astride, and dismounted by freeing both of her narrow booted feet from the stirrups and vaulting lightly to the ground; but then she had come up onto the stoep with an assured stride and smile, her right hand out like a man, and without waiting for her husband to introduce them had said: 'You must be Zouga Ballantyne. I'd recognize you anywhere by Mungo's description of you.'

Her hand was narrow, the skin warm but dry, but the grip of her fingers was unfemininely firm, the grip of a skilled horsewoman.

These leisurely Sunday luncheons at Zouga's camp were his one extravagance, and they had become one of the traditions of Kimberley, when excellent fare and good liquor and the company of intelligent men made for memorable afternoons.

Women were very seldom invited to these gatherings, and Louise St John would not have been there if Zouga had been able to have her husband come alone, but Mungo St John had replied pointedly to the invitation, 'General *and Mrs St John* have pleasure in accepting.'

The friendship between St John and Zouga had begun many years previously, and he was the kind of man whom Zouga could admire: a man like himself, hard and determined, one who lived by his own code without compromise. One who expected no preference nor favour, but whose triumphs were of his own engineering and whose disasters were met with fortitude, without plea or excuse, even when occasioned by cruel circumstances beyond his control.

In the late 'fifties St John had built up a commercial empire, a fleet of trading vessels which had carried the black ivory of slaves from the African continent to that of North America. Legend was that in three voyages, in the course of a single period of twelve months, across the notorious middle passage of the Atlantic, he had transported almost two million dollars' worth of slaves, and with those profits he had acquired vast estates in Louisiana.

It was at this time that Zouga had first met him. Zouga had travelled as a passenger on St John's magnificent clipper *Huron* out of the Port of Bristol in southern England to the Cape of Good Hope. The irony of that voyage had been that Zouga at the time had not been aware that St John was engaged in the trade, and Zouga had been accompanied on the voyage by his only sister, Robyn Ballantyne, a medical missionary whose declared goal in life was the extinction of the trade on the African continent.

When Robyn Ballantyne had discovered that St John was not sailing to Africa to barter beads and copper wire for ivory and ostrich feathers, for gumcopal and alluvial gold dust from the kingdom of Monomatapa, but was seeking richer, living black cargo, her hatred was rendered more implacable by her shame at having travelled in company with such a man.

It was Robyn Ballantyne who had called up the avenging spectre of the Royal Navy. She had been the chief instrument in delivering St John and his beautiful clipper *Huron*, with her cargo of five hundred prime slaves, to the gunboats of the British anti-slavery squadron.

St John, as was his right as an American captain, had resisted the British boarders, and in the savage action that followed, half his crew had been killed or maimed and his lovely ship so badly mauled that she had to be towed into Table Bay by her captors.

Though after imprisonment in Cape Town castle, the British governor had finally released St John and allowed him to sail away, still his cargo of slaves were seized and released from their chains, and the African coast was closed for ever to his ships.

It was then that Zouga had lost contact with him; but after Zouga's book *A Hunter's Odyssey* had been published, St John had written to him care of his London publishers, Messrs Rowland Ward, and since then they had corresponded at irregular intervals. Indeed it was Zouga's description of the diamond fields in one of these letters that was responsible for St John's presence here now.

Through the exchange of letters Zouga had been able to follow St John's career, and he learned how after his release from the Cape Town castle, St John had returned to Fairfields, his cotton and sugar estates near Baton Rouge, only weeks before the first cannon shots were fired at Fort Sumter.

Louisiana had voted for secession from the Union, and when the war began, Mungo raised his own force of irregular cavalry and led them in a brilliant series of hit-and-run raids against the supply lines and rear bases of the Federal army. So successful were these depredations that the northeners christened him 'Murdering Mungo', declared him an outlaw and placed a reward of fifty thousand dollars on his head. Promoted to major-general, he was later struck in the left eye by a red-hot splinter of shrapnel and dragged over a mile when his horse bolted. By the time he was discharged from the hospital, Vicksburg had fallen. Recognizing this as a fatal stab in the heart of the Confederacy, he had limped back along the empty road to Fairfields.

The reek of fermenting sugar juices mingled with that of charred flesh was more revolting than any battlefield Mungo had ever smelled. Four colonnades stood above the ashes of his homestead, like monuments to all his dreams.

Now, all these years later, St John had come up the road from Good Hope, driving a pair of magnificent pale gold horses with flowing white manes that he called 'Palaminos', a long black cigar between his white teeth, an eagle gleam in his single eye and this strangely disturbing woman on the seat of the phaeton beside him.

St John's first act in Kimberley had been to walk into the office of the Standard Bank on Market Square and present a letter of credit to the flabbergasted clerk. The letter of credit was on heavy, expensive paper, the printing embossed in rose and gold, the wax seal that of Messrs Coutts and Co. in the Strand, and the sum for which it was drawn was half a million of sterling.

St John had drawn a modest hundred pounds against that formidable total, and taken rooms for himself and his wife at the Craven Hotel, Kimberley's most fashionable and comfortable.

When he recovered from his shock, the bank-clerk had excitedly begun to spread the news. There was an American general on the fields who disposed of a half million pounds in cash.

The following noon St John had casually accepted an invitation to lunch at the Kimberley Club and smiled indulgently as his name was proposed for membership by Mr C. J. Rhodes and seconded by Dr Leander Starr Jameson. There were men, rich and influential men, who had tried in vain since the foundation of the Club to obtain membership.

St John was smiling that same indulgent smile now as he leaned back in his chair, twisting the stem of his champagne glass between his fingers and watching the other guests at the table fawning over his wife.

Even Mr Rhodes, who was famous for his immunity to female wiles, and who usually bluntly terminated any frivolous conversation, was responding to her artless questions and chuckling at her sallies.

With an effort, Zouga tore his own attention from Louise and turned to Mungo St John. Quite pointedly he changed the discussion from the split skirts which allowed his wife to ride astride to Mungo's own doings since their last meeting.

The reason for the change of subject was not missed by Louise. She shot a sharp speculative glance at Zouga, but then smiled graciously and relapsed into dutiful silence while the conversation became at last serious and important.

St John had been in Canada and Australia, and without being specific they all understood that both journeys had been rewarding, for St John spoke of wheat and opals and wool and gold, and they listened avidly, shooting their questions like arrows and nodding to the deft replies, until at last St John ended: 'Well, then I heard from my dear friend Zouga what you gentlemen have been doing here, and thought it was time to come and have a look.'

Almost on cue Ralph came down the verandah carrying the scrubbed carving board with its cargo of roasted venison enclosed in a crisp brown envelope of pastry. The company applauded with exclamations of delight and approbation.

Zouga stood up to carve the roast and while he stropped the hunting knife against steel, he glanced at Ralph who still lingered on the verandah.

'Are you feeling well?' he asked out of the side of his mouth, and Ralph roused himself, tearing his adoring gaze from Louise St John.

'Oh yes, Papa, I'm fine.'

'You don't look fine. You look as if you have a belly ache. Better get Jan Cheroot to give you a dose of sulphur and treacle.'

Jan Cheroot, dressed in his old regimental jacket with burnished buttons and his scarlet cap set at a rakish angle, brought in fresh bottles of champagne, the buckets packed with crushed white ice.

'Ice!' Louise clapped her hands with delight. 'I never expected such sophistication here.'

'Oh, we lack very little, ma'am,' Rhodes assured her. 'My ice-making factory has been in operation for a year or more. In a year or so the railway line will reach Kimberley and then we shall become a city, a real city.'

'And all this on woman's vanity.' Louise shook her long black tresses in mock dismay. 'A lady's baubles, a city built on engagement rings!'

Despite Zouga's best efforts, the focus of attention had shifted again. They were all hanging on her words with that slightly bemused expression which overcomes even the most sensible of men when he looks at a beautiful woman.

'Beautiful woman.' It was the first time Zouga had acknowledged that fact, even to himself, and for some reason it increased his resentment of her.

'Do you know, Mr Rhodes,' she leaned across the table confidentially, 'I have been here for five days now – and although I have searched the sidewalks diligently, I have not seen a single diamond – and I was assured the streets of Kimberley were paved with diamonds.'

They all laughed, more heartily than the witticism warranted, and Rhodes murmured a few words to Pickering before turning back to Louise.

'We shall do what we can to remedy that, Mrs St John,' and while he spoke Pickering scrawled a note and then summoned one of the coloured grooms who was lolling and smoking in the shade of the camel-thorn tree.

'Major, may I borrow one of your champagne buckets?' Pickering asked, and when Zouga agreed, he handed the empty bucket and the note to the groom.

Zouga was carving seconds off the roast when the groom returned. He was followed by a nondescript white man with an uncertain seat on his placid steed. He came up onto the verandah carrying the bucket as though it were filled with Mr Alfred Nobel's new-fangled blasting gelatine.

He placed the bucket on the table in front of Rhodes with a timid flourish, and then seemed to disappear from sight. With his thin colourless hair and myopic eyes behind pebble-lens wire-rimmed spectacles, his dark jacket shiny with wear at elbows and cuffs, he blended like a chameleon with his background.

'Where is young Jordan?' Rhodes asked. 'That boy loves diamonds as much as any of us do.'

Jordan came from the kitchen in his apron and with his colour high from the heat of his stove. He greeted Rhodes shyly.

'Ladies and Gentlemen, Mr Jordan Ballantyne is not only the finest chef on the diggings – but he is also one of the best diamond sorters that we have.' Rhodes was expansive as few of them had ever seen him. 'Come and stand by me, Jordan, where you can have a good view.'

When Jordan was beside his chair, Rhodes tipped the bucket carefully and even Zouga heard himself gasp with shock, while Louise St John cried out aloud.

The bucket was filled to the brim with uncut diamonds, and now they cascaded onto the white tablecloth in a sullenly glowing pyramid from which random darts of light sped to astound the eye.

'All right, Jordan. Tell us something about them,' Rhodes invited. And the boy stooped over the fabulous pile of treasure, his long tapered fingers flying lightly over the stones, spreading and sorting them into piles. While he worked he talked, and his voice was as lovely as his face, low and melodious. Fluently he explained the shapes of the crystals, pointed out the flaws in one, placed two side by side to compare the colours, twisting one to the light to bring up its smouldering fires.

Zouga was puzzled. This little act was too theatrical to be Rhodes' usual style, and he would never go to such lengths to impress a woman, even a beautiful one; for by jumbling up a bucket of stones he had given his own sorters many days of extra work. Every one of those stones would have to be re-graded and appraised and returned to its own little white envelope.

'Here is a perfect stone,' Jordan picked a diamond the size of a green pea. 'Look at that colour, blue as a bolt of lightning and as full of fire.'

Rhodes took it from him, considered it a moment, holding it between thumb and forefinger, then he leaned across the table and placed it before Louise St John.

'Madam, your first diamond. I sincerely hope not your last,' said Rhodes.

'Mr Rhodes, I cannot accept such a generous gift,' said Louise, her eyes wide with delight, and she turned to Mungo St John. 'Can I?'

'If I agreed with you, you would never forgive me,' Mungo St John murmured, and Louise turned back to Rhodes.

'Mr Rhodes, my husband insists, and I can find no words to express my gratitude.'

Zouga watched the scene attentively; there was so much happening here, so many nuances, so many undercurrents.

It was on the surface merely a demonstration of the remarkable effect that these bright hard pebbles had upon a woman. That was their true value, perhaps their only value. When he looked at Louise St John's face he could see that it was not avarice that lit it so, but a mystical emotion not far removed from love – the love of a living thing, a child, a horse, a man, a warming thing to watch.

Quite suddenly Zouga found himself wishing that he had been the author of such joy. That it had been he and not Rhodes who had made the gift which had transformed her, and it took a moment for him to free himself of that desire, so that he almost missed the glance that Rhodes shot beyond the woman's face.

Suddenly it was clear to Zouga. Rhodes was not baiting for the woman; he was fishing for the man. That display of treasure was for Mungo St John, the man with half a million sterling to dispose of.

Rhodes needed capital. When a man sets out to buy up every single claim on the Kimberley field, and when he is in a desperate hurry to do it, he must always be starved of capital. Rhodes' ambition was no secret. Zouga himself had been present at the long bar of the Kimberley Club when Rhodes had made the declaration of his intent.

'There is only one way to stabilize the price of the goods –' Rhodes' euphemism for diamonds – 'and that is an orderly, centralized marketing policy. There is only one way to stop the stealing of goods by the I.D.B., and that is through the institution of a rigorous security screen; and there is only one way to achieve both these objects, and that is to have every claim on the fields owned by one company.' Everyone listening to him had known who Rhodes intended that the head of that company should be.

That had been a year previously, and now the bucket of diamonds on Zouga's luncheon table was proof of how far Rhodes had made good his threat and had eaten up the field. Already he was more than halfway towards his goal, but he had been forced to take in partners and still he was short of capital, desperately short.

For the serious obstacle that stood between him and complete ownership of the field was Barney Barnato's company. He would need millions – literally millions of sterling – for that final step.

So the reason for the little charade was clear to Zouga now, and he was about to turn his head to study General Mungo St John's reaction to it when the tableau at the far end of the table struck him forcibly.

The untidily dressed young man, heavy in the shoulders, hunched forward in his chair, unruly curling hair spilling over onto the broad forehead above the florid meaty face, thick arms and square powerful hands enclosing a glittering mound of treasure. At his shoulder the slim and graceful figure of the boy with the bright and lovely face, and behind them both, towering above them, holding them both in its thrall, the graven statue of the falcon god.

Zouga shivered, touched for the first time in the presence of the falcon by a superstitious chill. For the first time he was aware of the sense of evil that the old Hottentot had immediately detected in the statue's stony eyes. For one horrifying instant Zouga was convinced that the bird was about to spread its sharp blade-shaped wings and hold them like a possessive canopy over the two human figures beneath it – and then the moment was past. The tableau broke up.

Rhodes was sweeping the gems back into the bucket, talking quietly to Jordan.

'Are you still studying the book of Mr Pitman's shorthand that I sent you, Jordan?'

'Yes, Mr Rhodes.'

'Good – you'll find it of great value one day.'

The boy understood the dismissal and slipped away down the verandah to his kitchen, while Rhodes casually handed the bucket of diamonds to his clerk and addressed General St John directly.

'In the section of the workings that we own we are recovering an average of ten carats to each ton of gravel that we process, to that we must add at least another two carats a ton which is being stolen by the labourers between the pit floor and the grading room. As our security system becomes more efficient and as we have better laws to control the I.D.B. we can expect to eliminate that wastage –' Rhodes was talking in that high-pitched voice so incongruous in such a big man, gesturing with strong square hands, persuasive and articulate. Reeling off figures for production costs and anticipated recovery, the expectations of profits on tonnage worked, returns on capital outlaid, he was addressing himself to one man only, the erect bearded figure with the black eye-patch, yet his manner was so persuasive that every one of them was listening with full attention, even Louise St John.

Zouga glanced at her and saw that she was concentrating on the confusing jumble of figures, and that she seemed to be able to absorb them. She proved that immediately.

'Mr Rhodes, you said earlier that working costs on the No. 9 Section were ten shillings and sixpence; now you use a new figure – twelve shillings?' She challenged unexpectedly, and Rhodes paused, gave a little nod of recognition for her perception before he replied.

'At the deeper levels the costs rise. Ten and six is our present cost, twelve shillings our projected cost for twelve months hence.' His voice had a new note of respect. 'I am flattered that you have followed my discourse so closely, madam.' Then he turned back to St John. 'From this you will see, General, that the returns on capital invested are about the best you will find anywhere: ten per cent is certain, fifteen per cent is possible.'

St John had been holding an unlit cigar between his teeth; now he removed it and stared hard at Rhodes with his single eye.

'So far, Mr Rhodes, you have not mentioned the blue.'

'The blue.' Every single one of them at the long table froze.

'The blue.' It was as if St John had spoken a gross obscenity, shocking them all into silence.

'The blue' was the main reason why Rhodes was hungry for capital.

'The blue' was the reason why the banks were calling on all diggers who had borrowed against the collateral of their claims to reduce their overdrafts by fifty per cent; and Rhodes had borrowed a million pounds to finance his attempt to acquire every single claim on the New Rush field. As he had acquired each block, Rhodes had immediately used it as security to borrow money to buy the next block, pyramiding loan upon loan, debt upon debt.

Zouga was one of the few who so far had resisted Rhodes' advances, resisted with pain and heart-searching an offer of £5,000 for his claims on the Devil's Own. The offer had been made six months before, before those dreaded words 'the blue' were whispered in the inner sanctum of the long bar of the Kimberley Club.

Nobody would offer Zouga £5,000 for his claims now. On the contrary, a week after he first heard those two dreaded words, the manager of the Standard Bank had sent a note asking him to call.

'Major Ballantyne, in view of recent developments, the bank has been forced to review the value of collateral securing our clients' overdrafts. We have calculated the present market value of your claims as five hundred pounds each.'

'That's ridiculous, sir.'

'Major, the blue has shown on the claims of the Orphen Company.' The bank manager did not have to elaborate. The Orphen block was only separated from the Devil's Own by a dozen intervening claims. 'I don't enjoy doing this, Major, but I must ask you to reduce your overdraft to one thousand pounds.'

'The blue' was the reason why many of the town's merchants were running down their stocks, preparing themselves to pull out.

'The blue' was the reason why many of the transport riders were re-routing their wagons to the new goldfields at Pilgrims' Rest.

'What is the blue?' asked Louise St John, and when none of the others spoke, Zouga's duty as host placed the burden of reply upon him.

'The blue is the diggers' name for a type of rock formation, Mrs St John. A volcanic conglomerate, dark blue in colour and very hard – too hard to work easily.' Zouga picked up his champagne glass, sipped the yellow wine and then studied the rising pinpricks of bubbles.

'Is that all?' Louise asked quietly.

'It has zircons in it, small zircons the size of sugar grains, but there is no market for zircons,' Zouga went on grudgingly.

'What is the significance of this – blue?' Louise persisted.

Zouga paused to pick his words with care.

'The diamondiferous earth is a friable yellow gravel – friable means crumbling.'

'Thank you,' Louise smiled without rancour. 'I do know the word.'

'Well, then, on some of the deeper claims in the northern section the yellow gravel has pinched out, and we have come up short against this hard blue floor, hard as marble and just as sterile.'

'That hasn't been proved,' Rhodes cut in sharply, and Zouga inclined his head in acceptance.

'No, it hasn't been proved, but that is what we all fear. That we have come to the end. That the fields are worked out.'

They were all silent then, contemplating that terrifying eventuality.

'When will you know for certain?' Mungo St John asked. 'When will you know that this blue ground underlies the entire field, and that there are no diamonds in it?'

'It will be many months still before the shallower claims can be worked down to the level of those that have run into the blue,' Rhodes answered. 'Then if we do find it covers the whole field, we will have to drive pot-holes through it to make sure that it is not a thin layer, and that the yellow gravel does not recur below it.'

'I see,' St John nodded. 'It seems that I was fortunate to delay my visit to Kimberley until after this blue ground was encountered, or I might have found myself the owner of a mountain of blue marble and no diamonds.'

'You have always been a fortunate man, Mungo.' Louise flashed a smile at him, and he replied to it gravely.

'You, my dear, are the greatest of all my good fortunes.'

With obvious relief the company abandoned the subject of the dreaded blue ground and turned to lighter topics. Only Rhodes did not join them, but sat silent and brooding at the head of the long table.

Though Zouga smiled and nodded at the repartee, he also was distracted by the talk of lurking disaster, and his thoughts were a barrier between him and the company, so that Louise St John had to repeat his name to gain his attention.

'Is that possible, Major Ballantyne?'

Zouga roused himself and turned to her. 'Forgive me, Mrs St John. Will you repeat the question?'

Louise was not accustomed to having a man's thoughts wander when she was talking to him. This cold and correct Englishman was truly beginning to irritate her, and she found herself wanting to shock some natural reaction out of him. She had thought of including a man's word, one of Mungo's soldier's words, in her conversation, but good sense warned her that he would merely raise an eyebrow at such gaucherie. She had thought of ignoring him, but intuition warned her that he would probably welcome that treatment. The best course open to her was to direct her queries at him and force him to recognize her existence, and let it nettle him.

'I was led to understand that you were the Chairman of the Kimberley Sporting Club?'

'I have that honour,' Zouga agreed.

'I have heard also that your steeplechases or point-to-point races – I am never quite sure of your British terminology – are the most popular diversions on the diamond fields.'

Zouga shook his head and smiled. 'I'm not sure of the terminology myself. They certainly are not steeplechases, we are critically short of steeples out here, and they are not point-to-point exactly, for we throw in a little rifle drill. So, we prefer to call them rough rides. A fairly accurate description, I think.'

'I thought to enter one of my horses – in a rough ride,' Louise said.

'We would welcome your participation,' Zouga agreed. 'I could prepare a list of our better riders from which you could choose.'

'I prefer to ride myself,' Louise shook her head.

'I am afraid that would not be possible, Mrs St John.'

'Why not?'

'Because you are a woman.'

Her expression gave Zouga his first truly satisfying moments in her company. She had turned waxen pale so that the freckles stood out boldly on her cheeks and her eyes glowed a lighter, brighter, angry blue.

Zouga waited for her retort, but she sensed his anticipation and, with a huge effort, denied him the satisfaction. Instead she turned to her husband.

'It's after three o'clock. It has been a very pleasant luncheon, but I should like to return to the hotel now.' She stood up quickly, and Mungo St John shrugged resignedly and stood up beside her.

'Please do not let us break up this delightful gathering.' His smile and his tone asked their indulgence for a womanly whim.

The groom brought her horse to her and she caressed its pale silken muzzle. Then she gathered the reins, looked up at the group of men on the stoep, held Zouga's eye for a moment, before deliberately turning away.

She placed one neat gloved hand on the stallion's withers where the long white mane rose into the crest of the shoulders, and then in the next instant she was seated on the broad and powerful back, her small feet thrust deeply into the silver-starred Mexican-type stirrups.

Zouga was astounded. He had never seen a woman vault to the saddle. Usually it took a groom to hold the head and another to form a bridge of linked fingers to boost her to the height of the horse's back.

Louise St John had gone up so lightly and easily that she might have flown, and the movement of her left hand that made the stallion rear was only apparent to someone looking for it.

The huge horse went up on its hind legs, walking backwards in a circle, cutting at the air with its forehooves, until it faced the five-foot barbed-wire fence that marked the division between Zouga's camp and the public road.

Then Louise moved her hand again and the stallion dropped into a dead run, straight at the fence.

The watching men exclaimed in alarm for the stallion had a bare twenty strides to build up momentum for the jump, yet he flew at it with his pink nostrils flaring and the serpentine veins beneath the burnished skin of his cheeks swelling with the pumping of the great heart.

Louise's thick black braids were flung out tautly behind her head by the power of the stallion's acceleration, and then she lifted him into the jump with her knees and her hands.

For an instant of time the horse and the tiny figure upon its back seemed to hang suspended against the pale blue of the sky, the horse with its forefeet drawn up beneath its noble head and the woman rising in the saddle to cushion the shock of take-off and landing – and then they were over.

The stallion landed neatly, with his rider in perfect balance, and the golden body flowed smoothly into the continuation of his run.

There was a soft involuntary sigh from the group on the verandah, and Zouga felt a surge of relief as powerful as the driving leap of the stallion. He had had a mental image of the woman caught up in the bloody strands of barbed wire, like a wild bird in the trapper's net, with torn body and broken wings.

Zouga stood on top of the central stagings. He was as high above the level of the plain as a three-storey building, and from his vantage point he could see as far north as the Vaal river. The dark-green stain of the lusher scrub and grass along its course looked like cloud shadow upon the dust-pale earth, but there were no clouds in the high vault of the sky, and the brutal sun threw stark shadows below the high stagings, geometrical patterns that parodied in two-dimensional plan the intricate structure of timber and iron and steel wire. The stagings clung perilously to the sheer precipice that fell into the depths.

It was as though a gigantic meteor had ploughed into the yellow earth, gouging this bowl-shaped dish through the earth's crust. In the deepest sections it was almost two hundred feet deep already, and each spadeful of gravel had been dug out by hand, lifted to the surface and laboriously picked over before being discarded in the mountainous waste dumps. It was a monument to the persistence of those antlike creatures that swarmed down there on the pit floor.

Zouga wiped the black grease off his hands with a wad of cotton waste, and nodded to the Matabele winchman who threw in the gear lever of the steam winch.

Once again the numbing clatter hammered against Zouga's skull and the slender thread of shining steel cable slithered in over the drums. The winch and steam boiler had cost Zouga over a thousand pounds, the entire winnings of an unusually productive week's labour when Jordan had picked eleven good diamonds off the sorting-table. That week's recovery had been one of the false promises that the Devil's Own had whispered to him, like an unfaithful wife.

Zouga moved to the front of the stagings to escape the painful sound of the winch. He was on an unguarded wooden balcony with the drop sucking seductively at him, but he ignored it.

He had ten minutes to rest now, the time that it took the gravel skip to travel up from the claims to the surface. He could see it lifting off the floor below like a fat spider creeping up its individual silken thread towards him, still too deep for him to recognize for certain the human figure riding on the enormous steel bucket.

Zouga lit a cheroot, and it tasted of engine grease from his fingers. He looked down again, and decided that instead of an ant's nest the pit reminded him more of a beehive. Even at these deep levels the precise shape of each claim had been maintained, and the geometrical shapes were like the individual cells in a honeycomb.

'If only mine would yield a little more honey,' he thought.

The skip was close enough now for there to be no doubt of the tall young figure standing casually on the lip of the steel bucket, balancing easily with both hands on his hips as the drop grew steadily deeper under him.

It was a matter of pride amongst the younger diggers to ride the skip in the most casual or spectacular manner possible. Zouga had forbidden Ralph to dance on the skip, a fad that had been started by a young Scot who had once danced between the floor and the stagings, accompanying himself on the bagpipes.

Ralph drew steadily closer, rising up through the glistening web of steel cables that hung over the pit like a silver cloud. Hundreds of cables, one for each individual claim, every strand polished by the pulley wheels, by the friction over the winding drums, until they caught the sunlight and shimmered into a silver mist that hung like an aura over the pit – ethereal and lovely, hiding the harsh reality of that gouged raw earth, with its dangers and disappointments.

While he waited for the skip to reach him, Zouga cast his mind back to that first day when he had led the single oxen into the sprawling encampment with Aletta on the wagon box beside him, and they had looked up at the riddled and torn kopje.

So much earth had been moved since then, so many men had died in this terrible pit where that kopje had once stood and so many dreams had perished with them.

Zouga lifted the wide-brimmed hat. Carefully he mopped the beads of sweat from the smoother paler skin along his hairline, and then he inspected the damp red stain on the silk bandanna and grimaced with distaste. It looked like blood.

He re-knotted the silk about his throat, still peering down into the depths, and his eyes clouded with disenchantment as he remembered the high hopes and bounding expectation that he had brought with him on that day – was it really ten years ago? It seemed like a day and an eternity.

He had found himself dreaming, the random events from those lost years replaying through his mind, the sorrows and the joys magnified by his imaginings and by the passage of time.

Then, after a few minutes, Zouga roused himself. Dreaming was an old man's vice. The past was beyond regret; today was all that counted. He straightened his shoulders and looked down at Ralph in the swinging skip. Something jarred him, scattering the last of his dreams.

The skip was riding differently, it did not have the accustomed weight to it, he could not yet make out the heaped yellow gravel, which, despite his orders, Ralph usually over-loaded high above the steel sides of the skip.

It was empty, and Ralph was alone. He was coming up without the Matabele gang to help run the skip over the bars and up-end its burden of gravel into the chute, down which it would be carried to the waiting cart.

Zouga cupped his hands to his mouth to shout an enquiry – but the words stayed in his throat.

Ralph was close enough now for Zouga to see the expression on his face. It was tragic, stricken with some terrible emotion.

Zouga lowered his hands and stared at his son in dread anticipation. The skip hit the end bars with an iron clash and the winchman threw out the gear lever, expertly braking the steel skip against the bars.

Ralph jumped lightly across the narrow gap onto the platform, and stood there, still staring at Zouga.

'What is it, my boy?' Zouga asked quietly, fearfully – and for answer Ralph turned away and glanced down into the empty body of the skip.

Zouga stepped up beside him, and followed his glance. He saw that he had been mistaken – the skip was not empty.

'It has taken us all morning to hack that out of the east face,' Ralph told him.

It looked like a roughly cut gravestone, before the inscription was chiselled in, as wide as the stretch of a man's arms and imperfectly squared up, the marks of the steel wedges and pickaxe still fresh upon it.

'We broke three pick handles on it,' Ralph went on grimly, 'and we only got it out because there was a natural fracture line that we could crack open with wedges.'

Zouga stared at the ugly cube of stone, not wanting to believe what it was, trying to close his ears against his son's voice.

'Underneath it's the same, solid, hard as a whore's heart, no faults, no cracks.'

The lump of stone was a dull ugly mottled thing, across which the steel tools had left paler weals and furrows.

'Sixteen of us,' Ralph went on. 'We worked on it all morning.' He opened his hands, and showed them palms upwards. The horny yellow calluses had been torn open, the raw flesh beneath was mushy and caked with dust and earth. 'All morning we broke our hearts and our picks on it – and that bloody little chip weighs less than half a ton.'

Slowly Zouga stooped over the edge of the skip and touched the stone. It was as cold as his heart felt – and its colour was dark mottled blue.

'The blue,' Ralph confirmed quietly. 'We have hit the blue.'

'Dynamite or blasting gelatine,' Ralph said. 'That's the only way we'll ever move it.'

He was stripped to the waist, a polish of sweat on his arms, and little drops of it hanging like dew in the thick hair of his chest.

The tombstone of blue marble lay at his feet, and Ralph rested on the shaft of the sledgehammer. The blows he had swung at the rock had raised bursts of sparks and tiny puffs of white dust that stung their nostrils like pepper – but had not cracked the rock through.

'We cannot blast in the pit,' Zouga said tiredly. 'Can you imagine two hundred diggers firing away dynamite, every one doing it when and how he wanted?' He shook his head.

'There is no other way,' Ralph said. 'No other way to get it out.'

'And if you do get it out?' Jordan asked from the verandah where he had stood without speaking for the past hour.

'What do you mean?' Zouga demanded. He could hear the strain in his own voice, and knew how close his anger and frustration were to the surface.

'What will you do with it when you do get it out?' Jordan persisted, and they all stared at the awful blue lump.

'There are no diamonds in that stuff.' Jordan said it for them.

'How do we know that?' Ralph snapped at him, his voice rough and ugly with the same tension that gripped Zouga.

'I know it,' Jordan said flatly. 'I can sense it – just look at it. It's hard and bleak and bare.'

Nobody replied to that, and Jordan shook his curls regretfully. 'Even if there were diamonds in it, how would you free them from the blue? You can't smash them out with sledgehammers. You'd end up with diamond dust.'

'Ralph,' Zouga turned away from Jordan, 'this stuff, this blue – it's only on the east face, isn't it?'

'So far.' Ralph nodded. 'But –'

'I want you to cover up the east face,' Zouga told him bluntly. 'Shovel gravel over the exposed rock. Nobody else must see it. Nobody else must know.'

Ralph nodded, and Zouga went on, 'We will keep on raising the yellow gravel from the other sections as though nothing has happened; and nobody, not one of you, is to say a word about – about us having struck the blue.' He looked directly at Jordan. 'Do you understand, not a word to anybody.'

Zouga sat easily in the saddle, riding with the long stirrups of a Boer hunter or of a born colonial.

He knew that Rhodes was leaving in the next few weeks, to keep his term at Oxford University. Perhaps his imminent departure would make his judgement hasty.

'Let's hope so, anyway.' And his mount flicked his ears back to listen to his voice.

'Steady, old man.' Zouga touched his withers, feeling a quick twist of guilt at his intentions. He knew he was going to try and sell faulty goods, and he steeled himself against his own conscience.

He touched his mount's flank with his knee and turned him off the rutted dusty track through the break in the milkwood fence and into Rhodes' camp.

Rhodes sat with his back to the mud wall of the shack, a mug in his hand, the big shaggy leonine head cocked to something that Pickering was saying.

The talk of the diggings was that he was already a multimillionaire, at least on paper, and Zouga had seen the champagne bucket of uncut diamonds poured out onto his lunch table. Yet here Rhodes was sitting on a soap box in the dusty yard, dressed in shabby ill-fitting clothes, drinking from a chipped enamel mug.

Zouga dropped his reins and his horse stopped obediently, and when he slipped off its back there was no need for him to tether it. It would stand as long as Zouga wanted it to.

He crossed the yard towards the small group of men, and Zouga smiled to himself. Rhodes' mug might be chipped – but it contained a twenty-year-old cognac. Rhodes' seat might be a soapbox, but he sat it as though it were a throne, and the men that sat around him like courtiers or supplicants were all rich and powerful men, the new aristocracy of the diggings.

One of these rose now and came to meet Zouga, laughing lightly and brandishing a rolled newspaper.

'By gad, Major, they say you need only speak of the devil.' He clapped Zouga's shoulder. 'I hope you are taking this assault on our masculine pride as seriously as we are – and have come to offer to champion our cause.'

'I don't understand.' Zouga's protest was lost in the laughter and friendly pummelling as they came to crowd around him. Only Rhodes had not left his seat against the wall, but even he was smiling.

'Let him read it for himself, Pickling,' Rhodes suggested mildly, and Pickering handed Zouga the news sheet with a flourish.

It was a copy of the *Diamond Fields Advertiser* – so newly printed that the ink smudged beneath Zouga's fingers.

'Front page,' said Pickering gleefully. 'The headline.'

GAUNTLET THROWN DOWN
LADY INSULTED
SEEKS SATISFACTION

This morning your editor was privileged to receive a visit from a beautiful and distinguished visitor to Kimberley. Mrs Louise St John is the wife of a hero of the American Civil War, and in her own right a noted equestrienne.

Her stallion 'Shooting Star' is a remarkable example of the recently developed American breed known as Palamino. He is a former Louisiana champion of breed, and quite one of the most magnificent animals ever to be seen on the Diamond Fields.

Mrs St John attempted to enter her mount in the regular point-to-point meetings organized by the Kimberley Sporting Club – but was informed by Major Ballantyne, the Club President, that she was barred from riding –

Zouga skipped quickly over the next few paragraphs:

'Simply because I happen to be a woman. . . . Insufferable masculine arrogance.'

He smiled and shook his head.

'Challenge the good major to ride against me over any course of his choice for any purse he stipulates.'

Now Zouga laughed delightedly, and tossed the paper back to Pickering.

'The lady has good bottom', he admitted, 'in both senses of the word.'

'I will lend you King Chaka,' Beit promised. He was a strong hunter, English and Arab blood, from one of the famous Cape studs. Beit had paid three hundred guineas for him.

Zouga shook his head and shot an affectionate glance at his own hunting horse standing across the yard. 'That won't be necessary, I shan't be riding.'

There was a howl of jovial protest from them all.

'By God, Ballantyne, you can't let us down.'

'This damned vixen will say you funked it, old man.'

'My wife will crow for a week – you'll ruin my marriage.'

Zouga held up his hands. 'I'm sorry, gentlemen. This is merely a bit of female nonsense – and you can quote me.'

'You won't ride, then?'

'Certainly not.' Zouga was smiling, but his voice had a brittle edge. 'I have more serious matters to concern me.'

'You are right, of course.' Rhodes' piping voice stilled them all into respectful silence. 'That pale brute is a flying devil and the lady rides like a witch – we have all seen that.'

The scar on Zouga's cheek turned pale pink, and there was a sudden green glint in his eye; but the smile stayed on his lips.

'That fancy high-stepper moves well on the flat, I grant you, but over the course I would choose he would be lucky to finish, let alone win.'

'You'll ride then?' They were clamouring again immediately.

'No, gentlemen. That's my final word.'

Long after the others had left, the three of them sat on: Pickering, Rhodes and Zouga. The sun had set, and just the orange glow of the fire lit their faces. The first bottle of cognac was empty and Pickering had opened another. Now Rhodes was staring into his mug, and he spoke without lifting his eyes.

'So, Major, at last you are ready to sell, and I ask myself a question, a simple little question – why?'

Zouga did not reply, and after a moment Rhodes lifted his head.

'Why, Major?' he repeated. 'Why now suddenly?'

Zouga found that the lie he had prepared would not come to his lips. He was dumb, but he held the gaze of those pale blue eyes – and it was Rhodes who broke the silence.

'I have trusted very few men in my life,' and involuntarily his eyes flickered to Pickering and then back to Zouga, 'but now, Major, you are one of them.'

He picked up the cognac bottle and spilled a little of the honey-dark liquor into Zouga's mug.

'Once you were offered a hundred thousand pounds in illicit diamonds – and you couldn't bring yourself to take them.' Rhodes was speaking so softly that Zouga had to lean forward to catch the words. 'Yesterday your son brought up the first hunk of blue ground from the Devil's Own – and still you could not bring yourself to lie.'

'You knew!' Zouga whispered, and Rhodes nodded and then sighed.

'By God, I wish I knew more like you.' He shook the big curling head and his voice was become brusque and businesslike. 'Once I offered you five thousand pounds for your claims. All right, I will make the same price –'and he lifted one meaty hand to still Zouga. 'Wait! Listen to the rest of it, before you thank me. The bird goes with the claims.'

'What?' For a moment Zouga did not understand.

'The stone bird, the statue. It becomes part of the deal.'

'Damn it!' Zouga half rose from the log on which he was sitting.

'Wait!' Rhodes stopped him again. 'Listen – before you refuse,' and Zouga sank back. 'You'll ride for it.'

Zouga shook his head, not understanding.

'You'll ride against this woman, St John, on her terms, and if you win you keep the claims and the bird and my five thousand.'

The silence stretched out for a full minute – and then Zouga asked with a harsh gravelly sound in the back of his throat:

'And if I lose?'

'You yourself have said there is little chance of that,' Rhodes reminded him.

'And if I lose?' Zouga persisted.

'Then you leave these fields as you came – with nothing.'

Zouga looked away to the horse standing at the edge of the shadows. He had named him Tom, after a friend, the old hunter who had first told Zouga about the land to the north and how to reach it, Tom Harkness, now dead these many years.

The horse was part of Zouga's dream of the north, the mount that would carry him back to Zambezia. Zouga had selected him with more care than a man usually gives to choosing his wife – and beauty was the last thing he looked for.

Tom was a mixture of many bloodlines, the wide nostrils and big chest of the Arab for staying power, the sturdy legs and sure feet of the Basuto, the canny eye and hammer head of a wild Mustang, the heart and strength of an English hunter. However, Tom was a drab unrelieved dun-colour. His coat was long and thick, brushed but not curried, protection from the night frost and the noon sun, from flying pebbles thrown by frantic hooves of the quarry in a stern chase or from the rip of red-tipped 'wait-a-bit' thorns.

Tom had proved that the intelligent gleam in his eye was no illusion. He learned swiftly and well. He learned to stand when the reins were dropped on his neck, giving his rider both hands for the rifle, and he remained stone-still while gunfire crashed about his head, only the twitching of his ears signalling his consternation.

When Zouga took him out into the open veld to continue his training, Tom displayed nimble feet on the rocky slopes of the kopje and a buffalo skin through the thorn bush; he learned to hunt, and seemed to enjoy it the way a good polo pony revels in the crack of the bamboo root and the riotous chase.

He seemed instinctively to understand stalking, keeping his own body between Zouga and the game, angling off his approach, never heading directly at the quarry, and the herds of springbuck let the seemingly riderless horse walk up into easy rifle shot. Then Tom would carry the freshly killed carcass on his back, without shying and fussing about the blood.

Tom was ugly, with a Roman nose, ears a little too long, legs a little too short, and he ran with an awkward hump-backed gait – which he could keep up all day, over any ground.

He was an incorrigible thief. Jordan's vegetable garden had to be fenced, but still

Tom left tufts of his drab hair on the spikes of the barbed wire. He had a trick of plucking the carrots out of the ground with a delicate grip between his square white teeth, and then knocking the earth off them against his forehooves.

He learned to push open the kitchen window and reach the fresh loaves of bread that were cooling on the marble sink, and once when Jan Cheroot left the door to the storeroom off the latch, Tom got in and ate half a bag of sugar – at twenty shillings a pound.

However, he would follow like a dog, and when ordered he would stand for hours – and Zouga, who was not sentimental about animals, had come to love him.

Zouga looked back from the horse to the young man across the log fire.

'Agreed,' he said without emphasis. 'Do we need to have further witnesses?'

'I don't think so, Major,' said Rhodes. 'Do you?'

'At the gun the competitor will ride out to the first flag –' Neville Pickering was the steward-in-chief, and his voice through the speaking trumpet carried to every member of the huge Sunday crowd that spilled out across the dry veld below the Magersfontein hills.

'At the first red flag they will fire upon the standing targets. When they have demolished all four targets to the satisfaction of the stewards, they will be free to round the second yellow flag, and thereafter to return to the finish line.' He pointed to the twin poles each with its crown of coloured bunting. 'The first rider to pass between them will be declared the winner.'

Pickering paused and drew fresh breath before going on.

'Are there any questions?'

'Would you recite the rules, please, Mr Pickering,' Louise St John called. She looked like a child on the great glistening pale stallion's back. She was walking him in circles, leaning forward to pat his neck for the crowds had made him nervous. He was chewing the light snaffle and sweating in dark patches on the rippling muscled shoulders.

'There are no other rules, ma'am.' Pickering answered her loudly enough for those at the back of the crowd to hear.

'No rules – barging and fouling?'

'There are no fouls, ma'am,' Pickering replied. 'Though if one of you deliberately shoots an opponent, he or she might have to face criminal charges, but not disqualification.'

Louise turned her head towards the figure on the front seat of the high-wheeled phaeton which was parked beyond the course markers. Her face was pale, the freckles standing out on her cheeks; and her head was bared so that the thick dark braid of hair thumped against her shoulder.

Mungo St John smiled back at her over the heads of the crowd, and shrugged slightly, so that Louise was forced to turn back to Pickering.

'Very well, then,' she agreed. 'But the stake. We have not agreed the stake.'

'Major Ballantyne,' Pickering called to where Zouga stood at Tom's head. 'You have laid out the course. Now will you be good enough to name the stake.'

Then a strange thing happened. For the first time since Zouga had met her, Louise

St John was uncertain of herself. Nobody else seemed to notice it, perhaps it was merely that Zouga had become highly receptive to every shade of her voice and expression. But he was certain that he saw something dark move in the blue depths of her eyes, like the shadow of a shark beneath the surface of the sea, and she took a pinch of her soft lower lip between her white teeth and again she glanced almost furtively at Mungo St John.

It was not Zouga's imagination. Mungo St John did not return Louise's glance with his usual amused indulgence. He was looking at Zouga and under his calm was a small undercurrent of unease, like an eddy at highwater when the tide turns.

Zouga raised his voice so that it would carry to St John.

'Firstly, the loser will publish at his or her own expense upon the front page of the *Advertiser* in terms dictated by the winner, an acknowledgement of defeat.'

'A composition I shall enjoy.' Louise had swiftly recovered her poise. 'And what else, Major?'

'A payment by the loser to a charity of the winner's choice of,' Zouga paused, and both man and woman watched his face with outward calm, 'of the sum of one shilling!'

'Done!'

There was a slightly jarring note in Louise's laugh, relief perhaps, and though Mungo St John's expression did not alter, the tension went out of his shoulders.

'Mrs St John. You are under starter's orders,' Pickering called through his speaking trumpet. 'Be so good as to bring your mount under control.'

'He is under perfect control, sir,' she called back, and Shooting Star put his head down and lashed out with both back hooves towards the crowd.

'If he is under control, Missus, then so is my mother-in-law,' called a wag, and there was a hoot of laughter.

'On the count of three then,' Pickering intoned, his voice hollow and solemn through the trumpet. 'One.'

Shooting Star backed up against the crowd, and they scattered as he bucked.

'Two.'

He went into a tortured high-stepping circle, so tight that his nose almost touched the toe of Louise's boot in the fancy silver stirrup.

'And three.' Louise lifted her left hand. Shooting Star came smoothly out of the circle, for the first time facing the start line, beginning to pace towards it majestically, and the pistol shot was a brief blurt of sound which sent the stallion sweeping away with an irresistible rush that made the slight figure on his wide back seem vulnerable and childlike.

There was no horse on the diamond fields that could match that first blazing burst of speed, the gap between the two horses opened, but not so dramatically as the watchers had expected. Tom's awkward gallop took him over the ground at surprising speed, and he was not following directly in Shooting Star's tracks.

'She's going wide, Thomas,' Zouga told him with satisfaction, and Tom cocked his ears back to listen. 'They aren't going to chance the river. Well, we didn't really think they would, did we?'

Directly ahead of Zouga the river started a lazy series of loops, symmetrical hairpin turns, winding back upon itself like a dying python.

Zouga had placed the red flag so that the direct line would cross the river-bed twice, and like most southern African rivers the banks were sheer, dropping ten feet to the dry sand and isolated rocky pools strung along the course. Each crossing was a trap in which a horse could break a leg and a rider his neck.

The alternative to the crossings was to ride wide, taking a circuit out beyond the meandering river course; but that almost doubled the distance to run to the first flag.

Already Shooting Star was a distant flying shape far out on the right, showing at intervals through gaps in the thorn scrub, marked by a little pale feather of dust flung up by his hooves.

'Here we are,' said Zouga, and under Tom's ugly Roman nose the ground opened abruptly.

Zouga gave him a slack rein, and Tom hardly checked on the brink of the steep clay bank. He sat down, and skidded over the edge on his fat round haunches, his forelegs sticking out stiffly ahead of him, and they tobogaoned down into the river bed and hit the sand in a scrambling tangle; and then Tom was up and lunging for the far bank, going half up before the dried clay crumbled under his hooves and they slid back again, Tom stiff-legged and trembling with exertion.

Zouga circled him once in the clinging white sand, and then put him to the bank again, and he went up in a determined series of buck-jumps, shifting his weight before the clay could break under his hooves, and they flew out over the top and were running again, the next bend of the river a quarter of a mile ahead.

At the next crossings Tom had the knack of it and they went down the bank and out the other side without a check. Under Tom's hooves the grass exploded into a whirl of noisy wings, and, with a wild harsh cry that would have panicked another horse, a big black-bellied bustard shot up into the air. Tom rolled a disdainful eye at the bird, steadied and gathered himself on the riverbank of the last crossing and went down into it in a slide of dust and rolling pebbles.

As they came up the far bank the red flag was two hundred paces dead ahead.

Zouga swivelled in the saddle and looked out on his right hand.

'Good for you, Tom,' he called. 'You've made a mile on them.'

Far out across the plain, the golden horse was just swinging wide of the last bend of the river, and Louise was bent low on his neck, pushing him at reckless speed over the rough going.

'If she rides like that for a shilling – 'Zouga broke off, and himself leaned into the rhythm of Tom's gallop. A mile was such a slim margin, and the stakes he was riding for were enormous. His fortune, his dream – nay his very existence – was at stake.

'Go, Thomas, go!' Zouga whispered grimly into the long furry ears, and Tom stabbed at the earth with his awkward hump-backed gait.

Zouga did not look back again; he knew the stallion was bearing down on them, fast, too fast, but Zouga dismissed them from his attention and slid the carbine from the leather boot at his knee and opened the breech, checking the load.

The targets were white china soup plates, the range two hundred yards, extreme range after a gallop like this. The stewards were waving their hats to guide him up to the firing line.

'This way, Major.'

Zouga dropped the reins as he reached the low barrier of thorn branches that marked the firing line, and Tom came up short. He swung up the carbine, and fired as the butt slapped into his shoulder. One of the far-off specks of white burst and vanished. He cranked another round into the chamber, and glanced over his shoulder. The stallion was still half a mile away, but coming on with a war drum of hooves.

Zouga fired again, but Tom was blowing between his knees, heaving with the effort of the wild gallop.

'Damn it to hell.'

Haste would be fatal now, but his fingers fumbled the reload and a shiny brass cartridge slipped and struck his boot before it fell into the sand. He thrust another into the breech, took a long slow breath, and judged Tom's movements beneath him.

The rifle jumped against his shoulder, and the acrid plume of gunsmoke blew into his face. The second target exploded.

'Two down, Major,' one of the stewards shouted, and then as he fired again,

'Three down – one to go!'

Then beside Zouga the golden stallion came plunging to a halt, coming back low on glossy bunched quarters.

Louise vaulted from his back in a swirl of beaded buckskin skirts. There was a flash of the silky skin of her upper calf above the boot, and the back of a dimpled knee. Even in the press of the moment, he found the pale beautiful flesh disturbing enough to spoil his aim – and he swore as his next shot flew wide.

Louise was shooting the latest model of the legendary '73 Winchester repeater, the original polished brass frame replaced by blued steel, and Zouga knew that the modern centre-fire ammunition drove the heavy lead bullet with amazing power and accuracy.

She threw the stallion's rein over her left shoulder, and braced herself to fire from a standing position, leaning forward to absorb the recoil of the Winchester, and let her first shot fly.

She shot in the American style, throwing the rifle to her shoulder and firing in the same movement, not holding her aim nor giving the barrel time to wander. It was fine shooting.

'One hit to Mrs St John,' yelled the steward. But the crash of the shot had startled Shooting Star and he reared wildly and backed off on his hind legs, heaving at the reins that were looped over Louise's shoulder, jerking her over backwards so that her second shot flew in a long spurt of powder smoke towards the sky; and then she was down on her back, being dragged away, her skirts tangled about her legs, and the Winchester rifle was flung from her hand.

The stallion came down on his forelegs again. One hoof, sharp as a woodman's axe, grazed the tender spot at the nape of Louise's neck, just below the thick plait of dark hair, leaving an angry pink blaze on the pale skin but not breaking it.

Zouga felt the sweat on his throat turn so cold that he could not swallow. He swung Tom around to head off the stallion.

For unholy seconds Louise's body was hidden by flying dust and trampling hooves; Zouga tried to shout to her to let the horse go, but his voice had choked, and then abruptly Louise was on her knees.

She was facing Shooting Star, clinging stubbornly to his reins with both hands, and when he reared again she used his strength to let him boost her to her feet.

'Steady!' she called to him. 'Steady, I tell you.'

She was dusty and a tendril of dark hair had escaped the plait and hung into her eyes, but she was safe and very angry. Her voice crackled like breaking ice. Zouga's

151

relief was immediate, but he mocked her as he swung Tom back to the firing line for his last target.

'I advise you to have that animal properly trained, madam.'

'To hell with you, Major Ballantyne!' she told him in the same tone as she had quelled her mount. Somehow the oath on her lips was not shocking at all, but strangely titillating.

Zouga gave Tom a few seconds to settle and regulate his breathing, and then swung up the rifle, held a full bead on the distant white speck and touched off the shot.

'Four hits – you are free to ride on, Major,' shouted the steward.

Louise was dragging Shooting Star by the reins to a wild plum tree, a tree with low and sturdy branches. Swiftly she lashed the stallion's reins to a branch, and now she was running back holding her skirts up to just below the knee, and the stewards gawked at her ankles in the tight-fitting buttoned boots.

She snatched the Winchester from a clump of sansevieria and ran up towards the firing line, reloading as she came. Zouga could see that there were little blisters of perspiration across her forehead, and knew that she was badly shaken, for when she threw up the rifle she held the shot and the heavy weapon wavered unsteadily.

She lowered it, and her shoulders were trembling. She took two long deep breaths and then lifted the Winchester again, firing on the toss up.

'Hit!' yelled the steward.

Louise's lower lip was quivering and she bit down on it fiercely, and shot again.

Zouga slid the carbine back into its leather scabbard, touched the brim of his helmet to Louise in a cavalier salute. 'Good shooting, ma'am.'

He turned Tom's head away from the firing line.

As they reached the wild plum, Zouga leaned out from the saddle. Louise had tied Shooting Star's reins to the branch with a slippery fisherman, it was a sailor's knot, a quick-release knot for a fast getaway.

Zouga twitched the loose end and the knot fell apart, then he slapped Shooting Star across the cheek with his open hand. 'Go on,' he said. 'Get out of it!'

The stallion jerked his head, found that he was free and kicked his heels high.

Zouga looked back as he reached the next low fold in the plain.

The stallion was grazing head down, but even at that distance it was apparent that he was keeping a wary eye on the lonely figure that ran after him in hampering skirts. As soon as Louise came within arm's length of his bridle, he tossed up his head and trotted away to the next clump of grass, leaving her blundering behind.

'Come, Tom.' He turned away, trying not to let his conscience trouble him. There were no rules, any ruse was acceptable, but it still felt bad – until he reminded himself of the stakes. A shilling against all he owned – and he set Tom to run in earnest.

Another mile and he glanced back, just in time to see Shooting Star and his rider come over the rise. They seemed to fly clear of the earth, borne along by the floating carpet of their own dust.

'Run! Tom! Run!' Zouga swept the hat off his head and slapped it against Tom's neck, goading him to his best speed.

Within another half mile Tom's shoulders were hot and slick with salt sweat. Ropes of saliva spilled from the corners of his lips and splattered onto Zouga's boots – but the yellow flag was in sight.

'Not far,' Zouga called to him anxiously. 'We must beat them to the flag.'

He looked back. He could not believe they were so close.

The stallion's head was driving like a hammer to each stride, and his neck and shoulders were black with sweat. She had pushed him fearfully. Louise was driving him with her arms and the rhythmic force of her body. Her hair was a wild tangle about her face, and her eyes were a blaze of blue.

Yet as she came up to them she straightened in the saddle, her chin lifted high, and she looked at Zouga coldly, expressionlessly, the way a queen might glance at an urchin running at the wheel of her coach.

Zouga lifted his right hand to salute her achievement. It had been a tremendous run, to make up so much ground. He was turned slightly towards her – and her expression of cold disinterest lulled him for the vital instant that it took her to bring Shooting Star level with Tom's shoulder.

Zouga never saw the command, probably the toe of her boot on the far side of Shooting Star's heaving chest; he had certainly not expected a show horse to have learned the low tricks of a polo pony. Shooting Star's huge sweat-streaked shoulder crashed into Tom, taking him in the short ribs with a force that drove the air out of him in a belching grunt, and as he was spun aside Tom chopped desperately to keep from falling, twisting and dropping to his knees, his nose on the ground, too tired and taken too unawares to meet the power of that ferocious barge.

Zouga lost a stirrup and was thrown onto Tom's neck. He clung desperately, feeling the saddle shift under the unequal transfer of weight; then Tom heaved again and Zouga went over, landing on his shoulders and the back of his neck.

He seemed to strike solid rock and blackness crushed down from the dome of his skull. When it cleared, he was standing again, swaying like a drunk, blinking uncertainly after the pounding stallion as he pulled away towards the last flag.

Zouga pulled Tom to his feet, and checked swiftly for strained sinew or broken bone, then threw himself back into the saddle.

'We're not beat yet,' he told Tom. 'There are still the thorns.'

Far ahead Shooting Star was making the turn around the last flag. From there Louise was free to make her way back to the finish line any way she wanted, but there were still the thorns.

Tom was winded, his chest shuddering with the effort of each laboured breath, and they reached the flag in an awkward jarring trot and made the turn. Ahead of them the thorns stretched in a solid green barrier. This was the last obstacle – and beyond it was a clear run to the finish.

A rider had a choice: go through the thorn, or ride wide.

'Which way did she go?' Zouga shouted at the stewards below the flag as he went past.

'She's gone for the gap,' one of them yelled back, and then Zouga saw the little feather of dust a mile or more out on the right subsiding only slowly as the stallion sped away.

The thorn barrier petered out on the rocky slopes of the Magersfontein hills, and there was an open gap below the steep ironstone cliffs – that was where the stallion was aimed.

Grimly Zouga swung Tom around the flag and pointed him directly at the thorns. This route was almost two miles shorter, but he would need every inch of it. Yet he stopped Tom when they reached the edge of the thorns and let him breathe as he untied the heavy greatcoat from the pommel of his saddle and shrugged into it. He buttoned it high at the throat and felt the sweat burst out on his forehead as he pulled on the leather gauntlets to protect his hands.

'Let's go,' he whispered, and lay flat on Tom's neck, as they crashed into the thorn.

The red-tipped hooked points of the thorns skidded over Zouga's thick felt hat with a rasping tearing sound, and tugged at the shoulders and skirts of the greatcoat.

The brush grew as high as a mounted man's head, the sturdy trunks just far enough apart to let a horse pass, but the barbed branches intertwined and exacted a cruel toll. However, Tom kept going, swinging and chopping from side to side; he dodged between the white barked trunks, ducking his head under the branches, his ears flat against his skull and his eyes closed to slits, maintaining just the right amount of momentum to snap the thorns off their triangular bases and showering both himself and Zouga with a confetti of feathery green leaves. Every few seconds he snorted at the sting of thorn that had penetrated his tough shaggy hide.

Shooting Star's burnished skin was so thin and finely bred that the network of veins and arteries showed through it. The thorns would have ripped it to bloody tatters.

Zouga felt blood trickling down his own neck from where a thorn had nicked his ear, but he crouched lower and let Tom pick his own way through. 'Poor Tom,' he encouraged him. 'Poor brave Tom.' The horse whickered with the pain of the stinging red needles, but did not check his stride. Yet his breathing was easier now, the slower gait had helped him; and the sweat was drying in salty white crystals on his shoulders.

Then abruptly they burst out of the thorn onto the open plain. Zouga tore off the leather gauntlets and threw them away. He ripped at the buttons of the greatcoat and let it fly away, flapping like a great black crow in the wind of Tom's gallop – and then he stood high in the stirrups and shaded his eyes with the brim of his hat.

Swiftly he searched the open ground, but it was empty as far as the tiny specks of colour in the distance: women's dresses and the gay bunting that marked the finish. His heart bounded with relief, and under him Tom lunged into a clumsy gallop.

Still standing in the stirrups, Zouga looked towards the line of hills out on his right hand, and he saw them.

The stallion had turned the far end of the thorn barrier where it ran into the hills and was coming down the rocky slope towards the level ground in a dangerous scramble.

The tiny figure on his back was being thrown about brutally. One instant she seemed to be on his neck, the next she was flung back onto his haunches, as Shooting Star plunged and heaved to keep his balance.

'We have them now, Tom. There it is. There is the line, right under your nose.' Zouga pointed his head. 'They cannot catch us now. Go, old man, go!'

Tom's hooves cracked on the hard earth like the beat of a joyous drummer. The crossing of the thorns had been cruel work, but it had rested him and he was pushing hard now.

' 'Ware hole!' Zouga called to him, and Tom flicked his ears reproachfully. He had seen it before Zouga had, and he jinked around the burrow neatly, while the heads of the curious little ground squirrels bobbed out of the earth as they passed.

The ground was rotten with their warrens, but Tom barely checked his gallop, swinging to avoid the mounds of freshly-turned earth, or occasionally stretching out to step over an entrance hole.

The ground squirrels were almost indistinguishable from their northern cousins, except for the stripe down their furry backs and their terrestrial habit. They stood on their hind legs, like small groups of spectators at the entrance of each warren, their expressions comically astonished and their long bushy tails curled over their backs as Tom pounded past them.

Zouga looked over his shoulder. Shooting Star was off the steep slope of the hills, down onto the open plain, and it was apparent that he was burning the last reserves of his great strength, coming on in a blazing run, driving out with his forelegs, and then bunching up his sweat-drenched hindquarters to hurl himself into the next stride. Louise was pushing him with her arms, like a washerwoman working over the scrubbing board, but she was too far behind for Zouga to see the expression on her face.

Much too far behind, half a mile behind – and there was less than a mile to run to the line of gaily coloured bunting that marked the finish.

Zouga could clearly see the crowds on each side of the posts, thick as bees at the entrance to the hive, and others were running for the wagons to join them.

He could hear the faint pop of gunfire, see the little spurts of gunsmoke jumping up above the heads of the crowd as his supporters fired into the air in jubilation.

Soon he would hear their voices, catch the sound of their cheers, even above the beat of Tom's hooves.

It was all over. He had won. He had won back his claims, the cherished image of the falcon god – and the five thousand pounds with which he could take his family away to a new life. He had taken on the gods of chance and won.

He had only one regret – that the courage of the horse and rider behind him had been in vain. Careful not to unbalance Tom's heavy unlovely gallop, he looked back under his own arm.

By God, she had not yet accepted defeat. She was driving with all her strength and all her heart, pushing the great horse as hard as she pushed herself, coming on so swiftly that Zouga glanced uneasily over Tom's pricked ears to reassure himself as to the proximity of the finish line. No, there was no chance – even at that tremendous speed – Shooting Star could never catch them.

Already he could hear the voices of the crowd, make out their individual faces, even recognize Pickering, the chief steward, on his seat on the wagon, and beside him Rhodes' unmistakable bulk and the mop of unruly hair. With him to witness it, Zouga's triumph was complete.

He turned for the last time to look back at Shooting Star – just in time to see him fall. It had been much too fast, too uncontrolled, that wild gallop across ground rotten with squirrel warrens. Shooting Star's front legs went from under him. Zouga imagined he could hear the bone break, like the crack of a pistol shot, and the huge horse went down from full gallop, shoulder first, neck twisted around in an agonized contortion like that of a dying flamingo; dust flew up in a cloud, blanketing them, and above it the stallion's hooves kicked spasmodically, convulsively, and then sagged.

The pale beige dust cloud drifted aside, revealing the tragic tangle of horse and rider. Shooting Star lay on his side and, as Zouga reined in and swung Tom's nose back the way he had come, the great stallion made a feeble effort to lift his head off the ground and then let it fall back weakly.

Louise's body had been flung clear. She lay curled like a sleeping child on the bare earth, very still, very small.

'Ha, Tom, ha!' Zouga urged him to greater speed. He was shocked at the sense of utter desolation that assailed him as he galloped back to where she lay. There was something so final, so terribly chilling in her stillness, in the complete relaxation, the lifelessness of that tiny crumpled body.

'Please God,' Zouga spoke aloud, his throat seared by dust and thirst and dread. 'Please don't let it be.'

He imagined the lovely delicate neck twisted at an impossible angle against the shattered vertebrae. He imagined the awful bloodless depression in the delicate dome of her skull; he imagined those huge dark eyes, open and staring, the inner glow fading – he imagined, oh God, he imagined – Then he was kicking his feet clear of the stirrups and jumping down even while Tom was at full gallop, stumbling to keep his balance and then running to where she lay.

Louise uncurled her body and rolled lightly to her feet.

'Come, darling, up darling,' she called to Shooting Star, as she ran to him. The stallion lunged once, twice and then he was standing, head up.

'What a clever darling,' Louise laughed, but with the huskiness of excitement and the tremor of heart-breaking exertion in the sound of it.

She did not have the strength left to vault for the saddle, and for a moment she hopped with one foot in the stirrup before she could find the energy to swing her other leg up over Shooting Star's back, while Zouga stood and gaped at her.

From the saddle she looked down at Zouga. 'Playing dead is an old Blackfoot Indian's trick, Major.'

Louise swung the stallion's head towards the finish line.

'Let's see you run the last lap on equal terms,' she challenged, and Shooting Star jumped away at full gallop.

For a moment Zouga could not bring himself to believe that she had taught the stallion to fall so convincingly, and to lie so still. Then suddenly his concern for her safety, the desolate feeling of believing her dead or maimed turned to fury and outrage.

As he ran back to where Tom stood, he yelled after her.

'Madam, you are a cheat – may God forgive you for that.'

She turned in the saddle and waved gaily. 'Sir, you are gullible, but I will forgive you for that.'

And Shooting Star bore her away towards the finish at a pace that poor Tom could never match.

Zouga Ballantyne was drunk. It was the first time in the twenty-two years they had been together that Jan Cheroot had seen him so.

He sat very erect on the high-backed deal chair, and his face above the beard had a strange waxen look to it. His eyes were glazed over with the same soapy sheen of uncut diamonds. The third bottle of Cape Brandy stood on the green baize of the table between them, and as Zouga fumbled for it, he knocked it over. The spirit glugged loudly from the mouth, and soaked into the cloth.

Jan Cheroot snatched it upright, with a shocked oath.

'Man, if you want to lose the Devil's Own, I don't mind – but, when you spill the brandy – that's another thing.'

Jan Cheroot stumbled a little over the words; they had been drinking since an hour before sundown.

'What am I going to tell the boys?' mumbled Zouga.

'Tell them that they are on holiday – for the first time in ten years. We are all on holiday.'

Jan Cheroot poured brandy into Zouga's mug, and pushed it closer to his hand. Then he poured a good dram into his own, thought about it for a moment, and added as much again.

'I have lost everything, Old Jan.'

'Ja,' Jan Cheroot said cheerfully. 'And that was not very much, was it.'

'I have lost the claims.'

'Good.' Jan Cheroot nodded. 'For ten years those double-damned squares of dirt ate our souls away – and starved us while they were doing it.'

'I have lost the bird.'

'Good again!' Jan Cheroot swigged his brandy, and smacked his lips with appreciation. 'Let Mr Rhodes have his share of bad luck now. That bird will finish him, as it nearly finished us. Send it to him as soon as you can, and thank God to be rid of it.'

Slowly Zouga lowered his face into his hands, covering his eyes and his mouth – so that his voice was muffled.

'Jan Cheroot. It's all over. For me the road to the north is closed. My dream is finished. It's all been for nothing.'

The bibulous grin faded slowly and Jan Cheroot's yellow face puckered with deep compassion.

'It is not finished – you are still young and strong – with two strong sons.'

'We shall lose them too – soon, very soon.'

'Then you will have me, old friend, like it has always been.'

Zouga lifted his head out of his hands and stared at the little Hottentot.

'What are we going to do, Jan Cheroot?'

'We are going to finish this bottle and then open another,' Jan Cheroot told him firmly.

In the morning they loaded the soapstone idol into the gravel cart, and laid it on a bed of straw; then Zouga spread a stained and tattered tarpaulin over it and Jordan helped him rope it down.

Neither of them spoke – until they were finished, and then Jordan whispered so softly that Zouga barely caught the words.

'You can't let it go, Papa.' And Zouga turned to look at his younger son, truly seeing him for the first time in many years.

With a small shock he realized that Jordan was a man. In imitation of Ralph perhaps, he also had grown a moustache. It was a dense coppery gold, and accentuated the gentle line of his mouth – yet, if anything, the man was more beautiful than the child had been.

'Is there no way we can keep it?' Jordan persisted, with a thin edge of desperation in his voice, and Zouga went on staring at him. How old was he now? Over nineteen years, and yesterday he had been a baby – little Jordie. Everything was changed.

Zouga turned away from him, and placed his hand on the tarpaulin-wrapped burden in the bottom of the cart.

'No, Jordan. It was a wager – a matter of honour.'

'But, Mama –' Jordan started and then broke off abruptly as Zouga looked back at him sharply.

'What about Aletta?' he demanded, and Jordan looked away and flushed, bringing up the colour under the velvety skin of his cheeks.

'Nothing,' he said quickly, and went to the head of the lead mule. 'I will take the bird to Mr Rhodes,' he volunteered, and Zouga nodded immediately, relieved that he would be spared this painful duty.

'Ask him when he will be free to sign the transfer of the claims.'

Zouga touched the wrapped statue again as though in farewell and then he pulled his hand away, went up the steps onto the verandah and into the bungalow without looking back.

Jordan led the mules out into the rutted road and swung them towards the settlement. He walked bareheaded in the sunlight. He was tall and slim and he moved with a peculiar grace, stepping lightly and lithely in the soft red dust. His chin was up, his eyes focused far ahead, with the dreaming, yet all-seeing, gaze of a poet.

Men and women, especially women, looked after him as he passed and their expressions softened, but Jordan walked on as though he were alone on a deserted street.

Though his lips never moved, the words of the invocation to the goddess Panes kept running through his mind.

' – Why did you run away? You would have been better with us –' So many times he had called to the goddess, the words were part of his very existence. 'Will you not come back to us, great Panes?'

The goddess was going – and Jordan did not believe he could support the agony of it. Statue, goddess and mother were all one in his mind, his last link with Aletta. Aletta who had become Panes.

He felt desolate, bereaved as though of his dearest love, and when he reached the milkwood fence of Rhodes' camp, he stopped and wild fancies seized him. He would take the goddess, run with her into the wilderness, hide her in some distant cave. His heart bounded. No, he would take her back to the ancient ruined city from which she had come, that far place in the north from which his father had stolen her, where she would be safe.

Then with a plunge of his spirits and a slide of despair in his guts he knew that these were childish dreamings and that he was no longer a child.

With a light touch on the lead mule's bridle, he guided her into the camp, and Rhodes was standing at the front door of his bungalow, bareheaded and in shirt-sleeves. He was talking quietly, urgently to a man below the stoep. Jordan recognized him as one of the Central Diamond Company overseers.

When Rhodes looked up and saw Jordan, he dismissed the overseer with a curt word and a nod.

'Jordan,' Rhodes' greeting was grave, perhaps he sensed the mood of the young man before him, 'you have brought it?'

When Jordan nodded, he turned back to the waiting overseer.

'Bring four of your best men,' he ordered. 'I want this cart unloaded – and carefully. It's a valuable work of art.'

He watched keenly as they untied the ropes that held the tarpaulin in place, but cocked the large curly head when Jordan spoke.

'If we have to lose it, then I'm glad it's you that it goes to, Mr Rhodes.'

'The bird means something to you also, Jordan?'

'Everything,' Jordan said simply, and then caught himself; that sounded ridiculous. Mr Rhodes would think him strange. 'I mean, it has been in my family since before I was born. I don't really know what it will be like without that goddess. I don't really want to think about losing it.'

'You don't have to lose it, Jordan.'

Jordan looked at him, unable to bring himself to ask the meaning.

'You can follow the goddess, Jordan.'

'Please don't tease me, Mr Rhodes.'

'You are bright and willing, you have studied Pitman's shorthand, and you have an excellent pen,' Rhodes said. 'I need a secretary – somebody who knows and loves diamonds as I do. Somebody whom I feel easy with. Somebody I know and whom I like. Somebody I can trust.'

Jordan felt a vast soaring rush of joy, something sharper, brighter and more poignant than he had ever known before. He could not speak; he stood rooted and stared into the pale blue and beautiful eyes of the man whom he had worshipped for so many years.

'Well, Jordan, I am offering you the position. Do you want it?'

'Yes,' Jordan said softly. 'More than anything on earth, Mr Rhodes.'

'Good, then your first task is to find a place to set up the bird.'

The white overseer had pulled the tarpaulin aside to expose the statue, and the sheet hung down over the side of the cart.

'Easy now,' he shouted at the gang of black labourers. 'Get a rope on it. Don't drop it. Watch that end, damn you.'

They swarmed over the statue, too many of them for the job, getting in one another's way – and Jordan's heady joy at Rhodes' offer was submerged in a quick stab of concern for the safety of the bird.

He started forward to set the ropes himself, but at that moment there was the clatter of hooves and Neville Pickering rode into the yard. He was astride his mare, a highly bred and finely mettled bay, and he reined her down to a walk.

He shot a glance at Jordan, and his face clouded for an instant – a quick show of irritation, or of something else. With a sudden intuitive flash Jordan realized that Pickering resented his presence here.

Then as quickly as it had come the shadow passed from Pickering's handsome features and he smiled that sunny charming smile of his and looked down at the statue in the cart.

'What have we here?' His tone was gay, his manner carefree and relaxed. As always he was elegantly dressed, the drape of broadcloth showing off his broad shoulders, the tooled leather belt emphasizing his narrow waist, as the polished half boots did the length and shape of his legs. The low-crowned, broad-brimmed hat was cocked forward over one eye, and he was smiling.

'Oh, the bird.' He looked up at Rhodes on the stoep of the bungalow. 'So you have it at last, as you said you would. I should congratulate you.'

The day had been still and too hot, it would change soon. The wind would come out of the south and the temperature would plunge, but until then the only movements of air were the sudden little dust devils that sprang out of nowhere, small but violent whirlwinds that lifted a high churning vortex of dust and dry grass and dead leaves a hundred or more feet into the still sky as they sped in a wildly erratic course across the plain, and then just as suddenly collapsed and disintegrated into nothingness again.

One of these dust devils rose now, on the open ground beyond the milkwood hedge. It tore a dense red cloud of spinning dust off the surface of the road, then swerved abruptly and raced into the yard of Rhodes' camp. Jordan felt his heart gripped in a cold vice of superstitious dread.

'Panes!' The cry was silent in his head. 'Great Panes!'

He knew what that wind was, he knew the presence of the goddess – for how many times had she come to his invocation? Suddenly the whole yard was filled with the swirling torrents of dust, and the wind battered them. It flew into Jordan's face, so that he must slit his eyes against it. It flung his soft shiny curls into his face, and it flattened his shirt against his chest and his lean flat belly.

The broad-brimmed hat sailed from Pickering's head, the tails of his coat flogged into the small of his back and he lifted one hand to protect his face from the stinging sand and sharp pieces of twig and grass.

Then the wind got under the ragged old tarpaulin, and filled it with a crack like a ship's mainsail gybing onto the opposite tack.

The harsh canvas lashed the bay mare's head, and she reared up on her back legs, whinnying shrilly with panic.

So high she went that Jordan thought she would go over on her back, and through the red raging curtain of dust, he jumped to catch her head; but he was an instant too late. Pickering had one hand to his face, and the mare's leap took him off balance; he went over backwards out of the saddle, and he hit hard earth with the back of his neck and one shoulder.

The rushing sound of the whirlwind, the grunt of air driven from Pickering's lungs and the meaty thump of his fall almost covered the tiny snapping sound of bone breaking somewhere deep in his body.

Then the mare came down from her high prancing dance, and she flattened immediately into full gallop. She flew at the gateway in the milkwood hedge, and Pickering was dragged after her, his ankle trapped in the steel of the stirrup, his body slithering and bouncing loosely across the earth.

As the mare swerved to take the gap in the hedge, Pickering was flung into the hedge, and the white thorns, each as long as a man's forefinger, were driven into his flesh like needles.

Then he was plucked away, out into the open ground, sledging over rocky earth, striking and flattening the small wiry bushes as the mare jumped them, his body totally relaxed and his arms flung out behind him.

One moment the back of his head was slapping against the earth, and the next his ankle had twisted in the stirrup and he was face down, the skin being smeared from his cheeks and forehead by the harsh abrasive earth.

Jordan found himself racing after him, his breath sobbing with horror – calling to the mare.

'Whoa, girl! Steady, girl!'

But she was maddened, firstly terrified by the wind and the flirt of canvas into her face, and now by the unfamiliar weight that dragged and slithered at her heels. She reached the slope of the trailing dumps and swerved again, and this time, mercifully, the stirrup leather parted with a twang. Freed of her burden, the mare galloped away down the pathway between the dumps.

Jordan dropped on his knees beside Pickering's inert crumpled body. He lay face down; the expensive broadcloth was ripped and dusty, the boots scuffed through to white leather beneath.

Gently, supporting his head in cupped hands, Jordan rolled him onto his back, turning his face out of the dust so that he could breathe. Pickering's face was a bloodied mask, caked with dust, a flap of white skin hanging off his cheek – but his eyes were wide open.

Despite the complete deathlike relaxation of his arms and body, Pickering was fully conscious. His eyes swivelled to Jordan's face, and his lips moved.

'Jordie,' he whispered. 'I can't feel anything, nothing at all. Numb – my hands, my feet, my whole body numb.'

They carried him back in a blanket, a man at each corner, and laid him gently on the narrow iron-framed cot in the bedroom next door to Rhodes' own room.

Dr Jameson came within the hour, and he nodded when he saw how Jordan had bathed and dressed his injuries and the arrangements he had made for his comfort.

'Good. Who taught you?' But he did not wait for an answer. 'Here!' he said. 'I'll need your help.' And he handed Jordan his bag, shrugged out of his jacket and rolled his sleeves.

'Get out,' he said to Rhodes. 'You'll be in the way here.'

It took Jameson only minutes to make certain that the paralysis below the neck was complete, and then he looked up at Jordan, making sure that he was out of sight of Pickering's alert, fever-bright eyes, and he shook his head curtly.

'I'll be a minute,' he said. 'I must speak with Mr Rhodes.'

'Jordie,' Pickering whispered painfully, the moment Jameson left the room, and Jordan stooped to his lips. 'It's my neck – it's broken.'

'No.'

'Be quiet. Listen.' Pickering frowned at the interruption. 'I think I always knew – that it would be you. One way or the other, it would be you –'

He broke off, fresh sweat blistered on his forehead, but he made another terrible effort to speak. 'I thought I hated you. But not any more – not now. There is not enough time left for hate.'

He did not speak again, not that night, nor the following day. But at dusk when the heat in the tiny iron-walled room abated a little, he opened his eyes again and looked up at Rhodes. It was frightening to see how low he had sunk. The fine bones of forehead and cheeks seemed to gleam through the translucent skin, and his eyes had receded into dark bruised cavities.

Rhodes leaned his great shaggy head over him until his ear touched Pickering's dry white lips. The whisper was so light, like a dead leaf blown softly across a roof at midnight, and Jordan could not hear the words, but Rhodes clenched his lids closed over his pale blue eyes as though in mortal anguish.

'Yes,' he answered, almost as softly as the dying man. 'Yes, I know, Pickling.'

When Rhodes opened his eyes again they were flooded with bright tears, and his colour was a frightening mottled purple.

'He's dead, Jordan,' he choked, and put one hand on his own chest, pressing hard as though to calm the beat of his swollen heart.

Then quite slowly, deliberately, he lowered his head again, and kissed the broken, torn lips of the man on the iron-framed cot.

Zouga thought the voice was part of his dream – so sweet, so low, and yet tremulous and filled with some dreadful appeal. Then he was awake, and the voice was still calling, and now there was a light tap on the window above the head of his bed.

'I'm coming,' Zouga answered, as low as he was called. He did not have to ask who it was.

He dressed swiftly, in total darkness, instinct warning him not to light a candle, and he carried his boots in his hand as he stepped out onto the stoep of the cottage.

The height of the moon told him that it was after midnight, but he barely glanced at it before turning to the figure that leaned against the wall beside the door.

'Are you alone?' he demanded softly. There was something in the way the figure slumped that frightened him.

'Yes.' The distress, the pain, were clear in her voice now that they were so close.

'You should not have come here – not alone, Mrs St John.'

'There was nobody else to turn to.'

'Where is Mungo. Where is your husband?'

'He is in trouble – terrible, terrible, trouble.'

'Where is he?'

'I left him out beyond the Cape crossroad.'

For a moment her voice choked on her, and then it came out with a forceful rush.

'He's hurt. Wounded, badly wounded.'

Her voice had risen, so that she might rouse Jan Cheroot and the boys. Zouga took her arm to calm and quieten her, and immediately she fell against him. The feel of her body shocked him, but he could not pull away.

'I'm afraid, Zouga. I'm afraid he might die.' It was the first time she had used his given name.

'What happened?'

'Oh God!' She was weeping now, clinging to him, and he realized how hard-pressed she was. He slipped his arm around her waist and led her down the verandah.

In the kitchen he seated her on one of the hard deal chairs, and then lit the candle. He was shocked again when he saw her face. She was pale and shaking, her hair in wild disorder, a smear of dirt on one cheek and her eyes red-rimmed and bloodshot.

He poured coffee from the blue enamel pot at the back of the stove. It was thick as molasses. He added a dram of brandy to it.

'Drink it.'

She shuddered and gasped at the potent black brew, but it seemed to steady her a little.

'I didn't want him to go. I tried to stop him. I was sick of it. I told him I couldn't take it any more, the cheating and lying. The shame and the running –'

'You aren't making sense,' he told her brusquely, and she took a deep breath and started again.

'Mungo went to meet a man tonight. The man was going to bring him a parcel of diamonds, a parcel of diamonds worth one hundred thousand pounds. And Mungo was going to buy them for two thousand.'

Zouga's face set grimly, and he sat down opposite her and stared at her. His expression intimidated her.

'Oh God, Zouga. I know. I hated it too. I have lived with it so long, but he promised me that this would be the last time.'

'Go on,' Zouga commanded.

'But he didn't have two thousand, Zouga. We are almost broke – a few pounds is all that we have left.'

This time Zouga could not contain himself and he broke in.

'The letter of credit, half a million pounds –'

'Forged,' she said quietly.

'Go on.'

'He didn't have the money to pay for the diamonds – and I knew what he was going to do. I tried to stop him, I swear it to you.'

'I believe you.'

'He arranged to meet this man tonight – at a place out on the Cape road.'

'Do you know the man's name?'

'I'm not sure. I think so.' She passed her hand over her eyes. 'He is a coloured man, a Griqua, Henry – no, Hendrick Somebody –'

'Hendrick Naaiman?'

'Yes. Naaiman, that's it.'

'He's an I.D.B. trap.'

'Police?'

'Yes, police.'

'Oh sweet God, it's even worse than I thought.'

'What happened?' Zouga insisted.

'Mungo made me wait for him at the crossroads and he went to the rendezvous alone. He said he needed to protect himself – he took his pistol. He went on my horse – on Shooting Star, and then I heard the gunfire.'

She took another gulp of the coffee and coughed at the burn of it.

'He came back. He had been shot, and so had Shooting Star. They couldn't go any further, neither of them. They were both hard hit, Zouga. I hid them near the road and I came to you.'

Zouga's voice was harsh. 'Did Mungo kill him?'

'I don't know, Zouga. Mungo says the other man fired first and he only tried to protect himself.'

'Mungo tried to hold him up and take the diamonds, without paying for them,' Zouga guessed. 'But Naaiman is a dangerous man.'

'There were four empty cartridges in Mungo's pistol, but I don't know what happened to the policeman. I only know that Mungo escaped, but he is hurt very badly.'

'Now keep quiet and rest for a while.' He stood up and paced up and down the kitchen, his bare feet making no sound, his hands clasped at the small of the back.

Louise St John watched him anxiously, almost fearfully, until he stopped abruptly and turned to her.

'We both know what I should do. Your husband is I.D.B.; he is a thief and by now he is probably a murderer.'

'He is also your friend,' she said simply. 'And he is very badly wounded.'

He resumed his pacing, but now he was muttering to himself, troubled and scowling, and Louise twisted her fingers in her lap.

'Very well,' he said at last. 'I'll help you to get him away.'

'Oh, Major Ballantyne – Zouga –'

He silenced her with a frown. 'Don't waste time talking. We'll need bandages, laudanum, food –' He was ticking off a list on his fingers. 'You can't go like that. They'll be watching for a woman. Jordan's cast-off clothes will fit you well enough – breeches, cap and coat –'

Zouga walked at the flank of the mule, and the gravel cart was loaded with bales of thatching grass.

Louise lay silently in the hollow between two bales, with another ready to pull over herself if the cart was stopped.

The iron-shod wheels crunched in the sand, but the night dew had damped down the dust. The lantern on the tailboard of the cart swung and jiggled to the motion.

They had just passed the last house on the Cape road, and were drawing level with the cemetery when there was the dust-muffled beat of hooves from behind them and Louise only just had time to drop down and cover herself before a small group of riders swept out of the darkness and overtook them.

As they galloped through the arc of lantern light, Zouga saw they were all armed. He stooped and lowered his chin into the collar of his greatcoat and the woollen cap was pulled low over his eyes. One of the riders pulled up his horse and shouted to Zouga.

'Hey, you! Have you seen anybody on this road tonight?'

'*Niemand nie*! Nobody!' Zouga answered in the taal, and the sound of the guttural dialect reassured the man.

He wheeled his horse and galloped on after his companions.

When the sound of hooves had died away Zouga spoke quietly.

'That means that Naaiman got away to spread the word. Unless he dies of his wounds later, it's not murder.'

'Please God,' Louise whispered.

'It also means that you cannot try to get out on either the Cape road or the road to the Transvaal. They will be watched.'

'Which way can we go?'

'If I were you I would take the track north, it goes to Kuruman. There is a mission station there – it's run by my grandfather. His name is Doctor Moffat. He will give you shelter, and Mungo will need a doctor. Then when Mungo is strong enough, you can try to reach German or Portuguese territory and get out through Lüderitz Bay or Lourenço Marques.'

Neither of them spoke for a long time as Zouga trudged on beside the mule, and Louise crawled out to sit on the bench of the cart. It was she who broke the silence.

'I am so tired of running. We seem to have run out of lands, America, Canada, Australia, we cannot go back to any of them.'

'You could go home to France,' Zouga said, 'to your sons.'

Louise's head jerked up. 'Why do you say that?'

'When Mungo and I first met he told me about you, his wife – that you were of a noble French family. He told me that you and he had three sons.'

Louise's chin sank onto her chest and Jordan's cloth cap covered her eyes.

'I have no sons,' she said. 'But oh how I pray that one day I may have. I belong to a noble family, yes – but not French. My grandmother was the daughter of Hawk Flies Lightly, the Blackfoot War Chief.'

'I don't understand, Mungo told me –'

'He told you about the woman who is his wife, Madame Solange de Montijo St John.'

Louise was silent again, and Zouga had to ask:

'She is dead?'

'Their marriage was unhappy. No, she is not dead. She returned with their three sons to France at the beginning of the Civil War. He has not seen her since.'

'Then she and Mungo are,' Zouga hesitated over the unsavoury word, 'divorced?'

'She is a Catholic,' Louise replied simply; and it was fully five minutes before either of them spoke again.

'Yes,' Louise said. 'What you are thinking is correct. Mungo and I are not married; we could not be.'

'It's not my business,' Zouga murmured, and yet what she had said did not shock him. He felt instead a strange lightness of spirit, a kind of glowing joy.

'It's a relief to speak completely honestly,' she explained. 'After all the lies. Somehow it had to be you, Zouga. I could never have admitted all this to anybody else.'

'Do you love him?' Zouga's voice was rough-edged, brusque.

'Once I loved him completely, without restraint, wildly – madly.'

'And now?'

'I do not know – there have been so many lies, so much shame, so much to hide.'

'Why do you stay with him, Louise?'

'Because now he needs me.'

'I understand that.' His voice was gentler. He did understand, he truly did. 'Duty is a harsh and unforgiving master. And yet you have a duty to yourself also.'

The mules plodded on in the darkness, and the swinging lantern did not light the face of the woman on the bench, but once she sighed, and it was a sound to twist Zouga's heart.

'Louise,' he spoke at last. 'I am not doing this for Mungo, even a friendship cannot condone deliberate robbery and premeditated murder.'

She did not reply.

'Many times you must have seen the way I have looked at you – for, God knows, I could not help myself.'

Still she was silent.

'You did know,' he insisted. 'You, as a woman, must know how I feel.'

'Yes,' she said at last.

'When I thought you were married to a friend, it was hopeless. Now, at least, I can tell you how I feel.'

'Zouga, please don't.'

'I would do anything you asked me to – even protect a murderer, that is how I feel for you.'

'Zouga –'

'I have never known anybody so beautiful and bright and brave –'

'I am not any of those things –'

'I could put you and Mungo on the road to Kuruman and then go back to Kimberley and tell the diamond police where to find you. They would take Mungo, and then you would be free.'

'You could,' she agreed. 'But you never would. Both of us are tied, Zouga, by our own peculiar sense of duty and of honour.'

'Louise –'

'We have arrived,' she said, with patent relief. 'The crossroads. Turn off the road here.'

From the bench she guided him as he threaded the cart through the scattered bush and the high wheels bumped over rock and rough ground. A quarter of a mile from the road there stood a massive camel-thorn tree, silver and high as a hill in the moonlight. Beneath its spread branches the moon shadow was black and impenetrable.

From the darkness a hoarse voice challenged.

'Stand where you are! Don't come any closer.'

'Mungo, it's me and Zouga is with me.'

Louise jumped down from the cart, lifted the lantern off its bracket and went forward, stooping under the branches. Zouga tethered the mules and then followed her. Louise was kneeling beside Mungo St John. He lay on a saddle blanket, propped on the silver ornamented Mexican saddle.

'Thank you for coming,' he greeted Zouga, and his voice was ragged with pain.

'How badly are you hit?'

'Badly enough,' he admitted. 'Do you have a cheroot?'

Zouga lit one from the lantern and handed it to him. Louise was unwrapping the torn strips of shirt and petticoat that were bound about his chest.

'Shotgun?' Zouga asked tersely.

'No, thank God,' Mungo said. 'Pistol.'

'You are lucky,' Zouga grunted. 'Naaiman's usual style is a sawed-off shotgun. He would have blown you in half.'

'You know him – Naaiman?'

'He's a police trap.'

'Police,' Mungo whispered. 'Oh God.'

'Yes,' Zouga nodded. 'You are in trouble.'

'I didn't know.'

'Does it really matter?' Zouga asked. 'You planned an I.D.B. switch, and you knew you might have to kill a man.'

'Don't preach to me, Zouga.'

'All right.' Zouga squatted next to Louise as she exposed the wound in Mungo's back. 'And it looks as though it missed the bloody lymph, set in a livid spread of bruise.'

Between them they lifted Mungo into a sitting position.

'Through and through,' Zouga murmured, as he saw the exit wound in Mungo's back. 'And it looks as though it missed the lung. You are luckier than you'll ever know.'

'One stayed in,' Mungo St John contradicted him, and reached down to his own leg. His breeches had been split down the leg, and now he pulled the bloodstained cloth aside to reveal a strip of pale thigh in the centre of which was another vicious little round opening from which fluid wept like blackcurrant juice.

'The bullet is still in,' Mungo repeated.

'Bone?' Zouga asked.

'No.' St John shook his head. 'I don't think so. I was still able to walk on it.'

'There is no chance of trying to cut the bullet out. Louise knows where she can find a doctor, and I have told her how to get there.'

'Louise?' Mungo asked with a sardonic twist of his lips.

She did not look up, concentrating on the task of painting the skin around the wounds with iodine.

Mungo was staring at Zouga, his single eye gleaming, and Zouga felt the scar on his cheek throb and he did not trouble to hide his anger.

'You don't think I am doing this for you,' he demanded. 'I hate I.D.B. as much as any digger on the workings, and I'm not that complacent about deliberate robbery and murder.' And he took the pistol from the blanket where it lay at Mungo's side.

He checked the load as he walked to where Shooting Star stood, head down in the moonlight beyond the camel-thorn tree.

The stallion lifted his head, and blew a fluttery breath through his nostrils as Zouga approached; then he shifted his weight awkwardly and painfully on three legs.

'There, boy. Easy, boy.' Zouga ran his hands down the animal's flank. It was sticky with drying blood, and Shooting Star whickered as he touched the wound.

Behind the ribs, bullet hole, and Zouga sniffed at it quickly. The bullet had pierced the bowel or the intestines – he could smell it.

Zouga went down on one knee and gently felt the foreleg that the stallion was favouring. He found the damage, another bullet wound. It had struck a few inches above the fetlock and the bone was shattered. Yet the horse had carried Mungo, a big heavy man, and it had brought him many miles. The agony must have been dreadful, but the stallion's great heart had carried them through.

Zouga shrugged off his greatcoat and wrapped it around the pistol in his right hand. A shot could alert the searching bands on the not too distant road.

'There, boy,' Zouga whispered, and touched the muzzle to the forehead between the horse's eyes.

The cloth muffled the shot. It was a dull blurt of sound, and the stallion dropped heavily on his side and never even kicked.

Louise was still bowed over Mungo, tying the knots in the bandage, but Zouga saw that her eyes were bright with tears in the moonlight.

'Thank you,' she whispered. 'I couldn't have done it myself.'

Zouga helped her lift Mungo to the cart. Mungo's breath whistled in his chest and the sweat of agony drenched his shirt and smelled rancid and gamey.

They settled him into the nest of thatching grass and spread a screen of it over him. Then Zouga led the mules on over the veld until they struck the track that led northwards towards the Vaal river, and beyond it Kuruman and the vast Kalahari Desert.

'Travel at night, and hobble the mules to graze during the day,' Zouga told her.

'There is more than enough meal and biltong; but you will have to spare the coffee and sugar.'

'Words cannot thank you enough,' she whispered.

'Don't attempt the main drift of the Vaal.'

'Somehow I know that this is not goodbye.' She seemed not to have heard the advice. 'And when we meet again,' she broke off.

'Go on,' he said, but she shook her head and took the reins from his hand and led the mules onto the track.

The cart seemed to merge into the night, and the wheels made no sound in the thick pale sand. Zouga stood staring after them, long after they had disappeared – and then Louise came back.

She came silent as a wraith, running with a kind of terrible desperation, the long tresses of hair had fallen out from under the cap and were streaming down her back. Her face was pale and stricken in the moonlight.

The grip of her arms about his neck was fierce, almost painful, and her mouth was shockingly hot and wet as it spread over his. But the taste of it he would never forget, and her sharp white teeth crushed his lips.

For seconds only they clung to each other, while Zouga thought his heart would burst; then she tore herself from his arms, and with neither a word nor a backward glance, she flew into the night – and was gone.

Ten days after Neville Pickering's funeral, Zouga signed the transfer deeds to the Devil's Own claims, and watched while one of Rhodes' secretaries registered them in favour of the Central Diamond Company. Then he walked out into the cold.

For the first time in living memory it was snowing over the diamond fields. Big soft flakes came twisting down like feathers from a shimmering white egret struck by birdshot.

The snowflakes vanished as they touched the earth, but the cold was a vindictive presence and Zouga's breath steamed in the air and condensed on his beard as he trudged up to the workings to watch the shift come off the Devil's Own claims for the last time. As he walked he tried to compose the words to tell Ralph that this was the last shift.

They were coming up in the skip. Zouga could make out Ralph, for he was the only man who wore a coat. The other men with him were almost naked.

Once again Zouga wondered idly that the men had not rebelled against the harsh measures of the new Diamond Trade Act, enforced by Colonel John Fry of the recently recruited Diamond Police, and aimed at stamping out I.D.B. on the fields.

Nowadays the black workers were compounded behind barbed wire; there were new curfew regulations to keep them in the compounds after nightfall; and there were spot searches and checks of the compounds, of men on the streets even during daylight, and body searches of each shift coming out of the pit.

Even the diggers, or at least a few of them, had protested at the most draconian of John Fry's new regulations. All black workers had been forced to go into the pit stark naked, so that they would not be able to hide stones in their clothing.

John Fry had been amazed when Zouga and a dozen other diggers had demanded to see him.

'Good Lord, Ballantyne, but they are a bunch of naked savages anyway. Modesty, forsooth!'

In the end, with the co-operation of Rhodes, they had forced him to compromise. Grudgingly Fry had allowed every worker a strip of seamless cotton 'limbo' to cover himself.

Thus Bazo and his Matabele wore only a strip of loin-cloth each as they rode up beside Ralph in the skip. The wind threw an icy noose about them, and Bazo shivered as goose-bumps rose upon the smooth dark skin of his chest and upper arms.

Above him stood Ralph Ballantyne, balancing easily on the rim of the steel skip, ignoring the wind and the deadly drop below him.

Ralph glanced down at Bazo crouching below the side of the steel bucket, and on impulse slipped the scrap of stained canvas off his own shoulders. Under it Ralph wore an old tweed jacket and dusty cardigan. He dropped the canvas over Bazo's neck.

'It's against the white man's law,' Bazo demurred, and made as if to shrug it off.

'There are no police in this skip,' Ralph grunted, and Bazo hesitated a moment and then crouched lower and gratefully pulled the canvas over his head and shoulders.

Ralph took the butt of a half-smoked cheroot from his breast pocket, and carefully reshaped it between his fingers; the dead ash flaked away on the wind and wafted down into the yawning depths below. He lit the butt and drew the smoke down deeply, exhaled and drew again, held the smoke and passed the butt to Bazo.

'You are not only cold, but you are unhappy,' Ralph said, and Bazo did not answer. He cupped the stubby cheroot in both hands and drew carefully upon it.

'Is it Donsela?' Ralph asked. 'He knew the law, Bazo. He knows what the law says of those who steal the stones.'

'It was a small stone,' murmured Bazo, the words and blue smoke mingled on his lips. 'And fifteen years is a long time.'

'He is alive,' Ralph pointed out and took the cheroot that Bazo passed back to him. 'In the old days before the Diamond Trade Act, he would be dead by now.'

'He might as well be dead,' Bazo whispered bitterly. 'They say that men work like animals, chained like monkeys, on the breakwater wall at Cape Town harbour.'

He drew again on the cheroot and it burned down with a fierce little glow that scorched his fingers. He crushed it out on the workhardened calluses of his palm and let the shreds of tobacco blow away.

'And you, Henshaw – are you then so happy?' he asked quietly, and Ralph shrugged.

'Happy? Who is happy?'

'Is not this pit' – with a gesture Bazo took in the mighty excavation over which they dangled – 'is not this your prison, does it not hold you as surely as the chains that hold Donsela as he places the rocks on the breakwater over the sea?'

They had almost reached the high stagings and Bazo slipped off his canvas covering before he could be spotted by one of the black constables who patrolled the area inside the new security fences.

'You ask me if I am unhappy.' Bazo stood up, and did not look at Ralph's face. 'I was thinking of the land in which I am a prince of the House of Kumalo. In that land the calves I tended as a boy have grown into bulls and have bred calves which I have never seen. Once I knew every beast in my father's herds, fifteen thousand head of prime cattle, and I knew each of them, the season of its birth, the twist of its horns and the markings of its hide.'

Bazo sighed and came to stand beside Ralph on the rim of the skip. They were of a height, two tall young men, well formed, and each, in the manner of his race, comely.

'Ten times I have not been with my impi when it danced the Festival of Fresh Fruits, ten times I did not witness my king throw the war-spear and send us out on the red road.'

Bazo's sombre mood deepened, and his voice sank lower.

'Boys have grown to men since I left, and some of them wear the cowtails of valour on their legs and arms.' Bazo glanced down at his own naked body with its single dirty rag at the waist. 'Little girls have grown into maidens, with ripe bellies, ready to be claimed by the warriors who have won the honour on the red road of war.' And both of them thought of the lonely nights when the phantoms came to haunt them. Then Bazo folded his arms across his wide chest and went on.

'I think of my father, and I wonder if the snows of age have yet settled upon his head. Every man of my tribe that comes down the road from the north brings me the words of Juba, the Dove, who is my mother. She has twelve sons, but I am the first and the eldest of them.'

'Why have you stayed so long?' Ralph asked harshly.

'Why have you stayed so long, Henshaw?' The young Matabele challenged him quietly, and Ralph had no answer.

'Have you found fame and riches in this hole?' Again they both glanced down into the pit, and from this height the off-shift waiting to come up in the skips were like columns of safari ants.

'Do you have a woman with hair as long and pale as the winter grass to give you comfort in the night, Henshaw? Do you have the music of your sons' laughter to cheer you, Henshaw? What keeps you here?'

Ralph lifted his eyes and stared at Bazo, but before he could find an answer the skip came level with the platform on the first ramp of the stagings. The jerk brought Ralph back to reality and he waved to his father on the platform above them.

The roar of the steam winch subsided. The skip slowed and Bazo led the party of Matabele workers onto the ramp. Ralph saw them all clear before he jumped across the narrow gap to the wooden platform and felt it tremble under the combined weight of twenty men.

Ralph signalled again. Then the winch growled, and the steel cable squealed in its sheaves. The heavy-laden skip ran on until it hit the striker blocks. Ralph and Bazo drove the jumper bars under it, and threw their full weight on them. The skip tipped over, and the load of gravel went roaring down the chute into the waiting cart.

Ralph looked up to see his father's encouraging smile and to hear his shouted congratulations.

'Well done, boy! Two hundred tons today!'

But the staging was deserted. Zouga had gone.

Zouga had packed a single chest, the chest that had belonged to Aletta and which had come up with her from the Cape. Now it was going back, and it was almost all that was going back.

Zouga put Aletta's Bible in the bottom of the chest, and with it her diary and the trinket box which contained the remaining pieces of her jewellery. The more valuable pieces had long ago been sold, to support the dying dream.

Over these few mementoes he packed his own diaries and maps, and his books. When he came to the bundled pile of his unfinished manuscript, he paused to weigh it in his hand.

'Perhaps I shall find time to finish it now,' he murmured, and laid it gently in the chest.

On top of that went his clothing, and there was so little of that – four shirts, a spare pair of boots – barely an armful.

The chest was only half-full, and he carried it easily down the steps into the yard. That was all that he was taking – the rest of it, the meagre furnishings of the bungalow he had sold to one of the auctioneers in Market Square. Ten pounds the lot. As Rhodes had predicted, he was leaving as he had come.

'Where is Ralph?' he demanded of Jan Cheroot, and the little Hottentot paused in chaining the cooking-pot and black iron kettle onto the tailboard of the cart.

'Perhaps he stopped at Diamond Lil's. The boy has got a right to his thirst – he worked hard enough for it.'

Zouga let it pass, and instead ran an appraising eye over the cart. It was the newest and strongest of the three vehicles he owned. One cart had gone with Louise St John, and she had taken the best mules – but this rig would get them back to Cape Town, even under the additional burden that he was planning to put into it.

Jan Cheroot ambled across to Zouga and took the other handle of the chest, ready to boost it up into the body of the cart.

'Wait,' Zouga told him. 'That first.' And he pointed to the roughly-hewn block of blue mottled rock that lay below the camel-thorn tree.

'My mother –' Jan Cheroot gaped. 'This I don't believe. In twenty-two years I've seen you do some stupid crazy things –'

Zouga strode across to the block of blue ground that Ralph had brought up from the Devil's Own and put his foot on it. 'We'll hoist it up with the block and tackle.' He glanced at the sturdy branch above his head from which the sheave block and manila rope hung. 'And we'll back the cart up under it.'

'That's it!' Jan Cheroot sat down on the chest and folded his arms. 'This time I refuse. Once before I broke my back for you, but that was when I was young and stupid.'

'Come on, Jan Cheroot, you are wasting time.'

'What do you want with that – piece of ugly bloody stone? With another piece of thundering nonsense.'

'I have lost the bird – I need a household god.'

'I have heard of someone putting up a monument to a brave man, or a great battle – but to put up a stone to stupidity,' Jan Cheroot mourned.

'Back the cart up.'

'I refuse – this time I refuse. I won't do it. Not for anything. Not for any price.'

'When we get it loaded – you can have a bottle of smoke all to yourself to celebrate.'

Jan Cheroot sighed, and stood up. 'That's my price.' He shook his head and came across to stand beside Zouga. He glared at the block of blue stone venomously. 'But don't expect me to like it.'

Zouga chuckled, for the first time in weeks, and in an unusual display of affection he put one arm around Jan Cheroot's shoulders.

'Now that you have something to hate again – just think how happy it will make you,' he said.

'You have been drinking,' Zouga said, and Ralph tossed his hat into the corner and agreed.

'Yes, I have had a beer or two.' He went to the black iron stove and warmed his hands. 'I would have had more – if I had had the money.'

'I have been waiting for you,' Zouga went on, and Ralph turned back to him truculently.

'I give you every hour of my day, Papa – let me have a little time at the end of it.'

'I have something of great importance to tell you,' Zouga nodded to the deal chair facing him. 'Sit down, Ralph.'

Zouga rubbed his eyes with forefinger and thumb as he collected his words. He had tried so often in the last days to find an easy way to tell Ralph that it was over, that they were destitute, that all that toil and heartbreak had been in vain – but there was no easy way. There were only the stark hard words of reality.

He dropped his hand, and looked at his son, and then slowly and carefully he told him, and when he had finished he waited for Ralph to speak. Ralph had not moved during the long recital, and now he stared at Zouga stonily.

Zouga was forced to speak again. 'We shall leave in the morning. Jan Cheroot and I have loaded the No. 2 wagon and we shall need all the mules, double team – it's a long haul.'

Again he waited, but there was still no reaction.

'You will be wondering where we are going and what we shall do. Well, once we get back to the Cape we still have the Harkness cottage.'

'You gambled it all.' Ralph spoke at last. 'Without telling me. You – you, who are always preaching to me about gambling, and honesty.'

'Ralph!'

'It wasn't yours, it belonged to all of us.'

'You are drunk,' Zouga said flatly.

'All these years I have listened to your promises. We shall go north, Ralph.' He mimicked Zouga with a sudden savagery in his tone. 'It's for all of us, Ralph. It's yours to share. There is a land waiting for us, Ralph. It will be yours as well as mine, Ralph.'

'It's not over – I still have the concession. When we get back to Cape Town–'

'You, not me.' Ralph's voice was flat, angry. 'You go back to Cape Town. Go dream your old man's dreams. I am sick of them.'

'You dare to use that tone to me?'

'Yes, I dare. And by God, I'll dare more than that. I'll dare what you are too weak or afraid to dare–'

'You insolent and stupid puppy!'

'You toothless old dog!'

Zouga threw himself half across the table, and his right arm lashed out. He caught Ralph open-handed across the face, and the crack of palm on flesh was stunning as a pistol shot.

Ralph's head snapped back, and then slowly he brought it upright again. 'That,' he said, 'is the last time you will strike me, ever.' He stood up and strode towards the door, and there he turned. 'Go dream your dreams – I will go live mine out.'

'Go then,' said Zouga, and the scar on his cheek was glassy and white as ice. 'Go and be damned to you.'

'Remember I took nothing with me, Papa, not even your blessing,' said Ralph, and stepped out into the night.

Bazo woke instantly at the touch on his cheek, and reached for the assegai at his side, his eyes wide in the faint glow of the ashes. A hand closed on his wrist, holding his spear hand from the weapon, and a voice spoke softly above him.

'Do you remember the road to Matabeleland, O Prince of Kumalo?'

It took Bazo a moment to gather his wits from where sleep had scattered them.

'I remember every running ford and every green hill, every sweet watering place along the way,' he whispered back, 'as clearly as I remember my father's voice and my mother's laughter.'

'Roll up your sleeping-mat, Bazo, the Axe, and show me the road,' said Ralph.

Diamond Lil did not smile so readily these days, not since the tooth that held the diamond had turned a dingy grey as the root died, and began to ache until Lil wept with the little explosion of agony against the top of her skull. The travelling dentist from the Cape had pulled the tooth and drained the virulent abscess beneath it.

Relief had been immediate, but it left a black gap in her smile.

She had put on flesh also, the consequence of good food and those little nips of gin which bolstered her day. Her breasts, always generous, had lost their individual definition and the cleavage that showed above the richly embroidered bodice was no longer a deeply sculptured crevasse but a thin line where abundant flesh packed against flesh.

The hand that held the bone china teacup was pudgy and dimpled over the knuckles, the rings that adorned each plump little finger had sunk into the flesh, but the diamonds and rubies and emeralds sparkled in a royal show of Lil's wealth.

Her hair was still lustrous gold, and crimped into long dangling ringlets with the hot-iron. Her skin was still smooth and rich as Devon cream, except around the eyes where it was just beginning to crack into little spider webs of lines.

She sat at the corner of the verandah, on the second floor above the street, where the eaves of the roof were of intricate white wrought-iron mouldings, pretty as Madeira lace. Although there were other double-storeyed buildings in Kimberley these days, not even the offices of the Central Diamond Company across the wide unpaved street boasted such affluent adornment.

Lil's chair was high-backed, and magnificently carved in dark red teak by oriental craftsmen, inlaid with mother-of-pearl and ivory and carried across the eastern oceans by the tall ships of the now long departed Dutch East India Company. It had cost her two hundred pounds, but from this throne she could watch every movement on the main thoroughfares that fed into Market Square, could sense the pulse of the diamond city, could check each coming and going, the scurry of a buyer with a good scent in his nostrils, the swagger of a digger who had turned up a bright one. She could watch the front of the four canteens around the square, all of which she now owned, and judge the volume of trade going through their doors.

Similarly, she could glance to her left, down De Beers Road to the red-brick cottage behind its white picket fence and discreet sign, 'French Dressmakers. Haute Couture. Six Continental Seamstresses. Specialities for individual tastes.' Business was always brisk there – from noon to midnight. Her girls seldom lasted the pace for more than six months or so – before taking the coach southward again, exhausted but considerably richer.

Lil herself worked her old trade only occasionally, perhaps once or twice a week with a favoured 'regular', just for old times' sake, and because it got her blood going and made her sleep better at night. There was too much else that required her constant attention.

Now she poured fresh tea from the rococo silver pot into the pretty bone china cups, hand-painted with pink roses and golden butterflies.

'How many spoons?' she asked.

Ralph sat on the cane-back chair opposite her. He smelled of shaving soap and cheap eau-de-Cologne. His chin shone with a burnish given it by the cut-throat razor, and his shirt was so crisply ironed and starched that it crackled at each movement.

Lil studied him speculatively over the rim of her teacup.

'Does the good major know your plans?' she asked quietly, and Ralph shook his head. Lil thought on that a while and it gave her a ripple of pleasure to have the son of a foundation member of the Kimberley Club sitting on her verandah. Son of one of the Kimberley gentlemen who would not greet her on the street, who had returned her donation towards the new hospital, who had not even replied to her invitation to attend the stone-laying ceremony of her new building – oh, the list of humiliations was too long to recite now.

'Why did you not go to your father?' she asked instead.

'My father is not a rich man.' Ralph would not say any more, too loyal to explain that Zouga was destitute, that he would soon leave Kimberley with a cartload of his meagre possessions. He did not want Lil to know that he and his father had turned from each other with harsh words.

Lil studied his face for a moment, then picked up the handwritten sheet of cheap notepaper from the tea tray and glanced down the list and the figures.

'Nine hundred pounds for oxen?'

'A full span of the biggest and best animals,' Ralph explained. 'The road to the Shashi river is sand veld, heavy going. I want to be able to haul a full load, eight thousand pounds weight.'

'Trade goods – fifteen thousand.' She looked up at him again.

'Guns, powder, brandy, beads and limbo cloth.'

'What type of guns?'

'Tower muskets. Five pounds ten shillings each.'

Lil shook her head. 'They have seen the breech-loaders. Your muskets won't have much pull.'

'I can't afford breech-loaders, and I wouldn't know where to find a load.'

'Ralph dearie, I could hire a bunch of Whitechapel hags to run my dressmakers' shop and I could get them cheap. But I don't. I pick them young and fresh and pretty. If you think small, your profits are small. Don't be cheap, Ralph darling, never be cheap.' She poured a little gin from the silver flask into the empty teacup before she went on. 'I can get Martini-Henry rifles but they will cost us fifteen hundred more.' Lil reached across and dipped her pen in the ink-well, then scratched out and re-wrote the figure.

'Brandy?'

'Cape Smoke in twenty-gallon casks.'

'I have heard that Lobengula likes Courvoisier cognac, and his sister Ningi drinks only Piper-Heidsieck champagne.'

'Another five hundred pounds – at least,' Ralph mourned.

'Three hundred,' Lil corrected the list. 'I can get it at wholesale prices. Now, ammunition – ten thousand rounds?'

'I'll need at least a thousand for my own account, and the rest to trade with the rifles.'

'If Lobengula gives you permission to hunt elephant,' Lil corrected.

'My grandfather is one of his oldest friends; my Aunty Robyn and her husband have been at Khami River Mission for almost twenty years.'

'Yes, I know that you have friends at court.' Lil pursed her lips approvingly. 'But I have heard that the elephant have been shot out across the whole of Matabeleland.'

'The herds have been driven into the fly belt on the Zambezi.'

'You cannot take horses into the fly and hunting elephant on foot in the fly is not work for a white man.'

'My father hunted on foot, and anyway I cannot afford a horse.'

'All right,' she agreed reluctantly, and made a tick on the sheet.

They worked on for an hour longer, going down the list item by item – and then starting again at the head and going over it all once more, Lil ticking and scratching with the pen – fining it down by ten pounds here and a hundred there, until at last she tossed the pen onto the tea tray, and then poured a little more gin into her tea cup and sipped it with a genteel flourish, her little finger raised, the spirit slurping softly through the gap in the front of her teeth.

'All right,' she said again.

'Does that mean you will lend me the money?'

'Yes.'

'I don't know what to say.' He leaned towards her, young and glowing and eager. 'Lil, I just don't–'

'Then don't say anything until you have heard my terms.' She smiled thinly, without lifting her upper lip.

'Twenty per cent per annum interest on the loan.'

'Twenty per cent!' he gasped. 'In God's name – that's usury, Lily!'

'Exactly,' she told him primly. 'But let me finish. Twenty per cent interest and half the profits.'

'And half, Lil – that's not usury, that's highway robbery.'

'Right again,' she agreed. 'At least you are bright enough to recognize it.'

'Can't we just –' he started desperately.

'No, we cannot. Those are my terms.' And Ralph remembered Scipio, his falcon, with her beautiful pouting breast and fierce cold eyes.

'I accept,' he said, and though she did not smile with her lips, her eyes were suddenly soft and merry.

'Partners,' she murmured, and placed her plump white hand on his forearm. His muscles were lean and sinewy, the skin brick-coloured from the sun. She stroked it slowly, sensually.

'It only remains to seal our bargain,' she told Ralph. 'Come!' She slid her hand down his arm and twined her fingers into his.

She led him through the stained-glass doors, and when she drew the velvet corded curtains it was cool and dark in the room. She turned back to him and reached up to unbutton his shirt at the throat. He stood still while she worked her way down slowly to his belt buckle, and then she placed one hand, palm down, upon his naked right breast.

'Ralph,' her voice was a husky tremor. 'I want you to do something for me.'

'What is it?' he asked, and she stood on her tiptoes, placed her lips against his ear and told him in a whisper. She felt him begin to pull back from under her hand.

'Partners?' she asked, and he hesitated a moment longer and then stooped and picked her up, one arm behind her knees, and carried her to the wide brass bed with the patchwork quilt.

'You will find it less arduous than hunting elephant on foot in the fly,' she told him, and it was dark enough in the room for her not to worry about the missing tooth.

She lifted her arms above her head, opened her mouth and chuckled in delicious anticipation.

'The good thing about life, dearie, is that you can have whatever you want, just as long as you are willing to pay the price,' she told him, still chuckling.

'These are not bullocks,' Bazo told Ralph. 'Each one is the son of a snake mated with the ghost of a Mashona dog.'

They were all strong oxen, big-boned, heavy in the shoulder, with wide straight horns for strength and even yellow teeth – hand-picked by Bazo, who was a Matabele and loved cattle, had lived with the great herds since he was old enough to toddle after the calves.

However, Bazo was not a trek man. He had never worked an eighteen-foot wagon, with an eight-thousand-pound load aboard. He had never tried to put twenty-four trek oxen into the traces.

The entire Matabele nation owned only a pair of wheeled vehicles, and those belonged to King Lobengula. To Bazo cattle were a store of wealth, a source of meat and milk – they were not draught animals. The closest that either he or Ralph had ever come to putting a team into the traces was working the little two-wheel gravel carts.

Ralph had assumed that the oxen he had purchased were trained and amiable, but within minutes of his and Bazo's first attempt to get them into span, the animals sensed their incompetence and became as spooky and wild as hunted buffalo.

It took two hours of wild chasing across the bleak grasslands beyond the town limits, two hours of running and cursing and whip-cracking to bring the bullocks together and get the yokes upon their necks. Half of them were badly winded by then and promptly lay down, and the others backed out and turned their great horned heads towards the load, tangling the trek chain and plunging the entire span into chaos.

The excitement had brought out most of the loafers and idlers from the canteens on Market Square, though they had enough forethought to bring their bottles with them. They formed an appreciative and jovial audience, greeting each new effort by Bazo and Ralph with delighted guffaws and facetious advice.

Bazo wiped the sweat from his face and chest, and looked broodingly down the dusty road to town.

'Soon Bakela will hear of this and come to see our disgrace,' he said.

Ralph had not seen his father since that stormy night, but he had visited Jordan in his tiny office next door to Mr Rhodes in the magnificent new Central Diamond Company building on De Beers Street.

Perhaps Zouga Ballantyne had not yet recovered from the shock of being deserted by both his sons, but Jordan said that he had not yet left for Cape Town.

The thought of his father witnessing this humiliating scene brought dark blood to Ralph's face, and he fired the long trek whip, at least that was one trick he had learned, and bellowed at the span.

'*Nkosana!*' There was a salutation at the level of Ralph's elbow, the mild tone belied by the mocking title.

'*Nkosi*' was a chief, and '*Nkosana*' was the condescending diminutive – usually reserved for a little white boy, an untried child.

Ralph turned and glared at the speaker, who went on to explain in the same condescending tone. 'Only one beast in ten will pull in front.' He pointed out one of the oxen. 'That one there is a lead ox. Any man who knows oxen can see that with both his eyes closed.'

He was a little black gnome, not as tall as Ralph's shoulder. His face was wrinkled and lined like that of a very old man, his eyes were mere slits in the merry smiling folds – but his cap of woolly hair and his little goatee beard were unmarred by a single strand of grey, and his teeth were even and white, the teeth of a man in his full flowering.

On his head was the polished black ring of the induna, and about his waist was a kilt of wild cat tails. Over that he wore a threadbare military-type tunic from which all insignia and buttons had been stripped, leaving small punctures in the fabric, some of which had enlarged into rents from which the lining peaked coyly. In the pierced lobe of one ear, he carried an ivory snuff-box, and in the other lobe a snuff spoon of the same material and a toothpick of porcupine quill. The language he used was very close to Matabele, but it preserved the ancient intonation and classic word structures of Zululand.

So when Ralph asked 'Zulu?' the question was redundant, and the little man shot a contemptuous glance at Bazo.

'Pure Zulu, not the treacherous house of Kumalo, of the traitor Mzilikazi who denied a king and whose blood is now so watered by Venda and Tswana and Mashona that they can no longer tell you if an ox grows horns on its head or on its testicles.'

Bazo bridled instantly. 'Hark!' He cocked his head. 'Do I hear a small baboon barking his boasts from the top of the kopjes?'

The little Zulu grinned at him mirthlessly, and took the stock whip from Ralph's sweaty hands. Then he walked to the tangled span with a jaunty step.

He touched the big black ox on the neck. 'Hau, Sathan!' he greeted him, and at the same time baptized him 'Devil'.

The great ox rolled one eye at him, seemed to recognize his assurance and immediately quietened. The little Zulu loosed him and took him forward, talking to him easily in a bizarre mixture of Zulu, English and the Cape Dutch taal, and chained him into the lead position.

He went back quickly and pulled the red ox out of the tangle by the rein about his horns.

'Dutchman –' he named him, for no good reason. 'Come, you red thunder!'

And he put him into the lead file beside Sathan and called to them quietly.

'*Donsa*, Sathan, pull. *Pakamisa*, Dutchman, pick up the chain!' Obediently the pair of bullocks straightened their forelegs and leaned forward against the yoke – and a miracle happened. The long heavy silver chain from the disselboom came up straight and hard as an iron bar, and those animals on the ground were forced to lunge up onto their feet, those that had backed out were pulled into the span, horns and heads pointing forward. In that moment Ralph learned the single most important rule of the open road, keep the chain straight and true, and all else is possible.

Now the little Zulu moved with a deceptively casual air along the double rank of bullocks, touching and talking and wheedling.

'Hey! Fransman, I can see by your wise and beautiful eyes that you were born to the wheel!' And the sturdy black and white beast was led back to his position at the off-wheel.

It took ten minutes, and then the Zulu put the long lash into the air. It hissed like a black mamba and then snaked forward over the ears of the team, not touching a single hair as it fired explosively. The heavy wagon jolted, the white canvas tent that covered the rear half of the long body shook like the unfurling mainsail of a tall ship and then it was rolling away smoothly.

The Zulu crinkled his eyes at Ralph and called a question. '*Yapi*? Where? Which way?'

'*Yakato!* North!' Ralph shouted back joyously, and despite himself Bazo snatched up his war shield and assegai and whirled into a frenzied challenge dance, leaping and stabbing at a host of imaginary enemies, shouting defiance and ecstasy to all the world.

The road to the Vaal river was the first leg of the journey, and the ruts were axle deep, and red soil raw as a fresh wound, the dust a fog in the windless air through which it was just possible to make out the horns of the two wheeler bullocks. The dust hid from Ralph his parting view of the sprawling town, and its high stagings above the gaping hole which had been his home and his prison for so many years, and by the time that the other traffic on the road had thinned sufficiently for the dust cloud to settle, they had made five miles and the stagings might have been merely a distant line of dead thorn trees silhouetted against the sunset.

The little Zulu called to his boy who led the front oxen, and the child swung them off the road, and the high rear wheels bumped out of the ruts and then crunched through crisp winter grass as the wagon rolled towards a spreading umbrella-shaped acacia which would give them shelter and firewood for the night.

Walking at the front wheel Ralph pondered the two unexpected additions to his company.

The child had come out of the curtain of red dust, naked except for the little flap of his *mutsha* in front, and with the roll of sleeping-mat and the cooking-pot balanced upon his head.

He had placed these meagre possessions on the tailboard of the wagon and then, at a nod and a word from the Zulu, had taken the lead rein and plodded solemnly ahead of the span, his bare feet sinking ankle-deep in the powder dust.

Ralph wondered how old he was, and decided he could not be more than ten years of age.

'What is his name?' he asked the Zulu.

'A name?' The little man shrugged. 'It is not important. Call him Umfaan – the Boy.'

'And what is your name?' Ralph went on, but the little driver suddenly had urgent business at the head of the span and perhaps the dust had clogged his ears for he did not seem to hear the question.

Ralph had to ask the question again, after the outspan, when the Zulu was squatting beside the cooking fire watching Umfaan stir the maize-meal in the black pot.

'What is your name?' And the Zulu smiled as though at a secret thought, and then he said:

'A name can be dangerous, it can hover over a man like a vulture and mark him for death. Before the soldiers came to the royal kraal at Ulundi, I was called one thing –'

Ralph stirred uncomfortably at the reference to the battle that had ended the Zulu War. The tattered tunic that the Zulu wore had once been the same dark blue as that of the Natal police uniform and one of those rents in the faded cloth might have been made by the stabbing blade. Lord Chelmsford had sent the Zulu king and most of his indunas in chains to the island of St Helena, where another emperor had died in captivity. However, some of his fighting chiefs had escaped from Zululand and now wandered homeless exiles across the vast continent. The driver wore the head-ring of an induna.

' – It was a name which men once spoke carefully, but I have not heard it for so long now that I have forgotten it,' the Zulu went on, and again Ralph wondered if there was a legend still alive amongst the defeated Zulu of a little induna, smaller than the tall warriors he commanded and wizened far beyond his years, who had led them in that terrible charge into the English camp below the Hill of the Little Hand.

In the firelight Ralph studied the Zulu's tunic again, and he told himself that it was unlikely that it had been taken from the corpse of an Englishman on that grisly field; yet he shivered briefly although the night was warm.

'Now you have forgotten that name?' he encouraged, and the Zulu crinkled his eyes again.

'Now I am called Isazi, the Wise One, for reasons that should be clear even to a Matabele.'

Across the fire Bazo snorted disdainfully, then stood and walked out of the fire-light, into the darkness where the jackals piped plaintively.

'My name is Henshaw,' Ralph told him. 'Will you stay with me and drive my wagon all the way?'

'Why not, Little Hawk?'

'You do not ask where I am going.'

'I need a road.' Isazi shrugged. 'The one to the north is no longer or harder than the road to the south.'

The jackal yipped again, but much closer this time, and Bazo paused, changed the assegai to his right hand, and answered the cry, cupping his palm over his mouth to give resonance to the sound; and then he moved on to where a small stone kopje shone in the moonlight like a pile of silver bullion.

'Bazo.' The greeting was a whisper, soft as the night wind in the pale grass, and a shadow stepped from amongst the moon shadows at the base of the kopje.

'Kamuza, my brother.' Bazo went to him and embraced him, open hands upon his shoulders.

'I have a stone in my belly, heavy with sorrow at this parting.'

'We will share the road again – one day, we will drink from the beer pot and fight with our shoulders touching–' Kamuza answered him quietly. 'But now we are both upon the king's business.'

Kamuza slipped the thongs that held his kilt in place, and it sagged heavily to his knees, leaving him naked.

'Hurry,' he said. 'I must return before the curfew bell.' Since the Diamond Trade Act, blacks were not allowed on the streets of Kimberley once the curfew bell had rung.

'You were not marked by the police?' Bazo asked, as he removed his own kilt and changed it with Kamuza.

'They are everywhere, like pepper ticks in the new spring grass,' Kamuza grunted. 'But I was not followed.'

Bazo weighed the fur kilt in both hands while Kamuza swiftly belted the replacement about his own waist.

'Show me,' Bazo said, and Kamuza took the kilt back from his hands and spread it on one of the flat moon-washed boulders.

He picked at the knotted thong that doubled the waistband, and as it came undone he opened the secret pouch of soft tanned leather, crusted with ceramic trade beads. The pouch ran the full length of the wide waistband, the opening concealed by the decorative beadwork, and the interior of the long pouch was divided into cells, like a wasp's nest.

In each stitched leather cell nestled a large pebble that glistened with a slick soapy sheen in the moonlight.

'Count them,' Kamuza instructed. 'Let us agree on the number – and let Lobengula, the great Black Elephant, count the same number into his mighty hands when you lay the belt before him at the kraal of GuBulawayo, the place of killing.'

Bazo touched each diamond with his fingertip, his lips moving silently. '*Amashumi amatatu*!'

'Thirty,' Kamuza repeated. 'It is agreed.'

And they were all large clean stones, the smallest the size of the first joint of a man's little finger.

Bazo tied the kilt about his waist, the fleecy tails of the bat-eared fox dangling to his knees.

'It looks well upon you,' Kamuza nodded, and then went on. 'Tell Lobengula, the Great Elephant, that I am his dog and I grovel in the dirt at his feet. Tell him that there will be more of the yellow coins and the bright stones. Tell him that his children labour each day in the pit – and there will be more, many more. Every man who takes the road north will bring him riches.' Kamuza stepped forward and laid his right hand on Bazo's shoulder.

'Go in peace, Bazo the Axe.'

'Stay in peace, my brother, and may the days disappear like raindrops into the desert sand until we smile upon each other once more.'

Isazi put the span to its first real test in the drift of the Vaal river.

The grey waters were barely flowing, but they covered the hubs of the tall iron-shod rear wheels, and the bottom was broken waterworn rock that clanked and rolled under pressure, threatening to jam the wheels and denying purchase to the driving hooves of the span.

Yet they ran the wagon through under load, leaning into the yokes, noses down almost touching the surface of the river, and the wagon tent jolting and rocking behind them.

Until, under the steep cut up the far bank, the rear wheels stuck and the wagon bed tilted alarmingly. Then Isazi showed his expertise. He swung the team wide, giving them a run at it, and when he called to his leaders and burst the air asunder with the thirty-foot lash that tapered to the thickness of twine they went in stiff-legged, jerked her clear, and took the load out of the river bed at a canter, while Isazi pranced and sang their praises and even Umfaan smiled.

Ralph ordered an early outspan under the tall trees on the far bank, for there was good grass and unlimited water, and the next leg of the road to his grandfather Moffat's mission station was a hundred and twenty miles, hard and dry going all the way.

'See, Little Hawk,' Isazi was still rapturous over the performance of his span. '- See how clever they are. They pick a good patch of grass and eat it up; they do not wander from patch to patch, wasting their time and strength, as lesser beasts might do. Soon they will settle with the cud, and in the morning they will be strong and rested. Each of them is a prince among cattle!'

'From tomorrow we begin night marches,' Ralph ordered, and Isazi's smile faded and he looked severe.

'I had already made that decision,' he said sternly, 'but where did you ever hear of night marching, Little Hawk? It is a trick of the wise ones.'

'Count me amongst them then, Isazi,' Ralph told him solemnly, and walked out of camp to find a place upon the riverbank from which to enjoy the sunset.

Here the banks of the Vaal were churned into mounds and irregular hollows, the old river workings, picked over by the first diggers and now abandoned and overgrown. It was a mass burial ground of men's dreams, and looking upon it Ralph's high spirits that had buoyed this first day's trek upon the open road began to evaporate.

It was the first day in his life that Ralph had been free and completely his own man. Walking at the wheel of his own wagon, he had woven dreams of fortune. He had imagined his wagons – fifty, a hundred – carrying his cargoes across the continent. He had seen them coming south again, loaded with ivory and bars of yellow gold. He had seen in his mind's eye the wide lands, the herds of elephant, the masses of native cattle, the riches that lay out there in the north beckoning to him, warbling the siren call in his ears.

He had been carried so high that now as his spirits turned they fell as low. He looked at the deserted diggings on the banks across the river, the vain scratchings where other men had attempted to turn this great brown slumbering giant of a continent to their own account.

Then suddenly he felt very small and lonely, and afraid. His thoughts turned to his father, and his spirits plunged lower still as he recalled the last words he had spoken.

'Go then! Go and be damned to you.'

That was not the way he had wanted it. Zouga Ballantyne had been the central figure in his life until that day. A colossus who overshadowed each of his actions, each of his thoughts.

Much as he had chafed under the shackles that his duty to his father had placed upon him, much as he had resented every one of his decisions being made for him, each of his actions ordered, yet now he felt as though the greater part of himself had been removed by some drastic surgery of the soul.

Until this moment he had not really thought of losing his father, he had not let the memory of their brutal parting cut him too deeply. Now suddenly this dirty slow river was the barrier between him and the life he had known. There was no going back – now or ever. He had lost his father and his brother and Jan Cheroot and he was alone and lonely. He felt the acid tears scald his eyelids.

His vision wavered, played him tricks, for across the wide river course, on the far bank was the figure of a horseman.

The horseman slouched easily in the saddle, one hand on his hip, the elbow cocked; and the set of the head upon the broad shoulders was unmistakable.

Slowly Ralph came to his feet, staring in disbelief, and then suddenly he was running and sliding down the sheer bank and splashing waist deep through the grey waters of the ford. Zouga swung down from Tom's back and ran forward to meet Ralph as he came up the bank.

Then both of them stopped and stared at each other. They had not embraced since the night of Aletta's funeral, and they could not bring themselves to do so now, though longing was naked in the eyes of both of them.

'I could not let you go, not like that,' said Zouga, but Ralph had no reply, for his throat had closed.

'It is time for you to go out on your own,' Zouga nodded his golden beard. 'Past time. You are like an eaglet that has outgrown the nest. I realized that before you did, Ralph, but I did not want it to be. That is why I spoke so cruelly.'

Zouga picked up Tom's reins and the pony nudged him affectionately. Zouga stroked his velvety muzzle.

'There are two parting gifts that I have for you.' He placed the reins in Ralph's hand. 'That is one,' he said evenly, but the green shadows in his eyes betrayed how dearly that gesture had cost him. 'The other is in Tom's saddle-bag. It's a book of notes. Read them at your leisure. You may find them of interest – even of value.'

Still Ralph could not speak. He held the reins awkwardly, and blinked back the stinging under his eyelids.

'There is one other small gift, but it has no real value. It is only my blessing.'

'That is all that I really wanted,' whispered Ralph.

It was six hundred miles to the Shashi river, to the border of Matabeleland.

Isazi inspanned at dusk each evening and they trekked through the cool of the night. When the moon went down and it was utterly dark, then Umfaan threw the lead rein over Dutchman's head, and the big black ox put his nose down and stayed on the track, like a hunting dog on the spoor, until the first glimmering of dawn signalled the outspan.

During a good night's trek they made fifteen miles – but when the going was heavy with sand they might make only five miles.

During the days, while the cattle grazed or chewed the cud in the shade, Ralph saddled up Tom and, with Bazo running beside his stirrup, they hunted.

They found herds of buffalo along the banks of the Zouga river, the river on whose bank Ralph's father had been born, big herds, two hundred beasts together.

The herd bulls were huge, bovine and bald with age, their backs crusted with the mud from the wallow, the spread of their armoured heads wider than the stretch of a man's arms, the tips of the polished black horns rising into symmetrical crescents like the points of the sickle moon, while the bosses above their broad foreheads were massively crenellated.

They ran them down, and Tom loved those wild flying chases every bit as much as his rider.

They chased the ghostly grey gemsbuck over the smoking red dunes, and in the thorn country they hunted the stilt-legged giraffe and sent their grotesque but stately bodies plunging and sliding to earth with the crack of rifle fire, the long graceful necks twisting in the agony of death like that of a swan.

They baited with the carcasses of zebra, and the coppery red Kalahari lions came to the taint of blood, and Tom stood down their charge. Though he trembled and snorted and rolled his eyes at the shockingly offensive cat smell, he stood for the shot which Ralph took from the saddle, aiming between the fierce yellow eyes or into the gape of rose-pink jaws starred with white fangs.

Thus, fifty days out from Kimberley they came at last to the Shashi river, and when they had made the crossing Bazo was on his native soil. He put on his war plumes and carrying his shield on his shoulder he walked with a new spring and joy in his stride as he led Ralph to a hilltop from which to survey the way ahead.

'See how the hills shine,' Bazo whispered with an almost religious fervour. And it was true. In the early sunlight the granite tops gleamed like precious jewels. Soft, dreaming, ruby, delicate sapphires and glossy pearl shaded like a peacock tail into a fanfare of colour.

The hills rolled away, rising gradually towards the high central plateau ahead of them, and the valleys were clad with virgin forest.

'You never saw such trees on the plains around Kimberley,' Bazo challenged him, and Ralph nodded. They stood on soaring trunks, some scaled like the crocodile, others white and smooth as though moulded from potter's clay, their tops sailing in traceries of green high above the open glades of yellow grass.

'See, the buffalo herds – thick as cattle.'

There was other game. There were small family groups of grey kudo, pale as ghosts, trumpet-eared, the bulls carrying the burden of their long black cork-screw horns with studied grace.

There were clouds of red impala antelope upon the woven silk carpet of golden grasses. There were the darkly massive statues of the rhinoceros seemingly graven from the solid granite of the hills, and there were the noblest antelope of all, the sable antelope, black and imperial as the name implied, the long horns curved and cruel as Saladin's scimitar, the belly blazing white, the neck of the herd bull arched haughtily as he led his lighter coloured females out of the open glade into the cool green sanctuary of the forest.

'Is it not beautiful, Henshaw?' Bazo asked.

'It is beautiful.'

There was the same awe in Ralph's voice, and a strange unformed longing in his throat, a wanting that he knew could never be satisfied – and suddenly he understood his own father's obsession with this fair land: 'My north,' as Zouga called it.

'My north,' Ralph whispered, and then, thinking of his father, the next question came immediately to mind.

'Elephant – *Indhlovu?* There are no elephant, Bazo. Where are the herds?'

'Ask Bakela – your own father,' Bazo grunted. 'He was the first to come for them with the gun, but others followed him, many others. When Gandang, my father, son of Mzilikazi the Destroyer, half brother of the great black bull Lobengula, when he crossed the Shashi as a child on his mother's hip, the elephant herds were black as midnight upon the land and their teeth shone like the stars. Now we will find their bones growing like white lilies in the forest.'

In the last hours of daylight, when Bazo and Isazi and Umfaan still slept to fortify themselves for the long night's trek, Ralph took the leather-bound notebook out of Tom's saddle-bag.

By now the pages were dog-eared and grubby from the constant perusal to which Ralph had subjected it. It was the gift that Zouga Ballantyne had given him on the bank of the Vaal river, and the inside cover was inscribed:

> To my son Ralph.
> May these few notes guide your feet
> northwards, and may they inspire you to

dare what I have not dared

Zouga Ballantyne

The first twenty pages were filled with hand-drawn sketch maps of those areas of the land between the Zambezi and the Limpopo and the Shashi rivers over which Zouga, and before him the old hunter Tom Harkness, had travelled.

Often the map was headed by the notation:

Copied from the original map drawn by Tom Harkness in 1851.

Ralph recognized the unique value of this information, but there was more. Page 21 of the notebook bore a terse explanation in Zouga's precise spiky hand:

In the winter of 1860 while on trek from Tete on the Zambezi river, to King Mzilikazi's town at Thabas Indunas I slew 216 elephant. Lacking porters or wagons I had perforce to cache the ivory along my route.

During my later expeditions to Zambezia, I was able to recover the bulk of this treasure.

There remain fifteen separate caches, containing eighty-four good tusks, which I was for various reasons unable to reach.

Here follows a list of these caches with directions and navigational notes to reach them:

And on page 22 the list began:

Cache made 16 September 1860.
Position by sun sight and dead reckoning:
30° 55' E.   17° 45' S.
A granite kopje which I named Mount Hampden. The largest for many miles in any direction. Distinct peak with three turrets. On the northern face between two large *ficus natalensis* trees there is a rock fissure. 18 large tusks total weight 426 pounds placed in fissure and covered with small boulders.

The current price of ivory was twenty-two shillings and sixpence the pound, and Ralph had added the total weights of the ivory still lying out in the veld. It exceeded three thousand pounds: a great fortune waiting merely to be picked up and loaded on his wagon.

Still that was not all. The final entry in the notebook read:

In my book *A Hunter's Odyssey* I described my discovery of the deserted city which the tribes call 'ZIMBABWE', a name which can be translated as 'The Grave-yard of the Kings'.

I described how I was able to glean fragments of gold from the inner court-yards of the walled ruins, a little over 50 lbs weight of the metal in all. I also carried away with me one of the ancient bird-like statues. A souvenir which has been with me from that time until very recently.

It is possible that there is precious metal which I overlooked, and certainly there remain within the walled enclosures six more bird carvings which I was unable to bring away.

In *Hunter's Odyssey* I deliberately refrained from giving the location of the ancient ruin. As far as I know, it has not been rediscovered by any other white man – while a superstitious taboo forbids any African to venture into the area.

Thus there is every reason to believe the statues lie where last I laid eyes upon them.

Bearing in mind that my chronometer had not been checked for many months when these observations were made, I now give you the position of the city as calculated by myself at that time.

The ruins lie on the same longitude as the kopje which I named Mount Hampden on 30° 55′ E. – but 175 miles farther south at 20° 0′ S.

There followed a detailed description of the route that Zouga had taken to reach Zimbabwe, and then the notes ended with this statement:

Mr Rhodes offered the sum of £1,000 for the statue which I rescued.

The following noon Ralph took the brass sextant from its travel-battered wooden case. He had bid ten shillings for it at one of the Saturday auctions in the Market Square of Kimberley – and Zouga had checked its accuracy against his own instrument and showed Ralph how to shoot an 'apparent local noon' to establish his latitude. Ralph had no chronometer to fix a longitude, but he could guess at it from his proximity to the confluence of the Shashi and Macloutsi rivers.

Half an hour's work with *Brown's Nautical Almanac* gave him an approximate position to compare with the one that his father had given in the notes for Zimbabwe.

'Less than one hundred and fifty miles,' he muttered to himself, still squatting over his father's map, but staring eastwards.

'Six thousand pounds just lying there,' Ralph said quietly, and shook his head in wonder. It was a sum difficult to imagine.

He packed away the sextant, rolled the map and went to join the slumbering trio beneath the wagon for what remained of the drowsy afternoon.

Ralph woke to a stentorian challenge that seemed to echo off the granite cliffs above the camp.

'Who dares take the king's road? Who chances the wrath of Lobengula?'

Ralph scrambled out from under the wagon. The day was almost gone, the sun flamed in the top branches of the forest, and the chill of evening prickled his bare chest. He stared about him wildly, but some instinct warned him not to reach for the loaded rifle propped against the rear wheel of the wagon. Below the trees the shadows were alive, blackness moved on blackness, dusky rank on rank.

'Stand forth, white man,' the voice commanded. 'Speak your business – lest the white spears of Lobengula turn to red.'

The speaker stepped forward, out of the forest to the edge of the camp. Behind him the ring of dappled black and white war-shields overlapped, edge to edge in an unbroken circle surrounding the entire outspan, the 'bull's horns' of the Matabele fighting formations.

There were many hundreds of warriors in that deadly circle, and the broad stabbing spears were held in an underhand grip so that the silver blades pointed forward at belly height between the shields.

Above each shield the frothy white ostrich-feather headdress trembled and swayed in the small evening breeze, the only movement in that silent multitude.

The man who had broken the ranks was one of the most impressive figures that Ralph had ever seen. The high crown of ostrich feathers turned him into a towering giant. The breadth of his chest was enhanced by the flowering bunches of white cowtails that he wore on his upper arms. Each separate tail had been awarded him by his king for an act of valour – and he wore them not only on his arms but around his knees also.

His broad intelligent face was lightly seamed by the passage of the years, as though by the chisel of a skilled carpenter, forming a frame for the dark penetrating sparkle of his eyes; yet his chest was covered with the elastic muscle of a man only just reaching his prime and his lean belly rippled with the same muscle as he moved forward.

His legs were long and straight under the kilt of black spotted civet tails, and the war-rattles bound about his ankles rustled softly at each pace.

'I come in peace,' Ralph called, hearing the catch in his own voice.

'Peace is a word that sits as lightly on the tongue as the sunbird sits upon the open flower, and as lightly does it fly.'

There was movement beside Ralph, and Bazo came from his bed under the wagon.

'Baba!' Bazo said reverently, and clapped his hands softly at the level of his face. 'I see you Baba! The sun has been dark all these years, but now it shines again, my father.'

The tall warrior started, took a swift pace forward, and for an instant a wonderful smile bloomed upon the sculptured ebony of his face; then he checked himself, and drew himself up to his full height again, his expression grave – but the feathers of his headdress trembled and there was a light in his tar-bright eyes that he could not extinguish. Still clapping his hands, stooping with respect, Bazo went forward and knelt on one knee.

'Gandang, son of Mzilikazi – your eldest son – Bazo the Axe, brings you the greetings and the duty of his heart.'

Gandang looked down at his son, and at that moment nothing else existed for him in all the world.

'Baba, I ask your blessing.'

Gandang placed his open hand on the short cropped fleecy cap of the young man's head.

'You have my blessing,' he said quietly, but the hand lingered, the gesture of blessing became a caress, and then slowly and reluctantly Gandang withdrew the hand.

'Rise up, my son.'

Bazo was as tall as his father, and for a quiet moment they looked steadily into each other's eyes. Then Gandang turned, and flirted his war-shield, a gesture of dismissal, and instantly the still and silent ring of warriors turned their own shields edge on, so that they seemed to fold like a woman's fan, and with miraculous swiftness they split into small platoons and disappeared into the forest.

Within seconds it seemed as though they had never been. Only Gandang and his son still remained at the edge of the camp, and then they too turned and slipped away like two shadows thrown by the moving branches of the mopani trees.

Isazi came out from under the wagon, naked except for the sheath of hollowed gourd covering the head of his penis, and he spat in the fire with a thoughtful and philosophical air.

'Chaka was too soft,' he said. 'He should have followed the traitor Mzilikazi, and taught him good manners. The Matabele are upstart bastards, with no breeding and less respect.'

'Would a Zulu induna have acted that way?' Ralph asked him, as he reached for his shirt.

'No,' Isazi admitted. 'He would certainly have stabbed us all to death. But he would have done so with greater respect and better manners.'

'What do we do now?' Ralph asked.

'We wait,' said Isazi. 'While that vaunting dandy, who should wear the induna headring not on his forehead but around his neck like the collar of a dog, decides what should become of us.' Isazi spat in the fire again, this time with contempt. 'We may have long to wait – a Matabele thinks at the same speed as a chameleon runs.' And he crawled back under the wagon and pulled the kaross over his head.

In the night the cooking fires from the camp of the Matabele impi down the valley glowed amber and russet on the tops of the mopani, and every time the fickle night wind shifted, the deep melodious sound of their singing carried down to Ralph's outspan.

In the grey dawn Bazo appeared again, as silently as he had disappeared.

'My father, Gandang, induna of the Inyati Regiment, summons you to *indaba*, Henshaw.'

Ralph bridled immediately. He could almost hear his father's voice. 'Remember always that you are an Englishman, my boy, and as such you are a direct representative of your Queen in this land.'

The reply rose swiftly to Ralph's lips: 'If he wants to see me, tell him to come to me.' But he held the words back.

Gandang was an induna of two thousand, the equivalent of a general. He was a son of an emperor and half brother of a king, the equivalent of an English duke, and this was the soil of Matabeleland on which Ralph was an intruder.

'Tell your father I will come directly.' And he went to fetch a fresh shirt and the spare pair of boots, which he had taught Umfaan to polish.

'You are Henshaw, the son of Bakela,' Gandang sat on a low stool, intricately carved from a single piece of ebony. Ralph had been offered no seat, and he squatted down on his heels. 'And Bakela is a man.' And there was a murmur of assent and a rustle of plumes as the massed ranks of warriors about them stirred.

'Tshedi is your great-grandfather, and in the king's name has given you the road to GuBulawayo. Tshedi has the right to do so – for he is Lobengula's friend and he was Mzilikazi's friend before that.'

Ralph made no reply. He realized that these statements about his great-grandfather, old Dr Moffat, whose Matabele name was Tshedi, were for the waiting warriors rather than for himself. Gandang was explaining his decision to his impi.

'But for what reason do you take the road to the king's kraal?'

'I come to see this fair land of which my father has told me.'

'Is that all?' Gandang asked.

'No, I come also to trade – and if the king is kind enough to give me his word, then I wish to hunt the elephant.'

Gandang did not smile, but there was a sparkle in his dark eyes. 'It is not for me to ask which you desire most, Henshaw. The view from a hilltop – or a wagonload of ivory.'

Ralph suppressed his own smile, and remained silent.

'Tell me, son of Bakela, what goods do you bring with you to trade?'

'I have twenty bales of the finest beads and cloth.'

Gandang made a gesture of disinterest. 'Women's fripperies,' he said.

'I have fifty cases of liquor – of the kind preferred by King Lobengula and his royal sister Ningi.'

This time the line of Gandang's mouth thinned and hardened. 'If it were my word on it, I would force those fifty cases of poison down your own throat.' His voice was almost a whisper, but then he spoke again in a natural tone. 'Yet Lobengula, the Great Elephant, will welcome your load.' And then he was silent and yet expectant. Ralph realized that Bazo would have reported to his father every detail of his little caravan.

'I have guns,' he said simply, and suddenly there was an intense hunger in Gandang's expression. His eyes narrowed slightly and his lips parted.

'Sting the mamba with his own venom,' he whispered, and beside him Bazo started. It was the Umlimo's prophecy that his father had repeated, and he wondered that Gandang could have uttered it in the presence of one who was not Matabele.

'I do not understand,' Ralph said.

'No matter.' Gandang waved it away with a graceful pink-palmed hand. 'Tell me, Henshaw. Are these guns of yours of the kind that swallow a round ball through the mouth and place the life of the man that fires them in more danger than the man who stands in front?'

Ralph smiled at the description of the ancient trade muskets, many of which had survived Wellington's Iberian campaign and some of which had seen action at Bull Run and Gettysburg before being shipped out to Africa in trade; the barrel worn paper thin, the priming pan and hammer mechanism so badly abused that each shot fired threatened to tear the head off any marksman bold enough to press the trigger.

'These guns are the finest,' he replied.

'With twisting snakes in the barrel?' Gandang asked, and it took Ralph a moment to recognize the allusion to the rifling in the barrel.

He nodded. 'And the barrel opens to take the bullet.'

'Bring me one of these guns,' Gandang ordered.

'The price of each is one large tusk of ivory,' Ralph told him, and Gandang stared at him impassively for a moment longer. Then he smiled for the first time – but the smile was sharp as the edge of his stabbing spear.

'Now,' he said. 'I truly believe that you have come to Matabeleland to see how tall stand the trees.'

'I am leaving you now, Henshaw,' Bazo said, without lifting his eyes from the thick yellow tusk that he had brought from his father in payment for the rifle.

'We knew it was not for ever,' Ralph answered him.

'The bond between us is for ever,' Bazo replied, 'but now I must go to join my regiment. My father will leave ten of his men to escort and guide you to GuBulawayo – where King Lobengula awaits you.'

'Is Lobengula not at Thabas Indunas, the Hills of the Chiefs?' Ralph asked.

'It is the same kraal, in the days of Mzilikazi it was Thabas Indunas, but now Lobengula has changed the name to GuBulawayo, the Place of Killing.'

'I see,' Ralph nodded, and then waited for it was clear that Bazo had more to say.

'Henshaw. You did not hear me say this – but the ten warriors who will go with you to the king's kraal are not only for your protection. Do not look too closely at the stones and rocks along the road, and do not dig a hole, even to bury your own excrement, else Lobengula will hear of it and believe that you are searching for the shiny pebbles and yellow metal. That is death.'

'I understand.'

'Henshaw, while you are in Matabeleland, give up your habit of travelling at night. Only magicians and sorcerers go abroad in the darkness, mounted on the backs of the hyena. The king will hear of it – and that is death.'

'Yes.'

'Do not hunt the hippopotamus. They are the king's beasts. To kill one – is death.'

'I understand.'

'When you enter the presence of the king, be sure that your head is always below that of the Great Elephant, even if you must crawl on your belly.'

'You have told me this already.'

'I will tell you again,' Bazo nodded. 'And I will tell you once more that the maidens of Matabeleland are the most beautiful in all the world. They light a raging fire in a man's loins, but to take one of them without the king's word is death for both man and maiden.'

For an hour they squatted opposite each other, occasionally taking a little snuff or passing one of Ralph's cheap black cheroots back and forth, but always with Bazo talking and Ralph listening.

Bazo spoke quietly, insistently, reciting the names of the most powerful indunas, the governors of each of Matabeleland's military provinces, listing those who had the king's ear and should be treated with care, explaining how a man should conduct himself so as not to give offence, advising how much tribute each would ask and finally accept, trying to give it all to Ralph in these last minutes, and then finally glancing up at the sky.

'It is time.' He stood. 'Go in peace, Henshaw.' And he walked out of Ralph's camp without looking back.

As Ralph's wagon, with its escort of warriors, climbed out of the low veld, so the heat abated. The air was so sweet and clean that it made Ralph feel as though the blood sparkled and fizzed in his veins.

Isazi was infected by the same elation. He composed new verses to sing to his bullocks, lauding their strength and beauty, and occasionally he slipped in a reference to a 'feathered baboon' or some other fanciful and unlovely creature, while rolling his eyes significantly in the direction of the bodyguard of Matabele warriors that preceded the wagon.

The forests thinned as they climbed, becoming open woodlands of shapely mimosa trees, the paper-thin bark peeling away to reveal the clear smooth underbark, and the branches loaded with the fluffy yellow flower heads. The grass cloaked the undulating earth, thick and sweet, so that the bullocks fleshed out after the enervating heat of the lowlands, and they stepped out with a new will against the yoke.

This was cattle country, the heartland of the Matabele, and they began to encounter the herds. Huge assemblies of multi-coloured animals, red and white and black and all the combinations of those colours. Smaller than the big Cape bullocks, but sturdy and agile as wild game, the bulls with the hump and heavy dewlap of their Egyptian forebears.

Isazi looked at them covetously, and came back to Ralph at the forewheel of the wagon to say:

'Such were the herds of Zululand, before the soldiers came.'

'There must be hundreds of thousands, and they would be worth twenty pounds a head.'

'Will you never learn, Little Hawk.' Isazi still returned to the diminutive when one of Ralph's stupidities exasperated him. 'A man cannot place a value on a fine breeding cow or a beautiful woman in little round coins.'

'Yet, as a Zulu you pay for a wife.'

'Yes, Little Hawk.' Isazi's voice was weary with Ralph's obtuse arguments. 'A Zulu pays for a wife; but he pays in cattle, not in coin, which is what I have been telling you all along.' And he ended the discussion with a thunderous clap of his long trek whip.

Small family kraals dotted the wide savannahs, each built around its own cattle stockade and fortified against predators – or against marauders. As they passed the settlements of thatched beehive-shaped huts, the little naked herd boys scampered to alert the kraals, and then the women came out, bare-legged and naked-breasted, balancing the clay pots and hollowed gourds upon their heads, an exercise that gave them a stately dignity of movement.

Then Ralph's bodyguard of warriors from Gandang's regiment paused to refresh themselves on the tart and bubbling millet beer or on the delicious soured milk, thick as yoghurt. The young women examined Ralph with bold and curious eyes. Totally unaware that he spoke the language, they speculated about him in such intimate terms that his ears turned bright red, and he challenged them:

'It is easy to speak the lion's name and question his size and his strength when he is hidden in the long grass, but will you be so brave when he raises himself in his rage to confront you face to face?'

The silence, stunned and incredulous, lasted only a second, then they covered their mouths and shrieked with delighted laughter, before the bravest came to wheedle coquettishly for a strip of ribbon or a handful of pretty beads.

As they drew closer to the stronghold of Lobengula, so they passed the great regimental kraals. Each of them was fifty miles from its neighbours, a day's travel at the rate of a marching impi, the ground-devouring trot that they could maintain for hour after hour.

Here there was no exchange of greeting and banter. The warriors came swarming from the kraal like bees from a disturbed hive, and they lined each side of the track and settled into a deathly stillness, watching Ralph's wagon pass in total silence. There was a blankness in their eyes, the inscrutable gaze with which the lion watches his prey before he begins the stalk.

Ralph passed between the massed ranks at a measured walk, sitting very upright on Tom's back, without deigning to glance left or right at the silent menacing ranks; but when they had passed out into the open grasslands again, his shirt was wet under the arms and between his shoulder blades, and there was a catch in his breathing and a chill in the pit of his belly.

The Khami was one of the last wide rivers to cross before reaching the king's kraal at GuBulawayo.

As soon as Ralph saw the denser and greener growth of mimosa trees that marked the river course, he threw the saddle on Tom's back and trotted ahead to survey the drift.

Ports had been cut into the steep sides of the riverbanks to enable a wagon to enter the watercourse, and the sandbank between two tranquil green pools had been corduroyed with carefully selected branches, cut to length and laid side by side across the softer going to prevent the narrow ironshod wheels from sinking.

Whoever had travelled this road ahead of Ralph had saved him a great deal of trouble. Ralph knee-haltered Tom on a patch of good grass and went down into the riverbed to check the crossing. It was obviously many months since the last wagon had crossed, and Ralph worked his way slowly over the corduroyed pathway, repairing the damage that time had wrought, kicking the dried branches back into place and refilling the hollows scooped by water and wind beneath them.

It was furnace-hot in the riverbed and the white sand bounced the sun's rays back at him so that by the time he reached the far bank he was sweating heavily, and he threw himself down in the shade of one of the trees and wiped his face and arms with his scarf moistened in the waters of the river pool.

Quite suddenly he was aware of being watched, and he scrambled quickly to his feet. There was someone standing on the bank above him at the head of the roadway.

With a shock of disbelief, he realized that it was a girl – a white girl, and she was dressed all in white: a loose cotton shift that reached to her ankle just above her bare feet. It was caught in at the waist with a ribbon of blue, and she was so slim that Ralph felt he could lift her with one hand.

The dress was buttoned with mother of pearl to the throat and the sleeves reached to her elbows; but the cotton had been washed, ironed and bleached so often that it seemed to have less substance than gossamer, and the light was behind her.

Ralph could clearly see the outline of her legs under the skirt, and it shocked him again so his breathing tripped. Her legs were long and so delicately shaped that he had to exercise his will to tear his eyes from them. With his heart still pounding he looked at her face.

It was pale as bone china, and seemed almost translucent, so that he thought he could see the sheen of fragile bone beneath the skin.

Her hair was pale shining silver blond, brushed into a fine cascade that flowed over her shoulders, and shimmered and shook with each breath that lifted the tiny girlish breasts under the thin cotton.

There were flowers on her brow, and a garland of them over her shoulders, and about the brim of the wide straw hat that she held in her hands at the level of her narrow hips – and Ralph felt a sense of unreality. The flowers were roses. The girl and the flowers seemed not to belong in this wilderness but in some gentle and cultivated English garden.

She came down the cutting; her bare feet were silent and seemed to glide over the sandy earth. Her eyes were huge and luminous blue in her pale face, and she was smiling. It was the sweetest smile that Ralph had ever seen, and yet it was neither shy nor simpering.

While Ralph still stood, self-conscious and gawking, the girl lifted her slim smooth arms and stood on tiptoe to kiss him full upon the mouth. Her lips were cool and soft, delicate as the rose petals at her brow.

'Oh Ralph, we are so glad to see you. Nobody has talked of anything else since first we heard that you were upon the road.'

'Who – who are you?' Ralph blurted, his surprise and embarrassment making him boorish; but she seemed unaffected by the gauche question.

'Salina,' she said, and slipped her hand into the crook of his elbow to lead him up the bank. 'Salina Codrington.'

'I don't understand.' He pulled against the hand so that she had to turn to face him again.

'Salina –' she repeated, laughing now, and her laughter was warm and sweet as her smile. 'I'm Salina Codrington.' And then when it was apparent that the name meant nothing, 'I'm your cousin, Ralph. My mother is your father's sister – Robyn Codrington – but she was Robyn Ballantyne.'

'Good God!' Ralph stared at her. 'I didn't know Aunt Robyn had a daughter.'

'I suppose not. Uncle Zouga never was a good correspondent.' But suddenly the smile was no longer on Salina's lips, and Ralph remembered abruptly that he had never taken the trouble to unravel the tangled skein of family history, except to comprehend vaguely that there was ill-feeling and unsettled scores between Zouga and his Aunt Robyn. Then it came back to him, he had overheard his father recalling bitterly how Robyn had taken unfair advantage by publishing her own version of their joint expedition to the Zambezi months before Zouga's *Hunter's Odyssey* - thereby robbing Zouga of his fair share of critical acclaim, and royalties.

Ralph's touching on the family enmities must account for Salina's quick change of mood, but it was fleeting. She took his arm again, and was smiling as they came up the bank.

'Not one daughter, Ralph. We Codringtons will not let you off so lightly. There are a whole tribe of us, four of us, all girls.' And she stopped, lifted the straw hat to shade her eyes and looked down the winding overgrown track that meandered away across the grassy savannah. 'Oh dear!' she exclaimed. 'I came ahead to warn you – and I was only just in time!'

Down the track towards them pelted three small figures, jostling one another for advantage, their faint squeaks of excitement gaining rapidly in volume, long hair flying wildly, fluttering skirts of faded and patched cloth lifted high above the knees so that bare legs flashed, faces freckled and flushed, contorted with exertion and excitement and recrimination.

'Salina! You promised to wait!'

They bore down on where Ralph stood with the lovely blond girl on his arm.

'Good God!' Ralph whispered again, and Salina squeezed his elbow.

'That's the second time that you have used the Lord's name, Cousin Ralph. Please don't.' So that was the reason for her faint displeasure.

'Oh – I'm terribly sorry.' And he remembered too late that Salina's parents were pious missionaries. 'I didn't mean – ' Again he was thick-tongued, for suddenly this girl's good opinion was the most important thing in all the world. 'I won't do it again. I promise.'

'Thank you,' she said softly, and before either of them could speak again they were surrounded by what appeared to be an ocean of small females, every one of which was bobbing up and down with remarkable rapidity, competing vocally for Ralph's attention and at the same time shrieking accusations at their eldest sister.

'You cheated, Salina. You told us –'

'Ralph, Cousin Ralph, I'm Victoria, the eldest twin.'

'Cousin Ralph, we prayed God to speed you to us.'

Salina clapped her hands, and there was a barely noticeable reduction in the volume of sound.

'In order of age!' she said calmly.

'You *always* say that because you are the eldest!'

Salina ignored the protest and picked out a dark-haired child with a hand on her shoulder.

'This is Catherine.' She drew her forward to face Ralph. 'Cathy is fourteen.'

'And a half, almost fifteen,' said Cathy, and her manner changed with this declaration, becoming ladylike and controlled.

She was thin, and as flat-chested as a boy, but the young body gave the immediate impression of strength and suppleness. Her nose and cheeks were peppered with freckles, but the mouth was full and frank, her eyes the same Ballantyne green as Ralph's own, and her thick dark brows were a frame for their bright intelligent gleam. Her chin was a little too large, as was her nose, but they had a determined set and thrust. Her thick dark hair was plaited and piled on top of her head, leaving her ears exposed, small and pointed and lying flat against her head.

'Welcome to Khami, Ralph,' she said evenly, and bobbed a small curtsey, holding her skirts up as she had obviously been coached; and Ralph realized that the skirt was made of old flour bags that had been stitched together and dyed a muddy green. The lettering still showed through: 'Cape Flour Mills'.

Then Cathy reached up and kissed him quickly, and it left a little wet spot on Ralph's lips. Kissing was obviously the accepted family salutation, and Ralph glanced with trepidation at the eager but grubby faces of the twins.

'I'm Victoria, the eldest.'

'And I'm Elizabeth, but if you call me "baby", I shall hate you, Cousin Ralph.'

'You won't hate anybody,' Salina said, and Elizabeth hurled herself at Ralph's neck, got a fair grip and hung on as she plastered her mouth to Ralph's.

'I was teasing, Ralph. I shall love you,' she whispered fiercely. 'Always! Always!'

'Me!' howled Victoria indignantly. 'I'm older than Lizzie. Me first.'

Salina led them with that gliding walk which did not move her shoulders and barely ruffled the white-gold curtain of her hair, and every once in a while she turned to smile at Ralph, and he thought he had never seen anything so lovely.

The twins each had hold of one of Ralph's hands, and they gabbled out all the things they had saved up for weeks to tell him, and skipped to keep pace with his stride. Cathy came up behind them all, leading Tom. She and the pony had formed an immediate accord.

'Oh, he's beautiful, Ralph,' she had said and kissed Tom's velvety muzzle.

'We don't have a horse,' Victoria explained. 'Daddy is a man of God, and men of God are too poor to have horses.'

The small party straggled over the first low rise beyond the river, and Salina stopped and pointed down into the shallow basin ahead of them.

'Khami!' she said simply, and all of them looked to Ralph for approbation.

There was a notch in the next line of granite hills, a natural divide and shed for underground water, which accounted for the spread of lush grass that carpeted the valley.

Like chickens under the hen, the small huddle of buildings crouched beneath the hills. They were neatly laid out, thatched with yellow grass and painted dazzlingly white with burnt limewash. The largest building had a wooden cross set proudly on the ridge of the roof.

'Daddy and Mummy built the church with their own hands. King Silly Cat would not allow any of his people to help them,' Victoria explained.

'Silly Cat?' Ralph asked, puzzled.

'King Mzilikazi,' Salina translated. 'You know Mama does not like you using fun names for the kings, Vicky,' she rebuked the child mildly; but Victoria was shaking Ralph's hand excitedly and pointing to a distant figure in the valley below them.

'Daddy!' shrieked the twins in unison. 'There's Daddy!'

He was working in the precise geometrically laid out gardens below the church, a lanky figure whose shoulders remained stooped even when he stood upright and looked towards them, stabbed his spade into the earth and came striding up the hill.

'Ralph!' He swept off the sweatstained hat, and he was bald – like a monk, with just a fringe of silky hair forming a halo around his pate at the level of his ears. It was immediately apparent from whom Salina had inherited her glorious white-gold tresses.

'Ralph,' the man repeated, and he wiped his right hand on the seat of his pants and then held it out. Despite the stoop, he was as tall as Ralph, his face deeply tanned, his bald dome as shiny as if it had been waxed and polished, his eyes pale blue as a summer sky, washed out by heat haze; but his smile was like Salina's – calm and tranquil, so that as he took the hand Ralph realized that this was the most contented and deeply happy man he had ever met in his life.

'I'm Clinton Codrington,' he said. 'And I suppose I must count as your uncle, though goodness knows I do not feel that old.'

'I would have known you anywhere, sir,' said Ralph.

'Would you indeed?'

'I have read Aunt Robyn's books, and I have always admired your exploits as a Royal Naval officer.'

'Oh dear.' Clinton shook his head in mock dismay. 'I thought to have left that all far behind me.'

'You were one of the most illustrious and courageous officers in the African anti-slavery squadron, sir.' Ralph's eyes shone with a still boyish hero worship.

'Your Aunt Robyn's account suffered a dreadful list to port, I'm afraid.'

'Daddy is the bravest man in the world,' Victoria declared stoutly, and she released Ralph's hand and ran to her father.

Clinton Codrington gathered her up and held her on his hip.

'And yours, young lady, is probably the most unbiased opinion in Matabeleland,' he chuckled, and Ralph was suddenly sharply jealous of this palpable aura of deep affection and love which welded the little group, from which he felt himself excluded. It was something beyond his experience, something he had never missed until that moment. Somehow Salina seemed to sense his pang of melancholy, and she took the hand that Victoria had relinquished.

'Come,' she said. 'Mama will be waiting. And there is one thing you will soon learn, Ralph. In this family, nobody keeps Mama waiting.'

They went down towards the church, passing between the beds of growing vegetables.

'You didn't bring any seed?' Clinton asked, and when Ralph shook his head, 'Well, how were you to know?' and he went on to point out with pride his flourishing crops. 'Maize, potatoes, beans, tomatoes do particularly well here.'

'We divide it this way,' Cathy told Ralph, teasing her father. 'One for the bugs, two for the baboons, three for the bushbuck – and one for Daddy.'

'Be good to all God's creatures.' Clinton reached out to ruffle her dark hair, and Ralph realized that these gentle people were always touching and kissing one another. He had never experienced anything like it.

Squatting patiently on the shady side against the wall of the church were twenty or more Matabele of all ages and sexes, from a skeleton-thin ancient with a completely white cap of wool on his bowed head and both his eyes turned to blind orbs of milky jelly by tropical ophthalmia to a new-born infant held against its mother's milk-swollen breasts with its tiny dark face screwed up with the terrible colic of infant dysentery.

Catherine tethered Tom beside the church door, and they all trooped into the cool interior, insulated by thatch and thick walls of unbaked brick from the outside heat. The church smelled of homemade soap, and of iodine. The pews of rough-hewn timber had been pushed aside to make way for an operating table of the same material.

There was a girl at work over the table, but as they came in she tied the last knot in a bandage and dismissed her semi-naked black patient with a word and a pat – then, wiping her hands on a clean but threadbare cloth, she came down the aisle of the church towards them.

Ralph was certain that she was Cathy's twin, for though she was a little taller, she was as slim and as flat-chested; her hair had the same dark brown colouring, though shot through with tones of russet and chestnut, her skin the same youthful lustre, and her nose and chin the same forceful size and thrust.

Then as she came closer, Ralph realized that he had been mistaken and that she was older than Cathy, perhaps even older than Salina, but not much.

'Hello, Ralph,' the girl said. 'I'm your Aunt Robyn.' Ralph felt the blasphemy of surprise leap to his lips again, but conscious of Salina's hand in his he suppressed it.

'You are so young,' he said instead.

'Bless you for that,' she laughed. 'You turn a prettier compliment than your daddy ever did.' She was the only one who made no effort to kiss him; instead she turned to the twins.

'Right!' she said. 'I want ten pages of copperplate written out before Evensong – and I don't want to see a single blot.'

'Oh Mama! Ralph –'

'Ralph has been your excuse for two weeks. Go – or you will eat in the kitchen hut tonight.'

Then, to Cathy: 'Have you finished the ironing, young lady?'

'Not yet, Mama.' Cathy followed the twins.

'Salina, your baking.'

'Yes, Mama.'

Then there were three of them alone in the little church, and Robyn ran a professional eye over her nephew.

'Well, Zouga has bred a likely boy,' she gave her opinion. 'But I never expected anything else.'

'How did you all know I was coming?' Ralph voiced his bewilderment at last.

'Grandpa Moffat sent a runner when you left Kuruman, and Induna Gandang passed here two weeks ago on his way to King Lobengula's kraal. His eldest son was with him, and Bazo's mother is an old friend of mine.'

'I see.'

'Nothing moves in Matabeleland but the whole nation knows of it immediately,' Clinton explained.

'Now, Ralph, how is your father? I was terribly distressed to hear of the death of Aletta, your mother. She was a lovely person, so good and gentle. I wrote to Zouga, but he never replied.'

Robyn seemed determined to catch up on the doings of a decade in the first ten minutes, and her questions were quick and incisive; but Clinton soon excused himself and left the two of them alone in the little church to return to his gardens.

Ralph replied dutifully to all her questions, while he reassessed his first impression of his aunt. Youthful she looked, but childlike she was not. Now at last he could understand the remarkable achievements of this forceful woman. How she had enrolled at a famous London hospital, one which would never accept a female on its student body, by impersonating a man. Dressed in breeches, she had kept her terms and been granted her doctorate when she was twenty-one years of age. The scandal which attended the discovery that a female had invaded an exclusive male preserve had rocked all England.

Then she had accompanied Zouga to Africa, equal partners in the expedition to find their father Fuller Ballantyne, who had been missing in the unexplored interior for eight years. When she and Zouga had fallen out over the conduct of the expedition, she had pushed on, a white woman alone with only primitive black tribesmen as companions, and achieved the main object of the expedition on her own.

Her book describing the expedition, entitled *Africa in My Blood*, had been a publishing phenomenon and had sold almost a quarter of a million copies – three times as many as Zouga Ballantyne's *A Hunter's Odyssey* published six months later.

Robyn had signed over all her royalties from the book to The London Missionary Society, and that august body had been so delighted by the donation that they had reinstated her as a society officer, had ordained her husband as her assistant, and had approved her heading a mission to Matabeleland.

Her two subsequent publications had not enjoyed the same success as the first. *The Sick African*, a practical study of tropical medicine, had contained ludicrous theories that had earned her the derision of her medical peers – she had even dared to suggest that malarial fever was not caused by breathing the foul night airs of tropical swamps, when this fact had been known since the time of Hippocrates.

Then her further account of her life as a medical missionary, *Blind Faith*, had been too homely in style and too prejudiced in championing the indigenous tribes. She had firmly embraced the beliefs of Jean-Jacques Rousseau and had added her own refinements to them. Her round condemnation of all settlers, hunters, prospectors and traders, and of their treatment of the noble savages, had been too salty for her European readers.

Indeed, scandal and contention seemed to follow Robyn Codrington as vultures and jackals follow the lion, and at each new provocation all her previous adventures would be recalled:

What decent female missionary would provoke men sufficiently to make them fight a bloody duel over her? Robyn Ballantyne had.

What God-fearing lady would sail aboard a notorious slaver, unchaperoned and with only slavers for company? Robyn Ballantyne had.

What lady would choose for husband a man who had been court-martialled, stripped of his naval rank and imprisoned for piracy and dereliction of duty? Robyn Codrington had.

What loyal subject of the Queen would hail the terrible reversal of British arms at Isandhlwana, the bloody death of hundreds of Englishmen at the hands of the savage Zulus, as a judgement of God – Robyn Codrington had, in a letter to the *Evening Standard*.

Who, other than Robyn Codrington, would write to Lord Kimberley demanding that half the profits of the diamond fields that bore his name should go to the Griqua captain, Nicholaas Waterboer?

Only Robyn Codrington would demand of Paulus Kruger, the newly-elected President of the little Transvaal Republic, that he return to Lobengula, King of the Matabele, the land below the Cashan mountains from which the Boer commandos had driven Mzilikazi, his father.

She spared no one. Nothing was sacred to her except her God, whom she treated rather like a senior partner in the business of running Africa.

Her enemies, and they were legion, hated her fiercely, and her friends loved her with equal passion. It was impossible to be unmoved by her, and Ralph found himself fascinated as she sat beside him on the church pew and subjected him to an exhaustive catechism that covered every aspect of his life and that of the family.

'You have a brother,' she seemed to know it all. 'Jordan? That is his name, isn't it? Tell me about him.' It was a command.

'Oh, Jordie is everybody's favourite; everybody loves him.'

Ralph had never met anybody like her. He doubted he could ever bring himself to like her, she was far too prickly. That was the exact word to describe her, but he would never doubt her strength and her determination.

Clinton Codrington came back into the church as the light outside was mellowing into late afternoon.

'My dear, you really must let the poor fellow go now.' He turned to Ralph. 'Your wagon has come up. I showed your driver where to outspan. He seems a first-rate chap, I must say.'

'You will sleep in the guest-house,' Robyn announced as she stood.

'Cathy has taken your soiled clothes from the wagon, and she has washed and ironed them,' Clinton went on.

'You will want to put on a fresh shirt before Evensong,' Robyn told him. 'We shall not begin the service until you return.'

He had liked it better on the open road, Ralph thought sourly; then he had made his own decisions as to when he made his ablutions, as to how he dressed and where he spent his evenings – but he went to change his shirt as he was bidden.

The distaff side of the Codrington family filled the front pew. Clinton Codrington faced them from the pulpit. Ralph was between the twins; there had been a brief but ferocious competition between Victoria and Elizabeth to decide who should sit closest to him.

Apart from the family, there was nobody else in the church, and Victoria saw his glance and explained to Ralph in a penetrating whisper, 'King Ben won't let any of his people come to our church.'

'King Lobengula,' Salina corrected her sweetly, 'not King Ben.'

Despite the full attendance, Clinton delayed the commencement of the evening service, finding and losing his place in the Book of Common Prayer half a dozen times – and glancing repeatedly towards the rear of the tiny church.

From this quarter there was a sudden commotion. A small retinue of Matabele women had arrived outside the church. Clearly they were servants, house slaves and ladies-in-waiting to the imposing female figure in their midst. She dismissed them with a royal gesture and came in through the doors of the church. Every one of the Codringtons turned their heads and their faces lit with pleasure.

The way in which this matron paced majestically down the aisle left not a doubt as to her high breeding and her place in the aristocracy of Matabeleland. She wore bangles and bracelets of beaten red copper, strings of highly prized sam-sam beads that only a chief would afford. Her cloak was of beautifully tanned leather, ornamented with feathers of the blue jay and worked with designs of chipped ostrich shell.

'I see you, Nomusa,' she declared.

Her huge naked breasts shone with an ointment of fat and red clay; they pushed out ponderously from under her tanned cloak and dangled weightily to the level of her navel.

Her arms were thick as a grown man's thigh, her thighs as thick as his waist. There were rolls of fat around her belly, and her face was a black full moon, the glossy skin stretched tightly over her abundant flesh. Her merry eyes sparkled from between creases of fat, and her teeth flashed like the sunlit surface of a lake as she smiled. All this size was evidence to the world of her station, of her amazing beauty, of her fecundity. It was also unassailable proof of the high regard of her husband, of his prosperity and importance in the councils of Matabeleland.

'I see you, Girlchild of Mercy,' she smiled at Robyn.

'I see you, Juba, the little dove.' Robyn answered her.

'I am not a Christian,' Juba intoned. 'Let no evil one bear false tidings to Lobengula, the Black and Mighty Elephant.'

'If you say so, Juba,' Robyn answered primly, and Juba pinioned her in a vast embrace while at the same time she called to Clinton in the pulpit.

'I see you also, Hlopi. I see you, White Head! But do not be deceived by my presence here, I am not a Christian.' She drew an elephantine breath and went on, 'I come merely to greet old friends – not to sing hymns and worship your God. Also I warn you, Hlopi, that if you read the story tonight of a man called the Rock who denied his God three times before the call of the cock, I shall be displeased.'

'I shall not read that story,' Clinton answered. 'For by now you should know it by heart.'

'Very well, Hlopi, then let the singing begin.' And led by Juba in a startlingly clear and beautiful soprano, the entire Codrington family rollicked into the first verse of 'Onward Christian Soldiers' – which Robyn had translated into the Matabele vernacular.

After the service Juba bore down on Ralph.

'You are Henshaw?' she demanded.

'*Nkosikazi*!' Ralph agreed, and Juba inclined her head to acknowledge the correct style of address to the senior wife of a great chief that Ralph had employed.

'Then you are the one whom Bazo, my first-born son, calls brother,' Juba said. 'You are very skinny and very white, Little Hawk – but if you are Bazo's brother, then you are my son.'

'You do me great honour, *Umame*!' Ralph said, and Juba took him in those mammoth arms. She smelled of clarified fat, and ochre and wood-smoke, but the embrace was strangely comforting, not at all unlike the feeling, only half remembered, that he had once experienced in Aletta's arms.

The twins knelt side-by-side at the low truckle cot, both in long nightdresses, their hands clasped before their eyes which were so tightly closed that they seemed to be in pain.

Salina, also in her nightdress, stood over them to supervise the last prayer of the day.

'Gentle Jesus meek and mild –'

Cathy was already in her own bed, hair ribboned for the night, writing the day's entry in her diary by the light of the guttering candle made from buffalo fat and cloth wick.

'Pity my simplicity –' gabbled the twins, at such a speed that it came out as, 'Pretty mice, and pretty me!'

Arriving at the 'Amen' in a dead heat, the twins leaped into the bed that they shared, pulled the blanket to their chins and watched with fascination as Salina began to brush her hair, one hundred strokes with each hand, so that it rippled and flamed with white fire in the candlelight. Then she came to kiss them, blew out the candle, and the thongs of her bed squeaked from across the small thatched hut as she climbed into it.

'Lina?' whispered Victoria.

'Vicky, go to sleep.'

'Just one question, please.'

'All right then, just one.'

'Does God allow a girl to marry her own cousin?'

The silence that followed the question seemed to hum in the darkened bedroom like a copper telegraph wire struck by a sword.

Cathy broke the silence.

'Yes, Vicky,' she answered quietly. 'God does allow it. Read the Table of Kindred and Affinity on the last page of your prayer book.'

The silence was contemplative now.

'Lina?'

'Lizzie, go to sleep.'

'You allowed Vicky to ask a question.'

'All right then, just one.'

'Does God get cross if you pray for something just for yourself – not for Daddy or Mama or your sisters, but just for you alone?'

'I don't think so,' Salina's voice was becoming drowsy. 'He might not give it to you but I don't think He will be cross. *Now* go to sleep, both of you.'

Cathy lay very still, on her back with her hands clenched at her sides, staring at the lighter oblong across the hut where the moon defined the single window.

'Please God,' she prayed. 'Let him look at me the way he looks at Salina, just once. Please.'

'What do you think of Zouga's boy?' Robyn took Clinton's arm as they stood together on the darkened stoep and looked out at the star-pricked black velvet curtain of the African night.

'He's a powerful lad – and I don't mean merely muscle.' Clinton took his pipe from between his teeth and peered into the bowl. 'His wagon is loaded with cases, long wooden cases from which the markings have been burned with a hot iron.'

'Guns?' Robyn asked.

'I think so.'

'There is no law against trading guns north of the Limpopo,' Robyn reminded him. 'And Lobengula needs all the power he can get to defend himself.'

'Still, guns! I mean, it does go against the grain.' Clinton sucked at his pipe, and each puff of smoke he exhaled was denser and ranker. They were both silent for a while.

'He has a hard and ruthless streak, like his father,' Robyn judged at last.

'A man needs that to survive in this land.'

Robyn shivered suddenly, and hugged her own arms.

'Are you cold?' Clinton was immediately solicitous.

'No. A grey goose walked over my grave.'

'Let's go off to bed.'

'A moment longer, Clinton. The night is so beautiful.'

Clinton put his arm about her shoulders.

'Sometimes I am so happy that it frightens me,' he said. 'So much happiness cannot go on for ever.'

His words seemed to precipitate the thick but formless dread that had hung over Robyn all this day like the pall of smoke above the winter bush fires. It weighed her down with the premonition that something had changed in all their lives.

'May God save us all,' she whispered.

'Amen to that,' said Clinton as softly, and took her in out of the night.

The interior of the thatched hall was domed and darkened, so that the patterns of latticed branches and lovingly knotted bark rope disappeared into the gloom above their heads like the arches of a medieval cathedral.

The only light was from the small fire on the clay hearth in the centre of the floor. One of the king's wives threw another handful of dried herbs upon it and oily blue tendrils of smoke twisted upwards towards the unseen roof.

Across the fire, on a low platform of dried clay covered with a thick mattress of furs, silver-backed jackal and blue monkey, bat-eared fox and spotted civet, sat the king.

He was a mountainous figure, stark naked, and his skin polished with fat so that he gleamed like an enormous Buddha carved from a solid block of washed anthracite. His head was round as a cannon ball, surmounted by the induna's ring. His arms were massive, bulging with muscle and fat, but the hands in his lap were strangely dainty, narrow across the pink palms, with long tapered fingers.

His trunk was thickened, his breasts pendulous. All this was flesh which he had carefully cultivated. The beer pots and beef dishes stood close at hand. The thick millet beer bubbled softly and the cuts of beef each had a thick rind of yellow fat. Every few minutes one of his wives responded to a nod or a small movement of one graceful hand by proffering a dish. Weight and size were the mark of a king. Not for nothing was Lobengula called the Great Black Elephant of Matabeleland.

His manner was slow, imbued with the vast dignity of his size and rank. Yet his eyes were thoughtful and deeply intelligent, his features despite the burden of fat which blurred them were handsome, lacking outward traits of the hideous cruelties which any Matabele king had to make part of his life.

'My people expect me to be strong and harsh. There are always those who look for the smallest weakness in me – as the young lions watch the black-maned leader of the pride,' Mzilikazi had explained to his son. 'See how my chickens follow me to be fed.' He had pointed with the toy spear of kingship at the high wheel of tiny specks turning slowly in the sky above the hills of Thabas Indunas. 'When my vultures desert me, I will be as dust.'

Lobengula, his son, had learned the lesson well – but it had not brutalized him. Indeed, there was a line to his mouth that was almost diffident, and a shadow behind the light of intelligence in his eyes that was hesitant, the confusion of a man tugged at by too many currents and winds – a man caught up by his destiny, and uncertain as to how he could break away from its remorseless toils.

Lobengula had never expected to take up his father's spear of kingship. He was never the heir apparent, there had been older brothers from mothers of higher rank and nobler blood.

He stared now across the fire at the man that squatted there. A magnificent warrior, his body tempered to black steel by long marches and savage warfare, his understanding and compassion expanded by close and intimate daily contact with common men, his courage and loyalty proven to all the world ten thousand times so there could be no doubts, not even in his own midnight watches, which is the time of doubts – and Lobengula found himself longing to rid himself of this fearsome burden of kingship and place it on the other man's shoulders. He found himself wishing for that quiet and secret cave in the Matopos hills where he had known the only happy days of his life.

The man opposite him was a half-brother; his blood line, like that of Lobengula himself, reaching back unsullied to the Zanzi of Zululand. He was a prince of the House of Kumalo, wise and brave and untroubled by doubts.

'Such a one should have been king,' Lobengula thought, and his love for his half-brother choked his throat so that he coughed. He moved one little finger, and a wife held the beer pot to his lips and he swallowed once and then signed for it to be taken away.

'I see you, Gandang.' His voice was throaty and low, the sadness still in it for he knew that he could not escape that way. He felt like a man on a solitary journey through the forest where the lions are hunting. His recognition released Gandang from his respectful silence. The induna clapped his hands softly and began to recite his half-brother's ritual praises, and Lobengula's mind wandered back across the years.

His earliest memory was of the road, the hard road up from the south – driven by the mounted men dressed all in brown, riding brown ponies. He remembered the popping sound of the guns, which he learned only later to fear, and the smell of gunsmoke, spicy and sour as the wind brought it down to where he clung to his mother, and he remembered the wailing of the women as they mourned the dead.

He remembered the heat and the dust, trotting naked as a puppy at his mother's heels. How tall she had seemed, the muscles of her back gleaming with sweat, and Ningi, his sister, in the sling upon her hip, clinging to one of his mother's fat jostling breasts with mouth and tiny determined fists.

He remembered toiling up the stony hills with his father's single wagon rolling and pitching along ahead of them. On it rode Mzilikazi's senior wife, and her son Nkulumane, three years older than Lobengula and heir apparent to the kingship of the Matabele. They were the only ones who did not walk.

He remembered how his mother's back had withered, the beautiful gleaming skin becoming loose and baggy, the ribcage beginning to show through as the famine wasted her substance, and Ningi screaming with hunger as the rich creamy flow from her teats dried up.

This was where the memory of 'Saala' began; it was mixed up at first with the shouting and singing as a band of raiding Matabele returned to the fleeing column. He had first seen Saala in the firelight, as the warriors slaughtered the captured cattle, and Lobengula could almost still feel the hot grease and the bloody juices of the beef running down his chin and dripping onto his naked chest as they feasted, breaking the long days and months of starvation on cattle taken from the white men, the *buni*.

Once his belly was bulging tightly with meat, Lobengula had joined the circle of curious Matabele princelings and princesses who surrounded the captives; but he had stood back from the teasing and jeering and prodding of the other children.

Saala was the eldest of the two little girls. It was only long afterwards that Lobengula learned that her name was Sarah, but even now he could not pronounce that sound. The Matabele raiding party had surprised a small caravan of Boer wagons, and had killed everybody except these two small white children.

Her whiteness was the first thing that had struck Lobengula. How white her face was in the firelight, as white as an egret's wing, and she had not wept as her younger sister wept.

After that the memories grew stronger, Saala walking ahead of him as the slow column wound through thick thorn forest. Saala taking the infant Ningi from his mother when she slipped and fell with weakness in the black mud of the swamps while the mosquitoes formed a dark whining cloud over them.

Exactly where Saala's little sister died, Lobengula could not recall. It might have been in the swamps. They left her small naked white body unburied, and the column marched on.

At last Lobengula's own mother fell and could not rise again, and with her last strength handed little Ningi to Saala; then she curled up quietly and died. All the weak ones died like that, and their infants died with them, for no other women would take the orphans, for each of them had her own infants to care for.

However, Saala strapped little Ningi on her own thin white back in the way that the Matabele carry their babies, then she took Lobengula's hand in hers and they toiled on after the fleeing nation.

By now Saala's clothing had long ago fallen off her thin white body, and she was as the other Matabele girls who had not yet reached puberty, completely naked. She had half forgotten her own language, and spoke only the language of the tribe. The sun had darkened her skin, and the soles of her bare feet had grown a thick covering, hard as rhinoceros skin, so she could march over razor flint and needle thorns.

Lobengula came to love Saala, transferring everything he had ever felt for his mother to her, and she stole extra food for him and protected him from the bullying of his older brothers – from Nkulumane the cruel one, and from Nkulumane's mother, who hated all that might one day stand in the way of her son's claim to the kingship of the Matabele.

Then the Matabele crossed the Limpopo, the River of Crocodiles, and the land beyond was fair, thick with game and running with sweet rivers. The wandering nation followed Mzilikazi into the magical hills of the Matopos. There on a lonely hilltop the king met the wizard of the Matopos, face to face.

Mzilikazi saw fire spring up at the Umlimo's bidding, and he heard the spirits speak from the very air about the Umlimo, a hundred different voices – voice of infant and crone, of man and of beast, the cry of the fish eagle, the snarl of the leopard – and from that day the Umlimo had the reverence and superstitious awe of the king and all his people.

The Umlimo pointed the way north again, and as the Matabele emerged from the broken hills of the Matopos, they saw spread before them a beautiful land, rich with grass and tall trees.

'This is my land,' said Mzilikazi, and built his kraal under the Hills of the Indunas.

However, the Matabele had lost nearly all their cattle and many of the women and children had died on that cruel journey northwards.

At Thabas Indunas Mzilikazi left his senior wife, mother of Nkulumane, as his regent, and he took five thousand of his finest warriors and went out against the tribes – for women and for cattle.

He went westwards into the land ruled by great Khama, and there was no word from him. The seasons came and changed, the rains followed the long dryness, the heat followed the frosts, and still there was no word of Mzilikazi.

Slowly the strict order of Matabele society began to break up, for the regent, Mzilikazi's senior wife, was unrestrained in her intercourses, and she rutted shamelessly with her lovers.

Some of the lesser wives followed her example, and then the common people took sexual licence, the youths, unblooded and without the royal permission to go into the women, lay in wait for the young girls on the path to the water-hole, and dragged them giggling into the bushes.

With the code of morality broken, other vices followed. The remaining cattle, the breeding herds – were slaughtered, and the feasting went on for months. Looseness and drunkenness swept through the nation like a plague, and in the midst of this debauchery, one of the Matabele patrols captured a little yellow Bushman who had wandered in out of the west, and the Bushman had momentous tidings.

'Mzilikazi is dead,' he told his captors. 'I have thrust my own fingers into the stab wound in his heart, and watched the hyena wolfing down his flesh and cracking his bones.'

The senior wife had her guards boil clay pots of water, and pour them over the Bushman until his flesh fell off his bones and he died, which is fitting treatment for one who brings news of the death of a king. Then she called the indunas into council, and urged them to proclaim Nkulumane king in place of his dead father. However, none of the indunas were fools. One whispered to the other, 'It would take more than a Tswana dog to kill Mzilikazi.'

While they procrastinated and talked, the senior wife grew wild with impatience and sent for the executioners, determined now that there would be no rival for her son. Saala was playing outside the queen's hut, moulding little clay oxen and figures of men and women for Ningi. Through the thatched wall she heard the queen giving her orders to the Black Ones. Frantic with terror for the safety of Lobengula, Saala ran to the other royal mothers.

'The Black Ones are coming for the royal sons. You must hide them.'

Then Saala left little Ningi, now weaned and strong, with one of the royal women who was barren and childless.

'Look after her,' she whispered, and ran out into the grasslands.

Lobengula was by now ten years of age, and was tending what remained of the royal herds: the duty of every Matabele boy, the essential service through which he learned the secrets of the veld and the ways of cattle, the nation's treasure.

Saala found him bringing in the herd to water. He was naked except for the little flap of leather over his loins, and armed only with two short fighting sticks with which he was expected to drive off any predator and to hold his own in competition with the other herd boys.

Holding hands again, the Matabele princeling and the little white girl fled, and instinctively they turned southwards, back the way they had come.

They lived on roots and berries, on the eggs of wild birds and the flesh of the iguana lizards. They competed with the jackals and vultures for the remains of the lion kill – and sometimes they went hungry, but at last they found themselves in the maze of the Matopos Hills where the Black Ones would not follow them. They slept under the single kaross that Saala had brought with her, and the nights crackled with frost so they slept in each other's arms, clinging together for warmth.

Early one morning the old man found them thus. He was thin and mad-looking, with strange charms and magical objects about his neck, and the children were terrified of him.

Saala pushed Lobengula behind her, and with a show of false courage faced the wizard.

'This is Lobengula. Favourite son of Mzilikazi,' she declared stoutly. 'Who harms him, harms the king.'

The old man rolled his mad eyes, and drooled horribly as he grinned with toothless gums. Then suddenly the air was full of the sound of ghost voices – and Saala screamed and Lobengula wailed with terror, and they clung to each other pitifully.

The wizard led the children, chastened, shivering and weeping, through secret passages and over precipitous trails, deeper and deeper into the hills, until at last they came to the caves which honeycombed the rock.

Here the old man began the instruction of the boy who would be king. He taught him many of the mysteries, but not how to control the ghost voices, nor how to throw fire by pointing his finger, nor how to see the future in a calabash of mountain water.

Here in the caves of the Matopos, Lobengula learned the scope and power of the magical order. He learned how the little wizards, the witchdoctors, were spread across the land, performing the small rites, making rain and giving charms for fertility and childbirth, smelling out the evil-doers, and sending back their reports to the cave in the Matopos.

Here the grand wizards, of which the old man was one, worked the great magics, called up the spirits of their ancestors, and looked into the mists of time to see what the future would bring. Above them all was the Umlimo. It was a name only for Lobengula, Umlimo, a name that even after he had lived five years in the cave could still make him shiver and sweat.

Then when he was sixteen, the mad old wizard took him to the cave of the Umlimo. And the Umlimo was a woman, a beautiful woman.

What Lobengula saw in the cave of the Umlimo he would never speak about, not even to Saala, but when he came back from the cave there was a sadness in his eyes, and the weight of knowledge seemed to bow his young shoulders.

There was a furious thunderstorm the night of Lobengula's return, and the blue lightning clanged upon the anvil of the hills with strokes that tortured their eardrums as they lay together under the kaross. Then it was that the little orphan white girl made the boy into a man, the princeling into a king; and when her term was run she gave him a son who was the colour of the early morning sunlight on the yellow winter grass, and Lobengula knew happiness for the only time in his life.

In their joy they paid little attention to tidings which the mad old wizard brought to their cave.

He told them how Mzilikazi, great with plunder, fat with cattle, had come back to Thabas Indunas, arriving suddenly with the blood barely dried on the spears of his impi, and red rage in his heart.

At Mzilikazi's nod the Black Ones gathered all those who had acted as if the king were dead. Some they hurled from the cliff of execution, some they pegged down upon the sandbanks of the river where the crocodiles sunned themselves, others they skewered with bamboo spikes through the secret openings of their bodies.

But when the mother of Nkulumane was led before the king, she wept so and tore her own flesh with her nails while she called on all the spirits of the dead to witness how faithful she had been to Mzilikazi in his absence, how constant had been her belief in his eventual safe return and how during his absence she had guarded the other royal sons from the Black Ones and had even sent Lobengula into the wilderness to save him that Mzilikazi, who at the bottom was only a man, believed her. However, the others died in their hundreds, victims of the king's wrath, and the nation rejoiced for the king had returned and the good old days were back.

Through all this Lobengula and Saala and their little yellow son stayed on in the cave of the Matopos and knew happiness.

Far away in the south below the Limpopo river, a Hottentot elephant hunter stopped to water his horse at the well beside a Boer homestead that stood not far from the battlefield where the Boer horsemen had long ago first defeated Mzilikazi before driving him out of this country.

'I saw a curious thing,' said the Hottentot to the big, solemn, bearded man who was his host. 'In the southern hills of Matabeleland, I saw a white woman, full grown and naked. She was shy as a wild buck and ran into the rocky ground where I could not follow her.'

Two months later, when the Boer farmer took his family into the service of Nachtmaal in the new church at Rustenberg, he repeated the strange story which the Hottentot hunter had brought from the north. Someone recalled the story of the massacre of the Van Heerden family, and the two little girls, Sarah and Hannah, taken by the murderous plundering savages.

Then Hendrik Potgieter, that doughty trekker and kaffir-fighter, stood up in the pulpit, and thundered:

'The heathen have a Christian woman as captive!' And the words offended much that the congregation held dear: God and their womankind.

'Commando!' roared Hendrik Potgieter. 'I call commando!'

The women filled the powder-horns and poured the lead into the bullet moulds, and the men picked out their best horses and elected Potgieter as their leader.

Not all of it was for God and womankind; for one whispered to another, 'Even if there is no white woman, I have heard that there are fine new herds in Matabeleland.'

Then the old wizard came to Lobengula's cave and rolled his eyes and cackled.

'The *buni* have crossed the river of crocodiles, riding on the backs of strange beasts. Many men, many men!'

Instinctively Lobengula knew why the Boer commando was coming, and he knew also what to do about it.

'Stay here, with the child,' he ordered Saala. 'I am going to my father's kraal, and I will lead his impis back here.'

But Saala was a woman, with a woman's curiosity, and blood called to blood. Vaguely she remembered that these strange white men had once been her kin.

When Lobengula had gone north to Thabas Indunas, she slung the baby on her back and crept out of the cave. At first the distant sound of gunfire guided her, for the Boer commando was living off the abundant herds of wild game. Then later she heard the shout of voices, and the whicker of horses, sounds that awakened a terrible nostalgia in her breast.

She crept closer and closer to the bivouac, with all the stealth of a wild animal, closer still until she could clearly see the tall sun-bronzed men, dressed to throat and wrists in brown homespun, the white-brimmed felt hats on their heads – closer still until she could hear their voices lifted in praise of their God as they sang their hymns around the camp fire.

She recognized the words, and memories flooded back to her. She was no longer Saala but Sarah, and she rose from her place of hiding to go down to her people. Then she looked down at her body – and she saw that she was naked. She looked at the child on her hip – and saw that it was yellow, and its features were neither hers nor yet those of its Matabele father.

The awareness of sin came upon her, as it had done to Eve in another Paradise, and Sarah was ashamed.

She crept away, and in the dawn she stood on the top of one of those soaring granite precipices that rend the Matopos hills.

She kissed her baby and then holding the little mite to her breast she stepped out into the void.

Lobengula found them at the bottom of the cliff. He found them before the vultures did, and they were still together, Sarah's grasp on the infant had not faltered during the long plunge from the top of the precipice.

Strangely, both she and the child seemed to be merely sleeping – quiet and at peace.

At the memory Lobengula sighed now, and returned his gaze to his half-brother, the Induna Gandang who still sat across him from the fire.

If only he had been able to escape the prophecy of the Umlimo – for she had foreseen this destiny for him:

Your name is Lobengula, the one who drives like the wind. Yet the winds will drive you, high as an eagle. Lobengula will hold the spear of Mzilikazi. Yet again the winds will drive you, down, down, down, and your nation with you.

Those were the words of that strange and beautiful woman of the cave, and already the first part of the prophecy had held true.

Mzilikazi, the mighty warrior, had died like an old woman – riddled with arthritis and dropsy and gout and liquor – in his royal hut.

His widows had wrapped him in the skin of a freshly-killed bull, and sat mourning over him for twelve days: until his remains were almost liquid with putrefaction in the summer heat.

After the mourning the regiments had carried his corpse into the Matopos Hills, the Sacred Hills, and they had seated Mzilikazi in the cave of the king. They placed all his possessions about him: his assegais, his guns, his ivory; even his wagon was taken down and the pieces piled in the crevices of the cave.

Then masons closed the opening with blocks of granite, and after the feasting and dancing the indunas of Matabele met to decide who would succeed Mzilikazi as king.

The argument and counter-argument lasted many weeks, until the indunas led by the princes of Kumalo returned into the Matopos bearing rich gifts to the cave of the Umlimo.

'Give us a king!' they pleaded.

'The one who drives like the wind!' replied the Umlimo, but Lobengula had fled, trying even at the last moment to escape his destiny.

The border impis captured him, and led him back to Thabas Indunas like a criminal to judgement. The indunas came to him one by one, and swore their allegiance and loyalty unto death.

'Black Bull of Matabele, The Thunderer! The Great Elephant. The one whose tread shakes the earth.'

Nkulumane was the first of his brothers to crawl before him, and Nkulumane's mother, the senior wife of Mzilikazi, followed her son on her knees.

Lobengula turned to the Black Ones who stood behind him, like hounds on the leash.

'I do not wish to look upon their faces again.'

It was Lobengula's first command, spoken like a true king, and the Black Ones took mother and son into the cattle stockade and twisted their necks, quickly and mercifully.

'He will be a great king,' the people told one another delightedly. 'Like his father.'

But Lobengula had never known happiness again. Now with a shudder he threw off the terrible burden of the past, and his voice was a deep but melodious bass.

'Rise up, Gandang my brother. Your countenance warms me like a watch-fire in the frosty night.'

They spoke then, easily and intimately, trusted companions of a lifetime, until at last Gandang passed the Martini-Henry rifle to his king and Lobengula held it in his lap and rubbed the cold blued metal of the block with one forefinger and then held the finger to his nose to smell the fresh grease.

'Sting the mamba with his own venom,' he murmured. 'This is the fang of the mamba.'

'The lad, Henshaw, son of Bakela, has a wagon filled with these.'

'Then he will be welcome,' Lobengula nodded. 'But now let me hear all this from the mouth of your own son. Bring him to me.'

Bazo lay face down on the hard clay floor of the king's hut, and he chanted the ritual praises with a catch in his throat, and brave as he was, he sweated with fear in the king's presence.

'Rise up, Bazo the Axe,' Lobengula broke in impatiently. 'Come closer.'

Bazo crept forward on all fours, and he offered the beaded kilt. Lobengula spilled the diamonds from it into a glowing puddle and he stirred them with his finger.

'There are prettier stones than these in every riverbed of my land,' he said. 'These are ugly.'

'The *buni* are mad for them. No other stone will satisfy them, but for these their hunger is so great that they will kill any who stand in their way.'

'Tear the lion with his own claws.' Lobengula repeated the prophecy of the Umlimo and then went on, 'Are these ugly little stones the claws of the lion? Then, if they are, let all men see how Lobengula is ready with claws.'

And he clapped his hands for his wives to come to him.

The royal hut was crowded now, rank upon rank of squatting men faced the low platform on which Lobengula lay. Every man of them except Bazo wore the headring of the induna, and their names were the rolls of glory of the Matabele nation.

There was Somabula, the lion-hearted old warrior, and beside him Babiaan, royal prince of Kumalo, and all the others. Their ranks were silent and attentive, their faces grave in the light of the fire which had been built up and whose flames leapt almost to the high-domed roof of the king's hut.

They were watching the king.

Lobengula lay on his back on the built-up platform beyond the fire. There was a low carved headrest under the nape of his neck. Only the tip of his penis was covered by the dried and hollowed-out gourd, otherwise he was stark naked. His great belly was mountainous and his limbs were like tree trunks.

Four of his wives squatted about him in a circle, each of them with a calabash of rendered white beef fat beside her. They anointed the king, smearing the fat thickly over his body from his throat to his ankles. Then when it was done they rose silently, and stooped out through the opening in the back of the hut which led to the women's quarters.

Singing softly, shuffling and swaying to the song, another file of younger wives began to wind into the hut; each of them carried upon her head a beer pot of fired clay; but these pots were not filled with the bubbling millet beer.

The wives knelt on each side of the king, and at a word from the senior wife they dipped into the clay pots and each of them came out with a large uncut diamond in her fingers. They began sticking the stones on the king's skin, and the thick coating of grease held them in the patterns that they built up to ornament Lobengula's gleaming limbs. They worked swiftly, for they had done this before, and under their fingers Lobengula was transformed. He became a creature of mythology: half man, half glittering scaled fish.

The diamonds caught the beam of the fire, and sent it spinning against the thatched walls and high roof, darting insects of golden light that flashed in the eyes of the watchers and dazzled them so that they grunted with amazement, and their voices went up like a choir in praise of their king.

At last the work was done and the wives crept away and left Lobengula lying on the thick soft furs, covered from throat to wrist to ankle in a silver burning coat of mail, each link of which was a priceless diamond; and as the king's chest and belly rose and subsided to the tide of his breathing, so this immense treasure burned and flamed.

'Indunas of Matabele, Princes of Kumalo, hail your King.'

'*Bayete! Bayete!*' The royal salute burst from their throats. '*Bayete!*'

Then the silence was complete but expectant, for it had become the king's custom that after this ritual display of the contents of the nation's treasury, he would dispense honours and rewards.

'Bazo,' Lobengula's voice was sonorous. 'Stand forward!'

The young man rose from his lowly position in the rearmost rank.

'*Bayete, Nkosi.*'

'Bazo, you have pleased me. I grant you a boon. What shall it be. Speak!'

'I crave only that the king should know the depth of my duty and love for him. Set me a task, I pray you, and if it should be fierce and hard and bloody, my heart and my mouth will sing the king's praises for ever.'

'On Chaka's royal buttocks, your pup is hungry for glory.' Lobengula looked to Gandang in the front rank of indunas. 'And he shames all those who ask for trinkets and cattle and women.'

He thought a moment, and then chuckled.

'In the direction of the sunrise, two days' march beyond the forests of Somabula, on a high hilltop lives a Mashona dog who deems himself such a great magician and rainmaker that he is beyond the king's arm. His name is Pemba.' And there was a hiss of indrawn breath from the squatting ranks of elders. Three times in the past season the king had sent impis to Pemba's hilltop, and three times they had returned empty-handed. The name Pemba mocked them all. 'Take fifty men from your old regiment, Little Axe, and fetch Pemba's head so that I can see his insolent smile with my own eyes.'

'*Bayete!*' Bazo's joy carried him in a single bound over the grey heads of the indunas. He landed lightly in the space before the fire and he whirled into the *giya*, the challenge dance:

> 'Thus will I stab the traitor dog –
> and thus will I rip out the bellies of his sons –'

The indunas grinned and nodded indulgently, but their smiles were tinged with regret for the fury and passion of their youth which had long ago cooled in their own breasts.

Lobengula sat on the bench of his wagon. It was a big twentyfour-foot four-wheeler built in Cape Town from good English oak, but it still showed all the marks of punishment from its long trek up from the south.

It had not moved in many years, so the grass had grown up through the wheel spokes and around the axle shafts. The canvas of the tent was bleached bone white and crusted with the dung of the hens which roosted on the hoops of the tent framework, but the canvas protected Lobengula from the sun and the seat on the box elevated his head above the level of his courtiers and guards and children and wives and supplicants who crowded the enclosed stockade.

The wagon was Lobengula's throne, and the open stockade his audience chamber. Because there would be white men and women in his audience, he had donned his European finery for this occasion. The long coat encrusted with gold lace had once belonged to a Portuguese diplomat. The lace was tarnished and one epaulette was missing, and the front could not be buttoned over the king's noble belly, not by twelve inches, and the cuffs reached only halfway down his forearms.

The toy spear of kingship, the haft of red wild mahogany and the blade of brightest silver, was in his right hand, and he used it to summon a young boy from out of the crush.

The child was shaking with terror, and his voice so tremulous that Lobengula had to lean forward to hear him.

'I waited until the leopard entered the goat house; then I crept up and closed the door and I barricaded it with stones.'

'How did you kill the beast?' Lobengula demanded.

'I stabbed him through the chinks in the wall with my father's assegai.'

The boy crept forward and laid the lustrous gold and black dappled skin at Lobengula's feet.

'Take your choice of three cows from my royal herds, little one, and drive them to your father's kraal and tell him that the king has given you a praise name. From this day you will be known as "The one who stares into the eyes of the leopard".'

The boy's voice cracked in an adolescent squeak as he backed away gabbling the praises.

Next was a Hollander, a big arrogant white man with a querulous voice.

'I have waited three weeks for the king to decide –'

This was translated for Lobengula, and he mused aloud.

'See how red the man's face becomes when he is angry, like the wattles on the head of the black vulture. Tell him that the king does not count days, perhaps he will have to wait as long again, who knows?' And he dismissed him with a flirt of the spear.

Lobengula took a pull from the bottle of champagne that stood on the wagon seat beside him. The wine fizzed and spilled onto the front of his gold-frogged jacket. Then suddenly his face lit into a beatific smile, but his voice was carping and querulous.

'I sent for you yesterday, Nomusa, Girlchild of Mercy. I am in great pain; why did you not come sooner?'

'An eagle flies, a cheetah runs, but I am limited to the pace of a mule, oh King,' said Robyn Codrington, as she picked her way through the offal that littered the earthen floor of the stockade, and with the fly switch in her hand cleared a path through the crowd towards the wagon, even dealing a stinging cut to one of the king's black-cloaked executioners.

'Out of my way, eater of human flesh,' she told him primly. 'Be gone, child stabber.' And the man leaped aside nimbly and scowled after her.

'What is it, Lobengula?' she asked as she reached the wagon. 'What ails you this time?'

'My feet are filled with burning coals.'

'Gout,' Robyn said as she touched the grotesquely swollen appendages. 'You drink too much beer, oh King, you drink too much brandy and champagne.' She opened her bag.

'You would have me die of thirst. You are not well named, Nomusa; there is no pity in your heart.'

'Nor yours, Lobengula,' Robyn snapped. 'They tell me you have sent another impi to murder the people of Pemba.'

'He is only a Mashona,' Lobengula chuckled. 'Save your sympathy for a king whose stomach feels as though it is filled with sharp stones.'

'Indigestion,' Robyn scolded. 'Gluttony killed your father, and it is killing you.'

'Now you would starve me also. You want me to be a skinny little man of no consequence.'

'A thin live one or a fat dead one,' Robyn told him. 'Open your mouth.'

Lobengula choked on the draught, and rolled his eyes theatrically.

'The pain is better than the taste of your medicine.'

'I will leave you five of these pills. Eat one when your feet swell and the pain becomes fierce.'

'Twenty,' said Lobengula. 'A box full. I, Lobengula, King of Matabele, command it. Leave me a box of these little white pills.'

'Five,' said Robyn firmly. 'Or you will eat them all at one time, as you did before.'

The king rocked with gargantuan laughter, and almost fell from the wagon seat.

'I think I will command you to leave those little white huts of yours at Khami, and come to live closer to me.'

'I should not obey.'

'That's why I do not command it,' Lobengula agreed, with another shout of laughter.

'This kraal is a disgrace, the dirt, the flies—'

'A few old bones and a little dog shit never killed a Matabele,' the king told her, and then was serious and motioned her closer, dropping his voice so that only she could hear.

'The Dutchman with the red face, you know he wishes to build a trade post at the ford of the Hunyani river —'

'The man is a cheat. The goods he brings are shoddy, and he will deceive your people.'

'A runner has brought this book.' He handed the folded and wafered sheet to Robyn. 'Read it for me.'

'It is from Sir Francis Good. He wishes —' For almost an hour, whispering hoarsely so that no other could hear, Lobengula consulted Robyn on fifty different matters ranging from the British Commissioner's letter to the menstrual problems of his youngest wife. Then at last he said, 'Your coming is like the first sweet rain at the end of the long dry. Is there aught I can do for your happiness?'

'You can let your people come to worship in my church.'

This time the king's chuckle was rueful. 'Nomusa, you are as persistent as the termites that gnaw away the poles of my hut.' He frowned with thought and then smiled again. 'Very well, I will let you take one of my people – as long as it is a woman, the wife of an induna of royal blood, and the mother of twelve sons. If you can find one of my people who meets all those conditions, you may take her and splash water on her and make your sign on her forehead; and she may sing songs to your three white gods if she so wishes.'

This time Robyn had to answer his sly and mischievous grin. 'You are a cruel man, Lobengula, and you eat and drink too much. But I love you.'

'And I love you also, Nomusa.'

'Then I will ask one more favour.'

'Ask it,' he commanded.

'There is a lad, son of my brother —'

'Henshaw.'

'The king knows all.'

'What of this boy?'

'Will the king listen to his petition?'

'Send him to me.'

*

Even from where he stood Bazo could see that the grain bins were overflowing with corn that had been sun-dried still on the cob. There was enough to feed an army, he decided bitterly. There was no chance of starving them out.

The grain bins were cylindrical in shape, their walls of plaited green saplings plastered with clay and cow dung. They stood on stilts of mopani poles to allow the air to circulate below them, and to keep out bush rats and other vermin.

They were perched on the very edge of the precipice.

'The dog has brought good rains to his own fields,' murmured Zama, Bazo's lieutenant. 'He is fat with corn. Perhaps he is a rain-doctor as he claims.'

'Water,' Bazo mused, staring up the sheer cliff. Beyond the grain bins he could make out the thatched roofs of the tribal huts. 'Can we drive them out with thirst?' he asked advice, for Zama had been a member of one of the previous abortive raids upon the stronghold.

'The three other indunas tried that at first,' Zama pointed out. 'But then one of the Mashona that they captured told them that there is a running spring from which they draw all the water they wish.'

The sun was beyond the summit of the hill, so Bazo squinted his eyes against it. 'There is lush green growth there – ' He pointed to a narrow gulley that cleft the top of the cliff like an axe stroke but was choked with growth. 'That would be it.'

As if to confirm his words the tiny distant figure of a girl appeared suddenly out of the gulley. She was foreshortened by her height above them, and the ledge along which she climbed was not apparent from where they stood.

She had a calabash gourd balanced on her head, with green leaves stuffed into its mouth to stop the water splashing out of it as she moved.

She disappeared over the top of the cliff.

'So,' grunted Bazo. 'We must climb up to them.'

'It would be easier to fly,' Zama grunted. 'That rock would daunt a baboon – or a klipspringer.'

The rock was pearly grey and marble smooth. There were streaks of lichen dashed across it, green and blue and red, like dry paint on an artist's palette.

'Come,' Bazo ordered, and they began a slow measured circuit of the hill – and as they went so the armed guards on the clifftop above kept pace with them, watching every move they made, and if they approached too close to the foot of the cliff, a hail of rocks fell upon them, striking sparks from the scree slope and caroming viciously past their heads, forcing them to shelve their dignity as they retired in haste.

'It is always the Mashona way,' Zama grumbled. 'Stones instead of spears.'

In places the cliff was riven by vertical cracks, yet none of these reached from base to crest, none of them offered a route to the summit. Bazo looked for a place that had been polished by the paws of wild baboon or marked by the hooves of the tiny little chamois-like klipspringer which might reveal a way up the rock face, but there was none. The cliff girded the entire hill, and transformed it into a fortress.

'There!' Zama pointed to a tiny irregularity in the face. 'That is where two warriors of the swimmers' impi tried to force a road to the top. They climbed as far as that little bush.' It grew in a crack in the face a hundred feet from the base of the cliff. 'And there the ledge narrowed and gave out. They could not go on, nor could they return. They hung there two days and three nights until their strength failed and they fell, one after the other, to be crushed like beetles on the rocks here where we stand.'

They went on, and as the sun was setting they came back to where they had started – the bivouac below the ladderway. Pemba's people had built a ladder of long straight mopani poles, bound together with bark rope, and they had used it to span the lowest point in the cliff – a place where a deep gully descended from the summit to within fifty feet of the surrounding plain. Like a drawbridge, the massive ladder was cunningly counter-weighted with round ironstone boulders, so that it had only to be drawn up on its ropes – as it was now – and the mountain stronghold was impregnable.

When the sun set, Bazo was still leaning on his long shield staring up the cliff, seemingly oblivious to the faint shouted insults of the Mashona that just reached him in the evening silence.

'Pustules on Lobengula's fat buttocks.'

'Puppies of the rabid dog Lobengula.'

'Dried turds of the spavined Matabele elephant.'

Only when it was too dark to make out the top of the cliff did Bazo turn away – but even then he sat late beside the watch-fire, and rolled into his kaross only after the rise of the big white star over the top of the kopje.

Even then his sleep was troubled with dreams. He dreamed of water, of streams and lakes and waterfalls.

He woke again before light and checked that his sentries were alert before he slipped from the camp and under cover of the darkness crept up to the base of the cliff – at the point directly below the gulley choked with green growth where they had seen the girl carry water the day before.

Bazo heard the liquid chuckling, and his spirits soared. Guided by the sound he groped through the darkness, and found the spring in the base of the cliff. It filled a small natural basin of grey rock and then overflowed to waste itself again in the dry earth of the plain. Bazo scooped a handful and it was icy cold and sweet on his tongue. The fountain came splashing out of a dark rent in the rock face. Bazo explored it in the short time that was left before the strengthening light threatened to expose him to the sentries on the cliff above.

'Up,' Bazo shouted as he strode into the bivouac. 'All of you, up!' And his men came off their sleeping-mats, leopard swift and with the stabbing spears in their fists.

'What is it?' Zama hissed.

'We are going to dance,' Bazo told them, and they looked from one to the other in amazed disbelief.

On the north side of the kopje, farthest from the spring in the rock cliff and from the long ladder drawbridge, they danced. While they danced, all Pemba's people lined the clifftop to watch them, first in puzzled silence and then yelling with ribald laughter, hurling down taunts and stones.

'I count four hundred – without the children,' Zama panted, as he stamped and leaped and stabbed at the air.

'There will be enough for each of us,' Bazo agreed, and pirouetted with his shield high over his head.

They danced until the sun was high and then Bazo led them back to the camp, and when he stretched out on his mat and fell instantly asleep, his warriors looked at Zama with exasperation, but Zama could only shrug and turn his eyes to the sky.

An hour before sunset Bazo woke. He ate a little maize cake and drank a small gourd of sour milk, then he called for Zama and spoke quietly with him until it was almost dark.

Zama listened and nodded and his eyes shone, and while he talked, Bazo was honing the silver blade of his assegai until the light twinkled like tiny stars along its cutting edge.

At dark Bazo rose to his feet, handed his long dappled war shield to Zama and, armed only with his assegai, strode out of the bivouac. At the spring in the base of the cliff, Bazo shed his kilt and cloak and headdress. He rolled them into a bundle and hid them in a rock crevice. Then stark naked with only his assegai tied to his back by a leather thong, he waded across the pool. The reflection of the stars on its surface exploded into chips of light.

The water cascaded over him from the fountain in the cliff and he shuddered and gasped with the cold and then reached up into the dark rocky opening, found a fingerhold, drew a deep breath, and then pulled himself upwards.

With a solid black jet of water racing over his head, he held his breath and wriggled frantically up into the hole in the cliff. The force of water opposed him, and it required all his strength to go against it. Inch by inch, his chest throbbing for air, he fought his way upwards – and then just when he knew he would have to let himself be washed back into the pool, his head broke out – and he could breathe.

He sucked air desperately, wedging shoulders and knees against the smooth water-polished rock to hold himself in the torrent. It was utterly dark, not the faintest glimmering of starlight, and the darkness seemed to have physical weight that threatened to crush him.

He reached as high as he could and found another smooth fingerhold, and with all the strength of his arms gained another few feet, rested a moment, and then reached up again. The rock was like glass, and in places coated with a thick beard of algae, slippery as an eel's skin. The cold was a terrible living thing that invaded his body. His bones ached and his fingers were so numbed that he could barely take his holds.

The water tore at him, battering his shoulders, forcing its way into his nose and mouth and ears, filling his head with its angry animal roaring. Still he went up in the irregular twisting tunnel, sometimes horizontal, wriggling forward on his belly, the roof cracking his skull if he lifted his head too quickly to find the few precious inches of air trapped beneath it. Mostly the tunnel climbed vertically, and he wedged with knees and elbows to hold himself against the cascade, while his skin, softened with water, was smeared and torn away in slabs against the stone; but the inches became yards, and the minutes became hours, and still he went up.

Then the tunnel narrowed so sharply that he was trapped, cold slippery rock at each shoulder and hard heavy rock cramming down between his shoulderblades. He could not go on, nor could he go back. He was trapped in the rocky maw of the mountain, and he screamed with terror, but his voice was lost in the thunder of water and the water gushed into his throat.

He fought with the last of his drowning, desperate strength, and suddenly he kicked himself forward into a narrow cavern where he could breathe again, and where the water swirled into little back-eddies so that he could rest a few moments from its drag.

Even while he coughed and choked on his flooded lungs, he realized that he had lost his assegai, and he groped for it until he felt the tug of the thong on his shoulder; there was still something tied to the other end. Hand over hand he drew in the thong and then his fingers closed on the familiar shaft and he sobbed with relief and pressed his lips to the beloved steel.

It took time for him to realize that the air in the tiny cavern was sweet, and he felt it moving like a lover's fingers on his skin, warm and soft – warmth, that was what made his heart soar. Warmth from the outside world, beyond this icy roaring tomb of water. He found the shaft down which the torrent was sucking air from the surface, and from somewhere came the strength to attempt it. He climbed slowly, agonizingly, and suddenly there was a white prick of light ahead of him, distorted by racing black water.

He thrust his head forward, and the night wind struck his cheek, and he smelled woodsmoke and grass and earth redolent of the lingering warmth of the sun, and the great white star stood in the night sky high above his head. That dreadful passage had connected the fountain at the base of the cliff to the one high above.

He did not have the strength to drag himself more than a few feet from the fountainhead, and there under a bush on the soft bed of leaf mould he lay and panted like a dog.

He must have drifted into an exhausted and cold-drugged sleep, for he woke with a start. The sky had paled. He could just see the branches of the bush above his head outlined against it. He dragged himself out, and he found that he ached down to the bones of his spine and his skinned elbows and knees burned even at the touch of the dawn wind.

There was a narrow path, well marked by many feet from the fountainhead up the last few feet of the cliff, and as he stepped out onto it he looked down and saw far below him the moonsilver forest and the tiny sparks that were the watch-fires of his own bivouac. As he moved, he felt his muscles easing and unknotting, felt the blood recharging his limbs.

Although he was ready for one, there was no sentry at the top of the path, and he peered out cautiously from behind the stone portals of the gulley onto the tranquil village.

'By Chaka's teeth, they sleep like fat and lazy dogs,' Bazo thought grimly. The doors were all tightly closed, and smoke oozed from every chink in the walls. They were half suffocating themselves to keep out the mosquitoes. He could hear a man coughing hoarsely in the nearest hut.

He was about to slip out from behind his rocky screen when faint movement in the gloom between the huts made him sink gently down again. A dark figure scurried directly towards where he hid. He shifted his grip on the assegai, but only a few paces from him the figure stopped.

It was swathed in a skin cloak against the pre-dawn chill, hunched up like an old woman, until it straightened and threw off the cloak. Bazo felt his breath hiss up his throat and he bit down to stop it reaching his lips.

The naked girl was in that lovely tender stage just past puberty, on the very brink of full womanhood. There were the last vulnerable vestiges of childhood in the plump little buttocks and in the kitten awkward way she stood with toes turned slightly inwards. She was naked and the first light touched her sable skin with a lemon glow. Then she turned her head.

She had a long slender neck and the neat little head balanced perfectly upon it. The dome of her skull was covered with an intricate pattern of closely woven plaits. Her forehead was high and smooth, her cheekbones vaulted in the Egyptian way, her lips chiselled into perfect sweeps, symmetrical as the wings of a beautiful butterfly, and the light glinted briefly in her huge slanted eyes as she looked about her.

Then she squatted briefly and her water tinkled against the earth. It was a sound that unaccountably filled Bazo's chest with a swollen tender feeling, for the act was so innocent and so natural.

She stood, and in the instant before she covered her head once more with the cloak, he had one more glimpse of her face. He knew then that he had never seen anything so beautiful in all his life – and he stared after her as she hurried back between the huts with a peculiar aching hunger consuming his very being.

It took him many minutes to rouse himself, and then as he crept forward he found that, hard as he tried, he could not drive the girl's image from his mind. The pathway that led from the village to the ladder drawbridge was unmistakable. It was broad and its surface beaten smooth. There were walls of worked stone on each side of it behind which the defenders could meet any thrust up the path. There were piles of stones at intervals along its course, placed ready to be hurled down at anybody attempting to force the ladder or fight their way up the path.

The pathway dropped steeply into the gulley, and then ended on a wide level stone platform. The light was stronger now and Bazo could see that there were sentries here; two of them stood on the lip watching the plain fifty feet below the platform, guarding the massive counterbalanced ladder. Farther back four other guards squatted around a small smoky fire, and Bazo's saliva flooded as he smelled the roasting maize cakes. The men were talking in the low sleepy tones of men who had stood a long watch, and their backs were turned to the gulley, for they would never expect an enemy to come from that direction.

Bazo crept closer. There was another pile of rocks at the corner of the platform, ready for the guards to hurl down the cliff. Bazo crawled into the shadows behind it.

He did not have long to wait. Very faintly on the morning wind he heard the singing. Zama had begun the dance below the cliff. The song was the fighting hymn of his regiment, and Bazo's blood thrilled in his veins. He felt the divine madness begin. It was a feeling that other lesser men got only from the hemp pipe.

He felt the sweat break on his skin, and the madness mount from his belly to his heart – felt the blood swell in his throat, felt his eyes burn and bulge.

The guards had left the fire now and crowded the edge of the cliff, peering downwards, laughing and pointing.

'Hear Lobengula's puppies yap!'

'Look at them dance like virgins at the Festival of First Fruits!'

The signal Bazo had agreed with Zama was the moment the battle song ended, but he could barely contain himself that long.

He rose from his crouch, and his muscles twitched, his head jerked like that of a maniac, and in the dawn light his eyes were glazed like shards of ceramic pottery, the red rage of the berserker. At that instant the distant song ended.

Bazo's cry froze the men on the edge of the cliff, it was the bellow of a heart-struck buffalo bull, the screech of the stooping eagle.

In the paralysed moment before they could turn, Bazo struck them. He charged with outstretched arms and swept four of them away into the void. They twisted and turned in the air as they fell, and they screamed the whole way down on a high receding note that was cut off abruptly at the end.

Bazo's charge had been so headlong that he almost followed them over the brink; for a giddy moment he tottered there, and then he caught his balance and spun to strike underhand at one of the survivors. The blade went into the man's belly and out the other side, cleaving his bowels and his kidneys, and crunching through his backbone; and when Bazo jerked the steel clear, the life blood sprayed hotly onto his forearm and his chest. The last sentry ran, silently and desperately, for the pathway, and Bazo let him go.

Bazo bounded along the edge of the cliff and reached the point where the top of the ladder was secured. The ropes that held it were of twisted and plaited bark, reinforced with liana and leather thongs. They were thick as Bazo's arm, and he changed his grip on the assegai to a chopping stroke.

The ropes popped and crackled as he hacked through them. He grunted at each stroke, slitting his eyes against the flying chips of wood and bark.

Behind him he heard the babble of many voices on the pathway. The sentry would call them down like hunting dogs – but Bazo scorned to turn until the work was done. One rope gave, and the massive unwieldy ladder sagged and twisted. He cut again, reversing his grip to swing back-handed, and the other ropes went.

The ladder swung outwards and downwards, gathering momentum, and the timbers crackled and squealed, drowning out the voices of the men coming down behind him. The bottom of the ladder struck the scree below the cliff with a shattering crash, and some of the uprights snapped under the impact. The head of the ladder was still secured at Bazo's feet, and the whole twisted mess hung down like the rigging of a dismasted ship.

Bazo stood long enough to watch Zama lead his warriors swarming up the dangling tangle of rope and timber. Then he turned.

They were coming down the pathway, a solid phalanx of black bodies and sparkling weapons; but their advance was hesitant enough for Bazo to race forward and reach the narrow gap in the wall before the leaders did. With solid rock to guard his flanks, he laughed at them, and it was a sound to stop them dead, those in front pushing back and those behind struggling forward.

One of them threw a long spear and it clashed sparks from the wall at the level of Bazo's head. He drove forward and stabbed into the press of bodies caught in the narrow gut between the stone walls. The screams and moans goaded him – and the blood from the gaping wounds splattered his face and sprayed into his open mouth, a ghastly draught that maddened him further. They broke and fled, leaving four of their number writhing and twisting on the pathway.

Bazo glanced behind him. None of his Matabele had reached the head of the ladder yet. He looked back up the pathway and saw that the real men were coming.

These would be the picked warriors, the best spearmen – there was no mistaking their superiority over the rabble that Bazo had just scattered; they were bigger and more powerful in body, their expressions grim and determined, and their formation ordered and controlled.

They came down in massed ranks to where Bazo stood, their shields raised, their spears poised, and at their head danced a skinny wizened old man with a face ravaged by some terrible disease, his nose and ears rotted away and his cheeks and forehead covered with silver white blotches.

He was hung about the waist and neck with the accoutrements of his magical trade, and he shrieked and gibbered like an enraged ape.

'Kill the Matabele dog.'

Bazo was naked, without a shield, but he hefted the assegai and stood to meet them and their horrid master and he laughed again, the wild joyous laughter of a man who was living a lifetime in his last few seconds.

'Bazo!' The cry reached him, even through his rage, and he turned.

Zama had crawled onto the platform, blown from that long scrambling climb up the swinging twisted ladder. He rose on his knees and sent the great dappled shield skimming across the platform. Like a falcon coming to bate it settled on Bazo's shoulder, and Bazo laughed and went springing forward.

His assegai drove through the wizard's rotting flesh as though it were soft as a boiled yam, and Pemba screeched one last time.

'Bazo, wait! Leave some of them for us!' The shouts of his fifty Matabele behind him, as they scrambled onto the platform, and then Zama's muscled shoulder was touching his as they locked shields and swept the pathway, the way the flash floods of summer scour the dry riverbeds.

It was a beautiful stabbing, a glory which men would sing about. The assegais seemed to hold their keen edge no matter how often they were buried and the spear arms never tired despite the heavy work. The line of Matabele swept the hilltop from end to end, roaring their frustration when the last of Pemba's men threw down their spears and leapt out over the cliff, grudging them that easy death for the assegais were still thirsty and the madness was still on them.

Then they turned and went back through the village, ransacking the huts, throwing a toddling infant high and catching it on the point as it fell, or sending the steel full length out between the withered dugs of some scurrying crone, for the divine madness does not pass swiftly.

With his shoulder, Bazo smashed open another hut, and Zama leaped in at his side, both of them were painted from throat to knee with red running crimson, their contorted faces hideous, blood-glutted masks. Someone tried to escape from the dark interior of the hut.

'Mine!' roared Zama and sped his long steel, and the low early sun struck a ray through the open doorway, sparkling on Zama's assegai and falling in the same instant on the huge slanted terrified eyes and high Egyptian cheekbones of the girl he was killing.

Zama's steel clashed against Bazo's great shield and was deflected past the girl's cheek by the width of a finger, so that the stroke died in the air. Before Zama could strike again Bazo stood over the girl, spreading the shield over her the way a heron covers its chick with a wing, and he snarled at Zama like a leopard whose cub is menaced.

After the first weary day of the return march, while the long file of roped captives was settling exhausted and miserable beneath the grove of msasa trees, Bazo strode down the line and stopped beside the girl.

'You!' he said, and with a careless stroke of his assegai severed the thong at her neck. 'Cook my meal!'

While she worked over the fire, Bazo joked loudly with Zama and his men, trying to prevent his eyes from straying from their faces. He ate what she cooked without showing either pleasure or displeasure, while she knelt at a respectful distance and watched every mouthful he took.

Then suddenly when he had finished eating, she came gliding to his side with that disconcerting silent grace, and she lifted the bunch of wilted leaves from the swollen and crusted spear wound in Bazo's flank. It was an impertinence, and he lifted his hand to strike her – and then let the hand fall. She had not flinched and her manner was assured and competent.

She cleaned the wound with deft fingers and then she unstoppered two of the little buck-horn containers that she wore on her belt and with the powder they contained made a poultice. It burned like fire for a few seconds, but then felt much easier.

Bazo made no acknowledgement, but when one of his Matabele came to rope her back with the other captives, Bazo frowned, and the man passed her by.

When Bazo lay on his sleeping-mat, she curled like a puppy at his feet. He was ready for her to try to escape once the camp settled, but after midnight she had not stirred and he fell asleep.

In the hour before dawn when he rose to check the sentries, there was frost on the grass, and he heard the girl's teeth chattering softly. He dropped his fur regimental cloak over her as he passed and she cuddled down into it quickly.

When he called for the day's march to begin, she had his bedding roll and cooking-pot balanced on her head, and a dozen times during the march, Bazo had to go back along the winding column for no reason that he could explain to Zama, and each time his steps slowed as he came up behind the girl, and he watched the play of muscle down her back, the roll of her plump black buttocks and the joggle of her glossy sable breasts. But when she turned her head and smiled shyly at him, his hauteur was frosty and he stalked back to the head of the column.

That night he permitted himself a nod of approval at the first taste of her cooking, and when she dressed the wound, he said, 'The heat has gone from it.'

She did not lift her eyes.

'Who taught you this skill?' he insisted.

'Pemba, the wizard,' she whispered.

'Why?'

'I was his apprentice.'

'Why you?'

'I have the gift.'

'So then, little witch, make me an oracle,' Bazo laughed, and she lifted her head and he looked into those disconcerting slanted tar-bright eyes.

'Do not scoff, lord.'

'*Nkosi* – lord,' she called him, but Bazo stopped laughing, and felt the spirits tickle the hair at the nape of his neck. That night, when he heard her shiver, he opened a fold of his kaross and she crept into it.

Bazo feigned sleep, but his body was tense and he was aware of each tiny movement that the girl made as she settled to sleep. It would have been so easy to reach out and hold her down with his arm across her chest while he forced his knee between hers. The thought made him twitch and grunt.

'Lord?' she whispered. 'Something troubles you.'

'What is your name?' he asked, for want of a reply, and found that he was whispering also.

'Tanase.'

'Tanase.' He measured it on his tongue, and it fitted well enough, although he recognized it was a Rozwi name, one of the splinter tribes of the Mashona, and he did not know the meaning.

'I know your name – everyone speaks it with respect,' she said. 'Bazo, the Axe.'

'I killed your master, Pemba. I struck him down with my own hand.' He did not know what compelled him to say that.

'I know,' she whispered.

'Do you hate me for that, little witch?'

'I praise you for that!' Her voice shook with quiet vehemence, and her hip touched his under the kaross.

'Praise? Did you not love Pemba as a dog loves its master?'

'I hated him, and when I foresaw his death in the magic calabash, I was filled with joy.'

'You saw his death?'

'I saw his death – as I saw your face, long before you came to take me.'

Bazo shuddered involuntarily, and she felt it.

'You are cold, lord.' She pressed a little closer to him. Her flesh was hot and soft, he felt his own flesh respond to its touch.

'Why did you hate Pemba?'

'He was evil beyond the telling. The things he forced me to do I will never forget.'

'He used your body?' There was a rough edge to Bazo's question.

'Not even Pemba would dare tamper with the body of one of the chosen ones, for to tear the veil of maidenhood is to destroy the gift.'

'The gift?'

'The gift of foresight which the likes of Pemba value so highly.'

'What then did he force upon you?'

'Dark things, midnight things, torture not of the body but of the spirit.'

Now it was her turn to shudder, and she turned towards him and clung to his broad smooth chest, hiding her face against it so that her voice was muffled and he could hardly catch her next words.

'I did not wish to be chosen, I hate and fear what still lies ahead of me if I follow that road.'

'Pemba is dead.'

'You do not understand. Pemba was but a little wizard, already he had taught me almost all he knew. Then I would have been called by the one whose name I dare not speak aloud. That call will still come – and I shall not be able to deny it.'

'You are under my protection.'

'There is only one way you can protect me, Bazo Lord.'

'How?'

'Make me worthless to them. Destroy this gift which is such a terrible burden.'

'How?'

'As you destroyed Pemba with the stabbing spear of steel, destroy it with your great spear of flesh, tear my veil and let this thing pass from me.'

She felt him, hot and fierce, pressing against her, and her body seemed to melt and become pliant and yielding.

'Ah yes, Lord. Make me as other women, so that I may feel your noble belly on mine in the nights, that I may feel your son kick in my womb and tug at my breast when I give him suck.'

'All these things you will have, Tanase.' Bazo's voice was hoarse with his wanting. 'When we reach GuBulawayo the king will reward me, and give me leave to go in to the women, and take a wife.'

'Lord, it is dangerous to wait.'

'I will not rut on you like a slave girl. You will be the first and senior of all my wives.'

'Lord –'

'Enough, Tanase, tempt me no further, for what you feel, hard though it may be, is not stone but flesh only.'

'*Nkosi*, you do not know the power of the wizards. Save me from them.'

'I know the law and custom of Matabele, and that is all a man should know and heed.'

Bazo's scout came in at a dead run, the sweat snaking down his back and chest, and he shouted his report the moment he came up to the head of the column.

Bazo whirled and barked three sharp orders. Immediately the column closed up, and the captives were forced to squat with a dozen warriors standing guard over them. The rest of the Matabele formed up behind Bazo and he led them away at that gait between a trot and a run which lifted the dust to their knees.

Bazo picked his ambush with an unerring eye. He chose a place where broken ground and thick bush allowed only one passage through, and the single horseman rode into it. The long shields were suddenly all around him, fencing him in as his dun-coloured pony snorted and skittered.

The rifle was half-way drawn from the leather boot at the horseman's knee when Bazo stopped him with a shout.

'Too late for that. You were dead, and the jackals feasting already. You grow careless, despite all that I taught you, Henshaw.'

Ralph let the rifle slide back into its scabbard, and he threw up his hands, pleasure and chagrin warring on his face.

'Shake any tree and a Matabele falls out of it.' His voice was mock-mournful, and he swung down off Tom's sturdy back and strode to meet Bazo.

'I expected to see the induna's ring on your forehead already, oh mighty slayer of Mashona,' he laughed as they embraced.

'Soon, Little Hawk, very soon. But you, I thought your wagon would be heavy with ivory –'

'Done, Little Axe, already done.' Ralph stepped back and looked at him. In the months since they had parted, both men had changed.

In Bazo there remained no trace of the young mine labourer who had worked his shifts in the pit and eaten Zouga Ballantyne's rations. Here was a warrior and a prince, tall and plumed and proud.

Ralph was no longer the callow lad, his every action ordered by his father. Instead he was a grown man, with a jaunty lift to his chin and a self-assured set to his shoulder. Yet though his clothes were travel-worn and stained the training of Zouga Ballantyne still showed, for they were recently washed and his jaws had been clean shaven that very morning. They looked at each other and the affection between them was tempered and hardened with respect.

'I shot a young buffalo cow, not two hours ago.'

'Yes,' Bazo nodded. 'It was the shot which brought us.'

'Then I am glad of it. The buffalo meat is fat, and there is enough even for a hungry Matabele.'

Bazo glanced at the sun. 'Though I am in haste, on the king's business, my prisoners are in need of rest. We will help you eat your buffalo, Henshaw, but in the dawn we will go on.'

'Then there is much to talk about – and little time to do so.'

There was the pop of a trek-whip, and Bazo glanced beyond Ralph's shoulder to see the oxen come plodding between the trees and the wagon lurching and wallowing behind them.

'You still keep bad company,' Bazo scolded with a grin as he recognized Umfaan at the head of the span and Isazi, the little Zulu, on the flank, 'but the load you carry is welcome.'

From the wagon box hung the raw quarters and shoulders of the freshly-butchered buffalo carcass.

'We have not tasted fresh meat since we left the king's kraal.'

Ralph and Bazo sat at a separate fire apart from their retinues, where they could talk freely.

'The king agreed to buy the guns and bottles that I carried up from Kimberley,' Ralph told Bazo, 'and he paid me generously.'

He did not go on to describe to Bazo the currency in which be had been paid. He did not describe his own astonishment when Lobengula had offered him an uncut diamond, a big bright first-water stone.

His surprise had immediately been tempered by conscience; he had no doubts about where that stone had come from. His conscience lasted about as long as his surprise, and he haggled with gusto, forcing up the price to six stones, which he had picked with an eye trained by many years on the diggings. He knew they would be worth £10,000 when he got them back to civilization.

Thus in a single stroke he had paid for the wagon and team, his entire debt to Diamond Lil – interest and all – and was already many thousands of pounds in profit.

'Then I asked Lobengula to let me hunt elephant, and he laughed and said I was too young and that the elephant would eat me up. He kept me waiting outside his kraal for ten days.'

'If he kept you such a short time, then you have found favour with the king,' Bazo interrupted. 'Some white men have waited from the beginning of the dry season to the middle of the wet, merely for permission to take the road out of Matabeleland.'

'Ten days was long enough for me,' Ralph grunted. 'But when I asked him in which part of his lands I was allowed to hunt, he laughed again and said, 'The elephant will be in so little danger from you, Little Hawk, that you may go where you wish, and kill as many as are stupid or lame enough to let you.'

Bazo chuckled delightedly. 'And how many lame stupid elephant have you found so far, Henshaw?'

'I have fifty good tusks in the wagon already.'

'Fifty!' Bazo's chuckles died and he stared at Ralph in amazement; then he stood up and crossed to the wagon. He untied one of the straps and lifted the canvas cover to peer in at the load, while Isazi looked up from his cooking fire, frowned and called to Ralph.

'This boy's great-grandfather, Mashobane, was a thief, his grandfather, Mzilikazi was a traitor – you have every reason to trust him with our ivory, Henshaw.'

Bazo did not look at him, but glanced up into the trees. 'The monkeys hereabout make a frightful chatter,' he murmured, and then came back to Ralph.

'Fine tusks!' he admitted. 'Like the ones the hunters took when I was still a child.'

Ralph did not tell him that most of those in the wagon were taken even before that time. He had discovered all but two of the caches that his father had bequeathed to him.

The ivory had dried out – lost almost a quarter of its green weight; but most of it was still in good condition, and would fetch the market price once he got it to the railhead.

Though Ralph had hunted diligently for his own elephant whilst he sought out Zouga's ancient dumps, he had had little success. He had killed five, only one of which was a bull and whose green tusks had weighed just over sixty pounds. The others had been small female ivory, barely worth taking.

The great herds that Zouga had described in *A Hunter's Odyssey* no longer existed. Since those days there had been many hunters, some of them inspired by Zouga's own writing. Boer and Briton, Hottentot and German, they had hunted and harried the huge grey beasts and left their white bones piled on the veld and in the forest.

'Yes, they are good tusks,' Ralph nodded. 'And my wagon is heavy laden now. I am on the road back to the king's kraal to ask him for permission to leave Matabeleland and go back to Kimberley.'

'Then when you have gone, we will see you no more,' Bazo said quietly. 'You will be like the other white men who come to Matabeleland. You will take what you want, and never come back.'

Ralph laughed. 'No, old friend, I will be back. I do not have everything I wish, not yet. I will come back with more wagons, perhaps six wagons, all loaded with trade goods. I will set up trading posts from the Shashi river to the Zambezi.'

'You will be a rich man, Henshaw. I am sure of it,' Bazo agreed. 'But rich men are not always happy men. This I have remarked often. Is there nothing else in Matabeleland for you but ivory and gold and diamonds?'

Ralph's expression changed. 'How did you know that?' he demanded.

'I asked, I did not know,' Bazo denied, still smiling. 'Though I do not have to throw the bones or look in the magic calabash to know it is a woman – you have suddenly the look of a dog that smells the bitch. Tell me, Henshaw, who is she and when will you take her to wife?' Then he laughed aloud. 'You have not yet asked her father? Or you have asked and he has refused?'

'It is not a matter for laughter,' Ralph said stiffly, and with an effort Bazo wiped the mirth from his face, though it twinkled still in his eyes.

'Forgive one who loves you as a brother, I did not know it was such a heavy matter.' And at last he managed to match Ralph's portentous expression, while he waited for him to speak again.

'Once, long ago, while we rode up in the skip, you spoke of a woman with hair as white and fine as the winter grass,' Ralph said at last, and Bazo nodded.

'It is she, Bazo. I have found her.'

'She wants you as much as you want her?' Bazo said firmly. 'If she does not, then she is so stupid that she does not deserve you.'

'I haven't asked her yet,' Ralph admitted.

'Do not ask her, tell her, and then ask her father. Show the father your tusks of ivory; that will settle the matter.'

'You are right, Bazo,' Ralph looked dubious. 'It will be that simple.' And then softly in English, so that Bazo could not understand. 'God knows what I shall do if it is not. I don't think I can live without her.'

If he did not follow the words, Bazo understood the sense and the mood. He sighed, and his eyes strayed to Tanase at the cooking fire.

'They are so soft and weak, but they wound more deeply than the sharpest steel.'

Ralph followed his eyes, and then suddenly his own expression cleared and it was his turn to guffaw and reach across to slap Bazo's shoulder.

'Now I recognize the look you spoke of earlier, the dog with the smell of the bitch in his nostrils.'

'It is not a matter for laughter,' said Bazo, haughtily.

Long after the last gnawed buffalo bone was thrown upon the fire and the last beer pot emptied; long after the Matabele warriors had tired of singing the song of Pemba, the ode to their own prowess and courage on the hill of the wizard, and rolled into their sleeping karosses; long after the last captive girl had ceased wailing, Bazo and Ralph sat on beside their own fire – and the drone of their voices and the munch of the oxen chewing the cud were the only sounds in the camp.

It was as though every last moment was precious to them for both sensed that when they met again they would be changed, and perhaps the world with them.

They relived their youth, remembering Scipio, the falcon, and Inkosikazi, the great spider; they smiled at the stinging memory of the fighting sticks, and Bakela's wrath when Bazo gave him the shattered diamond; they talked of Jordan and Jan Cheroot and Kamuza and all the others – until at last reluctantly Bazo rose.

'I will be gone before the sun, Henshaw,' he said.

'Go in peace, Bazo – and enjoy the honours that await you and the woman you have won.'

When Bazo reached his sleeping-mat, the girl was already wrapped in his kaross.

As soon as Bazo lay down beside her, she reached for him. She was as hot as though she was in high fever – her body burning and her skin dry. Silent sobs racked her and her grip was fierce.

'What is it, Tanase?' He was shocked and alarmed.

'A vision. A terrible vision.'

'A dream.' He was relieved. 'It was only a dream.'

'It was a vision,' she denied. 'Oh, Bazo, will you not take this terrible gift from me, before it destroys us both.'

He held her and could not answer her; her distress moved him deeply, but he was helpless to alleviate it.

After a while she was quiet, and he thought that she slept, but then she suddenly whispered.

'It was a terrible vision, Bazo Lord – and it will haunt me unto my grave.'

He did not answer, but he felt the superstitious chill in his guts.

'I saw you high upon a tree –' She broke off, and another single sob hit her like a blow. 'The white man, the one you call Henshaw, the Hawk – do not trust him.'

'He is as my brother, and like a brother I love him.'

'Then why did he not weep, Bazo, why did he not weep when he looked up at you upon the tree?'

Salina Codrington rolled out her pastry with long and expert strokes of the pin. The sleeves of her blouse were rolled high and she was floury to the elbows. Little blobs of pastry stuck to her hands and fingers.

The thatched ceiling of the kitchen at Khami Mission Station was sooty from the open iron stove, and the smell of the dough was yeasty and warm.

A single skein of white-gold hair had escaped the ribbon and now tickled her nose and chin. Salina pursed her lips and blew it away; it floated like gossamer and then gently settled across her face again, but she did not change the rhythm of the rolling-pin.

Ralph thought that little gesture the most poignant he had ever witnessed, but then everything she did fascinated him – even the way she cocked her head and smiled at him as he slouched against the jamb of the kitchen door.

Her smile was so gentle, so unaffected, that his chest squeezed again, and his voice sounded choked in his own ears.

'I am leaving tomorrow.'

'Yes,' Salina nodded. 'We shall all miss you dreadfully.'

'This is the first chance I have had to speak to you alone, without the monsters –'

'Oh Ralph, that's an unkind, if totally accurate, description of my darling sisters.' Her laughter had a surprising timbre and depth to it. 'If you wanted to speak to me, you should have asked.'

'I'm asking now, Salina.'

'And we are alone.'

'Will you not stop still for a moment.'

'The baking will spoil, but I can listen well enough while I work.'

Ralph shifted his feet, and hunched his shoulders uncertainly. It was not as he had planned it. It was going to be a feat of timing and dexterity to sweep her up in arms all covered with flour and dough and with a heavy rolling-pin clutched in her hands.

'Salina, you are the most beautiful girl – woman – I mean, lady, that I have ever seen.'

'That's kind, but untrue, Ralph. I do have a mirror, you know.'

'It's true, I swear –'

'Please don't swear, Ralph. In any event, there are much more important things in life than physical beauty – kindness, and goodness and understanding, for instance.'

'Oh yes, and you have all those.'

Suddenly Salina stopped in mid stroke, and she stared at him with an expression of dawning consternation.

'Ralph,' she whispered. 'Cousin Ralph –'

'Cousin I may be,' he was stammering slightly in his rush to have it all said, 'but I love you, Salina, I loved you from the first moment I saw you at the river.'

'Oh Ralph, my poor dear Ralph.' Consternation was mingled now with compassion.

'I would never have spoken, not before – but now, after this expedition I have some substance. I will be able to pay off my debts, and when I come back I will have my own wagons. I am not yet rich, but I will be.'

'If only I had known. Oh Ralph, if only I had suspected, I would have been able to –'

But he was gabbling it out now.

'I love you, Salina, oh how dearly I love you, and I want you to marry me.'

She came to him then, and her eyes filled with blue tears that trembled on her lower lids.

'Oh dear Ralph. I am so sorry. I would have given anything to save you from hurt. If only I had known.'

He stopped then, bewildered. 'You will not – does that mean you will not marry me?' The bewilderment faded, and his jaw thrust out and his mouth hardened. 'But why not, I will give you everything, I will cherish and –'

'Ralph.' She touched his lips, and left a little dab of flour upon them. 'Hush, Ralph, hush.'

'But, Salina, I love you! Don't you understand?'

'Yes, I do. But, dear Ralph, I don't love you!'

Cathy and the twins went as far as the river with Ralph. Vicky and Lizzie rode, two up, on Tom's back. They rode astride, with their skirts up around their thighs, and squealed with delight every few seconds, until Ralph thought his eardrums would split, and he scowled moodily ahead – not replying to Cathy's questions and comments as she skipped along beside him, until the spring went out of her step and she, too, fell silent.

The bank of the Khami river was where they would part. All of them knew that, without speaking about it. And when they reached it Isazi had already taken the wagon through the drift. The ironshod wheels had left deep scars in the far bank. He would be an hour or so ahead. They stopped on the near bank and now even the twins were silent. Ralph looked back along the track, lifting his hat and shading his eyes with the brim against the early sunlight.

'Salina isn't coming then?' he said flatly.

'She's got a belly ache,' said Vicky. 'She told me so.'

'If you ask me, it's more like the curse of Eve,' said Lizzie airily.

'That's rude,' Cathy said. 'And only silly little girls talk about things they don't understand.'

Lizzie looked chastened, and Vicky assumed a virtuous air of innocence.

'Now both of you say goodbye to Cousin Ralph.'

'I love you, Cousin Ralph,' said Vicky, and had to be prised off him like a leach.

'I love you, Cousin Ralph.'

Lizzie had counted the kisses that Vicky had bestowed on him, and she went for a new world record, a noble attempt, but frustrated by Cathy.

'Now, scat,' Cathy told them. 'Go, both of you.'

'Cathy is crying,' said Lizzie, and both twins were immediately entranced.

'I am not,' said Cathy furiously.

'Oh yes, you are,' said Vicky.

'I have something in my eye.'

'Both eyes?' asked Lizzie sceptically.

'I warn you,' Cathy told them. They knew that expression of old, and reluctantly they retired just out of range. Cathy turned her back to them so they missed half of what followed.

'They are right.' Her whisper was as blurred as her eyes. 'I am crying, Ralph. I hate so to see you go.'

Ralph had not truly looked at her, not ever, his eyes had been for Salina alone, but now her frank admission touched him and he saw her for the first time.

He had thought her a child, but he had been wrong, he realized suddenly. It was the thick dark eyebrows and the firm chin that gave strength to her face, so that he sensed that anything that made her cry was deeply felt. Surely she had not been so tall when first he met her almost a year before. Now the top of her head reached his chin.

The freckles on her cheeks kept her young, but her nose was set in the shape of maturity and the gaze of her green eyes below the arched brows, though flooded now with tears, was too wise and steady for childhood.

She still wore the muddy green dress of sewn flour sacks, but its fit had altered. Now it was baggy at the waist, while at the same time it was too tight across her chest. Yet it could not suppress the thrust of young firm breasts, and the seams strained across hips that he remembered being as narrow and bony as a boy's.

'You will come back, Ralph? Unless you promise, I cannot let you go.'

'I promise,' he said, and suddenly the pain of rejection by Salina, which he had thought might destroy him, was just supportable.

'I will pray for you each day until you do,' Cathy said, and came to kiss him. She no longer felt skinny and awkward in his arms, and Ralph was suddenly very aware of the softness of her against his chest – and lower.

Her mouth had a taste like chewing a stalk of green spring grass. Her lips formed a pillow for his. He had no burning desire to break the embrace, and Cathy also seemed content to let it persist. The pain of unrequited love ebbed a little more to be replaced by a warm and comforting sensation, a most pleasant glow, until with a shock Ralph realized two things.

Firstly, the twins were an avid audience, their eyes enormous and their grins impudent. Secondly, that the pleasant glow which had suffused him had its source considerably lower than his broken heart, and was accompanied by more tangible changes that must soon become apparent to the fresh young innocent in his arms.

He almost shoved her away, and vaulted up onto Tom's back with unnecessary violence. However, when he looked down at Cathy again, the tide of green tears in her eyes had receded and been replaced by a look of satisfaction, a knowingness that proved beyond doubt what he had just come to realize, that she was no longer a child.

'How long?' she asked.

'Not before the end of the rains,' he told her. 'Six or seven months from now.' And suddenly that seemed to Ralph to be a very long time indeed.

'Anyway,' she said. 'I have your promise.'

On the far bank of the river he looked back. The twins had lost interest and started home. They were racing each other down the track, skirts and plaits flying – but Cathy still stood staring after him. Now she lifted her hand and waved. She kept waving until horse and rider disappeared amongst the trees.

Then she sat down on a log beside the track. The sun made its noon and then sank into the misty smoke of the bush fires that blued the horizon and turned to a soft red orb that she could look at directly without paining her eyes.

In the gloaming a leopard sawed and hacked harshly from the dense dark riverine forest nearby. Cathy shivered and stood up. She cast one last lingering glance across the wide riverbed and then at last she turned for home.

Bazo could not sleep; hours ago he had left his sleeping-mat and come to squat by the fire in the centre of the hut. The others had not even stirred when he moved, Zama and Kamuza and Mondane, those who would accompany him tomorrow.

Their finery was piled beside their recumbent figures. The cloaks of feathers and furs and beads, the headdresses and kilts – the regalia reserved for only the most grave and momentous occasions – like the Festival of the First Fruits, or a personal report to the king, or, again, the ceremony for which they had gathered and which would start at the dawn of the morrow.

Bazo looked at them now, and his chest felt congested with his joy, joy so intense that it sang in his ears and fizzed in his blood. Joy even more intense in that these his companions of the years, with whom he had shared boyhood and youth and now manhood, would be there again at one of the most important days of his life.

Now Bazo sat alone at the fire while his companions snored and muttered in sleep, and he took each coin of his good fortune and, like a miser counting his treasure, fondled it with his mind, turning each memory over and gloating upon it.

He lived again every moment of his triumph when the lines of captive women had filed before Lobengula and piled the spoils in front of his wagon, the bars and coils of red copper, the axe heads, the leather bags of salt, the clay pots full of beads, for Pemba had been a famous wizard and had gathered his tribute from a host of fearful clients.

Lobengula had smiled when he saw his treasure, for that was what had been at the root of his feud with Pemba. The king was not above the jealousies of common men. When Lobengula smiled, all his indunas smiled in sympathy and made those little clucking sounds of approval.

Bazo remembered how the king had called him forward, and smiled again when

Bazo emptied the bag he carried over his shoulder, and the wizard's head, which by then was in an advanced state of decomposition, had rolled to the forewheel of the wagon and grinned up at Lobengula with ruined lips drawn back from uneven teeth stained by the hemp pipe.

A troop of the gaunt, mange-ridden pariah dogs that skulked about the king's kraal had come to snarl and squabble over the morsel, and when one of the black-cloaked executioners would have scattered them with blows of his knobkerrie, the king restrained him.

'The poor beasts are hungry, let them be.' And he turned back to Bazo. 'Tell me how it was done.'

Bazo relived in his mind every word with which he had described the expedition, and while he told it he had begun to *giya*, to dance and sing the ode to Pemba which he had composed:

> 'Like a mole in the earth's gut
> Bazo found the secret way –'

He sang, and in the front row of the senior indunas, Gandang, his father, sat grave and proud.

> 'Like the blind catfish
> that live in the caves of Sinoia
> Bazo swam through darkness –'

Then as the verses of the song mentioned them, Zama and his warriors sprang forward to whirl and dance at his side.

> 'Like the black mamba from under a stone
> Zama milked death from his silver fang –'

When the triumph dance was over, they threw themselves face down on the earth in front of the wagon.

'Bazo, son of Gandang, go out and choose two hundred head from the royal herds,' said Lobengula.

'*Bayete!*' shouted Bazo, still panting from the dance.

'Bazo, son of Gandang – you who commanded fifty so skilfully – now I give you one thousand to command.'

'*Nkosi!* Lord!'

'You will command the levy of young men waiting now at the royal kraal on the Shangani river. I give you the insignia for your new regiment. Your shields will be red, your kilts the tails of the genet cat, your plumes the wing feathers of the marabou stork, and your headband the fur of the burrowing mole,' Lobengula intoned, and then paused. 'The name of your regiment will be Izimvukuzane Ezembintaba – the moles that burrow under a mountain.'

'*Nkosi kakhula!* Great King!' Bazo roared.

'Now Bazo, rise up and go into the women to choose yourself a wife. Be sure that she is virtuous and fruitful, and let her first duty be to set the headring of the induna on your brow.'

'*Indhlovu! Ngi ya bonga!* Great Elephant, I praise you!'

Sitting his solitary watch by the fire, Bazo remembered every word, every change of tone, every pause and emphasis that the king had used to heap his honours upon him. He sighed with contentment and placed another log upon the fire, carefully so as not to wake his companions, and the sparks floated up through the opening in the highest point of the domed roof.

Then a distant sound interrupted his reverie; it was the single whoop of a hyena, not an unusual sound except that it was the first time that he had heard it since nightfall. On every other night the hideous cries of these loathsome animals began when they crept from their burrows at dusk and continued until sunrise.

They haunted the small woody copse beyond the cattle enclosure that all the inhabitants of Gandang's kraal used as a communal open-air latrine. The hyena cleansed the area of excrement during the hours of darkness. For this reason, Gandang's people tolerated the presence of an animal that they usually abhorred with a superstitious dread.

So tonight the single whooping cry at midnight drew attention to the silence that had preceded it. Bazo listened a few seconds longer and then let his thoughts stray to the morrow.

After the king, Gandang was one of the three most important personages in Matabeleland – only Somabula and Babiaan were his peers, so that a marriage at his kraal would have been a momentous event even if it were not his eldest son – himself a newly appointed induna of one thousand – who was to be the bridegroom.

Juba, senior wife of Gandang, and mother of Bazo the bridegroom, had supervised the brew of beer, watching with an expert eye for the bloom of yeast on the germinating sorghum, testing with her own plump finger the temperature of the ground meal gruel as it was malted, judging the addition of the final booster of yeast and then standing over the matrons as they strained the brewing through woven bamboo sieves into the huge black clay beer-pots. Now there were a thousand pots each holding half a gallon of her famous brew, ready to greet the guests as they arrived at Gandang's kraal. There would be a thousand invited guests.

Lobengula and his retinue were already on the road; they were sleeping tonight at the regimental kraal of the Intemba regiment, only five miles distant, and they would arrive before noon.

Somabula was with the king, while Babiaan was coming in from his kraal in the east with a hundred warriors in his bodyguard. Nomusa and Hlopi were coming from the mission station at Khami as Juba's special guests, and they were bringing all their daughters with them.

Gandang had picked fifty fat bullocks from his herds, and the bridegroom and his young companions would begin to slaughter and butcher them in the dawn – while the unmarried girls took the bride down to the river pool, bathed her and then anointed her with fat and clay until she glistened in the early sunlight. Then they would deck her with wild flowers.

The hyena called again much closer this time, sounding as if it were right outside the stockade – and then a strange thing happened. The single cry was answered by a chorus, as though a great multitude of the huge shaggy spotted dog-like beasts had surrounded Gandang's kraal.

Bazo started up from the fire in astonishment. He had never heard anything to equal this – there must be a hundred or more of the ungainly animals out there. He could imagine them, their high shoulders sloping down to meagre hindquarters, the flat snake-like heads held low as though the weight of massive underslung jaw and yellow carnassial teeth was too heavy for the neck.

One hundred at least, he could almost smell their breath as they opened those iron jaws, capable of crunching the thigh bone of a bull buffalo to splinters. They would reek of long-dead carrion and excrement and other filth, but it was the sound of their voices that chilled Bazo's guts and started the march of ghost feet along his spine.

It was as though all the souls of the dead had risen from their graves to clamour outside Gandang's stockade. They whooped and howled, beginning in a low moan and rising sharply in key.

'Oooh – wee!'

They shrieked like the ghost of a Mashona feeling again the steel cleave his breast, and the terrible cries woke the echoes amongst the kopjes along the river.

Almost humanly, they giggled, and they laughed – that maniacal and mirthless laughter. The peals of fiendish laughter mingled with the tormented shrieks, and then with them were the cries of the kraal's watchmen, the screeches of the waking women in their huts, the shouts of the men, still half-asleep, as they scrambled for their weapons.

'Do not go out,' Kamuza shouted across the hut as Bazo sprang to the door with his shield on his shoulder and his assegai in his right hand. 'Do not go into the dark, this is a witchcraft. Those are not animals out there.'

His words stopped Bazo at the threshold. There was nothing of flesh and blood he would not face, but this –

The fiendish chorus reached a climax, and then abruptly ceased. The silence that followed was even more chilling, and Bazo shrank away from the door. His companions crouched on their sleeping-mats, weapons in their hands, their eyes wide and white in the firelight – but not one of them moved towards the door.

All of Gandang's kraal was awake now, but silent, waiting, the women creeping away into the farthest recesses of their huts and covering their heads with their fur karosses, the men frozen with superstitious terror.

The silence lasted the time it would take for a man to run the full circle of the stockade, and then was broken by the call of a single hyena, the same whooping cry, starting low and rising to a shriek. The head of every one of the warriors in Bazo's hut lifted, and they all stared upwards to the roof and the star-pricked sky above it – for that was from where the ghostly cry emanated – from the very air high above Gandang's kraal.

'Sorcery.' Kamuza's voice shook, and Bazo choked down on the wail of terror that rose in his own throat.

As the animal cry died in the night, there was only one other sound. The voice of a young girl, raised in terrible distress.

'Bazo! Help me, Bazo!'

It was the only thing that could have roused him. Bazo shook himself like a dog that leaps from water to land, throwing off the terror that paralysed him.

'Do not go!' Kamuza yelled, after him. 'It is not the girl, it is a witch voice.'

But Bazo tore the locking bar from the door.

He saw her immediately. Tanase raced towards him from the women's quarters, from Juba's own great hut where she had been passing the last night before her nuptials.

Her dark naked body was without substance, like a moon shadow as she sped to him. Bazo leaped towards her, and they met in front of the main gate of the stockade, and Tanase clung to him.

No other person had left the huts; the kraal was deserted, the fearful silence oppressive. Bazo lifted his shield to cover both himself and the girl – and instinctively he turned to face the gateway. It was only then that he realized that the gate was open.

He tried to retreat towards the hut, taking the girl with him, but she was rigid in his arms, rooted to the earth like the stump of a wild ebony tree – and his own strength was sapped by terror.

'Bazo,' Tanase whispered. 'It is them, they have come.'

As she spoke the watch-fire beside the gate, which had long ago burned down to ash and charred logs, suddenly burst into flame once again. The flames sprang higher than a man's head, roaring like a waterfall, and the stockade and gateway were lit brightly by the yellow dancing light. Beyond the open gateway, at the very edge of the firelight stood a human figure. It was the figure of a very old man, with stick-like limbs and bowed back; his cap of hair was white as the salt from the Makarikari pan; his skin was grey and dusty with age. The whites of his eyes flashed as they squinted and rolled upwards into his skull, and glassy strings of spittle dribbled from his toothless mouth onto his chest, wetting the dry parchment skin through which each skeletal rib stood out clearly.

His voice was a quavering ancient squeal.

'Tanase!' he called. 'Tanase, daughter of the spirits.'

In the firelight all life went out of Tanase's eyes; they became blank.

'Do not heed –' Bazo croaked, but a bluish sheen appeared over Tanase's eyeballs like the nictitating membrane that covers the eye of a shark or the cataract of tropical ophthalmia, and blindly her head turned towards the spectral figure beyond the gates.

'Tanase, your destiny calls you!'

She broke out of Bazo's arms. It seemed to require no effort. He could not hold her. Her strength was superhuman.

She began to walk towards the gateway, and when Bazo tried to follow her, he found he could not lift a foot. He dropped his shield, and it clattered on the hard earth, but Tanase did not look back. She walked with a floating grace, light as river mist towards the ancient stooped figure.

'Tanase!' Bazo's voice was a despairing cry, and he fell upon his knees, yearning after her.

The old man held out one hand, and Tanase took it, and as she did so, the watch-fire died down as abruptly as it had flared, and the darkness beyond the gateway was instantly impenetrable.

'Tanase!' whispered Bazo, his arms outstretched – and far away, down by the river the hyena called one last time.

The twins came pelting into the church, tumbling over each other with eagerness to be the first to tell.

'Mama! Mama! –'

'Vicky, I saw first, let me!'

Robyn Codrington looked up from the black body stretched on the table and quelled them with a frown.

'Ladies don't push.'

They came up in a parody of demureness, but hopping with impatience.

'Very well, Vicky. What is it?'

They began together, and Robyn stopped them again.

'I said Vicky.'

And Victoria puffed up importantly.

'There is someone coming.'

'From Thabas Indunas?' Robyn asked.

'No, Mama, from the south.'

'It's probably one of the king's messengers.'

'No, Mama, it's a white man on a horse.'

Robyn's interest quickened; she would never have admitted even to herself how often the isolation palled. A white traveller would mean news, perhaps letters, stores and supplies, or even the most precious of all, books. Failing those treasures there would be the mere mental stimulation of a strange face and of conversation and ideas.

She was tempted to leave the patient on the table, it was not a serious burn, but she checked herself.

'Tell Papa I shall come directly,' she said, and the twins fled, jammed in the doorway for a moment, and then popped through like a cork from a champagne bottle.

By the time Robyn had finished dressing the burn, dismissed the patient, washed her hands and hurried out onto the porch of the church – the stranger was coming up the hill.

Clinton was leading the mule on which he was mounted. It was a big strong-looking grey animal, so the rider looked small and slim upon the broad back. He was a lad, dressed in an old tweed jacket and a boy's cloth cap. The twins danced on each side of the mule, and Clinton at its head was looking back over his shoulder, listening to something that the stranger was saying.

'Who is it, Mama?' Salina came out of the kitchen and called across the yard.

'We shall find out in a moment.'

Clinton led the mule to the porch, and the rider's head was on a level with Robyn's.

'Dr Ballantyne, your grandfather, Dr Moffat, sent me to you, I have letters and gifts from him for you.'

With a start Robyn realized that under the patched tweed coat and cap was a woman – and even in that moment of surprise she was aware that it was an extraordinarily handsome woman, younger than Robyn herself, not much over thirty years of age, with steady, dark eyes and almost Mongolian cheekbones.

She jumped down from the mule with the agility of an expert horsewoman, and came up the steps of the porch to seize Robyn's hands. Her grip was firm as a man's, and her expression was intense.

'My husband is ill and suffering. Dr Moffat says you are the only one who can help him. Will you do it? Oh please, will you?'

'I am a doctor.' Robyn gently twisted her fingers out of the other woman's painful grip – but it was not that which troubled her – there was something too intense, too passionate about her. 'I am a doctor, and I could never refuse to help anyone who is suffering. Of course, I shall do whatever I can.'

'Do you promise that?' the woman insisted, and Robyn bridled slightly.

'I have said I will help, there is no need to promise.'

'Oh, thank you.' The woman smiled with relief.

'Where is your husband?'

'Not far behind. I rode ahead to warn you – and to make sure that you would help us.'

'What is it that ails your husband?'

'Dr Moffat has explained it all in a letter. He sent gifts for you also.' The woman was evasive, turning away from Robyn's scrutiny and running back to the mule.

From the saddle-bags she lifted down two packages, wrapped in oilskin to protect them against the elements and bound up with rawhide thongs. They were so heavy and bulky that Clinton took them from her and carried them into the church.

'You are tired,' Robyn said. 'I am sorry I cannot offer you coffee, we used the last a month ago – but a glass of lemonade?'

'No.' The woman shook her head decidedly. 'I shall go back immediately, to be with my husband – but we shall arrive before nightfall.'

She ran back, and vaulted lightly to the mule's back. None of them had ever seen a woman do that.

'Thank you,' she repeated, and then trotted out of the yard, back down the hill.

Clinton came out of the church and put one arm around Robyn's shoulders.

'What a very beautiful and unusual woman,' he said, and Robyn nodded. That was one of the things that had troubled her. Robyn mistrusted beautiful women.

'What is her name?' she asked.

'I didn't have a chance to ask.'

'You were too busy looking, perhaps,' Robyn suggested tartly, and wriggled out from under his arm and went back into the church, while Clinton stared after her with a rueful expression.

After a moment he made a move as if to follow her – but then sighed and shook his head. It was always as well to let Robyn come round on her own, coaxing only angered her even more unreasonably.

In the quiet of the church Robyn untied the first package, and unpacked the contents onto the table.

There were five heavy bottles with glass stoppers, and she read the labels as she lifted out each one.

'Carbolic Acid.'

'Alum.'

'Quicksilver.'

'Iodine.'

And then the fifth bottle was labelled:

'Trichloromethane.'

'Bless you, Grandfather.' She smiled delightedly – but still she unstoppered the last bottle and sniffed cautiously at the mouth to confirm her good fortune.

The pungent sweet odour was unmistakable. Chloroform was to her more precious than her own life's blood; she would gladly have exchanged drop for drop.

Her own last supply had been exhausted months before and the London Missionary Society was as parsimonious as ever with its stores. She wished she had retained just a few hundred guineas of her enormous book royalties to enable her to purchase her own medicines rather than having to plead for them with the secretary in London by a correspondence which often took twelve months each way.

Sometimes, in a flagrantly unchristian manner, she wished she could have that bloodless myopic little man at her side when she removed an eye damaged by a blow with a knobkerrie and hanging out of its socket onto a black cheek, or when she went for a Caesarian section – all without anaesthetic.

She hugged the bottle to her chest for a moment.

'Darling Grandfather,' she repeated, then as reverently as if it were the fabulous Kohinoor diamond, she set the bottle of colourless but precious fluid aside, and turned to the second package.

A roll of newspapers – *The Cape Times* and *The Diamond Fields Advertiser*. In the weeks ahead every column would be read and re-read, down to the announcements of auction sales and the legal notices; then the newsprint itself would be used for a dozen domestic chores. Under the newspaper – books, wonderful fat leather-bound books.

'Bless you, Robert Moffat.'

She lifted out a translation of Ibsen's *An Enemy of the People*. She admired the Norwegian for his insight into the human mind, and the muted poetry of his prose. Robert Louis Stevenson's *Virginibus Puerisque*'; the title made her pause. She had four virgins in her household, and she intended maintaining that happy condition without allowing any inflammatory literature to thwart her. She flipped through the book. Despite the dubious title, it was merely a collection of essays – and the man was a good Calvinistic Scot. It might just do to let the girls read it, but she would vet it first.

Then there was Mark Twain's *Tom Sawyer*. Here she was less sanguine. She had heard of this American's frivolous and irreverent attitude towards adolescence, industry and filial duty. She would read it carefully before letting it anywhere near Salina or Catherine. Reluctantly she left the other books for future study and turned to her grandfather's letter.

There were many pages, written with sooty home-made ink, and the script was shaky and wavering. She skimmed swiftly through the salutations and the personal news until she reached the middle of the second page:

Robyn, they say a doctor buries his mistakes: blatantly untrue. I send mine to you. The patient who delivers this letter should long ago have sought the sanctuary of a modern hospital, such as that at Kimberley.

This he has steadfastly refused to do. His reasons are his own, and I have not pried. However, the fact that for over a year now he has had a pistol ball lodged in his body may point to his motives.

Twice I have cut for this foreign body, but at 87 years of age my eyes are not as bright nor my hand as steady as yours. Each time I have failed and I fear that I have done more harm than good.

I know that you have interest and skill in treatment of this type of injury, as so you should, for you have been provided by young Lobengula's warriors with endless opportunity to practise your technique. I recall with admiration your inspired reintroduction of the spoon of Diokles, after nearly 2,000 years, which you designed from the contemporary description by Celsus – and your successful removal of barbed arrowheads with it.

Thus I send you one more subject on which to demonstrate your art – and with him my last bottle of Chloroform; for the poor fellow – whatever his sins – has suffered enough under my knife.

The letter left her with a sense of foreboding – as did the woman who had delivered it. She folded the letter and thrust it into the pocket of her skirt as she left the church and hurried across the yard.

'Cathy,' she called. 'Where is that girl! She must set the guest-house to rights.'

'She's gone to it already, Mama.' Salina looked up as she stormed into the kitchen. 'Then where is your father?'

Within an hour the mission station was prepared to receive guests, and buzzing with anticipation; but they had to wait until mid-afternoon before a two-wheeled cart of unusually high and heavy construction appeared over the rise before the river. It was drawn by a pair of mules.

The entire family assembled on the front porch of the main building, and all of them had changed their clothing, while the girls had also brushed and dressed their hair with ribbons. A dozen times the twins had to be cautioned for improper comments and unrestrained behaviour, but finally the cart wheeled into the yard.

The woman had put her mule into the traces and now she walked beside the wheel of the cart, which reached almost as high as her head. There was a coloured servant in ragged cast-off clothes leading the mules, and over the body of the cart was rigged a makeshift sunshade of saplings and stained canvas.

Below the porch the cart stopped, and all of them craned forward as a man's head and upper body appeared above its side. He was laid on a straw mattress on the floor of the cart, and now he lifted himself on one elbow.

He was a gaunt wasted figure; the flesh seemed to have melted from the big bones of his shoulders. His cheeks had fallen in and turned a muddy yellow, the hand on the side of the cart was bony, and the veins were roped under the skin like blue serpents. His hair bushed wildly about his head, coarse dark hair that was shot through with strands of dead white. He had not shaved in days; thick stubble covered his jaws and was salted with the same white as his hair. One eye was sunk into a bruised cavity, and it had that feverish glitter that Robyn recognized instantly. It was the look of mortal illness.

The other eye was covered by a black piratical patch. There was something dreadfully familiar about the big aquiline nose and the wide mouth – yet it was only when he smiled that old mocking yet somehow tender smile that she had never forgotten that Robyn reeled backwards, one hand flying to her mouth too late to stop her cry.

She caught for support at one of the mopani poles that held the roof.

'Mama, are you all right?' But Robyn pushed Salina's hands away and went on staring at the man in the cart.

Only one memory out of so many rose up like a freak wave out of a storm-swept sea to overwhelm her. She saw again that dark bush of curls, devoid only of its silver lacing, bowing to her naked bosom. She saw above her the beamed roof of the great cabin in the sternquarters of the slave ship *Huron*, and she remembered as she had a thousand times in the twenty years since then – that pain. The deep splitting incursion that rocked her. Four childbirths since then had not eradicated the memory of it, the agony of passing from maiden to woman.

Her senses wavered, there was a rushing in her ears, she was going to fall, but then Clinton's voice steadied her. The hard fierce tone of it which she had not heard in years.

'You!' he said.

As Clinton drew himself erect, the years seemed to fall away from him. He was once again tall and lithe, stiff with anger as the young Royal Naval officer who had come up onto the slaver's quarter-deck with pistols and a naval cutlass on his hip to confront this same man.

Still clinging to the verandah pole, Robyn remembered the words he had spoken then in that same fierce tone:

'Captain Mungo St John, your reputation precedes you, sir. The first trader ever to transport more than three thousand souls across the middle passage in a single twelve-month period – I'd give five years' pay to have the hatches off your holds, sir.'

Robyn remembered then how it had taken another year for Clinton to get his wish, when off Good Hope he had come back onto *Huron*'s decks, boarding her over the stern in the cannon smoke with his fighting seamen at his back, and how this action had cost him more than a mere five years' pay. He had been court-martialled and cashiered from the Royal Navy and imprisoned for it.

'You dare to come here, to us.' Clinton was pale with rage; his blue eyes, so gentle for so long, were bleak and hating. 'You, you cruel and bloody slaver, you dare to come here.'

Mungo St John was still smiling, taunting him with that smile and the glitter in his single eye, but his voice was low and rough with his suffering.

'And you, you kind and sainted Christian gentleman, do you dare to turn me away?'

Clinton flinched as though he had been struck across the face, and he took a step backwards. Slowly the litheness and youth went out of his stance, his shoulders slumped into their habitual stoop. He shook his bald head uncertainly, and then instinctively he turned towards Robyn.

With a huge effort Robyn gathered herself, pushed away from the supporting pole. Despite the turmoil of her emotions she managed to keep her expression neutral.

'Dr Ballantyne,' Louise St John came to the steps of the verandah. She took the cap from her head, and the thick black plait tumbled out from under it.

'I find it difficult to beg,' she said. 'But I am begging now.'

'That is not necessary, madam. I gave you my word.' Robyn turned away. 'Clinton, please help Mrs St John to put this patient into the bed in the guest-house.'

'Yes, dear.'

'I shall be there directly to make an examination.'

'Thank you, Doctor, oh thank you.' Robyn ignored Louise, but when she had followed the mule cart across the yard to the guest-hut, she turned to face her daughters.

'None of you – not even you, Salina – will go near the guest-house while that man is here. You will not speak to him or the woman, you will not answer if they speak to you. You will do your best to avoid seeing either of them, and if you do by error find yourself in their presence, you will leave immediately.'

The twins were quivering with excitement, their eyes shone, and even their ears seemed to be pink and pricked like those of a pair of young bunny rabbits. They could not remember a day so wildly exciting.

'Why?' gasped Vicky, forgetting herself sufficiently in this incredible series of events to question her mother's order. For a moment it seemed that she would have to pay for the impertinence with a box on one pink ear, but Robyn's hand dropped back to her side.

'Because–' Robyn said softly, '–because he is the devil – the very devil.'

He was propped on the iron cot, with a bolster under his shoulders, and Louise rose from the other cot as Robyn entered the guest-hut carrying her bag.

'Madam, will you kindly wait outside,' Robyn ordered brusquely and, not deigning to see if she would obey, Robyn placed her bag on the chair beside his cot. Behind her the latch on the door clicked.

Mungo St John wore only a pair of baggy white trousers from which one leg had been hacked off high in the thigh. Like his face, his body was wasted by sickness, but there was still the width of shoulder and the solidity of bone that she remembered so well. His belly had sunk in like that of a greyhound, and his ribs stood out in a rack above it, but his skin retained the texture and silkiness of a far younger man, while the body hair that was crimped into curls upon his chest was not marred with silver as was his beard and the hair upon his head.

'Hello, Robyn,' he said.

'I will speak to you only when it is absolutely necessary for your treatment, and you will do the same,' she said, without looking at his face.

She started with the wounds in his flank and back – bullet wounds, she realized, but through and through – and completely healed. Then with a little start she noticed the other old, long-healed scar just below the bullet wound.

She recognized the little white pricks of the suture which had closed the knife-cut. Her own work was distinctive, there was nobody who could throw down those even and precise knotted sutures as she could, and before she realized what she was doing she touched the old hardened cicatrice.

'Yes,' Mungo nodded. 'Camacho made that.'

She jerked her hand away. Mungo had taken that knife-cut when he had intervened to protect her from the Portuguese slaver. He had saved her life that night.

'Do you remember this also?' Mungo asked, and showed her the pock mark on his forearm. That was where she had inoculated him when smallpox had swept through *Huron*.

'Do you remember?' Mungo insisted softly, but she kept her face averted and her lips compressed in a thin hard line as she lifted the dressing from his upper leg.

Then the horror showed on her face. Her grandfather's uneven knife strokes had lacerated the leg from knee to groin, where he had probed and searched for the ball, and his crude stitches had cobbled it all back together like a man repacking a valise in haste.

'Bad?' Mungo asked.

'It's a mess,' she said, and then hated herself for unbending that far, and by inference criticizing her grandfather's work.

The flesh of the leg had that unhealthy putty colour, and there was ulceration in the wounds, that awful sloughing of tissue that hinted at the corruption beneath.

Her grandfather had left drains in the wounds, thick black horse hairs that stuck stiffly out between the stitches. She drew one now, and Mungo gasped but did not flinch. A weak little trickle of watery pus followed the hair out. She stooped and sniffed it and grimaced. This was not the rich creamy pus that the ancients had called *'pus bonum et laudabile'*. From the stink of it, gangrene was not far off. She felt a little icy splinter of dread, and immediately wondered at it; surely there were no feelings left in her for this man.

'Tell me how it happened?'

'That, doctor, is my business.'

'Dirty business, I have no doubt,' she snapped. 'And I want no lurid account of it, but if I am to locate the ball I must know where you were in relationship to the weapon that was fired at you, the type of weapon, the weight and charge –'

'Of course,' he said quickly. 'Your grandfather did not bother to enquire.'

'Leave my grandfather out of it.'

'The man used a pistol; it looked like a single-action Remington army model, in which case the ball would be .44, of lead, cone-shaped, weight one fifty grains, and driven by black powder.'

'Low penetration, break up of the ball if it hit bone,' she muttered.

'The man was lying on the ground, about twenty-five paces distant, and I was in the act of dismounting from my horse, this leg raised – '

'He was ahead of you.'

'Slightly ahead and on my right hand.'

Robyn nodded. 'This will hurt.' And ten minutes later she stood back and called, 'Mrs St John.'

As soon as Louise entered, she said, 'I shall operate as soon as the light is good enough tomorrow morning. I shall need your assistance. I warn you now that even if I am successful, your husband will not recover full use of the leg. He will always have a pronounced limp.'

'And if you are unsuccessful?'

'The degeneration will accelerate, mortification and gangrene– '

'You are frank, doctor,' Louise whispered.

'Yes,' Robyn agreed. 'I always am.'

Robyn could not sleep, but she reminded herself that she seldom could on the eve of an operation under anaesthetic. Chloroform was such an unpredictable substance, the margins of safety were frighteningly narrow, overdosage, too high a concentration or inadequate oxygenation, would lead to primary collapse with fatal depression of the heart, lungs, liver and kidneys.

She lay beside Clinton in the darkness and ran through a mental list of her preparations for the morrow, and set her mind on the procedures she must adopt.

Firstly she must re-open and find the source of the mortification. She moved and Clinton stirred beside her and muttered in his sleep. She froze and waited for him to settle.

The distraction altered the direction of her thoughts, and she found she was thinking about the man and not the patient. For a while she tried to prevent it, and then gave in.

She remembered him on his quarter-deck, the white linen shirt open to the throat and his chest hair curling out of the V, his head thrown back to hail the masthead, the thick dark mane of his hair rippling in the wind.

Then suddenly she remembered that morning when she slipped out of her cabin and stepped out onto *Huron*'s main-deck. He had been under the deck pump, while two seamen worked the handles, and clear sea water hissed over him as he stood naked under the jet. She remembered his body and the way he smiled at her without attempting to cover it from her gaze. Then abruptly she remembered his eyes, those flecked yellow eyes above her in the gloom of the cabin, eyes like those of a leopard.

She moved again, and this time Clinton came half awake. He said her name and threw one arm across her at the level of her waist. For a while she lay quiescent under his arm and then slowly she reached down and drew up the hem of her nightdress. She took Clinton's wrist lightly and guided his hand downwards. She felt him come fully awake, heard his breathing change and his hand went on without her insistence.

Long ago she had learned, painfully, that there were limits to the restraint that she could exercise over her unruly sensuality. So now she closed her eyes, relaxed her limbs and let her imagination run unchecked.

She drank only a cup of the hot coffee substitute that she had concocted of roasted sorghum and wild honey – and while she did so she composed her mind by glancing through her notes.

She always found comfort in Celsus' injunctions, somehow the fact that they were written around the time of Christ made them more poignant.

> Now a surgeon, the chirugus, should be youthful or at any rate closer to youth than age, with a strong and steady hand that never trembles, ready to use left hand as well as right, with vision sharp and clear and spirit undaunted. . . .

Then there was Galen, the surgeon of the gladiators, the Roman who had stored all his experience in twenty-two volumes. Robyn had read them in the original Greek, and extracted the pearls of his genius, which she had used with great success in treating the gladiatorial-type wounds of Lobengula's young men. Though she had substituted alum for corn, iodine for pigeon dung, and carbolic acid for lamp black and oil in the fight against inflammation and mortification.

The kind of trauma that faced her now as she bowed over the long table in the church was much like those described by Galen, though caused by a different projectile. Mungo St John's hoarse, muffled breathing was the only sound in the quiet church. Robyn tested the depth of his coma by pricking his finger with a probe, and then immediately lifted the mask of plaited bamboo and lint from his nose and mouth.

Then she listened to his breathing as it eased, and found herself examining his face as she had not been able to while he was conscious. He was still a handsome man, despite the missing eye and marks of pain and of advancing age etched into his face. Louise St John had borrowed Clinton's straight razor the previous day. Mungo St John was clean-shaven now, and suddenly she realized that the new lines in his face and the silver wings above his temples accentuated the power of the man, while at the same time the relaxation of his mouth gave him a childlike innocence which made the breath catch in her throat.

Clinton looked across at her, and she turned her face away quickly before he could see her expression.

'Are you ready, madam?' Robyn made her voice cold and businesslike, and Louise nodded. She was very pale, the fine freckles standing out in sharp contrast on her cheeks and the bridge of her nose.

Still Robyn hesitated. She knew that she was squandering the moments during which the chloroform was having its blessed effect, but she was seized by a terrible dread. For the first time in her life she was afraid to wield the knife, and a thought transfixed her.

'If you once love a man, can you ever cease entirely to do so?'

She dared not look again at Mungo St John's sleeping face; she felt she must turn and run from the church.

'Are you unwell, doctor?' Louise St John's concern steeled her. She would not let this woman suspect weakness in her.

The leg was painted dark yellow brown with tincture of iodine. It looked like a rotten banana. She snipped her grandfather's stitches and the wound fell open. She saw the depth of the ulceration, and knew from dreadful experience that a wound like this would never heal, even by second intention. Her main task was not to find the pistol ball but to repair this damage.

She went in deeper, down past the thick pulsing snake of the femoral artery, down to the bone, the bared femur, and again she felt her spirits quail. The bone was malformed, yellow and cheesy.

She guessed at the cause, this was where the pistol ball had struck and been deflected away. It had struck a long splinter of bone off the femur, and she picked something out of the dead stinking tissue with the forceps and held it up to the light from the window.

It was a flake of black lead. She dropped it into the bucket under the table and bent once more over the open chasm in Mungo's flesh. There was hardly any blood, a few drops only from the stitches, and the rest of it was slimy yellow matter smelling like a corpse.

She knew the risks of attempting to remove this decomposing tissue surgically; she had tried it before – and killed in the process. It was drastic treatment which only a very strong man could survive, yet if she closed up, the macabre spectre of gangrene lurked close at hand.

She took up the scraper and it rasped over the exposed bone of the femur. Stinking pus welled up from out of the bone itself. Osteomyelitis, the mortification of the bony tissue. She worked at it grimly, the scraper was the only sound in the room until Louise St John choked.

'Madam, if you are going to throw up – please leave,' Robyn told her, without looking up.

'I shall be all right,' Louise whispered.

'Then use the swab as I instructed you,' Robyn snapped.

The rotten bone came away, curling off the blade in little yellow whorls like wood shavings from the carpenter's plane, until Robyn reached the porous core – and at last clean bright blood came up through it like wine from a sea sponge that had been squeezed, and the bone around the hole was hard and white as china.

Robyn sighed with relief, and at the same moment Mungo groaned and would have twitched the leg if Clinton had not been holding it at the ankle. Swiftly Robyn replaced the little bamboo basket over his nose and mouth then let a few drops of chloroform fall on the lint covering.

She cut away the rotten ulcerations, working perilously close to the artery and the white cord of the femoral nerve. She found more pockets of sepsis around the sutures with which her grandfather had closed the blood vessels. She cleaned these out and carefully cut away dead tissue.

There was blood now, plenty of it, but clean bright blood. Robyn had reached the most critical stage of the reparative surgery. She knew that there was still infection amongst the healthy tissue and as soon as she closed the wound it would blossom again.

She had mixed the antiseptic the night before, one part of carbolic acid to one hundred parts of rainwater. With this she washed out the open pit in Mungo's leg, and the astringent action of the mixture dried up the weeping blood from the vessels too small to tie off.

She could come out now, and sew up. She had left foreign bodies in before, and often they stabilized and became encysted, causing the patient little further discomfort, but instinct warned her not to do so this time.

She glanced at Clinton's big silver hunter watch, which he had placed beside her instrument case where she could see it readily. She had been in for twenty-five minutes, and experience had taught her that the longer she stayed in the greater the danger of primary or secondary collapse.

She looked up at Louise St John. She was still very pale, but the sweat of nausea had dried on her forehead. She had grit, Robyn conceded grudgingly, and that was one thing she could admire – much more than her exotic beauty.

'Madam, I am about to go after the ball now,' she said. 'I shall only have time for one attempt.'

She knew from Lister's writing and her own observation how risky it was to use her bare hands in a wound – but that risk was preferable to leading with a sharp instrument into the nest of veins, arteries and nerves in the groin.

She had guessed the location of the ball by the restricted movement of the femur within its pelvic socket, and by the focus of intense pain when she had palpated the area while Mungo was conscious. She probed with her forefinger, boldly up into the tissue above the raw scraped area of the bone. The direction of the shot, from ahead and upwards, must be on this line.

She met resistance and tried again, and then again. Suddenly her finger slid into a narrow canal in the hot meat of his thigh, right in to its full length, and then at the very limit of her reach she touched something hard. It could have been the head of the femur or the lower ridge of pelvic bone – but she took up the scalpel.

A fine needle jet of blood from a severed blood vessel sprayed her cheek and forehead before she could twist it closed, and she could hear Louise gagging again, but her hands with the swab barely shook as she wiped away the blood so that Robyn could cut again – and there was a rush of thick creamy yellow matter out of the cut like a dam burst by muddy flood waters. In the flood were little chips and fragments of shattered metal, rotting threads of woollen cloth and other detritus.

'Praise God!' whispered Robyn, and brought her hand out, dripping with the reeking yellow discharge, but with the distorted, misshapen lump of bluish lead held firmly between thumb and forefinger.

The twins had long ago discovered the literary treasure trove that Robyn kept in the locked cupboard against the far wall of her bedroom. Of course, they could only visit it when their parents and elder sisters were fully occupied elsewhere – for instance when King Ben had summoned them to GuBulawayo and Salina was cooking and Cathy was painting or reading.

Then they could sneak into the bedroom and push the chair against the wall so that Vicky standing on Lizzie's shoulders could reach the key.

There were more than fifty books in the cupboard. The great majority unfortunately contained no illustrations. These had proved unrewarding, as the twins' efforts at deciphering the text had been shipwrecked on too many rock-hard words; at other times, just when it was becoming intensely interesting, they would encounter a solid slab of foreign language which they suspected was either Latin or Greek.

The twins avoided these tomes, but the ones with pictures were a forbidden delight, greatly enhanced by danger and guilt. There was even one that had drawings of the inside of women, with and without a baby *in situ*, and another of the baby in the process of emerging.

However, their perennial favourite was the one they called 'The Devil Book' – for there was an illustration on each facing page vivid, lifelike and explicit, of souls in torment and the devils who attended them. The artist who had interpreted this edition of Dante's *Inferno* had dwelt ghoulishly on decapitation and disembowelment, on red-hot irons and hooks, lolling tongues and bulging eyes. Even the briefest stolen perusal of this masterpiece was enough to ensure that the twins would spend most of the following night clinging together in their bed, shivering with delicious terror.

However, this particular visit to the forbidden cupboard was in the interest of scientific research, otherwise they would never have taken the risk while Robyn Ballantyne was actually at Khami Mission.

They chose the time of morning clinic when Mama would certainly be in the church attending her patients, when Daddy would be mucking out the sties, and Salina and Cathy at their chores.

The raid went with the precision of repeated rehearsal. They left their open readers on the dining-room table, and were down the verandah and had the key within the time it takes to draw a long breath.

Lizzie took guard at the window from where she could cover kitchen, the church and the pigsties – while Vicky got the cupboard open and the 'Devil Book' out and open at the correct page.

'See!' she whispered. 'I told you so.'

There he was – Satan, Lucifer, King of the Underworld – and Vicky had been right. He did not have horns. All the lesser demons had horns, but not the Devil, not the very Devil himself. What he did have was a tail, a magnificent tail with a point like the blade of a Matabele assegai upon the end of it.

'He's got a beard in this picture,' Lizzie pointed out, reluctant to abandon her position.

'He probably shaved it off – to fool us,' Vicky told her. 'Now look!' She took a pin out of her hair and used the black round tip to cover one of Lucifer's eyes. Immediately the resemblance was undeniable, the thick dark curls, the broad forehead, the beaked nose and the piercing eye under arched brow, and the smile, the same satanically mocking smile.

Lizzie shuddered luxuriously. Vicky was right, it was him all right.

'Kitty Cat!' Vicky hissed a warning. Salina was coming out of the kitchen, and they had the book back on its shelf, the cupboard locked, the key back in its hiding-place, and were once more seated at the table poring over their readers by the time that Salina had crossed the yard and looked in upon them.

'Good.' She smiled at them tenderly, they were such an angelic pair – sometimes. 'Good girls,' she said, and went back towards the kitchen.

'Where does he put it?' Lizzie asked softly, without looking up from her reader.

'What?'

'His tail.'

'Watch!' Vicky ordered. 'And I'll show you.'

Napoleon, the aged yellow mongrel, was sleeping in the patch of sunlight on the verandah. He had a ridge down his back, and grey hair around his muzzle. Every few minutes a dream of rabbits and guineafowl made his back legs gallop spasmodically and he would puff off an evil-smelling fart of excitement.

'Bad dog!' Vicky said loudly. 'Napoleon, you are a bad, bad dog!'

Napoleon sprang to his feet, appalled by this unjust accusation, and wriggled his entire body ingratiatingly, while his upper lip lifted in a simpering sycophantic grin. At the same time his long whippy tail disappeared between his legs and curled up under his belly.

'That's how he tucks it away. Just like Napoleon,' Vicky announced.

'How do you know?'

'If you look carefully, you can see the bulge where it comes out in front of him.'

They worked on distractedly for a few seconds, then Lizzie could not restrain herself further.

'Do you think we could see his tail?'

'How?'

'What if we –' Halfway through propounding her scheme, Lizzie faltered. Even she realized that it would be impossible to modify the latrine, drilling a peephole through the back wall, without being apprehended; and their motives could never be convincingly explained, especially not to Mama.

'Anyway,' Vicky quashed the plan effectively, 'Devils are probably like fairies, they just don't go.'

Silence fell again. Obviously relieved that nobody had followed up the original accusation, Napoleon re-composed himself to his dreams, and it seemed the project was abandoned – until Vicky looked up with a determined gleam in her eyes.

'We are going to ask him.'

'But,' stammered Lizzie, 'but Mama forbade us to talk to him – ' She knew her protest to be unavailing; that gleam in Vicky's eye was familiar.

Ten days after she had removed the pistol ball, Robyn came down to the guest-house with a crutch carved from mopani wood.

'My husband made it for you,' she told Mungo St John. 'And you are going to use it every day from now on.'

The first day Mungo managed one halting circuit of the yard, and at the end of it he was pale and sweating. Robyn checked the leg and the stitches had all held, but the muscles of the thigh had withered and contracted, pulling the leg an inch shorter than the other. The next morning she was there to watch him at exercise. He moved more easily.

After fifteen days she removed the last catgut stitches, and though the scar was raised and thickened, a livid purplish red, yet there was no indication of mortification. It looked as though it had healed by first intention – the drastic use of strong antiseptic on living tissue seemed to have been justified.

After five weeks, Mungo abandoned the crutch in favour of a stout stick, and took the footpath that girded the kopje behind the Khami Mission.

Each day he walked farther and stayed out longer. It was a relief to be away from the bitter arguments with Louise which punctuated the long periods of her icy withdrawal.

He had found a viewpoint beyond the sharp northern ridge of the kopje, a natural platform and bench of dark serpentine rock under the spreading branches of a lovely old leadwood tree, where he could sit and brood out over the gently undulating grassland to the far blue silhouette of hills that marked the site of Lobengula's kraal.

His instinct warned him that there was an opportunity there. It was the instinct and the awareness of the cruising shark which could detect the presence of prey at distances and depths beyond the range of other senses. His instinct had seldom failed him, and there had been a time when he had seized every opportunity with boldness, with the ruthless application of all his skills and all his strength.

Sitting under the leadwood, his hands upon the head of the cane and his chin upon his hands, he cast his mind back to his triumphs: to the great ships that he had won and sailed to the ends of the oceans and brought back laden with treasures, with tea and coffee and spices or holds filled with black slaves. He remembered the rich fertile lands to which he had held title, and the sweet smell of sugar-cane fields when the harvest was being cut. He remembered piles of gold coins, carriages and beautiful horses – and women.

So many women, too many women perhaps; for they were the cause of his present low condition.

He let himself think of Louise at last. She had been a fire in his blood, which grew fiercer the more often he tried to slake it, and she had weakened him, distracted him, diverted him from his ruthless purpose of old.

She had been the daughter of one of his overseers on Fairfields, his vast Louisiana estate. When she was sixteen years of age he had allowed her to exercise his wife's Palamino horses; when she was seventeen he arranged for her to move into the big house as companion and maid to his wife and when she was eighteen he had raped her.

His wife was in the next-door bedroom, suffering from one of her black headaches, and he had torn Louise's clothes off her body, possessed by a madness that he had never known before. She had fought him with the savagery of one of her Blackfoot Indian ancestors, but in some perverse fashion her resistance maddened him as much as the glimpses of her hard young flesh, as it was revealed a gleaming flash at a time.

She had clawed red lines down his chest, and bitten him until he bled, but through it all she had not uttered a word or a sound, although a single scream would have brought her mistress or the house servants running.

In the end, he had borne her down onto the thick white pelt of a polar bear in the middle of the floor, naked except for the tatters of her petticoats hanging from her long fine legs, and with his full weight he had spread her and entered her.

Only then had she made any sound, she had gripped him with the same atavistic savagery, legs and arms encircling him, and she had whispered hoarsely, brokenly. 'I love you, I have always loved you, I shall always love you.'

When the armies of the North had marched against them, and his wife had fled with the children to her native France, Louise had stayed with him. When she could she had been in the field with him, and when she could not she had waited for him, filling in the days and most of the nights nursing the wounded at the Confederate Hospital in Galveston, and there she had nursed him when he was brought in half blinded and terribly hurt from the battlefield.

She had been with him when he went back to Fairfields for the last time, and shared his desolation at the burnt fields and ruined buildings, and she had been at his side ever since. Perhaps if she had not, things would have been different now, for she had weakened him; she had dulled the edge of his resolve.

So many times he had smelled out the opportunities – the chances for the coup which would restore it all, and each time she had caused him to waver.

'I could never respect you again,' she had said once. 'Not if you did that.'

'I never suspected you were capable of that, Mungo. It's wrong, morally wrong.'

Gradually it had changed, until sometimes, after another abortive attempt to restore his fortunes, she would look at him with a coldness – a kind of icy contempt.

'Why do you not leave me?' he had challenged her then.

'Because I love you,' she had replied. 'And, oh, sometimes how I wish I did not.'

In Perth, when he had forced her to bait the trap for him, luring in the intended victim – she had for the first time rebelled. She herself had ridden to warn the man, and they had been forced to run again, shipping out on a little trading schooner only an hour or so ahead of the constables with the warrant for Mungo's arrest.

He had never trusted her again, although he had never been able to make the decision to desert her. He found that he needed her still. At Cape Town a letter had finally caught up with Mungo. It was one of five copies sent out by his brother-in-law, the Duc de Montijo, a copy to each of the addresses that Mungo had occupied in the years since his wife had left him. Solange, his wife, had taken a chill while out riding and had died five days later of pneumonia. Her children were in the care of the

Duc, being educated with his own, and the Duc hinted that he would resist any attempt by Mungo St John to assume custody.

At last Mungo was free to make good his promise to Louise, the solemn promise he had made to her as they knelt hand in hand before the altar in London's church of St Martin-in-the-Fields. He had sworn in the sight of God that just as soon as he was able to do so, he would marry Louise.

Mungo had read through his brother-in-law's letter three times, and then held it in the flame of the candle. He had crushed the ashes to powder, and never mentioned the letter or its news to Louise. She had gone on believing that he was married, and their relationship had limped on, sickening and staling.

Yet still she could influence him even when she was not physically present. At the dark crossroads south of Kimberley, even when he had seen the diamonds gleam in Hendrick Naaiman's hands, he had not been able to banish Louise's image from his mind: Louise with contempt in her eyes and cold accusation on her lovely lips.

Expert marksman that he was, the shade of Louise had spoiled his aim. He had fired a wink too late, and a touch too wide. He had not killed the Bastaard, but if he had done so, Louise's reaction could have been no more severe.

When he rode back to where she waited, reeling in the saddle, the wounded stallion dragging under him, he had seen her face in the moonlight. Even though she caught him when he might have fallen, and though she had tended his wounds and gone for succour, he had realized that they had crossed a dividing line over which there was no return.

As if to confirm it, he had seen Zouga Ballantyne staring at her in the lantern light with that unmistakable look in his eyes. Many men had looked at her like that over the years, but this time she had returned Zouga's scrutiny openly, making no attempt to hide it from either man.

On the long road northwards, as she walked beside the cart in which he lay wounded, he had challenged her again and she had not denied it.

' – At least Zouga Ballantyne is a man of honour.'

'Then why do you not leave me?'

'You know I cannot leave you now, not as you are – ' She left it unfinished, and they had not spoken of it again, though in her icy silences he had sensed the presence in her mind of the other man, and he knew that no matter how desperately unhappy a woman might be she will seldom leave a relationship until she has the prospect of something better to replace it. Louise had that prospect now, and they were both aware of it.

He wondered if he would let Louise go if she finally made the decision. There had been a time not long ago when he would have killed her first; but since they had reached Khami, everything had begun altering even more swiftly. They were rushing towards some climax, and Mungo had sensed that it would be explosive.

For Mungo had forgotten the magnetism that Robyn Ballantyne had once exerted upon him, but now he had been vividly reminded by the mature woman, Robyn Codrington. She was even more attractive to him now than she had been as a girl. He sensed that her strength and assurance would provide a secure port for a man tired to his guts and the marrow of his bones by the storms of life.

He knew that she was the trusted confidante of the Matabele king, and that if his fortune awaited him here in the north, as he had come to suspect, then her intercession with the Matabele would be invaluable.

There was something else, some other darker need within him. Mungo St John never forgave or forgot an injury. Clinton Codrington had commanded the Royal Naval cruiser which had seized *Huron* off the Cape of Good Hope, an action which seemed to Mungo to mark the beginning of his long decline, and herald his dogged misfortune. Codrington was vulnerable. Through this woman Mungo could be avenged, and the prospect was strangely compelling.

He sighed and shook his head, roused himself and used the stick to push himself erect. He found himself confronted by the two small figures. Mungo St John liked all women of whatever age, and though he had not seen his own children in many years, the youngest would be about the same age as these two.

They were pretty little things. Though he had seen them only fleetingly or at a distance, he had felt the stirring of his paternal instincts; and now their presence was a welcome relief from his dark thoughts, and from the loneliness of the past weeks.

'Good afternoon, ladies.' He smiled, and bowed as low as his leg would allow. His smile was irresistible, and some of the rigidity went out of the two small bodies, but their expressions remained pale and fixed; their eyes, huge with trepidation, were fastened upon the fly of his breeches, so that after a few seconds silence even Mungo St John felt disconcerted, and he shifted uncomfortably.

'What service can I be to you?' he asked.

'We would like to see your tail, sir.'

'Ah!' Mungo knew never to show himself at a loss in front of a female, of no matter what age. 'You aren't supposed to know about that,' he said. 'Are you, now?'

They shook their heads in unison, but their eyes remained fixed with fascination below his waist. Vicky was right, there was definitely something there.

'Who told you about it?' Mungo sat down again, bringing his eyes to the level of theirs, and their disappointment was evident.

'Mama said you were the Devil – and we know the Devil has a tail.'

'I see.' Mungo nodded. With a huge effort, he fought back his laughter, and kept his expression serious, his tone conspiratorial.

'You are the only ones that know,' he told them. 'You won't tell anybody, will you?' Quite suddenly Mungo realized the value of having allies at Khami, two pairs of sharp bright eyes that saw everything and long ears that heard all.

'We won't tell anybody,' promised Vicky. 'If you show us.'

'I can't do that.' And there was an immediate wail of disappointment.

'Why not?'

'Didn't your mother teach you that it's a sin to show anybody under your clothes?'

They glanced at each other, and then Vicky admitted reluctantly. 'Yes, we aren't even really allowed to look at ourselves there. Lizzie got whacked for it.'

'There.' Mungo nodded. 'But I'll tell you what I will do – I'll tell you the story of how I got my tail.'

'Story!' Vicky clapped her hands, and they spread their skirts and squatted cross-legged at Mungo's feet. If there was one thing better than a secret, it was a story, and Mungo St John had stories, wonderful scary, blood-thirsty stories – the kind that guaranteed nightmares.

Each afternoon when he reached the lookout under the leadwood tree, they were waiting for him – captives of his charisma, addicted to those amazing stories of ghosts and dragons, of evil witches and beautiful princesses who always had Vicky's hair or Lizzie's eyes when Mungo St John described them.

Then after each of Mungo's stories, he would tactfully initiate a lively discussion of the affairs of Khami Mission. On a typical day he would learn that Cathy had begun painting a portrait of Cousin Ralph from memory, and that it was the considered and unanimous verdict of the twins that Cathy was not only 'soft' but, much worse, 'sloppy' about Cousin Ralph.

He learned that King Ben had commanded the entire family to attend the Chawala ceremony at the new moon, and the twins were ghoulishly anticipating the slaughter of the sacrificial black bull. 'They do it with their bare hands,' Vicky gloated. 'And this year we are going to be allowed to watch, now that we are eleven.'

He was told in detail how Papa had demanded from Mama at the dinner table how much longer 'that infamous pirate' was to remain at Khami, and Mungo had to explain to the twins what 'infamous' meant – 'famous, but only more so'.

Then on one such afternoon, Mungo learned from Lizzie that King Ben had once again '*khombisile*' with his indunas. Gandang, one of the king's brothers, had told Juba, who was his wife, and Juba had told Mama.

'*Khombisile?*' Mungo asked dutifully. 'What does that mean?'

'It means that he *showed* them.'

'Showed them what?'

'The treasure,' Vicky cut in, and Lizzie rounded on her.

'I'm telling him!'

'All right, Lizzie.' Mungo was leaning forward, interest tempering the indulgent smile. 'You tell me.'

'It's a secret. Mama says that if other people, bad people, heard about it, it would be terrible for King Ben. Robbers might come.'

'It's a secret then,' Mungo agreed.

'Cross your heart.'

And Lizzie was telling it before he had made the sign of good faith. Lizzie was determined that Vicky would not get in ahead of her, this time.

'He shows them the diamonds. His wives rub fat all over him, and then they stick the diamonds onto the fat.'

'Where did King Ben get all these diamonds?' Scepticism warred with the need to believe.

'His people bring them from Kimberley. Juba says it isn't really stealing. King Ben says it is only the tribute that a king should have.'

'Did Juba say how many diamonds?'

'Pots full, pots and pots of them.'

Mungo St John turned his single eye from her flushed and shining face and looked across the grassy golden plains to the Hills of the Indunas, and his eye was flecked golden yellow like one of the big predatory cats of Africa.

Jordan looked forward to this early hour of day. It was one of his duties to check each evening in the nautical almanac the time of sunrise, and to waken Mr Rhodes an hour beforehand.

Rhodes liked to see the sun come up, whether it was from the balcony of his magnificent private railway coach or drinking coffee in the dusty yard of the corrugated iron cottage that he still maintained behind Market Square in Kimberley, from the upper deck of an ocean-going liner or from the back of a horse as they rode the quiet pathways of his estate on the slopes of Table Mountain.

It was the time when Jordan was alone with his master, the time when ideas which Mr Rhodes called his 'thoughts' would come spilling out of him. Incredible ideas, sweeping and grand or wild and fanciful, but all fascinating.

It was the time when Jordan could feel that he was part of the vast genius of the man, as he scribbled down Mr Rhodes' draft speeches in his shorthand pad, speeches that would be made in the lofty halls of the Cape Parliament to which Mr Rhodes had been elected by the constituents of what had once been Griqualand, or at the board table of the governors of De Beers, of which he was chairman. De Beers was the mammoth diamond company which Mr Rhodes had welded together out of all the little diggers' claims and lesser competing companies. Like some mythical boa constrictor, he had swallowed them all – even Barney Barnato, the other giant of the fields. Mr Rhodes owned it all now.

On other mornings they would ride in silence, until Mr Rhodes would lift his chin from his chest and stare at Jordan with those stark blue eyes. Every time he had something startling to say. Once it was, 'You should thank God every day, Jordan, that you were born an Englishman.'

Another time it was, 'There is only one real purpose behind it all, Jordan. It is not the accumulation of wealth. I was fortunate to recognize it so early. The real purpose is to bring the whole civilized world under British rule, to recover North America to the crown, to make all the Anglo-Saxon race into one great empire.'

It was thrilling and intoxicating to be part of all this, especially as so often the big burly figure would rein his horse and turn his head and look to the north, towards a land that neither he nor Jordan had ever seen, but which, during the years that Jordan had been with him, had become a part of both their existences.

'My thought,' he called it. 'My north – my idea.'

'That's where it will really begin, Jordan. And when the time comes, I shall send you. The person I can trust beyond any other.'

It had never seemed strange to Jordan that those blue eyes had looked in that direction, that the open land to the north had come to loom so large in Mr Rhodes' imagination, that it had taken on the aura of a sacred quest.

Jordan could mark the day that it had begun, not only the day but the hour. For weeks after Pickering had been buried in the sprawling cemetery on the Cape Road, Jordan had respected Mr Rhodes' mourning. Then, one afternoon, he had left his office early. He had returned to the camp.

He retrieved the bird image from where it had been abandoned in the yard, and with the help of three black workmen, he moved it into the cottage. The living-room had been too small to hold it; it hindered access to both the dining-table and the front door.

In the small cottage, there was only one free wall, and that was in Mr Rhodes' bedroom, at the head of his narrow cot. The statue fitted perfectly into the space beyond the window. The next morning, when Jordan went to call him, Mr Rhodes had already left his cot and, wearing a dressing-gown, was standing before the statue.

In the fresh pink light of sunrise, as they rode down to the De Beers offices, Mr Rhodes had said, suddenly: 'I have had a thought, Jordan, one which I'd like to share with you. While I was studying that statue, it came to me that the north is the gateway, the north is the hinterland of this continent of ours.' That is how it had begun, in the shadow of the bird.

When the architect, Herbert Baker, had consulted Mr Rhodes on the decoration and furnishings of the mansion that they were building on his Cape Estate, 'Groote Schuur' – 'The Great Barn', Jordan had sat aside from the two men. As always in the presence of others he was unobtrusive and self-effacing, taking the notes that Mr Rhodes dictated, supplying a figure or a fact only when it was demanded, and then with his voice kept low, the natural lilt and music of his rich tenor subdued.

Mr Rhodes had jumped up from his seat on the box against the wall of the cottage and begun to pace, with that sudden excitable and voluble mood upon him.

'I have had a thought, Baker. I want there to be a theme for the place, something which is essentially me, which will be my motif long after I am gone, something that when men look at it, even in a thousand years' time, they will immediately recall the name Cecil John Rhodes.'

'A diamond, perhaps?' Baker had hazarded, sketching a stylized stone on his pad.

'No, no, Baker. Do be original, man! First I have to scold you for being stingy, for trying to build me a mean little hovel and now that I have prevailed on you for magnificently barbaric size and space, you want to spoil it.'

'The bird,' said Jordan. He had spoken despite himself, and both men looked at him with surprise.

'What did you say, Jordan?'

'The bird, Mr Rhodes. The stone bird. I think that should be your motif.'

Rhodes stared at him for a moment, and then punched his big fist into the palm of his left hand.

'That's it, Baker. The bird, sketch it for me. Sketch it now.'

So the bird had become the spirit of Groote Schuur. There was barely one of the huge cavernous rooms without its frieze or carved door jambs depicting it, even the bath, eleven tons of chiselled and polished granite, was adorned at its four corners with the image of the falcon.

The original statue had been shipped down from Kimberley, and a special niche prepared for it high above the baronial entrance hall, from where it stared down blindly upon everyone who came through the massive teak front doors of the mansion.

On this morning they had ridden out even earlier than usual, for Mr Rhodes had slept badly and had summoned Jordan from his small bedroom down the corridor.

It was cold. A vindictive wind came down off the mountains of the Hottentots Holland and as they took the path up towards the private zoo, Jordan looked back. Across the wide Cape flats he saw the snow on the distant peaks turning pink and gold in the early light.

Mr Rhodes was in a morose mood, silent and heavy in the saddle, his collar pulled up over his ears, and the broad hat jammed down to meet it. Jordan surreptitiously pushed his own mount level and studied his face.

Rhodes was still in his thirties, and yet this morning he looked fifteen years older. He took no notice of the first unseasonal flush of blue plumbago blooms beside the path, though on another morning he would have exclaimed with delight, for they were his favourite flowers. He did not stop at the zoo to watch the lions fed, but turned up into the forest; and on the prow of land that led to the steeper cliffs of the flat-topped massif they dismounted.

At this distance the thatched roof of Groote Schuur with its twirling barley-corn turrets looked like a fairy castle – but Rhodes looked beyond it.

'I feel like a racehorse,' he said suddenly. 'Like a thoroughbred Arab with the heart and the will and the need to run, but there is a dark horseman upon my back that checks me with a harsh curb of iron or pricks me with a cruel spur.' He rubbed his closed eyes with thumb and forefinger, and then massaged his cheeks as though to set the blood coursing in them again. 'He was with me again last night, Jordan. Long ago I fled from England to this land and I thought I had eluded him, but he is back in the saddle. His name is Death, Jordan, and he will give me so little time.' He pressed his hand to his chest, fingers spread as though to slow the racing of his damaged heart. 'There is so little time, Jordan. I must hurry.' He turned and took the hand from his heart and placed it on Jordan's shoulder. His expression became tender, a small sad smile touched his white lips. 'How I envy you, my boy – for you will see it all and I shall not.'

At that moment Jordan thought his own heart might break and, seeing his expression, Rhodes lifted his hand and touched his cheek.

'It's all too short, Jordan, life and glory – even love – it's all too short.' He turned back to his horse. 'Come, there is work to do.'

As they rode out of the forest, the course of that mercurial mind had changed again. Death had been pushed aside and he said suddenly:

'We shall have to square him, Jordan. I know he is your father – but we shall have to square him. Think about it and let me have your thoughts, but remember time is running short and we cannot move without him.'

The road over the neck between the main massif of Table Mountain and Signal Hill was well travelled and Jordan passed twenty coaches or more before he reached the top, but it was another two hours' ride beyond that and the road became steadily less populous, until at last it was a lonely deserted track which led into one of the ravines in the mountainside.

In this winter season the protea bushes on the slopes beyond the sprawling thatched building were drab and their blooms had withered and browned on the branches. The waterfall that smoked down off the mountain polished the rocks black and cold, and the spray dripped from the clustering trees about the pool.

However, the cottage had a neat cared-for look. The thatch had recently been renewed. It was still bright gold, and the thick walls had been whitewashed. With relief Jordan saw smoke curling from the chimney stack. His father was at home.

He knew that the property had once belonged to the old hunter and explorer Tom Harkness, and that his father had purchased it with £150 of his royalties from *A Hunter's Odyssey*. A sentimental gesture perhaps – for old Tom had been the one who had encouraged and counselled Zouga Ballantyne on his first expedition to Zambezia.

Jordan dismounted and hitched the big glossy hunter from the stables of Groote Schuur to the rail below the verandah, and he walked to the front steps.

He glanced at the pillar of blue marbled stone that stood at the head of the steps like a sentinel, and a little shadow flitted over his face as he remembered the fateful day that Ralph had hacked it out of the Devil's Own claims and brought it to the surface.

It was the only thing that remained to any of them from all those years of labour and travail. He wondered not only that his father had transported it so far with so much effort, but that he had placed it so prominently to rebuke him.

For a moment he laid his hand upon the stone, and he felt the faint satiny bloom that other hands had made on the same spot on the surface, like the marks of worshippers' hands on a holy relic. Perhaps Zouga also touched it every time he passed. Jordan dropped his hand and called towards the shuttered cottage.

'Is anybody there?'

There was a commotion in the front room, and the front door burst open.

'Jordan, my Jordie!' howled Jan Cheroot, and came bounding down the steps. His cap of peppercorn hair was pure white at last, but his eyes were bright and the web of wrinkles around them had not deepened.

He embraced Jordan with the wiry strength of brown arms; but even from the advantage of the verandah step he did not reach to Jordan's chin.

'So tall, Jordie,' he chuckled. 'Whoever thought you'd grow so tall, my little Jordie.'

He hopped back and stared up into Jordan's face. 'Look at you, I bet a guinea to a baboon turd that you've broken a few hearts already.'

'Not as many as you have.' Jordan pulled him close again, and hugged him.

'I had a start,' Jan Cheroot admitted, and then grinned wickedly. 'And I've still got the wind left for a sprint or two.'

'I was afraid that you and Papa might still be away.'

'We got home three days ago.'

'Where is Papa?'

'Jordan!'

The familiar, beloved voice made him start and he broke from Jan Cheroot's embrace and looked beyond him to Zouga Ballantyne standing in the doorway of the cottage.

He had never seen his father looking so well. It was not merely that he was lean and hard and sun-browned. He seemed to stand taller and straighter with an easy set to his shoulders, so different from the defeated slump with which he had left the diamond fields.

'Jordan!' he said again, and they came together and shook hands, and Jordan studied his father's face at closer range.

The pride and the purpose that had been burnt away in the diamond pit had returned, but with their quality subtly changed. Now he had the look of a man who had worked out the terms on which he was prepared to live. There were the shadows of a new thoughtfulness in his green eyes, the weight of understanding and compassion in his gaze. Here was a man who had tested himself almost to the point of destruction, had explored the frontiers of his soul and found them secure.

'Jordan,' he said again quietly for the third time, and then he did something that demonstrated the profound change he had undergone. He leaned forward and briefly he pressed the soft golden curls of his beard to Jordan's cheek.

'I have thought of you often,' he said without embarrassment. 'Thank you for coming.' Then with his arm about his shoulders he ushered Jordan into the front room.

This room always pleased Jordan, and he moved across to the log fire in the walk-in hearth and held out his hands to the blaze while he looked about him. It was a man's room – shelves filled with men's books, encyclopaedias and almanacs and thick leatherbound volumes of travel and exploration.

Weapons hung upon the walls, bows and quivers of poisoned Bushman arrows, shields and assegais of Matabele and Zulu, and, of course, the tools of the trade to which Zouga had reverted, firearms, heavy calibre sporting rifles by famous gun-smiths, Gibbs, Holland and Holland, Westley Richards. They were racked on the wall facing the fireplace, blued steel and lovingly carved wood.

With them were the souvenirs and trophies of Zouga's work, horns of antelope and buffalo, twisting or curved or straight as a lance, the zig-zag stripes of a zebra hide, the tawny gold bushed mane of the Kalahari lion, and ivory, great yellow arcs reaching higher than a man's head, yellow as fresh butter and translucent as candle-wax in the cold winter light from the doorway.

'You had a good trip?' Jordan asked, and Zouga shrugged.

'It gets more difficult each season to find good specimens for my clients.'

His clients were rich and aristocratic sportsmen, come out to Africa for the chase.

'But at least the Americans seem to have discovered Africa at last. I have a good party booked for next season – young fellow called Roosevelt, Secretary of the Navy.' He broke off. 'Yes, we are managing to keep body and soul together, old Jan Cheroot and I – but I don't have to ask about you.'

He glanced down at the expensive English cloth of Jordan's suit, the soft leather of his riding boots which creased perfectly around his ankles like the bellows of a concertina, the solid silver spurs and the gold watch chain in his fob pocket – and then his eye paused on the white sparkle of the diamond in his cravat.

'You made the right choice when you decided to go with Rhodes. My God, how that man's star rises higher and brighter with each passing day.'

'He is a great man, Papa.'

'Or a great rogue.' Then Zouga smiled apologetically. 'I am sorry, I know how highly you think of him. Let's have a glass of sherry, Jordie, while Jan Cheroot makes lunch for us.' He smiled again. 'We miss your cooking. You will find it poor fare, I'm afraid.'

While he poured sweet Cape sherry into long glasses, he asked over his shoulder:

'And Ralph, what do you hear of Ralph?'

'We meet often in Kimberley or at the railhead. He always asks after you.'

'How is he?'

'He will be a big man, Papa. Already his wagons run to Pilgrims' Rest and those new goldfields on the Witwatersrand. He has just won the fast coach contract from Algoa Bay. He has trading posts at Tati and on the Shashi river.'

They ate in front of the fire, sour bread and cheese, a cold joint of mutton and a black bottle of Constantia wine, and Jan Cheroot hovered over Jordan, scolding him fondly for his appetite and recharging his glass when it was barely a quarter empty.

At last they finished and stretched out their legs towards the fire, while Jan Cheroot brought a burning taper to light the cigars which Jordan produced from a gold pocket case.

Jordan spoke through the perfumed wreaths of smoke.

'Papa, the concession –' And for the first time an angry arrowhead creased the skin between Zouga's eyes.

'I had hoped that you came to see us,' he said coldly. 'I keep forgetting that you are Rhodes' man, ahead of being my son.'

'I am both,' Jordan contradicted him evenly. 'That's why I can talk to you like this.'

'What message has the famous Mr Rhodes for me this time?' Zouga demanded.

'Maund and Selous have both accepted his offers. They have sold their concessions to Mr Rhodes, and both are ten thousand pounds richer.'

Maund was a soldier and an adventurer. Fred Selous, like Zouga, a hunter and explorer. Also, like Zouga, Selous had written a well-received book on the African chase *A Hunter's Wanderings in Africa*. Both of these men had at different times prevailed on Lobengula to grant them concessions to ivory and minerals in his eastern dominions.

'Mr Rhodes wants me to point out to you that both the Maund and Selous concessions are over the same territory as the concession that Mzilikazi granted to you. He owns both of them now – the validity of all the treaties is hopelessly confused and hazy.'

'The Ballantyne concession was granted first – by Mzilikazi; the ones that followed have no force,' snapped Zouga.

'Mr Rhodes' lawyers have advised –'

'Damn Mr Rhodes and his lawyers. Damn them all to hell.'

Jordan dropped his eyes and was silent, and after a long pause Zouga sighed and stood up. He went to the yellow wood cupboard and took out a stained and dog-eared document, so ragged that it had been pasted onto a backing to prevent it falling to pieces.

The ink had faded to brown, but the script was bold and spiky, the hand of an arrogant and cocksure young man.

The document was headed:

EXCLUSIVE CONCESSION TO MINE GOLD AND HUNT IVORY
IN THE
SOVEREIGN TERRITORY OF MATABELELAND

And at its foot was a crude wax seal with the image of a bull elephant, and the words:

NKOSI NKHULU – GREAT KING

Below it a shaky cross in the same faded ink:

MZILIKAZI – *his mark*

Zouga laid the document on the table between them, and they both stared at it.

'All right,' Zouga capitulated. 'What do Mr Rhodes' lawyers advise?'

'That this concession could be set aside on five separate points of law.'

'I would fight him.'

'Papa. He is a determined man. His influence is enormous. He will be Prime Minister of the Cape Parliament at the next session, there is little doubt of that.' Jordan touched the red wax seal. 'His fortune is vast, perhaps ten million pounds –'

'Still I will fight him,' Zouga said, and then stopped Jordan speaking with a hand on his arm. 'Jordan, don't you understand. A man must have something, a dream, a light to follow in the darkness. I can never sell this, it has been all of my life for too long. Without it I shall have nothing.'

'Papa –'

'I know what you will say, that I can never make this into reality. I do not have the money it would need. You might even say that I no longer even have the strength of purpose. But, Jordan, while I have this piece of paper I can still hope, I still have my dream to follow. I can never sell it.'

'I told him that, and he understood immediately. He wants you to be a part of it.'

Zouga lifted his head and stared at his son.

'A seat on the Board of Governors of the company for which Mr Rhodes will petition a Royal Charter from Her Majesty. Then you will have grants of farm land, gold claims, and an active command in the field. Don't you see, Papa, he is not taking your dream away from you, he is making it come true at last.'

The silence drew out, a log crumbled and crashed softly in the hearth; sparks shot up and the flare lit Zouga's face.

'When will he see me?' he asked.

'We can be at Groote Schuur in four hours' ride.'

'It will be dark by then.'

'There are fifteen bedrooms for you to choose from,' Jordan smiled, and Zouga laughed like a man who has been given back all the excitement and eagerness of youth.

'Then why are we sitting here?' he asked. 'Jan Cheroot, bring my heavy coat.'

Zouga strode out onto the verandah of the cottage, and on the top step he checked and reached out with his right hand to the pillar of blue stone. He touched it with a strangely formal caress, and with the same hand touched his own lips and forehead, the gesture with which an Arab greets an old friend.

Then Zouga glanced at Jordan, and smiled.

'Superstition,' he explained. 'Good luck.'

'Good luck?' Jan Cheroot snorted from below the steps where he held Zouga's horse. 'Damn stone – all the way from Kimberley, trip over the thundering rubbish.' He went on muttering to himself as Zouga mounted.

'Jan Cheroot would pine away if he didn't have something to complain about.' Zouga winked at Jordan, and they trotted out from under the milkwood trees onto the track.

'I often think back to that day when we hit the blue,' Jordan said. 'If we had only known!'

'How could we know?'

'It was I – I feel sure of that. It was I who convinced you that the blue ground was barren.'

'Jordan, you were only a boy.'

'But I was supposed to be the diviner of diamonds. If I had not been so certain that it was dead ground, you would never have sold the Devil's Own.'

'I never sold it. I gambled it away.'

'Only because you thought it was worthless. You would never have accepted Mr Rhodes' bet if you had known that the blue was not the end – but only the beginning.'

'Nobody knew that, not then.'

'Mr Rhodes sensed it. He never lost faith. He knew what the blue was. He knew it with a certain instinct that nobody else had.'

'I have never been back to Kimberley, Jordie.' Zouga settled down in the saddle, riding with long stirrups like a Boer hunter. 'I never wanted to go back, but of course the news filters down the line of rail. I heard that when Rhodes and Barnato made their deal, they valued the Devil's Own claims at half a million pounds.'

'They were the keys to the field,' Jordie explained. 'It just happened that they were the central claims in the main enrichment. But you could never have guessed that, Papa.'

'Strange how right one man's instincts can be,' Zouga brooded. 'And how wrong another man's. I always *knew*, or thought I knew, that my road to the north began in that hole, that terrible hole.'

'Perhaps it still does. The money to take us all to the north will still come from it. Mr Rhodes' millions.'

'Tell me about the blue. You have been with Rhodes through it all. Tell me about it.'

'It changes,' Jordan said. 'It's as simple as that, it alters.'

Zouga shook his head. 'It's like some sort of miracle.'

'Yes,' Jordan nodded. 'Diamonds are nature's beautiful miracles. I'll never forget my own astonishment when Mr Rhodes showed it to me. That hard blue rock is unyielding as any granite when it comes out of the earth, and yet after it has been laid out in the stacking fields for a year or two it starts to crumble. It's the sunlight, we think, that does it. It crumbles up like a loaf of stale bread – and the diamonds, oh Papa, the diamonds. Incredible stones, eleven thousand carats of diamonds each day. The blue is the mother lode, the blue is the heart.' He broke off in embarrassment. 'Sometimes I run away with myself,' he confessed, and Zouga smiled with him. Who could resist this beautiful young man, that was the word to describe him – not handsome, not good-looking, but beautiful, with a quality of gentleness and goodness that seemed to form an aura about him.

'Papa.' Jordan sobered. 'Oh Papa, you will never know how happy I am that you are to be part of it, after all. You and Mr Rhodes.'

'Mr Rhodes,' Zouga thought indulgently. 'Always Mr Rhodes. And yet it's a good thing for a young man to have a hero. Pity this poor world of ours when the last hero passes.'

Can you judge a man by his books? Zouga wondered.

The library was choked with them. One complete wall packed to the ceiling with the sources and references which Gibbon had consulted for his *Decline and Fall*. So impressed had Rhodes been with this work that he had ordered Hatchards of London to collect and, if necessary, translate and bind the complete authorities. Jordan said it had cost him £8,000 thus far, and was not yet complete.

Ranked beside this formidable array were all the published lives of Alexander, of Julius Caesar and of Napoleon. What dreams of empire they must sustain. Zouga smiled inwardly as he listened to the high hypnotic voice of the burly figure with the flushed swollen face as he sat behind the vast desk into whose panels were chiselled the stylized figures of the bird, the falcon of Zimbabwe.

'You are an Englishman, Ballantyne, a man of honour and dedication; these things have always attracted me to you.' He was irresistible, able to conjure up a gamut of emotions with a few words, and Zouga smiled at himself again. He was in danger of the same hero worship as his own son.

'I want you even more than this concession of yours. You understand, you know what it is we seek, not merely wealth and personal aggrandizement. No, no, it is something beyond that, something sacred.'

Then he came to it abruptly, without flourish.

'There,' Rhodes said. 'You know what I need – you and your concession. What do you want from me in return?'

'What task will I perform?' Zouga asked.

'Good.' Rhodes nodded the untidy leonine head. 'Glory before gold. You please me, Ballantyne – but to business. I had thought to ask you to lead the occupying expedition, to guide it over the ground you know so well – but other men can do something as simple as that. I shall let Selous do it. I have something more important for you. You will be my alter-ego at the kraal of the Matabele king. The savages know and respect you, you speak their language, know their customs, you are a soldier, I have read your military paper on the tribe – and we must not deceive ourselves, Ballantyne, it may come to a military option. Few other men can do all these things, have all these qualities.'

They stared at each other across the desk, both men leaning forward, and then Rhodes spoke again.

'I am not a mean man, Ballantyne. Do the job for me and you can name your rewards. Money, ten thousand pounds – land, each land grant will be four thousand acres – gold claims, each will be five hundred yards square. How many shall we say – five of each – ten thousand pounds in cash, twenty thousand acres of prime land of your choice, five claims on the rich gold reef over which you shot the great elephant that you described in *Hunter's Odyssey*. What do you say, Ballantyne?'

'Ten of each,' said Zouga. 'Ten thousand pounds, ten land grants, ten gold claims.'

'Done!' Rhodes slapped the desk. 'Write it down, Jordan, write it down. But what of your salary while you are agent at Lobengula's kraal? Two thousand, four thousand per annum? I am not a mean man, Ballantyne.'

'And I am not a greedy one.'

'Four thousand, then – and we are all agreed, so we can go to lunch.'

Zouga stayed five days at Groote Schuur, days of talking and planning and listening.

It amused him to see the legend dispelled. The idea of Rhodes as a solitary and brooding man – withdrawn to some high Olympus where other men could not follow, was proved to be a myth.

For Rhodes surrounded himself with men; there was not a meal at which less than fifteen sat to his generous board. What men they were, clever or rich or both, belted earls or farm-born Boers, politicians and financiers, judges and soldiers. And if they were not wealthy, they were powerful or useful or merely amusing. At one dinner there was even a poet, a bespectacled little shrimp of a man on passage from Indian Service back to England. Jordan had read his *Plain Tales from the Hills* and secured an invitation for him, and despite his appearance, the company was quite taken with him. Rhodes invited him to return and write about Africa: 'The future is here, young Kipling, and we shall need a poet to sing it for us.'

Men by the dozen, and never a woman. Rhodes refused to have a woman servant in the house. There was not even a painting of a woman on the walls.

And the taciturn, brooding figure of legend never stopped talking. From the back of a horse as they rode through the estate, striding over the lawns with his clumsy unco-ordinated gait, seated behind the teak desk or at the head of the long, laden dining-table, he talked. Figures and facts and estimates poured from him without reference to notes, other than an occasional glance at Jordan for confirmation. Then came the ideas, fateful, ludicrous, prophetic, fascinating or fantastic – but never-ending.

To a visiting member of the British Parliament: 'We have to make a practical tie with the old country, for future generations will be born beyond its shores; it must be useful, physical and rewarding for both, or we shall drift apart.'

To an American senator: 'We could hold Parliament for five years in Westminster and for the next five in Washington.'

To a rival financier who enviously sniped at his monopoly of the diamond industry: 'Without me, the price of diamonds would not make it worthwhile turning over a stone to pick one up. Kimberley would revert to desert and thirty thousand would starve.'

When they began to plan the grand expedition to the north, Zouga had imagined that Rhodes would concern himself with each detail. He was wrong.

He defined the objective: 'We need a document from Lobengula, ratifying and consolidating all these grants into a single concession, that I can take to London.' Then he picked the man. 'Rudd, you have the legal mind.' And gave him *carte blanche*. 'Go and do it. Take Jordan with you. He speaks the language. Take anyone else you need.'

Then to Zouga: 'We need an occupying force, small enough to move fast, large enough to protect itself against Matabele treachery. Ballantyne, that will be your first concern. Let me know what you decide, but remember there is little time.'

What might have taken another man six months, was accomplished in five days, and when Zouga left Groote Schuur, Jordan rode with him as far as the neck of the mountain. The wind had gone up into the north-west, and then came down like a ravenous beast, roaring dully against the crags of the mountain and bringing in cold, steely-grey rain squalls off the Atlantic.

It could not blunt their spirits, and although their wind-driven oilskins flogged their bodies and the horses shivered and drooped their ears, they shouted above the wind.

'Isn't he a great man? Every minute spent in his company is like a draught of fine wine, intoxicating with excitement. He is so generous.'

'Though he is the one who profits most from his generosity,' Zouga laughed.

'That's mean, Papa.'

'A saint does not make such a fortune in so short a time. But if anybody can do this thing, then it is Rhodes, and for that I will follow him into hell itself.'

'Let's pray that won't be necessary.'

At the top of the pass the wind was stronger still, and Jordan had to turn his horse in until their knees touched.

'Papa, the column – the occupying column. There is one person who has the wagons, who knows the route, can requisition the supplies and recruit the men.'

'Who is that, Jordie?'

'Ralph.'

Zouga watched Jordan ride back down the pass, towards the wind-darkened waters of Table Bay and the sprawling white buildings that clung to the lower slopes of the mountain under the dingy scudding sky. Then he turned his own mount into the wind and went down the other side.

The excitement stayed with him. He realized that it was Rhodes' particular genius to awaken this feeling in men around him. Even though there were quicksands ahead in which he knew he might soon be engulfed, the enthusiasm and quickness of spirit persisted.

Ten land grants meant forty thousand acres of land, but it would take more than £10,000 to hold it. Homestead and wells and fences to build, cattle to stock it, men to work it – all that would cost money, a great deal of money.

The gold claims – he could not even begin to imagine how much it might cost to transport stamp mills and sluice boxes from the railhead. Of course, for lack of money to exploit them, he would have to pass by a hundred opportunities that the new land would offer. In the beginning the land grants of other men would be for sale at bargain prices, hundreds of thousands of acres of the land that he had always thought of as his own, and because he did not have the money, it would go to others.

None of this could break the mood, not the cold rain in his face that numbed his cheeks, not the realization that his dream was still merely a dream. For now at last they were on the move at the breakneck pace set by an impatient man – towards the realization of that dream. So Zouga could lift his chin and sit up straight in the saddle, ignoring the icy snakes of rainwater that wriggled down inside his collar, buoyed high above mundane doubts by the gambler's certainty that at last his luck had changed, the dice were hot for him and every time he rolled the aces would flash like spearheads.

The sheets of rain hid the cottage from Zouga until he turned in under the milk-wood grove; then a fluke of the wind opened the slanting silver sheets of water, and his mood popped like a bubble.

He had been mistaken, his luck had not changed, it had all been words and illusion, the caravan of his misfortunes rolled on unchecked – for before him his home was partially destroyed.

One of the ancient milkwoods, weary of resisting the gales of a hundred winters, had succumbed at last; it had come crashing down across the front of the cottage. The roof had given under the blow, and sagged in. The supports of the verandah had shattered and a tangle of fallen roof beams and milkwood branches blocked the front entrance. The living-room would be swamped with rain – his books, his papers.

Appalled at the havoc, he dismounted and stood before it, and his spirits slid further. He felt his ribs constricting his breathing and dread uncoiled in his guts like an awakening serpent. It was the superstitious terror of one who has offended the gods.

The pillar of blue marbled rock that he had set to guard his threshold had been thrown down. It lay half under the tumbled thatch with the shattered verandah support beside it. Once it had been hard and smooth as granite, but the sunlight and the air had rotted it and the fall had shattered it like chalk.

Zouga went down on one knee and touched a rough, irregular lump of the smashed blue ground. The destruction of his home was as nothing. This was the only one of his possessions that was irreplaceable, and the omen of its destruction struck frost into the secret places of his soul.

Almost as a chorus to his dread, a fresh rain squall came booming down the valley, thrashing the trees and ripping at the scattered thatch. Rain beat down onto the broken surface of the rock he was touching, and at Zouga's fingertips there was a tiny burst of white lightning, so dazzling, so searing, that it seemed it could flay the skin from his finger as he touched it. But it was cold, cold as a crystal of Arctic ice.

It had never been exposed to the light of day, not once in the two hundred million years since it had assumed its present form, and yet it seemed in itself to be a drop of distilled sunlight.

Zouga had never seen anything so beautiful, nor touched anything so sensual – for it was the beacon and the lodestone of his life. It made all the striving and the heartbreak seem worthwhile, it was justification for the years he had believed squandered, it exonerated his once firmly held belief that his road to the north began in the gaping chasm of De Beers New Rush.

With hands that shook like those of a very old man, he fumbled open the blade of his clasp knife and gently prised that rainbow of light from its niche in the shattered blue rock, and held it up before his own eyes.

'The Ballantyne diamond,' he whispered, and staring into its limpid liquid depths like a sorcerer into his divining ball of crystal, he saw light and shadow ripple and change and in his imagination become vistas of enchanted pastures rich with sweet grass; he saw slow herds of cattle and the headgear of winding wheels of fabulous gold mines spinning against a high blue sky.

They didn't expect him. He came so swiftly that no runner brought word ahead of him. He had left Rudd and the rest of the party to follow from the Shashi and ridden on ahead, leading two spare horses and changing as soon as the mount beneath him tired. The horses were the pick of De Beers' stables, and it took him five days from the frontier of Matabeleland to Khami Mission.

'I'm Jordan Ballantyne,' he said, and looked down on the family that had hastily assembled on the front verandah of the Mission. The siege was over without a shot fired; he walked in with his curls shining and that warm, almost shy, smile on his lips, and took their hearts, every one of them, by storm.

The gifts he brought had been chosen with obvious care, and spoke of a knowledge of each of them and their individual needs.

There were two dozen packets of seeds for Clinton – unusual vegetables and rare herbs – comfrey and okra, horseradish and turmeric, shallot and sou-sou. For Robyn a box of medicines, which included a bottle of chloroform, and a folding wallet of shiny, sharp surgical instruments.

The latest volume of Tennyson's poetry for Salina, a pair of marvellous lifelike china dogs with moving eyes for the twins, and for Cathy the best of all, a box of oil paints, a bundle of brushes, and a letter from Ralph.

In the first week, while he waited for Rudd and the rest of the party to come up from the Shashi, Jordan used a green twig to divine water, an art that Clinton had never acquired, and helped him dig the new well. They hit clear, sweet water ten feet down. He recited to Cathy a biography of Ralph from the day and hour of his birth, which was so minutely detailed that it took instalments over the entire week to complete, while she listened with a fixed avidity.

He rolled up his sleeves and from the black wood-burning stove produced a flow of culinary phenomena – quenelles and soufflés, croques-en-bouche and meringues, sauces both Hollandaise and Béarnaise – and while Salina hovered near him, eager to learn and help, he quoted to her the entire 'In Memoriam' of Alfred Lord Tennyson, from memory:

> 'So fret not, like an idle girl,
> That life is dash'd with flecks of sin.
> Abide: thy wealth is gathered in,
> When Time hath sunder'd shell from pearl.'

And she was utterly enchanted by his golden spell.

He showed the twins how to cut and fold from a piece of newspaper all manner of fantastic bird and animal shapes, and he told stories that were the best they had heard since Mungo St John had left Khami.

For Robyn he had the latest news from the Cape. He was able to describe for her the rising stars on the political horizon, and categorize their strengths and weaknesses. He had the latest assessments of the political scene at home. Members of both Houses of Parliament, Cape and home, were constant guests at Groote Schuur, so he could repeat the gossip of that 'wild and incomprehensible old man', as the Queen had called Gladstone. He could explain the Home Rule issue and tell her what the odds were for a Liberal victory at the next election, even after Gladstone's failure to rescue Gordon from Khartoum and his consequential loss of popularity.

'At the Queen's Jubilee the common people on the pavements cheered him, but the aristocracy hissed him from the balconies,' he told her.

For Robyn, this was nectar to a woman lost over twenty years in the wilderness.

Dinners at Khami usually finished by the fall of dark, and the family was abed an hour later, but after Jordan's arrival, the talk and laughter sometimes lasted until midnight.

'Jordan, there is no doubt that if we want Mashonaland, we shall have to square your aunt. I hear that Lobengula will not make a major decision without Dr Codrington. I want you to go on ahead of Rudd and the others. Go to Khami and talk to your aunt.' That had been Mr Rhodes' parting injunction to him, and Jordan's conscience found no conflict between this duty and his family loyalties.

Again and again in that week Jordan returned to extol Mr Rhodes to Robyn, his integrity and sincerity, his vision of a world at peace and united under one sovereign power.

Instinctively he knew which areas of Rhodes' character to emphasize to Robyn, patriotism, charity, his sympathetic treatment of his black workers, his opposition to the Stropping Act in the Cape Parliament which, if passed, would have given employers the right to lash their black servants, and only when he judged that she was swayed to his views, did Jordan mention the concession to her. Yet, despite his preparations, her opposition was immediate and ferocious.

'Not another tribe robbed of its lands,' she cried.

'We do not want Matabeleland, Aunty. Mr Rhodes would guarantee Lobengula's sovereignty and protect him –'

'I read the letter you wrote to the *Cape Times,* Aunty, expressing your concern over the Matabele raids into Mashonaland. With the British flag flying over the Shona tribes, they would be protected by British justice.'

'The Germans and Portuguese and Belgians are gathering like vultures – you know, Aunty, that there is only one nation fit to take on the sacred trust.'

Jordan's arguments were calculated and persuasive, his manner without guile and his trust in Cecil John Rhodes touching and infectious, and he kept returning to his most poignant argument.

'Aunty, you have seen the Matabele bucks returning from Mashonaland with the blood caked on their blades and the captured Shona girls roped together. Think of the havoc that they have left behind them, the burned villages, the murdered infants and grey heads, the slaughtered Shona warriors. You cannot deny the Shona people the protection that we will offer.'

That night she spoke to Clinton, lying beside him in the darkness in the narrow cot on the hard straw-filled mattress; and his reply was immediate and simple:

'My dear, it has always been clear to me as the African sun that God has prepared this continent for the protection of the only nation on earth that has the public virtue sufficient to govern it for the benefit of its native peoples.'

'Clinton, Mr Rhodes is not the British nation.'

'He is an Englishman.'

'So was Edward Teach, *alias* Blackbeard the pirate.'

They were silent for many minutes and then Robyn said suddenly:

'Clinton, have you noticed anything wrong with Salina?'

His concern was immediate. 'Is she sickening?'

'I'm afraid so, incurably. I think she is in love.'

'Good gracious.' He sat abruptly upright in the bed. 'Who on earth is she in love with?'

'How many young men are there at Khami at the present time?'

In the morning, on the way to her clinic in the church, she stopped at the kitchen. The previous evening Clinton had slaughtered a pig, and now Salina and Jordan were making sausages. He was turning the handle of the mincing machine while she forced lumps of pork into the funnel. They were so absorbed, chatting so gaily together, that while Robyn stood in the doorway watching them they were unaware of her presence.

They made a beautiful couple, so beautiful indeed, that Robyn felt a sense of unreality as she watched them, and it was followed immediately by uneasiness, nothing in life was that perfect.

Salina saw her, and started – and then unaccountably blushed so that her pixie pointed ears glowed.

'Oh Mama, you startled me.'

Robyn felt a rush of empathy, and, strangely, of envy for her eldest daughter. She wished that she were still capable of that pure and innocent emotion, and suddenly she had the contrasting image of Mungo St John, lean and scarred and unscrupulous, and what she felt shocked her so her voice was brusque.

'Jordan, I have made up my mind. When Mr Rudd arrives, I will go with you to Lobengula's kraal, and I will speak for your case.'

After a prolonged and unprofitable trading expedition as far as the Zambezi, Mungo had returned with Louise to the kraal at GuBulawayo, where they were kept almost seven months. But Lobengula's procrastinations worked in Mungo St John's favour.

Robyn Codrington had refused to speak to the king on Mungo's behalf, and consequently he was only one among dozens of white concession-seekers camped around Lobengula's royal kraal.

The king would not have let Mungo leave, even if he had wanted to. He seemed to enjoy talking to him, and listened eagerly to Mungo's accounts of the American War and of Mungo's sea voyages. Every week or so he would summon Mungo to an audience and question him through his interpreter, for hours at a time.

The destructive power of cannon fascinated him, and he demanded detailed descriptions of sundered walls and human bodies blown to nothingness. The sea was another source of intense interest, and he tried to grasp the immensity of waters and the blast of storm and gale across it. However, when Mungo delicately hinted at a land grant and trading concession, Lobengula smiled and sent him away.

'I will call for you again, One Bright Eye, when I have thought on it more heavily. Now is there aught you lack in food or drink? I will send my women to your camp with it.'

Once he gave Mungo permission to go out into the hunting veld so long as he stayed south of the Shangani river and killed neither elephant nor hippopotamus. On this expedition Mungo shot a huge cock ostrich and salted and dried the skin with its magnificent plumage intact.

On three other occasions the king allowed him to return to Khami Mission Station when Mungo complained that his leg was paining him. Mungo's predatory instinct was that Robyn Codrington was disturbed and excited by these returns, and each time he was able to draw out the visit for days, gradually consolidating his position with her so that when he again asked her to intercede with Lobengula on his behalf, she actually thought about it for a full day before refusing once more.

'I cannot set a cat upon a mouse, General St John.'

'Madam, I freed my own slaves many years ago.'

'When you were forced to,' she agreed. 'But who will control you here in Matabeleland?'

'You, Robyn, and gladly would I submit to that.'

She had flushed and turned her face away from him to hide the colour.

'Your familiarity is presumptuous, sir.' And she had left him so that he could keep his revived assignations under the leadwood tree with the twins. His absence since those first encounters in his convalescence had not dimmed their fascination for him. They had become invaluable allies. Nobody else could have extracted from Juba the vital information he needed for his planning. Mungo had expressed doubts as to the existence of the diamonds, and declared that he would only be convinced if the twins could tell him where Lobengula kept the treasure.

Juba never suspected danger from such an innocent pair, and in the late afternoon, when she had drunk a gallon pot of her own famous brew, she was always genial and garrulous.

'Ningi keeps the diamonds under her sleeping place,' Vicky informed Mungo.

'Who is Ningi?'

'The king's sister, and she is almost as fat as King Ben is.'

Ningi would be the most trusted of all Lobengula's people – and her hut in the sanctuary of the forbidden women's quarters was the most secure in all Matabeleland.

'I believe you now. You are clever girls, both of you,' Mungo told them, and they glowed with pleasure. There was nothing he could not ask of them.

'Vicky, I need some paint. It's for a secret thing, I will tell you about it later, if you can get the paint for me.'

'What colour?' Lizzie cut in. 'I'll get it for you.'

'Red, white and yellow.'

In the end Lizzie stood guard while Vicky raided Cathy's paintbox, and they delivered their offering to Mungo and basked in his extravagant praise.

In his planning, it was not enough merely to get the diamonds into his hands; even more vital was to escape the consequences. No man or woman could hope to reach the frontier without the king's permission; it was hundreds of miles of wild country patrolled by the border impis. He could not grab and run. He had to use guile and perhaps turn the Matabele dread of darkness and witchcraft to his own advantage.

So he planned with meticulous concentration, and waited for the right moment with the patience of the stalking leopard, for he knew that this was his last attempt. If he failed this time, then not even his white skin nor his status as a guest of the king could save him.

If he failed, the Black Ones would wield their knobkerries, crushing in his skull – and his corpse would be flung from the cliffs to the waiting vultures or into the flooded river pools where the crocodiles would rip it into chunks with their spiky yellow saurian teeth. Louise would suffer the same fate, he knew, but it was a chance he was prepared to take.

He was careful to conceal his preparations from her – and this was made easier by the distance that she had for long now been maintaining between them. Though they shared the thatched hut that Lobengula's men had built for them in the grove beyond the royal kraal, and though they ate the same meals of beef and sour milk and stone-ground maize cakes that the king sent down to them each evening, Louise spent her days alone, riding out on one of the mules in the early morning and not returning until dusk. Her mattress of straw in the farthest recesses of the hut she had screened with the tattered canvas sunshade from the cart, and he only once tried to pass the screen.

'Not again,' she hissed at him. 'Never again!' And she showed him the knife that she kept under her skirts.

So he was able to work uninterrupted, during the day, and to hide his equipment under his own mattress each evening. He carved the mask from the naturally curved portion of a hollow tree trunk, a hideous grimacing ape-like visage with staring eyes and a gaping mouth full of white fangs – and he painted it with the colours from Cathy's paintbox.

From the plumed ostrich skin he tailored a cloak that reached from neck to ankles, and for his feet and hands he made grotesque mittens of black goatskin. In full costume he was enough to paralyse even the bravest warrior with supernatural terror. He was the very embodiment of the *Tokoloshe* of Matabele mythology.

Robyn Codrington had given him repeated doses of laudanum for the persisting pain in his leg, but he had saved these for the occasion. He had decided on one of the Matabele festivals, and he waited until the third night when every man and woman of the entire nation, surfeited with beer and three days and nights of wild dancing, had fallen asleep where they fell.

At nightfall he gave the laudanum to Louise in a cup of soured milk, and the tart flavour concealed the musky taste of the drug. An hour after dark he crept across the hut, drew aside the screen and listened to her even breathing for a minute before leaning over her and slapping her cheeks lightly. She did not move nor murmur, and the rhythm of her breathing did not alter.

He dressed swiftly in the feather cloak, not yet donning the mask and mittens – but blackening his face and limbs with a mixture of crushed charcoal and fat. Then with the mask and a length of rope under one arm and a heavy assegai in the other hand, he crept out of the hut.

The grove was deserted, no Matabele would venture here when the spirits were abroad, so he hurried through it – and from the treeline surveyed the stockade of the royal kraal.

There was a sliver of the old moon rising, and it gave just enough light for him to pick his way, but not enough to betray him to watchful eyes. There would be few eyes open on this night. Even so he crouched low as he crossed the open ground; the cloak made a shaggy hyena shape that would excite no real interest.

At the outer stockade he paused to look and listen, then flicked the length of manila rope over the barrier of sharpened poles.

He climbed up carefully, favouring his bad leg, and peered into the kraal.

It was deserted, but a low watch-fire burned in front of the barred gateway.

Mungo slid down the rope and he crossed quickly to the shadows of the nearest hut, and there paused to pull on his mittens and settle the cumbersome mask over his head before creeping on again towards the inner stockade that guarded the women's quarters.

In the preceding weeks, using his brass telescope from the vantage point of the nearest hilltop, he had been able to see over the walls and to study the layout of the wives' quarters.

There was a double circle of huts, like the concentric rings of a target, but at the centre, the bull's-eye, was a larger hut with intricate patterns of thatch and lacing proclaiming its greater importance. His guess that this was the king's sister's residence had been confirmed when he had seen, through the telescope, Ningi's elephantine gleaming naked body, escorted by a dozen hand-maidens, emerging into the early sunlight from the low doorway.

Now he reached the gateway in the inner stockade, and studied it from around the sheltering wall of the nearest hut. Again his luck held. He had been prepared to use the assegai here, but both the guards were stretched out, wrapped in their furs, and neither of them moved as Mungo stepped over their prostrate bodies.

From inside one hut he heard the low regular snores of one fat wife, and in another a woman coughed and muttered in her sleep, but though his nerves jumped, he went on swiftly.

The door to Ningi's hut was closed. Mungo had honed the edge of the assegai to a razor edge, and with it he sawed through the fastenings of bark rope that secured the opening. The rasp and rustle of the blade sounded thunderous in his ears, and his skin prickled as he waited for a shouted challenge from within. It did not come, but he found that he was sweating as he stepped back and brought out the bladders of goats' blood from under the cloak.

He slit the bladders and splashed the stinking, congealing blood over the portals of the doorway. He had learned from the twins, who were authorities on the supernatural, that a *Tokoloshe* always spurted blood on any doorway through which it passed. It was one of the creature's more endearing characteristics.

Now with the assegai gripped in his right hand, Mungo stooped into the hut and, crouched in the doorway, he waited for his eyes to adjust to the gloom.

The fire in the centre of the large hut had burned low. There was just enough light to make out two figures curled like dogs on the sleeping-mats on each side of it – and beyond it the ponderous bulk of the princess under her furs.

Her snores started as a low grumbling like a volcano, and rose to a whistling crescendo that covered any sound Mungo might make as he slipped across to the first of the sleeping hand-maids.

Before she could stir he had slipped a gag of goat's skin into her mouth and trussed her at the ankles and wrists with a leather thong. She did not struggle, but stared up at his horrific mask with huge white eyes in the firelight. He tied and gagged the second woman before crossing to Ningi's sleeping platform.

That afternoon, as one of the king's guests, Mungo had watched Ningi sitting beside her brother and swilling pot after pot of French champagne. She went on snoring and grunting as he bound her arms and legs. Only when he thrust the gag into her gaping mouth did she snuffle and moan and come out of her alcoholic slumbers.

He rolled her off the platform and she fell with a thump to the clay floor. He dragged her across to where her bound servants lay. It was heavy work, for she weighed 300 pounds or more.

He threw a log on the fire, and when it flared he pranced and capered around his captives, thrusting his hideous mask into their faces and gibbeting at them in fiendish menace. In the firelight their sweat of fear burst out and ran in little rivulets down their bodies as they writhed and wriggled against their bonds.

Suddenly there was a spluttering explosive rush as Ningi voided her bowels with sheer terror, and the hot stink of faeces filled the hut. Mungo threw a fur kaross over them and immediately they were still, their grunts and muffled groans ceased.

He moved quickly then. Returning to the sleeping platform he threw the furs aside, and found a pallet of woven bamboo. It lifted like a trap door, and in the low recess below it were a dozen small clay pots.

His hands began to shake as he reached for one and lifted it out of the recess. His own sweat half blinded him – but through his blurred vision he saw the soapy gleam of reflected firelight in the mouth of the pot.

He could not take it all, there was too much for him to carry and too much for him later to conceal. Moreover, his survivor's instinct warned him that the more he took the more remorseless would be the search and pursuit.

He spilled the contents of all twelve pots into a glittering heap beside the fire, and in its uncertain light made his choice of the biggest and brightest stones from the hundreds that teased him with their twinkling smiles. Thirty of them filled the leather drawstring bag he had brought with him. He tied it back at his waist, snatched up the assegai and slipped out of the hut.

The guards at the inner stockade still slept, and he passed them silently. Below the wall of the outer stockade he stripped off his cloak, mittens and mask and dropped them on the untended watch-fire. Then he heaped branches over them – there would be only ash by morning.

He went up the rope swiftly, hand over hand, and pulled it up after him. The royal kraal behind him was silent in heavy midnight stupor, and he climbed lightly down the outer wall of the stockade.

He bathed in the pool below the camp, washing off the charcoal and fat, and then found his shirt and breeches where he had left them in the hollow of a tree trunk beside the pool.

In the hut he knelt beside Louise and placed one hand, still icy cold from the pool, upon her cheek. She sighed and rolled over onto her side. He felt like laughing and shouting his triumph out loud. Instead, he hid the bag of precious stones under his mattress and rolled into his blanket. He did not sleep for the rest of the night, and in the dawn he heard the hubbub of superstitious fear from the king's kraal, the screams of women and the shouts of men, loudly bolstering their courage against the spirits and the demons.

'This is a cruel thing for a good king to do,' Robyn told Lobengula bitterly.

'Nomusa, you are a wise woman, the wisest that I have ever known – but you do not understand the spirits and demons of Matabeleland.'

'I understand that the world is full of evil men, but that there are very few evil spirits.'

'The thing that entered my sister's hut came from the air. All the gates to the kraal were guarded by men unsleeping; they have sworn to me that they stood at their posts from dusk to dawn, with eyes wide and spears in their hands. Nothing passed them.'

'Even your best men can doze, and then lie to protect themselves.'

'Nobody dare lie to the king. It came from air, and it sprayed rotten stinking blood upon the portals of Ningi's hut.' Lobengula shuddered despite himself. 'On Chaka's scrawny buttocks, that is a *Tokoloshe* trick. No man can do that.'

'Except if he carry blood in a pot to hurl on the doorway.'

'Nomusa –' Lobengula shook his head sorrowfully. 'My sister and her servants saw this great hairy thing, black as midnight and stinking of the grave, with blood and not sweat oozing from its skin. Its eyes were like the full moon, and its voice that of lion and eagle, it had no hands and no feet, just hairy pads.' Lobengula shuddered again.

'And it stole diamonds,' Robyn told him. 'What does a demon want with diamonds?'

'Who knows what a demon needs for his spells or his magic, or to please his dark master?'

'Men lust after diamonds.'

'Nomusa, to black men diamonds have no value, so it could not have been a black man. On the other hand, if a white man had entered my sister's hut he would not have been satisfied with a few stones. A white man would have taken them all, for that is their way. So it could not have been either a white man or a black man – what is left but a demon?'

'Lobengula, Great King, you cannot allow this thing to happen.'

'Nomusa, there has been a terrible witchcraft perpetrated within the royal kraal. An evil person or many evil persons have conjured up a black demon, and I would be no king at all if I allowed them to live. The evil ones must be smelled out, and my birds must feast before we are cleansed of this filthy thing.'

'Lobengula –'

'Say no more, Girlchild of Mercy, words cannot divert my purpose, for you and your family and all the guests at my kraal are summoned to see justice done.'

It took ten days for the Matabele people to come in to GuBulawayo; they came in their regiments, warriors and maidens, ringed indunas and fruitful matrons – the toddlers and the greyheaded toothless old droolers – in their thousands and tens of thousands; and on the morning that Lobengula had appointed, the nation assembled, rank upon rank, regiment upon regiment, a black ocean of humanity that overflowed the great cattle stockade.

There was a peculiar stillness over such an immense gathering, only the plumed headdresses moved softly in the small restless breeze, and a pall of fear hung over them, so palpable that it seemed to take the heat from the sun and dim its very rays.

The silence was oppressive; it seemed to crush the breath from their lungs. Only once when a black crow flew low over the serried ranks and screeched its raucous cry into the silence, all their heads lifted and a soft sigh shook them, like the wind through the top branches of the forest.

Before the gates of the royal kraal, facing this huge concourse, were drawn up the senior indunas of the Matabele, Somabula and Babiaan and Gandang and the lesser princes of Kumalo, while behind them again, their backs to the poles of the stockade, were Lobengula's white guests, almost one hundred of them, Germans and Frenchmen, Dutchmen and Englishmen, hunters and scholars and businessmen and adventurers, petitioners and missionaries and traders. Soberly clad in broadcloth, wearing hunting leathers and bandoliers or dressed in spangled and gaudy uniform, they waited in the sweltering silence.

There were only two white women present, for Robyn had flatly refused to bring her daughters from Khami for the smelling-out ceremony, and Lobengula had relented and made an exception for them.

The king had given permission for the two women to be seated. Robyn sat beside the entrance to the stockade, and Clinton stood over her protectively while the members of Mr Rhodes' deputation flanked her. Mr Rudd, red-faced and whiskered, with his Derby hat set four square on his head, and Jordan Ballantyne, bare-headed and golden-haired at Robyn's other hand.

Further down the line of guests, Louise St John sat on a stool of leather thongs. Her thick sable plaits hung to the waist of her simple white dress, and the eyes of the men around her kept returning surreptitiously to her exotic high-cheeked beauty. Behind her stood Mungo St John, one eye hidden by the black patch, leaning easily on his cane and smiling to himself as he saw the direction of the eyes of the men about him.

The nation surged like a slumbering black sea struck by a sudden gale of wind, and the plumes tossed like spume. There was a single clap of sound like the volley of massed cannon as every right leg was lifted shoulder high and brought down to stamp the hard earth, and every throat corded and strained to the royal salute.

'*Bayete!*'

The Great Black Elephant of Matabele came through the gateway, and behind him his wives led by Ningi swayed and shuffled and sang his praises.

With the toy spear of kingship in his hand, Lobengula paced towards the mound of packed clay on which the bath chair, which had been his father's throne, was set, and Gandang and Babiaan, his brothers, came forward to help him ascend the steps.

From his platform, Lobengula looked upon his people, and those closest to him saw the terrible sorrow in his eyes.

'Let it begin,' he said, and slumped into his chair.

There was a ragged chorus of shrieks and whines and maniacal laughter from beyond the stockade walls, and through the gateway came a horrid procession of beldams and crones, of prancing hell-hags and gibbeting necromancers.

At their throats and waists were hung the trappings of their wizardry, skull of baboon and infant, skin of reptile, of python and iguana, carapace of tortoise, and stoppered horns, rattles of lucky bean pods and bones, and other grisly relics of man and animal and bird.

Wailing and hooting they assembled before Lobengula's throne.

'Dark sisters, can you smell the evil ones?'

'We smell their breaths – they are here! They are here!'

One of the witches collapsed in the dust, with froth bubbling over her toothless gums; her eyes rolled back into her skull and her limbs twitched spasmodically. One of her sisters dashed the red powder from a snuff-horn in her face, and she shrieked and leaped into the air.

'Dark sisters, will you bring forth the evil-doers?' Lobengula asked.

'We will bring them to you, Great Bull of Kumalo. We will deliver them up, son of Mzilikazi.'

'Go!' ordered Lobengula. 'Do what must be done!'

Some of them went whirling and cavorting, brandishing their divining rods, one the tail of a giraffe, another the inflated bladder of a jackal on a staff of red tambooti wood, still another the stretched and sun-dried penis of a black-maned lion, the rods with which they would point out the evil ones.

Others crept away, slinking and sly as the night-prowling hyena. Others again crawled on all fours, snuffling the earth like hunting hounds quartering for the scent as they spread out amongst the rows of waiting people.

One of the witches came down the line of white guests, hopping like an ancient baboon, her empty teats flapping against her withered belly, her skin crusty grey with filth and her charms clattering and jangling; and she stopped in front of Mungo St John and lifted her nose to sniff the air, then she howled like a bitch in season.

Mungo St John took the long black hand-rolled cheroot of native tobacco from between his lips and inspected the ash on its tip. The crone hopped closer and looked up into his face, and he returned the cheroot to his lips and returned her stare without interest.

She leapt up to thrust her face inches from his and noisily sniff the breath of his nostrils, and then she danced away – until she faced him again, lifted the long giraffe tail above her head, shrieked like a stooping owl and rushed at Mungo, the tail raised to strike into his face.

In front of him she froze in the act of striking, and Mungo St John took the cheroot from his mouth and he blew a perfect smoke ring, that spun upon itself until it broke in the witch's face and blew away in soft wisps.

She cackled, wildly, madly, and passed on down the line to pause in front of Robyn Codrington.

'You stink like the hyena that spawned you,' Robyn told her evenly in perfect Matabele, and the witch whirled and raced away to where Juba stood in the front line of noble matrons; she raised the switch to strike and looked back at Robyn, gloating loathsomely.

Robyn had gone white as bone, and came to her feet clutching her own bosom.

'No,' she whispered. 'Please, fair sister, let her be.'

The witch dropped her arm and came back to strut and preen in front of Robyn; then again she shrieked, whirled and rushed at Juba, this time she struck, and the tail hissed and snapped on black flesh – but at the very last second the witch had diverted her aim, and the blow flew into the startled face of the young woman who stood beside Juba.

'I smell evil,' shrieked the witch, and the woman fell to her knees. 'I smell blood.'

The witch struck again and again, the tail cutting stingingly into the woman's unprotected face until the tears started and ran down her cheeks.

The executioners came forward and pulled her to her feet. The woman's legs were paralysed, so they dragged her unprotesting before Lobengula, and he looked down on her, saddened and helplessly compassionate, before he lifted the forefinger of his right hand.

One of the executioners swung his war club, a full blow that stove in the back of the woman's skull. The bone crunched like a footstep in loose gravel, and the woman's eyes were driven from their sockets like over-ripe grapes by the force of it. When she fell face forward in the dust there was a bloodless depression in the back of her head into which a man could have placed his fist. The witch scurried away to continue the hunt, and Juba looked across at Robyn. Robyn had fallen back on her chair, trembling and pale, while Clinton put an arm around her shoulders to steady her.

In the packed ranks there was another triumphant shriek, and the executioners dragged a fine-looking young warrior from his place. He threw off their hands and strode to drop on one knee before Lobengula's throne.

'Father of the nation, hear my praises. Great Thunderer, Black Bull, let me die with your name on my lips. Oh Lobengula who drives like the wind –'

The king lifted his finger and the club fell with the flute of a goose's wing.

The chorus of howls and shrieks was unending now as the sisters warmed to their work, and the victims were dragged out and slaughtered – until their corpses were a high mound before the king's throne, a tangle of black limbs and shattered heads, that grew and grew.

A hundred, two hundred, were added to the pile, while the sun reached its zenith and the dust and heat and terror formed a suffocating miasma, and the blue metallic flies swarmed in the staring eyes and open mouths of the dead, and the witches cavorted and giggled and struck with their rods.

Here and there a maiden, overcome with the fear and the blazing heat, fell swooning from her place and the witches pounced upon this irrefutable evidence of guilt and rained blows upon her bare back or glossy breasts, and the executioners hurried to keep pace with their dreadful task.

The sun began its slow descent towards the western horizon, and at last one at a time the witches crept back to the mountain of death they had created. They staggered with exhaustion – the dust had caked on their running sweat, but they bayed and whined like dogs as they pored over the corpses, selecting those they would take with them – back to their caves and secret places – a sliver of the womb of a virgin was a powerful fertility charm, a slice of the heart of a blooded warrior was a wonderful talisman in battle.

'Is the work done?' Lobengula asked.

'It is done, oh king.'

'Are all the evil ones dead?'

'They are all dead, son of Mzilikazi.'

'Go then – and go in peace,' Lobengula said wearily.

'Stay in peace, Great King.' They chuckled and hooted and, bearing their gruesome plunder with them, they shuffled away through the gateway of the stockade.

Three times in as many weeks Mungo St John petitioned the king – asking him to 'give the road' to the south – but each time the king chatted affably for an hour and then waved him away. 'I will think on it, One Bright Eye, but are you unhappy here? Does the beef and beer I send you not fill your belly? Perhaps you would like to go once again on the hunt?'

'I want to go south, oh King.'

'Perhaps in the next full moon, One Bright Eye, and then again perhaps after the rain has passed, or after the Chawala Ceremony, who knows? We will see in good season.'

Then one morning Louise rode out early, as had become her custom – but after she had been gone some hours Mungo realized that this time she had the rifle and bandolier of ammunition, her blanket roll and the gallon water bottle with her.

He puzzled over her behaviour for the rest of that day, but he was not alarmed until night fell and she had not returned. He sat up beside the fire all that night, and at first light he took the second mule and crossed the river to where Rudd's party was camped in grand style in a pleasant glade of the forest. They had six wagons and as many tents made of best quality waterproof canvas, each with sun flysheets.

The horses on the picket line were all blood Arabs, one of which would carry Mungo and his small bag of precious stones to the Shashi river in six days or less. He was eyeing them hungrily, when Robyn Codrington stooped out of one of the tents. She saw him and would have gone in again, but he called to her and jumped down from the mule.

'Dr Codrington, please, it is a matter of extreme urgency.'

Reluctantly she turned back.

'My wife is missing, she did not come in last night.'

Immediately her distant expression changed to one of concern.

'Did she say where she was going?'

He shook his head. 'I can only think that she might have ridden back to Khami – you know she was becoming friendly with your elder daughter –'

'I shall send a servant to the mission.'

'Can you not ask the king to let me go?'

'The king has gone in to his wives – nobody, not even I, dare disturb him until he comes out from the women's quarters.'

'How long will that be?'

'A day, a week – there is no way of telling. I shall send word to you as soon as I have news.'

That night Mungo waited again, and then in the dawn as he crouched, haggard and bleary-eyed, over the smoky fire, listening for the hoof beats of the mule or the sound of Louise's voice out of the darkness – he was struck instead by a thought that chilled his blood and made his guts slide with dread.

He leapt up from the fire, ran into the hut and scrabbled frantically under the mattress. With a blessed soaring relief his fingers closed on the bag, and he pulled it out and fumbled the drawstring open. He poured the bright stones into the palm of his hand. They were all there, but with them was something that had not been there before. It was a folded sheet of paper – and he took it to the fire and held it to catch the light.

'When you find this you will know why I have gone. Even as I write this the memory of those poor wretches who died in their hundreds to pay for your greed rises before me to torment me. With them died the last of my love for you.

'I leave you those blood-spattered stones in the certain knowledge that they are accursed.

'Do not follow me. Do not send after me. Do not think of me again.'

She had not signed it.

Rudd's party was at breakfast under the open-sided dining-tent.

It was a fresh and cool morning. The conversation around the table was intelligent, informed and yet quick and witty, Robyn revelled in it.

She sat at the head of the trestle table and the gentlemen deferred to her. Mr Rudd had been very obviously taken with her from their first meeting, and addressed all his remarks to her directly.

Jordan had supervised the preparation of a gargantuan English breakfast, fresh eggs and grilled gammon, salted kippers and tinned pork sausage, potted shrimps and bloater paste, with freshly-churned yellow butter and hot scones.

Mr Rudd, quite carried away with the spontaneous festive mood, called for a bottle of champagne that had been hung overnight in a wet sack to cool.

'Well,' he lifted his glass to Robyn, 'I am sure we shall be able to survive this rough life and rude fare until the good king makes up his mind.'

Despite Robyn's intercession, Lobengula had not yet ratified the concession that they sought. His senior indunas had been in secret conclave for weeks, but could not reach a consensus of agreement – while Lobengula vacillated and reacted to Mr Rudd's insistence by retiring to his women's quarters where nobody could reach him.

'It may take months yet.' Robyn lifted her own glass and returned Rudd's salute. 'I would not expect Lobengula to make a decision on such an important matter without going into the Matopos Hills to consult the oracle, the Umlimo.'

Suddenly Clinton looked down towards the river, frowned and whispered to Robyn. 'It's that scoundrel St John, what does he want coming here?'

Mungo St John had dismounted at the periphery of the camp, but he did not approach the company under the open-sided marquee.

Robyn stood up quickly. 'Please excuse me, gentlemen. General St John's wife is missing, and he is naturally worried.'

'Thank you for coming,' Mungo said, as she hurried to him. 'I have nobody else to turn to, Robyn.'

She tried to ignore the intimacy of his appeal, and the little jolt that his use of her given name always gave her.

'Do you have news?' she asked.

'I have discovered a note that Louise left for me.'

'Let me see it.' Robyn held out her hand.

'I am sorry. It contains most personal and, I fear, embarrassing, references,' Mungo told her. 'But what is important is that Louise is trying to leave Matabeleland by the southern road.'

'That is madness,' Robyn whispered. 'Without the king's permission, without an escort. The road is obscure, the country wild and infested with lions, she cannot hope to pass the border impis – and they have orders to kill all who do not have the road from Lobengula.'

'She knows all this,' Mungo said.

'Then what possessed her to make the attempt?'

'We argued. She resented the feeling which she knows that I still have – for you.'

Robyn fell back a pace, her cheeks paling and her breath catching in her throat.

'General St John, I forbid you to talk in that fashion.'

'You asked me, Robyn, and once, long ago, I told you that I would never forget that night aboard *Huron* –'

'Stop it! Stop it, this instant! How can you speak like this when your wife is in dire danger?'

'Louise was never my wife,' he said quietly, staring into her green eyes with that single penetrating gaze. 'She was my travelling companion, never my wife.'

Robyn faltered, colour rushed back into her cheeks, and with it came a strange unaccountable pagan joy.

'You told me – once – that you were married.'

'I was, Robyn. Not to Louise. That other lady died many years ago in Navarre in France.'

Robyn confounded herself. She was married to a brave, kind man – in his own way a saintly man – while before her stood the embodiment of evil, the veritable serpent of Eden; and yet she could not suppress this wicked unconscionable elation at the knowledge that he was free – free for she knew not what, or could not bring herself to think on it.

'I shall go to the king,' she said, painfully aware of the quaver in her voice. 'I shall ask him to send men after your – after the lady. I shall ask him also to give you the road, General, and I would consider it full repayment if you would take it immediately, and never return to Matabeleland.'

'What is between us can never be denied, Robyn, as long as we both live.'

'I do not wish to see you again.' With an effort of all her will she steadied her voice and met his eye.

'Robyn –'

'I shall send a messenger to you with the king's reply.'

'Robyn –'

'Please.' Her voice cracked again. 'In God's holy name, please leave me alone.'

However, it was two more days before Robyn sent Jordan Ballantyne to Mungo's camp.

'Dr Codrington bids me tell you, sir, that the king has already sent one of his trusted indunas with a picked body of warriors after your wife. They have orders to protect her from the border guards and to escort her to the Shashi river.'

'Thank you, young man.'

'Furthermore, she asked me to tell you that the king has given you the road. You may follow your wife immediately.'

'Again my thanks to Dr Codrington.'

'General St John, you do not remember me –'

'I am afraid –' Mungo frowned up at Jordan on the back of the dancing Arab mare.

'Jordan – Zouga Ballantyne's son. We met in Kimberley some years ago.'

'Ah! Of course, forgive me. You have changed.'

'General, I know that it is none of my business, but as you are a trusted friend of my father's, it is my duty to warn you that there were unpleasant rumours after your departure from Kimberley.'

'I did not know,' Mungo told him indifferently. 'Still, it is one of life's unpleasant truths that the more prominent a man becomes, the more determined are the mean little men to tear him down.'

'I know that, General. I am associated with a great man –' Jordan checked himself. 'However, a police agent, a Griqua named Hendrick Naaiman claimed that you attended an I.D.B. rendezvous and that when you realized it was a trap you attempted to kill him.'

Mungo made an impatient gesture. 'Why should somebody of my standing, my estate, take such a ridiculous risk as to indulge in I.D.B?'

'That was what Mr Rhodes said, sir. He has repeatedly expressed certainty of your innocence.'

'After I have found my wife I shall return immediately to Kimberley to confront this Naaiman person.'

'General St John, that will be neither necessary nor possible. Naaiman was killed some months ago in a knife fight in one of the drinking canteens. He cannot give evidence for or against you. Without either witness or accuser, your innocence is presumed.'

'Damn it –' Mungo frowned to cover his immense relief. 'I should have welcomed the chance to force his words down his lying throat, now there will always be doubts in some men's minds.'

'Only in the minds of the mean little men.' Jordan touched the brim of his cap. 'I shall not detain you further; you must be anxious to follow and find your wife. Good luck and God speed. I am sure we shall meet again, General.'

Mungo St John stared after Jordan as he rode away. It was hard to grasp the extent of his good fortune – the spectre of unrelenting justice that had pursued him from the south had vanished; he had the road to leave Matabeleland, and an immense fortune in diamonds to carry with him.

An hour later he had visited one of the traders and exchanged the cart and the other meagre possessions he no longer needed for a good rifle and one hundred rounds of ammunition, and he sat the broad comfortable back of the mule, its head pointed southwards, as it skirted the granite hills of the indunas.

Mungo looked neither left nor right: his eye was fixed ahead, towards the south, so that he did not see the slim almost boyish figure on the slopes high above him. Robyn shaded her eyes with the brim of her bonnet and peered after him until the little feather of dust raised by the mule's big heavy hooves subsided into the mimosa forests.

Louise St John was driven on by her need to keep ahead of any pursuit, obsessed with the knowledge that she must avoid the kraals along the road, ridden by the guilt she knew she must share with Mungo, her senses and emotions in terrible turmoil – so that she did not have a chance to regret her hasty action, taken in the shock of discovering the diamonds, nor did she realize the depths of her loneliness – until she had successfully skirted the last of the great kraals and left the pleasant grasslands of the plateau.

Now ahead of her the escarpment fell into the wild land, hot and heavily forested, which she knew was teeming with wild animals and guarded by the merciless border impis.

It was a measure of her desperate need to be free of Mungo St John and all he stood for that she never once considered turning back – though she knew there was sanctuary for her at Khami Mission, though she knew that Robyn Codrington would go to the king on her behalf and he would give her an escort of warriors to the border.

She could not go back, she could not bear the prospect of being close to Mungo St John ever again. The love she had once borne him had sickened into a total revulsion. No risk was too high to escape him and she had to do it now. There was no going back.

She lay the last night beside the wagon ruts that were her tenuous link with civilization and life itself, her own thread through the maze of the Matabele Minotaur, and she listened to the mule cropping grass close at hand and, far away down the escarpment, the faint roar of a hunting lion, while she tried to reconstruct in her mind the map that had formed the frontispiece to Zouga Ballantyne's book *A Hunter's Odyssey*. The account of Zouga's journeys had fascinated her, even before she had met him, and she had studied the map with minute attention.

She judged that from where she now lay the Tati river was not more than one hundred miles due west. No pursuer would expect her to take that direction. No impi would guard that desolate untravelled quarter, and the Tati river was the border between Matabeleland and Khama's country. By all accounts King Khama was a gentle and honourable man; his country was under suzerainty of the British crown, and British justice was ensured by the presence of Sir Sidney Shippard at Khama's kraal.

If she could reach the Tati river and follow it south until she met some of Khama's people who could take her to Sir Sidney – then he would see to it that she was sent on southwards to Kimberley.

The thought of that town made her realize the true reason for her desperate haste. For the first time she became aware of the terrible hunger within her to be with a man whom she could trust, whose strength would shield her and make her strong again. The man to whom she could at last acknowledge she had transferred the love which Mungo St John had long ago forfeited. She must reach Zouga, and reach him soon – that was the only thing certain in her confusion, and her despair, but first there were a hundred miles of wilderness to cross.

She rose in the first pale light of day, kicked sand over the fire, saddled the mule, and slid the rifle into its scabbard, she buckled the water bottle and blanket to the pommel and swung up onto his back. With the unearthly red glow of the sunrise at her back, she urged the mule forward, and after fifty paces, when she glanced back, the faint double track of wagon wheels was no longer discernible.

The land through which she rode had a harsh and forbidding grandeur; the horizons were infinite and the sky was tall and milky blue. It was empty of all life, she saw no bird nor animal, and the sunlight was white and fierce. In the nights the stars filled the heavens with whorls and eddies of cold bright light and she felt herself shrinking under the immensity and loneliness of it all.

On the third evening, she knew that she was lost, hopelessly and irretrievably lost. She was barely certain of the direction of the sunset, but she had no idea of distances and her memories of the sketch map which she had thought vivid and clear, had become fuddled and confused.

The gallon water bottle was empty. She had drunk the last bloodwarm mouthful a little before noon. She had seen no game to provide meat, and she had eaten the last stale maize cake the previous evening. The mule was too exhausted and thirsty to graze. He stood miserably under the wild sycamore tree that she had chosen for her night's camp; but though she put the knee halter on him, she knew that he would not wander. His head hung to his knees. An arrowhead of flint had lacerated the frog of his left fore. He was dead lame, and she had no idea how much farther it was to the Tati, nor in which direction the river lay.

She put a little round white pebble under her tongue to draw her saliva and lay down next to the fire. Exhausted sleep came like sudden black death – and she woke as though she were struggling up from the depths of hell itself.

The moon was up, full and yellow, but it was the mule's fearful snorts and the stamp of his hooves on the stony earth that had roused her. She dragged herself up with the help of the sycamore trunk and peered about her. Something moved at the edge of her vision, something big and ghostly pale, and as she stared at it she caught the acrid ammoniacal whiff of cat. The mule whinnied with terror and broke into a maimed lunging gallop, the halters holding his forelegs so that he was awkward and slow, and the big pale thing came flashing lightly upon him, rising like a huge white bat against the moonlit sky, and settled upon the mule's back.

The mule screamed once and clearly Louise heard his spinal column break as the lioness on his back bit into his neck and in the same movement reached forward to sink her claws into his cheek and twist his head backwards against the hold of her jaws.

The mule went down with a thumping impact on the hard earth, and the lioness immediately flattened herself behind the shuddering and spasmodically kicking carcass and began ripping into the soft skin around the anus – making an opening into the belly cavity through which to reach the titbits of kidney and spleen and liver and guts.

Behind her Louise saw other pale cat shapes coming out of the shadows, and she had just presence of mind enough to snatch up the rifle before she scrambled up into the fork of the sycamore and climbed upwards, driven by a suffocating terror.

She clung to an upper branch and listened to the grisly feast below her, the growling and squabbling of a dozen lions over the carcass, the lapping sounds as they licked the meat off the bones with tongues like wood rasps, and the awful guttural purring and slurping.

As the light of day slowly strengthened, so the noises subsided. The big cats had eaten their fill and slunk away into the bush. Then Louise looked down the trunk of the sycamore into two implacable yellow orbs that seemed to search out new depths in her terror.

A full-maned lion stood at the base of the tree. He seemed as broad across the back as a carthorse, and his colour was a dark bluish-grey in the bad light. He was looking up at her, and as she stared in horror, the great black ruff of his mane came erect in excitation, so that he seemed to swell in size to fill the whole field of vision.

Suddenly he reared up on his hindlegs and reached up towards her, the long, curved, yellow claws unsheathing from their massive pads, and he ripped long parallel wounds down the bark of the sycamore from which the sap swelled in white milky beads.

Then the lion opened his jaws, and she stared into the deep pink cave of his throat. The long velvety tongue curled like the fleshy petal of some weird orchid, and each gleaming ivory fang was long as a man's forefinger and sharp as the point of a guardsman's pike.

The lion roared up at her. It was a gale of sound that struck her like a blow from a mailed fist. It drove in her eardrums and it jellied every muscle in her body. Then the huge beast came up the tree. It climbed in a series of lunges, the yellow claws raking slabs of wet bark off the trunk as it bunched its quarters and drove upwards, those painful gusts of sound still bursting from its throat, the enormous yellow eyes fastened upon her coldly and remorselessly.

Louise began to scream and the tree rocked, the branches tossed and crackled as the great tawny body forced its way through them with a speed and power she would never have believed possible. Still screaming, she pushed the long barrel of the rifle downwards, without aiming she jerked at the trigger and nothing happened except that the lion was closer still.

In her panic she had forgotten the safety catch of the rifle. It was almost too late; the lion reached up and struck the barrel with one enormous paw. The blow jarred her wrists and numbed her arms, but she kept her grip and slid the catch forward with her thumb and thrust the muzzle into the animal's jaws as she pulled the trigger again. The shot was almost drowned in the lion's roars.

The recoil broke her grip on the weapon and it went spinning away, clattered against the branches, leaving her utterly defenceless. Just below her perch the lion still clung to the tree trunk, but the huge shaggy head was thrown back on the arch of the thick neck, and a bright fountain of blood spurted up out of the open jaws, and the gleaming fangs turned rosy red as it washed over them.

Slowly the hooked claws released their deep grip on the bark of the tree trunk, and the cat fell, twisting and convulsing in mid-air until it struck the ground at the foot of the tree. Lying on its side, it stretched out its limbs and arched its back, one last breath choked with blood rattled up its throat – and then it slumped and softened into the total relaxation of death.

Timidly Louise clambered down from the sycamore and, keeping well clear of the carcass, she retrieved the rifle. The butt was cracked through and the breech block jammed solid. She struggled with it futilely for a few minutes, and then dropped it.

Terror still stifled her breathing, and congested her bladder – but she did not pause to relieve it. Frantically she snatched up the small canvas bag that contained her tinder-box and steel, a clasp knife and a few items of jewellery and other personal oddments. She left the bandolier and blanket and the empty water-bottle, for she was desperately driven by the need to leave this place, and she stumbled away from the sycamore.

Once only she looked back. A pair of jackals were already at the lion's carcass, and out of the lemon-pale morning sky the first vulture came planing down on wide elegant wings to roost, hump-backed, in the top branches of the sycamore. It bobbed its foul boiled-looking naked head in gluttonous anticipation.

Louise began to run. She ran with a panicky desperation, looking over her shoulder, so that the thorn bushes ripped at her and her high-heeled riding boots tottered over the broken ground. She almost exhausted herself in that wild run, and when she fell at last she lay face down, racked by the sob of each breath, and with the tears of fear and despair mingling with the sweat of her cheeks.

It took her until almost noon to recover her strength, and gather her determination and get her racing terror under control.

Then she went on.

In the mid-afternoon one heel broke off her boot, and she twisted her ankle painfully. She hobbled on until darkness gathered around her and with it all her fears returned.

She climbed to the high fork of a mopani tree. The cramped position on the hard trunk, the cold and her own fears prevented her from sleeping. In the dawn she climbed down. Her ankle had swollen and turned a deep purple-rose colour. She knew that if she removed her boot once more she would never get it on again. She pulled up the straps as hard as she could and cut a branch of mopani to use as a crutch.

The noon was windless and fiercely hot. The mucous membrane of her nostrils had dried out and swollen so that she was forced to breath through her mouth. Her lips cracked and began to bleed. The metallic salt of her own blood seemed to scald her tongue. The crutch of raw rough mopani rubbed the skin from her armpit and flank, and by mid-afternoon her tongue had swollen into a choking gag like a ball of oakum jammed into her mouth.

That night she did not have the strength to climb to a tree fork. She crouched at its base, and when at last exhausted sleep assailed her, she was tormented by dreams of running mountain streams – from which she woke mumbling and coughing to the worse torment of reality.

Somehow she dragged herself up again when the light woke her. Each step now was an effort to which she had to steel herself. She leaned on the staff, staring through bloodshot eyes and swollen lids at the spot where she would place her foot, then she lunged forward and swayed to catch her balance before she drew her injured foot up beside the other.

'Five hundred and four –' She counted each step, and then steeled herself for the next pace. At every count of 'one thousand' she rested and peered around her at the wavering heat mirage.

In mid-afternoon she lifted her head during one of the rest pauses and saw ahead of her a file of human figures. Her joy was so intense that for a moment her vision darkened, then she roused herself and tried to shout. No sound came out of her dry, cracked, swollen mouth.

She lifted the crutch and waved it at the oncoming figures – and realized at that moment that the mirage and her own hallucinations had tricked her. In her wavering, uncertain vision the line of human figures resolved into a troop of wild ostrich, and they scattered away across the plain.

There were no tears to tell the depths of her disappointment. Her tears had dried long ago. At dusk she fell face down, and her last conscious thought was, 'It's over. I cannot go on.'

But the dawn chill roused her and she lifted her head painfully and in front of her face she saw a stalk of grass curved under the weight of the drops of dew that hung from it, trembling precariously and sparkling like precious jewels. She reached out her hand and touched it, and instantly the lovely drops fell into the dry baked earth and left no trace of their going.

She crawled to the next stalk and this time let the liquid diamonds fall into her black swollen mouth. The pleasure was so intense as to change its shape to pain. The sun came up swiftly to dry the dew, but she had taken enough strength at least to push herself upright and go on.

The following night there was a small warm breeze that nagged at her while she slept, and because of it there was no dew, and she knew that this was the day she would die. It would be easier to do it here where she lay, and she closed her eyes – then opened them again and struggled into a sitting position.

Each thousand paces seemed to take an infinity, and she was hallucinating again. Once her grandfather walked beside her for a while. He wore his war bonnet of eagle feathers, and his beaded and tasselled buckskins. When she tried to talk to him he smiled sadly at her and his face folded into ancient leathery brown seams, and he disappeared.

At another time Mungo St John galloped past on Shooting Star. He did not look in her direction and the great golden stallion's hooves made no sound. They whirled way into the dusty distances. Then suddenly the earth opened under her and she fell, lightly as a feather from the breast of a goose, lightly as a snowflake, twisting and turning, down and down, then a jarring impact shocked her back to reality.

She lay face down in a bed of sugary white sand. For a moment she thought it was water, and she scooped a double handful and lifted it to her lips, but the dry sharp grains were like salt on her tongue. She looked about her and realized with a sort of bitter triumph that she had at last reached the Tati river and that she lay now in the parched riverbed. The fine sand, white as salt, reached from bank to bank – she was about to die of thirst in a river.

'A pool – ' she thought. 'There must be a pool.' She began to crawl through the sand, down towards the first bend in the course.

It opened to another long vista of tall banks, and overhanging trees – but the white glittering unbroken sand taunted her. She knew she did not have the strength to crawl as far as the next bend. Her vision was starring and breaking up again; but she frowned with concentration at the piles of brown ball-shaped lumps in the centre of the river bed, and vaguely realized that they were heaps of elephant dung, and that near them were mounds of sand, like children's sandcastles on the beach.

She remembered suddenly a description of the elephant digs from Zouga Ballantyne's book – and it gave her the final burst of strength to pull herself onto her feet and stagger to the nearest sandcastle. The elephants had kicked aside the sand, and made an excavation in the bottom of the riverbed as deep as a man's waist. She slid down into it and began frantically to dig with her bare hands. Within minutes her nails were broken and her fingertips bleeding, and the sand kept collapsing back into her hole, but she dug on doggedly.

Then the white sand changed colour, became damp and firm, and at last there was a glint in the very bottom. She tore a strip of cloth from the hem of her ragged skirt and pressed it down into the hole, then after a moment lifted it to her mouth, and with bleeding fingers squeezed out a drop of water onto her cracked and blackened tongue.

It was as Zouga had always imagined that it would be.

He crossed the Shashi river an hour before high noon on a hot windless day, with the silver and blue thunderheads piled on the far horizons and the teeming forests and hunting veld of Matabeleland ahead.

He sat astride a fine salted horse, and at his right hand rode his eldest son, a man full grown, straight and strong, a man to delight his father's heart.

'There she is, Papa.' Ralph swept his hat from his head and gestured with it to include the horizon of smoky-blue hills and green forests. 'There is your north at last. We are coming to take her now.'

Zouga laughed with him, his golden beard glowing in the sunlight and his teeth as white and even as his son's.

'Not quite yet, my boy. This time we have come to woo her – and the next time to take her as a bride.'

Zouga had broken his journey three months at Kimberley, and with the full resources of De Beers Diamond Mines at his disposal had done the planning that Rhodes had ordered.

He had decided on a band of two hundred men to take and hold Mashonaland, to ride the boundaries of the farms and peg the gold reefs. They were to be supported by a detachment of Sir Sidney Shippard's Bechuanaland Police from Khama's kraal – and another detachment of Rhodes' own police which he would raise. Zouga detailed the arms and equipment that they would need – one hundred and sixteen pages of schedules and lists – and Rhodes approved it with that bold sweeping signature and a curt injunction. 'Do it!'

Four days later Ralph had come into Kimberley with two dozen wagons from the Witwatersrand goldfields, and Zouga sat with him all night in his suite in Lil's new hotel.

In the morning Ralph had whistled with excitement.

'It's so big, so many men, so much equipment—'

'Can you do it, Ralph?'

'You want me to tender for a price to recruit the men, buy the equipment and assemble it here at Kimberley, provide the wagons and oxen to carry it all, horses for the men, rifles and ammunition, machine-guns, a steam engine to power a search-light; then you want me to tender to build a road to get it all to a map reference, a place which you call Mount Hampden, somewhere in the wilderness, and you want it all to be ready to leave in nine months?'

'You have grasped it fairly,' Zouga smiled. 'Can you do it?'

'Give me a week,' Ralph said, and five days later he was back.

'It's too big for me, I'm afraid, Papa,' he said, and then grinned mischievously at Zouga's expression of disappointment. 'I had to take in a partner – Frank Johnson.'

Johnson was another young man in a hurry, and, like Ralph, had already acquired a reputation for being able to get things done.

'Have you and young Johnson worked out a price?'

'We'll do it for eighty-eight thousand two hundred and eighty-five pounds and ten shillings.' Ralph handed him the signed tender and Zouga studied it in silence. When at last he looked up he asked:

'Tell me, Ralph, what is that ten shillings on the end for?'

'Why, Papa –' Ralph widened his eyes disarmingly. 'That is our profit on the deal.'

Zouga had cabled the tender price to Rhodes at Claridge's Hotel in London, and the following day Rhodes had cabled back his acceptance in principle.

All that was still needed was Lobengula's ratification of the consolidated concessions – and Zouga was under Rhodes' orders to go immediately to GuBulawayo and find out from Rudd the reasons for the delay.

Ralph had immediately elected to ride with Zouga.

'Once Mr Rhodes gives us the word to go – there will be no time for anything else. I have some unfinished business in Matabeleland, at Khami Mission and beyond –' And an uncharacteristic dreamy look had come into Ralph's eyes. 'This is the time to do it. While I still have the chance.'

So now, side by side, Zouga and Ralph spurred their mounts up the bank of the Shashi river and rode into Matabeleland.

'We will outspan here for a few days, Papa,' Ralph said; it was still strange for Zouga to have his son make decisions without deferring to him. 'The grazing is good and sweet, and we will rest the oxen and do a little hunting; there is still plenty of game up near the confluence of the Tati river.'

At the beginning of this long journey together, Zouga had been disconcerted by his son's competitive spirit that turned even the most mundane task into a contest. He had forgotten this trait of Ralph's in the time they had been separated but found now that it had grown stronger and fiercer during that period.

His energy daunted Zouga, who found that on this journey – for lack of other opposition – he was a foil for his son's need to compete.

They shot bird, on foot in heavy cover – guinea-fowl and francolin, Ralph counted the bag and scowled when Zouga outgunned him. They sat late at each outspan over the ivory dice, or the greasy dog-eared pack of cards, and Ralph glowed when he won a shilling, and growled when he lost one.

So now, when he said, 'We'll hunt together tomorrow, Papa,' Zouga knew he was in for an early start, and a long hard day.

They rode out from the wagons an hour before the first glimmer of dawn.

'Old Tom is getting *madala* – he's getting old – but I have a sovereign that says he'll run rings around that fancy beast of yours,' Ralph offered.

'I cannot afford that sort of money,' Zouga told him. He was hard and fit, his long professional hunting expeditions had kept him that way but the pace that Ralph set once he was aroused would be punishing. There was something else that troubled Zouga. When Ralph hunted competitively, he could be murderous. If he were challenged, there was only one consideration for him, the size of the bag.

Zouga had been a hunter for the greater part of his life. He had hunted for ivory, and for the peculiar fascination of the beautiful and noble animals he pursued. It was almost a form of love, that made a man want to study and understand and finally take the quarry irrevocably for his own.

These last seasons he had hunted, of necessity, with many men, but he had never yet met a man who hunted like his own son when his blood was up. It seemed as if the game were merely counters in another of Ralph's contests, the score all that counted. 'I don't want to be a sportsman, Papa. I leave that to you. I just want to be a winner.'

'I cannot afford that sort of money,' Zouga repeated, trying lightly to defuse Ralph's escalating tension.

'You can't afford a sovereign?' Ralph threw back his darkly handsome head, and his green eyes flashed as he laughed delighted. 'Papa, you have just sold that fat diamond of yours for thirty thousand pounds.'

'Ralph, let's make an easy day of it. If we get one giraffe, or a buffalo, that's all we need.'

'Papa, you are getting old. A sovereign. If you can't pay immediately, why then, your credit is always good!'

In mid-morning they cut the spoor of a troop of giraffe, feeding slowly eastward along the riverbank.

'I make out sixteen of them.' Ralph leaned from the saddle to examine the huge double bean-shaped spoor in the sandy earth. 'They'll not be an hour ahead of us.' And he put his heels into old Tom's flanks.

The forest alternated with open glades through which meandered little streams, draining the escarpment down to the Shashi river. They were dry at this season of the year, but that did not account for the paucity of game.

When Zouga had first travelled this road, going south from old King Mzilikazi's kraal, the herds had darkened every one of these open glades. In one day's ride he had counted over a hundred monstrous grey rhinoceros, but there had been no counting the silvery herds of fat zebra and clowning purple wildebeest.

In those days, after a man had fired a shot, the dust rising from the galloping herds had looked like the smoke from a bush fire – and yet this day they had ridden since dawn without seeing a single wild animal.

Zouga brooded on it as he rode stirrup for stirrup with his son. Of course, this area was on the direct road to Lobengula's kraal, over which steadily more and more wagons and travellers passed. There were still vast areas beyond where the herds were thick as the grass on which they grazed. But after the road they would cut into Mashonaland – and the railway line that would follow – he wondered what would remain.

Perhaps one day his grandchildren would live in a land of which every corner was as barren as this. He did not envy them the prospect; and even as he thought that, his trained hunter's eye picked up the tiny speck just above the forest line, far ahead.

For a moment he was reluctant to call Ralph's attention to it. It was the head of a giraffe, raised inquisitively high above the mimosa tree on which it was feeding.

For the first time in the hunting veld Zouga felt sick to the gut at the slaughter he knew was to follow – and he thought to distract Ralph's attention from the herd of huge spotted animals in the mimosa forest ahead. But at that moment Ralph shouted gaily:

'There they are, I'll be damned! They are shy as blushing virgins, they are off already.'

There had been a time when Zouga had been able to ride up to within two hundred yards of a herd before they took alarm. These were still a mile away and already galloping from the two horsemen.

'Come on, Papa. We'll catch them when they try to cross the Shashi,' and they tore into the stand of flowering mimosa.

'Tally-ho!' yelled Ralph. His hat came off and, hanging on its thong, it slapped against his back; while his long dark hair fluttered in the wind of their gallop. 'By God, Papa – you'll have to work to win your sovereign today,' he warned laughingly.

They crashed out of the forest onto another level open plain. The entire herd of huge vulnerable animals were spread before them: bulls and cows and calves, but that was not what caught Zouga's attention.

He pulled his horse down out of its gallop and swung his head away to the west.

'Ralph,' he shouted, 'let them go!'

Ralph looked back at him through the flying dust. His face was flushed with the hunter's fever.

'Warriors,' Zouga shouted. 'War party, Ralph. Close up!'

For a moment it seemed that Ralph would not obey, but then his good sense prevailed. It would be reckless to separate when there was a war party out, and he broke back to Zouga's side and let the panic-driven giraffe tear away towards the river.

He reined Tom to a halt. 'What do you make of them?' he asked, shading his eyes and peering through the heat-distorted air at the squiggly black line, like a shoal of tadpoles in the bottom of a rippling pool, which moved across the far side of the open plain. 'Khama's men? Bamangweto raiders? We are only a few miles from the frontier.'

'We won't take any chances until we know,' Zouga told him grimly. 'Let the horses blow. We may have to make a run –'

But Ralph interrupted him. 'Long shields! And they are red, those are the Moles, Bazo's fellows,' Ralph urged Tom towards the approaching impi. 'And I'll be damned if that isn't Bazo himself out front.'

By the time Zouga came up, Ralph had dismounted and, leaving Tom to stand, had run to embrace his old comrade – and he was already joshing Bazo cruelly.

'Lo, the Moles-that-burrow-under-a-mountain are returning from a raid without women or cattle. Did Khama's people give you the steel farewell?'

Bazo's delighted smile slid off his face at such levity, and he shook his plumes sternly.

'Not even in jest, Henshaw – do not talk like a giggling girl. If the king had sent us to Khama,' and he stabbed the air with his assegai, 'there would have been a beautiful killing.' He broke off as he recognized Zouga.

'Baba!' he said. 'Bakela – I see you, and my eyes are white with joy.'

'It has been too long, Bazo – but now you have the headring on your brow and an impi at your back – we shall shoot a beast and feast together this night.'

'Ah Bakela, it grieves me – but I am on the king's business. I return to GuBulawayo in haste to report the woman's death to the king.'

'Woman?' Zouga asked without real interest.

'A white woman. She ran from GuBulawayo without the king's word, and the king sent me after her –' Bazo broke off with an exclamation. 'Hau! But you know this woman, Bakela.'

'It is not Nomusa, my sister?' Zouga asked with quick concern. 'Not one of her daughters?'

'No, not them.'

'There are no other white women in Matabeleland.'

'She is the woman of One-Bright-Eye. The same woman who raced her horse against yours at Kimberley – and won. But now she is dead.'

'Dead?' All the blood had drained from Zouga's face, leaving his tan muddy and yellow. 'Dead?' he whispered, and swayed in the saddle so that, had he not grabbed at the pommel, he would have fallen.

'Louise – dead.'

*

Zouga found the sycamore that Bazo described to him, merely by back-tracking the impi.

They had left a good wide spoor, and Zouga reached the tree in the middle of the afternoon.

He did not know why he tortured himself so. There could be no reasonable doubt that she was dead. Bazo had showed him the pathetic relics he had retrieved. The damaged rifle and bandolier, the empty water bottle, and the tatters of cloth and saddlery ripped and chewed by the omnivorous jaws of the hyena.

The ground under the sycamore was beaten and swept of all traces of Louise by the pads of jackal and hyena, by the fluttering wings and the talons of hundreds of feeding, squabbling vultures. It smelled like a chicken coop, smeared with vulture dung, and loose feathers blew aimlessly hither and thither on the soft dry breeze.

Except for a few splinters of bone and tufts of hair, every trace of animal carcasses and the human body had been devoured. The hyena would have gobbled up even the leather of Louise's boots and belt, and the few remaining shreds of blanket and cloth were bloodstained.

It was quite easy to reconstruct what had happened. Louise had been set upon by a pride of lion. She had managed a single shot, there was an empty shell in the breech of the damaged rifle, and had killed one of the cats before being pulled off the mule.

Zouga could imagine every moment of her agony, almost hear her screams as the great jaws crunched through her bone and the yellow claws hooked into her flesh. It left him physically nauseated and weakened. He wanted to pray on the spot where she had died, but he did not seem to have the energy for even such small effort. It was as though the very force of life had gone out of him. Until that moment he had not realized what Louise's memory had meant to him, how the certainty that their lives were intertwined had sustained him while they were apart, how his belief in their eventual reunion had given his life purpose and direction. She had become part of his dream, and now it had been snuffed out on this wild and bloody patch of earth.

Twice he turned back to his horse to mount and leave, but each time he hesitated and then wandered back to sift through the reeking dust with his fingers for some last trace of her.

At last he looked at the sun. He could not reach the wagons before nightfall. He had told Ralph to leave Jan Cheroot and the spare horses at the drift of the Shashi when he went on with the wagons, so there was no urgency. There was no hurry. Without Louise there was no flavour in his life. Nothing really mattered any more, but he crossed to his horse, clinched the girth and mounted. He took one more lingering look at the trampled earth and then turned his horse's head back towards the Shashi and the wagons. He had not gone fifty yards when he found himself circling. It was not a conscious decision to begin casting for outgoing spoor. He knew it was futile, but his reluctance to leave the place dictated his actions.

Once he circled the sycamore, leaning out of the saddle and examining the broken and stony earth, then he moved farther out and circled again, then again, each time opening the radius of the circle. Suddenly his heart leaped against his ribs, and new hope flooded his devastated soul, but he had to steel himself to lean from the saddle and examine the thorn twig, in case he was to be disappointed once again.

The white tear had caught his eye, the twig had been broken half-through and now hung from the main branch at the level of a man's waist. The soft green leaves had wilted, the break was two or three days' old, but that was not what made Zouga's fingers shake.

From one of the curved red-tipped thorns hung a fine red thread of spun cotton. Zouga lifted it reverently and then touched it to his lips as though it were a sacred relic.

He was to the west of the sycamore; he could just make out the top branches above the surrounding bush, which meant that Louise had left that thread on the grasping thorn after she had run from the tree. The height above ground showed she had been on foot, and the broken twig and shredded cloth were evidence of her haste.

She had run from the sycamore and kept going in the direction which she had been stubbornly following, westwards, towards the Tati and Khama's country.

Zouga thumped his heels into the horse's flanks and galloped in the same direction. It was useless to look for spoor three days' old on this rocky ground. The wind had blown steadily for most of that time, and it would have scoured the last traces.

He must rely on luck and speed. He had seen the empty water bottle and he knew what were the chances of survival on foot, without water, in this country between the rivers. He galloped on the line of her flight, quartering from side to side, searching grimly – not allowing himself to doubt again, concentrating all his mind on the search for another tiny sign. In the last minutes of dusk he found it. It was the heel of a brown riding boot torn from the sole. The gleam of the steel nails had caught his eye. He drew the rifle from its holder and fired three spaced shots into the darkening sky.

He knew she had no rifle to reply – but if somewhere out ahead she heard his signal, it might give her hope and strength. He waited beside a small fire until the moon came up – and then by its light he went on, and every hour he stopped and fired signal shots into the great starry silence, and afterwards he listened intently, but there was only the shriek of a hunting owl overhead and the yipping of a jackal far out across the silvery plain.

In the dawn he reached the wide white course of the Tati river. It was dry as the dunes of the Kalahari Desert, and the hopes which he had kept alive all night began to wane.

He searched the morning sky for the high spiral of turning vultures which would show a kill, but all he saw was a brace of sand grouse slanting down on quick stabbing wings. Their presence proved that there was surface water – somewhere. She might have found it – that was the only chance. Unless she had found water she would be dead by now. He took a cautious mouthful from his own bottle, and his horse whickered when he smelt the precious liquid. Soon the thirst would begin wearing him down as well.

He had to believe that if Louise had reached the river, she would follow it downstream. She was part Indian, and she would surely be able to get her direction from the sun and to know that her only chance was southwards towards the confluence with the Shashi. He turned in that direction, staying up on the bank, watching the riverbed and the far bank and the sky.

Elephant had been digging in the bed, but their holes were dry now. He trotted on along the edge of the high bank. Ahead of him there was a rush of big purple-beige bodies as a herd of gemsbuck burst through the rank undergrowth on the far bank. Their long straight horns were like lances against the pale horizon sky, and the diamond-patterned face masks that gave their name seemed theatrical and frivolous. They galloped away into the deserts of Khama's country.

They could live without water for months at a time, and their presence gave Zouga no hope, but as he watched them go, his attention shifted to another distant movement much farther out on the flat open ground beyond the river.

There was a chacma baboon foraging there – the humanoid shape was quite distinctive. He looked for the rest of the troop – perhaps they were in the treeline beyond the plain. Chacma baboon would drink daily, and he shaded his eyes against the glare to watch the distant moving dark blob. It seemed to be feeding on the green fruit of the vine of the wild desert melons, but at this range it was difficult to be certain.

Then abruptly he realized that he had never before encountered baboon this far to the west, and at the same moment he was convinced that there was no troop. It was a solitary animal, unheard of with such a gregarious species, and immediately after that he saw that this animal was too big to be a baboon, and that its movements were uncharacteristic of an ape.

With a singing, soaring joy he launched into a full gallop, and the hooves beat an urgent staccato rhythm on the iron-hard earth, but as he dragged his horse down to a plunging halt and swung down out of the saddle, his joy shrivelled.

She was on her knees, and they were scratched bloody by the stony ground. Her clothing was mostly gone, and her tender flesh was exposed in the rents. The sun had burned her arms and legs into red raw blisters. Her feet were bound up in the remains of her skirt, but blood had soaked through the rags.

Her hair was a dry tangled bush about her head, powdered with dust and with the ends split and bleached. Her lips were black scabs, burned and cracked down into the living meat. Her eyelids were swollen as though stung by bees and she peered up at him like a blind old crone through slits that were caked with dried yellow mucus. The flesh had fallen off her body and her face. Her arms were skeletal and her cheekbones seemed to push through the skin. Her hands were blackened claws – the nails torn down into the quick.

She crouched like an animal over the flat leaves of the vine, and she had broken open one of the wild green melons with her fingers and stuffed pulp into her ruined mouth. The juice ran down her chin, cutting a runnel through the dirt that plastered her skin.

'Louise.' He went down on one knee, facing her. 'Louise –' His voice choked.

She made a little mewling sound in her throat and then touched her hair in a heart-breakingly feminine gesture, trying to smooth the stiff dust-caked tresses.

'Is it?' she croaked, peering at him with bloodshot eyes from slits of sun-swollen red lids. 'It isn't –'

Fumbling, she tried to cover one soft white breast with the rags of her blouse. She started to shake, wildly and uncontrollably, and then she closed her eyes tightly.

He reached out gently and at his touch she collapsed against his chest, still shaking, and he held her. She felt light and frail as a child.

'I knew –' she mumbled. 'It didn't make sense, but I knew somehow that you would come.'

*

'Will you not dowse the lantern, Ralph?' Cathy whispered, and her eyes were huge and dark and piteous as she crept in under the canvas of his wagon.

'Why?' he asked, smiling, propping himself on one elbow on the wagon cot.

'Somebody may come.'

'Your father and mother are still at Lobengula's kraal. There is nobody –'

'My sister – Salina –'

'Salina is long ago asleep, dreaming of brother Jordan, no doubt. We are alone, Cathy, all alone. So why should we put out the lantern?'

'Because I am shy, then,' she said, and blushed a new shade of scarlet. 'All you ever do is tease me. I wish I had never come.'

'Oh Cathy.' His chuckle was fond and indulgent, and he sat up on his cot, and the blanket slid to his waist. Quickly she averted her eyes from his naked chest and muscled upper arms. The skin was so white and marble-smooth in comparison to his brown forearms and face. It set strange unfamiliar emotions loose within her.

'Come!' He caught her wrist and drew her towards the cot, but she hung back until he jerked her forward and, taken off balance, she fell across his legs.

Before she could break free, he had taken a handful of the thick dark hair at the back of her head and turned her pale face up to his mouth. For a while she continued to struggle unconvincingly, and then her whole body softened, like wax in the candle flame, and seemed to melt over him.

'Do you still wish you had not come, Cathy?' he asked, but she could not reply; instead she tightened her arms around his neck convulsively. Once more she searched for his mouth with hers, and made a little moaning sound.

He goaded her with his mouth and tongue, the way Lil had first taught him so long ago, and she was defenceless as a beautiful soft-bodied insect in the spider's gossamer toils. It excited him as none of the practised and calculating women on whom he had spent his gold sovereigns ever had.

His own breathing started to hunt roughly, and his fingers shook at the lacings of her bodice. The skin of her shoulder was without blemish, silky and warm. He touched it with the tip of his tongue, and she shuddered and gasped, but when he pulled down the light cotton, she shrugged her shoulders to let the cloth come free. It caught for a moment and then slid to the level of her lowest rib.

He was unprepared for those tender and terribly vulnerable young breasts, so pale and rosy-tipped and yet at the same time hard and jubilant in their marvellous symmetry.

He stared at her body, and she watched him through half-closed lids, but made no effort to cover herself, though her cheeks were wildly flushed and her lips trembled as she whispered.

'No, Ralph, I don't want to go – not now, or ever.'

'The lantern –' He reached for it, but now she caught his hand.

'No, Ralph, I'm not ashamed of you and me. I don't want darkness, I want to see your dear face.'

She jerked the ribbon loose from her waist and then lifted her dress over her head and let it flutter to the wagon floor. Her limbs were long and coltish, her hips still bony as a boy's, and her belly concave as a greyhound's above the dark triangular bush of her womanhood. Her skin shone in the lanternlight with that peculiar lustre of healthy, vibrant youth. He stared at it for only an instant and then she had lifted the corner of the rough woollen blanket and slid in under it. The long slim arms and legs wrapped around him.

'There is nothing I would not do for you. I would steal and lie and cheat – and even kill for you, my wonderful, beautiful Ralph,' she whispered. 'I'm not sure what a man and woman do, but if you show me I will be the happiest girl on this earth to do it with you.'

'Cathy, I didn't mean this to happen –' He tried with a last sudden lash of his conscience to push her away.

'I did,' she said, clinging stubbornly to him. 'Why else do you think I came here?'

'Cathy –'

'I love you, Ralph, I loved you from the very first moment I ever saw you.'

'I love you, Cathy.' And he was amazed to find that what be said was the truth. 'I really and truly love you,' he said again, and then later, much later: 'I didn't realize how much until now.'

'I didn't know that it would be like this,' she whispered. 'I have thought about it often, every day since you first came to Khami. I even read about it in the Bible – it says that David *knew* her. Do we know each other now, Ralph?'

'I want to know you better – and more often,' he grinned at her, his tousled hair still damp with sweat.

'I felt as though I had fallen through a dark hole in my soul into another beautiful world, and I didn't want to come back again.' Cathy's voice was awed and marvelling, as though she were the first in all the infinite lists of creation to experience it. 'Didn't you feel that, Ralph?'

They held each other close under the blanket, and they talked softly, examining each other's faces in the yellow lantern light, breaking off every few minutes to kiss the other's throat and eyelids and lips.

It was Cathy who pulled away at last. 'I don't want to know the time, but listen to the birds, it will be light too soon.' Then, with a rush of words, 'Oh Ralph, I don't want you to go.'

'It will not be for long, I promise you. Then I will be back.'

'Take me with you.'

'You know I can't.'

'Why not – because it's dangerous, isn't it?'

But he avoided the question by trying to kiss her again. She put her hand over his mouth.

'I'll die a little every moment of the time you are gone, but I'll pray for you. I'll pray that Lobengula's warriors do not find you.'

'Don't worry about me,' he chuckled fondly. 'We'll fall through that dark hole in your soul again soon.'

'Promise,' she whispered, and brushed the damp curls off his forehead with her lips. 'Promise me you will come back, my beautiful, darling Ralph.'

Ralph started his wagon train south again on the road to the Shashi, and for the first morning he rode at the head of the unusually lightly loaded vehicles. At noon he gave the order to outspan. He and Isazi slept away the hot afternoon, while the bullocks and horses grazed and rested.

Then at dusk they cut the five chosen bullocks out of the herd and tied them to the wagon wheels by leather reins around the boss of their horns while they fitted the back packs. Ralph and Isazi had selected these beasts for their strength and willingness, and during the long trek up from Kimberley he had trained them to accept these unusual burdens with resigned docility.

Jordan had provided Ralph with the precise measurements and weight of the bird statue that now graced the entrance to Mr Rhodes' new mansion, Groote Schuur, and Ralph had used these figures to design the back packs and constructed them with his own hands, not trusting anyone else with his secret intentions.

Each pack could carry two statues like the one at Groote Schuur. They would be slung in woven nets of good mania rope on each side of the bullock, and Ralph had worked meticulously to ensure a perfect fit of the saddle to protect the beasts' back from galling, and prevent the load from shifting even over the roughest ground or on the steepest inclines.

Now, when Isazi, the little Zulu driver, led the file of three bullocks quietly out of the camp and disappeared into the darkening forest, they followed meekly. Ralph stayed behind just long enough to repeat his orders to the other drivers.

'You will double-march to the Shashi river. If the border impis question where I am, you will tell them I am hunting to the east with the king's permission, and that you expect me to rejoin the wagons at any time. Do you understand?'

'I understand, Nkosi,' said Umfaan, who, although now promoted from *voorlooper* to driver, still answered to the name of 'Boy'.

'Once you cross the Shashi, you will trek on as far as the Bushman wells, five days' march beyond the frontier. Lobengula's impis will not follow you that far. Wait there until I come, do you understand, Umfaan?'

'I understand, Nkosi.'

'Then repeat it to me.'

Satisfied at last, Ralph stepped up into Tom's stirrup and looked down at them from his back.

'Go swiftly,' he said.

'Go in peace, Nkosi.'

He trotted out of camp, following Isazi's bullock train and dragging behind him a bulky branch of thorn mimosa to sweep their spoor clean. By mid-morning the following day they were well clear of the wagon road and had entered the mystical Matopos Hills. While the oxen grazed and rested, Ralph rode ahead to mark a trail between the soaring granite kopjes, and through the deep and sullen gorges. At dark they resaddled the bullocks with their packs and went on.

The next day Ralph made a noon observation of the sun with the old brass sextant. From experience he made allowance for the cumulative error in his boxed chronometer, and worked out a position which he knew was accurate to within ten miles. Also from experience, he knew that his father's observations, made before he was born, were usually as accurate. Without them he would never have found the caches of ivory which had been the start of his growing fortune.

His calculations compared to his father's showed that he was one hundred and sixty miles west of the ancient ruined city that the Matabele called Zimbabwe, the burial place of the old kings.

Then, while he waited for darkness to resume the march, he took from his saddle-bags the sheaf of notes which Zouga had given him as a parting gift when he first left Kimberley. He read the description of the route to Zimbabwe, and of the city itself, for possibly the hundredth time.

'How much longer must we march through these hills?' Isazi broke his concentration. He was cooking maize cakes on a small smokeless fire of dry wood. 'My beasts suffer on these rocks and steep places,' he grumbled. 'We should have gone farther south and passed below the hills on the open ground.'

'Where Lobengula's bucks wait and pray every day for the chance to stick an assegai through a skinny little Zulu,' Ralph smiled.

'There is the same danger here.'

'No,' Ralph shook his head. 'No Matabele comes into these sacred hills without good reason. We will find no impi here, and once we come out on the far side, we will be beyond the farthest regimental kraals.'

'And this place of stone to which we go? There will be no impi waiting for us there?'

'Lobengula forbids any man even to look into the valley in which the stones stand. It is a death-marked place, cursed by Lobengula and his priests.'

Isazi shifted uncomfortably. 'Who sets store by the curse of a fat Matabele dog?' he demanded, and touched the charm on his belt which warded off devils and hobgoblins and other dark secret things.

Despite his assurances to Isazi, Ralph moved with utmost caution in threading the maze of the Matopos. During daylight he hid the bullocks in some thick patch of bush in a rock gorge, and he went ahead to reconnoitre every yard of the way and to mark it for Isazi to follow with a discreetly blazed tree trunk or a broken twig of green leaves at every turning or difficult place.

These precautions saved him from disaster. On the third day he had tied Tom in good cover and gone forward on foot to the ridge from where he could look into the next valley.

Just below the brow he was alerted by the raucous alarm call of a grey lourie, the 'Go-Away' bird of the African bush. The cry came from just beyond the ridge, and as he froze to listen he heard a gentle susurration like the wind in tall grass; he ducked and jumped off the path, sprawling on his belly with his rifle tucked into the crook of his elbows, and rolled under the spreading branches of a low red berry bush – just as the first rank of Matabele warriors came sweeping over the rise ahead of him, with their cloaks and kilts and headdresses rustling – the sound which had warned him.

From where he lay under the bush beside the path, Ralph could see only as high as their knees as they passed, but their gait was that determined businesslike trot which the Matabele call 'minza hlabathi', to eat the earth greedily.

He counted them. Two hundred warriors in all went past, and the soft rustle of their feet dwindled – but Ralph lay frozen beneath his bush, not daring even to creep deeper into the undergrowth. Minutes later, he heard the soft chant of bearers coming up from the next valley, and then they were trotting past his hiding-place, singing the praise song to the king in their deep melodious voices.

Ralph could tell by the spacing and weight of their gait that they were carrying a heavy litter.

He had guessed that the leading band was merely a vanguard. This was the main party, while the person on the litter was without any doubt Lobengula himself, and following him were his attendants, his high indunas and other important personages. After them again, more bearers carrying sleeping-mats and karosses of fur, beer pots and leather sacks of maize meal and other burdens. They filed past and disappeared, but still Ralph did not rise from hiding.

Another long silence, and then, with only a soft warning rustle, came the rear guard, two hundred more picked warriors trotting past. After five minutes Ralph felt it was safe to crawl out onto the path and dust the damp leaf mould from his knees and elbows.

From the top of the ridge he stared back in the direction which Lobengula's party had taken, puzzled as to where they were all headed and why. He knew from Cathy that Rudd and his party were still at GuBulawayo and that Clinton Codrington and Robyn were with them, negotiating the concession that Mr Rhodes so desperately needed.

Why would Lobengula leave such important guests at his kraal and come up here into these sacred and deserted hills?

There was no answer, and Ralph had to be content with having so narrowly escaped discovery, and to be now alerted to the presence of large parties of warriors in the area.

He moved forward with even more caution than before so that it took three more nights of travel at the pace of the bullocks before they came out of another pass between bald granite cliffs and saw the open forests of tall and lovely trees rolling away below them, silver and charcoal in the moonlight.

In the dawn Ralph climbed the cliff to the peak of the last of the Matopos Hills, and on the eastern horizon – almost exactly where he had hoped to find it – he picked out the far blue silhouette of a solitary kopje standing above the forested plain. It was still thirty miles distant, but the shape of a crouching lion was unmistakable, and it fitted exactly the description in Zouga Ballantyne's notes:

'The hill which I have named "Lion's Head" stands high above the surrounding terrain, and points the traveller unerringly towards great Zimbabwe – '

A man might have walked in the shadow of the massive stone walls and never known they were there, so dense was the growth that covered them. It was a jungle of liana and flowering creepers, while from the very walls themselves grew the twisting serpentine roots of the strangler figs, wedging open the mortarless joints of the stonework and bringing it down in screes of fallen blocks.

Above the level of the high walls soared the heads of other tall trees, grown to giants in the time since the last inhabitant had fled this place or died within its labyrinth of passages and courtyards. When Zouga Ballantyne had discovered this massive keep before Ralph's birth, it had taken him almost two days to find the narrow gateway under this mass of tangled vegetation, but now his directions and descriptions led Ralph immediately to it.

Ralph stood before the ancient portals and looked up at the pattern of chevron stone blocks which decorated the top of the wall thirty feet above his head, and was seized with a primeval superstitious awe.

Though he could see the marks of his father's axe, and the old stumps cut away on each side of the opening, a veil of trailing plants had regrown to screen the gateway – proof that no human being had entered it since Zouga's visit more than twenty-five years before.

The steps that led up to the gateway had been dished by the passage of the feet of the ancient inhabitants over the centuries. Ralph drew a deep breath, and silently reminded himself that he was a civilized Christian; but his superstitious fears lingered as he climbed the stairs, ducked under the trailing creepers and stepped through the gateway.

He found himself in a narrow twisted stone gut between high walls open to the sky. He followed the passage, clambering over fallen stonework blocks and forcing his way through brush and undergrowth that choked it, until abruptly he came out into a wide courtyard, dominated by an immense cylindrical tower of lichen-coated grey granite.

It was exactly as his father had described it, even to the damaged parapet of the tower where Zouga had broken in to discover whether the interior of the towering structure contained a secret treasure chamber. He knew that his father had ransacked the ruins for treasure, he had even torn up and sieved the earth of this temple enclosure for gold. He had retrieved almost a thousand ounces of the yellow metal, small beads and flakes of foil, finely woven gold wire and tiny ingots the size of an infant's finger, and Ralph knew that the only treasure left for him were the idols of green soapstone.

With a stoop of his spirits, Ralph thought for a moment that someone else had forestalled him. According to Zouga, the stone falcons should have been here in this courtyard, and he started forward, his superstitious chills forgotten in the bleaker fear of having been deprived of his booty.

He plunged into the waist-high undergrowth and waded through it towards the tower – and he tripped over the first of the statues, and almost fell. He crouched over it and with his hands tore away the tangle that covered it, and then he looked into the blank cruel eyes above the curved beak that he remembered so well from his childhood. It was the identical twin of the statue that had stood on the verandah of Zouga's cottage at Kimberley, but this falcon had been cast down and lay half buried by roots and brush.

He ran his hands over the satiny green soapstone, then with one finger traced the well-remembered shark's-tooth pattern around the plinth.

'I've come for you at last,' he whispered aloud, and then looked around him quickly. His voice had echoed eerily against the surrounding walls, and he shivered though the sun was still high. Then he stood up and went on searching.

There were six statues, as Zouga had counted them. One was shattered as though by the blows from a sledgehammer, the battered head lay beside it. Three others were damaged to a lesser extent, but the remaining two statues were perfect.

'This is an evil place,' a sepulchral voice intoned unexpectedly, and Ralph started and spun to face it.

Isazi had followed and stood close behind him, preferring the terrors of the narrow passages and ominous walls to the greater terror of remaining alone at the gateway to the city.

'When can we leave here, Nkosi?' Isazi shot restless little glances into the dismal corners of tumbled passageways. 'It is not a place where a man should stay overlong.'

'How soon can we load these onto the oxen?' Ralph squatted and patted one of the fallen images. 'Can we do it before nightfall?'

'*Yebho*, Nkosi.' Isazi promised fervently. 'By nightfall we will be a good march away from here. You have my word upon it.'

The king had once again chosen Bazo for a special task – and Bazo's heart was big with pride as he led the vanguard of his impi along the secret road that took them deeper and deeper into the dreaming Hills of the Matopos.

The road was well beaten, wide enough for two warriors to run abreast with their shields just touching, for it had been used since the time when Mzilikazi, the old king, had first brought the nation up from the south.

Mzilikazi himself had blazed the trail to the secret cavern of the Umlimo. At every crisis in the nation's history, the old king had followed this road – in drought or pestilence or plague, he had come to hear the words of the chosen one. Every season he had come for advice on the herds and the crops, or to help him decide in which direction to send his raiding impis.

Lobengula, himself an initiate of the lesser mysteries, had first entered the cavern of the Umlimo as a youth – led by the crazed old magician who had been his mentor and his tutor. It had been the Umlimo's word which had placed the toy spear of kingship in Lobengula's hand when Mzilikazi had let it fall from his grasp. It was the Umlimo who had chosen Lobengula in preference to Nkulumane or the other older brothers of nobler birth – and it was the Umlimo who had made him the favourite of the ancestral spirits and had sustained him in the darkest hours of his reign.

Thus it was that Lobengula, plagued by the importunate demands of the emissaries of a white man whom he had never seen, confused by scraps of paper whose signs he could not read, troubled by doubts and tormented by fears, badgered and pulled by the conflicting advice of his senior indunas – was at last returning to the secret cavern.

He lay on his litter, on a mattress of the soft yellow and black spotted furs of the leopard, rocked by the motion of the trotting bearers, so that the naked folds and bulges of his gross black body shook and rippled, and he looked ahead with dark and haunted eyes.

Lodzi – that was the name on every white man's lips. Everywhere he turned, Lobengula heard the name Lodzi.

'Is this Lodzi a king, as I am a king?' he had asked the white man with the red face; for Lobengula, as a Matabele, could not pronounce the 'R' of the name.

'Mr Rhodes is not a king, yet he is greater than a king,' Rudd had replied.

'Why does not Lodzi come to me himself?'

'Mr Rhodes has gone across the sea, he sends us lesser men to do this business.'

'If I could look upon the face of Lodzi, then I would know if his heart was great.'

But Rhodes would not come, and day after day Lobengula had listened to the insistence of Lodzi's minions, and in the nights his indunas cautioned and questioned him, and argued amongst themselves.

'If you give the white men a finger, they want the hand,' Gandang told him, 'and having the hand, they desire the arm and then the chest and the heart and the head.'

'Oh King, Lodzi is a man of pride and honour. His word is like Lobengula's own. He is a good man,' said Nomusa, whom he trusted as he trusted few others.

'Give each of the white men a little – and give the same thing to each of them,' counselled Kamuza, one of his youngest but most cunning indunas, a man who had lived with the white men and knew their ways. 'Thus every white man becomes the enemy of the other. Set one dog on the other, lest the pack set upon you.'

'Choose the strongest of the white men and make him our ally,' said Somabula. 'This Lodzi is the herd bull. Choose him.'

And Lobengula had cocked his ear to each of them in turn, and become more desperate and more confused with every conflicting view, until now there was only one path open to him, the path into the Matopos.

Behind his litter came the bearers with the gifts for the oracle, rolls of copper wire, leather bags of coarse salt, pots of trade beads, six great tusks of yellow ivory, bolts of bright cloth, knives made by his master smith with handles of rhinoceros horn, a considerable treasure to pay for the words which he hoped would give him solace.

The path twisted down like a maimed serpent into the gut of the hills, so that the sun was lost and there was only a narrow strip of blue sky showing between the tops of the granite cliffs.

The rank and thorny vegetation crowded the pathway and at last met overhead, forming a dreary tunnel, and the silence was a heavy oppressive presence, for no bird sang and no animal squeaked or scurried in the undergrowth.

But Bazo led on at the same pace, his head swinging from side to side, scanning for danger or menace, and his grip on the shaft of his stabbing spear was firm, his sweat-oiled muscles tense as the springs of a mantrap, ready to hurl his body forward to meet an enemy at any twist in the path.

There was a stream of slow green water and algae-slick boulders across the track, and Bazo leapt it easily with barely a break in his stride; and fifty paces farther on the bush thinned and the cliffs pinched in to form a natural gateway of stone that led into the looming precipice.

Here a determined spearman could hold a thousand and Bazo surveyed it with the swift appraisal of a soldier; and then he raised his gaze to the ledge high above on which was perched a small thatched watch-hut.

Bazo grounded the butt of his long red shield – and called up the cliff. 'I, Bazo, induna of one thousand, demand passage.' His voice boomed and broke into a myriad echoes against the stone walls.

'In whose name do you come to trouble the spirits of the air and earth?' a querulous old man's voice replied, and a sticklike figure, foreshortened by the height of the cliff, appeared upon the lip.

'I come in the king's name, Lobengula the Black Bull of Matabele.' Bazo scorned to wait on permission or favour and, sweeping his shield up onto his shoulder, he sprang forward through the ominous portals.

The passageway beyond was so narrow that his warriors could follow only in single file, and the grey sand that covered the floor sparkled with starry chips of mica and crunched under their bare feet. The passageway curved upon itself and then opened again without warning over a hidden valley.

The valley was completely enclosed by sheer cliffs, and this narrow passage was its only entrance. The bowl of the floor was lush with green grass, and watered by a clear fountain that sprang from the cliff face beside the gateway and meandered down into the valley bottom.

In the centre of the valley, a thousand paces ahead, was a tiny village, twenty or so thatched huts laid out in a neat circle. Bazo led his warriors down and, with a gesture of his assegai, formed them into a double rank on each side of the pathway that led to the huts.

They waited in stillness and silence until the distant chant of the litter-bearers grew louder, and at last the king's party emerged into the hidden valley – and Bazo led his men in a deep chorus of praise and salutation.

The royal party camped two days beside the tiny stream, waiting on the Umlimo's pleasure.

Each day her attendants came to Lobengula to receive gifts and tribute on the oracle's behalf. They were a strange and macabre motley of lesser wizards and witches; some of them, touched by the spirits they served, were crazed and wild-eyed, others were young nubile girls, their bodies painted and their eyes blank and empty like the smokers of the hemp pipe. There were children with wise old eyes who did not laugh or play like other children, and ancients with withered bodies and sly eyes who spoke with the king in low, wheedling tones and took his gifts and promised: 'Perhaps tomorrow; who knows when the power of divination will descend upon the Umlimo.'

Then on the dawn of the third day Lobengula sent for Bazo, and when he came to the king's camp fire, his father Gandang was already with the king, dressed in full regimentals, plume and fur and tassels of valour at elbow and knee, and with him were six of the other senior indunas.

'Bazo, my fine axe with a sharp edge, I have chosen you to stand by my shoulder when I face the Umlimo – to guard my back against treachery,' ordered Lobengula, and Bazo felt his chest swell with pride at such a mark of the king's trust.

A witch led them, prancing and mumbling and mouthing, through the village and up the far side of the valley. Burdened by his great bulk, Lobengula paused often on the climb, his breathing sobbing in his throat, and he rested on Gandang's arm before going on again, until at last they reached the foot of the sheer high cliff. Here there was a cave in the rock. Its entrance was a hundred paces wide, but its roof low enough for a man to reach up and touch. Some time long ago the entrance had been walled up with square blocks of dressed stone, but the wall had tumbled down, leaving dark gaps like the missing teeth in an old man's mouth.

At a nod from his father, Bazo placed the king's carved stool facing the cave and Lobengula lowered his great black haunches upon it gratefully. Bazo stood at the king's back, his assegai gripped underhand, and pointed forward towards the dark entrance in the rock.

Suddenly there came the terrible spitting, tearing snarl of an angry leopard from the cave mouth, so loud and close and real that the band of hardened old warriors started and swayed, and stood their ground only with an obvious effort of will. The old witch giggled and spittle ran down her chin.

The silence fell again, but charged with promise and the threat of an unseen presence watching them from the utter darkness of the cave's recesses.

Then there was a voice, the voice of a child, sweet and piping clear. It issued not from the cave but from the air above the king's head, so that all of them raised their eyes. There was nothing there except the voice.

'The stars will shine upon the hills, and the Black Bull will not quench them.'

The little group of indunas drew closer together as though to take comfort from one another, and the silence fell again. Bazo felt himself shivering, although his sweat tickled like an insect as it ran down between his shoulder blades. Then he jerked his head as another voice spoke. It came from the ground at the king's feet, and it used the liquid purring tones of a beautiful and seductive woman.

'The sun will shine at midnight, and the Great Elephant will not dim it.'

Again that fraught and frightening silence, before something croaked from the cliff high above them, a hoarse inhuman sound, like the croak of a carrion crow.

'Heed the wisdom of the vixen before that of the dogfox, Lobengula, King of – '
The voice broke off abruptly, and there was a scuffling sound deep in the black maw of the cave, and the old crone who had been nodding and grinning at Lobengula's feet scrambled up and shouted an order in an unknown tongue.

Now there was a flash of movement within the cave, and it caused consternation to Lobengula and his indunas, for they had visited the cave a hundred times and more but they had never seen the Umlimo nor had any glimpse of her presence in the depths of the cave.

This was something beyond ritual and custom, and the crone hopped forward, shouting angrily; and now they could make out what was happening in the gloom. It seemed that two of the macabre attendants of the Umlimo were trying to restrain a smaller and more agile figure. They were unsuccessful, for the person threw off their clutching, claw-like hands and ran forward to the threshold of the cave, where the early sunlight revealed the Umlimo at last.

She was so beautiful that all of them, even the king, gasped and stared. Her skin was oiled and polished to the colour of dark amber.

Her limbs were long and supple as a heron's neck, her feet and hands finely shaped. She was in the prime of her womanhood, her body not yet distorted by child-bearing; although her belly was luscious as a ripening fruit her waist was narrow as a lad's. All she wore was a single string of crimson beads about her waist, knotted at the level of the deeply sculptured pit of her navel. Her hips flared with a delicate line, forming a broad basin to contain the spade-shaped wedge of her sex. It nestled there like a dark furry little animal possessed of separate life and existence.

Her head was perfectly balanced on the long stem of her neck; the neat cap of her hair set off the marvellous domed contours of her skull and exposed the small neat shape of her ears. Her features were oriental, the huge eyes slanted, her cheekbones high and her nose delicate and straight – but her mouth was twisted with anguish and her eyes blinded with tears as she stared at the young induna who stood at the king's back.

Slowly she lifted one hand and reached out towards him; the long, delicate palm was pink and soft, the gesture infinitely sad.

'Tanase!' whispered Bazo, staring at her, and his hands shook so that the blade of his assegai clattered against the rim of his shield.

This was the woman he had chosen and who had been so cruelly taken from him. Since her going Bazo had sought no other to wife, though the king had chided him, and others whispered that it was unnatural, yet Bazo had held to the memory of this bright, sweet maid. He wanted to rush to her and seize her, to swing her high upon his shoulder and bear her away, but he stood rooted, her anguish reflected in his own eyes.

For though she stood before him, she was as remote as the full moon. She was a child of the spirits and protected by their horrid servants, far beyond the reach of his loving hands and constant heart.

Her attendants came now from the cave behind her, to scold and whine. Slowly Tanase lowered her arm, though for a moment longer her whole body yearned towards Bazo, and then her lovely head wilted like a flower upon the long, graceful stalk of her neck and she allowed them to take her arms.

'Tanase!' Bazo said her name for the last time, and her shoulders jerked at the sound of his voice.

Then a terrible thing happened. A shuddering convulsion ran up Tanase's back, from the perfect globes of her tight, hard buttocks to the nape of her neck, so that the nerves and muscles twitched and contracted on each side of her spine. Then her spine began to bend backwards like a hunter's bow.

'The spirit is upon her,' shrieked the old witch. 'Let the spirit take her!'

They let her be, drawing back from her wracked body.

Every muscle in her body was under such strain that it stood out in clear and separate definition under her glossy skin – and her spine arched to an impossible angle, the base of her skull almost touching the soft flesh at the back of her knees.

Her face was contorted with the unbearable agony of divination; her eyes rolled back into her head so that only the whites showed. Her lips were drawn back so that the small perfect white teeth were exposed in a frozen rictus and creamy froth bubbled from the corners of her mouth.

Though her lips did not move, a voice boomed from her tortured throat. It was the deep bass of a man, the stentorian voice of a warrior, and it bore no trace of the terrible travail of the young woman from whom it issued.

'The falcons! The white hawk has torn open the nest of stone. The falcons are flying. Save the falcons! The falcons!'

The voice rose abruptly into a wild shriek, and Tanase collapsed and writhed like a squashed insect upon the earth.

'No black man, neither Matabele nor Rozwi nor Karanga, none of them would dare desecrate the nest of the falcons,' said Lobengula, and the circle of indunas nodded. 'Only a white man would have the effrontery to defy the word of the king and chance the wrath of the spirits.'

He paused and took snuff, drawing out the little ritual to put off the moment of decision.

'If I send an impi to Zimbabwe and we take a white man in the red act of plundering the ancient place, dare I send steel through his heart?' Lobengula turned to Somabula, and the old man lifted his grey head and looked sadly at his king.

'Kill one of them, and the others will come swarming like ants,' he said. 'Set not a feast for the birds, when it will bring a pride of lions instead.'

Lobengula sighed and looked to Gandang:

'Speak, my father's son.'

'Oh King, Somabula is wise and his words have the same weight as boulders of black ironstone. Yet the king's words are heavier still, and the king's words have been given – *the despoilers of the ancient places must die*. Those are the words of Lobengula.'

The king nodded slowly.

'Bazo!' he said softly, and the young induna dropped on one knee before the king's stool.

'Take one of the wizards to guide your impi to the nest of the falcons. If the stone birds are gone, follow them. Find the despoiler. If it is a white man, take him where no other eyes can see you, not even those of your most trusted warriors. Kill the man and bury him in a secret place, and speak of it to no man but your king. Do you hear the words of Lobengula?'

'I hear, oh Great King, and to hear is to obey.'

Dutchman, the bullock with the narrowest spread of horns, was the only one which Isazi could coax down the narrow passageways and over the tumbled stonework into the temple enclosure of the ruins. In the baskets on his sturdy, dappled back, they ferried out the bird images, even the damaged ones, and repacked them onto the backs of the other oxen which waited outside the massive walls.

With Isazi's skilful handling of the bullocks and their burdens, the work was finished by mid-afternoon, and they roped the oxen in single file. With patent relief, Isazi led them away through the forest towards the south.

Ralph's relief was every bit as intense. He had been uneasy ever since that chance encounter with the Matabele impi in the hills. Now he let Isazi go on with the oxen, while he circled back across their incoming tracks to the north-west of the ruined city, examining the ground with the hunter's eye for any sign that they had been followed, or that there were any other human beings in the area. It need not be a war party – even a band of honey-gatherers or a hunter could carry word back to Lobengula's kraal or alert the border impis.

He knew what he would have to do if he found a wanderer or solitary hunter, and he eased the rifle in the leather boot at his knee. These forests were populous. He saw troops of big-eared striped kudu, sable antelope with snowy bellies and sweeping scimitar horns, big black bovine buffalo and spreading herds of plump zebra with alert pricked ears and stiff, black manes, but there was no sign of human presence.

He was only slightly mollified when he turned back and picked up the spoor of the bullock file five miles on the other side of the ruins. He trotted along the widely beaten sign, and his misgivings returned at full strength. This was too easy to follow.

He caught up with Isazi and his bullock train as the dusk was falling, and he helped him lift the heavy packs down from the backs of the oxen and examine them for galling or saddle sores, before hobbling them and letting them graze. More than once during the night he started awake, and listened for the sound of men's voices – but heard only the yipping of jackal.

In the early light they entered a wide grassy plain; the trees on the far side were a dark line on the horizon, and there were huge troops of zebra grazing out in the open. They lifted their heads to watch the strange little caravan go past, and sounded their curiosity and concern with their sharp, almost dog-like, barks.

Halfway across the plain Ralph turned the bullock train at a right angle to their track, and they marched due east until noon, when they re-entered the forest. Still Ralph headed on east until darkness fell and they camped.

Isazi muttered and complained about the wasted day, and the detour of so many miles out of their direct route towards the Limpopo river and the Bushman wells beyond, where Umfaan waited for them with the wagons.

'Why do we do this?'

'For the benefit of anyone who follows us.'

'They will still be able to follow the spoor we have laid,' Isazi protested.

'I will change that, in the morning,' Ralph assured him, and in the dawn he allowed Isazi to resume the southerly direction again.

'If I do not rejoin you, do not wait for me. Keep on until you reach the wagons, well beyond the frontier of the Matabele. Wait for me there,' he ordered, and he left Isazi and rode back on their spoor of the previous day.

He reached the open grassland where they had made such a dramatic change of direction the preceding morning, and the zebra barked at him. Their stripes were indistinguishable at this distance, and the herds were moving silver-grey masses on the yellow grassland.

'You are going to enjoy this, old Tom.' Ralph patted the horse's neck and then trotted out onto the plain towards the nearest herd of zebra. There were more than a hundred animals in the group, and they let horse and rider approach to within a few hundred paces before bunching up and galloping away.

'After them, Tom!' Ralph whooped, and they tore into the bellowing dust cloud, gaining swiftly on the chubby, striped ranks of bobbing hindquarters. Ralph quartered and turned them, and they gathered up another herd, and then another, until there were two or three thousand zebra in stampede ahead of them.

He rode out onto one flank and pushed the herd over the ground which his bullock train had crossed the previous day. Thousands of broad hooves churned the earth into soft explosions of dust. When they reached the far side of the plain, Ralph forced Tom ahead of the leading zebras and rode across their front, yelling and waving his hat about his head. The dense mass of animals turned like a living whirlpool, and the dust boiled up into the sky.

Back they went across the open ground with Tom delighting in the chase, and Ralph worked them northward until the zebra herds reached the forest line and swung parallel with the trees, and they scoured the earth with driving hooves in a swathe five hundred yards wide.

Back and forth again Ralph drove them, sheep-dogging them deliberately over the bullock tracks on each pass, until at last even Tom's pace was short and knocked up, and he was sweating in black streaks down his shoulders and flanks and blowing like a south-easterly gale over False Bay.

Ralph off-saddled in the shade of the treeline, while out on the plain the zebra herds, skittish and nervous at the harassment – still galloped in aimless circles, or snorted and pawed the torn earth.

'Nobody, not even a Bushman, will be able to pick the spoor through that,' Ralph told Tom, and stooped to lift each of his hooves in turn.

With his clasp knife Ralph prised off Tom's iron horseshoes and bundled them into the saddle-bag.

Without shoes, Tom's tracks were almost identical to those of a zebra stallion. He might go lame before they reached the wagons at Bushman wells, but they could limp in at their own speed, sure at last that there would be no pursuit. Once they reached the wagon, there was forge and anvil to re-shoe him, and Tom would suffer no lasting injury.

Ralph wiped Tom down with the saddle blanket and let him rest for another hour before re-saddling. Then he rode back amongst the scattered zebra herds to mingle and lose Tom's hoof prints amongst theirs before deliberately turning westwards, the opposite direction to Isazi's bullocks. He settled down in the saddle to lay a false trail into the forest before circling back southwards to find Isazi.

Ralph slept until sunrise the following morning, secure at last, and the temptation to drink coffee was too much for him. He chanced a small fire and delighted in the strong hot brew.

When they rode on, the sun was well up, and clear of the forest tops. Ralph let old Tom amble along at his own pace to save his unshod hooves, and he pushed his hat onto the back of his head and repeated the opening bars of Yankee Doodle over and over in a flat tuneless whistle.

The morning was cool and fresh. He felt elated at the success of his coup; already he was planning the sale of the statues. He would send letters to the British Museum and the Smithsonian Institution in Washington, D.C.

Out on his right a red-breasted cuckoo uttered its staccato call that sounded like a greeting 'Pete-my-friend!'.

Tom flicked his ears but Ralph went on whistling happily, slouched down in the saddle.

Old J. B. Robinson, one of the Kimberley millionaires who had made millions more on the new Witwatersrand goldfield, would buy at least one of the birds simply because Rhodes had one. He could not bear –

In the grassy glade ahead of Ralph a francolin called harshly, 'Kwali! Kwali!' only twice, and it rang falsely to Ralph's ear. These brown partridges usually called five or six times, not twice.

Ralph checked Tom and stood up in the stirrups. Carefully he surveyed the narrow open strip of head-high elephant grass. Suddenly a covey of brown partridge burst out of the grass and whirled away on noisy wings.

Ralph grinned and slouched down again in the saddle, and Tom trotted into the waving stand of coarse grass – and instantly it was full of dark figures of dancing plumes and red shields. They swarmed around Tom and the sunlight sparkled on the long silver blades.

'Go, Tom!' Ralph urged, and kicked his heels into his flank, while he jerked the rifle from its bucket and held it against his hip.

As Tom lunged forward, one of the plumed warriors leapt to catch his bridle, and Ralph fired. The heavy lead bullet hit the Matabele in the jaw and blew half of it away; for a moment teeth and white bone flashed in the shattered face, and then were smothered in an eruption of bright blood.

Tom bounded into the gap in their line that the man had left, but as he went through, one of them darted in from the side and grunted with the strength of his stroke.

With a thrill of horror Ralph saw the long steel blade go into Tom's ribs, an inch in front of his toe cap. He swung the empty rifle at the warrior's head, but the man ducked under it, and while Ralph twisted in the saddle, a second Matabele darted in, and Tom's whole body shuddered and convulsed between Ralph's knees as the man stabbed deep and hard into Tom's neck, an inch in front of his plunging shoulder.

Then they were through the line of Matabele, but the assegai had been plucked from the warrior's hand and the shaft stuck out of Tom's neck at a brutal angle that showed the point must be buried in his lungs. Still the gallant old pony carried his master on across the glade and into the first trees of the forest.

Then abruptly a double stream of frothy bright lung-blood burst from Tom's nostrils, and splattered back against Ralph's boots. Tom died in full run. His nose dropped to the earth and he went over in a somersault that pitched Ralph high over his head.

Ralph smashed into the earth, and he felt as though his ribs were stoved in and his teeth cracked from his jaws, but he crawled desperately to his fallen rifle and jammed a fresh cartridge into the breech.

When he looked up, they were almost upon him, a line of racing red shields and pounding bare feet below; the war rattles on their ankles clashed and the hunting chorus was like the deep baying of hounds.

One tall *indoda* lifted his shield high to clear his spear arm for the killing stroke, and the blade flashed as it started down, and then the movement froze.

'Henshaw!' The name exploded out of the warrior's straining throat, and then Bazo continued the stroke, but at the last instant rolled his wrist and the flat of the heavy blade smashed against Ralph's skull above his temple; and he pitched forwards, face down against the sandy earth, and lay still as death.

'You took the irons from the horse's hooves.' Bazo nodded approval. 'That was a good trick. If you had not slept so long this morning, we might never have caught up with you.'

'Tom is dead now,' replied Ralph.

He was propped against the trunk of a mopani tree. There was a bright scarlet smear of gravel rash on one cheek where he had hit the ground when he was thrown from the saddle. The hair above his temple was caked with black dried blood where the flat of Bazo's blade had knocked him senseless, and he was bound at ankles and wrists with thongs of rawhide. Already his hands were puffy and blue from the constriction of his bonds.

'Yes!' Bazo nodded again gravely, and looked at the carcass of the horse where it lay fifty paces away. 'He was a good horse, and now he is dead.' He looked back at Ralph. 'The *indoda* whom we will bury today was a good man – and now he is dead also.'

All about them squatted ranks of Matabele warriors, all Bazo's men drawn up in a dense black circle, sitting on their shields and listening intently to every word spoken.

'Your men fell upon me without warning, as though I were a thief or a murderer. I defended myself as any man would do.'

'And are you not a thief then, Henshaw?' Bazo interrupted.

'What question is that?' Ralph demanded.

'The birds, Henshaw. The stone birds.'

'I do not know what you speak of,' Ralph challenged angrily, pushing himself away from the tree trunk and staring arrogantly at Bazo.

'You know, Henshaw. You know about the birds, for we have spoken about them many times. You know also the king's warning that to despoil the ancient places is death to any man, for I myself have told you of it.'

Still Ralph glared his defiance.

'Your spoor led straight to the burial place of the kings and straight away from it – and the birds are gone. Where are they, Henshaw?'

A moment longer Ralph continued his show, and then he shrugged and smiled and sank back against the tree.

'They are gone, Bazo, flown afar where you cannot follow them. It was the prophecy of the Umlimo, beyond the powers of mortal men to prevent.'

At the mention of the prophetess, a shadow of sorrow passed over Bazo's face.

'Yes, it was part of the prophecy,' he agreed. 'And now it is time to carry out the orders of the king.' He stood up and addressed the squatting ranks of Matabele.

'All of you heard the king's word,' he said. 'What must be done, must be done in secret; it must be done by me alone, and no other may witness it, nor speak of it after, even in a whisper, on pain of slow and lingering death. You have heard the king's word.'

'We have heard the king's word,' they agreed in deep sonorous chorus.

'Go!' Bazo commanded. 'Wait for me at great Zimbabwe, and wipe from your eyes the things you have seen this day.'

His warriors sprang up and saluted him. They shouldered the body of the man that Ralph had slain, using their shields as a litter, and they bore him away. The double column of running warriors snaked away across the glade and into the forest.

Bazo watched them go, leaning on his own shield, and then he turned back to Ralph, heavily and unwillingly.

'I am the king's man,' he said softly. 'Strictly charged with your death. What I have to do today will leave a deep scar in my heart for all my life, though I live to be an old greyhead. The memory of this thing will keep me from sleep, and turn the food sour and heavy in my belly.' Slowly he paced to where Ralph lay and stood over him. 'I will never forget this deed, Henshaw, though I will never be able to speak of it, not to my father or my favourite wife. I must lock it in the darkness of my soul.'

'If you must do it, then do it swiftly,' Ralph challenged him, trying to show no fear, trying to keep his gaze steady.

'Yes,' Bazo nodded, and shifted his grip on the haft of the spear. 'Intercede for me with your God, Henshaw,' he said, and struck.

Ralph cried out at the stinging burn of razor steel, and his blood burst from the wound and spilled into the dry earth.

Bazo dropped to his knee beside him and scooped up the blood in his cupped hands. He splashed it on his arms and chest. He smeared it on the haft and blade of his spear, until the bright steel was dulled.

Then Bazo leapt up and ripped a strip of bark from the mopani tree. He plucked a bunch of green leaves and came back to Ralph's side. He held together the lips of the deep wound in Ralph's forearm, then he placed the bunch of leaves over it and bound it up with the strip of bark.

The bleeding slowed and stopped, and Bazo hacked the rawhide bonds from Ralph's ankles and wrists and stood back.

He gestured at his own blood-sullied arms and weapon.

'Who, seeing me thus, would believe that I am a traitor to my king?' he asked softly. 'Yet the love of a brother is stronger than the duty to a king.'

Ralph dragged himself upright against the mopani trunk, holding his wounded arm against his chest and staring at the young induna.

'Go in peace, Henshaw,' whispered Bazo. 'But pray to your God for me, for I have betrayed my king and forfeited my honour.'

Then Bazo whirled and ran back across the glade of yellow grass. When he reached the trees on the far side he neither paused nor looked back, but plunged into them with a kind of reckless despair.

Ten days later, with his boots scuffed through the uppers and the legs of his breeches ripped to tatters by arrow grass and thorn, with his inflamed and infected left arm strapped to his chest by a sling of bark, his face gaunt with starvation and his body bony and wasted, Ralph staggered into the circle of wagons that were outspanned beside the Bushman wells – and Isazi shouted for Umfaan and ran to catch Ralph before he fell.

'Isazi,' Ralph croaked, 'the birds, the stone birds?'

'I have them safe, Nkosi.'

Ralph grinned wickedly, so that his dried lips cracked and his bloodshot eyes slitted.

'By your own boast, Isazi, you are a wise man. Now I tell you also, that you are beautiful to behold, as beautiful as a falcon in flight,' Ralph told him, and then reeled so that he had to catch his balance with an arm around the little Zulu's shoulders.

Lobengula sat cross-legged on his sleeping-mat, alone in his great hut. Before him was a gourd of clear spring water. He stared into it fixedly.

Long ago, when he had lived in the cave of the Matopos with Saala, the white girl, the mad old witchdoctor had instructed him in the art of the gourd. Very occasionally, after many hours' staring into the limpid water, and after the utmost exercise of his concentration and will, he had been able to see snatches of the future, faces and events, but even then they had been murky and unclear, and soon after he left the Matopos this small gift had gone from him. Sometimes still, in desperation, he resorted to the gourd – although, as it was this night, nothing moved or roiled darkly beneath the still surface of the spring water, and his concentration kept slipping away. Tonight he kept toying with the words of the Umlimo.

Always the oracle spoke obliquely, always her counsel was shrouded in imagery and riddles. Often it was repetitive, on at least five previous visits to the cavern the witch had spoken of 'the stars shining on the hills' and 'the sun that burns at midnight'. No matter how doggedly Lobengula and his senior indunas had picked at the words, and tried to unravel the meaning that was tied up in them, they had found no answer.

Now Lobengula set aside the fruitless gourd, and lay back upon his kaross to consider the third prophecy, made in the croaking raven's voice from the cliff above the cavern.

'Heed the wisdom of the vixen before that of the dogfox.'

He took each word and weighed it separately, then he considered the whole, and twisted it and studied it from every angle.

In the dawn there remained only one possible solution that had survived the night. For once the oracle seemed to have given advice that was unequivocal. It was only for him to decide which female was the 'vixen' of the oracle.

He considered each of his senior wives – and there was not one of them that had any interest in anything beyond the begetting and suckling of infants, or the baubles and ribbons that the traders brought to GuBulawayo.

Ningi, his full-blooded sister, he loved still as his one link with the mother he barely remembered. Yet now when Ningi was sober she was elephantine and slow-witted, bad-tempered and cruel. When she was filled with the traders' champagne and cognac, she was giggling and silly to begin with, and then incontinent and comatose at the end. He had spoken with her for an hour and more the previous day. Little that she had said was sensible, and nothing she had said could possibly bear on the terrible pressures of Lodzi and his emissaries.

So at last Lobengula returned to what he had known all along must be the key to the riddle of the Umlimo.

'Guards!' he shouted suddenly, and there were quick and urgent footfalls, and one of his cloaked executioners stooped through the doorway and prostrated himself on the threshold.

'Go to Nomusa, the Girlchild of Mercy, bid her come to me with all speed,' said Lobengula.

Whereas I have been much molested of late by divers persons seeking and desiring to obtain grants and concessions of land and mining rights in my territories –

Now, therefore, for the following considerations:

Item One, payment by the grantee to the grantor of £100 per month in perpetuity.

Item Two, the provision by the grantee to the grantor of One Thousand Martini-

Henry rifles, together with One Hundred Thousand rounds of ammunition for the same.

Item Three, the provision by the grantee to the grantor of an armed steamboat to patrol the navigable reaches of the Zambezi river.

Now, therefore, I, Lobengula – King of the Matabele people, and Paramount Chief of Mashonaland, Monarch of all territories South of the Zambezi River and Northwards of the Shashi and Limpopo Rivers, do hereby grant –

Complete and exclusive charge over all metals and minerals in my Kingdom, Principalities and Dominions, together with full power to do all things that they may deem necessary to win and procure the same and to enjoy the profits and revenues, if any, derivable from the said metals and minerals.

In his fair hand, Jordan Ballantyne wrote out the document from Mr Rudd's dictation.

Robyn Codrington read the text to Lobengula, and explained it to him, then she helped him attach the Great Elephant seal. Finally, she witnessed the mark that Lobengula made beside it.

'Damn me, Jordan, there's none of us here that can ride the way you can.' Rudd made no effort to conceal his jubilation when they were alone. 'It's speed now that counts. If you leave immediately, you can reach Khami Mission by nightfall. Pick the three best horses from those that we left there, and go like the wind, my boy. Take the concession to Mr Rhodes – and tell him I will follow directly.'

The twins ran down the front steps of Khami Mission and surrounded Jordan as he stepped down from the stirrup.

At the head of the steps, Cathy held a lantern high, and Salina stood beside her with her hands clasped demurely in front of her, and her eyes shining with joy in the lantern light.

'Welcome, Jordan,' she called. 'We have all missed you so.'

Jordan came up the steps. 'I can rest one night only,' he told her, and a little of her delight died and her smile with it. 'I ride south tomorrow at first light.'

He was so beautiful, tall and straight, and fair, and though his shoulders were wide and his limbs finely muscled, yet he was lithe and light as a dancer and his expression gentle as a poet's as he looked down into Salina's face.

'Only one night,' she murmured. 'Then we must make the most of it.'

They ate a dinner of smoked ham and roasted sweet yams, and afterwards they sat on the verandah and Salina sang for them while Jordan smoked a cigar and listened with obvious pleasure, tapping the time on his knee and joining with the others in the chorus.

The moment Salina had finished, Vicky leapt to her feet.

'My turn,' she announced. 'Lizzie and I have written a poem.'

'Not tonight,' said Cathy.

'Why?' demanded Vicky.

'Cathy,' wailed the twins in unison. 'It's Jordan's last night.'

'That is precisely why.' Cathy stood up. 'Come on, both of you.'

Still they cajoled and procrastinated, until suddenly Cathy's eyes slitted viciously, and she hissed at them with a vehemence that startled them to their feet, to bestow hasty pecks on Jordan's face and then hurry off down the verandah, with Cathy close behind.

Jordan chuckled fondly and flicked the cigar over the verandah rail. 'Cathy is right, of course,' he said. 'I'll be in the saddle for twelve hours tomorrow – it's time we were all abed.'

Salina did not reply but moved to the end of the verandah farthest from the bedrooms and leaned on the rail, staring down across the starlit valley.

After a moment, Jordan followed her, and asked softly:

'Have I offended you?'

'No,' she answered quickly. 'It's just that I am a little sad. We all have such fun when you are here.'

Jordan did not reply, and after a minute she asked:

'What will you do now, Jordan?'

'I shall not know until I reach Kimberley. If Mr Rhodes is at Groote Schuur already, then I shall go there – but if he is still in London, then he will want me to join him.'

'How long will it take?'

'From Kimberley to London and back? Four months, if the sailings coincide.'

'Tell me about London, Jordan. I have read about it and dreamed about it.'

He talked quietly, but lucidly and fluently, so that she laughed and exclaimed at his descriptions and anecdotes, and the minutes turned to hours, until suddenly Jordan interrupted himself.

'What am I thinking of; it's almost midnight.'

She grasped at anything to keep him from going.

'You promised to tell me about Mr Rhodes' house at Groote Schuur.'

'It will have to wait for another time, Salina.'

'Will there be another time?' she asked.

'Oh, I am sure there will,' he answered lightly.

'You will go to England, and Cape Town, it could be years before you come back to Khami.'

'Even years will not dim our friendship, Salina.' And she stared at him as though he had struck her.

'Is that it – Jordan – are we friends, just friends?'

He took both her hands in his. 'The dearest, most precious friends,' he confirmed.

She was pale as ivory in the dim light, and her grip on his hands was like that of a drowning woman as she steeled herself to speak – but her voice, when at last she summoned it, was so strained that she was not sure he had understood her.

'Take me with you, Jordan.'

'Salina, I don't know what you mean.'

'I cannot bear to lose you – take me. Please take me.'

'But –' he was confused and shaken, 'but what would you do?'

'Whatever you tell me. I should be your slave, your loving slave, Jordan – for ever.'

He tried to free his hands from hers, but he did it gently.

'You cannot just go away and leave me, Jordan. When you came to Khami, it was like the sun rising into my life; and if you go you will take the light with you. I love you, Jordan, oh sweet Jesus, forgive me, but I love you more than life itself.'

'Salina, stop! Please stop now.' He pleaded with her, but she clung to his hands.

'I cannot let you go without telling you – I love you, Jordan, I shall always love you.'

'Salina.' His voice was stricken. 'Oh Salina, I love somebody else,' he said.

'It's not true,' she whispered. 'Oh, please say it's not true.'

'I am sorry, Salina. Terribly sorry.'

'Nobody else can love you as much as I do, nobody would sacrifice what I would.'

'Please stop, Salina. I don't want you to humiliate yourself.'

'Humiliate myself?' she asked. 'Oh, Jordan, that would be so small a price – you don't understand.'

'Salina, please.'

'Let me prove to you, Jordan, let me prove how joyfully I will make any sacrifice.' And when he tried to speak, she put her hand lightly over his mouth. 'We need not even have to wait for marriage. I will give myself to you this very night.'

When he shook his head, she tightened her grip to gag his words of denial.

> 'So fret not, like an idle girl,
> That life is dash'd with flecks of sin.'

She whispered the quotation, with quivering voice. 'Give me the chance, dear Jordan, please give me the chance to prove that I can love and cherish you more than any other woman in all the world. You will see how this other woman's love pales to nothing beside the flame of mine.'

He took her wrist and lifted her hand from his mouth, and his head bowed over hers with a terrible regret.

'Salina,' he said, 'it is not another woman.'

She stared up at him, both of them rooted and stricken, while the enormity of his words slowly spread across her soul like hoar frost.

'Not another woman?' she asked at last, and when he shook his head, 'Then I can never even hope – never?'

He did not reply, and at last she shook herself like a sleeper wakening from a dream to deathly reality.

'Will you kiss me goodbye, Jordan, just one last time?'

'It need not be the last –' But she reached up and crushed the words on his lips so fiercely that her teeth left a taste of blood on his tongue.

'Goodbye, Jordan,' she said, and turning from him she walked down the length of the verandah as infirmly as an invalid arising from a long sick-bed. At the door of her bedroom, she staggered and put out a hand to save herself, and then looked back at him.

Her lips moved, but no sound came from them. 'Goodbye, Jordan. Goodbye, my love.'

Ralph Ballantyne carried up the rifles, one thousand of them, brand new and still in their yellow grease, five in a wooden case, and twenty cases to a wagonload. There were another ten wagonloads of ammunition – all for the account of De Beers diamond mines – another three wagonloads of liquor for his own account, and a single wagon of furniture and household effects for the bungalow that Zouga was building for himself at GuBulawayo.

Ralph crossed the Shashi river with a certain thousand-pound profit from the convoy already safely deposited in the Standard Bank at Kimberley, but with a nagging hollow feeling in the pit of his stomach.

He had no way of knowing whether Bazo had reported him to Lobengula as the abductor of the stone falcons, or whether one of Bazo's warriors had recognized him and, despite the king's warning, had told a wife, who had told her mother, who had told her husband. 'Nothing moves in Matabeleland but the whole nation knows of it,' Clinton Codrington had warned him once. However, the profits on this run, and the prospect of visiting Khami Mission again, were worth the risk.

On the first day's march beyond the Shashi, that risk was vindicated, for it was Bazo himself at the head of his red shields who intercepted the convoy, and greeted Ralph inscrutably.

'Who dares the road? Who risks the wrath of Lobengula?' And after he had inspected the loaded wagons, as he and Ralph sat alone by the camp fire, Ralph asked him quietly:

'I heard that a white man died in the bush between great Zimbabwe and the Limpopo. What was that man's name?'

'Nobody knows of this matter, except Lobengula and one of his indunas,' Bazo replied, without lifting his gaze from the flames. 'And even the king does not know who the stranger was or where he came from, nor does he know the site of the grave of the nameless stranger.' Bazo took a little snuff and went on. 'Nor will we ever speak of this matter again, you and me.'

And now he lifted his eyes at last, and there was something in their dark depths that had never been there before, and Ralph thought that it was the look of a man destroyed, a man who would never trust a brother again.

In the morning, Bazo was gone, and Ralph faced northwards, with the doubts dispelled and his spirits soaring like the silver and mauve thunderheads that piled the horizon ahead of him. Zouga was waiting for him at the drift of the Khami river.

'You've made good time, my boy.'

'Nobody ever made better,' Ralph agreed, and twirled his thick dark moustache, 'and nobody is likely to, not until Mr Rhodes builds his railroad.'

'Did Mr Rhodes send the money?'

'In good gold sovereigns,' Ralph told him. 'I have carried them in my own saddle-bags.'

'All we have to do is get Lobengula to accept them.'

'That, Papa, is your job. You are Mr Rhodes' agent.'

Yet three weeks later the wagons still stood outside Lobengula's kraal, their loads roped down under the tarpaulins while Zouga waited each day from early morning until dusk in front of the king's great hut.

'The king is sick,' they said.

'The king is with his wives.'

'Perhaps the king will come tomorrow.'

'Who knows when the king will tire of his wives,' they said, and at last even Zouga, who knew and understood the ways of Africa, became angry.

'Tell the king that Bakela, the Fist, rides now to Lodzi to tell him that the king spurns his gifts,' he ordered Gandang, who had come to make the day's excuses, and Zouga called to Jan Cheroot to saddle the horses.

'The king has not given you the road.' Gandang was shocked and perturbed.

'Then tell Lobengula that his impis can kill the emissary of Lodzi on the road, but it will not take long for the word to be carried to Lodzi. Lodzi sits even now at the great kraal of the queen across the water, basking in her favour.'

The king's messengers caught up with Zouga before he reached Khami Mission, for his pace was deliberately leisurely.

'The king bids Bakela return at once, he will speak with him at the moment of his return.'

'Tell Lobengula that Bakela sleeps tonight at Khami Mission and perhaps the night after – for who knows when he will see fit to talk with the king again.'

Somebody at Khami must have put a spy-glass on the dust raised by Zouga's horses, for when they were still a mile from the hills, a rider came out to meet them at full gallop, a slim figure with long dark plaits streaming behind her lovely head.

When they met, Zouga jumped down from his saddle and lifted her from hers.

'Louise,' he whispered into her smiling mouth. 'You will never know how slowly the days pass when I am away from you.'

'It's a cross you make us both carry,' she told him. 'I am fully recovered now – thanks to Robyn – and still you make me loiter and pine at Khami. Oh, Zouga, will you not let me join you at GuBulawayo?'

'That I will, my dear, just as soon as we have a roof on the cottage, and a ring on your finger.'

'You are always so proper.' She pulled a face at him. 'Who would ever know?'

'I would,' he said, and kissed her again, before he lifted her back into the saddle of the bay Arab mare which had been his betrothal gift to her.

They rode with their knees touching and their fingers linked, while Jan Cheroot trailed them discreetly out of earshot.

'We shall have only days longer to wait,' Zouga assured her. 'I have forced Lobengula's hand. This matter of the rifles will be settled soon and then you can choose where you will make me the happiest man on earth, the cathedral at Cape Town perhaps?'

'Darling Zouga, your family at Khami has been so kind to me. The girls have become like my own sisters, and Robyn lavished care upon me when I was so ill, so burned and desiccated by the sun.'

'Why not?' Zouga agreed. 'I'm sure that Clinton will agree to say the words.'

'He has already, but there is more to it. The wedding is all planned, and it is to be a double wedding.'

'A double wedding – who are the others?'

'You would never guess, not in a thousand years.'

They looked more like brothers than father and son, as they stood before the carved altar in the little whitewashed church at Khami.

Zouga wore his full dress uniform, and the scarlet jacket, tailored twenty years before, still fitted him to perfection. The gold lace had been renewed to impress

Lobengula and his indunas, and now it sparkled bright and untarnished, even in the cool gloom of the church.

Ralph was dressed in expensive broadcloth with a high stock and cravat of watered grey silk that on this hot June day brought beads of sweat to his forehead. His thick dark hair was dressed with pomade to a glossy shine, and his magnificent moustache, twirled with beeswax, pricked out in two stiff points.

Both of them were rigid with expectation, staring fixedly at the altar candles which Clinton had hoarded for such an occasion, and lit only minutes before.

Behind them one of the twins fidgeted with excited anticipation, and Salina pumped up the little organ and launched into 'Here comes the Bride', while Ralph grinned with bravado and, out of the side of his mouth, muttered to his father, 'Well, here we go then, Papa. Fix bayonets and prepare to receive cavalry!'

They turned with parade ground precision to face the church door, just as the brides stepped through it.

Cathy wore the mail-order dress which Ralph had brought up from Kimberley, while Robyn had lifted her own wedding dress from its resting place in the leather-bound trunk and they had taken in the waist and let down the hem to fit Louise. The delicate lace had turned to the colour of old ivory, and she carried a bouquet of Clinton's yellow roses.

Afterwards they all straggled across the yard. The brides tottered on their high heels and tripped on their trains, clinging to the arms of their new husbands; and the twins pelted them with handfuls of rice, before running ahead to the verandah where the wedding board was piled with mountains of food and lined with regiments of bottles, the finest champagne from Ralph's wagons.

At one end of the table Ralph loosened his stock and held Cathy in the circle of his arm and a glass in his other hand as he made his speech:

'My wife –' he referred to her, and the company hooted with laughter and clapped with delight, while Cathy clung to him and looked up at his face in transparent adoration.

Then when the speeches were ended, Clinton looked across the table at his eldest daughter. His bald head shone with the heat and excitement and the good champagne.

'Will you not sing to us, my darling Salina?' he asked. 'Something happy and joyous?'

Salina nodded and smiled, and lifted her chin to sing in her gentle voice:

> 'However far you go, my love,
> I will follow too.
> The highest mountain top, my love,
> Across deepest ocean blue.'

Louise turned her face towards Zouga, and when she smiled the corners of her dark blue eyes slanted upwards and her lips parted and glistened. Below the tabletop Clinton reached for Robyn's hand, but his gaze stayed upon his daughter's face.

Even Ralph sobered, and sat attentively while Cathy laid her cheek upon his shoulder.

> 'No arctic night too cold, my love,
> No tropic noon too fierce.

> For I will cleave to you, my love,
> 'Til death my heart do pierce.'

Salina sat very straight on the wooden bench with her hands in her lap. She was smiling as she sang, a sweet serene smile, but a single tear broke from her lower lid and descended, with tortuous slowness, the velvet curve of her cheek, until it reached the corner of her mouth.

The song ended, and they were silent for a long moment, and then Ralph pounded on the table with the flat of his hand.

'Oh bravo, Salina, that was superb.'

Then they were all applauding, and Salina smiled at them and the single tear broke and fell to her breast, to leave a dark star upon the satin of her bodice.

'Excuse me,' she said. 'Please excuse me.'

And she stood up and, still smiling, glided down the verandah. Cathy sprang to her feet, her face twisted with concern, but Robyn caught her wrist before she could follow.

'Leave her be,' she whispered. 'The child needs to be alone a while. You will only upset her further.' And Cathy sank back beside Ralph.

'Shame on you, Louise,' with forced jocularity, Clinton called down the table. 'Your husband's glass is empty, are you neglecting him so soon?'

An hour later Salina had not returned, and Ralph's voice had become louder and even more assertive. 'Now that Mr Rhodes has got his charter, we can begin to assemble the column. Cathy and I will start back tomorrow with the empty wagons. Heaven knows we will need every pair of wheels, and I thought old King Ben would never take those rifles off my hands.'

But Cathy was for once not drinking in every one of his words; she kept looking down the verandah, and again she whispered to Robyn, who frowned and shook her head.

'You talk as though the whole affair was arranged for your personal profit, Ralph.' Robyn turned from Cathy to challenge her new son-in-law.

'Perish the thought, Aunty.' Ralph laughed, and winked at his father down the length of the table. 'It's all for the good of Empire and the glory of God.'

Cathy waited until they were once more embroiled in amiable argument, and then she slipped away so quietly that Robyn did not notice until Cathy reached the end of the verandah. For a moment she looked set to call her back, but instead she made a move of annoyance and addressed herself to Zouga.

'How long will you and Louise remain at GuBulawayo?'

'Until the column reaches Mount Hampden. Mr Rhodes doesn't want any misunderstanding between the volunteers and Lobengula's young bucks.'

'I will be able to send up fresh vegetables and even a few flowers while you are at the king's kraal, Louise,' Clinton offered.

'You've been too kind already,' Louise thanked him, and then broke off, and an expression of deep concern crossed her face.

They all turned hurriedly in the direction she was staring.

Cathy had returned and climbed the verandah steps. She leaned against one of the whitewashed columns. Her face was the muddy yellow of a malaria sufferer, and her brow and chin were blistered with droplets of sweat. Her eyes were tortured, and her mouth twisted with horror.

'In the church,' she said. 'She's in the church.' And then she doubled over, and retched with a terrible tearing sound, and it came up her throat in a solid yellow eruption that soaked the virginal white skirts of her wedding gown.

Robyn was the first to reach the church door. She stared for only a moment and then she whirled and hid her face against Clinton's chest.

'Take her away,' Zouga ordered Clinton brusquely, and then to Ralph. 'Help me!'

The garland of pink roses had fallen from Salina's head, and lay below her on the floor of the nave. She had thrown a halter rope over one of the roof beams, and she must have climbed up on the table that Robyn used for her surgery.

Her hands hung open at her sides. The toes of her slippers were turned in towards each other in a touchingly innocent stance, like those of a little girl standing on tiptoe; but they were suspended at the height of a man's waist above the flagged floor.

Zouga had to look up at her face. The rope had caught her under one ear and her head was twisted at an impossible angle to one side. To Zouga her face seemed swollen to twice its normal size, and it was mottled a dark mulberry hue.

At that moment a merciful little breeze came in through the doorway and turned her slowly on the rope to face the altar, so that Zouga could see only her lustrous golden hair which had come down and now hung to her waist. That was still beautiful.

Cathy Ballantyne had never known such happiness as the months spent in the British South Africa Company camp on the Macloutsi river.

She was the only woman among nearly seven hundred men, and a favourite of all of them. They called her 'Missus', and her presence was eagerly sought at every social activity with which officers and men diverted themselves during the long term of waiting.

The harsh conditions of camp life might have daunted another newly married girl of her age, but Cathy had known no others, and she turned the hut of daub and thatch that Ralph built for her into a cosy retreat with calico curtains in the glassless windows and woven grass native mats on the earth floor. She planted petunias on each side of the doorway, and the troopers of the column vied for the honour of watering them. She cooked over an open fire in the lean-to kitchen, and her invitations to dine were eagerly sought after by men who subsisted on canned bully beef and stamped maize meal.

She glowed with all the attention and excitement, so that from being merely pretty, she seemed to become beautiful – which made the men cherish her the more. Then, of course, she had Ralph, and she wondered some nights as she lay awake and listened to his breathing, how she had ever lived without him.

Ralph had the rank of major now, and he told her with a wink and an irreverent chuckle, 'We are all colonels and majors, my girl. I'm even thinking of making old Isazi a captain.' But he looked so handsome in his uniform with frogged coat and slouch hat and Sam Browne belt, that she wished he would wear it more often.

With each day Ralph seemed to her to become taller, his body more powerful and his energy more abundant. Even when he was away down the line hustling up the wagons, setting up the heliograph stations, or meeting with the other directors of the British South Africa Company in Kimberley, she was not lonely. Somehow his presence seemed always with her, and his absence made anticipation of his return a sort of secret joy.

Then suddenly he would be back, galloping into camp to sweep her up and toss her as high as if she were a child, before kissing her on the mouth.

'Not in public,' she would gasp and blush. 'People are watching, Ralph.'

'And turning green with envy,' he agreed, and carried her into the hut.

When he was there, everything was a breathless whirl. He was everywhere with his long assured stride and merry infectious laugh, driving his men along with a word of encouragement or of banter, and occasionally with sudden murderous black rages.

His rages terrified her, although they were never directed at her; and yet at the same time they excited her strangely. She would watch him with fearful fascination as his face swelled and darkened with passion, and his voice rose into a roar like a wounded bull. Then his fists and boots would fly and somebody would roll in the dust.

Afterwards she felt weak and trembly, and she would hurry away to the hut and draw the curtains and wait. When he came in, he would have that savage look on his face that made something flutter in the pit of her stomach, and it took all her will not to run to him – but to wait for him to come to her.

'By God, Katie my girl,' he said to her once as he leaned on his elbow over her, the sweat still glistening on his naked chest, and his breathing as rough as though he had run a race, 'you may look like an angel, but you could teach the devil himself a trick or two.'

Though she prayed afterwards for strength to control the wanton sensations and cravings of her body, the prayers were perfunctory and lacked real conviction, and that lovely smug and contented feeling just would not go away.

With Ralph it was excitement all the time, day and night, when they were alone and when they were in company. She loved to watch the deference with which other men treated him, rich and famous men older than he was like Colonel Pennefather and Dr Leander Starr Jameson, who were the leaders of the column. But then, she told herself, so they should. Ralph was already a director of the Chartered Company, Mr Rhodes' British South Africa Company, and when he sat down at the boardroom table in the De Beers building, it was in the company of lords and generals and of Mr Rhodes himself, though Ralph grinned and told her wickedly, 'Great men, Katie, but not one of them whose feet don't stink in hot weather – same as mine.'

'You are awful, Ralph Ballantyne,' she scolded, but she felt all puffed up with pride when she overheard two troopers talking of him and one said: 'Ralph Ballantyne, there's a man for you, and no mistake.'

Then at night, after they had made boisterous unashamed love, they would talk in the darkness, sometimes through most of the night, and his dreams and plans were the more enchanting for she knew that he would make them come true.

Her personal rapture was heightened by the mood of the seven hundred men around her, and each day's restraint as they waited for the word to move off increased the tension which gripped them all. Ralph's oxen brought up the guns, two seven-pounders, and the artillery fired shrapnel over the deserted veld beyond the camp, while the watchers cheered them as the fleecy cotton pods of smoking death opened prettily in the clear dry air.

The four Maxim machine-guns were unpacked from their cases and de-greased – and then, on a memorable day, the monstrous steam engine came chugging into the encampment, dragging behind it the electric generator and the naval searchlight which would be just another precaution against night attack by the Matabele hordes.

That night as she lay in his arms, Cathy asked Ralph the question they were all asking one another.

'What will Lobengula do?'

'What can he do?' Ralph stroked her hair, the way he might caress a favourite puppy. 'He has signed the concession, taken his gold and guns, and promised Papa the road to Mashonaland.'

'They say he has eighteen thousand men waiting across the Shashi.'

'Then let them come, Katie, my lass. There are not a few amongst us who would welcome the chance to teach King Ben's buckeroos a sharp lesson.'

'That's a terrible thing to say,' she said without conviction.

'But it's the truth, by God.'

She no longer chided him when he blasphemed so lightly, for the days and ways of Khami Mission seemed to be part of a fading dream.

Then one day, early in July of 1890, the mirror of a heliograph winked its eye across the dusty, sun-washed distances. It was the word for which they had waited all these months. The British Foreign Secretary had at last approved the occupation of Mashonaland by the representatives of the British South Africa Company.

The long ponderous column uncoiled like a serpent. At its head rode Colonel Pennefather in company uniform, and at his right hand the guide Frederick Selous, whose duty it would be to take the column wide of any Matabele settlements, to cross the low malarial lands before the rains broke and to lead them up the escarpment to the sweet and healthy airs of the high plateau.

The Union Jack unfurled above their heads and a bugler sounded the advance.

'Heroes every one of them,' Ralph grinned at Cathy. 'But it's up to the likes of me to see our heroes through.'

His shirtsleeves were rolled high on his muscled arms and a disgracefully stained hat was cocked over one eye.

'When I come back, we'll be richer by eighty thousand pounds,' he told her, and lifted her off the ground with his embrace.

'Oh Ralph, how I wish I were coming with you.'

'You know Mr Rhodes has forbidden any women to cross the frontier – and you'll be a damned sight safer and more comfortable at Lily's Hotel in Kimberley with Jordan to keep an eye on you.'

'Then be careful, my darling,' she cautioned him, breathless from his hug.

'No need for that, Katie, my sweet. The devil looks after his own.'

*

'These are not men coming to dig holes.' Gandang stood forth from the circle of indunas. 'They are dressed as soldiers; they bring guns that can break down the granite hills with their smoke.'

'What did the king promise Lodzi?' demanded Babiaan. 'That he may come in peace to look for gold. Why does he march against us like an army?'

Bazo spoke for the young men. 'Oh great King, the spears are bright and our eyes are red. We are fifteen thousand men; can the king's enemies stand against us?'

Lobengula looked at his handsome eager young face. 'Sometimes the most dangerous enemy is a hasty heart,' he said, softly.

'And at other times, Bull Elephant of Kumalo, it might be a tardy spear arm.'

A shadow of irritation at importunate youth passed behind the king's eyes; then he sighed. 'Who knows?' he agreed. 'Who knows where the enemy lies?'

'The enemy lies before you, great King; he has crossed the Shashi river and he has come to take your land from you,' Somabula told him. And then Gandang stood again:

'Let the spears go, Lobengula, Son of Mzilikazi, let your young men run – or as the sun will rise tomorrow, that surely will you live to regret it.'

'That I cannot do,' Lobengula said softly. 'Not yet. I cannot use the assegai when words may still suffice.' He roused himself and his voice firmed.

'Go, Gandang, my brother, take your hot-hearted son with you. Go to the leader of these soldiers and ask him why he comes into my lands in battle array, and bring his answer to me here.'

Frederick Selous rode ahead, a trooper with an axe following him, and he pointed out the trees to be cut.

The trooper blazed them with a slash of the axe, and followed Selous on. The axemen came up behind them, fifty of them, riding in pairs. One man dismounted, handed his reins to his partner, spat on his already callused hands and, hefting the axe, addressed himself to the trunk of the doomed tree.

While his axe thudded and the wood chips flew white as bone in the sunlight, the second man sat in the saddle, his rifle in his hands, and he watched the forest around him for the first plumed head and long tasselled shield to appear. When the tree crackled and toppled, the axeman mounted and they rode on to the next, where he took his turn on guard while his mate swung the axe. Behind them the bullock spans came plodding to chain the fallen trunks and drag them out of the road, and then the whole ponderous caravan rumbled forward.

It was slow work, and on the third day Ralph rode to the head of the column to discuss with Selous the possibility of using the steam engine to haul the smaller trees, roots and all, from the sandy earth. They had left their horses with a trooper and walked forward for a better view of the way ahead when Ralph said quietly: 'Stand your ground, Mr Selous. Do not draw your pistol, and, in God's name, do not show any agitation.'

There were dark and moving shadows in the forest all around them, and then suddenly the dreaded long shields were there, forming a wall across their front.

'Has the king killed any white men?' a deep voice challenged. 'If he has not, then why has this impi of warriors crossed his border?'

'Lobengula has killed nobody,' Ralph called back.

'Then have the white men mislaid something of value – that they come to seek it here?'

Ralph said quietly to Selous. 'I know this man. He is one of the king's senior indunas. The one with the red shield behind him is his son; between them they disposed of eight thousand men. It would be as well to tread warily, Mr Selous. We are surrounded by an army.'

Then he addressed himself to the watching and waiting warriors: 'The king has given us the road.'

'The king denies that he called an army to enter his domain.'

'We are not an army,' Ralph denied, and Gandang threw back his head and laughed briefly and bitterly. Then he spoke again:

'Hear me, Henshaw, no white man steps beyond this place without the word of Lobengula. Tell that to your masters.'

Ralph whispered briefly with Selous, and then faced Gandang again.

'We will wait,' he agreed, 'for the king's word.'

'And we will watch while you wait,' Gandang promised ominously, and at a gesture the warriors melted away into the forest again and it seemed they had never been.

'Pull in the pickets,' Colonel Pennefather ordered. 'Put the wagons into laager. Ballantyne, can you get a message back to Tuli on the heliograph and have someone post up to GuBulawayo to find what are Lobengula's real intentions.' And, as Ralph turned to hurry away, 'Oh, one other thing, Ballantyne, can you start the generator and have the searchlight ready to sweep the area around the camp tonight. We don't want those fellows creeping up on us in the dark.'

Gandang and his son stood together on the crest of one of the little rocky kopjes that dotted the wide hot plain between the rivers.

They were alone, although when Bazo turned his head and looked down the steep back-slope of the hill, he could see the bivouac of their combined impis. There were no cooking fires to disclose their presence to the white men; they would eat cold rations and sleep in darkness this night. The long, black ranks squatted with enforced patience, dense as hiving bees beneath the shading branches of the mopani.

Bazo knew that he had only to lift his right arm above his shield to bring them to their feet and send them racing away, silent and ferocious as hunting leopards, and the thought gave him a savage joy. Reluctantly he turned back, and stood quietly with his shield not quite touching his father's.

The little afternoon breeze coming up from the river stirred their war plumes, and they gazed down upon the laager of the white men.

The bullocks had been penned within the circle of the wagons, and they could see the field guns and the Maxim machine-guns posted at the points of the barricade, their positions fortified with biscuit boxes and ammunition cases from the wagonloads. The gun crews lounged near their weapons, yet somehow the whole scene appeared tranquil and unwarlike.

'In the dark hour before the dawn, we could take them before they could stand to their guns,' murmured Bazo. 'It would be so quick, so easy.'

'We will wait on the king's word,' his father replied, and then started and exclaimed.

'What is it, my father?'

Gandang lifted his assegai and pointed with it southwards, to the pale blue horizon, far beyond the Shashi river, to the faint line of hills, shaped as fantastically as the turreted towers of a fairy castle.

On those far pale hills, something flickered and sparkled, a tiny speck of brightest white light, like a fire-fly in flight, or like the twinkle of the morning star.

'The stars,' Gandang whispered with superstitious awe, 'the stars are shining on the hills.'

The little group of officers stood behind the tripod of the instrument and focused their telescopes on the distant twinkle of light.

The heliograph operator called the message aloud, at the same time scribbling it on his signal pad. 'Jove advises hold your position pending clarification Lobengula's intention.' Jove was the code for Mr Rhodes.

'Very well.' Pennefather closed his telescope with a snap. 'Acknowledge message received and understood.'

The operator bent to the prism of the instrument and made a minute adjustment in its focus, turning one mirror to catch the sunlight and the second to reflect it directly towards the line of distant hills; then he seized the handle and the shutter clattered as it blinked the beam of sunlight, speeding the dots and dashes of the Morse code instantaneously across fifty miles of wilderness.

Pennefather turned away and crossed briskly to the massive steam engine on its tall steel wheels. He looked up at Ralph on the footplate.

'Are you ready to light up, Ballantyne?'

Ralph removed the long black cheroot from between his teeth, and gave a parody of a military salute.

'We've got sixty pounds of pressure on the boiler. Another half hour and she'll be whistling out of the valve.'

'Very well.' Pennefather hid his mystification. He neither understood nor admired these demoniacal contraptions. 'Just as long as we have light by nightfall.'

Gandang sat on his shield with his fur kaross of monkey skins over his shoulders. The winter evenings were cold, even here in the lowlands. There were no fires in the bivouac – and he could barely make out the faces of his junior commanders who sat opposite him, for the last flush of the sunset was fading from the western sky.

'It was something that all of us saw, and something that we have never seen before.'

They murmured agreement.

'It was a star, fallen from the heavens, and it lay upon the hills. We all saw it.'

'In the morning I will send two of our swiftest runners to the king. He must know of this terrible witchcraft.' He stood up and let his kaross fall. 'Now I am going –' He did not finish the sentence.

Instead he dropped into a defensive crouch and flung up his shield to cover his head, and around him his warriors wailed like frightened children, their eyes wide and white, glinting in the flood of light that burst down upon them from the sky.

The evening stars were washed out by the brilliance of the great white beam that reached from earth to heaven, and threw the hills into crisp black silhouette.

'The sun has returned,' Gandang croaked in religious terror. 'It is the prophecy, the whole prophecy. The stone falcons have flown, the stars shine on the hills, and now the sun burns at midnight.'

> Fort Salisbury
> 20th Sept. 1890

My darling Kate,

Over two months since last I kissed you – and I am missing your cooking, amongst other things!

You will see by the address that we have reached our destination – although we lost a man drowned, another to drink, a third bitten by a mamba and a fourth eaten by a lion – the Matabele touched not one of us.

So Lobengula kept his word – to the surprise of all, and the disappointment of not a few. After one exchange of insults with old Gandang at the head of 8,000 of his bully boys, they let us pass – and the rest of it was rather tedious – just sweat and blisters!

The great Selous almost lost us once – but then I showed him the pass through the hills which Isazi and I found when we made our little foray to Great Zimbabwe. Selous called it Providential Pass (providential that I was with him, I'd say), and he took the kudos (to which he is welcome). He will probably write another book about his feat!

We reached Mount Hampden on the 6th instant, and it gave me a turn to think that Papa had been the first man here all those years ago.

However, Pennefather, in his great wisdom, decided there was insufficient water there and moved us all twelve miles across here. Of course the man is a new chum, fresh out from home, so how is he to know that this place will turn into a swamp with the first rains. (I intend to be well away by then!)

I have visited some God-forsaken places on my travels – but this one gets the coconut! It's infested with lions – and I've lost 15 oxen to them already. The grazing is sour-veld – the remaining beasts are losing condition – oh, how I long for the sweet-veld of Matabeleland. Trust the Matabele to pick the best stock country, so I'll not be too surprised when others start thinking about Lobengula's herds and pastures. If only the cunning old blighter had thrown his war spear and given us the excuse, we might be hoisting the flag over GuBulawayo now – rather than over this dreary spot.

Oh well! At least I am the only one here with whisky – two wagonloads of it – and doing a roaring trade at £10 the bottle. You shall have the prettiest bonnet in Kimberley when I return, Katie my heart.

The day Pennefather hoisted the flag the boys were free to go their own way – and what a stampede there was! Everyone intent to be the first to peg the gold reef we've heard so much about. Some of them are crawling back already, tail between their legs. This is no Eldorado – if there is gold, they'll have to work for it – and then, of course, Mr Rhodes and his British South Africa Company will take half of it. Of course, they all were happy enough about the Company's cut when they signed on – but they are starting to belly-ache about it now.

We had a message on the 'Helio' this morning that the British South Africa Company shares are selling for £3–15s-0d. each in London, and 5,000 new shareholders on the books in the first week. Well, all I can say is that whoever is paying that price has never seen Fort Salisbury!

'Young Ballantyne,' says Leander Starr Jameson to me, 'you were damnably lucky to take half your fees payable in B.S.A. shares valued at £1 each.'

'Jameson,' says I, 'it's strange how the harder I work and the harder I think, the luckier I get.'

So I have 40,000 B.S.A. shares, Katie my love, and you will find here attached a letter addressed to Aaron Fagan, my solicitor in Kimberley, instructing him to sell every last one of them. Take it around to him post-haste, that's a good girl. We'll be well rid of them at a profit of £2–15s-0d. each, and that's God's truth! Perhaps I'll buy you two bonnets when I come back!

Oh, if only we had Matabeleland – no wonder Lobengula left Mashonaland to the Mashonas! Though they don't call it that any more. The new name that is all the rage is Rhodesia – no less!

What an ungainly name it is, but no doubt Mr Rhodes will be flattered and my brother Jordan will be delighted. They are welcome to my share of Rhodesia – Don't forget to take the letter to Fagan, mind!

Nonetheless, there is still a penny to be made here. I have taken a partner, and we are building a General Store and Bar-room. He will run both businesses, as well as the Salisbury Depot for my wagons. He seems an honest lad, our Tom Meikle, and hard-working, so I have given him a wage of £5 a month and ten per cent of the profits – no point in spoiling him! Just as soon as we get the building up and the stocks on the shelves, I will leave him to it and be on my way back to you.

Mr Rhodes wants me to contract to erect the telegraph line from Kimberley to Fort Salisbury for him at a price of £25,000. I reckon there will be £10,000 profit in it. You shall have three bonnets, Katie, I swear it to you!

I must leave here by the 10th of next month if I am to beat the rains. Once they start the mosquitoes are going to take over Fort Salisbury, and every river between here and the Shashi will be a flood that would break even Noah's heart.

Thus I expect to reach Kimberley by the end of October, so take a good look at the floor, Katie my sweet, for when I get there you will be looking at nought but the ceiling for a week – and my word on it!

Your loving husband,
Ralph Ballantyne
(Ex Major B.S.A. Police Retired!)

*

'We must have Matabeleland. It is as simple as that,' said Zouga Ballantyne, and Jordan looked up sharply from his pad of Pitman's shorthand.

His father sat in one of the deep buttoned leather chairs facing Mr Rhodes' desk. Beyond him the green velvet curtains were open and held with yellow tasselled ropes of silk. The view from this top floor of the De Beers Company buildings took in a wide sweep of the dry Griqualand plain dotted with camel-thorn trees, and closer to hand the stacking ground where the blue earth from the Kimberley mine was left to deteriorate in the brilliant sunshine before being made to yield up its precious diamonds.

Jordan had no eyes for the view now; his father's words had shocked him. But Mr Rhodes merely hooded his eyes and slumped massively at his desk, gesturing for Zouga to continue.

'The Company shares are six shillings in London, against three pounds fifteen on the day we raised the flag at Fort Salisbury three years ago –'

'I know, I know,' Rhodes nodded.

'I have spoken with the men that remain; I have spent the last three months travelling from Fort Victoria to Salisbury as you bid me. They won't stay, Mr Rhodes. They won't stay unless you let them go in and finish it.'

'Matabeleland.' Rhodes lifted his great shaggy head, and Jordan thought how terribly he had aged in these last three years. 'Matabeleland,' he repeated softly.

'They are sick of the constant menace of Lobengula's hordes upon their borders; they have convinced themselves that the gold they did not find in Mashonaland lies under Lobengula's earth; they have seen Lobengula's fat herds of choice cattle and compared them to their own lean beasts that starve on the thin sour veld to which they are restricted–'

'Go on,' Rhodes nodded.

'They know that to reach them the telegraph and the railroad must come through Matabeleland. They are sick to the guts with malaria and the constant fear of the Matabele. If you want to keep Rhodesia, you must give them Matabeleland.'

'I have known this all along. I think we all have. Yet we must move carefully. We must be careful of the Imperial Factor, of Gladstone and of Whitehall.' Rhodes stood up and began to pace back and forth before the shelves laden with leather-bound books titled in gold leaf.

'We need to prepare ourselves. You must remember, Ballantyne, that we have technically only the right to dig for gold. As long as Lobengula does not molest us, we cannot declare war upon him.'

'But if Lobengula were to interfere in any way with our people and their rights?'

'That would be another matter.' Rhodes stopped in front of Zouga's chair. 'Then I should certainly end his game for him.'

'In the meantime the company's shares are six shillings each,' Zouga reminded him.

'We need an incident,' said Rhodes. 'But in the meantime we have to prepare and I dare not put it on the wires. I want you to leave immediately for Fort Victoria to speak to Jameson.' Rhodes swung his big head towards Jordan. 'Do not make notes of this, Jordan,' he ordered, and Jordan dutifully lifted his pencil from the pad. 'Instruct Jameson to send me a series of telegrams on the new wires. Telegrams advising against war, that we can show the British Government and people when it is all over – but in the meantime tell him to prepare for war.'

Rhodes turned back to Jordan. 'Take an instruction, Jordan. Sell fifty thousand B.S.A. Company shares for what they will fetch. Jameson must have what he needs to do the business. Tell him that, Ballantyne. I shall be behind him all the way – but we need an incident.'

Ralph Ballantyne sat his horse on the heights of the escarpment which fell away before him, in a tumbled splendour of rocky hills and forests. The spring foliage turned the groves of msasa trees into clouds of pink and swelling scarlets, and the air was so clear and bright that he could pick out the telegraph line all the way to the horizon.

The wires were a gossamer thread that glistened red gold in the sunlight, so fragile, so insubstantial, that it seemed impossible that they ran, arrow straight, six hundred miles and more to meet the railhead at Kimberley.

Ralph's men had laid this line. The surveyors riding ahead to set up the beacons, the axemen following to clear the line, then the wagons bringing up the poles and finally the enormous spools of gleaming copper wire uncoiling endlessly.

Ralph had hired good men, paid them well, and visited them less than once a month. Yet he was proud as he saw the wires sparkle and thought of the importance and significance of this achievement.

Beside him his foreman cursed suddenly. 'There it is! The thieving bastards!' And he pointed to where the line of telegraph poles marched up the side of one forested hill. Ralph had thought that cloud shadow had dimmed the sparkle of the copper wire up this slope, but now when he focused his binoculars upon them he saw that the poles had been stripped bare.

'Come on,' he said grimly, and rode forward. When they reached the bottom of the slope they found that one of the telegraph poles had been chopped through at the base, and felled like timber. The wires had been hacked through, and the scuff marks in the earth where it had been rolled into bundles had not yet been erased by the wind.

Slowly they rode on up the slope, and Ralph did not have to dismount to read the sign of bare feet.

'There were at least twenty of them,' he said. 'Women and children with them – a family outing, damn them to hell.'

'It's the women that put them up to it,' the foreman agreed. 'That wire makes beautiful bracelets and bangles. The black girls just love it.'

At the top of the slope another telegraph pole had been felled and the wire snipped through.

'They have got away with five hundred yards of wire,' Ralph scowled. 'But next time it could be five thousand. Do you know who they are?'

The foreman shrugged. 'The local Mashona chief is Matanka. His village is just the other side of the valley. You can see the smoke from here.'

Ralph slipped his rifle out of its boot under his knee. It was a magnificent new Winchester Repeater Model 1890 with his name engraved and chased with gold into the metal of the block. He levered a round into the breech.

'Let's go to see brother Matanka.'

325

He was an old man, with legs like a stork and a cap of pure white wool covering his head. He trembled with fear and fell on his knees before this furious young white man with a rifle in his hand.

'Fifty head,' Ralph told him. 'And next time your people touch the wires it will be a hundred.'

Ralph and his foreman cut the fattest cattle out of Matanka's herds and drove them ahead of them, up the escarpment and into the little white settlement of Fort Victoria which had grown up mid-way between the Shashi river and Fort Salisbury.

'All right,' Ralph told his foreman. 'You can take them from here. Turn them over to the auctioneer, we should get ten pounds a head for them.'

'That will cover the cost of replacing the wires fifty times over,' the foreman grinned.

'I don't believe in taking a loss when I don't have to,' Ralph laughed. 'Get on with you, I'll have to go down and square it with the good doctor.'

Doctor Jameson's office, as administrator of the Charterlands of the British South Africa Company, was a wood and iron building with an untidily thatched roof directly opposite the only canteen in Fort Victoria.

'Ah, young Ballantyne,' Jameson greeted Ralph, and secretly enjoyed Ralph's frown of annoyance. He did not share the general high opinion of this youngster. He was too bumptious and too successful by a half, while physically he was all that Jameson was not; tall and broad-shouldered, with a striking appearance and forceful presence.

The wags were saying that one day Ralph Ballantyne would own the half of the Charterland that Rhodes did not already have his brand on. However, even Jameson had to grant that if you wanted something done, no matter how difficult, and if you wanted it done swiftly and thoroughly, and if you were prepared to pay top dollar, then Ralph Ballantyne was your man.

'Ah, Jameson.' Ralph retaliated by dropping the mousy little doctor's title from the greeting, and by turning immediately to the other man in the room.

'General St John.' Ralph flashed that compelling smile. 'How good to see you, sir! When did you get into Fort Victoria?'

Mungo St John limped across the room to take Ralph's hand, and his single eye gleamed.

'Got in this very morning.'

'Congratulations on your appointment, sir. We need a good soldier up here, the way things are going.' Ralph's compliment was an oblique jibe at Dr Jameson's own military aspirations. Rhodes had very recently appointed Mungo St John as the Company's Chief of Staff. He would be under Jameson's administration, naturally, but would be directly responsible for police and military affairs in the Charterlands of Rhodesia.

'Did your men find the break in the wires?' Jameson interrupted them.

'Bangles and bracelets,' Ralph nodded. 'That's what happened to the wires. I have given the local chief a lesson that I hope will teach him to behave himself. I fined him fifty head of cattle.'

Jameson frowned quickly.

'Lobengula considers Matanka to be his vassal. He owns those cattle, the Mashona merely tend the herds on the king's behalf.'

Ralph shrugged. 'Then Matanka will have some explaining to do, and rather him than me, and that's the truth.'

'Lobengula won't let this pass –' Jameson broke off, and the frown cleared. He began to pace up and down behind his desk with excited, hopping, bird-like steps. 'Perhaps,' he twitched at his scraggly little moustache, 'perhaps this is what we have been waiting for. Lobengula will not let it pass – nor, by God, will we.' He paused and looked at Ralph. 'How soon will you have the wires restored?'

'By noon tomorrow,' Ralph told him promptly.

'Good! Good! We must get a message through to your father at GuBulawayo. If he protests to Lobengula that his vassals are stealing Company property, and informs him that we have fined him in cattle, what will Lobengula do?'

'He will send an impi to punish Matanka.'

'Punish him?'

'Cut his head off, kill his men, rape his women and burn his village.'

'Exactly.' Jameson punched his fist into his palm. 'And Matanka is on Company ground and under protection of the British flag. It will be our duty, our bounden duty, to drive off Lobengula's men.'

'War!' said Ralph.

'War,' agreed St John softly. 'Well done, young fellow. This is what we have been waiting for.'

'Ballantyne, can you give me a tender to provide wagons and supplies for an expeditionary force, say five hundred men; we'll need twenty-five wagons, six hundred horses, when we drive for GuBulawayo.'

'When do you expect to march?'

'Before the rains.' Jameson was decisive. 'If we go, then we'll have to finish it before the rains break.'

'I will have a tender for you by the time the telegraph is reopened tomorrow.'

Ralph jumped down from the saddle and tossed his reins to the groom who came running.

Although it was only a temporary lodging which Ralph used on his infrequent visits to check the progress of his construction gangs, his transport stages and his trading posts – yet it was the grandest house in Fort Victoria, with glass in the windows and insect mesh screening the doors.

His spurs clattered on the steps as he stormed up onto the verandah, and Cathy heard him and came running with the baby on her hip.

'You are home so soon,' she cried delightedly, rebuttoning her bodice from the feeding.

'Couldn't stay away from you two.' He laughed and smacked a kiss on her mouth, then snatched the baby from her and tossed him high.

'Do be careful.' Cathy hopped anxiously to try and take him back, but Jonathan gurgled joyously and kicked with excitement, and a trickle of milk reappeared and ran down his chin.

'Mucky little devil.' Ralph held him high and sniffed at his son. 'Both ends at once, by God. Here, Katie.' He handed the infant to her and held her around the waist.

'We are going to GuBulawayo,' he said.

'Who?' She looked up at him in confusion.

'St John and the good doctor and I, and when we get there B.S.A. shares will go to five pounds. Last price I heard before the wires were cut was five shillings. The first message that goes out tomorrow is my buying order to Aaron Fagan – for fifty thousand British South Africans!'

Bazo's impi came sweeping down out of the western forests, silent as shadows and murderous as wild hunting dogs.

'Kill that dog Matanka,' the king had ordered. 'Kill him and all his men.' And Bazo caught them in the dawn, as the first of them came out of their huts yawning and rubbing the sleep from their eyes, and then they chased the young girls cackling and shrieking like hens amongst the huts, and roped them in bunches.

'And all his men,' had been the king's order, and some of Matanka's men were working for the white men, at the Prince Mine, one of the very few paying gold reefs in Mashonaland. They were breaking and carrying the rock.

'Do not interfere,' Bazo told the mine overseer. 'This is the king's business. No white man will be hurt, that is the king's order.' And they chased the Mashona labourers into the crushing plant and stabbed them as they hid under the sorting-tables.

They came racing down the telegraph line, five hundred red shields. The Mashona wiremen were unwinding the huge drums and stringing the shining strands.

'No white men will be hurt,' Bazo shouted as he let his young men run. 'Stand aside, white men.' But now Bazo was mad with blood and boastful with the killing fever. 'This is not for you, white men. Not yet, white men, but your day will come.'

They dragged the Mashona down from the telegraph poles, and bayed about them like hounds tearing a fox to pieces, while the Mashona screamed to their white masters for protection.

'Bring in the cattle, all Matanka's cattle,' the king had ordered, and Bazo's men swept the Mashona pastures, and drove the sprawling multi-coloured herds back into the west in the clouds of their own dust; and with the herds were mingled some of the white men's cattle – for one beast looks like another, and the marks burned by hot iron into the hide meant nothing to the Matabele warriors.

It was all done so swiftly that Jameson had to ride hard with his band of hastily assembled volunteers to catch them before they reached the frontier of the Charterland.

He had thirty-eight men with him, and when he saw the horsemen, Bazo turned back and with the massed warriors at his back he greeted Jameson.

'Sakubona, Daketela! I see you, Doctor! Fear not, by the king's orders no white man will be molested.'

But the volunteers bunched their horses, and there was the snick of breech blocks and the rattle of bolts as they loaded. Thirty-eight against five hundred, and they were jumpy and white-faced.

The little doctor spurred forward, and Ralph murmured to St John: 'By God, the man is a bantam cock, and he'll get us all into it yet.'

But Jameson showed no agitation as he stood in the stirrups and called: 'Men of Matabele, why have you crossed the border?'

'*Hau, Daketela!*' Bazo answered him with mock astonishment. 'What border is this you speak of? Surely this land, all of it, belongs to Lobengula. There are no borders.'

'The men you have slaughtered are under my protection.'

'The men we killed were Mashona,' Bazo replied scornfully. 'And the Mashona are Lobengula's dogs – to kill or keep as he wishes.'

'The cattle you have stolen belong to my people.'

'All the Mashona cattle belong to the king.'

Then St John shouted over him, 'Careful, Jameson, there is treachery here, watch those men on your left.'

Some of Bazo's men had pressed forward, the better to see and to hear. A few of them were armed with ancient Martini-Henry rifles, probably those with which Rhodes had paid the king for his concession.

Jameson swung his horse to face them.

'Back!' he shouted. 'Back, I say.' He lifted his rifle to enforce his order, and one of the Matabele instinctively copied the gesture, half threatening the little group of mounted white men with his rifle.

Mungo St John flung up his rifle, and as it touched his shoulder he fired. The shot was a thunderous burst of sound in the heated dusty air, and the heavy bullet smashed into the Matabele's naked chest. His rifle clattered on the ground, and a little feather of bright crimson sprayed from his chest. The warrior pirouetted slowly, almost gracefully, until they looked into the shocking gape of the exit wound between his shoulder blades. Then the warrior collapsed, and his legs kicked convulsively.

'Do not touch a white man!' Bazo bellowed into the terrible silence, but not more than half a dozen of the horsemen understood the language. To the others it sounded like a killing order. The crash of volleyed rifle fire mingled with the trample of hooves and whinny of panicky horses. The banks of blue gunsmoke blended with the billowing pale dust and the rippling plumes of running warriors.

Bazo's impi was streaming away into the forest, carrying their wounded with them, and slowly the rifle fire stuttered and faded, and the horses quietened. The little group sat, silent and appalled, and stared at the Matabele dead strewn across the open ground ahead of them. They looked like the abandoned toys of a petulant child.

Ralph Ballantyne had not drawn the gold-engraved Winchester from its boot, and there was a long unlit cheroot between his white teeth. He spoke around it, smiling ironically, but his eyes were cold and green and hard.

'I count thirty-three of 'em down, Doctor Jim,' he said loudly. 'Not a bad bag really, even though they were sitting birds.' And he struck a Vesta against the thigh of his riding breeches and lit the cheroot; then he gathered the reins and turned his horses's head back towards the fort.

*

Lobengula turned the small canvas bag of sovereigns in his narrow graceful hands. He stood in the centre of the goat kraal, and there were only three Matabele with him, Gandang and Somabula and Babiaan. The others he had sent away.

Before him stood a little white group. Zouga had brought Louise with him to the meeting. He had not dared leave her alone in the cottage beyond the stockade of the royal kraal, not with the mood of the Matabele as it had been ever since Jameson's massacre at Fort Victoria.

Facing the king also, but a little separated from the other couple, stood Robyn and Clinton Codrington.

Still fingering the bag of gold, Lobengula turned his face to Robyn.

'See, Nomusa, these are the gold queens that you advised me to accept from Lodzi.'

'I am deeply ashamed, oh King,' Robyn whispered.

'Tell me faithfully, did I give away my land when I signed the paper?'

'No, King, you gave away only the gold beneath it.'

'But how can men dig for gold without the land over it?' Lobengula asked, and Robyn was silent and miserable.

'Nomusa, you said that Lodzi was a man of honour. So why does he do these things to me? His young men swagger across my land and call it their own. They shoot down my warriors, and now they gather a great army against me, with wagons and guns and thousands of soldiers. How can Lodzi do this to me, Nomusa?'

'I cannot answer you, oh King. I deceived you as I was myself deceived.'

Lobengula sighed. 'I believe you, Nomusa. There is still no quarrel between us. Bring your family, all your people here to my kraal that I may protect you through the dark times that lie ahead.'

'I do not deserve the king's consideration.' She choked on the words.

'No harm will come to you, Nomusa. You have Lobengula's word upon it.' He turned slowly back to Zouga.

'This gold, Bakela. Does it pay me for the blood of my young men?' And he threw the bag at Zouga's feet. 'Pick up your gold, Bakela, and take it back to Lodzi.'

'Lobengula, I am your friend – and I tell you this as a friend. If you refuse the monthly payment, then Lodzi will look upon it as a breaking of faith.'

'Was not the killing of my young men a breaking of faith, Bakela?' Lobengula asked sadly. 'If it was not, then my people believe it to be so. The regiments are gathered, so that they darken the Hills of the Indunas; they wear their plumes and carry their assegais and their guns, and their eyes are red. The blood of Matabele has been spilled, Bakela, and the enemies of the king gather against him.'

'Hear me, oh King, think a while before you let your young men run. What do they know of fighting Englishmen?' Zouga was angry now, and the scar on his cheek burned red as a welt raised by the lash of a whip.

'My young men will eat them up,' said Lobengula simply. 'As did the Zulu at the Hill of the Little Hand.'

'After the Little Hand came Ulundi,' Zouga reminded him. 'The earth was black with the Zulu dead, and they put chains on the legs of the Zulu King and sent him to an island far across the sea.'

'Bakela, it is too late. I cannot hold my young men, I have held them too long. They must run now.'

'Your young men are brave when there are old Mashona women to stab, and young babies to disembowel, but they have never met real men.'

Gandang hissed with anger behind the king's shoulder, but Zouga went on firmly.

'Send them home to dally with their women and preen their feathers, for if you let them run, then you will be lucky if you live to see your kraal burning and your herds being driven off.'

This time all three of the senior indunas hissed, and Gandang started forward impulsively, but Lobengula spread his hand to restrain him.

'Bakela is a guest of the king,' Lobengula said. 'While he stands in my kraal, every hair of his head is sacred.' But the king's eyes had never left Zouga's face. 'Go, Bakela, leave this day and take your woman with you. Go to Daketela and tell him that my impis are ready. If he crosses the Gwelo river, I will let my young men go.'

'Lobengula, if I leave then the last link between black men and white men is broken. There will be no more talking. It will be war.'

'Then let it be so, Bakela.'

It was hard riding. They took the road that Ralph Ballantyne's wagons had recently pioneered from Fort Salisbury to GuBulawayo. They left all their furniture and possessions in the cottage outside the stockade of the king's kraal – and they rode light, with a blanket roll on the pommel of the saddle and a food bag on one of the spare horses that Jan Cheroot brought up behind on a lead rein.

Louise rode like a man, astride and uncomplaining, and on the fifth day, unexpectedly, they came up with Jameson's column in camp around the skeletal headgear of Iron Mine Hill, where the volunteers from Salisbury and Fort Victoria had joined up.

'Zouga, is that how Jameson is going to challenge Lobengula's impi?'

The little encampment looked pathetically inadequate. There were two dozen wagons, and on the canvas tents of most of them Zouga could make out the insignia of Ralph's transport company. But he pointed to the corners of the laager.

'Machine-guns,' he said. 'Six of them, and they are worth five hundred men each. They have field guns also, look at their emplacements.'

'Oh Zouga, do you have to go with them?'

'You know that I do.'

They rode down into the camp, and as they passed the pickets there was a hail that startled the sentries and made Louise's horse shy and skitter.

'Papa!' Ralph came hurrying from the nearest wagon.

'My boy.' Zouga jumped down from the saddle, and they embraced happily. 'I should have known you would be wherever there was something doing.'

Louise bent from the saddle and Ralph brushed her cheek with his fine moustache. 'I still find it difficult to believe that I have a stepmother so young and beautiful.'

'You are my favourite son,' she laughed. 'But I'd love you more if you could arrange a hot bath–'

From behind the canvas screen Louise kept calling for more buckets of hot water, and Zouga had to carry them from the fire and top-up the galvanized hip-bath in which she sat with her thick, dark braids piled on top of her head, glowing pinkly from the almost boiling water and taking full part in the conversation beyond the screen.

Ralph and Zouga sat at a camp table with a blue enamel pot of coffee and a bottle of whisky between them.

'We have six hundred and eighty-five men all in.'

'I warned Rhodes that he would need fifteen hundred,' Zouga frowned.

'Well, there are another five hundred volunteers under Major Goold-Adams ready to move off from Macloutsi.'

'They would never get here in time to take a part in the fighting.' Zouga shook his head. 'What about lines of supply and reinforcements? What happens if we get into trouble with the Matabele? What chance of a relieving force?'

Ralph grinned devilishly. 'I am the whole commissariat – you don't think I would split the profits with anyone else, do you?'

'Re-supply? Relieving force?'

Ralph spread his hands in negation. 'The doctor informs me that we don't need them. God and Mr Rhodes are on our side.'

'If it goes against us, it will be death and mutilation for every man, woman and child this side of the Shashi river. Lobengula's impis are mad for war now. Neither the king nor his indunas will be able to control them once they begin.'

'That thought had occurred to me,' Ralph admitted. 'I have Cathy and Jonathan at Fort Victoria, packed and ready, old Isazi is with them and one of my best young men. I have fresh relays of mules posted all the way from Fort Vicky to the Shashi. The hour Jameson gives the word for the column to march, my family will be on their way south.'

'Ralph, I am taking Louise to Fort Victoria. Can she stay with Cathy and leave with her?'

'Nobody asked me,' Louise called from behind the screen, and there was an angry splash of water. 'I took a vow, until death us do part – Zouga Ballantyne.'

'You also vowed to love, honour and obey,' Zouga reminded her, and winked at Ralph. 'I hope you don't suffer the same insubordination from your wife.'

'Beat them regularly and give them plenty of babies,' Ralph advised. 'Of course, Louise must go with Katie, but you had better leave for Fort Vicky right away – the Doctor is champing at the bit to settle Lobengula's hash.' He broke off, and gestured at a trooper who was hurrying towards their wagon across the laager. 'And it looks as though he has heard of your arrival at last.'

The trooper saluted Zouga breathlessly. 'Are you Major Zouga Ballantyne, sir? Dr Jameson asks you please to come to his tent at your earliest convenience.'

Dr Jameson jumped up from the travelling-desk and bustled across the tent to meet Zouga.

'Ballantyne, I was worried about you. Have you come directly from Lobengula? What are the chances? What force do you reckon he disposes?' He broke off and scolded himself with a deprecatory chuckle. 'What am I thinking of. Let me get you a drink, man!'

He led Zouga into the tent. 'You know General St John, of course –' And Zouga stiffened, his face expressionless.

'Zouga.' Mungo St John lounged in a canvas camp chair – but he made no effort to rise or offer his hand. 'How long it is. But you are looking well. Marriage agrees with you – I have not had the opportunity to congratulate you.'

'Thank you.' Zouga nodded. Naturally he had known that Mungo was the Doctor's Chief of Staff – but still he was not ready for his anger and bitterness at the confrontation. This was the man who had kept Louise as a mistress, had held her tender precious body. He found that he was trembling, and he thrust the picture from his mind, but it was replaced instantly by the image of Louise as he had found her in the desert, her skin burned off her in slabs by the sun – and it was Mungo St John who had let her go and made no effort to follow her.

'I have heard that your wife is in camp with you –' St John's single eye glowed maliciously. 'You must dine with me tonight; it will be gratifying to discuss old times.'

'My wife has had a long, hard journey.' Zouga kept his voice level; he did not want to give Mungo the satisfaction of knowing how angry he was. 'And in the morning I am taking her into Fort Victoria.'

'Good!' Jameson cut in briskly. 'That suits my own plans – I need a trustworthy man to put a message on the telegraph line for Mr Rhodes. But now, Ballantyne, what is the news from GuBulawayo, and how do you rate our chances?'

'Well, Doctor Jim, Lobengula's ready for you – his young men are spoiling for a fight – and you have a scanty enough force here. In the ordinary way I would say that to take it into Matabeleland without reinforcements or a relieving force in the offing would be suicide. However –'

'However?' Jameson demanded eagerly.

'Four of Lobengula's regiments, those he sent against Lewanika, the king of the Barotse, are still on the Zambezi, and Lobengula will not be able to use them.'

'Why not?'

'Smallpox,' Zouga said. 'It's broken out in those regiments, and he dare not recall them to the south. They can take no part in the fighting.'

'Half the Matabele army out of it,' Jameson exulted. 'That's a nudge from on high, St John – what do you think?'

'I would say it's still a risk, a damnable risk. But think of the stake. A whole country to be won with all its lands and herds and gold. I'd say if we are ever to march, we must march now.'

'Ballantyne, your sister – the missionary woman, what's her name – Codrington, is she still at Khami? Is her family there with her?'

Zouga nodded, mystified, and Jameson snatched up a pencil and scribbled a message on his pad. Then he tore off the sheet and handed it to Mungo St John. Mungo read it and smiled. He looked like a bird of prey, beak-nosed and fierce.

'Yes,' he said. 'Perfect.' He passed the sheet to Zouga. Jameson had written in block capitals.

URGENT FOR JOVE MATABELE REGIMENTS MASSED TO ATTACK STOP ENGLISH WOMEN AND CHILDREN IN THE POWER OF THE MATABELE TYRANT STOP IMPERATIVE WE MARCH AT ONCE TO SAVE THEM REPLY SOONEST

'Even Labouchère couldn't quibble with that,' Zouga remarked wryly. Labouchère was the London editor of *Truth* magazine, a champion of the oppressed and one of Rhodes' most eloquent and persistent adversaries. Zouga proffered the sheet, but Jameson waved it back.

'Keep it. Send it. I don't suppose you could leave this evening?' Jameson asked wistfully.

'It will be dark in an hour, and my wife is exhausted.'

'Very well,' Jameson agreed. 'But you will return here as soon as you can with Mr Rhodes' reply?'

'Of course.'

'And there will be something else I want you to do on your return, a most important assignment.'

'What is it?'

'General St John will explain.' And Zouga turned suspiciously to Mungo.

Mungo's manner was suddenly placatory. 'Zouga, there's not one of us who hasn't read your book *Hunter's Odyssey*. I would say that it's the bible of anybody wanting to know about this country and its people.'

'Thank you.' Zouga was unbending still.

'And one of the most interesting sections is the description of your visit to the oracle of the Umlimo in the hills south of GuBulawayo.'

'The Matopos,' Zouga told him.

'Yes, of course, the Matopos. Could you find your way back to the witch's cavern? After all, it has been over twenty-five years?'

'Yes, I could find it again.' Zouga did not hesitate.

'Excellent,' Jameson interrupted. 'Come along, St John, do tell him why.' But Mungo seemed to digress.

'You know the old Zulu who works for your son – '

'Isazi, Ralph's head driver?' Zouga asked.

'That's the one. Well, we captured four Matabele scouts and we put Isazi in the stockade with them. He can pass for a Matabele, so the prisoners spoke freely in front of him. One of the things we learnt is that the Umlimo has called all the witch doctors of the nation to a ritual in the hills.'

'Yes,' Zouga agreed. 'I heard of it before I left GuBulawayo. The Umlimo is preaching war, and promises a charm to the impis that will turn our bullets to water.'

'Ah, so it's true then.' Mungo nodded – and then, thoughtfully: 'Just what influence does this prophetess have?'

'The Umlimo is a hereditary figure, a sort of virgin demi-deity that has her origins long before the arrival of the Matabele in this land, perhaps a thousand years or more ago. First Mzilikazi and then Lobengula have fallen under her spell. I have even heard it whispered that Lobengula served an apprenticeship in sorcery under the Umlimo's guidance, in the Matopos.'

'Then she does wield power over the Matabele?'

'Immense power. Lobengula makes no important decision without her oracle. No impi would march without her charms to protect them.'

'If she were to die on the day we march into Matabeleland?'

'It would throw the king and his warriors into consternation. They would probably act recklessly. The Umlimo's charms would perish with her; her advice might turn like a serpent and strike the receiver. They would be demoralized – and it would take at least three months to choose a prophetess to replace her. During that time the nation would be vulnerable.'

'Zouga, I want you to take a party of mounted men – the toughest and the best we have. I want you to ride to the witch's cave and destroy her and all her witch doctors.'

*

Will Daniel was Zouga's sergeant. He was a Canadian who had been twenty years in Africa without losing his accent. He had fought the tribes on the Fish river and in Zululand. He boasted that he had killed three of Cetewayo's men with a single shot at Ulundi and made his tobacco pouch from the scalp of one of them. He had been in the Gazaland rebellion and fought at the Hill of the Doves against the free burghers of the Transvaal Republic. Wherever there had been trouble and shooting, Will Daniel had forged his bloody reputation. He was a big man, heavy in the gut, prematurely bald with large round ears that stood out from his polished scalp like those of a wild dog. His fists were gnarled, his legs bowed from the saddle, and he wore a perpetual wide white grin which never touched his cold little eyes.

'You don't have to like or trust him,' Mungo St John had advised Zouga. 'But he is the man for the job.'

With Will Daniel went his henchman, Jim Thorn, half Will's size but every bit as vicious. A skinny little Cockney with the grey tones of the slum-dweller so deeply etched into his gaunt melancholy face that five thousand African suns had been unable to erase them. Dr Jameson had released him from the Fort Victoria gaol, where he was waiting trial for beating a Mashona servant to death with a rhinoceros-hide *sjambok*. His pardon depended on his conduct during the campaign. 'So you can rely on him to do whatever needs doing,' Mungo had pointed out to Zouga.

The other thirteen troopers were men of a similar type. They had all volunteered under Doctor Jim's Victoria Agreement and signed the enlistment document, a document which Jameson made sure remained secret. No copy of it went to the High Commissioner in Cape Town nor to Gladstone's Government in Whitehall, for it promised the volunteers a share of Lobengula's land and cattle and treasures; the word 'loot' was specifically mentioned in the text.

On the first night out Will Daniel had come silently to where Zouga slept a little apart and, as he stooped over Zouga's recumbent form, a wiry arm had whipped suddenly around his neck and the muzzle of a Webley revolver was thrust under his ribs with sufficient force to drive the air from his lungs.

'Next time you creep up on me, I'll kill you,' Zouga hissed into his face; and Will's teeth flashed in the moonlight as he grinned appreciatively.

'They told me you were a sharp one.'

'What do you want?'

'Me and the boys want to sell our land rights – three thousand *morgen* each, that's ninety thousand acres. You can have them for a hundred each.'

'You haven't earned them yet.'

'That's a chance you gotta take, skipper.'

'I thought you were on guard duty, sergeant.'

'Well, it was just for a moment, sir.'

'Next time you leave your post, I'll shoot you myself, without bothering about a court-martial.'

Daniel stared into his face for a moment.

'Yep, I reckon you would too,' Will grinned mirthlessly.

Zouga led the patrol south and westwards through the forests where once long ago he had hunted the wandering herds of elephant. Now the tuskers were all gone, and even the herds of lesser game were wild from the unrestrained hunting of the new settlers and they scattered at the first approach of the small party of horsemen.

Zouga avoided the established roads between the Matabele regimental towns, and when they had to pass close to a settlement or the cultivated lands surrounding it, they did so at night. Though he knew that the impis had all answered Lobengula's call and were already assembled at Thabas Indunas, still he felt a vast relief when the granite domes of the Matopos rose above the treetops ahead of them and in single file his horsemen followed him into one of the steep-sided valleys.

That night there was a deputation of four troopers led by Will Daniel and Jim Thorn.

'The boys have all voted, skipper. We will take a hundred for the lot.' Will grinned ingratiatingly. 'There's not one of us have the price of a drink to celebrate when we get home – and you have that money belt around your belly. It must be damned heavy by now, and no good it will do you if a Matabele sniper puts a bullet in your back.'

The smile was still on Will's face, but the threat was naked in his eyes. If Zouga did not buy their land grants, it might be a bullet in the back. They would divide up the contents of his money belt anyway.

Zouga considered defying the big ugly sergeant, but there were fifteen of them. The gold in his belt could be his death warrant. He was in enough danger from the Matabele.

'I have seventy-five sovereigns in my belt,' he said grimly.

'Fine,' Will agreed. 'You've got yourself a bargain, Major.'

Zouga wrote out a contract of land grant sale on the back page of his message pad, and twelve of them signed it. Will Daniel and two other illiterates made their marks, and then they squabbled over the division of the gold sovereigns from Zouga's belt. Zouga was relieved to be rid of them, and as he returned the pad to his saddle-bag, he realized abruptly that, if those grants were valid, then Will Daniel was right. He had got a bargain. He decided that when he rejoined Jameson's column, he would buy up all the other grants that were on offer from any of the rootless drifters who wanted to sell for the price of a bottle of whisky.

Zouga had forgotten just how intense were the peculiar brooding silences of the magical Matopos hills. The silence was a thing of weight and substance that made their spirits quail. No bird twittered or danced upon a twig in the dense undergrowth that pressed in upon the narrow path, and no breeze reached into the depths of the granite-sided valleys.

The silence and the heat weighed even upon the hard and unsusceptible men who followed Zouga in single file. They rode with their rifles held across their laps, their eyes narrowed against the glare from the sparkling chips of mica in the granite walls, watchful and anxious, the dense dark green bush about them charged with a nameless menace.

At times the narrow game trails they were following pinched out or ended abruptly in the gut of a valley, and they were forced to retrace their route and try another; but always Zouga kept working south and west. Then, on the third day, he was rewarded.

He cut the broad beaten road that led from GuBulawayo to the hidden valley of the Umlimo. It was wide and smooth enough for Zouga to spur his horse into a canter. At Zouga's orders, his troopers had muffled their equipment, and put leathers over the hooves of their mounts, so the only sound was the creak of saddlery and the occasional brush and whip of an overhanging branch.

The earlier uneasiness was gone now, and they leaned forward in their saddles, eager as hunting dogs on the leash with a hot scent in their nostrils. Jameson had promised them a bonus of twenty guineas each and all the loot that they could carry away from the valley of the Umlimo.

Zouga began to recognize landmarks that he passed. There was a pile of rocks, the largest of them the size of St Paul's dome, and three others, graded down in size, all of them weathered to almost perfect spheres and balanced one upon the other, and he knew they would reach the entrance to the valley before noon. He halted the patrol and let them snatch a quick meal standing at their horses' heads as he went down the line checking their equipment and assigning each of them a separate task.

'Sergeant, you and trooper Thorn are to stay close behind me. We will be the first through the pass and into the valley. There is a small village in the centre of it, and there may be Matabele amongst the huts. Don't stop for them – even if there are warriors with them, leave them for the others. Ride straight on to the cave at the end of the valley; we must find the witch before she can escape.'

'This witch, what does she look like, skipper?'

'I am not sure, she may be quite young, probably naked.'

'You leave 'er to me, mate.' Jim Thorn grinned lasciviously and nudged Will, but Zouga ignored him.

'Any woman you find in the cave will be the witch. Now don't be put off by the sound of wild animals, or strange voices – she is a skilled ventriloquist.' He went on, giving precise details, and ended grimly: 'Our orders are harsh, but they may eventually save the lives of many of our comrades by breaking the morale of the Matabele fighting impis.'

They mounted again, and almost immediately the road began to narrow so that the branches brushed their stirrups as they passed, and Zouga's horse stumbled in a narrow stream, clumsy with the leathers over its hooves. Then he was through and he looked up the sheer granite cliff that blocked their way. The entrance to the passage through the rock was a dark vertical cleft and high above it a thatched watch-hut was perched in a niche of the granite.

As he stared up at it, Zouga saw an indistinct movement on the ledge.

'Look out above!' Even as he yelled, a dozen black men appeared on the lip of the cliff, and each of them hurled a bundle of what looked like staves out over the edge. They scattered as they fell, and the steel sparkled as the weighted heads dropped, points first, towards them. There was a fluting sound in the air all around them, soft as swallows' wings, then the rattle of steel against rock and the thud of the points into the earth beneath the hooves of the horses.

One of the steel-headed javelins caught a trooper in the side of his neck, driving down behind the collar bone, deep into one lung so that when he tried to scream the blood gagged him and bubbled out over his chin. His horse reared and whinnied wildly, and he fell backwards out of the saddle; and then all was milling, shouting confusion on the narrow track.

Through it Zouga craned to watch the ledge, and saw the defenders lining the lip again, each with another bundle of javelins on his shoulder. Zouga dropped his reins and used both hands to aim his rifle vertically upwards.

He emptied the magazine, firing as rapidly as he could pump cartridges into the breech, and though his aim was spoiled by the dancing horse under him, one of the men on the ledge arched over backwards with his arms windmilling wildly and then fell free, writhing and twisting and shrieking in the air until he hit the rock in front of Zouga's horse, and his screams and struggles ceased abruptly.

The rest of the men on the ledge scattered away, and Zouga waved the empty rifle over his head.

'Forward!' he yelled. 'Follow me!' And he plunged into the forbidding crevice that split the cliff vertically from base to crest.

The passage was so narrow that his stirrup irons struck sparks from the rock walls on each side of him, but he looked back and saw Will Daniel pounding along behind. He had lost his slouch hat. His bald head was washed with sweat, and he was grinning like a hungry hyena as he reloaded his rifle from the bandolier across his chest.

The passage turned sharply, and the white sand that floored it splashed up under the hooves, and the mica chips sparkled even in the gloom. Ahead of Zouga a tiny freshet of clear water fountained from the rock, and his horse gathered its front feet under its chest and jumped the stream easily; then suddenly they burst out from the narrow passage, back into the sunlight again.

The hidden valley of the Umlimo lay in a green basin below them, the little village of huts at its centre; and in the base of the cliff beyond it, a mile or so away, Zouga could make out the low entrance of the cavern, dark as the eye cavity in a bleached skull. It was all exactly as he remembered it.

'Troop, into line wheel!' he shouted as his horsemen galloped out into the open behind him; and they swung into extended formation, facing the valley, the rifles unsheathed and cocked, impatient and fierce as they saw before them the prize they had come so far to find.

'*Amadoda!*' shouted Will Daniel, pointing at the band of warriors that were trotting out of the village to face the line of horsemen.

'Twenty of them,' Zouga counted swiftly. 'They'll give us no trouble.' And then he stood in his stirrups. 'Walk march, forward!'

The horsemen moved down the slope, keeping their line – while the warriors lifted their shields high and raced to meet them.

'Troop, halt.' Zouga ordered when the nearest Matabele was a hundred paces ahead. 'Pick your targets.'

The first volley, carefully aimed by hard and experienced soldiers, scythed the line of charging warriors like the reaper's steel; and they went down, falling over their shields, plumes tumbling from their heads, assegais pinning harmlessly into the earth, and yet a handful of them came on without checking.

'Fire at will!' Zouga called, and looked over the sights of his rifle at a bounding Matabele, watching him grow in size with every pace, seized by a strange reluctance to kill a brave man such as this one.

'Jee! Jee!' the Matabele yelled defiantly, and raised his shield to clear his spear arm. Zouga shot him in the notch of bone at the base of his throat and the Matabele spun sharply round, hit the ground with one shoulder and rolled against the legs of Zouga's horse.

Half a dozen of the Matabele had broken in the face of those deadly volleys, and were running back towards the village. The others were strewn about in front of the line of horsemen.

'After them.' Zouga hardly raised his voice above a conversational tone. 'Forward! Charge!'

'Sergeant Daniel. Trooper Thorn, to the cave.' He swung his horse's head to gallop clear of the cluster of huts, and there was the body of one of the fallen Matabele directly in his path. He altered course again to miss it, and both Thorn and Daniel pulled a length ahead of him.

Then the Matabele rolled lithely to his feet, and dodged in front of Zouga. Playing dead was an old Zulu trick, and Zouga should have been ready for it. But his rifle was in his left hand, and he tried to get it across, at the same time trying to turn his horse and shouting an impotent challenge at the warrior.

The Matabele extended his spear arm stiffly and let the running horse impale itself upon the broad silver blade. It went deeply into the heaving chest between the front legs, and the horse reeled from the blow and then went over on its side.

Zouga barely had time to kick his feet out of the irons and jump clear before the carcass hit the earth with all four legs kicking briefly at the sky.

Zouga landed badly, but gathered himself and whirled to face the warrior. He was only just in time to deflect the blood-smeared assegai as the Matabele struck at his belly. The steel rang against the barrel of his rifle and then they were straining chest to chest.

The man smelled of woodsmoke and ochre and fat, and his body was hard as carved ebony and slippery as a freshly caught catfish. Zouga knew he could not hold him for more than a few seconds, and with one hand on the muzzle and the other on the breech, Zouga rammed the barrel of the rifle up under the man's chin into his bulging corded throat, and hooked desperately with the rowel of his spur for the ankle.

They went over backwards, Zouga on top, and he threw all his weight onto the rifle at the moment they hit the hard earth, savagely driving it into the Matabele's throat, and the neck broke with a crunch like a walnut in a silver nutcracker. The warrior's lids fluttered down over the smoky bloodshot eyes and the body went limp under Zouga's chest.

Zouga pushed himself to his feet and looked around him quickly. His troopers were amongst the huts, and there was the thudding of scattered rifle fire as they finished off the survivors of that gallant but futile charge. He saw one of his men chase a scampering old naked crone, her empty dugs swinging and her thin legs almost giving under her with terror. He rode her down, and then backed his horse up to trample her – shouting and swearing with excitement and firing down into the frail, withered body that lay crushed against the earth.

Beyond the village, Zouga saw two horses going up the slope towards the base of the cliff at full gallop, and even as he started forward, they reached it and Daniel and Thorn jumped from the saddles and disappeared into the mouth of the cavern.

It was half a mile from where Zouga had fallen to the base of the cliff. He reloaded his rifle as he ran. The fight with the Matabele had shaken him, and his riding boots hampered each step. It took him many long minutes to toil up the slope to where Daniel and Thorn had left their horses, and by then he was badly winded.

He leaned against the stone portal of the cavern, peering into the black and threatening depths, while each breath he drew jarred his whole body. Tumultuous echoes boomed out of the blackness of the cavern, the shouts of men and the bellowing and snarling of wild animals, the screams of a woman in terrible anguish and the crash of rifle fire.

Zouga pushed himself away from the cliff and stooped through the entrance. Almost immediately he stumbled over a body. It was that of an old man, his hair pure white and his skin wrinkled like a dried prune. Zouga stepped over him, into a puddle of his dark, sticky blood.

As he moved forward, Zouga's eyes accustomed to the gloom, and he peered about him at the mummified bodies of ancient dead piled haphazard against the walls of the cavern. Here and there white bone gleamed through the parchment of leathery dried flesh, and an arm was raised in a macabre salutation or a gesture of supplication.

Zouga moved on through this grisly catacomb, and ahead of him there was a diffused source of light. He quickened his pace as another gale of wild screams was this time mingled with booming inhuman laughter that bounced from the rocky walls and roof.

He turned a corner of jagged rock and looked down into a natural amphitheatre in the floor of the cavern. It was lit by the flames of a flickering orange fire, and from above by a single beam of sunlight that came in through a narrow crack in the high arched roof. The sunbeam was dimmed to an unearthly blue by the tendrils of curling smoke from the fire, and like the limelights of a theatre stage it dramatized the group of struggling figures on the floor of the amphitheatre beyond the fire.

Zouga ran down the natural steps, and had almost reached them before he realized what they were doing.

Between them Daniel and Thorn had the body of a young black girl stretched out on the rocky floor, the girl was naked, on her back with her limbs spreadeagled. Her oiled body was as glossy as the pelt of a panther, her limbs were long and shapely. She was struggling with the desperation of a wild animal in a trap. But her screams were muted by the fur kaross wrapped about her head, and Jim Thorn knelt upon her shoulders, pinning her helplessly while he twisted her arms back against the joint of the elbows and roared with cruel laughter that was too loud for his skinny body.

Will Daniel was over the girl, his face swollen and dark with congested blood. His belt and breeches were down across the back of his knees. He was grunting and snuffling like a boar at the trough. His pale buttocks were covered with a fuzz of sparse curly black hair. He drove against the girl with a wet slapping sound like a washerwoman pounding laundry on a slab.

Before Zouga could reach him, Will Daniel's whole body stiffened and jerked spasmodically and then he rolled off the tender young body, and he was bloodied from the knees to the navel of his sagging, hairy paunch.

'By God, Jim my lad,' he panted at the little trooper, 'that was better than a belly ache. Get up on the bitch for your turn—' Then he saw Zouga coming out of the shadows, and he grinned at him. 'First come, first served, Major—'

Zouga took two strides to reach him, and then he kicked him in his smiling mouth with the heel of his riding boot. Will Daniel's bottom lip split open like the petals of a rose, and he scrambled to his feet, spitting out white chips of tooth, and hauling up his breeches over his monstrous nakedness.

'I'll kill you for that.' He tugged at the knife on his dangling unclinched belt, but Zouga thrust the muzzle of his rifle into his belly, doubling him over at the waist, and then whirled to slam the butt against Jim Thorn's temple, as Thorn was reaching for his abandoned rifle.

'Get on your feet,' Zouga told him coldly, and, swaying and clutching the swelling above his ear, Jim Thorn backed off against the wall of the cave.

'I'll get you for this,' Will Daniel wheezed painfully, still holding his belly, and Zouga turned the rifle back onto him.

'Get out,' he said softly. 'Get out of here you filthy bloody animals.'

They shuffled up the steps of the amphitheatre; and from the shadows of the cavern entrance, Will Daniel yelled again, his voice blustering and angry.

'I'll not forget this, Major bloody Ballantyne. I'll get you yet!'

Zouga turned back to the girl. She had pulled the kaross off her head, and she crouched on the stone floor with her legs curled up under her. She was trying to staunch the flow of her virgin blood with her hands, but she stared at Zouga with the tortured ferocity of a leopard held by the serrated jaws of a spring trap.

Zouga felt an overwhelming compassion sweep over him – yet he knew there was no succour he could give her.

'You, who were Umlimo, are Umlimo no longer,' he said at last, and she drew back her head and spat at him. The frothy spittle splattered against his boots, but the effort made her whimper with pain and press her hands against her lower belly. A fresh trickle of bright arterial blood snaked down her thigh.

'I came to destroy the Umlimo,' he said. 'But she is destroyed not by a bullet from a gun. Go, child. The gift of the spirits has been taken from you. Go swiftly, but go in peace.'

Like a wounded animal she crept on her hands and knees into the dark maze of tunnels beyond the amphitheatre, leaving a speckle of bloody drops upon the stone floor.

She looked back at him once. 'Peace, you say, white man. There will be no peace, ever!'

And then she was gone into the shadows.

The rains had not yet come – but their heralds soared up to the heavens, great ranges of cumulus cloud, their heads shaped like mushrooms. Silver and blue and imperial purple, they stood above the Hills of the Indunas.

The heat seemed trapped beneath them. It clanged down upon the iron hills like a blacksmith's hammer on the anvil. The impis were thick as safari ants upon the slopes; they squatted in dense ranks their shields under them, their assegais and guns laid on the rocky earth before them – thousands upon thousands they waited, every plumed head craning down towards the royal kraal at the foot of the hills.

There was the beat of a single drum. Tap – tap! Tap – tap! – And the great black mass of warriors stirred like an amorphous sea monster rising from the depths.

'The Elephant comes! He comes! He comes!' It was a soft growl in all their throats.

Through the gates of the stockade filed a small procession, twenty men wearing the tassels of valour, twenty men walking proud, the blood royal of Kumalo, and at their head the huge heavy figure of the king.

Lobengula had thrown off all the European gee-gaws, the brass buttons and mirrors, the gold brocaded coat – and he was dressed in the regalia of a Matabele king.

The headring was on his brow, and heron feathers in his hair. His cloak was royal leopardskin, spotted gold, and his kilt was of leopard tails. His swollen ankles, crippled with gout, were covered by the war rattles, but he mastered the agony of the disease, striding out with ponderous dignity, so the waiting impis gasped with the splendour of his presence.

'See the Great Bull whose tread shakes the earth.'

In his right hand he carried the toy spear of polished redwood, the spear of kingship. Now he raised the puny weapon high, and the nation came bounding upright; and the shields, the long shields that gave them their name, bloomed upon the slope of the hill, covering it like a garden of exotic deadly flowers.

'*Bayete!*' The royal salute roared like the surf of a winter sea breaking on a rocky headland.

'*Bayete!* Lobengula, son of Mzilikazi.'

After that great burst of sound, the silence was daunting, but Lobengula paced slowly along the ranks, and in his eyes was the terrible sorrow of a father for the sons who must die. This was the hour which he had dreaded from the first day he took the little redwood spear in his right hand. This was the destiny which he had tried to avoid – and now it had overtaken him.

His voice boomed, and he lifted the spear and pointed to the east. 'The enemy that comes upon us now is like –' the spear shook in his hand, 'like the leopard in the goat kraal, like the white termites in the kingpost of a hut. They will not stop until all is destroyed.'

The massed regiments of Matabele growled, straining like hunting dogs against the leash, and Lobengula stopped in the centre of their lines and threw the leopardskin cloak back from his right arm.

He turned slowly until he faced into the east, where Jameson's columns were massing far over the horizon, and his spear arm went back to its full stretch. He stood poised in the classic stance of the javelin-thrower, and there was a soft susurration in the air as ten thousand lungs filled with breath and held it.

Then, with a heart-stopping shout, the cry of a man crushed under the iron wheel of his own destiny, Lobengula hurled the war spear into the east, and his shout was echoed by ten thousand throats.

'Jee! Jee!' They roared, and stabbed at the air with the broad silver blades, stabbing at the still invisible enemy.

Then the impis formed, one behind the other. Led by their indunas, their matched shields overlapping, they swept past the king, fierce in their pride, leaping high and flashing their assegais, and Lobengula saluted them: the Imbezu and the Inyati, the Ingubu and the Izimvukuzane, the 'Moles-that-burrow-under-a-mountain', with their matt red shields held high and Bazo, the Axe, prancing at their head. They wound away into the eastern grasslands, and Lobengula could still hear their singing, faintly on the heated air, long after the last of them had disappeared from view.

A little group of indunas and guards still attended the king, but they waited below at the gate of the stockade.

Lobengula was alone upon the deserted hillside; all the dignity and regal pride had gone out of his bearing. His grossly swollen body slumped like that of a very old and sick man. His eyes were rheumy with unshed tears, and he stared out into the east without moving, listening to the fading war chants.

At last he sighed, shook himself, and hobbled forward on his crippled distorted feet.

Painfully he stooped to retrieve the little redwood spear, but he paused before his fingers touched it.

The blade of the spear of kingship had snapped through. He picked up the broken pieces and held them in his hands, and then he turned and shuffled slowly down from the Hills of the Indunas.

The Company flag stood high above the laager on a slightly crooked pole of mopani.

It had hung limply in the stupefying heat all that morning, but now as the patrol rode in across the open ground above the river bank, it unfurled briefly on a random current of air, snapped as though to draw attention to itself, and then extended its full glory for a moment, before sagging wearily once again.

At the head of the patrol, Ralph Ballantyne turned to his father who rode at his side. 'That flag makes no bones about it, Papa.'

The pretty crosses of St George, St Andrew and St Patrick that made up the Union Jack, had the Company insignia superimposed upon them, the lion gardant with a tusk of ivory held in its claw and the letters under it 'B.S.A.C.' – British South Africa Company.

'Servants of the Company first, and of the queen a good deal later.'

'You're a cynical rascal, Ralph.' Zouga could hardly suppress his smile. 'Are you suggesting that there is a man in all our Company here for personal gain rather than glory of Empire?'

'Perish the thought.' This time Ralph chuckled. 'By the way, Papa, how many land grants have you bought up so far? I am losing count – is it thirty or thirty-five?'

'This is a dream I worked for all my life, Ralph. It's coming true before our eyes – and when it does, I'll have my fair reward, and nothing more.'

The laager was drawn up in its rigid square three hundred yards from the steep banks of the Shangani river, in the centre of a dried-out clay pan. The surface was as flat and bare as a tennis court. The clay had cracked into irregular briquettes that curled up at the edges. They crunched under the horses' hooves as Zouga led the patrol in.

They had been out for two days, scouting the road beyond the river, and Zouga was pleased to see that during his absence St John had taken Zouga's advice and had his axemen hack down the brush around the edges of the pan to open the field of fire. Now any attacker would have to cross three hundred yards of bare clay to reach the square of wagons, all of it under the evil little Cyclopean scrutiny of the Maxims.

As they cantered up, a party unchained the wheels of one of the wagons and dragged it aside to allow them to enter, and a sergeant in Company uniform saluted Zouga as he passed and called after him.

'General St John's compliments, sir, and will you report to him directly.'

'My bet is that you need a drink.' Mungo St John took one look at the dust that clung like flour in Zouga's beard and the dark patches of sweat that had soaked through his shirt. Coldly Zouga nodded his thanks and poured from the bottle that held down one corner of the map.

'The impis are out in full array,' he said, and let the whisky soak the cloying dust from the back of his throat before going on. 'I have identified most of them. There's Gandang's Inyati, and Manonda's Insukamini –' He reeled off the names of the indunas and their impis, glancing at the notes he had made on his pad. 'We had a brush with the 'Moles' and had to shoot our way out and ride for it, but still we reached the Bembesi river before turning back.'

'Where are the impis, Ballantyne? Damn it, man, we have advanced seventy miles from Iron Mine Hill and seen neither hide nor hair of them,' Jameson demanded almost petulantly.

'They are all around us, Doctor. A thousand or more in the trees just across the river, and I cut tracks that showed that two more impis have circled out behind us. They are probably lying across the Longiwe Hills watching every move we make.'

'We must bring them to battle,' Jameson fretted. 'Every day the campaign lasts is costing the shareholders money.'

'They won't attack us here, not while we are in laager, not across open ground.'

'Where then?'

'They will attack in the Zulu way, in broken ground, or thick bush. I have marked four likely defiles ahead of us, places where they will be able to creep up close on either side or lay to ambush the wagons as we pass.'

'You want us to walk into their trap – rather than draw them out?' Mungo asked.

'You'll not draw them out. I think their commander here is Gandang, the king's half-brother. He is far too cunning to come at us in the open. If you want to fight them, it must be in the bad ground.'

'When the serpent is coiled, with his head drawn back and his mouth agape to show the venom hanging like drops of dew upon his fangs – then the wise man does not stretch out his hands towards him.' Gandang spoke softly, and the other indunas cocked their heads to listen to his words. 'The wise man waits until the serpent uncoils and begins to creep away, then he steps upon the head and crushes it. We must wait. We must wait to take them in the forests, when the wagons are strung out, and the outriders cannot see one another. Then we cut the column into pieces and swallow each one, a mouthful at a time.'

'Yet my young men are tired of waiting,' said Manonda, facing Gandang across the fire. Manonda was the commander of the elite Insukamini impi, and though there was silver on his head, there was still fire in his heart. They all knew him to be brave to the edge of folly, quick to take an insult, and quicker still to revenge it. 'These white barbarians have marched unopposed across our lands, while we trail around them like timid girls guarding our maidenheads and giggling behind our hands. My young men grow weary of waiting, Gandang, and I with them.'

'There is a time for timidity, Manonda, my cousin, and there is a time to be brave.'

'The time to be brave is when your enemy stands brazenly before you. They are six hundred, you have counted them yourself, Gandang, and we are six thousand.' Manonda grinned mockingly around the circle of listening men. On the brow of each was the headring of high office, and on their arms and legs the tassels of courage. 'Shame on those that hesitate,' said Manonda, the Bold. 'Shame on you, Bazo. Shame on you, Ntabene. Shame on you, Gambo.' His voice was filled with scorn, and as he said each of their names they hissed with angry denial.

Then suddenly there was a sound from beyond the circle of squatting indunas, a sound in the night that chilled and silenced them all. It was the eerie wail of mourning for the dead, and as they listened it came closer, and with it were many other voices.

Gandang sprang to his feet and challenged loudly. 'Who comes?'

And out of the darkness a dozen guards, half dragged and half carried an old woman. She wore only a skirt of untanned hyena skin, and around her neck the grisly accoutrements and trappings of the witch's trade. Her eyes were rolled up into her head so that the whites flashed in the firelight, and her spittle foamed on her slack lips. From her throat issued the wails of mourning for the dead.

'What is it, witch?' Gandang demanded, his superstitious fears twisting his mouth and darkening his eyes. 'What tidings do you bring?'

'The white men have desecrated the holy places. They have destroyed the chosen one of the spirits. They have slaughtered the priests of the nation. They have entered the cave of the Umlimo in the sacred hills – and her blood is splashed upon the ancient rocks. Woe unto all of us. Woe unto those who do not seek revenge. Kill the white men. Kill them all!'

The witch threw off the restraining hands of the guard and, with a wild shriek, hurled herself into the midst of the leaping flames of the watch-fire.

Her skirt burst into flames. Her wild bush of hair burned like a torch. They drew back in horror.

'Kill the white men,' screamed the witch from out of the flames, and they stared as her skin blackened and her flesh peeled from off her bones. She collapsed and a torrent of sparks flew up into the overhanging branches of the forest, and then there was only the crackle and drum of the fire.

Bazo stood in the stunned silence, and he felt the rage rising from deep within his soul. Staring into the flames at the black and twisted remains of the witch, he felt the same need of sacrifice – an atonement and a surcease from the rage and the grief.

He saw in the yellow flames an image of Tanase's beloved face, and something seemed to tear in his chest.

'Jee!' he said, drawing out the war cry, giving expression to his rage. 'Jee!' He lifted the assegai and pointed the blade in the direction of the river and the white men's laager which lay not more than a mile beyond the dark silhouette of the hills. 'Jee!' and the night breeze turned the tears cold as the snow-melt from the Drakensberg mountains upon his cheeks.

'Jee.' Manonda took up the chant, and stabbed towards the enemy, and the divine madness descended upon them. Gandang was the only one who had reason and fear of consequence left to him.

'Wait!' he cried. 'Wait, my children and my brothers.' But they were gone already, racing away into the darkness to rouse their sleeping impis.

*

345

Zouga Ballantyne could not sleep, though his back and thighs still ached for rest from hard riding, and the earth under his blanket was no harder than that on which he had passed a thousand other nights. He lay and listened to the snores and occasional dreamers' gabble from the men around him, while vague forebodings and dark thoughts kept him from joining them in slumber.

Once again vivid memories of the little tragedy in the cave of the Umlimo returned to plague him – and he wondered how long it would be before the news of the atrocity reached the king and his indunas. It might take weeks for a witness to come down from the cave of the Matopos, but when that happened, he would know it by the actions of the Matabele indunas.

From the opposite side of the laager a sky-rocket went hissing up into the night sky, and popped into little red stars high in the heavens. The pickets had been firing a rocket every hour, to guide a missing patrol into the laager.

Now Zouga reached under the saddle that was his pillow and brought out the gold hunter watch. In the light of the sky-rocket he checked the time. It was three o'clock in the morning. He threw off his blanket, and groped for his boots. While he pulled them on, his premonition of lurking evil grew stronger.

He strapped on his bandolier and checked the Webley service revolver hanging on the webbing. Then he stepped over the sleeping blanket-wrapped forms around him and went down to the horse lines. The bay gelding whickered as it recognized him, and Jan Cheroot woke.

'It is all right,' Zouga told him quietly, but the little Hottentot yawned and, with the blanket over his shoulders like a shawl, hobbled across to stir the ashes of his cooking-fire. He set the blue enamel coffee pot on the coals and, while it was heating, they sat side by side and talked quietly like the old friends that they were.

'Less than sixty miles to GuBulawayo,' Jan Cheroot murmured. 'It's taken us more than thirty years – but now at last I feel we are coming home.'

'I have bought up almost forty land grants,' Zouga agreed. 'That is nearly a quarter of a million acres. Yes, Jan Cheroot, we are coming home at last. By God, it's been a long, hard road, though, from the pit of Kimberley mine to the Zambezi –' Zouga broke off and listened. There had been a faint cry, almost like a night bird, from beyond the laager.

'The Mashona,' Jan Cheroot grunted. 'The general should have let them stay in the laager.'

During the slow trek up from Iron Mine Hill, many small groups of Mashona had come to the wagons, begging protection from the assembling Matabele. They knew from bitter experience what to expect when the impis swept across the land in battle array.

'The general could not take that chance.' Zouga shook his head. 'There may be Matabele spies amongst them, he has to guard against treachery.'

Mungo St John had ordered the refugees to keep clear of the laager, and now there were three or four hundred, mostly black women and children, camped amongst the thorn trees on the riverbank, five hundred yards from the nearest wagon.

Zouga lifted the coffee pot from the coals and poured the steaming black brew into his mug, then he cocked his head again to listen. There was a faint hubbub, a distant chorus of shrieks and shouts from the direction of the river. With the mug in his hand Zouga strolled across to the nearest wagon in the square, and climbed up onto the disselboom. He peered out of the laager, towards the river.

The open expanse of flat clay was ghostly pale in the starlight, and the treeline beyond it was solid blackness. There was nothing to be seen – except – he blinked his eyes rapidly, for they were playing him false. Nothing, except the blackness of the treeline seemed to be closer, the blackness was spreading towards the laager across the pale clay, like spilled oil or a pool of blood.

Now there was a sound, a rustle like locust wings when the swarms pass overhead, and the engulfing blackness was coming closer, with eerie swiftness.

At that moment another sky-rocket went swooshing up into the night sky, and when it burst, it flooded the pan with a soft, pink light and Zouga dropped the mug of steaming coffee.

The earth was black with the Matabele horde. It swept like a black tide towards the wagons, rank upon rank of great oval shields, and the assegais twinkled in the reflection of the rocket flare.

Zouga pulled the pistol from its holster, and fired towards the racing black wall of shields.

'Stand to your guns,' he bellowed, the heavy revolver bouncing and crashing in his fist. 'The Matabele are coming! Stand to your guns.' And from the black tide swelled a sound like a swarm of bees when the hive is overturned.

The hammer of Zouga's revolver clicked on a spent cartridge, and he jumped down from the disselboom and raced down the line of wagons to where the nearest Maxim was emplaced.

Throughout the laager there was a rush of bodies and the shouts of frightened men running to their posts, and as Zouga reached the corner of the square, the machine-gunner came stumbling out from his bed under a wagon body. His face was a pale blob, and his hair was hanging into his eyes. He was in stockinged feet and his braces dangled down his legs as he hitched his breeches and plumped himself down on the little seat that was built onto the rear leg of the Maxim tripod.

His number two loader was nowhere to be seen, perhaps lost in the milling con-fusion of newly-awakened bodies, so Zouga stuffed the revolver into his belt and dropped upon his knees beside the ungainly weapon. He yanked the top off the ammunition box and lifted out the first length of the canvas belt.

'Good-oh, mate!' muttered the gunner, as Zouga lifted the shutter in the side of the breech and passed the brass tag loader of the belt through the block.

'Ready! Load one!' he snapped, and the gunner jerked back the crank handle on the opposite side of the block and let it fly home, and the gib at the top of the extractor gripped the first round.

The spears were drumming on the rawhide shields now, and the deep humming chorus of the running warriors was almost deafening. They could only be yards from the barricade of wagons, but Zouga did not look up. He concentrated all his attention on the intricate task of loading the Maxim.

'Load two!' The gunner cranked again, and the feed block clattered. Zouga jerked the brass tag leader and the gunner let the handle fly back the second time. The first round shot smoothly into the breech.

'Loaded and cocked!' Zouga said, and tapped the gunner on the shoulder. Now they both looked up. The front rank of shields and war plumes seemed to curl over where they squatted beside the weapon, like a wave breaking on a beach.

It was the moment of the 'closing in' that the *amadoda* loved and lived for, already the shields were going up on high to free the spear arms and the steel rasped as the blades were cleared for the stabbing.

The joyous roar of the killing chant sundered the night; they were at the wagons, breaking into the laager, and the gunner sat stiffly upright with the gun between his knees and both hands on the traversing handles. He hooked his fingers through the rings of the safety guard, and as it lifted, he pressed his thumbs down on the chequered firing button.

The muzzle was almost touching the belly of a tall plumed warrior coming in between the wagons when the thick barrel shuddered, and a bright bar of flickering light sprang from the muzzle and the hammering clatter dinned upon Zouga's eardrums. It sounded as though a giant was drawing a steel bar horizontally across a sheet of corrugated iron, and miraculously the warrior was blown away.

The gunner traversed the Maxim back and forth, like a meticulous housewife sweeping a dusty floor, and the continuous muzzle flashes lit the open clay pan with a dancing unearthly light.

The black tide of Matabele was no longer advancing; it stood static in front of the wagons; and though its crest foamed with dancing plumes and the shields that formed the body of the wave heaved and clattered and tumbled, they came no closer. They were dammed by the stroking, flickering bar of light that sprang from the Maxim gun. The solid stream of bullets played like a jet of water from a firehose upon them, and as each of the chanting warriors came racing up, he died on the same spot as the man in front of him had died, and he fell upon his corpse, while another warrior appeared in the space he had left, and the gun swung back, hammering and jerking, and that man went down, his shield clattering on the baked clay of the pan and the flash of the gun reflected from the burnished steel of his assegai as it went spinning from his nerveless hand.

All around the square the Maxims ripped and roared, and six hundred repeating rifles underscored that hellish chorus. The air was blue with gunsmoke, and the reek of cordite burned the throats of the troopers and made their eyes run, so that they seemed to be weeping for the terrible butchery in which they were engaged.

Still the Matabele came on, though now they had to clamber over a shapeless barricade of their own dead, and the gunner beside Zouga lifted his thumbs from the button trigger and twirled the elevation wheel of the Maxim, lifting the muzzle an inch so as to keep the fire on the belly line of the warriors as they climbed over the mounds of corpses.

Then once again the gun fluttered and roared, the glossy black bodies jerked and twitched and bucked as the stream of bullets tore into them.

Still the Matabele came on.

'By God, will they never stop!' yelled the gunner. The muzzle of the gun glowed cherry red, like a horseshoe fresh from the forge, and the steam from the water jacket whistled shrilly as the coolant boiled. The bright brass cases spewed from the extractor; they pinged and pattered against the iron-shod wheel of the wagon and formed a glittering mound beneath it.

'Empty gun!' Zouga yelled, as the end of the belt whipped into the clattering breech. They had been firing for less than sixty seconds, and the case of five hundred belted cartridges was empty.

Zouga kicked it aside and dragged up a fresh case, and the Matabele surged towards the silent gun.

'Ready, load one!' Zouga yelled.

'Load two!' They were swarming into the gap between the wagons.

'Loaded and cocked!' And once again that fluttering beat like the wings of a dark angel dulled their senses, and the barrel swung back and forth, back and forth, washing them away into the darkness.

'They're running,' shouted the gunner. 'Look at them run!'

In front of the wagons lay nothing but the piles of bodies. Here and there a dying man made feeble little movements, groping for a lost assegai or trying to staunch one of the awful holes in his flesh with fumbling fingers.

Beyond the massed corpses, the wounded and maimed were dragging themselves back towards the treeline, leaving dark wet smears on the clay. One of them was on his feet, staggering in aimless circles, using both hands to hold his bulging entrails from falling out of the open pouch of his belly. The Maxim had gutted him like a fish.

Beyond the trees the sky was a marvellous shade of ashes of roses, and the clouds were picked out in smoking scarlets and pipings of pale gold as the dawn came up in silent fury over the reeking field.

'Them black bastards have had enough.' The Maxim gunner giggled with mirthless, nervous reaction to that glimpse that he had just had into hell itself.

'They'll be back,' said Zouga quietly, as he dragged up another case of belted ammunition and knocked off the lid.

'You did all right, mate,' the gunner giggled again, staring with wide horrified eyes at the piles of dead.

'Refill the water in your condenser, soldier,' Zouga ordered him. 'The gun's overheating, you'll have a jam when the next wave hits.'

'Sir!' The gunner realized suddenly who Zouga was. 'Sorry, sir.'

'Here is your loader.' The number two came up breathlessly. He was a fresh-faced lad, curly-headed and pink-cheeked. He looked more like a choirboy than a machine-gunner.

'Where were you, trooper?' Zouga demanded.

'Checking the horses, sir. It was all over so quickly.'

'Listen!' Zouga ordered, as the boy took his place at the gun.

From the treeline, across the bloodied clay pan, came the sound of singing – deep and sonorous in the dawn. It was the praise song of the 'Moles-who-burrow-under-a-mountain'.

'Stand to your gun, trooper,' Zouga ordered. 'It's not over yet.' And he turned on his heel and went striding down the line of wagons, reloading the revolver from his belt as he went.

*

Singing, Bazo strode down the squatting lines of his impi, and they sang with him.

He had held their shattered ranks just beyond the edge of the treeline as they came streaming back from the square of wagons. They were re-grouped now, singing as they screwed their courage for the next assault. What remained of Manonda's impi was mingled with his. They had been in the first wave of the attack, and very few of them were left.

Suddenly there was a great rushing sound in the air above the treetops, like the onrush of the first wild storm of summer. Then in the midst of the squatting ranks a tall column of smoke and dust and flame sprang into the air, and the bodies of men were flung high with it.

'Kill the smoke devil,' somebody screamed, and another shell burst amongst them, and another, leaping fountains of smoke and flame; and the maddened warriors fired their ancient Martini-Henry rifles at these smoke devils, killing and wounding their comrades on the far side.

'They are not devils,' shouted Bazo, but his voice was lost in the barrage of artillery fire, and the pandemonium of warriors trying to defend themselves against something they did not understand.

'Come!' Bazo bellowed. There was only one way to bring them under control again. 'To the wagons. Forward to the wagons.'And those close enough to hear him followed, and the others, seeing them go, went bounding after them. They came out of the treeline in a swarm, and the other shattered impis heard the war chant go up, and turned again back onto the open pan of pale grey clay – and immediately that terrible clattering din, like the laughter of maniacs, began again and the air was filled with the flute and crack of a thousand whiplashes.

'They are coming again,' Zouga said quietly, almost to himself. 'This is the fifth time.'

'It's madness.' Mungo St John murmured, as the racing ranks came out of the trees and over the lip of the riverbank, their plumes seething like the surface of boiling milk as they came onto the guns.

The field guns were depressed to the limit of their travel, the fuses screwed down to their shortest range, and the shrapnel bursts were strangely beautiful in the morning sky, popping open like pods of new cotton, shot through with pretty red fire.

The storm of small-arms fire was like the monsoon rains beating on an iron roof, and as the impis came into the drifting banks of gunsmoke, the dense ranks thinned out, and lost momentum, like a wave sliding up a steep beach.

Once again the wave faltered, and just short of the wagons it stopped, hesitated and then was going back, and the storm of gunfire continued long after the last of them had disappeared amongst the trees. In a kind of insensate fury the Maxim bullets tore wet white slabs of bark off the tree trunks, and then one after the other fell silent.

Standing beside Zouga, Dr Jameson scrubbed his hands together gleefully. 'It's all over. Their impis are destroyed, shattered, blown away. It's better than we could ever have hoped for. Tell me, St John, as a military man, what do you estimate their losses to be so far?'

Mungo St John considered the question seriously, climbing up onto one of the wagons the better to survey the field, ignoring the spattering of Martini-Henry rifle fire from the edge of the treeline where a few Matabele snipers were making very poor practice; convinced that raising their sights to the maximum made the bullets more powerful, most of their fire crackled high over the heads of the men manning the wagons.

Standing on the wagon Mungo St John lit a cheroot without transferring his attention from the carnage which surrounded them. At last he said gravely, 'Not less than two thousand casualties – perhaps as many as three.'

'Why don't you send a party out to count the bag, Doctor?' Zouga suggested, and Jameson did not recognize the sarcasm.

'We cannot spare the delay – more is the pity. We can still get in a full day's trek. That will look good in the Company report.' He pulled the gold chain from his fob pocket and sprang the lid of his watch with his thumbnail. 'Eight o'clock,' he marvelled. 'It's only eight o'clock in the morning. Do you realize that we have won a decisive battle before breakfast, gentlemen, and that by ten o'clock we can be on our way to Lobengula's royal kraal? I think we have done our shareholders rather proud.'

'I think,' Zouga cut in gently. 'That we still have a little more work to do. They are coming again.'

'I don't believe this,' Mungo St John marvelled.

Bazo paced slowly down the sparse ranks. This was no longer an impi. It was a pathetic little band of desperate survivors. Most of them had bound up their wounds with bloody bunches of green leaves, and their eyes had that strange fixed stare of men who had just looked into eternity. They were no longer singing, they squatted in silence – but they were still facing towards the white men's laager.

Bazo passed beyond the shortened line and paused under the spreading branches of a wild teak tree. He looked up.

Manonda, the commander of what had once been the glorious Insukamini impi, hung by his neck from one of the main branches. There was a thong of rawhide around his throat, and his eyes were still open, bulging in a defiant glare towards his enemies. His right leg, shattered above the knee by machine-gun fire, was twisted at an ugly angle and hung lower than his other leg.

Bazo lifted his assegai in a salute to the dead induna.

'I greet you, Manonda, who chose death rather than to drink the bitter draught of defeat,' he shouted.

The Insukamini impi was no more. Its warriors lay in deep windrows in front of the wagons.

'I praise you, Manonda, who chose death rather than to live a cripple and a slave. Go in peace, Manonda – and speak sweetly to the spirits on our behalf.'

Bazo turned back and stood before the waiting, silent ranks. The early morning sun, just clearing the treetops, threw long black shadows in front of them.

'Are the eyes still red, my children?' Bazo sang out in a high clear voice.

'They are still red, Baba!' they answered him in bass chorus.

'Then let us go to do the work which still waits to be done.'

Where ten *amadoda* had raced in that first wave, now two made the last charge across the blood-soaked clay. Only one of that pitiful band went more than halfway between the treelines and the wagons. The rest of them turned back and left Bazo to run on alone. He was sobbing with each stride, his mouth open, the sweat running in oily snakes down his naked chest. He did not feel the first bullet that struck him. It was just a sudden numbness as though part of his body was missing, and he ran on, jumping over a pile of twisted corpses, and now the sound of the guns seemed muted and far-off, and there was another greater dinning in his ears that boomed and echoed strangely like the thunder of a mighty waterfall.

He felt another sharp tug, like the curved red-tipped thorn of the 'wait-a-bit' tree hooking into his flesh, but there was no pain. The roaring in his head was louder, and his vision narrowed so that he seemed to be looking down a long tunnel in the darkness.

Again he felt that irritating but painless jerk and tug in his flesh, and he was suddenly weary. He just wanted to lie down and rest, but he kept on towards the flashing white canvas of the wagon tents. Yet again that sharp insistent pull as though he was held on a leash, and his legs buckled under him. Quite gently he toppled forward and lay with his face against the hard sun-baked clay.

The sound of the guns had ceased, but in its place was another sound, it was the sound of cheering; behind the wall of wagons the white men were cheering themselves.

Bazo was tired, so utterly deathly tired. He closed his eyes and let the darkness come.

The wind had swung suddenly and unseasonably into the east, and there was a cold dank mist lying on the hills. the fine *guti* which made the trees drip dismally and chilled every bone in Tanase's body as she trudged up a narrow path that led to a saddle between two pearly grey granite peaks. Over her shoulders was a leather cloak and on her head she balanced a bundle of possessions which she had salvaged from the cave of the Umlimo.

She reached the saddle and looked down into yet another valley choked with dense, dark green undergrowth. She searched it eagerly, but then her spirits slowly fell again. Like all the others, it was devoid of any human presence.

Since she had left the secret valley, the moon had reached its full, and waned to nothingness, and was once again a curved yellow sliver in the night sky. All that time she had searched for the women and children of the Matabele nation. She knew they were here, hiding somewhere in the Matopos, for it was always the way. When a powerful enemy threatened the nation, the women and children were sent into the hills – but it was such a vast area, so many valleys and deep labyrinthine caves that she might search a lifetime without finding them.

Tanase started slowly down into the deserted valley. Her legs felt leaden, and another spasm of nausea brought saliva flooding from under her tongue. She swallowed it down, but when she reached the floor of the valley, she sank down onto a moss-covered rock beside the little stream.

She knew what was the cause of her malady; though she had missed her courses by only a few days, she knew that the loathsome seed that her pale, hairy, balloon-bellied ravisher had pumped into her had struck and taken hold, and she knew what she must do.

She laid aside her load and searched for dry kindling under the trees where the *guti* had not yet dampened it. She piled it in the protected lee of a sheltering rock, and crouched over it.

For many long minutes she concentrated all her will upon it. Then at last she sighed, and her shoulders slumped. Even this minor power, this small magic of fire-making, had gone from her. As the white man with the golden beard had warned her, she was Umlimo no longer. She was just a young woman, without strange gifts or terrible duties, and she was free. The spirits could make no demands upon her, she was free at last to seek out the man she loved.

As she prepared to make fire in the conventional manner, with the tiny bow for twirling the dry twig, two passions gave her strength to face the ordeal ahead of her – her love and her equally fierce hatred.

When the contents of the little clay pot boiled, she added the shreds of dried bark of the tambooti to it, and immediately the sweet odour of the poisonous steam cloyed upon the back of her throat.

The straight sharp black horn of the gemsbuck had been clipped off at the tip so that it could be used for cupping blood, or as a funnel for introducing fluids into the body.

Tanase spread the leather cloak below the rock shelter and lay on it, flat upon her back, with her feet braced high against rough granite. She had lubricated the horn with fat, and she took a deep breath, clenched her jaw upon it, and then slid the horn into herself. When it met resistance, she manipulated it carefully, but firmly, and then her breath burst from her in a gasp of agony as the point found the opening and forced its way still farther into her secret depths.

The pain gave her a strange unholy joy, as though she were inflicting it upon the hated thing that had taken root within her. She lifted herself on one elbow, and tested the contents of the little clay pot. It was just cool enough for her to be able to bear the heat when she plunged her forefinger into it.

She took up the pot and poured it into the mouth of the long black funnel, and this time she moaned, and her back arched involuntarily, but she poured until the pot was empty. There was the coppery salt taste of blood in her mouth, and she realized that she had bitten through her own lip. She seized the horn and plucked it out of herself, and then she curled up on the leather cloak and hugged her knees to her bosom, shuddering and moaning at the fire in her womb.

In the night the first terrible cramps seized her, and she felt her belly muscles spasm up hard as a cannon ball under her clutching hands.

She wished there had been something formed, a tiny replica of that white animal that had rutted upon her, so that she could have wreaked a form of vengeance upon it. She would have delighted in mutilating and burning it, but there was nothing substantial on which to expend her hatred. So despite the purging of her body, she carried her hatred with her still, fierce and unabated, as she toiled on deeper and deeper into the Matopos.

*

The joyful cries and sweet laughter of children at play guided her, and Tanase crept along the river verge, using the tall cotton-tipped reeds as a screen until she overlooked the green pool between its sugary sandbanks. They were girls sent to fetch water. The big, black clay pots stood in a row on the white sand with green leaves stuffed in the mouths to stop them slopping over when carried balanced on the girls' heads.

However, once the pots were filled, they had not been able to resist the temptation of the cool, green waters, and they had thrown off their skirts and were shrieking and sporting in the pool. The eldest girls were pubescent with swelling breast buds, and one of them spotted Tanase in the reeds and screamed a warning.

Tanase was just able to catch the youngest and slowest child as she was disappearing over the far bank, and she held the wriggling little body, glossy black and wet from the river, against her bosom while the child wailed and struggled with terror.

Tanase cooed reassurances and stroked the little girl with gentling hands until she quietened.

'I am of the people,' she whispered. 'Don't be afraid, little one.'

Half an hour later the child was chattering gaily and leading Tanase by the hand.

The mothers came swarming out of the caves at the head of the valley to greet Tanase, and they crowded about her.

'Is it true that there have been two great battles?' they begged her.

'We have heard that the impis were broken at Shangani and again those that remained were butchered like cattle on the banks of the Bembesi?'

'Our husbands and our sons are dead – please tell us it is not so,' they pleaded.

'They say the king has fled from his royal kraal, and that we are children without a father. Is it true, can you tell us if it is true?'

'I know nothing,' Tanase told them. 'I come to hear news, not to bear it. Is there not one amongst you who can tell me where I may find Juba, senior wife of Gandang, brother of the king?'

They pointed over the hills, and Tanase went on, and found another group of women hiding in the thick bush. These children did not laugh and play, their limbs were thin as sticks, but their bellies were swollen little pots.

'There is no food,' the women told Tanase. 'Soon we will starve.' And they sent her stumbling back northwards, seeking and questioning, trying to blind herself to the agonies of a defeated nation, until one day she stooped in through the entrance of a dim and smoky cave, and a vaguely familiar figure rose to greet her.

'Tanase, my child, my daughter.'

Only then did Tanase recognize her, for the abundant flesh had melted off the woman's frame and her once bounteous breasts hung slack as empty pouches against her belly.

'Juba, my mother,' Tanase cried, and ran into her embrace. It was a long time after that before she could speak through her sobs.

'Oh my mother, do you know what has become of Bazo?'

Juba pushed her gently to arm's length and looked into her face. When Tanase saw the devastating sorrow in Juba's eyes, she cried out with dread.

'He is not dead!'

'Come, my daughter,' Juba whispered, and led her deeper into the cave, along a natural passageway through the living rock – and there was a graveyard smell on the cool dark air, the odour of corruption and rotting flesh.

The second cavern was lit only by a burning wick floating in a bowl of oil. There was a litter against the far wall. On it lay a wasted skeletal body, and the smell of death was overpowering.

Fearfully Tanase knelt beside the litter and lifted a bunch of leaves off one of the stinking wounds.

'He is not dead,' Tanase repeated. 'Bazo is not dead.'

'Not yet,' agreed Juba. 'His father and those of his men who survived the white men's bullets, carried my son to me on his shield. They bid me save him – but nobody can save him.'

'He will not die,' said Tanase fiercely. 'I will not let him die.' And she leaned over his wasted body and pressed her lips to the fever-hot flesh. 'I will not let you die,' she whispered.

The Hills of the Indunas were deserted; no beast grazed upon them for the herds had long ago been driven afar to try to save them from the invaders. There were no vultures or crows sailing high above the hills, for the Maxim guns had laid a richer feast for them barely twenty-five miles eastwards at the Bembesi crossing.

The royal kraal of GuBulawayo was almost deserted. The women's quarters were silent. No child cried, no young girl sang, no crone scolded. They were all hiding in the magical Matopos hills.

The barracks of the fighting regiments were deserted. Two thousand dead on the Shangani, three thousand more at Bembesi – and nobody would ever count those who had crawled away to die like animals in the caves and thickets.

The survivors had scattered, some to join the women in the hills, the others to cower, bewildered and demoralized, wherever they could find shelter.

Of all the fighting impis of Matabele, only one remained intact, the Inyati regiment of Induna Gandang, the king's half-brother. Gandang alone had been able to resist the madness of hurling his men over open ground at the waiting Maxim guns, and now he waited for his king's orders in the hills just north of the royal kraal with his impi gathered about him.

In all of GuBulawayo, there was one small group remaining. Twenty-six of these were white men and women. They were the traders and concession-hunters who had been at the kraal when Jameson had marched from Iron Mine Hill. With them, were the Codrington family, Clinton and Robyn and the twins. Lobengula had ordered them all to remain under his protection, while the impis were out in battle array, and now he had called them to the goat kraal for his last audience.

Drawn up before the two new brick-built houses which had replaced the great thatched hut, were Lobengula's four Cape wagons with the teams already in the traces.

About the wagons were a small party of the royal retainers: two of the king's senior wives, four elderly indunas, and a dozen or so slaves and servants.

The king himself sat on the box of the leading wagon. In that wagon were all Lobengula's treasures, a hundred big tusks of ivory, the little sealed pots of uncut diamonds, and the canvas bags stencilled with the name 'The Standard Bank Ltd' containing the sovereigns paid to him during the four years since he had granted the concession to the British South Africa Company, four thousand sovereigns, less than a sovereign for every one of his dead warriors.

Around the wagon were gathered the white men, and Lobengula looked down upon them. The king had become an old man in the few short weeks since he had thrown the war spear on the Hills of the Indunas. There were deep lines of sorrow and despair carved around his mouth and eyes. His eyes were rheumy and shortsighted, his hair bleached silver-grey, his body bloated and misshapen, and his breathing was racked and irregular like that of a dying animal.

'Tell your queen, white men, that Lobengula kept his word. Not one of you has been harmed,' he wheezed. 'Daketela and his soldiers will be here tomorrow. If you go out upon the eastern road, you will even meet them before nightfall.' Lobengula paused to catch his breath, and then went on. 'Go now. There is nothing more I have to say to you.'

They were silent, subdued, and strangely chastened, as they trooped out of the goat kraal. Only Robyn and her family remained.

The twins stood on each side of Robyn. At twenty-one years of age, they were as tall as she. It seemed that the three of them were sisters – for they all had the clear eyes and glossy hair of healthy young women.

Clinton Codrington, standing behind them, stooped and bald, dressed in sober broadcloth that was mossy green with age and shiny at the cuffs and elbows, seemed father to Robyn as well as to the twins.

The king looked down upon them with a terrible regret.

'It is the last time that you will make my eyes glad, Nomusa,' he said.

'Oh King, my heart is on fire for you. I think of what has happened and how I advised you.'

Lobengula held up his hand to silence her. 'Do not torture yourself, Nomusa. You have been a true friend of many years, and what you did was done in friendship. Nothing you or I could have done would have changed the manner of it. It was the prophecy; it was as certain as the fall of the leaves from the msasa trees when the frosts are on the hills.'

Robyn ran forward to the wagon, and Lobengula stooped to take her hand.

'Pray to your three gods that are one god for me, Nomusa.'

'He will hear you, Lobengula, you are a good man.'

'No man is all goodness or all evil,' the king sighed. 'Now, Nomusa, soon Daketela and his soldiers will be here. Tell him that Lobengula says thus. "I am beaten, white men, my impis are eaten up. Let me go now, do not hunt me further, for I am an old sick man. I wish only to find a place where I may mourn my people – and at last die in peace." '

'I will tell them, Lobengula.'

'And will they listen, Nomusa?'

She could not face him, and she dropped her eyes. 'You know they will not listen.'

'My poor people,' whispered Lobengula. 'Will you look after my poor people when I am gone, Nomusa?'

'I swear it to you, oh King,' Robyn said fiercely. 'I will stay at Khami Mission until the day that I die, and I will devote my life to your people.'

Then Lobengula smiled, and once again there was a flash of the old mischievous twinkle in his eye.

'I give you the royal permission which I denied you all these years, Nomusa. From this day forward any of my people – man or woman or child of Matabele who wish it of you – you may pour water on their heads and make the cross of your three gods over them.'

Robyn could not reply.

'Stay in peace, Nomusa,' said Lobengula, and his wagon rumbled slowly out through the gates of the stockade.

Clinton Codrington reined in the mule on the crest of the rise above the royal kraal, and he groped for Robyn's hand. They sat silently on the seat of the little Scotch cart, watching the last pale shreds of dust thrown up by the king's wagons disappearing away in the north across the grassy plain.

'They will never leave him in peace,'Robyn said softly.

'Lobengula is the prize,' Clinton agreed. 'Without him, Jameson and Rhodes will have no victory.'

'What will they do with him?' she asked sadly. 'If they catch him.'

'Exile, certainly,' Clinton said. 'St Helena Island, probably. It's where they sent Cetewayo.'

'Poor tragic man,' Robyn whispered. 'Caught between two ages, half savage and half civilized man, half cruel despot and half a shy and sensitive dreamer. Poor Lobengula.'

'Do look, Papa!' Vicky called suddenly, pointing down the rude track towards the east. There was a thick column of dust rising above the tops of the thorn trees, and even as they watched, a distant troop of mounted men rode out onto the grassy plain with badges and weapons twinkling in the sunlight.

'Soldiers,' whispered Lizzie.

'Soldiers,' repeated Vicky gleefully. 'Hundreds of them.' And the twins exchanged a bright ecstatic glance of complete understanding and accord.

Clinton picked up the reins – but Robyn tightened her grip on his hand to restrain him.

'Wait,' she said. 'I want to watch it happen. Somehow it will be the end of an age, the end of a cruel but innocent age.'

Lobengula had left one of his trusted indunas in the royal kraal, with instructions to lay fire to the train as soon as the last wagons were clear. In the mud-brick building behind the king's new residence were the remains of the hundred thousand rounds of Martini-Henry ammunition for which he had sold his land and his people. There were also twenty barrels of black powder.

'There!' said Robyn, as the pillar of black smoke and flame shot hundreds of feet straight up into the still air.

Only many seconds later did the shock wave and the great clap of sound pass over where they watched from the ridge, and the smoke, still spinning upon itself, blossomed into an anvil head high above the shattered kraal.

Lobengula's house that had given him such pleasure and pride was only a shell, the roof blown away and the walls fallen in.

The beehive huts of the women's quarters were ablaze, and even as they watched, the flames jumped the stockade and caught in the roofs beyond. Within minutes the whole of GuBulawayo was in leaping, swirling flames.

'Now we can go on,' Robyn said quietly, and Clinton shook up the mule.

There were thirty horsemen in the advance scouting party – and as they galloped up, the tall straight figure leading them was unmistakable.

'Thank God that you are safe!' Zouga called to them. He was handsome and heroic in the frogged uniform with his brass badges of rank ablaze in the sunlight, and the slouch hat cocked forward over his handsome, gravely concerned features.

'We were never in any danger,' Robyn told him. 'And well you knew that.'

'Where is Lobengula?' Zouga sought to divert her scorn, but she shook her head.

'I am guilty of one act of treachery against Lobengula –'

'You are an Englishwoman,' Zouga reminded her. 'You should know where your loyalties lie.'

'Yes, I am an Englishwoman,' she agreed icily, 'but I am ashamed of that today. I will not tell you where the king is.'

'As you wish.' Zouga looked at Clinton. 'You know that it is for the good of every one in this land. Until we have Lobengula, there will be no peace.'

Clinton bowed his bald head. 'The king has gone to the north with his wagons and wives and the Inyati regiment.'

'Thank you,' Zouga nodded. 'I will send an escort with you to the main column. They are not far behind us. Sergeant!'

A young trooper with triple chevrons on his sleeve spurred forward. He was a fine-looking lad, with high English colour in his cheeks and broad shoulders.

'Sergeant Acutt. Take the six men from the rear three files and see this party to safety.'

Zouga saluted his sister and brother-in-law curtly and then ordered. 'Troop, at the gallop. Forward!'

The first two dozen troopers went clattering away towards GuBulawayo, while the sergeant and his six men wheeled in alongside the cart.

Vicky turned her head and looked directly into the young sergeant's eyes. She took a long slow breath that pushed her bosom out under the faded cotton of her blouse. The sergeant stared, and the flush of dark blood rose from the high stock of his tunic and suffused his cheeks.

Vicky wetted her pouting lips with the tip of a pink tongue, and slanted her eyes at him – and Sergeant Acutt seemed about to fall out of the saddle, for Vicky's gaze had struck him from a range of less than six feet.

'Victoria!' Robyn snapped sharply, without looking back over her shoulder.

'Yes, Mama.' Hurriedly, Vicky slumped her shoulders forward to alter the cheeky thrust of her bosom to a more demure angle, and composed her expression into dutiful gravity.

*

TELEGRAM MESSAGE RECEIVED FORT VICTORIA 10TH NOVEMBER 1893 RELAYED BY HELIOGRAPH TO GUBULAWAYO:

FOR JAMESON STOP HER MAJESTY'S GOVERNMENT DECLINES TO DECLARE MATABELE A CROWN COLONY OR PLACE IT UNDER THE JURISDICTION OF THE HIGH COMMISSIONER STOP HER MAJESTY'S FOREIGN SECRETARY AGREES THAT THE CHARTER COMPANY IS TO PROVIDE THE MACHINERY OF GOVERNMENT FOR THE NEW TERRITORY STOP BOTH MASHONALAND AND MATABELELAND NOW FALL WITHIN THE ADMINISTRATIVE AREA OF THE COMPANY STOP COMPANY SHARES QUOTED AT £8 LONDON CLOSE STOP HEARTIEST CONGRATULATIONS TO YOU YOUR OFFICERS AND MEN FROM JOVE

FOR JAMESON URGENT AND CONFIDENTIAL DESTROY ALL COPIES STOP WE MUST HAVE LOBENGULA STOP NO RISK TOO GREAT NO PRICE TOO HIGH FROM JOVE

'Reverend Codrington, I am sending out a considerable force to escort Lobengula in.' Jameson stood at the fly of his tent, looking out beyond the laager to the blackened ruins of the royal kraal. 'I have already sent this message after the king.' Jameson came back to his desk and read from his pad:

'Now, to stop this useless killing, you must at once come back to me at GuBula-wayo. I guarantee that your life will be safe and that you will be kindly treated.'

'Has the king sent you a reply?' Clinton asked. He had declined a seat and stood stiffly in front of the camp table that served Jameson as a desk.

'Here.' The doctor handed Clinton a grubby, folded scrap of paper. Clinton scanned it swiftly:

I have the honour to inform you that I have received your letter and have heard all what you have said, so I will come. . . .

'This is written by a half-caste rogue, named Jacobs, who has joined up with Lobengula,' Clinton muttered, as he glanced through the rest of the wandering, misspelt and barely literate note. 'I know his handwriting.'

'Do you think the king means it?' Mungo St John asked. 'Do you think he means to come in?'

Clinton did not turn his head towards where Mungo lolled in a canvas camp chair across the tent.

'Dr Jameson, I do not condone your actions or those of your infamous Chartered Company, but I came here at your bidding in order to do what little I can to redress the terrible wrongs that have been perpetrated on the Matabele people. However, I draw the line at having to speak or in any way communicate with this henchman of yours.'

Jameson frowned irritably. 'Reverend, I would like you to bear in mind that I have appointed General St John as Administrator and Chief Magistrate of Matabeleland –'

Clinton cut in brusquely. 'You are, of course, aware that your Chief Magistrate was once a notorious slave-trader, buying and selling the black people over whom you now give him supreme powers?'

'Yes, thank you, Reverend, I am aware that General St John was once a legitimate trader, and I am also fully aware that while a serving officer of Her Majesty's navy, you led an attack on his ship – an action which led to your being court-martialled, imprisoned and cashiered from the service. Now let us continue, Reverend. If you do not wish to talk directly to General St John, you may address me instead.'

In the camp chair Mungo St John crossed his beautifully polished riding boots and smiled lazily, but his eye was bright and sharp as a bared blade. 'Doctor Jameson, would you ask the good priest if he is of the opinion that Lobengula will give himself up?'

'Would you?' Clinton asked, still without a glance in St John's direction.

'No,' Mungo replied, and nodded his head significantly at Jameson.

'Reverend, General St John is taking out a flying column to bring Lobengula in. I want you to go with him, please,' Jameson said.

'Why me, Doctor?'

'You speak the language fluently.'

'So do many others – Zouga Ballantyne is one of them. He is also a soldier.'

'Your brother-in-law has other important work to do –'

'Stealing the king's cattle,' Clinton cut in acidly.

It was already common knowledge that Zouga Ballantyne had been given the task of rounding up the vast Matabele herds and bringing them in to GuBulawayo for distribution.

However, Jameson might not have heard the remark, and he went on smoothly. 'Besides, Reverend, you and your wife have been close friends of Lobengula for many years, he trusts and likes you. But, since it was Major Ballantyne who delivered our ultimatum, Lobengula looks upon him as an enemy.'

'Not without reason,' Clinton murmured dryly. 'However, Doctor, I refuse to be your Judas goat.'

'Your presence with the column may help to avert another bloody conflict, with the inevitable result of hundreds if not thousands more Matabele slaughtered. I would think it your Christian duty to try to prevent that.'

Clinton hesitated, and Mungo murmured. 'Do point out, Doctor Jim, that after Lobengula surrenders, Reverend Codrington will be in a position to comfort and protect him, to ensure that the king is kindly treated and that no harm befalls him. I give him my word on that.'

'Very well,' Clinton capitulated sadly. 'On the understanding that I am to be the king's protector and advisor, I will go with your column.'

'They follow,' Gandang said softly. 'They still follow.' And Lobengula lifted his face and looked at the sky. The rain drops, heavy and hard as newly minted silver shillings, struck his cheeks and forehead.

'The rain,' said Lobengula. 'Who said they could not follow us in the rain?'

'It was me, my King, but I was wrong,' Gandang admitted. 'When he marched from GuBulawayo, One Bright Eye had three hundred men and four of the little guns with three legs which chatter like old women. He also had wagons and one big cannon.'

'I know this,' said the king.

'When the rains came, I thought that they had turned back, but now my scouts have come in with heavy news to tell. One Bright Eye has sent back half of his men and the wagons, the cannon and two of the little three-legged guns. They could not ride over the mud – but–' Gandang paused.

'Do not try to spare me, my brother, tell me it all.'

'He comes on with half his men, and two little machine-guns drawn by horses. They are travelling fast, even in the mud.'

'How fast?' the king asked quietly.

'They are a day's march behind us, tomorrow evening they will camp here on this very river.'

The king pulled the tattered old coat around his shoulders. It was cold in the rain, but he did not have the energy to crawl under the canvas of his wagon tent. He looked out across the watercourse. They were camped on the Shangani river, but almost a hundred and fifty miles higher than where the first battle of the war had been fought upon the headwaters of this same river.

They were in thick mopani forest, so thick that a road had to be chopped through it to allow the king's wagons to pass. The terrain was flat and relieved only by the clay hills of the termite nests that dotted the forest, some of them as large as houses, others the size of a beer keg, just big enough to smash the axle of a wagon.

The sky, grey and heavy as the belly of a pregnant sow, pressed down upon the tops of the mopani. Soon it would rain heavily again, these fat drops were merely a warning of the next deluge to come, and that trickle of muddy water, the colour of a drunkard's bile, down the middle of the watercourse would be a roaring torrent again within minutes of the onslaught.

'One hundred and fifty men, Gandang,' the king sighed. 'How many have we?'

'Two thousand,' said Gandang. 'And perhaps tomorrow or the next day Gambo may come to join us with a thousand more.'

'Yet we cannot stand against them?'

'The men we would eat. It is those little guns with three legs, oh King, not even ten thousand warriors, each with the liver of a lion, could prevail when they begin to laugh. But if the king commands, we will run –'

'No! It is the gold,' Lobengula said suddenly. 'The white men will never let me be until they have the gold. I will send it to them. Perhaps then they will leave me in peace. Where is Kamuza, my young induna? He speaks the language of the white men. I will send him to them.'

Kamuza came swiftly to the king's bidding. He stood attentively in the spattering rain beside the front wheel of the wagon.

'Place the little bags of gold in the hands of the white men, Kamuza, my trusted induna, and say to them thus, "You have eaten up my regiments and killed my young men, you have burned my kraals and scattered the women and children of Matabeleland into the hills where they burrow for roots like wild animals, you have seized my royal herds, and now you have my gold. White men, you have it all, will you now leave me in peace to mourn my lost people?" '

There were ten bags of white canvas, stamped with black lettering. They made a heavy burden for one man to carry. Kamuza knelt and tied them together in bunches, and then packed each bunch into a leather grain bag.

'To hear is to obey, Great Elephant,' Kamuza saluted his king.

'Go swiftly, Kamuza,' Lobengula ordered softly. 'For they are close upon us.'

Will Daniel sat his own horse, with the brim of his hat pulled down to protect the bowl of his clay pipe from the drizzling rain, and over his shoulders he wore a rubber groundsheet which glistened with moisture and gave him a pregnant, clumsy look as he slumped barrel-bellied in the saddle.

On lead reins he held two other horses, one was a pack animal whose burden was covered by a white canvas sheet. Daniel no longer bore the lofty rank of sergeant. After his conduct at the secret valley of the Umlimo, Zouga Ballantyne had seen him reduced to trooper, and as an additional mortification, he was now acting as batman to one of the officers of the flying column. The packhorse carried Captain Coventry's traps.

The other horse belonged to Will's old comrade in arms, Jim Thorn. That worthy was crouched behind a thorny shrub a short way off, with his belt hanging around his neck and cursing bitterly in a low monotone.

'Filthy bleeding water, stinking bloody rain – God-forsaken country – '

'Hey, Jimmo, your backside must be on fire by now. That's the twelfth time today.'

'Shut your ugly face, Will Daniel,' Jim shouted back, and then dropped back into his dismal monotone. 'Bloody gut-breaking trots –'

'Come on, Jim my lad.' Will lifted the brim of his hat to peer about him. 'We can't fall too far behind the rest, not with the bush crawling with bloody black savages.'

Jim Thorn came out from behind the bush re-buckling his belt, but wincing with another bout of stomach cramps. He climbed gingerly up into the saddle, and the three horses plodded along in the deep yellow muddy ruts of the horse-drawn carts which carried the two Maxim machine-guns.

The rear of the column was out of sight ahead of them amongst the dripping mopani trees. The two of them had soon learned to loiter at the back away from the scrutiny of the officers, so that they would not be ordered into the thigh-deep mud when the Maxim carts bogged down and had to be man-handled through one of the glutinous 'mopani holes'.

'Look out, Will!' Jim Thorn yelled suddenly, and his oilskins flapped like the wings of a startled rooster as he tried to draw his rifle from its scabbard. 'Look out, bloody savages!'

A Matabele had stepped silently out of the thick bush alongside the cart tracks, and now he stood directly in front of the horses and held up his empty hands to show the white men that he was unarmed.

'Wait, Jimmo!' Will Daniel called. 'Let's see what the bastard wants.'

'I don't like it, man. It's a trap.' Jim searched the bush around them nervously. 'Let's shoot the black bugger and get out of it.'

'I come in peace!' the Matabele called in English. He wore only a fur kilt, without armlets and leg tassels, and the rain shone on his smoothly muscled torso. On his head was the headring of an induna.

The two mounted men both had their rifles out now, and were aiming from the hip, covering Kamuza at point-blank range.

'I have a message from the king.'

'Well, spit it out then,' Will snapped.

'Lobengula says take my gold, and go back to GuBulawayo.'

'Gold?' demanded Jim Thorn. 'What gold?'

Kamuza stepped back into the scrub, picked up the leather grain bag, and carried it to them.

Will Daniel was laughing excitedly as he pulled out the little canvas bags. They jingled softly in his hands.

'By God, that's the sweetest music I ever heard!'

'What will you do, white men?' Kamuza demanded. 'Will you take the gold to your chief?'

'Don't fret yourself, my friend.' Will Daniel clapped him delightedly on the shoulder. 'It will go to the right person, you have the word of William Daniel hisself on it.'

Jim Thorn was unbuckling his saddle-bags and stuffing the canvas sacks into it.

'Christmas and my birthday all in one,' he winked at Will.

'White men, will you turn and go back to GuBulawayo now?' Kamuza called anxiously.

'Don't worry about it another minute,' Will assured him, and ferreted a loaf of hard bread out of his own saddle-bag. 'Here's a present for you, *bonsela*, present, you understand?' Then to Jim. 'Come on, Mr Thorn, it's Mister I'll be calling you now that you are rich.'

'Lead on, Mr Daniel,' Jim grinned at him, and they spurred past Kamuza, leaving him standing in the muddy pathway with the mouldy loaf of bread in his hands.

Clinton Codrington came slipping and sloshing along the bank of the Shangani river. The lowering clouds were bringing on the night prematurely, and the forests on the far bank were dank and gloomy.

The thunder rumbled sullenly, as though boulders were being rolled across the roof of the sky, and for a few seconds the rain spurted down thickly and then sank once more to a fine drizzle. Clinton shivered and pulled up the collar of his sheepskin coat as he hurried on to where the Maxim carts stood at the head of the column.

There was a tarpaulin draped between the two carts and beneath it squatted a small group of officers. Mungo St John looked up as Clinton approached.

'Ah, parson!' he greeted him. Mungo had learned that this address irritated Clinton inordinately. 'You took your time.' Clinton did not reply; he stood hunched in the rain and none of the officers made room for him beneath the canvas.

'Major Wilson is going to make a reconnaissance across the river with a dozen men. I want you to go with him to translate, if he meets any of the enemy.'

'It will be dark in less than two hours,' Clinton pointed out stolidly.

'Then you had best hurry.'

'The rains will break at any minute,' Clinton persisted. 'Your forces could be split –'

'Parson, you bother about brimstone and salvation – let us do the soldiering.' Mungo turned back to his officers. 'Are you ready to go, Wilson?'

Allan Wilson was a bluff Scot, with long, dark moustaches and an accent that burred with the tang of heather and highlands.

'You'll be giving me detailed orders then, sir?' he demanded stiffly. There had been ill-feeling between him and St John ever since they had left GuBulawayo.

'I want you to use your common sense, man,' St John snapped. 'If you can catch Lobengula, then grab him, put him on a horse, and get back here. If you are attacked, fall back immediately. If you let yourself be cut off, I will not be able to cross the river to support you with the Maxims until first light, do you understand that?'

'I do, General.' Wilson touched the brim of his slouch hat. 'Come on, Reverend,' he said to Clinton. 'We do not have much time.'

Burnham and Ingram, the two American scouts, led the patrol down the steep bank of the Shangani; Wilson and Clinton followed immediately behind.

Clinton's lanky, stooped frame, in the scuffed sheepskin jacket and with a shapeless stained hat pulled down over his ears, looked oddly out of place in the middle of the uniformed patrol of armed men. As he came level with Mungo St John, standing on the top of the bank with his hands clasped behind his back, Clinton bent low from the saddle of his borrowed horse and said, so quietly that only Mungo heard him, 'Read II Samuel, chapter eleven, verse fifteen.' Then Clinton straightened, gathered the old grey gelding with which he had been provided by the Company, and the two of them went sliding untidily down the cutting in the steep bank which the Matabele had dug to take Lobengula's wagons across.

At this point, the Shangani river was two hundred yards across, and as the little patrol waded the deepest part of the channel, the muddy waters reached to their stirrup irons. They climbed the far bank and almost immediately were lost from view in the dripping woods and poor light.

Mungo St John stood for many minutes, staring across the river, ignoring the fine, drizzling rain. He was wondering at himself, wondering why he had sent such a puny force across the river, with only hours of daylight left. The priest was right, of course, it would rain again soon. The heavens were leaden and charged with it. The Matabele were in force. The priest had seen the Inyati impi under its old and crafty commander, Gandang, escorting the wagons away from GuBulawayo.

If he were going to reconnoitre the lie of the land beyond the river, then he knew that he should have used the last of the daylight to ford his entire force. It was the correct tactical disposition. That way the patrol could fall back under the protection of the Maxims at any time during the night, or he could go forward to relieve them if they ran into trouble.

Some demon had possessed him when he gave the orders. Perhaps Wilson had finally irritated him beyond all restraint. The man had argued with him at every opportunity, and had done his best to subvert Mungo's authority amongst the other officers, who resented the fact that he was an American over British officers. It was mostly Wilson's fault that this was such an unhappy and divided little expedition. He was well rid of the overbearing and blunt Scotsman, he decided. Perhaps a night spent in company with the Inyati regiment would take some of the pepper out of him; and he would be a little more tractable in the future – if there was a future for him. Mungo turned back to the sheltering tarpaulin strung between the gun carriages.

Suddenly a thought struck him, and he called down the line. 'Captain Borrow.'

'Sir?

'You have a Bible, don't you? Let me have it, will you?'

Mungo's batman had a fire going, and coffee brewing in the shelter, and he took Mungo's coat to dry and spread a grey woollen blanket over his shoulders as Mungo squatted beside the fire and paged slowly through the little leather-bound, travel-battered Bible.

He found the reference and stared at it thoughtfully:

And he wrote in the letter, saying, Set ye Uriah in the forefront of the hottest battle, and retire ye from him, that he may be smitten, and die.

Mungo wondered that he was still capable of surprising himself. There were still strange places in his soul that he had never explored.

He took a burning stick from the fire and lit his cigar, then plunged the glowing red of the brand into the black coffee to enhance the taste of the brew.

'Well, well, Parson!' he murmured aloud. 'You have a sharper instinct than I ever gave you credit for.'

Then he thought of Robyn Codrington, trying to consider his feelings objectively, and without passion.

'Do I love her?' he asked, and the answer was immediate.

'I have never loved a woman, and by God's grace, I never will.'

'Do I want her, then?' And again there was no hesitation. 'Yes, I want her. I want her badly enough to send anybody who stands in my way to his death.'

'Why do I want her?' he pondered. 'When I have never loved a woman – why do I want this one? She is no longer young, and God knows, I have had my pick of a hundred more beautiful. Why do I want her?' and he grinned at his own perception. 'I want her because she is the only one whom I have never had, and whom I will never have completely.'

He closed the Bible with a snap, and grinned wickedly across the wide river at the dark and silent mopani forest.

'Well done, Parson. You saw it long before I did.'

*

The tracks of Lobengula's wagons were clear to follow, even in the worsening light, and Wilson pushed the pace to a canter.

Clinton's aged grey was exhausted by two weeks of hard trekking. He fell back little by little, until after five miles they were loping along with Captain Napier's rear file. The mud thrown up by the hooves ahead speckled Clinton's face as though he was suffering from some strange disease.

The mopani thinned out dramatically ahead of the tiny patrol, and there were low bare hills on either hand.

'Look at them, Padre,' Wilson called to Clinton, and gestured at the hills. 'There must be hundreds of them.'

'Women and old men,' Clinton grunted. The slopes were scattered with silent watching figures. 'The fighting men will be with the king.'

The twelve riders cantered on without a check, and the thunder muttered and shook the sky above the low, swirling clouds.

Suddenly Wilson raised his right hand high.

'Troop, halt!'

Clinton's grey stood, head hanging and chest heaving between his knees – and Clinton was as grateful. At his best he was no horseman, and he was unaccustomed to such hard riding.

'Reverend Codrington to the front!' The order was passed back, and Clinton kicked the grey into a plodding walk.

At that moment a squall of rain stung his face like a handful of thrown rock-salt, and he wiped it off with the palm of his right hand.

'There they are!' said Wilson tersely, and through the drizzle Clinton could make out the stained and ragged canvas tent of a wagon rising above the scrub, not more than two hundred paces ahead.

'You know what to say, Padre.' Wilson's Scots accent seemed even stronger and was incongruous at this place and in these circumstances.

Clinton walked the grey forward another few paces, and then drew a deep breath.

'Lobengula, King of the Matabele, it is me – Hlopi. These men wish you to come to GuBulawayo to parley with Dakatela and Lodzi. Do you hear me, oh King?'

The silence was broken only by the scraping of a windblown branch and the rustle of the rain on the brim of Clinton's old hat.

Then quite clearly, he heard the snick of a Martini-Henry rifle being loaded; and a young voice asked in whispered Matabele from the scrub near the wagon:

'Must we shoot, Baba?'

A deeper, firmer voice replied in the same language. 'Not yet. Let them come closer so there can be no mistake.'

And then the voices were blotted out by a grumbling roll of thunder overhead, and Clinton backed the grey up.

'It is a trap, Major. There are armed Matabele in ambush about the wagons. I heard them talking.'

'Do you think the king is there?'

'I would not think so, but what I am sure of is that even now the main impi is circling back between us and the river.'

'What makes you think that?'

'It is always the Zulu way, the encirclement and then the closing in.'

'What do you advise, Padre?'

Clinton shrugged and smiled. 'I gave my advice on the bank of the river –' He was interrupted by a shouted warning from the rear of the column. It was one of the Americans, his accent unmistakable.

'There is a force moving in behind us.'

'How many?' Wilson shouted back.

'Plenty, I can see their plumes.'

'Troop, about wheel!' Wilson ordered. 'At the gallop, forward!'

As the horses plunged back down the rough trail, the rain that had been threatening so long burst upon them in an icy silver cascade. It slashed at their faces, and stung their eyes, and drummed on their oilskins.

'This will cover our retreat,' Wilson grunted, and Clinton flogged the grey's neck with the loose end of the reins, for the old horse was falling back again.

Through the thick silver lances of falling rain, he caught a glimpse of waving war-plumes above the scrub; they were racing in to head off the patrol. At that moment the grey stumbled and Clinton was thrown onto his neck.

'Jee!' He heard the war chant go up, and he clung desperately to the grey's neck as it plunged to regain its balance.

'Come on, Padre!' somebody yelled, as the other troopers went pounding past him in the mud and the rain.

Then his horse was running again. Clinton had lost a stirrup, and he bumped painfully on the wet saddle, clinging to the pommel for a grip, but they were through. There were no shields or plumes in the bush around them, only the twisting streamers of rain and the gloom of gathering night.

'Are you telling me, Napier, that Major Wilson has deliberately chosen to spend the night on the far bank, despite my direct orders to return before nightfall?' Mungo St John asked. The only light was that of a storm lantern. The rain had washed out the fires.

The tarpaulin over the heads of the two officers flogged in the wind, spilling gouts of rainwater over them, and the lantern flame fluttered uncertainly in its glass chimney, lighting Captain Napier's face from below so that he looked like a skull.

'We got so close to Lobengula, General, within hail of the wagons. Major Wilson considered a retreat would not be justified. In any event, sir, the bush is swarming with the enemy. The patrol has a better chance of surviving the night by stopping in thick bush and waiting for daylight.'

'That is Wilson's estimate, is it?' Mungo demanded, putting on a grim expression. Yet inwardly, he congratulated himself on such an accurate assessment of the Scotsman's impetuous character.

'You must reinforce the patrol, sir. You must send at least one of the Maxims across – now, this very hour.'

'Listen carefully, Captain,' Mungo ordered him. 'What do you hear?'

Even over the rain and the wind there was an echo like the sound in a seashell held to the ear.

'The river, Captain,' Mungo told him. 'The river is spating!'

'I have just forded it. You can still get across, sir. If you give the order now! If you wait until dawn, it may well be in full flood.'

'Thank you for your advice, Napier. I will not risk the Maxims.'

'Sir, sir – you can take at least one Maxim off its carriage. We can carry it in a blanket and swim across.'

'Thank you, Captain. I will send Borrow across with twenty men to reinforce Wilson until morning – and this force will follow, with both Maxims, only when it is light enough to see the ford and make the crossing in safety.'

'General St John, you are signing the death warrant of those men.'

'Captain Napier, you are overwrought. I shall expect an apology from you when you have recovered yourself.'

Clinton sat with his back against the bole of a mopani tree. He had one hand thrust into the front of his sheepskin jacket, to hold his travelling Bible out of the rain. He wished above any other creature needs that he had light enough to read it.

All around him the rest of the tiny patrol lay stretched out on the muddy earth, bundled up in their rubber groundsheets and oilskins, though Clinton was certain that, like himself, none of them was asleep – nor would any of them sleep that night.

Clutching the Bible above his heart, he had the certain prescience of his own death, and he made the astonishing discovery that it had no terrors for him. Once, long ago, before he had discovered how close at hand was God's comfort, he had been afraid, and now the release from fear was a blessed gift.

Sitting in darkness, he thought of love, the love of his God and his woman and his daughters – and that was all that he would regret leaving behind him.

He thought of Robyn as he had first seen her, standing on the deck of the American slaver *Huron* with her dark hair aflutter on the wind and her green eyes flashing.

He remembered her upon the rumpled sweat-soaked childbed as she struggled to give birth, and he remembered the hot slippery and totally enchanting feeling of his first infant daughter's body as it slithered from Robyn's body into his waiting hands.

He remembered the first petulant birth wail, and how beautiful Robyn had been as she smiled at him, exhausted and racked and proud.

There were other small regrets – one that he would never dandle a grandchild, another that Robyn had never come to love him the same way he loved her. Suddenly Clinton sat up straighter against the mopani, and inclined his head to listen, peering out into the utter blackness from whence the sound had come.

No, it was not really a sound – the only true sound was the rain. It was more like a vibration in the air. Carefully, he returned the precious book to his inside pocket, then he made a trumpet of his bare hands and pressed them to the wet earth, listening intently with his ear to the funnel.

The vibration coming up from the ground was that of running feet, horny bare feet, thousands of feet, trotting to the rhythm of an impi on the march. It sounded like the very pulse of the earth.

Clinton crawled and groped his way across to where he had last seen Major Wilson lie down under his plaid. There was no glimmering of light under the midnight clouds, and when his fingers touched coarse woven cloth, Clinton asked softly:

'Is that you, Major?'

'What is it, Padre?'

'They are here, all around us, moving back to get between us and the river.'

They stood-to while the dawn tried vainly to penetrate the low roof of cloud above them. The saddled horses were merely humped shapes just a little darker than the night around them. They were drawn up in a circle, with the men standing on the inside, rifles resting on the saddles as they peered out into the thick bush that surrounded them, straining for the first glimpse as the grey light settled gently, like a sprinkling of pearl dust upon their dark, wet world.

In the centre of the circle of horses, Clinton knelt in the mud. With one hand he held the reins of the grey horse, and with the other he held the Bible to his chest. His calm voice carried clearly to every man in the dark waiting circle.

> 'Our Father which art in heaven,
> Hallowed be thy name –'

The light grew stronger; they could make out the shape of the nearest bushes. One of the horses, perhaps infected by the tension of the waiting men, whickered and scissored its ears.

> 'Thy will be done
> in earth, as it is in heaven –'

Now they all heard what had alarmed the horse. The faint drumming approached from the direction of the river, growing stronger with the dawn light.

> ' – for thine is the Kingdom,
> the Power and the glory –'

There was the metallic clash of a rifle breech from the silent waiting circle of dismounted men, and half a dozen gruff voices echoed Clinton's quiet 'Amen!'

Then suddenly someone shouted. 'Horses! Those are horses out there!'

And a ragged little cheer went up as they recognized the shape of slouch hats bobbing against the sullen grey sky.

'Who is it?' Wilson challenged.

'Borrow, Sir, Captain Borrow!'

'By God, you're welcome.' Wilson laughed as the column of horsemen rode out of the forest into their defensive circle. 'Where is General St John; where are the Maxims?'

The two officers shook hands as Borrow dismounted, but he did not return Wilson's smile.

'The general is still on the south bank.'

Wilson stared at him incredulous, the smile sliding off his face.

'I have twenty men, rifles only, no Maxims,' Borrow went on.

'When will the column cross?'

'We had to swim our horses across. By now the river is ten feet deep.' Borrow lowered his voice so as not to alarm the men. 'They won't be coming.'

'Did you make contact with the enemy?' Wilson demanded.

'We heard them all around us. They called to each other as we passed, and we heard them keeping pace with us in the forest on either hand.'

'So they are massed between us and the river, and even if we cut our way through to the river, the ford is impassable. Is that it?'

'I am afraid so, sir.'

Wilson took his hat from his head and against his thigh he beat the raindrops from its brim. Then he settled it again carefully on his head at a jaunty angle.

'Then it seems there is only one direction that we can take, one direction in which the Matabele will not expect us to move.' He turned back to Borrow. 'Our orders were to seize the king, and now our very lives depend on it. We must have Lobengula as a hostage. We have to go forward – and that right smartly.' He raised his voice. 'Troop, mount! Walk march, Trot!'

They rode closed up, tense and silent. Clinton's old grey had benefited from the night's rest, and kept his place in the third file.

A young trooper rode at Clinton's right hand.

'What is your name, son?' he asked quietly.

'Dillon, sir – I mean, Reverend.' He was smooth-cheeked, and fresh-faced.

'How old are you, Dillon?'

'Eighteen, Reverend.'

They are all so young, Clinton thought. Even Major Allan Wilson himself is barely thirty years of age. If only, he thought, if only –

'Padre!'

Clinton looked up sharply, his attention had been wandering. They had long ago emerged from the thick bush, and were now coming up to the same spot from which they had retreated the previous evening.

The wagons were still standing abandoned beside the rude track; the tents made pale geometrical oblongs of solid canvas against the dark wet scrub.

Once again, Wilson halted the patrol, and Clinton walked the grey forward.

'Tell them we do not wish to fight,' Wilson ordered.

'There is nobody here.'

'Try anyway,' Wilson urged. 'If the wagons are deserted, then we will ride on until we catch up with the king.'

Clinton rode forward, shouting as he went:

'Lobengula, do not be afraid. It is me. Hlopi.'

There was no reply, only the flutter of the wind in the torn wagon canvas.

'Warriors of Matabele – children of Mashobane, we do not wish to fight – ' Clinton called again; and this time he was answered by a bellowing bull voice, haughty and angry and proud. It came out of the gloom and rain, seeming to emanate from the very air, for there was no man to be seen.

'Hau, white men! You do not wish to fight – but we do, for our eyes are red and our steel is thirsty.'

The last word was blown away on a great gust of sound, and the shrub about them misted over with blue gunsmoke and the air about their heads was torn by a gale of shot.

It was twenty-five years and more since Clinton had stood to receive volleyed gunfire; yet he could still clearly differentiate between the crack of high-powered rifles and the whistle of ball thrown from ancient muzzle loaders, and in the storm the 'whirr-whirr' of beaten pot-legs tumbling as they flew; so that, glancing up, Clinton expected to actually see one come over like a rising pheasant.

'Back! Fall back!' Wilson was shouting, and the horses were all rearing and plunging. The fire was, most of it, flying overhead. As always, the Matabele had raised their sights to the maximum; but there must have been a hundred or more of them hidden in the shrub and random bullets were scoring.

One of the troopers was hit in both eyes, the bridge of his nose shot away. He was reeling in the saddle, clutching his face with blood spurting out between his fingers.

His number two spurred in to catch him before he fell, and with an arm around his shoulder led him at a gallop back along the trail.

Young Dillon's horse was hit in the neck, and he was thrown in the mud, but he came up with his rifle in his hands, and Clinton yelled at him as he galloped back.

'Cut off your saddle-bags. You'll need every round in them, lad.'

Clinton came in for the pick-up, but Wilson rode him off like a polo player.

'Your moke's half done, Padre. He'll not carry two. Get on with you!'

They tried to make a stand in the thicket where they had spent the night, but the hidden Matabele riflemen crept in so close that four of the horses went down, kicking and struggling, exposing the men who had been standing behind them, firing over their backs, and three of the men were hit. One of them, a young Afrikander from the Cape, had a pot-leg slug shatter the bone above his right elbow. The arm was hanging on a tattered ribbon of flesh, and Clinton used the sleeves of his shirt to make a sling for it.

'Well, Padre, we are for it now – and that's no mistake.' The trooper grinned at him, white face speckled with his own blood, like a thrush's egg.

'We can't stand here,' Wilson called. 'Two wounded to a horse and a man to lead them. They'll go in the centre with those who have lost their own horses. The rest of us will ride in a box around them.'

Clinton helped the young Afrikander up onto the grey's back, and one of the lads from Borrow's volunteers up behind him. The sharp slivers of his shin bone were sticking out of the meat of his leg.

They started back slowly, at the pace of the walkers, and from the thickets beside the track the muskets banged and smoked; but the Matabele were all of them well hidden. Clearly, they were taking no chances, even with this tiny band of thirty-odd men.

Clinton walked beside the grey, holding the good leg of the wounded man to prevent him slipping from the saddle. He carried the two rifles belonging to the wounded men slung over his shoulder.

'Padre!' Clinton looked up to find Wilson above him. 'We have three horses that are fresh enough to try a run for the river. I have ordered Burnham and Ingram to try and get back to the main camp and warn St John of our predicament. There is one horse for you. They will take you with them.'

'Thank you, Major,' Clinton answered without a moment's hesitation. 'I am a sailor and a priest, not a horseman; besides, I rather think I have work to do here. Let somebody else go.'

Wilson nodded. 'I expected you to say that.' He pushed his horse to a trot and went up to the head of the dismal little column. Minutes later, Clinton heard the quick beat of flying hooves and he looked up to see three horsemen wheel out of the straggling line and plunge into the brush that surrounded them.

There was a chorus of angry yells and the low humming 'Jee!' as the Matabele tried to head them, but Clinton saw their hats bobbing away above the low bush, and he called after them.

'God speed you, boys!'

Then, as he trudged on in the mud that was balling to the soles of his riding boots – he began silently to pray.

On the outside of the column, another horse fell, throwing its rider over its head, and then lunged up again to stand on three legs, shivering miserably in the rain, its off-fore hanging limply as a sock on a laundry line. The trooper limped back, drawing his revolver from its webbing holster, and shot the animal between the eyes.

'That's a wasted bullet,' Wilson called clearly. 'Don't waste any more.'

They went on slowly, and after a while Clinton became aware that they were no longer following the wagon tracks. Wilson seemed to be leading them gradually more towards the east, but it was hard to tell, for the sun was still hidden by low, grey cloud.

Then abruptly the column stopped again, and now for the first time the insistent banging of muskets from hidden skirmishers in the mopani scrub was silenced.

Wilson had led them into a lovely parklike forest, with short, green grass below the stately mopani trees. Some of these trees stood sixty feet high and their trunks were fluted and twisted as though moulded from potter's clay.

They could see deep into the forest, between the widely spaced trunks. There, directly ahead of the patrol, stretched across their front, waited the army of Lobengula. How many thousands, it was impossible to tell, for their rearguard was hidden in the forest; and even as the little band of white men stared at their host, the *Jikela* began, the 'surrounding' which had been the Zulu way ever since great Chaka's time.

The 'horns' were being spread, the youngest and swiftest warriors running out on the flanks, their naked skins burning like black fire through the forest. A net around a shoal of sardines, they were thrown out until the tips of the horns met to the rear of the band of white men – and again all movement ceased.

Facing the patrol was the 'chest of the bull', the hard and seasoned veterans; when the 'horns' tightened, it was the 'chest' that would close and crush, but now they waited, massed rank upon rank, silent and watchful. Their shields were of dappled black and white, their plumes were of the ostrich, jet black and frothing white, and their kilts of spotted civet tails. In their silence and stillness, it was not necessary for Wilson to raise his voice above conversational tones.

'Well, gentlemen. We will not be going any farther – not for a while anyway. Kindly dismount and form the circle.'

Quietly the horses were led into a ring, so that they stood with their noses touching the rump of the one ahead. Behind each horse, his rider crouched with the stock of his rifle resting on the saddle, aiming across at the surrounding wall of silent, waiting black and white dappled shields.

'Padre!' Wilson called softly, and Clinton left the wounded whom he was tending in the centre and crossed quickly to his side.

'I want you here to translate, if they want to parley.'

'There will be no more talking,' Clinton assured him, and as he said it the massed ranks of the 'chest' parted and a tall induna came through. Even at a distance of two hundred paces, he was an imposing figure in his plumes and tassels of valour.

'Gandang,' said Clinton quietly. 'The king's half-brother.'

For long seconds Gandang stared across at the circle of rain-streaked horses and the grim, white faces that peered over them, and then he lifted his broad assegai above his head. It was almost a gladiatorial salute, and he held it for a dozen beats of Clinton's heart. Then his voice carried clearly to where they waited.

'Let it begin!' he called, and his spear arm dropped.

Instantly, the horns came racing in, tightening like a strangler's grip on the throat.

'Steady!' Wilson called. 'Hold your fire! No bullets to waste, lads! Hold your fire, wait to make sure.'

The blades came out of the thongs that held them to the grip of the shields with a rasping growl, and the war chant rose, deep and resonant:

'Jee! Jee!' And now the silver blades drummed on the dappled rawhide, so that the horses stamped and threw their heads.

'Wait lads.' The front rank was fifty yards away, sweeping in out of the gentle silky grey rain mist.

'Pick your man! Pick your man!' Twenty yards, chanting and drumming to the rhythm of their pounding bare feet.

'Fire!' Gunfire rippled around the tight little circle, not a single blast but with the spacing that told that every shot had been aimed, and the front rank of attackers melted into the soggy earth.

The breech blocks clashed, and the gunfire was continuous, like strings of Chinese crackers, and an echo came back, the slapping sound of lead bullets striking naked black flesh.

At two places the warriors burst into the ring, and for desperate seconds there were knots of milling men, and the banging of revolvers held point blank to chest and belly. Then the black wave lost its impetus, hesitated and finally drew back, the surviving warriors slipping back into the forest, leaving their dead scattered in the wet grass.

'We did it, we sent them off!' someone yelled, and then they were all cheering.

'A little early to celebrate,' Clinton murmured drily.

'Let them shout,' Wilson was reloading his pistol. 'Let them keep their courage up.' He looked up from the weapon at Clinton. 'You'll not be joining us then?' he asked. 'You were a fighting man once.'

Clinton shook his head. 'I killed my last man over twenty-five years ago, but I will look to the wounded and do anything else you want of me.'

'Go around to each man. Collect all the spare ammunition. Fill the bandoliers and dole 'em out as they are needed.'

Clinton turned back to the centre of the circle, and there were three new men there – one was dead, shot in the head – another with a broken hip – and the third with the shaft of an assegai protruding from his chest.

'Take it out!' his voice rose as he tugged ineffectually at the handle. 'Take it out! I can't stand it.'

Clinton knelt in front of him and judged the angle of the blade. The point must lie near the heart. 'It's better to leave it,' he advised gently.

'No! No!' The man's voice rose, and the men in the outer circle looked back, their faces stricken by that hysterical shriek. 'Take it out!'

Perhaps it was best after all – better than lingering, shrieking death to unnerve the men around him.

'Hold his shoulders,' Clinton ordered quietly, and a trooper knelt behind the dying man. Clinton gripped the shaft. It was a beautiful weapon, bound in decorative patterns with hair from an elephant's tail and bright copper wire.

He pulled and the wide blade sucked with the sound of a boot in thick mud, and it came free. The trooper shrieked only once more, as his heart's blood followed the steel out in a bright torrent.

*

The waves of warriors came again four times before noon. Each time it seemed impossible that they could fail to overwhelm the waiting circle, but each time they swirled and broke upon it like a tide upon a rock, and then were sucked back into the forest.

After each assault the circle had to be drawn a little smaller, to take up the gaps left by fallen horses and dead and wounded men, and then the Matabele musketeers would creep in again, moving like quick and silent shadows from mopani to mopani, offering meagre targets, the bulge of a shoulder around the stem of a mopani trunk, little cotton pods of gunsmoke in the patches of green grass, the black bead of a head bobbing above the summit of one of the scattered termite nests as a warrior rose to fire.

Wilson walked quietly around the circle, talking calmly to each man in turn, stroking the muzzle of a restless horse, and then coming back into the centre.

'Are you coping, Padre?'

'We are doing fine, Major.'

The dead were laid out with what little dignity was left to them, and Clinton had covered their faces with saddle blankets. There were twelve of them now – and it was only a little past noon, another seven hours of daylight.

The lad who had lost his eyes in the first volley was talking to somebody from long ago in his delirium, but the words were jumbled and made little sense. Clinton had bound his head in a clean white bandage from the saddle-bag of the grey – but the bandage was now muddied, and the blood had seeped through.

Two others lay still, one breathing noisily through the hole in his throat from which the air bubbled and whistled, the other silent and pale, except for a little dry cough at intervals. He had been hit low in the back, and there was no use nor feeling in his lower body. The others, too gravely wounded to stand in the circle, were breaking open the waxed paper packages of cartridges and refilling the bandoliers.

Wilson squatted on his haunches beside Clinton. 'Ammunition?' he asked softly.

'Four hundred rounds,' Clinton replied as softly.

'Less than thirty rounds a man,' Wilson calculated swiftly. 'Not counting the wounded, of course.'

'Well, look at it this way, Major, at least it is no longer raining.'

'Do you know, Padre, I hadn't even noticed.' Wilson smiled faintly, and looked up at the sky. The cloud belly had risen and at that moment a pale ghostly silhouette of the sun appeared through it; but it was without warmth and so mild that they stared at it without paining their eyes.

'You are hit, Major,' Clinton exclaimed suddenly. He had not realized it until that moment. 'Let me look at it.'

'It's almost stopped bleeding. Let it be.' Wilson shook his head 'Keep your bandages for those others.'

He was interrupted by a shout from one of the troopers in the outer circle.

'There he is again!' And immediately firing rifles whipcracked, and the same voice swore angrily.

'The bastard, the bloody bastard –'

'What is it, soldier?'

'That big induna – he's moving about again out there; but he's got the devil's luck, sir. We just wasted a packet of bullets on him.'

As he spoke, Clinton's old grey horse threw up his head and fell on his knees, hit in the neck. He struggled to rise again, then rolled over on his side.

'Poor old fellow!' Clinton murmured, and immediately another horse reared up, thrashed frantically at the air with his fore hooves and then crashed over on his back.

'They're shooting better now,' Wilson said quietly.

'I would guess that is Gandang's work,' Clinton agreed. 'He's moving from sniper to sniper, setting their sights for them and coaching their fire.'

'Well, it's time to close the circle again.'

There were only ten horses still standing; the others lay where they had fallen, and their troopers lay belly down behind them, waiting patiently for a certain shot at one of the hundreds of elusive figures amongst the trees.

'Close up.' Wilson stood and gestured to the ring of troopers. 'Come in on the centre –'

He broke off abruptly, spun in a half circle and clutched his shoulder, but still he kept his feet.

'You're hit again!' Clinton jumped up to help him and immediately both his legs were struck out from under him, and he dropped back onto the muddy earth and stared at his smashed knee caps.

It must have been one of the ancient elephant guns, the four-to-the-pounders that some of the Matabele were using. It was a weapon that threw a ball of soft lead weighing a quarter of a pound. It had hit him in one knee and torn through into the other.

Both his legs were gone; one was twisted up under his buttocks, and he was sitting on his own muddy riding boot. The other leg was reversed, the toe-cap of his boot was dug into the mud and the silver spur stuck up towards the swirling cloud belly of the sky.

Gandang knelt behind the trunk of the mopani tree and snatched the Martini-Henry rifle out of the hands of a young brave.

'Even a baboon remembers a lesson he is taught,' Gandang fumed. 'How often have you been told not to do this.'

The long leaf sight on top of the blued barrel was at maximum extension, set for one thousand yards.

Under Gandang's quiet instructions, the young Matabele rested the rifle in a crotch of the mopani, and fired.

The rifle kicked back viciously, and he shouted joyously. In the little circle a big sway-backed grey horse dropped to its knees, fought briefly to rise and then flopped over on its side.

'Did you see me, my brothers?' howled the warrior. 'Did you see me kill the grey horse?'

Vamba's hands were shaking with excitement as he reloaded and rested the rifle again.

He fired, and this time a bay gelding reared up and then crashed over on its back.

'Jee!' sang Vamba, and brandished the smoking rifle over his head, and the war chant was taken up by a hundred other hidden riflemen, and the volley of their fire flared up.

'They are almost ready,' Gandang thought, as he glimpsed another of the defenders struck down in the renewed gale of gunfire. 'There can be few of them who still can shoot. Soon now it will be time to send the spears for the closing-in, and tonight I will have a victory to take to my brother the king. One little victory in all the terrible defeats – and so hard bought.'

He slipped away from the shelter of the mopani trunk, and loped swiftly across towards where another of his riflemen was firing away as fast as he could re-load. Halfway there Gandang felt the jarring impact in his upper arm, but he covered the open ground to shelter without a check in his stride, and then leaned against the bole of the mopani, and examined the wound. The bullet had gone in the side of his biceps and out the back of his arm. The blood was dripping from his elbow, like thick black treacle. Gandang scooped a handful of mud and slapped it over the wounds, plugging and masking them.

Then he said scornfully to the kneeling warrior at his side. 'You shoot like an old woman husking maize.' And he took the rifle out of his hands.

Clinton dragged himself backwards on his elbows, and his legs slithered loosely after him through the mud. He had used the webbing belt from one of the dead men as a tourniquet, and there was very little bleeding. The numbness of the shock still persisted, so the pain was just bearable, though the sound of the shattered ends of bone grating together as he moved brought up the nausea in a bitter-acid flood in the back of his throat.

He reached the blind boy, and paused for his breathing to settle before he spoke. 'The others are writing letters, afterwards somebody may find them. Is there anybody at home? I'll write for you.'

The boy was silent, did not seem to have heard. An hour earlier Clinton had given him one of the precious laudanum pills from the kit which Robyn had prepared for him before he left GuBulawayo.

'Did you hear, lad?'

'I heard, Padre. I was thinking. Yes, there is a girl.'

Clinton turned a fresh page of his notebook and licked the point of his pencil, and the boy thought again and mumbled shyly:

'Well then, Mary. You'll have read in the papers, we had quite a scrap here today. It's nearly over now, and I was thinking about that day on the river –'

Clinton wrote quickly, to keep up.

'I'll be saying cheerio, then Mary. Isn't one of us afraid. I reckon as how we just want to do it right – when the time comes –'

Quite suddenly, Clinton found his vision blurring as he wrote the final salutation, and he glanced up at the pale beardless face. The eyes were swathed in bloody bandages, but his lips were quivering and the boy gulped hard as he finished.

'What is her name, lad? I have to address it.'

'Mary Swayne. The Red Boar at Falmouth.'

She was a barmaid then, Clinton thought, as he buttoned the folded page into the boy's breast pocket. She would probably laugh at the note if she ever got it, and pass it around the regulars in the saloon bar.

'Padre, I was lying,' the boy whispered. 'I am afraid.'

'We all are.' Clinton squeezed his hand. 'I tell you what, lad. If you like, you can load for Dillon here. He's got eyes to shoot, but only one arm – you're got two good arms.'

'Bully on you, Padre,' Dillon grinned. 'Why didn't we think of that.'

Clinton draped a bandolier across the blind boy's legs. There were only fifteen cartridges in the loops – and at that moment, out in the mopani, the singing started.

It was slow and deep and very beautiful, echoing and ringing through the forest. The praise song of the Inyati. And Clinton turned his head and looked slowly around the circle.

All the horses were dead; they lay in a litter of saddlery and broken equipment, of crumpled yellow scraps of waxed paper from the ammunition packets, of empty brass cartridge cases and discarded rifles. In the confusion, only the row of dead men was orderly. How long was that row, Clinton thought, oh God, what a waste this is, what a cruel waste.

He raised his eyes, and the clouds were at last breaking up. There were valleys of sweet blue sky between the soaring ranges of cumulus. Already the sunset was licking the cloud mountains with soft, fleshy tones of pink and rose, while the depths of the billowing masses were the colour of burnt antimony and tarnished silver.

They had fought all day on this bloody patch of mud. In another hour it would be dark, but even now there were dark specks moving like dust motes against the high singing blue of the evening sky. The tiny specks turned in slow eddies, like a lazy whirlpool, for the vultures were still very high, waiting and watching with the infinite patience of Africa.

Clinton lowered his eyes, and across the circle Wilson was watching him.

He sat with his back against the belly of one of the dead horses. His right arm hung uselessly at his side, and the wadding over the wound in his stomach was crimson with seeping blood, but he held his revolver in his lap.

The two men held each other's gaze while the singing soared and fell and soared again.

'They'll be coming now – for the last time,' Wilson said.

Clinton nodded, and then he lifted his chin, and he, too, began to sing:

> 'Nearer my God to Thee,
> Nearer to Thee – '

His voice was surprisingly clear and true, and Wilson was singing with him, holding the wadding to his stomach wound.

> ' – Darkness comes over me,
> My rest a stone – '

The blind boy's voice cracked and quavered. Dillon was beside him; though his ankle and elbow were shot through, he lay upon his back with a rifle propped on his crossed knees, ready to fire one-handed when they came. His voice was flat and tuneless, but he winked cheekily at Clinton and grinned:

' – Angels to beckon me – '

Eight of them, all that were left, every one of them wounded more than once, but all of them singing in the wilderness of the mopani forests – their voices tinny and thin, almost lost in the great crashing chords of the praise song of the Inyati regiment.

Then there was thunder in the air, the drumming of two thousand assegais on black and white dappled shields, and the thunder came rolling down upon their little circle.

Allan Wilson dragged himself to his feet to face them. Because of his stomach wound, he could not stand erect, and the one arm dangled at his side. His service revolver made a strangely unwarlike popping sound in the roar of the war chant and the drumming blades.

Dillon was still singing, snatching the loaded rifles and firing, and singing, and grabbing the next rifle. The blind boy felt the last cartridge into a rifle breech, and passed the hot rifle back to Dillon, and then he groped for another round, his fingers becoming frantic as he realized the bandolier was empty.

'They're finished,' he cried. 'They are all finished!'

Dillon pushed himself erect on his one good leg, and hopped forward, holding the empty rifle by the muzzle, and he swung the butt at the wave of shields and plumes that reared over him, but the blow lacked power and was deflected harmlessly aside by one of the tall oval shields; and then quite miraculously a long, broad blade sprang from between his shoulder blades, driven through from breast bone to spine, and the silver steel was misted pink.

'I don't want to die,' screamed the blind boy. 'Please hold me, Padre.'

And Clinton put his arm around his shoulders and squeezed with all his strength.

'It's all right, lad,' he said. 'It's going to be all right.'

The bodies were stripped naked. Their skin, never touched by the sun, was snowy white and strangely delicate-looking, like the smooth petals of the arum lily. Upon this whiteness, the wounds were the shocking colour of crushed mulberries.

Around the killing ground was gathered a vast concourse of warriors, some of them already wearing items of the looted uniforms, all of them still panting with the exhilaration of that last wild charge and the stabbing with which it had ended.

From the dense ranks, an old grizzle-headed warrior stepped forward with his assegai held under-handed, like a butcher's knife. He stooped over the naked corpse of Clinton Codrington. It was the time to let the spirits of the white men free, to let them escape from their bodies and fly, lest they remain on earth to trouble the living. It was time for the ritual disembowelment. The old warrior placed the point of his blade on the skin of Clinton's stomach, just above the pathetic shrivelled cluster of his genitals, and gathered himself to make the deep upward stroke.

'Hold!' A clear voice stopped him, and the warrior stood back and saluted respectfully as Gandang came striding through the parting ranks of his warriors.

In the centre of that awful field, Gandang stopped, and looked down at the naked bodies of his enemies. His face was impassive, but his eyes were terrible, as though he mourned for all the earth.

'Let them lie,' he said quietly. 'These were men of men, for their fathers were men before them.'

Then he turned and strode back the way he had come, and his men formed up behind him and trotted away into the north.

Lobengula had come to the end of his domains. Below him the earth opened into the steep escarpment of the Zambezi valley, wild infernal place of broken rocky gorges and impenetrable thickets, of savage animals and a smouldering crushing heat.

At the limit of the eye the dark serpentine growth of riverine bush outlined the course of the father of all waters, and in the west a tall silver cloud of spray stood against the sky: it marked the place where the Zambezi river went crashing over a sheer ledge of rock in an awesome, creaming torrent, falling over three hundred feet into the narrow gorge below.

Lobengula sat upon the box of the leading wagon and looked upon all this savage grandeur with listless eyes. The wagon was drawn by two hundred of his warriors. The oxen were all dead, the ground had been too rugged and rocky for most of them and they had broken down and died in the traces.

Then the migration had run into the first belt of the tsetse fly, and the dreaded little insects had come to swarm on the dappled hides of the remaining bullocks and plague the men and women in Lobengula's sprawling caravan. Within weeks, the last of the fly-struck beasts was dead, and men, more resistant to the sting of the tsetse, had taken their places in the span and drawn their king onwards in his hopeless, aimless flight.

Now even they were daunted by what lay ahead, and they rested on the yokes and looked back at Lobengula.

'We will sleep here this night,' said the king, and immediately the weary, starving host that followed the wagons spread out to begin the chores of making camp, the young girls to carry water in the clay pots, the men to build the temporary lean-to shelters and cut the wood for the fires, and the women to eke out the contents of the almost empty grain bags and the few shreds of dried meat that remained. The fly had killed the last of the slaughter beasts with the draught bullocks, and game was scarce and shy.

Gandang went forward to the lead wagon and saluted his half-brother.

'Your bed will be ready soon, Nkosi Nkulu.'

But Lobengula was staring dreamily up at the steep rocky kopje that towered above their bivouac. The great bloated trunks of the cream-of-tartar trees had forced the black boulders apart. The little twisted branches, loaded with smooth furry pods, reached towards the uncaring sky like the maimed arms of a cripple.

'Is that a cave up there, my brother?' Lobengula asked softly. A dark cleft was riven into the rock face that girdled the crest of the hill. 'I wish to go up to that cave.'

Twenty men carried Lobengula on a litter of poles and furs, and he winced at each jolt, his great swollen body riddled with gout and arthritis, but his eyes were fastened on the crest high above him.

Just below the rock face Gandang made a sign to the bearers and they lay the litter gently upon the rocky slope while Gandang shifted his shield onto his shoulder and freed his broad blade from its thong as he went ahead.

The cave was narrow but deep and dark. The small ledge at its mouth was littered with the furry remains and chewed bones of small animals, the hydrax and baboon, gazelle and klipspringer. The cave itself gave out the fetid odour of the cage of a carnivorous animal, and when Gandang squatted at the entrance and peered into the sombre depths, there was the sudden vicious spitting snarl of a leopard, and dimly he saw the beast move in the shadows and caught the glint of its fierce golden eyes.

Gandang moved slowly out of the sunlight, and paused to let his eyes adjust to the gloom. The leopard warned him again with a terrifying crackle of anger in the confined spaces of the cavern. It had crept closer and was lying flat upon a narrow ledge above the level of Gandang's head. He could just make out the shape of its broad adder-like brow; the ears were laid back flat and the eyes slitted with rage.

Carefully, Gandang moved into position below the ledge, for he did not want to trigger the charge until he was ready to receive it. Balanced lightly in a half crouch, with the assegai's point lifted and lined up on the enraged animal's throat, Gandang flirted his shield and called to it.

'Come, evil one! Come, devil spawn.' And with another stunning burst of rage, the leopard launched itself, a blurr of gold, upon the tall dappled shield. But as it dropped, so Gandang lifted the point and took the leopard upon it, letting its own weight drive the steel through its heart; and then he rolled backwards under the shield and the cruel hooked talons raked the cured iron-hard hide unavailingly.

The blade was still buried in the leopard's chest. It coughed once, choking on its own blood, and then it wrenched itself free of the steel and bounded out through the mouth of the cavern. When Gandang followed it cautiously into the sunlight, the beautiful beast was stretched out on the rocky ledge in a spreading puddle of its own blood. It was a magnificent old male, the pelt unscarred. The sable rosettes upon its back were not much darker than the dark amber ground, that shaded down to a pure buttery cream on the underbelly. A noble animal, and only a king might wear its fur.

'The way is safe, oh King,' Gandang called down the slope, and the litter-bearers carried Lobengula up and set him gently upon the ledge.

The king dismissed the bearers, and he and his half-brother were alone on the hillside, high above this harsh and barbaric land. Lobengula looked at the dead leopard and then at the dark mouth of the cavern.

'This would be a fitting tomb for a king,' said Lobengula reflectively, and Gandang could not answer him. They were silent for a long while.

'I am a dead man,' said Lobengula at last, and raised a graceful hand to still Gandang's protest. 'I walk, I speak still, but my heart is dead within me.'

Gandang was silent, and he could not look upon the king's face.

'Gandang, my brother. I want only peace. Will you grant me that? When I order it, will you bring your spear to me and by piercing my dead heart let my spirit free to find that peace?'

'My King, my brother, never once have I disobeyed your order. Ever your word was the centre of my existence. Ask anything of me, my brother, anything but this. Never can I lift my hand towards you, son of Mzilikazi, my father, grandson of Mashobane, my grandfather.'

Lobengula sighed. 'Oh Gandang, I am so weary and sick with grief. If you will not give me surcease, then will you send for my senior witchdoctor?'

The witchdoctor came and listened gravely to the king's command; then he rose and went to the carcass of the leopard.

He clipped off the long, stiff, white whiskers and burned them to powder in a tiny clay pot over a small fire. To make the potion stronger still, he pounded a dozen seeds of the poison rope shrub to a paste and mixed it with the lethal ashes. Then from a stoppered buck-horn on his belt, he poured and stirred an acrid green liquid.

On his knees, with face to the ground, he wriggled towards the king like an obsequious cur-dog and placed the pot on the rocky ledge before him. As his withered claw-like fingers released the deadly vessel, Gandang rose silently behind him and drove his assegai between the witchdoctor's bony shoulder blades and out of his pigeon chest.

Then he picked up the wizened skeletal body and carried it into the recesses of the cavern. When he came back he knelt again before Lobengula.

'You are right,' Lobengula nodded. 'No man but you should know the manner of the king's going.'

He picked up the pot and held it between his cupped pink palms.

'Now you will be the father of my poor people. Stay in peace, my brother,' said Lobengula, and lifted the pot to his lips and drained it at a single draught.

Then he lay back on the litter and pulled a fur kaross over his head.

'Go sweetly, my beloved brother,' said Gandang. His noble features were set like weathered granite, but as he sat beside the king's bier the tears coursed down his cheeks and wet the great battle-scarred muscles of his chest.

They buried Lobengula in the cavern, sitting upright on the stone floor and wrapped in the wet green skin of the leopard. They dismantled his wagons and carried them up the hill and stacked the parts at the back of the cave.

They piled Lobengula's tusks of yellow ivory at each hand, and at his feet Gandang placed his toy spear of kingship and his beer pots and eating plates, his knives and mirrors and snuff-horn, his beads and ornaments, a bag of salt and another of grain for the journey – and finally the little sealed clay pots of uncut diamonds to pay his way into the spirit world of his forefathers.

Under Gandang's supervision, they sealed the mouth of the cavern with heavy slabs of black ironstone, then, dolefully singing the king's praises, they went back down the hill.

There were no cattle to slaughter for the funeral feast, nor grain for the beer pots. Gandang called the leaders of the mourning people to him.

'A mountain has fallen,' he said simply. 'And an age is past. I have left behind me my wife and my son and the land that I loved. Without those things a man is nothing. I am going back. No man need follow me. Each must choose his own path, but mine is south again to GuBulawayo and the magical hills of the Matopos – to meet and talk with this man Lodzi.'

In the morning, when Gandang started southwards again, he looked back and saw what was left of the Matabele nation straggling along behind him, no longer a great and warlike people, but a bewildered and broken rabble.

Robyn Codrington stood on the cool shaded verandah of Khami Mission. It had rained that morning, and the air was washed sparkling clean and the wet earth smelled like newly baked bread as the bright sunshine warmed it.

Robyn wore the black ribbons of mourning sewn on her sleeves.

'Why do you come here?' she demanded quietly, but unsmilingly, of the man who mounted the front steps of the verandah.

'I had no choice,' Mungo St John answered her. He stopped on the top step, and studied her for a moment without any trace of mockery on his face.

Her skin was scrubbed and fresh, devoid of either rouge or powder. It was smooth and fine-textured. There was no pouching below her clear green eyes, no blurring of her jawline, and her hair drawn back from her temples and forehead was innocent of silver lacing. Her body was small-breasted and narrow-hipped, tall and supple, but when she saw the direction of his gaze, the line of Robyn's lips hardened and set.

'I should be grateful, sir, if you would state your business and leave.'

'Robyn, I am sorry, but perhaps it is best that the uncertainty is over.'

In the four months since the return of the flying column from the Shangani, a dozen rumours had come out of the bush.

That fateful morning, Mungo St John's column, cut off by the flooded river, had heard heavy firing on the opposite bank. Then almost immediately they had themselves come under fierce attack by elements of the Matabele army. They had been forced to retire, a long weary fighting retreat in the rain that had taken weeks of starvation and privation, until at last the harrying impis had let them go, but not before the gun carriages had been abandoned and half the horses lost.

Nobody had known what had happened to Allan Wilson's patrol on the north bank of the Shangani, but then the word had reached GuBulawayo that the little band had cut their way through the impis, gained the Zambezi, and rafted down it to the Portuguese settlement of Tete, three hundred miles downstream. Later that was denied by the Portuguese and hopes plunged, to be revived again when a Matabele induna coming in to surrender suggested that the white men had been taken prisoner by the Inyati regiment – rumour, denial and counter-rumour for four harrowing months, and now Mungo St John was standing before Robyn.

'It's certain,' he said. 'I did not want a stranger to bring the news to you.'

'They are dead,' she said flatly.

'All of them. Dawson reached the battlefield and found them.'

'He would not have been able to recognize them or be certain of how many bodies. Not after all these months, not after the hyena and vultures –'

'Robyn, please.' Mungo held out a hand to her, but she recoiled from him.

'I won't believe it, Clinton could have escaped.'

'In the bush Dawson met the senior induna of the Matabele. He is coming in with all his people to surrender. He described to Dawson the patrol's last stand, and how in the end they all died.'

'Clinton could have – ' She was very pale, shaking her head firmly.

'Robyn, it was Gandang. He knew your husband well. "Hlopi" he called him, the man with white hair. He saw him lying with the other dead. It is certain. There can be no more hope.'

'You can go now,' she said, and then quite suddenly she was weeping. Standing very erect and chewing her lower lip to try and stop herself, but her face had crumpled and the rims of her eyelids turned rosy-pink with grief.

'I cannot leave you like this,' he said and limped down the stoep towards her.

'Don't come near me,' she husked through her tears, and she retreated before him. 'Please don't touch me.'

He came on, lean and rangy as an old tom-leopard; but the cruel and swarthy planes of his face had softened with an expression she had never seen upon them before, and his one good eye held her swimming green ones with a deep and tender concern.

'Don't, oh please don't –' Now she held up both hands as if to ward him off, and she turned her face away. She had reached the end of the verandah; her back was pressed to the door of the bedroom which Cathy and Salina had once shared, and she began to pray, her voice muffled by her own tears.

'Oh Gentle Jesus, help me to be strong –' His hands fell upon her shoulders; they were hard as bone and cool through the thin cotton of her blouse. She shuddered, and gasped.

' – Have pity. I beg you. Let me be.'

He took her chin in the cup of his hand and forced her face up to his.

'Will you give me no peace, ever?' she mumbled brokenly, and then his mouth covered hers and she could not speak again. Slowly the rigidity went out of her body, and she swayed against him. She sobbed once, and began to slump into the embrace of his hard muscled arms. He caught her behind the knees, and around the shoulders, and lifted her like a sleeping child against his chest.

He kicked open the door to the bedroom, stepped through and pushed it closed with his heel.

There was a dustsheet on the bed, but no pillow or eiderdown. He laid her upon it, and knelt beside her, still holding her to his chest.

'He was a saint,' she choked. 'And you sent him to his death. You are the very devil.'

Then with the shaking, frantic fingers of a drowning woman, she unfastened the mother-of-pearl buttons down the front of his linen shirt.

His chest was hard and smooth, the olive skin covered with crisp, dark curls. She pressed her open lips to it, breathing deeply the man-smell of him.

'Forgive me,' she sobbed. 'Oh God, forgive me.'

*

From his cubbyhole beside the pantries, Jordan Ballantyne could overlook the cavernous kitchens of Groote Schuur.

There were three chefs at work over the gleaming, anthracite-burning Aga ranges, and one of them hurried across to Jordan with the enamelled double-boiler and a silver spoon. With it Jordan tasted the Béarnaise sauce that would go with the

383

galjoen. The galjoen was a fish of the stormy Cape waters; fancifully its shape could be likened to that of a Spanish galleon, and its delicate greenish flesh was one of the great African delicacies.

'Perfect,' Jordan nodded. *'Parfait, Monsieur Galliard, comme toujours.'* The little Frenchman scurried away beaming, and Jordan turned to the heavy teak door leading to the wine cellars below the kitchens.

Jordan had personally decanted the port that afternoon, ten bottles of the forty-year-old Vilanova de Gaia of the 1853 vintage; it had faded to the beautiful tawny colour of wild honey. Now a Malay waiter in long white Kanzu robes, with crimson sash and pillbox fez, came up the stone steps, reverently carrying the first Waterford glass decanter on a Georgian silver tray.

Jordan poured a thimbleful into the chased silver *tastevin* which he wore on the chain about his neck. He sipped, rolled it on his tongue and then drew breath sharply through pursed lips to let the wine declare itself.

'I was right,' he murmured. 'What a fortunate purchase.'

Jordan opened the heavy leatherbound wine register, and noted with pleasure that they still had twelve dozen bottles of the Vilanova, after he had deducted today's decanting. In the 'remarks' column he wrote. 'Extraordinary. Keep for best,' and then turned back to the Malay steward.

'So then, Ramallah, we will offer a choice of Sherry Finos Palma or Madeira with the soup, with the fish the Chablis or the 1889 Krug –' Quickly Jordan ran down the menu, and then dismissed him. 'The company will be coming through presently, kindly see that everyone takes their places now.'

The twelve waiters stood with their backs to the oak panelling of the dining-hall, their white-gloved hands clasped in front of them, expressionless as guardsmen, and Jordan gave each one a quick appraisal as he passed, looking for a stain on the brilliant white robes or a sloppily knotted sash.

At the head of the long table, he paused. The service was the silver gilt queen's pattern presented to Mr Rhodes by the directors of the Chartered Company, the glass was long, finely stemmed Venetian, lipped with twenty-two carat gold to complement the gilt. There were twenty-two settings this evening, and Jordan had agonized over the seating arrangements. Finally he had decided to place Dr Jameson at the bottom of the table and put Sir Henry Loch, the High Commissioner, on Mr Rhodes' right. He nodded his satisfaction at that arrangement, and took one of the Alphonso Havanas from the silver humidor and sniffed it before crackling it against his ear – that too was perfect; he replaced it and took one last lingering look around the hall.

The flowers had been arranged by Jordan's own hands, great banks of protea blooms from the slopes of Table Mountain. In the centrepiece, yellow English roses from the gardens of Groote Schuur, and of course Mr Rhodes' favourite flowers, the lovely blue plumbago blossom.

From beyond the double doors came the clatter of many feet on the marble floor of the hall and the high, almost querulous, voice which Jordan knew and loved so well carried to him.

'And we shall just have to square the old man.' Jordan smiled fondly at the words, the old man was certainly Kruger, the President of the Boer Republic, and 'square' was still one of the central words in Mr Rhodes' vocabulary. Just before the doors swung open to admit the company of brilliant and famous men clad in sombre dinner jackets, Jordan slipped out of the hall, back to his little cubbyhole – but he raised the hatch beside his desk an inch, so that he could hear the conversation at the long, glittering table in the hall beyond.

It gave him a glorious feeling of power, to be sitting so close to the centre of all this and to listen to the pulse of history beating, to know that it was within him subtly to alter and direct, and to do so in secrecy. A word here, a hint there, even something so trivial as the placing of two powerful men side by side at the long dinner table. On occasions, in privacy, Mr Rhodes would actually ask, 'What do you think, Jordan?' and would listen attentively to his reply.

The tumultuous excitement of this life had become a drug to Jordan, and barely a day passed that he did not drink the heady draught to the fill. There were special moments that he treasured and whose memory he stored. When the meal ended, and the company settled down to the port and cigars, Jordan could sit alone and gloat over these special memories of his.

He remembered that it had been he who had written out that legendary cheque in his own fair hand for Mr Rhodes to sign the day that they had bought out the Kimberley Central Company. The amount had been £5,338,650, the largest cheque ever drawn anywhere in the world.

He remembered sitting in the visitor's gallery of Parliament as Mr Rhodes rose to make his acceptance speech as Prime Minister of Cape Colony, how Mr Rhodes had looked up and caught his eye and smiled before he began speaking.

He remembered after that wild ride down from Matabeleland when he had handed the Rudd Concession with Lobengula's seal upon it to Mr Rhodes, how he had clasped Jordan's shoulder and with those pale blue eyes conveyed in an instant more than a thousand carefully chosen words ever could.

He remembered riding beside Mr Rhodes' carriage down the Mall to Buckingham Palace and dinner with the queen, while the Union Castle mailship delayed its sacred sailing by twenty-four hours to wait for them.

This very morning had added another memory to Jordan's store, for he had read aloud the cable from Queen Victoria to 'Our well-beloved Cecil John Rhodes', appointing him one of Her Majesty's Privy Councillors.

Jordan started back to the present.

It was after midnight, and in the dining-hall Mr Rhodes was abruptly breaking up the dinner in his characteristic fashion.

'Well, gentlemen, I'll bid you all a good night's rest.'

Quickly Jordan rose from his desk and slipped down the servants' passageway.

At the end he opened the door a crack and anxiously watched the burly, appealingly awkward figure mount the stairs. The company had done justice to Jordan's choice of wine, but still Mr Rhodes' tread was steady enough. Though he stumbled once at the top of the sweeping marble staircase, he caught his balance, and Jordan shook his head with relief.

When the last servant left, Jordan locked the wine cellar and the pantry. There was a silver tray left upon his desk, and on it a glass of the Vilanova and two water biscuits spread thickly with salted Beluga caviar. Jordan carried the tray through the silent mansion. A single candle burned in the lofty entrance hall. It stood upon the massive carved teak table in the centre of the floor.

Jordan paced slowly across the chequer board of black and white marble paving, like a priest approaching the altar, and reverently he laid the silver tray upon the table. Then he looked up at the carved image high in its shadowy niche, and his lips moved as he silently began the invocation to the bird goddess, Panes.

When he had finished, he stood silent and expectant in the fluttering light of the candle, and the great house slept around him. The falcon-headed goddess stared with cruel blind eyes into the north, a thousand miles and more towards an ancient land, now blessed, or cursed, with a new name, Rhodesia.

Jordan waited quietly, staring up at the bird like a worshipper before a statue of the Virgin, and then suddenly in the silence, from the bottom of the gardens, where grew the tall dark oak trees that Governor van der Stel had planted almost two hundred years before, came the sad and eerie cry of an eagle owl. Jordan relaxed and backed away from the offering that he left upon the table. Then he turned and went bounding up the marble staircase.

In his own small room he quickly stripped off his clothing that was impregnated with the odours of the kitchen. Naked, he sponged down his body with cold water, admiring his own lithe form in the full-length mirror on the far wall. He scrubbed himself dry with a rough towel, and then rinsed his hands in eau-de-Cologne.

With a pair of silver-backed brushes he burnished his hair until his curls shone like whorls of pure gold wire in the lamplight; then he slipped his arms into the brocaded gown of midnight blue satin, belted it around his waist, picked up the lamp to light his way and stepped out into the passage.

He closed the door to his bedroom quietly and listened for a few seconds. The house was still silent, their guests slept. On silent, bare feet, Jordan glided down the thick carpet to the double doors at the end of the passage to tap lightly on one of the panels, twice then twice again, and a voice called to him softly,

'Enter!'

'These are a pastoral people. You cannot take their herds away from them.' Robyn Ballantyne spoke with a low controlled intensity, but her face was pale and her eyes sparkled with furious green lights.

'Please, won't you be seated, Robyn.'

Mungo St John indicated the chair of rough raw lumber, one of the few furnishings in this adobe mud hut that was the office of the Administrator of Matabeleland. 'You will be more comfortable, and I will feel more at ease.'

Nothing could make him appear more at ease, she thought wryly. He lolled back in his swivel chair, and his booted ankles were crossed on the desk in front of him. He was in shirtsleeves, without a tie or cravat, and his waistcoat was unbuttoned.

'Thank you, General. I shall continue to stand until I receive your answer.'

'The costs of the relief of Matabeleland and the conduct of the war were born entirely by the Chartered Company. Even you must see that there must be reparation.'

'You have taken everything. My brother, Zouga Ballantyne, has rounded up over a hundred and twenty-five thousand head of Matabele cattle –'

'The war cost us a hundred thousand pounds.'

'All right.' Robyn nodded. 'If you will not listen to the voice of humanity, then perhaps hard cash will convince you. The Matabele people are scattered and bewildered; their tribal organizations have broken down; the smallpox is rife amongst them –'

'A conquered nation always suffers privation, Robyn. Oh, do sit down, you are giving me a crick in the neck.'

'Unless you return part of their herds to them, at least enough for milk and slaughter, you are going to be faced with a famine that will cost you more than your neat little war ever did.'

The smile slipped from Mungo St John's face, and he inclined his head slightly and studied the ash of his cigar.

'Think about this, General. When the Imperial Government realizes the extent of the famine, it will force your famous Chartered Company to feed the Matabele. What is the cost of transporting grain from the Cape? A hundred pounds a load. Or is it more now? If the famine approaches the proportions of genocide, then I will see to it that Her Majesty's Government is faced with such a public outcry, led by humanitarians like Labouchère and Blunt, that they may be obliged to revoke the charter and make Matabeleland a crown colony after all.'

Mungo St John took his bottle off the desk and sat upright in his chair.

'Who appointed you champion of these savages, anyway?' he asked. But she ignored his question.

'I suggest, General, that you relay these thoughts to Mr Rhodes before the famine takes a hold.'

She gloried in the visible effort it took him to regain his equanimity.

'You may well be right, Robyn.' His smile was light and mocking again. 'I will point this out to the directors of the Company.'

'Immediately,' she insisted.

'Immediately,' he capitulated, and spread his hands in a parody of helplessness. 'Now is there anything else you want of me?'

'Yes,' she said. 'I want you to marry me.'

He stood up slowly and stared at her.

'You may not believe this, my dear, but nothing would give me greater pleasure. Yet, I am confused. I asked you that day at Khami Mission. Why now have you changed your mind?'

'I need a father for the bastard you have got on me. It was conceived four months after Clinton's death.'

'A son,' he said. 'It will be a son.' He came around the desk towards her.

'You must know that I hate you,' she said.

His single eye crinkled as he smiled at her.

'Yes, and that is probably the reason that I love you.'

'Never say that again,' she hissed at him.

'Oh, but I must. You see I did not even realize it myself. I always believed that I was proof from such a mundane emotion as love. I was deceiving myself. You and I must now bravely face up to that fact. I love you.'

'I want nothing from you but your name, and you shall have nothing from me but hatred and contempt.'

'Marry me first, my love, and later we will decide who gets what from whom.'

'Do not touch me,' she said, and Mungo St John kissed her full on the mouth.

*

It had taken almost ten full days of leisurely riding to make a circuit of the boundaries of the ranch lands that Zouga had claimed with his land grants.

It stretched eastwards from the Khami river, almost as far as the Bembesi crossing and southwards to the outskirts of GuBulawayo, an area the size of the county of Surrey, rich grasslands with stretches of parklike forests and low golden hills. Through it meandered a dozen lesser rivers and streams, which watered the herds that Zouga was already grazing.

Mr Rhodes had appointed Zouga the custodian of enemy property – with powers to take possession of the royal herds of Lobengula. The hundred troopers who volunteered for the duty rounded up almost 130,000 head of prime cattle.

Half of these belonged to the Chartered Company, but that left 65,000 to be distributed as loot to the men who had ridden in to GuBulawayo with Jameson and St John. However, at the very last minute, Mr Rhodes had changed his mind, and telegraphed St John with instructions to redistribute 40,000 head to the Matabele tribe.

The volunteers were incensed at having lost more than a third of their rightful loot, and word was soon spreading through the improvised bars and canteens of GuBulawayo that the cattle had been given back to the tribe after threats and representations by the woman doctor of Khami Mission. Credence was given to the rumour by the fact that the same telegraph message authorized the grant of six thousand acres of land to Khami Mission. Mr Rhodes was squaring the God-botherers, and the volunteers were not going to stand for it.

Fifty troopers, all full of whisky, rode out to burn down the mission and string up the hag responsible for their loss. Zouga Ballantyne and Mungo St John met them at the foot of the hills. With a few salty sallies, they had them laughing; then they took it in turn to curse them fluently and roundly, and finally they drove them back to town, where they stood them a dozen rounds of drinks.

Despite the redistribution to the tribe, still the flood of cattle upon the market brought the price down to two pounds a head, and Zouga used half the proceeds of the Ballantyne diamond to buy up ten thousand of them to stock his new estates.

Now as Zouga and Louise rode together, with Jan Cheroot following them in the Scotch cart with the tent and camping equipment, they passed small herds of the cattle tended by Matabele herders that Zouga had hired.

Zouga had been able to select only the best animals, and he had graded them by colour, so that one herd might consist of all red beasts while the next of only black ones.

Ralph had contracted to bring up all the materials for the new homestead from the railhead at Kimberley – and with the same convoy would be twenty thoroughbred bulls of Hereford stock that Zouga intended running with his cows.

'This is the place,' Louise exclaimed with delight.

'How can you be so certain – so soon?' Zouga laughed.

'Oh, darling, it's perfect. I can spend the rest of my life looking at that view.'

Below them the land fell away steeply to deep green pools of the river.

'At least there will be good water – and that bottom land will grow excellent vegetables –'

'Don't be so unromantic,' she chided him. 'Look at the trees.'

They soared above their heads like the arched and vaulted spans of a great cathedral, and the autumn foliage was a thousand shades of reds and golds, murmurous with bees and merry with bird song.

'They will give good shade in the hot season,' Zouga agreed.

'Shame on you,' she laughed. 'If you cannot see their beauty, then look at the Thabas Indunas.'

The Hills of the Indunas were whalebacked and dreaming blue beneath the tall silver clouds. The grassy plains between were scattered with small groups of Zouga's cattle, and of wild game – zebra and blue wildebeest.

'They are close enough,' Zouga nodded. 'When Ralph's construction company finally reaches GuBulawayo with the railway line, then we shall be a few hours' ride from the railhead and all the amenities of civilization.'

'So you will build me a home here – on this very spot?'

'Not until you give it a name.'

'What would you like to call it, my darling husband?'

'I'd like to have a touch of the old country – King's Lynn was where I spent my childhood.'

'That's it then.'

'King's Lynn.' Zouga tested the name. 'Yes, that will do very nicely. Now you shall have the home you want.'

Louise took his hand, and they walked down under the trees towards the river.

A man and a woman came down the narrow winding pathway through the thick riverine bush.

The man carried his shield on his left shoulder, with the broad-bladed assegai secured to it by the rawhide thongs; but his right arm was shortened and deformed, twisted out from his shoulder as though the bone had been broken and badly set.

There was no superfluous flesh upon his powerfully boned frame; the rack of his ribs showed through, and his skin lacked the lustre of health. It was the dull lifeless colour of lamp-black – as though he had just risen from a long sickbed. On his trunk and back gleamed the satiny rosettes of freshly healed gunshot wounds, like newly-minted coins of pure blue cobalt.

The woman who followed him was young and straight. Her eyes were slanted and her features those of an Egyptian princess. Her breasts were fat and full with milk, and her infant son was strapped tightly to her back so that his head would not jerk or wobble to her long, swinging gait.

Bazo reached the bank of the river and turned to his wife.

'We will rest here, Tanase.'

She loosened the knot and swung the child onto her hip. She took one of her swollen nipples between thumb and forefinger until milk spurted from it, and then she touched it to the boy's lips. Immediately he began to feed with little pig-like snuffles and grunts.

'When will we reach the next village?' she asked.

'When the sun is there.' Bazo pointed halfway down the sky. 'Are you not weary of the road, we have travelled so far, so long.'

'I will never weary, not until we have delivered the word to every man and woman and child in Matabeleland,' she replied, and she began to joggle the baby and croon to it:

'Tungata is your name, for you will be a seeker.

'Zebiwe is your name, for what you will seek is that which has been stolen from you and your people.

'Drink my words Tungata Zebiwe, even as you drink my milk. Remember them all your days, Tungata, and teach them to your own children. Remember the wounds on your father's breast, and the wounds in your mother's heart – and teach your children to hate.'

She changed the infant to her other hip, and her other breast, and she went on crooning until he had drunk his fill and his little head drooped sleepily. Then she slung him upon her back once more, and they crossed the river and went on.

They reached the village an hour before the setting of the sun. There were less than a hundred people living in the scattered huts. They saw the young couple from afar and a dozen of the men came out to greet them with respect and lead them in.

The women brought them grilled maize cakes and thick soured milk in calabash gourds, and the children came to stare at the strangers and to whisper to one another. 'These are the wanderers – these are the people from the Hills of the Matopos.'

When they had eaten, and the sun had set, the villagers built up the fire. Tanase stood in the firelight, and they squatted in a circle about her, silent and intent.

'I am called Tanase,' she said. 'And once I was the Umlimo.'

There was a low gasp of shock at her mention of that name.

'I was the Umlimo,' Tanase repeated. 'But then the powers of the spirits were taken from me.'

They sighed softly and stirred like dead leaves when a random breeze passes.

'There is another who is now the Umlimo and lives in the secret place in the hills, for the Umlimo never dies.'

There was a little hum of assent.

'Now I am the voice of the Umlimo only. I am the messenger who brings you the word of the Umlimo. Listen well, my children, for the Umlimo prophesies thus.' She paused and now the silence was charged with religious terror.

'When the noon sun goes dark with wings, and the trees are bare of leaves in the springtime – then warriors of Matabele put an edge to your steel.'

Tanase paused and the firelight gleamed on the hundreds of eyes that watched her.

'When the cattle lie with their heads twisted to touch their flank and cannot rise – then will be the time to rise up and to strike with the steel.'

She spread her arms like a crucifix and cried out:

'That is the prophecy. Harken to it, children of Mashobane; Harken to the voice of the Umlimo. For the Matabele will be great once again.'

In the dawn the two wanderers, carrying the infant who was named the 'Seeker after what has been stolen', went on towards the next village, where the elders came out to greet them.

*

In the southern springtime of 1896 on the shores of a lake near the southern extremity of the Rift Valley, that mighty geological fault which splits the African Continental Shield like an axe stroke, a bizarre hatching occurred.

The huge egg masses of *schistocerca gregaria*, the desert locust, that were buried in the loose earth along the border of the lake, released countless multitudes of flightless nymphs. The eggs had been laid by females in the solitary phase of the locust's life cycle; but so vast was the hatching of their progeny that the earth could not contain them, and though they spread out over an area of almost fifty square miles, they were forced to crawl upon one another's backs.

The constant agitation and stimulation of contact with other nymphs wrought a miraculous change in this teeming tide of insects. Their colour turned to a vivid orange and midnight black, unlike their parents' drab brown. Their metabolic rate surged and they became hyperactive and nervous. Their legs grew longer and stronger, their gregarious instincts more powerful, so that they flowed in a compact body that seemed to be a single monstrous organism. They had entered the gregarious phase of the life cycle, and when at last they moulted for the last time and their newly-fledged wings had dried, the entire swarm took spontaneously to the air.

In that first baptism of flight, they were spurred by their high body temperature, which was raised further by their muscular activity. They could not stop until the cool of evening, and then they settled in such dense swarms that the branches of the forest snapped under their weight. They fed voraciously all night, and in the morning the rising heat spurred them into flight once more.

They rose in a cloud so dense that the sound of their wings was the drumming roar of hurricane winds. The trees they left behind were stripped completely of their tender springtime foliage. As they passed overhead, their wings eclipsed the noonday sun, and a deep shadow fell over the land.

They were headed south towards the Zambezi river.

From the Great Sud where the infant Nile river weaves its way through fathomless swamps of floating papyrus, southwards over the wide savannahs of eastern and central Africa, down to the Zambezi and beyond, roamed vast herds of buffalo.

They had never been hunted by the primitive tribes, who preferred easier game; only a few Europeans with sophisticated weapons had ventured into these remote lands, and even the lions which followed the herds could not check their natural multiplication.

The grasslands were black with the huge bovine black beasts. Twenty or thirty thousand strong, the herds were so dense that the animals in the rear literally starved, for the pasture was destroyed before they could reach it. Weakened by their own vast multitudes, they were ripe for the pestilence that came out of the north.

It was the same plague that Moses' God had inflicted on the Pharaoh of Egypt, the rinderpest, the *peste bovine*, a virus disease which attacks cattle and all other ruminants. The stricken animals were blinded by the discharge of thick mucus from their eyes. It poured in ropes from their gaping jaws and nostrils to contaminate the pastures and infect any other animal that passed over them.

Their emaciated bodies were wracked by spasms of profuse diarrhoea and dysentery. When at last they dropped, the convulsions twisted their heads back upon their tortured necks, so that their noses touched one of their flanks – and they could never rise again.

So swift was the passage of the disease that a herd of ten thousand great horned black beasts was wiped out between dawn and sunset. Their carcasses lay so thickly that they touched each other, and the characteristic fetid odour of the disease mingled with the stench of rotting flesh; for although the vultures gorged, they could not devour one thousandth part of this dreadful harvest of death.

Swiftly, carried by the vultures and the blundering, bellowing herds, the plague swept southwards towards the Zambezi river.

On the banks of that mighty river Tanase stood beside another watch-fire and repeated the prophecy of the Umlimo:

> 'When the noon sun goes dark with wings,
> and the trees are bare of leaves in the
> springtime –
> 'When the cattle lie with their heads
> twisted to touch their flank, and cannot
> rise –'

Thus she cried, and the people of the Matabele listened and took new heart and looked to their steel.

Shout at the
Devil

Foreword

I will not deny that this story was suggested to me by the action in World War I, when the German mercantile raider *Königsberg* was sunk in the Kikunya channel of the Rufiji delta by ships of the Royal Navy.

However, I will most emphatically deny that the rogues and scoundrels depicted in my tale bear the slightest resemblance to any members of the company of men that operated to the destruction of *Königsberg*. In particular, I would strongly resist the suggestion that Flynn Patrick O'Flynn is based on the character of the gallant Colonel 'Jungle Man' Pretorius, who actually went aboard *Königsberg*, disguised as a native bearer, and paced out the ranges for the guns of His Majesty's warships *Severn* and *Mersey*.

I would like to express my thanks to Lieutenant Commander Mathers (R.N. retired) for his assistance in my researches.

Part One

1

Flynn Patrick O'Flynn was an ivory poacher by profession, and modestly he admitted that he was the best on the east coast of Africa.

Rachid El Keb was an exporter of precious stones, of women for the harems and great houses of Arabia and India, and of illicit ivory. This he admitted only to his trusted clients; to the rest he was a rich and respectable owner of coastal shipping.

In an afternoon during the monsoon of 1912, drawn together by their mutual interest in pachyderms, Flynn and Rachid sat in the back room of El Keb's shop in the Arab quarter of Zanzibar, and drank tea from tiny brass thimbles. The hot tea made Flynn O'Flynn perspire even more than usual. It was so humid hot in the room that the flies sat in languid stupor upon the low ceiling.

'Listen, Kebby, you lend me just one of those stinking little ships of yours and I'll fill her so high with tusks, she'll damn nigh sink.'

'Ah!' replied El Keb carefully, and went on waving the palm-leaf fan in his own face – a face that resembled that of a suspicious parrot with a straggly, goatee beard.

'Have I ever let you down yet?' Flynn demanded aggressively, and a drop of sweat fell from the tip of his nose onto his already damp shirt.

'Ah!' El Keb repeated.

'This scheme has a flair. It has the touch of greatness to it. This scheme . . .' Flynn paused to find a suitable adjective, '. . . this scheme is Napoleonic. It is Caesarian!'

'Ah!' El Keb said again, and refilled his tea cup. Lifting it delicately between thumb and forefinger, he sipped before speaking. 'It is necessary only that I should risk the total destruction of a sixty-foot dhow worth . . .' prudently he inflated the figure, '. . . two thousand English pounds?'

'Against an almost certain recovery of twenty thousand,' Flynn cut in quickly, and El Keb smiled a little, almost dreamily.

'You'd put the profits so high?' he asked.

'That's the lowest figure. Good God, Kebby! There hasn't been a shot fired in the Rufiji basin for twenty years. You know damn well it's the Kaiser's private hunting reserve. The Jumbo are so thick in there I could round them up and drive them in like sheep.' Involuntarily Flynn's right forefinger crooked and twitched as though it were already curled around a trigger.

'Madness,' whispered El Keb, with the gold gloat softening the shape of his lips. 'You'd sail into the Rufiji river from the sea, hoist the Union Jack on one of the islands in the delta and fill the dhow with German ivory. Madness.'

'The Germans have formally annexed none of those islands. I'd be in and out again before Berlin had sent their first cable to London. With ten of my gun-boys hunting, we'd fill the dhow in two weeks.'

'The Germans would have a gunboat there in a week. They've got the *Blücher* lying at Dar es Salaam under steam, heavy cruiser with nine-inch guns.'

'We'd be under protection of the British flag. They couldn't dare touch us – not on the high seas – not with things the way they are now between England and Germany.'

'Mr O'Flynn, I was led to believe you were a citizen of the United States of America.'

'You damn right I am.' Flynn sat up a little straighter, a little more proudly.

'You'd need a British captain for the dhow,' El Keb mused, and stroked his beard thoughtfully.

'Jesus, Kebby, you didn't think I was fool enough to sail that cow in myself?' Flynn looked pained. 'I'll find someone else to do that, and to sail her out again through the Imperial German navy. Me, I'm going to walk in from my base camp in Portuguese Mozambique and go out the same way.'

'Forgive me.' El Keb smiled again. 'I underestimated you.' He stood up quickly. The splendour of the great jewelled dagger at his waist was somewhat spoiled by the unwashed white of his ankle-length robe. 'Mr O'Flynn, I think I have just the man to captain your dhow for you. But first it is necessary to alter his financial circumstances so that he might be willing to accept employment.'

2

T he leather purse of gold sovereigns had been the pivot on which the gentle confusion of Sebastian Oldsmith's life turned. It had been presented to him by his father when Sebastian had announced to the family his intention of sailing to Australia to make his fortune in the wool trade. It had comforted him during the voyage from Liverpool to the Cape of Good Hope where the captain had unceremoniously deposited him after Sebastian's misalliance with the daughter of the gentleman who was proceeding to Sydney to take up his appointment as Governor of New South Wales.

In gradually dwindling quantity the sovereigns had remained with him through the series of misfortunes that ended in Zanzibar, when he awoke from heat-drugged sleep in a shoddy room to find that the leather purse and its contents were gone, and with them were gone the letters of introduction from his father to certain prominent wool-brokers of Sydney.

It occurred to Sebastian as he sat on the edge of his bed that the letters had little real value in Zanzibar, and with increasing bewilderment, he reviewed the events that had blown him so far off his intended course. Slowly his forehead creased in the effort of thought. It was the high, intelligent forehead of a philosopher crowned by a splendid mass of shiny black curls; his eyes were dark brown, his nose long and straight, his jaw firm, and his mouth sensitive. In his twenty-second year, Sebastian had the face of a young Oxford don; which proves, perhaps, how misleading looks can be. Those who knew him well would have been surprised that Sebastian, in setting out for Australia, had come as close to it as Zanzibar.

Abandoning the mental exercise that was already giving him a slight headache, Sebastian stood up from the bed and, with the skirt of his nightshirt flapping around his calves, began his third minute search of the hotel room. Although the purse had been under his mattress when he went to sleep the preceding evening, this time Sebastian emptied the water jug and peered into it hopefully. He unpacked his valise and shook out each shirt. He crawled under the bed, lifted the coconut matting and probed every hole in the rotten flooring before giving way to despair.

Shaved, the bed-bug bites on his person anointed with saliva, and dressed in the grey three-piece suit which was showing signs of travel fatigue, he brushed his derby hat and placed it carefully over his curls, picked up his cane in one hand, and lugging his valise in the other, he went down the stairs into the hot noisy lobby of the Hotel Royal.

'I say,' he greeted the little Arab at the desk with the most cheerful smile he could muster. 'I say, I seem to have lost my money.'

A silence fell upon the room. The waiters carrying trays out to the hotel veranda slowed and stopped, heads turned towards Sebastian with the same hostile curiosity as if he had announced that he was suffering from a mild attack of leprosy.

'Stolen, I should imagine,' Sebastian went on, grinning. 'Nasty bit of luck, really.'

The silence exploded as the bead curtains from the office were thrown open and the Hindu proprietor erupted into the room with a loud cry of, 'Mr Oldsmith, what about your bill?'

'Oh, the bill. Yes, well, let's not get excited. I mean, it won't help, now, will it?'

And the proprietor proceeded to become very excited indeed. His cries of anguish and indignation carried to the veranda where a dozen persons were already beginning the daily fight against heat and thirst. They crowded into the lobby to watch with interest.

'Ten days you owe. Nearly one hundred rupees.'

'Yes, it's jolly unfortunate, I know.' Sebastian was grinning desperately, when a new voice added itself to the uproar.

'Now just hold on a shake.' Together Sebastian and the Hindu turned to the big red-faced, middle-aged man with the pleasantly mixed American and Irish accent. 'Did I hear you called Mr Oldsmith?'

'That is correct, sir.' Sebastian knew instinctively that here was an ally.

'An unusual name. You wouldn't be related to Mister Francis Oldsmith, wool merchant of Liverpool, England?' Flynn O'Flynn inquired politely. He had perused Sebastian's letters of introduction passed on to him by Rachid El Keb.

'Good Lord!' Sebastian cried with joy. 'Do you know my pater?'

'Do I know Francis Oldsmith?' Flynn laughed easily, and then checked himself. His acquaintance was limited to the letterheads. 'Well, I don't exactly know him person to person, you understand, but I think I can say I know of him. Used to be in the wool business myself once.' Flynn turned genially to the hotel proprietor and breathed on him a mixture of gin fumes and goodfellowship. 'One hundred rupees was the sum you mentioned.'

'That's the sum, Mr O'Flynn.' The proprietor was easily soothed.

'Mr Oldsmith and I will be having a drink on the veranda. You can bring the receipt to us there.' Flynn placed two sovereigns on the counter; sovereigns that had so recently reposed beneath Sebastian's mattress.

With his boots propped on the low veranda wall, Sebastian regarded the harbour over the rim of his glass. Sebastian was not a drinking man but in view of Flynn

O'Flynn's guardianship he could not be churlish and refuse hospitality. The number of craft in the bay suddenly multiplied miraculously before his eyes. Where a moment before one stubby little dhow had been tacking in through the entrance, there were now three identical boats sailing in formation. Sebastian closed one eye and by focusing determinedly, he reduced the three back to one. Mildly elated with his success, he turned his attention to his new friend and business partner who had pressed such large quantities of gin upon him.

'Mr O'Flynn,' he said with deliberation, slurring the words slightly.

'Forget that mister, Bassie, call me Flynn. Just plain Flynn, the same as in gin.'

'Flynn,' said Sebastian. 'There isn't anything – well, there isn't anything funny about this?'

'How do you mean *funny*, boy?'

'I mean' – and Sebastian blushed slightly. 'There isn't anything illegal, is there?'

'Bassie.' Flynn shook his head sorrowfully. 'What do you take me for, Bassie? You think I'm a crook or something, boy?'

'Oh, no, of course not, Flynn,' and Sebastian blushed a shade deeper. 'I just thought – well, all these elephants we're going to shoot. They must belong to somebody. Aren't they German elephants?'

'Bassie, I want to show you something.' Flynn set down his glass and groping in the inside pocket of his wilted tropical suit, he produced an envelope. 'Read that, boy!'

The address at the head of the sheet of cheap notepaper was 'The Kaiserhof. Berlin. Dated June 10, 1912', and the body of the letter read:

> Dear Mr Flynn O'Flynn,
> I am worried about all those elephants down in the Rufiji basin eating up all the grass and smashing up all the trees and things, so if you've got time, would you go down there and shoot some of them as they're eating up all the grass and smashing up all the trees and things.
> > Yours sincerely,
> > Kaiser Willem III.
> > Emperor of Germany.

A vague uneasiness formed through the clouds of gin in Sebastian's skull. 'Why did he write to you?'

'Because he knows I'm the best goddamned elephant hunter in the world.'

'You'd expect him to use better English, wouldn't you?' Sebastian murmured.

'What's wrong with his English?' Flynn demanded truculently. He had spent some time in composing the letter.

'Well, I mean that bit about eating up all the grass – he said that twice.'

'Well, you got to remember he's a German. They don't write English too good.'

'Of course! I hadn't thought of that.' Sebastian looked relieved and lifted his glass. 'Well, good hunting!'

'I'll drink to that,' and Flynn emptied his glass.

3

S ebastian stood with both hands gripping the wooden rail of the dhow and stared out across a dozen miles of water at the loom of the African mainland. The monsoon wind had ruffled the sea to a dark indigo and it flipped spray from the white-caps into Sebastian's face. Overlaying the clean salt of the ocean was the taint of the mangrove swamps, an evil smell as though an animal had died in its own cage. Sebastian sniffed it with distaste as he searched the low, green line of the coast for the entrance to the maze of the Rufiji delta.

Frowning, he tried to reconstruct the admiralty chart in his mind. The Rufiji river came to the sea through a dozen channels spread over forty miles, and in doing so, carved fifty, maybe a hundred, islands out of the mainland.

Tidal water washed fifteen miles upstream, past the mangroves to where the vast grass swampland began. It was there in the swampland that the elephant herds had taken shelter from the guns and arrows of the ivory hunters, protected by Imperial decree and by a formidable terrain.

The murderous-looking ruffian who captained the dhow uttered a string of sing-song orders, and Sebastian turned to watch the complicated manoeuvre of tacking the ungainly craft. Half-naked seamen dropped out of the rigging like over-ripe brown fruit and swarmed around the sixty-foot teak boom. Bare feet padding on the filthy deck, they ran the boom back and forward again. The dhow creaked like an old man with arthritis, came round wearily on to the wind, and butted its nose in towards the land. The new motion, combined with the swamp smell and the smell of freshly-stirred bilges, moved something deep within Sebastian. His grip upon the rail increased, and new sweat popped out like little blisters on his brow. He leaned forward, and, to shouts of encouragement from the crew, made another sacrifice to the sea gods. He was still draped worshipfully across the rail as the dhow wallowed and slid in the turbulent waters of the entrance, and then passed into the calm of the southernmost channel of the Rufiji basin.

Four days later, Sebastian sat cross-legged with the dhow captain on a thick Bokhara carpet spread upon the deck, and they explained to each other in sign language that neither of them had the vaguest idea where they were. The dhow was anchored in a narrow water-way hemmed in by the twisted and deformed trunks of the mangroves. The sensation of being lost was not new to Sebastian and he accepted it with resignation, but the dhow captain, who could run from Aden to Calcutta and back to Zanzibar with the certainty of a man visiting his own outhouse, was not so stoical. He lifted his eyes to the heavens and called upon Allah to intercede with the djinn who guarded this stinking labyrinth, who made the waters flow in strange, unnatural ways, who changed the shape of each island, and thrust mud banks in their path. Driven on by his own eloquence, he leapt to the rail and screamed defiance into the brooding mangroves until flocks of ibis rose and milled in the heat mists above the dhow. Then he flung himself down on the carpet and fixed Sebastian with a stare of sullen malevolence.

'It's not really my fault, you know.' Sebastian wriggled with embarrassment under the stare. Then once again he produced his admiralty chart, spread it on the deck, and placed his finger on the island which Flynn O'Flynn had ringed in blue pencil as the rendezvous. 'I mean, it *is* rather your cup of tea, finding the place. After all, you *are* the navigator, aren't you?'

The captain spat fiercely on his deck, and Sebastian flushed.

'Now that sort of thing isn't going to get us anywhere. Let's try and behave like gentlemen.'

This time the captain hawked it up from deep down in his throat and spat a lump of yellow phlegm into the blue pencil circle on Sebastian's map, then he rose to his feet and stalked away to where his crew squatted in a group under the poop.

In the short dusk, while the mosquitoes whined in a thin mist about Sebastian's head, he listened to the Arabic muttering and saw the glances that were directed at him down the length of the dhow. So when the night closed over the ship like a bank of black steam, he took up a defensive position on the foredeck and waited for them to come. As a weapon he had his cane of solid ebony. He laid it across his lap and sat against the rail until the darkness was complete, then, silently, he changed his position and crouched beside one of the water barrels that was lashed to the base of the mast.

They were a long time coming. Half the night had wasted away before he heard the stealthy scuff of bare feet on the planking. The absolute blackness of the night was filled with the din of the swamp; the boom and tonk of frogs, the muted buzz of insects and the occasional snort and splash of a hippo, so that Sebastian had difficulty in deciding how many they had sent against him. Crouching by the water barrel he strained his eyes unavailingly into the utter blackness and tuned his hearing to filter out the swamp noises and catch only those soft little sounds that death made as it came down the deck towards him.

Although Sebastian had never scaled any academic heights, he had boxed light heavyweight for Rugby, and fast-bowled for Sussex the previous cricket season when he had led the county bowling averages. So, although he was afraid now, Sebastian had a sublime confidence in his own physical prowess and it was not the kind of fear that filled his belly with oily warmth, nor turned his ego to jelly, but rather, it keyed him to a point where every muscle in his body quivered on the edge of exploding. Crouching in the night he groped for the cane that he had laid on the deck beside him. His hands fell on the bulky sackful of green coconuts that made up part of the dhow's deck cargo. They were carried to supplement, with their milk, the meagre supply of fresh water on board. Quickly Sebastian tore open the fastenings of the sack and hefted one of the hard round fruits.

'Not quite as handy as a cricket ball, but – ' murmured Sebastian and came to his feet. Using the short run up he delivered the fast ball with which he had shattered the Yorkshire first innings the previous year. It had the same effect on the Arab first innings. The coconut whirred and cracked against the skull of one of the approaching assassins and the rest retired in confusion.

'Now send the men,' roared Sebastian and bowled a short lifter that hastened the retreat.

He selected another coconut and was about to deliver that also when there was a flash and a report from aft, and something howled over Sebastian's head. Hastily he ducked behind the sack of coconuts.

'My God, they've got a gun up there!' Sebastian remembered then the ancient muzzle-loading Jezail he had seen the captain polishing lovingly on their first day out from Zanzibar, and he felt his anger rising in earnest.

He jumped to his feet and hurled his next coconut with fury.

'Fight fair, you dirty swine!' he yelled.

There was a delay while the dhow captain went through the complicated process of loading his piece. Then a cannon report, a burst of flame, and another potleg howled over Sebastian's head.

Through the dark hours before dawn the lively exchange of jeers and curses, of coconuts and potlegs continued. Sebastian more than held his own for he scored four howls of pain and a yelp, while the dhow captain succeeded only in shooting away a great deal of his own standing rigging. But as the light of the new day increased, so Sebastian's advantage waned. The Arab captain's shooting improved to such an extent that Sebastian spent most of his time crouching behind the sack of coconuts. Sebastian was nearly exhausted. His right arm and shoulder ached unmercifully, and he could hear the first stealthy advance of the Arab crew as they crept down towards his hide. In daylight they could surround him and use their numbers to drag him down.

While he rested for the final effort, Sebastian looked out at the morning. It was a red dawn, angry and beautiful through the swamp mists so the water glowed with a pink sheen and the mangroves stood very dark around the ship.

Something splashed farther up the channel, a water bird perhaps. Sebastian looked for it without interest, and heard it splash again and then again. He stirred and sat up a little straighter. The sound was too regular for that of a bird or a fish.

Then around the bend in the channel, from behind the wall of mangroves, driven on by urgent paddles, shot a dug-out canoe. Standing in the bow with a double-barrelled elephant gun under his arm and a clay pipe sticking out of his red face, was Flynn O'Flynn.

'What the hell's going on here?' he roared. 'Are you fighting a goddamned war? I've been waiting a week for you lot!'

'Look out, Flynn!' Sebastian yelled a warning. 'That swine has got a gun!'

The Arab captain had jumped to his feet and was looking around uncertainly. Long ago he had regretted his impulse to rid himself of the Englishman and escape from this evil swamp, and now his misgivings were truly justified. Having committed himself, however, there was only one course open to him. He lifted the Jezail to his shoulder and aimed at O'Flynn in the canoe. The discharge blew a long grey spurt of powder from the muzzle, and the potleg lifted a burst of spray from the surface of the water beyond the canoe. The echoes of the shot were drowned by the bellow of O'Flynn's rifle. He fired without moving the pipe from his mouth and the narrow dug-out rocked dangerously with the recoil.

The heavy bullet picked up the Arab captain's scrawny body, his robe fluttered like a piece of old paper and his turban flew from his head and unwound in mid-air as he was flung clear of the rail to drop with a tall splash alongside. He floated face down, trapped air ballooning his robe about him and then he drifted away slowly on the sluggish current. His crew, stunned and silent, stood by the rail and watched him depart.

Dismissing the neat execution as though it had never happened, O'Flynn glared up at Sebastian and roared, 'You're a week late. I haven't been able to do a goddamned thing until you got here. Now let's get the flag up and start doing some work!'

4

T he formal annexation of Flynn O'Flynn's island took place in the relatively cool of the following morning. It had taken some hours for Flynn to convince Sebastian of the necessity of occupying the island for the British crown, and he succeeded only by casting Sebastian in the role of empire builder. He made some flattering comparisons between Clive of India and Sebastian Oldsmith of Liverpool.

The next problem was the choice of a name. This stirred up a little Anglo-American enmity, with Flynn O'Flynn campaigning aggressively for 'New Boston'. Sebastian was horrified, his patriotic ardour burned brightly.

'Now hold on a jiffy, old chap,' he protested.

'What's wrong with it? You just tell me what's wrong with it!'

'Well, first of all this is going to be one of His Britannic Majesty's possessions, you know.'

'New Boston,' O'Flynn repeated. 'That sounds good. That sounds real good.'

Sebastian shuddered. 'I think it would be – well, not quite suitable. I mean, Boston was the place where they had that tea thing, you know.'

The argument raged more savagely as Flynn lowered the level in the gin bottle, until finally Sebastian stood up from the carpet on the floor of the dhow cabin, his eyes blazing with patriotic outrage. 'If you would care to step outside, sir,' he enunciated with care as he stood over the older man, 'we can settle this matter.' The dignity of the challenge was spoiled by the low roof of the cabin which made it necessary for Sebastian to stoop.

'Man, I'd eat you without spitting the bones.'

'That, sir, is your opinion. But I must warn you I was highly thought of in the light heavyweight division.'

'Oh, goddamn it,' Flynn shook his head wearily and capitulated. 'What difference does it make what we call the mother-loving place. Sit down, for God's sake. Here! Let's drink to whatever you want to call it.'

Sebastian sat on the carpet and accepted the mug that Flynn handed him. 'We shall call it – ' he paused dramatically, 'we shall call it New Liverpool,' and he lifted the mug.

'You know,' said Flynn, 'for a limey, you aren't a bad guy,' and the rest of the night was devoted to celebrating the birth of the new colony.

In the dawn the empire builders were paddled ashore in the dug-out by two of Flynn's gun-bearers.

The canoe ran aground on the narrow muddy beach of New Liverpool, and the sudden halt threw both of them off-balance. They collapsed gently together on to the floor of the dug-out, and had to be assisted ashore by the paddlers.

Sebastian was formally dressed for the occasion but had buttoned his waistcoat awry and he kept tugging at it as he peered about him.

Now at high tide, New Liverpool was about a thousand yards long and half as broad. At the highest point it rose not more than ten feet above the level of the Rufiji river. Fifteen miles from the mouth the water was only slightly tainted with salt and the mangrove trees had thinned out and given way to tall matted elephant grass and slender bottle palms.

Flynn's gun-bearers and porters had cleared a small opening above the beach, and had erected a dozen grass huts around one of the palm trees. It was a dead palm, its crown leaves long gone and Flynn pointed an unsteady finger at it.

'Flag pole,' he said indistinctly, took Sebastian's elbow and led him towards it.

Tugging at his waistcoat with one hand and clutching the bundled Union Jack that Flynn had provided in the other, Sebastian felt a surge of emotion within him as he looked up at the slender column of the palm tree.

'Leave me,' he mumbled and shook off Flynn's guiding hand. 'We got to do this right. Solemn occasion – very solemn.'

'Have a drink.' Flynn offered him the gin bottle, and when Sebastian waved it away, he lifted it to his own lips.

'Shouldn't drink on parade.' Sebastian frowned at him. 'Bad form.'

Flynn coughed at the vicious sting of the liquor and smote himself on the chest with his free hand.

'Should draw the men up in a hollow square,' Sebastian went on. 'Ready to salute the flag.'

'Jesus, man, get on with it,' grumbled Flynn.

'Got to do it right.'

'Oh, hell,' Flynn shrugged with resignation, then issued a string of orders in Swahili.

Puzzled and amused, Flynn's fifteen retainers gathered in a ragged circle about the flag pole. They were a curious band, gathered from half a dozen tribes, dressed in an assortment of cast-off western clothing, half of them armed with ancient double-barrelled elephant rifles from which Flynn had carefully filed the serial numbers so they could never be traced back to him.

'Fine body of men,' Sebastian beamed at them in alcoholic goodwill, unconsciously using the words of a Brigadier who had inspected Sebastian's cadet parade at Rugby.

'Let's get this show on the road,' Flynn suggested.

'My friends,' Sebastian obliged, 'we are gathered here today . . .' It was a longish speech but Flynn weathered it by nipping away quietly at the gin bottle, and at last Sebastian ended with his voice ringing and tears of great emotion prickling his eyelids, '. . . In the sight of God and man, I hereby declare this island part of the glorious Empire of His Majesty, George V, King of England, Emperor of India, Protector of the Faith . . .' His voice wavered as he tried to remember the correct form, and he ended lamely, '. . . and all that sort of thing.'

A silence fell on the assembly and Sebastian fidgeted with embarrassment. 'What do I do now?' he enquired of Flynn O'Flynn in a stage whisper.

'Get that goddamned flag up.'

'Ah, the flag!' Sebastian exclaimed with relief, and the uncertainly, 'How?'

Flynn considered this at length. 'I guess you have to climb up the palm tree.'

With shrill cries of encouragement from the gun-bearers, and with Flynn shoving and cursing from below, the Governor of New Liverpool managed to scale the flag pole to a height of about fifteen feet. There he secured the flag and descended again so swiftly he tore the buttons off the front of his waistcoat, and twisted his ankle. He was borne away to one of the grass huts singing, 'God save our Gracious King' in a voice broken with gin, pain and patriotism.

For the rest of their stay on the island, the Union Jack flew at half mast above the encampment.

Carried initially by two Wakamba fishermen, it took fully ten days for the word of the annexation to reach the outpost of the German Empire one hundred miles away at Mahenge.

5

M ahenge was in the bush country above the coastal lowlands. It consisted, in its entirety, of four trading posts owned by Indian shopkeepers – and the German boma.

The German boma was a large stone building, thatched, set about with wide verandas over which purple bougainvillaea climbed in profusion. Behind it stood the barracks and parade ground of the African Askari, and before it a lonely flag pole from which streamed the black, red and yellow of the empire. A speck in the vastness of the African bush, seat of government for an area the size of France. An area that spread south to the Rovuma river and the border of Portuguese Mozambique, east to the Indian Ocean, and west to the uplands of Sao Hill and Mbeya.

From this stronghold the German Commissioner (Southern Province) wielded the limitless powers of a medieval robber baron. One of the Kaiser's arms, or, more realistically, one of his little fingers, he was answerable only to Governor Schee in Dar es Salaam. But Dar es Salaam was many torturous miles away, and Governor Schee was a busy man not to be troubled with trivialities. Just as long as the Herr Commissioner Herman Fleischer collected the taxes, he was free to collect them in his own sweet way; though very few of the indigenous inhabitants of the southern province would have described Herman Fleischer's ways as sweet.

At the time that the messenger, carrying the news of the British annexation of New Liverpool, trotted up over the last skyline and saw through the acacia thorn trees ahead of him the tiny clustered buildings of Mahenge, Herr Fleischer was finishing his midday meal.

A man of large appetite, his luncheon consisted of approximately two pounds of *Eisbein*, as much pickled cabbage, and a dozen potatoes, all swimming in thick gravy. Having aroused his taste-buds, he then went on to the sausage. The sausage came by weekly fast-runner from Dodoma in the north, and was manufactured by a man of genius, a Westphalian immigrant who made sausage with the taste of the Black Forest in them. The sausage, and the Hansa beer cooling in its earthernware jug, aroused in Herr Fleischer a delicious nostalgia. He ate not quietly but steadily, and, these quantities of food confined within the thick grey corduroy of his tunic and breeches, built up a pressure that squeezed the perspiration from his face and neck, forcing him to pause and mop up at regular intervals.

When he sighed at last and sagged back in his chair, the leather thongs squeaked a little under him. A bubble of trapped gas found its way up through the sausage and passed in genteel eruption between his lips. Tasting it, he sighed again in happiness and squinted out from the deep shade of the veranda into the flat shimmering glare of the sunlight.

Then he saw the messenger coming. The man reached the steps of the veranda and squatted down in the sun with his loin-cloth drawn up modestly between his legs. His body was washed shiny black with sweat but his legs were powdered with fine dust to the knees, and his chest swelled and subsided as he drank the thin hot air. His eyes were downcast, he could not look directly at the Bwana Mkuba until his presence was formally acknowledged.

Herman Fleischer watched him broodingly, his mood evaporating for he had been looking forward to his afternoon siesta – and the messenger had spoiled that. He looked away at the low cloud above the hills in the south and sipped his beer. Then he selected a cheroot from the box before him and lit it. The cheroot burned slowly and evenly, restoring a little of his good humour. He smoked it short before flicking the stub over the veranda wall.

'Speak,' he grunted, and the messenger lifted his eyes, and gasped with wonder and awe at the beauty and dignity of the Commissioner's person. Although this was ritual admiration, it never failed to stir a faint pleasure in Herr Fleischer.

'I see you, Bwana Mkuba – Great Lord,' and Fleischer inclined his head slightly. 'I bring you greetings from Kalani, headman of Batja, on the Rufiji. You are his father, and he crawls on his belly before you. Your hair of yellow, and the great fatness of your body, blind him with beauty.'

Herr Fleischer stirred restlessly in his chair. References to his corpulence, however well-intentioned, always annoyed him. 'Speak,' he repeated.

'Kalani says thus: "Ten suns ago, a ship came into the delta of the Rufiji, and stopped by the Island of the Dogs, Inja. On the island, the men of this ship have built houses, and above the houses, they have placed on a dead palm tree the cloth of the Insingeese which is of blue and white and red, having many crosses within crosses." '

Herr Fleischer struggled upright in his chair and stared at the messenger. The pink of his complexion slowly became cross-veined with red and purple.

'Kalani says also: "Since their coming the voices of their guns have never ceased to speak along the Rufiji river, and there has been a great killing of elephants so that in the noonday the sky is dark with the birds that come for the meat." '

Herr Fleischer was thrashing around in his chair, speech was locked in his throat and his face had swollen so it threatened to burst like an over-ripe fruit.

'Kalani says further: "Two white men are on the island. One is a man who is very thin and young and is therefore of no account. The other white man Kalani has seen only at a great distance but by the redness of this man's face, and by his bulk, he knows in his heart it is Fini." '

At the name Herr Fleischer became articulate, if not coherent – he bellowed like a bull in rut. The messenger winced, such a bellow from the Bwana Mkuba usually preceded a multiple hanging.

'Sergeant!' The next bellow had form, and Herr Fleischer was on his feet, struggling to clinch the buckle of his belt.

'Rasch!' he roared again. O'Flynn was in German territory again; O'Flynn was stealing German ivory once more – and compounding the insult by flying the Union Jack over the Kaiser's domain.

'Sergeant, where the thunder of God are you?' With incredible speed for a fat man Herr Fleischer raced down the long length of the veranda. For three years now, ever since his arrival in Mahenge, the name of Flynn O'Flynn had been enough to ruin his appetite, and produce in him a condition very close to epilepsy.

Around the corner of the veranda appeared the sergeant of the Askari, and Herr Fleischer braked just in time to avert collision.

'A storm patrol,' bellowed the Commissioner, blowing a cloud of spittle in his agitation. 'Twenty men. Full field packs, and one hundred pounds of ammunition. We leave in an hour.'

The sergeant saluted and doubled away across the parade ground. A minute later a bugle began singing with desperate urgency.

Slowly, through the black mists of rage, reason returned to Herman Fleischer. He stood with shoulders hunched, breathing heavily through his mouth, and mentally digested the full import of Kalani's message.

This was not just another of O'Flynn's will-o'-the-wisp forays across the Rovuma from Mozambique. This time he had sailed brazenly into the Rufiji delta, with a full-scale expedition, and hoisted the British flag. A queasy sensation, not attributable to the pickled pork, settled on Herr Fleischer's stomach. He knew the makings of an international incident when he saw one.

This, perhaps, was the goad that would launch the fatherland on the road to its true destiny. He gulped with excitement. They had flapped that hated flag in the Kaiser's face just once too often. This was history being made, and Herman Fleischer stood in the centre of it.

Trembling a little, he hurried into his office, and began drafting the report to Governor Schee that might plunge the world into a holocaust from which the German people would rise as the rulers of creation.

An hour later, he rode out of the boma on a white donkey with his slouch uniform hat set well forward on his head to shield his eyes from the glare. Behind him his black Askari marched with their rifles at the slope. Smart in their pillbox kepis with the backflaps hanging to the shoulder, khaki uniforms freshly pressed, and putteed legs rising and falling in unison, they made as gallant a show as any commander could wish.

A day and a half march would bring them to the confluence of the Kilombero and Rufiji rivers where the Commissioner's steam launch was moored.

As the buildings of Mahenge vanished behind him, Herr Fleischer relaxed and let his ample backside conform to the shape of the saddle.

6

'**N**ow, have you got it straight?' Flynn asked without conviction. The past eight days of hunting together had given him no confidence in Sebastian's ability to carry out a simple set of instructions without introducing some remarkable variation of his own. 'You go down the river to the island, and you load the ivory onto the dhow. Then you come back here with all the canoes to pick up the next batch.' Flynn paused to allow his words to absorb into the spongy tissue of Sebastian's head before he went on. 'And for Chrissake don't forget the gin.'

'Right you are, old chap.' With eight days' growth of black beard, and the skin peeling from the tip of his sunburned nose, Sebastian was beginning to fit the role of ivory poacher. The wide brimmed terai hat that Flynn had loaned him came down to his ears, and the razor edges of the elephant grass had shredded his trouser legs and stripped the polish from his boots. His wrists and the soft skin behind his ears were puffy and speckled with spots of angry red where the mosquitoes had drunk deep, but he had lost a little weight in the heat and the ceaseless walking, so now he was lean and hard-looking.

They stood together under a monkey-bean tree on the bank of the Rufiji, while at the water's edge the bearers were loading the last tusks into the canoes. There was a purple-greenish smell hanging over them in the steamy heat, a smell which Sebastian hardly noticed now – for the last eight days had seen a great killing of elephant and the stink of green ivory was as familiar to him as the smell of the sea to a mariner.

'By the time you get back tomorrow morning the boys will have brought in the last of the ivory. We'll have a full dhow-load and you can set off for Zanzibar.'

'What about you? Are you staying on here?'

'Not bloody likely. I'll light out for my base camp in Mozambique.'

'Wouldn't it be easier for you to come along on the dhow? It's nearly two hundred miles to walk.' Sebastian was solicitous; in these last days he had conceived a burning admiration for Flynn.

'Well, you see, it's like this . . .' Flynn hesitated. This was no time to trouble Sebastian with talk of German gunboats waiting off the mouth of the Rufiji. 'I have to get back to my camp, because . . .' Suddenly inspiration came to Flynn O'Flynn. 'Because my poor little daughter is there all alone.'

'You've got a daughter?' Sebastian was taken by surprise.

'You damn right I have.' Flynn experienced a sudden rush of paternal affection and duty. 'And the poor little thing is there all alone.'

'Well, when will I see you again?' The thought of parting from Flynn, of being left to try and find his own way to Australia saddened Sebastian.

'Well,' Flynn was tactful. 'I hadn't really given that much thought.' This was a lie. Flynn had thought about it ceaselessly for the last eight days. He was eagerly anticipating waving farewell to Sebastian Oldsmith for all time.

'Couldn't we . . .' Sebastian blushed a little under his sun-reddened cheeks. 'Couldn't we sort of team up together. I could work for you, sort of as an apprentice?'

The idea made Flynn wince. He almost panicked at the thought of Sebastian permanently trailing along behind him and discharging his rifle at random intervals. 'Well now, Bassie boy,' he clasped a thick arm around Sebastian's shoulders, 'first you sail that old dhow back to Zanzibar and old Kebby El Keb will pay you out your share. Then you write to me, hey? How about that? You write me, and we'll work something out.'

Sebastian grinned happily. 'I'd like that, Flynn. I'd truly like that.'

'All right, then, off you go. And don't forget the gin.'

With Sebastian standing in the bows of the lead canoe, the double-barrelled rifle clutched in his hands, and the terai hat pulled down firmly over his ears, the little flotilla of heavily laden canoes pulled out from the bank and caught the current. Paddles dipped and gleamed in the evening sunlight as they arrowed away towards the first bend downstream.

Still standing unsteadily in the frail craft, Sebastian looked back and waved his rifle at Flynn on the bank.

'For Chrissake, be careful with that goddamn piece,' Flynn bellowed too late. The rifle fired, and the recoil toppled Sebastian sprawling onto the pile of ivory behind him. The canoe rocked dangerously while the paddlers struggled to keep it from capsizing, and then disappeared around the bend.

Twelve hours later, the canoes reappeared around the same bend, and headed towards the lone monkey-bean tree on the bank. The canoes rode lightly, empty of ivory, and the paddlers were singing one of the old river chants.

Freshly shaved, wearing a clean shirt and his other pair of boots, a case of Flynn's liquor between his knees, Sebastian peered eagerly ahead for his first glimpse of the big American.

A fine blue tendril of camp-fire smoke smeared out across the river, but there were no figures waving a welcome from the bank. Suddenly Sebastian frowned as he realized that the silhouette of the monkey-bean tree had altered. He wrinkled his eyes, peering ahead uncertainly.

Behind him rang the first cry of alarm from his boatmen. 'Allemand!' And the canoe served under him.

He glanced back and saw the other canoes wheel away in tight circles aimed downstream, the boatmen jabbering in terror as they leaned forward to thrust against the paddles.

His own canoe was in swift pursuit of the others as they darted beyond the bend.

'Hey!' Sebastian shouted at the sweat-shiny backs of his paddlers. 'What do you think you're doing?'

They gave him no answer but the muscles beneath their black skins bunched and rippled in their frantic efforts to drive the canoe faster.

'Stop that immediately!' Sebastian yelled at them. 'Take me back, dash it all. Take me to the camp.'

In desperation Sebastian lifted the rifle and aimed at the nearest man. 'I'm not joking,' he yelled again. The native glanced over his shoulder into the gaping twin muzzles and his face, already twisted with fear, now convulsed into a mask of terror. They had all developed a healthy reverence for the way Sebastian handled that rifle.

The man stopped paddling, and one by one the others followed his example. Sitting frozen under the hypnotic eyes of Sebastian's rifle.

'Back!' said Sebastian and gestured eloquently upstream. Reluctantly the man nearest him dipped his paddle and the canoe turned broadside across the current. 'Back!' Sebastian repeated and the men dipped again.

Slowly, warily, the single canoe crept upstream towards the monkey-bean tree and the grotesque new fruit that hung from its branches.

The hull slid in onto the firm mud and Sebastian stepped ashore.

'Out!' he ordered the boatmen and gestured again. He wanted them well away from the canoe for he knew that, otherwise, the moment his back was turned they would set off downstream again with renewed enthusiasm. 'Out!' and he herded them up the steep bank into Flynn O'Flynn's camp.

The two bearers who had died of gunshot wounds lay beside the smouldering fire. But the four men in the monkey-bean tree had been less fortunate. The ropes had cut deeply into the flesh of their necks and their faces were swollen, mouths wide in the last breath that had never been taken. On the lolling tongues the flies crawled like metallic green bees.

'Cut them down!' Sebastian roused himself from the nausea that was bubbling queasily up from his stomach. The boatmen stood paralysed and Sebastian felt anger now mixed with his revulsion. Roughly he shoved one of the men towards the tree. 'Cut them down,' he repeated, and thrust the handle of his hunting knife into the man's hand. Sebastian turned away as the native shinned up into the fork of the tree with the knife blade clamped between his teeth. Behind him he heard the heavy meaty thuds as the dead men dropped from the tree. Again his stomach heaved, and he concentrated on his search of the trampled grass around the camp.

'Flynn!' he called softly. 'Flynn. I say Flynn! Where are you?' There were the prints of hobnailed boots in the soft earth, and at one place he stooped and picked up the shiny brass cylinder of an empty cartridge case. Stamped into the metal of the base around the detonator cap were the words *Mauser Fabriken. 7 mm.*

'Flynn!' more urgently now as the horror of it came home to him. 'Flynn!' and he heard the grass rustle near him. He swung towards it, half raising the rifle.

'Master!' and Sebastian felt disappointment swoop in his chest.

'Mohammed. Is that you, Mohammed?' and he recognized the wizened little figure with the eternal fez perched on the woolly head as it emerged. Flynn's chief gun-boy, the only one with a little English.

'Mohammed,' with relief, and then quickly, 'Fini? Where is Fini?'

'They shot him, master. The Askari came in the early morning before the sun. Fini was washing. They shot him and he fell into the water.'

'Where? Show me where.'

Below the camp, a few yards from where the canoe was drawn up, they found the pathetic little bundle of Flynn's clothing. Beside it was a half-consumed cake of cheap soap and a metal hand-mirror. There were the deep imprints of naked feet in the mud, and Mohammed stooped and broke off one of the green reeds at the water's edge. Wordlessly he handed it to Sebastian. A drop of blood had dried black on the leaf, and it crumbled as Sebastian touched it with his thumb-nail.

'We must find him. He might still be alive. Call the others. We'll search the banks downstream.'

In an agony of loss, Sebastian picked up Flynn's soiled shirt and crumpled it in his fist.

7

F lynn shucked off his pants and the filthy bush-shirt. Shivering briefly in the chill of dawn, he hugged himself and massaged his upper arms while he peered into the shallow water, searching the bottom for the tell-tale chicken-wire pattern that would mean a crocodile was buried in the mud waiting for him.

His body was porcelain-white where clothing had protected it from the sun, but his arms were chocolate-brown, and a deep vee of the same brown dipped down from his throat onto his chest. Above it the battered red face was creased and puffy with sleep, and his long, greying hair was tangled and matted. He belched thunderously, and grimaced at the taste of old gin and pipe tobacco, then, satisfied that no reptile lay in ambush, he stepped into the water and lowered his massive hams to sit waist-deep. Snorting, he scooped water with his cupped hands over his head, then lumbered out onto the bank again. Sixty seconds is a long time to stay in a river like the Rifiji, for the crocodiles come quickly to the sound of splashing.

Naked, dripping, hair plastered down across his face, Flynn began to soap himself, working up a thick lather at his crotch and tenderly massaging his abundant genitalia, he washed away the sloth of sleep and his appetite stirred. He called up at the camp, 'Mohammed, beloved of Allah and son of his prophet, shake your black arse out of the sack and get the coffee brewing.' Then as an afterthought, he added, 'And put a little gin in it.'

Soapsuds filled Flynn's armpits, and coated the melancholy sag of his belly when Mohammed came down the bank to him. Mohammed was balancing a large enamel mug from which curled little wisps of aromatic steam, and Flynn grinned at him, and spoke in Swahili. 'Thou art kind and merciful; this charity will be writ against your name in the Book of Paradise.'

He reached for the mug but before his fingers touched it, there was a fusillade of gun-fire above them and a bullet hit Flynn high up in the thigh. It spun him sideways so he sprawled half in mud and half in water.

Lying stunned with the shock, he heard the rush of Askari into the camp, heard their shouted triumph as they clubbed with the gun-butt those who had survived the first volley. Flynn wriggled into a sitting position.

Mohammed was coming to him anxiously.

'Run,' grunted Flynn. 'Run, damn you.'

'Lord . . .'

'Get out of here,' savagely Flynn lashed out at him, and Mohammed recoiled. 'The rope, you fool. They'll give you the rope and wrap you in a pigskin.'

A second longer Mohammed hesitated, then he ducked and scampered into the reeds.

'Find Fini,' roared a bull voice in German. 'Find the white man.'

Flynn realized then that it was a stray bullet that had hit him – perhaps even a ricochet. His leg was numb from the hip down, but he dragged himself into the water. He could not run, so he must swim.

'Where is he? Find him!' raged the voice, and suddenly the grass on the bank burst open and Flynn looked up.

For the first time they confronted each other. These two who had played murderous hide-and-seek for three long years across ten thousand square miles of bush.

'Ja!' Fleischer's jubilant bellow as he swung and sighted the pistol at the man in the water below him. 'This time!' aiming carefully, steadying the Luger with both hands.

The brittle snapping sound of the shot, and the slap of the bullet into the water a foot from Flynn's head were followed by Fleischer's snarl of disappointment.

Filling his lungs, Flynn ducked below the surface. Frog-kicking with his good leg, trailing the wounded one, he turned with the current and swam. He swam until his trapped breath threatened to explode his chest, and coloured lights flashed and twinkled behind his clenched eyelids. Then he clawed to the surface. On the bank Fleischer was waiting for him with a dozen of his Askari. 'There he is!' as Flynn blew like a whale thirty yards downstream. Gun-fire crackled and the water whipped and leaped and creamed around Flynn's head.

'Shoot straight!' Howling in frustration and blazing wildly with the Luger, Fleischer watched the head disappear and Flynn's fat white buttocks break the surface for an instant as he dived. Sobbing with anger and exertion, Fleischer turned his fury on the Askari around him. 'Pigs! Stupid black pig dogs!' And he swung the empty pistol against the nearest head, knocking the man to his knees. Intent on avoiding the flailing pistol, none of them were ready when Flynn surfaced for the second time. A desultory volley kicked fountains no closer than ten feet to Flynn's bobbing head, and he dived again.

'Come on! Chase him!' Herding his Askari ahead of him, Fleischer trotted along the bank in pursuit. Twenty yards of good going, then they came to the first swamp hole and waded through it to be confronted by a solid barrier of elephant grass. They plunged into it and were swallowed so they no longer had sight of the river.

'Schnell! Schnell! He'll get away,' gasped Fleischer and the thick stems wrapped his ankles so that he fell headlong in the mud. Two of his Askari dragged him up and they staggered on until the thicket of tall grass ended, and they stood on the elbow of the river bend with a clear view a thousand yards downstream.

Disturbed by the gun-fire, the birds were up, milling in confused flight above the reed-beds. Their alarm cries blended into a harsh chorus that spoiled the peace of the brooding dawn. They were the only living things in sight. From bank to far bank, the curved expanse of water was broken only by a few floating islands of papyrus grass; rafts of matted vegetation cut loose by the current and floating unhurriedly down towards the sea.

Panting, Herman Fleischer shook off the supporting hands of his two Askari and searched desperately for a glimpse of Flynn's bobbing head. 'Where did he go?' His fingers trembled as he fitted a new clip of ammunition into the Luger. 'Where did he go?' he demanded again, but none of his Askari drew attention to himself by venturing a reply.

'He must be on this side!' The Rufiji was half a mile wide here, Flynn could not have crossed it in the few minutes since they had last seen him. 'Search the bank!' Fleischer ordered. 'Find him!'

With relief the sergeant of his Askari turned on his men, quickly splitting them into two parties and sending them up and downstream to scour the water's edge.

Slowly Fleischer returned the pistol to its holster and fastened the flap, then he took a handkerchief from his pocket and mopped at his face and neck.

'Come on!' he snapped at his sergeant, and set off back towards the camp.

When he reached it, his men had already set out the folding table and chair. New life had been stirred into Flynn's camp-fire, and the Askari cook was preparing breakfast.

Sitting at the table with the front of his tunic open, spooning up oatmeal porridge and wild honey, Fleischer was soothed into a better humour by the food, and by the thorough manner in which the execution of the four captives was conducted.

When the last of them had stopped twitching and kicking and hung quietly with his comrades in the monkey-bean tree, Herman wiped up the bacon grease in his plate with a hunk of black bread and popped it into his mouth. The cook removed the plate and replaced it with a mug of steaming coffee at the exact moment when the two parties of searchers straggled into the clearing to report that a few drops of blood at the water's edge was the only sign they had found of Flynn O'Flynn.

'Ja,' Herman nodded, 'the crocodiles have eaten him.' He sipped appreciatively at his coffee mug before he gave his next orders. 'Sergeant, take this up to the launch.' He pointed at the stack of ivory on the edge of the clearing. 'Then we will go down to the Island of the Dogs and find this other white man with his English flag.'

8

T here was only the entry wound, a dark red hole from which watery blood still oozed slowly. Flynn could have thrust his thumb into it but instead he groped gently around the back of his leg and located the lump in his flesh where the spent slug had come to rest just below the skin.

'God damn it, God damn it to hell,' he whispered in pain, and in anger, at the unlikely chance which had deflected the ricochet downwards to where he had stood below the bank, deflecting it with just sufficient velocity to lodge the bullet in his thigh instead of delivering a clean in-and-out wound.

Slowly he straightened his leg, testing it for broken bone. At the movement, the matt of drifting papyrus on which he lay rocked slightly.

'Might have touched the bone, but it's still in one piece,' he grunted with relief, and felt the first giddy swing of weakness in his head. In his ears was the faint rushing sound of a waterfall heard far off. 'Lost a bit of the old juice,' and from the wound a fresh trickle of bright blood broke and mingled with the water-drops to snake down his leg and drip into the dry matted papyrus. 'Got to stop that,' he whispered.

He was naked, his body still wet from the river. No belt or cloth to use as a tourniquet but he must staunch the bleeding. His fingers clumsy with the weakness of the wound, he tore a bunch of the long sword blade leaves from the reeds around him and began twisting them into a rope. Binding it around his leg above the wound, he pulled it tight and knotted it. The dribble of blood slowed and almost stopped before Flynn sank back and closed his eyes.

Beneath him the island swung and undulated with the eddy of the current and the wavelets pushed up by the rising morning wind. It was a soothing motion, and he was tired – terribly, achingly, tired. He slept.

The pain and the cessation of motion woke him at last. The pain was a dull persistent throb, a pulse that beat through his leg and groin and his lower belly. Groggily he pulled himself on to his elbows and looked down on his own body. The leg was swollen, bluish-looking from the constriction of the grass rope. He stared at it dully, without comprehension, for a full minute before memory flooded back.

'Gangrene!' he spoke aloud, and tore at the knot. The rope fell away and he gasped at the agony of new blood flowing into the leg, clenching his fists and grinding his teeth against it. The pain slowed and settled into a steady beat, and he breathed again, wheezy as a man with asthma.

Then the change of his circumstances came through to the conscious level of his mind and he peered around short-sightedly. The river had carried him down into the mangrove swamps again, down into the maze of little islands and water-ways of the delta. His raft of papyrus had been washed in and stranded against a mud bank by the falling tide. The mud stank of rotting vegetation and sulphur. Near him a gathering of big green river crabs were clicking and bubbling over the body of a dead fish, their little eye-stalks raised in perpetual surprise. At Flynn's movement they sidled away towards the water with their red-tipped claws raised defensively.

Water! Instantly Flynn was aware of the gummy saliva that glued his tongue to the roof of his mouth. Reddened by the harsh sunlight, heated by the first fever of his wound, his body was a furnace that craved moisture.

Flynn moved and instantly cried out in pain. His leg had stiffened while he slept. It was now a heavy anchor, shackling him helplessly to the papyrus raft. He tried again, easing himself backwards on his hands and his buttocks, dragging the leg after him. Each breath was a sob in his dry throat, each movement a white-hot lance into his thigh. But he must drink, he had to drink. Inch by inch, he worked his way to the edge of the raft and slid from it on to the mud bank.

The water had receded with the tide, and he was still fifty paces from the edge. With the motion of a man swimming on his back, he moved across the slimy evil-smelling mud, and his leg slithered after him. It was beginning to bleed again, not copiously but a bright wine-drop at a time.

He reached the water at last, and rolled onto his side with the bad leg uppermost in an attempt to keep the wound out of the mud. On one elbow he buried his face in the water, drinking greedily. The water was warm, tainted with sea salt, and musky with rotted mangroves so it tasted like animal urine. But he gulped it noisily with his mouth and his nostrils and his eyes below the surface. At last he must breathe, and he lifted his head, panting for breath, coughing so the water shot up his throat, out through his nose and dimmed his vision with tears. Gradually his breathing steadied and his eyes cleared. Before he bowed his head to drink again, he glanced out across the channel and saw it coming.

It was on the surface, still a hundred yards away but swimming fast, driving towards him with the great tail churning the water. A big one – at least fifteen feet of it – showing like the rough bark of a pine log, leaving a wide wake across the surface as it came.

And Flynn screamed, just once, but shrill and high and achingly clear. Forgetting the wound in his panic, he tried to get to his feet, pushing himself up with his hands – but the leg pinned him. He screamed again, in pain and in fear.

Belly down, he wriggled in frantic haste from the shallow water back onto the mud bank, dragging himself across the glutinous slime, clawing and threshing towards the papyrus raft where it lay stranded among the mangrove roots fifty yards away. Expecting each moment to hear the slithering rush of the huge reptile across the mud behind him, he reached the first of the mangroves and rolled on his side, looking back, coated with black mud, his face working in his terror and the sound of it spilling in an incoherent babble through his lips.

The crocodile was at the edge of the mud bank, still in the river. Only its head showed above the surface and the little piggy bright eyes watched him unwinkingly, each set on its knot of horny scale.

Desperately Flynn looked about him. The mud bank was a tiny island with this grove of a dozen mangroves set in the centre of it. The trunks of the mangroves were twice as thick as a man's chest, but without branches for the first ten feet of their height; smooth bark slimy with mud and encrusted with little colonies of fresh water mussels. Unwounded Flynn would not have been able to climb any of them – with his leg those branches above him were doubly inaccessible.

Wildly now he searched for a weapon – anything, no matter how puny – to defend himself. But there was nothing. Not a branch of driftwood, not a rock – only the thick black sheet of mud around him.

He looked back at the crocodile. It had not moved. His first feeble hope that it might not come out onto the mud bank withered almost before it was born. It would come. Cowardly, loathsome creature it was – but in time it would gather its courage. It had smelled his blood; it knew him to be wounded, helpless. It would come.

Painfully Flynn leaned his back against the roots of the mangrove, and his terror settled down to a steady, pulsing fear – as steady as the pain in his leg. During the frantic flight across the bank, stiff mud had plugged the bullet hole and stopped the bleeding. But it does not matter now, Flynn thought, nothing matters. Only the creature out there, waiting while its appetite overcomes its timidity, swamps its reluctance to leave its natural element. It might take five minutes, or half a day – but, inevitably, it will come.

There was a tiny ripple around its snout, the first sign of its movement, and the long scaly head inched in towards the edge. Flynn stiffened.

The back showed, its scales like the patterned teeth of a file, and beyond it, the tail with the coxcomb double crest. Cautiously, on its short bowed legs, it waddled through the shallows. Wet and shiny, as broad across the back as a percheron stallion, more than a ton of cold, armoured flesh, it emerged from the water. Sinking elbow-deep into the soft mud, so its belly left a slide mark behind it. Grinning savagely, but with the jagged, irregular teeth lying yellow and long on its lips, and the small eyes watching him.

It came so slowly that Flynn lay passively against the tree, mesmerized by the deliberate waddling approach.

When it was half-way across the bank, it stopped – crouching, grinning – and he smelled it. The heavy odour of stale fish and musk on the warm air.

'Get away!' Flynn yelled at it, and it stood unmoving, unblinking. 'Get away!' He snatched up a handful of mud and hurled it. It crouched a little lower on its stubby legs and the fat crested tail stiffened, arching slightly.

Sobbing now, Flynn threw another handful of mud. The long grinning jaws opened an inch, then shut again. He heard the click as its teeth met, and it charged. Incredibly fast through the mud, grinning still, it slithered towards him.

This time Flynn's voice was a lunatic babble of horror and he writhed helplessly against the mangrove roots.

The deep booming note of the gun seemed not part of reality, but the crocodile reared up on its tail, drowning the echoes of the shot with its own hissing bellow, and above the next boom of the gun, Flynn heard the bullet strike the scaly body with a thump.

Mud sprayed as the reptile rolled in convulsions, and then, lifting itself high on its legs, it lumbered in ungainly flight towards the water. Again and again the heavy rifle fired, but the crocodile never faltered in its rush, and the surface of the water exploded like blown glass, as it launched itself from the bank and was gone in the spreading ripples.

Standing in the bows of the canoe with the smoking rifle in his hands, while the paddlers drove in towards the bank, Sebastian Oldsmith shouted anxiously, 'Flynn, Flynn – did it get you? Are you all right?'

Flynn's reply was a croak. 'Bassie. Oh, Bassie boy, for the first time in my life I'm real pleased to see you,' and he sagged only half conscious against the mangrove roots.

9

The sun burned down on the dhow where it lay at anchor off the Island of the Dogs, yet a steady breeze came down the narrow waterway between the mangroves and plucked at the furled sail on the boom.

With a rope sling under his armpits, they lifted Flynn from the canoe and swung him, legs dangling, over the bulwark. Sebastian was ready to receive him and lower him gently to the deck.

'Get that goddamn sail up, and let's get the hell out of the river,' gasped Flynn.

'I must tend to your leg.'

'That can wait. We've got to get out into the open sea. The Germans have got a steam launch. They'll be looking for us. We can expect them to drop in on us at any minute.'

'They can't touch us – we're under the protection of the flag,' Sebastian protested.

'Listen, you stupid, bloody limey,' Flynn's voice was a squawk of pain and impatience. 'That murdering Hun will give us a rope dance with or without the flag. Don't argue, get that sail up!'

They laid him on a blanket in the shadow of the high poop before Sebastian hurried forward to release the Arab crew from the hold. They came up shiny with sweat and blinking in the dazzle of the sun. It took perhaps fifteen seconds for Mohammed to explain to them the urgency of the situation, and this invoked a few seconds of paralysed horror before they scattered to their stations. Four of them were hauling ineffectively at the anchor rope, but the great lump of coral was buried in the gluey mud of the bottom. Sebastian pushed them aside impatiently and with one knife stroke, severed the rope.

The crew, with the enthusiastic assistance of Flynn's bearers and gun-boys, ran up the faded and patched old sail. The wind caught it and bellied it. The deck canted slightly and two Arabs ran back to the tiller. From under the bows came the faint giggle of water, and from the stern spread a wide oily wake. With a cluster of the Arabs and bearers calling directions in the bows to the steersman at the rudder, the ancient dhow pointed downstream and ambled towards the sea.

When Sebastian went back to Flynn, he found old Mohammed squatting anxiously beside him and watching, as Flynn drank from the square bottle. Already a quarter of its contents had disappeared.

Flynn lowered the gin bottle, and breathed heavily through his mouth. 'Tastes like honey,' he gasped.

'Let's look at that leg,' Sebastian stooped over Flynn's naked, mud-besmeared body. 'My God, what a mess! Mohammed, get a basin of water and try and find some clean cloth.'

10

With the coming of evening, the breeze gathered strength, kicking up a chop on the widening water-ways of the delta. All afternoon the little dhow had butted against the run of the tide, but now began the ebb and it helped push her down towards the sea.

'With any luck we'll reach the mouth before sunset.' Sebastian was sitting beside Flynn's blanket-wrapped form under the poop. Flynn grunted. He was weak with pain, and groggy with gin. 'If we don't, we'll have to moor somewhere for the night. Can't risk the channel in the dark.' He received no reply from Flynn and himself fell silent.

Except for the gurgle of the bow-wave and the sing-song chant of the pilot, a lazy silence blanketed the dhow. Most of the crew and the bearers were strewn in sleep about the deck, although two of them worked quietly over the open galley as they prepared the evening meal.

The heavy miasma of the swamps blended poorly with the stench of the bilges and the cargo of green ivory in the holds. It seemed to act as a drug, increasing Sebastian's fatigue. His head sagged forward on his chest and his hands slipped from the rifle in his lap. He slept.

The magpie chatter of the crew, and Mohammed's urgent hands on his shoulder, shook him awake. He came to his feet and gazed blearily around him. 'What is it? What is the trouble, Mohammed?'

For answer, Mohammed shouted the crew into silence, and turned back to Sebastian. 'Listen, master.'

Sebastian shook the remnants of sleep from his head, then cocked it slightly. 'I can't hear . . .' He stopped, an expression of uncertainty on his face.

Very faintly in the still of the evening he heard it, a faint huffing rhythm, as though a train passed in the distance. 'Yes,' he said, still uncertain. 'What is it?'

'The toot-toot boat, she comes.'

Sebastian stared at him without comprehension.

'The Allemand. The Germans.' Mohammed's hands fluttered with agitation. 'They follow us. They chase. They catch. They . . .' He clutched his own throat with both hands and rolled his eyes. His tongue protruded from the corner of his mouth.

Flynn's entire retinue was gathered in a mob around Sebastian, and at Mohammed's graphic little charade, they burst once more into a frightened chorus. Every eye was on Sebastian, waiting for his lead, and he felt confused, uncertain. Instinctively he turned to Flynn. Flynn lay on his back, his mouth open, snoring. Quickly Sebastian knelt beside him. 'Flynn! Flynn!' Flynn opened his eyes but they were focused beyond Sebastian's face. 'The Germans are coming.'

'The Campbells are coming. Hurrah! Hurrah!' muttered Flynn and closed his eyes again. His usually red face was flushed hot-scarlet with fever.

'What must I do?' pleaded Sebastian.

'Drink it!' advised Flynn. 'Never hesitate. Drink it!' his eyes still closed, his voice slurred.

'Please, Flynn. Please tell me.'

'Tell you?' muttered Flynn in delirium. 'Sure! Have you heard the one about the camel and the missionary?'

Sebastian jumped to his feet and looked wildly about him. The sun was low, perhaps another two hours to nightfall. *If only we can hold them off until then.* 'Mohammed. Get the gun-boys up into the stern,' he snapped, and Mohammed, recognizing the new crispness in his voice, turned on the mob about him to relay the order.

The ten gun-boys scattered to gather their weapons and then crowded up on to the poop. Sebastian followed them, gazing anxiously back along the channel. He could see two thousand yards to the bend behind them and the channel was empty, but he was sure the sound of the steam engine was louder.

'Spread them along the rail,' he ordered Mohammed. He was thinking hard now; always a difficult task for Sebastian. Stubborn as a mule, his mind began to sulk as soon as he flogged it. He wrinkled his high scholar's forehead and his next thought emerged slowly. 'A barricade,' he said. The thin planking of the bulwark would offer little protection against the high-powered Mausers. 'Mohammed, get the others to carry up everything they can find, and pile it here to shield the steersmen and the gun-boys. Bring everything – water barrels, the sacks of coconuts, those old fishing-nets.'

While they hurried to obey the order, Sebastian stood in frowning concentration, prodding the mass within his skull and finding it as responsive as a lump of freshly kneaded dough. He tried to estimate the relative speeds of the dhow and a modern steam launch. Perhaps they were moving at half the speed of their pursuers. With a sliding sensation, he decided that even in this wind, sail could not hope to out-run a propeller-driven craft.

The word *propeller*, and the chance that at that moment he was forced to move aside to allow four of the men to drag an untidy bundle of old fishing-nets past, eased the next idea to the surface of his mind.

Humbled by the brilliance of his idea, he clung to it desperately, lest it somehow sink once more below the surface to be lost. 'Mohammed . . .' he stammered in his excitement. 'Mohammed, those nets . . .' He looked back again along the wide channel, and saw it still empty. He looked ahead and saw the next bend coming towards them; already the helmsman was chanting the orders preparatory to tacking the dhow. 'Those nets. I want to lay them across the channel.'

Mohammed stared at him aghast, his wizened face crinkling deeper in disbelief.

'Cut off the corks. Leave every fourth one.' Sebastian grabbed his shoulders and shook him in agitation. 'I want the net to sag. I don't want them to spot it too soon.'

They were almost up to the bend now, and Sebastian pointed ahead. 'We'll lay it just around the corner.'

'Why, master?' pleaded Mohammed. 'We must run. They are close now.'

'The propeller,' Sebastian shouted in his face. He made a churning motion with his hands. 'I want to snag the propeller.'

A moment longer Mohammed stared at him, then he began to grin, exposing his bald gums.

While they worked in frantic haste the muffled engine beat from upstream grew steadily louder, more insistent.

The dhow wallowed and balked at the efforts of the helmsman to work her across the channel. Her head kept falling away before the wind, threatening to snarl the net in her own rudder, but slowly the line of bobbing corks spread from the mangroves on one side towards the far bank, while in grim concentration Sebastian and a group led by Mohammed paid the net out over the stern. Every few minutes they lifted their faces to glance at the bend upstream, expecting to see the German launch appear and hear the crackle of Mauser fire.

Gradually the dhow edged in towards the north bank, sowing the row of corks behind her, and abruptly Sebastian realized that the net was too short – too short by fifty yards. There would be a gap in their defence. If the launch cut the bend fine, hugging the bank as it came, then they were lost. Already the note of its engine was so close that he could hear the metallic whine of the drive shaft.

Now also there was a new problem. How to anchor the loose end of the net? To let it float free would allow the current to wash it away, and open the gap still further.

'Mohammed. Fetch one of the tusks. The biggest one you can find. Quickly. Go quickly.'

Mohammed scampered away and returned immediately, the two bearers with him staggering under the weight of the long curved shaft of ivory.

His hands clumsy with haste, Sebastian lashed the end rope of the net to the tusk. Then grunting with the effort, he and Mohammed hoisted it to the side rail, and pushed it overboard. As it splashed, Sebastian shouted at the helmsman, 'Go!' and pointed downstream. Thankfully the Arab wrenched the tiller across. The dhow spun on her heel and pointed once more towards the sea.

Silently, anxiously, Sebastian and his gun-boys lined the stern and gazed back at the bend of the channel. In the fists of each of them were clutched the short-barrelled elephant rifles, and their faces were set intently.

The chug of the steam engine rose louder and still louder.

'Shout as soon as it shows,' Sebastian ordered. 'Shoot as fast as you can. Keep them looking at us, so they don't see the net.'

And the launch came around the bend; flying a ribbon of grey smoke from its single stack and the bold red, yellow and black flag of the Empire at its bows. A neat little craft, forty-footer, low in the waist, small deck-house aft, gleaming white in the sunlight, and the white moustache of the bow wave curled about her bows.

'Shoot!' bellowed Sebastian as he saw the Askari clustered on the foredeck. 'Shoot!' and his voice was lost in the concerted blast of the heavy calibre rifles around him. One of the Askari was flung backwards against the deck-house, his arms spread wide as he hung there a moment in the attitude of crucifixion before subsiding gently on to the deck. His comrades scattered and dropped into cover behind the steel bulwark. A single figure was left alone on the deck; a massive figure in the light grey uniform of the German colonial service, with his wide-brimmed slouch hat, and gold gleaming at the shoulders of his tunic.

Sebastian took him in the notch of his rear sight, held the bead on his chest, and jerked the trigger. The rifle jumped joyously against his shoulder, and he saw a fountain of spray leap from the surface of the river a hundred yards beyond the launch. Sebastian fired again, closing his eyes in anticipation of the savage recoil of the rifle. When he opened them, the German officer was still on his feet, shooting back at Sebastian with a pistol in his outstretched right hand. He was making better practice than Sebastian. The fluting hum of his fire whipped about Sebastian's head, or smacked into the planking of the dhow.

Hastily Sebastian ducked behind the water barrel and clawed a pair of cartridges from his belt. Sharper, higher than the dull booming of the elephant rifles, climbed the brittle crackle of the Mauser fire as the Askari joined in.

Cautiously Sebastian lifted his eyes above the water barrel. The launch was cutting the bend fine, and with a sudden swoop of dismay, he knew it was going to clear the fishnet by twenty feet. He dropped his rifle on to the deck and jumped to his feet. A Mauser bullet missed his ear by so little that it nearly burst his eardrum. Instinctively he ducked, then checked the movement and instead ran to the helmsman. 'Get out of the way!' he yelled in his excitement and his fear. Roughly he shoved the man aside and, grasping the tiller, pushed it across. Perilously close to the jibe, the dhow veered across the channel, opening the angle between it and the launch. Looking back Sebastian saw the fat German officer turn and shout an order towards the wheel-house. Almost immediately the bows of the launch swung, following the dhow's manoeuvre and Sebastian felt triumph flare in his chest. Now directly in the path of the launch lay the line of tiny black dots that marked the net.

His deep-drawn breath trapped in his lungs, Sebastian watched the launch sweep over the net. His grip on the tiller tightened until his knuckles threatened to push out through the skin, and then he expelled his breath in a howl of joy and relief.

For the line of corks was suddenly plucked below the surface, leaving the small disturbance of ripples where each had stood. For ten seconds the launch sped on, then abruptly the even sound of her passage altered, a harsh clattering intruded, and her bows swung suddenly as she slowed.

The gap between the two craft widened. Sebastian saw the German officer drag a frightened Askari from the wheel-house and club him unmercifully about the head, but the squeals of Teutonic fury were muted by the swiftly increasing distance, and then drowned by the tumultuous clamour of his own crew, as they pranced and danced about the deck.

The Arab helmsman hopped up on to the water barrel and hoisted the skirts of his dirty grey robe to expose his naked posterior at the launch in calculated mockery.

11

Long after the dhow had sailed sedately first out of rifle range, and then out of sight, Herman Fleischer gave himself over completely to the epilepsy of frustrated anger. He raved about the tiny deck, lashing out with ham-sized fists while his Askari skittled around him trying to keep out of range. Repeatedly he returned to the unconscious form of his helmsman to kick him as he lay. At last his fury burned itself down to the level where it allowed him to trundle aft and hang over the stern rail peering down at the sodden bundle of netting which was wrapped around the propeller.

'Sergeant!' His voice was hoarse with strain. 'Get two men with knives over the side to cut that away!'

And a stillness fell upon them all. Every man tried to shrink himself down into insignificance, so that the choice might not fall on him. Two volunteers were selected, divested of their uniforms and hustled to the stern, despite their terrified entreaties.

'Tell them to hurry,' grunted Herman, and went to his folding chair. His personal boy placed the evening meal with its attendant pitcher of beer on the table before him and Herman fell to.

Once from the stern there was a squeak and a splash, following by a furious burst of rifle fire. Herman frowned and looked up from his plate.

'A crocodile has taken one of the men,' his sergeant reported in agitation.

'Well, put another one over,' said Herman and returned with unabated relish to his meal. This last batch of sausage was particularly tasty.

The netting had wound so tightly about the blades and shaft of the propeller, that it was an hour after midnight when the last of it was hacked away by lantern light.

The drive shaft had twisted slightly and run one of its bearings, so even at quarter speed there was a fearsome clattering and threshing sound from the stern as the launch limped slowly down the channel towards the sea.

In the grey and pallid pink of dawn they crept past the last island of mangroves and the launch lifted her head to the sluggish thrust of the Indian Ocean. It was a windless morning of flat calm, and Herman peered without hope into the misty half light that obscured the ocean's far horizon. He had come this far only on the slight chance that the dhow might have gone aground on a mud bank during her night run down the river.

'Stop!' he shouted at his battered helmsman. Immediately the agonized clatter of the propeller ceased, and the launch rose and fell uneasily on the long oily swells.

So they had got clear away then. He could not risk his damaged launch on the open sea. He must go back, and leave the dhow and its ivory and its many candidates for the rope, to head unmolested for that pest-hole of rogues and pirates on Zanzibar island.

Moodily he looked out across the sea and mourned that cargo of ivory. There had been perhaps a million Reichsmarks of it aboard, of which his unofficial handling fee would have been considerable.

Also he mourned the departure of the Englishman. He had never hanged one before.

He sighed and tried to comfort himself with the thought of that damned American, now well digested in the maw of a crocodile, but truly it would have been more satisfying to see him kick and spin on the rope.

He sighed again. Ah, well! At least he would no longer have the perpetual worry of Flynn O'Flynn's presence on his border, nor would he have to suffer the nagging of Governor Schee and his endless demands for O'Flynn's head.

Now it was breakfast time. He was about to turn away when something out there in the lightening dawn caught his attention.

A long low shape, its outline becoming crisper as he watched. There were cries from his Askari as they saw it also, huge in the dawn. The stark square turrets with their slim gun-barrels, the tall triple stacks and the neat geometrical patterns of its rigging.

'The *Blücher*!' roared Herman in savage elation. 'The *Blücher*, by God!' He recognized the cruiser, for he had seen her not six months before, lying in Dar es Salaam harbour. 'Sergeant, bring the signal pistol!' He was capering with excitement. In reply to Herman's hasty message, Governor Schee must have sent the *Blücher* racing southwards to blockade the Rufiji mouth. 'Start the engine. Schnell! Run out to her,' he shouted at the helmsman as he slid one of the fat Verey cartridges into the gaping breech of the pistol, snapped it closed and pointed the muzzle to the sky.

Beside the tall bulk of the cruiser the launch was as tiny as a floating leaf, and Herman looked up with apprehension at the frail rope ladder he was expected to climb. His Askari assisted him across the narrow strip of water between the two vessels and he hung for a desperate minute until his feet found the rungs and he began his ponderous ascent. Sweating profusely he was helped on to the deck by two seamen and faced an honour guard of a dozen or more. Heading them was a young lieutenant in crisp, smart tropical whites.

Herman shrugged off the helping hands, drew himself to attention with a click of heels. 'Commissioner Fleischer.' His voice shaky with exertion.

'Lieutenant Kyller.' The officer clicked and saluted.

'I must see your captain immediately. A matter of extreme urgency.'

12

K apitän zur See Count Otto von Kleine inclined his head gravely as he greeted Herman. He was a tall, thin man, who wore a neat, pointed blond beard with just a few threads of grey to give it dignity. 'The English have landed a full-scale expeditionary force in the Rufiji delta, supported by capital ships? This is correct?' he asked immediately.

'The report was exaggerated.' Herman regretted bitterly the impetuous wording of his message to the Governor; he had been fired with patriotic ardour at the time. 'In fact, it was only . . . ah,' he hesitated, 'one vessel.'

'Of what strength? What is her armament?' demanded von Kleine.

'Well, it was an unarmed vessel.'

And von Kleine frowned. 'Of what type?'

Herman flushed with embarrassment. 'An Arab dhow. Of about twenty-two metres.'

'But this is impossible. Ridiculous. The Kaiser has delivered an ultimatum to the British Consul in Berlin. He has issued mobilization orders to five divisions.' The captain spun on his heel and began to pace restlessly about his bridge, clapping his hands together in agitation. 'What was the purpose of this British invasion? Where is this . . . this dhow? What explanation must I send to Berlin?'

'I have since learned that the expedition was led by a notorious ivory poacher named O'Flynn. He was shot resisting arrest by my Askari, but his accessory, an unknown Englishman, escaped down the river last night in the dhow.'

'Where will they be headed?' The captain stopped pacing and glared at Herman.

'Zanzibar.'

'This is stupidity, utter stupidity. We will be a laughing stock! A battle cruiser to catch a pair of common criminals!'

'But, Captain, you must pursue them.'

'To what purpose?'

'If they escape to tell their story, the dignity of the Emperor will be lowered throughout the length of Africa. Think if the British Press were to hear of this! Also, these men are dangerous criminals.'

'But I cannot board a foreign ship on the high seas. Especially if she flies the Union Jack. It would be an act of war – an act of piracy.'

'But, Captain, if she were to sink with all hands, sink without a trace?'

And Captain von Kleine nodded thoughtfully. Then abruptly he snapped his fingers and turned to his pilot. 'Plot me a course for Zanzibar Island.'

13

They lay becalmed below a sky of brazen cobalt, and every hour of the calm allowed the Mozambique current to push the little dhow another three miles off its course. Aimlessly she swung her head to meet each of the long swells, and then let it fall away into the troughs.

For the twentieth time since dawn, Sebastian climbed up on to the poop-deck and surveyed the endless waters, searching for a ruffle on the glassy surface that would herald the wind. But there was never any sign of it. He looked towards the west, but the blue line of the coast had long since sunk below the horizon.

'I'm an old dog, *Fisi*,' bellowed Flynn from the lower deck. 'Hear me laugh,' and he imitated faithfully the yammering cry of an hyena. All day Flynn had regaled the company with snatches of song and animal imitations. Yet his delirium was interspaced with periods of lucidity. 'I reckon this time old Fleischer got me good, Bassie. There's a sack of poison forming round that bullet. I can feel it there. A fat, hot sack of it. Reckon we've got to dig for it pretty soon. Reckon if we can't make it back to Zanzibar pretty soon, we're going to have to dig for it.' Then his mind escaped once more into the hot land of delirium.

'My little girl, I'll bring you a pretty ribbon. There, don't cry. A pretty ribbon for a pretty girl.' His voice syrupy, then suddenly harsh. 'You cheeky little bitch. You're just like that goddamned mother of yours. Don't know why I don't chase you out,' this last followed immediately by the hyena imitation again.

Now Sebastian turned away from the poop rail and looked down on Flynn. Beside him the faithful Mohammed was dipping strips of cloth in a bucket of sea water, wringing them out and then laying them on Flynn's flushed forehead in a futile attempt to reduce the fever.

Sebastian sighed. His responsibilities lay heavily. The command of the expedition had devolved squarely upon him. And yet, there was a sneaky sensation of pleasure, of pride in his execution of that command to the present. He went back and replayed in his mind the episode of the fish-net, remembering the quick decision that had altered the launch's course and lured it into the trap. He smiled at the memory, and the smile was not his usual self-effacing grin, but something harder. When he turned away to pace the narrow deck there was more spring in his step, and he set his shoulders square.

Again he stopped by the rail and looked towards the west. There was a cloud on the horizon, a tiny dark figure of it. And he watched it with hope that it might herald the start of the afternoon sea breeze. Yet it seemed unnatural. As he watched, it moved. He could swear it moved. Now his whole attention was fastened upon it. Realization began to flicker in him, building up until it was certainty.

A ship. By God, a ship!

He ran to the poop ladder, and slid down into the waist, across it to the mast.

The crew and the bearers watched him with awakening interest. Some of them got to their feet.

Sebastian jumped on to the boom, balancing there a moment before he started to shin up the mast. Using the mainsail hoops like the rungs of a ladder, he reached the masthead and clung there, peering eagerly into the west.

There she was – no doubt about it. He could see the tips of the triple stacks, each with its feather of dark smoke, and he began to cheer.

Below him the rail was lined with his men, all peering out in the direction they took from him. Sebastian slid down the mast, the friction burning his hands in his haste. His feet hit the deck and he ran to Flynn. 'A ship. A big ship coming up fast.' Flynn rolled his head and looked at him vaguely. 'Listen to me, Flynn. There'll be a doctor aboard. We'll get you to a port in no time.'

'That's good, Bassie.' Flynn's brain clicked back into focus. 'You've done real good.'

She came up over the horizon with astonishing rapidity, and her silhouette changed as she altered course towards them. But not before Sebastian had seen the gun turrets.

'A warship!' he shouted. To his mind this proved her British – only one nation ruled the waves. 'They've seen us!' He waved his hands above his head.

Bows on, each second growing in size, grey and big, she bore down upon the little dhow.

Gradually the cheering of the crew faltered and subsided into an uneasy silence. Magnified by the still, hot air, huge on the velvety gloss of the ocean, lifting a bow wave of pearling white, the warship came on. No check in her speed, the ensign at her masthead streaming away from them so they could not see the colours.

'What are they going to do?' Sebastian asked aloud, and was answered by Flynn's voice. Sebastian glanced around. Balancing on his good leg with one arm draped around Mohammed's neck, Flynn was hopping across the deck towards him.

'I'll tell you what they're going to do! They're going to hit us smack-bang up the arse!' Flynn roared. 'That's the *Blücher*! That's a German cruiser!'

'They can't do that!' Sebastian protested.

'You'd like to bet? She's coming straight from the Rufiji delta – and my guess is she's had a chat with Fleischer. He's probably aboard her.' Flynn swayed against Mohammed, gasping with the pain of his leg before he went on. 'They're going to ram us, and then machine-gun anyone still floating.'

'We've got to make a life raft.'

'No time, Bassie. Look at her come!'

Less than five miles away, but swiftly narrowing the distance, the *Blücher's* tall bows knifed towards them. Wildly Sebastian looked around the crowded deck, and he saw the pile of cork floats they had cut from the fish nets.

Drawing his knife, he ran to one of the sacks of coconuts and cut the twine that closed the mouth. He slipped the knife back into its sheath, stooped, and up-ended the sack, spilling coconuts on to the deck. Then with the empty sack in his hand he ran to the pile of floats and dropped on his knees. In frantic haste he shovelled them into the sack, half filling it before he looked up again. The *Blücher* was two miles away, a tall tower of murderous grey steel.

With a length of rope Sebastian tied the sack closed and dragged it to where Flynn stood supported by Mohammed.

'What are you doing?' Flynn demanded.

'Fixing you up! Lift your arms!' Flynn obeyed and Sebastian tied the free end of the rope around his chest at the level of his armpits. He paused to unlace and kick off his boots before speaking again. 'Mohammed, you stay with him. Hang on to the sack and don't let go.' He left them, trotting on bare feet to find his rifle propped against the poop. Buckling on his cartridge belt, he hurried back to the rail.

Sebastian Oldsmith was about to engage a nine-inch battle cruiser with a double-barrelled Gibbs .500.

She was close now, hanging over them like a high cliff of steel. Even Sebastian could not miss a battle cruiser at two hundred yards, and the heavy bullets clanged against the armoured hull, ringing loudly above the hissing rush of the bow wave.

While he reloaded, Sebastian looked up at the line of heads in the bows of the *Blücher*; grinning faces below the white caps with their little swallow-tailed black ribbons. 'You bloody swines,' he shouted at them. Hatred stronger than he had ever dreamed possible, choked his voice. 'You filthy, bloody swine.' He lifted the rifle and fired without effect, and the *Blücher* hit the dhow.

It struck with a crash and the crackling roar of rending timber. It crushed her side and cut through in the screaming of dying men and the squeal of planking against steel.

It trod the dhow under, breaking her back, forcing her far below the surface. At the initial shock, Sebastian was hurled overboard, the rifle thrown from his hands. He struck the armoured plate of the cruiser a glancing blow and then dropped into the sea beside her. The thrust of the bow wave tumbled him aside, else he would have been dragged along the hull and his body shredded against the steel plate.

He surfaced just in time to suck a lungful of air before the turbulence of the great screws caught him and plucked him under again, driving him deep so the pressure stabbed like red-hot needles in his eardrums. He felt himself swirled end over end, buffeted, shaken vigorously as the water tore at his body.

Colour flashed and zigzagged behind his closed eyelids. There was a suffocating pain in his chest and his lungs pumped, urgently craving air, but he sealed his lips and kicked out with his legs, clawing at the water with his hands.

The churning wake of the cruiser released its grip upon him, and he was shot to the surface with such force that he broke clear to the waist before dropping back to drink air greedily. He unbuckled the heavy cartridge belt and let it sink before he looked about him.

The surface of the sea was scattered with floating debris, and a few bobbing human heads. Near him a section of torn planking rose in a burst of trapped air bubbles. Sebastian struck out for it and clung there, his legs hanging in the clear green water.

'Flynn,' he gasped. 'Flynn, where are you?'

A quarter of a mile away, the *Blücher* was circling slowly, long and menacing and shark-like, and he stared at it in hatred and in fear.

'Master!' Mohammed's voice behind him.

Sebastian turned quickly and saw the black face and the red face beside the floating sack of corks a hundred yards away. 'Flynn!'

'Good-bye, Bassie,' Flynn called. 'The old Hun is coming back to finish us off. Look! They've got machine guns set up on the bridge. See you on the other side, boy.'

Quickly Sebastian looked back at the cruiser and saw the clusters of white uniforms on the angle of her bridge.

'Ja, there are still some of them alive.' Through borrowed binoculars, Fleischer scanned the littered area of the wreck. 'You will use the Maxims, of course, Captain? It will be quicker than picking them off with rifles.'

Captain von Kleine did not answer. He stood tall on his bridge, slightly round-shouldered, staring out at the wreckage with his hands clasped behind him. 'There is something sad in the death of a ship,' he murmured. 'Even such a dirty little one as this.' Suddenly he straightened his shoulders and turned to Fleischer. 'Your launch is waiting for you at the mouth of the Rufiji. I will take you there, Commissioner.'

'But first the business of the survivors.'

Von Kleine's expression hardened. 'Commissioner, I sank that dhow in what I believed to be my duty. But now I am not sure that my judgement was not clouded by anger. I will not trespass further on my conscience by machine-gunning swimming civilians.'

'You will then pick them up. I must arrest them and give them trial.'

'I am not a policeman,' he paused and his expression softened a little. 'That one who fired the rifle at us. I think he must be a brave man. He is a criminal, perhaps, but I am not so old in the ways of the world that I do not love courage merely for its own sake. I would not like to know I have saved this man for the noose. Let the sea be the judge and the executioner.' He turned to his lieutenant. 'Kyller, prepare to drop one of the life rafts.' The lieutenant stared at him in disbelief. 'You heard me?'

'Yes, my Captain.'

'Then do it.' Ignoring Fleischer's squawks of protest, von Kleine crossed to the pilot. 'Alter course to pass the survivors at a distance of fifty metres.'

'Here she comes.' Flynn grinned tightly, without humour, and watched the cruiser swing ponderously towards them.

The cries of the swimmers around him, pleading mercy, were plaintive as the voices of sea birds – tiny on the immensity of the ocean.

'Flynn. Look at the bridge!' Sebastian's voice floated across to him. 'See him there. The grey uniform.'

Tears from the sting of sea salt in his wound, and the distortion of fever had blurred Flynn's vision, yet he could make out the spot of grey among the speckling of white uniforms on the bridge of the cruiser.

'Who is it?'

'You were right. It's Fleischer,' Sebastian shouted back, and Flynn began to curse.

'Hey, you filthy, fat butcher,' he bellowed, trying to drag himself up onto the floating sack of corks. 'Hey, you whore's chamber pot.' His voice carried above the murmur of the cruiser's engines running at dead-slow. 'Come on, you blood-smeared little pig.'

The tall hull of the cruiser was close now, so close he could see the bulky figure in grey turn to the tall white-uniformed officer beside him, gesticulating in what was clearly entreaty.

The officer turned away, and moved to the rail of the bridge. He leaned out and waved to a group of seamen on the deck below him.

'That's right. Tell them to shoot. Let's get it over with. Tell them . . .'

A large square object was lifted over the rail by the gang below the bridge. It dropped and fell with a splash alongside.

Flynn's voice dried up, and he watched in disbelief as the white-clad officer lifted his right arm in a gesture that might have been a salute. The beat of the cruiser's engines mounted as it increased speed, and she swung away towards the west.

Flynn O'Flynn began to laugh, the cackling hysteria of relief and delirium. He rolled off the sack of corks and his head dropped forward, so the warm green water smothered his laughter. Mohammed took a handful of the grey hair and lifted his face to prevent him drowning.

14

S| ebastian reached the raft, and grasped the rope that hung in loops around its
sides. He paused to regain his breath before hauling himself up to lie gasping,
the blood-warm sea-water streaming from his sodden clothing, and watched the
shape of the battle cruiser recede into the west.

'Master! Help me!'

The voice roused him and he sat up. Mohammed was struggling, dragging Flynn
and the sack through the water. Among the floating wreckage a dozen others of the
crew and the bearers were flapping their way towards the raft; the weaker swimmers
were already failing, their cries becoming more pitiful, and their splashing more
frenzied.

There were oars roped to the slatted deck of the raft. Quickly Sebastian cut one
loose with his hunting knife and began rowing towards the pair. His progress was
slow, for the raft was an ungainly bitch that balked and swung away from the thrust
of the oar.

An Arab crewman reached the raft and scrambled aboard, then another, and
another. Each of them freed an oar and helped with the rowing. They passed the
body of one of the bearers floating just below the surface, both its legs cut off above
the knees and the bones sticking out of the ragged meat of the stumps. This was
not the only one – there was other human flotsam among the scattered wreckage,
and the pinky-brown stains that drifted away on the current attracted the sharks.

The Arab beside Sebastian saw the first one and called out, pointing with the oar.

It came hunting, its fin waggling from side to side as it tacked up against the
current, so that they could sense its excitation, the cold, unthinking excitement of
Euselachii hunger. Below the surface, distorted and dark, showed the tapering length
of its body. Not a big one. Perhaps nine feet in length and four hundred pounds in
weight, but big enough to chop a leg with one bite. No longer guided by the drift of
blood-taste, picking up the vibrations of the swimmers, it straightened and came in
on its first run.

'Shark!' Sebastian yelled at Flynn and Mohammed where they floundered ten
yards away. And both of them panicked; no longer making for the raft, they tried to
clamber on to the sack of corks. Terror has no logic. Their only concern was to lift
their dangling legs from the water, but the sack was too small, too unstable and their
panic attracted the shark's attention. It veered towards them, showing the full height
of its curved triangular fin, each sweep of its tail breaking the surface as it drove in.

'This way,' shouted Sebastian. 'Come to the raft!' He was hacking at the water with
the oar, while beside him the Arabs worked in equal dedication. 'This way, Flynn.
For God's sake, this way.'

His voice penetrated their panic, and once more they struck out for the raft. But
the shark was closing fast, long and dappled by sunlight through the surface ripple.

The sack was still tied to Flynn's body, and its resistance to the water slowed them

431

as it dragged behind. The shark swerved and made its first pass; it seemed to hump up out of the water, and its mouth opened. The upper jaw bulged out, the lower jaw gaped, and the multiple rows of teeth came erect like the quills of a porcupine, *and it hit the sack*. Locking its jaws into the coarse jute material, worrying it, still humped out of the water, shaking its blunt head clumsily, scattering a spray of water drops that flew like shattered glass in the sun.

'Grab here!' commanded Sebastian, leaning out to offer the blade of the oar to the pair in the water. They clutched at it with the strength of fear, and Sebastian drew them in.

But the sack and the shark were still attached to Flynn, its threshing threatening to break Flynn's hold on the life-line around the raft.

Dropping to his knees, Sebastian fumbled the knife from its sheath and sawed at the rope. It parted. The shark, still worrying the sack, worked away from the raft and Sebastian helped the Arabs to drag first Flynn, and then Mohammed, over the side.

They were not finished yet. There were still half a dozen men in the water.

Realizing its error at last, the shark relinquished its hold on the sack. It backed away. For a moment it hung motionless, puzzled, then it circled out towards the nearest sound of splashing. One of the gun-boys, clawing at the water in exhausted dog-paddle. The shark hit him in the side, and pulled him under. Moments later he reappeared, his mouth an open pink cave as he screamed, the water about him clouded dark red-brown by his own blood. Again he was pulled under as the shark hit his legs, but again he floated. This time face down, wriggling feebly, and the shark circled him, dashing in to chop off a mouthful of his flesh, backing away to gulp it down before coming in again.

Then there was another shark, two more, ten, so many that Sebastian could not count them, as they circled and dove in ecstatic greed, until the sea around the raft trembled and swirled in agitation.

Sebastian and his Arabs managed to drag two more of the crew into the raft and they had a third half out of the water when a six-foot white-pointer shot up from the depths, and fastened on his thigh with such violence that it almost jerked all of them overboard. But they steadied themselves and held on to the man's arms, frozen in this gruesome tug-of-war, while the shark worried the leg, so dog-like in its determination that Sebastian expected it to growl.

Little Mohammed staggered to his feet, snatched up an oar and swung it against the pointed snout with all his strength. They had dragged the shark's head from the water, and the oar fell on it with a series of rubbery thumps, but the shark held on. Fresh, bright blood squirted and trickled from the leg in its jaws, running down the shark's glistening snake-like head into the open slits of its gill covers.

'Hold him!' gasped Sebastian, and drew his knife. The raft rocking crazily under him, he leaned over the man's outstretched body and drove the knife blade into the shark's expressionless little eye. It popped in a burst of clear fluid, and the shark stiffened and trembled. Sebastian withdrew the blade and stabbed into the other eye. With a convulsive gulp the shark opened its jaws and slid back into the sea to meander blindly away.

There were no more swimmers. The little group on the raft huddled together and watched the shark pack milling hungrily, seeming to sniff at the tainted water as they gathered the last morsels of meat.

The shark victim hosed the deck with his severed femoral artery and died before any of them could rouse themselves to apply a tourniquet.

'Push him over,' grunted Flynn.

'No,' Sebastian shook his head.

'Chrissake, we're crowded enough as it is. Chuck the poor bastard over.'

'Later on, not now.' Sebastian could not stand to watch the sharks squabble over the corpse.

'Mohammed, get a couple of your lads on the oars. I want to pick up as many of those coconuts as we can.'

By the time darkness stopped them, they had retrieved fifty-two of the floating coconuts, sufficient to keep the seven of them thirst-free for a week.

It was cold that night. They crowded together for warmth and watched the underwater pyrotechnics, as the shark pack circled the raft in phosphorescent splendour.

15

Y ou've got to cut for it,' Flynn whispered, and he shivered with cold in the burning heat of the midday sun.

'I don't know anything about it,' Sebastian protested, yet he could see that Flynn was dying.

'No more do I. But this is certain – you've got to do it soon . . . Flynn's eyes had sunk into plum-coloured cavities and the smell of his breath was that of something long dead.

Staring at the leg, Sebastian had difficulty controlling his nausea. It was swollen fat and purple. The bullet hole was covered with a crusty black scab, but Sebastian caught a whiff of the putrefaction under it – and this time his nausea came up acid-sweet into the back of his throat. He swallowed it.

'You've got to do it, Bassie boy.'

Sebastian nodded, and tentatively laid his hand on the leg. Immediately he jerked his fingers away, surprised by the heat of the skin.

'You've got to do it,' urged Flynn. 'Feel for the slug. It's not deep. Just under the skin.'

He felt the lump. It moved under his fingers, the size of a green acorn in the taut hot flesh.

'It's going to hurt like Billy-o.' Sebastian's voice was hoarse.

The rowers were resting on their oars, watching with frank curiosity, while the raft eddied and swung in the drift of the Mozambique current. Above them the sail that Sebastian had rigged from salvaged planking and canvas, flapped wearily, throwing a shadow across the leg.

'Mohammed, you and one other to hold the master's shoulders. Two others to keep his legs still.'

Flynn lay quiescent, pinioned beneath them on the slats of the deck.

Sebastian knelt over him, gathering his resolve. The knife he had sharpened against the metal edge of the raft, and then scrubbed clean with coconut fibre and sea-water. He had sluiced the leg also, and washed his hands until the skin tingled. Beside him on the deck stood half a coconut shell containing perhaps an ounce of evaporated salt scraped from the deck and the sail, ready to pack into the open wound. 'Ready?' he whispered.

'Ready,' grunted Flynn, and Sebastian located the lump of the bullet and drew the edge of the blade across it timidly. Flynn gasped, but human skin was tougher than Sebastian allowed. It did not part.

'Goddamn you!' Flynn was sweating already. 'Don't play with it. Cut, man, cut!'

This time Sebastian slashed, and the flesh split open under the blade. He dropped the knife and drew back in horror as the infection bubbled up through the lips of the knife wound. It looked like yellow custard mixed with prune juice – and the smell of it filled his nostrils and his throat.

'Go for the slug. Go for it with your fingers.' Flynn writhed beneath the men who held him. 'Hurry. Hurry. I can't take much more.'

Steeling himself, closing his throat against the vomit that threatened to vent at any moment, Sebastian slipped his little finger into the slit. Hooking with it for the bullet, finding it, easing it up although tissue clung to it reluctantly, until it popped from the wound and dropped on to the deck. A fresh gush of warm poison followed it out, flowing over Sebastian's hand, and he crawled to the edge of the raft, choking and gagging.

16

'If only we had some red cloth.' Flynn sat against the rickety mast. He was still very weak but four days ago the fever had broken with the release of the poison.

'What would you do with it?' Sebastian asked.

'Catch me one of those dolphins. Man, I'm so goddamned hungry I'd eat it raw.'

A four-day diet of coconut pulp and milk had left all their bellies grumbling.

'Why red?'

'They go for red. Make a lure.'

'You haven't any hooks or line.'

'Tie it to a bit of twine from the sack and tease them up to the surface – then harpoon one with your knife tied to an oar.'

Sebastian was silent, peering thoughtfully over the side at the deep flashes of gold where the shoal of dolphin played under the raft. 'It's got to be red, hey?' he asked, and Flynn looked at him sharply.

'Yeah. It's got to be red.'

'Well . . .' Sebastian hesitated, and then flushed with embarrassment under his tropical sunburn.

'What's wrong with you?'

Still blushing, Sebastian stood up and loosened his belt – then, shyly as a bride on her wedding night, he drew down his pants.

'My God,' breathed Flynn in shock, as he held up his hand to shield his eyes.

'Hau! Hau!' was the chorus of admiration from the crew.

'Got them at Harrods,' said Sebastian with becoming modesty.

Red, Flynn had asked for – but Sebastian's underpants were the brightest, most beautiful red; the most vivid sunset and roses red, he could have imagined. They hung in oriental splendour to Sebastian's knees.

'Pure silk,' said Sebastian, fingering the cloth. 'Ten shillings a pair.'

'Whoa now! Come on, little fishy. Come on there,' Flynn whispered as he lay on his belly, head and shoulders over the edge of the raft. On its thread of twine, the scrap of red danced deep in the green water. A long, slithering flash of gold shot towards it, and Flynn jerked the twine away at the last instant. The dolphin swirled and darted back. Again Flynn jerked the twine. Chameleon lines and dots of excitement showed against the gold of the dolphin's body. 'That's it, fishy. Chase it.' The other fish of the shoal joined hunt, forming a sparkling planetary system of movement around the lure. 'Get ready!'

'I'm ready.' Sebastian stood over him, poised like a javelin thrower. In the excitement he had forgotten to don his pants and his shirt-tails flapped around his thighs in a most undignified manner. But his legs were long and finely muscled, the legs of an athlete. 'Get back!' he snapped at the crew who were crowded around him so that the raft was listing dangerously. 'Get back – give me room,' and he hefted the oar with the long hunting knife lashed to the tip.

'Here they come.' Flynn's voice trembled with excitement as he worked the scrap of red cloth upwards, and the shoal followed it. 'Now!' he shouted as a single fish broke the surface – four feet of flashing gold, and Sebastian lunged. The steady hand and eye that had once clean-bowled the great Frank Woolley directed the oar. Sebastian hit the dolphin an inch behind the eye, and the blade slipped through to lacerate the gills.

For a few seconds the oar came alive in his hands as the dolphin twitched and fought on the blade, but there were no barbs to hold in the flesh, and the fish slipped from the knife.

'God damn it to hell!' bellowed Flynn.

'Dash it all!' echoed Sebastian.

But ten feet down the dolphin was mortally wounded; it jigged and whipped like a golden kite in a high wind while the rest of the shoal scattered.

Sebastian dropped the oar and began stripping his shirt.

'What are you doing?' demanded Flynn.

'Going after it.'

'You're mad. Sharks!'

'I'm so hungry, I'll eat a shark also,' and he dived over the side. Thirty seconds later he surfaced, blowing like a grampus but grinning triumphantly, with the dead dolphin clasped lovingly to his bosom.

They ate strips of raw fish seasoned with evaporated salt, squatting around the mutilated carcass of the dolphin.

'Well, I've paid a guinea for worse meals than this,' said Sebastian, and belched softly. 'Oh, I beg your pardon.'

'Granted,' Flynn grunted with his mouth full of fish; and then eyeing Sebastian's nudity with a world-weary eye, 'Stop boasting and put your pants on before you trip over it.'

Flynn O'Flynn was slowly, very slowly, revising his estimate of Sebastian Oldsmith.

17

T he rowers had long since lost any enthusiasm they might have had for the task. They kept at it only in response to offers of bodily violence by Flynn – and the example set by Sebastian, who worked tirelessly. The thin layer of fat that had sheathed Sebastian's muscles was long since consumed, and his sun-baked body was a Michelangelo sculpture, as he leaned and dug and pulled the oar.

Six days they had dragged the raft across the southward push of the current. Six days of sun-blazing calm, with the sea flattening, until now in the late afternoon, it looked like an endless sheet of smooth green velvet.

'No,' said Mohammed. 'That means, *The two porcupines make love under the blanket.*'

'Oh!' Sebastian repeated the phrase without interrupting the rhythm of his rowing. Sebastian was a dogged pupil of Swahili, making up in determination what he lacked in brilliance. Mohammed was proud of him, and opposed any attempt by the other members of the crew to usurp his position as chief tutor.

'That's all right about the porcupines shagging themselves to a standstill,' grunted Flynn. 'But what does this mean . . .?' and he spoke in Swahili.

'It means, *Big winds will blow across the sea,*' interpreted Sebastian, and glowed with achievement.

'And I'm not joking either.' Flynn stood up, crouching to favour his bad leg, and shaded his eyes to peer into the east. 'You see that line of cloud?'

Laying aside the oar, Sebastian stood beside him and flexed the aching muscles of his back and shoulders. Immediately all activity ceased among the other rowers.

'Keep going, me beauties!' growled Flynn, and reluctantly they obeyed. Flynn turned back to Sebastian. 'You see it?'

'Yes.' It was drawn like a kohl line across the eyelid of a Hindu woman, smeared black along the horizon.

'Well, Bassie, there's the wind you've been griping about. But, my friend, I think it's a little more than you bargained for.'

In the darkness they heard it coming from far away, a muted sibilance in the night. One by one, the fat stars were blotted out in the east as dark cloud spread out to fill half the midnight sky.

A single gust hit the raft and flogged the makeshift sail with a clap like a shotgun, and the sleepers woke and sat up.

'Hang on to those fancy underpants,' muttered Flynn, 'or you'll get them blown right up your backside.'

Another gust, another lull, but already there was the boisterous slapping of small waves against the sides of the raft.

'I'd better get that sail down.'

'You had, and all,' agreed Flynn, 'and while you're at it, use the rope to fix life-lines for us.' In haste, spurred on by the rising hiss of the wind, they lashed themselves to the slats of the deck.

The main force of the wind spun the raft like a top, splattering them with spray; the spray was icy cold in the warm rush of the wind. The wind was steady now and the raft moved uneasily – the jerky motion of an animal restless at the prick of spur.

'At least it will push us towards the land,' Sebastian shouted across at Flynn.

'Bassie, boy, you think of the cutest things,' and the first wave came aboard, smothering Flynn's voice, breaking over their prostrate bodies, and then streaming out through the slatted deck. The raft wallowed in dismay, then gathered itself to meet the next rush of the sea.

Under the steady fury of the wind, the sea came up more swiftly than Sebastian believed was possible. Within minutes the waves were breaking over the raft with such weight as to squeeze the breath from their lungs, submerging them completely, driving the raft under before its buoyancy reasserted itself and lifted it, canting crazily, and they could gasp for air in the smother of spray.

Waiting for the lulls, Sebastian inched his way across the deck until he reached Flynn. 'How are you bearing up?' he bellowed.

'Great, just great,' and another wave drove them under.

'Your leg?' spluttered Sebastian as they came up.

'For Chrissake, stop yapping,' and they went under again.

It was completely dark, no star, no sliver of moon, but each line of breaking water glowed in dull, phosphorescent malevolence as it dashed down upon them, warning them to suck air and cling with cramped fingers hooked into the slats.

For all eternity Sebastian lived in darkness, battered by the wind and the wild, flying water. The aching chill of his body dulled out into numbness. Slowly his mind emptied of conscious thought, so when a bigger wave scoured them, he heard the tearing sound of deck slats pulling loose, and the lost wail as one of the Arabs was washed away into the night sea – but the sound had no meaning to him.

Twice he vomited sea water that he had swallowed, but it had no taste in his mouth, and he let it run heedlessly down his chin and warm on to his chest, to be washed away by the next torrential wave.

His eyes burned without pain from the harsh rake of windflung spray, and he blinked them owlishly at each advancing wave. It seemed, in time, that he could see more clearly, and he turned his head slowly. Beside him, Flynn's face was a leprous blotch in the darkness. This puzzled him, and he lay and thought about it but no solution came, until he looked beyond the next wave, and saw the faint promise of a new day show pale through the black massed cloud-banks.

He tried to speak, but no sound came for his throat was swollen closed with the salt, and his tongue was tingling numb. Again, he tried. 'Dawn coming,' he croaked, but beside him Flynn lay like a corpse frozen in rigor mortis.

Slowly the light grew over that mad, grey sea but the scudding black cloud-banks tried desperately to oppose its coming.

Now the seas were more awesome in their raging insanity. Each mountain of glassy grey rose high above the raft, shielding it for a few seconds from the whip of the wind, its crest blowing off like the plume of an Etruscan helmet, before it slid down, collapsing upon itself in the tumbling roar of breaking water.

Each time, the men on the raft shrank flat on the deck, and waited in bovine acceptance to be smothered again beneath the white deluge.

Once, the raft rode high and clear in a freak flat of the storm, and Sebastian looked about him. The canvas and rope, the coconuts and the other pathetic accumulation of their possessions were all gone. The sea had ripped away many of the deck slats so that the metal floats of the raft were exposed; it had torn the very clothing from them so they were clad in sodden tatters. Of the seven men who had ridden the raft the previous day, only he and Flynn, Mohammed and one more, were left – the other three were gone, gobbled up by the hungry sea.

Then the storm struck again, so that the raft reeled and reared to the point of capsizing.

Sebastian sensed it first in the altered action of the waves; they were steeper, marching closer together. Then, through the clamour of the storm, a new sound, like that of a cannon fired at irregular intervals with varying charges of gunpowder. He realized suddenly that he had been hearing this sound for some time, but only now had it penetrated the stupor of his fatigue.

He lifted his head, and every nerve of his being shrieked in protest at the effort. He looked about, but the sea stood up around him like a series of grey walls that limited his vision to a circle of fifty yards. Yet that discordant boom, boom, boom, was louder now and more insistent.

In the short, choppy waves, a side-break caught the raft and tossed it high – lifting him so he could see the land; so close that the palm trees showed sharply, bending their stems to the wind and threshing their long fronds in panic. He saw the beach, grey-white in the gloom and, beyond it, far beyond it, rose the watery blue of the high ground.

These things had small comfort for him when he saw the reef. It bared its black teeth at him, snarling through the white water that burst like cannon-fire upon it before cascading on into the comparative quiet of the lagoon. The raft was riding down towards it.

'Flynn,' he croaked. 'Flynn, listen to me!' but the older man did not move, His eyes were fixed open and only the movement of his chest, as he breathed, proved him still alive. 'Flynn.' Sebastian released one of his clawed hands from its grip on the wooden slatting. 'Flynn!' he said, and struck him across the cheek.

'Flynn!' The head turned towards Sebastian, the eyes blinked, the mouth opened, but no voice spoke.

Another wave broke over the raft. This time the cold, malicious rush of it stirred Sebastian, roused a little of his failing strength. He shook the water from his head. 'Land,' he whispered. 'Land,' and Flynn stared at him dully.

Two lines of surf away, the reef showed its ragged back again. Clinging with only one hand to the slatting, Sebastian fumbled the knife from its sheath and hacked clumsily at the life-line that bound him to the deck. It parted. He reached over and cut Flynn's line, sawing frantically at the wet hemp. That done, he slid back on his belly until he reached Mohammed and freed him also. The little African stared at him with bloodshot eyes from his wrinkled monkey face.

'Swim,' whispered Sebastian. 'Must swim,' and re-sheathing the knife, he tried to crawl over Mohammed to reach the Arab but the next wave caught the raft, rearing up under it as it felt the push of the land, rearing so steeply that this time the raft was overturned and they were thrown from it into the seething turmoil of the reef.

Sebastian hit the water flat, and was hardly under, before he had surfaced again. Beside him, close enough to touch, Flynn emerged. In the strength born of the fear of death, Flynn caught at Sebastian, locking both arms around his chest. The same wave that had capsized them, had poured over the reef and covered it completely, so that where the coral fangs had been was now only a frothy area of disturbed water. In it bobbed the debris of the raft, shattered into pieces against the reef. The muti-lated corpse of the Arab was still roped to a piece of the wreckage. Flynn and Sebastian were locked like lovers in each other's arms and the next wave, following close upon the first, lifted them, and shot them forward over the submerged reef.

In one great swoop that left their guts behind them, they were carried over the coral which could have minced them into jelly, and tumbled into the quiet lagoon. With them went little Mohammed, and what remained of the raft.

The lagoon was covered by a thick scum of wind spume, creamy as the head of a good beer. So when the three of them staggered waist-deep towards the beach, supporting each other with arms around shoulders, they were coated with white froth. It made them look like a party of drunken snowmen returning home after a long night out.

18

Mohammed squatted with a pile of madafu, the shiny green coconuts, beside him. The beach was littered with them, for the storm had stripped the trees. He worked in feverish haste with Sebastian's hunting knife, his face frosted with dried salt, mumbling to himself through cracked and swollen lips, shaving down through the white, fibrous material of the shell, until he exposed the hollow centre filled with its white custard and effervescent milk. At this point the madafu was snatched from his hands by either Flynn or Sebastian. His despair growing deeper, he watched for a second the two white men drinking with heads thrown back, throats pulsing as they swallowed, spilled milk trickling from the corners of their mouths, eyes closed tight in their intense pleasure; then he picked up another nut and got to work on it. He opened a dozen before he was able to satiate the other two, and he held the next nut to his own mouth and whimpered with eagerness.

Then they slept. Bellies filled with the sweet, rich milk, they sagged backwards on the sand and slept the rest of that day and that night, and when they woke, the wind had dropped, although the sea still burst like an artillery bombardment on the reef.

'Now,' said Flynn, 'where, in the name of the devil and all his angels, are we?' Neither Sebastian nor Mohammed answered him. 'We were six days on the raft. We could have drifted hundreds of miles south before the storm pushed us in.' He frowned as he considered the problem. 'We might even have reached Portuguese Mozambique. We could be as far as the Zambezi river.'

Flynn focused his attention on Mohammed. 'Go!' he said. 'Search for a river, or a mountain that you know. Better still, find a village where we can get food – and bearers.'

'I'll go also,' Sebastian volunteered.

'You wouldn't know the difference between the Zambezi and the Mississippi,' Flynn grunted impatiently. 'You'd be lost after the first hundred yards.'

Mohammed was gone for two days and a half, but Sebastian and Flynn ate well in his absence.

Under a sun shelter of palm fronds they feasted three times a day on crab and sand-clams, and big green rock-lobster which Sebastian fished from the lagoon, baking them in their shells over the fire that Flynn coaxed from two dry sticks.

On the first night the entertainment was provided by Flynn. For some years now, Flynn's intake of gin had averaged a daily two bottles. The abrupt cessation of supply resulted in a delayed but classic visitation of *delirium tremens*. He spent half the night hobbling up and down the beach brandishing a branch of driftwood and hurling obscenities at the phantoms that had come to plague him. There was one purple cobra in particular which pursued him doggedly, and it was only after Flynn had beaten it noisily to death behind a palm tree, that he allowed Sebastian to lead him back to the shelter and seat him beside the camp-fire. Then he got the shakes. He shook like a man on a jack-hammer. His teeth rattled together with such violence that Sebastian was sure they must shatter. Gradually, however, the shakes subsided and by the following noon he was able to eat three large rock-lobsters and then collapse into a death-like sleep.

He woke in the late evening, looking as well as Sebastian had ever seen him, to greet the returning Mohammed and the dozen tall Angoni tribesmen who accompanied him. They returned Flynn's greeting with respect. From Beira to Dar es Salaam, the name 'Fini' was held in universal awe by the indigenous peoples. Legend credited him with powers far above the natural order. His exploits, his skill with the rifle, his volcanic temper and his seeming immunity from death and retribution, had formed the foundation of a belief that Flynn had carefully fostered. They said in whispers around the night fires when the women and the children were not listening that 'Fini' was in truth a reincarnation of the Monomatapa. They said further that in the intervening period between his death as the Great King and his latest birth as 'Fini', he had been first a monstrous crocodile, and then *Mowana Lisa*, the most notorious man-eating lion in the history of East Africa, a predator responsible for at least three hundred human killings. The day, twenty-five years previously, that Flynn had stepped ashore at Port Amelia was the exact day that *Mowana Lisa* had been shot dead by the Portuguese Chef D'Post at Sofala. All men knew these things – and only an idiot would take chances with 'Fini' – hence the respect with which they greeted him now.

Flynn recognized one of the men. 'Luti,' he roared, 'you scab on an hyena's backside!'

Luti smiled broadly, and bobbed his head in pleasure at being singled out by Flynn.

'Mohammed,' Flynn turned to his man. 'Where did you find him? Are we near his village?'

'We are a day's march away.'

'In which direction?'

'North.'

'Then we are in Portuguese territory!' exalted Flynn. 'We must have drifted down past the Rovuma river.'

The Rovuma river was the frontier between Portuguese Mozambique and German East Africa. Once in Portuguese territory, Flynn was immune from the wrath of the Germans. All their efforts at extraditing him from the Portuguese had proved unsuccessful, for Flynn had a working agreement with the Chef D'Post, Mozambique, and through him with the Governor in Lourenco Marques. In a manner of speaking, these two officials were sleeping partners in Flynn's business, and were entitled to a quarterly financial statement of Flynn's activities, and an agreed percentage of the profits.

'You can relax, Bassie boy. Old Fleischer can't touch us now. And in three or four days we'll be home.'

The first leg of the journey took them to Luti's village. Lolling in their maschilles, hammock-like litters slung beneath a long pole and carried by four of Luti's men at a synchronized jog trot, Flynn and Sebastian were borne smoothly out of the coastal lowland into the hills and bush country.

The litter-bearers sang as they ran, and their deep melodious voices, coupled with the swinging motion of the maschille, lulled Sebastian into a mood of deep contentment. Occasionally he dozed. Where the path was wide enough to allow the maschilles to travel side by side, he lay and chatted with Flynn, at other times he watched the changing country and the animal life along the way. It was better than London Zoo.

Each time Sebastian saw something new, he called across for Flynn to identify it.

In every glade and clearing were herds of the golden brown impala; delicate little creatures that watched them in wide-eyed curiosity as they passed.

Troops of guinea-fowl, like a dark cloud shadow on the earth, scratched and chittered on the banks of every stream.

Heavy, yellow eland, with their stubby horns and swinging dewlaps, trotting in Indian file, formed a regal frieze along the edge of the bush.

Sable and roan antelope; purple-brown waterbuck, with a perfect circle of white branded on their rumps; buffalo, big and black and ugly; giraffe, dainty little klipspringer, standing like chamois on the tumbled granite boulders of a kopje. The whole land seethed and skittered with life.

There were trees so strange in shape and size and foliage that Sebastian could hardly credit them as existing. Swollen baobabs, fifty feet in circumference, standing awkwardly as prehistoric monsters, fat pods filled with cream of tartar hanging from their deformed branches. There were forests of msasa trees, leaves not green as leaves should be, but rose and chocolate and red. Fever trees sixty feet high, with bright yellow trunks, shedding their bark like the brittle parchment of a snake's skin. Groves of mopani, whose massed foliage glittered a shiny, metallic green in the sun; and in the jungle growth along the river banks, the lianas climbed up like long, grey worms and hung in loops and festoons among the wild fig and the buffalo-bean vines and the tree ferns.

'Why haven't we seen any sign of elephant?' Sebastian asked.

'Me and my boys worked this territory over about six months ago,' Flynn explained. 'I guess they just moved on a little – probably up north across the Rovuma.'

In the late afternoon they descended a stony path into a valley, and for the first time Sebastian saw the permanent habitations of man. In irregular shaped plots, the bottom land of the valley was cultivated, and the rich black soil threw up lush green stands of millet, while on the banks of the little stream stood Luti's village; shaggy grass huts, shaped like beehives, each with a circular mud-walled granary standing on stilts beside it. The huts were arranged in a rough circle around an open space where the earth was packed hard by the passage of bare feet.

The entire population turned out to welcome Flynn: three hundred souls, from hobbling old white heads with grinning toothless gums, down to infants held on mothers' naked hip, who did not interrupt their feeding but clung like fat black limpets with hands and mouth to the breast.

Through the crowd that ululated and clapped hands in welcome, Flynn and Sebastian were carried to the chief's hut and there they descended from the maschilles.

Flynn and the old chief greeted each other affectionately; Flynn because of favours received and because of future favours yet to be asked for, and the chief because of Flynn's reputation and the fact that wherever Flynn travelled, he usually left behind him large quantities of good, red meat.

'You come to hunt elephant?' the chief asked, looking hopefully for Flynn's rifle.

'No.' Flynn shook his head. 'I return from a journey to a far place.'

'From where?'

In answer, Flynn looked significantly at the sky and repeated, 'From a far place.'

There was an awed murmur from the crowd and the chief nodded sagely. It was clear to all of them that 'Fini' must have been to visit and commune with his *alter ego*, Monomatapa.

'Will you stay long at our village?' again hopefully.

'I will stay tonight only. I leave again in the dawn.'

'Ah!' Disappointment. 'We had hoped to welcome you with a dance. Since we heard of your coming, we have prepared.'

'No,' Flynn repeated. He knew a dance could last three or four days.

'There is a great brewing of palm wine which is only now ready for drinking,' the chief tried again, and this time his argument hit Flynn like a charging rhinoceros. Flynn had been many days without liquor.

'My friend,' said Flynn, and he could feel the saliva spurting out from under his tongue in anticipation. 'I cannot stay to dance with you but I will drink a small gourd of palm wine to show my love for you and your village.' Then turning to Sebastian he warned, 'I wouldn't touch this stuff, Bassie, if I were you – it's real poison.'

'Right,' agreed Sebastian. 'I'm going down to the river to wash.'

'You do that,' and Flynn lifted the first gourd of palm wine lovingly to his lips.

Sebastian's progress to the river resembled a Roman triumph. The entire village lined the bank to watch his necessarily limited ablutions with avid interest, and a buzz of awe went up when he disrobed to his underpants.

'Bwana Manali,' they chorused. 'Lord of the Red Cloth,' and the name stuck.

As a farewell gift the headman presented Flynn with four gourds of palm wine, and begged him to return soon – bringing his rifle with him.

They marched hard all that day and when they camped at nightfall, Flynn was semi-paralysed with palm wine, while Sebastian shivered and his teeth chattered uncontrollably.

From the swamps of the Rufigi delta, Sebastian had brought with him a souvenir of his visit – his first full go of malaria.

They reached Lalapanzi the following day, a few hours before the crisis of Sebastian's fever. Lalapanzi was Flynn's base camp and the name meant 'Lie Down', or more accurately, 'The Place of Rest'.

It was in the hills on a tiny tributary of the great Rovuma river, a hundred miles from the Indian Ocean, but only ten miles from German territory across the river. Flynn believed in living close to his principle place of business.

Had Sebastian been in full possession of his senses, and not wandering in the hot shadow land of malaria, he would have been surprised by the camp at Lalapanzi. It was not what anybody who knew Flynn O'Flynn would have expected.

Behind a palisade of split bamboo to protect the lawns and gardens from the attentions of the duiker and steenbok and kudu, it glowed like a green jewel in the sombre brown of the hills. Much hard work and patience must have gone into damming the stream, and digging the irrigation furrows, which suckled the lawns and flower-beds and the vegetable garden. Three indigenous fig trees dwarfed the buildings, crimson frangipani burst like fireworks against the green kikuyu grass, beds of bright barberton daisies ringed the gentle terraces that fell away to the stream, and a bougainvillaea creeper smothered the main building in a profusion of dark green and purple.

Behind the long bungalow, with its wide, open veranda, stood half a dozen circular rondavels, all neatly capped with golden thatch and gleaming painfully white, with burned limestone paint, in the sunlight.

The whole had about it an air of feminine order and neatness. Only a woman, and a determined one at that, could have devoted so much time and pain to building up such a speck of prettiness in the midst of brown rock and harsh thorn veld.

She stood on the veranda in the shade like a valkyrie, tall and sun-browned and angry. The full-length dress of faded blue was crisp with new ironing, and the neat mends in the fabric invisible except at close range. Gathered close about her waist, her skirt ballooned out over her woman's hips and fell to her ankles, slyly concealing the long straight legs beneath. Folded across her stomach, her arms were an amber brown frame for the proud double bulge of her bosom, and the thick braid of black hair that hung to her waist twitched like the tail of an angry lioness. A face too young for the marks of hardship and loneliness that were chiselled into it, was harder now by the expression of distaste it wore as she watched Flynn and Sebastian arriving.

They lolled in their maschilles, unshaven, dressed in filthy rags, hair matted with sweat and dust; Flynn full of palm wine, and Sebastian full of fever – although it was impossible to distinguish the symptoms of their separate disorders.

'May I ask where you've been these last two months, Flynn Patrick O'Flynn?' Although she tried to speak like a man, yet her voice had a lift and a ring to it.

'You may not ask, daughter!' Flynn shouted back defiantly.

'You're drunk again!'

'And if I am?' roared Flynn. 'You're as bad as that mother of yours (may her soul rest in peace), always going on and on. Never a civil word of welcome for your old Daddy, who's been away trying to earn an honest crust.'

The girl's eyes switched to the maschille that carried Sebastian, and narrowed in mounting outrage. 'Sweet merciful heavens, and what's this you've brought home with you now?'

Sebastian grinned inanely, and tried valiantly to sit up as Flynn introduced him. 'That is Sebastian Oldsmith. My very dear friend, Sebastian Oldsmith.'

'He's also drunk!'

'Listen, Rosa. You show some respect.' Flynn struggled to climb from his maschille.

'He's drunk,' Rosa repeated grimly. 'Drunk as a pig. You can take him straight back and leave him where you found him. He's not coming in this house.' She turned away, pausing only a moment at the front door to add, 'That goes for you also, Flynn O'Flynn. I'll be waiting with the shotgun. You just put one foot on the veranda before you're sober – and I'll blow it clean off.'

'Rosa – wait – he isn't drunk, please,' wailed Flynn, but the fly-screen door had slammed closed behind her.

Flynn teetered uncertainly at the foot of the veranda stairs, for a moment it looked as though he might be foolhardy enough to put his daughter's threat to the test, but he was not that drunk.

'Women,' he mourned. 'The good Lord protect us,' and he led his little caravan around the back of the bungalow to the farthest of the rondavel huts. This room was sparsely furnished in anticipation of Flynn's regular periods of exile from the main building.

19

R osa O'Flynn closed the front door behind her and leaned back against it wearily. Slowly her chin sagged down to her chest, and she closed her eyes to imprison the itchy tears beneath the lids, but one of them squeezed through and quivered like a fat, glistening grape on her lashes, before falling to splash on the stone floor.

'Oh, Daddy, Daddy,' she whispered. It was an expression of those months of aching loneliness. The long, slow slide of days when she had searched desperately for work to fill her hands and her mind. The nights when, locked alone in her room with a loaded shotgun beside the bed, she had lain and listened to the sounds of the African bush beyond the window, afraid then of everything, even the four devoted African servants sleeping soundly with their families in their little compound behind the bungalow.

Waiting, waiting for Flynn to return. Lifting her head in the noonday and standing listening, hoping to hear the singing of his bearers as they came down the valley. And each hour the fear and the resentment building up within her. Fear that he might not come, and resentment that he left her for so long.

Now he had come. He had come drunk and filthy, with some oafish ruffian as a companion, and all her loneliness and fear had vented itself in that shrewish outburst. She straightened and pushed herself away from the door. Listlessly she walked through the shady cool rooms of the bungalow, spread with a rich profusion of animal skins and rough native-made furniture, until she reached her own room and sank down on the bed.

Beneath her unhappiness was a restlessness, a formless, undirected longing for something she did not understand. It was a new thing; only in these last few years had she become aware of it. Before that she had gloried in the companionship of her father, never having experienced and, therefore, never missing the society of others. She had taken it as the natural order of things that much of her time must be spent completely alone with only the wife of old Mohammed to replace her natural mother – the young Portuguese girl who had died in the struggle to give life to Rosa.

She knew the land as a slum child knows the city. It was her land and she loved it.

Now all of it was changing, she was uncertain, without bearings in this sea of new emotion. Lonely, irritable – and afraid.

A timid knocking on the back door of the bungalow roused her, and she felt a leap of hope within her. Her anger at Flynn had long ago abated – now he had made the first overture she would welcome him to the bungalow without sacrifice of pride.

Quickly she bathed her face in the china wash-basin beside her bed, and patted her hair into order before the mirror, before going through to answer the knock.

Old Mohammed stood outside, shuffling his feet and grinning ingratiatingly. He stood in almost as great an awe of Rosa's temper as that of Flynn himself. It was with relief, therefore, that he saw her smile.

'Mohammed, you old rascal,' and he bobbed his head with pleasure.

'You are well, Little Long Hair?'

'I am well, Mohammed – and I can see you are also.'

'The Lord Fini asks that you send blankets and quinine.'

'Why?' Rosa frowned quickly. 'Is the fever on him?'

'Not on him, but on Manali, his friend.'

'Is he bad?'

'He is very bad.'

The rich hostility that her first glimpse of Sebastian had invoked in Rosa, wavered a little. She felt the woman in her irresistibly drawn towards anything wounded or sick, even such an uncouth and filthy specimen as she had seen Sebastian to be.

'I will come,' she decided aloud, while silently qualifying her surrender by deciding that under no circumstances would she let him in the house. Sick or healthy, he would stay out there in the rondavel.

Armed with a pitcher of boiled drinking water, and a bottle of quinine tablets, closely attended by Mohammed carrying an armful of cheap trade blankets, she crossed to the rondavel and entered.

She entered it at an unpropitious moment. For Flynn had spent the last ten minutes exhuming the bottle he had so carefully buried some months before beneath the earthen floor of the rondavel. Being a man of foresight, he had caches of gin scattered in unlikely places around the camp, and now, in delicious anticipation, he was carefully wiping damp earth from the neck of the bottle with the the tail of his shirt. So engrossed with this labour he was not aware of Rosa's presence until the bottle was snatched from his hands, and thrown through the open side window to pop and tinkle as it burst.

'Now what did you do that for?' Flynn was hurt as deeply as a mother deprived of her infant.

'For the good of your soul.' Icily Rosa turned from him to the inert figure on the bed, and her nose wrinkled as she caught the whiff of unwashed body and fever. 'Where did you find this one?' she asked without expecting an answer.

20

F ive grains of quinine washed down Sebastian's throat with scalding tea, heated stones were packed around his body, and half a dozen blankets swaddled him to begin the sweat.

The malarial parasite has a thirty-six hour life cycle, and now at the crisis, Rosa was attempting to raise his body temperature sufficiently to interrupt the cycle and break the fever. Heat radiated from the bed, filling the single room of the rondavel as though it were a kitchen. Only Sebastian's head showed from the pile of blankets, and his face was flushed a dusky brick colour. Although sweat spurted from every pore of his skin and ran back in heavy drops to soak his hair and his pillow, yet his teeth rattled together and he shivered so that the camp-bed shook.

Rosa sat beside his bed and watched him. Occasionally she leaned forward with a cloth in her hand and wiped the perspiration from his eyes and upper lip. Her expression had softened and become almost broody. One of Sebastian's curls had plastered itself wetly across his forehead, and, with her finger-tips, Rosa combed it back. She repeated the gesture, and then did it again, stroking her fingers through his damp hair, instinctively gentling and soothing him.

He opened his eyes, and Rosa snatched her hand away guiltily. His eyes were misty grey, unfocused as a new-born puppy's, and Rosa felt something squirm in her stomach.

'Please don't stop.' His voice was slurred with the fever, but even so Rosa was surprised at the timbre and inflection. It was the first time she had heard him speak and it was not the voice of a ruffian. Hesitating a moment, she glanced at the door of the hut to make sure they were alone before she reached forward to touch his face.

'You are kind – good and kind.'

'Sshh!' she admonished him.

'Thank you.'

'Sshh! Close your eyes.'

His eyes flickered down and he sighed, a gusty, broken sound.

The crisis came like a big wind and shook him as though he were a tree in its path. His body temperature rocketed, and he tossed and writhed in the camp-bed, trying to throw off the weight of blankets upon him, so that Rosa called for Mohammed's wife to help her restrain him. His perspiration soaked through the thin mattress and dripped to form a puddle on the earth floor beneath the bed, and he cried out in the fantasy of his fever.

Then, miraculously, the crisis was past, and he slumped into relaxation. He lay still and exhausted so that only the shallow flutter of his breathing showed there was life in him. Rosa could feel his skin cooling under her hand, and she saw the yellowish tinge with which the fever had coloured it.

'The first time it is always bad,' Mohammed's wife released her grip on the blanket-wrapped legs.

'Yes,' said Rosa. 'Now bring the basin. We must wash him and change his blankets, Nanny.'

She had worked many times with men who were sick or badly hurt; the servants and the bearers and the gun-boys, and, of course, with her father. But now, as Nanny peeled back the blankets and Rosa swabbed Sebastian's unconscious body with the moist cloth, she felt an inexplicable tension within her – a sense of dread mingled with tight excitement. She could feel new blood warming her cheeks, and she leaned forward, so that Nanny could not see her face as she worked.

The skin of his chest and upper arms was creamy-smooth as polished alabaster, where the sun had not stained it. Beneath her fingers it had an elastic hardness, a rubbery sensuality and warmth that disturbed her. When she realized suddenly that she was no longer wiping with the flannel but using it to caress the shape of hard muscle beneath the pale skin, she checked herself and made her actions brusque and businesslike.

They dried his upper body, and Nanny reached to jerk the blankets down below Sebastian's waist.

'Wait!' It came out of Rosa as a cry, and Nanny paused with her hand on the bedclothes and her head held at an angle, quizzical, birdlike. Her wizened old features crinkling in sly amusement.

'Wait,' Rosa repeated in confusion. 'First help me get the night-shirt on him,' and she snatched up one of Flynn's freshly ironed but threadbare old night-shirts from the chair beside the bed.

'It cannot bite you, Little Long Hair,' the old woman teased her gently. 'It has no teeth.'

'You just stop that kind of talk,' snapped Rosa with unnecessary violence. 'Help me sit him up.'

Between them they lifted Sebastian and slipped the night-shirt down over his head, before lowering him to the pillow again.

'And now?' Nanny asked innocently. For answer, Rosa handed her the flannel, and turned to stare fixedly out of the rondavel window. Behind her she heard the rustle of blankets and then Nanny's voice.

'Hau! Hau!' The age-old expression of deep admiration, followed by a cackle of delighted laughter, as Nanny saw the back of Rosa's neck turning bright pink with embarrassment.

Nanny had smuggled Flynn's cut-throat razor out of the bungalow, and was supervising critically as Rosa stroked it gingerly over Sebastian's soapy cheeks. There was no sound medical reason why a malaria patient should be shaved immediately after emerging from the crisis, but Rosa had advanced the theory that it would make him feel more comfortable and Nanny had agreed enthusiastically. Both of them were enjoying themselves with all the sober delight of two small girls playing with a doll.

Despite Nanny's cautionary clucks and sharp hisses of in-drawn breath, Rosa succeeded in removing the hair that covered Sebastian's face like the black pelt of an otter without inflicting any serious wounds. There was a nick on the chin and another below the left nostril, but neither of these bled more than a drop or two.

Rosa rinsed the razor and then narrowed her eyes thoughtfully as she surveyed her handiwork, and that thing squirmed in her stomach again. 'I think,' she muttered, 'we should move him into the main bungalow. It will be more comfortable.'

'I will call the servants to carry him,' said Nanny.

21

F lynn O'Flynn was a busy man during the period of Sebastian's convalescence. His band of followers had been seriously depleted during the recent exchange with Herman Fleischer on the Rufiji, so to replace his losses, he press-ganged all the maschille-bearers who had carried them home from Luti's village. These he put through a preliminary course of training and at the end of four days selected a dozen of the most promising, to become gun-boys. The remainder he despatched homeward despite their protests; they would dearly have loved to stay for the glamour and reward that they were certain would be heaped upon their more fortunate fellows.

Thereafter the chosen few were entered upon the second part of their training. Securely locked in one of the rondavels behind the bungalow, Flynn kept the tools of his trade. It was an impressive arsenal.

Rack upon rack of cheap Martini Henry .450 rifles, a score of W. D. Lee-Metfords that had survived the Anglo-Boer war, a lesser number of German Mausers salvaged from his encounters with Askari across the Rovuma, and a very few of the expensive hand-made doubles by Gibbs and Messrs Greener of London. Not a single weapon had a serial number on it. Above these, neatly stacked on the wooden shelves, were bulk packages of cartridges, wrapped and soldered in lead foil – enough of them to fight a small battle.

The room reeked with the slick, mineral smell of gun oil.

Flynn issued his recruits with Mausers, and set about instructing them in the art of handling a rifle. Again he weeded out those who showed no aptitude and he was left finally with eight men who could hit an elephant at fifty paces. This group passed into the third and last period of training.

Many years previously, Mohammed had been recruited into the German Askari. He had even won a medal during the Salito rebellion of 1904, and from there had risen to the rank of sergeant and overseer of the officers' mess. During a visit by the army auditor to Mbeya, where Mohammed was at that time stationed, there had been discovered a stock discrepancy of some twenty dozen bottles of schnapps, and a hole in the mess funds amounting to a little over a thousand Reichsmarks. This was a hanging matter, and Mohammed had resigned without ceremony from the Imperial army and reached the Portuguese border by a series of forced marches. In Portuguese territory he had met Flynn, and solicited and received employment from him. However, he was still an authority on German army drill procedure and retained a command of the language.

The recruits were handed over to him, for it was part of Flynn's plans that they be able to masquerade as a squad of German Askari. For days thereafter the camp at Lalapanzi reverberated to Mohammed's Teutonic cries, as he goose-stepped about the lawns at the head of his band of nearly naked troopers, with his fez set squarely on the grey wool of his head.

This left Flynn free to make further preparations. Seated on the stoep of the bungalow, he pored sweatily over his correspondence for many days. First there was a letter to:

His Excellency, The Governor,
German Administration of East Africa,
Dar Es Salaam.

Sir,
I enclose my account for damages, as follows, herewith:

1 Dhow (Market value)	£1,500.—.—.
10 Rifles	£200.—.—.
Various stores and provisions etcetera (too numerous to list)	£100.—.—.
Injury, suffering and hardships (estimated)	£200.—.—.
TOTAL	£2,000.—.—.

This claim arises from the sinking of the above-said dhow off the mouth of the Rufiji, 10th July, 1912, which was an act of piracy by your gunboat, the *Blücher*.

I would appreciate payment in gold, on or before 25th September, 1912, otherwise I will take the necessary steps to collect same personally.
Yours sincerely,
Flynn Patrick O'Flynn, Esq.,
(Citizen of The United States of America).

After much heavy thought, Flynn had decided not to include a claim for the ivory as he was not too certain of its legality. Best not to mention it.

He had considered signing himself 'United States Ambassador to Africa,' but had discarded the idea on the grounds that Governor Schee knew damned well that he was no such thing. However, there was no harm in reminding him of Flynn's nationality – it might make the old rogue hesitate before hanging Flynn out of hand if ever he got his hooks into him.

Satisfied that the only response to his demands would be a significant increase in Governor Schee's blood pressure, Flynn proceeded with his preparations to make good his threat of collecting the debt *personally*.

Flynn used this word lightly – he had long ago selected a representative debt collector in the form of Sebastian Oldsmith. It now remained to have him suitably outfitted for the occasion, and, armed with a tape-measure from Rosa's work-basket, Flynn visited Sebastian's sick bed. These days, visiting Sebastian was much like trying to arrange an interview with the Pope. Sebastian was securely under the maternal protection of Rosa O'Flynn.

Flynn knocked discreetly on the door of the guest bedroom, paused for a count of five, and entered.

'What do you want?' Rosa greeted him affectionately. She was sitting on the foot of Sebastian's bed.

'Hello, hello,' said Flynn, and then again lamely, 'Hello.'

'I suppose you're looking for a drinking companion,' accused Rosa.

'Good Lord, no!' Flynn was genuinely horrified by the accusation. What with Rosa's depredations his stock of gin was running perilously low, and he had no intention of sharing it with anyone. 'I just called in to see how he was doing.' Flynn transferred his attention to Sebastian. 'How you feeling, old Bassie boy?'

'Much better, thank you.' In fact, Sebastian was looking very chirpy indeed. Freshly shaved, dressed in one of Flynn's best night-shirts, he lay like a Roman emperor on clean sheets. On the low table beside his bed stood a vase of frangipani blooms, and there were other floral tributes standing about the room – all of them cut and carefully arranged by Rosa O'Flynn.

He was steadily putting on weight again as Rosa and Nanny stuffed food into him and colour was starting to drive the yellowish fever stains from his skin. Flynn felt a prickle of irritation at the way Sebastian was being pampered like a stud stallion, while Flynn himself was barely tolerated in his own home.

The metaphor which had come naturally into Flynn's mind, now sparked a further train of thought, and a sharper prickle of irritation. *Stud stallion!* Flynn looked at Rosa with attention, and noticed that the dress she wore was the white one with gauzy sleeves, that had belonged to her mother – a garment that Rosa usually kept securely locked away, a garment she had worn perhaps twice before in her life. Furthermore, her feet, which were usually bare about the house, were now neatly clad in store-bought patent leather, and, by Jesus, she was wearing a sprig of bougainvillaea tucked into the shiny black slick of her hair. The tip of her long braid, which was usually tied carelessly with a thong of leather, flaunted a silk ribbon.

Now, Flynn O'Flynn was not a sentimental man but suddenly he recognized in his daughter a strange new glow, and a demure air that had never been there before, and within himself he became aware of an unusual sensation, so unfamiliar that he did not recognize it as paternal jealousy. He did, however, recognize that the sooner he sent Sebastian on his way, the safer it would be.

'Well, that's fine, Bassie,' he boomed genially. 'That's just fine. Now, I'm sending bearers down to Beira to pick up supplies, and I just thought they might as well get some clothes for you while they were there.'

'Well, thank you very much, Flynn.' Sebastian was touched by the kindness of his friend.

'Might as well do it properly.' Flynn produced his tape-measure with a flourish. 'We'll send your measurements down to old Parbhoo and he can tailor-make some stuff for you.'

'I say, that *is* jolly decent of you.'

And completely out of character, thought Rosa O'Flynn as she watched her father carefully noting the length of Sebastian's legs and arms, and the girth of his neck, chest and waist.

'The boots and the hat will be a problem,' Flynn mused aloud when he had finished. 'But I'll find something.'

'And what do you mean by that, Flynn O'Flynn?' Rosa demanded suspiciously.

'Nothing, just nothing at all.' Hurriedly Flynn gathered his notes and his tape, and fled from further interrogation.

Some time later, Mohammed and the bearers returned from the shopping expedition to Beira, and he and Flynn immediately closeted themselves in secret conclave in the arsenal.

'Did you get it?' demanded Flynn eagerly.

'Five boxes of gin I left in the cave behind the waterfall at the top of the valley,' whispered Mohammed, and Flynn sighed with relief. 'But one bottle I brought with me.' Mohammed produced it from under his tunic. Flynn took it from him and drew the cork with his teeth, before spilling a little into the enamel mug that was standing ready.

'And the other purchases?'

'It was difficult – especially the hat.'

'But did you get it?' Flynn demanded.

'It was a direct intervention of Allah.' Mohammed refused to be hurried. 'In the harbour was a German ship, stopped at Beira on its way north to Dar es Salaam. On the boat were three German officers. I saw them walking upon the deck.' Mohammed paused and cleared his throat portentously. 'That night a man who is my friend rowed me out to the ship, and I visited the cabin of one of the soldiers.'

'Where is it?' Flynn could not hold his patience. Mohammed stood up, went to the door of the rondavel and called to one of the bearers. He returned and set a bundle on the table in front of Flynn. Grinning proudly, he waited while Flynn unwrapped the bundle.

'Good God Almighty,' breathed Flynn.

'Is it not beautiful?'

'Call Manali. Tell him to come here immediately.'

Ten minutes later Sebastian, whom Rosa had at last reluctantly placed on the list of walking wounded, entered the rondavel, to be greeted effusively by Flynn. 'Sit down, Bassie boy. I've got a present for you.'

Reluctantly, Sebastian obeyed, eyeing the covered object on the table. Flynn stood over it and whisked away the cloth. Then, with the same ceremony as the Archbishop of Canterbury placing the crown, he lifted the helmet above Sebastian's head and lowered it reverently.

On the summit a golden eagle cocked its wings on the point of flight and opened its beak in a silent squawk of menace, the black enamel of the helmet shone with a polished gloss, and the golden chain drooped heavily under Sebastian's chin.

It was indeed a thing of beauty. A thing of such presence that it completely overwhelmed Sebastian, enveloping his head to the bridge of his nose so that his eyes were just visible below the jutting brim.

'A few sizes too large,' Flynn conceded. 'But we can stuff some cloth into the crown to keep it up.' He backed away a few paces and cocked his head on one side as he examined the effect. 'Bassie boy, you'll slay them.'

'What's this for?' Sebastian asked in concern from under the steel helmet.

'You'll see. Just hold on a shake.' Flynn turned to Mohammed who was cooing with admiration in the doorway. 'The clothes?' he asked, and Mohammed beckoned imperiously to the bearers to bring in the boxes they had carried all the way from Beira.

Parbhoo, the Indian tailor, had obviously laboured with dedication and enthusiasm. The task set him by Flynn had touched the soul of the creative artist in him.

Ten minutes later, Sebastian stood self-consciously in the centre of the rondavel while Flynn and Mohammed circled him slowly, exclaiming with delight and self-congratulation.

Below the massive helmet, which was now propped high with a wad of cloth between steel and scalp, Sebastian was dressed in the sky-blue tunic and riding breeches. The cuffs of the jacket were ringed with yellow silk – a stripe of the same material ran down the outside of the breeches – and the high collar was covered with embroidered metal thread. Complete with spurs, the tall black boots pinched his toes so painfully that Sebastian stood pigeon-toed and blushed with bewilderment. 'I say, Flynn,' he pleaded, 'what's all this about?'

'Bassie boy.' Flynn laid a hand fondly on his shoulder. 'You're going to go in there and collect hut tax for . . .' he almost said *me*, but altered it quickly to '. . . us.'

'What is hut tax?'

'Hut tax is the annual sum of five shillings, paid by the headmen to the German Governor for each hut in his village.' Flynn led Sebastian to the chair and seated him as gently as though he were pregnant. He lifted a hand to still Sebastian's further enquiries and protests. 'Yes, I know you don't understand. But I'll explain it to you carefully. Just keep your mouth shut and listen.' He sat down opposite Sebastian and leaned forward earnestly. 'Now! The Germans owe us for the dhow and that, like we agreed – right?'

Sebastian nodded, and the helmet slid forward over his eyes. He pushed it back.

'Well, you are going to go across the river with the gun-bearers dressed as Askari. You are going to visit each of the villages before the real tax-collector gets there and picks up the money that they owe us. Do you follow me so far?'

'Are you coming with me?'

'Now, how can I do that? Me with my leg not properly healed yet?' Flynn protested impatiently. 'Besides that, every headman on the other side knows who I am. Not one of them has ever laid eyes on you before. You just tell them you're a new officer – straight out from Germany. One look at that uniform, and they'll pay up sharpish.'

'What happens if the real tax-inspector has already been?'

'They don't start collecting until September usually – and then they start in the north and work down this way. You'll have plenty of time.'

Frowning below the rim of the helmet, Sebastian brought forward a series of objections – each one progressively weaker than its predecessor, and, one by one, Flynn annihilated them. Finally there was a long silence while Sebastian's brain ground to a standstill.

'Well?' Flynn asked. 'Are you going to do it?'

And the question was answered from an unexpected quarter in feminine, but not dulcet tones. 'He is certainly *not* going to do it!'

Guiltily as small boys caught smoking in the school latrines, Flynn and Sebastian wheeled to face the door which had carelessly been left ajar.

Rosa's suspicions had been aroused by all the surreptitious activity around the rondavel, and when she had seen Sebastian join in, she had not the slightest qualms about listening outside the window. Her active intervention was not on ethical grounds. Rosa O'Flynn had acquired a rather elastic definition of honesty from her father. Like him, she believed that German property belonged to anybody who could get their hands on it. The fact that Sebastian was involved in a scheme based on dubious moral foundations in no way lowered her opinion of him – rather, in a sneaking sort of way, it heightened her estimate of him as a potential breadwinner. To date, this was the only area in which she had held misgivings about Sebastian Oldsmith.

From experience she knew that those of her father's business enterprises in which Flynn was not eager to participate personally always involved a great deal of risk. The thought of Sebastian Oldsmith dressed in a sky-blue uniform, marching across the Rovuma and never coming back – roused in her the same instincts as those of a lioness shortly to be deprived of her cubs.

'He is certainly *not* going to do it,' she repeated, and then to Sebastian. 'Do you hear me? I forbid it. I forbid it absolutely.'

This was the wrong approach.

Sebastian had, in turn, acquired from his father very Victorian views on the rights and privileges of women. Mr Oldsmith, the senior, was a courteous domestic tyrant, a man whose infallibility had never been challenged by his wife. A man who regarded sex deviates, Bolsheviks, trade union organizers, and suffragettes, in that descending order of repugnance.

Sebastian's mother, a meek little lady with a perpetually harassed expression, would no more have contemplated *absolutely forbidding* Mr Oldsmith a course of action, than she would have contemplated denying the existence of God. Her belief in the divine rights of man had extended to her sons. From a very tender age Sebastian had grown accustomed to worshipful obedience, not only from his mother, but also from his large flock of sisters.

Rosa's present attitude and manner of speech came as a shock. It took him but a few seconds to recover and then he rose to his feet and adjusted the helmet. 'I beg your pardon?' he asked coldly.

'You heard me,' snapped Rosa. 'I'm not going to allow this.'

Sebastian nodded thoughtfully, and then hastily grabbed at the helmet as it threatened to spoil his dignity by blind-folding him again. Ignoring Rosa he turned to Flynn. 'I will leave as soon as possible – tomorrow?'

'It will take a couple more days to get organized,' Flynn demurred.

'Very well then.' Sebastian stalked from the room, and the sunlight lit his uniform with dazzling splendour.

With a triumphant guffaw, Flynn reached for the enamel mug at his elbow. 'You made a mess of that one,' he gloated, and then his expression changed to unease.

Standing in the doorway, Rosa O'Flynn's shoulders had sagged, the angry line of her lips drooped.

'Oh, come on now!' gruffed Flynn.

'He won't come back. You know what you are doing to him. You're sending him in there to die.'

'Don't talk silly. He's a big boy, he can look after himself.'

'Oh, I hate you. Both of you – I hate you both!' and she was gone, running across the yard to the bungalow.

22

I n a red dawn Flynn and Sebastian stood together on the stoep of the bungalow, talking together quietly.

'Now listen, Bassie. I reckon the best thing you can do is send back the collection from each village, as you make it. No sense in carrying all that money round with you.' Tactfully Flynn refrained from pointing out that by following this procedure, in the event of Sebastian running into trouble half-way through the expedition, the profits to that time would be safeguarded.

Sebastian was not really listening – he was more preoccupied with the whereabouts of Rosa O'Flynn. He had seen very little of her in the last few days.

'Now you listen to old Mohammed. He knows which are the biggest villages. Let him do the talking – those headmen are the biggest bunch of rogues you'll ever meet. They'll all plead poverty and famine, so you've got to be tough. Do you hear me? Tough, Bassie, tough!!'

'Tough,' agreed Sebastian absent-mindedly, glancing surreptitiously into the windows of the bungalow for a glimpse of Rosa.

'Now another thing,' Flynn went on. 'Remember to keep moving fast. March until nightfall. Make your cooking fire, eat, and then march again in the dark before you camp. Never sleep at your first camp, that's asking for trouble. Then get away again before first light in the morning.' There were many other instructions, and Sebastian listened to them without attention. 'Remember the sound of gun-fire carries for miles. Don't use your rifle except in emergency, and if you do fire a shot, then don't hang about afterwards. Now the route I've planned for you will never take you more than twenty miles beyond the Rovuma. At the first sign of trouble, you run for the river. If any of your men get hurt, leave them. Don't play hero, leave them and run like hell for the river.'

'Very well,' muttered Sebastian unhappily. The prospect of leaving Lalapanzi was becoming less attractive each minute. Where on earth was she?

'Now remember, don't let those headmen talk you out of anything. You might even have to . . .' Here Flynn paused to find the least offensive phraseology, '. . . you might even have to hang one or two of them.'

'Good God, Flynn. You're not serious.' Sebastian's full attention jerked back to Flynn.

'Ha! Ha!' Flynn laughed away the suggestion. 'I was joking, of course. But . . .' he went on wistfully, 'the Germans do it, and it gets results, you know.'

'Well, I'd better be on my way.' Sebastian changed the subject ostentatiously and picked up his helmet. He placed it upon his head and descended the steps to where his Askari, with rifles at the slope, were drawn up on the lawn. All of them, including Mohammed, were dressed in authentic uniform, complete with puttees and the little pillbox kepis. Sebastian had prudently refrained from asking Flynn how he had obtained these uniforms. The answer was evident in the neatly patched circular punctures in most of the tunics, and the faint brownish stain around each mend.

In single file, the blazing eagle on Sebastian's head-piece leading like a beacon, they marched past the massive solitary figure of Flynn O'Flynn on the veranda. Mohammed called for a salute and the response was enthusiastic, but ragged. Sebastian tripped on his spurs and with an effort, regained his equilibrium and plodded on gamely.

Shading his eyes against the glare, Flynn watched the gallant little column wind away down the valley towards the Rovuma river. Flynn's voice was without conviction as he spoke aloud, 'I hope to God he doesn't mess this one up.'

23

O nce out of sight of the bungalow, Sebastian halted the column. Sitting beside the footpath, he sighed with relief as he removed the weight of the metal helmet from his head and replaced it with a sombrero of plaited grass, then he eased the spurred boots from his already aching feet, and slipped on a pair of rawhide sandals. He handed the discarded equipment to his personal bearer, stood up, and in his best Swahili ordered the march to continue.

Three miles down the valley the footpath crossed the stream above a tiny waterfall. It was a place of jyshade where great trees reached out towards each other across the narrow watercourse. Clear water trickled and gurgled between a tumble of lichen-covered boulders, before jumping like white lace in the sunlight down the slippery black slope of the falls.

Sebastian paused on the bank and allowed his men to proceed. He watched them hop from boulder to boulder, the bearers balancing their loads without effort, and then scramble up the far bank and disappear into the dense river bush. He listened to their voices becoming fainter with distance, and suddenly he was sad and alone.

Instinctively he turned and looked back up the valley towards Lalapanzi, and the sense of loss was a great emptiness inside him. The urge to return burned up so strongly, that he took a step back along the path before he could check himself.

He stood irresolute. The voices of his men were very faint now, muted by the dense vegetation, overlaid by the drowsy droning of insects, the wind murmur in the top branches of the trees, and the purl of falling water.

Then the soft rustle beside him, and he turned to it quickly. She stood near him and the sunlight through the leaves threw a golden dapple on her, giving a sense of unreality, a fairy quality, to her presence.

'I wanted to give you something to take with you, a farewell present for you to remember,' she said softly. 'But there was nothing I could think of,' and she came forward, reached up to him with her arms and her mouth, and she kissed him.

24

S ebastian Oldsmith crossed the Rovuma river in a mood of dreamy goodwill towards all men.

Mohammed was worried about him. He suspected that Sebastian had suffered a malarial relapse and he watched him carefully for evidence of further symptoms.

Mohammed at the head of the column of Askari and bearers had reached the crossing place on the Rovuma, before he realized that Sebastian was missing. In wild concern he had taken two armed Askari with him and hurried back along the path through the thorn scrub and broken rock – expecting at any moment to find a pride of lions growling over Sebastian's dismembered corpse. They had almost reached the waterfall when they met Sebastian ambling benignly along the path towards them, an expression of ethereal contentment lighting his classic features. His magnificent uniform was not a little rumpled; there were fresh grass stains on the knees and elbows, and dead leaves and bits of dried grass clung to the expensive material. From this Mohammed deduced that Sebastian had either fallen, or in sickness had lain down to rest.

'Manali,' Mohammed cried in concern. 'Are you well?'

'Never better – never in all my life,' Sebastian assured him.

'You have been lying down,' Mohammed accused.

'Son of a gun,' Sebastian borrowed from the vocabulary of Flynn O'Flynn. 'Son of a gun, you can say that again – and then repeat it!' and he clapped Mohammed between the shoulder blades with such well-intentioned violence that it almost floored him. Since then, Sebastian had not spoken again, but every few minutes he would smile and shake his head in wonder. Mohammed was truly worried.

They crossed the Rovuma in hired canoes and camped that night on the far bank. Twice during the night Mohammed awoke, slipped out of his blanket, and crept across to Sebastian to check his condition. Each time Sebastian was sleeping easily and the silver moonlight showed just a suggestion of a smile on his lips.

In the middle of the next morning, Mohammed halted the column in thick cover and came back from the head to confer with Sebastian. 'The village of M'topo lies just beyond,' he pointed ahead. 'You can see the smoke from the fires.'

There was a greyish smear of it above the trees, and faintly a dog began yapping.

'Good. Let's go.' Sebastian had donned his eagle helmet and was struggling into his boots.

'First I will send the Askari to surround the village.'

'Why?' Sebastian looked up in surprise.

'Otherwise there will be nobody there when we arrive.' During his service with the German Imperial army, Mohammed had been on tax expeditions before.

'Well – if you think it necessary,' Sebastian agreed dubiously.

Half an hour later Sebastian swaggered in burlesque of a German officer into the village of M'topo, and was dismayed by the reception he received. The lamentations of two hundred human beings made a hideous chorus for his entry. Some of them were on their knees and all of them were wringing their hands, smiting their breasts or showing other signs of deep distress. At the far end of the village M'topo, the headman, waited under guard by Mohammed and two of his Askari.

M'topo was an old man, with a cap of pure white wool, and an emaciated body covered with a parchment of dry skin. One eye was glazed over with tropical opthalmia, and he was clearly very agitated. 'I crawl on my belly before you, Splendid and Merciful Lord,' he greeted Sebastian, and prostrated himself in the dust.

'I say, that isn't necessary, you know,' murmured Sebastian.

'My poor village welcomes you,' whimpered M'topo. Bitterly he recriminated himself for thus being taken unawares. He had not expected the tax expedition for another two months, and had taken no pains with the disposal of his wealth. Buried under the earthen floor of his hut was nearly a thousand silver Portuguese escudos and half again as many golden Deutsche Marks. The traffic of his villagers in dried fish, netted in the Rovuma river, was highly organized and lucrative.

Now he dragged himself pitifully to his old knees and signalled two of his wives to bring forward stools and gourds of palm wine.

'It has been a year of great pestilence, disease and famine,' M'topo began his prepared speech, when Sebastian was seated and refreshed. The rest of it took fifteen minutes to deliver, and Sebastian's Swahili was now strong enough for him to follow the argument. He was deeply touched. Under the spell of palm wine and his new rosy outlook on life, he felt his heart going out to the old man.

While M'topo spoke, the other villagers had dispersed quietly and barricaded themselves in their huts. It was best not to draw attention to oneself when candidates for the rope were being selected. Now a mournful silence hung over the village, broken only by the mewling of an infant and the squabbling of a pair of mangy mongrels, contesting the ownership of a piece of offal.

'Manali,' impatiently Mohammed interrupted the old man's catalogue of misfortune. 'Let me search his hut.'

'Wait,' Sebastian stopped him. He had been looking about, and beneath the single baobab tree in the centre of the village he had noticed a dozen or so crude litters. Now he stood up and walked across to them.

When he saw what they contained, his throat contracted with horror. In each litter lay a human skeleton, the bones still covered with a thin layer of living flesh and skin. Naked men and women mixed indiscriminately, but their bodies so wasted that it was almost impossible to tell their sex. The pelvic girdles were gaunt basins of bone, elbows and knees great deformed knobs distorting the stick-like limbs, each rib standing out in clear definition, the faces were skulls whose lips had shrunk to expose the teeth in a perpetual sardonic grin. But the real horror was contained in the sunken eye cavities; the lids were fixed wide open – and the eyeballs glared like red marbles. There was no pupil nor iris, just those polished orbs the colour of blood.

Sebastian stepped back hurriedly, feeling his belly heave and the taste of it in his throat. Not trusting himself to speak, he beckoned for M'topo to come to him, and pointed at the bodies in the litters.

M'topo glanced at them without interest. They were so much part of the ordinary scene that for many days he had not consciously been aware of their existence. The village was situated on the edge of a tsetse fly belt, and since his childhood there had always been the sleeping sickness cases lying under the baobab tree, deep in the coma which precedes death. He could not understand Sebastian's concern.

'When . . .?' Sebastian's voice faltered, and he swallowed before going on. 'When did these people last eat?' he asked.

'Not for a long time.' M'topo was puzzled by the question. Everybody knew that once the sleeping time came they never ate again.

Sebastian had heard of people dying of starvation. It happened in places like India, but here he was confronted with the actual fact. A revulsion of feeling swept over him. This was irrefutable proof that all M'topo had told him was true. This was famine as he had not believed really could exist – and he had been trying to extort money from these people!

Sebastian walked slowly back to his stool and sank down upon it. He removed the heavy helmet from his head, held it in his lap and sat staring miserably at his own feet. He was helpless with guilt and compassion.

Flynn O'Flynn had reluctantly provided Sebastian with one hundred escudos as travelling expenses to meet any emergency that might arise before he could make his first collection. Some of this had been expended on the hire of canoes to cross the Rovuma, but there was still eighty escudos left.

From his hip-pocket, Sebastian produced the tobacco pouch containing the money and counted out half of it. 'M'topo,' his voice was subdued. 'Take this money. Buy food for them.'

'Manali,' screeched Mohammed in protest. 'Manali. Do not do it.'

'Shut up!' Sebastian snapped at him, and prodded the handful of coins towards M'topo. 'Take it!'

M'topo stared at him as though he offered a live scorpion. It was as unnatural as though a man-eating lion had walked up and rubbed itself against his leg.

'Take it,' Sebastian insisted impatiently, and in disbelief, M'topo extended his cupped hands.

'Mohammed,' Sebastian stood up and replaced his helmet, 'we'll move on immediately to the next village.'

Long after Sebastian's column had disappeared into the bush again, old M'topo squatted alone, clutching the coins, too stunned to move. At last he roused himself and shouted for one of his sons.

'Go quickly to the village of Saali, who is my brother. Tell him that a madman comes to him. A German lord who comes to collect the hut tax and stays to offer gifts. Tell him . . .' here his voice broke as though he could not believe what he was about to say, '. . . tell him that this lord should be shown the ones who sleep, and that the madness will then come upon him, and he will give you forty escudos of the Portuguese. And, furthermore, there will be no hangings.'

'Saali, my uncle, will not believe these things.'

'No,' M'topo admitted. 'It is true that he will not believe. But tell him anyway.'

25

Saali received the message from his elder brother, and it induced in him a state of terror bordering on paralysis. M'topo, he knew, had a vicious sense of humour – and there was between them that matter of the woman Gita, a luscious little fourteen-year-old who had deserted the village of M'topo within two days of taking up her duties as M'topo's junior wife, on the grounds that he was impotent and smelled like an hyena. She was now a notable addition to Saali's household. Saali was convinced that the true interpretation of his brother's message was that the new German commissioner was a rampaging lion who would not be content with merely hanging a few of the old men but who might extend his attentions to Saali himself. Even should he escape the noose, he would be left destitute; his carefully accumulated hoard of silver, his six fine tusks of ivory, his goat herd, his dozen bags of white salt, the bar of copper, his two European-made axes, the bolts of trade cloth – all of his treasures gone! It required an heroic effort to rouse himself from the stupor of despair and make his few futile preparations for flight.

Mohammed's Askari caught him as he was heading for the bush at a trot, and when they led him back to meet Sebastian Oldsmith, the tears that coursed freely down his cheeks and dripped on to his chest were genuine.

Sebastian was very susceptible to tears. Despite the protests of Mohammed, Sebastian pressed upon Saali twenty silver escudos. It took Saali about twenty minutes to recover from the shock, at the end of which time he, in turn, shocked Sebastian profoundly by offering him on a temporary basis the unrestricted services of the girl, Gita. This young lady was witness to the offer made by her husband, and was obviously wholeheartedly in favour of it.

Sebastian set off again hurriedly, with his retinue straggling along behind him in a state of deep depression. Mohammed now had a bad case of the mutters.

Drums tap-tap-tapped, runners scurried along the network of footpaths that crossed and criss-crossed the bush; from hilltop to hilltop men called one to the other in the high-pitched wail that carries for miles. The news spread. Village after village buzzed with incredulous excitement, and then the inhabitants flocked out to meet the mad German commissioner.

By this time Sebastian was thoroughly enjoying himself. He was carried away with the pleasure of giving, delighted with these simple lovable people who welcomed him sincerely and pressed humble little gifts upon him. Here a scrawny fowl, there a dozen half-incubated eggs, a basin of sweet potatoes, a gourd of palm wine.

But Santa Claus's bag, or, more accurately, his tobacco pouch, was soon empty – and Sebastian was at a loss for some way to help alleviate the misery and poverty he saw in each village. He considered issuing indulgences from future tax . . . *the bearer is hereby excused from the payment of hut tax for five years* . . . but realized that this was a lethal gift. He shuddered at what Herman Fleischer might do to anybody he caught in possession of one of these.

Finally he struck on the solution. These people were starving. He would give them food. He would give them meat.

In fact, this was one of the most desirable commodities Sebastian could have offered. Despite the abundance of wild life, the great herds of game that spread across the plains and hills, these people were starved for protein. The primitive hunting methods they employed were so ineffectual, that the killing of a single animal was an event that happened infrequently, and then almost by accident. When the carcass was shared out among two or three hundred hungry mouths, there was only a few ounces of meat for each. Men and women would risk their lives in attempting to drive a pride of lions from their kill, for just a few mouthfuls of this precious stuff.

Sebastian's Askari joined in the sport with delight. Even old Mohammed perked up a little. Unfortunately, their marksmanship was about the same standard as Sebastian's own, and a day's hunting usually resulted in the expenditure of thirty or forty rounds of Mauser ammunition, and a bag of sometimes as little as one half-grown zebra. But there were good days also, like the memorable occasion when a herd of buffalo virtually committed suicide by running down on the line of Askari. In the resulting chaos one of Sebastian's men was shot dead by his comrades, but eight full-grown buffalo followed him to the happy hunting grounds.

So Sebastian's tax tour proceeded triumphantly, leaving behind a trail of empty cartridge cases, racks of meat drying in the sun, full bellies, and smiling faces.

26

T hree months after crossing the Rovuma river, Sebastian found himself back at the village of his good friend, M'topo. He had by-passed Saali's in order to avoid the offended Gita.

Sitting alone in the night within the hut that M'topo placed at his disposal, Sebastian was having his first misgivings. On the morrow, he would begin the return to Lalapanzi, where Flynn O'Flynn was waiting for him. Sebastian was acutely aware that from Flynn's point of view the expedition had not been a success – and Flynn would have a great deal to say on the subject. Once more Sebastian puzzled on the fates which took his best intentions, and manipulated them in such a manner that they became completely unrecognizable from the original.

Then his thoughts kicked off at a tangent. Soon, the day after tomorrow, if all went well, he would be back with Rosa. The deep yearning that had been his constant companion these last three months throbbed through Sebastian's whole body. Staring into the wood-fire on the hearth of the hut, it seemed as though the embers formed a picture of her face, and in his memory he heard her voice again.

'Come back, Sebastian. Come back soon.'

And he whispered the words aloud, watching her face in the fire. Gloating on each detail of it. He saw her smile, and her nose wrinkled a little, the dark eyes slanted upwards at the corners.

'Come back, Sebastian.'

The need of her was a physical pain so intense that he could hardly breathe, and his imagination reconstructed every detail of their parting beside the waterfall. Each subtle change and inflection of her voice, the very sound of her breathing, and the bitter salt taste of her tears upon his lips. He felt again the touch of her hands, her mouth – and through the woodsmoke that filled the hut, his nostrils flared at the warm woman smell of her body.

'I'm coming, Rosa. I'm coming back,' he whispered, and stood up restlessly from beside the fire. At that moment his attention was jerked back to the present by a soft scratching at the door of the hut.

'Lord. Lord.' He recognized old M'topo's hoarse croaking.

'What is it?'

'We seek your protection.'

'What is the trouble?' Sebastian crossed to the door and lifted the cross-bar. 'What is it?'

In the moonlight M'topo stood with a skin blanket draped around his frail shoulders. Behind him a dozen of the villagers huddled in trepidation.

'The elephant are in our gardens. They will destroy them before morning. There will be nothing, not a single stalk of millet left standing.' He swung away and stood with his head cocked. 'Listen, you may hear them now.'

It was an eerie sound in the night, the high-pitched elephant squeal, and Sebastian's skin crawled. He could feel the hair on his forearms become erect.

'There are two of them.' M'topo's voice was a scratchy whisper. 'Two old bulls. We know them well. They came last season and laid waste our corn. They killed one of my sons who tried to drive them off.' In entreaty, the old man clawed hold of Sebastian's arm and tugged at it. 'Avenge my son, lord. Avenge my son for me, and save our millet that the children will not go hungry again this year.'

Sebastian responded to the appeal in the same manner that St George would have done.

In haste he buttoned his tunic and went to fetch his rifle. On his return he found his entire command armed to the teeth, and as eager for the hunt as a pack of foxhounds. Mohammed waited at their head.

'Lord Manali, we are ready.'

'Now, steady on, old chap.' Sebastian had no intention of sharing the glory. 'This is my shauri. Too many cooks, what?'

M'topo stood by, wringing his hands with impatience, listening alternately first to the distant sounds of the garden raiders feeding contentedly in his lands, and then to the undignified wrangling between Sebastian and his Askari, until at last he could bear it no longer. 'Lord, already half the millet is eaten. In an hour it will all be gone.'

'You're right,' Sebastian agreed, and turned angrily on his men. 'Shut up, all of you. Shut up!'

They were unaccustomed to this tone of command from Sebastian, and it surprised them into silence.

'Only Mohammed shall accompany me. The rest of you go to your huts and stay there.'

It was a working compromise, Sebastian now had Mohammed as an ally. Mohammed turned on his comrades and scattered them before falling in beside Sebastian. 'Let us go.'

At the head of the main gardens, high on its stilts of poles, stood a rickety platform. This was the watch-tower from which, night and day, a guard was kept over the ripening millet. It was now deserted, the two young guards had left hurriedly at the first sight of the garden raiders. Kudu or waterbuck were one thing, a pair of bad-tempered old elephant bulls were another matter entirely.

Sebastian and Mohammed reached the watch-tower and paused beneath it. Quite clearly now they could hear the rustling and ripping sound of the millet stalks being torn up and trampled.

'Wait here,' whispered Sebastian, slinging his rifle over his shoulder, as he turned to the ladder beside him. He climbed slowly and silently to the platform, and from it, looked out over the gardens.

The moon was so brilliant as to throw sharply defined shadows below the tower and the trees. Its light was a soft silver that distorted distance and size, reducing all things to a cold, homogeneous grey.

Beyond the clearing the forest rose like frozen smoke clouds, while the field of standing millet moved in the small night wind, rippling like the surface of a lake.

Humped big and darker grey, standing high above the millet, two great islands in the soft sea of vegetation, the old bulls grazed slowly. Although the nearest elephant was two hundred paces from the tower, the moon was so bright that Sebastian could see clearly as he reached forward with his trunk, coiled it about a clump of the leafy stalks and plucked them easily. Then swaying gently, rocking his massive bulk lazily from side to side, he beat the millet against his lifted foreleg to shake the clinging earth from the roots before lifting it and stuffing it into his mouth. The tattered banners of his ears flapped gently, an untidy tangle of millet leaves hanging from his lips between the long curved shafts of ivory, he moved on, feeding and trampling so that behind him he left a wide path of devastation.

On the open platform of the tower, Sebastian felt his stomach contracting, convulsing itself into a hard ball, and his hands on the rifle were unsteady; his breathing whistled softly in his own ears as the elephant thrill came upon him. Watching those two huge beasts, he found himself held motionless with an almost mystic sense of awe; a realization of his own insignificance, his presumption in going out against them, armed with this puny weapon of steel and wood. But beneath his reluctance was the tingle of tight nerves – that strange blend of fear and eagerness – the age-old lust of the hunter. He roused himself and climbed down to where Mohammed waited.

Through the standing corn that reached above their heads, stepping with care between the rows so that they disturb not a single leaf, they moved in towards the centre of the garden. Ears and eyes tuned to their finest limit, breathing controlled so that it did not match the wild pump of his heart, Sebastian homed in on the crackle and rustle made by the nearest bull.

Even though the millet screened him, he could feel the weak wash of the wind move his hair softly, and the first whiff of elephant smell hit him like an open-handed blow in the face. He stooped so suddenly that Mohammed almost bumped into him from behind. They stood crouching, peering ahead into the moving wall of vegetation. Sebastian felt Mohammed lean forward beside him, and heard his whisper breathed softer than the sound of the wind. 'Very close now.'

Sebastian nodded, and then swallowed jerkily. He could hear clearly the soft slithering scrape of leaves brushing against the rough hide of the old bull. It was feeding down towards them. They were standing directly in the path of its leisurely approach, at any moment now – at any moment!

Standing with the rifle lifted protectively, sweat starting to prickle his forehead and upper lip in the cool of the night, his eyes watering with the intensity of his gaze, Sebastian was suddenly aware of massive movement ahead of him. A solid shape through the bank of dancing leaves, and he looked up. High above him it loomed, black and big so that the night sky was blotted out by the spread of its ears, so near that he stood beneath the forward thrust of its tusks, and he could see the trunk uncoil like a fat grey python and grope forward blindly towards him; and beneath it the mouth gaped a little, spilling leaves at the corners.

He lifted the rifle, pointing it upwards without aiming, almost touching the elephant's hanging lower lip with the muzzle, and he fired. The shot was a blunt burst of sound in the night.

The bullet angled up through the pink palate of the animal's mouth, up through the spongy bone of the skull; mushrooming and exploding, it tore into the fist-sized cell that contained the brain, and burst it into a grey jelly.

Had it passed four inches to either side; had it been deflected by one of the larger bones, Sebastian would have died before he had time to work the bolt of the Mauser, for he stood directly below the outstretched tusks and trunk. But the old bull reeled backwards from the shot, his trunk falling flabbily against his chest, his forelegs spreading, and his head unbalanced by long tusks sagged forwards, knees collapsed suddenly under him, and he fell so heavily that they heard the thump in the village half a mile away.

'Son of a gun!' gasped Sebastian, staring in disbelief at the dead mountain of flesh. 'I did it. Son of a gun, I did it!' Jubilation, a delirious release from fear and tension, mounted giddily within him. He lifted an arm to hit Mohammed across the back, but he froze in that attitude.

Like the shriek of steam escaping from a burst boiler, the other bull squealed in the moonlight nearby. And they heard the crackling rush of his run in the corn.

'He's coming!' Sebastian looked frantically about him for the sound had no direction.

'No,' squawked Mohammed. 'He turns against the wind. First he seeks for the smell of us, and then he will come.' He grabbed Sebastian's arm and clung to him, while they listened to the elephant circling to get down-wind of them.

'Perhaps he will run,' whispered Sebastian.

'Not this one. He is old and evil-tempered, and he has killed men before. Now he will hunt us.' Mohammed pulled at Sebastian's arm. 'We must get out into the open. In this stuff we will have no chance, he will be on top of us before we see him.'

They started to run. There is no more piquant sauce for fear than flying feet. Once he starts to run, even a brave man becomes a coward. Within twenty paces, both of them were in headlong flight towards the village. They ran without regard for stealth, fighting their way through the tangle of leaves and stalks, panting wildly. The noise of their flight blanketed the sounds made by the elephant, so they lost all idea of his whereabouts. This sharpened the spurs of terror that drove them, for at any moment he might loom over them.

At last they stumbled out into the open, and paused, panting, sweating heavily, heads swinging from side to side as they tried to place the second bull.

'There!' shouted Mohammed. 'He comes,' and they heard the shrill pig-squealing, the noisy rush of his charge through the millet.

'Run!' yelled Sebastian, still in the grip of panic, and they ran.

Around a freshly lit bonfire at the edge of the village, waited the rejected Askari and a hundred of M'topo's men. They waited in anxiety for they had heard the shot and the fall of the first bull – but since then, the squealing and shouting and crashing had left them in some doubt as to what was happening in the gardens.

This doubt was quickly dispelled as Mohammed, closely followed by Sebastian, came down the path towards them, giving a fair imitation of two dogs whose backsides had been dipped in turpentine. A hundred yards behind them the bank of standing millet burst open, and the second bull came out in full charge.

Immense in the great light, hump-back, shambling in the deceptive speed of his run, streaming his huge ears, each squeal of rage enough to burst the eardrums – he bore down on the village.

'Get out! Run!' Sebastian's shouted warning was as wheezy as it was unnecessary. The waiting crowd was no longer waiting, it scattered like a shoal of sardines at the approach of a barracuda.

Men threw aside their blankets and ran naked; they fell over each other and ran headlong into trees. Two of them ran straight through the middle of the bonfire and emerged on the other side trailing sparks with live coals sticking to their feet. In a wailing hubbub they swept back through the village, and from each hut women with infants bundled under their arms, or slung over their backs, scurried out to join the terrified torrent of humanity.

Still making good time, Sebastian and Mohammed were passing the weaker runners among the villagers, while from behind, the elephant was gaining rapidly on all of them.

With the force and velocity of a great boulder rolling down a steep hillside, the bull reached the first hut of the village and ran into it. The flimsy structure of grass and light poles exploded, bursting asunder without diminishing the fury of the animal's charge. A second hut disintegrated, then a third, before the elephant caught the first human straggler.

She was an old woman, tottering on thin legs, the empty pouches of her breasts flopping against her wrinkled belly, a long monotonous wail of fear keening from the toothless pit of her mouth as she ran.

The bull uncoiled his trunk from his chest, lifted it high above the woman and struck her across the shoulder. The force of the blow crumpled her, bones snapped in her chest like old dry sticks, and she died before she hit the ground.

The next was a girl. Groggy with sleep, yet her naked body was silver-smooth and graceful in the moonlight, as she emerged from a hut into the path of the bull's charge. Lightly the thick trunk enfolded her, and then with an effortless flick threw her forty feet into the air.

She screamed, and the sound of the scream knifed through Sebastian's panic. He glanced over his shoulder in time to see the girl thrown high in the night sky. Her limbs were spread-eagled and she spun in the air like a cartwheel before she dropped back to earth – falling heavily so that the scream was cut off abruptly. Sebastian stopped running.

Deliberately the elephant knelt over the girl's feebly squirming body, and driving down with his tusks, impaled her through the chest. She hung from the shaft of ivory, squashed and broken, no longer recognizable as human, until the elephant shook his head irritably and threw her off.

It needed a sight as horrible as this to rally Sebastian's shattered nerves – to summon the reserves of his manhood from the far places that fear had scattered them. The rifle was still in his hands, but he was shaking with fear and exertion; sweat had drenched his tunic and plastered his curly hair on to his forehead, and his breath sawed hoarsely in his throat. He stood irresolute, fighting the driving urge to run again.

The bull came on, and now his one tusk was painted glistening black with the girl's blood, and gouts of the same stuff were splattered across his bulging forehead and the bridge of his trunk. It was this that changed Sebastian's fear first to disgust, and then to anger.

He lifted the rifle and it weaved unsteadily in his hands. He sighted along the barrel and suddenly his vision snapped into sharp focus and his nerves stilled their clamour. He was a man again.

Coldly he moved the blob of the foresight on to the bull's head, holding it on the deep lateral crease at the root of the trunk, and he squeezed the trigger. The butt jumped solidly into his shoulder, the report stung his eardrums, but he saw the bullet strike exactly where he had aimed it – a spurt of dust from the crust of dried mud that caked the animal's head and the skin around it, twitched, the eyelids quivered shut for an instant, then blinked open again.

Without lowering the rifle Sebastian jerked the bolt open, and the empty case ejected crisply, pinging away into the dust. He levered another cartridge into the breach and held his aim into the massive head. Again he fired and the elephant staggered drunkenly. The ears which had been cocked half back, now fanned open and the head swung vaguely in his direction.

He fired again, and the bull winced as the bullet lanced into the bone and gristle of his head, then he turned and came for Sebastian – but there was a slackness, a lack of determination in his charge. Aiming now for the chest, handling the rifle with cold method, Sebastian fired again and again, leaning forward against the recoil of the rifle, sighting every shot with care, knowing that each of them was raking the chest cavity, tearing through lung and heart and liver.

And the bull broke his run into a shuffling, uncertain walk, losing direction, turning away from Sebastian to stand broadside, the barrel of his chest heaving against the agony of his torn vitals.

Sebastian lowered the rifle and with steady fingers pressed fresh cartridges down into the empty magazine. The bull groaned softly and from the tip of his trunk, blood hosed up from the haemorrhaging lungs.

Without pity, cold in his anger, Sebastian lifted the reloaded rifle, and aimed for the dark cavity that nestled in the centre of the huge ear. The bullet struck with the sharp thwack of an axe swung against a tree trunk, and the elephant sagged and fell forward to the brain shot. His weight drove his tusks into the earth, burying them to the lip.

27

Four tons of meat delivered fresh to the very centre of the village was good value. The price paid was not exorbitant, M'topo decided. Three huts could be rebuilt in two days, and only four acres of millet had been destroyed. Furthermore, of the women who had died, one was very old and the other, although she was almost eighteen years old, had never conceived. There was good reason, therefore, to believe she was barren and not a great loss to the community.

Warmed by the early sun, M'topo was a satisfied man. With Sebastian beside him, he sat on his carved wooden stool and grinned widely as he watched the fun.

Two dozen of his men, armed with short-handled, long-bladed spears, and divested of all clothing, were to act as butchers. They were gathered beside the mountainous carcass arguing good-naturedly as they waited for Mohammed and his four assistants to remove the tusks. Around them, in a wider circle, waited the rest of the villagers, and while they waited, they sang. A drum hammered out the rhythm for them, and the clap of hands and the stamp of feet confirmed it. The masculine bass was a foundation from which the clear, sweet soprano of the women soared, and sank, and soared again.

Beneath Mohammed's patiently chipping axe, first the one tusk and then the other were freed from the bone that held them, and, with two Askari staggering under the weight, they were carried to where Sebastian sat, and laid with ceremony at his feet.

It occurred to Sebastian that four big tusks carried home to Lalapanzi might in some measure mollify Flynn O'Flynn. They would at least cover the costs of the expedition. The thought cheered him up considerably, and he turned to M'topo. 'Old one, you may take the meat.'

'Lord.' In gratitude, M'topo clapped his hands at the level of his chest, and then turned to squawk an order at the waiting butchers.

A roar of excitement and meat hunger went up from the crowd as one of them scrambled up on to the carcass, and drove his spear though the thick grey hide behind the last rib. Then walking backwards, he drew it down towards the haunch and the razor steel sliced deep. Two others made the lateral incisions, opening a square flap – a trapdoor into the belly cavity from which the fat coils of the viscera bulged, pink and blue and glossy wet in the early morning sunlight. In mounting eagerness, four others dragged from the square hole the contents of the belly, and then, while Sebastian stared in disbelief, they wriggled into the opening and disappeared. He could hear their muffled shouts reverberating within the carcass as they competed for the prize of the liver. Within minutes one of them reappeared, clutching against his chest a slippery lump of tattered, purple liver. Like a maggot, he came squirming out of the wound, painted over-all with a thick coating of dark red blood. It had matted in the woolly cap of his hair, and turned his face into a gruesome mask from which only his teeth and his eyes gleamed white. Carrying the mutilated liver, laughing in triumph, he ran through the crowd to where Sebastian sat.

The offering embarrassed Sebastian. More than that, it made his gorge rise, and he felt his stomach heave as it was thrust almost into his lap.

'Eat,' M'topo encouraged him. 'It will make you strong. It will sharpen the spear of your manhood. Ten, twenty women will not tire you.'

It was M'topo's opinion that Sebastian needed this type of tonic. He had heard from his brother Saali, and from the chiefs along the river, about Sebastian's lack of initiative.

'Like this.' M'topo cut a hunk of the liver and popped it into his mouth. He chewed heartily, and the juice wet his lips as he grinned in appreciation. 'Very good.' He thrust a piece into Sebastian's face. 'Eat.'

'No.' Sebastian's gorge pressed heavily on the back of his throat, and he stood up hurriedly. M'topo shrugged, and ate it himself. Then he shouted to the butchers to continue their work.

In a miraculously short space of time the huge carcass disintegrated under the blades of the spears and machetes. It was a labour in which the entire village joined. With a dozen strokes of the knife, a butcher would free a large hunk of flesh and throw it down to one of the women. She, in turn, would hack it into smaller pieces and pass these on to the children. Squealing with excitement, they would run with them to the hastily erected drying racks, deposit them and come scampering back for more.

Sebastian had recovered from his initial revulsion and now he laughed to see how every mouth was busy, chewing as they worked and yet at the same time managing to emit a surprising volume of noise.

Among the milling feet the dogs snarled and yipped, and gulped the scraps. Without interrupting their feeding, they dodged the casual kicks and blows that were aimed at them.

Into the midst of this cosy, domestic scene entered Commissioner Herman Fleischer with ten armed Askari.

28

H erman Fleischer was tired and there were blisters on his feet from the series of forced marches that had brought him to M'topo's village.

A month before he had left his headquarters at Mahenge to begin the annual tax tour of his area. As was his custom, he had started in the northern province, and it had been an unusually successful expedition. The wooden chest with the rampant black eagle painted on its lid had grown heavier with each day's journey. Herman had amused himself by calculating how many more years service in Africa would be necessary before he could resign and return home to Plaven and settle down on the estate he planned to buy. Three more years as fruitful as this, he decided, would be sufficient. It was a bitter shame that he had not been able to capture O'Flynn's dhow on the Rufiji thirteen months previously – that would have advanced his date of departure by a full twelve months. Thinking about it stirred his residual anger at that episode, and he placated it by doubling the hut tax on the next village he visited. This raised such a howl of protest from the village headman that Herman nodded at his sergeant of Askari, who began ostentatiously to unpack the rope from his saddle-bag.

'O fat and beautiful bull elephant,' the headman changed his mind hastily. 'If you will wait but a little while, I will bring the money to you. There is a new hut, without lice or fleas, in which you may rest your lovely body, and I will send a young girl to you with beer for your thirst.'

'Good,' agreed Herman. 'While I rest, my Askari will stay with you.' He nodded at the sergeant to bind the chief, then waddled away to the hut.

The headman sent two of his sons to dig beneath a certain tree in the forest, and they returned an hour later with mournful faces, carrying a heavy skin bag.

Contentedly Herman Fleischer signed an official receipt for ninety per cent of the contents of the bag – Fleischer allowed himself a ten per cent handling fee – and the headman, who could not read a word of German, accepted it with relief.

'I will stay tonight in your village,' Herman announced. 'Send the same girl to cook my food.'

The runner from the south arrived in the night, and disturbed Herman Fleischer at a most inopportune moment. The news he carried was even more disturbing. From his description of the new German commissioner who was doing Herman's job for him in the southern province, and shooting up the countryside in the process, Herman immediately recognized the young Englishman whom he had last seen on the deck of a dhow in the Rufiji delta.

Leaving the bulk of his retinue, including the bearers of the tax chest, to follow him at their best speed, Herman mounted at midnight on his white donkey and, taking ten Askari with him, he rode southwards on a storm patrol.

Five nights later, in those still dark hours that precede the dawn, Herman was camped near the Rovuma river when he was awakened by his sergeant.

'What is it?' Grumpy with fatigue, Herman sat up and lifted the side of his mosquito net.

'We heard the sound of gun-fire. A single shot.'

'Where?' He was instantly awake, and reaching for his boots.

'From the south, towards the village of M'topo on the Rovuma.'

Fully dressed now, Herman waited anxiously, straining his ears against the small sounds of the African night. 'Are you sure . . .?' he began as he turned to his sergeant, but he did not finish. Faintly, but unmistakable in the darkness, they heard the pop, pop, pop, of a distant rifle – a pause and then another shot.

'Break camp,' bellowed Herman. 'Rasch! You black heathen. Rasch!'

The sun was well up by the time they reached M'topo's village. They came upon it suddenly through the gardens of tall millet that screened their approach. Herman Fleischer paused to throw out his Askari in a line of skirmishers before closing in on the cluster of huts, but when he reached the fringe, he stopped once more in surprise at the extraordinary spectacle which was being enacted in the open square of the village.

The dense knot of half-naked black people that swarmed over the remains of the elephant was perfectly oblivious of Herman's presence until at last he filled his lungs, and then emptied them again in a roar that carried over the hubbub of shouts and laughter. Instantly a vast silence fell upon the gathering, every head turned towards Herman and from each head eyes bulged in horrific disbelief.

'Bwana Intambu,' a small voice broke the silence at last. 'Lord of the rope.' They knew him well.

'What . . .?' Herman began, and then gasped in outrage as he noticed in the crowd a black man he had never seen before, dressed in the full uniform of German Askari. 'You!' he shouted, pointing an accusing finger, but the man whirled and ducked away behind the screen of blood-smeared black bodies. 'Stop him!' Herman fumbled with the flap of his holster.

Movement caught his eye and he turned to see another pseudo-Askari running away between the huts. 'There's another one! Stop him! Sergeant, Sergeant, get your men here!'

The initial shock that had held them frozen was now past, and the crowd broke and scattered. Once again, Herman Fleischer gasped in outrage as he saw, for the first time, a figure sitting on a carved native stool on the far side of the square. A figure in an outlandish uniform of bright but travel-stained blue, frogged with gold, his legs clad in high jackboots, and on his head the dress helmet of an illustrious Prussian regiment.

'Englishman!' Despite the disguise, Herman recognized him. He had finally succeeded in unbuttoning the flap of his holster, and now he withdrew his Luger. 'Englishman!' He repeated the insult and lifted the pistol.

With the quickness of mind for which he was noted, Sebastian sat bewildered by this unforeseen turn of events, but when Herman showed him the working end of the Luger, he realized that it was time to take his leave, and he attempted to leap nimbly to his feet. However, the spurs on his boots became entangled once more and he went backwards over the stool. The bullet hissed harmlessly through the empty space where he would have been standing.

'God damn!' Herman fired again, and the bullet kicked a burst of splinters out of the heavy wooden stool behind which Sebastian was lying. This second failure aroused in Herman Fleischer the blinding rage which spoiled his aim for the next two shots he fired, as Sebastian went on hands and knees around the corner of the nearest hut.

Behind the hut, Sebastian jumped to his feet and set off at a run. His main concern was to get out of the village and into the bush. In his ears echoed Flynn O'Flynn's advice.

'Make for the river. Go straight for the river.'

And he was so occupied with it that, when he charged around the side of the next hut, he could not check himself in time to avoid collision with one of Herman Fleischer's Askari, who was coming in the opposite direction. Both of them went down together in an untidy heap, and the steel helmet fell forward over Sebastian's eyes. As he struggled into a sitting position, he removed the helmet and found the man's woolly black head in front of him. It was ideally placed and Sebastian was holding the heavy helmet above it. With the strength of both his arms, he brought the helmet down again, and it clanged loudly against the Askari's skull. With a grunt the Askari sagged backwards and lay quietly in the dust. Sebastian placed the helmet over his sleeping face, picked up the man's rifle from beside him and got to his feet once more.

He stood crouching in the shelter of the hut while he tried to make sense of the chaos around him. Through the pandemonium set up by the panic-stricken villagers, who were milling about with all the purpose of a flock of sheep attacked by wolves, Sebastian could hear the bellowed commands of Herman Fleischer, and the answering shouts of the German Askari. Rifle-fire cracked and whined, to be answered by renewed outbursts of screaming.

Sebastian's first impulse was to hide in one of the huts but he realized this would be futile. At the best it would only delay his capture.

No, he must get out of the village. But the thought of covering the hundred yards of open ground to the shelter of the nearest trees, while a dozen Askari shot at him, was most unattractive.

At this moment Sebastian became aware of an unpleasant warmth in his feet, and he looked down to find that he was standing in the live ashes of a cooking fire. The leather of his jackboots was already beginning to char and smoke. He stepped back hurriedly, and the smell of burning leather acted as a laxative for the constipation of his brain.

From the hut beside him he snatched a handful of thatch and stooped to thrust it into the fire. The dry grass burst into flame, and Sebastian held the torch to the wall of the hut. Instantly fire bloomed and shot upwards. With the torch in his hand, Sebastian ducked across the narrow opening to the next hut and set fire to that also.

'Son of a gun!' exulted Sebastian as great oily billows of smoke obscured the sun and limited his field of vision to ten paces.

Slowly he moved forward in the rolling cloud of smoke, setting fire to each hut he passed, and delighted in the frustrated bellows of Germanic rage he heard behind him. Occasionally ghostly figures scampered past him in the acrid half-darkness but none of them paid him the slightest attention, and each time Sebastian relaxed the pressure of his forefinger on the trigger of the Mauser, and moved on.

He reached the last hut and paused there to gather himself for the final sprint across open ground to the edge of the millet garden. Through the eddying bank of smoke, the mass of dark green vegetation from which he had fled in terror not many hours before, now seemed as welcoming as the arms of his mother.

Movement near him in the smoke, and he swung the Mauser to cover it; he saw the square outline of a kepi and the sparkle of metal buttons, and his finger tightened on the trigger.

'Manali!'

'Mohammed! Good God, I nearly killed you.' Sebastian threw up the rifle barrel as he recognized him.

'Quickly! They are close behind me.' Mohammed snatched at his arm and dragged him forward. The jackboots pinched his toes and thumped like the hooves of a galloping buffalo as Sebastian ran. From the huts behind them a voice shouted urgently and, immediately afterwards, came the vicious crack of a Mauser and the shrill whinny of the ricochet.

Sebastian had a lead of ten paces on Mohammed as he plunged into the bank of leaves and millet stalks.

29

'What should we do now, Manali?' Mohammed asked, and the expression on the faces of the two other men echoed the question with pathetic trust. A benevolent chance had reunited Sebastian with the remnants of his command. During the flight through the millet gardens, with random rifle-fire clipping the leaves about their heads, Sebastian had literally fallen over these two. At the time they were engaged in pressing their bellies and their faces hard against the earth, and it had taken a number of lusty kicks with the jackboot to get them up and moving.

Since then Sebastian, mindful of Flynn's advice, had cautiously and circuitously led them down to the landing-place on the bank of the Rovuma. He arrived to find that Fleisher's Askari, by using the direct route and without the necessity of concealing themselves, had arrived before him. From the cover of the reed-banks Sebastian watched dejectedly, as they used an axe to knock the bottoms out of the dug-out canoes that were drawn up on the little white beach.

'Can we swim across?' he asked Mohammed in a whisper, and Mohammed's face crumpled with horror, as he considered the suggestion. Both of them peered out through the reeds across a quarter of a mile of deep water that flowed so fast, its surface was dimpled with tiny whirlpools.

'No,' said Mohammed with finality.

'Too far?' asked Sebastian hopelessly.

'Too far. Too fast. Too deep. Too many crocodiles,' agreed Mohammed, and in an unspoken, but mutual desire to get away from the river and the Askari, they crawled out of the reed-bank and crept away inland.

In the late afternoon they were lying up in a bushy gully about two miles from the river and an equal distance from M'topo's village.

'What should we do now, Manali?' Mohammed repeated his question, and Sebastian cleared his throat before answering.

'Well . . .' he said and paused while his wide brow wrinkled in the agony of creative thought. Then it came to him with all the splendour of a sunrise. 'We'll just jolly well have to find some other way of getting across the river.' He said it with the air of a man well pleased with his own perspicacity. 'What do you suggest, Mohammed.'

A little surprised to find the ball returned so neatly into his own court, Mohammed remained silent.

'A raft?' hazarded Sebastian. The lack of tools, material and opportunity to build one was so obvious, that Mohammed did not deign to reply. He shook his head.

'No,' agreed Sebastian. 'Perhaps you are right.' Again the classic beauty of his features was marred by a scowl of concentration. At last he demanded, 'There are other villages along the river?'

'Yes,' Mohammed conceded. 'But the Askari will visit each of them and destroy the canoes. Also they will tell the headmen who we are, and threaten them with the rope.'

'But they cannot cover the whole river. It has a frontier of five or six hundred miles. We'll just keep walking until we find a canoe. It may take us a long time but we'll find one eventually.'

'If the Askari don't catch us first.'

'They'll expect us to stay close to the border. We'll make a detour well inland, and march for five or six days before we come back to the river again. We'll rest now and move tonight.'

Heading on a diagonal line of march away from the Rovuma and deeper into German territory, moving north-west along a well defined footpath, the four of them kept walking all that night. As the slow hours passed so the pace flagged and twice Sebastian noticed one or other of his men wander off the path at an angle until suddenly they started and looked about in surprise, before hurrying back to join the others. It puzzled him and he meant to ask them what they were doing, but he was tired and the effort of speech was too great. An hour later he found the reason for their behaviour.

Plodding along with the movement of his legs became completely automatic, Sebastian was slowly overcome by a state of gentle well-being. He surrendered to it and let the warm, dark mists of oblivion wash over his mind.

The sting of a thorn branch across his cheek jerked him back to consciousness and he looked about in bewilderment. Ten yards away on his flank, Mohammed and the two gun-boys walked along the path in single file, their faces turned towards him with expressions of mild interest in the moonlight. It took some moments for Sebastian to realize that he had fallen asleep on his feet. Feeling a complete ass, he trotted back to take his place at the head of the line.

When the fat silver moon sank below the trees, they kept going by the faint glow of reflected light, but slowly that waned until the footpath hardly showed at their feet. Sebastian decided that dawn could be only an hour away and it was time to halt. He stopped and was about to speak when Mohammed's clutching hand on his shoulder prevented him.

'Manali!' There was a tone in Mohammed's whisper that cautioned him, and Sebastian felt his nerves jerk taut.

'What is it?' he breathed, protectively unslinging the Mauser.

'Look. There – ahead of us.'

Screwing up his eyes Sebastian searched the blackness ahead, and it was a long time before the faint ruddiness in the solid blanket of darkness registered itself upon the exhausted retinas of his eyes. 'Yes!' he whispered. 'What is it?'

'A fire,' breathed Mohammed. 'There is someone camped across the path in front of us.'

'Askari?' asked Sebastian.

'Perhaps.'

Peering at the ruby puddle of dying coals, Sebastian felt the hair on the back of his neck stir and come erect with alarm. He was fully awake now. 'We must go around them.'

'No. They will see our spoor in the dust of the path and they will follow us,' Mohammed demurred.

'What then?'

'First let me see how many there are.'

Without waiting for Sebastian's permission, Mohammed slipped away and disappeared into the night like a leopard. Five anxious minutes Sebastian waited. Once he thought he heard a scuffling sound but he was not certain. Mohammed's shape materialized again beside him. 'Ten of them,' he reported. 'Two Askari and eight bearers. One of the Askari sat guard by the fire. He saw me, so I killed him.'

'Good God!' Sebastian's voice rose higher. 'You did what?'

'I killed him. But do not speak so loud.'

'How?'

'With my knife.'

'Why?'

'Lest he kill me first.'

'And the other?'

'Him also.'

'You killed both of them?' Sebastian was appalled.

'Yes, and took their rifles. Now it is safe to go on. But the bearers have with them many cases. It comes to me that this party follows after Bwana Intambu, the German commissioner, and that they carry with them all his goods.'

'But you shouldn't have killed them,' protested Sebastian. 'You could have just tied them up or something.'

'Manali, you argue like a woman,' Mohammed snapped impatiently, and then went on with his original line of thought. 'Among the cases is one that by its size I think is the box for the tax money. The one Askari slept with his back against it as though to give it special care.'

'The tax money?'

'Yes.'

'Well, son of a gun!' Sebastian's scruples dissolved and in the darkness his expression was suddenly transformed into that of a small boy on Christmas morning.

They woke the German bearers by standing over them and prodding them with the rifle barrels. Then they hustled them out of their blankets and herded them into a small group, bewildered and shivering miserably in the chill of dawn. Wood was heaped on the fire; it burned up brightly, and by its light Sebastian examined the booty.

The one Askari had bled profusely from the throat on to the small wooden chest. Mohammed took him by the heels and dragged him out of the way, then used his blanket to wipe the chest clean.

'Manali,' he said with reverence. 'See the big lock. See the bird of the Kaiser painted on the lid . . .' He stooped over the chest and took a grip on the handles, '. . . but most of all, feel the weight of it!'

Amongst the other equipment around the fire, Mohammed found a thick coil of one-inch manila rope. A commodity which was essential equipment on any of Herman Fleischer's safaris. With it, Mohammed roped the bearers together, at waist level, allowing enough line between each of them to make concerted movement possible but preventing individual flight.

'Why are you doing that?' Sebastian asked with interest, through a mouthful of blood sausage and black bread. Most of the other boxes were filled with food, and Sebastian was breakfasting well and heartily.

'So they cannot escape.'

'We're not taking them with us – are we?'

'Who else will carry all this?' Mohammed asked patiently.

Five days later Sebastian was seated in the bows of a long dugout canoe, with the charred soles of his boots set firmly on the chest that lay in the bilges. He was eating with relish a thick sandwich of polony and picked onions, wearing a change of clean underwear and socks that were a few sizes too large, and there was clutched in his left hand an open bottle of Hansa beer – all these with the courtesy of Commissioner Fleischer.

The paddlers were singing with unforced gaiety, for the hiring fee that Sebastian had paid them would buy each of them a new wife at least.

Hugging the bank of the Rovuma on the Portuguese side, driven on by willing paddles and the eager current, in twelve hours they covered the distance that it had taken Sebastian and his heavily-laden bearers five days on foot.

The canoe deposited Sebastian's party at the landing opposite M'topo's village, only ten miles from Lalapanzi. They walked that distance without resting and arrived after nightfall.

30

The windows of the bungalow were darkened, and the whole camp slept. After cautioning them to silence, Sebastian drew his depleted band up on the front lawn with the tax chest set prominently in front of them. He was proud of his success and wanted to achieve the appropriate mood for his home-coming. Having set the stage, he went up on to the stoep of the bungalow and tip-toed towards the front door with the intention of awakening the household by hammering upon it dramatically.

However, there was a chair on the stoep, and Sebastian tripped over it. He fell heavily. The chair clattered and the rifle slipped from his shoulder and rang on the stone flags.

Before Sebastian could recover his feet, the door was flung open and through it appeared Flynn O'Flynn in his night-shirt and armed with a double-barrelled shotgun. 'Caught you, you bastard!' he roared and lifted the shotgun.

Sebastian heard the click of the safety-catch and scrambled to his knees. 'Don't shoot! Flynn, it's me.'

The shotgun wavered a little. 'Who are you – and what do you want?'

'It's me – Sebastian.'

'Bassie?' Flynn lowered the shotgun uncertainly. 'It can't be. Stand up, let's have a look at you.'

Sebastian obeyed with alacrity.

'Good God,' Flynn swore in amazement. 'It *is* you. Good God! We heard that Fleischer caught you at M'topo's village a week ago. We heard he'd nobbled you for keeps!' He came forward with his right hand extended in welcome. 'You made it, did you? Well done, Bassie boy.'

Before Sebastian could accept Flynn's hand, Rosa came through the doorway, brushed past Flynn, and almost knocked Sebastian down again. With her arms locked around his chest and her cheek pressed to his unshaven cheek, she kept repeating, 'You're safe! Oh Sebastian, you're safe.'

Acutely aware of the fact that Rosa wore nothing under the thin night-gown, and that everywhere he put his hands they came in contact with thinly-veiled warm flesh, Sebastian grinned sheepishly at Flynn over her shoulder.

'Excuse me,' he said.

His first two kisses were off target for she was moving around a lot. One caught her on the ear, the next on her eyebrow, but the third was right between the lips.

When at last they were forced to separate or suffocate, Rosa gasped, 'I thought you were dead.'

'All right, missie,' growled Flynn. 'You can go and put some clothes on now.'

Breakfast at Lalapanzi that morning was a festive affair. Flynn took advantage of his daughter's weakened condition and brought a bottle of gin to the table. Her protests were half-hearted, and later with her own hands she poured a little into Sebastian's tea to brace it.

They ate on the stoep in golden sunshine that filtered through the bougainvillaea creeper. A flock of glossy starlings hopped and chirruped on the lawns, and an oriel sang from the wild fig-trees. All nature conspired to make Sebastian's victory feast a success, while Rosa and Nanny did their best from the kitchen – drawing upon the remains of Herman Fleischer's supplies that Sebastian had brought home with him.

Flynn O'Flynn's eyes were bloodshot and underhung with plum-coloured pouches, for he had been up all night counting the contents of the German tax chest and working out his accounts by the light of a hurricane lamp. Nevertheless, he was in a merry mood made merrier by the cups of fortified tea on which he was breakfasting. He joined warmly in the chorus of praise and felicitation to Sebastian Oldsmith that was being sung by Rosa O'Flynn.

'You turned up one for the book, so help me, Bassie,' he chortled at the end of the meal. 'I'd just love to hear how Fleischer is going to explain this one to Governor Schee. Oh, I'd love to be there when he tells him about the tax money – son of a gun, it'll nigh kill them both.'

'While you're on the subject of money,' Rosa smiled at Flynn, 'have you worked out how much Sebastian's share comes to, Daddy?' Rosa only used Flynn's paternal title when she was extremely well-disposed towards him.

'That I have,' admitted Flynn, and the sudden shiftiness of his eyes aroused Rosa's suspicions. Her lips pursed a little.

'And how much is it?' she asked in the syrupy tone which Flynn recognized as the equivalent of the blood roar of a wounded lioness.

'Sure now, and who wants to be spoiling a lovely day with the talking of business?' Under pressure, Flynn exaggerated the brogue in his voice in the hope that Rosa would find it beguiling. A forlorn hope.

'How much?' demanded Rosa, and he told her.

There was a sickly silence. Sebastian paled under his sunburn and opened his mouth to protest. On the strength of his half share, he had the previous night made to Rosa O'Flynn a serious proposal, which she had accepted.

'Leave this to me, Sebastian,' she whispered and laid a restraining hand on his knee as she turned back to her father. 'You'll let us have a look at the accounts, won't you?' Still syrupy sweet.

'Sure and I will. They're all straight and square.'

The document that Flynn O'Flynn produced under the main heading, 'Joint Venture Between F. O'Flynn, Esq., S. Oldsmith, Esq., and Others. German East Africa. Period May 15, 1913, to August 21, 1913,' showed that he belonged to an unorthodox school of accountancy.

The contents of the tax chest had been converted to English sterling at the rates laid down by Pear's Almanac for 1893. Flynn set great store by this particular publication.

From the gross proceeds of £4,652. 18s. 6d., Flynn had deducted his own fifty per cent share and the ten per cent of the other partners – the Portuguese Chef D'Post and the Governor of Mozambique. From the balance he had then deducted the losses incurred on the Rufiji expedition (for which see separate account addressed to German East African Administration). From there he had gone on to charge the expenses of the second expedition, not forgetting such items as:

To L. Parbhoo (Tailor)	£15.10. —.
To One German Dress Helmet (say)	£ 5.10. —.
To Five Uniforms (Askari) £ 2.10. —. each	£12.10. —.
To Five Mauser Rifles £10. —. —. each	£50. —. —.
To Six Hundred and Twenty-Five Rounds 7mm Ammunition	£22.10. —.
To Advance re travelling expenses, One Hundred Escudos made to S. Oldsmith, Esq.	£ 1. 5. —.

Finally, Sebastian's half share of the net losses amounted to a little under twenty pounds.

'Don't worry,' Flynn assured him magnanimously. 'I don't expect you to pay it now – we'll just deduct it from your share of the profits of the next expedition.'

'But, Flynn, I thought you said – well, I mean, you told me I had a half share.'

'And so you have, Bassie, and so you have.'

'You said we were equal partners.'

'You must have misunderstood me, boy. I said a half share – and that means after expenses. It's just a great pity there was such a large accumulated loss to bring forward.'

While they discussed this, Rosa was busy with a stub of indelible pencil on the reverse side of Flynn's account. Two minutes later she thrust the result across the breakfast table at Flynn. She said, 'And that's the way I work it out.'

Rosa O'Flynn was a student of the 'One-for-you-one-for-me' school, and her reckonings were much simpler than those of her father.

With a cry of anguish, Flynn O'Flynn lodged objection. 'You don't understand business.'

'But I recognize crookery when I see it,' Rosa flashed back.

'You'd call your old father a crook?'

'Yes.'

'I've a damn good mind to take the kiboko to you. You're not too big and uppity that I can't warm your tail up good.'

'You just try it!' said Rosa, and Flynn backpedalled.

'Anyway, what would Bassie do with all that money? It's not good for a youngster. It would spoil him.'

'He'd marry me with it. That's what he'd do with it.'

Flynn made a noise as though there were a fish-bone stuck in his throat, his face mottled over with emotion and he swung ominously in Sebastian's direction. 'So!' he rasped. 'I thought so!'

'Now steady on, old chap,' Sebastian tried to soothe him.

'You come into my home and act like the king of bloody England. You try to fraudulently embezzle my money – but that's not enough! Oh no! That's not a bloody 'nough. You've also got to start tampering with my daughter just to round things off.'

'Don't be coarse,' said Rosa.

'That's rich – *don't be coarse*, she says, and just what exactly have you two been up to behind my back?'

Sebastian stood up from the breakfast table with dignity. 'I will not have you speak so of a lady in my presence, sir. Especially of the lady who has done me the great honour of consenting to become my wife.' He begun unbuttoning his jacket. 'Will you step into the garden with me, and give me satisfaction?'

'Come along, then.' As Flynn lumbered out of his chair he made as if to pass Sebastian, but at the moment Sebastian's arms were behind him, still bound by the sleeves of his jacket as he attempted to shrug it off. Flynn side-stepped swiftly, paused a moment as he took his aim, and the drove his left fist into Sebastian's stomach.

'Oof!' said Sebastian, and leaned forward involuntarily to meet Flynn's other fist as it came up from the level of his knees. It took Sebastian between the eyes, and he changed direction abruptly and ran backwards across the veranda. The low wooden railing caught him behind the knees and he toppled slowly into the flower-beds below the stoep.

'You've killed him,' wailed Rosa, and picked up the heavy china tea-pot.

'I hope so,' said Flynn, and ducked as the pot flew towards his head, passed over it and burst against the wall of the stoep, spraying tea and steam.

There was an ominous stirring among Rosa's flowers, and presently Sebastian's head emerged with blue hydrangea petals festively strewn in his hair and the skin around both eyes fast swelling and chameleoning to a creditable match with the petals. 'I say, Flynn. That wasn't fair,' he announced.

'He wasn't looking,' Rosa accused. 'You hit him before he was ready.'

'Well, he's looking now,' roared Flynn and went down the veranda stairs like a charging hippopotamus. From the hydrangeas, Sebastian rose to meet him and took up the classic stance of the ring fighter. 'Marquis of Queensberry rules?' he cautioned as Flynn closed in.

Flynn signified his rejection of the Marquis's code by kicking Sebastian on the shin. Sebastian yelped and hopped one-legged out of the flower-bed, while Flynn pursued him with a further series of lusty kicks. Placing his boot twice in succession into Sebastian's posterior, the third kick, however, missed and the force behind it was sufficient to throw Flynn on to his back. He sprawled on the lawn, and the pause while he scrambled to his knees, gave Sebastian respite to ready himself for the next round.

Both his eyes had puffed and he was experiencing discomfort from his rear end; nevertheless, he stood once again with his left arm extended and the right crossed over his chest. Glancing beyond Flynn, Sebastian saw his fiancée descending from the veranda. She was armed with a bread-knife.

'Rosa!' Sebastian was alarmed. It was clear that Rosa would not stop at patricide to protect her love. 'Rosa! What are you doing with that knife?'

'I'm going to stick him with it!'

'You'll do no such thing,' said Sebastian, but Flynn did not have the same faith in his daughter's restraint. Very hurriedly, he moved into a defensive position behind Sebastian. From there he listened with attention to the argument between Sebastian and Rosa. It took a full minute for Sebastian to persuade Rosa that her assistance was not necessary and that he was capable of handling the situation on his own. Reluctantly, Rosa retreated to the veranda.

'Thanks, Bassie,' said Flynn, and kicked him in his already bruised behind. It was extremely painful.

Very few people had ever seen Sebastian Oldsmith lose his temper. The last time it had happened was eight years previously; the two sixth-formers who had invoked it by forcing Sebastian's head into a toilet bowl and flushing the cistern, were both hospitalized for a short period.

This time there were more witnesses. Attracted by the cries and crash of breaking crockery, Flynn's entire following, including Mohammed and his Askari, had arrived from the compound and were assembled at the top of the lawn. They watched in breathless wonder.

From the grandstand of the veranda, Rosa, her eyes sparkling with the strange feminine ferocity that arises in even the mildest women when their man fights for them, exhorted Sebastian to even greater violence.

Like all great storms, it did not last long, and when it was over the silence was appalling. Flynn lay stretched full-length on the lawn. His eyes closed and his breathing snoring softly in his throat, and bursting from his nose in a froth of red bubbles.

Mohammed and five of his men carried him towards the bungalow. He lay massive on their shoulders with the bulge of his belly rising and falling softly, and an expression of unusual peace on his bloody face.

Standing alone on the lawn, Sebastian's features were contorted with savagery and his whole body shook as though he was in high fever. Then, watching them carry the huge, inert body, suddenly Sebastian's mood was past. His expression changed first to concern, and then to gentle dismay. 'I say . . .' his voice was husky and he took a pace after them. 'You shouldn't have kicked me.' His hands opened helplessly, and he lifted them in a gesture of appeal. 'You shouldn't have done it.'

Rosa came down from the veranda and walked slowly towards him. She stopped and looked up at him, half in awe, half in glowing pride. 'You were magnificent,' she whispered. 'Like a lion.' She reached up with both arms around his neck, and before she kissed him she spoke again. 'I love you,' she said.

Sebastian had very little luggage to take with him. He was wearing everything he possessed. Rosa on the other hand, had boxes of it, enough to give full employment to the dozen bearers that were assembled on the lawn in front of the bungalow.

'Well,' murmured Sebastian, 'I suppose we should start moving.'

'Yes,' whispered Rosa, and looked at the gardens of Lalapanzi. Although she had suggested this departure, now that the time had come she was uncertain. This place had been her home since childhood. Here she had spun a cocoon that had shielded and protected her, and now that the time had come to emerge from it, she was afraid. She took Sebastian's arm, drawing strength from him.

'Don't you want to say good-bye to your father?' Sebastian looked down at her with the tender protectiveness that was such a new and delightful sensation for him.

Rosa hesitated a moment, and then realized that it would take very little to weaken her resolve. Her dutiful affection for Flynn, which at the moment was submerged beneath the tide of anger and resentment, could easily re-emerge should Flynn employ a little of his celebrated blarney. 'No,' she said.

'I suppose it's best,' Sebastian agreed. He glanced guiltily towards the bungalow where Flynn was, presumably, still lying in state – attended by the faithful Mohammed. 'But do you think he'll be all right? I mean, I did hit him rather hard, you know.'

'He'll be all right,' Rosa said without conviction, and tugged at his sleeve. Together they moved to take their places at the head of the little column of bearers.

Kneeling on the floor of the bedroom, below the window sill, peering with one swollen eye through a slit in the curtain, Flynn saw this decisive move. 'My God,' he whispered in concern. 'The young idiots are really leaving.'

Rosa O'Flynn was his last link with that frail little Portuguese girl. The one person in his life that Flynn had truly loved. Now that he was about to lose her also, Flynn was suddenly aware of his feeling for his daughter. The prospect of never seeing her again filled him with dismay.

As for Sebastian Oldsmith, here no sentiment clouded his reasoning. Sebastian was a valuable business asset. Through him, Flynn could put into operation a number of schemes that he had shelved as involving disproportionate personal risk. In these last few years Flynn had become increasingly aware of the depreciation that time and large quantities of raw spirit had wrought in his eyes and legs and nerves. Sebastian Oldsmith had eyes like a fish eagle, legs like a prize fighter, and no nerves at all that Flynn could discern. Flynn needed him.

Flynn opened his mouth and groaned. It was the throaty death rattle of an old bull buffalo. Peering through the curtain, Flynn grinned as he saw the young couple freeze, and stand tense and still in the sunlight. Their faces were turned towards the bungalow, and in spite of himself, Flynn had to admit they made a handsome pair; Sebastian tall above her with the body of a gladiator and the face of a poet; Rosa small beside him but with the full bosom and wide hips of womanhood. The slippery black cascade of her hair glowed in the sun, and her dark eyes were big with concern.

Flynn groaned again but softly this time. A breathless, husky sound, the last breath of a dying man, and instantly Rosa and Sebastian were running towards the bungalow. Her skirts gathered up above her knees, long legs flying, Rosa led Sebastian up onto the veranda.

Flynn had just sufficient time to return to his bed and compose his limbs and his face into the attitude of one fast sinking towards the abyss.

'Daddy!' Rosa leaned over him, and Flynn opened his eyes uncertainly. For a moment he did not seem to recognize her, then he whispered, 'My little girl,' so faintly she hardly caught the words.

'Oh, Daddy, what is it?' She knelt beside him.

'My heart.' His hand crawled up like a hairy spider across his belly and clutched weakly at his hairy chest. 'Like a knife. A hot knife.'

There was a terrible silence in the room, and then Flynn spoke again. 'I wanted to . . . give you my . . . my blessing. I wish happiness for you . . . wherever you go.' The effort of speech was too much, and for a while he lay gasping. 'Think of your old Daddy sometimes. Say a prayer for him.'

A fat, tiny tear broke from the corner of Rosa's eye and slid down her cheek.

'Bassie, my boy.' Slowly Flynn's eyes sought him, found him, and focused with difficulty. 'Don't blame yourself for this. I was an old man anyway – I've had my life.' He panted a little and then went on painfully. 'Look after her. Look after my little Rosa. You are my son now. I've never had a son.'

'I didn't know . . . I had no idea that your heart . . . Flynn, I'm dreadfully sorry. Forgive me.'

Flynn smiled, a brave little smile that just touched his lips. He lifted his hand weakly and held it out towards Sebastian. While Sebastian clasped his hand, Flynn considered offering him the money that had been the cause of the dispute as a dying man's gift but he manfully restrained himself from such extravagance. Instead he whispered, 'I would like to have seen my grandson, but no matter. Good-bye, my boy.'

'You'll see him, Flynn. I promise you that. We'll stay, won't we, Rosa? We'll stay with him.'

'Yes, we'll stay,' said Rosa. 'We won't leave you, Daddy.'

'My children.' Flynn sank back and closed his eyes. Thank God, he hadn't offered the money. A peaceful little smile hovered around his mouth. 'You've made an old man very happy.'

31

Flynn made a strong come-back from the edge of death, so strong, in fact, that it aroused Rosa's suspicions. However, she let it pass for she was happy to have avoided the necessity of leaving Lalapanzi. In addition, there was another matter which was taking up a lot of her attention.

Since she had said good-bye to Sebastian at the start of his tax tour, Rosa had been aware of the cessation of certain womanly functions of her body. She consulted Nanny who, in turn, consulted the local nungane who, in his turn, opened the belly of a chicken, and consulted its entrails. His findings were conclusive, and Nanny reported back to Rosa, without disclosing the source of her information, for Little Long Hair had an almost blasphemous lack of faith in the occult.

Delighted, Rosa took Sebastian for a walk down the valley, and when they reached the waterfall where it had all begun, she stood on top-toe, put both arms around his neck and whispered in his ear. She had to repeat herself for her voice was muffled with breathless laughter.

'You're joking,' gasped Sebastian, and then blushed bright crimson.

'I'm not, you know.'

'Good grief,' said Sebastian; and then, groping for something more expressive, 'Son of a gun!'

'Aren't you pleased?' Rosa pouted playfully. 'I did it for you.'

'But we aren't even married.'

'That can be arranged.'

'And quickly, too,' agreed Sebastian. He grabbed her wrist. 'Come on!'

'Sebastian, remember my condition.'

'Good grief, I'm sorry.'

He took her back to Lalapanzi, handing her over the rough ground with as much care as though she was a case of sweating gelignite.

'What's the big hurry?' asked Flynn jovially at dinner that evening. 'I've got a little job for Bassie first. I want him to slip across the river . . .'

'No, you don't,' said Rosa. 'We are going to see the priest at Beira.'

'It would only take Bassie a couple of weeks. Then we could talk about it when he gets back.'

'We are going to Beira – tomorrow!'

'What's the rush?' Flynn asked again.

'Well, the truth is, Flynn, old boy . . .' Wriggling in his chair, colouring up vividly, Sebastian relapsed into silence.

'The truth is I'm going to have a baby,' Rosa finished for him.

'You're *what*?!' Flynn stared at her in horror.

'You said that you wanted to see your grandchild,' Rosa pointed out.

'But I didn't mean you to start work on it right away,' roared Flynn, and he rounded on Sebastian. 'You dirty young bugger!'

'Father, your heart!' Rosa restrained him. 'Anyway, don't pick on Sebastian, I did my share as well.'

'You shameless . . . You brazen little . . .'

Rosa reached behind the seat cushion where Flynn had hidden the gin bottle. 'Have a little of this – it will help calm you.'

They left for Beira the following morning. Rosa was carried in a maschille with Sebastian trotting beside it in anxious attendance, ready to help ease the litter over the fords and rough places, and to curse any of the bearers who stumbled.

When they left Lalapanzi, Flynn O'Flynn brought up the rear of the column, lying in his maschille with a square-faced bottle for company, scowling and muttering darkly about 'fornication' and 'sin'.

But both Rosa and Sebastian ignored him, and when they camped that night the two of them sat across the camp-fire from him, and whispered and laughed secretly together. They pitched their voices at such a tantalizing level that even by straining his ears, Flynn could not overhear their conversation. It infuriated him to such an extent that finally he made a loud remark about '. . . beating the hell out of the person who had repaid his hospitality by violating his daughter.'

Rosa said that she would give anything to see him try it *again*. In her opinion it would be better than a visit to the circus. And Flynn gathered his dignity and his gin bottle and stalked away to where Mohammed had laid out his bedding under a lean-to of thorn bushes.

During the dark hours before dawn they were visited by an old lion. He came with a rush from the darkness beyond the fire-light, grunting like an angry boar, the great black bush of his mane erect, snaking with incredible speed towards the huddle of blanket-wrapped figures about the fire.

Flynn was the only one not asleep. He had waited all night, watching Sebastian's reclining figure; just waiting for him to move across to the temporary thorn-bush shelter that gave Rosa privacy. Lying beside Flynn was his shotgun, double-loaded with big loopers, lion shot, and he had every intention of using it.

When the lion charged into the camp, Flynn sat up quickly and fired both barrels of the shotgun at point-blank range into the man-eater's head and chest, killing it instantly. But the momentum of its rush bowled it forward, sent it sliding full into Sebastian, and both of them rolled into the camp-fire.

Sebastian awoke to lion noises, and gun-fire, and the violent collision of a big body into his, and red-hot coals sticking to various parts of his anatomy. With a single bound, and a wild cry, he threw off his blanket, came to his feet, and went into such a lively song and dance routine, yodelling and high-kicking, and striking out at his imaginary assailants that Flynn was reduced to a jelly of helpless laughter.

The laughter, and the praise and thanks showered on him by Sebastian, Rosa, and the bearers, cleared the air.

'You saved my life,' said Sebastian soulfully.

'Oh Daddy, you're wonderful,' said Rosa. 'Thank you. Thank you,' and she hugged him.

The mantle of the hero felt snug and comfortable on Flynn's shoulders. He became almost human – and the improvement continued as each day's march brought them closer to the little Portuguese port of Beira, for Flynn greatly enjoyed his rare visits to civilization.

The last night they camped a mile from the outskirts of the town, and after a private conference with Flynn, old Mohammed went ahead armed with a small purse of escudos to make the arrangements for Flynn's formal entry on the morrow.

Flynn was up with the dawn, and while he shaved with care, and dressed in clean moleskin jacket and trousers, one of the bearers polished his boots with hippo fat, and two others scaled the tall bottle palm tree near the camp and cut fronds from its head.

All things being ready, Flynn ascended his maschille and lay back elegantly on the leopard-skin rugs. On each side of Flynn a bearer took his position, armed with a palm-frond, and began to fan him gently. Behind Flynn, in single file, followed other servants bearing tusks of ivory and the still-green lion skin. Behind this, with instructions from Flynn not to draw undue attention to themselves, followed Sebastian and Rosa, and the baggage bearers.

With a languid gesture such as might have been used by Nero to signal the start of a Roman circus, Flynn gave the order to move.

Along the rough road through the thick coastal bush, they came at last to Beira and entered the main street in procession.

'Good Lord,' Sebastian expressed his surprise when he saw the reception that awaited them, 'where did they all come from?'

Both sides of the street were lined with cheering crowds, mainly natives, but with here and there a Portuguese or an Indian trader come out of his shop to find the cause of the disturbance.

'Fini!' chanted the crowd, clapping their hands in unison. 'Bwana Mkuba! Great Lord! Slayer of elephant. Killer of lions!'

'I didn't realize that Flynn was so well regarded.' Sebastian was impressed.

'Most of them have never heard of him,' Rosa disillusioned him. 'He sent Mohammed in last night to gather a claque of about a hundred or so. Pays them one escudo each to come and cheer – they make so much noise that the entire population turns out to see what is going on. They fall for it every time.'

'What on earth does he go to so much trouble for?'

'Because he enjoys it. Just look at him!'

Lying in his maschille, graciously acknowledging the applause, Flynn was very obviously loving every minute of it.

The head of the procession reached the only hotel in Beira and halted. Madame da Souza, the portly, well-moustached widow who was the proprietress of the hotel, rushed down to welcome Flynn with a smacking kiss and usher him ceremoniously through the shabby portals. Flynn was the kind of customer she had always dreamed about.

When Rosa and Sebastian at last fought their way through the crowd into the hotel, Flynn was already seated at the bar counter and half way through a tall glass of Laurentia beer. The man sitting on the stool beside his was the Governor of Mozambique's aide-de-camp, who had come to deliver His Excellency's invitation for Flynn O'Flynn to dine at Government House that evening. It was settlement day in the partnership of 'Flynn O'Flynn and Others'. His Excellency José De Clare Don Felezardo da Silva Marques had received from Governor Schee, in Dar es Salaam, an agitated report, in the form of an official protest and an extradition demand, of the success of the partnership's operations during the last few months – and His Excellency was delighted to see Flynn.

In fact, so pleased was His Excellency with the progress of the partnership's affairs, that he exercised his authority to waive the formalities required by law to precede a marriage under Portuguese jurisdiction. This saved a week, and the afternoon after their arrival in Beira, Rosa and Sebastian stood before the altar in the stucco and thatch cathedral, while Sebastian tried with little success to remember enough of his schoolroom Latin to understand just what he was getting himself into.

The wedding veil, that had belonged to Rosa's mother, was yellowed by many years of storage under tropical conditions, but it served well enough to keep off the flies which were always bad during the hot season in Beira.

Towards the end of the long ceremony, Flynn was so overcome by the heat, the gin he had taken at lunch, and an unusually fine flood of Irish feeling, that he began snuffling loudly. While he mopped at his eyes and nose with a grubby handkerchief, the Governor's aide-de-camp patted his shoulder soothingly and murmured encouragement.

The priest declared them husband and wife, and the congregation launched into a faltering rendition of the *Te Deum*. His voice quivering with emotion and alcohol, Flynn kept repeating, 'My little girl, my poor little girl.' Rosa lifted her veil and turned to Sebastian who immediately forgot his misgivings as to the form of the ceremony, and enfolded her enthusiastically in his arms.

Still maintaining his chorus of 'My little girl,' Flynn was led away by the aide-de-camp to the hotel where the proprietress had prepared the wedding feast. In deference to Flynn O'Flynn's mood this started on a sombre note but as the champagne, which Madame da Souza had specially bottled the previous evening, started to do its work, so the tempo changed. Among his other actions, Flynn gave Sebastian a wedding present of ten pounds and poured a full glass of beer over the aide-de-camp's head.

When, later that evening, Rosa and Sebastian slipped away to the bridal suite above the bar, Flynn was giving lusty tongue in the chorus of 'They are jolly good fellows', Madame da Souza was seated on his lap, and over-flowing it in all directions. Every time Flynn pinched her posterior, great gusts of laughter made her shake like a stranded jellyfish.

Later the pleasure of Rosa and Sebastian's wedding-bed was disturbed by the fact that, in the bar-room directly below them, Flynn O'Flynn was shooting the bottles off the shelves with a double-barrelled elephant rifle. Every direct hit was greeted by thunderous applause from the other guests. Madame da Souza, still palpitating with laughter, sat in a corner of the bar-room dutifully making such entries in her note-book as, 'One bottle of Grandio London Dry Gin 14.50 escudos; one bottle Grandio French Cognac Five Star 14.50 escudos; one bottle Grandio Scotch whisky 30.00 escudos; I magnum Grandio French Champagne 75.90 escudos.' 'Grandio' was the brand-name of the house, and signified that the liquor each bottle contained had been brewed and bottled on the premises under the personal supervision of Madame da Souza.

Once the newly-wed couple realized that the uproar from the room below was sufficient to mask the protests of their rickety brass bedstead, they no longer grudged Flynn his amusements.

For everyone involved it was a night of great pleasure, a night to be looked back upon with nostalgia and wistful smiles.

32

E ven at Flynn's prodigious rate of expenditure, his share of the profits from Sebastian's tax expedition lasted another two weeks.

During this period Rosa and Sebastian spent a little of their time wandering hand in hand through the streets and bazaars of Beira, or sitting, still hand in hand, on the beach and watching the sea. Their happiness radiated from them so strongly that it affected anyone who came within fifty feet of them. A worried stranger hurrying towards them along the narrow little street with his face creased in a frown would come under the spell; his pace would slacken, his step losing its urgency, the frown would smooth away to be replaced by an indulgent grin as he passed them. But mostly they remained closeted in the bridal suite above the bar – entering it in the early afternoon and not reappearing until nearly noon the following day.

Neither Rosa nor Sebastian had imagined such happiness could exist.

At the expiry of the two weeks Flynn was waiting for them in the bar-room as they came down to lunch. He hurried out to join them as they passed the door. 'Greetings! Greetings!' He threw an arm around each of their shoulders. 'And how are you this morning?' He listened without attention as Sebastian replied at length on how well he felt, how well Rosa was, and how well both of them had slept. 'Sure! Sure!' Flynn interrupted his rhapsodizing. 'Listen, Bassie, my boy, you remember that £10 I gave you?'

'Yes.' Sebastian was immediately wary.

'Let me have it back, will you?'

'I've spent it, Flynn.'

'You've *what*?' bellowed Flynn.

'I've spent it.'

'Good God Almighty! All of it? You've squandered ten pounds in as many days?' Flynn was horrified by his son-in-law's extravagance and Sebastian, who had honestly believed the money was his to do with as he wished, was very apologetic.

They left for Lalapanzi that afternoon. Madame da Souza had accepted Flynn's note of hand for the balance outstanding on her bill.

At the head of the column Flynn, broke to the wide, and nursing a burning hangover, was in evil temper. The line of bearers behind him, bedraggled and bilious from two weeks spent in the flesh-pots, were in similar straits. At the rear of the doleful little caravan, Rosa and Sebastian chirruped and cooed together – an island of sunshine in the sea of gloom.

The months passed quickly at Lalapanzi during the monsoon of 1913. Gradually, as its girth increased, Rosa's belly became the centre of Lalapanzi. The pivot upon which the whole community turned. The debates in the servants' quarters, led by Nanny, the accepted authority, dealt almost exclusively with the contents thereof. All of them were hot for a man-child, although secretly Nanny cherished a treacherous hope that it might be another Little Long Hair.

Even Flynn, during the long months of enforced inactivity while the driving monsoon rains turned the land into a quagmire and the rivers into seething brown torrents, felt his grand-paternal instincts stirred. Unlike Nanny, he had no doubts as to the unborn child's sex, and he decided to name it Patrick Flynn O'Flynn Oldsmith.

He conveyed his decision to Sebastian while the two of them were hunting for the pot in the kopjes above the homestead.

By dint of diligent application and practice, Sebastian's marksmanship had improved beyond all reasonable expectation. He had just demonstrated it. They were jump-shooting in thick cat-bush among the broken rock and twisted ravines of the kopjes. Constant rain had softened the ground and enabled them to move silently down-wind along one of the ravines. Flynn was fifty yards out on Sebastian's right, moving heavily but deceptively fast through the sodden grass and undergrowth.

The kudu were lying in dense cover below the lip of the ravine. Two young bulls, bluish-gold in colour, striped with thin chalk lines across the body, pendulent dewlaps heavily fringed with yellow hair, two and a half twists in each of the corkscrew horns – big as polo ponies but heavier. They broke left across the ravine when Flynn jumped them from their hide, and the intervening bush denied him a shot.

'Breaking your way, Bassie,' Flynn shouted and Sebastian took two swift paces around the bush in front of him, shook the clinging raindrops from his lashes, and slipped the safety-catch. He heard the tap of big horn against a branch, and the first bull came out of the ravine at full run across his front. Yet it seemed to float, unreal, intangible, through the blue-grey rain mist. It blended ghostlike into the background of dark rain-soaked vegetation, and the clumps of bush and the tree trunks between them made it an almost impossible shot. In the instant that the bull flashed across a gap between two clumps of buffalo thorn, Sebastian's bullet broke its neck a hand's width in front of the shoulder.

At the sound of the shot, the second bull swerved in dead run, gathered its forelegs beneath its chest and went up in a high, driving leap over the thorn bush that stood in its path. Sebastian traversed his rifle smoothly without taking the butt from his shoulder, his right hand flicked the bolt open and closed, and he fired as a continuation of the movement.

The heavy bullet caught the kudu in mid-air and threw it sideways. Kicking and thrashing, it struck the ground and rolled down the bank of the ravine.

Whooping like a red indian, Mohammed galloped past Sebastian, brandishing a long knife, racing to reach the second bull and cut its throat before it died so that the dictates of the Koran might be observed.

Flynn ambled across to Sebastian. 'Nice shooting, Bassie boy. Salted and dried and pickled, there's meat there for a month.'

And Sebastian grinned in modest recognition of the compliment. Together they walked across to watch Mohammed and his gang begin paunching and quartering the big animals.

With the skill of a master tactician, Flynn chose this moment to inform Sebastian of the name he had selected for his grandson. He was not prepared for the fierce opposition he encountered from Sebastian. It seemed that Sebastian had expected to name the child Francis Sebastian Oldsmith. Flynn laughed easily, and then in his most reasonable and persuasive brogue he started pointing out to Sebastian just how cruel it would be to saddle the child with a name like that.

It was a lance in the pride of the Oldsmiths, and Sebastian rose to the defence. By the time they returned to Lalapanzi, the discussion needed about six hot words to reach the stage of single combat.

Rosa heard them coming. Flynn's bellow carried across the lawns. 'I'll no have my grandson called a pewling, milksop name like that!'

'Francis is the name of kings and warriors and gentlemen!' cried Sebastian.

'My aching buttocks, it is!'

Rosa came out on to the wide veranda and stood there with her arms folded over the beautiful bulge that housed the cause of the controversy.

They saw her and started an undignified race across the lawns, each trying to reach her first to enlist her support for their respective causes.

She listened to the pleadings, a small and secret smile upon her lips, and then said with finality, 'Her name will be Maria Rosa Oldsmith.'

Some time later Flynn and Sebastian were together on the veranda.

Ten days before the last rains of the season had come roaring in from the Indian Ocean and broken upon the unyielding shield of the continent. Now the land was drying out; the rivers regaining their sanity and returning, chastened to the confines of their banks. New grass lifted from the red earth to welcome the return of the sun.

For this brief period the whole land was alive and green; even the gnarled and crabbed thorn trees wore a pale fuzz of tender leaves. Behind each pair of guinea-fowl that clinked and scratched on the bottom lawns of Lalapanzi, there paraded a file of dappled chicks. Early that morning a herd of eland had moved along the skyline across the valley, and beside each cow had trotted a calf. Everywhere was new life, or the expectation of new life.

'Now, stop worrying!' said Flynn, as his impatient pacing brought him level with Sebastian's chair.

'I'm not worrying,' Sebastian said mildly. 'Everything will be all right.'

'How do you know that?' challenged Flynn.

'Well . . .'

'You know the child could be stillborn, or something.' Flynn shook his finger in Sebastian's face. 'It could have six fingers on each hand – how about that? I heard about one that was born with . . .'

While Flynn related a long list of horrors, Sebastian's expression of proud and eager anticipation crumbled slowly. He rose from his chair and fell into step beside Flynn. 'Have you got any gin left?' he asked hoarsely, glancing at the shuttered windows of Rosa's bedroom. Flynn produced the bottle from the inside pocket of his jacket.

An hour later, Sebastian was hunched forward in his chair, clutching a half-full tumbler of gin with both hands. He stared into it miserably. 'I don't know what I'd do if it was born with . . .' He could not go on. He shuddered and lifted the tumbler to his lips. At that instant a long, petulant wail issued from the closed bedroom. Sebastian leapt as though he had been bayoneted from behind, and spilled the gin down his shirt. His next leap was in the direction of the bedroom, a direction Flynn had also chosen. They collided heavily and then set off together at a gallop along the veranda. They reached the locked door and hammered upon it for admission. But Nanny, who had evicted them in the first instance, still adamantly refused to lift the locking bar or to give them any information as to the progress of the birthing. Her decision was endorsed by Rosa.

'Don't you dare let them in until everything is ready,' she whispered huskily, and roused herself from the stupor of exhaustion, to help Nanny with washing and wrapping the infant.

When at last everything was ready, she lay propped on the pillows with her child held against her chest, and nodded to Nanny. 'Open the door,' she said.

The delay had confirmed Flynn's worst suspicions. The door flew open, and he and Sebastian fell into the room, wild with anxiety.

'Oh, thank God, Rosa. You're still alive!' Sebastian reached the bed and fell on his knees beside it.

'You check his feet,' instructed Flynn. 'I'll do his hands and head,' and before Rosa could prevent him, he had lifted the infant out of her arms.

'His fingers are all right. Two arms, one head,' Flynn muttered above Rosa's protests and the infant's muffled squawls of indignation.

'This end is fine. Just fine!' Sebastian spoke in rising relief and delight. 'He's beautiful, Flynn!' And he lifted the shawl that swaddled the child's body. His expression cracked and his voice choked. 'Oh, my God!'

'What's wrong?' Flynn asked sharply.

'You were right, Flynn. He's deformed.'

'What? Where?'

'There!' Sebastian pointed. 'He hasn't got a what-ye-ma-call-it,' and they both stared in horror.

It was many long seconds before they realized simultaneously that the tiny cleft was no deformity but very much as nature had intended it.

'It's a girl!' said Flynn in dismay.

'A girl!' echoed Sebastian, and quickly pulled down the shawl to preserve his daughter's modesty.

'It's a girl,' Rosa smiled, wan and happy.

'It's a girl,' cackled Nanny in triumph.

Maria Rosa Oldsmith had arrived without fuss and with the minimum of inconvenience to her mother, so that Rosa was on her feet again within twenty-four hours. All her other activities were conducted with the same consideration and dispatch. She cried once every four hours; a single angry howl which was cut off the instant the breast was thrust into her mouth. Her bowel movements were equally regular and of the correct volume and consistency, and the rest of her days and nights were devoted almost entirely to sleeping.

She was beautiful; without the parboiled, purple look of most new-borns; without the squashed-in pug features or the vague, squinty eyes.

From the curly cap of silk hair to the tips of her pink toes, she was perfection.

It took Flynn two days to recover from the disappointment of having been cheated out of a grandson. He sulked in the arsenal or sat solitary at the end of the veranda. On the second evening Rosa pitched her voice just high enough to carry the length of the veranda.

'Don't you think Maria looks just like Daddy – the same mouth and nose? Look at her eyes.'

Sebastian opened his mouth to deny the resemblance emphatically but closed it again, as Rosa kicked him painfully on the ankle.

'She is the image of him. There's no doubting who her grandfather is.'

'Well, I suppose. . . . If you look closely,' Sebastian agreed unhappily.

At the end of the veranda, Flynn sat with his head cocked in an attitude of attention. Half an hour later Flynn had sidled up to the cradle and was studying the contents thoughtfully. By the following evening he had moved his chair alongside and was leading the discussion with such remarks as, 'There is quite a strong family resemblance. Look at those eyes – no doubt who her Granddaddy is!'

Interspersing his observations with warnings and instructions, 'Don't get so close, Bassie. You're breathing germs all over her.' 'Rosa, this child needs another blanket. When did she have her last feed?'

It was not long before he started bringing pressure to bear on Sebastian.

'You've got responsibilities now. Have you thought about that?'

'How do you mean, Flynn?'

'Just answer me this. What have you got in this world?'

'Rosa and Maria,' Sebastian answered promptly.

'Fine. That's just great! And how are you going to feed them and clothe them and . . . and look after them?'

Sebastian expressed himself well satisfied with the existing arrangements.

'I bet you are! It isn't costing you a thing. But I reckon it's about time you got up off your bum and did something.'

'Like what?'

'Like going and shooting some ivory.'

Three days later, armed and equipped for a full-scale poaching expedition, Sebastian led a column of gun-boys and bearers down the valley towards the Rovuma river.

Fourteen hours later, in the dusk of evening, he led them back.

'What in the name of all that's holy, are you doing back here?' Flynn demanded.

'I had this premonition,' Sebastian was sheepish.

'What premonition?'

'That I should come back,' muttered Sebastian.

He left again two days later. This time he actually crossed the Rovuma before the premonition over-powered him once more, and he came back to Rosa and Maria.

'Well,' Flynn sighed with resignation. 'I reckon I'll just have to go along with you and make sure you do it.' He shook his head. 'You've been a big disappointment to me, Bassie.' The biggest disappointment being the fact that he had hoped to have his granddaughter to himself for a few weeks.

'Mohammed,' he bellowed. 'Get my gear packed.'

33

F lynn sent his scouts across the river and when they reported back that the far bank was clear of German patrols, Flynn made the crossing.

This expedition was a far cry from Sebastian's amiable and aimless wandering in German territory. Flynn was a professional. They crossed in the night. They crossed in strictest silence and landed two miles downstream from M'topo's village. There was no lingering on the beach, but an urgent night march that began immediately and went on in grim silence until an hour before dawn; a march that took them fifteen miles inland from the river, and ended in a grove of elephant thorn, carefully chosen for the kopjes and ravines around it that afforded multiple avenues of escape in each direction.

Sebastian was impressed by the elaborate precautions that Flynn took before going into camp; the jinking and counter-marching, the careful sweeping of their spoor with brushes of dry grass, and the placing of sentries on the kopje above the camp.

During the ten days they waited there, not a single branch was broken from a tree, not a single axe-stroke swung to leave a tell-tale white blaze on the dark bush. The tiny night fire fed with dry trash and dead wood was carefully screened, and before dawn was smothered with sand so that not a wisp of smoke was left to mark them in the day.

Voices were never raised above conversational tones, and even the clatter of a bucket brought such a swift and ferocious reprimand from Flynn, that on all of them was a nervous awareness, an expectancy of danger, a tuning of the minds and bodies to action.

On the eighth night the scouts that Flynn had thrown out began drifting back to the camp. They came in with all the stealth and secrecy of night animals and huddled over the fire to tell what they had seen.

'. . . Last night three old bulls drank at the water-hole of the sick hyena. They carried teeth so, and so, and so . . .' showing the arm to measure the length of ivory, '. . . apart from them, ten cows left their feet in the mud, six of them young with calves. Yesterday, at the place where the hill of Inhosana breaks and turns its arms, I saw where another herd had crossed, moving towards the dawn; five young bulls, twenty-three cows and . . .'

The reports were jumbled, unintelligible to Sebastian who did not carry a map of the land in his head. But Flynn, sitting beside the fire listening, fitted the fragments together and built them into an exact picture of how the game was moving. He saw that the big bulls were still separated from the breeding herds – that they lingered on the high ground while the cows had started moving back towards the swamps from which the floods had driven them, anxious to take their young away from the dangers that the savannah forests would offer once the dry season set in.

He noted the estimates of thickness and length of tusk. Immature ivory was hardly worth carrying home, good only for carving into billiard balls and piano keys. The market was glutted with it.

But on the other hand, a prime tusk, over one hundred pounds in weight, seven foot long and twice the thickness of a fat woman's thigh, would fetch fifty shillings a pound avoirdupois.

An animal carrying such a tusk in each side of his face was worth four or five hundred pounds in good, gold sovereigns.

One by one Flynn discarded the possible areas in which he would hunt. This year there were no elephant in the M'bahora hills. There was good reason for this; thirty piles of great sun-bleached bones lay scattered along the ridge, marking the path that Flynn's rifles had followed two years before. The memory of gun-fire was too fresh and the herds shunned that place.

There were no elephant on the Tabora escarpment. A blight had struck the groves of mapundu trees, and withered the fruit before it could ripen. Dearly the elephant loved mapundu berries and they had gone elsewhere to find them.

They had gone up to the Sania Heights, to Kilombera, and to the Salito hills.

Salito was an easy day's march from the German boma at Mahenge. Flynn struck it from his mental list.

As each of the scouts finished his report, Flynn asked the question which would influence his final decision.

'What of *Plough the Earth*?'

And they said, 'We saw nothing. We heard nothing.'

The last scout came in two days after the others. He looked sheepish and more than a little guilty.

'Where the hell have you been?' Flynn demanded, and the gun-boy had his excuse ready.

'Knowing that the great Lord Fini would ask of certain matters, I turned aside in my journey to the village of Yetu, who is my uncle. My uncle is a fundi. No wild thing walks, no lion kills, no elephant breaks a branch from a tree but my uncle knows of it. Thus I went to ask him of these things.'

'Thy uncle is a famous fundi, he is also a famous breeder of daughters,' Flynn remarked drily. 'He breeds daughters the way the moon breeds stars.'

'Indeed, my uncle Yetu is a man of fame.' Hurriedly the scout went on to turn Flynn aside from this line of discussion. 'My uncle sends his greetings to the Lord Fini and bids me speak thus: "This season there are many fine elephants on the Sania Heights. They walk by twos and threes. With my own eyes I have seen twelve which show ivory as long as the shaft of a throwing spear, and I have seen signs of as many more." My uncle bids me speak further: "There is one among them of which the Lord Fini knows for he has asked of him many times. This one is a bull among great bulls. One who moves in such majesty that men have named him *Plough the Earth*." '

'You do not bring a story from the honey-bird to cool my anger against you?' Flynn demanded harshly. 'Did you dream of *Plough the Earth* while you were plough-ing the bellies of your uncle's many daughters?' His eagerness was soured by scepti-cism. Too many times he had followed wild stories in his pursuit of the great bull. He leaned forward across the fire to watch the gun-bearer's eyes as he replied, 'It is true, lord.' Flynn watched him carefully but found no hint of guile in his face. Flynn grunted, rocked back on his hams, and lowered his gaze to the small flames of the camp-fire.

For his first ten years in Africa, Flynn had heard the legend of the elephant whose tusks were of such length that their points touched the ground and left a double furrow along his spoor. He had smiled at this story as he had at the story of the rhinoceros who fifty years before had killed an Arab slaver, and now wore around his horn a massive gold bangle studded with precious stones. They said the bangle had lodged there as he gored the Arab. There were a thousand other romantic tales come out of Africa; from Solomon's treasure to the legend of the elephants' graveyard, and Flynn believed none of them.

Then he saw a myth come alive. One evening, camped near the Zambezi in Portuguese territory, he had taken a bird-gun and walked along the bank hoping for a brace of sand-grouse. Two miles from the camp he had seen a flight of birds coming in to the water, fly fast as racing pigeons, whistling in on backswept wings, and he had ducked into a thick bank of reeds and watched them come.

As they banked steeply overhead, dropping towards the sand-banks of the river, Flynn jumped to his feet and fired left and right, folding the lead bird and the second, so they crumpled in mid-air and tumbled, leaving a pale flurry of feathers to mark their fall.

But Flynn never saw the birds hit the ground. For, while the double blast of the shotgun still echoed along the river, the reed-bed below where he stood swayed and crashed and burst open, then an elephant came out into the open.

It was a bull elephant that stood fourteen feet high at the shoulder. An elephant so old that his ears were shredded to half their original size. The hide that covered his body hung in folds and deep wrinkles, baggy at the knees and the throat. The tuft of his tail long ago worn bald. The rheumy tears of great age staining his seared and dusty cheeks.

He came out of the reed-bed in a shambling, hump-backed run, and his head was tilted at an awkward, unnatural angle.

Flynn could hardly credit his vision when he saw the reason why the old bull cocked his head back in that fashion. From each side of the head extended two identical shafts of ivory, perfectly matched, straight as the columns of a Greek temple, with not an inch of taper from lip to bluntly rounded tip. They were stained to the colour of tobacco juice, fourteen long feet of ivory that would have touched the ground, if the elephant had carried his head relaxed.

As Flynn stood frozen in disbelief, the bull passed him by a mere fifty yards and lumbered on into the forest.

It took Flynn thirty minutes to get back to camp and exchange the bird-gun for the double-barrelled Gibbs, snatch up a water bottle, shout for his gun-boys, and return to the river.

He put Mohammed to the spoor. At first there were only the round pad marks in the dusty earth, smooth pad marks the size of a dustbin lid; the graining on the old bull's hooves had long been worn away. Then after five miles of flight there were other marks to follow. On each side of the spoor a double line scuffed through dead leaves and grass and soft earth where the tips of the tusks touched, and Flynn learned why the old bull was called *Plough the Earth*.

They lost the spoor on the third day in the rain, but a dozen times in the years since then, Flynn had followed and lost those double furrows, and once, through his binoculars, he had seen the old bull again, standing dozing beneath a grove of marula trees at a distance of three miles, his eroded old head propped up by the mythical tusks. When Flynn reached the spot on which he had seen the bull, it was deserted.

In all his life Flynn had never wanted anything with such obsessive passion as he wanted those tusks.

Now he sat silently staring into the camp-fire, remembering all these things, and the lust within him was tighter and more compelling than he had ever felt for a woman.

At last he looked up at the scout and said huskily, 'Tomorrow, with the first light, we will go to the village of Yetu, at Sania.'

A fly settled on Herman Fleischer's cheek and rubbed its front feet together in delight, as it savoured the prospect of drinking from the droplet of sweat that quivered precariously at the level of his ear lobe.

The Askari standing behind Herman's chair flicked the zebra tail switch with such skill, that not one of the long black hairs touched the Commissioner's face, and the fly darted away to take its place in the circuit that orbited around Herman's head.

Herman hardly noticed the interruption. He was sunk down in the chair, glowering at the two old men who squatted on the dusty parade ground below the veranda. The silence was a blanket that lay on them all in the stupefying heat. The two headmen waited patiently. They had spoken, and now they waited for the Bwana Mkuba to reply.

'How many have been killed?' Herman asked at last, and the senior of the two headmen answered.

'Lord, as many as the fingers of both your hands. But these are the ones of which we are certain, there may be others.'

Herman's concern was not for the dead, but their numbers would be a measure of the seriousness of the situation. Ritual murder was the first stage on the road to rebellion. It started with a dozen men meeting in the moonlight, dressed in cloaks of leopard skin, with designs of white clay painted on their faces. With the crude iron claws strapped to their hands, they would ceremoniously mutilate a young girl, and then devour certain parts of her body. This was harmless entertainment in Herman's view, but when it happened more frequently, it generated in the district a mood of abject terror. This was the climate of revolt. Then the leopard priests would walk through the villages in the night, walk openly in procession with the torches burning, and the men who lay shivering within the barricaded huts would listen to the chanted instructions from the macabre little procession – and they would obey.

It had happened ten years earlier at Salito. The priests had ordered them to resist the tax expedition that year. They had slaughtered the visiting Commissioner and twenty of his Askari, and they cut the bodies into small pieces with which they festooned the thorn trees.

Three months later a battalion of German infantry had disembarked at Dar es Salaam and marched to Salito. They burned the villages and they shot everything – men, women, children, chickens, dogs and goats. The final casualty list could only be estimated, but the officer commanding the battalion boasted that they had killed two thousand human beings. He was probably exaggerating. Nevertheless, the Salito hills were still devoid of human life and habitation to this day. The whole episode was irritating and costly – and Herman Fleischer wanted no repetition of it during his term of office.

On the principle that prevention was better than cure, he decided to go down and conduct a few ritual sacrifices of his own. He humped himself forward in his chair, and spoke to his sergeant of Askari.

'Twenty men. We will leave for the village of Yetu, at Sania, tomorrow before dawn. Do not forget the ropes.'

34

O n the Sania Heights, in the heat of the day, an elephant stood under the wide branches of a wild fig-tree. He was asleep on his feet but his head was propped up by two long columns of stained ivory. He slept as an old man sleeps, fitfully, never sinking very deep below the level of consciousness. Occasionally the tattered grey ears flapped, and each time a fine haze of flies rose around his head. They hung in the hot air and then settled again. The rims of the elephant's ears were raw where the flies had eaten down through the thick skin. The flies were everywhere. The humid green shade beneath the wild fig was murmurous with the sound of their wings.

Across the divide of the Sania Heights, four miles from the spot where the old bull slept, three men were moving up one of the bush-choked gulleys towards the ridge.

Mohammed was leading. He moved fast, half-crouched to peer at the ground, glancing up occasionally to anticipate the run of the spoor he was following. He stopped at a place where a grove of mapundu trees had carpeted the ground beneath them with a stinking, jellified mass of rotten berries. He looked back at the two white men and indicated the marks in the earth, and the pyramid of bright yellow dung that lay upon it. 'He stopped here for the first time in the heat, but it was not to his liking, and he has gone on.'

Flynn was sweating. It ran down his flushed jowls and dripped on to his already sodden shirt. 'Yes,' he nodded and a small cloud-burst of sweat scattered from his head at the movement. 'He will have crossed the ridge.'

'What makes you so certain?' Sebastian spoke in the same sepulchral whisper as the others.

'The cool evening breeze will come from the east – he will cross to the other side of the ridge to wait for it.' Flynn spoke with irritation and wiped his face on the short sleeve of his shirt. 'Now, you just remember, Bassie. This is my elephant, you understand that? You try for it and, so help me God, I'll shoot you dead.'

Flynn nodded to Mohammed and they moved on up the slope, following the spoor that meandered between outcrops of grey granite and scrub.

The crest of the ridge was well defined, sharp as the spine of a starving ox. They paused below it, squatting to rest in the coarse brown grass. Flynn opened the binocular case that hung on his chest, lifted out the instrument and began to polish the lens with a scrap of cloth.

'Stay here!' Flynn ordered the other two, then on his belly he wriggled up towards the skyline. Using the cover of a tree stump, he lifted his head cautiously and peered over.

Below him the Sania Heights fell away at a gentle slope, fifteen hundred feet and ten miles to the plain below. The slope was broken and crenellated, riven into a thousand gulleys and ravines, covered over-all with a mantle of coarse brown scrub and dotted with clumps of bigger trees.

Flynn settled himself comfortably on his elbows and lifted the binoculars to his eyes. Systematically he began to examine each of the groves below him.

'Yes!' he whispered aloud, wriggling a little on his belly, staring at the picture puzzle beneath the spread branches of the tree, a mile away. In the shade there were shapes that made no sense, a mass too diffuse to be the trunk of the tree.

He lowered the glasses and wiped away the sweat that clung in his eyebrows. He closed his eyes to rest them from the glare, then he opened them again and lifted the glasses.

For two long minutes he stared before suddenly the puzzle made sense. The bull was standing half away from him, merging with the trunk of the wild fig, the head and half the body obscured by the lower branches of the tree – and what he had taken to be the stem of a lesser tree was, in fact, a tusk of ivory.

A spasm of excitement closed on his chest.

'Yes!' he said. 'Yes!'

Flynn planned his stalk with care, taking every precaution against the intervention of fate that twenty years of elephant hunting had taught him.

He had gone back to where Sebastian and Mohammed waited.

'He's there,' he told them.

'Can I come with you?' Sebastian pleaded.

'In a barrel you can,' snarled Flynn as he sat and pulled off his heavy boots to replace them with the light sandals that Mohammed produced from the pack. 'You stay here until you hear my shot. You so much as stick your nose over the ridge before that – and, so help me God, I'll shoot it off.'

While Mohammed knelt in front of Flynn and strapped the leather pads to his knees to protect them as he crawled over rock and thorn, Flynn fortified himself from the gin bottle. As he recorked it, he glowered at Sebastian again. 'That's a promise!' he said.

At the top of the ridge Flynn paused again with only his eyes lifted over the skyline, while he plotted his stalk, fixing in his memory a procession of landmarks – an ant-hill, an outcrop of white quartz, a tree festooned with weaver birds' nests – so that as he reached each of these he would know his exact position in relation to that of the elephant.

Then with the rifle cradled across the crook of his elbows he slid on his belly to begin the stalk.

Now, an hour after he had left the ridge, he saw before him through the grass a slab of granite like a headstone in an ancient cemetery. It stood square and weathered brown, and it was the end of the stalk.

He had marked it from the ridge as the point from which he would fire. It stood fifty yards from the wild fig-tree, at a right angle from the old bull's position. It would give him cover as he rose to his knees to make the shot.

Anxious now, suddenly overcome with a premonition of disaster – sensing that somehow the cup would be dashed from his lips, the maid plucked from under him before the moment of fulfillment, Flynn started forward. Slithering towards the granite headstone, his face set hard in nervous anticipation, he reached the rock.

He rolled carefully on to his side and, holding the heavy rifle against his chest, he slipped the catch across and eased the rifle open, so that the click of the mechanism was muted. From the belt around his waist he selected two fat cartridges and examined the brass casings for tarnish or denting; with relief he saw the fingers that held them were steadier. He slipped the cartridges into the blank eyes of the breeches, and they slid home against the seatings with a soft metallic plong. And now his breathing was faintly ragged at the end of each inhalation. He closed the rifle, and with his thumb pushed the safety-catch forward into the 'fire' position.

His shoulder against the rough, sun-heated granite, he drew up his legs against his belly and rolled gently on to his knees. With his head bowed low and the rifle in his lap, he knelt behind the rock, and for the first time in an hour he lifted his head. He brought it up with inching deliberation. Slowly the crystalline texture of the granite passed before his eyes, then suddenly he looked across fifty yards of open ground at his elephant.

It stood broadside to him but the head was hidden by the leaves and branches of the wild fig. The brain shot was impossible from here. His eyes moved down on to the shoulder and he saw the outline of the bone beneath the thick grey skin. He picked out the point of the elbow and his eyes moved back into the barrel of the chest. He could visualize the heart pulsing softly there beneath the ribs, pink and soft and vital, throbbing like a giant sea anemone.

He lifted the rifle, and laid it across the rock in front of him. He looked along the barrels, and saw the blade of dry grass that was wound around the bead of the foresight, obscuring it. He lowered the rifle and with his thumb-nail picked away the shred of grass. Again he lifted and sighted.

The black blob of the foresight lay snugly in the deep, wide vee of the backsight, he moved the gun, riding the bead down across the old bull's shoulder then back on to the chest. It lay there ready to kill, and he took up the slack in the trigger, gently, lovingly, with his forefinger.

The shout was faint, a tiny sound in the drowsy immensity of the hot African air. It came from the high ground above him.

'Flynn!' and again, 'Flynn!'

In an explosive burst of movement under the wild fig-tree, the old bull swung his body with unbelievable speed, his great tusks riding high, he went away from Flynn at an awkward shambling run, his flight covered by the trunk of the fig-tree.

For stunned seconds, Flynn crouched behind the boulder, and with each second the chances of a shot dwindled. Flynn jumped to his feet and ran out to one side of the fig-tree, opening his field of fire for a snap shot at the bull as he fled, a try for the spine where it curved down between the massive haunches to the tuftless tail.

Spiked agony stabbed up through the ball of his lightly shod foot, as he trod squarely on a three-inch buffalo thorn. Red-tipped, wickedly barbed, it buried its full length in his flesh, and he stumbled to his knees crying a protest at the pain.

Two hundred yards away, the old bull disappeared into one of the wooded ravines, and was gone.

'Flynn! Flynn!'

Sobbing in pain and frustration, his injured foot twisted up into his lap, Flynn sat in the grass and waited for Sebastian Oldsmith to come down to him.

'I'll let him get real close,' Flynn told himself. Sebastian was approaching with the long awkward strides of a man running downhill. He had lost his hat and the black tangled curls danced on his head at each stride. He was still shouting.

'I'll give it to him in the belly,' Flynn decided. 'Both barrels!' and he groped for the rifle that lay beside him.

Sebastian saw him and swerved in his run.

Flynn hefted the rifle. 'I warned him. I said I'd do it,' and his right hand settled around the pistol grip of the rifle, his forefinger instinctively hooking forward for the trigger.

'Flynn! Germans! A whole army of them. Just over the hill. Coming this way.'

'Christ!' said Flynn, immediately abandoning his homicidal intentions.

35

L ifting himself in the stirrups, Herman Fleischer reached behind to massage himself. His buttocks were of a plump, almost feminine, quantity and quality. After five hours in the saddle Herman longed to rest them. He had just crossed the ridge of the Sania Heights on his donkey, and it was cool here beneath the outspread branches of the wild fig-tree. He flirted with the temptation, decided to indulge himself, and turned to give the order to the troop of twenty Askari who stood behind him. All of them were watching him avidly, anticipating the order that would allow them to throw themselves down and relax.

'Lazy dogs!' thought Herman as he scowled at them. He turned away from them, settled his aching posterior gently on to the saddle and growled. 'Akwende! Let us go!' His heels thumped against the flanks of his donkey and it started forward at a trot.

From a crotch in the trunk of the fig-tree ten feet above Herman's head, Flynn O'Flynn viewed his departure over the double barrels of his rifle. He watched the patrol wind away down the slope and drop from sight over a fold in the ground before he put up the gun.

'Phew! That was close.' Sebastian's voice came from the leafy mass above Flynn.

'If he'd touched one foot to the ground, I'd have blown his bloody head off,' said Flynn. He sounded as though he regretted missing the opportunity. 'All right, Bassie, get me down out of this frigging tree.'

Fully dressed, except for his boots, Flynn sat against the base of the fig-tree and proffered his right foot to Sebastian. '. . . I had him right there in my sights.'

'Who?' asked Sebastian.

'The elephant, you idiot. For the first time I had him cold. And then . . . Yeow! What the hell are you doing?'

'I'm trying to get the thorn out, Flynn.'

'Feels like you're trying to knock it in with a hammer.'

'I can't get a grip on it.'

'Use your teeth. That's the only way,' Flynn instructed, and Sebastian paled a little at the thought. He considered Flynn's foot. It was a large foot; corns on the toes, flakes of loose skin and other darker matter between them. Sebastian could smell it at a range of three feet. 'Couldn't you reach it with your own teeth, Flynn?' he hedged.

'You think I'm a goddamned contortionist?'

'Mohammed?' Sebastian's eyes lit up with relief as he turned on the little gun-bearer. In answer to the question Mohammed drew back his lips in a death's head grin, exposing his smooth, pink toothless gums. 'Yes,' agreed Sebastian. 'I see what you mean.' He returned his gaze to the foot, and studied it with sickened fascination. His adam's apple bobbed as he swallowed.

'Get on with it,' said Flynn, and Sebastian stooped. There was a howl from Flynn, and Sebastian straightened up with the wet thorn gripped in his teeth. He spat it out explosively, and Mohammed handed him the gin bottle. Sebastian gargled from it loudly but when he lifted the bottle to his lips again, Flynn laid a restraining hand on his forearm. 'Now don't overdo it, Bassie boy,' he remonstrated mildly, retrieved the bottle and placed it to his own mouth. It seemed to refuel Flynn's anger, for when he removed the bottle his voice had fire in it. 'That goddamn sneaking, sausage-eating slug. He spoiled the only chance I've ever had at that elephant.' He paused to breathe heavily. 'I'd like to do something really nasty to him, like . . . like . . .' he searched for some atrocity to commit upon Herman Fleischer, and suddenly he found one. 'My God!' he said, and his scowl changed to a lovely smile. 'That's it!'

'What?' Sebastian was alarmed. He was certain that he would be selected as the vehicle of Flynn's revenge. 'What?' he repeated.

'We will go . . .' said Flynn, '. . . to Mahenge!'

'Good Lord, that's the German headquarters!'

'Yes,' said Flynn. 'With no Commissioner and no Askari to guard it! They've just passed us, heading in the opposite direction.'

36

They hit Mahenge two hours before dawn, in that time of utter darkness when mankind's vitality is at its lowest ebb. The defence put up by the corporal and five Askari whom Fleischer had left to guard his headquarters was hardly heroic. In fact, they were only half awakened by the lusty and indiscriminate use of Flynn's boot, and by the time they were fully conscious, they found themselves securely locked behind the bars of the jail-house. There was only one casualty. It was, of course, Sebastian Oldsmith, who, in the excitement, ran into a half-open door. It was fortunate, as Flynn pointed out, that he struck the door with his head, otherwise he may have done himself injury. But as it was, he had recovered sufficiently by sunrise to watch the orgy of looting and vandalism in which Flynn and his gun-bearers indulged themselves.

They began in the office of the Commissioner. Built into the thick adobe wall of the room was an enormous iron safe.

'We will open that first,' decreed Flynn as he eyed it greedily. 'See if you can find some tools.'

Sebastian remembered the blacksmith shop at the end of the parade ground. He returned from there laden with sledge-hammers and crow-bars.

Two hours later they were sweating and swearing in an atmosphere heavy with plaster dust. They had torn the safe from the wall, and it lay in the centre of the floor. Three of Flynn's gun-boys were beating on it with sledge-hammers in a steadily diminishing display of enthusiasm, while Sebastian worked with a crow-bar at the hinge joints. He had succeeded in inflicting a few bright scratches upon the metal. Flynn was seated on the Commissioner's desk, steadily working himself into a fury of frustration; for the last hour his contribution to the assault on the safe had been limited to consuming half a bottle of schnapps that he had found in a drawer of the desk.

'It's no use, Flynn.' Sebastian's curls were slick with perspiration, and he licked at the blisters on the palms of his hands. 'We will just have to forget about it.'

'Stand back!' roared Flynn. 'I'll shoot the goddamned thing open.' He rose from the desk wild-eyed, his double-barrelled Gibbs clutched in his hands.

'Wait!' shouted Sebastian and he and the gun-bearers scattered for cover.

The detonations of the heavy rifle were thunderous in the confined space of the office; gun-smoke mingled with the plaster dust, and the bullets ricocheted off the metal of the safe, leaving long smears of lead upon it, before whining away to embed themselves in the floor, wall and furniture.

This act of violence seemed to placate Flynn. He lost interest in the safe. 'Let's go and find something to eat,' he said mildly, and they trooped through to the kitchens.

Once Flynn had shot away the lock, Herman Fleischer's larder proved to be an Aladdin's cave of delight. The roof was hung with hams and polonies and sausages, there were barrels of pickled meats, stacks of fat round cheeses, cases of Hansa beer, cases of cognac, pyramids of canned truffles, asparagus tips, pâté, shrimps, mushrooms, olives in oil, and other rarities.

They stared at this profusion in awe, and then moved forward together. Each man to his own particular tastes, they fell upon Herman Fleischer's treasure house. The gun-boys rolled out a cask of pickled pork, Sebastian started with his hunting knife on the cans, while Flynn devoted himself on the case of Steinhager in the corner.

It took two hours of dedicated eating and drinking for them to reach saturation point.

'We'd better get ready to move on now,' Sebastian belched softly, and Flynn nodded owlish agreement, the movement spilling a little Steinhager down his bush jacket. He wiped at it with his hand and then licked his fingers.

'Yep! Best we are gone before Fleischer gets home.' He looked at Mohammed. 'Make up full loads of food for each of the bearers. What you can't carry away we'll dump in the latrine buckets.' He stood up carefully. 'I'll just have a look round, and make sure we haven't missed anything important,' and he went out through the door with unsteady dignity.

In Fleischer's office he stood for a minute regarding the invulnerable safe balefully. It was certainly much too heavy to carry away, and abandoning the notion with regret, he looked around for some outlet for his frustration.

There was a portrait of the Kaiser on the entrance wall, a colour print showing the Emperor in full dress, mounted on a magnificent cavalry charger. Flynn picked up an indelible pencil from the desk and walked across to the picture. With a dozen strokes of the pencil he drastically altered the relationship between horse and rider. Then, beginning to chuckle, he printed on the whitewashed wall below the picture, 'The Kaiser loves horses.'

This struck him as being such a pearl of wit, that he had to summon Sebastian and show it to him. 'That's what you call being subtle Bassie, boy. All good jokes are subtle.'

It seemed to Sebastian that Flynn's graffiti were as subtle as the charge of an enraged rhinoceros but he laughed dutifully. This encouraged Flynn to a further essay in humour. He had two of the gun bearers carry in a bucket from the latrines, and under his supervision, they propped it above the half-open door of Herman Fleischer's bedroom.

An hour later, heavily laden with booty, the raiding party left Mahenge and began the first of a series of forced marches aimed at the Rovuma river.

37

I n a state of mental confusion induced by a superfluity of adrenalin in the bloodstream, Herman Fleischer wandered through his ransacked boma. As he discovered each new outrage he regarded it with slitted eyes and laboured breathing. But first it was necessary to effect a jail-break in reverse in order to free his own captive Askari. When they emerged through the hole in the prison wall, Herman curtly ordered his sergeant to administer twenty strokes of the kiboko to each of them, as a token rebuke for their inefficiency. He stood by and drew a little comfort from the solid slap of the kiboko on bare flesh and the shrieks of the recipient.

However, the calming effect of the floggings evaporated when Herman entered the kitchen area of his establishment, and found that his larder of painstakingly accumulated foodstuffs was now empty. This nearly broke his spirit. His jowls quivered with self-pity, and from under his tongue saliva oozed in melancholic nostalgia. It would take a month to replace the sausages alone, heaven knew how long to replace the cheeses imported from the fatherland.

From the larder he went through to his office and found Flynn's subtleties. Herman's sense of humour was not equal to the occasion.

'Pig-swine, English bastard,' he muttered dejectedly, and a dark wave of despair and fatigue washed over him as he realized the futility of setting out in pursuit of the raiders. With two days start he could never hope to catch them before they reached the Rovuma. If only Governor Schee, who was so forthcoming with criticism, would allow him to cross the river one night with his Askari and visit the community at Lalapanzi. There would be no one left the following morning to make complaint to the Portuguese Government about breach of sovereignty.

Herman sighed. He was tired and depressed. He would go to his bed now and rest a while before supervising the tidying up of his headquarters. He left the office and plodded heavily along the stoep to his private quarters, and pushed open the door of his bedroom.

His bedroom temporarily uninhabitable, Herman reposed that night on the open stoep. But his sleep was disturbed by a dream in which he pursued Flynn O'Flynn across an endless plain without ever narrowing the gap between them, while above him circled two huge birds – one with the austere face of Governor Schee, and the other with the face of the young English bandit – at regular intervals these two voided their bowels on him. After the previous afternoon's experience the olfactory hallucinations which formed part of the dream were horribly realistic.

He was tactfully awakened by one of his household servants, and struggled up in bed with an ache behind his eyes and a foul taste in his mouth.

'What is it?' he growled.

'There is a bearer from Dodoma who brings a book with the red mark of the Bwana Mkuba upon it.'

Herman groaned. An envelope with Governor Schee's seal affixed to it usually meant trouble. Surely he could not so speedily have learned about Flynn O'Flynn's latest escapade.

'Bring coffee!'

'Lord, there is no coffee. It was all stolen,' and Herman groaned again.

'Very well. Bring the messenger.' He would have to endure the ordeal of Governor Schee's rebukes without the fortifying therapy of a cup of coffee. He broke the seal and began to read:

4th August, 1914.
The Residency,
Dar es Salaam.

To The Commissioner (Southern Province)
At: Mahenge.
Sir,

It is my duty to inform you that a state of war now exists between the Empire and the Governments of England, France, Russia, and Portugal.

You are hereby appointed temporary Military Commander of the Southern Province of German East Africa, with orders to take whatever steps you deem necessary for the protection of our borders, and the confusion of the enemy.

In due course a military force, now being assembled at Dar es Salaam, will be despatched to your area. But I fear that there will be a delay before this can be achieved.

In the meantime, you must operate with the force presently at your disposal.

There was more, much more, but Herman Fleischer read the detailed instructions with perfunctory attention. His headache was forgotten, the taste in his mouth unnoticed in the fierce surge of warrior passions that arose within him.

His chubby features puckered with smiles, he looked up from the letter and spoke aloud. 'Ja, O'Flynn, now I will pay you for the bucket.'

He turned back to the first page of the letter, and his mouth formed the words as he read '. . . whatever steps you deem necessary for the protection of our borders, and the confusion of the enemy.'

At last. At last he had the order for which he had pleaded so many times. He shouted for his sergeant.

38

'**P**erhaps they will come home tonight.' Rosa Oldsmith looked up from the child's smock she was embroidering.

'Tonight, or tomorrow, or the next day,' Nanny replied philosophically. 'There is no profit in guessing at the coming or going of men. They all have worms in their heads,' and she began again to rock the cradle, squatting beside it on the leopard-skin rugs like an animated mummy. The child snuffled a little in its sleep.

'I'm sure it will be tonight. I can feel it – something good is going to happen.' Rosa laid aside her sewing and crossed to the door that led out on to the stoep. In the last few minutes the sun had gone down below the trees, and the land was ghostly quiet in the brief African dusk.

Rosa went out on to the stoep, and hugging her arms across her chest at the chill of evening, she stared out down the darkening length of the valley. She stood there, waiting restlessly, and as the day passed swiftly into darkness, so her mood changed from anticipation to a formless foreboding.

Quietly, but with an edge to her voice, she called back into the room, 'Light the lamps please, Nanny.'

Behind her she heard the sounds of metal on glass, then the flare of a sulphur match, and a feeble yellow square of light was thrown out on to the veranda to fall around her feet.

The first puff of the night wind was cold on her bare arms. She felt the prickle of goose-flesh and she shivered unexpectedly.

'Come inside, Little Long Hair,' Nanny ordered. 'The night is for mosquitoes and leopards – and other things.'

But Rosa lingered, straining her eyes into the darkness until she could no longer see the shape of the fig-trees at the bottom of the lawn. Then abruptly she turned away and went into the bungalow. She closed the door and slid the bolt across.

Later she woke. There was no moon outside and the room was dark. Beside her bed she could hear the soft, piglet sounds that little Maria made in her sleep.

Again the disquieting mood of the early evening returned to her and she lay still in her bed, waiting and listening in the utter blackness, and the darkness bore down upon her so that she felt herself shrinking, receding, becoming remote from reality, small and lonely in the night.

In fear then she lifted the mosquito netting and groped for the cradle. The baby whimpered as she lifted her and brought her into the bed beside her, but Rosa's arms quietened her and soon she slept against the breast, and the warmth of the tiny body stilled Rosa's own agitation.

The shouting woke her, and she opened her eyes with a surge of joy, for the shouts would be Sebastian's bearers. Before she was fully awake she had thrown aside the bedclothes, struggled out from under the mosquito netting, and was standing in her night-dress with the baby clasped to her chest.

It was then that she realized that the room was no longer in darkness. From the window into the yard it was lit by a red-gold glow that flared, and flickered, and faded.

The last tarnish of sleep was cleaned from her brain, so she could hear that the shouts from outside were not those of welcome, and on a lower key, there were other sounds – a whispering, rustling, and popping, that she could not identify.

She crossed to the window, moving slowly, with dread for what she might find, but before she reached it a scream froze her. It came from the kitchen yard, a scream that quivered on the air long after it had ended, a scream of terror and of pain.

'Merciful God!' she whispered, and forced herself to peer out.

The servants' quarters and the outhouses were on fire. From the thatch of each the flames stood up in writhing yellow columns, lighting the darkness.

There were men in the yard, many men, and all of them wore the khaki uniform of German Askari. Each of them carried a rifle, and the bayonet blades glittered in the glare of the flames.

'They have crossed the river – No, oh please God, no!' and Rosa hugged the baby to her, crouching down below the window sill.

The scream rang out again, but weaker now, and she saw a knot of four Askari crowded around something that squirmed in the dust of the yard. She heard their laughter, the excited laughter of men who kill for fun, as they stabbed down on the squirming thing with their bayonets.

At that moment another of the servants broke from the burning outbuildings and ran for the darkness beyond the circle of the flames. Shouting again, the Askari left the dying man and chased the other. They turned him like a pack of trained grey-hounds coursing a gazelle, laughing and shouting in their excitement, and drove him back into the daylight glare of the flames.

Bewildered, surrounded, the servant stopped and looked wildly about him, his face convulsed with terror. Then the Askari swarmed over him, clubbing and hacking with their rifles.

'Oh, oh God, no,' Rosa's whisper sobbed in her throat, but she could not drag her eyes away.

Suddenly in the uproar she heard a new voice, a bull-bellow of authority. She could not understand the words for they were shouted in German but from around the angle of the bungalow appeared a white man, a massive figure in the blue corduroy uniform of the German Colonial Service, with a slouch hat pulled low down on his head, and a pistol brandished in one hand. From the description that Sebastian had given her, she recognized the German Commissioner.

'Stop them!' Rosa did not speak aloud, the appeal was in her mind only. 'Please, stop them burning and killing.'

The white man was railing at his Askari, his face turned towards where Rosa crouched and she saw it was round and pink like that of an overweight baby. In the fire-light it glistened with a fine sheen of sweat.

'Stop them. Please stop them,' Rosa pleaded silently, but under the Commissioner's direction three of the Askari ran to where, in the excitement of the chase, they had dropped their torches of dry grass. While they lit them from the flaming outbuildings, the other Askari left the corpses of the two servants and spread out in a circle around the bungalow, facing inwards, with their rifles held at high port. Most of the bayonets were dulled with blood.

'I want Fini and the Singese – not bearers and gun-boys – I want the white men! Burn them out!' shouted Fleischer, but Rosa recognized only her father's name. She wanted to cry out that he was not here, that it was only her and the child.

The three Askari were running in towards the bungalow now, sparks and fire smeared back from the torches they carried. In turn each man checked his run, poised himself like a javelin thrower, then hurled his torch in a high, smoking arc towards the bungalow. Rosa heard them thump, thump, thump, on to the thatched roof above her.

'I must get my baby away, before the fire catches,' and she hurried across the room, out into the passage. It was dark here and she groped along the wall until she found the entrance to the main room. At the front door she fumbled with the bolts, and opened it a crack. Peering through to the fire-lit lawns beyond the stoep, she saw the dark forms of Askari waiting there also, and she drew back.

'The side windows of the kitchen,' she told herself. 'They're closest to the bush. That's the best chance,' and she stumbled back into the passage.

Above her now there was a sound like high wind and water, a rushing sound blending with the crackle of burning thatch, and the first taint of smoke stung her nostrils.

'If only I can reach the bush,' she whispered desperately, and the child in her arms began to cry.

'Hush, my darling, hush now,' but her voice was scratchy with fear. Maria seemed to sense it; her petulant whimperings changed to lusty high-pitched yells and she struggled in Rosa's grasp.

From the side windows of the kitchen Rosa saw the familiar waiting figures of the Askari hovering at the edge of the fire-light. She felt despair catch her stomach in a cold grip and squeeze the resolve from her. Suddenly her legs were weak under her and her whole body was shaking.

From within the bungalow behind her there came a thunderous roar as part of the burning roof collapsed. A blast of scalding air blew through the kitchen and the tall column of sparks and flames thrown up by the collapse lit the surroundings even more vividly. It showed another figure beyond the line of Askari, scampering in from the edge of the bush like a little black monkey, and Rosa heard Nanny's voice.

'Little Long Hair! Little Long Hair.' A plaintive, ancient wail.

Nanny had escaped into the bush during the first minutes of the attack. She had lain there watching until the roof of the bungalow fell in – then she could no longer contain herself. Insensible of her own danger, caring for nothing except her precious charges, she was coming back.

The Askari saw her also. Their rigid, well-spaced line crumpled as all of them ran to head her off. Suddenly the ground between Rosa and the edge of the bush was clear. Now there was a chance – just the smallest chance that she could get the child away. She flung the window open and dropped through it to the earth.

One moment she hesitated and glanced towards the confusion of running men away on her right hand. In that moment she saw one of the Askari catch up with the old woman and lunge forward with his bayonet. Nanny reeled from the force of the blow in her back. Involuntarily her arms were flung wide open, and for a fleeting second Rosa saw the point of the bayonet appear miraculously from the centre of her chest, as it impaled her.

Then Rosa was running towards the wall of bush and scrub fifty yards ahead of her, while Maria howled in her arms. The sound attracted the attention of the Askari. One of them shouted a warning, and then the whole pack was after her in full tongue.

Rosa's senses were overwrought by her terror, so finely tuned that it seemed the passage of time was lagging. Weighed down by the child, each pace she took dragged on for ever, as though she waded through waist-deep water. The long night-dress around her legs hampered her, and there was rough stone and thorn beneath her bare feet. The wall of bush ahead of her seemed to come no closer, and she ran with the cold hand of fear squeezing her chest and cramping her breathing.

Then into her line of vision from the side came a man, an Askari, a big man bounding towards her with the long loping gallop of a bull baboon, cutting across her line of flight, his open mouth, an obscene pink pit in the shiny black of his face.

Rosa screamed and swung away from him. Now she was running parallel to the edge of the bush and behind her she heard the slap of feet upon the earth, closing fast, and the babbling chorus of the pursuit.

A hand snatched at her shoulder, and she twisted away from it, feeling the stuff of her night-gown tear beneath the clutching fingers.

Blind with terror she stumbled a dozen paces back towards the burning homestead. She felt the vast waves of heat from it in her face and through her thin clothing – and then a rifle butt struck her in the small of the back, and a bright burst of agony paralysed her legs. She dropped to her knees, still holding Maria.

They ringed her in, a palisade of human bodies and gloating, blood-crazed faces.

The big one who had felled her with the rifle butt stooped over her and before she recognized his intention, he had snatched Maria from her arms and stepped back again.

He stood laughing, holding the child by her ankles, letting her swing head downwards, so her tiny face was suffused with blood, scarlet in the light of the flames.

'No, please, no!' Rosa crawled painfully towards the man. 'Give her back to me. My baby. Please give her back,' and she lifted her arms towards him.

The Askari dangled the child tantalizingly in front of her, retreating slowly as she crawled towards him. The others were laughing, hoarse sensual laughter, crowding around her, faces contorted with enjoyment, and polished ebony black with the sweat of excitement, as they jostled each other for a better view of the sport.

Then with a wild yell, the Askari swung Maria high, whirled her twice above his head as he pivoted to face the bungalow – and threw Maria up towards the burning roof.

The tiny body flew with the looseness of a rag doll through the air, her night-dress fluttered as she dropped and struck the roof, rolled awkwardly down the slope of it with her clothing blooming into instant flame, until she reached a weak spot in the burning thatch. It sucked Maria in like a fiery mouth and blew a belch of sparks as it swallowed her. At that instant Rosa heard the voice of her child for the last time. It was a sound she was never to forget.

For a moment the men about her were hushed, and then as though wind blew through trees, they moved a little with a sound that was half sigh, half moan.

Still kneeling, facing the burning building which was now a pyre, Rosa slumped forward and lifted her hands to cover her face as though in prayer.

The Askari who had thrown the child snatched up his rifle from where it lay at his feet and stood over her. He lifted it above his head the way a harpooner holds his steel with the point of the bayonet aimed at the base of Rosa's neck where her hair had fallen open to expose the pale skin.

In the moment that the Askari paused to take his aim, Herman Fleischer shot him in the back of the head with the Luger.

'Mad dog!' the Commissioner shouted at the Askari's corpse. 'I told you to take them alive.'

Then, breathing like an asthma case from the exertion of his run to intervene, he turned to Rosa.

'Fräulein, my apologies,' he doffed the slouch hat with ponderous courtesy, and spoke in German that Rosa did not understand. 'We do not make war on women and babies.'

She did not look up at him. She was crying quietly into her cupped hands.

39

'E arly in the year for a bush fire,' Flynn muttered. He sat with an enamel mug cupped in his hands and blew steam from the hot coffee. His blanket had slid down to his waist.

Across the camp-fire from him Sebastian was also sitting in a muddle of bedding, and cooling his own pre-dawn mug of coffee. At Flynn's words he looked up from his labour, and out into the dark south.

False dawn had paled the sky just enough to define the hills below it as an undulating mass that seemed much closer than it was. That way lay Lalapanzi – and Rosa and Maria.

Without real interest Sebastian saw the radiated glow at one point along the spine of the ridge; a fan of pink light no larger than a thumb-nail.

'Not a very big one,' he said.

'No,' agreed Flynn. 'Hope she doesn't spread though,' and he gulped noisily at his mug.

As Sebastian watched it idly, the glow diminished, shrinking into insignificance at the coming of the sun, and above it the stars paled out also.

'We'd best get moving. It's a long day's march and we've wasted enough time on this trip already.'

'You're a regular bloody fire-eater when it comes to getting your home comforts.' Flynn feigned disinterest, yet secretly the thought of returning to his granddaughter had strong appeal. He hurried the coffee a little and scalded his tongue.

Sebastian was right. They had wasted a lot of time on the return trip from the Mahenge raid.

First, there was a detour to avoid a party of German Askari that one of the native headmen had warned them was at M'topo's village. They had trekked upstream for three days before finding a safe crossing, and a village willing to hire canoes.

Then there was the brush with the hippo which had cost them almost a week. As was usual practice, the four hired canoes, loaded to within a few inches of free-board with Flynn, Sebastian, their retinue and loot, had slipped across the Rovuma and were hugging the Portuguese bank as they headed downstream towards the landing opposite M'topo's village when the hippo had disputed their passage.

She was an old cow hippo who a few hours earlier had given birth to her calf in a tiny island of reeds, separated from the south bank by twenty feet of lily-padded water. When the four canoes entered this channel in line astern with the paddlers chanting happily, she took it as a direct threat to her offspring and she threw a tantrum.

Two tons of hippo in a tantrum has the destructive force of a localized hurricane. Surfacing violently from under the leading canoe, she had thrown Sebastian, two gun-boys, four paddlers, and all their equipment, ten feet in the air. The canoe, rotted with beetle, had snapped in half and sunk immediately.

The mother hippo had then treated the three following canoes with the same consideration, and within the space of a few minutes, the canal was clogged with floating debris, and struggling, panic-stricken men. Fortunately they were no more than ten feet from the bank. Sebastian was first ashore. None of them, however, was very far behind him, and they all took off like the start of a cross-country race over the veld, when the hippo emerged from the river and signified that, not satisfied with wrecking the flotilla, she intended chopping a few of them in half with her guillotine jaws.

A hundred yards later she abandoned the pursuit, and trotted back to the water, wiggling her little ears and snorting in triumph. Half a mile farther on the survivors had stopped running.

They camped there that night without food, bedding or weapons, and the following morning, after a heated council of war, Sebastian was elected to return to the river and ascertain whether the hippo was still in control of the channel. He came back at high speed to report that she was.

Three more days they waited for the hippo and her calf to move away. During this time they suffered the miseries of cold nights and hungry days, but the greatest misery was inflicted on Flynn O'Flynn whose case of gin was under eight feet of water – and by the third morning he was threatening *delirium tremens* again. Just before Sebastian set off for his morning reconnaissance of the channel, Flynn informed him agitatedly that there were three blue scorpions sitting on his head. After the initial alarm, Sebastian went through the motions of removing the imaginary scorpions and stamping them to death, and Flynn was satisfied.

Sebastian returned from the river with the news that the hippo and her calf had evacuated the island, and it was now possible to begin salvage operations.

Protesting mildly and talking about crocodiles, Sebastian was stripped naked and coaxed into the water. On his first dive, he retrieved the precious case of gin.

'Bless you, my boy,' Flynn murmured fervently as he eased the cork out of a bottle.

By the following morning Sebastian had recovered nearly all their equipment and booty, without being eaten by crocodiles, and they set off for Lalapanzi on foot.

Now they were in their last camp before Lalapanzi, and Sebastian felt his impatience rising. He wanted to get home to Rosa and baby Maria. He should be home by evening.

'Come on, Flynn. Let's go.' He flicked the coffee grounds from his mug, threw aside his blanket, and shouted to Mohammed and the bearers who were huddled around the other fire.

'Safari! Let us march.'

Nine hours later, with the daylight dying around him, he breasted the last rise and paused at the top.

All that day eagerness had lengthened his stride, and he had left Flynn and the column of heavily laden bearers far behind.

Now he stood alone, and stared without comprehension at the smoke-blackened ruins of Lalapanzi from which a few thin tendrils of smoke still drifted.

'Rosa!' Her name was a harsh bellow of fear, and he ran wildly.

'Rosa!' he shouted as he crossed the scorched and trampled lawns.

'Rosa! Rosa! Rosa!' the echo from the kopje above the homestead shouted back.

'Rosa!' He saw something amongst the bushes at the edge of the lawn, and he ran to it. Old Nanny lying dead with the blood dried black on the floral stuff of her nightgown.

'Rosa!' He ran back towards the bungalow. The ash swirled in a warm mist around his legs as he crossed the stoep.

'Rosa!' His voice rang hollowly through the roofless shell of the house, as he stumbled over the fallen beams that littered the main room. The reek of burned cloth and hair and wood almost choked him, so that his voice was husky as he called again.

'Rosa!'

He found her in the burnt-out kitchen block and he thought she was dead. She was slumped against the cracked and blackened wall. Her night-gown was torn and scorched, and the snarled skeins of hair, that hid her face, were powdered with white wood ash.

'My darling. Oh, my darling.' He knelt beside her, and timidly touched her shoulder. Her flesh was warm and alive beneath his fingers, and he felt relief leap up into his throat, blocking it so he could not speak again. Instead, he brushed the tangle of hair from her face and looked at it.

Beneath the charcoal smears of dirt her skin was pale as grey marble. Her eyes, tight closed, were heavily underscored with blue, and rimmed with crusty red.

He touched her lips with the tips of his fingers, and she opened her eyes, But they looked beyond him; unseeing, dead eyes. They frightened him. He did not want to look into them, and he drew her head towards his shoulder.

There was no resistance in her. She lay against him quietly, and he pressed his face into her hair. Her hair was impregnated with the smell of smoke.

'Are you hurt?' he asked her in a whisper, not wanting to hear the answer. But she made no answer, lying inert in his arms.

'Tell me, Rosa. Speak to me. Where is Maria?'

At the mention of the child's name, she reacted for the first time. She began to tremble.

'Where is she?' more urgency in his voice now.

She rolled her head against his shoulder and looked across the floor of the room. He followed the direction of her gaze.

Near the far wall an area of the floor had been swept clear of debris and ash. Rosa had done it with her bare hands while the ash was still hot. Her fingers were blistered and burned raw in places, and her arms were black to the elbows. Lying in the centre of this cleared space was a small, charred thing.

'Maria?' Sebastian whispered, and Rosa shuddered against him.

'Oh, God,' he said, and lifted Rosa. Carrying her against his chest, he staggered from the ruins of the bungalow out into the cool, sweet evening air, but in his nostrils lingered the smell of smoke and burned flesh. He wanted to escape from it. He ran blindly along the path and Rosa lay unresisting in his arms.

40

T he following day Flynn buried their dead on the kopje above Lalapanzi. He placed a thick slab of granite over the small grave that stood apart from the others, and when it was done he sent a bearer to the camp to fetch Rosa and Sebastian.

When they came, they found him standing alone by Maria's grave under the marula trees. His face was puffy and purply red. The thinning grey hair hung limply over his ears and forehead, like the wet feathers of an old rooster. His body looked as though it was melting. It sagged at the shoulders and the belly. Sweat had soaked through his clothing across the shoulders, and at the armpits and crotch. He was sick with drink and sorrow.

Sebastian stood beside Rosa, and the three of them took their silent farewell of the child.

'There is nothing else to do now,' Sebastian spoke huskily.

'Yes,' said Flynn. He stooped slowly and took a handful of the new earth from the grave. 'Yes, there is.' He crumbled the earth between his fingers. 'We still have to find the man who did this – and kill him.'

Beside Sebastian, Rosa straightened up. She turned to Sebastian, lifted her chin, and spoke for the first time since he had come home.

'Kill him!' she repeated softly.

Part Two

41

W ith his hands clasped behind his back, and his chin thrust forward aggressively, Rear-Admiral Sir Percy Howe sucked in his lower lip and nibbled it reflectively. 'What was our last substantiated sighting on *Blücher*?' he asked at last.

'A month ago, sir. Two days before the outbreak of war. Sighting reported by *S.S. Tygerberg*. Latitude 0°27hN. Longitude 52°16hE. Headed south-west; estimated speed, eighteen knots.'

'And a hell of a lot of good that does us,' Sir Percy interrupted his flag-captain and glared at the vast Admiralty plot of the Indian Ocean. 'She could be back in Bremerhaven by now.'

'She could be, sir,' the flag-captain nodded, and Sir Percy glanced at him and permitted himself a wintry smile.

'But you don't believe that, do you, Henry?'

'No, sir, I don't. During the last thirty days, eight merchantmen have disappeared between Aden and Lourenco Marques. Nearly a quarter of a million tons of shipping. That's the *Blücher*'s work.'

'Yes, it's the *Blücher*, all right,' agreed the Admiral, and reached across the plot to pick up the black counter labelled '*Blücher*', that lay on the wide green expanse of the Indian Ocean.

A respectful silence held the personnel of the plotting room South Atlantic and Indian Oceans while they waited for the great man to reach his decision. It was a long time coming. He stood bouncing the '*Blücher*' in the palm of his right hand, his grey eyebrows erect like the spines of a hedgehog's back, as his forehead creased in thought. A full minute they waited.

'Refresh my memory of her class and commission.' Like most successful men Sir Percy would not hurry a decision when there was time to think, and the duty lieutenant who had anticipated his request, stepped forward with the German Imperial Navy list open at the correct page.

' "*Blücher*. Commissioned August 16, 1905. 'B' Class heavy cruiser. Main armament, eight nine-inch guns. Secondary armament, six six-inch guns." '

The lieutenant finished his reading and waited quietly.

'Who is her captain?' Sir Percy asked, and the lieutenant consulted an addendum to the list.

' "Otto von Kleine (Count). Previously commanded the light cruiser *Sturm Vogel*." '

'Yes,' said Sir Percy. 'I've heard of him,' and he replaced the counter on the plot, keeping his hand on it. 'A dangerous man to have here, south of Suez,' and he pushed the counter up towards the Red Sea and the entrance to the canal, where the tiny red shipping lanes amalgamated into a thick artery, ' – or here,' and he pushed it down towards the Cape of Good Hope, around which were curved the same red threads that joined London to Australia and India. Sir Percy lifted his hand from the black counter and left it sitting menacingly upon the shipping lanes.

'What force have we deployed against him so far?' and in answer the flag-captain picked up a wooden pointer and touched in turn the red counters that were scattered about the Indian Ocean.

'*Pegasus* and *Renounce* in the north. *Eagle* and *Plunger* sweeping the southern waters, sir.'

'What further force can we spare, Henry?'

'Well, sir, *Orion* and *Bloodhound* are at Simonstown,' and he touched the nose of the African continent with the pointer.

'*Orion* – that's Manderson, isn't it?'

'Yes, sir.'

'And who has *Bloodhound*?'

'Little, sir.'

'Good,' Sir Percy nodded with satisfaction. 'A six-inch cruiser and a destroyer should be able to deal with *Blücher*', and he smiled again. 'Especially with a hellion like Charles Little handling the *Bloodhound*. I played golf with him last summer – he damn nigh drove the sixteenth green at St Andrews!'

The flag-captain glanced at the Admiral and, on the strength of the destroyer captain's reputation, decided to permit himself an inanity. 'The young ladies of Cape Town will mourn his departure, sir.'

'We must hope that Kapitän zur See Otto von Kleine will mourn his arrival,' chuckled Sir Percy.

'Daddy likes you very much.'

'Your father is a man of exquisite good taste,' Commander the Honourable Charles Little conceded gallantly, and rolled his head to smile at the young lady who lay beside him on a rug, in the dappled shade beneath the pine trees.

'Can't you ever be serious?'

'Helen, my sweet, at times I can be deadly serious.'

'Oh, you!' and his companion blushed prettily as she remembered certain of Charles's recent actions, which would make her father hastily revise his judgement.

'I value your father's good opinion, but my chief concern is that you endorse it.'

The girl sat up slowly and while she stared at him her hands were busy, brushing the pine needles from the glorious tangle of her hair, readjusting the fastenings of her blouse, spreading the skirts of her riding-habit to cover sweet legs clad in dark, tall polished leather boots.

She stared at Charles Little and ached with the strength of her want. It was not a sensual need she felt, but an over-powering obsession to have this man as her very own. To own him in the same way as she already owned diamonds, and furs, and silk, and horses, and peacocks, and other beautiful things.

His body sprawled out on the rug with all the unconscious grace of a reclining leopard. A secret little smile tugged at the corners of his lips and his eyelids drooped to mask the sparkle of his eyes. His recent exertions had dampened the hair that flopped forward onto his forehead.

There was something satanical about him, an air of wickedness, and Helen decided it was the slant of the eyebrows and the way his ears lay flat against his temples, but were pointed like those of a satyr, yet they were pink and smooth as those of an infant.

'I think you have devil's ears,' she said, and then she blushed again, and scrambled to her feet avoiding Charles' arm that reached out for her. 'Enough of that!' she giggled and ran to the thoroughbred hunter that was tied near them in the forest. 'Come on,' she called as she mounted.

Charles stood up lazily and stretched. He tucked the tail of his shirt into his breeches, folded the rug on which they had lain, and went to his own horse.

At the edge of the pine forest, they checked their mounts and sat looking down over the Constantia valley.

'Isn't it beautiful?' she said.

'It is indeed,' he agreed.

'I meant the view.'

'And so did I.' Twice in the six days he had known her, she had led him up this mountain and subjected him to the temptation. Below them lay six thousand acres of the richest land in all of Africa.

'When my brother Hubert was killed there was no one left to carry it on. Just my sister and I – and we are only girls. Poor Daddy isn't so well any more – he finds it such a strain.'

Charles let his eyes move lazily from the great squat buttress of Table Mountain on their left, across the lush basin of vineyards below them, and then on to where the glittering wedge of False Bay drove into the mountains.

'Doesn't the homestead look lovely from here?' Helen drew his attention to the massive Dutch-gabled residence with its attendant outbuildings, grouped in servility behind it.

'I am truly impressed by the magnificence of the stud fee,' Charles murmured, purposefully slurring the last two words, and the girl glanced at him in surprise, beginning to bridle.

'I beg your pardon?'

'It is truly magnificent scenery,' he amended. Her persistent efforts at ensnaring him were beginning to bore Charles. He had teased and avoided more artful huntresses.

'Charles,' she whispered. 'How would you like to live here. I mean, forever?'

And Charles was shocked. This little provincial had no understanding whatsoever of the rules governing the game of flirtation. He was so shocked that he threw back his head and laughed.

When Charles laughed it sent shivers of delight through every woman within a hundred yards. It was a merry sound with underlying tones of sensuality. His teeth were very white against the sea-tan of his face, and the muscles of his chest and upper arms tensed into bold relief beneath the silk shirt he wore.

Helen was the only witness of this particular performance, and she was helpless as a sparrow in a hurricane. Eagerly she leaned across the space between their horses and touched his arm. 'You would like it, Charles. Wouldn't you?'

She did not know that Charles Little had a private income of twenty thousand pounds a year, that when his father died he would inherit the title Viscount Sutherton and the estates that went with it. She did not know that one of those estates would swallow her father's own three times over; nor did she know that Charles had passed by willing young ladies with twice her looks, ten times her fortune, and a hundred times her breeding.

'You would, Charles. I know you would!'

So young, so vulnerable, that he stopped the flippant reply before it reached his lips.

'Helen,' he took her hand. 'I am a sea creature. We move with the wind and the waves,' and he lifted her hand to his lips.

A while she sat, feeling the warm pressure of his lips upon her flesh, and the burn of tears behind her eyes. Then she snatched her hand away, and wheeled her horse. She lifted the leather riding-crop and slashed the glossy black shoulder between her knees. Startled, the stallion jumped forward into a dead run back along the road towards the Constantia valley.

Charles shook his head and grimaced with regret. He had not meant to hurt her. It had been an escapade, something to fill the waiting days while *Bloodhound* went through the final stages of her refit. But Charles had learned to harden himself to the ending of his adventures – to the tears and tragedy.

'Shame on you, you heartless cad,' he said aloud, and touching his mount with his heels ambled in pursuit of the galloping stallion.

He caught up with the stallion in the stable yards. A groom was walking it, and there were darker sweat patches on its coat, and the barrel of its chest still heaved with laboured breathing.

Helen was nowhere in sight, but her father stood at the stable gates – a big man, with a square-cut black beard picked out with grey.

'Enjoy your ride?'

'Thank you, Mr Uys.' Charles was noncommittal, and the older man glanced significantly at the blown stallion before going on.

'There's one of your sailors been waiting for you for an hour.'

'Where is he?' Charles's manner altered abruptly, became instantly businesslike.

'Here, sir.' From the deep shade of the stable doorway, a young seaman stepped out into the bright sunlight.

'What is it, man?' Impatiently Charles acknowledged his salute.

'Captain Manderson's compliments, sir, and you're to report aboard H.M.S. *Orion* with all possible speed. There's a motor car waiting to take you to the base, sir.'

'An untimely summons, Commander.' Uys gave his opinion lounging against the worked stone gateway. 'I fear we will see no more of you for a long time.'

But Charles was not listening. His body seemed to quiver with suppressed excitement, the way a good gun-dog reacts to the scent of the bird. 'Sailing orders,' he whispered, ' — at last. At last!'

There was a heavy south-east swell battering Cape Point, so the sea spray wreathed the beam of the lighthouse on the cliffs above. A flight of malgas came in so high towards the land that they caught the last of the sun, and glowed pink above the dark water.

Bloodhound cleared Cape Hangklip and took the press of the South Atlantic on her shoulder, staggered from it with a welter of white water running waist-deep past her foredeck gun-turrets. Then in retaliation she hurled herself at the next swell, and Charles Little on her bridge exulted at the vital movement of the deck beneath his feet.

'Bring her round to oh-five-oh.'

'Oh-five-oh, sir,' repeated his navigating lieutenant.

'Revolutions for seventeen knots, pilot.'

Almost immediately the beat of the engines changed, and her action through the water became more abandoned.

Charles crossed to the angle of the flimsy little bridge and looked back into the dark, mountain-lined maw of False Bay. Two miles astern the shape of H.M.S. *Orion* melted into the dying light.

'Come along, old girl. Do try and keep up,' murmured Charles Little with the scorn that a destroyer man feels for any vessel that cannot cruise at twenty knots. Then he looked beyond *Orion* at the land. Below the massif of Table Mountain, near the head of the Constantia valley a single pin prick of light showed.

'There'll be fog tonight, sir,' the pilot spoke at Charles's elbow, and Charles turned without regret to peer over the bows into the gathering night.

'Yes, a good night for pirates.'

42

T he fog condensed on the grey metal of the bridge, so the footplates were slippery underfoot. It soaked into the overcoats of the men huddled against the rail, and it dewed in minute pearls on the eyebrows and the beard of Kapitän zur See Otto von Kleine. It gave him an air of derring-do, the reckless look of a scholarly pirate.

Every few seconds Lieutenant Kyller glanced anxiously at his captain, wondering when the order to turn would come. He hated this business of creeping inshore in the fog, with a flood tide pushing them towards a hostile coast.

'Stop all engines,' said von Kleine, and Kyller repeated the order to the helm with alacrity. The muted throbbing died beneath their feet, and afterwards the fog-blanketed air was heavy with a sepulchral hush.

'Ask masthead what he makes of the land.' Von Kleine spoke without turning his head, and after a pause Kyller reported back.

'Masthead is in the fog. No visibility,' he paused. 'Foredeck reports fifty fathoms shoaling rapidly.'

And von Kleine nodded. The sounding tended to confirm his estimate that they were sitting five miles off the breakwater of Durban harbour. When the morning wind swept the fog aside he hoped to see the low coastal hills of Natal ahead of him, terraced with gardens and whitewashed buildings – but most of all he hoped to see at least six British merchantmen anchored off the beach waiting their turn to enter the congested harbour, plump and sleepy under the protection of the shore batteries; unaware just how feeble was the protection afforded by half a dozen obsolete ten-pounders manned by old men and boys of the militia.

German naval intelligence had submitted a very detailed report of the defences and conditions prevailing in Durban. After careful perusal of this report, von Kleine had decided that he could trade certain betrayal of his exact position to the English for such a rich prize. There was little actual risk involved. One pass across the entrance of the harbour at high speed, a single broadside for each of the anchored merchantmen, and he could be over the horizon again before the shore gunners had loaded their weapons.

The risk, of course, was in showing *Blücher* to the entire population of Durban city and thereby supplying the Royal Navy with its first accurate sighting since the declaration of war. Within minutes of his first broadside, the British squadrons, which were hunting him, would be racing in from all directions to block each of his escape routes. He hoped to counter this by swinging away towards the south, down into that watery wilderness of wind and ice below latitude 40°, to the rendezvous with *Esther*, his supply ship. Then on to Australia or South America, as the opportunity arose.

He turned to glance at the chronometer above the ship's compass. Sunrise in three minutes, then they could expect the morning wind.

'Masthead reports the fog dispersing, sir.'

Von Kleine aroused himself, and looked out into the fog banks. They were moving now, twisting upon themselves in agitation at the warmth of the sun. 'All engines slow ahead together,' he said.

'Masthead,' warbled one of the voice-pipes in the battery in front of Kyller. 'Land bearing green four-oh. Range, ten thousand metres. A big headland.'

That would be the bluff above Durban, that massive whale-backed mountain that sheltered the harbour. But in the fog von Kleine had misjudged his approach; he was twice as far from the shore as he had intended.

'All engines full ahead together. New course. Oh-oh-six.' He waited for the order to be relayed to the helm before strolling across to the voice-pipes. 'Guns. Captain.'

'Guns,' the voice from far away acknowledged.

'I will be opening fire with high explosives in about ten minutes. The target will be massed merchant shipping on an approximate mark of three hundred degrees. Range, five thousand metres. You may fire as soon as you bear.'

'Mark three hundred degrees. Range, five thousand metres. Sir,' repeated the pipe, and von Kleine snapped the voice-tube cover shut and returned to his original position, facing forward with his hands clasped loosely behind his back.

Below him the gun-turrets revolved ponderously and the long barrels lifted slightly, pointing out into the mist with impassive menace.

A burst of dazzling sunshine struck the bridge so fiercely that Kyller lifted his hand to shield his eyes, but it was gone instantly as the *Blücher* dashed into another clammy cold bank of fog. Then as though they had passed through a curtain on to a brilliantly lit stage, they came out into a gay summer's morning.

Behind them the fog rolled away in a sodden grey wall from horizon to horizon. Ahead rose the green hills of Africa, rimmed with white beach and surf and speckled with thousands of whiter flecks that were the buildings of Durban town. The scaffolding of the cranes along the harbour wall looked like derelict sets of gallows.

Humped on the smooth green mirror of water between them and the shore, lay four ungainly shapes looking like a troop of basking hippo. The British merchantmen.

'Four only,' muttered von Kleine in chagrin. 'I had hoped for more.'

The forty-foot barrels of the nine-inch guns moved restlessly, seeming to sniff for their prey, and the *Blücher* raced on, lifting a hissing white wave at her bows, vibrating and shuddering to the thrust of her engines as they built up to full speed.

'Masthead,' the voice-tube beside Kyller squawked urgently.

'Bridge,' said Kyller but the reply was lost in the deafening detonation of the first broadside, the long thunderous roll of heavy gun-fire. He jumped involuntarily, taken unawares, and then quickly lifted the binoculars from his chest to train them on the British merchantmen.

All attention, every eye on the bridge was concentrated ahead, waiting for the fall of shot upon the doomed vessels.

In the comparative silence that followed the bellow of the broadside, a shriek from the masthead voice-pipe carried clearly.

'Warships! Enemy warships dead astern!'

'Starboard ten.' Von Kleine raised his voice a little louder than was his wont, and still under full power, *Blücher* swerved away from the land, leaning out from the turn, with her wake curved like an ostrich plume on the surface of the sea behind her, and ran for the shelter of the fog banks, leaving the rich prize of cargo shipping unscathed. On her bridge von Kleine and his officers were staring aft, the merchantmen forgotten as they searched for this new threat.

'Two warships.' The masthead look-out was elaborating his sighting report. 'A destroyer and a cruiser. Bearing ninety degrees. Range, five-oh-seven-oh. Destroyer leading.'

In the spherical field of von Kleine's binoculars the neat little triangle of the leading destroyer's superstructure popped up above the horizon. The cruiser was not yet in sight from the bridge.

'If they'd been an hour later,' lamented Kyller, 'we'd have finished the business and . . .'

'What does masthead see of the cruiser?' von Kleine interrupted him impatiently. He had no time to mourn this chance of fate – his only concern was to evaluate the force that was pursuing him, and then make the decision whether to run, or to turn back and engage them immediately.

'Cruiser is a medium, six or nine-inch. Either "O" class, or an "R". She's four miles behind her escort. Both ships still out of range.'

The destroyer was of no consequence; he could run down on her and blast her into a burning wreck, before her feeble little 4.7-inch guns were able to drop a shell within a mile of *Blücher*, but the cruiser was another matter entirely. To tackle her, *Blücher* would be engaging with her own class; victory would only be won after a severe mauling, and she was six thousand miles from the nearest friendly port where she could effect major repairs.

There was a further consideration. These two British ships might be the vanguard of a battle squadron. If he turned now and challenged action, engaged the cruiser in a single ship action, he might suddenly find himself pitted against imponderable odds. There could very well be another cruiser, or two, or three – even a battleship, below the southern horizon.

His duty and his orders dictated instant flight, avoiding action, and so prolonging *Blücher*'s fighting life.

'Enemy are streaming their colours, sir,' Kyller reported.

Von Kleine lifted his binoculars again. At the destroyer's masthead flew the tiny spots of white and red. This time he must leave the challenge to combat unanswered. 'Very well,' he said, and turned away to his stool in the corner of the bridge. He slumped into it and hunched his shoulders in thought. There were many interesting problems to occupy him, not least of them was how long he could run at full speed towards the north while his boilers devoured coal ravenously, and each minute widened the gap between *Blücher* and *Esther*.

He swivelled his stool and looked back over his stern. The destroyer was visible to the unaided eye now, and von Kleine frowned at it in irritation. She would yap at his heels like a terrier, clinging to him and shouting his course and speed across the ether to the hungry British squadrons, that must even now be closing with him from every direction. For days now he could expect to see her sitting in his wake.

43

'**C**ome on! Come on!' Charles Little slapped his hand impatiently against the padded arm of his stool as he watched *Orion*.

For a night and a day he had watched her gaining on *Blücher* but so infinitesimally slowly that it required his range finder to confirm the gain every thirty minutes.

Orion's bows were unnaturally high, and the waves she lifted with the passage of her hull through the water were the white wings of a seagull in the tropical sunlight; for Manderson, her captain, had pumped out her forward fresh-water tanks and fired away half the shell and explosive propellent from her forward magazines. Every man whose presence in the front half of the ship was not essential to her operation had been ordered aft to stand on the open deck as human ballast – all this in an effort to lift *Orion*'s bows and to coax another inch of speed from the cruiser.

Now she faced the most dangerous hour of her life, for she was creeping within extreme range of *Blücher*'s terrible nine-inch armament, and, taking into account the discrepancy in their speeds, it would be another hour before she could bring her own six-inch guns to bear. During that time she would be under fire from *Blücher*'s after turrets and would have no answer to them.

It was heart-breaking for Charles to watch the chase, for *Bloodhound* had not once been asked to extend herself. Below there was a reserve of speed that would allow her to close with *Blücher* in fifty minutes of steaming – always provided she was not smashed into a fiery shambles long before.

Thus the three vessels fled towards the ever-receding northern horizon. The two long shapes of the cruisers flying arrow straight, solid columns of reeking smoke pouring from the triple funnels to besmear the gay, glittering surface of the sea with a long double bank of black that dispersed only slowly on the easterly breeze; while, like a water beetle, the diminutive *Bloodhound* circled out to the side of *Blücher* from where, when the time came, she could spot the fall of *Orion*'s shells more accurately and signal the corrections to her. But always *Bloodhound* tactfully kept outside the fifteen mile radius which marked the length of *Blücher*'s talons.

'We can expect *Blücher* to open fire at any moment now, sir,' the navigating lieutenant commented as he straightened up from the sextant, over which he had been measuring the angle subtended by the two cruisers.

Charles nodded in agreement. 'Yes. Von Kleine must try for a few lucky hits, even at that range.'

'This isn't going to be very pretty to watch.'

'We'll just have to sit tight, keep our fingers crossed, and hope old *Orion* can – ' He stopped abruptly, and then jumped up from his stool. 'Hello! *Blücher's* up to something!'

The silhouette of the German cruiser had altered drastically in the last few seconds. The gap between her funnels widened and now Charles could see the humped menace of her forward turrets.

'By God, she's altering course! The bloody bastard is bringing all his turrets to bear!'

Lieutenant Kyller studied his captain's face. In sleep there was an air of serenity about the man. It reminded Kyller of a painting he had seen in the cathedral at Nürnberg, a portrait of Saint Luke by Holbein. The same fine bone structure, the golden blond beard and moustache that framed the mobile and sensitive lips. He pushed the idea aside and leaned forward. Gently he touched von Kleine's shoulder.

'Captain. My Captain,' and von Kleine opened his eyes. They were smoky blue with sleep but his voice was crisp.

'What is it, Kyller?'

'The gunnery officer reports the enemy will be within range in fifteen minutes.'

Von Kleine swivelled his stool and looked quickly about his ship. Above him the smoke poured from every funnel, and from the mouth of each stack a volcano of sparks and shimmering heat blew steadily. The paint had blistered and peeled from the metal of the funnels and they glowed red hot, even in the sunlight. *Blücher* was straining herself far beyond the limits her makers had set. God alone knew what injury this constant running at full speed was doing her, and von Kleine winced as he felt her tremble in protest beneath him.

He turned his eyes astern. The British cruiser was hull up on the horizon now. The difference in their speeds must be a small fraction of a knot, but *Blücher's* superiority in fire power was enormous.

For a moment he allowed himself to ponder the arrogance of a nation that constantly, almost by choice, matched their men and ships against unnatural odds. Always they sent terriers to fight against wolfhounds. Then he smiled, you had to be English or mad, to understand the English.

He glanced out to starboard. The British destroyer had worked out on to his flank. It could do little harm from there.

'Very well, Kyller . . .' He stood as he spoke.

'Bridge – Engine Room,' the voice-tube squealed.

'Engine Room – Bridge.' Kyller turned to it.

'Our port main bearing is running red hot. I must shut down our port engine!'

The words struck von Kleine like a bucket of iced water thrown down his back. He leaped to the voice-tube.

'This is the Captain. I must have full power for another hour!'

'I can't do it, sir. Another fifteen minutes and the main drive shaft will seize up. God knows what damage it will do.'

For five seconds von Kleine hunched silently over the voice-tube. His mind raced. On one engine *Blücher* would lose ten knots on her speed. The enemy would be able to manoeuvre about him freely – possibly hold off until nightfall and then. . . . He must attack immediately; turn on them and press his attack home with all his armament.

'Give me full power for as long as you can,' he snapped, and then turning to the gunnery officer's tube. 'This is the Captain. I am turning four points to starboard, and will keep the enemy directly on our starboard beam for the next fifteen minutes. After that I will be forced to reduce speed. Open fire when you bear.' Von Kleine snapped the cover closed and turned to his yeoman of signals. 'Hoist the battle ensign!'

He spoke softly, without heat, but there were lights in his eyes like those in a blue sapphire.

44

'T here she goes!' whispered Charles Little without lowering his glasses. Upon the black turrets of *Blücher* the gun-fire gleamed and sparkled without sound. Quickly he traversed his glasses across the surface of the sea until he found *Orion*. She was plunging in eagerly, narrowing the gap very rapidly between herself and *Blücher*. In another seven minutes she would be able to return the German's fire.

Suddenly, a quarter of a mile ahead of her, there rose from the sea a series of tall columns, stately as the columns of a Greek temple, slender and beautiful, shining like white marble in the sun. Then slowly they dropped back.

'Short,' grunted the navigating lieutenant.

'Her guns are still cold,' Charles commented. 'Please God let old *Orion* get within range.'

Again *Blücher*'s shells fell short, and short again, but each time they were closer to the low bulk of *Orion*, and the next broadside dropped all around her, partially screening her with spray, and *Orion* started to zigzag.

'Another three minutes,' the navigating lieutenant spoke with tension making his voice husky.

At regular intervals of fifteen seconds the German salvos fell around *Orion* – once within fifty feet of her bows so that as she tore into the standing columns of spray, they blew back over her and mingled with the black smoke of her funnels.

'Come on, old girl! Go in and get her. Go on! Go on!' Charles was gripping the rail in front of him and cheering like a maniac, all the dignity of his rank and his thirty-five years gone in the tense excitement of the battle. It had infected all of them on the bridge of the destroyer, and they capered and shouted with him.

'There she blows!' howled the lieutenant.

'She's opened fire!'

'Go it, *Orion*, go it!'

On *Orion*'s forward turrets gun-fire sparkled, then again and again. The harsh roll of the broadsides carried to them against the light wind.

'Short,' groaned Charles. 'She's still out of range.'

'Short again!'

'Still short.'

Each time the call of shot was signalled by the chief yeoman at the Aldis lamp, and briefly acknowledged from *Orion*'s bridge-works.

'Oh my God,' moaned Charles.

'She's hit!' echoed his lieutenant.

A flat yellow glare, like sheet lightning on a summer's day, lit *Orion*'s afterdeck, and almost immediately a ball of yellowish grey smoke enveloped her. Through it Charles saw her after-funnel sag drunkenly and hang back at an unnatural angle.

'She's holding on!'

Orion emerged from the shell smoke and dragged it after her like a funeral cloak, but her speed seemed unabated, and the regular salvos burned briefly and brightly on her forward turrets.

'Now she's hitting,' exulted the lieutenant, and Charles turned quickly to see shell-fire burst on *Blücher*, and his wide grin split his face.

'Kill her! Kill her!' he roared, knowing that though *Blücher* was better armed yet she was as vulnerable as *Orion*. Her plating was egg-shell thin and the six-inch shells that crashed through it would be doing her terrible damage.

Now the two cruisers were pounding each other. The range was closing so rapidly that soon they must hit with every broadside. This was a contest from which only one ship, or neither of them, would emerge.

Charles was trying to estimate the damage that had been inflicted upon *Blücher* during the last few minutes. She was on fire forward. Sulphur-yellow flames poured from her, her upperworks were riven into a grotesque sculpture of destruction, and a pall of smoke enveloped her, so her profile was shadowy and vague, yet every fifteen seconds her turrets lit with those deadly little flashes.

Charles turned to assess the relative damage that *Orion* had suffered. He found and held her with his binoculars – and at that moment *Orion* ceased to exist.

Her boilers, pierced by high explosive shell, burst and tore her in half. A cloud of white steam spurted five hundred feet into the air, completely blanketing her. The steam hung for thirty seconds then sagged wearily, and rolled aside. *Orion* was gone. A wide circle of oil slick and floating debris marked her grave. The speed of her charge had run her clean under.

On the bridge of *Bloodhound*, the cheering strangled into deathly silence. The silence was not spoiled but rather accentuated by the mournful note of the wind in her rigging and the muted throb of her engines.

45

For eight long hours Charles Little had ridden his anger and his hatred, using the curb to hold it on the right side of madness, resisting the consuming and suicidal urge to hurl his ship at the German cruiser and die as *Orion* had died.

Immediately after the sinking of *Orion*, the *Blücher* had reduced speed sharply and turned due south. With her fires still raging, she had limped along like a gun-shot lion. The battle ensigns at her masthead were tattered by shrapnel and blackened by smoke.

As soon as she had passed, *Bloodhound* altered course and cruised slowly over the area of water that was still rainbowed by floating oil and speckled with wreckage. There were no survivors from *Orion*; all of them had died with her.

Bloodhound turned and trailed after the crippled German cruiser, and the hatred that emanated from the destroyer was of such strength that it should have reached out across the sea as a physical force and destroyed *Blücher*.

But as Charles Little stood at the rail of his bridge, he saw the smoke and flame upon *Blücher*'s decks reduce perceptibly every minute as her damage control teams fought it to a standstill. The last wisp of smoke from her shrivelled.

'Fire's out,' said the pilot, and Charles made no answer. He had hoped that the flames would eat their way into one of *Blücher*'s magazines and blow her into the same oblivion into which she had sent *Orion*.

'But she isn't making more than six knots. *Orion* must have hit her in the engine room.' Hopefully the navigating lieutenant went on, 'My bet is that she's got major damage below. At this speed we can expect *Pegasus* and *Renounce* to catch up with us by midday tomorrow. Then *Blücher* will stand no chance!'

'Yes,' agreed Charles softly.

Summoned by *Bloodhound*'s frantic radio transmissions, *Pegasus* and *Renounce*, the two heavy cruisers of the northern squadron, were racing down the East African coast, cutting through the five hundred miles of water that separated them.

46

'**K**yller. Ask the chief how he's making out.' Von Kleine was fretting beneath the calm set of his features. Night was closing, and in the darkness, even the frail little English destroyer was a danger to him. There was danger all around, danger must each minute be approaching from every quarter of the sea. He must have power on his port side engine before nightfall; it was a matter of survival; he must have speed to carry him south through the hunting packs of the British – south to where *Esther* waited to give him succour, to replace the shell he had fired away, to replenish his coal bunkers which were now dangerously depleted. Then once more *Blücher* would be a force to reckon with. But first he must have speed.

'Captain.' Kyller was beside him again. 'Commander Lochtkamper reports they have cleared the oil line to the main bearing. They have stripped the bearing and there is no damage to the shaft. He is fitting new half shells. The work is well advanced, sir.'

The words conjured up for von Kleine a picture of half-naked men, smeared to the elbows with black grease, sweating in the confined heat of the drive shaft tunnel as they worked. 'How much longer?' he asked.

'He promised full power on both engines within two hours, sir.'

Von Kleine sighed with relief, and glanced over his stern at the British destroyer that was shadowing him. He began to smile.

'I hope, my friend, that you are a brave man. I hope that when you see me increase speed, you will not be able to control your disappointment. I hope tonight you will try with your torpedoes, so that I can crush you, for your eyes always on me are a dangerous embarrassment.' He spoke so softly that his lips barely moved, then he turned back to Kyller. 'I want all the battle lights checked and reported.'

'Aye, aye, sir.'

Von Kleine crossed to the voice-tubes. 'Gunnery officer,' he said. 'I want "X" turret guns loaded with star shell and trained to maximum elevation . . .' He went on listing his preparations for night action and then he ended, '. . . stand all your gun crews down. Let them eat and rest. From dusk action stations onwards they will be held in the first degree of readiness.'

'Commander, sir!'

The urgent call startled Commander Charles Little, and he spilled his mug of cocoa. This was the first period of rest he had allowed himself all day, and now it was interrupted within ten minutes. 'What is it?' He flung open the door of the chart room, and ran out on to the bridge.

'*Blücher* is increasing speed rapidly.'

'No!' It was too cruel a blow, and the exclamation of protest was wrung from Charles. He darted to the voice-pipe.

'Gunnery officer. Report your target.'

A moment's delay, and then the reply. 'Bearing mark, green oh-oh. Range, one-five-oh-five-oh. Speed, seventeen knots.'

It was true. *Blücher* was under full power again, with all her guns still operable. *Orion* had died in vain.

Charles wiped his mouth with the open palm of his hand, and felt the brittle stubble of his new beard rasp under his fingers. Beneath the tan, his face was sickly pale with strain and fatigue. There were smears of dark blue beneath his eyes, and in their corners were tiny lumps of yellow mucus. His eyes were bloodshot, and the wisp of hair that escaped from under the brim of his cap was matted on to his forehead by the salt spray, as he peered into the gathering dusk.

The fighting madness which had threatened all that day to overwhelm him, rose slowly from the depth of his belly and his loins. He no longer struggled to suppress it.

'Turn two points to starboard, pilot. All engines full ahead together.' The engine telegraph clanged, and *Bloodhound* pivoted like a polo pony. It would take her thirty minutes to work up to full speed, and by that time it would be dark.

'Sound action stations.' Charles wanted to attack in the hour of darkness before the moon came up. Through the ship the alarm bells thrilled, and without taking his eyes from the dark dot on the darkening horizon, Charles listened to the reports coming into the bridge, until the one for which he waited, 'Torpedo party closed up, sir!'

Now he turned and went to the voice-tube. 'Torps,' he said, 'I hope to give you a chance at *Blücher* with both port and starboard tubes. I am going to take you in as close as possible.'

The men grouped around Charles on the bridge listened to him say 'as close as possible', and knew that he had pronounced sentence of death upon them.

Henry Sargent, the navigating lieutenant, was afraid. Stealthily he groped in the pocket of his overcoat until he found the little silver crucifix that Lynette had given him. It was warm from his own body heat. He held it tightly.

He remembered it hanging between her breasts on its silver chain, and the way she had lifted both hands to the back of her neck as she unclasped it. The chain had caught in the shiny cascade of hair as she had tried to free it, kneeling on the bed facing him. He had leaned forward to help her, and she had clung to him, pressing the warm smooth bulge of her pregnant stomach against him.

'God protect you, my darling husband,' she had whispered. 'Please God bring you back safely to us.'

And now he was afraid for her and the daughter he had never seen.

'Hold your course, damn you!' he snapped at Herbert Cryer, the helmsman.

'Aye, aye, sir,' Herbert Cryer replied with just a trace of injured innocence in his tone. No man could hold *Bloodhound* true when she hurled herself from swell to swell with such abandoned violence, she must yaw and throw her head that fraction before the helm could correct her. The reprimand was unjustified, uttered in fear and tension. 'Give it a flipping break, mate,' Herbert retorted silently. 'You're not the only one who is going to catch it. Tighten up the old arsehole like a bloody officer and a ruddy gentleman.'

In these wordless exchanges of repartee with his officers, Herbert Cryer was never bested. They were wonderful release for resentments and pent-up emotion, and now because he was also afraid, he became silently lyrical.

'Climb-aboard-Romeo's one way express to flipping glory.' Commander Little's reputation with the ladies had resulted in him being irreverently but affectionately baptized by his crew. 'Come along with us. We're off to shout at the devil, while Charlie kisses his daughter.'

Herbert glanced sideways at his commander and grinned. Fear made the grin wolfish, and Charles Little saw it and misinterpreted it. He read it as a mark of the same berserk fury that possessed him. The two of them grinned at each other for an instant in complete misunderstanding, before Herbert refocused his attention on *Bloodhound*'s next wild crabbing lunge.

Charles was afraid as well. He was afraid of finding a weakness in himself – but this was the fear that had walked at his right hand all his life, close beside him, whispering to him, 'Harder, try harder. You must do it better, you must do it quicker, or bigger than they do, or they'll laugh at you. You mustn't fail – not in one thing, not for one moment, you mustn't fail. You mustn't fail!' This fear was the eternal companion and partner in every venture on which he embarked.

It had stood beside the thirteen-year-old Charles in a duck blind, while he fired a twelve gauge shotgun, and wept slow fat tears of agony every time the recoil smashed into his bruised bicep and shoulder.

It had stooped over him as he lay in the mud hugging a broken collar bone. 'Get up!' it hissed at him. 'Get up!' It had forced him to his feet and led him back to the unbroken colt to mount again, and again, and again.

So conditioned was he to respond to its voice that when it crouched beside him now, twisted and misshapen on the footplates of the bridge, its presence almost tangible, and croaked so Charles alone could hear it, 'Prove it! Prove it!' there was only one course open to Charles Little; a peregrine stooping at a golden eagle, he took his ship in against the *Blücher*.

47

'T he turn to starboard was a feint.' Otto von Kleine spoke with certainty, staring out to where the dusk had obliterated the frail silhouette of the English destroyer. 'Even now he is turning again to cross our stern. He will attack on our port side.'

'Captain, it could be the double bluff,' Kyller answered dubiously.

'No.' Von Kleine shook his golden beard. 'He must try to outline us against the last of the light from the sunset. He will attack from the east.' A moment longer he frowned in thought, as he anticipated his opponent's moves across the chessboard of the ocean. 'Kyller, plot me his course, assuming a speed of twenty-five knots, a turn four points to port three minutes after our last sighting, a run of fifteen miles across our stern, and then a turn of four points to starboard. If we hold our present course and speed, where will he be in relation to us, in ninety minutes' time?'

Working quickly, Kyller completed the problem. Von Kleine had been mentally checking every step of the calculation. 'Yes,' he agreed with Kyller's solution, and already he had formulated the orders for change of course and speed to place *Bloodhound* in ambush.

48

U nder full power, *Bloodhound* threw a bow-wave ten feet high, and a wake that boiled out for a quarter of a mile behind her, a long, faintly phosphorescent smear in the darkness.

Aboard *Blücher* a hundred pairs of eyes were straining out into the night, watching for that phosphorescence. Behind the battle lights on her upperworks men waited, in the dimly-lit turrets men waited, on the open bridge, at the masthead, deep in her belly, the crew of *Blücher* waited.

Von Kleine had reduced speed to lessen his own wake, and turned away from the land at an angle of forty-five degrees. He wanted to catch the Englishman on his starboard beam, out of torpedo range.

He stood peering out across the dark sea, with the fur-lined collar of his overcoat drawn up to his ears. The night was cool. The sea was a black immensity, vast as the sky that was lined in glowing ivory by the whorls and smears of the star patterns.

A dozen men saw it at the same instant; pale, ethereal, seeming to float upon the darkness of the sea like a plume of iridescent mist – the wake of the Englishman.

'Star shell!' Von Kleine snapped the order to the waiting guns. He was alarmed by the English destroyer's proximity. He had hoped to spot her at greater range.

High above the ocean, the star shells burst blue-white, so intensely bright as to sear the retina of the eye that looked directly at them. Beneath them the surface of the sea was polished ebony, sculptured and scooped with the pattern of the swells. The two ships were starkly and crisply lit, steaming on converging courses, already so close to each other that the mile-long, solid white beams of their battle lights jumped out to join, fumbling together like the hands of hesitant lovers.

In almost the same second both ships opened fire, but the banging of *Bloodhound*'s little 4.7-inch guns were lost in the bellow of the cruiser's broadside.

Blücher was firing over open sights with her guns depressed until the long barrels were horizontal to the surface of the sea. Her first salvo was aimed a fraction high, and the huge shells howled over *Bloodhound*'s open bridge.

The wind of their passage, the fierce draught of disrupted air they threw out, caught Charles Little and sent him reeling against the compass pinnacle. He felt the ribs below his armpit crack.

The command he shouted at the helm was hoarse with pain.

'Turn four points to port! Steer for the enemy!' and *Bloodhound* spun like a ballet dancer, and charged straight at *Blücher*.

The cruiser's next broadside was high again but now her secondary armament had joined in, and a four-pound shell from one of the quick-firing pom-poms burst on the director tower above *Bloodhound*'s bridge. It swept the exposed area with a buzzing hailstorm of shrapnel.

It killed the navigating lieutenant instantly, cutting away the top of his head as though it were the shell of a soft-boiled egg. He fell on the deck and splattered the footplates with the warm custard of his brains.

A piece of the red hot shell casing, the size of a thumb-nail entered the point of Herbert Cryer's right elbow and shattered the bone to splinters. He gasped at the shock and sprawled against the wheel.

'Hold her. Hold her true!' The order from Commander Little was blurred as the speech of a spastic. Herbert Cryer pulled himself up and with his left hand spun the wheel to meet *Bloodhound*'s wild swing, but with his right arm hanging useless, his steering was clumsy and awkward.

'Steady her, man. Hold her steady!' Again that thick slurring voice, and Cryer was aware of Charles Little beside him, his hands on the helm, helping to hold *Bloodhound*'s frantic head.

'Aye, aye, sir.' Cryer glanced at his commander and gasped again. This time in horror. Razor-sharp steel had sliced off Charles Little's ear, then gone on to cut his cheek away, and expose the bone of his jaw and the white teeth that lined it. A flap of tattered flesh hung down on to his chest, and from a dozen severed blood vessels dark blood dripped and spurted and dribbled.

The two of them crouched wounded over the wheel, with the dead men at their feet, and aimed *Bloodhound* at the long low bulk of the German cruiser.

Now in the daylight glare of the star shells, the sea around them was thrashed and whipped into seething life by the cacophony of *Blücher*'s guns. Tall towers of white water rose briefly and majestically about them, then dropped back to leave the surface troubled and restless with foam.

And *Bloodhound* drove on until suddenly it seemed she had run into a cliff of solid granite. Beneath their feet, she jarred and bucked violently. A nine-inch shell had taken her full in the bows.

'Port full rudder.' Charles Little's voice was sloshy sounding, wet with the blood that filled his mouth, and together they spun the wheel to full left lock.

But *Bloodhound* was dying. The shell had split her bows wide open, torn her plating and fanned it open like the petals of a macabre orchid. The black night sea rushed through her. Already her bows were sinking, slumping wearily, lifting her stern so the rudder no longer had full purchase. But even in death she was trying desperately to obey. Slowly she swung, inchingly, achingly, she swung.

Charles Little left the helm and tottered towards the starboard rail. His legs were numb and heavy under him, and the weakness of his lost blood drummed in his ears. He reached the rail and clung there, peering down on the torpedo tubes that stood on the deck below him.

The tubes looked like a rack of fat cigars, and with weary jubilation Charles saw that there were men still tending them, crouching behind the sheet of armour plate, waiting for *Bloodhound* to turn and bring *Blücher* on to her starboard beam.

'Turn, old girl. Come on! That's it! Turn!' Charles croaked through the blood.

Another shell struck *Bloodhound*, and she heaved in mortal agony. Perhaps this movement, combined with a chance push of the sea swell, was enough to swing her those last few degrees.

There, full in the track of the torpedo tubes, lit by her own star shells and the gun-fire from her turrets, a scant thousand yards across the black water, lay the German cruiser.

Charles heard the whoosh, whoosh, whoosh, whoosh, of the tubes as they fired. He saw the long sharklike shapes of the torpedoes leap out from the deck and strike the water, saw the four white wakes arrowing away in formation, and behind him he heard the torpedo officer's triumphant shout, distorted by the voice-pipe.

'All four fired, and running true!'

Charles never saw his torpedoes strike, for one of *Blücher*'s nine-inch shells hit the bridgework three feet below him. For one brief unholy instant, he stood in the centre of a furnace as hot as the flames of the sun.

49

Otto von Kleine watched the English destroyer explode. Towering orange flames erupted from her, and a solid ball of black smoke spun upon itself, blooming on the dark ocean like a flower from the gardens of hell. The surface of the sea around her was dimpled by the fall of thrown debris and the cruiser's shells – for all of *Blücher*'s guns were still blazing.

'Cease fire,' he said, without taking his eyes from the awesome pageant of destruction that he had created.

Another salvo of star shell burst above, and von Kleine lifted his hand to his eyes and pressed his thumb and forefinger into the closed lids, shielding them from the stabbing brilliance of the light. It was finished, and he was tired.

He was tired, drained of nervous and physical energy, overwhelmed by the back-wash of fatigue that followed these last two days and nights of ceaseless strain. And he was sad – sad for the brave men he had killed, and the terrible destruction he had wrought.

Still holding his eyes, he opened his mouth to give the order that would send *Blücher* once more thrashing southward, but before the words reached his lips, a wild shout from the look-out interrupted him.

'Torpedoes! Close on the starboard beam!'

Long seconds von Kleine hesitated. He had let his brain relax, let the numbness wash over it. The battle was over, and he had dropped back from the high pinnacle of alertness on which he had balanced these last desperate hours. It needed a conscious physical effort to call up his reserves, and during those seconds, the torpedoes fired by *Bloodhound* in her death throes were knifing in to revenge her.

At last von Kleine snapped the bonds of inertia that bound his mind. He leaped to the starboard rail of the bridge, and saw in the light of the star shells the pale phosphorescent trails of the four torpedoes. Against the dark water they looked like the tails of meteors on a night sky.

'Full port rudder. All engines full astern together!' he shouted, his voice pitched high with consternation.

He felt his ship swerve beneath him, thrown violently over as the great propellers clawed at the sea to hold her from crossing the path of the torpedoes.

Hopelessly he stood and reviled himself. *I should have anticipated this. I should have known the destroyer had fired.*

Helplessly he stood and watched the four white lines drawn swiftly across the surface towards him.

In the last moments he felt a fierce upward surge of hope. Three of the English torpedoes would miss. That was certain. They would cross *Blücher*'s bows as she side-stepped. And the fourth torpedo it was just possible would miss also.

His fingers upon the bridge rail clenched, until it felt as though they must press into the metal. His breath jammed in his throat and choked him.

Ponderously, *Blücher* swung her bows away. If he had given the order for the turn only five seconds earlier . . .

The torpedo struck *Blücher* five feet below the surface, on the very tip of her curved keel.

The explosion shot a mountain of white water one hundred and fifty feet into the air. It slammed *Blücher* back onto her haunches with such violence that Otto von Kleine and his officers were thrown heavily to the steel deck.

Von Kleine scrabbled to his knees and looked forward. A fine veil of spray, like pearl dust in the light of the star shells, hung over *Blücher*. As he watched, it subsided slowly.

All that night they struggled to keep *Blücher* afloat.

They sealed off her bows with the five-inch steel doors in the watertight bulkhead, and behind those doors they locked thirty German seamen whose battle stations were in the bows. At intervals during the frenzied activity of the night, von Kleine had visions of those men floating face-down in the flooded compartments.

While the pumps clanged throughout the ship to free her of the hundreds of tons of sea-water that washed through her, von Kleine left the bridge and, with his engineer commander and damage control officer, they listed the injuries that *Blücher* had received.

In the dawn they assembled grimly in the chart-room behind the bridge, and assessed their plight.

'What power can you give me, Lochtkamper?' von Kleine demanded of his engineer.

'I can give you as much as you ask.' A reddish-purple bruise covered half the engineer's face where he had been thrown against a steam cock-valve when the torpedo struck. 'But anything over five knots will carry away the watertight bulkheads forward. They will take the full brunt of the sea.'

Von Kleine swivelled his stool, and looked at the damage control officer. 'What repairs can you effect at sea?'

'None, sir. We have braced and propped the watertight bulkhead. We have patched and jammed the holes made by the British cruiser's guns. But I can do nothing about the underwater damage without a dry dock – or calm water where I can put divers over the side. We must enter a port.'

Von Kleine leaned back in his stool and closed his eyes to think.

The only friendly port within six thousand miles was Dar es Salaam, the capital of German East Africa, but he knew the British were blockading it. He discarded it from his list of possible refuges.

An island? Zanzibar? – The Seychelles? – Mauritius? – All hostile territories with no anchorage safe from bombardment by a British squadron.

A river mouth? The Zambezi? No, that was in Portuguese territory, navigable for only the first few miles of its length.

Suddenly he opened his eyes. There was one ideal haven situated in German territory, navigable even by a ship of *Blücher*'s tonnage for twenty miles. It was guarded from overland approach by formidable terrain, yet he could call upon the German Commissioner for stores and labour and protection.

'Kyller,' he said. 'Plot me a course for the Kikunya mouth of the Rufiji delta.'

Five days later the *Blücher* crawled painfully as a crippled centipede into the north-ernmost channel of the Rufiji delta. She was blackened with battle smoke, her rigging hung in tatters, and at a thousand places shell splinters had pierced her upperworks. Her bows were swollen and distorted, and the sea washed through her forward compartments and then boiled and spilled out of the ghastly rents in her plating.

As she passed between the forests of mangroves that lined the channel, they seemed to enfold her like welcoming arms.

Overside she lowered two picket boats and these darted ahead of her like busy little water beetles as they sounded the channel, and searched for a secure anchorage. Gradually *Blücher* wriggled and twisted her way deeper and deeper into the wilderness of the delta. At a place where the flood waters of the Rufiji had cut a deep bay between two islands, and formed a natural jetty on both sides, the *Blücher* came to rest.

50

H erman Fleischer wiped his face and neck with a hand towel and then looked at the sodden material. God, how he hated the Rufiji basin. As soon as he entered its humid and malodorous heat, a thousand tiny taps opened under his skin and out gushed the juices of his body.

The prospect of an extended stay aroused in him a dark resentment to all things, but especially to this young snob who stood beside him on the foredeck of the steam launch. Herman darted a glance at him now. Cool he looked, as though he were sauntering down Unter den Linden in June. The shimmering white of his tropical uniform was unwrinkled and dry, not like the thick corduroy that bunched damply at Herman's armpits and crotch. Mother of a dog, it would start the rash again; he could feel it beginning to itch and he scratched at it moodily, then checked his hand as he saw the lieutenant smile.

'How far are we from *Blücher*?' and then as an afterthought he used the lieuten-ant's surname without rank, 'How far, Kyller?' It was as well to keep reminding the man that as the equivalent of a full colonel, he far outranked him.

'Around the next bend, Commissioner.' Kyller's voice carried the lazy inflection that made Fleischer think of champagne and opera houses, of skiing parties, and boar hunts.

'I hope that Captain von Kleine has made adequate preparation to defend her against enemy attack?'

'She is safe.' For the first time there was a brittle undertone to Kyller's reply, and Fleischer pounced on it. He sensed an advantage. For the last two days, ever since Kyller had met him at the confluence of the Ruhaha river, Herman had been need-ling him to find a weakness.

'Tell me, Kyller,' he dropped his voice to an intimate, confidential level. 'This is in strict confidence, of course, but do you really feel that Captain von Kleine is able to handle this situation? I mean, do you feel that someone else may have been able to reach a more satisfactory result?' Ah! Yes! That was it! Look at him flush, look at the anger stain those cool brown cheeks. For the first time the advantage was with Herman Fleischer.

'Commissioner Fleischer,' Kyller spoke softly but Herman exulted to hear his tone. 'Captain von Kleine is the most skilful, efficient, and courageous officer under which I have had the honour to serve. He is, furthermore, a gentleman.'

'So?' Herman grunted. 'Then why is this paragon hiding in the Rufiji basin with his buttocks shot full of holes?' Then he threw back his head and guffawed in triumph.

'At another time, sir, and in different circumstances, I would ask you to withdraw those words.' Kyller turned from him and walked to the forward rail. He stood there staring ahead, while the launch chugged around another bend in the river, opening the same dreary vista of dark water and mangrove forest. Kyller spoke without turning his head. 'There is the *Blücher*,' he said.

There was nothing but the sweep of water and the massed fuzzy heads of the mangroves below a hump of higher ground upon the bank. The laughter faded from Herman's chubby face as he searched, then a small scowl replaced it as he realized that the lieutenant was baiting him. There was certainly no battle cruiser anchored in the water-way. 'Lieutenant . . .' he began angrily, then checked himself. The high ground was divided by a narrow channel, not more than a hundred yards wide, fenced in by the mangrove forest, but the channel was blocked by a shapeless and ungainly mound of vegetation. He stared at it uncomprehendingly until suddenly beneath the netting that was festooned with branches of mangroves, he saw the blurred outline of turrets and superstructure.

The camouflage had been laid with fascinating ingenuity. From a distance of three hundred yards the *Blücher* was invisible.

51

The bubbles came up slowly through the dark water as though it had the same viscosity as warm honey. They burst on the surface in a boiling white rash.

Captain von Kleine leaned across the foredeck rail of the *Blücher* and peered at the disturbance below him, with the absorption of a man attempting to read his own future in the murky mirror of the Rufiji waters. For almost two hours he had waited like this, drawing quietly on a succession of little black cheroots, occasionally easing his body into a more comfortable position.

Although his body was at rest, his brain was busy, endlessly reviewing his preparations and his plans. His preparations were complete, he had mentally listed them and found no omissions.

A party of six seamen had been despatched fifteen miles downstream by picket boat to the entrance of the delta. They were encamped on a hummock of high ground above the channel to watch the sea for the British blockade squadron.

As *Blücher* crept up the channel she had sown the last of her globular multi-horned mines behind her. No British ship could follow her.

Remote as the chances of overland attack seemed, yet von Kleine had set up a system of defence around the *Blücher*. Half his seamen were ashore now, spread in a network to guard each of the possible approaches. Fields of fire had been cut through the mangroves for his Maxim guns. Crude fortifications of log and earth had been built and manned, communication lines set up, and he was ready.

After long discussions with his medical officer, von Kleine had issued orders to protect the health of his men. Orders for the purification of water, the disposal of sanitation and waste, for the issue of five grains of quinine daily to each man, and fifty other safeguards to health and morale.

He had ordered an inventory made of stocks of food and supplies, and he was satisfied that with care he could subsist for a further four months. Thereafter he would be reduced to fishing and hunting, and foraging.

He had despatched Kyller upstream to make contact with the German Commissioner, and solicit his full co-operation.

Four days had been spent in hiding the *Blücher* under her camouflage, in setting up a complete workshop on the foredeck under sun awnings, so that the engineers could work in comparative comfort.

Now at last they had begun a full underwater appraisal of *Blücher*'s wounds.

Behind him he heard the petty officer pass an order to the team at the winch. 'Bring him up – slowly.'

The donkey engine spluttered into life, and the winch clattered and whined shrilly. Von Kleine stirred against the rail and focused his full attention on the water below him.

The heavy line and airpipe reeled in smoothly, then suddenly the surface bulged and the body of the diver was lifted dangling on the line. Black in shiny wet rubber, the three brass-bound cyclopean eyes of his helmet glaring, grotesque as a sea monster, he was swung inboard and lowered to the deck.

Two seamen hurried forward and unscrewed the bolts at the neck, lifted off the heavy helmet, and exposed the head of the engineering commander, Lochtkamper. The heavy face, flat and lined as that of a mastiff, was made heavier than usual by the thoughtful frown it now wore. He looked across at his captain and shook his head slightly.

'Come to my cabin when you are ready, Commander,' said von Kleine, and walked away.

'A small glass of cognac?' von Kleine suggested.

'I'd like that, sir.' Commander Lochtkamper looked out of place in the elegance of the cabin. The hands that accepted the glass were big, knuckles scarred and enlarged by constant violent contact with metal, the skin etched deeply with oil and engine filth. When he sank into the chair at his captain's invitation, his legs seemed to have too many knees.

'Well?' asked von Kleine, and Lochtkamper launched into his report. He spoke for ten minutes and von Kleine followed him slowly through the maze of technicalities where strange and irrelevant obscenities grew along the way. In moments of deep concentration such as these Lochtkamper fell back on the gutter idiom of his native Hamburg, and von Kleine was unable to suppress a smile when he learned that the copulatory torpedo had committed a perversion on one of the main frames, springing the plating whose morals were definitely suspect. The damage sounded like that suffered in a brothel during a Saturday night brawl.

'Can you repair it?' von Kleine asked at last.

'It will mean cutting away all the obscenely damaged plating, lifting it to the deck, recutting it, welding and shaping it. But we will still be short of at least eight hundred obscene square feet of plate, sir.'

'A commodity not readily obtainable in the delta of the Rufiji river,' von Kleine mused.

'No, sir.'

'How long will it take you – if I can get the plating for you?'

'Two months, perhaps.'

'When can you start?'

'Now, sir.'

'Do it then,' said von Kleine, and Lochtkamper drained his glass, smacked his lips, and stood up. 'Very good cognac, sir,' he complimented his captain, and shambled out of the cabin.

52

S taring upward at the massive warship, Herman Fleischer surveyed the battle damage with the uncomprehending curiosity of a landsman. He saw the gaping ulcers where *Orion*'s shells had struck, the black blight where the flames had raged through her, the irregular rash with which the splinters had pierced and peppered her upperworks, and then he dropped his eyes to the bows. Work cradles were suspended a few feet above the water, and upon them clutters of seamen were illuminated by the crackling blue glare of the welding torches.

'God in heaven, what a beating!' He spoke with sadistic relish.

Kyller ignored the remark. He was directing the native helmsman of the launch to the landing ladder that had been rigged down the side of *Blücher*. Not even the presence of this sweaty peasant, Fleischer, could spoil his pleasure in this moment of homecoming. To Ernst Kyller, the *Blücher* was home in the deep sense of the word; it contained all that he valued in life, including the man for whom he bore a devotion surpassing the natural duty of a son to his father. He was savouring the anticipation of von Kleine's smile and words of commendation for another task well done.

'Ah, Kyller!' Von Kleine rose from behind his desk and moved around it to greet his lieutenant.

'Back so soon? Did you find Fleischer?'

'He is waiting outside, sir.'

'Good, good. Bring him in.'

Herman Fleischer paused in the companion-way and blinked suspiciously around the cabin. His mind was automatically converting the furnishings into Reichsmarks, the rugs were silk Teheran in blue and gold and red, the chairs were in dark buttoned leather, all the heavy furniture, including the panelling, was polished mahogany. The light fittings were worked in brass, the glasses in the liquor cabinet were sparkling diamond crystal flanked by a platoon of bottles that wore the uniforms of the great houses of Champagne and Alsace and the Rhine. There was a portrait in oils opposite the desk of two women, both beautiful golden women, clearly mother and daughter. The portholes were curtained with forest green velvet, corded and tasselled in gold.

Herman decided that the Count must be a rich man. He had a proper respect for wealth, and it showed in the way he stepped forward, drew himself up, brought his heels together sharply, and then creased his bulging belly in a bow.

'Captain. I came as soon as I received your message.'

'I am grateful, Commissioner.' Von Kleine returned the salutation. 'You will take refreshment?'

'A glass of beer, and . . .' Herman hesitated, he was certain that somewhere aboard

Blücher there must be a treasure trove of rare foods, '. . . a bite to eat. I have not eaten since noon.'

It was now the middle of the afternoon. Von Kleine saw nothing unusual in a two-hour period of abstinence, yet he passed the word for his steward while he opened a bottle of beer for his guest.

'I must congratulate you on your victory over the two English warships, Captain. Magnificent, truly magnificent!'

Lying back in one of the leather chairs Fleischer was engaged in mopping his face and neck, and Kyller grinned cynically as he listened to this new tune.

'A victory that was dearly bought,' murmured von Kleine, bringing the glass to Fleischer's chair. 'And now I need your help.'

'Of course! You need only ask.'

Von Kleine went to his desk, sat down and drew towards him a sheaf of notes. From their chamois leather case, he produced a pair of gold-rimmed spectacles and placed them on his nose.

'Commissioner . . .' he started, but at that moment he completely lost Fleischer's attention. For with a discreet knock the Captain's steward returned with a large, heavily laden carving-plate. He placed it on the table beside Fleischer's chair.

'Sweet Mother of God!' whispered Herman, his eyes glittering, and a fresh sweat of excitement breaking out on his upper lip.

'Smoked salmon!'

Neither von Kleine nor Kyller had ever been privileged to watch Herman eat before. They did so now in awed silence. This was a specialist working with skill and dedication. After a while von Kleine made another effort to attract Herman's attention by coughing and rustling his sheaf of notes, but the Commissioner's snufflings and small moans of sensual pleasure continued. Von Kleine glanced at his lieutenant and lifted a golden eyebrow, Kyller half smiled in embarrassment. It was like watching a man in orgasm, so intimate that von Kleine was obliged to light a cheroot and concentrate his attention on the portrait of his wife and daughter across the cabin.

A gusty sigh signalled Herman's climax, and von Kleine looked at him again. He sagged back in the chair, a vague and dreamy smile playing over the ruddy curves of his face. The plate was empty, and with the sweet sorrow of a man remembering a lost love, Herman dabbed a forefinger on to the last shred of pink flesh and lifted it to his mouth.

'That was the best salmon I have ever tasted.'

'I am pleased that you found it so.' Von Kleine's voice crackled a little. He felt slightly nauseated by the exhibition.

'I wonder if I might trouble you for another glass of beer, Captain.'

Von Kleine nodded at Kyller, and the lieutenant went to refill Fleischer's glass.

'Commissioner. I need at least eight hundred square feet of $1\frac{1}{2}$-inch steel plate delivered to me here. I want it within six weeks,' von Kleine said, and Herman Fleischer laughed. He laughed the way a man laughs at a children's tale of fairies and witches, then suddenly he noticed von Kleine's eyes . . . and he stopped abruptly.

'Lying in Dar es Salaam harbour under British blockade is the steamer *Rheinlander*.' Von Kleine went on speaking softly and clearly. 'You will proceed there as fast as you can. I will send one of my engineers with you. He will beach the *Rheinlander* and dismantle her hull. You will then arrange to convey the plating to me here.'

'Dar es Salaam is one hundred kilometres away.' Herman was aghast.

'According to the admiralty chart it is seventy-five kilometres,' von Kleine corrected him.

'The plating will weigh many tons!' he cried.

'In German East Africa there are many hundreds of thousands of indigenes. I doubt not that you will be able to persuade them to serve as porters.'

'The route is impossible . . . and what is more, there is a band of enemy guerrillas operating in the area north of here. Guerrillas led by those same bandits that you allowed to escape from the dhow, off the mouth of this river.' In agitation Fleischer had risen from his chair and now he pointed a fat accusing forefinger at von Kleine. 'You allowed them to escape. Now they are ravaging the whole province. If I try to bring a heavily laden, slow moving caravan of porters down from Dar es Salaam, word will reach them before I have marched five kilometres. It's madness – I won't do it!'

'It seems then, that you have a choice.' Von Kleine smiled with his mouth only. 'The English marauders, or a firing party on the afterdeck of this ship.'

'What do you mean?' howled Fleischer.

'I mean that my request is no longer a request, it is now an order. If you defy it, I will immediately convene a court martial.'

Von Kleine drew his gold watch and checked the time.

'We should be able to dispose of the formalities and shoot you before dark. What do you think, Kyller?'

'It will be cutting things fine, sir. But I think we could manage it.'

53

When the Governor of Mozambique had offered Flynn a captaincy in the army of Portugal, there had been an ugly scene. Flynn felt strongly that he deserved at least the rank of colonel. He had suggested terminating their business relationship. The Governor had countered with an offer of major – and signalled to his aide-de-camp to refill Flynn's glass. Flynn had accepted both offers, but the one under protest. That was seven months ago, a few short weeks after the massacre at Lalapanzi.

Since then Flynn's army, a mixed bag of a hundred native troops, officered by himself, Sebastian and Rosa Oldsmith, had been operating almost continually in German territory.

There had been a raid on the Songea railway siding where Flynn had burned five hundred tons of sugar, and nearly a thousand of millet that was in the warehouses awaiting shipment to Dar es Salaam, supplies badly needed by Governor Schee and Colonel Lettow von Vorbeck who were assembling an army in the coastal area.

There had been another brilliant success when they had ambushed and wiped out a band of thirty Askari at a river crossing. Flynn released the three hundred native recruits that the Askari were escorting, and advised them to get the hell back to their villages and forsake any ambitions of military glory – using the corpses of the Askari that littered the banks of the ford as tangible argument.

Apart from cutting every telegraph line, and blowing up the railway tracks they came across, three other raids had met with mixed results. Twice they had captured supply columns of bearers carrying in provisions to the massing German forces. Each time they had been forced to run as German reinforcements came up to drive them off. The third effort had been an abject failure, the ignominy of it being compounded by the fact that they had almost had the person of Commissioner Fleischer in their grasp.

Carried on the swift feet of the runners who were part of Flynn's intelligence system came the news that Herman Fleischer and a party of Askari had left Mahenge boma and marched to the confluence of the Ruhaha and Rufiji rivers. There they had gone aboard the steam launch and disappeared into the fastness of the Rufiji delta on a mysterious errand.

'What goes up must come down,' Flynn pointed out to Sebastian. 'And what goes down the Rufiji must come up again. We will go to the Ruhaha and wait for Herr Fleischer to return.'

For once there was no argument from either Sebastian or Rosa. Between the three of them it was understood without discussion that Flynn's army existed chiefly to act as the vehicle of retribution. They had made a vow over the grave of the child, and now they fought not so much from a sense of duty or patriotism, but from a burning desire for revenge. They wanted the life of Herman Fleischer in part payment for that of Maria Oldsmith.

They set out for the Ruhaha river. As happened so often these days, Rosa marched at the head of the column. There was only the long braid of dark hair hanging down her back to show she was a woman, for she was dressed in bush jacket and long khaki cotton trousers that concealed the feminine fullness of her hips. She stepped out long-legged, and from her shoulder the loaded Mauser hung on its strap and bumped lightly against her flank at each pace.

The change in her was so startling as to leave Sebastian bewildered. The new hard line of her mouth, her eyes that gave off the dark hot glow of a fanatic, the voice that had lost the underlying ripple of laughter. She spoke seldom, but when she did, both Flynn and Sebastian were forced to hear her with respect. Sometimes listening to that flat deadly tone Sebastian could feel a prickle of horror under his skin.

They reached the landing-place and the jetty on the Ruhaha river and waited for the launch to return. It came three days later, heralding its approach by the soft chugging of its engine. When it came round the river bend, pushing briskly against the current, headed for the wooden jetty, they were lying in wait for it.

'There he is!' Sebastian's voice was thick with emotion as he recognized the plump grey-clad figure in the bows.

'The swine, oh, the bloody swine!' and he jerked the bolt of his rifle open then snapped it shut.

'Wait!' Rosa's hand closed on his wrist before he could lift the butt to his shoulder.

'I can get him from here!' protested Sebastian.

'No. I want him to see us. I want to tell him first. I want him to know why he must die.'

The launch swung in broadside to the current, losing its way, until it came in gently to nudge the jetty. Two of the Askari jumped ashore, laying back on the lines to hold her while the Commissioner disembarked.

Fleischer stood on the jetty for a minute, looking back down the river. This action should have warned Flynn, but he did not see its significance. Then the Commissioner shrugged slightly and trudged up the jetty towards the boat-house.

'Tell your men to drop their weapons into the river,' said Flynn in his best German as he stood up from the patch of reeds beside the jetty.

Herman Fleischer froze in mid-stride, but his belly quivered and his head turned slowly towards Flynn. His blue eyes seemed to spread until they filled his face, and he made a clucking noise in his throat.

'Tell them quickly, or I will shoot you through the stomach,' said Flynn, and Fleischer found his voice. He relayed Flynn's order to the Askari, and there were a series of splashes around the launch as it was obeyed.

Movement in the corner of his eye made Fleischer swing his head, and he was face to face with Rosa Oldsmith. Beyond her in a half circle stood Sebastian and a dozen armed Africans, but some instinct warned Fleischer that the woman was the danger. There was a merciless quality about her, some undefinable air of deadly purpose. It was to her he addressed his question.

'What do you want?' His voice was husky with apprehension.

'What did he say?' Rosa asked her father.

'He wants to know what you want.'

'Ask him if he remembers me.'

As he heard the question, Fleischer remembered her in her night-dress, kneeling in the fire-light, and with the memory came real fear.

'It was a mistake,' he whispered. 'The child! I did not order it.'

'Tell him . . .' said Rosa, 'tell him that I am going to kill him.' And her hands moved deliberately on the Mauser, slipping the safety-catch across, but her eyes never left his face.

'It was a mistake,' Herman repeated and he stepped backwards, lifting his hands to ward off the bullet that he knew must come.

At that moment Sebastian shouted behind Rosa, just one word.

'Look!'

Around the bend of the Ruhaha river, only two hundred yards from where they stood, another launch swept into view. It came silently, swiftly and at its stubby masthead flew the ensign of the German navy. There were men in crisp white uniforms clustered around the Maxim machine gun in its bows.

Flynn's party stared at it in complete disbelief. Its presence was as unbelievable as that of the Loch Ness monster in the Serpentine or a man-eating lion in St Paul's Cathedral, and in the long seconds that they stood paralysed the launch closed in quickly on the jetty.

Herman Fleischer broke the spell. He opened his mouth and from the barrel of his chest issued a bellow that rang clearly across the water.

'Kyller, they are Englishmen!'

Then he moved, with three light steps he danced sideways, incredibly quickly he moved his gross body from under the threatening muzzle of Rosa's rifle and dived from the jetty into the dark green swirl of water below the boards.

The splash of his dive was immediately followed by the tack, tack, tack of the launch's machine gun – and the air was filled with the swishing crack of a hundred whips. The launch drove straight in towards them with the Maxim blazing on its prow. Around Flynn, and Rosa and Sebastian the earth erupted in a rapid series of dust fountains, a ricochet howled dementedly, one of the gun-boys spun on his heels in a brief dervish dance and then sprawled down the bank, with his rifle clattering on the wooden boards of the jetty, and the frozen party on the bank exploded into violent movement. Flynn and his black troopers ducked and dodged away up the bank, but Rosa ran forward. She reached the edge of the jetty unscathed through the hailstorm of Maxim fire, there she checked and aimed the Mauser at the wallowing body of Herman Fleischer in the water below her.

'You killed my baby!' Rosa shrieked, and Fleischer looked up at her and knew he was about to die. A Maxim bullet struck the metal of the rifle, tearing it from Rosa's hands, and she staggered off balance, her arms windmilling as she tottered on the edge of the jetty.

Sebastian reached her as she fell. He caught her and swung her up on to his shoulder, whirled with her and bounded away up the bank, running with all the reserves of his strength unlocked by the key of his terror.

With ten of the gun-boys Sebastian took the rearguard; for that day and the next they skirmished back along the line of the retreat, briefly holding each natural defensive point until the Germans brought up the Maxim gun. Then they dropped back, retreating slowly while Flynn and Rosa made a straight run of it. In the second night Sebastian broke contact with the pursuers and fled north towards the rendezvous at the stream below the ruins of Lalapanzi.

Forty-eight hours later he reached it. In the moonlight he staggered into the camp, and Rosa threw off her blankets and came running to him with a low joyous cry of greeting. She knelt before him, unlaced and gently drew off each of his boots. While Sebastian gulped the mug of coffee and hot gin that Flynn brewed for him, Rosa bathed and tended the blisters that had burst on his feet. Then she dried her hands, stood and picked up her blankets.

'Come,' she said, and together they walked away along the bank of the stream. Behind a curtain of hanging creepers, on a nest of dry grass and blankets, while the jewelled night sky glowed above them, they gave each other the comfort of their bodies for the first time since the death of the child. Afterwards they slept entwined until the low sun woke them. Then they rose and went down the bank together naked into the stream. The water was cold when she splashed him, and she giggled like a little girl and ran through the shallows across the sandbank with the water bursting in a sparkling spray around her legs, drops of it glittering like sequins on her skin, her waist was the neck of a Venetian vase flaring down into full double rounds on her lower body.

He chased and caught her and they fell together and knelt facing each other, spluttering and laughing, and with each gust of laughter her bosom jumped and bounced. Sebastian leaned forward with the laughter drying in his throat and cupped them in his hands.

Instantly her own laughter ceased, she looked at him a moment, then suddenly her face hardened and she struck his hands away.

'No!' she hissed at him, and jumping to her feet she waded to where her clothing lay on the bank. Swiftly she covered her femininity, and as she strapped the heavy bandolier of ammunition around her body the last soft memory of their loving was gone from her face.

54

I t was that stinking Rufiji water, Herman Fleischer decided, and moved painfully in his maschille as another cramp took him.

The hot hand of dysentery that closed on his stomach added to his mood of dark resentment. His present discomfort was directly linked to the arrival of *Blücher* in his territory, the indignities he had experienced at the hands of her captain, the danger he had run into in his brush with the English bandits at the start of this expedition, and since then the constant gruelling work and ever-present fear of another attack, the nagging of the engineer whom von Kleine had placed over him – he hated everything to do with that cursed warship, he hated every man aboard her.

The jogging motion of the maschille bearers stirred the contents of his belly, making it gurgle and squeak. He would have to stop again, and he looked ahead for a suitable place in which to find privacy.

Ahead of him the caravan of porters was toiling along the shallow bottom of a valley between two sparsely wooded ridges of shale and broken rock.

The column was spread out in an untidy straggle half a mile long, for it comprised just under a thousand men.

In the van a hundred of them, stripped to loin-cloths and shiny with sweat, were wielding their long pangas on the scrub. The blades glinting as they rose and fell, the thudding of the blows muted in the lazy heat of afternoon. Working under the supervision of Gunther Raube, the young engineering officer from *Blücher*, they were cutting out the narrow track, widening it for the passage of the bulky objects that followed.

Dwarfing the men that swarmed around them, these four objects rolled slowly along, rocking and swaying over patches of uneven ground. Now and then halting as they came up against a tree stump or an outcrop of rock, before the animal exertions of two hundred black men could get them rolling again.

Three weeks previously they had beached the freighter *Rheinlander* in Dar es Salaam harbour and dismantled eight slabs of her plating. Then from the metal frames of her hull, Raube had shaped eight enormous wheel rims, fourteen feet in diameter, into each of these he had welded a sheet of $1\frac{1}{2}$-inch plating ten foot square. Using the freighter's bollards as axles, he had linked these eight discs in four pairs. Thus each of these contraptions looked like the wheel and axle assembly of a gigantic Roman chariot.

Herman Fleischer had made a swift recruitment tour, and secured nine hundred able-bodied volunteers from the town of Dar es Salaam and its outlying villages. These nine hundred were now engaged in trundling the four sets of wheels southward towards the Rufiji delta. While they worked, Herman's Askari stood by with loaded Mausers to discourage any of the volunteers from succumbing to an attack of homesickness; a malady which was fast reaching epidemic proportions, aggravated as it was by shoulders rubbed raw by contact with harsh sun-heated metal, and by palms whose outer layers of skin had been smeared away on the rough hemp ropes. They had been two weeks at their labours and they were still thirty torturous miles from the river.

Herman Fleischer squirmed again in his maschille as the amoebic dysentery gnawed at his guts.

'Mother of a pig!' he moaned, and then shouted at the bearers, 'Quickly, take me to those trees.' He pointed to a clump of wild ebony that smothered one of the side draws of the valley.

With alacrity, the maschille bearers swung off the path and trotted up the draw. Within the screen of wild ebony they paused while the Commissioner alighted from the hammock and hurried into the deepest recess of the bush to be alone. Then they drew themselves down with a communal sigh and gave themselves up to a session of African callisthenics.

When the Commissioner came out of retreat he was hungry. It was cool and restful in the shade, an ideal place to take his mid-afternoon snack. Raube would have to fend for himself for an hour or so. Herman nodded to his personal servant to set up the camp table and open the food box. His mouth was full of sausage when the first rifle shot clapped dully in the dusty dry air.

55

Where is he? He must be here. The scouts said he was here. Can you see him?' Rosa Oldsmith spoke through lips that were chapped dry by sun and wind, white flakes of skin had come loose from the raw red patches of sunburn on her nose, and her eyes were bloodshot from the dust and the glare.

She lay on her stomach behind a bank of shale and coarse grass with the Mauser probing out in front of her.

'Can you see him?' she demanded again impatiently, turning her head towards her father.

Flynn grunted noncommittally, holding the binoculars to his eyes, panning them slowly down the length of the valley then back again to the head of the strange caravan.

'There is a white man there,' he said.

'Is it Fleischer, is it?'

'No,' doubtfully Flynn gave the negative.

'No, I don't think só.'

'Look for him. He must be there somewhere.'

'I wonder what the hell those things are.'

Flynn concentrated on the four huge sets of wheels. The lens of the binoculars magnified the heat distortion through the still air, making them change shape and size so that one second they were insignificant and the next they were monstrous.

'Look for Fleischer. Damn those things, look for Fleischer,' Rosa snapped at him.

'He's not with them.'

'He must be. He must be there.' Rosa rolled on her side and reached out to snatch the binoculars from Flynn's hands. Eagerly she scanned the long column that moved slowly towards them up the valley.

'He must be there. Please God, he must be there,' she whispered her hatred through cracked dry lips.

'We will have to attack soon. They are nearly in position now.'

'We must find Fleischer.' Desperately Rosa searched, her knuckles showing white through sun-brown skin as she clutched the binoculars.

'We can't let it go much longer. Sebastian is in position, he will be expecting my signal.'

'Wait! You must wait.'

'No. We can't let them get closer.' Flynn half lifted his body, and called softly.

'Mohammed! Are you ready?'

'We are ready.' The reply came from farther down the slope where the line of riflemen lay.

'Remember my words, oh, thou chosen of Allah. Kill the Askari first and the others will run.'

'Your words ring in my ears with the brightness and the beauty of golden bells,' Mohammed replied.

'Up yours!' said Flynn and unbuttoned the pocket flap of his tunic. He fumbled out the hand-mirror and held it slanted to catch the sun, deflecting a bright splinter of light towards the far slope of the valley. From the jumble of rock and bush there was an immediate answering flash as Sebastian acknowledged the signal.

'Ah!' Flynn breathed theatrical relief, 'I was afraid our Bassie might have fallen asleep over there.' And he picked up the Mauser from the rock in front of him.

'Wait,' pleaded Rosa. 'Please wait.'

'We can't. You know we can't – if Fleischer is down there then we'll get him. If he isn't, then waiting any longer isn't going to help us.'

'You don't care,' she accused. 'You have forgotten about Maria already.'

'No,' said Flynn. 'No, I haven't forgotten,' and he cuddled the Mauser into his shoulder. There was an Askari he had been watching. A big man who moved ahead of the column. Even at this range Flynn sensed that this man was dangerous. He moved with a leopard's slouching awareness, head cocked and alert.

Flynn picked him up in the notch of the rear sight and rode the pip down his body, aiming low to compensate for the downhill shot, taking him in the belly. He gathered the slack in the trigger, squeezing it up gently. The Mauser cracked viciously and the recoil jumped back into his shoulder.

Incredulously Flynn saw the bullet throw a jump of dust from the slope below the Askari. A clean miss at four hundred yards from a carefully aimed shot – By Christ, he was getting old.

Frantically he worked the bolt of the rifle, but already the Askari had ducked for cover, unslinging his rifle as he disappeared into a bank of grey thorn bush, and Flynn's next shot ripped ineffectively into the coarse dry vegetation.

'Damn it to hell!' howled Flynn, and his voice was small in the storm of gun-fire that blew around him. From both slopes all his riflemen were shooting down into the solid pack of humanity that clogged the valley floor.

For startled seconds the mass of native bearers stood quiescent under the lash of the Mausers, each man frozen in the attitude in which the attack had caught him;

bent to the giant wheels, leaning forward against the ropes, panga raised to strike at a branch, or merely standing watching while others worked. Every head lifted to stare up at the slopes from which Flynn's hidden rifles menaced them, then with a sound like a rising wind a single voice climbed in a wail of terror, to be lost almost instantly in the babble from a thousand throats.

Without regard for Flynn's orders to single out only the armed Askari, his men were firing blindly into the mass of men around the wheels, bullets striking with a meaty thump, thump, thump, or whining from rock to inflict the ghastly secondary wounds of a ricochet.

Then the bearers broke. Flowing back like flood water along the valley, carrying the Askari whose khaki uniforms bobbed with them like driftwood in the torrent.

Beside Flynn in the donga, Rosa was firing also. Her hands on the rifle incongruously feminine, fingers long and sensitive working the bolt as though it were the shuttle of a loom, weaving death, her eyes slitted behind the gunsight, her lips barely moving as they formed the name which had become her battle hymn.

'Maria! Maria!' With each shot she said it softly.

As he fumbled a fresh clip of cartridges from his bandolier, Flynn glanced sideways at her. Even in this moment of hot excitement Flynn felt the prickle of disquiet as he saw his daughter's face. There was a madness in her eyes, the madness of grief too long sustained, the madness of hatred too carefully nourished.

His rifle was loaded and he switched his attention back to the valley. The scene had changed. From the rush of fear-crazed bearers, the German, whom Flynn had earlier watched through the binoculars, was rallying a defence. With him was the big Askari, the one that Flynn had missed with his first shot. These two stood to hold the guards who were being carried away on the rush of panic-stricken bearers, stopping them, turning them back, pushing and shoving them into defensive cover around the four huge wheels. Now they were returning the fire of Flynn's men.

'Mohammed! Get that man! The white man – get him!' roared Flynn, and fired twice, missing with each shot. But his bullets passed so close that the German dodged back behind the metal shield of the nearest wheel.

'That's done it,' lamented Flynn, as his hopes of quick success faded. 'They're getting settled in down there. We are going to have to prise them loose.'

The prospect was unattractive. Flynn had found from experience that while every man in his motley band was a hero when firing from ambush, and a master in the art of strategic retreat, yet their weak suit was frontal assault, or any other manoeuvre that involved exposure to the enemy. Of the hundred under his command, there were a dozen whom he could rely on to obey an order to attack. Flynn was understandably reluctant to issue such an order, for there are few situations more humiliating than bellowing, 'Charge!' – then having everybody look at you with a 'Who, me? You must be joking!' expression.

Now he steeled himself to do it, aware that with every second the battle madness of his men was cooling and being replaced by sanity and caution. He filled his lungs and opened his mouth, but Rosa saved him.

She rolled and lifted her knees, coming on to her feet with one fluid motion whose continuation was a catlike leap that carried her over the shale bank and into the open. Boyish, big hipped, but graceful – the rifle across her hip, firing. Long hair streaming, long legs flying, she went down the slope.

'Rosa!' roared Flynn in consternation, and jumped up to chase her in an ungainly lumbering run like the charge of an old bull buffalo.

'Fini!' shouted Mohammed, and scampered after his master.

'My goodness!' Sebastian gasped where he lay on the opposite side of the valley. 'It's Rosa!' and in a completely reflex response he found himself on his feet and bounding down the rocky slope.

'Akwende!' yelled the man beside him, carried away in his excitement, and before any of them had time to think, fifty of them were up and following. After the first half-dozen paces they were committed, for once they had started to run down the steep incline they could not stop without falling flat on their faces, they could only accelerate.

Down both slopes of the valley, scrambling, sliding on loose stone, pell-mell through thorn bush, screaming, shouting, they poured down on the cluster of Askari around the wheels.

From opposite sides, Rosa and Sebastian were first to reach the perimeter of the German position. Their momentum carried them unscathed through the first line of the defenders, and then with the empty rifle in her hands Rosa ran chest to chest against the big Askari who rose from behind a boulder to meet her. She shrieked as he caught her, and the sound exploded within Sebastian's brain in a red burst of fury.

Twenty yards away Rosa struggled with the man, but she was helpless as a baby in his arms. He lifted her, changing his grip on her body, snatching her up above his head, steadying himself to hurl her down on to the pointed rock behind which he had hidden. There was such animal power in the bunched muscles of his arms, in the thick sweat-slimy neck, in the muscular straddled legs, that Sebastian knew that when he dashed Rosa against the rock he would kill her. Her spine, her ribs must shatter with the force of it; the soft vital organs within her trunk must bruise or burst.

Sebastian went for him. Brushing from his path two lesser men of the bewildered defenders, clubbing the Mauser in his hands because he could not fire for fear of hitting Rosa, silently saving his breath for physical effort, he crossed the distance that separated them and reached them in the moment that the Askari began the first downward movement of his arms.

'Aah!' A gusty grunt was forced up Sebastian's throat by the force with which he swung the rifle, he used it like an axe, swinging it low with the full weight of his body behind it. The blade of the butt hit the Askari across the small of his back, and within his body cavity the kidneys popped like overripe satsuma plums. He was dying as he toppled backwards. As he hit the ground Rosa fell on top of him, his body cushioning her fall.

Sebastian dropped the rifle and stooped to gather her in his arms, crouching over her protectively.

Around them Flynn led his men boiling over the defenders, swamping them, knocking the rifles from their hands and dragging them to their feet, laughing in awe of their own courageous assault, chattering in excitement and relief.

Sebastian was on the point of straightening up and lifting Rosa to her feet, he glanced around quickly to assure himself that all danger was past – and his breathing jammed in his throat.

Ten paces away, kneeling in the shadow of one of the huge steel wheels was the white officer. He was a young man, swarthy for a German, but with pale green eyes. The tropical white of his uniform was patchy with damp sweat stains, and smeared with dust; his cap was pushed back, the gold braid on its peak sparkling with incongruous gaiety, for beneath it the face was taut and angry, the mouth pulled tight by the clenched jaws.

There was a Luger pistol clutched in his right hand. He lifted it and aimed.

'No!' croaked Sebastian, clumsily trying to shield Rosa with his own body, but he knew the German was going to fire.

'Mädchen!' cried Sebastian in his schoolboy German. 'Nein shutzen dis ein Mädchen!' and he saw the change in the young officer's expression, the pale green glitter of his eyes softening as he responded automatically to the appeal to his chivalry. Yet still the Luger was levelled, and over it Sebastian and the officer stared at each other. All this in seconds, but the delay was enough. While the officer still hesitated, suddenly it was too late, for Flynn stood over him and pressed the muzzle of his rifle into the back of the German's neck.

'Drop it, me beauty. Else I'll shoot your tonsils clean out through your Adam's apple.'

56

Strewn along the floor of the valley were the loads dropped by the native bearers, in their anxiety to leave for far places and fairer climes. Many of the packs had burst open and all had been trampled in the rush, so the contents littered the ground and discarded clothing flapped in the lower branches of the thorn trees.

Flynn's men were looting, a pastime in which they demonstrated a marked aptitude and industry. Busy as jackals around a lion's kill they gleaned the spoils and bickered over them.

The German officer sat quietly against the metal wheel. In front of him stood Rosa; she had in her hand the Luger pistol. The two of them watched each other steadily and expressionlessly. To one side Flynn squatted and pored over the contents of the German's pockets. Beside him Sebastian was ready to give his assistance.

'He's a naval officer,' said Sebastian, looking at the German with interest. 'He's got an anchor on his cap badge.'

'Do me a favour, Bassie,' pleaded Flynn.

'Of course.' Sebastian was ever anxious to please.

'Shut up!' said Flynn, without looking up from the contents of the officer's wallet which he had piled on the ground in front of him. In his dealings with Flynn, Sebastian had built up a thick layer of scar tissue around his sensitivity. He went on without a change of tone or expression.

'I wonder what on earth a naval officer is doing in the middle of the bush – pushing these funny contraptions around.' Sebastian examined the wheel with interest, before addressing himself to the German. 'Bitte, was it das?' He pointed at the wheel. The young officer did not even glance at him. He was watching Rosa with almost hypnotic concentration.

Sebastian repeated his question and when he found that he was again ignored he shrugged slightly, and leaned across to lift a sheet of paper from the small pile in front of Flynn.

'Leave it,' Flynn slapped his hand away. 'I'm reading.'

'Can I look at this, then?' He touched a photograph.

'Don't lose it,' cautioned Flynn, and Sebastian held it in his lap and examined it. It showed three young men in white overalls and naval peaked caps. They were smiling broadly into the camera with their arms linked together. In the background loomed the superstructure of a warship, the gun-turrets showed clearly. One of the men in the photograph was their prisoner who now sat against the wheel.

Sebastian reversed the square of heavy cardboard and read the inscription on the back of it.

' "Bremerhaven. 6 Aug. 1911." '

Both Flynn and Sebastian were absorbed in their studies, and Rosa and the German were alone. Completely alone, isolated by an intimate relationship.

Gunther Raube was fascinated. Staring into the girl's face, he had never known this sensation of mingled dread and elation which she invoked within him. Though her expression was flat and neutral, he could sense in her a hunger and a promise. He knew that they were bound together by something he did not understand, between them there was something very important to happen. It excited him, he felt it crawling like a living thing in his loins, ghost-walking along his spine, and his breathing was cramped and painful. Yet there was fear with it, fear that was as cloying as warm olive oil in his belly.

'What is it?' he whispered huskily as a lover. 'I do not understand. Tell me.'

And he sensed that she could not understand his language, but his tone made something move in her eyes. They darkened like cloud shadow on a green sea, and he saw she was beautiful. With a pang he thought how close he had been to firing the Luger she now held in her hand.

I might have killed her, and he wanted to reach out and touch her. Slowly he leaned forward, and Rosa shot him in the centre of his chest. The impact of the bullet threw him back against the metal frame of the wheel. He lay there looking at her.

Deliberately, each shot spaced, she emptied the magazine of the pistol. The Luger jumped and steadied and jumped again in her hand. Each blurt of gun-fire shockingly loud, and the wounds appeared like magic on the white front of his shirt, beginning to weep blood as he slumped sideways, and he lay with his eyes still fastened on her face as he died.

The pistol clicked empty and she let it drop from her hand.

57

S ir Percy held the square of cardboard at arm's length to read the inscription on the back of it.

' "Bremerhaven. 6 Aug. 1911," ' he said. Across the desk from him his flag-captain sat uncomfortably on the edge of the hard-backed H.M. issue chair. His right hand reached for his pocket, checked, then withdrew guiltily.

'For God's sake, Henry. Smoke that damned thing if you must,' grunted Sir Percy.

'Thank you, sir.' Gratefully Captain Henry Green completed the reach for his pocket, brought out a gnarled briar and began stuffing it with tobacco.

Laying aside the photograph, Sir Percy took up the bedraggled sheet of paper and studied the crude hand-drawn circles upon it, reading the descriptions that were linked by arrows to the circles. This sample of primitive art had been laboriously drawn by Flynn Patrick O'Flynn as an addendum to his report.

'You say this lot came in the diplomatic bag from the Embassy in Lourenco Marques?'

'That's right, sir.'

'Who is this fellow . . .' Sir Percy checked the name, 'Flynn Patrick O'Flynn?'

'It seems that he is a major in the Portuguese army, sir.'

'With a name like that?'

'You find these Irishmen everywhere, sir.' The captain smiled. 'He commands a group of scouts who raid across the border into German territory. They have built up something of a reputation for derring-do.'

Sir Percy grunted again, dropped the paper, clasped his hands behind his head and stared across the room at the portrait of Lord Nelson.

'All right, Henry. Let's hear what you make of it.'

The captain held a flaring match to the bowl of his pipe and sucked noisily, waved the match to extinguish it, and spoke through wreaths of smoke.

'The photograph first. It shows three German engineering officers on the foredeck of a cruiser. The one in the centre was the man killed by the scouts.' He puffed again. 'Intelligence reports that the cruiser is a "B" class. Nine-inch guns in raked turrets.'

' "B" class?' asked Sir Percy. 'They only launched two vessels of that class.'

'*Battenberg* and *Blücher*, sir.'

'*Blücher*!' said Sir Percy softly.

'*Blücher*!' agreed Henry Green. 'Presumed destroyed in a surface action with His Majesty's ships *Bloodhound* and *Orion* off the east coast of Africa between 16 and 20 September.'

'Go on.'

'Well, this officer could have been a survivor from *Blücher* who was lucky enough to come ashore in German East Africa – and is now serving with von Vorbeck's army.'

'Still dressed in full naval uniform, trundling strange round objects about the continent?' asked Sir Percy sceptically.

'An unusual duty, I agree, sir.'

'Now what do you make of these things?' With one finger Sir Percy prodded Flynn's diagram in front of him.

'Wheels,' said Green.

'For what?'

'Transporting material.'

'What material?'

'Steel plate.'

'Now who would want steel plate on the east coast of Africa?' mused Sir Percy.

'Perhaps the captain of a damaged battle cruiser.'

'Let's go down into the plotting room.' Sir Percy heaved his bulk out of the chair, and headed for the door.

His shoulders hunched, massive jaw jutting, Admiral Howe brooded over the plot of the Indian Ocean.

'Where was this column intercepted?' he asked.

'Here, sir.' Green touched the vast map with the pointer. 'About fifteen miles south-east of Kibiti. It was moving southwards towards . . .' He did not finish the statement but let the tip of the marker slide down on to the complexity of islands that clustered about the mouth of the long black snake that was the Rufiji river.

'Admiralty plot for East Africa, please.' Sir Percy turned to the lieutenant in charge of the plot, and the lieutenant selected Volume II of the blue-jacketed books that lined the shelf on the far wall.

'What are the sailing directions for the Rufiji mouth?' demanded the Admiral, and the lieutenant began to read.

'*Ras Pombwe to Kikunya mouth, including Mto Rufiji and Rufiji delta (Latitude 8° 17hS, Longitude 39° 20hE).* For fifty miles the coast is a maze of low, swampy, mangrove-covered islands, intersected by creeks comprising the delta of Mto Rufiji. During the rainy season the whole area of the delta is frequently inundated.

'The coast of the delta is broken by ten large mouths, eight of which are connected at all times with Mto Rufiji.'

Sir Percy interrupted peevishly, 'What is all this *Mto* business?'

'Arabic word for "river", sir.'

'Well, why don't they say so? Carry on.'

'With the exception of *Simba Uranga mouth* and *Kikunya mouth*, all other entrances are heavily shoaled and navigable only by craft drawing one metre or less.'

'Concentrate on those two then,' grunted Sir Percy, and the lieutenant turned the page.

'*Simba Uranga mouth.* Used by coasting vessels engaged in the timber trade. There is no defined bar and, in 1911, the channel was reported by the German Admiralty as having a low river level mean of ten fathoms.

'The channel is bifurcated by a wedge-shaped island, *Rufiji-ya-wake*, and both arms afford secure anchorage to vessels of large burden. However, holding ground is bad and securing to trees on the bank is more satisfactory. Floating islands of grass and weed are common.'

'All right!' Sir Percy halted the recitation, and every person in the plotting room looked expectantly at him. Sir Percy was glowering at the plot, breathing heavily through his nose. 'Where is *Blücher's* plaque?' he demanded harshly.

The lieutenant went to the locker behind him, and came back with the black wooden disc he had removed from the plot two months previously. Sir Percy took it from him, and rubbed it slowly between thumb and forefinger. There was complete silence in the room.

Slowly Sir Percy leaned forward across the map and placed the disc with a click upon the glass top. They all stared at it. It sat sinister as a black cancer where the green land met the blue ocean.

'Communications!' grunted Sir Percy and the yeoman of signals stepped forward with his pad ready.

'Despatch to Commodore Commanding Indian Ocean. Captain Joyce. H.M.S.

Renounce. Maximum Priority. Message reads: Intelligence reports indicate high probability . . .'

58

You know something, Captain Joyce, this is bloody good gin.' Flynn O'Flynn pointed the base of the glass at the ceiling, and in his eagerness to engulf the liquid, he did the same for the slice of lemon that the steward had placed in his glass. He gurgled like an air-locked geyser, his face changed swiftly to a deeper shade of red, then he expelled the lemon and with it a fine spray of gin and Indian tonic in a burst of explosive coughing.

'Are you all right?' Anxiously Captain Joyce leapt across the cabin and begun pounding Flynn between the shoulder-blades. He had visions of his key tool in the coming operation being asphyxiated before they had started.

'Pips!' gasped Flynn. 'Goddamned lemon pips.'

'Steward!' Captain Joyce called over his shoulder without interrupting the tattoo he was playing on Flynn's back. 'Bring the major a glass of water. Hurry!'

'Water?' wheezed Flynn in horror and the shock was sufficient to diminish the strength of his paroxysm.

The steward, who from experience could recognize a drinking man when he saw one, rose nobly to the occasion. He hurried across the cabin with a glass in his hand. A mouthful of the raw spirit effected a near miraculous cure, Flynn lay back in his chair his face still bright purple but his breathing easing, and Joyce withdrew to the far side of the cabin to inhale with relief the moist warm tropical air that oozed sluggishly through the open porthole. After a close range whiff of Flynn's body smell, it was as sweet as a bunch of tulips.

Flynn had been in the field for six weeks, and during that time it had not occurred to him to change his clothing. He smelled like a Roquefort cheese.

There was a pause while everybody recovered their breath, then Joyce picked up where he had left off.

'I was saying, Major, how good it was of you to return so promptly to meet me here.'

'I came the moment I received your message. The runner was waiting for us in M'topo's village. I left my command camped south of the Rovuma, and pushed through in forced marches. A hundred and fifty miles in three days! Not bad going, hey?'

'Damn good show!' agreed Joyce, and looked across at the other two men in the cabin for confirmation. With the Portuguese Governor's aide-de-camp was a young army lieutenant. Neither of them could understand a word of English. The aide-de-camp was wearing a politely non-committal expression, and the lieutenant had loosened the top button of his tunic and was lolling on the cabin's day couch with a little black cigarette drooping from his lips. Yet he contrived to look as gracefully insolent as a matador.

'The English captain asks that you recommend me to the Governor for the Star of St Peter.' Flynn translated Captain Joyce's speech to the aide-de-camp. Flynn wanted a medal. He had been hounding the Governor for one these last six months.

'Will you please tell the English captain that I would be delighted to convey his written citation to the Governor.' The aide-de-camp smiled blandly. Through their business association he knew better than to take Flynn's translation literally. Flynn scowled at him, and Joyce sensed the strain in the cabin. He went on quickly.

'I asked you to meet me here to discuss a matter of very great importance.' He paused. 'Two months ago your scouts attacked a German supply column near the village of Kibiti.'

'That's right.' Flynn sat up in his chair. 'A hell of a fight. We fought like madmen. Hand-to-hand stuff.'

'Quite,' Joyce agreed quickly. 'Quite so. With this column was a German naval officer . . .'

'I didn't do it,' interjected Flynn with alarm. 'It wasn't me. He was trying to escape. You can't pin that one on me.'

Joyce looked startled.

'I beg your pardon.'

'He was shot trying to escape – and you try and prove different,' Flynn challenged him hotly.

'Yes, I know. I have a copy of your report. A pity. A great pity. We would dearly have liked to interrogate the man.'

'You calling me a liar?'

'Good Lord, Major O'Flynn. Nothing is further from my mind.' Joyce was finding that conversation with Flynn O'Flynn was similar to feeling your way blindfolded through a hawthorn bush. 'Your glass is empty, may I offer you a drink?'

Flynn's mouth was open to emit further truculent denials, but the offer of hospitality took him unawares and he subsided.

'Thank you. It's damn good gin, haven't tasted anything like it in years. I don't suppose you could spare a case or two?'

Again Joyce was startled.

'I'm sure the wardroom secretary will be able to arrange something for you.'

'Bloody good stuff,' said Flynn, and sipped at his recharged glass. Joyce decided on a different approach.

'Major O'Flynn, have you heard of a German warship, a cruiser, named *Blücher*?'

'Have I, hell!' bellowed Flynn with such vehemence that Joyce was left in no doubt that he had struck another jarring note. 'The bastard sank me!'

These words conjured up in the eye of Captain Joyce's mind a brief but macabre picture of a Flynn floating on his back, while a battle cruiser fired on him with nine-inch guns.

'Sank you?' asked Joyce.

'Rammed me! There I was sailing along in this dhow peaceful as anything when up she comes and – bang, right up the arse.'

'I see,' murmured Joyce. 'Was it intentional?'

'You bloody tooting it was.'

'Why?'

'Well . . .' started Flynn, and then changed his mind. 'It's a long story.'

'Where did this happen?'

'About fifty miles off the mouth of the Rufiji river.'

'The Rufiji?' Joyce leaned forward eagerly. 'Do you know it? Do you know the Rufiji delta?'

'Do I know the Rufiji delta?' chucked Flynn. 'I know it like you know the way to your own Thunder Box. I used to do a lot of business there before the war.'

'Excellent! Wonderful!' Joyce could not restrain himself from pursing his lips and whistling the first two bars of 'Tipperary'. From him this was expression of unadulterated joy.

'Yeah? What's so wonderful about that?' Flynn was immediately suspicious.

'Major O'Flynn. On the basis of your report, Naval Intelligence considers it highly probable that the *Blücher* is anchored somewhere in the Rufiji delta.'

'Who are you kidding? The *Blücher* was sunk months ago – everybody knows that.'

'Presumed sunk. She, and the two British warships that pursued her, disappeared off the face of the earth – or more correctly the ocean. Certain pieces of floating wreckage were recovered that indicated that a battle had been fought by the three ships. It was thought that all three had gone down.' Joyce paused and smoothed the grey wings of hair along his temples. 'But now it seems certain that *Blücher* was badly damaged during the engagement, and that she was holed up in the delta.'

'Those wheels! Steel plating for repairs!'

'Precisely, Major, precisely. But . . .' Joyce smiled at Flynn, '. . . thanks to you, they did not get the plating through.'

'Yes, they did.' Flynn growled a denial.

'They did?' demanded Joyce harshly.

'Yeah. We left them lying in the veld. My spies told me that after we had gone the Germans sent another party of bearers up and took them away.'

'Why didn't you prevent it?'

'What the hell for? They've got no value,' Flynn retorted.

'The enemy's insistence must have demonstrated their value.'

'Yeah. The enemy were so insistent they sent up a couple of Maxim guns with the second party. In my book the more Maxims there are guarding something, the less value it is.'

'Well, why didn't you destroy them while you had the chance?'

'Listen, friend, how do you reckon to destroy twenty tons of steel – swallow it perhaps?'

'Do you realize just what a threat this ship will be once it is seaworthy?' Joyce hesitated. 'I tell you now in strict confidence that there will be an invasion of German East Africa in the very near future. Can you imagine the havoc if *Blücher* were to slip out of the Rufiji and get among the troop convoys.'

'Yeah – all of us have got troubles.'

'Major.' The captain's voice was hoarse with the effort of checking his temper. 'Major. I want you to do a reconnaissance and locate the *Blücher* for us.'

'Is that so?' boomed Flynn. 'You want me to go galloping round in the delta when there's a Maxim behind every mangrove tree. It might take a year to search that delta, you've got no idea what it's like in there.'

'That won't be necessary.' Joyce swivelled his chair, he nodded at the Portuguese lieutenant. 'This officer is an aviator.'

'What's that mean?'

'He is a flyer.'

'Yeah? Is that so good? I did a bit of sleeping around when I was young – still get it up now and then.'

Joyce coughed.

'He flies an aircraft. A flying-machine.'

'Oh!' said Flynn. He was impressed. 'Jeez! is that so?' He looked at the Portuguese lieutenant with respect.

'With the co-operation of the Portuguese army I intend conducting an aerial reconnaissance of the Rufiji delta.'

'You mean flying over it in a flying-machine?'

'Precisely.'

'That's a bloody good idea.' Flynn was enthusiastic.

'When can you be ready?'

'What for?'

'For the reconnaissance.'

'Now just hold on a shake, friend!' Flynn was aghast. 'You not getting me into one of those flying things.'

Two hours later they were still arguing on the bridge of H.M.S. *Renounce*, as Joyce conned her back towards the land to deposit Flynn and the two Portuguese on the beach from which his launch had picked them up that morning. The British cruiser steamed over a sea that was oil-slick calm and purple blue, and the land lay as a dark irregular line on the horizon.

'It is essential that someone who knows the delta flies with the pilot. He has just arrived from Portugal, besides which he will be fully occupied in piloting the machine. He must have an observer.' Joyce was trying again.

Flynn had lost all interest in the discussion, he was now occupied with weightier matters.

'Captain,' he started, and Joyce recognized the new tone of his voice and turned to him hopefully.

'Captain, that other business. 'What about it?'

'I'm sorry – I don't follow you.'

'That gin you promised me, what about it?'

Captain Arthur Joyce R.N was a man of gentle mien. His face was smooth and unlined, his mouth full but grave, his eyes thoughtful, the streaks of silver grey at his temples gave him dignity. There was only one pointer to his true temperament, his eyebrows grew in one solid continuous line across his face; they were as thick and furry across the bridge of his nose as they were above his eyes. Despite his appearance he was a man of dark and violent temper. Ten years on his own bridge, wielding the limitless power and authority of a Royal Naval Captain had not mellowed him, but had taught him how to use the curb on his temper. Since early that morning when he had first shaken Flynn O'Flynn's large hairy paw, Arthur Joyce had been exercising every bit of restraint he possessed – now he had exhausted it all.

Flynn found himself standing speechless beneath the full blaze of Captain Joyce's anger. In a staccato, low-pitched speech, Arthur Joyce told him his opinion of Flynn's courage, character, reliability, drinking habits and sense of personal hygiene.

Flynn was shocked and deeply hurt.

'Listen . . .' he said.

'*YOU* listen,' said Joyce. 'Nothing will give me more pleasure than to see you leave this ship. And when you do so you can rest content in the knowledge that a full report of your conduct will go to my superiors – with copies to the Governor of Mozambique, and the Portuguese War Office.'

'Hold on!' cried Flynn. Not only was he going to leave the cruiser without the gin, but he could imagine that the wording of Joyce's report would ensure that he never got that medal. They might even withdraw his commission. In this moment of terrible stress the solution came to him.

'There is one man. *Only* one man who knows the delta better than I do. He's young, plenty of guts – and he's got eyes like a hawk.'

Joyce glared at him, breathing hard as he fought to check the headlong run of his rage.

'Who?' he demanded.

'My own son,' intoned Flynn, it sounded better than son-in-law.

'Will he do it?'

'He'll do it. I'll see to that,' Flynn assured him.

59

'I t's as safe as a horse and cart,' boomed Flynn, he liked the simile, and repeated it.

'How safe is a horse and cart when it's up in the clouds?' asked Sebastian, without lowering his eyes from the sky.

'I'm disappointed in you, Bassie. Most young fellows would jump at this chance.' Flynn was literally in excellent spirits. Joyce had come through with three cases of best Beefeater gin. He sat on one of the gasoline drums that lay beneath the shade of the palm trees above the beach, around him in various attitudes of relaxation lay twenty of his scouts, for it was a drowsy, warm and windless morning. A bright sun burned down from a clear sky, and the white sand was dazzling against the dark green of the sea. The low surf sighed softly against the beach, and half a mile out, a cloud of seabirds were milling and diving on a shoal of bait-fish. Their cries blending with the sound of the sea.

Even though they were a hundred miles north of the Rovuma mouth, deep in German territory, a holiday atmosphere prevailed. Heightened by anticipation of the imminent arrival of the flying-machine they were enjoying themselves – all of them except Sebastian and Rosa. They were holding each other's hands and looking into the southern sky.

'You must find it for us.' Rosa's voice was low, but not low enough to cover her intensity. For the last ten days, since Flynn had returned from his meeting with Joyce on board the *Renounce*, she had spoken of little else but the German warship. It had become another cup to catch the hatred that overflowed from her.

'I'll try,' said Sebastian.

'You must,' she said. 'You must.'

'Should be able to get a good view from up there. Like standing on a mountain –

only with no mountain under you,' said Sebastian and he felt his skin crawl at the thought.

'Listen!' said Rosa.

'What?'

'Ssh!'

And he heard it, an insect drone that swelled and sank and swelled again. They heard it under the trees also, and some of them came out into the sun and stood peering towards the south.

Suddenly in the sky there was a flash of reflected sunlight off metal or glass, and a shout went up from the watchers.

It came in towards them, low on wobbly wings, the clatter of its engine rising to a crescendo, its shadow racing ahead of it along the white beach. The group of native scouts exploded in panic-stricken retreat, Sebastian dropped on his face in the sand, only Rosa stood unmoving as it roared a few feet over her head, and then rose and banked away in a curve out over the sea.

Sebastian stood up and sheepishly brushed sand from his bush-jacket, as the aircraft levelled in and sank down on to the hard-packed sand near the water's edge. The beat of its engine faded to a spluttering burble, and it waddled slowly towards them, the backwash of the propeller sending a misty plume of sand scudding out behind. The wings looked as though they were about to fall off.

'All right,' bellowed Flynn at his men who were standing well back in the palm grove. 'Get these drums down there.'

The pilot switched off the motor, and the silence was stunning. He climbed stiffly out of the cockpit on to the lower wing, dumpy and awkward in his thick leather jacket, helmet and goggles. He jumped down on to the beach and shrugged out of the jacket, pulled off the helmet and was revealed as the suave young Portuguese lieutenant.

'Da Silva,' he said offering his right hand as Sebastian ran forward to greet him. 'Hernandez da Silva.'

While Flynn and Sebastian supervised the refuelling of the aircraft, Rosa sat with the pilot under the palms, while he breakfasted on garlic polony and a bottle of white wine that he had brought with him – suitably exotic food for a dashing knight of the air.

Although his mouth was busy, the pilot's eyes were free and he used them on Rosa. Even at a distance of fifty yards Sebastian became aware with mounting disquiet that Rosa was suddenly a woman again. Where before there had been a lifted chin and the straightforward masculine gaze; now there were downcast eyes broken with quick bright glances and secret smiles, now there were soft rose colours that glowed and faded beneath the sun-browned skin of her cheeks and neck. She touched her hair with a finger, pushing a strand back behind her ear. She tugged at the front of her bush-jacket to straighten it, then drew her long khaki-clad legs up sideways beneath her as she sat in the sand. The pilot's eyes followed the movement. He wiped the neck of the wine bottle on his sleeve, and then with a flourish offered it to Rosa.

Rosa murmured her thanks and accepted the bottle to sip at it delicately. With the freckles across her cheeks and the skin peeling from her nose she looked as fresh and as innocent as a little girl, Sebastian thought.

The Portuguese lieutenant on the other hand looked neither fresh nor innocent.

He was handsome, if you liked the slimy continental type with that slightly jaded tom cat look. Sebastian decided that there was something obscenely erotic about that little black moustache, that lay upon his upper lip and accentuated the cherry-pink lips beneath.

Watching him take the bottle back from Rosa and lift it towards her in salutation before drinking, Sebastian was overcome with two strong desires. One was to take the wine bottle and thrust it down the lieutenant's throat, the other was to get him into the flying-machine and away from Rosa just as quickly as was possible.

'Paci. Paci,' he growled at Mohammed's gang who were slopping gasoline into the funnel on the upper wing. 'Get a move on, for cat's sake!'

'Get your clobber into this thing, Bassie, and stop giving orders – you know it just confuses everybody.'

'I don't know where to put it – you'd better tell that greaser to come and show me. I can't speak his language.'

'Put it in the front cockpit – the observer's cockpit.'

'Tell that damned Portuguese to come here.' Sebastian dug in stubbornly. 'Tell him to leave Rosa alone and come here.'

Rosa followed the pilot to the aircraft and the expression of awed respect on her face, as she listened to him throwing out orders in Portuguese, infuriated Sebastian. The ritual of starting the aircraft completed, it stood clattering and quivering on the beach, and the pilot waved imperiously at Sebastian from the cockpit to come aboard.

Instead he went to Rosa and took her possessively in his arms.

'Do you love me?' he asked.

'What?' she shouted above the bellow of the engine.

'Do you love me?' he roared.

'Of course I do, you fool,' she shouted back and smiled up into his face before going up on tip-toe to kiss him while the slipstream of the propeller howled around them. Her embrace had passion in it that had not been there these many months, and Sebastian wondered sickly how much of it had been engendered by an outside agency.

'You can do that when you get back.' Flynn prised him loose from Rosa's grip, and boosted him up into the cockpit. The machine jerked forward and Sebastian clutched desperately to retain his balance, then glanced back. Rosa was waving and smiling, he was not certain if the smile was directed at him or at the helmeted head in the cockpit behind him, but his jealousy was swamped by the primeval instinct of survival.

Clutching with both hands at the sides of the cockpit, even his toes curling in their boots as though to grip the floorboards of the cockpit, Sebastian stared ahead.

The beach disappeared beneath the fuselage in a solid white blur; the palm trees whipped past on one side, the sea on the other; the wind tore at his face and tears streamed back along his cheeks, the machine bumped and bucked and jounced, and then leaped upwards under him, dropped back to bounce once more and then was airborne. The earth fell away gently beneath them as they soared, and Sebastian's spirits soared with them. His misgivings melted away.

Sebastian remembered at last to pull the goggles down over his eyes to protect them from the stinging wind, and godlike he looked down through them at a world that was small and tranquil.

When at last he looked back over his shoulder at the pilot, this strange and wonderful shared experience of immortality had lifted him above the petty passions of mere men, and they smiled at each other.

The pilot pointed out over the right wing tip, and Sebastian followed the direction of his arm.

Far, far out on the crenellated blue blanket of the sea, tiny beneath vast fluffy piles of thunderhead cloud, he saw the grey shape of the British cruiser *Renounce* with the pale white feather of its wake fanning on the surface of the ocean behind it.

He nodded and smiled at his companion. Again the pilot pointed, this time ahead.

Still misty in the blue haze of distance, haphazard as the unfitted pieces of a jigsaw puzzle, the islands of the Rufiji delta were spilled and scattered between ocean and mainland.

In the rackety little cockpit, Sebastian squatted over his pack and took from it binoculars, pencil and map-case.

60

I t was hot. Moist itchy hot. Even in the shade beneath the festooned camouflage-nets the decks of *Blücher* were smothered with hot sticky waves of swamp air. The sweat that oozed and trickled down the glistening bodies of the half-naked men who slaved on her foredeck gave them no relief, for the air was too humid to evaporate the moisture. They moved like sleep-walkers, with slow mechanical determination, manhandling the thick sheet of steel plate into its slings beneath the high arm of the crane.

Even the flow of obscenity from the lips of Lochtkamper, the engineering commander, had dried up like a spring in drought season. He worked with his men, like them stripped to the waist, and the tattoos on his upper arms and across his chest heaved and bulged as they rode on an undulating sea of muscles.

'Rest,' he grunted; and they straightened up from their labour, mouths gaping as they sucked in the stale air, massaging aching backs, glowering at the sheet of steel with true hatred.

'Captain.' Lochtkamper became aware of von Kleine for the first time. He stood against the forward gun-turret, tall in full whites, the blond beard half concealing the cross of black enamel and silver that hung at his throat. Lochtkamper crossed to him.

'It goes well?' von Kleine asked, and the engineer shook his head.

'Not as well as I had hoped.' He wiped one huge hand across his forehead, leaving a smudge of grease and rust scale on his own face. 'Slow,' he said. 'Too slow.'

'You have encountered difficulties?'

'Everywhere,' growled the engineer, and he looked around at the heat mist and the mangroves, at the sluggish black waters and the mud banks. 'Nothing works here – the welding equipment, the winch engines, even the men – everything sickens in this obscene heat.'

'How much longer?'

'I do not know, Captain. I truly do not know.'

Von Kleine would not press him. If any man could get *Blücher* seaworthy, it would be this man. When Lochtkamper slept at all, it was here on the foredeck, curled like a dog on a mattress thrown on the planking. He slept a few exhausted hours amid the whine and groan of the winches, the blue hissing glare of the welding torches and the drum splitting hammering of the riveters, then he was up again bullying, leading, coaxing and threatening.

'Another three weeks,' Lochtkamper estimated reluctantly. 'A month at the most — if all goes as it does now.'

They were both silent, standing together, two men from different worlds drawn together by a common goal, united by respect for each other's ability.

A mile up the channel, movement caught their attention. It was one of the launches returning to the cruiser, yet it looked like a hayrick under its bulky cargo. It came slowly against the sluggish current, sitting so low in the water that only a few inches of freeboard showed, while its load was a great shaggy hump on which sat a dozen black men.

Von Kleine and Lochtkamper watched it approaching.

'I still do not know about that obscene wood, Captain.' Lochtkamper shook his big untidy head again. 'It is so soft, so much ash, it could clog the furnace.'

'There is nothing else we can do,' von Kleine reminded him.

When *Blücher* entered the Rufiji, her coal-bunkers were almost empty. There was enough fuel for perhaps four thousand miles of steaming. Hardly enough to carry her in a straight run down into latitude 45° south, where her mother ship, *Esther*, waited to refuel her, and fill her magazines with shell.

There was not the faintest chance of obtaining coal. Instead von Kleine had set Commissioner Fleischer and his thousand native porters to cutting cordwood from the forests, that grew at the apex of the delta. It was a duty that Commissioner Fleischer had opposed with every argument and excuse he could muster. He felt that in delivering safely to Captain von Kleine the steel plating from Dar es Salaam, he had discharged any obligation that he might have towards the *Blücher*. His eloquence availed him not at all — Lochtkamper had fashioned two hundred primitive axe heads from the steel plate, and von Kleine had sent Lieutenant Kyller up-river with Fleischer to help him keep his enthusiasm for wood-cutting burning brightly.

For three weeks now, the *Blücher*'s launches had been plying steadily back and forth. Up to the present they had delivered some five hundred tons of timber. The problem was finding storage for this unwieldly cargo once the coal-bunkers were filled.

'We will have to begin deck loading the cordwood soon,' von Kleine muttered, and Lochtkamper opened his mouth to reply when the alarm bells began to clamour an emergency, and the loudhailer boomed.

'Captain to the bridge. Captain to the bridge.'

Von Kleine turned and ran.

On the companion ladder he collided with one of his lieutenants. They caught at each other for balance and the lieutenant shouted into von Kleine's face.

'Captain — an aircraft. Flying low. Coming this way. Portuguese markings.'

'Damn it to hell!' Von Kleine pushed past him, and bounded up the ladder. He burst on to the bridge, panting.

'Where is it?' he shouted.

The officer of the watch dropped his binoculars and turned to von Kleine with relief.

'There it is, sir!' He pointed through a hole in the tangled screen of camouflage that hung like a veranda roof over the bridge.

Von Kleine snatched the binoculars from him and, as he trained them on the distant winged shape in the mist haze above the mangroves, he issued his orders.

'Warn the men ashore. Everybody under cover,' he barked. 'All guns trained to maximum elevation. Pom-poms loaded with shrapnel. Machine gun crews closed up – but no firing until my orders.'

He held the aircraft in the round field of the field glasses.

'Portuguese, all right,' he grunted; the green and red insignia showed clearly against the brown body of the aircraft.

'She's searching . . .' The aircraft was sweeping back and forth, banking over and turning back at the end of each leg of her search pattern, like a farmer ploughing a field. Von Kleine could make out the head and shoulders of a man crouched forward in the squat round nose of the aircraft. '. . . Now we'll find out how effective is our camouflage.'

So the enemy have guessed at last. They must have reported the convoy of steel plate – or perhaps the chopping of the cordwood has alerted them, he thought, watching the aircraft tacking slowly towards him. *We could not hope to go undetected for ever – but I did not expect them to send an aircraft.*

Then suddenly the thought struck him so hard that he gasped with the danger of it. He whirled and ran to the forward rail of the bridge and peered out through the camouflage net.

Still half a mile distant, trundling slowly down the centre of the channel with the wide rippling V of her wake spread on the current behind her, clumsy as a pregnant hippo with her load of cordwood, the launch was aimed straight at *Blücher*. From the air she would be as conspicuous as a fat tick on a white sheet.

'The launch . . .' shouted von Kleine, '. . . hail her. Order her to run for the bank – get her under cover.'

But he knew it was useless. By the time she was within hail, it would be too late. He thought of ordering his forward turrets to fire on the launch and sink her – but discarded the idea immediately, the fall of shell would immediately draw the enemy's attention.

Impatiently he stood gripping the rail of the bridge, and mouthing his anger and his frustration at the approaching launch.

61

S| ebastian hung over the edge of the cockpit. The wind buffeted him, flapping his jacket wildly about his body, whipping his hair into a black tangle. With his usual dexterity Sebastian had managed to drop the binoculars overboard. They were the property of Flynn Patrick O'Flynn, and Sebastian knew that he would be expected to pay for them. This spoiled Sebastian's enjoyment of the flight to some extent, he already owed Flynn a little over three hundred pounds. Rosa would have something to say also. However, the loss of the binoculars was no handicap, the aircraft was flying too low and was so unstable that the unaided eye was much more effective.

From a height of five hundred feet the mangrove forest looked like a fluffy over-stuffed mattress, a sickly fever green in colour, with the channels and the water-ways between them dark gun-metal veins that flashed the sunlight back like a heliograph. The clouds of white egrets that rose in alarm as the aircraft approached looked like drifts of torn paper scraps. A fish eagle hung suspended in silent flight ahead of them, the wide span of its wings flared at the tips like the fingers of a hand. It dipped away, sliding past the aircraft's wing tip so close, that Sebastian saw the fierce yellow eyes in its white hooded head.

Sebastian laughed with delight, and then grabbed at the side of the cockpit to steady himself, as the machine rocked violently under him. This was the pilot's method of attracting Sebastian's attention, and Sebastian wished he would think up some other way of doing it.

He looked back angrily shouting in the howl of wind and engine.

'Watch it! You stupid dago.'

Da Silva was gesticulating wildly, his pink mouth working under the black moustache, his eyes wild behind the panes of his goggles, his right hand stabbing urgently out over the starboard wing.

Sebastian saw it immediately on the wide water-way, the launch was so glaringly conspicuous that he wondered why he had not seen it before, then he recalled that his attention had been concentrated on the terrain directly beneath the aircraft – and he excused himself.

Yet there was little to justify da Silva's excitement, he thought. This was no battle cruiser, it was a tiny vessel of perhaps twenty-five feet. Quickly he ran his eyes down the channel, following it to the open sea in the blue distance. It was empty.

He glanced back at the pilot and shook his head. But da Silva's excitement had, if anything, increased. He was making another frenzied hand-signal that Sebastian could not understand. To save argument Sebastian nodded in agreement, and instantly the machine dropped away under him so that Sebastian's belly was left behind and he clutched desperately at the side of the cockpit once more.

In a shallow turning dive, da Silva took the machine down and then levelled out with the landing-wheels almost brushing the tops of the mangroves. They rushed towards the channel, and as the last mangroves whipped away under them da Silva eased the nose down still farther and they dropped to within a few feet of the surface of the water. It was a display of fine flying that was completely wasted on Sebastian. He was cursing da Silva quietly, his eyes starting from their sockets.

A mile ahead of them across the open water bobbed the overladen launch. It was only a few feet below their own level, and they raced towards it with the wash of the propeller blowing a squall of ripples across the surface behind them.

'My God!' The blasphemy was wrung from Sebastian in his distress. 'He's going to fly right into it!'

It was an opinion that seemed to be shared by the crew of the launch. As the machine roared in on them, they began to abandon ship. Sebastian saw two men leap from the high piled load of timber and hit the water with small white splashes.

At the last second da Silva lifted the plane and they hopped over the launch. For a fleeting instant Sebastian stared at a range of fifteen feet into the face of the German naval officer who crouched down over the tiller bar at the stern of the launch. They were then past and climbing sharply, banking and turning back.

Sebastian saw the launch had rounded to, and that her crew were clambering aboard and splashing around her sides. Once more the aircraft dropped towards the channel, but da Silva had throttled back and the engine was burbling under half power. He leveled out fifty feet above the water, and flew sedately, keeping away from the launch and well towards the northern side of the channel.

'What are you doing?' Sebastian mouthed the question at da Silva. In reply the pilot made a sweeping gesture with his right hand at the thick bank of mangroves alongside.

Puzzled, Sebastian stared into the mangroves. What was the fool doing, surely he didn't think that . . .

There was a hump of high ground on the bank, a hump that rose perhaps one hundred and fifty feet above the level of the river. They came up to it.

Like a hunter following a wounded buffalo, moving carelessly through thin scattered bush which could not possibly give cover to such a large animal, and then suddenly coming face to face with it – so close, that he sees the minute detail of crenellation on the massive bosses of the horns, sees the blood dripping from moist black nostrils, and the dull furnace glare of the piggy little eyes – in the same fashion Sebastian found the *Blücher*.

She was so close he could see the pattern of rivets on her plating, the joints in the planking of her foredeck, the individual strands of the canopy of camouflage netting spread over her. He saw the men on her bridge, and the gun-crews behind the pom-poms and the Maxim machine guns on the balconies of her upperworks. From her squatting turrets her big guns gaped at him with hungry mouths, revolving to follow the flight of the machine.

She was monstrous, grey and sinister among the mangroves, crouching in her lair, and Sebastian cried aloud in surprise and alarm, a sound without shape or coherence, and at the same moment the engine of the aeroplane bellowed in full power, as da Silva thrust the throttle wide and hauled the joystick back into his crotch.

As the aircraft rocketed upwards, the deck of the *Blücher* erupted in a thunderous volcano of flame. Flame flew in great bell-shaped ejaculations from the muzzles of her nine-inch guns. Flame spat viciously from the multi-barrelled pom-poms and the machine guns on her upperworks.

Around the little aircraft the air boiled and hissed, disrupted, churned into violent turbulence by the passage of the big shells.

Something struck the plane, and she was whirled upwards like a burning leaf from a garden bonfire. Wing over wing she rolled, her engine surging wildly, her rigging groaning and creaking at the strain.

Sebastian was flung forward, the bridge of his nose cracked against the edge of the cockpit and instantly twin jets of blood spurted from his nostrils to douse the front of his jacket.

The machine stood on her tail, propeller clawing ineffectively at the air, engine wailing in over rev. Then she dropped away on one wing and one side swooped sickeningly downwards.

Da Silva fought her, feeling the sloppiness of the stall in her controls come alive again as she regained air-speed. The fluffy tops of the mangroves rushed up to meet him, and desperately he tried to ease her off. She was trying to respond, the fabric wrinkling along her wings as they flexed to the enormous pressure. He felt her lurch again as she touched the top branches, heard above the howl of the engine the faint crackling brush of the vegetation against her belly. Then suddenly, miraculously, she was clear; flying straight and level, climbing slowly up and away from the hungry swamp.

She was sluggish and heavy, and there was something loose under her. It banged and thumped and slapped in the slipstream, jarring the whole fuselage. Da Silva could not dare to manoeuvre her. He held her on the course she had chosen, easing her nose slightly upwards, slowly gaining precious altitude.

At a thousand feet he brought her round in a wide gentle turn to the south, and banging and thumping, one wing heavy, she staggered drunkenly through the sky towards her rendezvous with Flynn O'Flynn.

62

Flynn stood up with slow dignity from where he had been leaning against the bole of the palm tree.

'Where are you going?' Rosa opened her eyes and looked up at him.

'To do something you can't do for me.'

'That's the third time in an hour!' Rosa was suspicious.

'That's why they call it the East African quickstep,' said Flynn, and moved off ponderously into the undergrowth. He reached the lantana bush, and looked around carefully. He couldn't trust Rosa not to follow him. Satisfied, he dropped to his knees and dug with his hands in the loose sand.

With the air of an old-time pirate unearthing a chest of doubloons, he lifted the bottle from its grave, and withdrew the cork.

The neck of the bottle was in his mouth, when he heard the muted beat of the returning aircraft. The bottle stayed there a while longer, Flynn's Adam's apple pulsing up and down his throat as he swallowed, but his eyes swivelled upwards and creased in concentration.

With a sigh of intense pleasure he recorked, and laid the bottle once more to rest, kicked sand over it, and set course for the beach.

'Can you see them?' he shouted the question at Rosa as he came down through the palms. She was standing out in the open. Her head was thrown back so that the long braid of her hair hung down to her waist behind. She did not answer him, but the set of her expression was hard and strained with anxiety. The men standing about her were silent also, held by an expectant dread.

Flynn looked up and saw it coming in like a wounded bird, the engine stuttering and surging irregularly, streaming a long bluish streak of oily smoke from the exhaust manifold, the wings rocking crazily, and a loose tangle of wreckage hanging and swinging under the belly where one of the landing-wheels had been shot away.

It sagged wearily towards the beach, the broken beat of the engine failing so they could hear the whisper of the wind in her rigging.

The single landing-wheel touched down on the hard sand and for fifty yards she ran true, then with a jerk she toppled sideways. The port wing bit into the sand, slewing her towards the edge of the sea, the tail came up and over. There was a crackling, ripping, tearing sound; and in a dust storm of flying sand she cartwheeled, stern over stem.

The propeller tore into the beach, disintegrating in a blur of flying splinters, and from the forward cockpit a human body was flung clear, spinning in the air so that the outflung limbs were the spokes of a wheel. It fell with a splash in the shallow water at the edge of the beach, while the aircraft careened onwards, tearing herself to pieces. A lower wing broke off – the guy wires snapping with a sound like a volley of musketry. The body of the machine slowed as it hit the water, skidding to a standstill on its back, with the surf washing around it. Da Silva hung motionless in the back cockpit, suspended upside down by his safety-straps, his arms dangling.

The next few seconds of silence were appalling.

'Help the pilot! I'll get Sebastian.' Rosa broke it at last. Mohammed and two other Askari ran with her towards where Sebastian was lying awash, a piece of flotsam at the water's edge.

'Come on!' Flynn shouted at the men near him, and lumbered through the soft fluffy sand towards the wreck. They never reached it.

There was a concussion, a vast disturbance in the air that sucked at their eardrums, as the gasoline ignited in explosive combustion. The machine and the surface of the sea about it was instantly transformed into a roaring, raging sheet of flame.

They backed away from the heat. The flames were dark red laced with satanic black smoke, and they ate the canvas skin from the body of the aircraft, exposing the wooden framework beneath.

In the heart of the flames da Silva still hung in his cockpit, a blackened monkey-like shape as his clothing burned. Then the fire ate through the straps of his harness and he dropped heavily into the shallow water, hissing and sizzling as the flames were quenched.

The fire was still smouldering by the time Sebastian regained consciousness, and was able to lift himself on one elbow. Muzzily he stared down the beach at the smoking wreckage. The shadows of the palms lay like the stripes of a tiger on the sand that the low evening sun had softened to a dull gold.

'Da Silva?' Sebastian's voice was thick and slurred. His nose was broken and squashed across his face. Although Rosa had wiped most of the blood away, there were still little black crusts of it in his nostrils and at the corners of his mouth. Both his eyes were slits in the swollen plum-coloured bruises that bulged from the sockets.

'No!' Flynn shook his head. 'He didn't make it.'

'Dead?' whispered Sebastian.

'We buried him back in the bush.'

'What happened?' asked Rosa. 'What on earth happened out there?' She sat close beside him, protective as a mother over her child. Slowly Sebastian turned his head to look at her.

'We found the *Blücher*,' he said.

63

Captain Arthur Joyce, R.N., was a happy man. He stooped over his cabin desk, his hands placed open and flat on either side of the spread admiralty chart. He glowed with satisfaction as he looked down at the hand-drawn circle in crude blue pencil as though it were the signature of the President of the Bank of England on a cheque for a million sterling.

'Good!' he said. 'Oh, very good,' and he pursed his lips as though he were about to whistle 'Tipperary'. Instead he made a sucking sound, and smiled across at Sebastian. Behind his flattened nose and blue-ringed eyes, Sebastian smiled back at him.

'A damn good show, Oldsmith!' Joyce's expression changed, the little lights of recognition sparkled suddenly in his eyes. 'Oldsmith?' he repeated. 'I say, didn't you open the bowling for Sussex in the 1911 cricket season?'

'That's right, sir.'

'Good Lord!' Joyce beamed at him. 'I'll never forget your opening over to Yorkshire in the first match of the season. You dismissed Graham and Penridge for two runs – two for two, hey?'

'Two for two, it was,' Sebastian liked this man.

'Fiery stuff! And then you made fifty-five runs?'

'Sixty-five,' Sebastian corrected him. 'A record ninth wicket partnership with Clifford Dumont of – one hundred and eighty-six!'

'Yes! Yes! I remember it well. Fiery stuff! You were damned unlucky not to play for England.'

'Oh, I don't know about that,' said Sebastian in modest agreement.

'Yes, you were.' Joyce pursed his lips again. '*Damned* unlucky.'

Flynn O'Flynn had not understood a word of this. He was thrashing around in his chair like an old buffalo in a trap, bored to the point of pain. Rosa Oldsmith had understood no more than he had, but she was fascinated. It was clear that Captain Joyce knew of some outstanding accomplishment of Sebastian's, and if a man like Joyce knew of it – then Sebastian was famous. She felt pride swell in her chest and she smiled on Sebastian also.

'I didn't know, Sebastian. Why didn't you tell me?' She glowed warmly at him.

'Some other time,' Joyce interrupted quickly. 'Now we must get on with this other business.' And he returned his attention to the chart on the desk.

'Now I want you to cast your mind back. Shut your eyes and try to see it again.

Every detail you can remember, every little detail – it might be important. Did you see any signs of damage?'

Obediently Sebastian closed his eyes, and was surprised at how vividly the acid of fear had engraved the picture of *Blücher* on his mind.

'Yes,' he said. 'There were holes in her. Hundreds of holes, little black ones. And at the front end – the bows – there were trapezes hanging down on ropes, near the water. You know the kind that they use when they paint a high building . . .'

Joyce nodded at his secretary to record every word of it.

64

The single fan suspended over the table in the wardroom hummed quietly, the blades stirred the air that was moist and warm as the bedding of a malarial patient.

Except for the soft clink of cutlery on china, the only other sound was that of Commissioner Fleischer drinking his soup. It was thick, green pea soup, scalding hot, so that Fleischer found it necessary to blow heavily on each spoonful before ingesting it with a noise, not of the same volume as, but with the delicate tonal quality, of a flushing water closet. During the pause while he crumbled a slice of black bread into his soup, Fleischer looked across the board at Lieutenant Kyller.

'So you did not find the enemy flying-machine, then?'

'No.' Kyller went on fiddling with his wine glass without looking up. For forty-eight hours he and his patrols had searched the swamps and channels and mangrove forests for the wreckage of the aircraft. He was exhausted and covered with insect bites.

'Ja,' Fleischer nodded solemnly. 'It fell only a short way, but it did not hit the trees. I was sure of that. I have seen sand-grouse do the same thing sometimes when you shoot them with a shot-gun. Pow! They come tumbling down like this . . .' He fluttered his hand in the air, letting it fall towards his soup, '. . . then suddenly they do this.' The hand took flight again in the direction of Commander (Engineering) Lochtkamper's rugged Neanderthal face. They all watched it.

'The little bird flies away home. It was bad shooting from so close,' said Fleischer, and ended the demonstration by picking up his soup spoon, and the moist warm silence once more gripped the wardroom.

Commander Lochtkamper stoked his mouth as though it were one of his furnaces. The knuckles of both his hands were knocked raw by contact with steel plate and wire rope. Even when Fleischer's hand had flown into his face, he had not been distracted from his thoughts. His mind was wholly occupied with steel and machinery, weights and points of balance. He wanted to achieve twenty degrees of starboard list on *Blücher*, so that a greater area of her bottom would be exposed to his welders. This meant displacing one thousand tons of dead weight. It seemed an impossibility – unless we flood the port magazines, he thought, and take the guns from their turrets and move them. Then we could rig camels under her . . .

'It was not bad shooting,' said the gunnery lieutenant. 'She was flying too close, the rate of track was . . .' He broke off, wiped the side of his long pointed nose with his forefinger, and regarded balefully the sweat that came away on it. This fat peasant would not understand, he would not waste energy in explaining the technicalities. He contented himself with repeating, 'It was not bad shooting.'

'I think we must accept that the enemy machine has returned safely to her base,' said Lieutenant Kyller. 'Therefore we can expect the enemy to mount some form of offensive action against us in the very near future.' Kyller enjoyed a position of privilege in the wardroom. No other of the junior officers would have dared to express his opinions so freely. Yet none of them would have made as much sense as Kyller. When he spoke his senior officers listened, if not respectfully, at least attentively. Kyller had passed out sword of honour cadet from Bremerhaven Naval Academy in 1910. His father was a Baron, a personal friend of the Kaiser's, and an Admiral of the Imperial Fleet. Kyller was wardroom favourite, not only because of his dark good looks and courteous manner – but also because of his appetite for hard work, his meticulous attention to detail, and his ready mind. He was a good officer to have aboard – a credit to the ship.

'What can the enemy do?' Fleischer asked with scorn. He did not share the general opinion of Ernst Kyller. 'We are safe here – what can he do?'

'A superficial study of naval history will reveal, sir, that the English can be expected to do what you least expect them to do. And that they will do it, quickly, efficiently and with iron purpose.' Kyller scratched the lumpy red insect bites behind his left ear.

'Bah!' said Fleischer, and sprayed a little pea soup with the violence of his disgust. 'The English are fools and cowards – at the worst, they will skulk off the mouth of the river. They would not dare come in here after us.'

'I have no doubt that time will prove you correct, sir.' This was Kyller's phrase of violent disagreement with a senior officer, and from experience Captain von Kleine and his commanders recognized it. They smiled a little.

'This soup is bitter,' said Fleischer, satisfied that he had carried the argument. 'The cook has used sea-water in it.'

The accusation was so outrageous, that even von Kleine looked up from his plate.

'Please do not let our humble hospitality delay you, Herr Commissioner. You must be anxious to return up-river to your wood-cutting duties.'

And Fleischer subsided quickly, hunching over his food. Von Kleine transferred his gaze to Kyller.

'Kyller, you will not be returning with the Herr Commissioner. I am sending Ensign Proust with him this trip. You will be in command of the first line of defence that I plan to place at the mouth of the delta, in readiness for the English attack. You will attend the conference in my cabin after this meal, please.'

'Thank you, sir.' His voice was husky with gratitude for the honour his captain was conferring upon him. Von Kleine looked from him to his gunnery lieutenant.

'You also, please, Guns. I want to relieve you of your beloved upper deck pom-poms.'

'You mean to take them off their mountings, sir?' The gunnery lieutenant asked, looking at von Kleine dolefully over his long doleful nose.

'I regret the necessity,' von Kleine told him sympathetically.

65

'W'ell, Henry. We were right. *Blücher*'s there.'
    'Unfortunately, sir.'

'Two heavy cruisers tied up indefinitely on blockade service.'

Admiral Sir Percy thrust out his lower lip lugubriously as he regarded the plaques of *Renounce* and *Pegasus* on the Indian Ocean plot. 'There is work for them elsewhere.'

'There is, at that,' agreed Henry Green.

'That request of Joyce's for two motor torpedo-boats . . .'

'Yes, sir?'

'We must suppose he intends mounting a torpedo attack into the delta.'

'It looks like it, sir.'

'It might work – worth a try anyway. What can we scratch together for him?'

'There is a full squadron at Bombay, and another at Aden, sir.'

For five seconds, Sir Percy Howe reviewed the meagre forces with which he was expected to guard two oceans. With this new submarine menace, he could not detach a single ship from the approaches to the Suez Canal – it would have to be Bombay. 'Send him an M. T. B. from the Bombay squadron.'

'He asked for two, sir.'

'Joyce knows full well that I only let him have half of anything he requests. He always doubles up.'

'What about this recommendation for a decoration, sir?'

'The fellow who spotted the *Blücher*?'

'Yes, sir.'

'A bit tricky – Portuguese irregular and all that sort of thing.'

'He's a British subject, sir.'

'Then he shouldn't be with the dagos,' said Sir Percy. 'Leave it over until the operation is completed. We'll think about it after we've sunk the *Blücher*.'

66

'T'he sunset was blood and roses, nude pink and tarnished gold as the British blockade squadron stood in towards the land.

Renounce led with the commodore's penant flying at her masthead. In the smooth wide road of her wake, *Pegasus* slid over the water. Their silhouettes were crisp and black against the garish colours of the sunset. There was something prim and old-maidish about the lines of a heavy cruiser – none of the solid majesty of a battle-ship, nor the jaunty devil-may-care rake of a destroyer.

Close in under *Pegasus*'s beam, screened by her hull from the land, like a signet swimming beside the swan, rode the motor torpedo-boat.

Even in this light surface chop she was taking in water. Each wave puffed up over her bows and then streamed back greenish and cream along her decks. The spray rattled against the thin canvas that screened the open bridge.

Flynn O'Flynn crouched behind the screen and cursed the vaunting ambition that had led him to volunteer as pilot for this expedition. He glanced across at Sebastian who stood in the open wing of the bridge, behind the canvas-shrouded batteries of Lewis guns. Sebastian was grinning as the warm spray flew back into his face and trickled down his cheeks.

Joyce had recommended Sebastian for a Distinguished Service Order. This was almost more than Flynn could bear. He wanted one also. He had decided to go along now for that reason alone. Therefore Sebastian was directly to blame for Flynn's present discomfort, and Flynn felt a small warmth of satisfaction as he looked at the flattened, almost negroid contours of Sebastian's new nose. The young bastard deserved it, and he found himself wishing further punishment on his son-in-law.

'Distinguished Service Order and all . . .' he grunted. 'A half-trained chimpanzee could have done what he did. Yet who was it who found the wheels in the first place? No, Flynn Patrick, there just ain't no justice in this world, but we'll show the sons of bitches this time . . .'

His thoughts were interrupted by the small bustle of activity on the bridge around him. An Aldis lamp was winking from the high dark bulk of *Renounce* ahead of them.

The lieutenant commanding the torpedo-boat spelled the message aloud.

'Flag to YN2. D . . . P departure point. Good luck.' He was a dumpy amorphous figure in his duffle coat with the collar turned up. 'Thanks a lot, old chap – and one up your pipe also. No, Signaller, don't make that.' He went on quickly, 'YN2 to Flag. Acknowledged! Then turning to the engine voice-pipe. 'Both engines stop,' he said.

The beat of her engines faded away, and she wallowed in the trough of the next wave. *Renounce* and *Pegasus* sailed on sedately, leaving the tiny vessel rolling crazily in the turbulence of their wakes. A lonely speck five miles off the mouth of the Rufiji delta, too far off for the shorewatchers to see her in the fading evening light.

67

Lieutenant Ernst Kyller watched through his binoculars as the two British cruisers turned in succession away from the land and coalesced with the darkness that fell so swiftly over the ocean and the land. They were gone.

'Every day it is the same.' Kyller let the binoculars fall against his chest and pulled his watch from the pocket of his tunic. 'Fifteen minutes before sunset, and again fifteen minutes before sun-up they sail past to show us that they are still waiting.'

'Yes, sir,' agreed the seaman who was squeezed into the crow's-nest beside Kyller.

'I will go down now. Moon comes up at 11.44 tonight – keep awake.'

'Yes, sir.'

Kyller swung his legs over the side and groped with his feet for the rungs of the rope ladder. Then he climbed down the palm tree to the beach fifty feet below. By the time he reached it the light had gone, and the beach was a vague white blur down to the green lights of phosphorus in the surf.

The sand crunched like sugar under his boots as he set off to where the launch was moored. As he walked, his mind was wholly absorbed with the details of his defence system.

There were only two of the many mouths of the Rufiji, up which the English could attack. They were separated by a low wedge-shaped island of sand and mud and mangrove. It was on the seaward side of this island that Kyller had sited the four-pounder pom-poms taken from their mountings on *Blucher's* upper deck.

He had sunk a raft of logs into the soft mud to give them a firm foundation on which to stand, and he had cut out the mangroves so they commanded an arc of fire across both channels. His search-lights he sited with equal care – so they could sweep left or right without blinding his gunners.

From Commander Lochtkamper he had solicited a length of four-inch steel hawser. This was rather like an unrehabilitated insolvent raising an unsecured loan from a money-lender, for Commander Locktkamper was not easily parted from his stores. Far up river Ensign Proust had diverted some of his axe-men to felling fifty giant African mahogany trees. They had floated the trunks down on the tide; logs the size of the columns of a Greek temple. With these and the cable Kyller had fashioned a boom that stretched across both channels, an obstacle so formidable that it would rip the belly out of even a heavy cruiser coming down on it at speed.

Not satisfied with this, for Kyller had highly developed the Teutonic capacity for taking infinite pains, he lifted the fat globular mines with their sinister horns that *Blücher* had sown haphazardly behind her on her journey up-river. These he rearranged into neat geometrical ranks behind his log boom, a labour that left his men almost prostrated with nervous exhaustion.

This work had taken ten days to complete, and immediately Kyller had begun building observation posts. He placed them on every hump of high ground that commanded a view of the ocean, he built them in the tops of the palm trees, and on the smaller islands that stood out at sea. He arranged a system of signals with his observers – flags and heliographs for the day, sky-rockets for the night.

During the hours of darkness, two whale boats rowed steadily back and forth along the log boom, manned by seamen who slapped steadily and sulkily at the light cloud of mosquitoes that haloed their heads, and made occasional brief but vitriolic statements about Lieutenant Kyller's ancestry, present worth and future prospects.

At 2200 hours on the moonless night of 16 June 1915, the British motor torpedo-boat YN2 crept with both engines running dead slow into the centre of Lieutenant Kyller's elaborate reception arrangements.

68

After the clean cool air on the open sea, the smell was like entering the monkey-house of London Zoo. The land masked the breeze, and the frolic of the surface chop died away. As the torpedo-boat groped its way into the delta, the miasma of the swamps spread out to meet her.

'My God, that smell,' Sebastian twitched his flattened nose. 'It brings back pleasant memories.'

'Lovely, isn't it?' agreed Flynn.

'We must be almost into the channel.' Sebastian peered into the night, sensing rather than seeing the loom of the mangroves ahead and on either hand.

'I don't know what the hell I'm doing on this barge,' grunted Flynn. 'This is raving bloody madness. We've got more chance of catching a clap than finding our way up to where *Blücher* is anchored.'

'Faith! Major O'Flynn, and shame on ye!' The commander of the torpedo-boat exclaimed in his best music-hall brogue. 'We put our trust in you and the Lord.' His tone changed and he spoke crisply to the helmsman beside him. 'Lay her off a point to starboard.'

The long nose of the boat, with the torpedo tubes lying like a rack of gigantic champagne bottles on her foredeck, swung fractionally. The commander cocked his head to listen to the whispered soundings relayed from the leadsman in the bows.

'Twelve fathoms,' he repeated thoughtfully. 'So far so good.' Then he turned back to Flynn.

'Now, Major, I heard you shooting the blarney to Captain Joyce about how well you know this river, I think your exact words were, "Like you know the way to your own Thunder Box." You don't seem so certain about it any longer. Why is that?'

'It's dark,' said Flynn sulkily.

'My, so it is. But that shouldn't fluster an old river pilot like you.'

'Well, it sure as hell does.'

'If we get into the channel and lay up until the moon rises, would that help?'

'It wouldn't do any harm.'

That exchange seemed to exhaust the subject and for a further fifteen minutes the tense silence on the bridge was spoiled only by the commander's quiet orders to the helm, as he kept his ship within the ten fathom line of the channel.

Then Sebastian made a contribution.

'I say, there's something dead ahead of us.'

A patch of deeper darkness in the night; a low blurred shape that showed against the faint sheen of the star reflections on the surface. A reef perhaps? No, there was a splash alongside it as an oar dipped and pulled.

'Guard boat!' said the commander, and stooped to the voice-pipe. 'Both engines full ahead together.'

The deck canted sharply under their feet as the bows lifted, the whisper of the engines rose to a dull bellow and the torpedo-boat plunged forward like a bull at the cape.

'Hold on! I'm going to ram it.' The commander's voice was pitched at conversational level, and a hubbub of shouts broke out ahead, oars splashed frantically as the guard boat tried to pull out of their line of charge.

'Steer for them,' said the commander pleasantly, and the helmsman put her over a little.

Flash and crack, flash and crack, someone in the guard boat fired a rifle just as the torpedo-boat struck her. It was a glancing blow, taken on her shoulder, that spun the little whale boat aside, shearing off the protruding oars with a crackling popping sound.

She scraped down the gunwhale of the torpedo-boat, and then was left astern bobbing and rocking wildly as the larger vessel surged ahead.

Then abruptly it was no longer dark. From all around them sparkling trails of fire shot into the sky and burst in balls of blue, that lit it all with an eerie flickering glow.

'Sky rockets, be Jesus. Guy Fawkes, Guy,' said the commander.

They could see the banks of mangrove massed on either hand, and ahead of them the double mouths of the two channels.

'Steer for the southern channel.' This time the commander lifted his voice a little, and the ship plunged onward, throwing out white wings of water from under her bows, bucking and jarring as she leapt over the low swells pushed up by the out-flowing tide, so the men on the bridge hung on to the hand rail to steady themselves.

Then all of them gasped together in the pain of seared eyeballs as a solid shaft of dazzling white light struck them. It leapt out from the dark wedge of land that divided the two channels, and almost immediately two other searchlights on the outer banks of the channels joined in the hunt. Their beams fastened on the ship like the tentacles of a squid on the carcass of a flying fish.

'Get those lights!' This time the commander shouted the order at the gunners behind the Lewis guns at the corners of the bridge. The tracer that hosed out in a gentle arc towards the base of the searchlight beams was anaemic and pinkly pale, in contrast to the brilliance they were trying to quench.

The torpedo-boat roared on into the channel.

Then there was another sound. A regular thump, thump, thump like the working of a distant water pump. Lieutenant Kyller had opened up with his quick firing pom-pom.

The four-pound tracer emanated from the dark blob of the island. Seeming to float slowly towards the torpedo-boat, but gaining speed as it approached, until it flashed past with the whirr of a rocketing pheasant.

'Jesus!' said Flynn as though he meant it. He sat down hurriedly on the deck and began to unlace his boots.

Still held in the cold white grip of the searchlights, the torpedo-boat roared on with four-pounder shells streaking around her, and bursting in flurries of spray on the surface near her. The long dotted tendrils of tracer from her own Lewis guns still arched out in delicate lines towards the shore, and suddenly they had effect.

The beam of one of the searchlights snapped off as a bullet shattered the glass, for a few seconds the filaments continued to glow dull red as they burned themselves out.

In the relief from the blinding glare, Sebastian could see ahead, and he saw a sea serpent. It lay across the channel, undulating in the swells, bellied from bank to bank by the push of the tide, showing its back at the top of the swells and then ducking into the troughs; long and sinuous and menacing, Lieutenant Kyller's log boom waited to welcome them.

'Good God, what's that?'

'Full port rudder!' the commander bellowed. 'Both engines full astern together.'

And before the ship could answer her helm or the drag of her propellers, she ran into a log four feet thick and a hundred feet long. A log as unyielding as a reef of solid granite that stopped her dead in the water and crunched in her bows.

The men in the well of her bridge were thrown into a heap of tangled bodies on the deck. A heap from which the bull figure of Flynn Patrick O'Flynn was the first to emerge. On stockinged feet he made for the side of the ship.

'Flynn, where are you going?' Sebastian shouted after him.

'Home,' said Flynn.

'Wait for me.' Sebastian scrambled to his knees.

The engines roaring in reverse pulled the torpedo-boat back off the log-boom, her plywood hull crackling and squeaking, but she was mortally wounded. She was sinking with a rapidity that amazed Sebastian. Already her cockpit was flooding.

'Abandon ship,' shouted the commander.

'You damned tooting,' said Flynn O'Flynn and leaped in an untidy tangle of arms and legs into the water.

Like a playful seal the torpedo-boat rolled over on its side, and Sebastian jumped. Drawing his breath while he was in the air, steeling himself against the cold of the water.

He was surprised at how warm it was.

69

F rom the bridge of H.M.S. *Renounce*, the survivors looked like a cluster of bedraggled water rats. In the dawn they floundered and splashed around the edge of the balloon of stained and filthy water where the Rufiji had washed them out, like the effluent from the sewer outlet of a city. *Renounce* found them before the sharks did, for there was no blood. There was one broken leg, a fractured collar bone and a few cracked ribs – but miraculously there was no blood. So from a crew of fourteen, *Renounce* recovered every man – including the two pilots.

They came aboard with their hair matted, their faces streaked, and their eyes swollen and inflamed with engine oil. With a man on either hand to guide them, leaving a trail of malodorous Rufiji water across the deck, they shuffled down to the sick-bay, a sodden and sorrowful-looking assembly of humanity.

'Well,' said Flynn O'Flynn, 'if we don't get a medal for *that*, then I'm going back to my old job – and the hell with them.'

'That,' said Captain Arthur Joyce, sitting hunched behind his desk, 'was not a roaring success.' He showed no inclination to whistle 'Tipperary'.

'It wasn't even a good try, sir,' agreed the torpedo-boat commander. 'The Boche had everything ready to throw at our heads.'

'A log boom — ' Joyce shook his head, ' — good Lord, they went out with the Napoleonic War!' He said it in a tone that implied that he was a victim of unfair play.

'It was extraordinarily effective, sir.'

'Yes, it must have been.' Joyce sighed. 'Well, at the very least we have established that an attack up the channel is not practical.'

'During the few minutes before the tide swept us away from the boom I looked beyond it, and I saw what I took to be a mine. I think it certain that the Boche have laid a minefield beyond the boom, sir.'

'Thank you, Commander,' Joyce nodded. 'I will see to it that their Lordships receive a full account of your conduct. I consider it excellent.' Then he went on, 'I would value your opinion of Major O'Flynn and his son – do you think they are reliable men?'

'Well . . .' the commander hesitated, he did not want to be unfair, ' — they can both swim and the young one seems to have good eyesight. Apart from that I am not really in a position to give a judgement.'

'No, I don't suppose you are. Still I wish I knew more about them. For the next phase in this operation I am going to rely quite heavily on them.' He stood up. 'I think I will talk to them now.'

'You mean you actually want someone to go on board *Blücher*!' Flynn was appalled.

'I have explained to you, Major, how important it is for me to know exactly what state she is in. I must be able to estimate when she is likely to break out of the delta. I must know how much time I have.'

'Madness,' whispered Flynn. 'Stark raving bloody madness.' He stared at Joyce in disbelief.

'You have told me how well organized is your intelligence system ashore, of the reliable men who work for you. Indeed it is through you that we know that the Germans are cutting cordwood and taking it aboard. We know that they have recruited an army of native labourers and are using them not only for wood-cutting, but also for heavy work aboard the *Blücher*.'

'So?' Into that single word Flynn put a wealth of caution.

'One of your men could infiltrate the labour gangs and get aboard *Blücher*.'

And Flynn perked up immediately; he had anticipated that Joyce would suggest that Flynn Patrick O'Flynn should personally conduct a survey of *Blücher*'s damage.

'It might be done.' There was a lengthy pause while Flynn considered every aspect of the business. 'Of course, Captain, my men aren't fighting patriots like you and I. They work for money. They are . . .' Flynn searched for the word. 'They are . . .'

'Mercenaries?'

'Yes,' said Flynn. 'That's exactly what they are.'

'Hmm,' said Joyce. 'You mean they would want payment?'

'They'd want a big dollop of lolly – and you can't blame them, can you?'

'The person you send would have to be a first-class man.'

'He would be,' Flynn assured him.

'On behalf of His Majesty's Government, I could undertake to purchase a complete and competent report on the disposition of the German cruiser *Blücher*, for the sum of . . .' he thought about it a moment, '. . . one thousand pounds.'

'Gold?'

'Gold,' agreed Joyce.

'That would cover it nicely.' Flynn nodded, then allowed his eyes to move across the cabin to where Sebastian and Rosa sat side by side on the day couch. They were holding hands, and showing more interest in each other than in the bargainings of Flynn and Captain Joyce.

It was a good thing, Flynn decided, that the Wakamba tribe from which Commissioner Fleischer had recruited the majority of his labour force, effected clean-shaven pates. It would be impossible for a person of European descent to dress his straight hair to resemble the woollen cap of an African.

It was also a good thing about the M'senga tree. From the bark of the M'senga tree the fishermen of Central Africa decocted a liquid in which they soaked their nets. It toughened the fibres of the netting and it also stained the skin. Once Flynn had dipped his finger into a basin of the stuff, and despite constant scrubbing, it was fifteen days before the black stain faded.

It was finally a good thing about Sebastian's nose. Its new contours were decidedly negroid.

70

'A thousand pounds!' said Flynn O'Flynn as though it were a benediction, and he scooped another mugful of the black liquid and poured it over Sebastian Oldsmith's clean-shaven scalp. 'Think of it, Bassie, me lad, a thousand pounds! Your half share of that is five hundred. Why! You'll be in a position to pay me back every penny you owe me. You'll be out of debt at last.'

They were camped on the Abati river, one of the tributaries of the Rufiji. Six miles downstream was Commissioner Fleischer's wood-cutting camp.

'It's money for jam,' opined Flynn. He was sitting comfortably in a riempie chair beside the galvanized iron tub, in which Sebastian Oldsmith squatted with his knees drawn up under his chin, Sebastian had the dejected look of a spaniel taking a bath in flea shampoo. The liquid in which he sat was the colour and viscosity of strong Turkish coffee and already his face and body were a dark purply chocolate colour.

'Sebastian isn't interested in the money,' said Rosa Oldsmith. She knelt beside the tub and, tenderly as a mother bathing her infant, she was ladling the M'senga juice over Sebastian's shoulders and back.

'I know, I know!' Flynn agreed quickly. 'We are all doing our duty. We all remember little Maria – may the Lord bless and keep her tiny soul. But the money won't hurt us either.'

Sebastian closed his eyes as another mugful cascaded over his head.

'Rub it into the creases round your eyes – and under your chin,' said Flynn, and Sebastian obeyed. 'Now, let's go over it again, Bassie, so you don't get it all balled up.

One of Mohammed's cousins is boss-boy of the gang loading the timber into the launches. They are camped on the bank of the Rufiji. Mohammed will slip you in tonight, and tomorrow his cousin will get you on to one of the launches going down with a load for *Blücher*. All you've got to do is keep your eyes open. Joyce just wants to know what work they are doing to repair her; whether or not they've got the boilers fired; things like that. You understand?'

Sebastian nodded glumly.

'You'll come back up-river tomorrow evening, slip out of camp soon as it's dark and meet us here. Simple as a pimple, right?'

'Right,' murmured Sebastian.

'Right then. Out you get and dry off.'

As the dry wind from the uplands blew over his naked body, the purply tint of the dye faded into a matt chocolate. Rosa had modestly moved away into the grove of Marula trees behind the camp. Every few minutes Flynn came across to Sebastian and touched his skin.

'Coming along nicely,' he said, and, 'Nearly done,' and, 'Jeez, you look better than real.' Then finally in Swahili, 'Right, Mohammed, mark his face.'

Mohammed squatted in front of Sebastian with a tiny gourd of cosmetics; a mixture of animal fat and ash and ochre. With his fingers he daubed Sebastian's cheeks and nose and forehead with the tribal patterns. His head held on one side in artistic concentration, making soft clucking sounds of concentration as he worked, until at last Mohammed was satisfied.

'He is ready.'

'Get the clothes,' said Flynn. This was an exaggeration. Sebastian's attire could hardly be called clothing.

A string of bark around his neck from which was suspended a plugged duiker horn filled with snuff, a cloak of animal skin that smelled of woodsmoke and man-sweat, draped over his shoulders.

'It stinks!' said Sebastian cringing from contact with the garment. 'And it's probably got lice.'

'The real thing,' agreed Flynn jovially. 'All right, Mohammed. show him how to fit the istopo – the hat.'

'I don't have to wear that also,' Sebastian protested, staring in horror as Mohammed came towards him, grinning.

'Of course you've got to wear it.' Impatiently Flynn brushed aside his protest.

The hat was a hollow six-inch length cut from the neck of a calabash gourd. An anthropologist would have called it a penis-sheath. It had two purposes; firstly to protect the wearer from the scratches of thorns and the bites of insect pests, and secondly as a boost to his masculinity.

Once in position it looked impressive, enhancing Sebastian's already considerable muscular development.

Rosa said nothing when she returned. She took one long startled look at the hat and then quickly averted her gaze, but her cheeks and neck flared bright scarlet.

'For God's sake, Bassie. Act like you're proud of it. Stand up straight and take your hands away.' Flynn coached his son-in-law.

Mohammed knelt to slip the rawhide sandals on to Sebastian's feet, and then hand him the small blanket roll tied with a bark string. Sebastian slung it over one shoulder then picked up the long-handled throwing-spear.

Automatically he grounded the butt and leaned his weight on the shaft; lifting his left leg and placing the sole of his foot against the calf of his right leg, he stood in the stork posture of rest.

In every detail he was a Wakamba tribesman.

'You'll do,' said Flynn.

71

In the dawn, little wisps of river mist swirled around Commissioner Fleischer's legs as he came down the bank and on to the improvised jetty of logs.

He ran his eyes over the two launches, checking the ropes that held down the cargoes of timber. The launches sat low in the water, their exhausts puttering and blowing pale blue smoke that drifted away across the slick surface of the river.

'Are you ready?' he called to his sergeant of Askari.

'The men are eating, Bwana Mkuba.'

'Tell them to hurry,' growled Fleischer. It was a futile order and he stepped to the edge of the jetty, unbuttoning his trousers. He urinated noisily into the river, and the circle of men who squatted around the three-legged pot on the jetty watched him with interest, but without interrupting their breakfast.

With leather cloaks folded around their shoulders against the chill air off the water, they reached in turn into the pot and took a handful of the thick white maize porridge, moulding it into a mouth-size ball and then with the thumb forming a cup in the ball, dipping the ball into the smaller enamel dish and filling the depression with the creamy yellow gravy it contained, a tantalizing mixture of stewed catfish and tree caterpillars.

It was the first time that Sebastian had tasted this delicacy. He sat with the others and imitated their eating routine, forcing himself to place a lump of the spiced maize meal in his mouth. His gorge rose and gagged him, it tasted like fish oil and new-mown grass, not really offensive – it was just the thought of those fat yellow caterpillars. But had he been eating ham sandwiches, his appetite would not have been hearty.

His stomach was cramped with apprehension. He was a spy. A word from one of his companions, and Commissioner Fleischer would shout for the hanging ropes. Sebastian remembered the men he had seen in the monkey-bean tree on the bank of this same river, he remembered the flies clustered on their swollen, lolling tongues. It was not a mental picture conducive to enjoyment of breakfast.

Now, pretending to eat, he watched Commissioner Fleischer instead. It was the first time he had done so at leisure. The bulky figure in grey corduroy uniform, the pink-boiled face with pale golden eyelashes, the full petulant lips, the big freckled hands, all these revolted him. He felt his uneasiness swamped by a revival of the emotions that had possessed him as he stood beside the newly filled grave of his daughter on the heights above Lalapanzi.

'Black pig-animals,' shouted Herman Fleischer in Swahili, as he rebuttoned his clothing. 'That is enough! You do nothing but eat and sleep. It is time now for work.' He waddled across the logs of the jetty, into the little circle of porters. His first kick sent the three-legged pot clattering, his second kick caught Sebastian in the back and threw him forward on to his knees.

'Rasch!' He aimed another kick at one of them, but it was dodged, and the porters scattered to the launches.

Sebastian scrambled up. He had been kicked only once before in his life, and Flynn O'Flynn had learned not to do it again. For Sebastian there was nothing so humiliating as the contact of another man's foot against his person, also it had hurt.

Herman Fleischer had turned away to chivvy the others, so he did not see the hatred nor the way that Sebastian snarled at him, crouching like a leopard. Another second and he would have been on him. He might have killed Fleischer before the Askari shot him down – but he never made the attempt.

A hand on his arm. Mohammed's cousin beside him, his voice very low.

'Come! Let it pass. They will kill us also.'

And when Fleischer turned back the two of them had gone to the launch.

On the run down-river, Sebastian huddled with the others. Like them, drawing his cloak over his head to keep off the sun, but unlike them, he did not sleep. Through half-hooded eyes he was still watching Herman Fleischer, and his thoughts were hate-ugly.

Even with the current, the run in the deep-laden launches took almost four hours, and it was noon before they chugged around the last bend in the channel and turned in towards the mangrove forests.

Sebastian saw Herman Fleischer swallow the last bite of sausage and carefully repack the remainder into his haversack. He stood up and spoke to the man at the rudder, and both of them peered ahead.

'We have arrived,' said Mohammed's cousin, and removed his cloak from over his head. The little huddle of porters stirred into wakefulness and Sebastian stood up with them.

This time he knew what to look for, and he saw the muzzy silhouette of the *Blücher* skulking under her camouflage. From low down on the water she looked mountainous, and Sebastian's spine tingled as he remembered when last he had seen her from this angle, driving down to ram them with those axe-sharp blows. But now she floated awry, listing heavily.

'The boat leans over to one side.'

'Yes,' agreed Mohammed's cousin. 'The Allemand wanted it so. There has been a great carrying of goods within her, they have moved everything to make the boat lean over.'

'Why?'

The man shrugged and pointed with his chin. 'They have lifted her belly from the water, see how they work with fire on the holes in her skin.'

Tiny as beetles, men swarmed on the exposed hull, and even in the bright glare of midday, the welding torches flared and sparkled with blue-white flame. The new plating was conspicious in its coat of dull brown zinc oxide paint, against the battle-ship-grey of the original hull.

As the launch approached, Sebastian studied the work carefully. He could see that it was nearing completion, the welders were running closed the last seams in the new plating. Already there were painters covering the oxide red with the matt grey final coat.

The pock marks of the shell splinters in her upperworks had been closed, and here again men hung on the flimsy trapezes of rope and planks, their arms lifting and falling as they plied the paint brushes.

An air of bustle and intent activity gripped the *Blücher*. Everywhere men moved about fifty different tasks, while the uniforms of the officers were restless white spots roving about her decks.

'They have closed all the holes in her belly?' Sebastian asked.

'All of them,' Mohammed's cousin confirmed. 'See how she spits out the water that was in her womb.' And he pointed again with his chin. From a dozen outlet vents, *Blücher*'s pumps were expelling solid streams of brown water as she emptied the flooded compartments.

'There is smoke from her chimneys,' Sebastian exclaimed, as he noticed for the first time the faint shimmer of heat at the mouths of her stacks.

'Yes. They have built fire in the iron boxes deep inside her. My brother Walaka works there now. He is helping to tend the fires. At first the fires were small, but each day they feed them higher.'

Sebastian nodded thoughtfully, he knew it took time to heat cold furnaces without cracking the linings of fireclay.

The launch nosed in and bumped against the cliff-high side of the cruiser.

'Come,' said Mohammed's cousin. 'We will climb up and work with the gangs carrying the wood down into her. You will see more up there.'

A new wave of dread flooded over Sebastian. He didn't want to go up there among the enemy. But already his guide was scrambling up the catwalk that hung down *Blücher*'s flank.

Sebastian adjusted his penis-sheath, hitched up his cloak, took a deep breath and followed him.

72

'S ometimes it goes like that. In the beginning everything is an obscene shambles; nothing but snags and accidents and delays. Then suddenly everything drops into place and the job is finished.' Standing under the awning on the foredeck, Commander (Engineering) Lochtkamper was a satisfied man, as he looked around the ship. 'Two weeks ago it looked as though we would still be messing around when the war was over – but now!'

'You have done well,' von Kleine understated the facts. 'Again you have justified my confidence. But now I have another task to add to your burdens.'

'What is it, Captain?' Lochtkamper kept his voice noncommittal, but there was a wariness in his eyes.

'I want to alter the ship's profile – change it to resemble that of a British heavy cruiser.'

'How?'

'A dummy stack abaft the radio office. Canvas on a wooden frame. Then mask "X" turret, and block in the dip of our waist. If we run into the British blockade squadron in the night, it may give us the few extra minutes that will make the difference between success or failure.' Von Kleine spoke again as he turned away, 'Come, I will show you what I mean.'

Lochtkamper fell in beside him and they started aft, an incongruous pair; the engineer swaddled in soiled overalls, long arms dangling, shambling along beside his captain like a trained ape. Von Kleine tall over him, his tropical whites crisp and sterile, hands clasped behind his back and golden beard bowed forward on to his chest, leaning slightly against the steeply canted angle of the deck.

He spoke carefully. 'When can I sail, Commander? I must know precisely. Is the work so far advanced that you can say with certainty?'

Lochtkamper was silent, considering his reply as they picked their way side by side through the milling jostle of seamen and native porters.

'I will have full pressure on my boilers by tomorrow night, another day after that to complete the work on the hull, two more days to adjust the trim of the ship and to make the alterations to the superstructure,' he mused aloud. Then he looked up. Von Kleine was watching him. 'Four days,' he said. 'I will be ready in four days.'

'Four days. You are certain of that?'

'Yes.'

'Four days,' repeated von Kleine, and he stopped in mid-stride to think. This morning he had received a message from Governor Schee in Dar es Salaam, a message relayed from the Admiralty in Berlin. Naval Intelligence reported that three days ago a convoy of twelve troop ships, carrying Indian and South African infantry, had left Durban harbour. Their destination was not known, but it was an educated guess that the British were about to open a new theatre of war. The campaign in German West Africa had been brought to a swift and decisive conclusion by the South Africans. Botha and Smuts had launched a double-pronged offensive, driving in along the railroads to the German capital of Windhoek. The capitulation of the German West African army had released the South African forces for work elsewhere. It was almost certain that those troopships were trundling up the east coast at this very moment, intent on a landing at one of the little harbours that dotted the coast of East Africa. Tanga perhaps, or Kilwa Kvinje – possibly even Dar as Salaam itself.

He must have his ship seaworthy and battle-ready to break out through the blockade squadron, and destroy that convoy.

'The big job will be readjusting the ship's trim. There is much to be done. Stores to be manhandled, shell from the magazines, the guns remounted . . .' Lochtkamper interrupted his thoughts, 'We will need labour.'

'I will order Fleischer to bring all his forced labour down to assist with the work,' von Kleine muttered. 'But we must sail in four days. The moon will be right on the night of the thirtieth, we must break out then.' The saintly face was ruffled by the force of his concentration, he paced slowly, the golden beard sunk on his chest as he formulated his plans, speaking aloud. 'Kyller has buoyed the channel. He must start clearing the minefield at the entrance. We can cut the boom at the last moment – and the current will sweep it aside.'

They had reached the waist of the cruiser. Von Kleine was so deep in his thoughts that it took Lochtkamper's restraining hand on his arm, to return him to reality.

'Careful, sir.'

With a start von Kleine looked up. They had walked into a knot of African porters. Wild tribesmen, naked beneath their filthy leather cloaks, faces daubed with yellow ochre. They were man-handling the faggots of cordwood that were coming aboard from the launch that lay alongside *Blücher*. One of the heavy bundles was suspended from the boom of the derrick, it was swaying twenty feet above the deck and von Kleine had been about to walk under it. Lochtkamper's warning stopped him.

While he waited for them to clear away the faggot, von Kleine idly watched the native gang of workers.

One of the porters caught his attention. He was taller than his companions, his body sleeker, lacking the bunched and knotty muscle. His legs also were sturdier and finely moulded. The man lifted his head from his labours, and von Kleine looked into his face. The features were delicate; the lips not as full as, the forehead broader and deeper than, the typical African.

But it was the eyes that jerked von Kleine's attention back from the troop convoy. They were brown, dark brown and shifty. Von Kleine had learned to recognize guilt in the faces of his subordinates, it showed in the eyes. This man was guilty. It was only an instant that von Kleine saw it, then the porter dropped his gaze and stooped to take a grip on the bundle of timber. The man worried him, left him feeling vaguely uneasy, he wanted to speak with him – question him. He started towards him.

'Captain! Captain!' Commissioner Fleischer had come puffing up the catwalk from the launch, plump and sweaty he was pawing von Kleine's arm.

'I must speak with you, Captain.'

'Ah, Commissioner,' von Kleine greeted him coolly, trying to avoid the damp paw. 'One moment, please. I wish to . . .'

'It is a matter of the utmost importance. Ensign Proust . . .'

'In a moment, Commissioner.' Von Kleine pulled away, but Fleischer was determined. He stepped in front of von Kleine, blocking his path.

'Ensign Proust, the cowardly little prig . . .' and von Kleine found himself embroiled in a long report about Ensign Proust's lack of respect for the dignity of the Commissioner. He had been insubordinate, he had argued with Herr Fleischer, and further he had told Herr Fleischer that he considered him 'fat'.

'I will speak to Proust,' said von Kleine. It was a trivial matter and he wanted no part of it. Then Commander Lochtkamper was beside them. Would the Captain speak to the Herr Commissioner about labour for the handling of ballast? They fell into a long discussion and while they talked, the gang of porters lugged the bundle of timber aft and were absorbed by the bustling hordes of workmen.

Sebastian was sweating with fright; trembling, giddy with fright. Clearly he had sensed the German officer's suspicions. Those cold blue eyes had burned like dry ice. Now he stooped under his load, trying to shrink himself into insignificance, trying to overcome the grey clammy sense of dread that threatened to crush him.

'He saw you,' wheezed Mohammed's cousin, shuffling along beside Sebastian.

'Yes.' Sebastian bent lower. 'Is he still watching?'

The old man glanced back over his shoulder.

'No. He speaks with Mafuta, the fat one.'

'Good.' Sebastian felt a lift of relief. 'We must get back on the launch.'

'The loading is almost finished, but we must first speak with my brother. He waits for us.'

They turned the corner of the aft gun-turrets. On the deck was a mountain of cordwood. Stacked neatly and lashed down with rope. Black men swarmed over it, between them spreading a huge green tarpaulin over the wood pile.

They reached the wood pile and added the faggots they carried to the stack. Then, in the custom of Africa, they paused to rest and talk. A man clambered down from the wood pile to join them, a sprightly old gentleman with woolly grey hair, impeccably turned out in cloak and penis-sheath. Mohammed's cousin greeted him with courteous affection, and they took snuff together.

'This man is my brother,' he told Sebastian. 'His name is Walaka. When he was a young man he killed a lion with a spear. It was a big lion with a black mane.' To Sebastian this information seemed to be slightly irrelevant, his fear of discovery was making him nervously impatient. There were Germans all around them, big blond Germans bellowing orders as they chivvied on the labour gangs, Germans looking down on them from the tall superstructure above them, Germans elbowing them aside as they passed. Sebastian found it difficult to concentrate.

His two accomplices were involved in a family discussion. It seemed that Walaka's youngest daughter had given birth to a fine son, but that during his absence a leopard had raided Walaka's village and killed three of his goats. The new grandson did not seem to compensate Walaka for the loss of his goats. He was distressed.

'Leopards are the excrement of dead lepers,' he said, and would have enlarged on the subject but Sebastian interrupted him.

'Tell me of the things you have seen on this canoe. Say swiftly, there is little time. I must go before the Allemand comes for all of us with the ropes.'

Mention of the ropes brought the meeting to order, and Walaka launched into his report.

There were fires burning in the iron boxes in the belly of the canoe. Fires of such heat that they pained the eye when the door of the box was opened, fires with a breath like that of a hundred bush fires, fires that consumed . . .

'Yes, yes.' Sebastian cut short the lyrical description. 'What else?'

There had been a great carrying of goods, moving of them to one side of the canoe to make it lean in the water. They had carried boxes and bales, unbolted machinery and guns. See how they had been moved. They had taken from the rooms under her roof a great quantity of the huge bullets, also the white bags of powder for the guns and placed them in other rooms on the far side.

'What else?'

There was more, much more to tell. Walaka enthused about meat which came out of little tins, of lanterns that burned without wick, flame or oil, of great wheels that spun, and boxes of steel that screamed and hummed, of clean fresh water that gushed from the mouths of long rubber snakes, sometimes cold and at other times hot as though it had been boiled over a fire. There were marvels so numerous that it confused a man.

'These things I know. Is there nothing else that you have seen?'

Indeed there was. The Allemand had shot three native porters, lining them up and covering their eyes with strips of white cloth. The men had jumped and wriggled and fallen in a most comical fashion, and afterwards the Germans had washed the blood from the deck with water from the long snakes. Since then none of the other porters had helped themselves to blankets and buckets and other small moveables – the price was exorbitant.

Walaka's description of the execution had a chilling effect on Sebastian. He had done what he had come to do and now his urge to leave *Blücher* became overpowering. It was helped on by a German petty officer who joined the group uninvited.

'You lazy black baboons,' he bellowed. 'This is not a bloody Sunday-school outing – move, you swine, move!' And his boots flew. Led by Mohammed's cousin they left Walaka without farewell and scampered back along the deck. Just before they reached the entry port, Sebastian checked. The two German officers stood where he had left them, but now they were looking up at the high smoke stacks. The tall officer with the golden beard was describing sweeping motions with his outstretched hand, talking while the stocky one listened intently.

Mohammed's cousin scurried past them and disappeared over the side into the launch, leaving Sebastian hesitant and reluctant to run the gauntlet of those pale blue eyes.

'Manali, come quickly. The boat swims, you will be left!' Mohammed's cousin called from down below, his voice faint but urgent above the chug of the launch's engine.

Sebastian started forward again, his stomach a cold lump under his ribs. A dozen paces and he had reached the entry port.

The German officer turned and saw him. He challenged with raised voice, and came towards Sebastian, one arm outstretched as though to hold him.

Sebastian whirled and dived down the catwalk. Below him the launch was casting off her lines, water churning back from her propeller.

Sebastian reached the grating at the bottom of the catwalk. There was a gap of ten feet between him and the launch. He jumped, hung for a moment in the air, then hit the gunwale of the launch. His clutching fingers found a grip while his legs dangled in the warm water.

Mohammed's cousin caught his shoulder and dragged him aboard. They tumbled together in a heap on the deck of the launch.

'Bloody kaffir,' said Herman Fleischer and stooped to cuff them both heavily around the ears. Then he went back to his seat in the stern, and Sebastian smiled at him with something close to affection. After those deadly blue eyes, Herman Fleischer seemed as dangerous as a teddy-bear.

Then he looked back at *Blücher*. The German officer stood at the top of the catwalk, watching them as they drew away, and set a course upstream. Then he turned away from the rail and disappeared.

73

S ebastian sat on the day couch in the master cabin of H.M.S. *Renounce*, he sagged against the arm-rest and fought off the grey waves of exhaustion that washed over his mind.

He had not slept in thirty hours. After his escape from *Blücher* there had been the long launch journey up-river during which he had remained awake and jittery with the after-effects of tension.

After disembarking he had sneaked out of Fleischer's camp, avoiding the Askari guards, and trotted through the moonlight to meet Flynn and Rosa.

A hurried meal, and then all three of them had mounted on bicycles supplied with the compliments of the Royal Navy, and ridden all night along a rough elephant path to where they had left a canoe hidden among the reeds on the bank of one of the Rufiji tributaries.

In the dawn they had paddled out of one of the unguarded channels of the delta and made their rendezvous with the little whaler from H.M.S. *Renounce*.

Two long days of activity without rest, and Sebastian was groggy. Rosa sat beside him on the couch. She leaned across and touched his arm, her eyes dark with concern. Neither of them were taking any part in the conference in which the other persons in the crowded cabin were deeply involved.

Joyce sat as chairman, and beside him an older heavier man with bushy grey eyebrows and a truculent jaw, hair brushed in streaks across his pate in an ineffectual attempt to conceal his baldness. This was Armstrong, Captain of H.M.S. *Pegasus*, the other cruiser of the blockade squadron.

'Well, it looks as though *Blücher* has made good her damage, then. If she has fired her boilers, we can expect her to break out any day now – von Kleine would not burn up good fuel to keep his stokers warm.' He said it with relish, a fighting man anticipating a good hard fight. 'There's a message I'd like to give her from *Bloodhound* and *Orion* – an old account to settle.'

But Joyce also had a message, one that had its origin at the desk of Admiral Sir Percy Howe, Commander-in-Chief, South Atlantic and Indian Oceans. In part this message read:

'The safety of your squadron considered secondary to containing *Blücher*. Risk involved in delaying until *Blücher* leaves the delta before engaging her is too high. Absolutely imperative that she be either destroyed or blocked at her present anchorage. Consequences of *Blücher* running blockade and attacking the troop convoy conveying landing forces to invasion of Tanga will be catastrophic. Efforts being made to send you two tramp steamers to act as block ships, but failing their arrival, and failing also effective offensive action against *Blücher* before 30 July 1915, you are hereby ordered to scuttle *Renounce* and *Pegasus* in the channel of the Rufiji to block *Blücher*'s exit.'

It was a command that left Captain Arthur Joyce sick with dread. To scuttle his splendid ships – a thought as repulsive and loathsome as that of incest, of patricide, of human sacrifice. Today was 26 July, he had four days in which to find an alternative before the order became effective,

'She'll come out at night, of course, bound to!' Armstrong's voice was thick with battle lust. 'This time she'll not have an old girl and a baby like *Orion* and *Bloodhound* to deal with.' His tone changed slightly. 'We'll have to look lively. New moon in three days so *Blücher* will have dark nights. There could be a change in the weather . . .' Armstrong was looking a little worried now, '. . . we'll have to tighten up . . .'

'Read this,' said Joyce, and passed the flimsy to Armstrong. He read it.

'My God!' he gasped. 'Scuttle. Oh, my God!'

'There are two channels that *Blücher* could use.' Joyce spoke softly. 'We would have to block both of them – *Renounce* and *Pegasus*!'

'Jesus God!' swore Armstrong in horror. 'There must be another way.'

'I think there is,' said Joyce, and looked across at Sebastian. 'Mr Oldsmith,' he spoke gently, 'would it be possible for you to get on board the German cruiser once again?'

There were tiny lumps of yellow mucus in the corner of Sebastian's bloodshot eyes, but the stain that darkened his skin concealed the rings of fatigue under them.

'I'd rather not, old chap.' He ran his hand thoughtfully over his shaven scalp and the stubble of new hair rasped under his fingers. 'It was one of the most unpleasant hours of my life.'

'Quite,' said Captain Joyce. 'Quite so! I wouldn't have asked you, had I not considered it to be of prime importance.' Joyce paused and pursed his lips to whistle softly the first bar of Chopin's 'Funeral March', then he sighed and shook his head. 'If I were to tell you that you alone have it in your power to save both the cruisers of this squadron from destruction and to protect the lives of fifteen thousand British soldiers and seamen – how would you answer then?'

Glumly, Sebastian sagged back against the couch and closed his eyes.

'Can I have a few hours sleep first?'

74

It was exactly the size of a box of twenty-four Monte Cristo Havana Cigars, for that had been its contents before *Renounce*'s chief engine room artificer and the gunnery lieutenant had set to work on it.

It lay on the centre of Captain Joyce's desk, while the artificer explained its purpose to the respectful audience that stood around him.

'It's verra simple,' started the artificer in an accent that was as bracing as the fragrance of heather and highland whisky.

'It would have to be . . .' commented Flynn O'Flynn, '. . . for Bassie to understand it.'

'All you do is lift the lid.' The artificer suited action to the words, and even Flynn craned forward to examine the contents of the cigar box. Packed neatly into it were six yellow sticks of gelignite, looking like candles wrapped in grease-proof paper. There was also the flat dry cell battery from a bull's eye lantern, and a travelling-clock in a pigskin case. All of these were connected by loops and twists of fine copper wire. Engraved into the metal of the clock base were the words:

> 'To my dear husband Arthur,
> With love,
> Iris.
> Christmas 1914.'

Captain Arthur Joyce stilled a sentimental pang of regret with the thought that Iris would understand.

'Then . . .' said the artificer, clearly enjoying the hold he had on his audience, '. . . you wind the knob on the clock.' He touched it with his forefinger, '. . . close the lid,' he closed it, '. . . wait twelve hours, and – Boom!' The enthusiasm with which the Scotsman simulated an explosion blew a fine spray of spittle across the desk, and Flynn withdrew hurriedly out of range.

'Wait twelve hours?' asked Flynn, dabbing at the droplets on his cheeks. 'Why so long?'

'I ordered a twelve-hour delay on the fusing of the charge.' Joyce answered the question. 'If Mr Oldsmith is to gain access to the *Blücher*'s magazines, he will have to infiltrate the native labour gangs engaged in transferring the explosives. Once he is a member of the gang he might find difficulty in extricating himself and getting away from the ship after he has placed the charge. I am sure that Mr Oldsmith would be reluctant to make this attempt unless we could ensure that there is time for him to escape from *Blücher*, when his efforts . . . ah,' he sought the correct phraseology, '. . . ah . . . come to fruition.' Joyce was pleased with this speech, and he turned to Sebastian for endorsement. 'Am I correct in my assumption, Mr Oldsmith?'

Not to be outdone in verbosity, Sebastian pondered his reply for a second. Five hours of deathlike sleep curled in Rosa'a arms had refreshed his body and sharpened his wit to the edge of a Toledo steel blade.

'Indubitably,' he replied, and beamed in triumph.

75

They sat together in the time when the sun was dying and bleeding on the clouds. They sat together on a kaross of monkey skin in a thicket of wild ebony, at the head of one of the draws that wrinkled down into the valley of the Rufiji. They sat in silence. Rosa bent forward over her needlework, as she stitched a concealed pocket into the filthy cloak of leather that lay across her lap. The pocket would hold the cigar box. Sebastian watched her, and his eyes upon her were a caress. She pulled the last stitch tight, knotted it, then leaned forward to bite the thread.

'There!' she said. 'It's finished.' And looked up into his eyes.

'Thank you,' said Sebastian. They sat together quietly and Rosa reached out to touch his shoulder. The muscle under the black stained skin was rubber hard, and warm.

'Come,' she said and drew his head down to her so that their cheeks touched, and they held each other while the last light faded. The African dusk thickened the shadows in the wild ebony, and down the draw a jackal yipped plaintively.

'Are you ready?' Flynn stood near them, a dark bulky figure, with Mohammed beside him.

'Yes.' Sebastian looked up at him.

'Kiss me,' whispered Rosa, 'and come back safely.'

Gently Sebastian broke from her embrace. He stood tall above her, and draped the cloak over his naked body. The cigar box hung heavily between his shoulder blades.

'Wait for me,' he said, and walked away.

Flynn Patrick O'Flynn moved restlessly under his single blanket and belched. Heartburn moved acid sour in his throat, and he was cold. The earth under him had long since lost the warmth it had sucked from yesterday's sun. A small slice of the old moon gave a little silver light to the night.

Unsleeping he lay and listened to the soft sound of Rosa sleeping near him. The sound irritated him, he lacked only an excuse to waken her and make her talk to him. Instead he reached into the haversack that served as his pillow and his fingers closed round the cold smooth glass of the bottle.

A night-bird hooted softly down the draw, and Flynn released the bottle and sat up quickly. He placed two fingers between his lips and repeated the night-bird's cry.

Minutes later Mohammed drifted like a small black ghost into camp and came to squat beside Flynn's bed.

'I see you, Fini.'

'You I see also, Mohammed. It went well?'

'It went well.'

'Manali has entered the camp of the Allemand?'

'He sleeps now beside the man who is my cousin, and in the dawn they will go down the Rufiji, to the big boat of the Allemand once again.'

'Good!' grunted Flynn. 'You have done well.'

Mohammed coughed softly to signify that there was more to tell.

'What is it?' Flynn demanded.

'When I had seen Manali safely into the care of my cousin, I came back along the valley and . . .' he hesitated, '. . . perhaps it is not fitting to speak of such matters at a time when our Lord Manali goes unarmed and alone into the camp of the Allemand.'

'Speak,' said Flynn.

'As I walked without sound, I came to a place where this valley falls down to the little river called Abati. You know the place?'

'Yes, about a mile down the draw from here.'

'That is the place.' Mohammed nodded. 'It was here that I saw something move in the night. It was as though a mountain walked.'

A sliver of ice was thrust down Flynn's spine, and his breathing snagged painfully in his throat.

'Yes?' he breathed.

'It was a mountain armed with teeth of ivory that grew from its face to touch the ground as it walked.'

'*Plough the Earth.*' Flynn whispered the name, and his hand fell on to the rifle that lay loaded beside his bed.

'It was that one.' Mohammed nodded again. 'He feeds quietly, moving towards the Rufiji. But the voice of a rifle would carry down to the ears of the Allemand.'

'I won't fire,' whispered Flynn. 'I just want to have a look at him. I just want to see him again.' And the hand on the rifle shook like that of a man in high fever.

76

T he sun pushed up and sat fat and fiery as molten gold, on the hills of the Rufiji basin. Its warmth lifted streamers of mist from the swamps and reed-beds that bounded the Abati river, and they smoked like the ashes of a dying fire.

Under the fever trees the air was still cool with the memory of the night, but the sun sent long yellow shafts of light probing through the branches to disperse and warm it.

Three old eland bulls came up from the river, bigger than domestic cattle, light bluey-brown in colour with faint chalk stripes across the barrel of their bodies, they walked in single file, heavy dewlaps swinging, thick stubby horns held erect, and the tuft of darker hair on their foreheads standing out clearly. They reached the grove of fever trees and the lead bull stopped, suddenly alert. For long seconds they stood absolutely still, staring into the open palisade of fever tree trunks where the light was still vague beneath the canopy of interlaced leaves and branches.

The lead bull blew softly through his nostrils, and swung off the game path that led into the grove. Stepping lightly for such large animals, the three eland skirted the grove and moved away to blend into the dry thorn scrub higher up the slope.

'He is in there,' whispered Mohammed. 'The eland saw him, and turned aside.'

'Yes,' agreed Flynn. 'It is such a place as he would choose to lie up for the day.' He sat in the crotch of a M'banga tree, wedged securely ten feet above the ground, and peered across three hundred yards of open grassland at the dense stand of fever trees. The hands that held the binoculars to his eyes were unsteady with gin and excitement, and he was sweating, a droplet broke from his hair-line and slid down his cheek, tickling like an insect. He brushed it away.

'A wise man would leave him, and walk away even as the eland did.' Mohammed gave his opinion. He leaned against the base of the tree, holding Flynn's rifle across his chest. Flynn did not reply. He peered through the binoculars, swinging them slowly in an arc as he searched.

'He must be deep among the trees, I cannot see him from here.' And he loosened his leg grip from the crotch and clambered down to where Mohammed waited. He took his rifle and checked the load.

'Leave him, Fini,' Mohammed urged softly. 'There is no profit in it. We cannot carry the teeth away.'

'Stay here,' said Flynn.

'Fini, the Allemand will hear you. They are close – very close.'

'I will not shoot,' said Flynn. 'I must see him again – that is all. I will not shoot.'

Mohammed took the gin bottle from the haversack and handed it to him. Flynn drank.

'Stay here,' he repeated, his voice husky from the burn of the raw spirit.

'Be careful, Fini. He is an old one of evil temper – be careful.' Mohammed watched Flynn start out across the clearing. He walked with the slow deliberation of a man who goes in good time to a meeting that has long been prearranged. He reached the grove of fever trees and walked on into them without checking.

Plough the Earth was sleeping on his feet. His little eyes closed tightly in their wrinkled pouches. Tears had oozed in a long dark stain down his cheeks, and a fine haze of midges hovered about them. Tattered as battle-riven banners on a windless day, his ears lay back against his shoulders. His tusks were crutches that propped up the gnarled old head, and his trunk hung down between them, grey and slack and heavy.

Flynn saw him, and picked his way towards him between the trunks of the fever trees. The setting had an unreal quality, for the light effect of the low sun through the branches was golden beams reflected in shimmering misty green from the leaves of the fever trees. The grove was resonant with the whine of cicada beetles.

Flynn circled out until he was head on to the sleeping elephant, and then he moved in again. Twenty paces from him Flynn stopped. He stood with his feet set apart, the rifle held ready across one hip, and his head thrown back as he looked up at the unbelievable bulk of the old bull.

Up to this moment Flynn still believed that he would not shoot. He had come only to look at him once more, but it was as futile as an alcoholic who promised himself just one taste. He felt the madness begin at the base of his spine, hot and hard it poured into his body, filling him as though he were a container. The level rose to his throat and he tried to check it there, but the rifle was coming up. He felt the butt in his shoulder. Then he heard with surprise a voice, a voice that rang clearly through the grove and instantly stilled the whine of the cicadas. It was his own voice, crying out in defiance of his conscious resolve.

'Come on, then,' he shouted. And the old elephant burst from massive quiescence into full charge. It came down on him like a dynamited cliff of black rock. He saw it over the open rear sight of his rifle, saw it beyond the minute pip of the foresight that rode unwaveringly in the centre of the old bull's bulging brow – between the eyes, where the crease of skin at the base of its trunk was a deep lateral line.

The shot was thunderous, shattering into a thousand echoes against the boles of the fever trees. The elephant died in the fullness of his run. Legs buckled, and he came toppling forward, carried by his own momentum, a loose avalanche of flesh and bone and long ivory.

Flynn turned aside like a matador from the run of the bull, three quick dancing steps and then one of the tusks hit him. It took him across the hip with a force that hurled him twenty feet, the rifle spinning from his hands so that as he fell and rolled in the soft bed of loose trash and leaf mould, his lower body twisted away from his trunk at an impossible angle. His brittle old bones had broken like china; the ball of the femur snapping off in its socket, his pelvis fracturing clean through.

Lying face down, Flynn was mildly surprised that there was no pain. He could feel the jagged edges of bone rasping together deep in his flesh at his slightest movement, but there was no pain.

Slowly, pulling himself forward on his elbows so that his legs slithered uselessly after him, he crawled towards the carcass of the old bull.

He reached it, and with one hand stroked the yellowed shaft of ivory that had crippled him.

'Now,' he whispered, fondling the smoothly polished tusk the way a man might touch his firstborn son. 'Now, at last you are mine.'

And then the pain started, and he closed his eyes and cowered down, huddled beneath the hillock of dead and cooling flesh that had been *Plough the Earth*. The pain buzzed in his ears like cicada beetles, but through it he heard Mohammed's voice.

'Fini. It was not wise.'

He opened his eyes and saw Mohammed's monkey face puckered with concern.

'Call Rosa,' he croaked. 'Call Little Long Hair. Tell her to come.'

Then he closed his eyes again, and rode the pain. The tempo of the pain changed constantly – first it was drums, tom-toms that throbbed and beat within him. Then it was the sea, long undulating swells of agony. Then again it was night, cold black night that chilled him so he shivered and moaned – and the night gave way to the sun. A great fiery ball of pain that burned and shot out lances of blinding light that burst against his clenched eyelids. Then the drums began again.

Time was of no significance. He rode the pain for a minute and a million years, then through the beat of the drums of agony he heard movement near him. The shuffle of feet through the dead leaves, the murmur of voices that were not part of his consuming anguish.

'Rosa,' Flynn whispered, 'you have come!'

He rolled his head and forced his eyelids open.

Herman Fleischer stood over him. He was grinning. His face flushed as a rose petal, fresh sweat clinging in his pale eyebrows, breathing quickly and heavily with exertion as though he had been running, but he was grinning.

'So!' he wheezed. 'So!'

The shock of his presence was muted for Flynn by the haze of pain in which he lay. There were smears of dust dulling the gloss of Fleischer's jackboots, and dark patches of sweat had soaked through the thick grey corduroy tunic at the armpits. He held a Luger pistol in his right hand and with his left hand he pushed the slouch hat to the back of his head.

'Herr Flynn!' he said and chuckled. It was the fat infectious chuckle of a healthy baby.

Mildly Flynn wondered how Fleischer had found him so quickly in the broken terrain and thick bush. The shot would have alerted him, but what had led him directly to the grove of fever trees?

Then he heard a rustling fluting rush in the air above him, and he looked upwards. Through the lacework of branches he saw the vultures spiralling against the aching blue of the sky. They turned and dipped on spread black wings, cocking their heads sideways in flight to look down with bright beady eyes on the elephant carcass.

'Ja! The birds. We followed the birds.'

'Jackals always follow the birds,' whispered Flynn, and Fleischer laughed. He threw back his head and laughed with genuine delight.

'Good. Oh, ja. That is good.' And he kicked Flynn. He swung the jackboot lazily into Flynn's body, and Flynn shrieked. The laughter dried instantly in Fleischer's throat, and he bent quickly to examine Flynn.

He noticed for the first time how his lower body was grotesquely twisted and distorted. And he dropped to his knees beside him. Gently he touched Flynn's forehead, and deep concern flashed across his chubby features at the clammy cold feeling of the skin.

'Sergeant!' There was a desperate edge to his voice now. 'This man is badly injured. He will not last long. Be quick! Get the rope! We must hang him before he loses consciousness.'

77

R osa awoke in the dawn and found that she was alone. Beside Flynn's personal pack, his discarded blanket had been carelessly flung aside. His rifle was gone.

She was not alarmed, not at first. She guessed that he had gone into the bush on one of his regular excursions to be alone while he drank his breakfast. But an hour later when he had not returned she grew anxious. She sat with her rifle across her lap, and every bird noise or animal scuffle in the ebony thicket jarred her nerves.

Another hour and she was fretting. Every few minutes she stood up and walked to the edge of the clearing to listen. Then she went back to sit and worry.

Where on earth was Flynn? Why had Mohammed not returned? What had happened to Sebastian? Was he safe, or had he been discovered? Had Flynn gone to assist him? Should she wait here, or follow them down the draw?

Her eyes haunted, her mouth hard set with doubts, she sat and twisted the braid of her hair around one finger in a nervously restless gesture.

Then Mohammed came. Suddenly he appeared out of the thicket beside her, and Rosa jumped up with a low cry of relief. The cry died in her throat as she saw his face.

'Fini!' he said. 'He is hurt. The great elephant has broken his bones and he lies in pain. He asks for you.'

Rosa stared at him, appalled, not understanding.

'An elephant?'

'He followed *Plough the Earth*, the great elephant, and killed him. But in dying the elephant struck him, breaking him.'

'The fool. Oh, the fool!' Rosa whispered. 'Now of all times. With Sebastian in danger, he must . . .' And then she caught herself and broke off her futile lament. 'Where is he, Mohammed? Take me to him.'

Mohammed led along one of the game paths, Rosa ran behind him. There was no time for caution, no thought of it as they hurried to find Flynn. They came to the stream of the Abati, and swung off the path, staying on the near bank. They plunged through a field of arrow grass, skirted around a tiny swamp and ran on into a stand of buffalo thorn. As they emerged on the far side Mohammed stopped abruptly and looked at the sky.

The vultures turned in a high wheel against the blue, like debris in a lazy whirlwind. The spot above which they circled lay half a mile ahead.

'Daddy!' Rosa choked on the word. In an instant all the hardness accumulated since that night at Lalapanzi disappeared from her face.

'Daddy!' she said again, and then she ran in earnest. Brushing past Mohammed, throwing her rifle aside so it clattered on the earth, she darted out of the buffalo thorn and into the open.

'Wait, Little Long Hair. Be careful.' Mohammed started after her. In his agitation he stepped carelessly, full on to a fallen twig from the buffalo thorn. There was a worn spot on the sole of his sandal, and three inches of cruel red-tipped thorn drove up through it and buried in his foot.

For a dozen paces he struggled on after Rosa, hopping on one leg, flapping his arms to maintain his balance and calling, but not too loudly.

'Wait! Be careful, Little Long Hair.'

But she took not the least heed, and went away from him, leaving him at last to sink down and tend to his wounded foot.

She crossed the open ground before the fever tree grove with the slack, blundering steps of exhaustion. Running silently, saving her breath for the effort of reaching her father. She ran into the grove, and a drop of perspiration fell into her eye, blurring her vision so she staggered against one of the trunks. She recovered her balance and ran on into the midst of them.

She recognized Herman Fleischer instantly. She had run almost against his chest, and his huge body towered over her. She screamed with shock and twisted away from the bear-like arms outspread to clutch her.

Two of the native Askari who were working over the crude litter on which lay Flynn O'Flynn, jumped up. As she ran they closed on her from either side, the way a pair of trained greyhounds will course a hare. They caught her between them, and dragged her struggling and screaming to where Herman Fleischer waited.

'Ah, so!' Fleischer nodded pleasantly in greeting. 'You have come in time for the fun.' Then he turned to his sergeant. 'Have them tie the woman.'

Rosa's screams penetrated the light mists of insensibility that screened Flynn's brain. He stirred on the litter, muttering incoherently, rolling his head from side to side, then he opened his eyes and focused them with difficulty. He saw her struggling between the Askari and he snapped back into full consciousness.

'Leave her!' he roared. 'Call those bloody animals off her. Leave her, your murderous bloody German bastard.'

'Good!' said Herman Fleischer. 'You are awake now.' Then he lifted his voice above Flynn's bellows. 'Hurry, Sergeant, tie the woman – and get the rope up.'

While they secured Rosa, one of the Askari shinned up the smooth yellow trunk of a fever tree. With his bayonet he hacked the twigs from the thick horizontal branch above their heads. The sergeant threw the end of the rope up to him, and at the second attempt the Askari caught it and passed it over the branch. Then he dropped back to earth.

There was a hangman's knot fixed in the rope, ready for use.

'Set the knot,' said Fleischer, and the sergeant went to where Flynn lay. With poles cut from a small tree they had rigged a combination litter and splints. The poles had been laid down Flynn's flanks from ankle to armpit, with bark strips they had bound them firmly so that Flynn's body was held rigidly as that of an Egyptian mummy, only his head and neck were free.

The sergeant stooped over him, and Flynn fell silent, watching him venomously.

591

As his hands came down with the noose to loop it over Flynn's head, Flynn moved suddenly. He darted his head forward like a striking adder and fastened his teeth in the man's wrist. With a howl the sergeant tried to pull away, but Flynn held on, his head jerking and wrenching as the man struggled.

'Fool,' grunted Fleischer, and strode over to the litter. He lifted his foot and placed it on Flynn's lower body. As he brought his weight down on it Flynn stiffened and gasped with pain, releasing the Askari's wrist.

'Do it this way.' Fleischer lunged forward and took a handful of Flynn's hair, roughly he yanked Flynn's head forward. 'Now, the rope, quickly.'

The Askari dropped the noose over Flynn's head and drew the slip-knot tight until it lay snugly under Flynn's ear.

'Good.' Fleischer stepped back. 'Four men on the rope,' he ordered. 'Gently. Do not jerk the rope. Walk away with it slowly. I don't want to break his neck.'

Rosa's hysteria had stilled into cold horror as she watched the preparations for the execution, and now she found her voice again.

'Please,' she whispered. 'He's my father. Please don't. Oh, no, please don't.'

'Hush, girl,' roared Flynn. 'You'd not shame me now by pleading with this fat bag of pus.' He swivelled his head, his eyes rolled towards the four Askari who stood ready with the rope end. 'Pull! You black sons of bitches. Pull! And damn you. I'll beat you to hell, and speak to the devil so he'll have you castrated and smeared with pig's fat.'

'You heard what Fini told you,' smiled Fleischer at his Askari. 'Pull!'

And they walked backwards in single file, shuffling through the dead leaves, leaning against the rope.

The litter lifted slowly at one end, came upright and then left the ground.

Rosa turned away and clenched her eyelids tight closed, but her hands were bound so she could not stop her ears, she could not keep out the sounds that Flynn Patrick O'Flynn made as he died.

When at last there was silence, Rosa was shivering. Hard spasms that shuddered through her whole body.

'All right,' said Herman Fleischer. 'That's it. Bring the woman. We can get back to camp in time for lunch if we hurry.'

When they were gone, the litter and its contents still hung in the fever tree. Swinging a little and turning slowly on the end of the rope. Near it lay the carcass of the elephant, and a vulture planed down slowly and made a flapping ungainly landing in the top branches of the fever tree. It sat hunched and suspicious, then suddenly squawked and launched again into noisy flight, for it had seen the man coming.

The little old man limped slowly into the grove. He stopped beside the dead elephant and looked up at the man who had been his master and his friend.

'Go in peace, Fini!' said Mohammed.

78

T he alleyway was a narrow low-roofed corridor, the bulkheads were painted a pale grey that glistened in the harsh light of the electric globes set in small wire cages at regular intervals along the roof.

At the end of the corridor, a guard stood outside the heavy watertight door in the bulkhead that led through into the handling room of the forward magazine. The guard wore only a thin white singlet and white flannel trousers, but his waist was belted in a blancoed webbing from which hung a sheathed bayonet, and there was a Mauser rifle slung from his shoulder.

From his position he could look into the handling room, and he could keep the full length of the alleyway under surveillance.

A double file of Wakamba tribesmen filled the alleyway, living chains along one of which passed the cordite charges; along the other the nine-inch shells.

The Africans worked with the stoical indifference of draught animals, turning to grip the ugly cylindro-conical shells, hugging a hundred and twenty pounds' weight of steel and explosive to their chests while they moved it on to the next man in the chain.

The cordite charges, each wrapped in thick paper, were not so weighty and moved more swiftly along their line. Each man bobbed and swung as he handled his load, so it seemed that the two ranks were sets in a complicated dance pattern.

From this mass of moving humanity rose clouds of warm body odour, that filled the alleyway and defeated the efforts of the air-conditioning fans.

Sebastian felt sweat trickling down his chest and back under the leather cloak, he felt also the tug of weight within the folds of the cloak each time he swung to receive a fresh cordite charge from his neighbour.

He stood just outside the door of the handling room, and each time he passed a charge through, he looked into the interior of the magazine where another gang was at work, packing the charges into the shelves that lined the bulkheads, and easing the nine-inch shells into their steel racks. Here there was another armed guard.

The work had been in progress since early that morning, with a half-hour's break at noon, so the German guards had relaxed their vigilance. They were restless in anticipation of relief. The one in the magazine was a fat middle-aged man who at intervals during the day had broken the monotony by releasing sudden ear-splitting posterior discharges of gas. With each salvo he had clapped the nearest African porter on the back and shouted happily.

'Have a bite at that one!' or, 'Cheer up – it doesn't smell.'

But at last he also was deflated. He slouched across the handling room, and leaned against the angle of the door to address his colleague in the alleyway.

'It's hot as hell, and smells like a zoo. These savages stink.'

'You've been doing your share.'

'I'll be glad when it's finished.'

'It's cooler in the magazine with the fans running – you are all right.'

'Jesus, I'd like to sit down for a few minutes.'

'Better not, Lieutenant Kyller is on the prowl.'

This exchange was taking place within a few feet of Sebastian. He followed the German conversation with more ease now that he had been able to exercise his rusty vocabulary, but he kept his head down in a renewed burst of energy. He was worried. In a short while the day's shift would end and the African porters would be herded on deck and into the launches to be transported to their camp on one of the islands. None of the native labour force were allowed to spend the night aboard *Blücher*.

He had waited since noon for an opportunity to enter the magazine and place the time charge. But he had been frustrated by the activities of the two German guards. It must be nearly seven o'clock in the evening now. It would have to be soon, very soon. He glanced once more into the magazine, and he caught the eye of Walaka, Mohammed's cousin. Walaka stood by the cordite shelves, supervising the packing, and now he shrugged at Sebastian in eloquent helplessness.

Suddenly there was a thud of a heavy object being dropped to the deck, and a commotion of shouts in the alleyway behind Sebastian. He glanced round quickly. One of the bearers had fainted in the heat and fallen with a shell in his arms, the shell had rolled and knocked down another man. Now there was a milling confusion clogging the alleyway. The two guards moved forward, forcing their way into the press of black bodies, shouting hoarsely and clubbing with the rifle butts. It was the opportunity for which Sebastian had waited.

He stepped over the threshold of the magazine, and went to Walaka beside the cordite shelves.

'Send one of your men to take my place,' he whispered, and reaching up into the folds of his cloak he brought out the cigar box.

With his back towards the door of the magazine, using the cloak as a screen to hide his movements, he slipped the catch of the box and opened the lid.

His hands trembled with haste and nervous agitation as he fumbled with the winder of the travelling-clock. It clicked, and he saw the second hand begin its endless circuit of the dial. Even over the shouts and scuffling in the alleyway, the muted ticking of its mechanism seemed offensively loud to Sebastian. Hastily he shut the lid and glanced guiltily over his shoulder at the doorway. Walaka stood there, and his face was sickly grey with the tension of imminent discovery, but he nodded to Sebastian, a signal that the guards were still occupied without.

Reaching up to the nearest shelf, Sebastian wedged the cigar box between two of the paper-wrapped cylinders of cordite. Then he packed others over it, covering it completely.

He stood back and found with surprise that he was panting, his breathing whistling in his throat. He could feel the little drops of sweat prickling on his shaven head. In the white electric light they shone like glass beads on his velvety, black-stained skin.

'Is it done?' Walaka croaked beside him.

'It is done,' Sebastian croaked back at him, and suddenly he was overcome with a driving compulsion to be out of this steel room, out of this box-packed room with the ingredients of violent death and destruction; out of the stifling press of bodies that had surrounded him all day. A dreadful thought seized his imagination, suppose the artificer had erred in his assembly of the time charge, suppose that even now the battery was heating the wires of the detonator and bringing them to explosion point. He felt panic as he looked around wildly at the tons of cordite and shell around him. He wanted to run, to fight his way out and up into the open air. He made the first move, and then froze.

The commotion in the alleyway had subsided miraculously, and now only one voice was raised. It came from just outside the doorway, using the curt inflection of authority. Sebastian had heard that voice repeatedly during that long day, and he had come to dread it. It heralded danger.

'Get them back to work immediately,' snapped Lieutenant Kyller as he stepped over the threshold into the magazine. He drew a gold watch from the pocket of his tunic and read the time. 'It is five minutes after seven. There is still almost half an hour before you knock off.' He tucked the watch away, and swept the magazine with a gaze that missed no detail. He was a tall young man, immaculate in his tropical whites. Behind him the two guards were hurriedly straightening their dishevelled uniforms and trying to look efficient and intelligent.

'Yes, sir,' they said in unison.

For a moment Kyller's eyes rested on Sebastian. It was probably because Sebastian was the finest physical specimen among the bearers, he stood taller than the rest of them – as tall as Kyller himself. But Sebastian felt his interest was deeper. He felt that Kyller was searching beneath the stain on his skin, that he was naked of disguise beneath those eyes. He felt that Kyller would remember him, had marked him down in his memory.

'That shelf.' Kyller turned away from Sebastian and crossed the magazine. He went directly to the shelf on which Sebastian had placed his time charge, and he patted the cordite cylinders that Sebastian had handled. They were slightly awry. 'Have it repacked immediately,' said Kyller.

'Right away, sir,' said the fat guard.

Again Kyller's eyes rested on Sebastian. It seemed that he was about to speak, then he changed his mind. He stooped through the doorway and disappeared.

Sebastian stood stony still, appalled by the order that Kyller had given. The fat guard grimaced sulkily.

'Christ, that one is a busy bastard.' And he glared at the cordite shelf. 'There's nothing wrong there.' He crossed to it and fiddled ineffectually. After a moment he asked the guard at the door. 'Has Kyller gone yet?'

'Yes. He's gone down the companion-way into the sick-bay.'

'Good!' grunted the fat one. 'I'm damned if I'm going to waste half an hour repacking this whole batch.' He hunched his shoulders, and screwed up his face with effort. There was a bagpipe squeal, and the guard relaxed and grinned. 'That one was for Lieutenant Kyller, God bless him!'

79

D arkness was falling, and with it the temperature dropped a few degrees into the high eighties and created an illusion that the faint evening breeze was chilly.

Sebastian hugged his cloak around his body, and shuffled along in the slow column of native labourers that dribbled over the side of the German battle cruiser into the waiting launches.

He was exhausted both in body and in mind from the strain of the day's labour in the magazine, so that he went down the catwalk and took his place in the whaler, moving in a state of stupor. When the boat shoved off and puttered up the channel towards the labour camp on the nearest island, Sebastian looked back at *Blücher* with the same dumb stare as the men who squatted beside him on the floorboards of the whaler. Mechanically he registered the fact that Commissioner Fleischer's steam launch was tied up alongside the cruiser.

'Perhaps the fat swine will be aboard when the whole lot blows to hell,' he thought wearily. 'I can at least hope for that.'

He had no way of knowing who else Herman Fleischer had taken aboard the cruiser with him. Sebastian had been below decks toiling in the handling room of the magazine when the launch arrived from up-river, and Rosa Oldsmith had been ushered up the catwalk by the Commissioner in person.

'Come along, Mädchen. We will take you to see the gallant captain of this fine ship.' Fleischer puffed jovially as he mounted the steps behind her. 'I am sure there are many interesting things that you can tell him.'

Bedraggled and exhausted with grief, pale with the horror of her father's death, and with cold hatred for the man who had engineered it, Rosa stumbled as she stepped from the catwalk on to the deck. Her hands were still bound in front of her so she could not check herself. She fell forward, letting herself fall uncaring, and with mild surprise felt hands hold and steady her.

She looked up at the man who had caught her, and in her confusion of mind she thought it was Sebastian. He was tall and dark and his hands were strong. Then she saw the peaked uniform cap with its golden insignia, and she jerked away from him in revulsion.

'Ah! Lieutenant Kyller.' Commissioner Fleischer spoke behind her. 'I have brought you a visitor – a lovely lady.'

'Who is she?' Kyller was appraising Rosa. Rosa could not understand a word that was spoken. She stood in quiet acceptance, her whole body drooping.

'This . . .' answered Fleischer proudly, '. . . is the most dangerous young lady in the whole of Africa. She is one of the leaders of the gang of English bandits that raided the column bringing down the steel plate from Dar es Salaam. It was she who shot and killed your engineer. I captured her and her father this morning. Her father was the notorious O'Flynn.'

'Where is he?' Kyller snapped.

'I hanged him.'

'You hanged him?' demanded Kyller. 'Without trial?'

'No trial was necessary.'

'Without interrogating him?'

'I brought in the woman for interrogation.'

Kyller was angry now, his voice crackled with it.

'I will leave it to Captain von Kleine to judge the wisdom of your actions,' and he turned to Rosa; his eyes dropped to her hands, and, with an exclamation of concern, he took her by the wrist.

'Commissioner Fleischer, how long has this woman been bound?'

Fleischer shrugged. 'I could take no chances on her escaping.'

'Look at this!' Kyller indicated Rosa's hands. They were swollen, the fingers puffy and blue, sticking out stiffly, dead-looking and useless.

'I could take no chances.' Fleischer bridled at the implied criticism.

'Give me your knife,' Kyller snapped at the petty officer in charge of the gangway, and the man produced a large clasp knife. He opened it and handed it to the lieutenant.

Carefully Kyller ran the blade between Rosa's wrists and sawed at the rope. As her bonds dropped away Rosa cried out in pain of fresh blood flowing into her hands.

'You will be lucky if you have not done her permanent damage,' Kyller muttered furiously as he massaged Rosa's bloated hands.

'She is a criminal. A dangerous criminal,' growled Fleischer.

'She is a woman, and therefore deserving of your consideration. Not of this barbarous treatment.'

'She will hang.'

'Her crimes she will answer for, in due course – but until she has stood trial she will be treated as a woman.'

Rosa did not understand the harsh German argument that raged around her. She stood quietly and her eyes were fastened on the knife in Lieutenant Kyller's hand. The hilt brushed her fingers as he worked to restore the circulation of her blood. The blade was long and silver bright, she had seen how keen was its edge by the way in which it had cut through the rope. As she stared at it, it seemed to her fevered fancy that there were two names engraved in the steel of the blade. The names of the two persons she had loved. The names of her father and her child.

With an effort she tore her gaze from the knife and looked at the man she hated. Fleischer had come close up to her, as though to take her away from Lieutenant Kyller's attention. His face was flushed with anger and the fold of flesh under his chin wobbled flabbily as he argued.

Rosa flexed her fingers. They were still numb and stiff, but she could feel the strength flowing back into them. She let her gaze drop down to Fleischer's belly.

It jutted out round and full, soft-looking under the grey corduroy tunic, and again her fevered imagination formed a picture of the blade going into that belly. Slipping in silently, smoothly, burying itself to the hilt and then drawing upwards to open the flesh like a pouch. The picture was so vivid that Rosa shuddered with the intense sensual pleasure of it.

Kyller was completely occupied with Fleischer. He felt the girl's fingers slide into the cupped palm of his right hand, but before he could pull away she had scooped the knife deftly from his grip. He lunged at her, but she pirouetted lightly away from him. Her knife hand dropped and then darted forward, driven by the full weight of her body at the bulging belly of Herman Fleischer.

Rosa thought that because he was fat he would be slow. She expected him to be stunned by the unexpected attack, to stand and take the knife in his vitals.

Herman Fleischer was fully alert before she even started her thrust. He was fast as a striking mamba, and strong beyond credibility. He did not make the mistake of intercepting the knife with his bare hands. Instead he struck her right shoulder with a clenched fist the size of a carpenter's mallet. The force of the blow knocked her sideways, deflecting the blade from its target. Her arm from the shoulder downwards was paralysed, and the knife flew from her hand and slithered away across the deck.

'Ja!' roared Fleischer triumphantly. 'Ja! So! Now you see how I was right to tie the bitch. She is vicious, dangerous.'

And he lifted the huge fist again to smash it into Rosa's face as she crouched, hugging her hurt shoulder and sobbing with pain and disappointment.

'Enough!' Kyller stepped between them. 'Leave her.'

'She must be tied up like an animal – she is dangerous,' bellowed Fleischer, but Kyller put a protective arm around Rosa's bowed shoulders.

'Petty Officer,' he said. 'Take this woman to the sick-bay. Have Surgeon Commander Buchholz see to her. Guard her carefully, but be gentle with her. Do you hear me?' And they took her away below.

'I must see Captain von Kleine,' Fleischer demanded. 'I must make a full report to him.'

'Come,' said Kyller, 'I will take you to him.'

80

S ebastian lay on his side beside the smoky little fire with his cloak draped over him. Outside he heard the night sounds of the swamp, the faint splash of a fish or a crocodile in the channel, the clink and boom of the tree frogs, the singing of insects, and the lap and sigh of wavelets on the mud bank below the hut.

The hut was one of twenty crude open-sided shelters that housed the native labour force. The earth floor was thickly strewn with sleeping bodies. The sound of their breathing was a restless murmur, broken by the cough and stir of dreamers.

Despite his fatigue, Sebastian was not sleeping, he could not relax from the state of tension in which he had been held all that day. He thought of the little travelling-clock ticking away in its nest of high explosive, measuring out the minutes and the hours, and then his mind side-stepped and went to Rosa. The muscles of his arms tightened with longing. Tomorrow, he thought, tomorrow I will see her and we will go away from this stinking river. Up into the sweet air of the highlands. Again his mind jumped. Seven o'clock, seven o'clock tomorrow morning and it will be over. He remembered Lieutenant Kyller's voice as he stood in the doorway of the magazine with the gold watch in his hand. '. . . The time is five minutes past seven . . .' he had said. So that Sebastian knew to within a few minutes when the time fuse would explode.

He must stop the porters going aboard *Blücher* in the morning. He had impressed on old Walaka that they must refuse to turn out for the next day's shift. They must . . .

'Manali! Manali!' his name was whispered close by in the gloom, and Sebastian lifted himself on one elbow. In the flickering light from the fire there was a shadowy figure, crawling on hands and knees across the earthen floor, and searching the faces of the sleeping men.

'Manali, where are you?'

'Who is it?' Sebastian answered softly, and the man jumped up and scurried to where he lay.

'It is I, Mohammed.'

'Mohammed?' Sebastian was startled. 'Why are you here? You should be with Fini at the camp on the Abati.'

'Fini is dead.' Mohammed's whisper was low with sorrow, so low that Sebastian thought he had misunderstood.

'What? What did you say?'

'Fini is dead. The Allemand came with the ropes. They hung him in the fever trees beside the Abati, and when he was dead they left him for the birds.'

'What talk is this?' Sebastian demanded.

'It is true,' mourned Mohammed. 'I saw it, and when the Allemand had gone, I cut the rope and brought him down. I wrapped him in my own blanket and buried him in an ant-bear hole.'

'Dead? Flynn dead? It isn't true!'

'It is true, Manali.' In the red glow of the camp-fire Mohammed's face was old and raddled and gaunt. He licked his lips. 'There is more, Manali. There is more to tell.'

But Sebastian was not listening. He was trying to force his mind to accept the reality of Flynn's death, but it balked. It would not accept the picture of Flynn swinging at the rope's end, Flynn with the rope burns at his throat and his face swollen and empurpled, Flynn wrapped in a dirty blanket and crammed into an ant-bear hole. Flynn dead? No! Flynn was too big, too vital – they could not kill Flynn.

'Manali, hear me.'

Sebastian shook his head, bemused, denying it. It could not be true.

'Manali, the Allemand, they have taken Little Long Hair. They have bound her with ropes and taken her.'

Sebastian winced, and jerked away as though he had been struck open-handed across the face.

'No!' He tried to close his mind against the words.

'They caught her this morning early as she went to Fini. They took her down-river in the small boat, and she is now on the great ship of the Allemand.'

'*Blücher*? Rosa is aboard the *Blücher*?'

'Yes. She is there.'

'No. Oh, God, *no*!'

In five hours *Blücher* would blow up. In five hours Rosa would die. Sebastian swung his head and looked out into the night, he looked through the open side of the hut, down the channel to where *Blücher* lay at her moorings half a mile away. There was a dim glow of light across the water from the hooded lanterns on *Blücher*'s main deck. But her form was indistinguishable against the dark mass of the mangroves. Between her and the island, the channel was a smooth expanse of velvety blackness on which the reflection of the stars were scattered sequins of light.

'I must go to her,' said Sebastian. 'I cannot let her die there alone.' His voice gathered strength and resolve. 'I cannot let her die. I'll tell the Germans where to find the charge – I'll tell them . . .' Then he faltered. 'I can't. No, I can't. I'd be a traitor then, but, but . . .'

He threw aside his cloak.

'Mohammed, how did you come here? Did you bring the canoe? Where is it?'

Mohammed shook his head. 'No. I swam. My cousin brought me close to the island in the canoe, but he has gone away. We could not leave the canoe here, lest the Askari find it. They would have seen the canoe.'

'There isn't a boat on the island – nothing,' muttered Sebastian. The Germans were careful to guard against desertion. Each night the labour force was marooned on the island – and the Askari patrolled the mud banks.

'Mohammed, hear me now,' Sebastian reached across and laid his hand on the old man's shoulder. 'You are my friend. I thank you that you have come to tell me these things.'

'You are going to Little Long Hair?'

'Yes.'

'Go in peace, Manali.'

'Take my place here, Mohammed. When the guards count tomorrow morning, you will stand for me.' Sebastian tightened his grip on the bony shoulder. 'Stay in peace, Mohammed.'

His blackened body blending into the darkness, Sebastian crouched beneath the spread branches of a clump of pampa scrub, and the Askari guard almost brushed against him as he passed. The Askari slouched along with his rifle slung so that the barrel stood up behind his shoulder. The constant patrolling had beaten a path around the circumference of the island, the guard followed it mechanically. Half asleep on his feet, completely unaware of Sebastian's presence. He stumbled in the darkness and swore sleepily, and moved on.

Sebastian crossed the path on his hands and knees, then stretched out on his belly into a reptilian slither as he reached the mud bank. Had he tried to walk across it, the glutinous mud would have sucked so loudly around his feet that every guard within a hundred yards would have heard him.

The mud coated his chest and belly and legs with its coldly loathsome, clinging oiliness, and the reek of it filled his nostrils so he gagged. Then he was into the water. The water was blood warm, he felt the tug of the current and the bottom dropped away beneath him. He swam on his side, careful that neither legs nor arms should break the surface. His head alone showed, like the head of a swimming otter, and he felt the mud washing off his body.

He swam across the current, guided by the distant glimmer of *Blücher's* deck lights. He swam slowly, husbanding his strength, for he knew he would need all of it later.

His mind was filled with layers of awareness. The lowest layer was a lurking undirected terror of the dark water in which he swam, his dangling legs were vulnerable to the scaly predators which infested the Rufiji river. The current must be carrying his scent down to them. Soon they would come hunting up to find him. But he kept up the easy stroke of arms and legs. It was a chance, one chance of the many he was taking and he tried to ignore it and grapple with the practical problems of his attempt. When he reached *Blücher*, how was he to get aboard her? Her sides were fifty feet high, and the catwalks were the only means of access. These were both heavily guarded. It was a problem without solution, and yet he harried it.

Over this was a thick layer of hopeless sorrow. Sorrow for Flynn.

But the uppermost layer was thickest, strongest. Rosa, Rosa and Rosa.

He found with surprise that he was saying it aloud.

'Rosa!' with each forward thrust of his body through the water.

'Rosa!' each time he drew breath.

'Rosa!' as his legs kicked out and pushed him towards the *Blücher*.

He did not know what he would do if he reached her. Perhaps there was some half-formed idea of escaping with her, of fighting his way out of *Blücher* with his woman. Getting her away before that moment when the ship would vanish in a holocaust of flame. He did not know, but he swam on quietly.

Then he was under *Blücher's* side. The towering mass of steel blotted out the starry night sky, and he stopped swimming and hung in the warm water looking up at her.

There were small sounds. The hum of machinery within her, the faint clang of metal struck against metal, the low guttural murmur of voices at her gangway, the thump of a rifle butt against the wooden deck, the soft wash of water around the hull – and then a closer, clearer sound, a regular creak and tap, creak and tap.

He swam in towards the hull, searching for the source of this new sound. It came from near the bows, creak and tap. The creak of rope, and the tap of wood against the steel hull. He saw it then, just above his head. He almost cried out with joy.

The cradles! The platforms still suspended above the water on which the welders and the painters had worked.

He reached up and gripped the wooden edge and drew himself on to the platform. He rested a few seconds and then began to climb the rope. Hand over hand, gripping the rope between the insides of his bare feet, he went up.

His head came level with the deck and he hung there, searching carefully. Fifty yards away he saw two seamen at the gangway. Neither was looking his way.

At intervals the hooded lanterns threw puddles of yellow light upon the deck, but there were concealing shadows beyond them. It was dark around the base of the forward gun-turrets, and there were piles of material, abandoned welding equipment, heaps of rope and canvas in the shadows which would hide him when he had crossed the deck.

Once more he checked the two guards at the gangway, their backs were turned to him.

Sebastian filled his lungs and steeled himself to act. Then with one fluid movement he drew himself up and rolled over the side. He landed lightly on his feet and darted across the exposed deck into the shadows. He ducked down behind a pile of canvas and rope netting, and struggled to control his breathing. He could feel his legs trembling violently under him, so he sat down on the planking and huddled against the protecting pile of canvas. River water trickled from his shaven pate over his forehead and into his eyes. He wiped it away.

'Now what?' He was aboard *Blücher*, but what should he do next?

Where would they hold Rosa? Was there some sort of guard-room for prisoners? Would they put her in one of the officer's cabins? The sick-bay?

He knew roughly where the sick-bay was located. While he was working in the magazine he had heard the one German guard say, 'He has gone down the companion-way to the sick-bay.'

It must be somewhere just below the forward magazine – oh, God! If they had her there she would be almost at the centre of the explosion.

He came up on his knees, and peered over the pile of canvas. It was lighter now. Through the screen of camouflage netting, he could see the night sky had paled a little in the east. Dawn was not far off. The night had passed so swiftly, morning was on its way and there were but a few scant hours before the hands of the travelling-clock completed their journey, and made the electrical connection that would seal the *Blücher's* fate, and the fate of all those aboard her.

He must move. He rose slowly and then froze. The guards at the gangway had come to attention. They stood stiffly with their rifles at the slope, and into the light stepped a tall, white-clad figure.

There was no mistaking him. It was the officer that Sebastian had last seen in the forward magazine. Kyller, they had called him, Lieutenant Kyller.

Kyller acknowledged the salutes of the two guards, and he spoke with them a while. Their voices were low and indistinct. Kyller saluted again, and then left them. He came down the deck towards the bows; he walked briskly, and his face below the peak of his cap was in darkness.

Sebastian crouched down again, only his eyes lifted above the piled canvas. He watched the officer and he was afraid.

Kyller stopped in mid-stride. He half stooped to look at the deck at his feet, and then in the same movement, straightened with his right hand dropping to the holstered pistol on his belt.

'Guard!' he bellowed. 'Here! At the double!'

On the holystoned white planking, the wet footprints that Sebastian had left behind him glittered in the lantern light. Kyller stared in the direction that they led, coming directly towards Sebastian's hiding-place.

The boots of the two guards pounded heavily along the deck. They had unslung their rifles as they ran to join Kyller.

'Someone has come aboard here. Spread out and search . . .' Kyller shouted at them, as he closed in on Sebastian.

Sebastian panicked. He jumped up and ran, trying to reach the corner of the gun-turret.

'There he is!' Kyller's voice. 'Stop! Stop or I'll fire.'

Sebastian ran. His legs driving powerfully, his elbows pumping, head down, bare feet slapping on the planking, he raced through shadow.

'Stop!' Kyller was balanced on the balls of his feet, legs braced, right shoulder thrust forward and right arm outflung in the classic stance of the pistol marksman. The arm dropped slowly and then kicked up violently, as the shot spouted from the Luger in a bell of yellow flame. The bullet spanged against the plating of the turret and then glanced off in whining ricochet.

Sebastian felt the wind of the bullet pass his head and he jinked his run. The corner of the turret was very close, and he dodged towards it.

Then Kyller's next shot blurted loudly in the night, and simultaneously something struck Sebastian a heavy blow under his left shoulder-blade. It threw him forward off balance and he reeled against the turret, his hands scrabbled at the smooth steel without finding purchase. His body flattened against the side of the turret, so that the blood from the exit hole that the bullet had torn in his breast sprayed on to the pale grey, painted turret.

His legs buckled and he slid down, slowly, still trying to find purchase with the hooked claws of his fingers, so that as his knees touched the deck he was in the attitude of devout prayer. Forehead pressed against the turret, kneeling, arms spread high and wide.

Then the arms sank down, and he slid sideways, collapsed onto the deck and rolled on to his back.

Kyller came and stood over him. The pistol hanging slackly in the hand at his side.

'Oh, my God,' there was genuine regret in Kyller's voice. 'It's only one of the porters. Why did the fool run! I wouldn't have fired if he had stood.'

Sebastian wanted to ask him where Rosa was. He wanted to explain that Rosa was his wife, that he loved her, and that he had come to find her.

He concentrated his vision on Kyller's face as it hung over him, and he summoned his school-boy German, marshalling the sentences in his mind.

But as he opened his mouth the blood welled up in his throat and choked him. He coughed, racking, and the blood bubbled through his lips in a pink froth.

'Lung shot!' said Kyller, and then to the guards as they came up, 'Get a stretcher. Hurry. We must take him down to the sick-bay.'

81

There were twelve bunks in *Blücher*'s sick-bay, six down each side of the narrow cabin. In eight of them lay German seamen; five malaria cases and three men injured in the work of repairing her bows.

Rosa Oldsmith was in the bunk farthest from the door. She lay behind a movable screen, and a guard sat outside the screen. He wore a pistol at his belt and was wholly absorbed in a year-old variety magazine, the cover of which depicted a buxom blonde woman in a black corset and high boots, with a horse whip in one hand.

The cabin was brightly lit and smelled of antiseptic. One of the malarial cases was in delirium, and he laughed and shouted. The medical orderly moved along the rows of bunks carrying a metal tray from which he administered the morning dosages of quinine. The time was 5 a.m.

Rosa had slept only intermittently during the night. She lay on top of the blankets and she wore a striped towelling dressing-gown over the blue flannel night-gown. The gown was many sizes too large and she had rolled back the cuffs of the sleeves. Her hair was loose on the pillows, and damp at the temples with sweat. Her face was pale and drawn, with bluish smudges of fatigue under her eyes, and her shoulder ached dully where Fleischer had struck her.

She was awake now. She lay staring up at the low roof of the cabin, playing over in her mind fragments from the happenings of the last twenty-four hours.

She recalled the interrogation with Captain von Kleine. He had sat opposite her in his luxuriously furnished cabin, and his manner had been kindly, his voice gentle, pronouncing the English words with blurring of the consonants and a hardening of the vowel sounds. His English was good.

'When did you last eat?' he asked her.

'I am not hungry,' she replied, making no attempt to conceal her hatred. Hating them all – this handsome, gentle man, the tall lieutenant who stood beside him, and Herman Fleischer who sat across the cabin from her, with his knees spread apart to accommodate the full hang of his belly.

'I will send for food.' Von Kleine ignored her protest and rang for his steward. When the food came, she could not deny the demands of her body and she ate, trying to show no enjoyment. The sausage and pickles were delicious, for she had not eaten since the previous noon.

Courteously von Kleine turned his attention to a discussion with Lieutenant Kyller until she had finished, but when the steward removed the empty tray he came back to her.

'Herr Fleischer tells me you are the daughter of Major O'Flynn, the commander of the Portuguese irregulars operating in German territory?'

'I was until he was hanged, murdered! He was injured and helpless. They tied him to a stretcher . . .' Rosa flared at him, tears starting in her eyes.

'Yes,' von Kleine stopped her, 'I know. I am not pleased. That is now a matter between myself and Commissioner Fleischer. I can only say that I am sorry. I offer you my condolence.' He paused and glanced at Herman Fleischer. Rosa could see by the angry blue of his eyes that he meant what he said.

'But now there are some questions I must ask you . . .'

Rosa had planned her replies, for she knew what he would ask. She replied frankly and truthfully to anything that did not jeopardize Sebastian's attempt to place the time fuse aboard *Blücher*.

What were she and Flynn doing when they were captured? Keeping the *Blücher* under surveillance. Waiting to signal her departure to the blockading cruisers.

How did the British know that Blücher was in the Rufiji? The steel plate, of course. Then confirmation by aerial reconnaissance.

Were they contemplating offensive action against Blücher? No, they would wait until she sailed.

What was the strength of the blockade squadron? Two cruisers that she had seen, she did not know if there were other warships waiting over the horizon.

Von Kleine phrased his questions carefully, and listened attentively to her replies. For an hour the interrogation continued, until Rosa was yawning openly, and her voice was slurred with exhaustion. Von Kleine realized that there was nothing to be learned from her, all she had told him he already knew or had guessed.

'Thank you,' he finished. 'I am keeping you aboard my ship. There will be danger here, for soon I will be going out to meet the British warships. But I believe that it will be better for you than if I handed you over to the German administration ashore.' He hesitated a moment and glanced at Commissioner Fleischer. 'In every nation there are evil men, fools and barbarians. Do not judge us all by one man.'

With distaste at her own treachery, Rosa found that she could not hate this man. A weary smile tugged her mouth and she answered him.

'You are kind.'

'Lieutenant Kyller will see you to the hospital. I am sorry I can offer you no better quarters, but this is a crowded vessel.'

When she had gone, von Kleine lit a cheroot and while he tasted its comforting fragrance, he allowed his eyes to rest on the portrait of the two golden women across the cabin. Then he sat up in his chair and his voice had lost its gentleness as he spoke to the man who lolled on the couch.

'Herr Fleischer, I find it difficult to express fully my extreme displeasure at your handling of this affair . . .'

After a night of fitful sleep, Rosa lay on her hospital bunk behind the screen and she thought of her husband. If things had gone well Sebastian must by now have placed the time charge and escaped from *Blücher*. Perhaps he was already on his way to the rendezvous on the Abati river. If this were so, then she would not see him again. It was her one regret. She imagined him in his ludicrous disguise, and she smiled a little. Dear lovable Sebastian. Would he ever know what had happened to her? Would he know that she had died with those whom she hated? She hoped that he would never know – that he would never torture himself with the knowledge that he had placed the instrument of her death with his own hands.

I wish I could see him just once more to tell him that my death is unimportant beside the death of Herman Fleischer, beside the destruction of this German warship. I wish only that when the time comes, I could see it. I wish there were some way I could know the exact time of the explosion so I could tell Herman Fleischer a minute before, when it is too late for him to escape, and watch him. Perhaps he would blubber, perhaps he would scream with fear. I would like that. I would like that very much.

The strength of her hatred was such that she could no longer lie still. She sat up and tied the belt of her gown around her waist. She was filled with a restless itchy exhilaration. It would be today – she felt sure – sometime today she would slake this burning thirst for vengeance that had tormented her for so long.

She threw her legs over the side of the bunk and pulled open the screen. The guard dropped his magazine and started up from his chair, his hand dropping to the pistol at his hip.

'I will not harm you . . .' Rosa smiled at him, '. . . . not yet!'

She pointed to the door which led into the tiny shower cabinet and toilet. The guard relaxed and nodded acquiescence. He followed her as she crossed the cabin.

Rosa walked slowly between the bunks, looking at the sick men that lay in them.

'All of you,' she thought happily. 'All of you!'

She slid the tongue of the lock across, and was alone in the bathroom. She undressed, and leaned across the wash-basin to the small mirror set above it. She could see the reflection of her head and shoulders. There was a purple and red bruise spreading down from her neck and staining the white swell of her right breast. She touched it tenderly with her finger-tips.

'Herman Fleischer,' she said the name gloatingly, 'it will be today – I promise you that. Today you will die.'

And then suddenly she was crying.

'I only wish you could burn as my baby burned – I wish you could choke and swing on the rope as my father did.' And the tears fell fat and slow, sliding down her cheeks to drop into the basin. She started to sob, dry convulsive gasps of grief and hatred. She turned blindly to the shower cabinet, and turned both taps full on so that the rush of the water would cover the sound of her weeping. She did not want them to hear it.

Later, when she had bathed her face and body and combed her hair and dressed again, she unlocked the door and stepped through it. She stopped abruptly and through puffy reddened eyes tried to make sense of what was happening in the sick-bay.

It was crowded. The surgeon was there, two orderlies, four German seamen, and the young lieutenant. All of them hovered about the stretcher that was being manoeuvred between the bunks. There was a man on the stretcher, she could see his form under the single grey blanket that covered him, but Lieutenant Kyller's back obscured her view of the man's face. There was blood on the blanket, and a brown smear of blood on the sleeve of Kyller's white tunic.

She moved along the bulkhead of the cabin and craned her head to see around Kyller, but at that moment one of the orderlies leaned across to swab the mouth of the man on the stretcher with a white cloth. The cloth obscured the wounded man's face. Bright frothy blood soaked through the material, and the sight of it nauseated Rosa. She averted her gaze and slipped away towards her own bunk at the end of the cabin. She reached the screen, and behind her somebody groaned. It was a low delirious groan, but the sound of it stopped Rosa instantly. She felt as though something within her chest was swelling to stifle her. Slowly, fearfully, she turned back.

They were lifting the man from the stretcher to lay him on an empty bunk. The head lolled sideways, and beneath its stain of bark juice Rosa saw that dear, well loved face.

'Sebastian!' she cried, and she ran to him, pushing past Kyller, throwing herself on to the blanket-draped body, trying to get her arms around him to hug him.

'Sebastian! What have they done to you!'

82

'**S**ebastian! Sebastian!' Rosa leaned across him and held her mouth to his ear.

'Sebastian!' She called his name quietly but urgently, then brushed his forehead with her lips. The skin was cold and damp.

He lay on his back with the bed clothes turned back to his waist. His chest was swathed in bandages, and his breathing sawed and gurgled.

'Sebastian. It's Rosa. It's Rosa. Wake up, Sebastian. Wake up, it's Rosa.'

'Rosa?' At last her name had reached him. He whispered it painfully, wetly, and fresh blood stained his lips.

Rosa had been on the edge of despair. Two hours she had been sitting beside him. Since the surgeon had finished dressing the wound, she had sat with him – touching him, calling to him. This was the first sign of recognition he had given her.

'Yes! Yes! It's Rosa. Wake up, Sebastian.' Her voice lifted with relief.

'Rosa?' His eyelashes trembled.

'Wake up.' She pinched his cold cheek and he winced. His eyelids fluttered open.

'Rosa?' on a shallow, sawing breath.

'Here, Sebastian. I'm here.' His eyes rolled in their sockets, searching, trying desperately to focus.

'Here,' she said, leaning over him and taking his face between her hands. She looked into his eyes.

'Here, my darling, here.'

'Rosa!' His lips convulsed into a dreadful parody of a smile.

'Sebastian, did you set the bomb?'

His breathing changed, hoarser, and his mouth twitched with the effort.

'Tell them,' he whispered.

'Tell them what?'

'Seven. Must stop it.'

'Seven o'clock?'

'Don't – want – you — '

'Will it explode at seven o'clock?'

'You — ' It was too much and he coughed.

'Seven o'clock? Is that it, Sebastian?'

'You will . . .' He squeezed his eyes closed, putting all his strength into the effort of speaking. 'Please. Don't die. Stop it.'

'Did you set it for seven o'clock?' In her impatience she tugged his head towards her. 'Tell me, for God's sake, tell me!'

'Seven o'clock. Tell them – tell them.'

Still holding him, she looked at the clock set high up on the bulkhead of the sick-bay.

On the white dial, the ornate black hands stood at fifteen minutes before the hour.

'Don't die, please don't die,' mumbled Sebastian.

She hardly heard the pain-muted pleading. A fierce surge of triumph lifted her – she knew the hour. The exact minute. Now she could send for Herman Fleischer, and have him with her.

Gently she laid Sebastian's head back on the pillow. On the table below the clock she had seen a pad and pencil among the bottles and jars, and trays of instruments. She went to it, and while the guard watched her suspiciously she scribbled a note.

'Captain,

My husband is conscious. He has a message of vital importance for Commissioner Fleischer. He will speak to no one but Commissioner Fleischer. The message could save your ship.

Rosa Oldsmith.'

She folded the sheet of paper and pushed it into the guard's hand.

'For the Captain. Captain.'

'Kapitän,' repeated the guard. 'Jawohl.' And he went to the door of the sick-bay. She saw him speak with the second guard outside the door, and then pass him the note.

Rosa sank down on the edge of Sebastian's bunk. She ran her hand tenderly over his shaven head. The new hair was stiff and bristly under her fingers.

'Wait for me. I'm coming with you, my darling. Wait for me.'

But he had lapsed back into unconsciousness. Crooning softly, she gentled him. Smiling to herself, happily, she waited for the minute hand of the clock to creep up to the zenith of the dial.

83

Captain Arthur Joyce had personally supervised the placing of the scuttling charges. Perhaps, long ago, another man had felt the way he did – hearing the command spoken from the burning bush, and knowing he must obey.

The charges were small, but laid in twenty places against the bare plating, they would rip *Renounce*'s belly out of her cleanly. The watertight bulkhead had been opened to let the water rush through her. The magazines had all of them been flooded to minimize the danger of explosion. The furnaces had been damped down, and he had blown the pressure on his boilers – retaining a head of steam, just sufficient to take *Renounce* in on her last run into the channel of the Rufiji.

The cruiser had been stripped of her crew. Twenty men left aboard her to handle the ship. The rest of them trans-shipped aboard *Pegasus*.

Joyce was going to attempt to force the log boom, take *Renounce* through the minefield, and sink her higher up, where the double mouth of the channel merged into a single thoroughfare.

If he succeeded he would effectively have blocked *Blücher*, and sacrificed a single ship.

If he failed, if *Renounce* sank in the minefield before she reached the confluence of the two channels, then Armstrong would have to take *Pegasus* in and scuttle her also. On his bridge Joyce sat hunched in his canvas deck chair, looking out at the land; the green line of Africa which the morning sun lit in harsh golden brilliance.

Renounce was running parallel to the coast, five miles off shore. Behind her *Pegasus* trailed like a mourner at a funeral.

'06.45 hours, sir.' The officer of the watch saluted.

'Very well.' Joyce roused himself. Until this moment he had hoped. Now the time had come and *Renounce* must die.

'Yeoman of Signals,' he spoke quietly, 'make this signal with *Pegasus* number "Plan A Effective".' This was the code that *Renounce* was to stand in for the channel. 'Stand by to pick up survivors.'

'*Pegasus* acknowledges, sir.'

Joyce was glad that Armstrong had not sent some inane message such as 'Good luck'. A curt acknowledgement, that was as it should be.

'All right, Pilot,' he said, 'take us in, please.'

84

I t was a beautiful morning and a flat sea. The captain of the escort destroyer wished it were not, he would have forfeited a year's seniority for a week of fog and rain.

As his ship tore down the line of transports to administer a rebuke to the steamer at the end of the column for not keeping proper station, he looked out at the western horizon. Visibility was perfect, a German masthead would be able to pick out this convoy of fat sluggish transports at a distance of thirty miles.

Twelve ships, fifteen thousand men – and *Blücher* could be out. At any moment she could come hurtling up over the horizon, with those long nine-inch guns blazing. The thought gave him the creeps. He jumped up from his stool, and crossed to the port rail of his bridge to glower at the convoy.

Close alongside wallowed one of the transports. They were playing cricket on her afterdeck. As he watched, a sun-bronzed giant of a South African clad only in short khaki pants swung the bat and clearly he heard the crack as it struck the ball. The ball soared up and dropped into the sea with a tiny splash.

'Oh, good shot, sir!' applauded the lieutenant who stood beside the captain.

'This is not the members' enclosure at Lords, Mr Parkinson,' snarled the destroyer captain. 'If you have nothing to occupy you, I can find duties for you.'

The lieutenant retired hurt, and the captain glanced along the line of troopships.

'Oh, no!' he groaned. Number Three was making smoke again. Ever since leaving Durban harbour Number Three had been giving periodic impersonations of Mount Vesuvius. It would be a give-away to the look-out at *Blücher*'s masthead.

He reached for his megaphone, ready to hurl the most scathing reprimand he could muster at Number Three as he passed her.

'This is worse than being a teacher in a kindergarten. They'll break me yet.' And he lifted the megaphone to his lips as Number Three came abreast.

The infantrymen that lined the troopship's rail cheered his eloquence to the echo.

'The fools. Let them cheer *Blücher* when she comes,' growled the captain and crossed the bridge to gaze apprehensively into the west where Africa lay just below the horizon.

'Strength to *Renounce* and *Pegasus*.' He made the wish fervently. 'God grant they hold *Blücher*. If she gets through . . .'

85

'I t's no use, Bwana. They won't move,' the sergeant of Askari reported·to Ensign Proust.

'What is the trouble?' demanded Proust.

'They say there is a bad magic on the ship. They will not go to her today.'

Proust looked over the mass of black humanity. They squatted sullenly among the huts and palm trees, rank upon rank of them, huddled in their cloaks, faces closed and secretive.

Drawn up on the mud bank of the island were the two motor launches, ready to ferry the bearers downstream to the day's labour aboard *Blücher*. The German seamen tending the launches were watching with interest this charade of dumb rebellion, and Ensign Proust was very conscious of their attention.

Proust was at the age where he had an iron-clad faith in his own sagacity, the dignity of a patriarch, and pimples.

He was, in other words, nineteen years of age.

It was clear to him that these native tribesmen had embarked on their present course of action for no other reason than to embarrass Ensign Proust. It was a direct and personal attack on his standing and authority.

He lifted his right hand to his mouth and began to feed thoughtfully on his fingernails. His rather prominent Adam's apple moved in sympathy with the working of his jaws. Suddenly he realized what he was doing. It was a habit he was trying to cure, and he jerked his hand away and linked it with its mate behind his back, in a faithful imitation of Captain Otto von Kleine, a man whom he held in high admiration. It had hurt him deeply when Lieutenant Kyller had greeted his request for permission to grow a beard like Captain von Kleine's with ribald laughter.

Now he sank his bare chin on to his chest and began to pace solemnly up and down the small clearing above the mud bank. The sergeant of Askari waited respectfully with his men drawn up behind him for Ensign Proust to reach a decision.

He could send one of the launches back to *Blücher*, to fetch Commissioner Fleischer. After all, this was really the Herr Commissioner's shauri (Proust had taken to using odd Swahili words like an old Africa hand). Yet he realized that to call for Fleischer would be an admission that he was unable to handle the situation. Commissioner Fleischer would jeer at him, Commissioner Fleischer had shown an increasing tendency to jeer at Ensign Proust.

'No,' he thought, flushing so that the red spots on his skin were less noticeable, 'I will not send for that fat peasant.' He stopped pacing and addressed himself to the sergeant of Askari.

'Tell them . . .' he started, and his voice squeaked alarmingly. He adjusted the timbre to a deep throaty rumble, 'Tell them I take a very serious view of this matter.'

The sergeant saluted, did a showy about-face with much feet stamping, and passed on Ensign Proust's message in loud Swahili. From the dark ranks of bearers there was no reaction whatsoever, not so much as a raised eyebrow. The crews of the launches were more responsive. One of them laughed.

Ensign Proust's Adam's apple bobbed, and his ears chameleoned to the colour of a good burgundy.

'Tell them that it is *mutiny*!' The last word squeaked again, and the sergeant hesitated while he groped for the Swahili equivalent. Finally he settled for:

'Bwana Heron is very angry.' Proust had been nicknamed for his pointed nose and long thin legs. The tribesmen bore up valiantly under this intelligence.

'Tell them I will take drastic steps.'

Now, thought the sergeant, he is making sense. He allowed himself literary licence in his translation.

'Bwana Heron says that there are trees on this island for all of you – and he has sufficient rope.'

A sigh blew through them, soft and restless as a small wind in a field of wheat. Heads turned slowly until they were all looking at Walaka.

Reluctantly Walaka stood up to reply. He realized that it was foolhardy to draw attention to himself when there was talk of ropes in the air, but the damage had already been done. The hundreds of eyes upon him had singled him out to the Allemand. Bwana Intambu always hanged the man that everyone looked at.

Walaka began to speak. His voice had the soothing quality of a rusty gate squeaking in the wind. It went on and on, as Walaka attempted a one-man filibust.

'What is he talking about?' demanded Ensign Proust.

'He is talking about leopards,' the sergeant told him.

'What is he saying about them?'

'He says, among other things, that they are the excrement of dead lepers.'

Proust looked stunned, he had expected Walaka's speech to have at least some bearing on the business in hand. He rallied gamely.

'Tell him that he is a wise old man, and that I look to him to lead the others to their duties.'

And the sergeant gazed upon Walaka sternly.

'Bwana Heron says that you, Walaka, are the son of a diseased porcupine and that you feed on offal with the vultures. He says further that you he has chosen to lead the others in the dance of the rope.'

Walaka stopped talking. He sighed in resignation and started down towards the waiting launch. Five hundred men stood up and followed him.

The two vessels chugged sedately down to *Blücher*'s moorings. Standing in the bows of the leading launch with his hands on his hips, Ensign Proust had the proud bearing of a Viking returning from a successful raid.

'I understand these people,' he would tell Lieutenant Kyller. 'You must pick out their leader and appeal to his sense of duty.'

He took his watch from his breast pocket.

'Fifteen minutes to seven,' he murmured. 'I'll have them aboard on the hour.' He turned and smiled fondly at Walaka who squatted miserably beside the wheel-house.

'Good man, that! I'll bring his conduct to Lieutenant Kyller's attention.'

86

L ieutenant Ernst Kyller shrugged out of his tunic and sat down on his bunk. He held the tunic in his lap and fingered the sleeve. The smear of blood had dried, and as he rubbed the material between thumb and forefinger, the blood crumbled and flaked.

'He should not have run. I had to shoot.'

He stood up and hung the tunic in the little cupboard at the head of his bunk. Then he took his watch from the pocket and sat down again to wind it.

'Fifteen minutes to seven.' He noted the time mechanically, and laid the gold hunter on the flap table beside the bunk. Then he lay back and arranged the pillows under his head, he crossed his still-booted feet and regarded them dispassionately.

'He came aboard to try and rescue his wife. It was the natural thing to do. But that disguise – the shaven head, and stained skin – that must have been carefully thought out. It must have taken time to arrange.'

Kyller closed his eyes. He was tired. It had been a long and eventful watch. Yet there was something nagging him, a feeling that there was an important detail that he had overlooked, a detail of vital – no, of deadly importance.

Within two minutes of the girl's recognition of the wounded man, Kyller and the surgeon commander had established that he was not a native, but a white man disguised as one.

Kyller's English was sketchy, but he had understood the girl's cries of love and concern and accusation.

'You've killed him also. You've killed them all. My baby, my father – and now my husband. You murderers, you filthy murdering swines!'

Kyller grimaced and pressed his knuckles into his aching eyes. Yes, he had understood her.

When he had reported to Captain von Kleine, the captain had placed little importance on the incident.

'Is the man conscious?'

'No, sir.'

'What does the surgeon say his chances are?'

'He will die. Probably before midday.'

'You did the right thing, Kyller.' Von Kleine touched his shoulder in a show of understanding. 'Do not reproach yourself. It was your duty.'

'Thank you, sir.'

'You are off watch now. Go to your cabin and rest – that is an order. I want you fresh and alert by nightfall.'

'Is it tonight then, sir?'

'Yes. Tonight we sail. The minefield has been cleared and I have given the order for the boom to be destroyed. The new moon sets at 11.47. We will sail at midnight.'

But Kyller could not rest. The girl's face, pale, smeared with her tears, haunted him. The strangled breathing of the dying man echoed in his ears, and that nagging doubt scratched against his nerves.

There was something he must remember. He flogged his tired brain, and it balked.

Why was the man disguised? If he came as soon as he had heard that his wife was a prisoner he would not have had time to effect the disguise.

Where had the man been when Fleischer had captured his wife? He had not been there to protect her. Where had he been? It must have been somewhere near at hand.

Kyller rolled on to his stomach and pressed his face into the pillow. He must rest. He must sleep now for tonight they would go out to break through the blockading English warships.

A single ship against a squadron. Their chances of slipping through unchallenged were small. There would be a night action. His imagination was heightened by fatigue, and behind his closed eyelids he saw the English cruisers, lit by the flashes of their own broadsides as they closed with *Blücher*. The enemy intent on vengeance. The enemy in overwhelming strength. The enemy strong and freshly provisioned, their coal-bunkers glutted, their magazines crammed with shell, their crews uncontaminated by the fever miasma of the Rufiji.

Against them a single ship with her battle damage hastily patched, half her men sick with malaria, burning green cordwood in her furnaces, her fire-power hampered by the desperate shortage of shell.

He remembered the tiers of empty shell racks, the depleted cordite shelves in the forward magazine.

The magazine? That was it! The magazine! It was something about the magazine that he must remember. That was the thing that had been nagging him. The magazine!

'Oh, my God!' he shouted in horror. In one abrupt movement he had leapt from his prone position on the bunk to stand in the centre of the cabin.

The skin on his bare upper arms prickled with goose-flesh.

That was where he had seen the Englishman before. He had been with the labour party – in the forward magazine.

He would have been there for one reason only – sabotage.

Kyller burst from his cabin, and raced, half dressed, along the corridor.

'I must get hold of Commander Lochtkamper. We'll need a dozen men – strong men – stokers. There are tons of explosive to move, we'll have to handle it all to find whatever the Englishman placed there. Please, God, give us time. Give us time!'

87

C aptain Otto von Kleine bit the tip from the end of his cheroot, and removed a flake of black tobacco from the tip of his tongue with thumb and forefinger. His steward held a match for him and von Kleine lit the cheroot. At the wardroom table, the chairs of Lochtkamper, Kyller, Proust and one other were empty.

'Thank you, Schmidt,' he said through the smoke. He pushed his chair back and stretched out his legs, crossing his ankles and laying his shoulders against the padded back-rest. The breakfast had not been of gourmet standard; bread without butter, fish taken from the river and strong with the taste of the mud, washed down with black unsweetened coffee. Nevertheless, Herr Fleischer seemed to be enjoying it. He was beginning his third plateful.

Von Kleine found his appreciative snuffling distracting. This would be the last period of relaxation that von Kleine could anticipate in the next many days. He wanted to savour it along with his cheroot, the wardroom was not the place to do so. Apart from the gusto with which the Herr Commissioner was demolishing his breakfast, and the smell of fish – there was a mood among his officers that was almost tangible. This was the last day and it was heavy with the prospect of what the night might bring. They were all of them edgy and tense. They ate in silence, keeping their attention on their plates, and it was obvious that most of them had slept badly. Von Kleine decided to finish his cheroot alone in his cabin. He stood up.

'Excuse me please, gentlemen.'

A polite murmur, and von Kleine turned to leave.

'Yes, Schmidt. What is it?' His steward was standing deferentially in his path.

'For you, sir.'

Von Kleine clamped the cheroot between his teeth and took the note in both hands, screwing up his eyes against the blue spiral of tobacco smoke. He frowned.

This woman, and the man she claimed was her husband, worried him. They were a drain on the attention which he should be devoting entirely to the problem of getting *Blücher* ready for tonight. Now this message – what could she mean by 'could save your ship'? He felt a prickle of apprehension.

He swung around.

'Herr Commissioner, a moment of your time, please.'

Fleischer looked up from his food with a smear of grease on his chin.

'Ja?'

'Come with me.'

'I will just finish . . .'

'Immediately, please.' And to avert argument von Kleine stooped out of the wardroom, leaving Herman Fleischer in terrible indecision, but he was a man for the occasion, he took the remaining piece of fish on his plate and put it in his mouth. It was a tight fit, but he still found space for the half cup of coffee as well. Then he scooped up a slice of bread and wiped his plate hurriedly. With the bread in his hand he lumbered after von Kleine.

He was still masticating as he entered the sick-bay behind von Kleine. He stopped in surprise.

The woman sat on one of the bunks. She had a cloth in her hand and with it she wiped the mouth of a black man who lay there. There was blood on the cloth. She looked up at Fleischer. Her expression was soft with compassion and sorrow, but it changed the moment she saw Fleischer. She stood up quickly.

'Oh, thank God, you've come,' she cried with joy as though she were greeting a dear friend. Then incongruously she looked up at the clock.

Keeping warily away from her, Fleischer worked his way around to the opposite side of the bunk by which she stood. He leaned over and studied the face of the dying man. There was something very familiar about it. He chewed stolidly as he puzzled over it. It was the association with the woman that triggered his memory.

He made a choking sound, and bits of half chewed bread flew from his mouth.

'Captain!' he shouted, 'this is one of them – one of the English bandits.'

'I know,' said von Kleine.

'Why wasn't I told? This man must be executed immediately. Even now it might be too late. Justice will be cheated.'

'Please, Herr Commissioner. The woman has an important message for you.'

'This is monstrous. I should have been told . . .'

'Be still,' snapped von Kleine. Then to Rosa, 'You sent for me? What is it you have to tell us?'

With one hand Rosa was stroking Sebastian's head, but she was looking up at the clock.

'You must tell Herr Fleischer that the time is one minute before seven.'

'I beg your pardon?'

'Tell him exactly as I say it.'

'Is this a joke?'

'Tell him, quickly. There is very little time.'

'She says the time is one minute to seven,' von Kleine rattled out the translation. Then in English, 'I have told him.'

'Tell him that at seven o'clock he will die.'

'What is the meaning of that?'

'Tell him first. Tell him!' insisted Rosa.

'She says that you will die at seven o'clock.' And Fleischer interrupted his impatient gobbling over the prone form of Sebastian. He stared at the woman for a moment, then he giggled uncertainly.

'Tell her I feel very well,' he said, and laughed again, 'better than this one here.' He prodded Sebastian. 'Ja, much better.' And his laughter came full and strong, booming in the confined space of the sick-bay.

'Tell him my husband has placed a bomb in this ship, and it will explode at seven o'clock.'

'Where?' demanded von Kleine.

'Tell him first.'

'If this is true you are in danger also – where is it?'

'Tell Fleischer what I said.'

'There is a bomb in the ship.' And Fleischer stopped laughing.

'She is lying,' he spluttered. 'English lies.'

'Where is the bomb?' von Kleine had grasped Rosa's arm.

'It is too late,' Rosa smiled complacently. 'Look at the clock.'

'Where is it?' Von Kleine shook her wildly in his agitation.

'In the magazine. The forward magazine.'

'In the *magazine*! Sweet merciful Jesus!' von Kleine swore in German, and turned for the door.

'The magazine?' shouted Fleischer and started after him. 'It is impossible – it can't be.' But he was running, wildly, desperately, and behind him he heard Rosa Oldsmith's triumphant laughter.

'You are dead. Like my baby – dead, like my father. It is too late to run, much too late!'

88

Von Kleine went up the companion-way steps three at a time. He came out into the alleyway that led to the magazine, and stopped abruptly.

The alleyway was almost blocked by a mountain of cordite charges thrown haphazard from the magazine by a knot of frantically busy stokers.

'What are you doing?' he shouted.

'Lieutenant Kyller is looking for a bomb.'

'Has he found it?' von Kleine demanded as he brushed past them.

'Not yet, sir.'

Von Kleine paused again in the entrance to the magazine. It was a shambles. Led by Kyller, men were tearing at the stacks of cordite, sweeping them from the shelves, ransacking the magazine.

Von Kleine jumped forward to help.

'Why didn't you send for me?' he asked as he reached up to the racks above his head.

'No time, sir,' grunted Kyller beside him.

'How did you know about the bomb?'

'It's a guess – I could be wrong, sir.'

'You're right! The woman told us. It's set for seven o'clock.'

'Help us God! Help us!' pleaded Kyller, and hurled himself at the next shelf.

'It could be anywhere – anywhere!' Captain von Kleine worked like a stevedore, knee-deep in spilled cylinders of cordite.

'We should clear the ship. Get the men off.' Kyller attacked the next rack.

'No time. We've got to find it.'

Then in the uproar there was a small sound, a muffled tinny buzz. The alarm bell of a travelling-clock.

'There!' shouted Kyller. 'That's it!' And he dived across the magazine at the same moment as von Kleine did. They collided and fell, but Kyller was up instantly, dragging himself on to his feet with hands clawing at the orderly rack of cordite cylinders.

The buzz of the alarm clock seemed to roar in his ears. He reached out and his hands fell on the smoothly paper wrapped parcels of death, and at that instant the two copper terminals within the leather case of the clock that had been creeping infinitesimally slowly towards each other for the past twelve hours, made contact.

Electricity stored in the dry cell battery flowed through the circuit, reached the hair-thin filament in the detonator cap, and heated it white-hot. The detonator fired, transferring its energy into the sticks of gelignite that were packed into the cigar box. The wave of explosion leapt from molecule to molecule with the speed of light so that the entire contents of *Blücher's* magazine were consumed in one hundredth part of a second. With it were consumed Lieutenant Kyller and Captain von Kleine and the men about them.

In the centre of that fiery holocaust they burned to vapour.

The blast swept through *Blücher*. Downwards through two decks with a force that blew the belly out of her as easily as popping a paper bag, down through ten fathoms of water to strike the bottom of the river and the shock wave bounced up to raise fifteen-foot waves along the surface.

It blew sideways through *Blücher's* watertight bulkheads, crumpling and tearing them like silver paper.

It caught Rosa Oldsmith as she lay across Sebastian's chest, hugging him. She did not even hear it come.

It caught Herman Fleischer just as he reached the deck, and shredded him to nothingness.

It swept through the engine room and burst the great boilers, releasing millions of cubic feet of scalding steam to race through the ship.

It blew upwards through the deck, lifting the forward gun-turret off its seating, tossing the hundreds of tons of steel high in a cloud of steam and smoke and debris.

It killed every single human being aboard. It did more than merely kill them, it reduced them to gas and minute particles of flesh or bone. Then still unsatisfied, its fury unabated, it blew outwards from *Blücher's* shattered hulk, a mighty wind that tore the branches from the mangrove forest and stripped it of leaves.

It lifted a column of smoke and flame writhing and twisting into the bright morning sky above the Rufiji delta, and the waves swept out across the river as though from the eye of a hurricane.

They overwhelmed the two launches that were approaching *Blücher*, pouring over them and capsizing them, swirling them over and over and spilling their human cargo into the frightened frothing water.

And the shock waves rolled on across the delta to burst thunderously against the far hills, or to dissipate out on the vastness of the Indian Ocean.

They passed over the British cruiser *Renounce* as she entered the channel between the mangroves. They rolled overhead like giant cannon-balls across the roof of the sky.

Captain Arthur Joyce leapt to the rail of his bridge, and he saw the column of agonized smoke rise from the swamps ahead of him. A grotesque living thing, unbelievable in its size, black and silver and shot through with flame.

'They've done it!' shouted Arthur Joyce. 'By Jove, they've done it!'

He was shaking; his whole body juddering, his face white as ice, and his eyes which he could not drag from that spinning column of destruction that rose into the sky, filled slowly with tears. He let them overflow his eyelids and run unashamedly down his cheeks.

89

Two old men walked into a grove of fever trees that stood on the south bank of the Abati river. They stopped beside a pile of gargantuan bones from which the scavengers had picked the flesh, leaving them scattered and white.

'The tusks are gone,' said Walaka.

'Yes,' agreed Mohammed, 'the Askari came back and stole them.'

Together they walked on through the fever trees and then they stopped again. There was a low mound of earth at the edge of the grove. Already it had settled and new grass was growing upon it.

'He was a man,' said Walaka.

'Leave me, my cousin. I will stay here a while.'

'Stay in peace, then,' said Walaka, and settled the string of his blanket roll more comfortably over his shoulder before he walked on.

Mohammed squatted down beside the grave. He sat there unmoving all that day. Then in the evening Mohammed stood up and walked away towards the south.

The Diamond Hunters

For DEE

His flight had been delayed for three hours at Nairobi, and despite four large whiskies he slept only fitfully until the intercontinental Boeing touched down at Heathrow. Johnny Lance felt as though someone had thrown a handful of grit in each eye, and his mood was ugly as he came through the indignity of Customs and Immigration into the main hall of the international terminus.

The Van Der Byl Diamond Company's London agent was there to meet him.

'Pleasant trip, Johnny?'

'Like the one to Hell,' Johnny grunted.

'Good practice for you.' The agent grinned. The two of them had seen some riotous times together.

Reluctantly Johnny grinned back at him.

'You got me a room and a car?'

'Dorchester – and Jag.' The agent handed over the car keys. 'And I've got two first-class seats reserved on tomorrow's nine o'clock flight back to Cape Town. Tickets at the hotel reception desk.'

'Good boy.' Johnny dropped the keys into the pocket of his cashmere overcoat and they started for the exit. 'Now where is Tracey van der Byl?'

The agent shrugged. 'Since I wrote to you she has dropped out of sight. I don't know where you can start looking.'

'Great, just great!' said Johnny bitterly as they came out into the car park. 'I'll start with Benedict.'

'Does the Old Man know about Tracey?'

Johnny shook his head. 'He's a sick man. I didn't tell him.'

'Here's your car.' The agent stopped by the pearl-grey Jaguar. 'Any chance of a drink together?'

'Not this trip, sorry.' Johnny slipped in behind the wheel. 'Next time.'

'I'll hold you to that,' said the agent and walked away.

It was almost dark by the time Johnny crossed the Hammersmith flyover in the moist smoky grey of the evening, and he lost himself twice in the maze of Belgravia before he found the narrow mews behind Belgrave Square and parked the Jaguar.

The exterior of the flat had been lavishly redecorated since his last visit, and Johnny's mouth twisted. He might not be so hot at earning the stuff – but our boy Benedict certainly was a dab hand at spending it.

There were lights burning and Johnny hit the door knocker half a dozen lusty cracks. It echoed hollowly about the mews, and in the silence that followed Johnny heard the whisper of voices from behind the curtains, and a shadow passed quickly across the window.

Johnny waited three minutes in the cold, then he stepped back into the middle of the mews.

'Benedict van der Byl,' he bellowed. 'I'll give you a count of ten to get this door open. Then I'll kick the bloody thing down.'

He drew breath, and bellowed again.

'This is Johnny Lance – and you know I mean it.'

The door opened almost immediately. Johnny pushed his way through it, not glancing at the man who held it, and started for the lounge.

'Dammit, Lance. You can't go in there.' Benedict van der Byl started after him.

'Why not?' Johnny glanced back at him. 'It is a Company flat – and I'm the General Manager.'

Before Benedict could reply, Johnny was through the door.

One of the girls picked up her clothing from the floor and ran naked into the bedroom passage. The other pulled a full-length caftan over her head and glared at Johnny sulkily. Her hair was in wild disorder, fluffed out into a grotesque halo of stiff curls.

'Nice party,' said Johnny. He glanced at the movie projector on the side table, and then at the screen across the room. 'Films and all.'

'Are you the Fuzz?' demanded the girl.

'You've got an infernal cheek, Lance.' Benedict van der Byl was beside him, tying the belt of his silk dressing-gown.

'Is he Fuzz?' the girl demanded again.

'No,' Benedict assured her. 'He works for my father.' With the statement he seemed to gather self-assurance, drawing himself up to his full height and smoothing his long dark hair with one hand. His voice regained its polish and lazy inflection. 'Actually, he is Daddy's messenger boy.'

Johnny turned to him, but he addressed the girl without looking at her.

'Beat it, girlie. Follow your friend.'

She hesitated.

'Beat it!' Johnny's voice crackled like a bush fire, and she went.

The two men stood facing each other. They were the same age, in their early thirties – both tall, both dark-haired – but different in every other way.

Johnny was big in the shoulder and lean across the hips and belly, his skin polished and browned by the desert sun. The line of his heavy jawbone stood out clearly, and his eyes seemed still to seek far horizons. His voice clipped and twanged with the accents of the other land.

'Where is Tracey?' he asked.

Benedict lifted one eyebrow in a pantomine of arrogant surprise. His skin was pale olive, unstained by sunlight for it was months since he had last visited Africa. His lips were very red, as though they had been painted, the classical lines of his features were blurred by flesh. There were soft little pouches under his eyes, and a plumpness beneath the silk dressing-gown that suggested he ate and drank often and exercised infrequently.

'My dear chap, what on earth makes you think I know where my sister is? I haven't seen her for weeks.'

Johnny turned away and crossed to one of the paintings on the far wall. The room was hung with good original South African artists – Alexis Preller, Irma Stern and Tretchikof – an unusual mixture of techniques and styles, but someone had convinced the Old Man they were sound investments.

Johnny turned back to face Benedict van der Byl. He studied him as he had the paintings, comparing him with the clean young athlete he had been a few years before. A clear mental image in his mind pictured Benedict moving with leopard grace across the green field of play under the packed grandstands, turning smoothly beneath the high floating arc of the ball to gather it neatly, head high, and break back in field to open the line for the return kick.

'You're getting fat, Laddy Buck,' he said softly, and Benedict's anger stained his cheeks dull red.

'Get out of here,' he snapped.

'In a minute – tell me about Tracey first.'

'I've told you – I don't know where she is. Whoring it up around Chelsea, I expect.' Johnny felt his own anger surge fiercely, but his voice remained level.

'Where is she getting the money, Benedict?'

'I don't know – the Old Man – '

Johnny cut him short. 'The Old Man is keeping her on an allowance of ten pounds a week. From what I hear she's throwing more than that around.'

'Christ, Johnny,' Benedict's tone became conciliatory, 'I don't know. It's not my business. Perhaps Kenny Hartford is – '

Again Johnny interrupted impatiently. 'Kenny Hartford is giving her nothing. That was part of the divorce agreement when they split up. Now I want to know who is subsidizing her trip to oblivion. How about it, big brother?'

'Me?' Benedict was indignant. 'You know there is no love wasted between us.'

'Must I spell it out?' Johnny asked. 'All right, then. The Old Man is dying – without losing his horror of all weakness and sin. If Tracey turns into a drug-soaked little tramp – then there's a good chance that our boy Benedict will come back into full favour. It would be a good gamble on your part to lay out a few thousand now, to send Tracey to Hell. Cut her off completely from her father – and all those nice fat millions.'

'Who said anything about drugs?' Benedict blustered.

'I did.' Johnny stepped up to him. 'You and I have a little unfinished business. It would give me intense pleasure to take you to pieces and see what makes you work.'

He held Benedict's eyes for long seconds, then Benedict looked down and fiddled with the cord of his dressing-gown.

'Where is she, Benedict?'

'I don't know, damn you!'

Johnny moved softly across to the movie projector and picked up a reel of film from the table beside it. He peeled off a few feet of celluloid from the reel and held it up to the light.

'Pretty!' he said, but the line of his mouth tightened with disgust.

'Put that down,' snapped Benedict.

'You know what the Old Man thinks about this sort of thing, don't you, Benedict?'

Suddenly Benedict went pale.

'He wouldn't believe you.'

'Yes, he would.' Johnny tossed the reel on the table and turned back to Benedict. 'He believes me because I've never lied to him.'

Benedict hesitated, wiped his lips nervously with the back of his hand.

'I haven't seen her for two weeks. She was renting a place in Chelsea. Stark Street. No. 23. She came to see me.'

'What for?'

'I lent her a couple of pounds,' Benedict muttered sulkily.

'A couple of pounds?' Johnny asked.

'All right, a couple of hundred. After all, she is my sister.'

'Damn decent of you,' Johnny lauded him. 'Write down the address.'

Benedict crossed to the leather-topped writing desk and scribbled on a card. He came back and handed the card to Johnny.

'You like to think you're big and dangerous, Lance.' His voice was pitched low but it shook with fury. 'Well, I'm dangerous too – in a different sort of way. The Old Man can't live for ever, Lance. When he's gone I'm coming after you.'

'You frighten the hell out of me.' Johnny grinned at him, and went down to the car.

The traffic was solid in Sloane Square as Johnny eased the Jaguar slowly down towards Chelsea. There was plenty of time to think; to remember how close they had been – the three of them. He and Tracey and Benedict.

Running together as wild young things with the endless beaches and mountains and sun-washed plains of Namaqualand as their playground. That was before the Old Man made the big strike on the Slang River, before there was money for shoes. When Tracey wore dresses made from flour sacks sewn together, and they rode to school each day, all three of them bare-back on a single pony like a row of bedraggled little brown sparrows on a fence.

He remembered how the long sun-drenched weeks while the Old Man was away were spent in laughter and secret games. How they climbed the *kopje* behind the mud-walled shack each evening and looked towards the north across the limitless land, flesh-coloured and purple in the sunset, searching for the wisp of dust in the distance that would mean the Old Man was coming home.

Then the almost painful excitement when the dusty, rackety Ford truck with its mudguards tied on with wire was suddenly there in the yard, and the Old Man was climbing down from the cab, a sweat-stained hat on the back of his head and the dust thick in the stubble of his beard, swinging Tracey squealing above his head. Then turning to Benedict, and lastly to Johnny. Always in that order – Tracey, Benedict, Johnny.

Johnny had never wondered why sometimes he was not first. It was always that way. Tracey, Benedict, Johnny. The same way as he had never wondered why his name was Lance and not van der Byl. Then it had come to an end suddenly, the whole brightly sunlit dream of childhood was gone and lost.

'Johnny, I'm not your real father. Your father and mother died when you were very young.' And Johnny had stared at the Old Man in disbelief.

'Do you understand, Johnny?'

'Yes, Pa.'

Tracey's hand groped for his beneath the table top like a little warm animal. He jerked his own hand away from it.

'I think you'd better not call me that any more, Johnny.' He could remember the exact tone of the Old Man's voice, neutral, matter of fact, as it splintered the fragile crystal of his childhood to fragments. The loneliness had begun.

Johnny accelerated the Jaguar forward and swung into the King's Road. He was surprised that the memory hurt so intensely – time should have mellowed and softened it.

His life from then on had become a ceaseless contest to win the Old Man's approval – he dare not hope for his love.

Soon there were other changes, for a week later the old Ford had come roaring unexpectedly out of the desert in the night, and the barking of the dogs and the Old Man's shouted laughter had brought them, sleepy-eyed, tumbling from their bunks.

The Old Man had lit the Petromax lamp and sat them on the kitchen chairs about the scrubbed deal table. Then with the air of a conjurer he had lain something that looked like a big lump of broken glass on the table.

The three sleepy children had stared at it solemnly, not understanding. The harsh glare of the Petromax was captured within the crystal, captured, repeated, magnified and thrown back at them in fire and blue lightning.

'Twelve carats –' gloated the Old Man, 'blue-white and perfect, and there is a cartload more where that came from.'

After that there were new clothes and motor cars, the move to Cape Town, the new school and the big house on Wynberg Hill – but always the contest. The contest that did not earn the Old Man's approval as it was designed to do, but earned instead Benedict van der Byl's jealousy and hatred. Without his drive and purpose, Benedict could not hope to match Johnny's achievements in the classroom and on the sports field. He fell far behind the pace that Johnny set – and hated him for it.

The Old Man did not notice for he was seldom with them now. They lived alone in the big house with the thin silent woman who was their housekeeper, and the Old Man came infrequently and for short periods. Always he seemed tired and distracted. Sometimes he brought presents for them from London and Amsterdam and Kimberley, but the presents meant very little to them. They would have liked it better had it stayed the way it was in the desert.

In the void left by the Old Man the hostility and rivalry between Johnny and Benedict flourished to such proportions that Tracy was forced to choose between them. She chose Johnny.

In their loneliness they clung to each other.

The grave little girl and the big gangling boy built together a castle against the loneliness. It was a bright secure place where the sadness could not reach them – and Benedict was excluded from it.

Johnny swung the Jaguar out of the line of traffic into Old Church Street, down towards the river in Chelsea. He drove automatically and the memories came crowding back.

He tried to recapture and hold the castle of warmth and love that he and Tracey had built so long ago, but instantly his mind leapt to the night on which it had collapsed.

One night in the old house on Wynberg Hill Johnny had come awake to the sound of distant weeping. He had gone barefooted in his pyjamas, following that heart-rending whisper of grief. He was afraid, fourteen years old and afraid in the dark house.

Tracey was weeping into her pillow and he had stooped over her.

'Tracey. What is it? Why are you crying?'

She had jumped up, kneeling on the bed, and flung both arms about his neck.

'Oh, Johnny. I had a dream, a terrible dream. Hold me, please. Don't go away, don't leave me.' Her whisper was still thick and muffled with tears. He had gone into her bed and held her until at last she slept.

Every night after that he had gone to her room. It was innocent and completely childlike, the twelve-year-old girl and the boy who was her brother, in fact if not in name. They held each other in the bed, and whispered and laughed secretly until sleep carried them both away.

Then suddenly the castle was blasted by the bright electric glare of the overhead light. The Old Man was standing in the door of the bedroom, and Benedict was behind him in his pyjamas dancing with excitement and chanting triumphantly.

'I told you, Pa! I told you so!'

The Old Man was shaking with rage, the bush of grey hair standing erect like the mane of a wounded lion. He had dragged Johnny from the bed, and struck away Tracey's clinging hands.

'You little whore,' he bellowed, holding the terrified boy easily with one hand and leaning forward to strike his daughter in the face with his open hand. Leaving her sobbing, face down on the bed, he dragged Johnny down the passages to the study on the ground floor. He threw him into the room with a violence that sent him staggering against the desk.

The Old Man had gone to the rack and taken out a light Malacca cane. He came to Johnny and, taking a handful of his hair, threw him face down over the desk.

The Old Man had beaten him before, but never like this. Mad with rage the Old Man's blows had been unaimed, some fell across Johnny's back.

Yet in the agony it was deadly important to the boy that he should not cry out. He bit through his lip so the taste of blood was salt and copper in his mouth. He must not hear me cry! And he choked back the moans feeling his pyjama trousers hanging heavy and sodden with blood.

His silence served only as a goad to the Old Man's fury. Flinging the cane aside, he pulled the boy upright and attacked him with his hands. Slamming Johnny's head from side to side with full, open-handed blows that burst in Johnny's skull with blinding flashes of light.

Still Johnny kept on his feet, clinging to the edge of the desk. His lips broken and swollen and his face bloated and darkening with bruises, until at last the Old Man was driven far beyond the borders of sanity. He bunched his fist and drove it into Johnny's face – and with a wonderful sense of relief Johnny felt the pain go out in a warm flood of darkness.

Johnny heard voices first. A strange voice:

' – As though he's been savaged by a wild beast. I'll have to inform the police.'

Then a voice he recognized. It took him a little time to place it. He tried to open his eyes but they seemed locked tight, his face felt enormous, swollen and hot. He forced the fat lids of his eyes back and recognized Michael Shapiro, the Old Man's secretary. He was talking quietly to the other man.

There was the smell of antiseptic and the doctor's bag lay open on the table beside the bed.

'Listen, Doctor. I know it looks bad – but hadn't you better talk to the boy before you stir up the police?'

They both looked towards the bed.

'He's conscious.' The doctor came to him quickly. 'What happened to you, Johnny? Tell us what happened. Whoever did this to you will be punished – I promise you.'

The words were wrong. Nobody must ever punish the Old Man.

Johnny tried to speak but his lips were stiff and swollen. He tried again.

'I fell,' he said. 'I fell. Nobody! Nobody! I fell down.'

When the doctor had gone Mike Shapiro came and stood over him. His Jewish eyes were dark with pity, and something else – anger perhaps, or admiration. 'I'm taking you to my house, Johnny. You will be all right now.'

He stayed two weeks under the care of Michael Shapiro's wife, Helen. The scabs came away, the bruises faded to a dirty yellow, but his nose stayed crooked with a lump at the bridge. He studied his new nose in the mirror, and liked it. It made him look like a boxer, he thought, or a pirate, but it was many months before the tenderness passed and he could finger it freely.

'Listen, Johnny, you are going to a new school. A fine boarding-school in Graham-stown.' Michael Shapiro tried to sound enthusiastic. Grahamstown was five hundred miles away. 'In the holidays you'll be going to work in Namaqualand – learning all about diamonds and how to mine them. You'll enjoy that, won't you?'

Johnny had thought about it for a minute, watching Michael's face and reading in it his shame.

'I won't be going home again then?' By home he meant the house on Wynberg Hill. Michael shook his head.

'When will I see – ' Johnny hesitated as he tried to find the right words, ' – when will I see them again?'

'I don't know, Johnny,' Michael answered him honestly.

As Michael had promised it was a fine school.

On his first Sunday after the church service, he had followed the other boys back to their classroom for the session of compulsory letter-writing. The others had immediately begun dashing off hasty scribbles to their parents. Johnny sat miserably until the master in charge stopped at his desk.

'Aren't you going to write home, Lance?' he asked kindly. 'I'm sure they'll all want to hear how you are.'

Johnny picked up his pen obediently, and puzzled over the blank writing-pad.

He wrote at last:

Dear Sir,

I hope you will be pleased to hear that I am now at school. The food is good, but the beds are very hard.

We go to church every day and play rugby football.

Yours faithfully,
Johnny.

From then until he left school and went up to University three years later, he wrote every week to the Old Man. Every letter began with the same salutation and went on, 'I hope you will be pleased to hear – ' There was never a reply to any of these letters.

Once each term he received a typewritten letter from Michael Shapiro setting out the arrangements that had been made for the school holidays. Usually these involved a train journey hundreds of miles across the Karroo to some remote village in the vast dry wasteland, where a light aircraft belonging to Van Der Byl Diamonds was waiting to fly him still deeper into the desert to one of the Company's concession areas. Again as Michael Shapiro had promised he learned about diamonds and how to mine them.

When the time to move on to University arrived, it was completely natural that he chose to take a degree in Geology.

During all that time he was an outcast from the van der Byl family. He had seen none of them – not the Old Man, nor Tracey, nor even Benedict.

Then, in one long eventful afternoon, he saw all three of them. It was his final year at University. His degree was a certainty. He had headed the lists at every examination from his first year onwards. He had been elected the senior student of Stellenbosch University, but now there was a further honour almost within his grasp.

In ten days' time the National Selectors would announce the Rugby team to meet the New Zealand All Black touring team – and Johnny's place at flank forward was as certain as his degree in Geology.

The sporting press had nicknamed Johnny 'Jag Hond' after that ferocious predator of the African wilds, the Cape hunting dog; an animal of incredible stamina and determination that savages its prey on the run. The nickname had stuck fast, and Johnny was a favourite of the crowds.

In the line-up of the team from Cape Town University was another crowd-pleaser whose place in the National Side to meet the All Blacks seemed equally assured. From his position at full back Benedict van der Byl dominated the field of play with a grace and artistry that was almost god-like. He had grown tall and wide-shouldered, with long powerful legs and dark brooding good looks.

Johnny led the visiting team out on to the smooth green velvet field, and while he jogged and flexed his back and shoulders he looked up at the packed stands seeking assurance that the high priests of rugby football were all there. He saw Doctor Danie Craven sitting with the other selectors in their privileged position below the Press enclosure. While in front of the Doctor, leaning back to exchange a few words with him, sat the Prime Minister.

This meeting between the two universities was one of the high spots of the rugby season, and the *aficionados* travelled thousands of miles to watch it.

The Prime Minister smiled and nodded, then leaned forward to touch the shoulder of the big white-headed figure that sat in the row below him.

Johnny felt an electric tingle run up his spine as the white head lifted and looked directly at him. It was the first time he had seen the Old Man in the seven years since that terrible night.

Johnny lifted an arm in salute, and the Old Man stared at him for long seconds before he turned away to speak with the Prime Minister.

Now the drum majorettes came out in ranks on to the field. White-booted, dressed in Cape Town University colours with short swinging skirts and tall hats, they high-stepped and paraded, lovely young girls flushed with excitement and exertion.

The roar of the crowd drummed with the blood in Johnny's ears, for Tracey van der Byl was leading the first rank. He knew her instantly, despite the passage of years in which she had grown to young womanhood. Her legs and arms were sun-bronzed and her dark hair hung glossily to her shoulders. She cavorted and kicked and stamped shouting the traditional cheers, jiggling her firm young bottom with innocent abandon while the crowds screamed and writhed, beginning already to work themselves into an hysterical frenzy. Johnny watched Tracey. He stood completely still in the thunderous uproar. She was the most beautiful woman he had ever seen.

Then the show was over, the drum majorettes retreating back through the stadium entrance, and the home team trotted on to the field.

The presence of the Old Man and Tracey added intensity to the glare of hatred that Johnny turned on the tall white-clad figure that fell back to take control of the Cape Town back field.

Benedict van der Byl reached his position and turned. From inside his calf-length sock he took a comb and ran it through his dark hair. The crowd bellowed and whistled, loving this little theatrical gesture. Benedict returned the comb to his sock and posed with one hand on his hip, his chin lifted arrogantly as he surveyed the opposition.

Suddenly he intercepted Johnny's glare, and the pose altered as he dropped his eyes and shuffled his feet a little.

The whistle fluted, and play began. It was everything the crowds had hoped for, a match that would long be remembered and gloated over. Massive Panzer offensives by the forwards, long probing raids by the backs with the oval ball flickering from hand to hand, until a bone-jarring tackle smashed the carrier to the turf. Hard and fast and clean play swung from side to side, a hundred times the crowd came up on its feet as one, eyes and mouths wide in screaming unbearable tension, to sink back with a groan as the ball was held by a desperate defence within inches of the goal line.

No score and three minutes of play left, Cape Town attacking from a set scrummage, driving through a gap in the defence and then putting the ball in the air with a long raking pass, taken cleanly by the Cape Town wing without a break in his stride. His feet twinkled across the green turf, and again the crowd came up with a gasp.

Johnny hit him low, just above the knee, with his shoulder. The two of them rolled together out of the field of play lifting a puff of white lime from the line and the crowd groaned and sank back.

While they waited to receive the throw, Johnny whispered hoarse orders. His gold and maroon jersey was soaked with sweat, and blood from a grazed hip stained his white shorts.

'Get it back fast. Don't run with it. Give it to Dawie. Kick high and deep, Dawie.'

Johnny leaped high to the flight of the thrown ball, with a bunched fist he punched it back accurately into Dawie's hands, at the same moment twisting his body to block the attackers.

Dawie fell back two paces and kicked. The power of the kick swung his right foot above his head, and the impetus flung him forward to put his forwards 'on side'.

The ball climbed slowly, flying like a dart with no wobble or roll in the air, reaching the zenith of its trajectory high over mid-field, then floating back to earth.

Twenty thousand heads followed its flight, a hush had fallen over the field – and in the unnatural silence Benedict van der Byl was drifting back deep into his own territory, anticipating the drop of the ball with deceptively unhurried strides, yet timing it with the precision of the gifted athlete.

The ball slotted neatly into his arms, and he began moving lazily infield to open his angle for the return kick. Still a tense throbbing mesmeric hush hung over the field, Benedict van der Byl was at the focus of attention.

'Jag Hond!' A single voice in the crowd alerted them, and twenty thousand heads swung downfield.

'Jag Hond!' A roar now. Johnny was well clear of the pack, arms pumping and legs churning as he bore down on Benedict. It was a futile effort, he could not hope to intercept a player of Benedict's calibre from such long range, yet Johnny was burning the last of his physical reserves in that charge. His face was a sweat-shining mask of determination, and clods of torn grass flew from under his savagely driving boots.

Then something happened which was unaccountable, almost past belief. Benedict van der Byl glanced round and saw Johnny. He broke his stride, two clumsy shuffling paces, and tried to pivot away deeper into his own ground. All the assurance had gone from his body, all the skill and grace. He tripped and stumbled, almost fell and the ball popped out of his hands, bouncing awkwardly.

Benedict scrambled after it, groping blindly, looking back over his shoulder. Now on his face was an expression of naked terror. Johnny was very close. Grunting at each stride like a gut-shot lion, massive shoulders already bunching for the strike, his lips drawn back into a murderous parody of a grin.

Benedict van der Byl dropped to his knees and covered his head with both arms, cringing down on to the green turf.

Johnny swept past him without a check, stooping easily in his run to gather the bouncing ball.

When Benedict uncovered his head and, still kneeling, looked up, Johnny stood ten yards away between the goal posts watching him. Then deliberately Johnny placed the ball between his feet to complete the formality of the touch-down.

Now, as if by agreement, both Johnny and Benedict looked towards the main grandstand. They saw the Old Man rise from his seat and make his way slowly through the ecstatic crowds towards the exit.

The day after the match, Johnny went back into the desert.

He was down in the bottom of a fifteen-foot prospect trench that had been dug across the gain of the country rock. It was oppressively hot in the confines of the trench and Johnny was stripped to a skimpy pair of khaki shorts, his sun-browned muscles oily with sweat, but he worked steadily at his sampling. He was establishing the contours and profile of an ancient marine terrace that the ages had buried beneath the sand. It was here on the bedrock that he expected to find the thin layer of diamond-bearing gravel.

He heard the Jeep pull up at ground level above him, and the crunch of footsteps. Johnny straightened up and held his aching back muscles.

The Old Man stood at the edge of the trench and looked down at him. He held a folded newspaper in his hand. This was the first time Johnny had seen him at close range in all the years, and he was shocked at the change. The mass of bushy hair was so white, and his features were folded and creased like those of a mastiff, leaving the big hooked nose standing like a hillock from his face. But there was no wasting or deterioration in his body, and his eyes were still that chilling enigmatic blue.

He dropped the newspaper into the trench and Johnny caught it, still staring up at the Old Man.

'Read it!' said the Old Man. The paper was folded to the sports page, and the headline was thick and bold.

'JAG HOND IN. VAN DER BYL OUT.'

The shock was as delicious as the plunge into a mountain stream. He was in – he would carry the gold and green, and wear the leaping Springbok on his blazer pocket.

He looked up, proud and happy, standing bare-headed in the sun waiting for the Old Man to speak.

'Make up your mind,' said the Old Man softly. 'Do you want to play ball – or work for Van Der Byl Diamonds? You can't do both.' And he walked back to the Jeep and drove away.

Johnny cabled his withdrawal from the team to the Doctor personally. The storm of outraged protest and abuse in the national press, and the hundreds of viperous letters Johnny received accusing him of cowardice and treachery and worse made him thankful for the sanctuary of the desert.

Neither Johnny nor Benedict had ever played the game again. Thinking about it, even at this remove of time, Johnny felt the sting of disappointment. He had wanted that green and gold badge of honour so very deeply. Brusquely he pulled the Jaguar off the road and scanned the street map of London and found Stark Street tucked away off the King's Road. He drove on remembering how it had been after the Old Man had taken it from him. The agony of mind had been scarcely endurable.

His companions in the desert were Ovambo tribesmen from the north, and a few of those taciturn white men that the desert produces, as hardy and uncompromising as her vegetation or her mountain ranges.

The deserts of the Namib and the Kalahari are amongst the loneliest places on earth, and the desert nights are long. Not even the day's unremitting physical labour could tire Johnny sufficiently to drug his dreams of a lovely girl in a short white skirt and high boots – or an old white-headed man with a face like a granite cliff.

Out of those long days and longer nights came solid achievements to stand like milestones marking the road of his career. He brought in a new diamond field, small but rich, in country which no one else had believed would yield diamonds. He pegged a uranium lode which Van Der Byl Diamonds sold for two and a half million, and there were other fruits from his efforts as valuable if not as spectacular.

At twenty-five, Johnny Lance's name was whispered in the closed and forbidding halls of the diamond industry as one of the bright young comers.

There were approaches – a junior partnership in a firm of consulting geologists, field manager for one of the struggling little companies working marginal ground in the Murderers' Karroo. Johnny turned them down. They were good offers, but he stayed on with the Old Man.

Then the big Company noticed him. A century ago the first payable pipe of 'blue ground' in Southern Africa was discovered on a hard scrabble farm owned by a Boer named De Beer. Old De Beer sold his farm for £6,000, never dreaming that a treasure worth £300,000,000 lay beneath the bleak dry earth. The strike was named De Beers New Rush, and a horde of miners, small businessmen, drifters, chancers, rogues and scoundrels moved in to purchase and work minute claims, each the size of a large room.

From this pretty company of fortune's soldiers two men rose high above the others, until between them they owned most of the claims in De Beers New Rush. When these two, Cecil John Rhodes and Barney Barnato, at last combined their resources, a formidable financial enterprise was born. From such humble beginnings the company has grown to awesome respectability and dignity. Its wealth is fabled, its influence immeasurable, its income is astronomical. It controls the diamond supply to the world. It controls also mineral concessions over areas of Central and Southern Africa which total hundreds of thousands of square miles, and its reserves of unmined precious and base minerals cannot be calculated. Small diamond companies are allowed to co-exist with the giant until they reach a certain size – then suddenly they become part of it, gobbled up as a tiger shark might swallow any of its pilot fish who become too large and daring. The big Company can afford to buy the best prospects, equipment – and men. It reached out one of its myriad tentacles to draw in Johnny Lance. The price they set on him was twice his present salary, and three times his future prospects.

Johnny turned it down flat. Perhaps the Old Man did not notice, perhaps it was mere coincidence that a week later Johnny was promoted Field Manager of Beach Operation. The nickname that went with the job was 'King Canute'.

Van Der Byl Diamonds had thirty-seven miles of beach concession. The tiny ribbon of shoreline, one hundred and twenty feet above high-water mark, and one hundred and twenty feet below low-water mark. Inland the concession belonged to the big Company. It had purchased the land, a dozen vast ranches, simply to obtain the mineral rights. The sea concessions, territorial up to waters twelve miles off shore, belonged to them also. Granted to them by Government charter twenty years before. But Van Der Byl Diamonds had the Admiralty strip – and it was 'King Canute's' job to work it.

The sea-mist came smoking in like ground pearl dust off the cold waters of the Benguela current. From out of the mist bank the high unhurried swells marched in towards the bright yellow sands and the tall wave-cut cliffs of Namaqualand.

The swells peaked up sharply as they felt the land. Their crests trembled and turned luminous green, began to dissolve in plumes of wind-blown spray, arched over and slid down upon themselves in the roar and rumble of white water.

Johnny stood on the driver's seat of the open Land-Rover. He wore a sheepskin jacket against the chill of the dawn mist, but his head was bare and his dark hair fluttered nervously against his forehead in the wind.

His heavy jaw was thrust forward, and his hands in the pockets of the sheepskin jacket were balled into fists. He scowled aggressively as he measured the height and push of the surf. With his crooked nose he looked like a boxer waiting for the gong.

Suddenly with an awkward angry movement he jerked his left hand from his pocket and looked down at the dial of his wrist watch. Two hours and three minutes to low tide, He pushed his fist back into his pocket, and swivelled quickly to look at his bulldozers.

There were eleven of them, bit bright yellow D.8 Caterpillars, lined up along the high-water mark. The operators sat goggled and tense in their high stern seats. They were all watching him anxiously.

Beyond them, standing well back, were the earthloaders. They were ungainly, pregnant-looking machines with swollen bellies, and heavily lugged tyres that stood taller than a man. When the time came they would rush in at thirty miles an hour, drop a steel blade beneath their bellies and scrape up a fifteen-ton load of sand or gravel, race back inland and drop their load, turn and rush back for another gargantuan bite out of the earth.

Johnny was steeling himself, judging the exact moment in which to hurl a quarter of a million pounds' worth of machinery into the Atlantic Ocean, in the hope of recovering a handful of bright pebbles.

The moment came, and Johnny spent half a minute of precious time in scrutinizing his preparations before committing himself to action.

Then 'GO!' he shouted into his loudhailer and windmilled his right arm in the unmistakable command to advance.

'Go!" he shouted again, but his voice was lost. Even the sound of the wild surf was lost in the bull bellow of the diesels. Lowering their massive steel blades, a chorus line of steel monsters, they crawled forward.

Now the golden sand curled before the scooped blades, like butter from the knife. It built up before the monstrous machines, becoming a pile and then a high wall. Thrusting, pulling back, butting, worrying, the bulldozers swept the wall of sand forward. The arms of the operators pumping the handles of the controls like mad barmen drawing a thousand pints of beer, the diesels roaring and muttering and roaring again.

The wall of sand met the first low push of seawater up the beach and smothered it. In seeming astonishment and uncertainty the sea pulled back, swirling and creaming before the advancing dyke of sand.

The bulldozers were performing a complicated but smoothly practised ballet now. Weaving and crossing, blades lifting and falling, backing and advancing, all under the supervision of the master choreographer, Johnny Lance.

The Land-Rover darted back and forward along the edge of the huge pit that was forming, with Johnny roaring orders and instructions through the electric loudhailer.

Gradually a sickle-shaped dyke of sand was thrown out into the sea, while behind it the bulldozer blades cut down, six, ten, fifteen feet through the loose yellow sand.

Then suddenly they hit the oyster line, that thin layer of fossilized oyster shell that so often covers the diamond gravels of South West Africa.

Johnny saw the change in the character of his pit, saw the shell curling from the blades of the bulldozers.

With half a dozen orders and hand signals he had his dozers flatten a ramp at each end of his pit, to give the earthloaders access. Then he ordered them away to hold the dyke against the sea.

He glanced at his watch. 'One hour thirteen minutes,' he muttered. 'We're running tight!'

Quickly he checked his pit. Two hundred yards long, fifteen feet deep, the overburden of sand stripped away, the oyster line showing clean and white in the sun, the bulldozers clear of the pit bottom – fighting back the sea.

'Right,' he grunted. 'Let's see what we've got.'

He turned to face the two earthmovers waiting expectantly above the high-water mark.

'Go in and get it!' he shouted, and gave the windmill arm signal.

Nose to tail the earthloaders roared forward, swinging wide at the head of the pit, then swooping down the ramp and dashing along the bottom. They scooped up a load of shell and gravel without checking their speed and went bellowing up the far ramp, swinging again to race up and deposit their load below the cliff, but above the high-water mark.

Round they went, and round again, chasing their tails, while the bulldozers held back the sea which was now becoming angry – sending its cohorts to skirmish along the dyke, seeking a weak place to attack.

Johnny glanced at his watch again.

'Three minutes to low water,' he spoke aloud, and grinned. 'We're going to make it – I think!'

He lit a cigarette, relaxing a little now. He dropped into the driving-seat and swung the Land-Rover up the beach, parking it beyond the mountain of gravel that the earth-loaders were building.

He climbed out and took up a handful of the gravel.

'Lovely!' he whispered. 'Oh sweet! Sweet!'

It was right. All the signs were good. In the single handful he identified a small garnet, and a larger lump of agate.

He scooped another handful.

'Jasper,' he gloated. 'And banded ironstone!'

All these stones were the team-mates of the diamond, you found them together.

The shape was right also, the stones polished round and shiny as marbles, not flattened like coins which would mean they had washed in only one direction. Round stones meant a wave action zone – a diamond trap!

'We've hit a jewel box – I'll take Lysol on that!'

From thirty-seven miles of beach Johnny had picked a two-hundred yard stretch, and hit it right on the nose. A choice not by luck, but by careful study of the configuration of the coastline. aerial photographs of the wave patterns and bottom contours of the sea, an analysis of the beach sands, and finally by that indefinable 'feel' for ground that a good diamond man has.

Johnny Lance was mightily delighted with himself as he climbed back into the Land-Rover. The earthloaders had scraped the gravel down to bed-rock. Their job was finished, and they pulled out of the pit and stood with panting exhausts beside the enormous pile of gravel they had recovered.

'Bottom boys!' roared Johnny, and the patient army of Ovambo tribesmen who had been squatting above the beach came swarming down into the pit. Their job was to sweep and clean the pit bottom, for a high proportion of the diamonds would have worked their way down through the gravel into the crevices and irregularities of the bedrock.

The sea changed its mood, furious at the brutal rape of its beaches it came hissing and tearing at the sand dyke. The tide was making now, and the bulldozers had to redouble their efforts to keep it out.

In the pit the Ovambos worked in a frenzy of activity, sparing only an occasional apprehensive glance for the wall of sand that held the Atlantic at bay.

Now Johnny was tensing up again. If he pulled them out early he would be leaving diamonds down there, if he left them in too late he might drown machinery – and men.

He cut it fine, just a fraction too fine. He pulled the bottom boys out with the sea beginning to break over the dyke, and to seep through under it.

Then he began to pull out his bulldozers, ten of them out – one still coming infinitely slowly, waddling across the wide bottom of the empty pit.

The sea broke through, it broke simultaneously in two places and came boiling into the pit in a waist-high wave.

The bulldozer operator saw it, hesitated one second, then his spirit failed him and he jumped down from his machine; abandoning it to the sea he sprinted ahead of the wave, making for the steep nearest side of the pit.

'Bastard!' swore Johnny as he watched the operator scramble to safety. 'He could have made it.' But his anger was against himself also. His decision to withdraw had been too long delayed, that was £20,000 worth of machinery he had sacrificed to the sea.

He slammed the Land-Rover into gear, and put her to the pit. She went off the edge like a ski jump, falling fifteen feet before she hit the bottom, but her fall was cushioned by the slope of sand and she sprang forward bravely to meet the rush of sea water.

It broke over the bonnet, slewing the vehicle viciously, but Johnny fought her head round and kept her going towards the stranded bulldozer.

The engine of the Land-Rover had been sealed and water-proofed against just such an emergency, and now she ploughed forward throwing a sheet of water to each side. But her forward rush faltered as the green water poured over her.

Now suddenly the entire sand dyke collapsed under the white surf and the Atlantic took control. The tall wave of green water that raced across the pit hit the Land-Rover, upending her, throwing Johnny into the jubilant frothing water, while the Land-Rover rolled over on her back, pointing all four wheels to the sky in surrender.

Johnny went under but came up immediately. Half swimming, half wading, battered by the boisterous sea he struggled on towards the yellow island of steel.

The sea struck him down, and he went under again. Found his feet for a moment, then had them cut from under him once more.

Then suddenly he had reached the bulldozer and was dragging himself up over the tracks to the driver's seat. He was coughing and vomiting sea water, as he reached the controls.

The bulldozer sat immovable, held down by her own twenty-six tons of dead weight on to the hard bed-rock of the pit. Although the sea burst over her, and swirled through her tracks, it could not move her.

Through eyes blurred and swimming with salt water and his own tears, Johnny briefly checked the gauges on the instrument panels. She had oil pressure and engine revs, and high above his head the exhaust pipe chugged blue smoke.

Johnny coughed again. Vomit and sea water shot up his throat in a scalding jet, but he pushed the throttle wide and threw in both clutch levers.

Ponderously the great machine ground forward, almost contemptuously shouldering the sea aside, her tracks solidly gripping the bed-rock.

Johnny looked about him quickly. The sand ramps at each end of the pit were washed away. The sides were sheer now, and behind him the sea was rushing unimpeded into the pit.

A wave broke over his head, and Johnny shook the water from his hair like a spaniel and looked around with mounting desperation for an avenue of escape.

With a shock of surprise he saw the Old Man. He had thought him to be four hundred miles away in Cape Town, but here he was on the edge of the pit. The white hair shone like a beacon.

Instinctively Johnny swung the bulldozer towards him, crawling through the turbulent waters towards him.

The Old Man was directing two of the other bulldozers, reversing them as close as he dared to the lip of the bank of sand, while from the service truck parked below the cliff a line of Ovambos came staggering down the beach with the heavy tractor tow chain over their shoulders. They shuffled bow-legged under the tremendous weight of the chain, sinking ankle deep into the sand with each step.

The Old Man roared at them, urging them on, but the words were lost in the thunder of diesel engines and the ranting of the wind and the sea. Now he turned back to Johnny.

'Get her in close,' the Old Man yelled through cupped hands. 'I'll bring the end of the chain down to you!'

Johnny waved an acknowledgement, then grabbed at the controls as the force of the next wave pushed even the giant tractor off its line, and Johnny felt the diesel falter for the first time – the water had found its way in through the seals at last.

Then he was under the high bank of yellow sand that towered twenty feet above him and he scrambled forward over the engine bonnet to meet the Old Man.

The Old Man was poised on the lip of the pit with the end of the chain draped in a loop over both shoulders. He was stooped beneath its weight, and when he stepped forward the sand crumpled away beneath him and he came sliding and slipping down the steep incline, buried waist deep, the great chain snaking after him.

Judging the rush of the sea Johnny jumped down to help him. Together, battered by the sea, they dragged the chain to the bulldozer.

'Fix it on to the blade arm,' grunted the Old Man, and they got a double turn of chain around the thick steel arm.

'Shackle!' Johnny snapped at him, and while the Old Man untied the length of rope which secured the steel shackle around his waist, Johnny looked up at the cliff of sand that hung over them.

'Christ!' he said softly, the sea was attacking it – and now it was soft and trembling above them, ready to collapse and smother them.

The Old Man passed him the huge shackle, and Johnny began with numbed hands to secure the end of the chain. He must pass the thick case-hardened pin through two links and then screw it closed. It was a Herculean task under these conditions, with the surf bursting over his head, the drag of the sea on the chain, and the cliff of sand threatening to fall on them at any moment. From twenty feet above them Johnny's foreman was watching anxiously, ready to pass the word to the two waiting bulldozers to throw their combined weights on the chain.

The thread of the pin caught, half a dozen turns would secure it, he would have finished the job by the time the word was passed to the 'dozer operators.

'Okay,' he nodded and gasped at the Old Man.'Pull!'

The Old Man lifted his head and bellowed up the bank, 'Pull!'

The foreman acknowledged with a wave.

'Okay.' And his head disappeared behind the bank as he ran back to the bulldozers, and at that moment the surf swung the chain. A movement of a few inches, but enough to catch Johnny's left index finger between two of the links.

The Old Man saw his face, saw him struggling to free himself.

'What is it?'

Then the water sucked back for a moment, and he saw what had happened. He waded forward to help – but from above them came the throaty roar of the diesels and the chain began running away, snaking and twisting up the bank like a python.

The Old Man reached Johnny and caught him about the shoulders to steady him. They braced themselves in horror, staring at the captive hand.

The chain jerked taut, severing the finger cleanly in a bright burst of scarlet, and Johnny reeled back into the Old Man's arms. The great yellow bulk of the bulldozer was dragged relentlessly down on top of them, threatening to crush them both, but using the next break and push of the sea the Old Man dragged Johnny clear – and they were carried sideways along the bank, tumbled helplessly by the strength of the water out of the bulldozer's path.

Johnny clutched his injured hand to his chest, but it hosed a bright stream of blood that discoloured the water about them. His head went under and salt water shot down his throat into his lungs. He felt himself drowning, the strength oozing out of him.

He surfaced again, and through bleary eyes saw the glistening wet bulldozer half-way up the sand bank. He felt the Old Man's arms about his chest and he went under again relaxing as the darkness closed over his eyes and brain.

When the darkness cleared from his eyes, he was lying on the dry sand of the beach and the first thing he saw was the Old Man's face above him, furrowed and pouched, his silver white hair plastered across his forehead.

'Did we get her out?' Johnny asked thickly.

'Ja,' the Old Man answered. 'We got her out.' And he stood up, walked to the Jeep, and drove away, leaving the foreman to tend to Johnny.

Johnny grinned at the memory, and lifting his left hand off the driving-wheel of the Jaguar he licked the shiny stump of his index finger.

'It was worth a finger,' he murmured aloud, and still searching for road signs he drove on slowly.

He smiled again comfortably, shaking his head with amusement as he remembered his hurt and disappointment when the Old Man had walked away and left him lying on the beach. He had not expected the Old Man to fall on his shoulders sobbing his gratitude and begging forgiveness for all the years of misery and loneliness – but he had expected something more than that.

After a two-hundred-mile round Jeep-journey through the desert night to the nearest hospital where they had trimmed and bound the stump, Johnny was back at the workings the next day in time to watch the first run of gravel from the beach.

In his absence, the gravel had been screened to sieve off all the over-size rock and stone, then it had been puddled through a tank of silicon mud to float off all the material with a specific gravity less than 2.5, then finally what was left had been run through a ball mill – a long steel cylinder containing steel balls the size of a baseball. The cylinder revolved continually and the steel balls crushed to powder all substance softer than 4 on Mohs hardness scale.

Now there was a residue, a thousandth part of the gravel they had won from the sea. In this remainder would be the diamonds – if diamonds there were.

When Johnny arrived back at the shed of galvanized iron and wood on the cliff above the beach that housed his separation plant, he was still half groggy from the anaesthetic and lack of sleep.

His hand throbbed with the persistence of a lighthouse, his eyes were reddened and a thick black stubble covered his jaws.

He went to stand beside the grease table that filled half the shed. He was swaying a little on his feet, as he looked around at the preparations. The massive bin at the head of the table was filled with the concentrated diamond gravels, the plates greased down, and his crew was standing ready.

'Let's go!' Johnny nodded at his foreman, who immediately threw in the lever that set the table shaking like an old man with palsy.

The table was a series of steel plates, each slightly inclined and thickly coated with dirty yellow grease. From the bin at the head of the shuddering table a mixture of gravel and water began to dribble, its consistency and rate of flow carefully regulated by the foreman. It spread over the greased table like spilled treacle, dropping from one plate to the next, and finally into the waste bin at the end of the table.

A diamond is unwettable, immerse it in water, scrub it, – but it comes out dry. A coat of grease on a steel plate is also unwettable, so wet gravel and sea shell will slide over it and keep moving across the agitating, sloping table.

But a diamond when it hits grease sticks like a half-sucked toffee to a woollen blanket.

In the excitement and anxiety of the moment Johnny felt his weariness recede, even the pain in his stump was muted by it. His eyes and whole attention were fastened on that glistening yellow sheet of grease.

The little stuff under a carat in weight, or the industrial black diamond and boart would not be visible on the table; the agitation was too rapid – blurring with speed, and the flow of loose material would disguise them.

So complete was his absorption that it was some seconds before he was aware of a presence beside him. He glanced up quickly.

The Old Man was there, standing with the wide stance and tension-charged attitude that was his own special way.

Johnny was acutely conscious of the Old Man's bulk beside him – and he felt the first flicker of alarm. What if this was a barren run? He needed diamonds now – as he had never needed anything in his life. He scanned the blurring plates of yellow grease, seeking the purchase price that could buy back the Old Man's esteem. The speckled gravel flowed imperturbably across the plates, and Johnny felt a flutter of panic.

Then from across the table the foreman let out a whoop, and pointed.

'Thar she blows!'

Johnny's eyes darted to the head of the table. There beneath the outlet from the bin, half buried in the thick grease by its own weight, anchored solidly while the worthless gravel washed past it, was a diamond.

A big fat five-carat thing, that glowed sulky and yellow, like a wild animal resenting its captivity.

Johnny sighed softly and darted a sideways glance at the Old Man. The Old Man was watching the table without expression, and though he must have been conscious of Johnny's scrutiny, he did not look up. Johnny's eyes were dragged irresistibly back to the table.

By some freakish chance, the next diamond fell from the bin directly on to the one already anchored in the grease.

When diamond strikes diamond it bounces like a golf ball off a tarmac road.

The second diamond, a white beauty the size of a peach pip, clicked loudly as it struck the other then spun head high in the air.

Both Johnny and the foreman laughed involuntarily with delight at the beauty of that twinkling drop of solid sunlight.

Johnny reached across the table with his good hand, and snatched it out of the air. He rubbed it between his fingers – revelling in the soapy feel of it, then turned and offered it to the Old Man.

The Old Man looked at the diamond, nodded in acknowledgement. Then he pulled back the cuff of his coat and checked his wrist watch.

'It's late. I must get back to Cape Town.'

'Won't you stay for the rest of the run, sir?' Johnny realized his tone was too eager. 'We could have a drink together afterwards.' He remembered after he had spoken, that the Old Man abhorred alcohol.

'No.' The Old Man shook his head. 'I have to get back by this evening.' Now he looked steadily into Johnny's eyes. 'You see, Tracey is getting married tomorrow afternoon and I must be there.'

Then he smiled, watching Johnny's face, but nobody could ever guess the meaning of a smile on the Old Man's lips – for it never showed in his eyes.

'Didn't you know?' he asked, still smiling. 'I thought you had received an invitation.' And he went out of the shed to where his Jeep stood in the bright sunshine waiting to take him out to the aircraft landing-strip among the sand dunes.

The pain in his injured hand, and the Old Man's words denied Johnny the sleep he so desperately needed, but it was two o'clock in the morning before he threw back his blankets and lit the lamp beside his camp bed.

'He said I had been invited – and, by God, I'll be there.'

He drove through the night, and the next morning. The first two hundred miles were on desert tracks of sand and stone, then he reached the metalled highway in the dawn and turned south across the great plains and over the mountains. It was noon before he saw the squat blue silhouette of Table Mountain on the skyline dwarfing the city that huddled beneath it.

He checked in at the Vineyard Hotel, and hurried to his room to bath and shave and change into a suit.

The grounds of the old house were crowded with expensive automobiles, and the overflow was parked along both sides of the street outside, but he found a space for the dusty Land-Rover. He walked up through the white gates and across the green lawns.

There was a band playing in the house, and a hubbub of voices and laughter drifted out through the windows of the ballroom.

He went in through the side door. The passages were thronged with guests, and he made his way amongst them seeking a familiar face in the groups of loud-voiced gesticulating men and giggling women. At last he found one.

'Michael.' And Michael Shapiro looked round, recognizing him and letting the conflicting emotions of pleasure, surprise and alarm show clearly on his face.

'Johnny. It's good to see you.'

'Is the ceremony over?'

'Yes, and the speeches also – thank God.' He took Johnny's arm and led him aside. 'Let me get you a glass of champagne.' Michael hailed a waiter and put a crystal glass into Johnny's hand.

'Here's to the bride,' Johnny murmured and drank.

'Does the Old Man know you are here?' Michael came out with the question that was burning his mouth, and when Johnny shook his head, Michael's expression became thoughtful.

'What's he like, Michael, Tracey's husband?'

'Kenny Hartford?' Michael considered the question. 'He's all right, I suppose. Nice-looking boy, plenty of money.'

'What's he do for a crust of bread?'

'His daddy left him the whole loaf – but to fill in the time he does fashion photography.' And Johnny pulled down the corners of his mouth.

Michael frowned. 'He's all right, Johnny. The Old Man picked him carefully.'

'The Old Man?' Johnny's jaw thrust out.

'Of course, you know him – he wouldn't leave an important decision like that to anybody else.'

Johnny finished his champagne in silence, and Michael watched his face anxiously.

'Where is she? Have they left yet?'

'No.' Michael shook his head. 'They're still in the ballroom.'

'I think I'll go and wish luck to the bride.'

'Johnny.' Michael caught hold of his elbow. 'Don't do anything stupid – will you?'

Johnny stood at the head of the marble staircase that led down into the ballroom. The floor was crowded with dancing couples and the music was loud and merry. The bridal party sat at a raised table across the floor.

Benedict van der Byl saw Johnny first. His face flushed and he leaned quickly to whisper to the Old Man, then began to rise from his seat. The Old Man placed a restraining hand on Benedict's shoulder, and smiled across the room at Johnny.

Johnny went down the stairs and made his way through the dancers. Tracey had not seen him. She was talking to the silky-faced young man who sat beside her. He had wavy blond hair.

'Hello, Tracey.' She looked up at Johnny and caught her breath. She was more beautiful than he remembered.

'Hello, Johnny.' Her voice was almost a whisper.

'May I dance with you?' She was pale now, and her eyes went to the Old Man, not to her new husband. The gleaming white bush of hair nodded slightly, and Tracey stood up.

They made one circuit of the dance floor before the band stopped playing. Johnny had planned a hundred different things to say to her, but he was dumb until the music ended and the opportunity was passing. Hurriedly now in the few seconds that were left Johnny told her: 'I hope you will be happy, Tracey. But if you ever need help – ever – I will come, I promise you that.'

'Thank you.' Her voice was husky, and for a moment she looked like the little girl who had cried in the night. Then he took her back to her husband.

The promise had been made five years ago, and now he had come to London to honour it.

Number 23 Stark Street was a neat double-storied cottage with a narrow front. He parked outside it. It was dark now and lights burned on both floors. He sat in the parked Jaguar, suddenly reluctant to go further. Somehow he knew that Tracey was here, and he knew it would not be pretty. For a moment he recaptured the image of her as a lovely young woman in a wedding dress of white satin, then he climbed out of the Jaguar and went up the steps to the front door. He reached for the bell before he noticed with surprise that the door was ajar. He pushed it open and walked into a small sitting-room furnished with feminine taste.

The room had been hastily ransacked, one of the curtains was spread on the floor and on it were piled books and ornaments. Pictures had been taken down from the walls and stacked ready for removal.

Johnny picked up one of the books, and opened the cover. On the fly leaf was a handwritten name. 'Tracey van der Byl.' He dropped it back on the pile as he heard footsteps on the stairs from the floor above.

A man came down the stairs. He was dressed in soiled green velvet trousers, sheepskin boots, and shabby frock coat of military cut frogged with tarnished gold braid. He was carrying an armful of women's dresses.

He saw Johnny and stopped nervously, his pink lips opened in vacant surprise but his eyes were beady and bright under the thatch of lank blond hair.

'Hello,' Johnny smiled pleasantly. 'Are you moving out?' And he drifted quietly closer to the man on the stairs and stood looking up at him.

Suddenly from the floor above a low wail echoed down the stairs. It was an eerie sound, without passion or pain, as though steam were escaping from a jet, only just recognizable as human. Johnny went rigid at the sound, and the man on the stairs glanced nervously over his shoulder.

'What have you done to her?' Johnny asked softly, without menace.

'No. Nothing! She's on a trip. A bad trip.' The man's denial was frantic. 'It's her first time on acid.'

'So you're cleaning the place out, are you?' Johnny asked mildly.

'She owes me plenty. She can't pay. She promised – and she can't pay.'

'Oh,' said Johnny. 'That's different. I thought you were hitting the place.' He reached into his overcoat and brought out his wallet, riffling the wad of banknotes. 'I'm a friend of hers. How much does she owe you.'

'Fifty nicker.' The man's eyes sparkled when he saw the wallet. 'I gave her credit.'

Johnny counted off ten fivers, and held them out. The man dropped the bundle of clothing over the banisters and came eagerly down the last few stairs.

'Did you sell her the stuff – the acid?' Johnny asked, and the man stopped a pace from him, his expression stiffening with suspicion.

'Oh, for God's sake.' Johnny grinned. 'We are not children – I know the score.' He offered the banknotes. 'Did you get the stuff for her?'

The man grinned back at him weakly, and nodded as he reached for the money. Johnny's free hand snapped closed on the thin wrist and he swung him off his feet, forcing his wrist up between his shoulder-blades.

Johnny stuffed the money into his pocket, and marched him up the stairs.

'Let's go and have a look, shall we?'

There was a mattress on the iron bedstead covered with a grey army blanket. Tracey sat cross-legged on the blanket. She wore only a thin cotton slip and her hair hung lank and lustreless to her waist. Her arms crossed over her chest were thin and white as sticks of chalk. Her face also was pale, the skin translucent in the light of the electric bulb. She was rocking gently back and forth and wailing softly, her breath steaming in the icy cold room.

It was her eyes that shocked Johnny the most. They seemed to have expanded to an enormous size, and beneath each was a dark bruised-looking smear. The pupils of the eyes were distended and glittery with the same adamant sheen as uncut diamonds.

The big glittery green eyes fastened on Johnny and the man in the doorway, and the wail rose abruptly to a shriek. The shriek died away, and she bowed forward and buried her face in her hands covering her eyes.

'Tracey,' said Johnny softly. 'Oh God, Tracey!'

'She'll be all right,' the man whimpered and twisted in his grip. 'It's the first time – she'll be all right.'

'Come.' Johnny dragged him out of the room, and pushed the door closed with his foot. He held him against the wall, and his face was set and pale, his eyes merciless – but he spoke quietly, patiently as though he was explaining to a child.

'I'm going to hurt you now. I'm going to hurt you very badly. Just as badly as I can without killing you. Not because I enjoy it, but because that girl is a very special person to me. In the future when you think about giving poison to another girl – I want you to remember what I did to you tonight.'

Johnny held him with his left hand against the wall and he used his right hand, punching up under the ribs at an angle to tear the stomach muscles. With three or four blows he was too high, and he felt ribs crack and snap under his fist.

When he stepped back the man sagged slowly face forward, and Johnny caught him cleanly in the mouth snapping his teeth off at the gums, splitting his lips open like the petals of a rose. The man had made a lot of noise. Johnny looked into Tracey's room to make sure she had not been disturbed, but she was still bowed forward, rocking rhythmically on her haunches.

He found the bathroom and dampened his handkerchief to wipe the blood off his hands and the front of his overcoat. He came out into the passage again and stopped over the unconscious body to check the pulse. It was strong and regular, and he felt a lift of relief as he dragged the man's face out of the puddle of his own vomit and blood to prevent him drowning.

He went through to Tracey and, despite her frantic struggles, wrapped her in the greasy army blanket and carried her down to the Jaguar.

She quietened down and lay like a sleeping child in the back seat while he tucked the blanket round her, then he went back into the house and phoned 999, giving the address and hanging up immediately.

He left Tracey in the car outside the Dorchester, while he went in to speak to the reception clerk. Within minutes Tracey was in a wheelchair on her way up to the two-bedroom suite on the second floor. The doctor was there fifteen minutes later.

After the doctor had gone Johnny bathed, and carrying a tumbler of Chivas Regal in one hand he went into Tracey's room and stood by her bed. Whatever the doctor had given her had put her out cleanly. She lay gaunt and pale – yet with a strangely fragile beauty that seemed enhanced by the bruised discoloration of her eye sockets.

He stooped to brush the hair from her cheek, and her breath was light and warm on his hand. He felt such an infinity of tenderness for her then as he had never known for any other person, he was amazed by the strength of it.

He stooped over her and gently brushed her lips with his own. Her lips were dry and flaky white, and their touch was harsh as sandpaper.

Johnny straightened up and went to the armchair across the room. He sank into it wearily, and sipped the whisky, feeling its warmth spread from his belly and untie the knots in his muscles. He watched the pale ruined face on the pillows.

'We are in a hell of a mess, you and I' he spoke aloud, and felt anger again. For long minutes it was undirected, but slowly it gelled and found an object to focus on.

For the first time in his life he was angry with the Old Man.

'He has brought you to this,' he said to the girl on the bed. 'And me – '

The reaction was swift, his loyalty was a thing grown part of his existence. Always he had trained himself to believe that the Old Man's machinations were just and wise – even if at times the justice and wisdom were hidden from him. Mortal man does not doubt the omnipotence of his gods.

Sickened by his own treachery, he began to examine the Old Man's motives and actions under the bright light of reason.

Why had the Old Man sent Michael Shapiro to fetch him out of the desert?

'He wants you in Cape Town, Johnny. Benedict didn't measure up. The Old Man has given him the London Office, it's a form of exile. He's picked you to take over the Company,' Michael explained. 'Tracey is out of the way. She and her husband are in London also. I guess the Old Man thinks it's safe to have you back in Cape Town now.'

Michael watched Johnny's undisguised joy and went on slowly.

'I'm speaking out of turn, perhaps. Mr van der Byl is a strange man. He's not like other people. I know how you feel about him, I've watched it all, you know – but listen, Johnny, you can go anywhere on your own now. There are a lot of other companies that want you – ' But he had seen the expression on Johnny's face, and stopped ' – okay, Johnny. Forget I ever said it. I only spoke because I like you.'

Thinking on it now, there had been substance in Michael's warning. Certainly he was General Manager of Van Der Byl Diamonds, but he was no nearer to the Old Man than he had ever been. He lived under the mountain but the mountain was remote and he had not been able to scale the lowest slopes.

He had found the city as lonely as the desert, and he was ripe for the first attractive woman who set her snares for him.

Ruby Grange was tall and slim with hair the colour they call 'Second Cape' in a diamond, like sunlight through a crystal glass of champagne.

He wondered now at his own naïvety. That he should be so easily misled, and should have rushed so headlong into her web. After the wedding she had revealed herself, exposing the deeply calculating greed, the driving hunger for flattery and material possessions which was her mainspring, and her complete absorption with herself – Johnny had not been able to believe it. For months he fought off the growing certainty until it could be denied no longer, and he looked with chilled dismay on the shallow selfish little creature he had married.

He had withdrawn from her and flung all his energies into the Company.

This, then, was his life and he saw that it was an empty thing, hollowed out by the Old Man's hand.

For the first time his mind skirted the idea that it was a carefully calculated and sadistic revenge for the innocent action of a half-grown boy.

As though it were an escape from thoughts too dreadful to be borne, he fell asleep in the chair and the glass fell from his hand.

Jacobus Isaac van der Byl sat in a leather chair before the X-ray viewer. Fear had blasted the granite of his features, leaving them cracked and sagging, recognizable but subtly alerted below the gleaming white mane.

Fear was in his eyes also, moving below the surface like slimy water creatures in the pale blue pools. With the fear chilling and numbing his limbs he watched the cloudy and swirling images on the screen.

The specialist was talking softly, impersonally, as though he were lecturing one of his classes.

' – enveloping the thymus here, and extending beyond the trachea.'

The point of his gold pencil followed the ghostly outline on the screen. The Old Man swallowed with an effort. It seemed to be swelling in his throat as he listened, and his voice was hoarse and blurred to his own ears.

'You will operate?' he asked, and the specialist paused in his explanation. He glanced at the surgeon across the desk. The exchange was as guilty as that of conspirators.

The Old Man swivelled his chair and faced the surgeon.

'Well?' he demanded harshly.

'No.' The surgeon shook his head apologetically. 'It's too late. If only you had – '

'How long?' The Old Man overrode his explanation.

'Six months, not more.'

'You are certain?'

'Yes.'

The Old Man's chin sank onto his chest and he closed his eyes. There was complete silence in the room, they watched him with professional pity and interest as he reached his own personal acceptance of death.

At last the Old Man opened his eyes and stood up slowly. He tried to smile but his lips would not hold the shape.

'Thank you, Gentlemen,' he croaked in this new rough voice. 'Will you excuse me, please. There are many things to arrange now.'

He went down to where the Rolls waited at the entrance. He walked slowly, shuffling his feet and the chauffeur came to him quickly, but the Old Man shrugged away his helping hands and climbed into the back seat of the car.

Michael Shapiro was waiting for him in the study of the big house. He saw the change in him immediately and jumped up from his chair. The Old Man stood in the doorway, his body seemed to have shrunk.

'Six months,' he said. 'They give me six months.' He said it as though he had expected to buy off death, and they had tricked him. He closed his eyes again, and when he opened them there was a glint of cunning in them, even his face had a pinched foxy look to it.

'Where is he? Is he back yet?'

'Yes, the Boeing got in at nine this morning. He's at the office now.' Michael was shocked, it was the first time he had seen the Old Man without the mask.

'And the girl?' He had not called her 'daughter' since the divorce.

'Johnny has her in a private nursing-home.'

'Worthless slut,' said the Old Man softly, and Michael stilled the protest before it reached his lips. 'Get your pad. I want you to take something down.' The Old Man chuckled hoarsely. 'We'll see!' he said, making it sound like a threat. 'We'll see!'

Johnny's doctor was waiting at Cape Town airport.

'Take her, Robin. Dry her out, and fatten her up. She's up to her gills with drugs and she probably hasn't eaten for a month.'

Tracey showed her first spark of spirit.

'Where do you think – '

'Into a nursing-home.' Johnny anticipated her questions. 'For as long as is necessary.'

'I'm not – '

'Oh, yes, you bloody well are.' He took her arm, and Robin grabbed the other. They walked her, still protesting weakly to the car park.

'Thanks, Robin Old Soldier, give her the full work-out.'

'I'll send her back to you like new,' Robin promised and drove away. Johnny took a few moments to look at the massive square silhouette of the mountain – his own private home-coming ceremony. Then he fetched the Mercedes from the airport garage, and hesitated between home or the office, decided he was not up to an interrogation from Ruby and chose the office. He kept a clean shirt and shaving tackle in his private bathroom there.

They descended on him like a tribe of man-eating Amazons as he came in through the glass doors into the lusciously furnished and carpeted reception area of Van Der Byl Diamonds head office.

The two pretty little receptionists began yipping joyously in chorus.

'Oh, Mr Lance, I have a whole sheaf of messages – '

'Oh, Mr Lance, your wife – '

Trying not to run he made it to within ten feet of his own door, when the Old Man's secretary popped out of ambush from behind her frosted-glass panel.

'Mr Lance, where on earth have you been? Mr van der Byl has been asking – '

Which alerted Lettie Pienaar, his own secretary.

'Mr Lance, thank goodness you're back.'

Johnny stopped and held up his hands in an attitude of surrender.

'One at a time, ladies. There is enough to go round – don't panic.'

Which broke the reception team into a quivering jelly of giggles, and sent the Old Man's watchdog back behind her panel sniffing disgustedly,

'Which is the most important, Lettie?' he asked as he went to his desk and flipped through his mail, shrugged out of his coat and began stripping tie and shirt as he headed for his bathroom.

They shouted at each other through the open door of the bathroom, as Johnny shaved quickly and showered, Lettie bringing him up to date on every aspect of company and domestic business.

'Mrs Lance has phoned regularly. She called me a liar when I told her you were at Cartridge Bay.' Lettie was silent a moment, then as Johnny came out of the bathroom she asked, 'By the way, where have you been?'

'Don't *you* start that.' Johnny stood over the desk, and began flipping through the accumulated papers. 'Get my wife on the phone, please – no, hold it. Tell her I'll be home at seven.'

Lettie saw she had lost his attention, and she stood and went out. Johnny settled down behind his desk.

Van Der Byl Diamonds was a sick company. Despite Johnny's protests the Old Man had been drawing off its reserves and feeding them into his other ventures – the property-developing company, the clothing factory, Van Der Byl fisheries, the big irrigation scheme on the Orange River – and now the cupboard was almost bare.

The beach concessions were reaching the end of a short but glorious life. They were starting to work break-even ground. The Old Man had sold the Huib Hoch concession to the big Company for a quick profit – but the profit had been just as quickly transferred out of Johnny's control.

There was only one really fat goose left in his pen, and it wasn't laying eggs yet.

Eighteen months earlier Johnny had purchased two offshore diamond grounds from a company which had died in attempting to work them. It had been strangled by its own inefficiency.

Taking diamonds from the sea is about eight times more expensive than working them from a dry open-cast. One must dredge the gravel from the wild and unpredictable waters of the Skeleton Coast, load it into dumb barges, tow the barges to a safe base, off-load it and then begin the recovery process – or rather, that was the method the defunct company had attempted.

Johnny had dreamed up, and then ordered a vessel which was completely self-contained. It could lie out at sea, suck up the gravel and process it, spilling the waste gravel back into the sea as rapidly as it was sucked aboard. It was fitted with a sophisticated recovery plant that was completely computerized and contained within the ocean-going hull. It needed only a small crew, and it could work in all weather conditions short of a full tornado.

The *Kingfisher* was lying at Portsmouth dockyards rapidly nearing completion. Her trials were scheduled for early August.

Financing the building of this vessel had been a nightmare for Johnny. The Old Man had been unhelpful, when he wasn't being downright obstructive. He never discussed the venture without that little smile twitching at his lips. He had restricted Van Der Byl Diamonds' monetary involvement in the project so severely that Johnny had been forced to raise two millions outside the company.

He had found the money, and the Old Man had smiled again.

Kingfisher should have been lying on the grounds three months ago, sucking up diamonds. The whole financial structure of the scheme was based on her completion on schedule, but *Kingfisher* was running six months behind and now the foundations were shivering.

Sitting at his desk Johnny was working out how to shore up the whole edifice and keep it from collapsing before he could get *Kingfisher* working. The creditors were rumbling and creaking, and Johnny had only his own enthusiasm and reputation left to keep them quiet.

Now he must ask them to defer their interest payments for another three months. He picked up the telephone.

'Get me Mr Larsen at Credit Finance,' he said, steeling himself as he did so, jutting out his jaw and thrusting one bunched fist into his coat pocket.

At five o'clock he stood up from his desk and went to the cabinet. He poured three fingers of whisky and went back to lower himself wearily into his swivel chair. He felt no elation at having won another reprieve, he was too tired.

The unlisted telephone on his desk rang and he picked it up.

'Lance,' he said.

'How was London?' he recognized the voice instantly, feeling no surprise that the Old Man knew about his journey. The Old Man knew everything. Before he could answer the hoarse croak came again, 'Come up to the house – now!' And the receiver clicked dead.

Johnny looked at the whisky in his hand regretfully and set it down untouched. The Old Man would smell it and smile.

Cloud was blowing over the mountain, and the setting sun turned it to the colour of tangerine and peaches. The Old Man stood at the window and watched the cloud cascade down into the valley, dispersing as it fell.

He turned from the window as Johnny entered the study and instantly Johnny was aware that something momentous had taken place in his absence.

He glanced quickly at Michael Shapiro for a cue, but Michael's grey-streaked head was bowed over the papers he held on his lap.

'Good evening.' Johnny addressed the Old Man.

'Sit there.' The Old Man indicated the Spanish leather chair opposite his desk.

'Read it,' the Old Man ordered Michael, and Michael cleared his throat and patted the papers into a neat square before he began.

The Old Man sat with his eyes on Johnny's face. It was a candid, intimate scrutiny, but Johnny felt no discomfort under it. It was almost as though the Old Man's eyes were caressing him.

Mike Shapiro read intelligently, bringing out the meaning of the involved and convoluted legal phrases. The document was the Old Man's Last Will and Testament, and it took twenty minutes for Mike to complete the reading of it. When he had finished there was silence in the room, and the Old Man broke it at last.

'Do you understand?' he asked. There was a gentleness about him that there had never been before. He seemed to have shrunk, the flesh withering on his bones and leaving them dry and light – like the sun-dried bones of a long dead seabird.

'Yes, I understand.' Johnny nodded.

'Explain it to us simply, not in your lawyer's gobbledy-gook, just to be certain.' the Old Man insisted, and Mike began to speak.

'Mr van der Byl's private estate, with the exception of his shares in Van Der Byl Diamond Co. Ltd, after taxes and expenses, is placed in Trust for his two children, Tracey – '

The Old Man interrupted impatiently, swatting Mike's words out of the air as though they were flies.

'Not that. The Company. Tell him about the shares in the Company.'

'Mr van der Byl's shares in the Company are to be divided equally between you and the two van der Byl children, Tracey – '

Again the Old Man interrupted.

'He knows their names, dammit.'

It was the first time ever that either of them had heard him swear. Mike grinned ruefully at Johnny, as though asking for his sympathy, but Johnny was intent on the Old Man, studying his face, feeling the deep satisfying thrill swelling within his chest.

A third share in Van Der Byl Diamonds was no great fortune – nobody knew that better than Johnny.

However, by placing Johnny's name on the list with Tracey and Benedict – he had made him his own. This was what he had worked for all these years. The declaration was public, an acknowledgement to the world.

Johnny Lance had a father at last. He wanted to reach out and touch the Old Man. His chest felt swollen, tight with emotion. Behind his eyelids was a slow soft burning. Johnny blinked.

'This is – ' His voice was ragged, and he coughed. 'I just don't know how to tell you – '

The Old Man interrupted him impatiently, silencing him with an imperious gesture, and he croaked at Mike.

'Now read him the codicil to the Will. No, don't read it. Explain it to him.'

Michael's expression changed; he looked down at his papers as he spoke, as though reluctant to meet Johnny's eyes. He cleared his throat unnecessarily and shifted in his seat.

' "By the codicil to the Will, dated the same date, and duly signed by Mr van der Byl the bequest of shares in Van Der Byl Diamond Co. Ltd to JOHN RIGBY LANCE, is made conditional on the issue by the said JOHN RIGBY LANCE of a personal guarantee for the debts of the company, including the present loan account and amounts outstanding to tributary companies for royalties and options." '

'Christ,' said Johnny, stiffening in his chair and turning to stare incredulously at the Old Man. The tightness in his chest was gone. 'What are you trying to do to me?'

The Old Man dismissed Mike Shapiro quietly, without even looking at him. 'I'll call you when I want you.' And when he had gone he repeated Johnny's question.

'What am I trying to do to you?' he asked. 'I am trying to make you responsible for debts totalling about two and a half million Rand.'

'No creditor would come to me for half a million, I would be hard pressed to raise ten thousand on my personal account.' Johnny shook his head irritably, the whole thing was nonsensical.

'There is one creditor who could come to you, and subject you to the full process of law. Not to receive payment in cash – but in personal satisfaction. He would smash you – and delight in doing so.'

Johnny's eyes narrowed disbelievingly. 'Benedict?'

The Old Man nodded. 'For once Benedict will hold the top cards. He won't be able to dislodge you from the management of the company, because Tracey will support you as she always has done – but he will be able to watch every move you make from his seat on the Board of Directors. He will be able to hound you, bring you and the company down without suffering financial loss himself. And when you fall – you know better than to expect mercy from him. You will be devoured by the ogre you have created.'

'Created?' Johnny's voice was shocked. 'What do you mean?'

'You turned him into what he is now. You broke his heart, made him weak and useless – '

'You are crazy.' Johnny came to his feet. 'I have never done anything to Benedict. It was he who – '

But the Old Man's husky croak brushed aside Johnny's protests. 'He tried to run with you – but could not. He gave up, became small and vicious. Oh, I know about the way he is – how you made him.'

'Please, listen to me. I did not – '

But the Old Man went on remorselessly. 'Tracey also, you have ruined her life. You enslaved her, in your sin – '

'That night!' Johnny shouted at him. 'You never let me explain. We never – '

Now the Old Man's voice was a whiplash.

'Silence!' And Johnny could not defy him, the habit was too deeply engrained. The Old Man was trembling, his eyes glittering with passion. 'Both my children! You have plagued me and my family. My son is a weak-willed drifter, trying to hide his hurt in a hunt for pleasure. I have given him the instruments to destroy you, and when he does so perhaps he will become a man.'

The Old Man's voice was strained now, rusty and pain-racked. He swallowed with an effort, his throat convulsing – but there was no softening of the glitter in his eyes.

'My daughter also, tortured by her lust. A lust which you awakened – she also seeks an escape from her guilty passion. Your destruction will be her release.'

'You're wrong,' Johnny cried out, half in protest, half in entreaty. 'Please, let me explain – '

'This is how it will work. I have made you vulnerable, linking you to a crippled and foundering enterprise. This time we will be rid of you.' He stopped to pant quickly, like a running dog. His breathing was strangled, harsh-sounding. 'Benedict will cut you down, and Tracey will have to watch you go. She cannot help you, her inheritance is carefully tied up, she has no control of the capital. Your only hope is the *Kingfisher*. The *Kingfisher* will turn into a vampire and suck your life blood! You asked why I was systematically transferring the assets of Van Der Byl Diamonds to my other companies? Well, now you know the answer.'

Johnny's lips moved. He was very pale. His voice came out small and whispery.

'I could refuse to sign the guarantee.'

The Old Man smiled bleakly, a drawing back of the lips that was without warmth or humour.

'You will sign it.' His voice was wheezy. 'Your pride and conceit will not let you do otherwise. You see, I know you. I've studied you all these years. But if you refuse to sign the guarantee, I will still have smashed you. Your shares will go to Benedict. You will be out. Out! Gone! We will be finished with you at last.' Then his voice dropped, 'But you will sign. I know it.'

Involuntarily Johnny lifted his hands towards the Old Man, a gesture of supplication. 'In all this time. When I stayed with you, when I – ' His voice went husky and dried up. 'Did you never feel anything for me – anything at all?'

The Old Man sat up in his chair. He seemed to regain his bulk and he began to smile. He spoke quietly now, he did not have to shout.

'Get out of my nest, Cuckoo. Get out and fly!' he said.

Slowly Johnny's expression changed, the line of his jaw hardened, thrusting out aggressively. His shoulders went back. He pushed his hands into his pockets, balling his fists into bony hammers.

He nodded once in understanding.

'I see.' He nodded again, and then he started to grin. It was an unconvincing grin, that twisted his mouth out of shape and left his eyes dark and haunted.

'All right, you mean old bastard, I'll show you.'

He turned and walked from the room without looking back.

The Old Man's expression lit in deep satisfaction. He chuckled, then his breath caught. He began to cough, and the pain ripped his throat with a violence that left him clinging weakly to the edge of his desk.

He felt the crab of death move within his flesh, sinking its claws more deeply into his throat and lungs – and he was afraid.

He called out in his pain and fear, but there was nobody in the old house to hear him.

Kingfisher was launched in August and ran her trials in the North Sea. Benedict was aboard, by the Old Man's express command. With a vessel of such complexity, and of such revolutionary design, it would have been a miracle had she functioned perfectly. August that year was not the month for miracles. At the end of the trials Johnny had compiled a list of twenty-three modifications that were necessary.

'How long?' he asked the representative of the shipyard.

'A month.' The reply was hesitant.

'You mean two,' said Benedict and laughed out loud. Johnny looked at him thoughtfully, he guessed that the Old Man had spoken to him.

'I'll tell you something, Johnny.' Benedict was still laughing. 'I'm glad this cow isn't my dream of paradise.'

Johnny froze. Those words were the Old Man's, repeated parrot fashion. It was all the confirmation that he needed.

Johnny flew back to Cape Town to find his creditors on the verge of mutiny. They wanted to sell out, and take the loss.

Johnny spent two whole precious days on Larsen's wine farm at Stellenbosch calming his fears. When Fifi Larsen, twenty years younger than her husband, squeezed Johnny's thigh under the lunch table he knew it would be all right – for another two months.

During the next hectic, strength-sapping week of argument and negotiation, Johnny made time to see Tracey.

She had been out of the nursing-home for a month now, staying with friends on a small farm near Somerset West.

When Johnny climbed out of the Mercedes, and Tracey came down from the stoop to greet him, he had his first real lift of pleasure in a long time.

'God,' he said. 'You look great.'

She was dressed in a cotton summer dress with open sandals on her feet. Her friends were away for the day, so they walked through the orchards. He studied her openly, noticing how her cheeks and arms had filled out and the colour had come back into them. Her hair was bright and springing with lights in the sun, but there were still the dark smears under her eyes, and she smiled only once when he picked a sprig of peach blossoms for her. She seemed to be afraid of him, and unsure of herself.

At last he faced her and placed his hands on her shoulders. 'All right. What's eating you?'

It came out in a quick staccato rush of words.

'I want to thank you for coming to find me. I want to explain why I was – like that. In that state. I don't want you to believe – well, bad things about me.'

'Tracey, you don't have to explain to me.'

'I want to. I must.' And she told him, not looking at his face, twisting and tearing the blossoms in her hands.

'You see, I didn't understand, I thought all men were like that. Not wanting, I mean not doing it – ' She broke off, and started again. 'He was kind, you understand. And there were lots of parties and friends around all the time, every night. Then he wanted to go to London – for his career. There was not enough scope here. Even then I didn't know. Well, I knew he had lots of men friends and that some of them were different – but . . . Then I went to his studio and found them, and they laughed, Kenny and the boy twined together like snakes. "But you must have known," he said. Something just snapped in my head, I felt spoiled, dirty and horrible and I wanted to die. There was nobody to go to and I didn't want anybody – I just wanted to die.' She stopped and stood waiting for him to speak.

'Do you still want to die?' he asked gently, and she looked up startled and shook her shining hair.

'I don't want you to die either.' And suddenly they were both laughing. After that it was good between them and they talked with all the strangeness gone until it was almost dark.

'I must go,' Johnny said.

'Your wife?' she asked, the laughter fading.

'Yes. My wife.'

It was dark when Johnny went in through the front door of the new split-level ranch type in Bishopscourt which was his house but not his home; the telephone was ringing. He picked up the receiver.

'Johnny?'

'Hello Michael.' He recognized the voice.

'Johnny, get up here to the old house right away.' Michael Shapiro's voice was strained.

'Is it the Old Man?' Johnny asked anxiously.

'No talk – just come, quickly!'

The curtains were drawn, and a log fire roared on the stone hearth. But the Old Man was cold. The coldness was deep inside him where the flames could not warm it. His hands shook as he picked sheets of paper from the open document box, glanced at them and then dropped them into the fire. They exploded into orange flame, then curled and blackened to ash. At last the box was empty but for a thick wad of multi-coloured envelopes bound together with a ribbon. He loosened the knot, picked out the first envelope, and slipped from it a single sheet of writing-paper.

'Dear sir,
I hope you will be pleased to hear that I am now at school. The food is good but the beds are very hard –'

He dropped both envelope and letter on the fire and selected another. One at a time he read and then burned them.

' – that I have been selected to play for the first fifteen –' Sometimes he smiled, once he chuckled.

' – I was top in all subjects except history and religious teaching. I hope to do better next –'

When there was one envelope left he held it a long time in his blue-veined bony hands. Then with an impatient flick of his wrist he threw it on to the fire and reached up to the mantelpiece to pull himself to his feet. As he stood he looked into the gilt-framed mirror above the fireplace.

He stared at his reflection, mildly surprised by the change that the last few weeks had wrought in his appearance. His eyes had lost the sparkle of life, fading to a pale dirty brownish blue – the colour of putrefaction. They bulged from the sockets, in the glassy startled stare which is peculiar to the later stages of terminal cancer.

The watery feeling of limb, and the coldness were not the result of the pain-killing drugs, he knew. Nor was the shuffling feet-dragging gait with which he crossed the thick Bokhara carpet to the stinkwood desk.

He looked down at the oblong leather case with its brass-bound corners, and he coughed, a single flesh-tearing bark. He caught at the desk to steady himself, waiting for the pain to pass before he sprang the catch on the case and lay the lid back.

His hands were quite steady as he took the barrel and butt section of the Purdey Royal twelve-bore shotgun from the case and fitted them together.

He died the way he had lived – alone.

'God, how I hate black.' Ruby Lance stood in the centre of the bedroom floor, staring at the clothing laid out on the double bed. 'It makes me look so washed out.'

She swung her head from side to side, setting the champagne-coloured cascade of her hair swinging. She turned and moved lazily across the room to the tall mirrors. She smiled at herself, a languid slanting of the eyes, and then she spoke over the shoulder of her own image.

'You say that Benedict van der Byl has arrived from England?'

'Yes,' Johnny nodded. He sat slumped in the chair beside his dressing-room door, pressing his fingers into his eyes.

Ruby came up on her toes, pulling in her stomach and pushing forward her small hard breasts.

'Who else will be there?' she asked, cupping her hands under her breasts and squeezing out the nipples between thumb and forefinger, inspecting them critically. Johnny took his hand from his eyes.

'Did you hear me?' Ruby's voice took on a sharp admonishing note. 'I'm not talking to myself, you know.'

She turned away from the mirror to face him. Standing long and slim and golden as a leopard, even her eyes had the yellow intentness of a leopard's stare. She gave the impression that at any moment she would draw her lips back in a snarl.

'It's a funeral,' he said quietly. 'Not a cocktail party.'

'Well, you can't expect me to die of sorrow. I couldn't stand him.' She crossed to the bed and picked up the pair of peach-coloured panties and rubbed the glossy material against her cheek. Then she stepped into them with two long-legged strides.

'At least I can wear something pretty under the weeds.' She snapped the elastic against her sun-gilt belly, and the almost colourless blonde curls were flattened beneath the sheer silk.

Johnny stood up slowly, and went into his dressing-room. Scornfully she called after him. 'Oh for God's sake, Johnny Lance, stop dragging that long face around as though it's the end of the world. Nobody owes that old devil a thing – he collected all his debts long before they fell due.'

They were a few minutes early, and they stood together beneath the pinetrees outside the entrance to the chapel.

When the pearl-grey Rolls drew up at the gate and brother and sister stepped down and came up the paved path, Ruby could not contain her interest.

'Is that Benedict van der Byl?'

Johnny nodded.

'He's very good-looking.'

But Johnny was looking at Tracey. The change in her appearance since he had last seen her was startling. She walked like a desert girl again, straight and proud. She came directly to Johnny and stopped in front of him. She removed her dark glasses, and he could see she had been weeping, for her eyes were slightly puffy. She wore no make-up, and with the dark scarf framing her face she looked like a nun. The marks that sorrow had left gave her face maturity.

'I did not think this day would ever come,' she said softly.

'No,' Johnny agreed. 'It was as though he would live for ever.'

Tracey moved a step closer to him, she reached out as if to touch Johnny's arm but her fingers stopped within inches of his sleeve. Johnny understood the gesture, it was a sharing of sorrow, an understanding of mutual loss, and an unstated offer of comfort.

'I don't think we have met.' Ruby used her sugar and arsenic tone. 'It is Miss van der Byl, isn't it?'

Tracey turned her head and her expression went flat and neutral. She replaced the dark glasses, masking her eyes.

'Mrs Hartford,' she said. 'How do you do.'

Mike Shapiro stood beside Johnny in the pew. He spoke without moving his lips, just loud enough for Johnny to catch the words.

'Benedict knows the conditions of the Will. You can expect his first move immediately.'

'Thanks, Mike.'

Johnny kept his eyes on the massive black coffin. The candlelight glinted and sparkled on the elaborate silver handles.

As yet he could find no interest for the conflict that lay ahead. That would come.

Now he was too deeply involved in the passing of an era, his life had reached another point of major departure. He knew it would change, had already changed.

He looked across the aisle suddenly, his gaze drawn intuitively.

Benedict van der Byl was watching him, and at that moment the priest asked for the pallbearers.

They went to stand beside the coffin, Benedict and Johnny on opposite sides of the polished black casket among the massed display of arum lilies. They watched each other warily. It seemed to Johnny that the whole scene was significant. The two of them standing over the Old Man's corpse, facing each other, with Tracey looking on anxiously.

Johnny glanced back into the body of the church, looking for Tracey. Instead he found Ruby. She was watching them both, and Johnny knew suddenly that the board had changed more than he realized. A new piece had been added to the game.

He felt Mike Shapiro nudge him, and he stooped forward and grasped the silver handle. Between them they carried the Old Man out into the sunshine.

The handle had cut into his palm with the weight of the coffin. He went on massaging it, even after the coffin had gone down into the pit. The crude mounds of fresh earth were covered with blankets of bright green artificial grass. The mourners began to drift away, but Johnny went on standing there bareheaded. Until Ruby came to touch his arm.

'Come on.' Her voice pitched low, but stinging. 'You're making a fool of yourself.'

Benedict and Tracey were waiting under the pinetrees by the churchyard gate, shaking hands and talking quietly to the departing mourners.

'You are Ruby, of course.' Benedict took her hand, smiling a little, urbane and charming. 'The flattering reports I've had of you hardly do you justice.' And Ruby glowed, seeming like a butterfly to spread her wings to the sun.

'Johnny.' Benedict turned to him, and Johnny was taken off balance by the friendly warmth of his smile and the grip of his hand. 'Michael Shapiro tells me that you have accepted my father's legacy and the conditions attached to it – you have signed the guarantee. It's wonderful news. I don't know what we would have done without you in Van Der Byl Diamonds. You are the only one that can pull the company though this difficult period. I want you to know I am behind you all the way, Johnny. I intend becoming much more involved with the company now, giving you all the help you need.'

'I knew I could depend on you, Benedict.' Johnny accepted the challenge as smoothly as it was thrown down. 'I think everything is going to turn out all right.'

'We have a meeting on Monday, then I must return to London on Thursday – but I hope you can have dinner with me before then – you and your lovely wife, of course.'

'Thank you.' Ruby seeing the refusal on Johnny's lips, interrupted quickly. 'We'd enjoy that.'

'You were going to refuse, weren't you?' She sat with her legs curled up sideways under her, watching him from the passenger seat of the Mercedes with the slanting eyes of a Persian cat.

'You're damn right.' Johnny nodded grimly.

'Why?'

'Benedict van der Byl is poison.'

'You say so.'

'Yes, I say so.'

'Could be you're jealous of him.' Ruby lit one of her gold-tipped cigarettes, putting the smoke through her lips.

'Good God!' Johnny gave one harsh snort of laughter, then they were silent awhile, both staring ahead.

'I think he's pretty dreamy.'

'You can have him.' Johnny's tone was disinterested, but her retort was shrill.

'I could too – if I wanted to. Anyway you and that Tracey creature mooning – '

'Cut it out, Ruby.'

'Oh my, I've said the wrong thing. The precious Mrs Hartford – '

'Cut it out, I said.' Johnny's tone was sharp.

'Little Miss Fancy Pants – God! She almost had them down for you in the bloody graveyard – '

'Shut up, damn you.'

'Don't you swear at me.' And she lashed out at him flat-handed, leaning forward across the seat to strike him in the mouth. His lower lip smeared against his teeth, and the taste of blood seeped into his mouth. He took the handkerchief from his breast pocket and held it to his mouth, steering the Mercedes with one hand.

Ruby sat curled in her corner of the seat, puffing quickly at the cigarette. Neither of them spoke again until he drew up in front of the double garages. Then Ruby slipped out of the Mercedes and ran across the lawns to the front door. She slammed it behind her, with a force that rattled the full-length glass panel.

Johnny parked the Mercedes, closed the garage door and followed her slowly into the house. She had kicked off her shoes on the wall-to-wall carpet in the lounge, and run through on to the patio beside the swimming pool. She stood barefooted staring down into the clear water, hugging herself about the shoulders.

'Ruby.' He came up behind her, forcing the anger out of his voice with an effort, trying to keep it conciliatory. 'Listen to me – '

She spun around to face him, eyes blazing like a cornered leopard.

'Don't try and gentle talk me, you bastard. What do you think I am – your damned servant. When did I last get to do anything I wanted?'

With Ruby he had long ago realized that placation was the short cut to peace, so he was roused by the implication.

'I've never stopped you from – '

'Good! That's just fine! Then you won't stop me going away.'

'What do you mean?' He was caught between shock and a sneaking sense of hope. 'Are you talking about divorce – '

'Divorce? Are you out of your little mind! I know all about the big bagful of goodies the Old Man left you in his Will. Well, little Ruby is getting her pinkies into that bag – starting right now.'

'What do you want exactly?' His voice was cold and flat.

'A new wardrobe, and a quick whip around all those nice places you go to all the time – London, Paris and the rest. That will do for a start.'

He thought a moment, assessing how far he could stretch his overdraft; since his marriage his bank statement had seldom been typed in black. It was worth it, he decided. He could afford no distraction over the next few months. He could move faster and think quicker without having Ruby Lance sitting between his shoulder-blades – much better she should go.

'All right,' he nodded. 'If that's what you want.'

Her eyes narrowed slightly and her mouth pinched in as she studied his face.

'That was too easy,' she said. 'You want to get rid of me? Don't get any ideas, Johnny boy, you put one finger – or anything else – out of line and I'll chop it off.'

'There is a Mrs Hartford to see you, sir.' Lettie Pienaar's voice whispered through on the intercom, then just audibly she added, 'Lucky you!'

Johnny grinned. 'You're fired for insolence – but send her in before you go.'

He stood up as Tracey came in, and went around his desk to meet her. She wore a no-nonsense grey suit, with her hair scraped back from her face. She should have looked like a school marm – but she didn't.

'You've got your times mixed up, Tracey. The Directors' meeting is at two this afternoon.'

'That's a sweet greeting.' She sat down in an egg-shaped swivel chair, crossing long legs which Johnny dragged his eyes off with an effort. 'I've come looking for a job.'

'A job?' He stared at her blankly.

'Yes, a job. You know – work? Employment?'

'What on earth for?'

'Well, now that you've dragged me back from the bright lights with all the finesse of a caveman – you don't expect me to sit around until I drop dead of boredom. Besides, your tame doctor feels that good healthy employment is essential to the completion of my – ah – cure.'

'I see.' He sank back into his own chair. 'Well – what can you do?'

'Mr Lance.' Tracey widened her eyes suggestively, but made her voice prim. ' – Really!'

'All right,' Johnny chuckled. 'What are your qualifications?'

'You may or may not know that I have a law degree from the University of Cape Town.'

'I didn't.'

'Also, it occurred to me that during the next few months you might need someone around whom you can trust.' She was serious now, and Johnny's smile faded also. 'Like the old days.' She added quietly. They were silent for a few seconds.

'It just so happens that we are looking for a personal assistant in our legal depart-ment.' Johnny murmured, and then softly, 'Thanks, Tracey.'

The Board Room of Van Der Byl Diamonds was furnished in soft forest colours, browns and greens. A long luxurious room that reflected the opulence of the days when the Company had been glutted with capital. But now the air was charged with a tension that crackled in the air like static electricity.

The subject of debate was the diamond recovery vessel, *Kingfisher*. The Company's last hope. Her only substantial asset, and Johnny's personal cross.

'This vessel should have been in operation nine months ago. All the estimates were based on that assumption – yet, she is still lying awaiting completion on the slips at Portsmouth.' Benedict was speaking with unconcealed relish. 'In consequence, the interest charges that are accruing put us in a position – '

'The shipyard was out on strike for a total of four months during construction – in addition they were working to rule for – ' Johnny's jaw was thrust out, he was ready to fight.

'Ah! I don't think we are particularly interested in the unpredictability of the British workman – the contract should have gone to the Japanese Company. Their tender was lower – '

'It would have,' grated Johnny, 'If your father had not insisted – '

'Please, let us not attempt to lay the blame at the door of a dead man.' Benedict's tone was sanctimonious. 'Let us rather try and rectify a grievous situation. When will *Kingfisher* be ready for sea?'

'On the thirteenth of September.'

'It had better be.' Benedict dropped his eyes to his notes. 'Now, this man whom you have engaged to captain the vessel – Sergio Caporetti – let us hear a little about him, please.'

'Fifteen years' experience on offshore oil-drilling vessels in the Red Sea. Three years as Captain of Atlantis Diamonds offshore dredger operating off the West Coast. He's one of the best, no doubt about it.'

'All right.' Almost reluctantly Benedict accepted this, and consulted his notes. 'Now, we have two sea-concession areas. No. 1 area off Cartridge Bay; No. 2 some twenty miles north of that. Judging by your prospecting results you will elect to work No. 1 area first.

Johnny nodded, waiting for the next attack to develop. Benedict sat back in his chair.

'Atlantis Diamonds Ltd went broke working our No. 1 area – what makes you think you can succeed where they failed?'

'We've been over this before,' Johnny snapped.

'I wasn't there, remember? Humour me, please. Go over it again.'

Quickly Johnny explained that Atlantis Diamonds' costs had been inflated by their method of operation. Their dredgers were not self-propelled but had to be towed by tugs. The gravel they recovered had been stored, taken into Cartridge Bay in bulk, transhipped ashore to be processed at a land-based plant. *Kingfisher* was a self-propelled and self-contained vessel. She would suck up the gravel, process it through the most sophisticated system of cyclone and X-ray equipment and dump the waste overboard.

'Our costs will be one quarter those of Atlantis Diamonds,' he finished.

'And our loan account is a mere two millions,' Benedict murmured dryly. Then he looked towards Mike Shapiro at the bottom of the table. 'Mr Secretary, please note the following motion – "That this Company proceed to sell the vessel *Kingfisher* presently building at Portsmouth. That it then sells all diamond concessions at the most advantageous terms negotiable, and goes into voluntary liquidation forthwith." Have you got that?'

It was a direct frontal attack. Clearly if the motion succeeded the Company was worthless. They could not recover the price of the *Kingfisher* on a forced sale. There would be a shortfall – and Johnny had signed the guarantee. It was a straight test that Benedict was making. A setting of the lines of battle. Tracey held the balance between Johnny and Benedict. He was forcing her to declare herself.

Benedict watched her while the motion was put to the vote. He leaned forward in the padded leather chair, a slightly amused smile on the full red lips. Beautifully groomed and tailored, with the grace that wealth and position give to a man and which cannot be counterfeited. But the clean athletic lines of his body were fractionally blurred by indulgence, and there was a little too much flesh along the line of his jaw that gave him the petulant look of a spoilt child.

Tracey voted with Johnny Lance, not hesitating a second before lifting her hand. Returning Benedict's smile levelly, and watching her brother's smile alter subtly – become wolfish, for Benedict did not like to lose.

'Very well, my darling sister. Now we know how we stand at least.' He turned easily to Johnny. 'I presume you wish me to continue with my duties in London.'

For years now Benedict had handled the London sales of the Company's stones. It was an unexacting task, which the Old Man had judged within his capabilities.

'Thank you, Benedict,' Johnny nodded. 'Now, I have a proposal to put to the meeting – "That the Directors of this Company, as a gesture of solidarity, agree to waive their rights to Directors' fees until such time as the Company's financial position is on a more sound footing." '

It was a puny counter attack, but the best he could mount at the moment.

Take-off was in the first light from Youngsfield, and Johnny swung the twin-engined Beechcraft on to a northerly heading, leaving the blue massif of Table Mountain on the left hand.

Tracey wore an anorak over her rose-coloured shirt, and the bottoms of her denim pants were tucked into soft leather boots, her dark hair caught at the nape of her neck with a leather thong.

She sat very still, looking ahead through the aircraft's windshield at the dawn-touched contours of the land ahead. At the bleak lilac and purple mountains and the great lion-coloured plains spreading down to meet the mists that hung over the cold Atlantic.

In her stillness Johnny sensed her excitement and found it infectious.

The sun exploded over the horizon, washing golden and bright over the plains, and tipping the mountains with flame.

'Namaqualand.' Johnny pointed ahead.

She laughed with excitement, like a child at Christmas, turning in the seat to face him.

'Do you remember – ' She began, then stopped in confusion.

'Yes,' said Johnny. 'I remember.'

They landed before noon on a rough air-strip bulldozed out of the wilderness.

There was a Land-Rover waiting to take them down to the beach to inspect the progress of the workings.

There was little remaining along the thirty-seven-mile Admiralty strip worth working. It was a clean-up and shut-down operation.

When the reigning 'King Canute' handed over the parcel of diamonds that made up the month's recovery, he was apologetic.

'You took out all the plums, Johnny. It's not like the old days.'

Johnny prodded the pathetic pile of small, low-grade stones with his forefinger.

'No, it's not,' he agreed. 'But every little bit helps.'

They climbed back into the Beechcraft and flew on northwards.

Now they passed over areas where the desert had been scratched and torn over wide areas.

The tractors had left centipede tracks in the soft earth.

'Ours?' asked Tracey.

'I wish they were. We'd have no worries then. No, all this belongs to the big Company.'

Johnny checked his watch, automatically comparing the progress of the flight to his estimates. Then he lifted the microphone from the R/T set.

'Alexandra Bay Control. This is Zulu Sugar Peter Tango Baker.'

He knew that they had him on the radar plot, and were watching him – not because they were worried about his safety, but because he was now over the Proclaimed Diamond Area of South West Africa – that vast jealously guarded tract of nothingness.

The radio crackled back at him instantly, demanding his permit number, his flight plan, querying his intentions and his destination.

Having convinced Control of his innocence, and received their permission to continue his flight, he switched off his R/T set, and grimaced at Tracey.

He felt ruffled by this small brush with Olympus. He knew that most of it was professional jealousy. He smarted under the knowledge that he was working ground that the big Company would despise as not sufficiently lucrative to bother about.

Sometimes Johnny dreamed about discovering a fault in a land title, or an error in a survey that had been casually performed seventy years previously before the value of this parched denuded earth had been realized. He imagined himself being able to claim the mineral rights to a few square miles plumb in the middle of the big Company's richest field. He shivered voluptuously at the thought, and Tracey looked at him enquiringly.

He shook his head, then his line of thought took him on to a further destination.

He banked the aircraft, crossing the coastline with its creamy lines of surf running in on the freezing white sands of the beach.

'What?' She was expectant, receptive to the new tone in his voice.

'Thunderbolt and Suicide,' he said, and she made a small grimace of incomprehension.

'There.' He pointed ahead, and through the light smoke of the sea mist she saw them show bare – white and shiny, like a pair of Albino whales.

'Islands?' she asked. 'What's so special about them?'

'Their shape,' he answered. 'See how they lie like the mouth of a funnel, with a small opening between them.'

She nodded. The two islands were almost identical twins, two narrow wedges of smooth granite, each about three miles long, lying in a chevron pattern to each other – but not quite meeting at the peak. The mighty Atlantic swells bore up from the south and ran into the mouth of the funnel. Finding themselves trapped in this granite corral, the swells reared up wildly and hurled themselves on the cliffs in massive bomb-bursts of spray before streaming out in white foam through the narrow opening between the two islands.

'I can see how Thunderbolt gets its name.' Tracey eyed the wild booming surf with awe. 'But how about Suicide?'

'The old guano collectors must have called it that, after they tried landing on it.'

'Guano,' Tracey nodded. 'That accounts for the colour.'

Johnny put the Beechcraft into a shallow dive, hurtling in low over the green water. Ahead of them the seabirds rose in alarm, streaming in a long black smear into the sky, the cormorants and gannets whose excreta through the ages had painted the rocks that glaring white.

As they flashed through the gap below the level of the cliffs, Tracey exclaimed, 'There's some sort of tower there – look! In the back of the island.'

'Yes,' Johnny agreed. 'It's an old wooden gantry they used for loading the guano into the longboats.'

He pulled the Beechcraft up in a climbing turn, gaining height to look down on the two islands.

'Do you see where the surf comes through the gap? Now look beneath the surface, can you see the reefs under the water?'

They lay like long dark shadows through the green water, at right angles to the drift of white foam.

'Well, you are looking at the most beautifully designed natural diamond trap in the world.'

'Explain,' Tracey invited.

'Down there,' he pointed south, 'are the big rivers. Some of them dried up a million years ago, but not before they had spat the diamonds they carried into the sea. The tide and the wind has been working them up towards the north for all these ages. Throwing some of them back on the beach but carrying others up this way.'

He levelled the Beechcraft out and resumed their interrupted flight northwards.

'Then suddenly they run up against Thunderbolt and Suicide. They are concentrated and squeezed through the gap, then they are confronted by a series of sharp reefs across their path. They cannot cross them – they just settle down in the gullies and wait for someone to come and suck them out.'

He sighed like a man crossed in love.

'My God, Tracey. The smell of those diamonds reeks in my nostrils. I can almost see the shine of them through a hundred and sixty feet of water.'

He shook himself as though waking from a dream.

'I've been in the game all my life, Tracey. I've got the "feel", the same as a water-diviner has. I tell you with absolute certainty there are millions of carats of diamonds lying in the crotch of Thunderbolt and Suicide.'

'What's the snag?' Tracey asked.

'The concession was granted twenty years ago to the big Company.'

'By whom?'

'The Government of South West Africa.'

'Why aren't they mining it?'

'They will – sometime in the next twenty years. They aren't in any hurry.'

They lapsed into silence, staring ahead, though once Johnny clucked his tongue irritably and shook his head – still thinking about Thunderbolt and Suicide.

To distract him Tracey asked, 'Where do they come from in the first place – the diamonds?'

'Volcanic pipes,' Johnny answered. 'There are more than a hundred known pipes in Southern Africa. Not all yield stones, but then some do. New Rush – Finsch – Dutoitspan – Bulfontein – Premier – Mwadui. Great oval-shaped treasure chests, filled with the legendary "Blue Ground" – the mother lode of the diamond.'

'There are no pipes here – surely?' Tracey turned towards him in his seat.

'No,' Johnny agreed. 'We are after the alluvial stones. Some of those ancient pipes exploded with the force of a hydrogen bomb, spraying diamonds over hundreds of square miles. Others were sub-marine pipes that discharged their treasure into the restless sea. Others of the more passive volcanic pipes were simply eroded away by wind and water and the diamonds were exposed.'

'Then they were washed down to the sea?' she guessed.

Johnny nodded. 'That's right. Over millions of years they were moved infinitely slowly by landslides, floods, rivers and rainwater. Where all the other pebbles and stones were abraded and worn away to nothingness – the diamonds, four hundred times harder than any other natural substance on earth, were unmarked. So at last they reached the sea and mingled with the others from the sub-marine pipes, to be laid down by wave action on the beaches, or finally to come up against a place like Thunderbolt and Suicide.'

Tracey opened her mouth to ask another question, but Johnny interrupted.

'Here we are. There is Cartridge Bay.' And he pushed the nose of the aircraft down slightly. It was more a lagoon than a bay. Separated from the sea by a narrow sandspit, it spread away into the treeless waste, an enormous extent of quiet shallow water in tranquil contrast to the unchecked surf that burst on the sandspit. There was a deep water entrance through the sandspit, and a channel meandered across the lagoon to where a cluster of lonely whitewashed buildings sprang up on the edge of the desert.

Johnny banked steeply towards the buildings, and below them flocks of black and white pelicans and pink flamingo rose in panic from the shallows.

Johnny landed and taxied across to the waiting Land-Rover with the white lightning insignia of Van Der Byl Diamonds painted on its side.

Lugging the cool box that contained their lunch, Johnny led Tracey to the vehicle and introduced her to his foreman. Then they climbed in and went bumping down to the buildings on the lagoon. Johnny received from his foreman a report on progress of the work. The buildings had been abandoned by the defunct Atlantis Diamond Company. Johnny was renovating them to serve as a base for the *Kingfisher*; a rest and recreation centre for the crew, a radio centre, a refuelling depot and a workshop to handle running maintenance and repairs. In addition he was putting a jetty out into the lagoon for the converted seventy-foot pilchard trawler that would be *Kingfisher*'s service boat – acting as tender and ferry.

They ran an extensive inspection of the base. Johnny was pleased with the interest Tracey showed, and he enjoyed answering her questions for his own enthusiasm was high. It was nearly two o'clock before they had finished.

'How are the watchtowers coming?' Johnny asked.

'All up, ready and waiting.'

And suddenly Johnny had a two-edged inspiration.

'Might as well go and have a look.' He made it casual.

'Okay, I'll fetch the Land-Rover,' the foreman agreed.

'I know the way.' Johnny put him off. 'You go and get your lunch.'

'It's no trouble –' the foreman began, caught Johnny's frown, cut himself short, then glanced at Tracey. 'Yeah! Sure! Fine! Okay – here are the keys.' He handed Johnny the Land-Rover keys, and disappeared into his own quarters.

Johnny checked the grub box, and they climbed into the open Land-Rover.

'Where are we going?' Tracey asked.

'Inspect the watchtowers along the sandspit.'

'Watchtowers?'

'We've put up a line of fifty-foot wooden towers along the beach. From them we will take continual bearings on *Kingfisher* when she is working offshore. By radio we will be able at any time to give her the exact position over the bottom to within a few feet, as a check to the computer.'

'My, you are clever.' Tracey fluttered her eyelashes at him in mock admiration.

'Silly wench,' said Johnny, and let out the clutch. He swung down past the radio shack on to the hard wet sand at the edge of the lagoon; accelerating he hit second then third and they went away around the curve of the lagoon, headed towards the great yellow wind-carved dunes that lined the coast.

Tracey stood up on her seat, clutching the edge of the windscreen, and the wind snatched at her hair. She pulled the retaining throng from it, and shook it out into a shiny black flag that snapped and snaked behind her.

'Look! Look!' she cried as the flocks of startled flamingoes lurched into flight, streaming white and pink and black over the glossy silver water.

Johnny laughed with her, and swung the Land-Rover towards the dunes.

'Hold on!' he shouted, and she clung to the windscreen, shrieking in delicious terror as they flew up the steep side of a dune, spinning a cloud of sand from the rear wheels and then dropped over the crest in a stomach-churning swoop. They crossed the sandspit and hit the beach, racing along it, playing tag with the waves that shot up the sand.

Five miles up the beach Johnny parked above the high watermark and they ate cold chicken and drank a bottle of chilled white wine sitting side by side in the sand, leaning against the seat cushions from the Land-Rover. Then they went down to the edge of the sea to wash the chicken grease from their fingers.

'Yipes! It's cold.' Tracey scooped a double handful of seawater. Then she looked at Johnny and her expression became devilish.

He backed away, but not quickly enough. The icy water hit him in the chest, and he gasped.

'War!' It was their childhood cry.

Tracey whirled and went off long-legged along the beach, with Johnny pounding after her. She sensed him gaining on her, and shouted.

'It was a mistake! I didn't mean it! I'm sorry!'

At the last moment as he reached out to grip her shoulder, she jinked and ran knee-deep into the sea. Turning at bay to face him, she kicked a spray of water at him, shouting defiance and laughter.

'All right, come on then!'

Braving the flying spray, he reached her and picked her up kicking and struggling and waded out waist deep.

'No, no – please. Johnny. I give in – I'll do anything.'

At that moment a freak wave, bigger and stronger than the others, knocked Johnny's legs out from under him. They went under, and were rolled up the beach, to stagger out, completely soaked, clinging together, helpless with laughter.

They stood beside the Land-Rover trying to wring the water out of their clothing.

'Oh, you beast!' sobbed Tracey through her laughter. Her hair was a sodden mass, and drops of sea-water clung in her eyelashes like dew.

Johnny took her in his arms and kissed her, and they stopped laughing.

She went loose against his chest, her eyes tightly closed and her lips, salty with sea-water, opened against his.

The radio telephone in the Land-Rover beside them began to bleat fretfully, flashing its little red warning light.

They drew apart slowly, reluctantly, and stared at each other with dazed, bemused eyes.

Johnny reached the Land-Rover, unhooked the microphone and lifted it to his lips.

'Yes?' his voice cracked. He cleared his throat and repeated. 'Yes?'

The foreman's voice was distorted and scratchy through the speaker.

'Mr Lance, I'm sorry to have – ' he was clearly about to finish ' – interrupted you.' But he stopped abruptly, and began again. 'It's just that I think you should know we've had a gale warning. Northerly gale building up quickly. If you want to get back to Cape Town you had better get airborne before it hits us – otherwise you could be shut in for days.'

'Thanks. We'll be back right away.' He hung up, and Tracey smiled shakily. Her voice was also husky and unnatural-sounding.

'And a damn good thing too!'

Tracey's hair was still damp, and the borrowed polo-neck jersey swamped her. The grey trousers were also borrowed, rolled up to show her bare feet.

She sat very quietly and thoughtfully in the passenger seat of the Beechcraft. Far below them a small fishing vessel lay with a white cloud of seabirds hovering over it, and she watched it with exaggerated attention. There was a heavy feeling of restraint between them now, they could no longer meet each other's eyes.

'Pilchard trawler.' Johnny noticed her gaze.

'Yes,' said Tracey, and they were silent again.

'Nothing happened.' Johnny spoke again gruffly.

'No,' she agreed. 'Nothing happened.' Then shyly she reached out and took his hand. Lightly she rubbed the stump of his missing finger.

'Still friends?' she asked.

'Still friends.' He grinned at her with relief, and they flew on towards Cape Town.

Hugo Kramer watched the aircraft through his binoculars, balancing easily against the roll and pitch of the bridge.

'Police patrol?' asked the man at the helm beside him.

'No,' Hugo replied without lowering the glasses. 'Red and white twin Beechcraft. Registration ZS – PTB. Private aircraft, probably one of the diamond companies.'

He lowered the glasses, and crossed to the wing of the bridge. 'Anyway, we are well outside territorial waters.'

The drone of the aircraft engine faded away, and Hugo transferred his attention to the frantic activity on the deck below him.

The trawler, *Wild Goose*, lay heeled over under the weight of fish that filled her purse seine-net; at least a hundred tons of seething silver pilchards bulging the net out alongside the trawler into a round bag fifty feet across. While above it a shrieking canopy of seabirds swirled and wheeled and dived, frantic with greed.

Three of the crew on a scoop-net which hung from the overhead derrick were dipping the fish out of the net, swinging a ton of fish at each scoop over the side, and dropping them like a silver cloudburst into the trawler's hold. The donkey engine on the winch clattered harshly in time to their movements.

Hugo watched with satisfaction. He had a good crew, and although the fishing was only a cover for the *Wild Goose* – yet Hugo took pride in his teutonic thoroughness which dictated that the cover should be as solid as possible. In any case, all profits from fishing were for his personal account. It was part of the agreement with the Ring.

He packed the binoculars carefully into their leather case, and hung them behind the chartroom door. Then he clambered swiftly down the steel ladder to deck level, moving with catlike grace despite the heavy rubber hip boots he wore.

'I'll take her here for a while,' he told the man at the winch controls. He spoke in Afrikaans, but his accent was shaded with the German of South West Africa.

Wide-shouldered under the blue fisherman's jersey, he worked with smooth economic movements. His hands on the winch control were rough and reddened by wind and sun, for his skin was too fair to weather. The skin of his face was also red, and half-boiled, peeling so there were pinky raw places on his cheeks and black scabs on his lips.

The hair that hung out under his cap was white as bleached sisal, and his eyelashes were thick and colourless, giving him a mild near-sighted look. His eyes were the palest of cornflower blue, yet without being weak and watery as those of most Albinos; they were slitted now, as he judged the roll and dip of the boat – engaging the clutch to meet the movement, or pulling on the drum brake.

'Skipper!' A shout from the bridge above him.

'Ja.' Hugo did not allow his attention to waver as he replied. 'What is it?'

'Gale warning! There is a northerly buster building up.'

And Hugo grinned, pulled on the brake and shut the throttle.

'All right, clean up. Cut the purse rope, let the fish go free.'

He turned and swarmed up the ladder to the bridge, and went to his chart table.

'It will take us three hours to get in position,' he muttered aloud, leaning over the chart, then he barged out on to the wing of the bridge again to chase up his crew.

They had cut the purse rope on the net, allowing the net to fall open like a woman's skirt, and the fish were pouring out, a dark spreading stain through the gap.

Two men had the pressure hose on, washing loose fish from the deck into the sea, others were slamming the hatch-covers closed.

Within forty minutes *Wild Goose* was running south under full throttle to take up her waiting station.

The diamond coast of South West Africa lies in the belt of the Trades. The prevailing wind is the south-easter, but periodically the wind system is completely reversed and a gale comes out of the north, off the land.

It is a Scirocco-type wind like the 'Khamsin' of the Libyan desert, or the 'Simoom' of Tripoli.

It was the same searing dry wind out of the desert, filling the sky with brooding dust and sand clouds, smothering everything beneath a hellish pall like the smoke from a great battlefield.

The dust clouds were part of the design, the Ring had taken account of them when they planned the system – for the north wind lifted into the sky such a quantity of mica dust that the radar screens of the diamond security police were cluttered and confused, throwing up phantom echoes and making it impossible to pick up the presence of a small airborne object.

Turn Back Point was three miles inland, and sixty miles north of the Orange River. The name was given by the first travellers, and expressed their views on continuing a journey northwards. Those old travellers had not known that they stood in the centre of an elevated marine terrace, an ancient beach now lifted above the level of the sea, and that it was the richest prospect of an area so diamond-rich that it was to be ring-fenced, patrolled by Jeep and dog and aircraft, guarded by gun and radar, a laager so secure that a man leaving it would have to submit to X-ray, and take nothing out with him but the clothes he wore.

At Turn Back Point was one of the four big separation plants where all the gravel from the big Company's workings from miles around was processed. The settlement was comparatively large, with plant, workshops and stores, and accommodation for five hundred men and their families. Yet not all the Company's efforts to make it attractive and livable could alter the fact that Turn Back Point was a hell-hole in a savage and forbidding desert.

Now with the north wind blowing, what had been unpleasant before was almost unbearable. The buildings were tightly sealed, even the joints around the windows and doors were plugged with cloth or paper – and yet the red dust seeped in to powder the furniture, the desks, the bed linen, even the interior of the refrigerators, with a thin gritty film. It settled in the hair, was sugary between the teeth, clogged the nostrils – and with it came that searing heat that seemed to dry the moisture from the eyeballs.

Outside the dust was a red glittering fog which reduced visibility to a dozen yards. Men who were forced out into that choking dry soup wore dust goggles to protect their eyes, and the mica dust covered their clothing with a shiny coating that glittered even in that dun light.

Beyond the settlement a man moved now through the fog, carrying a small cylindrical object. He leaned forward into the wind, moving slowly away into the desert.

He reached a shallow depression and went down into it. Setting his burden on the sand, he rested a moment. Then he knelt over the cylinder. He appeared monstrous under his leather jacket and cap, his face covered by goggles and a scarf.

The fibre-glass cylinder was painted with yellow-fluorescent paint. At one end was a transparent plastic bubble which housed an electric globe, at the other end was a folded envelope of rubberized nylon material attached to the cylinder by a stainless steel coupling, and linked to the coupling was a small steel bottle of hydrogen gas. The whole assembly was eighteen inches long, and three inches in diameter. It weighed a few ounces more than fifteen pounds.

Within the cylinder were two separate compartments. The larger contained a highly sophisticated piece of transistorized electronic equipment which would transmit a homing signal, light or extinguish its lamp on long-distance radio signal command, and also at command it would control the inflow of hydrogen gas into the nylon balloon through the connecting coupling.

The smaller compartment held simply a sealed plastic container into which were packed twenty-seven diamonds. The smallest of these stones weighed fourteen carats, the largest a formidable fifty-six carats. Each of these stones had been selected by experts for colour, brilliance, and perfection. These were all first-water diamonds, and once they were cut they would fetch in the open market between seven hundred thousand and a million pounds – depending on the skill of the cutting.

There were four members of the Ring at Turn Back Point. Two of them were long service and trusted diamond sorters employed behind the guarded walls of the processing plant. They worked together, to check each other, for the Company operated a system of employee double check – which was completely useless when there was collusion. These men selected the finest stones and got them out of the plant.

The third member of the Ring was a diesel mechanic in the Company workshops. It was his job to receive and assemble the equipment which arrived concealed in a marked drum of tractor grease. He also packed the stones into the cylinder and passed it on to the man who was now kneeling out in the desert, preparing to launch the cylinder into the swirling dust fog.

His final check completed, the man stood up and went to the lip of the depression and peered out into the dust storm. At last he seemed satisfied, and hurried back to the yellow cylinder. With an incisive twist of the bevelled release ring he opened the valve on the bottle of hydrogen gas. There was a snakelike hiss, and the nylon balloon began to inflate. The folds of material crackled as they filled. The balloon lifted, eager to be gone, but the man restrained it with difficulty until the balloon was smooth and tight. He let go, and the balloon with its dangling cylinder leapt into the sky, and almost instantly was gone into the dust clouds.

The man stood with his face lifted to the dark furnace-red sky. His goggles glinted blindly, but his attitude was one of triumph, and when he turned away he walked lightly with the step of a man freshly released from danger.

'One more package,' he promised himself. 'Just one more, and I'll pull out. Buy that farm on the Olifants River, do a bit of fishing, take a shooting trip every year – '

He was still dreaming when he reached the parked Land-Rover and climbed into the driver's seat. He started the engine, switched on the headlights, and drove slowly down the track towards the settlement.

The sign on the rear of the departing Land-Rover was in white paint so that it showed clearly through the haze of red dust.

'SECURITY PATROL,' it read.

Wild Goose lay on station, with her diesels throbbing softly, ticking over to hold her head into the wind. Even twenty miles out at sea the wind was searing hot and the occasional splatter of spray on Hugo's face was refreshing.

He stood in the corner of the bridge where he could watch the sea and the helmsman, but he was anxious. *Wild Goose* had been lying on station for fifteen hours now, during ten of which the norther had howled dismally through her rigging.

He was always anxious at the beginning of a pick-up. There was so much that could have gone wrong, anything from a police sweep to a tiny electrical fault in the equipment.

'What time is it, Hansie?' he shouted and the helmsman glanced up at the chronometer above his head.

'Three minutes after six, skipper.'

'Dark in half an hour,' Hugo grunted disgustedly, slitted those pale-lashed eyes into the wind once more, then shrugged and ambled back into the bridge house.

He stopped at the console beside his chart table. Even to an experienced eye the machine was an ordinary 'Fish-Finder', an adaptation of the old wartime antisubmarine device, the ASDIC, to the more prosaic business of plotting the depth and position of the pilchard shoals beneath the surface.

However, this model had undergone a costly and specialized conversion. The Ring had flown an expert out from Japan to do the work.

Now that the set hummed softly, its control panel lit soft green by the internal light, but the sound was neutral, and the circular glass screen was blank.

'You want some coffee, Hansie?' Hugo asked the old coloured man at the wheel. His crew were handpicked, loyal and trusted. They had to be – one loud mouth could blow a multi-million pound business.

'Ja dankie, skipper.' The old man creased his weather-battered face in appreciation, and Hugo shouted down the companionway to the galley.

'Cooky, how's it for a pot of coffee?'

But the reply was lost, for at that moment the console came to life dramatically. A row of lights blinked on above the control panel, the muted hum changed to a rapid beep-beep signal, and the screen glowed ghostly green.

'She's up!' Hugo shouted his relief, and ran to the set. His first mate rushed through from his cabin behind the bridge, tucking his shirt into unbuttoned trousers, his face puckered with sleep.

'About bloody time,' he blurted, groggily.

'Take over from Hansie,' Hugo told him, and he settled into the padded seat in front of the ASDIC set.

'Right, bring her round two points to port and open her up.'

The *Wild Goose* swung her head into the sea, and her motion changed from easy swoop and glide to a crabbing butting lunge, and the spray burst over the glass of the bridge.

Sitting before the console Hugo was tracking the flight of the balloon and keeping *Wild Goose* on an interception course.

Driven by the forty-knot norther the balloon crossed the coastline, climbing swiftly to three thousand feet. Hugo manipulated the knob on the console which sent the balloon a command to release gas and maintain altitude. Her response was recorded immediately on the screen.

'Good,' Hugo whispered. 'Good girl.' Then louder. 'Bring her round a bit, Oscar – the balloon is drifting to the south.'

For twenty minutes more they butted through the swells.

'Okay,' Hugo broke the silence. 'I'm going to ditch her.' He twisted the knob clockwise slowly, expelling all the gas from the nylon balloon.

'Ja. That's it. She's down.' He looked out of the window above the set. The dust-laden clouds had brought the night on prematurely. It was dark outside, with a low black ceiling through which no star showed.

Hugo turned his attention back to the set.

'That's it, Oscar. You're right on course. Hold her there.'

Then he glanced across at old Hansie and another younger crewman. They were sitting patiently on the bench against the far bulkhead. Both of them were clad in full oilskins, shiny yellow plastic from head to ankle, with gumboots below that.

'Okay, Hansie,' Hugo nodded. 'You can get up in the bows. We are only a mile or so away now.'

They climbed down on to the wave-swept deck, and Hugo watched them scuttling forward between each green burst of water and crouching in the bows. Both of them ducking each time another swell poured over the top of them, their yellow plastic suits showing clearly in the murky deck lights.

'I'm going to switch her on now,' Hugo warned the helm. 'We should have her visual.'

'Right.' Oscar peered ahead, and Hugo flicked a switch on the panel, commanding the balloon to turn on her guide light.

Almost immediately there was a shout from Oscar.

'There she is. Dead ahead!'

Hugo jumped up and ran forward. It took a few seconds for his eyes to adjust, then he made out the tiny red firefly of light ahead of them in the vast blackness of sea and sky. It showed for a second then was gone in the trough of the next wave.

'I'll take her.' Hugo replaced Oscar at the wheel. 'You get on the spotlight.'

The beam of the spotlight was a solid white shaft through the darkness. The fluorescent yellow paint of the cylinder glowed in the circle of the spot.

Hugo lay *Wild Goose* upwind of the cylinder, and then allowed her to drift down gently on it. Hansie and his assistant were ready with the twenty-foot boat-hook.

Delicately Hugo manoeuvred down over the bobbing yellow cylinder, and grunted with satisfaction as the boat-hook slipped through the recovery ring and the cylinder was hauled in over the bows.

He watched while the two dripping oilskin-clad figures clambered back up the ladder into the wheelhouse, and laid the cylinder on the chart table.

'Good! Good!' Hugo slapped their backs heartily. 'Now, go and get dry – both of you!' They climbed down the companionway, and Hugo handed the wheel over to Oscar.

'Home!' he instructed him. 'As quick as you like.' And he carried the cylinder through into his cabin.

Sitting at the fold-down table in his cabin, Hugo unscrewed the lower section of the cylinder and took out the plastic container. He opened it and spilled the contents out on the table-top.

He whistled softly, and picked up the biggest stone. Although he was no expert he knew instinctively that it was a brilliant of exceptional quality. Even the roughness of its exterior could not mask the fire in its depths.

To him it was worthless, there was nowhere he could market a stone like that. There was no temptation to take it out of the Ring – all it would mean for him was fifteen years at hard labour.

The Ring was based on this mutual reliance, no one part of it could function without all the others – yet each part was self-contained and watertight. Only one man knew all its parts, and nobody knew who that one man was.

From the drawer beside him Hugo took out his tools and set them on the table. He lit the spirit stove and set the pot of paraffin wax in the gimbal above it to heat.

Then he poured the diamonds into a shiny metal can. It was the type of ordinary commercial can used for packing and preserving foodstuffs.

Balancing against the ship's motion, he lifted the pot from the stove, and poured the steaming liquid wax over the diamonds, filling the can to rim level.

The wax cooled and solidified quickly, turning opaque and white. The stones were now incorporated in a cake of wax that would prevent them rattling, and would give the sealed can authentic weight.

Hugo lit a cigarette and crossed the cabin to look out into the wheelhouse. The helmsman winked at him and Hugo smiled.

He went back to the table, the can was cool enough to handle. He placed the circular lid over it, and moved to the portable Jenny bolted to a chest of drawers. Carefully he clinched the lid into place, his eyes squinting at the smoke from the cigarette that dangled from his lips.

Satisfied at last he set the sealed can on the table, while he went to where his jacket hung on the door. From the inside pocket he pulled out a manilla envelope, then from the envelope he drew a printed, colour-screened label. He came back to the bench and meticulously pasted the label around the can. On the label was a highly glamorized artist's conception of a leaping pilchard, making it look like a Scottish salmon.

'Pilchards in Tomato Sauce.' Hugo read the label aloud, as he leaned back to admire his work. 'A product of South West Africa.' He smiled with satisfaction and began packing his equipment away.

'How much?' The foreman of the fish pump called across the narrowing gap between _Wild Goose_ and the jetty.

'About fifty tons,' Hugo shouted back. 'Then the norther chased us home.'

'Ja. None of the boats stayed out.' The foreman watched his gang secure the mooring ropes, and swing the hose of the vacuum pump over _Wild Goose's_ hold to begin pumping out her pilchards.

'Take over, Oscar.' Hugo picked up his jacket and cap. 'I'll be back tomorrow.' He jumped down on to the jetty and strode down towards the canning factory with its awesome stink of pilchard oil. His jacket was slung over his shoulder, one finger hooked through the tag.

He went down an alley between the boiler rooms and the fish-drying plant, across a wide yard where the bags of fish meal were piled to the height of a double-storey building. He turned in through the double doors of the cavernous warehouse filled to roof height with cardboard cartons, each stencilled with the words:

'1 gross cans.   Pilchards in tomato sauce.
Consign to: Vee Dee Bee Agencies Ltd.
                          32, Bermondsey Street,
                          London, S.E.1.'

He went into the cubicle that served the warehouse storeman as an office.

'Hello, Hugo. Good trip?' The storeman was Hugo's brother-in-law.

'Fifty ton.' Hugo hung his coat casually on the hook behind the door. 'I've got to take a leak,' he said, and went to the latrine across the floor of the warehouse.

He came back, and drank a cup of tea with his brother-in-law. Then he stood and said, 'Jeannie will be waiting.'

'Give her my love.'

'She don't need yours. She's going to get plenty of mine!' Hugo winked, and took his coat from the hook. It was lighter now, the can was gone from the pocket.

He went through the main gates of the harbour, exchanging a casual greeting with the customs officer, and went to the battered early model convertible in the car park.

He kissed the girl at the driving-wheel, threw his coat on the back seat and climbed in over the door.

'You drive,' he told her, grinning. 'I want both hands free.'

She squeaked and pulled his hand out of her skirts.

'Can't you wait till we get home?'

'I've been at sea for five days and I'm hungry as hell.'

'You're a caution, you are.' She laughed at him and started the car.

This was Sergio Caporetti, the man Johnny had chosen to captain *Kingfisher*. He was a round man, the same shape as a snowman. He filled the doorway of Johnny's office, and his great belly bulging into the room ahead of him. His face was round also, like a baby's – but he had beautiful dark Italian eyes fringed with thick lashes like a girl's.

'Come in, Sergio,' Johnny greeted him. 'Nice to see you.'

The Italian crossed the room deceptively quickly, and Johnny's hand was completely engulfed by the enormous hairy paw.

'So, at last we are ready,' Sergio grunted. 'Three months I sit on bum – do nothing. Look at me – ' He slapped his belly with a sound like a pistol shot. ' – fat! No good.'

'Well, not quite ready.' Johnny qualified the statement. He was flying Sergio and his crew over to England well ahead of time. He wanted the big Italian to have plenty of opportunity to study and get to know the revolutionary new equipment with which *Kingfisher* was fitted. Then when the vessel was ready for sea, Sergio would sail her out to Africa.

'Sit down, Sergio. Let's go over the crew list – '

When Sergio left an hour later, Johnny went as far as the lift with him.

'If you have any problems phone me, Sergio.'

'Si.' Sergio shook hands. 'Don't worry – Caporetti is in charge. All is well.'

On his way back Johnny stopped at the reception desk.

'Is Mrs Hartford in today?' he asked one of the little receptionists, and both of them replied in chorus like Tweedledum and Tweedledee.

'No, Mr Lance.'

'Has she phoned to say where she is?'

'No, Mr Lance.'

Tracey had disappeared. Five days now there had been no sign of her, her new office was deserted and unused. Johnny was worried and angry. He was worried that she had gone on another binge, and he was angry because he missed her.

He was scowling ferociously as he went back into his office.

'Goodness me.' Lettie Pienaar stood beside his desk with a batch of mail in her hand. 'We do look happy. Here's something to cheer you.'

She handed him a postcard with a colour picture of the Eiffel Tower. It was the first word from Ruby since she had left. Johnny read it quickly.

'Paris – ' he said, ' – is fun, it seems.' He tossed the card on to the desk and plunged back into the day's work.

He worked late, stopped at a steakhouse to eat, then drove back to the silent house in Bishopscourt.

The crunch of tyres on the gravel drive and headlights flashing across the bedroom wall woke him. He sat up in bed as the front-door bell began a series of urgent peals and he switched on the bedside light. Two o'clock – Christ!

He pulled a dressing-gown over his nudity and tottered down the passage, switching on lights as he went. The doorbell kept ringing.

He turned the front door key. The door flew open and Tracey came in like a strong wind, clutching a briefcase to her chest.

'Where the hell have you been?' Johnny was suddenly fully awake, angry and relieved.

'Johnny! Johnny!' She was dancing with excitement, incoherent, her cheeks flaming and eyes shining. 'I've got them – at least, it, both of them.'

'Where have you been?' Johnny was not to be so easily sidetracked, and with an obvious effort Tracey brought her excitement under control, but she was still smiling and gave the impression of humming like an electric motor.

'Come.' She took his hand and dragged him into the lounge. 'Get yourself a large whisky and sit down,' she ordered, imperious as a queen.

'I don't want a whisky, and I don't – '

'You'll need one,' she interrupted, and went to the open liquor cabinet, poured a massive whisky into a crystal glass, squirted soda into it, and brought it back to Johnny.

'Tracey, what the hell is going on?'

'Please, Johnny. It's so wonderful, don't spoil it for me. Just sit there, please!'

Johnny sank reluctantly into the chair, and Tracey slipped the catch on her brief-case and drew out a sheaf of documents. She stood in the centre of the floor, and took up the pose of a Victorian actress.

'This – ' she explained, ' – is a translation from the original German of a procla-mation by Governor in Council dated 3rd May 1899 and issued at Windhoek. I will leave out the preamble and go straight to the meat.'

She cleared her throat and began reading:

'In consideration of the sum of 10,000 marks which is hereby paid and received, the rights to mine, win, recover, collect or carry away all metals, whether base or precious, stones whether base, semi-precious or precious, minerals, guano, veg-etation and other substances organic or in-organic for a period of Nine Hundred and Ninety-Nine years is granted to Messrs Farben, Hendryck and Mosenthal S.A., Guano Merchants of 14 Bergenstrasse, Windhoek, in respect of a circular area ten kilometres in radius whose centre shall be a point situate at the highest elevation of the island lying on latitude 23° 15′ South and longitude 15° 12′ East.'

Tracey paused and looked at Johnny. He was frozen, stony-faced, staring at her with all his attention. She went on quickly, gabbling it out.

'All the old German mineral concessions and rights were ratified by the Union Parliament when the Union of South Africa took over the mandate after the Great War.'

He nodded, unable to speak. Tracey's smile kept breaking out.

'That concession still has all the force of law behind it. The grant of any subsequent rights is invalid, and although the original grant was mainly for the recovery of guano – yet it covers precious stones also.'

Again Johnny nodded, and Tracey put the document at the bottom of the sheaf of papers in her hand.

'The concession Company, Farben, Hendryck and Mosenthal S.A., is still in exist-ence. The Company's only remaining asset, apart from any long-forgotten con-cessions, is an old building at 14 Bergenstrasse, Windhoek.'

Tracey seemed to change the subject suddenly.

'You asked me where I have been, Johnny. Well I've been to Windhoek, and over most of the worst roads in South West Africa.

'The Farben, Hendryck and Mosenthal Company is owned by the brothers Hend-ryck, a couple of karakul fur farmers. They are a pair of horrible old men, and when I saw them slitting the throats of those poor little Persian lambs just to prevent the fur uncurling, well – ' Tracey paused, and gulped. 'Well, I didn't explain to them about the concession. I just offered to buy the Company, and they asked twenty thousand and I said "sign", and they signed and I left them chuckling with glee. They thought they'd been terribly clever. There! It's all yours!'

Tracey handed the Agreement to Johnny and while he read it she went on.

'I made the Agreement in the name of van der Byl Diamonds, I signed it as a Director – I hope you don't mind.'

'Christ!' Johnny took a long deep swallow of whisky, then set the glass down and stood up.

'Mind?' he repeated. 'You bring me the concession to Thunderbolt and Suicide – and ask me if I mind.'

He reached for her and eagerly she went to him.

'Tracey, you're wonderful.' They hugged each other ecstatically, and Johnny swung her off her feet. Without either of them planning it they were suddenly lying, still in each other's arms, on the couch. Then they were kissing, and the laughter dwindled into small murmurs and incoherent sounds.

Tracey pulled away from him at last, and slipped off the couch. She stood in the centre of the floor. Her breathing was ragged. Her hair was a dark tangle.

'Whoa! That's enough.'

'Tracey.' He started up from the couch, wild for her, but she held him at the full stretch of her arms, her hands flat on his chest, backing away in front of him.

'No, Johnny, no!' She shook her head urgently. 'Listen to me.'

He stopped. The wild look faded from his eyes.

'Look, Johnny, God knows I'm no saint, but – well, I don't want us to – well, not on a couch in some other woman's house. That's not how I want it to be.'

Benedict eased the big honey-coloured Bentley out of the traffic stream that clogged Bermondsey Street and turned into the gates of the warehouse. He parked beside the loading bay and climbed out.

As he pulled off his gloves, he glanced along the bank. Mountains of goods were stacked ready for distribution. Cases of Cape wine and spirits, canned fruit in brown cartons, canned fish, forty gallon drums of fish oil, bundles of raw hides stiff as boards, and cases of indefinable goods – all of it the produce of Southern Africa.

Vee Dee Bee Agencies had grown out of all recognition in the ten years since Benedict had launched it.

Benedict climbed the steps to the bank three at a time, and strode down between the towering stacks of goods that reached up into the murk of the high ceiling. He walked with the assurance of a man on his own ground, the skirts of his overcoat swirling about his knees, broad-shouldered and tall. The storemen and porters greeted him deferentially as he passed, and when he entered the main office there was a stirring and whispering among the ranks of typists as though a wind had blown through a forest.

The Managing Director hurried out of his office to greet Benedict and usher him in.

'How are you, Mr van der Byl? There's tea coming now.' And he stood behind Benedict to take his coat.

The meeting lasted half an hour, Benedict reading through the weekly sales and cost reports, querying an item here, remarking on a figure with pleasure or displeasure as it deserved. Many people watching him work would have been startled. This was not the indolent playboy they thought they knew, this was a hard-eyed businessman coldly and unemotionally milking the maximum profit from his enterprise.

There would have been others who wondered where Benedict had found the capital to finance a business of this magnitude, especially if they had known that he owned the premises, and that Vee Dee Bee Agencies was by no means his only stake in the world of business. He had not received money from his father – the Old Man had not believed Benedict capable of successfully negotiating the purchase of a pound of butter.

The meeting ended, and Benedict stood up and shrugged on his overcoat, while his Managing Director went to the grey steel safe in the corner, tumbled the combination and swung the heavy door open.

'The shipment arrived yesterday,' he explained as he reached into the safe and brought out the can. 'On the S.S. *Loch Elsinore* from Walvis Bay.'

He handed the can to Benedict, who examined it briefly, smiling a little at the painting of the leaping fish and the lettering 'Pilchards in Tomato Sauce'.

'Thank you.' He slipped the can into his briefcase, and the Managing Director walked with him back to the Bentley.

Benedict left the Bentley in a garage in Broadwick Street, and walked through the jostle of Soho until he reached the grimy brick building behind the square. He pressed the bell opposite the card that read Aaron Cohen, Manufacturing Jeweller, and when the door opened he climbed the stairs to the top and fourth floor. Again he rang, and after a while an eye peeped at him through the peephole – but the door opened almost immediately.

'Hello, Mr van der Byl. Come in! Come in!' The young doorman welcomed him in and locked the door behind him. 'Papa is expecting you!' He went on as they both looked up at the eye of the closed-circuit TV camera above the wrought-iron grille that barred the passage.

Whoever was viewing the screen was satisfied, for there was an electrical buzz and the grille swung open. The doorman led Benedict down the passage.

'You know the way. Papa is in his office.'

Benedict was in a shabby little reception room, with a threadbare carpet and a pair of chairs that looked like Ministry of Works rejects. He turned to the right-hand door and went through it into a long room that clearly occupied most of the top floor of the building.

Along one side of the room ran a narrow bench, to which were bolted twenty small lathes. Each machine ran off a belt from a central drive below the bench. The man tending the machines wore a white dust jacket, and he grinned at Benedict. 'Hello, Mr van der Byl, Papa is expecting you.' But Benedict delayed a moment to watch the operation of the saws. In the jaws of each lathe was set a diamond, and spinning against the diamond was a circular blade of phosphor bronze. As Benedict watched, the man turned back to the task of spreading a fine paste of olive oil and diamond dust on to the cutting edge of each blade – for it was not the bronze that cut. Only a diamond will cut a diamond.

'Some nice stones, Larry,' Benedict remarked, and Larry Cohen nodded.

'All of them between four and five carats.'

Benedict leaned close and examined one of the diamonds. The line of the cut was marked with Indian ink on the stone. Benedict knew what heart-searching and discussion, what examination and drawing upon the rich storehouses of experience had preceded the positioning of that ink line. It might take two days to saw through each diamond, so Benedict left the bench and moved on.

In a row down the other side of the room sat the other Cohen brothers. Eight of them. Old Aaron was a great breeder of boys. They ranged in age from nearly forty to nineteen years and there were a couple who were still in school and hadn't yet come into the business.

'How do you like this one, Mr van der Byl?' Michael Cohen looked up as Benedict approached. Michael was shaping a fine diamond, cutting it into a round using a lesser stone as a blade. A small tray beneath the lathe caught the dust from the two stones. This dust would be used later for sawing and polishing.

'A beauty,' said Benedict. These men were of the brotherhood, working with diamonds all their lives and loving them as other men loved women or horses and fine paintings.

He moved on down the room, greeting each of the brothers, stopping to watch for a minute the loving care with which the elder boys, master craftsmen each of them, were cutting the precisely-angled facets that make up the perfect round brilliant. The fifty-eight facets – table, stars, pavilions and the others which endow a cut stone with its mystic 'life' and 'fire'.

Leaving them crouched over their wheels, so similar to those of a potter, he went through the door at the end of the room.

'Benedict, my friend.' Aaron Cohen came from his desk to embrace him. He was a tall thin man in his late sixties with a thick silver-grey mane of hair, round-shouldered from years of crouching over a diamond wheel. 'I did not know you were in London, they told me you were in Cape Town. Yesterday was Ruby's birthday. If we had known – '

Benedict took the envelope from his pocket and shook twenty-seven diamonds on to the blotter of the desk.

'What do you think of those, Papa?'

'Shu! Shu!' Papa patted his own cheeks with delight, and he reached instinctively for the biggest stone.

'I should live to see such a stone!' He screwed a jeweller's *loupe* into his eye, turning to catch the natural light from the high windows, and scrutinized the diamond through the eyepiece.

'Ah, yes. There is a feather*, but small. V.V.S.I.† But we will cut through it. Yes, we will take two gems from this stone. Two perfect diamonds of ten or twelve carats each, and perhaps five smaller ones.' More than half a diamond's bulk is lost in the cutting.

'Yes! Yes! From this stone we will sell a hundred thousand pounds' worth of polished diamonds!'

Aaron crossed to the door. 'Boys! Come see! I will show you a prince among diamonds.' And his sons crowded into the office. Michael took it first and gave his opinion. 'A good stone, yes. But not of the same water as the stone we had in the last batch. You remember that octahedron crystal – '

'What you talking!' his father interrupted. 'You wouldn't know a diamond from a piece of gorgonzola cheese already!'

'He is right, Papa.' Larry joined in the discussion. 'The other stone was better.'

'So the Big Lover agues with his father! Little shiksas with skirts up around their tochis you know all about. Dancing the Watsui and the Cha-Cha. Yes! But diamonds

---

*Semi-transparent veinlike flaw.
†Very very slight imperfection.

you know from nothing.' This declaration precipitated a full-scale, family argument in which each of the brothers joined with gusto.

'Shuddup! Shuddup! Back to work all of you! Out! Out!' Aaron broke up the meeting, driving his sons from the office and slamming the door behind them.

'Shu!' He looked to heaven. 'What a business! Now we can weigh the stones.'

When they had weighed and tallied the stones, and Aaron had locked them into the safe, Benedict told him:

'I am thinking of breaking up the Ring.'

Aaron froze and looked across the desk at Benedict. Between them there was always the pretence that their relationship was legitimate. They never spoke about the Ring, or where the unregistered stones came from, or how the finished gems were sent to Switzerland.

'Why?' Aaron asked carefully.

'I am a rich man now. With my father's money, and what I have made from the Ring and invested. A very rich man. I no longer need to take the risks.'

'Such problems I wish I had. But perhaps you are wise – I would not think to argue with you.'

'There will be one or two more packages. Then it will be finished.'

Aaron nodded. 'I understand,' he said. 'Like all good things it must end.'

It was a little after noon when Benedict parked the Bentley outside the mews flat off Belgrave Square. He went to shower immediately he was home. In all the years he had lived here he had never grown accustomed to London's grime-laden atmosphere, and he bathed or showered at least three times a day.

He sang in the shower, and then enveloped in a huge bath towel he left a string of damp footprints through to the lounge where he mixed a Martini, and screwed up his eyes at the first stinging taste of the drink.

The phone rang.

'Van der Byl,' he said into the mouthpiece, and then his expression changed as he listened. Quickly he put down the glass and used both hands to hold the telephone receiver.

'What on earth are you doing here?' His tone of astonishment was not faked.

'What a wonderful surprise. When can I see you? How about right now – for lunch? That's great! No, nothing I can't put off – this is a pretty special occasion, you know. Where are you staying? The Lancaster. Fine. Look, give me forty-five minutes, and I'll meet you in the Looking-Glass Room on the top floor. Yes, ten past one. God, what a delightful – I've said that already. See you in three-quarters of an hour.'

He replaced the receiver, swallowed the remains of his Martini and headed for his bedroom suite. This would make a good day into a truly remarkable one, he thought, as he quickly selected a silk shirt. He looked at his reflection in the mirror and grinned.

'The ball has really started bouncing your way, Benedict,' he whispered.

She was not at the bar, nor in the Looking-Glass Room. Benedict crossed to the tall picture windows for a glimpse of one of London's finest views across Hyde Park and the Serpentine. It was a smoky blue day, and the pale sun added bronze to the autumn shades of gold and red in the park.

He turned from the windows, and she was crossing the room towards him. His stomach swooped with delight for she also was pale gold with the coppery sheen of sun on her long legs and bare arms. The grace of her carriage was as he remembered it, the precise lifting and laying down of narrow feet on the thick pile of the carpet.

He stood quite still, letting her come to him. Heads turned all across the room, for she was a splendid golden creature. Benedict knew suddenly and clearly that he wanted this woman for himself.

'Hello, Benedict,' she said, and he stepped forward to take her hand in both of his.

'Ruby Lance!' He squeezed her long fingers gently. 'It's so good to see you again.'

The use of her surname was the clue to the strength of his reaction. She belonged to the one man in the world that Benedict most envied and hated. For this reason she was infinitely desirable.

'Let us celebrate with a little drink. I think the occasion deserves at the very least a champagne cocktail.'

She sat with those long slim legs neatly crossed, leaning back in her chair, holding the stemmed glass with tapering fingers. Her hair hung straight to her shoulders, like some rare silken tapestry in white gold, and her eyes watched him with a catlike candour, a calm feline intentness that seemed to look into his soul.

'I should not have bothered you,' she said. 'But I know so few people here.'

'How long can you stay?' He brushed aside the disclaimer. 'I must cancel my other arrangements.'

'A week.' She made it sound like an offer that was subject to negotiation.

'Oh, no!' His voice was mock distressed. 'You can do better than that – we won't be able to do half what I had planned in so short a time. You can stay longer, surely?'

'Perhaps,' she agreed, and lifted the glass an inch. 'It's good to see you.'

'And you.' Benedict agreed with emphasis. They sipped the sparkling wine watching each other's eyes.

Where others must wait weeks and months Benedict went in immediately as though it were his right. A smile and a murmured word, and theatre tickets were his or the doors of fashionable restaurants opened magically.

That first night he took her to the National Theatre, then for dinner at Le Coeur de France where a very famous movie actor stopped at their table.

'Hello, Benedict. We are all going on to the yacht later for a bit of a party. Join us, won't you?' And those legendary eyes turned to Ruby. 'And bring your beautiful friend with you.'

They ate breakfast under the awning on the afterdeck of the yacht, eggs and bacon and Veuve Clicquot champagne, and watched the hubbub of dawn traffic on the wondrously smelly old Thames. Ruby was the only girl in the party without a fur to cheat the chill of the river dawn. Benedict made a mental note of the fact.

On the way home she sat with those long legs curled under her in the seat of the Bentley, still sleek and golden despite the night's exertions, but with the lightest touch of blue beneath her eyes.

'I can't remember having enjoyed an evening so much, Benedict. She patted a tiny pink-lipped yawn. 'You're a wonderful companion.'

'Tonight again?' he asked.

'Yes, please,' she murmured.

She sensed an urgency in him, when she came down into the lobby of the Lancaster that evening. He came quickly to meet her as she stepped out of the lift, and the quiet assurance with which he kissed her cheek and took her arm surprised her.

They were silent as he snaked the Bentley through the evening traffic. Ruby realized that at the tips of her long tapered fingers, within touching distance, was a fortune such as she had never before allowed herself to dream about. She was deadly afraid. A wrong move, even a wrong word might drive that fortune beyond her grasp for ever. She would never have a chance like this again, and she was afraid to move, almost paralysed with fear. The decision she knew she would have to make very soon would be fateful. Must she encounter his advance with withdrawal, or must she meet it as frankly as it was made.

She was so deeply involved with her thoughts that when the Bentley came to a standstill she looked up with surprise. They were parked in a mews outside an expensive-looking flat.

Benedict came round and opened her door, and led her without protest into the flat.

She looked about her curiously, recognizing some of the art works on display in the entrance hall. Benedict took her through into the long lounge and settled her solicitously into the tapestry-covered chair which dominated the room like a throne, and suddenly her fear was gone. She felt queenlike in her control. She knew with certainty that this would all be hers.

Benedict stood in the centre of the room, almost a petitioner in his attitude, and he began to speak. She listened quietly, her expression showing no hint of the triumphant surge of her spirits, and when he stopped to wait for her reply she did not hesitate.

'Yes,' she said.

'I will be with you when you tell him,' Benedict promised.

'It won't be necessary,' Ruby assured him. 'I can handle Johnny Lance.'

'No.' Swiftly Benedict crossed to her chair and took her hands, drawing her to her feet. 'I must be there with you. Promise me that.'

Then it became suddenly evident to Ruby that the strength of her position was unassailable. Benedict needed her not for any physical reasons – but merely because she belonged to Johnny Lance.

Looking steadily into Benedict's eyes she determined to test her intuition.

'He does not have to know about you,' she said. 'I could arrange a divorce with him.'

'He *must* know about me. That's what I want, don't you see?'

'Yes, I see.' She was secure.

'It is agreed?' He could barely conceal his anxiety.

'Yes,' she nodded. 'It's agreed.' And they smiled at each other – each completely satisfied.

'Come.' He led her almost reverently into his bedroom, and Ruby stopped in the doorway with a little cry of delight.

The double bed was a mountain of glowing fur in a score of shades ranging from soft pinkish cream, through beige and oyster, pale smoky blue to midnight and jet glossy black.

'Choose one!' he ordered her. 'To seal our bargain.'

She moved like a sleepwalker towards the bed, but as she reached the centre of the Khedive carpet Benedict called out softly.

'Wait.'

She stopped obediently and he came up behind her. She felt his hands on the back of her neck, and she lowered her chin, shaking her hair forward so that he could unhook the clasp and draw down the fastening of her dress.

She stepped out of the dress as it dropped around her ankles, then waited passively as he carefully removed her brassiere.

'Now,' he said. 'Try them on.'

In her stockings and high-heeled shoes she went to the bed, subtly emphasizing the lilt of her movements, and took up the first fur.

Benedict was sprawled in the wing-back chair across the room as she glanced back at him. His face was gloating and flushed, so that his features seemed swollen and coarsened as he stared at her. She understood now that this was a form of ritual in which they were engaged. Like a victorious Roman general, Benedict was conducting his own personal triumph, reviewing the spoils and the plunder. It had no basis in sexual or physical desire, but was rather a service of worship to Benedict himself. She was the priestess of this rite.

Yet, knowing this, Ruby felt no resentment. Rather she found herself excited by the cold perversity of the pageant. As she paraded and postured, turned and swirled and flared the skirts of a wild mink, she was very conscious of his eyes upon her body. She knew it was perfect, and his scrutiny stirred her physically for the first time in her life. She felt her blood quicken and pound, felt her heart flutter within its cage of ribs like a captive bird, and her loins tighten like a clenching fist. For her also the ritual was narcissistic – satisfying her own deep emotional need.

As she discarded each of the coats she dropped it in the centre of the floor, until there was a knee-high pile of precious fur.

At last she faced him, hugging the soft creamy cloud tightly about her body. Then she opened her arms, and the coat also, standing on tip-toe to tighten and highlight the hard muscle in her legs and flanks.

'This one,' she whispered, and he came out of the chair, picked her up in his arms and laid her, still wrapped in mink, on the great pile of mink.

*

Ruby woke in the double bed to a feeling of excitement and enormous well-being such as she had not experienced since she was a schoolgirl on the first morning of a holiday.

The morning was far advanced, pale sunshine in a square shaft poured through the open window like a stage effect.

Benedict in a yellow silk dressing-gown stood beside the bed watching her with an unfathomable expression which changed immediately he realized that she was awake.

'My man has collected your luggage from the Lancaster. Your toilet things are in the bathroom, your clothing in the dressing-room.'

He sat down carefully on the edge of the bed, and leaned forward to kiss her forehead and then each cheek.

'We will breakfast when you are ready.' He sat back and watched her eyes; clearly he was waiting for her to say something important. Immediately she was on guard, wary of making a mistake, seeking a clue in his expression.

'Last night,' he asked. 'Was it as good for you, as it was for me?'

Understanding washed over her in a warm wave. He wanted assurance, a comparison between himself and Johnny Lance.

'I have never in my life – ' She placed the emphasis carefully. ' – experienced anything like it.'

He nodded, relieved, pleased – and stood up.

'After breakfast we will go to town.'

This morning, Edmund, Benedict's man, chauffeured the Bentley. When they alighted at the north end of Bond Street and walked arm in arm along the pavement, Edmund tailed them at a dignified crawl, steadfastly ignoring the abuse of other drivers.

The morning was cool enough for Ruby to wear her new cream mink, and the looks of admiration and envy she drew from the other strollers delighted Benedict. He wanted to impress her, he wanted to flaunt his wealth.

'The wife of a diamond man must have diamonds.' He spoke on impulse as they came up to an expensive-looking jewellers. Ruby squeezed his arm and turned to look into the window.

'Good Lord,' Benedict laughed. 'Not here!' And Ruby looked at him with surprise.

Mockingly Benedict began reading the signs in the window.

' "Paradise Jewellers. A large selection of blue-white gems. Certificate of flawlessness with every diamond. Perfect flawless stones at bargain prices as advertised on T.V. and in the national Press. Small deposit secures your ring now. A diamond is forever – show her you really care." '

'But they are such a well-known firm. They have branches all over the world – even in South Africa!' Ruby protested, and bridled a little as Benedict smiled patronizingly.

'Let me explain about diamonds. They are bought for two reasons by two different types of people. Firstly by rich men as investments that will not erode and can only increase in value. These men buy notable stones on the advice of experts, the best of the gem diamond production goes to them. So when Richard Burton buys Liz a £300,000 diamond he is not being extravagant – on the contrary he is being ultra-conservative and thrifty with his money.'

'That's the kind of meanness I like,' Ruby laughed, and Benedict smiled at her honesty.

'You may find me as thrifty,' he promised.

'Go on,' she said, 'tell me more about diamonds.'

'Well, there is another type who buys diamonds. Usually just one in his life, luckily for him – and he very seldom tries to resell it again or he would get a nasty shock. This type is Joe Everybody – who wants to get married. He usually goes to somebody like Paradise Jewellers.' Benedict poked a derisive finger at the sign in the window. 'Because he has seen it on Telly and he can get a ring on the instalment plan. In many cases the deposit covers the dealer for the cost of the stone – the rest goes on advertising, finance charges and, of course, profit.'

'How do you know Paradise Jewellers are that type?' Ruby's attention was wide-eyed and girlish.

'You recognize them firstly by the big advertising splurge, then by their language.' Again he studied the notices in the window. ' "A large selection of blue-white gems" – of every thousand stones of jewellery quality produced only one is fine enough in colour to be termed blue-white. It is unlikely they have a large selection. "Gem" is a special term reserved for a diamond which is in every way superb. "Flawless stones at bargain prices" – the lack of flaws in a diamond is only one of many factors governing its value. As for bargain prices – there ain't no such animal. Prices are maintained at the lowest level by fierce competition among expert and canny dealers, and there are no "sales" or special prices for anyone.'

'But where should a person buy a diamond?' Ruby was impressed and dismayed despite herself.

'Not here.' Benedict chuckled. 'Come, I will show you.' And before she could protest he had taken her arm and swept her into the shop, to be greeted with enthusiasm by the manager who must have noticed Ruby's mink and the attendant Bentley, which was causing a small traffic jam outside the shop.

'Good morning, madam and sir. May I be of service to you?'

'Yes,' Benedict turned to Ruby, as they settled down in the manager's office with a tray of diamond rings in front of them. 'You cannot examine a diamond properly in its setting.'

He selected the biggest diamond, took from his pocket a gold-plated penknife fitted with a special tool and prised open the claws of the setting to a chorus of horrified squeals from the staff.

'I will make good any damage,' he snapped, and they subsided as Benedict took the loose stone and laid it on the velvet-covered tray.

'Firstly, size. This stone is about one carat.' He looked for confirmation to the manager who nodded. 'Let us say the value of this stone is £500. Ten similar stones will be worth £5,000, right? However, a ten-carat stone may be worth as much as £75,000. So the price per carat rises sharply as the total weight of the stone increases. If I were investing I would not touch a stone under three carats.'

The staff were listening now with as much attention as Ruby.

'Next, colour,' said Benedict, and glanced at the manager. 'A sheet of clean white paper, please.'

The manager scratched in his drawer and laid a sheet of paper in front of Benedict who placed the stone upon it, bottom upwards.

'We compare the colour it "draws" from white paper in good natural light.' He looked up at the manager. 'Switch off the fluorescent lights, and open those curtains, please.'

The manager obeyed with alacrity.

'This is a matter of experience. The colour is judged by a standard. We forget about the fancy rare colours like blue and red and green, and take our top standard as blue-white. A stone so white as to appear slightly blue, after which the distinctions drop to "fine white", and "white". Then stones which "draw" a yellowish tinge which we call "Cape" – in different shades, then finally stones which "draw" a brown colour – which will reduce the value of a stone by up to eighty per cent.'

Benedict fished in his fob pocket and pulled out a guinea case which he opened.

'Every expert carries a special diamond which he uses as a gauge for colour by which to judge all other stones. This is mine.'

The staff exchanged apprehensive looks as Benedict placed a small diamond beside the other. He studied them a moment then replaced his gauge in the case.

'Second Silver Cape, I'd say,' he grunted, and the staff looked suitably abashed. 'Now we consider the stone's perfection.' He looked at the manager. 'Please lend me your *loupe*.'

'*Loupe*?' The manager was mystified.

'Yes, your jeweller's glass.'

'I – ' the manager was deeply embarrassed.

'You sell diamonds – yet you do not own a *loupe*.' Benedict shook his head in disapproval. 'No matter, I have my own.'

Benedict took the glass from his inner pocket and placed it in his eye.

'Imperfections can be almost negligible – a "natural" at the girdle, or a bubble or pinpoint of carbon in the stone, on the other hand they can be gross "cracks", "clouds", "ice", or "feathers" which will ruin the value of the stone. But this one is flawless – so when the certificate of flawlessness is issued there will be no misrepresentation.' Benedict closed the glass and tucked it back into his pocket. 'However, in order to produce a flawless stone, the cut has been squeezed.'

He held up the stone between thumb and forefinger.

'The cut or "make" of a stone is the fourth and final decider of its value. The "make" should conform closely to the "ideal". This stone has been cut to exclude a flaw, and in consequence it is badly proportioned – heavy and out of round. I would prefer to see a graceful stone which includes a slight imperfection rather than a grotesque little cripple like this.'

He put the diamond down on the desk.

'The asking price by Paradise Jewellers for this stone is £500 – which would be fair and correct for a gem. However, the colour is poor and although it is flawless it is of ungainly make. Its true value would be about – ah, let's see – £185 approximately.'

There was another chorus of protest from the assembled staff, led by the manager.

'I assure you, sir, that all our stones have been most carefully appraised.'

'How long have you been with Paradise Jewellers?' Benedict demanded brusquely. 'Four months, isn't it?'

The manager gaped at him.

'Before that you were a salesman in the showroom of a large firm of embalmers and undertakers.'

'I, well – I mean.' The manager fluttered his hands weakly. 'How did you know that?'

'I like to know about all my employees.'

'Employees?' The manager looked stunned.

'That's correct. My name is Benedict van der Byl. I own Paradise Jewellers.'
Ruby clapped her hands and cooed her applause.
'What a bundle of surprises you are!' she exclaimed.
Benedict smiled in acknowledgement and inclined his head.
'Now,' he said, as he rose and helped Ruby to her feet. 'We will go and buy some real diamonds.'
Aaron Cohen sold them two fine white twin marquise-cut brilliants, and Ruby chose the mounting for a pair of white-gold earrings from a leather-bound catalogue.
Benedict gave Aaron his cheque for twenty thousand pounds, then turned to Ruby.
'Now,' he said. 'We'll have lunch at the Celeste Grillroom. The food is bloody awful – but the decor is stupendous. We had best phone and reserve a table – it isn't really necessary but they get terribly hurt if you don't.'
As they settled back in the lush upholstery of the Bentley, Benedict instructed the chauffeur.
'Go past Trafalgar Square, Edmund. I want to pick up the newspapers from South Africa House.'
Edmund double-parked outside the Ambassador's entrance, and the doorman recognised the car and hurried inside to fetch the bundle of newspapers.
As they pulled away around the square towards Haymarket, Benedict selected a copy of the *Cape Argus*.
'Let's see what's happened at home.' He glanced at the front page, and stiffened perceptibly.
'What is it?' Ruby leaned towards him anxiously, but he ignored her. His eyes were darting across the page like the shuttle of a loom. She saw the colour fade from his face, leaving it white and intent. He finished reading, and pushed the paper towards her. She spread the page.

'VAN DER BYL DIAMONDS WIN VALUABLE CONCESSION.
APPEAL COURT SUPPORTS KAISER'S MINERAL GRANT.
LANCE GETS THUNDERBOLT AND SUICIDE.
    Bloemfontein, Thursday.

In an urgent application by the Central Diamond Mines Ltd, to prevent Van Der Byl Diamonds Ltd. prospecting and mining a concession area off the South West African Coast, Mr Justice Tromp today dismissed the application with costs stating in his judgement: "The original concession granted by German Imperial Decree in 1899, and subsequently ratified by Act of the Union Parliament in Act 24 of the 1920 must hold good in law, and will take precedent over any subsequent grant or concession purporting to have been made by the Minister of Mines to any other party."
The area in dispute covers 100 square kilometres surrounding two small islands lying some fifteen miles south of Cartridge Bay and five miles offshore. The islands are known as Thunderbolt Island and Suicide Island, and at the turn of the century were the site of considerable exploitation by a German Guano Company. Mr John Rigby Lance, the General Manger of Van Der Byl Diamond Co. Ltd., acquired the rights to the concession when he took over the inoperative guano company.
In Cape Town today Mr Lance stated: "It's the opportunity I have waited for all my

life. All indications are that Thunderbolt and Suicide will prove to be one of the richest marine diamond fields in the world."

Van Der Byl Diamond Co. had a diamond-dredging vessel nearing completion in the United Kingdom, and Mr Lance stated that he hoped to begin recovery operations off Thunderbolt and Suicide Islands before the end of the year.'

Ruby lowered the paper and looked at Benedict. What she saw was an intense physical shock.

Benedict had crumpled down in the seat. Gone was all the assurance and *savoir faire*. His face was deathly pale, but now his lips trembled and with disgust she saw that his eyes were swimming with tears. He hunched forward over his hands, shaking his head gently and hopelessly.

'The bastard' he whispered, and his voice was soggy and muffled. 'He does it every time. I thought that I had him at last but – Oh God, I hate him.'

He looked at her, his face soft with self-pity. 'He does it every time. Often I've thought I had him, but he just – '

She was mystified by his reaction.

'Aren't you pleased? Van Der Byl Diamonds will make millions – '

'No! No!' he cut in savagely, and then the years of hatred and frustration and humiliation began pouring out. Ruby listened quietly, slowly beginning to understand it all, marvelling at the accumulation of pain and hatred that he exposed for her. He remembered conversations from twenty years ago. Small childhood episodes, innocent remarks that had festered and rankled for a decade.

'You don't want him to succeed, is that it?' she asked.

'I want to crush him, break him, humiliate him.'

For ten seconds Ruby was silent.

'Well, what are we going to do about it?' she asked flatly.

'Nothing, I suppose.' Benedict's tone irritated her. 'He always comes out on top, you just can't – '

'Nonsense,' Ruby snapped. She was angry now. 'Let's go over it carefully, and see how we can stop him. He is only human, and you have shown me enough to prove you are a brilliant and successful businessman.'

Benedict's expression changed, becoming trusting and animated. He turned to her almost eagerly: He blinked his eyes. 'Do you really believe that?'

The bunk was too narrow, Sergio Caporetti decided, much too narrow. He would have one of the carpenters alter it today.

He lay on his back, wedged in firmly, with the blanket-covered mound of his belly blocking his view southwards. He lay and assessed his physical condition. It was surprisingly good. There was but a small blurred pain behind his eyes and the taste of stale cigars and rank wine in the back of his throat was bearable. The leaden feeling in his lower limbs alarmed him until he realized that he was still wearing his heavy fisherman's boots. He remembered one of the girls complaining about that.

He hoisted himself on one elbow, and looked at the girls. One on each side of him, jamming him solidly into the bunk with magnificent hillocks of pink flesh. Big strong girls both of them, he had chosen them with care, neither of them an ounce under twelve stone. Sergio sighed happily – it had been a wonderful weekend. The girls were snoring, in such harmony that it might have been a rehearsed stage act. He listened to them with mild admiration for a few minutes, then crawled over the outside girl and stood in the centre of the cabin, clad only in his heavy boots. He yawned extravagantly, scratching the thick black wiry curls that covered his chest and belly, and cocked an eye at the bulkhead clock. Four o'clock on a Monday morning, but it had been a truly memorable weekend.

The table was hidden under a forest of empty wine bottles, and dirty plates. There was a congealed mass of cold spaghetti bolognaise in a dish and he picked it up. As he clumped out of the cabin on to *Kingfisher*'s bridge he was scooping up spaghetti with his fingers and cramming it into his mouth.

He stood at the rail of the bridge, a naked hairy figure in tall black boots clutching a dish of spaghetti to his chest, and looked around the dockyard.

Kingfisher was in stocks undergoing the modifications that Johnny Lance had ordered. She was standing high above the level she would attain when she was launched. Although she was a vessel of a mere 3,000 ton displacement, she appeared black and monstrous in the floodlights that illuminated the ship-builders' yard. It was obvious from her unusual silhouette that she was designed for a special purpose. Her superstructure was situated well aft like that of an oil tanker, while her foredeck was crowded by the huge gantry which would control the dredge, and by the massive storage tanks for the compressed air.

At this hour of the morning the shipyard was deserted, and wisps and tendrils of sea mist drifted about *Kingfisher*'s bulk.

Standing fifty feet above the dry dock, still wolfing cold spaghetti, Sergio urinated over the rail – deriving a simple honest pleasure from the long arching stream and the tinkle of liquid striking the concrete far below.

He clumped back into his cabin, and looked down fondly on his two sleeping Valkyries while he finished the last of the spaghetti. Then he wiped his fingers carefully on his chest hair and called to them gently.

'Come, my kittens, my little doves, the time for play she has passed – the time for work she commences.'

With Latin gallantry he bundled them into a taxi at the dockyard gates, pressing on to each of them a lusty buss, a bank-note, a bottle of Chianti, protestations of deep affection, and the promise of another party next Friday night.

He picked his way back through the dockyard jungle of machinery and buildings, lighting a long black cigar and inhaling smoke pleasurably until he came in sight of *Kingfisher* and halted with surprise and annoyance. There was a big honey-coloured Bentley parked near the gangway that led up to *Kingfisher*'s deck. He resented visits from the Company bosses, especially this one, and especially at this ridiculous hour on a Monday morning.

*

The hose spiralled down into greenness, and they followed it down holding hands. Tracey was still a little nervous. This was not like the Mediterranean, a warm blue friendly embrace of waters to welcome the diver – it was the wild Atlantic, coldly menacing, green and untamed. It frightened her, and Johnny's hand gave her comfort.

Their Draeger demand valves repeated their breathing in a singing metallic wheeze, and icy leaks and rivulets kept finding their way into the cuffs and neck of Tracey's rubber suit.

Sixty feet below the surface Johnny paused, and peered into the glass window of her mask. He grinned at her, his mouth distorted by the bulky mouthpiece, and she gave him a thumbs-up sign. They both looked upwards. The surface was silvered like an imperfect mirror, and the black cigar shape of the boat was lapped in strange light. The hose and anchor chain pierced the silver ceiling and hung down into the shady green depths.

Johnny pointed downwards, and she nodded. They put their heads down, pointed their flippers to the surface, and still hand in hand they paddled steadily towards the sea bed.

Tracey was aware of a crackling hissing sound now, and from out of the greeny blackness below them scudded clouds of silver bubbles twisting and writhing towards the surface. She strained her eyes downwards, following the line of the hose, and slowly out of the murk materialized the black rubber-clad forms of the two men working at the end of the hose; they appeared weird and mystical like black priests performing a satanical mass.

She and Johnny reached the sea bed and hung just above it, a little way off from the two men on the hose. Johnny indicated the depth gauge that he wore like a wrist-watch. It showed a depth of 120 feet. Then he turned and by a hand signal showed her the direction of the reefs.

They were in a valley between these long peaked underwater ridges of black rocks, the same reefs that Tracey had seen from the air. There was a distinct pull of water as the current drifted at right angles to the direction of the reefs.

Johnny squeezed her hand, and then pulled her down. They lay on their bellies on the floor of the sea, and Johnny scooped a handful of the white sand, washed it quickly so that the smaller particles were carried away in a cloud on the current, then he showed her the coarse gravel which remained. Again he grinned, and she returned his smile.

Still leading her by the hand, he swam slowly towards the two men working on the hose, and stopped to watch them.

Attached to the end of the hose was a rigid steel pipe two inches in diameter, and twenty feet long – although now only half of its length was visible above the sand bottom. The two divers were forcing it down through sand and gravel to reach bedrock. The hose itself was attached to a compressor on the deck of the boat which was generating a vacuum in the hose and sucking up the sand and gravel as the steel pipe was forced downwards.

They were prospecting the Thunderbolt and Suicide field. Taking these two-inch samples at five-hundred-foot intervals to ascertain the depth of water, the thickness of the over-burden, and the content of the gravel beds. They were also mapping and plotting the reefs, so that by the time *Kingfisher* arrived they would have a fairly clear picture of the topography and aspect of the field. They would know where to begin dredging, and roughly what to expect when they did.

So far the results had endorsed Johnny's most optimistic expectations. There was a good thick catchment of gravel in all the gullies between the reefs. As he had expected, the heavier gravels had been laid down in the gullies closest to the gap between Thunderbolt and Suicide, and the smaller and lighter gravels had been carried further. In some of the gullies the gravel beds were fifteen feet deep, and the types of stone present were all highly promising. He had isolated garnet, jasper, ironstone, beryl chips and titanium dust.

However, the conclusive and definite proof had also come up through that two-inch hose out of the depths. They had already pulled the first diamonds from the Thunderbolt and Suicide fields. When you considered the odds against finding a stone in a two-inch sample at five-hundred-foot centres and that payable gravel contained one part diamond in fifty million, it was exciting and encouraging that they had already recovered four diamonds. Small stones, to be sure, not one of them more than half a carat, but diamonds for all that, and some of them of excellent quality.

One of the men on the hose turned and gave Johnny a flat-handed cut-out sign. The pipe was on bed-rock. Johnny nodded and jerked a thumb upwards, and drawing Tracey with him started for the surface.

They climbed the ladder over the survey boat's counter moving clumsily under the weight of the air bottles strapped to their backs, but there were willing hands to help them aboard and strip off the heavy equipment, and unzip the clinging rubber suits.

Tracey accepted a towel gratefully from one of the crew, and while she tilted her head to dry her sodden mane of hair, she looked across half a mile of green sea to the two white whale-backed islands with their attendant clouds of sea birds. The wave bursts on the cliffs sounded like distant artillery, or far thunder.

'God, this is a wild and exciting place.' Her voice bubbled with excitement as she scrubbed at her hair. 'It makes one come alive.'

Johnny understood her feelings, it was the forbidding restless sea and the harsh land that promised danger and adventure. He was about to reply, but the two hose men came aboard at that moment, the taller of them spitting out his mouthpiece and letting it fall to his chest.

'We'll move up to the next point, if it's okay by you, Mr Lance?' The man pulled off his mask and hood, exposing white-blond hair and a sun-broiled face.

'Fine, Hugo,' Johnny agreed, and watched approvingly as Hugo Kramer gave the orders to get the anchor and the hose up before taking *Wild Goose* seawards to her next prospecting point. Johnny had been reluctant to charter *Wild Goose* as the prospecting vessel and as the service boat for *Kingfisher*. He did not know Hugo Kramer, and Benedict van der Byl's insistence on the man had made him suspicious.

However, it was natural that they should use a skipper from the van der Byl fleet and Johnny was now prepared to admit he had been wrong. Kramer was an intelligent and willing worker, resourceful and trustworthy, a fine seaman who handled *Wild Goose* with all the skill it would need to bring her alongside *Kingfisher* in a heavy sea. His unfortunate physical appearance Johnny hardly noticed any more, although the original shock of that pink face, white hair and those blind-looking eyes had been considerable.

Tracey was not so charitable. The man made her uneasy. There was a wild-animal ferocity about him, a barely controlled violence. The way he looked at her sometimes made her skin prickle. He did it now; turning back from issuing his orders he ran his eyes over her body. In the black silk costume her good round breasts showed at their best, and Hugo Kramer looked at them with those white-fringed bland eyes. Instinctively she covered them with the towel, and it seemed as though his lips twitched with amusement as he turned to Johnny.

'They tell me this dredger of yours is something special, Mr. Lance?'

'She is, Hugo. Not like the other half-baked barges and bastardized conversions that have been tried by other companies. She's the first diamond recovery vessel designed expressly for the job.'

'What's different about her?'

'Nearly everything. Her hose is operated off a gantry on the foredeck, it goes out through a well pierced through her hull.'

'What kind of hose?'

'Eighteen-inch armoured woven steel with rubber liner. We can get it down to a hundred fathoms, and it has a compensating section in it to stop it plunging with the wave action of the hull.'

'Eighteen inches is pretty big. How will you build up vacuum?'

'That's the point, Hugo. We don't suck – we blow! We evacuate water from the hose by purging it with compressed air, the inrush of water into the opening of the hose sucks in the gravel.'

'Hey, that's neat. So the deeper you work the more effective it will be!'

'Right.'

'What about the actual recovery? Are you going to have the usual screening, ball mill, and grease table arrangement?'

'That's what killed the other companies – trying to separate by the old methods. No. We've got a cyclone to start with.'

'Cyclone?'

'You know a cream separator?'

'Yeah.'

'Same principle. Just spin the gravel in a circular tank and float off everything with a specific gravity of less than 2.5. Take what is left, dry it, spread it on a conveyor belt and run it under an X-ray machine which pinpoints every single diamond. As you know, diamonds fluoresce under X-rays and they show up crisply. The X-ray machine reports the diamond to the central computer – ' Johnny's voice and whole attitude was charged with enthusiasm which was impossible for his listeners to resist. Tracey was carried along with him, watching his eyes and his mouth as he talked, smiling when he smiled, her lips following his faithfully.

'This is the cyclone room,' Benedict van der Byl explained as, with a hand on her elbow, he helped Ruby Lance down off the last rung of the ladder. 'I explained to you how it worked.'

'Yes.' Ruby nodded, and looked around the room with interest. The roughly riveted and grey painted plating of *Kingfisher*'s hull formed a square metal box, in the centre of which stood the cyclone. It was also painted battleship grey, a ten-foot-high cone-shaped circular tower.

'The gravel is blown in through here.' Benedict indicated the eighteen-inch pipe which entered the cyclone room through the forward bulkhead, then connected to the bottom of the cyclone. 'Up it goes.' Benedict flung his hand upwards. 'And round it goes.' He made a stirring motion. 'The heavy stuff is thrown off and led away through that.' A smaller pipe emerged from the shoulder of the cyclone and disappeared through the farther bulkhead. 'While the lighter stuff shoots out through the top and is sprayed overboard again.'

'I understand. Now, where is the weak spot?' Ruby asked.

'Come.' Benedict led her across the room, picking their way among the litter left by the workmen who still swarmed through *Kingfisher*. They reached a steel door in the bulkhead.

'Watch your head.' They ducked into a long passageway with doors at both ends. On their right hand was an enclosed tunnel that ran the length of the room.

'This is the conveyor room,' Benedict explained. 'The concentrated gravels fall through a hot air draught from an electric furnace to dry them. They are gathered on a conveyor belt, concealed in that tunnel, and carried through into the X-ray room.'

'This is where you will fit it?' Ruby asked.

'Yes. In the conveyor tunnel. It will mean moving that inspection hatch back twelve feet to give us the space.'

Ruby nodded. 'The man who will do the work – can you trust him?'

'Yes. He has worked for me before.' Benedict did not add that the same man had designed the electronic equipment for the balloons used by the Ring, and had flown out from Japan to convert the ASDIC equipment on *Wild Goose*.

'All right.' Ruby seemed satisfied. More and more she was becoming the driving force in the alliance, bolstering Benedict's resolution when he showed timidity or when he tried to evade the actions which must, in time, lead to a confrontation with Johnny Lance.

'Let's see the X-ray room.'

It was a tiny cupboard-like compartment. The floor, roof and all four walls were clad with thick sheet lead. Suspended from the roof was the X-ray machine, and under it a circular table whose surface was covered with a honeycomb-patterned stainless steel sheet.

'The concentrated gravel spills on to the table, and the table revolves under the X-ray machine which flouresces each diamond and the computer picks it up and reports its size and exact position on the table. The computer then commands one of those – ' Benedict pointed to a forest of hard plastic tubes, each attached to a metal arm. ' – to swing out over the table exactly above the diamond and suck it up. The computer selects the correct diameter of tube for the size of the diamond – and, after the tube has obeyed the computer, the table passes under a second X-ray machine which confirms that the diamond has been collected. If, by chance, the tube fails to suck up the stone, then the computer automatically sends the table on another circuit. If, however, the diamond is safely gathered then the waste material is scraped from the table and it swings round to pick up more gravel from the cyclone room – and repeat the whole process. The system is 100 per cent effective. Every single diamond is recovered by it. Even stones as small as sugar grains.'

'Where is the computer?' Ruby asked.

'There.' Benedict pointed through the small leaded glass window which over-looked the X-ray table. Beyond it was another small compartment. Ruby flattened her nose against the glass, and peered in. The computer occupied most of the room, a huge glossy enamelled cabinet not unlike a refrigerator despite the switches and dials. Benedict peered in beside her.

'The computer runs the entire operation. It controls the flow of compressed air into the dredger pipe, it regulates the cyclone, runs the X-ray machine and the table, it weighs and counts the diamonds recovered before depositing them in a safe, and it even navigates the *Kingfisher* and reports to the bridge her exact position over the seabed, it checks the lubrication and temperature of the engines and power plant and on request will make a complete and immediate report of the whole or any part of the operation.'

Ruby was still peering into the computer room.

'What happens to the diamonds once they have been picked off the revolving table?' she asked.

'They are sucked through an electronic scale which weighs each stone, then they are carried through into the computer room and deposited in that safe.' Benedict pointed out the steel door set in the bulkhead. 'The safe has a time and combination lock. So the system works without a diamond being touched by human hand.'

'Let's go and talk to the Italian peasant,' suggested Ruby, and as she turned from the window Benedict slipped his arm about her shoulders and hugged her pos-sessively.

'Not now,' snapped Ruby irritably, shrugging off his arm, and she led the way out of the X-ray compartment, passing the locked door of the computer control room opposite the door to the conveyor room. She was impressed with the ingenuity of the system – but the fact that it had been constructed by Johnny Lance made her angry.

Her loyalties had changed completely, going to the highest bidder.

Sergio Caporetti felt a small twinge of pity when he looked at Ruby Lance. So thin, and with a backside like a boy. She would be little comfort to a man on a cold night. Sergio worked the cheroot from one corner of his mouth to the other, anointing the stub with saliva in the process. Also she was cold-blooded, he decided. Sergio had a very sensitive intuition when it came to judging the temperature of a woman's passion. Cold like a snake, he decided, his pity giving way to revulsion. He repressed a small shudder as he watched her settle on to the day couch in his cabin, and cross her long golden legs precisely. Just like a snake, she would eat a man as though he were a little hopping frog. Sergio had admiration for Johnny Lance, but – he decided – not even he would be safe with a woman like this.

'You like my ship?' he asked, an attempt at friendliness. 'She is *very* fine ship.'

Sergio actually used a more forceful adjective than *very*, one that suggested *Kingfisher* was capable of procreation, and Ruby's lips curled with disgust. She ignored the question and lit a cigarette, swinging one leg impatiently, and turned her head to stare through the porthole.

Sergio was hurt by the rebuff, but he had no time to brood on it for Benedict van der Byl came to stand in the centre of the cabin with his hands clasped lightly behind his back.

'Mr Caporetti – ' he asked quietly. 'How much do you like money?'

Sergio grinned, and pushed the grubby maritime cap to the back of his head. 'I like it pretty good, I like it better than my mother – and I love my mother like my life,' he said.

'Would you like to become a rich man?' Benedict asked, and Sergio sighed wistfully.

'Si!' he nodded. 'But it is the impossible thing. There is too much *vino*, too much lovely girls, and the cards they are cruel like – ' Sergio paused to find a suitable simile and glanced at Ruby, ' – like a thin woman. No. Money she does not stay long, she comes and she goes.'

'What would you do for twenty-five thousand pounds?' Benedict asked.

'For twenty-five thousand – ' Sergio's eyes were dark liquid and lovely as those of a dying gazelle or a woman in love, ' – there is nothing I will not do.'

Kingfisher sailed for Africa on the 4th of October. As the representative of the owners, Benedict van der Byl drove down from London to bid her *bon voyage*, and he spent an hour behind locked doors with Sergio Caporetti before the departure of the vessel.

Kingfisher made good time southwards on her first leg of the voyage, but the unscheduled delay of ten days at the island of Las Palmas infuriated Johnny. His urgently cabled enquiries from Cape Town elicited the reply that there were teething troubles in *Kingfisher*'s engine room which were being attended to in the Las Palmas dockyards. The voyage would be resumed as soon as the repairs had been effected.

The Japanese gentleman who welcomed *Kingfisher* to Las Palmas was named Kaminikoto. This was too much for Sergio's tongue, so he called him 'Kammy'.

Sergio's crew was sent ashore with the excuse that the work on *Kingfisher* was dangerous. They were installed in the best tourist hotel and liberally supplied with intoxicating liquor. Sergio did not see them for the next ten days that he and Kammy were busy on the modifications to *Kingfisher*'s computer, and recovery equipment.

During those ten days Sergio and Kammy discovered that despite physical appearances they were brothers.

Kammy had mysterious packing-cases brought on board and they worked like furies from dawn until after dark each day. Then they relaxed.

Kammy was half Sergio's size with a face like a mischievous monkey. At all times he wore a Homburg hat. On the one occasion that Sergio saw him in his bath without his headgear he discovered that Kammy was as bald as St Peter's dome.

Kammy's abundant tastes in women were identical to Sergio's. This made the hiring of partners an easy matter, for what suited the one suited the other. Sergio took south with him fond memories of the little Japanese clad only in his Homburg hat, uttering birdlike cries of encouragement and excitement, while perched like a jockey on top of a percheron mare.

When at last Sergio shepherded his debauched crew back aboard *Kingfisher* the only obvious sign of their labours was that the inspection hatch on the conveyor tunnel had been moved back twelve feet.

'It is my best work,' Kammy told Sergio. Already he was sad at the prospect of parting. They were brothers. 'I signed my name. You will remember me when you see it.'

'You good guy, Kammy. The best!' Sergio embraced him, lifting him off his feet and kissing him heartily on each cheek while Kammy clutched desperately at his Homburg.

They left him standing on the wharf, a forlorn and solitary figure, while *Kingfisher* butted out into the Atlantic and swung away southwards.

Ruefully Johnny Lance glanced over at the mountain of empty champagne bottles beyond the barbecue pits. The bill for this little party would be in the thousands, but it was not an extravagance. The guest list included all Van Der Byl Diamond Company's major creditors and their wives. Johnny Lance was showing them all what they were getting for their money. To appear prosperous was almost as reassuring to a creditor as being prosperous. He was going to stuff them full of food and champagne, show them over the *Kingfisher* and fly them back home, hoping sincerely that they would be sufficiently impressed to stop badgering him for a while – and let him get on with the business of taking the Company out into the clear.

Tracey caught his eye. Her humorous roll of the eyes was a plea for sympathy, for she was surrounded by a pack of middle-aged bankers and financiers whom champagne had made susceptible to her charms. Johnny winked at her in reply, then glanced around guiltily to find Ruby, and was relieved that she was in deep conversation with Benedict van der Byl in a far corner of the marquee.

He made his way out of the crowd to the edge of the dune, and lit a cigarette while he looked back across Cartridge Bay.

The chartered Dakotas that had flown the guests and caterers up from Cape Town were standing on the air-strip beyond the buildings.

The marquee was situated on the crest of a sand-dune overlooking the narrow entrance to the bay. The dune had been bulldozed to accommodate the tent, the laden tables, and the barbecue pits around which white-clad servants were busy, and the spitted carcasses of three sheep and a young ox were already browning crisply and emitting a cloud of fragrant steam.

Tracey watched Johnny standing out on the edge of the dune. He looked tired, she thought. The strain of the last few months had worn him. Looking back on it now she realized that every few days had thrust a crisis upon him. The terrible worry of the court case that had won them Thunderbolt and Suicide had barely ended before Johnny had faced the delays in the construction of *Kingfisher*, the bullying of creditors, the sniping of Benedict and a hundred other worries and frustrations.

He was like a prize-fighter coming out to the bell of the last round, she thought tenderly, as she studied the profile of his face now staring out to sea. His stance was still aggressive, the big jaw pushed out and the hand with the missing finger that held the cigarette balled into a fist, but there were blue shadows under his eyes and lines of tension at the corners of his mouth.

Suddenly, there was an alertness in Johnny's attitude, he shaded his eyes with a hand before turning back towards the marquee.

'All right, everyone!' he called, stilling the babble of their voices. 'Here she comes.'

Immediately the uproar was redoubled and the whole party trooped out into the sunlight, their excitement and the shrillness of their voices enhanced by the Pommery they had been walloping back since mid-morning.

'Look! There she is!'

'Where? Where?'

'I can't see her.'

'Just to the left of that cloud on the horizon.'

'Oh yes! Look! Look!'

Tracey took a second glass of champagne from one of the waiters, and carried it across to Johnny.

'Thanks.' He smiled at her with the ease that now existed between them.

'It's taken her long enough to get here.' Tracey picked out the faraway speck on the green ocean that was *Kingfisher*. 'When will she begin working?'

'Tomorrow.'

'How long will it be before we know – well, if it has come off?'

'A week.' Johnny turned to her. 'A week to be certain, but we'll know in a day or two how it's shaping up.'

They were silent then, staring out at the gradually approaching speck. The crowd lost interest quickly and drifted back to the liquor, and the fragrant steaming platters of golden-brown meat that were coming from the barbecue pits.

Tracey broke the long friendly silence at last. She spoke hesitantly, as though reluctant to bring up a painful subject.

'How long has Ruby been back now – ten days?'

'About that,' Johnny agreed, glancing at her quickly. 'I haven't seen much of her,' he admitted. 'But she seems to be a lot more relaxed – and at least she's kept off my back.'

'She and Benedict seem to have become very pally.' Tracey glanced across to where the other couple were now included in a boisterous circle of revellers.

'She bumped into him in London.' Johnny agreed, sounding offhand. 'She tells me they had lunch a couple of times.'

She waited for him to continue, to express some suspicion or reservation, but he seemed to have no further interest in the subject; instead he began running over the day's further arrangements with her.

'I'm relying on you to take charge of the wives when we go aboard. Keep an eye on Mrs Larsen particularly – she's up to her gills in bubbly.'

For the next two hours that it took *Kingfisher* to make her approach and enter the channel of Cartridge Bay, Johnny hardly took his eyes from her unusual silhouette. She was not a pretty vessel but the white lightning insignia of Van Der Byl Diamonds on her funnel gave her a special beauty in his eyes. As she passed below them and entered the bay, Larsen proposed a toast to her successful career, then they all descended the dune and climbed into the waiting Land-Rovers and drove round the bay to meet her. By the time they arrived *Kingfisher* had made fast alongside the jetty, and Captain Sergio Caporetti was waiting to welcome them aboard.

He stood at the head of the gangway, and sensible to the importance of the moment he was decked in his finest and best; a double-breasted suit with a cream and lilac pinstripe set off the tomato-red silk tie, but his two-tone black and white crocodile skin shoes drew attention to his large feet and his gait was that of an emperor penguin. A liberal application of a hair pomade with a penetrating smell of violets had flattened his black hair into a shiny slick, bisected by the ruler-straight line of white scalp which was his parting. However, the aroma of the pomade was at odds with the particularly stinky cheroot of a brand which Sergio reserved for weddings, funerals and other special occasions.

His beautiful gazelle eyes became passionate and dark as they lit on Fifi Larsen. Mrs Larsen's tight-fitting slacks moved as though they were full of live rabbits and her pink sweater was straining its seams. Her eyes were sparkling with champagne and she giggled without apparent reason, flushing under Sergio's scrutiny.

The tour of *Kingfisher* began, Sergio Caporetti taking up an escort position directly behind Mrs Larsen. They had hardly descended the first ladder when Mrs Larsen let out a small squeak and shot about eighteen inches into the air, before coming back to earth with all her plentiful woman-hood aquiver.

'My dear Fifi, whatever is wrong?' Her husband was all solicitude, while behind her Sergio Caporetti wore an expression of cherubic innocence. Johnny felt dizzy with alarm, for he had seen Sergio's great hairy paw settling comfortably on to those majestic buttocks. Mrs Fifi Larsen had been thoroughly goosed.

In relieved disbelief Johnny heard her reply, which was preceded by another giggle.

'I seem to have twisted my ankle. Perhaps there is somewhere I could sit down.'

Johnny looked around frantically for Tracey to get Mrs Larsen out of Sergio's clutching range, but before he could signal her, Fifi was limping away on Sergio Caporetti's arm, bravely declining all offers of help.

'Please don't let me spoil your fun. I'll just sit in the Captain's cabin for a few minutes.'

Quickly Johnny moved up beside the silver-haired Larsen and resolved to stay close beside him. Even if he could not prevent Fifi visiting Sergio's quarters, he was going to make good and sure that the husband didn't join the party.

'This is the explosives locker.' Johnny took Larsen's arm and led him away. 'We keep a store of plastique explosives for underwater blasting – '

Larsen's concern at his wife's injury dissolved and he became immersed in the tour of *Kingfisher*. Johnny followed the line of production for him from the moment the gravel was sucked in through the dredge.

As they left the cyclone room Johnny preceded him, holding the steel door open for Larsen.

'From the cyclone the concentrates pass through here into – ' He stopped with surprise as they entered the narrow compartment beyond the cyclone.

'What's wrong, Lance?' Larsen demanded.

'No. It's nothing,' Johnny assured him. After the surprise of finding that the inspection plate in the conveyor tunnel had been moved he realized that it was as well from a security angle. Probably the marine architects had ordered the modification. 'The concentrates are carried through into the next compartment to the X-ray room. This way, please.'

As Johnny led the way to the next door he resolved to check with the architects. Larsen asked a question and he replied and the conveyor tunnel was forgotten. They went through into the X-ray room.

'He noticed it.' Benedict puffed quickly and nervously at the cigarette cupped in his hand. 'He doesn't miss a thing. The bastard.'

'He noticed it, yes. But he accepted it.' Ruby was definite. 'I know him. I was watching him. He was disturbed for a second then he rationalized it. I could almost see his mind work. He accepted it.'

They stood together on the exposed angle of *Kingfisher*'s bridge. Suddenly Ruby laughed.

'Don't look so worried,' she warned him merrily. 'We are being watched by your sister again. She's down on the foredeck. Come.'

Still smiling she led him around the angle of the bridge house, and out of sight she was immediately deadly serious again.

'That sister of yours is getting suspicious. We must keep away from each other until you tell Johnny.'

Benedict nodded.

'When are you going to tell him?' she demanded.

'Soon.'

'How soon?' Ruby would not be able to rest until it was out in the open, until Benedict had committed himself, yet she must not push him too hard.

'As soon as *Kingfisher* runs the Company under. I will pick the moment that he is beaten financially, then I will tell him. I want it to be the *coup de grâce*.'

'When will it be, Benedict darling? I am so anxious to be with you – without all this subterfuge.'

Benedict opened his mouth to reply and froze like that, his expression changing slowly into that of a man who doubts the evidence of his own eyes. He was staring over Ruby's shoulder.

Ruby turned quickly. The curtain across the Captain's porthole behind her was open a chink. She looked in upon a spectacle of such whole-hearted rubicund magnitude that it should have occurred only to Olympus between Jupiter and Juno.

In the cabin Fifi Larsen was receiving treatment for her sprained ankle.

'Well, you've got your toy now. Let's hope for all our sakes you can do something with it,' Benedict smiled pleasantly as he came across to where Johnny stood with Larsen under the great gallows-shaped gantry on the foredeck of *Kingfisher* that would raise and lower the dredging head.

'Toy, Mr van der Byl?' Larsen's white eyebrows bristled. 'Surely you have no doubts? I mean, now that you've got this Thunderbolt and Suicide concession?'

'Oh, I wouldn't say doubts, Mr Larsen. Reservations perhaps, but not really doubts. Mr Lance has been the champion of this venture. His enthusiasm has carried it – in the face of all opposition. Even that of my late father.' Benedict turned to Larsen smoothly.

'Your father opposed the scheme? I didn't know that!' Larsen was perturbed.

'Not opposed it, Mr Larsen.' Benedict smiled reassuringly. 'Not really opposed it. But you will notice that he was prepared to risk your money – not his own. That will give you some idea of how he felt.'

There was a chilled silence, before Larsen turned to Johnny.

'Well, Lance, thank you for an interesting day. Very interesting. I'll be watching your progress with attention – close attention.' And he turned away and strode to where a subdued and demure Fifi was waiting with a group of the other wives.

'Thanks.' Johnny gave Benedict a bleak grin.

'Don't mention it.' Benedict smiled that charming boyish smile.

'At the end of this week I'll take that little speech of yours, roll it into a ball and ram it down your throat,' Johnny promised him softly, and Benedict's expression changed. His eyes slitted and his grin showed his teeth and tightened the soft line of his jaw.

'You're pretty slick with your mouth, Lance.'

They glared at each other, the antagonism so apparent, as elemental as a pair of rutting stags, that they were suddenly the centre of all attention. The guests stared curiously, aware of the drama but not understanding it.

Ruby started forward quickly to intervene, taking Johnny's elbow, her voice sugary.

'Oh, Benedict, do you mind if I talk to Johnny a moment? I have to know if he's returning to Cape Town with me this evening.'

She led him away, and the tension dissolved. The disappointed guests began drifting to the gangplank and filing down on to the jetty.

In the confusion of embarkation aboard the two Dakotas, Johnny managed to exchange a last word with Tracey.

'You'll stay here until you know?' she asked. He nodded.

'Good luck, Johnny. I'll pray for you,' she whispered, then followed Ruby Lance up into the fuselage of the Dakota.

Johnny watched the two big aircraft taxi down to the end of the strip, turn in succession and roar away into the purple and red sky of evening.

After they had gone it was very still, and the silence of the desert was complete. Johnny sat in the open Land-Rover and smoked a cigarette while the night came down around him.

He was uneasy, aware of a deep-down tickle of apprehension and foreboding which he could not pin down.

The last glow of sunset faded from the western sky, and the desert stars were bright and hard and close to the earth, silvering the dome of space with the splendour that the city-dweller would never guess at.

Still Johnny hunched in the seat of the open Land-Rover trying to explore the source of his uneasiness, but with so little success that at last he must attribute it to the strain and fatigue of the last few months, his involvement with Tracey, his steadily worsening relationship with Ruby – and the latest clash with Benedict.

He flicked the stub of his cigarette away, watching morosely the explosion of red sparks as it struck the earth, then he started the Land-Rover and drove slowly down towards the jetty.

Kingfisher's lights were smeared in paths of yellow and silver across the still waters of the bay. Every porthole was lit brightly, giving her the festive air of a cruise ship.

Johnny left the Land-Rover at the head of the jetty, and walked out to her. The muted throb of her engines cheered him a little, the knowledge that the vessel was preparing for the morrow.

On deck he paused beside the gigantic compressed air tanks, each the size of a steam locomotive, and checked the pressure gauges. The needles were moving perceptibly around the dials, and his mood lightened a little.

He went up the ladder to the bridge, and into the chart-room where Sergio and Hugo were drinking coffee.

'Not my fault, Mr Lance,' Sergio began defensively. 'I am a gentleman – I cannot refuse a lady.'

'You'll dig your own grave with that spade of yours one day,' Johnny warned him grimly, as he went to the chart table and hung over it.

'Now let's get cracking.' Johnny's sense of dread lifted completely as he looked down at the large-scale Admiralty chart. The twin humps of Thunderbolt and Suicide were clearly marked. 'Hugo, have you got the prospecting schedules?'

'There, on the table.' Hugo and Sergio came to stand on each side of Johnny while he opened the bound file of typewritten sheets.

'The soundings we made differ from the Admiralty chart. We'll put in our figures, before we plot the dredging pattern.'

The three of them settled over the chart with dividers and parallel to begin marking in the path that *Kingfisher* would follow through the maze of reefs and gullies.

It was long after midnight before Johnny made his way wearily to the guest cabin below the bridge. He kicked off his shoes, lay on the bunk to rest a moment before undressing and fell into a deathlike sleep of exhaustion.

He was awakened by one of the crew with a mug of coffee and he pulled on a windbreaker before hurrying on to the bridge.

Kingfisher was just passing out through the channel of Cartridge Bay into the open sea, and Sergio grinned at him from where he stood beside the helm.

Dawn was only a lemon-coloured promise over the desert behind them, and the sea was black as washed anthracite, kicked into a chop by the small morning wind. They stood on the darkened bridge and sipped steaming coffee, cupping their hands around the enamel mugs.

Then they turned and ran south, parallel to the desert which was now touched with hot orange and violet. The sea birds were up, a flight of malgas turned to glowing darts of fire by the early sun as they winged swiftly across the bows.

With a dramatic suddenness the sun came up over the horizon, and highlighted the chalk-white cliffs of Thunderbolt and Suicide far ahead so that they shone like beacons on the cold green sea. The curtains of spray that burst on the islands flashed and faded as they shot into the sky and fell again.

Wild Goose was waiting for them lying under the lee of the islands, but she came out to meet them, staggering and plunging theatrically over the short uneasy sea that hooked around the islands or boiled through the gap between them.

The radio telephone began crackling and squawking as the sighting reports from Johnny's watch towers on the shore started coming in, cross referencing to give *Kingfisher* her position over the ground. There were short exchanges between Sergio and Hugo on *Wild Goose* as they came together, and the little trawler worked in close, ready to give assistance with the laying of the cables if she were needed.

But standing in the angle of the bridge, Sergio Caporetti had the situation under his control. The grubby marine cap pushed to the back of his head and a long black cheroot stuck in the side of his mouth, he stood balanced on the balls of his feet, his eyes darting from judging the set of the sea surf to the repeater of the computer which was feeding him his soundings and position – yet attentive to the R/T reports from shore and from *Wild Goose*.

Johnny was contented with his choice of man as he watched Sergio at work. *Kingfisher* crept slowly up into the lee of Suicide Island, half a mile from the pearly white cliffs, then she hung there a moment before Sergio punched one of the buttons on her control panel.

From forward there was the harsh metallic roar of an anchor cable running out, and as *Kingfisher* backed away leaving a yellow painted buoy the size of a barrage balloon bobbing under the cliffs of Suicide so one of the massive deck winches began automatically paying out its six-inch steel cable.

Kingfisher backed and crept forward, drifted down on the current or butted up against it while she went through the laborious but delicate operation of laying her four anchors at each point of the compass. Chained above each anchor floated the huge yellow buoys, and from each buoy the steel cables led to the winches on *Kingfisher*'s deck. On instructions from the computer the winches on each quarter would pay out or reel in the cable to hold *Kingfisher* steady over the ground while she worked.

It was mid afternoon before *Kingfisher* was ready, pinned down like an insect to a board, and the computer reported that she was directly over the gully that Johnny had selected as the starting point. She had twenty-five fathoms of water under her – and then the thick bank of gravel.

'All is ready.' Sergio turned to Johnny, who had stood by quietly all this time – not interfering in the task of positioning. 'You will begin the programme now?'

'Yes.' Johnny stirred himself.

'I would like to watch,' Sergio suggested, and Johnny nodded.

'All right, come.' Sergio handed over the bridge to the helmsman and they went down to the armoured door of the computer room.

Johnny opened the lock. There were only two keys to this compartment. Johnny had one and Benedict van der Byl had the other. He had insisted on having the duplicate, and Johnny had reluctantly agreed not knowing that the key would be used in Las Palmas.

The heavy steel door swung back, and Johnny stepped over the coaming and seated himself before the console of the computer. Covered in cellophane and suspended on a clip above the keyboard of the computer were the cards containing the various programme codes.

Johnny selected the sheet headed: PRIMARY OPERATION: DREDGING AND RECOVERY, and began feeding the code into the computer, punching it on the keyboard.

'Beta, stroke, oh, oh, seven, alpha.'

And within the enamelled console, a change of sound heralded the beginning of the new programme, the hum of her reels and the click of the selectors, while on her control panel the lights blinked and flashed.

Now the computer's screen began to answer the instruction, spelling out her response like a typewriter.

'New programme.'
'Primary Operation. Dredging and Recovery.'
'Phase One.'

'Initiate safety procedure:–
a) Report air pressure . . . 1
b) Report air pressure . . . 2'

Johnny leaned back in the padded stool and watched the exhaustive check that the computer now made of *Kingfisher*'s equipment, typing out the results on the screen.

'What she do now?' Sergio asked curiously, as though he had never spent ten days in this compartment assisting his Japanese friend. Johnny explained the procedure briefly.

'How come you know this so good?' Sergio enquired.

'I spent a month at the Computer Company's head office in America last year while they designed this machine.'

'You the only one in the Company who can work it?'

'Mr Benedict van der Byl has done the course as well as I.' Johnny told him, then he leaned forward again. 'Now she is set.'

The screen on the computer reported itself satisfied.

'Phase One Completed.
Initiate Phase Two.
Lowering and siting of dredge head.'

Johnny stood up. 'Okay, let's get upstairs.'

He locked the door of the computer room and followed Sergio up to the bridge.

Johnny went to stand beside the repeater screen on the bridge, which was relaying the computer's signals exactly as they were printed on the main screen in the compartment below. He could see out through the windows of the wheelhouse, and he watched the automatic response of the heavy equipment on the foredeck.

The gantry swung forward, and the steel arms picked the dredge head from its chocks, and lifted it with the armoured suction hose dangling behind it. Then the gantry swung back, and with a jerky mechanical movement lowered the head through the square opening in the deck. This well pierced the hull, and through it the hose began to snake – a monstrous black python sliding into its hole. The huge reels that held the hose revolved smoothly, as the dredge was lowered to the sea bed.

'Head on bottom.'

The computer screen reported, and the hose reels stopped abruptly.

'Phase Two Completed.
Initiate Phase Three.
Cyclone Revolutions 300.
Vent dredge pump.'

There was a rising high-pitched whine now, like the approach of a jet aircraft. The sound reached a peak, and steadied – and immediately another sound overlaid it. The dull roar of high-pressure air through water, a sound of such power and excitement that Johnny felt the hair on his forearms prickle erect. He stood still as a statue, his expression rapt and his lips set in a small secret smile. That sound was the culmination of two years of planning and endeavour, the sweet reward of the driving dedication that had made a dream into reality.

Suddenly he wished that Tracey was with him to share this moment, and then he knew instinctively that she had deliberately left him alone to savour his moment of triumph.

He grinned then, as he watched the thick black hose engorge and pulse with internal life, like a great artery – pumping, pumping, pumping.

In his imagination Johnny could see the rich porridgy mixture of sea-water and mud and gravel that shot up the hose into the spinning cyclone, he could imagine the steel head on the sea bed below the hull surging rhythmically to stir the sand and pound loose any gravel that pressure had welded into a conglomerate.

From the waste pipe over *Kingfisher's* stern poured a solid steam of dirty yellow water mixed with the sand and gravel that had been rejected and spun out of the cyclone. It stained the green sea with a cloudy fecal discharge, like the effluent from a sewage outlet.

For three days and two nights *Kingfisher's* pumps roared, and she inched forward along the marine gully like a fussy housewife vacuuming every speck of dust from her floor. As the third evening spread its dark cloak over her, Johnny Lance sat on the padded seat in front of the computer console. He sat forward on the stool with his elbows on his knees and his face in his hands for a full hour. He sat like that in the attitude of despair.

When he lifted his head, his face was haggard and the lines of defeat were clearly cut into his features with the cold chisel of failure.

From the meagre recovery of small diamonds that *Kingfisher* had made in the last three days it was clear beyond reasonable doubt that despite all the indications the Thunderbolt and Suicide field would not support the running costs of the vessel let alone cover the overheads, or the interest charges and capital repayments on the loan account.

Van Der Byl Diamond Company was finished – and Johnny Lance was financially ruined beyond any possibility of ever finding redemption.

It remained only for the jackals to assemble and squabble over the carcass.

Sergio Caporetti leaned over the railing of the bridge, blowing long streamers of blue cheroot smoke from mouth and nostrils to help foul a morning which was already thick and grey with sea-fret. The islands of Thunderbolt and Suicide were blanketed by the mist, but the surf broke against their hidden cliffs like distant artillery and the sea birds' voices were plaintive and small lost souls in the void.

Wild Goose came bustling up out of the mist, swinging in under *Kingfisher's* side to hover there under power with two of her crew fending off.

Hugo Kramer stuck his white blond head out of the wheelhouse window, and shouted up at the deck.

'Okay, boss. Come on!'

Sergio watched the tall figure on *Kingfisher's* deck rouse and look around like a man waking from sleep. Johnny Lance lifted his head and looked up at the bridge, and Sergio noticed that he was unshaven, a new beard darkened his jaw and emphasized its prominence. He looked as though he had not slept, and he hunched into the wind-breaker with the collar turned up against the mist. He did not smile, but lifted one hand in farewell salute to Sergio – who noticed incongruously that the index finger was missing from the hand. Somehow, that pathetic little detail struck Sergio. He was sorry, truly sorry. But there is always a loser in every game, and twenty-five thousand pounds is a lot of money.

'Good luck, Johnny.'

'Thanks, Sergio.' Johnny went to the rail lugging his briefcase and swung over it; he dropped swiftly down the steel rungs set in *Kingfisher*'s hull and jumped the narrow gap of surging water to *Wild Goose*'s deck.

The trawler's engine bellowed, and she pulled away, rounding on to a course for Cartridge Bay. Johnny Lance stood on her open deck looking back at *Kingfisher*.

'He's a good guy.' Sergio shook his head with regret.

'He's a boss,' the helmsman grunted. 'No boss is any good.'

'Hey, you! I am also a boss,' Sergio challenged him.

'Like I said.' The helmsman suppressed a grin.

'I kiss your mother,' Sergio insulted him with dignity, then changed the subject. 'I go below now, take over.'

Sergio opened the door to the control room with the duplicate key. He closed the door behind him, seated himself at the console and took from his pocket a sheet of paper headed: KAMINIKOTO SECONDARY RECOVERY PROGRAMME.

Ten minutes later he came out of the control room and locked the door.

'Kammy, I love you,' he chuckled as he closed off the water-tight doors that isolated this deck from the one above. He wound the locking bars into position to ensure that he was not interrupted by one of his own crew.

From the tool cupboard on the bulkhead he selected a pair of set spanners and went through into the conveyor room. It took him twenty minutes to unscrew the heavy, deeply threaded bolts that secured the hatch. It had been designed to resist easy entry – a deterrent to casual investigation, but at last Sergio could lift the steel plate off its seating.

He eyed the small square opening with distaste, and reflexively sucked in his pendulous belly. The hatch had not been designed to afford passage to a man of his dimensions.

He took off his cap and jacket and hung them on the cock of one of the pipes, then he ground out his cheroot under his heel and brushed back the hair from his forehead with both hands, checked that his flashlight was in his pocket, and committed himself to the hatch.

He wriggled and kicked, and grunted and built up a heavy sweat for five minutes before he had squeezed through into the conveyor belt tunnel. He squatted on his haunches, panting heavily and flashed his torch along the tunnel. Above his head the conveyor belt carrying the gravel ran smoothly, but the residual heat from the driers made it unbearably hot. He began to crawl rapidly to the end of the tunnel.

From the inside it was impossible to tell, without measuring, that the conveyor belt tunnel was shorter by twelve feet than the external length.

The end of the tunnel was false, and beyond it was a secret cubicle only just large enough to house Kaminikoto's equipment through which all the gravel passed on its journey to the X-ray room.

The Japanese genius for miniaturization was demonstrated by the equipment in this secret cubicle. It was an almost exact copy of the sorting equipment in the main X-ray compartment – except that it had been scaled down to one tenth of the size without affecting its efficiency; in addition, this miniature plant could discriminate in the diamonds it selected. It would not allow a stone over four carats to pass through, and it screened out fixed percentages of the smaller stones – allowing only a proportion of the smaller and less valuable diamonds to proceed through into the main X-ray room.

It was an amazing piece of electronic engineering, but Sergio was unimpressed as he lay on his side in the cramped hot tunnel and began laboriously to unscrew another smaller plate in the false bulkhead.

At last it was open, and he reached through the opening; after a few seconds of fiddling and groping and heavy breathing he brought out a stainless steel cup with a capacity of about two pints. There were clamps on the cup to hold it in position below the chute under Kaminikoto's machine.

The metal cup was heavy, and Sergio placed it carefully on the deck beside him before propping himself on an elbow and shining the flashlight into the cup and took something out of it, stared at it a moment then dropped it back.

'By the blood of all the martyrs!' he gasped with shock, and then immediately contrite for his blasphemy he crossed himself awkwardly with the hand holding the flashlight. Then again he shone the torch into the cup, and shook his head in disbelief. Quickly he pulled a canvas drawstring bag from his pocket, and lying on his side he carefully poured the contents of the cup into the bag, drew the string tight and stuffed it back into his pocket where it made a big hard bulge on his hip like a paper sack of rock-candy. He clamped the stainless steel cup back into position, screwed the coverplate over the opening, and backed away down the tunnel on hands and knees.

He very badly needed a cheroot.

Four hours later Hugo Kramer shinned up the ladder on to *Kingfisher*'s deck while his helmsman took the trawler down to leeward to wait for him.

Sergio shouted down from the bridge.

'Johnny he has gone?'

'Ja!' Hugo shouted back. 'He should almost be in Cape Town by now. That Beechcraft is a fast plane.'

'Good.'

'How did it go with you?' Hugo countered.

'Come up – I'll show you.'

Sergio led him into his cabin behind the bridge and locked the door carefully. Then he went to each of the port-holes and drew the curtains across them, before crossing to his desk and switching on the reading lamp.

'Sit down.' Sergio indicated the chair opposite the desk. 'You want a drink, or something?'

'Come on,' Hugo grated impatiently. 'Stop mucking around, let's have a look.'

'Ah!' Sergio looked at him sadly. 'You Germans, you are always too much hurry. You cannot rest, enjoy life – '

'Cut the crap!' Hugo's pale eyes were on his face, and Sergio was suddenly aware that this man was dangerous, like a tiger-shark. Coldly dangerous, without malice or passion. Sergio was surprised he had not noticed it before. I must be careful with this one, he thought, and he unlocked the drawer of his desk and took out the canvas bag.

He loosened the drawstring and poured the diamonds on to the blotter. The smallest was the size of a match head – perhaps point one of a carat, and the poorest quality was black and granular-looking, ugly little industrial stones, for Kammy had been careful not to take out only the best and so distort the *Kingfisher's* recovery as to arouse suspicion. There were hundreds of these tiny crystals and chips which would fetch a few pounds in the industrial market; but there were other stones in the full range of quality and shapes and sizes – as big as green peas, or as marbles, and a few bigger than that. Some of them were perfect octahedron crystals, others water-worn, chipped or amorphous in shape.

They formed a dully glittering pile in the centre of the blotter, in all perhaps five hundred diamonds, yet all of these were dwarfed by one single stone that lay in the centre of the pile, rising out of it the way Mount Everest rises from her foothills.

There are freak diamonds so large or unusual that they become legend. Diamonds who have their own names and whose histories are recorded and invested with romance. The great 'paragons' – stones of the first water whose cut and finished weight exceed one hundred metric carats.

Africa has produced many of them: The *Jonker Diamond*, a 726–carat rough cut to a brilliant of 125 carats that hangs about the throat of the Queen of Nepal; The *Jubilee Diamond*, a superb 245–carat cushion of unearthly fire fashioned out of 650–carat rough – then the biggest of them all, a monstrous rough stone of 3,106 carats, the *Cullinan* which yielded not one, but two paragons. The *Great Star of Africa* at 530 carats and *The Cullinan II* at 317 carats. Both these stones grace the Crown Jewels of England.

Now on Sergio Caporetti's desk lay a rough stone which would add yet another paragon to the list.

'Have you weighed it?' asked Hugo, and Sergio nodded.

'How much?'

'Three hundred and twenty carats,' Sergio said softly.

'Jesus!' whispered Hugo, and Sergio crossed himself quickly to dissociate from the use of names.

Reverently Hugo Kramer leaned forward and picked up the big diamond. It filled the palm of his hand, the cleavage plane that formed its base was smooth and clean as an axe-stroke. There were bigger diamonds in history, but this diamond had a special feature which would set it in a niche of its own and endow it with peculiar value.

Its colour was the serene blue of a high summer sky.

This stone could pay half the total bill for *Kingfisher's* construction – if it were ever used for that purpose.

Hugo replaced the blue diamond on the desk and lit a cigarette without taking his eyes from it.

'This field – it is bigger – richer, far richer than we had guessed.'

Sergio nodded.

'In three days we have taken diamonds that I hoped to see once in five years,' Hugo went on as he began picking out the larger diamonds from the pile and laying them in a line across the desktop in approximate order of size, while Sergio opened his desk drawer and took out a box of his special occasion cheroots.

'We must tell the boss,' Hugo decided. He began arranging the diamonds in a neat circle about the big Blue, thinking deeply. 'He must know how rich it is before he talks to Lance. He must make arrangements. He will know what to do – he's a clever one.'

'What about these?' Sergio indicated the treasure on the desk. 'Are you going to take them off?'

Hugo hesitated. 'No,' he decided. 'We could never get rid of this big Blue through the usual channel, it is too big, too distinctive. We will keep it aboard. When the boss takes over the Company again – then we will just declare it all nice and legal. No trouble.' He stood up. 'Look after them. I must hurry if I am to get a message to Cape Town in time.'

'The Company bears my father's name, Mr Larsen. It's as simple as that.' Benedict's voice was husky with emotion, and he looked down at his hands. 'I have a duty to my father's memory.'

'My boy, well – ' Larsen came to lay his hand on Benedict's arm. 'Well, I just don't know what to say. Honour is a rare and precious thing these days.' With his free hand he was groping almost frantically for the bell on the desk behind him. He must get this signed up solid before the youngster changed his mind.

'I tried to warn you, Mr Larsen. My father and I never had any faith in this marine recovery scheme. Lance pushed it through – '

'Yes, quite so,' Larsen agreed, and turned to his assistant who came into the office at the trot in response to the bell. 'Ah, Simon. The Van Der Byl Diamond loan. Will you have an agreement made out immediately – Mr van der Byl will take over the capital amounts, and the outstanding interest as well.' By rolling his eyes Larsen tried to convey to his assistant the deadly urgency of the situation. The young man understood and fifteen minutes later laid the Agreement on Larsen's desk. Larsen unscrewed the cap of his pen and handed it to Benedict.

Larsen and three of his young men ushered Benedict out through the glass doors of the bank and across the pavement to where the Rolls stood in the reserved parking bay in Adderley Street.

Benedict settled into the back seat, acknowledged the bank official's farewells, and tapped on the chauffeur's window. As they pulled away, Ruby Lance slipped her hand through his arm and squeezed it.

'Did you get it?' she asked.

Benedict grinned happily. 'I frightened five years' growth out of old Larsen. He almost broke his neck in the hurry to give it to me.'

'Now you've got it all.' Ruby snuggled a little closer to him on the soft leather upholstery. Benedict nodded, and checked his watch.

'The meeting is set for fifteen minutes' time. I'll go up the front way, but I want you to go up in the private lift from the basement garage, and wait in my office. We will be in the Board Room. I will ring you at the right moment.'

The Rolls picked its way slowly down around the Heerengracht and double-parked outside the building. The chauffeur came to open the door, but before he alighted Benedict smiled into Ruby's face.

'This will be one of the high moments of my life,' he said softly. 'This time I've got the bastard cold.'

'I'll be waiting for you,' Ruby said, and he climbed out of the Rolls. He waited until it had turned into the entrance ramp of the basement garage, then he crossed the pavement into the main lobby of the skyscraper. He strode to the elevator with long eager strides, and his mouth kept pulling into a small excited smile.

The Board Room was set high, and the picture windows looked up at the great squat mountain, whose sheer cliffs dropped directly to the wooded slopes up which the first buildings of the city straggled.

Johnny Lance stood at the head of the table. He had lost weight in the last few days, so that his shoulders appeared bony and gaunt under the white silk shirt. He had discarded his jacket, and pulled the knot of his tie down an inch. The bones of his cheeks and jaw made harsh angles that were accentuated and not softened by the deep shades of fatigue that darkened his eyes. His hands were thrust deep into his pockets, and he spoke without reference to the sheaf of paper that lay on the table before him.

'Our working costs are as close as dammit to a hundred pounds an hour; right Mike?' And Michael Shapiro nodded. 'Well, we worked the Suicide main gully for sixty-six hours, and we recovered a princely 200 carats of the lousiest pile of junk I've ever seen. If we get a thousand quid for the lot we'll be doing well. This for an expenditure of six and a half thousand.'

Johnny paused, and looked around the table. Michael Shapiro was doodling on his note pad with fierce concentrations, Tracey van der Byl was pale, her eyes never left Johnny's face and her expression ached with pity and helpless compassion; Benedict van der Byl was looking out of the window at the mountain, he was slumped comfortably in his chair, smiling a little and listening politely.

'The Suicide main gully is one of the five most likely parts of the entire concession. It's no good, so the rest of the field may be useless. We have the two other concessions, the original fields, to try. However, it will take three or four days to get *Kingfisher* moved up the coast.' Johnny paused, and Benedict swivelled his chair, still with the small smile on his lips.

'The interest payments fall due on the 30th – three days' time. Where are you going to find one hundred and fifty thousand Rand?'

'Yes,' Johnny nodded. 'I think I can persuade Larsen to extend for a few weeks; he will bloody well have to if he wants to protect his – '

'Hold on,' Benedict murmured. 'Larsen has got nothing to do with it.'

Johnny was silent, watching him warily. 'Explain,' he invited.

'I've taken over the loan from Larsen,' Benedict told him. 'I'm not interested in extending.'

'Larsen wouldn't have negotiated without warning me.' Johnny was stricken, his disclaimer was wrung from him in pain.

'Shapiro?' Benedict turned to Michael Shapiro for confirmation.

'Sorry, Johnny. It's true. I've seen the documents.'

'Thanks, Michael.' Johnny's voice was bitter with accusations. 'Thanks for letting me know.'

'He showed me a few minutes before the meeting, Johnny. I swear I didn't know.' Michael's expression was distressed.

'Right.' Benedict straightened up in his chair, his voice was brisk. 'Let's get down to first principles. You've ruined my father's Company, Lance – but, thank God, I may be able to retrieve the situation. Call it sentiment or what you like, but I want your shares and yours.' He turned to Tracey and nodded at her.

'No,' said Tracey sharply.

'Right.' Benedict smiled at her. 'Then I'm going to hammer Johnny Lance for his full obligations. That way I get the Company anyway, but I'll make damn sure he remains an unrehabilitated bankrupt for the rest of his life.'

Tracey lifted her hand to her throat, and turned her eyes to Johnny. Waiting for him to set a lead. There was a long stark silence, then Johnny Lance dropped his eyes.

'I've still got three days.' His voice was gruff and tired.

'Three days you have.' Benedict grinned coldly. 'And you're welcome to them.'

Johnny picked up his papers and put them under one arm; he took his jacket off the back of the chair and swung it over his shoulder.

'Wait,' ordered Benedict.

'What for?' Johnny's grin was twisted. 'You've had your fun.'

Benedict lifted the receiver of the telephone on the table and dialled swiftly.

'Come through, please, darling.' He spoke into the mouthpiece and smiled at Johnny as he hung up. Then as the door opened he went to meet Ruby Lance, and kissed her on the mouth. The two of them stood, arm in arm, and looked at Johnny.

'The Company is not the only thing I've taken from you,' Benedict said softly.

'I want a divorce.' Ruby looked steadily into Johnny's face. 'Benedict and I are going to get married.'

They were all watching Johnny, and they saw him flinch. He looked from one face to the other, then his mouth tightened and his forehead furrowed.

Tracey saw his anger mounting, and her eyes flicked to Benedict's face. He was leaning forward expectantly, his lips quivering with expectation, his eyes alight with triumph. Tracey wanted to scream out a warning to Johnny, stop him falling into the trap that Benedict had set so carefully.

Johnny took a pace forward, coming up on to the balls of his feet. He was about to make his defeat total and ineradicable. Then Benedict spoiled it for himself, he goaded once more.

'Game, set and match, Johnny Lance,' he crowed.

The effort of will that Johnny made to recover his reason was not shown on his face, he made the step forward seem natural and he continued towards the door.

'The house is in your name, of course, Ruby, so would you please send my things down to the Tulbagh Hotel,' he asked quietly.

He stopped in front of the couple and spoke to Ruby.

'You'll want to protect your reputation, of course, so I'll not sue for adultery. We'll call it desertion.'

'You're eating your guts out,' jeered Benedict. 'Lance can't keep his woman. Van der Byl took her away from him. Go on, sue for adultery – let the world hear it.'

'As you wish,' Johnny agreed.

And he walked out of the Board Room to the elevators.

Johnny flopped on to the bed fully dressed, and rubbed his closed eyes with his finger-tips. He felt confused and off-balance, the edge of his mind which usually slashed quickly and incisively through a problem was dulled. This problem was so multiplied and tangled that he felt like a man in a thicket of African ebony trying to cut his way out with a blunt machete.

Without opening his eyes he groped for the telephone, and the girl on the hotel switchboard downstairs answered. He gave her a number in Kimberley.

'Person to person, Mr Ralph Ellison.'

'Fifteen minutes' delay, Mr Lance,' the girl told him.

'Okay,' Johnny replied. 'Ask room service to send me up a Chivas Regal and soda.' He suddenly needed liquor, something to dull the pain. 'Make that a double, honey – no, make it two doubles.'

He had drained both glasses by the time his Kimberley call came through.

'Ralph?' Johnny spoke into the receiver.

'Johnny, how nice of you to call.' There was an echo like distant laughter beneath those cool ambassadorial tones in Ralph Ellison's voice and Johnny knew instantly that the word was out. Damn it, he was slow – of course Benedict would have blocked him.

'Are you still interested in a deal on the Thunderbolt and Suicide Concession?' Johnny loosed a despairing long-range shot.

'Of course, you know we are always interested,' Ralph replied.

'The price is two million.' Johnny lost interest and lay back on the bed, closing his eyes again. He knew Ralph was having his revenge – you didn't take this boy to court and win without sowing yourself a minefield to retreat over.

'Two million,' Ralph murmured. 'Now that's a little high – for a field that's yielding 200 carats of small industrial diamonds per 10,000 loads, that's definitely on the high side. Of course we wouldn't want that battleship of yours either – we are not starting our own navy.' Ralph chuckled juicily. 'We could talk around fifty to a hundred grand – no more than that, Johnny.'

'Okay, Ralph.' Johnny spoke wearily. 'Thanks all the same. We'll have a drink together sometime.'

'Any time, Johnny,' Ralph agreed. 'Any time at all. You call me.'

Johnny dropped the receiver back on its hook and looked at the ceiling. He had heard that a gunshot wound was numb at first – he felt numb now. All that energy had seeped out of him, he had lost direction.

The telephone shrilled and he picked it up. The girl on the switchboard asked politely:

'Are you finished, Mr Lance?'

'Yes,' said Johnny. 'You might say that.'

'Is there anything else you require?' The girl sounded puzzled.

'Yes, honey, send up the hemlock.'

'I beg your pardon?'

'Two more big fat whiskies, please.'

He drank them in the bath, and while he dried himself the doorbell tinkled. He wound the bath towel round his waist and went through to open the door.

Tracey stepped into the bedroom and closed the door behind her. They stood looking at each other for a long moment. Her eyes were big and dark, reflecting his agony faithfully.

'Johnny –' Her voice was husky, and she reached out and laid the palm of her hand on his cheek. His shoulders sagged, and he moved close to her, his forehead sinking on to her shoulder. He sighed, a ragged broken exhalation of breath.

'Come,' she said, and led him to the bed. Leaving him there she went to the windows and closed the curtains.

It was warm and safe in the half dark of the curtained room, and they held each other as they had done long years before. Clinging together, so their breathing mingled, and it was not necessary to speak.

When they became lovers it seemed that they had waited all their lives for that moment.

Afterwards he lay in her arms and he felt strength flowing back into him drawing it from her. When he sat up in the bed the bemused, almost dazed expression had gone. His jaw was out and his eyes were bright.

'We've still got three days,' he said.

'Yes.' She sat up beside him. 'Go, Johnny. Go quickly, don't waste another moment.'

'I'll pull *Kingfisher* out of the main gully. I'll find those diamonds. They are there. I *know* they are there. I'll take her right down into the jaws of Thunderbolt and Suicide, I'll find those bloody diamonds – damned if I won't.' He swung his legs off the bed, reached for his clothes, glancing at his wrist-watch as he did so. 'Four o'clock. I can get to Cartridge Bay a few minutes after dark. Will you call the communications office, ask them to radio Cartridge Bay and have a flare path set for me, and *Wild Goose* standing by to run me out?'

'I'll phone them from here. Then I'll take a bath – you go on. Don't waste time.' Tracey nodded eagerly, and Johnny let his eyes drop down over her body. He reached out and touched one big white breast almost diffidently.

'You are beautiful – I hate to go.'

'It will all be here, waiting for you, when you get back.'

'It wasn't the way I'd planned it. It wasn't good the way I'd dreamed about it.' Benedict paced angrily over the floor of the Old Man's study, swinging towards the windows and pausing to stare out at the mountain across the valley.

'You hurt him. You crushed him.' Ruby moved restlessly in her chair across the room from him, curling her long golden legs defensively under her, sitting like a cat in the big chair. She was worried, and it showed in the tiny crows' feet at the corners of her eyes and the way she held her lips pursed. She should have anticipated this reaction from him, she should have known that this moment of triumph could never match his anticipation of it – and that revenge must always be followed by sour distaste and a feeling of disappointment. She realized that her safest course was to leave him alone now, she should never have returned with him to the old house on Wynberg Hill. She stood up.

'Darling.' She crossed to him. 'I'm going home now. I want to pack his clothes and get rid of them. I want to wipe out every memory of him. From now on it's you and I – together.'

She stretched up to kiss him, but Benedict turned his face away.

'Oh! So you're going, are you?' His expression was petulant, his lips pouting spitefully.

'We're both tired, darling. Let us both rest a while – and I'll come back later this evening.'

'So now you're giving the orders, are you?' He laughed nastily.

'Darling – '

'And cut out all the darlings. We pulled a deal and it didn't work out. You were meant to be a club to break his skull – and do you know something? He didn't give a damn. I was watching him, he was pleased – yes! He was bloody well delighted to get rid of you.'

'Benedict – ' She stepped back.

'Listen.' He stepped close to her, and pushed his face towards hers. 'If you're so bloody anxious to go, why don't you bloody well go – and keep going. If he doesn't want you – then I sure as hell don't want you either.'

'Benedict,' she whispered. The colour faded from her face, leaving it washed white as beach sand. She stared at him in horror, as her dreams began to fall into ruins around her. 'You don't mean that.'

'I don't? Is that so?' He threw back his head and laughed again. 'Listen, you got some nice diamonds and a mink coat. You got a big house in Bishopscourt – now, that's pretty good pay for a whore.'

'Benedict – ' She gasped at the insult, but he wasn't listening.

'I proved I could have you, didn't I? I proved I could take you away from him – and that's what it was all about. Now, why don't you go on home like a good girl.'

'The machine. I know about that thing in *Kingfisher*.' It was a mistake. Until then she still had a chance. His face changed shape and the blood flooded into it. His voice when he spoke was unsteady, thick with rage for his lips seemed to have swollen.

'Try it,' he whispered back at her. 'Go on, try it. They'll give you fifteen years in a woman's prison, my beauty. And think about this also – ' He showed her his hand, holding it like a blade before her eyes. 'I'll kill you. I swear before God, I'll kill you with my bare hands. You know I'll do it – you know enough about me now.'

She backed away from him, and he followed her still holding his hand at her throat.

'You've been paid. Now get out.'

A few seconds longer she stood before him, and he was not too far gone in rage to see the fear in her eyes mingle with something else that made her eyes slit and drew her lips back to show the little white teeth.

'All right,' she said. 'I'll go.' And she walked from the room, stepping daintily, the long yellow hair swinging against her shoulders.

Ruby drove slowly for her vision was blurred with her tears. Twice other drivers hooted at her but she kept both hands clenched on the wheel and stared ahead, following the De Waal Drive around the lower slopes of the mountain. Before she reached the University she swung off the road and drove up through the pine forests until she reached the car park behind the Cecil Rhodes Memorial. She left the car and walked down on to the wide paved terrace below the Greek columns and stone steps where the mounted statue eternally searched the horizon with one hand lifted to shade his eyes.

She went to the parapet and looked across to the far blue mountains of the Helderberg. She hugged herself about the shoulders for the wind through her silk summer dress was as cold as her misery.

Now the tears broke over her lids and slid down her cheeks to fall unheeded on to the silken front of her dress. They were tears of self-pity, but also the tears of an anger as searing cold as dry ice.

'The swine,' she whispered through lips that trembled. Near her two young students sitting on the parapet, kicking their legs over the drop beneath them and hugging each other in the abandon of first love, turned to glance at her.

The boy whispered to the girl, and she giggled in unthinking cruelty – but looked away as Ruby directed a long venomous glare at her. Then in embarrassment the couple scrambled off the parapet and moved away, leaving her alone.

Never for one moment did she consider standing aside, Benedict's threats meant nothing – her only concern was to take the action which would injure him most severely. The consequences to herself were not part of her calculations. She wanted only to select the swiftest and most terrible vehicle of retribution. As the dark clouds that fogged her reason slowly cleared, the means came to her readily.

Johnny was staying at the Tulbagh Hotel.

She turned and ran back to her car, the long yellow banner of her hair floating behind her like the pennant at the tip of a cavalry lance. She drove fast until she hit the down town rush-hour crowds. The tears dried on her face as she crawled, fuming with impatience, along the slow river of traffic.

It was after five when she parked in a loading zone outside the entrance to the Tulbagh and ran into the lobby.

'What room is Mr Lance in?' she demanded of the girl at the desk.

'Mr Lance checked out an hour ago.' Curiously the girl examined Ruby's ruined make-up.

'Did he say where he was going?' Ruby snapped at her, feeling the sickening slide of disappointment within her.

'No, madam.' The girl shook her head. 'But he was in a hurry.'

'Damn! Damn!' Ruby swore bitterly. She turned from the desk undecided where next to look. Perhaps Johnny had gone back to the office.

Across the lobby the elevator doors slid open and Tracey Hartford stepped out. Even in her impatience Ruby recognized in the glow that seemed to emanate from her that Tracey was a girl freshly risen from the bed of the man she loved. There was not a vestige of doubt in Ruby's mind as to the identity of that man.

The shock of it paralysed her for a moment. Then she felt the urge to cross the floor and claw that smug smile from Tracey's face. She fought it down, and instead she stepped into her path as Tracey started for the glass outer doors.

'Where is Johnny?' she demanded, and Tracey came up short. Her little gasp of guilt confirmed Ruby's suspicion.

'Where is he damn you!' Ruby's voice was pitched low but brittle with emotion.

'He's not here.' Tracey recovered herself, quickly masking her expression.

'Where has he gone? I must see him.'

'He's flown up to Cartridge Bay.'

'When did he leave? It's important – terribly important.'

'An hour ago. He'll be airborne already.'

'Can you get a message to him?' In her impatience Ruby caught Tracey's wrist, holding her in a grip that marked the skin.

'I can radio him – ' Tracey pulled her hand free.

'No,' Ruby cut in quickly. She could not have her message shouted across the ether for all to hear. 'Can you follow him – charter a plane?'

Tracey shook her head. 'They won't fly to an unscheduled airfield after dark.'

'Then you must follow him – by car. You must drive up there.'

'Why?' Tracey stared at her, puzzled by this strange insistence, noticing the dried tears and the wild look in Ruby's eyes. 'It's an eight-hour drive.'

'I'll tell you. Can we use Johnny's room?'

Tracey he hesitated, remembering the unmade bed. Then the hotel manager came into the lobby and Tracey turned to him with relief.

The Beechcraft bucked suddenly and dropped a wing, instinctively Johnny corrected the lunge with stick and rudder then glanced quickly at his instrument panel for an explanation. There was none to be found there, so he looked over the wing and for the first time noticed the dust on the great plains below him; it was moving low against the earth in long streamers like mist, and the setting sun turned it to mauve and old gold. With a prickle of alarm he scanned the horizon ahead, and saw it coming down from the north like a great moving range of blue mountains. Even as he watched it, it rolled across the low sun, turning it into a sullen red orb. The light in the cockpit changed to a weird glow as though the door to a furnace had been thrown open.

Again the Beechcraft crabbed awkwardly as another gust of high wind hit her, and at the same moment the radio crackled and came alive.

'Zulu Sugar Peter Tango Baker this is Alexandra Bay Control, come in please.'

The voice of the controller was almost unintelligible with storm static. Johnny reached for the transmit switch of the radio, then stopped his hand. He thought quickly. He could guess they were trying to reach him to cancel his flight approval. That was a big northern boiling down out of the desert. They would abort his flight, and divert him out of the path of the storm.

He checked his wrist-watch. Twenty minutes' flying time to Cartridge Bay. No – he was flying full into the eye of the wind, say twenty-five or thirty minutes. Quickly he searched the coast on his port side and saw the long white lines of surf stretched ahead into the thickening purple gloom. The coast was still clear, it might stay that way for another thirty minutes.

'Zulu Sugar Peter Tango Baker this is Alexandra Bay. I say again – come in. Come in. Zulu Sugar Peter Tango Baker.' The agitation in the controller's voice came through over the static.

There was a fair chance of getting in to Cartridge Bay, racing the storm and winning. He could edge out to the westward and come in from the sea, pick up *Kingfisher*'s riding lights as a beacon and sneak in under the leading edge of the dust clouds. If he missed he could turn and run with the wind for home. The radio was hissing and crackling angrily now, the controller's voice sometimes lost in the interference, sometimes coming through strongly.

' – Cancelled. I say again: your flight approval is cancelled. Do you read me, Zulu Sugar Peter Tango Baker. Come in, please. – Beaufort force seven. – visibility in the storm area – I say again, there is nil visibility in – '

The norther would roar for days now and with it would blow away his last chance of working the gap at Thunderbolt and Suicide.

Johnny switched off the radio, cut off contact with Control and immediately it was strangely quiet in the cockpit. He settled himself down into the bucket seat, and eased open the throttles, watching the needles creep up around the dials of the rev counters.

Now he was down to an altitude of three hundred feet and the Beechcraft was leaping about like a hooked marlin. He was flying her on instruments for outside the cockpit it was completely dark. He could not see his own wingtips, but above him the stars still showed. He was riding the vanguard of the storm, and the dust clouds were ahead, racing to meet him and blanket the flare path at Cartridge Bay.

Every few seconds he darted a quick glance ahead, hoping to pick up the lights, then his eyes flew back to the instrument panel.

'Now,' he thought grimly. 'It should be now. I should be over the grounds. Thirty seconds more and I'll know I've missed her.'

He looked up again, and there was *Kingfisher* dead ahead. All her lights were ablaze, a burning beacon of hope in the darkness. She appeared to be riding easily, for the wind had not yet had time to thrash the sea into a frenzy.

He flashed over her, seeming to graze her superstructure in passing, and now he was searching anxiously for the glow of the flare path on the land beyond.

It came up as a path of lesser darkness in the absolute blackness of the night. He steadied on course towards it, watching it change to a long double line of oil-burning flares that smoked and fluttered in the wind.

He flew her in fast, high above the stall and the shock of touch down threatened to tear the under-carriage off her.

Then he was jolting and trundling down the earthen runway with the flares flashing past his wingtips.

'Lance, old man,' he murmured thankfully, 'that was a very shaky do!'

The wind hum against the body of the car, and the snarl of rubber on tarmac as the Mercedes snaked through the bends of the twisting mountain road were sounds to match the racing of Tracey's blood and the hammer of her heart.

She drove with an inspired abandon, watching the bends leap out at her out of the darkness, sensing the massive crags and cliffs that hung over the road and blotted out half the night sky.

The silver sheet of Clanwilliam Lake reflected the stars, and then was left behind. Down from the mountains she went and over the Olifants River to make a brief fuel stop at Vanrynsdorp and scan the road map anxiously in the light of the gasoline pumps. She read with a sinking feeling the mileage figures printed along the little red ribbon of the road, and knew that for her each mile would be multiplied by her own urgency.

Then once more behind the wheel she faced the vast emptiness of Namaqualand – and sent the Mercedes flying across it.

'— There is some type of machine, I don't know how it works, but it filters out the diamonds. Benedict had it installed at Las Palmas – '

The headlights were puny little white shafts, and the road a long blue smear that went on endlessly. Tracey lit a cigarette with one hand, hearing Ruby's voice again in her ears.

'— There is one diamond amongst them. He called it "The Big Blue". Benedict says it's worth a million – '

Tracey was not sure she believed it. It was the enormity of the treachery and deceit that she could not accept.

'— The Italian, the Captain, be careful of him. He works for Benedict. The other one also – Hugo – they are all in it. Warn Johnny.'

Benedict! Weak, spoiled Benedict, the playboy, the spendthrift. Could he have planned and carried this through?

A gust of wind hit the car from the side, taking her unawares, pushing the Mercedes off the tar on to the gravel. Tracey fought to hold the skid. Dust and gravel roared out in a cloud from under the wheels. Then she was back on the road, hurtling northwards.

'Warn Johnny! Warn Johnny!'

Benedict van der Byl sat in his father's chair, in his father's house, and he was alone. His loneliness ate deep into the fibres of his whole being. Before him on the stinkwood desk stood a crystal glass and a decanter. The brandy was no comfort, its warmth in his throat and belly seemed only to accentuate the icy cold of his loneliness. His fantasy showed him as a hollow man. He thought of himself as a husk, filled only with the cold of melancholia.

He looked about the room with its dark panelled woodwork and he smelled the musty dead smell. He wondered how many times his father had sat in this chair alone and lonely. Lonely and afraid as the cancer ate him alive.

He stood up and moved listlessly about the room, touching the furniture as if he were trying to communicate with the man who had lived and died here. He moved across and stood in front of the curtained windows. The rug was new. It replaced the other that they had been unable to clean.

'The Old Man had the right idea.' He spoke aloud, his voice sounding strange in his own ears.

Then on an impulse he crossed quickly to the cupboard that flanked the massive stone fireplace, and tried the door. It was locked.

Without passion he stood back and kicked in the panel. The wood splintered and he kicked again, smashing the door from its hinges.

The oblong leather case was on the top shelf, and he took it down and carried it to the desk. He sprang the catches and laid back the lid.

He lifted out the blue metalled double barrels of the Purdey Royal, and the gun oil was greasy on his hands.

'Jacobus Isaac van der Byl.' He read aloud the name in gold inlay set into the steel among the engraved pheasants and gundogs.

He smiled then.

'The old devil.' He shook his head smiling as though at some private joke, and began slowly to assemble the shotgun. He weighed it in his hands, feeling the sweet pure balance of the weapon.

'The old bastard made his own decisions.' And still smiling he carried the gun across to the new carpet. He placed it butt down between his feet with the barrels pointed at the ceiling and leaning slowly forward he opened his mouth and placed the muzzles between his lips, then reaching farther down he placed a thumb on each trigger and pushed them simultaneously.

'Click! Click!'

The firing pins fell on the empty chambers, and Benedict straightened up and wiped the taste of gun oil from his lips. He grinned again.

'That's the way he did it. Both barrels in the back of the throat. What a cure for tonsils!' he chuckled, and glanced across at the shattered cupboard door. The square packets of cartridges were on the second shelf.

He tucked the gun under his arm and went to the cupboard again, moving more purposefully now. He snatched down a packet of S.S.G. and broke it open. Suddenly his hands were shaking and the fat red cartridges spilled on to the floor. He stooped and picked up two of them.

With mounting excitement and dread he broke open the shotgun and slipped the cartridges into the blank eyes of the breeches. They slid home against the seating with a solid double thunk, and he hurried back to the spot in front of the window.

His eyes were bright and his breathing quick as he pushed the safety catch on to 'Fire' and placed the butt between his feet once more.

He took the muzzles in his mouth again, in an obscene soul kiss and reached down for the triggers. They were cold and oily. He caressed them lightly, feeling the fine grooving in the curves of metal, thrilling to the touch and feel of them as he had never thrilled to the feel of a woman's body.

Then abruptly he stood up again. He was gasping for breath.

Unsteadily he carried the weapon back to the desk and laid it on the dark polished wood.

As he poured brandy into the crystal glass his eyes were fastened with perverse fascination on the beautiful glistening weapon.

The steam had fogged the mirrored walls of the bathroom, so her image was dewed and misty. Ruby Lance dried herself slowly with one of the thick fluffy towels. She was in no hurry; she wanted Tracey to have a start of at least four hours on her journey to Cartridge Bay. With a deep narcissistic pleasure she noticed in the mirrors how her whole body glowed with soft pink highlights from the hot waters of the bath.

Wrapping herself in the towel she went through into the dressing-room and picking up one of the silver-backed brushes began stroking it through her hair, moving across to the open wardrobe to select a dress for the occasion. It must be something special, perhaps the unworn full-length Louis Feraud of daffodil satin.

Still undecided she went back to seat herself at the dressing-table and began the complicated ritual of applying her make-up. She worked with meticulous care until at last she smiled at her reflection with satisfaction.

She dropped the towel, went back to the wardrobe, and stood slim and naked before it. Pouting slightly with concentration she decided against the Feraud. Then suddenly she smiled, and reached for Benedict's mink.

She wrapped herself in the pale cloud of fur, fluffing up the collar to frame her face. It was perfect. Just the fur and a pair of golden slippers, pale gold, a perfect match for her hair.

Now suddenly she was eager to go. She ran from the house to where her car was parked in the driveway.

She switched off the headlights as she turned into the driveway that curved up to where the old house crouched on the top of Wynberg Hill. The whisper of the engine was unobtrusive and blended with the whimper of the night breeze in the chestnut trees that flanked the driveway.

She parked in the courtyard, and saw that Benedict's Rolls was still in the garage and a light burned in the window of the study, a yellow oblong behind the curtains. The front door was open. Her slippered feet made no sound along the gloomy passages, and when she tried the door to the study it swung open readily. She stepped into the room, and closed the door behind her. She stood with her back to the dark panelled wood. A single shaded lamp lit the room dimly.

Benedict sat behind the desk. The room was heavy with the smell of cigar smoke and brandy fumes. He had been drinking. His face was flushed, and the top button of his shirt was undone. On the desk in front of him lay a shotgun. Ruby was surprised at the presence of the weapon, it disconcerted her and the words she had prepared were forgotten.

Benedict looked up at her. His eyes were slightly unfocused; and he blinked slowly. Then he grinned; it twisted his mouth and his voice when he spoke was slurred.

'So you've come back.'

Instantly her hatred returned in full flood. But she kept her face impassive. 'Yes,' she agreed. 'I've come back.'

'Come here.' He swivelled his chair to the side of the desk. Ruby did not move, she leaned back against the door.

'Come here.' Benedict's voice was stronger now, and suddenly Ruby smiled and obeyed.

She stood in front of him, huddled in the fur.

'Kneel down,' commanded Benedict, and she hesitated.

'Down!' his voice crackled. 'Down, damn you!'

Ruby sank to her knees in front of him, and he straightened up in the chair. She knelt in front of him in the attitude of submission, with her head forward so the golden hair hung like a curtain over her face.

'Say it,' he gloated. 'Ask me to forgive you.'

Slowly she lifted her face and looked up at him. She spoke softly.

'Tracey left for Cartridge Bay at five-thirty this evening.'

Benedict's expression changed.

'She has a start of four hours – she is half-way there already.'

He stared at her with his lips parting, soft and red and slack.

'She is going to Johnny,' Ruby went on. 'She knows about the thing in *Kingfisher*. She knows about the big blue diamond.'

He began to shake his head in disbelief.

'By dawn tomorrow Johnny will know also. So you see, my darling, you have lost again – haven't you? You can never beat him, can you, Benedict? Can you, my darling?'

Her voice was rising, ringing with triumph.

'You?' he croaked. 'You?'

And she laughed, nodding her head in agreement, unable to speak through her laughter.

Benedict lunged clumsily out of the chair, his hands going for her throat. She went over backwards with him on top of her. Her laughter died gurgling in her throat.

They rolled together on the floor. Benedict's hands locked on her neck, his voice rising in a scream of fury and despair. Her long legs kicking and thrashing, clawing at his face and hands, she fought him with the strength of a cornered animal.

They rolled back suddenly and Benedict's head struck the solid leg of the desk with a crack that jarred his whole body. His grip on her throat loosened and she tore herself free with fresh breath hissing into her open mouth. She rolled away from him and in one fluid movement gained her feet, reeling back from him with the front of the mink torn open and her hair tangled across her face.

Benedict dragged himself up the desk on to his knees. He was still screaming, a high keening note without form or coherence, as Ruby spun away from him and stumbled to the door.

Blinded by her own hair, fighting for strangled breath, she fumbled for the door handle with her back turned to him.

Benedict reached up and lifted the shotgun off the desk. Still kneeling beside the desk he held the weapon across his hip. The recoil was a liquid pulsing jolt in his hands and the muzzle blast was thunderous in the confines of the room, the long yellow flame lighting the scene like a photographer's flash-bulb.

The heavy charge caught Ruby in the small of her back. At that range there was no spread of shot and it went through spine and pelvis in a solid shattering ball. It tore out through the front of her belly, spinning her sideways along the wall. She slid down into a sitting position, facing him with the mink flared open about her.

On his knees Benedict swung the gun to follow her fall and he fired the second barrel; again the brief thunder and flame of the muzzle blast flashed across the room.

At even closer range than the first charge it struck her full in her beautiful golden face.

Benedict stood in the garage with his forehead pressed against the cold metal of the Rolls-Royce. The shotgun was still in his hands, and his pockets were crammed with cartridges that he had picked up from the floor before leaving the study.

He was shivering violently, like a man in high fever.

'No!' he moaned to himself, repeating the single negative over and over again, leaning against the big car.

Abruptly he gagged, remembering the carnage he had created. Then he retched, still leaning against the Rolls, bringing up the brandy mingled with his horror.

It left him pale and weak, but steadier. Through the open window he threw the gun on to the back seat of the Rolls, and climbed shakily into the driver's seat.

He sat there bowed over the steering-wheel, and now his instinct of self-preservation took hold of him.

It seemed to him there was but one avenue of escape still open to him. *Wild Goose* had the range to take him across an ocean – South America perhaps, and there was money in Switzerland.

He started the Rolls and reversed out of the garage, the spin of tyres against concrete burning blue smoke into the beams of the headlights.

The Mercedes crawled through the thick sand, the headlights probing ineffectually into the bright orange fog of dust that whipped endlessly over the track ahead. The hot gritty wind buffeted the car, rocking it on its suspension.

Tracey sat forward in the driver's seat peering ahead through eyes that felt raw and swollen with fatigue and mica dust.

From the main road to the coast this Jeep track was the only land access to Cartridge Bay. It was a hundred miles of tortuous trail, made up of deep sandy ruts and broken stone where it crossed one of the many rocky ridges.

The radiator of the Mercedes was boiling furiously, over-heating in the searing wind and the slogging low-gear grind through thick sand. In places Tracey followed the track only by driving through gaps in the stunted knee-high growth of desert bush. Every few minutes a tumbleweed, driven by the wind, would bowl across the track like a frightened furry animal.

At times she was sure she had missed a turning and was now grinding aimlessly out into the desert, then reassuringly the twin ruts would show up in the lights ahead of her. Once she did drive off the road, and immediately the Mercedes came to a gentle standstill with its rear wheels spinning helplessly in the soft sand. She had to climb out of the cab and, with her bare hands, scoop away the sand from behind the wheels and stuff bundles of tumbleweed into the depressions to give the wheels purchase. She almost wept with relief when the Mercedes pulled back sluggishly on to the trail again.

The slow dawn broke through the dustclouds and Tracey switched off the headlights and drove on until suddenly, and quite unexpectedly, she reached Cartridge Bay. The depot buildings loomed suddenly before her, and she left the Mercedes and ran to the living quarters. The foreman opened the door to her insistent hammering, and stared at her in astonishment before ushering her in. Tracey cut off his questions with her own.

'Where is *Wild Goose*?'

'She took Mr Lance out to *Kingfisher*, but she's back now lying at the jetty.'

'Hugo Kramer – the Captain?'

'He's aboard, holed up in his cabin.'

'Thanks.' Tracey left him, pushed the door open against the wind and ran out into the storm.

Wild Goose lay at her moorings, secured by heavy lines to the bollards, but fidgeting and fretting at the push of the wind. There was a gangplank laid to her deck, and lights showed at her portholes. Tracey went aboard.

Hugo Kramer came to the doorway of his cabin in a suit of rumpled striped pyjamas. Tracey pushed past him.

'You took Lance out to *Kingfisher*?' she accused him, her voice sharp and anxious.

'Yes.'

'You idiot, didn't you realize there was something up? Good God, why otherwise would he fly in through this weather?'

Hugo stared at her, and instinctively she knew that what Ruby had told her was true.

'I don't know what you're talking about,' he blurted.

'You'll know all right when we are all sitting behind bars – we'll have fifteen long years to think about it. Lance has tumbled to it, you fool, I've got to stop him. Take me out to *Kingfisher*.'

He was confused – and afraid.

'I know nothing about – ' Hugo started again.

'You're wasting time.' Brusquely Tracey brushed his protests aside. 'Take me out to *Kingfisher*.'

'Your brother – where is he? Why didn't he come?'

Tracey had anticipated the question. 'Lance beat him up – badly. He's in hospital. He sent me.'

Suddenly Hugo was convinced.

'*Gott!*' he swore. 'What are we going to do? This storm – I may be able to get you out there, but I won't be able to leave *Wild Goose*. My crew can't handle her in this sea. What can you do on your own?'

'Get me out there,' said Tracey. 'Get me aboard *Kingfisher* and you can come back. The Italian, Caporetti, he and I will take care of Lance. In this storm a man can be washed overboard very easily.'

'Ja.' Hugo's face lit with relief. 'That's it. The Italian!' And he a reached for his oilskins hanging on the bulkhead. As he pulled them on over his pyjamas he looked at Tracey with new respect.

'You,' he said. 'I didn't know you were in it.'

'Did you think my brother and I would stand by and let a stranger take our birthright from us?'

Hugo grinned. 'You're a cool one, I'll say that for you. You had me fooled.' And he went out on to the bridge.

Johnny Lance and Sergio Caporetti stood shoulder to shoulder on *Kingfisher*'s bridge. The ship was taking the big green seas over her bows, solid walls of water, and the wind whipped spray that spattered the armoured glass windows of the bridge house.

Kingfisher had slipped her moorings the previous evening, leaving the big yellow buoys floating on their anchor cables and she was working free of her fetters. She was on computer navigation, holding her position over the ground against the swells and the wind by use of her engine and rudder.

'She is no good.' Sergio spoke morosely. 'We come too close to the rocks. I get sick in my heart looking at them.'

The dust clouds did not carry this far out to sea despite the vicious screeching of the wind. The visibility was a mile or more, quite enough to show the brooding twin hulks of Thunderbolt and Suicide. The storm-crazed swells burst against them, throwing white spray two hundred feet into the gloomy sky, then surging back to expose the gleaming white rock.

'Hold her,' growled Johnny. Twice during the night they had changed position, each time edging down closer on the gap between the two islands. *Kingfisher* was battling gamely to hold her ground against the insidious sucking current that added its pull to that of the swell and the wind.

Johnny was not attempting to work any one of the gullys extensively, he wanted only to sample as much of the field as possible in the time that was left to him. The storm would not stop him – for *Kingfisher* was constructed to work in worse weather than this. Her compensating hose section was keeping the dredge-head on the bottom despite the lift and fall of her hull.

'Calm down, Sergio.' Johnny relented a little. 'The computer is foolproof.'

'The goddamned computer she no got eyes to see those rocks. Me, I got eyes – and it gives me a sick heart.'

Twice during the night Johnny had gone down into the control room and ordered the computer to report its recovery of diamonds. Each time the reply had been consistent – not a single stone over four carats, and a very precious few of any others.

'I'm going through to the plot. Watch her,' Johnny told Sergio, and staggering against the pitch and roll he went through the door behind the bridge.

He paused behind the repeater screen of the computer, and at a glance saw that *Kingfisher* was holding her primary operation and all departments were running normally. He passed the screen and leaned over the chart table.

The large scale chart of the South West African coast between Luderitz and Walvis Bay was pinned down on the board. The *Wild Goose* soundings were pencilled in, and the pattern of *Kingfisher*'s sweeps were carefully plotted around the islands of Thunderbolt and Suicide.

Johnny picked up a pair of dividers and stared moodily at the chart. Suddenly a surge of anger rose in him against those two names. They had promised so much and delivered so little.

He stared at the names Thunderbolt and Suicide printed in italics among the maze of soundings, and his anger turned to blind red hatred.

With the points of the dividers he slashed at the chart, ripping the thick linen paper once, and twice, in a ragged cross-shaped tear.

This small act of violence dissipated his anger. He felt embarrassed, it had been a petty childish gesture. He tried to smooth the edges of the tear, and through the gap he felt another loose scrap of paper which someone had slipped under the chart. He probed a finger through the tear in the chart and wormed the scrap out. He glanced at the scribbled title and the lines of figures and numbers that followed.

The sheet was headed: KAMINIKOTO SECONDARY RECOVERY PROGRAMME.'

He studied it, puzzled by the title but recognizing the numbers as a computer programme. The writing was in Sergio Caporetti's pointed continental style. The easiest way to resolve the mystery was to ask Sergio. Johnny started back for the bridge.

'Boss,' Sergio called anxiously, as Johnny stepped through the door. 'Look!'

He was pointing ahead into the eye of the wind. Johnny hurried to his side, the paper crumpled and forgotten in his hand.

'*Wild Goose*.' Sergio identified the small craft that was staggering and plunging towards them out of the gloom.

'What the hell is he doing here?' Johnny wondered aloud. *Wild Goose* was lost for long seconds behind the walls of green sea, then again she was lifted high into unnatural prominence, showing the red lead of her bottom as she rode the crests; water poured from her scuppers, before she shot down the steep slope of the next wave to bury her nose deep in frothing water. She came down swiftly on the wind, rounding to and beginning to edge in under *Kingfisher*'s counter.

'What the hell is he playing at?' Johnny protested, and then in disbelief he saw a slim figure dart from *Wild Goose*'s wheelhouse and run to the side nearest *Kingfisher*.

'It's Tracey,' shouted Johnny.

She reached the rail just as another swell burst over the bows and smothered her. Johnny expected to see her washed away, but she was still there clinging to the rail.

Thrusting the page of paper into his pocket, Johnny went out through the wing of the bridge and swarmed down the steel ladder to the deck, jumping the last ten feet and running the instant he landed.

He reached the side and looked down on the drowned-kitten figure of Tracey.

'Go back,' he yelled. 'Go back. Don't try it.'

She shouted something that was lost in the next smother of spray, and when it cleared he saw her poising herself to jump the gap of surging water between the two vessels.

He flung himself over *Kingfisher*'s side and climbed swiftly down the steel rungs.

He was still ten feet above her as she gathered herself for the leap.

'Go back,' he shouted desperately.

She jumped, missed her hold and fell into the murderous stretch of water between the hulls. Her head bobbed below Johnny, and he was aware of the next swell bearing down on them. It would throw *Wild Goose* against the steel cliff of *Kingfisher*, crushing Tracey between them.

Johnny went down those last ten feet and hanging outwards by one arm he got his other arm around her, and with a heave that crackled in his muscles and joints he plucked her from the water just as the two vessels dashed together with a crunching impact that tore splinters from *Wild Goose*'s planking, and left a smear of alien paint on *Kingfisher*'s steel plating.

Wild Goose swung away, and with her diesels bellowing went bucking off into the wind.

With puddles of sea water forming around her feet from her sodden clothing, Tracey stood in the centre of *Kingfisher*'s guest cabin. Her dark hair was plastered down her face and neck, and she was shivering so violently from shock and the icy water that she could not talk. Her teeth chattered together, and her lips were blue with cold.

Desperately she was trying to form words, her eyes never leaving Johnny's face.

Quickly he stripped off her clothing and throwing one towel round her shoulders he began roughly to chafe warmth back into her with another.

'You little idiot,' he berated her. 'Are you stark staring bloody mad?'

'Johnny,' she gasped through her chattering teeth.

'Christ – that was so close,' he snarled at her as he knelt to rub her legs.

'Johnny, listen.'

'Shut up and dry your hair.'

Humbly she obeyed him, her shivers became controllable as he crossed to the locker and found a thick jersey which he pulled over her head. It hung almost to her knees.

'Now,' he said, taking her roughly by the shoulders. 'What the hell is this all about?'

And she told him in a rush of words that poured out like water from a broken dam. Then she burst into tears and stood there forlornly in the voluminous jersey with her damp hair dangling about her shoulders, sobbing as though her heart was breaking.

Johnny took her in his arms.

For a long minute Tracey revelled in his warmth and strength, but she was the first to pull away.

'Do something, Johnny,' she implored him, her voice still thick with tears. 'Stop them. You mustn't let them get away with it.'

He went back to the locker, and while he ransacked it for clothing that might fit her, Johnny's mind was racing over the story she had told him.

He watched her pull on a pair of blue serge trousers and tie them at the waist with a length of cord. She folded back the cuffs and tucked them into thick woollen socks, before thrusting her feet into a pair of sea-boots that were only a few sizes too large for her.

'Where do we start?' she asked, and he remembered the sheet of paper. He fished it out of his pocket and flattened it on the table beside the bunk. Quickly he ran his eyes over the columns of figures. His first guess was right – it *was* a computer programme.

'Stay here,' he ordered Tracey.

'No.' Her response was immediate, and he grinned.

'Listen, I'm just going up on to the bridge to keep them busy there. I'll come back for you, I promise. You won't miss anything.'

'How is she, boss?' Sergio Caporetti's concern was genuine. Johnny realized that he must be worrying himself into a frenzy trying to guess the reason for Tracey's arrival.

'She is pretty shaken up,' Johnny answered.

'What she want – that was big chance she takes. Nearly fish food.'

'I don't know,' Johnny said. 'I want you to take over up here. Keep *Kingfisher* working. I'm going to get her to bed – I'll let you know what it's all about as soon as I find out.'

'Okay, boss.'

'Oh, and Sergio – keep an eye on those rocks. Don't let her drift down any closer.'

Johnny chose a powerful incentive to keep Sergio up on the bridge.

Johnny left him and went below, stopping only at the guest cabin.

'Come on.'

Tracey followed him, lurching unsteadily with *Kingfisher's* antics in the high sea.

Two decks down they reached the computer control room and Johnny unlocked the heavy steel door, then locked it again behind them.

Tracey wedged herself against the bulkhead and watched as Johnny seated himself at the console and clipped the rumpled sheet into the board.

Reading from the sheet he typed the first line of figures on the keyboard. Immediately the computer registered a protest.

'Operator error,' it typed back. Johnny ignored its denial and typed the second line. This time it was more emphatic.

'No procedure. Operator error.'

And Johnny typed the next line of figures. He guessed that whoever had stored this programme in the computer's memory would have placed a series of blocks to prevent accidental discovery. Again the denial flashed back at him.

'Operator error.'

And Johnny muttered, 'Thrice before the cock crows,' striking an incongruously biblical note in the tense atmosphere of the control room.

He typed the last line of figures and the denial faded from the screen. The console clicked like a monstrous crab, then suddenly it started to print again.

'KAMINIKOTO SECONDARY RECOVERY PROGRAMME.
INSTALLED OCTOBER 1969. AT LAS PALMAS BY
HIDEKI KAMINIKOTO. DOCTOR OF SCIENCE.
TOKYO UNIVERSITY.'

The little Japanese had been unable to resist autographing his masterpiece. Tracey and Johnny crouched over the screen, staring at it with awful fascination as the computer began spelling out its report. It began with the number of hours worked, and the weight of gravel processed during that time. Next it reported the weight of concentrates recovered from the cyclone and finally, in a series of columns, it printed out the weights and sizes of all the diamonds won from the sea. The big Blue showed up in the place of honour, and wordlessly Tracey touched the figure 320 with a forefinger. Johnny nodded grimly.

The computer ended by giving the grand total of carats recovered, and Johnny spoke for the first time.

'It's true,' he said softly. 'It doesn't seem possible – but it is.'

The click and hum of the computer ceased, and the screen went blank.

Johnny straightened up in the chair.

'Where would they put it?' he asked himself, as he ran quickly over the line of recovery. He stood up from the chair and peered through the leaded glass peephole into the X-ray room. 'It must be this side of the cyclone, this side of the drier – ' He was speaking aloud. ' – Between the drier and the X-ray room.'

Then there bobbed to the surface of memory the modification in design which he had meant to query, but which he had forgotten.

'The inspection plate on the conveyor tunnel!' He punched his fist into his palm. 'They moved the inspection plate! That's it! It's in the conveyor tunnel.'

His hands were frantic with haste as he unlocked the steel-door of the control room.

Sergio Caporetti paced his bridge like a captive bear, puffing so furiously on his cheroot that sparks flew from its tip. The wind howled hungrily around the wheel-house, and the swells still marched in from the north.

Suddenly he reached a decision and turned to the helmsman.

'Watch those goddamn rocks – watch them good.'

The helmsman nodded and Sergio shambled through the chartroom to his own cabin. He locked the door behind him, and crossed to his desk. Fumbling with his keys he opened the bottom drawer of his desk and reaching under the pile of cheroot packets he brought out the canvas bag.

Weighing it thoughtfully in his hand, he looked about the cabin for a more secure hiding-place. Through the canvas he could feel the nutty irregular shape of the stones.

'That Johnny, he a clever bastard,' he muttered. 'It better be good place.'

Then he reached a decision. 'Best place where I can watch them all a time.'

He opened his jacket and stuffed the bag into his inside pocket. He buttoned the jacket and patted the bulge over his heart.

'Fine!' he said. 'Good!' And stood up from the desk. He hurried back, unlocking the door into the chartroom, and headed for the bridge. He stopped in the middle of the chart-room, and his head swung towards the repeater screen of the computer. The buzzer was going like a rattlesnake, and the red bulb that warned of a new procedure was blinking softly.

Fearfully Sergio approached the screen and stooped over it. A single glance was enough, and he rushed from it to the chart table. He saw the cross-shaped tear in the chart.

'Mary Mother!'

He ripped back the thick crackling paper and searched under it. He stepped back from the table and hit himself across the chest.

'Fool!' he said. 'Idiot!' He spent ten seconds in self-castigation, then he looked about for a weapon. The locking handle of the cabin was a twelve-inch steel bar with a heavy head. He pulled out the pin and worked it loose. He slipped it into the waistband of his trousers.

'I'm going below,' he told the helmsman curtly, and clambered down the companionway. Swiftly he moved through the ship, balancing easily to her roll and pitch.

When he reached the lowest deck he became more stealthy, creeping silently forward. Now he carried the steel bar in his right hand. Every few paces he stopped to listen, but Kingfisher's hull was groaning and popping as she worked in the swells.

He could hear no other sound. He crept up to the door of the control room and cautiously peered through the small armoured glass window. The control room was empty. He tried the handle, and found it locked.

Then he heard voices – from the open doorway of the conveyor room behind him. Quickly he crossed to it and flattened himself against the jamb.

Johnny's voice came muffled and indistinct:

'There's another hatch in here. Get me a half-inch spanner from the tool cupboard.'

'What's a half-inch spanner look like?'

'It's a big one. The size is stamped on it.'

Sergio glanced one-eyed around the door jamb. The cover was off the inspection hatch in the conveyor tunnel, and Tracey's head was thrust into the opening. It was clear that Johnny Lance was in there, and that he had found the secret compartment.

Tracey drew her head out of the hatch, and Sergio ducked back and looked down the passageway. The tool cupboard was bolted to the bulkhead under the stairs from the deck above. He turned and darted around the corner of the passageway. Tracey came out of the conveyor room, and went to the cupboard. She opened the doors on the glittering array of tools, each clipped securely to its rack.

While she stood before the cupboard, completely absorbed in her search for a half-inch spanner, Sergio came from around the corner and crept up silently behind her.

He lifted the steel bar over his shoulder and came up on his toes, poised to strike.

Tracey was muttering softly to herself, head bowed slightly, handling the spanners – and Sergio knew the blow would crush her skull.

He closed his mind to the thought, and aimed carefully at the base of her skull. He started the blow, and then checked it. For a second that seemed to last for a long time he remained frozen. He couldn't do it.

With an exclamation of satisfaction Tracey found what she was searching for. As she turned away from the cupboard Sergio shrank back behind the angle of the bulkhead, and Tracey hurried back into the conveyor room.

'I've got it, Johnny,' she shouted into the hatch.

'Bring it to me. Hurry, Tracey. Sergio will be getting suspicious,' he shouted back, and Tracey hitched up her voluminous trousers and wriggled into the hatch.

On hands and knees she crawled up beside him. It was cramped and hot in the narrow tunnel. He took the spanner from her.

'Hold the flashlight.' She took it from him, holding the beam on the panel while he unscrewed the retaining bolts and lifted off the cover.

Lying on his side he peered into the opening.

'There's a container of sorts,' he grunted, and reached in. For a minute he struggled with the clamps, then slowly he lifted out the stainless steel cup.

At that moment *Kingfisher* reared and plunged to a freak wave and the cup slipped from Johnny's fingers, and from it spilled the diamonds. They cascaded over both of them, a glittering shower of stones of all sizes and colours. Some lodged in Tracey's damp hair, the rest rolled and bounced and scattered about them, catching the light from the torch and throwing it back in splinters of sunshine.

'Yipes!' gasped Tracey and laughed at Johnny's whoop of triumph.

Lying side by side they scrabbled and snatched at the treasure scattered around them.

'Look at this one,' exulted Tracey.

'And this.' They were crazy with excitement, hands filled with diamonds. They hugged each other and kissed ecstatically, laughing into each other's mouths.

Johnny sobered first, 'Come on. Let's get out of here.'

'What about the diamonds?'

'Leave them. There'll be plenty of time later.'

They crawled backwards down the tunnel, still laughing and exclaiming, and one after the other emerged into the conveyor room. While they straightened their clothing, and regained their breath, Tracey asked, 'What now?'

'First thing is to get young Sergio safely under lock and key, his crew also.' Johnny's face hardened. 'The bloody bastards,' he added angrily.

'Then?' Tracey asked.

'Then we'll pull up the hose, and sail *Kingfisher* back into Cartridge Bay. Then we'll call up the police on the radio. There's going to be an accounting with the whole gang of the bastards – your darling brother included.'

Johnny started for the door, asking as he crossed the deck:

'Why did you close the door, Tracey?'

'I didn't,' she replied as she hurried after him, and Johnny's expression changed. He ran to the heavy steel door and threw his weight on it. It did not move, and he swung round to face the door that led into the cyclone room.

It was closed also. He charged across the room and grabbed the handle, heaving at it with all his strength.

He stood back at last, and looked wildly about the long narrow cabin. There was no other opening, no hatch or porthole – nothing except the tiny square peephole in the centre of the steel door that led into the cyclone room beyond. The peephole was covered with three-inch armoured glass that was as strong as the steel that surrounded it. He looked through it.

The tall cyclone reached from floor to roof, dominating the room. Beyond it the steel pipe that carried the gravel from the sea bed pierced the roof from the deck above, but the cyclone room was deserted.

Johnny turned slowly back to Tracey and put an arm around her shoulders.

'We've got problems,' he said.

*

After closing and locking both the doors that led into the conveyor room, Sergio climbed quickly back to his bridge. The helmsman looked at him curiously.

'How's the lady?'

'Fine,' Sergio snapped at him. 'She's safe.' And then with unnecessary violence, 'Why you no mind your own business, hey? You think you Captain for this ship?'

Startled, the helmsman quickly transferred his attention back to the storm which still raged lustily about them. Sergio began to pace up and down the bridge, balancing easily and instinctively to her exaggerated motion. His smooth baby face was crumpled into a massive scowl, and he puffed on one of his cheroots. With all his soul Sergio Caporetti was lamenting his involvement in this business. He wished that he had never heard of *Kingfisher*. He would have traded his hopes of a life hereafter to be sitting on the seafront at Ostia, sipping *grappa* and watching the girls go by.

Impulsively he pulled open the storm doors at the angle of the bridge and went out on to the exposed wing. The wind buffeted him and set his soft hair dancing and flickering.

From inside his jacket he pulled the canvas bag.

'This is the trouble,' he muttered, looking at the bag in his hand. 'Bloody little stones.'

He threw back his arm like a baseball pitcher, set to hurl the bag out into that hissing green sea below him, but again he could not make the gesture. Swearing quietly to himself, he stuffed the stones back into his jacket, and went back into the wheelhouse.

'Call the radio operator,' he ordered, and the helmsman reached quickly for the voice tube.

The radio operator reached the bridge still owl-eyed with sleep and buttoning his clothing.

'Get on to *Wild Goose*,' Sergio told him.

'I won't be able to raise her in this,' the man protested, glancing out at the storm.

'Call her.' Sergio stepped towards him threateningly. 'Keep calling until you get her.'

Wild Goose staggered and wallowed through the turbulence at the entrance to Cartridge Bay, then fought her way into the sanctuary of the channel.

Hugo relaxed perceptibly. It had been a long hard run back from Thunderbolt and Suicide. Yet there was an uneasy feeling that still persisted. He hoped that the girl was able to handle Lance. He was a tough cooky that Lance, he wished that he had been able to go along with her and make sure of the business. Fifteen years was one hell of a long time – he would be almost fifty years old at the end of it.

Hugo followed the channel markers that appeared like milestones out of the dust clouds, until ahead he made out the loom of the jetty and the depot buildings.

There was a figure on the jetty, crouched beside the mountain of dieseline drums. With a prickle of alarm, Hugo strained his eyes in the bad visibility.

'Who the hell is it?' he puzzled aloud. The figure straightened and came forward to stand on the edge of the jetty. Bareheaded, dressed in rumpled dark business suit, the man carried a shotgun in one hand – and it was another few seconds before Hugo recognized him.

'Christ! It's the boss!' Hugo felt alarm flare in his stomach and chest, it tightened his breathing.

Benedict van der Byl jumped down on to the deck of *Wild Goose* at the moment she touched the jetty.

'What's happened?' Benedict demanded as he barged into the wheelhouse.

'I thought you were in hospital,' Hugo countered.

'Who told you that?'

'Your sister.'

'You've seen her? Where is she?'

'I took her out to *Kingfisher*. Like you said. She went out to deal with Lance.'

'Deal with Lance! She's with him, you idiot, she's not with us. She knows the whole deal. Everything!'

'She told me – ' Hugo was appalled. But Benedict cut him short.

'The whole thing's blown up. We've got to clear out. Get your crew to load those drums of dieseline into the hold. How are your water tanks?'

'Full.'

'Food?'

'We are stocked up.'

'For how long?'

'Three weeks – at a push, four.'

'Thank God for that.' Benedict looked relieved. 'This storm will blow another three days – we'll have that much start. They'll never find us in this. By the time it clears we'll be well on our way.'

'Where to – Angola?'

'God, no! We have to get well clear. South America.'

'South America!'

'Yes – we can do it, carrying extra fuel.'

Hugo was silent a moment, becoming accustomed to the idea.

'We can do it,' Benedict repeated.

'Yes.' Hugo nodded. 'We can do it,' he agreed thoughtfully. For the first time he examined Benedict closely. He saw that he was in an emotional and physical mess, his bloodshot eyes were sunk into deep plum-coloured hollows, dark new beard covered his jowls, and there was a gaunt hunted look to him – like some fugitive animal.

He was filthy with dust, and there was a streak of something that could have been dried vomit down the front of his jacket.

'But what do we do when we get there?' For the first time since he had known Benedict he felt in control. This was the time to deal, to make bargains.

'We'll get ashore on some deserted spot, and then we split up and disappear.'

'What about money?' Hugo spoke carefully. He glanced down at the shotgun. Benedict's hands were fidgety and restless on the weapon.

'I've got money.'

'How much?' Hugo asked.

'Enough.' Benedict blinked cautiously.

'For me also?' Hugo prodded him, and Benedict nodded.

'How much for me?' Hugo went on.

'Ten thousand.'

'Pounds?'

'Pounds,' Benedict agreed.

'That's not enough.' Hugo shook his head. 'I'll need more than that.'

'Twenty.' Benedict increased his bid, but he knew he was playing from weakness into strength. Ruby was lying mutilated in his study, the net was probably being spread for him already.

'Fifty,' said Hugo decisively.

'I haven't that much.'

'Who are you kidding, Buster!' Hugo snorted. 'You've been stacking it away for years.'

Benedict let the barrels of the shotgun swing towards Hugo's belly suggestively.

'Go ahead,' Hugo grinned at him, screwing up his pale albino eyes. 'That'll leave you to paddle this canoe – you want to try it? You'd pile her up on the bar at the entrance – that's how far you'd get.'

Benedict swung the barrels aside.

'Fifty,' he agreed.

'Right!' Hugo spoke briskly. 'Let's get the hell out of here.'

Wild Goose was clear of the land, and of the towering blinding dust clouds. The following seas came sweeping up under her stern urging her on her westward flight, while the high-pitched shriek of the wind in her rigging cried to her to hasten.

'Why don't you get down below and grab some sleep?' Hugo said. He found Benedict's restless haunting presence in the crowded wheelhouse disconcerting.

Benedict ignored the suggestion. 'Switch on the radio,' he said.

'What for? You'll get nothing on the set.'

'We are out of the dust,' Benedict replied. 'We might pick up a police message.'

The image of Ruby was so clear in his mind. He wanted to know if they'd found her yet. He felt his gorge rising again. That head – oh God – that head! He crossed quickly to the radio set and switched it on.

'They won't be on to us yet,' said Hugo, but Benedict was manipulating the dials – searching the tortured radio waves. The static wailed and gibbered and shrieked like a maniac.

'Turn it off,' snapped Hugo, and at that moment a voice cut in on them.

'– *Wild Goose*,' said the voice from the loud-speaker quite clearly. Benedict crouched eagerly over the set, his hands busy on the dials, and Hugo came up beside him.

'— Come in, *Wild Goose*. This is *Kingfisher*. I repeat, come in *Wild Goose* –'

Benedict and Hugo looked at each other. 'Don't answer,' said Hugo, but he made no move to intervene as Benedict lifted the microphone off its hook.

'*Kingfisher*, this is *Wild Goose*.'

'Stand by, *Wild Goose*.' The answer came back immediately. 'Stand by for Captain Caporetti.'

'*Wild Goose* standing by.'

Hugo caught Benedict's shoulder and his voice was angrily uncertain.

'Leave it, don't be a fool.'

Benedict shrugged off the hand, and Sergio's voice boomed out of the speaker.

'This is Caporetti – who dat?'

'No names,' Benedict cautioned him. 'Where are your guests?'

'They safe – battened down nicely.'

'Safe? Are you certain? Both of them safe?'

'Si. I have them safe and sure.'

'Stand by.' Benedict crouched over the set, and his mind was racing. Johnny Lance was in his power. This was the last chance he would ever have. Plans began to form, gelling quickly in his mind.

'The diamonds. Caporetti has the diamonds. That big Blue is worth a million on its own,' said Hugo. 'If Caporetti has taken care of the others – it would be worth the risk.'

'Yes.' Benedict turned to him, he had been puzzling how he could make Hugo turn back. He had forgotten the diamonds. 'It would be worth it,' he agreed.

'Just a quick pass alongside *Kingfisher* – pick up Caporetti with the diamonds and we'd be on our way.'

'I have to go aboard.' Benedict qualified the suggestion.

'Why?' Hugo asked.

'Wipe out the reel on the computer that carries the programme – it's got the Jap's name on it. They could trace him. I paid him on my Swiss bank. They'll find the account.'

Hugo hesitated. 'No killing – or anything like that. We've got enough trouble without that.'

'You think I'm crazy?' Benedict demanded.

'Okay, then,' Hugo agreed.

'*Kingfisher*,' Benedict spoke into the microphone. 'We are coming to you. I'll be coming on board to finalize matters.'

'Fine.' Through the static they could hear the relief in Sergio's voice. 'I'll be standing by.'

It took nearly two hours for *Wild Goose* to slug her way back to where *Kingfisher* lay beneath the ghostly white shapes of Thunderbolt and Suicide, and it was after midday before Hugo began manoeuvring *Wild Goose* into the big ship's lee.

'Don't waste time,' Hugo cautioned Benedict. 'The sooner we get on our way – the better for all of us.'

'I'll be about half an hour,' Benedict answered. 'You lay off and wait for us.'

'Are you taking that bloody shotgun?' Benedict nodded.

'What for?' But Benedict did not reply, he looked up at the sky. The sun was merely a luminous patch of silver light through the ceiling of sea-fret and wind-driven mist, and still the storm hunted hungrily across the sea.

'It will slow you up on the ladder.' Hugo harped on the shotgun. He wanted very much to part Benedict from it, he wanted it over the side – for its presence aboard would prejudice the plans that Hugo had been forming during the last few hours – plans that took into account the ready market for diamonds in South America, and the undesirability of sharing the proceeds with two partners.

'I'll take it.' Benedict tightened his grip on the stock of the weapon. Without it he would feel naked and vulnerable – and it was part of his own private plans for the future. Benedict's brain had also been busy during the last two hours.

'Suit yourself.' Hugo resigned himself to Benedict's refusal; there would be an opportunity later, during the long passage across the Southern Atlantic. 'You better get up for'ard.'

This time Hugo's approach was neatly executed; in a lull between the colossal swells he touched *Wild Goose*'s bows to the steel side of the factory ship. Benedict stepped across the gap and was up the landing ladder and standing at *Kingfisher*'s rail before the next wave came marching down on them.

He waved Hugo off, then hanging on to the rail, made his way aft to *Kingfisher's* bridge works.

'Where is Lance?' he demanded of Sergio the moment he stepped on to the bridge, but Sergio glanced significantly at the inquisitively listening helmsman and led Benedict through into his cabin.

'Where is Lance?' Benedict repeated the moment the door was locked.

'He and your sister they are in the conveyor room.'

'The conveyor room?' Benedict was incredulous.

'Si. They find out about Kammy's machine. They open the hatch and go inside. I close both doors. Lock them good.'

'They are in there now?' Benedict asked to gain time to reconstruct his plans.

'Si. Still there.'

'All right.' Benedict reached his decision. 'Now listen, Caporetti, this is what we are going to do. The whole thing has blown up on us. We are going to wipe out as much of the evidence against us as possible, then we are clearing out. We are going to run for South America in *Wild Goose*. You have got the diamonds – haven't you?'

'Si.' Sergio patted the breast of his jacket.

'Give them to me.' Benedict held out his hand, and Sergio grinned.

'I tink I look after them. They keep my heart warm.'

A frown of annoyance narrowed Benedict's eyes, but he let the moment pass.

'All right.' His tone was still friendly. 'Now, what you have to do is get down to the control room and wipe out Kaminikoto's programme. Get his name off that reel. He showed you how to do that?'

'Si.' Sergio nodded.

'How long will it take?'

'Half an hour, not longer,' Sergio answered, and Benedict checked his wrist-watch that this would give him time enough to do what he had to do.

'Good! Get cracking.'

'Boss.' Sergio hesitated at the cabin door. 'What about my boys, my crew. They good boys, no trouble for them?'

'They're clean,' Benedict pointed out irritably. 'I'll get them together now, and explain that you have to go ashore. They can keep *Kingfisher* hove to waiting for you to come back. After the storm blows out they are bound to radio base and find out we have disappeared. They'll be all right.'

Sergio nodded his satisfaction.

'I'll call them all to the bridge now. You talk to them.'

The five crew members were gathered on *Kingfisher's* bridge, and Sergio had disappeared down below.

'Any of you speak English?' Benedict demanded, and two of them affirmed that they did.

'Right,' Benedict addressed them. 'You will have been wondering about all the coming and going in this weather. I want you all to be ready to leave the ship. I want you to get all your valuables – now!'

Quickly they translated to the others, who looked apprehensively at Benedict. He was a strange wild-eyed figure with the shotgun tucked under his arm.

'Right – let's go.' And there was no dissent from any of them as they trooped to the companionway.

Benedict followed them along the passage-way towards the crew quarters, and glanced quickly at his wrist-watch. Seven minutes had elapsed. He looked at the men ahead of him.

The backs of their heads formed a solid target. He had shot guineafowl like that in Namaqualand when they were on the ground running away from him in a thick file, down on one knee and aim for the thicket of heads, knocking down half the flock with both barrels.

He knew he could take all five of these men with two shots. Just let them get a little further ahead so the shot could spread. But he remembered Ruby and his stomach heaved. The other way was just as sure.

'Stop!' he commanded as the five men came level with the paint store. They obeyed and turned back to face him. Now he held the shotgun so that there was no mistaking its menace. They stared at the gun fearfully.

'Open that door.' He pointed at the paint store. Nobody moved.

'You.' Benedict picked on one of those who spoke English. Like a man in a trance he went to the steel door and spun the locking handle. He pulled the door open.

'In!' Eloquently Benedict gestured with the shotgun. Reluctantly the five of them filed into the small windowless cubicle, and Benedict slammed the door on them. He spun the lock, throwing all his weight on the handle to set it.

Now he had a clear field, and his wrist-watch gave him another twenty minutes. He hurried for'ard, he wanted to keep well clear of the control room and Sergio Caporetti.

Using the forward companionway he dropped down to the working deck, fumbling out his duplicate set of keys.

'WARNING. EXPLOSIVES. NO UNAUTHORIZED ENTRY.'

He unlocked the door, and laying the shotgun flat on the deck he lifted a twenty-five pound drum of plastique down from its rack.

In his haste he tore a fingernail on the lid of the drum, but hardly felt the pain. He uncoiled a six-foot length of the soft dark toffee-coloured material and slung it around his neck. Next he selected a cardboard box of pencil time fuses. He read the label.

'Fourteen-minute delay. That's about right.'

Blood from his torn nail left brown blotches on the cardboard as he took four of the pencils from the box, picked up the shotgun and hurried aft. The jet engine whine of the cyclone mounted deafeningly as he came closer to it.

Tracey was curled on the bare steel plating of the deck with Johnny's jacket folded under her head. She was in a fatigue-drugged sleep, so deep as to be almost deathlike.

Every few minutes Johnny interrupted his restless patrol of the conveyor room to stand over her and look down on her unconscious form. His worried expression softened a little each time he studied her pale lovely face. Once he stooped over her and tenderly lifted a strand of dark hair from her cheek, before resuming his pacing up and down the narrow cabin.

Each time he reached the door of the conveyor room he glanced through the tiny window. The glass had resisted his attempts to smash it with one of the spanners. He had wanted to open the window to call for help, but his efforts had not marked the thick armoured glass.

There was no way out of the cabin. Johnny had tried every possible outlet. The apertures for the conveyor system were guarded at one end by the furnace, and at the other by moving machinery which would ferociously chew to tatters anyone who became entangled in it. They were caged securely, and Johnny paced his cage.

Again he stopped before the peephole, but this time he flung himself at the door with clenched fists. The steel plate smeared the skin from his knuckles as he hammered on it and the pain sobered him. He pressed his face to the glass and through it watched Benedict van der Byl enter the conveyor room and, without glancing at the window, cross to the cyclone.

Benedict laid aside the shotgun he carried and for a moment stood looking up at the thick steel pipe that carried the gravel down from the deck pumps above. As he lifted the thick rope of plastique from around his neck, Johnny knew exactly what he was going to do.

He watched in fascination as Benedict mounted the steel ladder up the side of the cyclone. Hanging with one hand to the ladder, Benedict reached out with the other and clumsily tied the rope of plastique around the gravel pipe. It hung there like a necklace about the throat of some obscene prehistoric monster.

'You bastard! You murdering bloody swine!' Johnny shouted, and again he beat on the steel door with his fists. But the thickness of the door and the whine of the cyclone drowned his voice. Benedict showed no sign of hearing him – but Tracey sat up and looked about her blearily. Then she came to her feet and staggering to the roll and pitch of the ship she went to Johnny and pressed her face to the window beside her.

Benedict was sticking the time pencils into the soft dark explosive. He used all four fuses, taking no chances on a misfire.

'What's he doing?' Tracey asked after she had recovered from the surprise of recognizing her brother.

'He's going to cut the pipe, and let *Kingfisher* pump herself full of gravel.'

'Sink her?' Tracey's voice was sharp with alarm.

'She'll pump water and gravel into herself at pressures that will tear away all the inner bulkheads.'

'This one?' Tracey patted the steel plate.

'It'll pop like a paper bag. God, you have no idea of the power in those pumps.'

'No.' Tracey shook her head. 'He's my brother. He won't do it, Johnny. He couldn't murder us.'

'By the time he's finished –' Johnny contradicted her grimly, ' – *Kingfisher* will be lying in 200 feet of water. Her hull will be packed so tightly with gravel that it will be like a block of cement. We, and everything in her, including his little machine, will be so flattened as to be unrecognizable. It would cost millions to salvage *King-fisher* – and no one will care that much.'

'No, not Benedict.' Tracey was almost pleading. 'He's not that bad.'

Johnny interrupted her brusquely. 'He could get away with it. It's a good try – his best chance. Encase all the evidence against him in concrete, and bury it deep.'

'No, Benedict.' Tracey was watching her brother as he climbed down the cyclone ladder and picked up the shotgun. 'Please, Benedict, don't do it.'

Almost as if he had heard her, Benedict turned suddenly and saw the two faces at the window. The shock of guilt held him rigid for a moment as he stared at them – Tracey's pale lips forming words he could not hear, Johnny's eyes burning with accusation.

Benedict dropped his eyes, he made a gesture that was indecisive, almost pathetic. He looked up at the fused and charged rope of explosive – and then he grinned. A sardonic twitching of the lips, and he stumbled out of the cyclone room and was gone.

'He'll come back,' whispered Tracey. 'He won't let it happen.'

'I wouldn't bet on that – if I were you,' said Johnny.

Benedict reached *Kingfisher*'s rail and clung to it. He looked out to where *Wild Goose* bobbed and hung on the swells. He saw Hugo's face as a white blob behind the wheelhouse window, but as the little trawler began closing in for the pick-up Benedict waved it away. He glanced at his watch again, then looked back anxiously at the bridge.

The long minutes dragged by. Where the hell was the Italian? Benedict could not leave him – not while he still had that diamond; not while he could stop the dredge pumps and release the prisoners locked below.

Again Benedict checked his watch, twelve minutes since he had set the time pencils. He must go back and find Caporetti. He started back along the rail, and at that moment Sergio appeared on the wing of the bridge. He shouted a question at Benedict that was lost in the wind.

'Come on!' Frantically Benedict beckoned to him. 'Come on! Hurry!'

With another last look about the bridge, Sergio ran to the ladder and climbed down to deck level.

'Where my boys?' he shouted at Benedict. 'Why nobody at the con? What you do with them?'

'They are all right,' Benedict assured him. He had turned to the rail and was signalling *Wild Goose* to come alongside.

'Where they?' Sergio demanded. 'Where my boys?'

'I sent them to – ' Benedict's reply was cut off as *Kingfisher*'s deck jarred under their feet. The explosion was a dull concussion in her belly, and Sergio's jaw hung open. Benedict backed away from him along the rail.

'Filth!' Sergio's jaw snapped closed, his whole body appeared to swell with anger.

'You kill them, dirty pig. You kill my boys. You kill Johnny – the girl.'

'Keep away from me.' Benedict braced himself against the rail, leaving both hands free to use the gun.

Not even Sergio would advance into the deadly blank eyes of those muzzles. He paused uncertainly.

'I'll blow your guts all over the deck,' Benedict warned him, and his forefinger was hooked around the trigger.

They stared at each other, and the wind fluttered their hair and tore at their clothing.

'Give me those diamonds,' Benedict commanded, and when Sergio stood unmoving, he went on urgently, 'Don't be a hero, Caporetti. I can gun you down and take them anyway. Give them to me – and our deal is still on. You'll come with us. I'll get you out of here. I swear it.'

Sergio's expression of outrage faded. A moment longer he hesitated.

'Come on, Caporetti. We haven't got much time.' It may have been his imagination, but to Benedict it seemed that *Kingfisher*'s action in the water had altered, she was sluggish to meet the swells and her roll was more pronounced.

'Okay,' said Sergio, and began unbuttoning his jacket. 'You win. I give you.'

Benedict relaxed with relief, and Sergio thrust his hand into his jacket and stepped towards him. He grasped the canvas bag by its neck, and brought it out held like a cosh.

Sergio was close to him, too close for Benedict to swing the shotgun on to him. Sergio's expression became savage, his intentions blazed in his dark eyes as he lifted the canvas bag and poised himself to deliver a blow at Benedict's head, but he had not reckoned with the extraordinary reflexes of the natural athlete he was facing.

As Sergio launched the blow, Benedict rolled his shoulders and head away from it, lifting the butt of the shotgun as a guard. Sergio's wrist struck the seasoned walnut, and he grunted with the pain. His fingers opened nervelessly and the canvas bag flew from his grip, glanced off Benedict's temple and flew on down the deck, sliding to stop against one of the compressed air tanks thirty feet away.

Benedict danced back, dropping the barrels of the shotgun until Sergio looked into the muzzles.

'Hold it, you bastard,' Benedict snarled at him. 'You've made your choice. Now let's see what your guts look like.'

Sergio was hugging his injured wrist to his belly, crouching over it. Benedict was backing away to where the bag lay against the tank. His face was flushed and hectic with anger, but he kept darting side glances at the canvas bag.

At that moment *Kingfisher* took another wave over her bows, and the water came swooshing down the deck, picking up the bag and washing it towards the scuppers.

'Look out!' Sergio shouted. 'The bag! It's going.'

Benedict lunged for it, sprawling full length. With his free hand he grabbed the sodden canvas as it was disappearing over the side. But he was thirty feet away from Sergio, and he still held the shotgun in his other fist. Sergio could not hope to reach him without getting both charges of buckshot in his belly.

Instead Sergio spun round and sprinted back along the deck towards the bridge.

Benedict was on his knees frantically stuffing the bag of diamonds into the side pocket of his jacket and shouting after Sergio.

'Stop! Stop or I'll shoot!'

Sergio did not look back nor check his run, and Benedict had the bag in his pocket and now both hands were free. He lifted the shotgun, and tried to balance himself against *Kingfisher*'s wallowing motion as he aimed.

At the shot, Sergio stumbled slightly but kept on running. He reached the ladder and went up it.

Again Benedict aimed, and the shotgun clapped dully in the wind. This time a spasm of pain shuddered through Sergio's big body, and he froze on the ladder.

Benedict fumbled in his pocket for fresh shells, but before he could reload Sergio had begun climbing again. Benedict broke the gun and thrust the shells into the breech. He snapped the gun closed and looked up just as Sergio disappeared through the storm doors – and the two shots that Benedict loosed after him merely pockmarked the paintwork and starred the glass of the wheelhouse.

'The stupid bastard.' Hugo watched from the wheelhouse of *Wild Goose*. 'He's gone berserk.'

Hugo had heard the explosion and seen the shooting.

'Fifteen years is enough – but not the rope as well.'

He swung the wheel and *Wild Goose* sheered in towards *Kingfisher*'s side. Peering through the spray and salt smattered windows, he saw Benedict drag himself to his feet and start after Sergio along the deck.

Hugo snatched the electric loudhailer from its bracket and pulled open the side window of the wheelhouse, holding the hailer to his lips.

'Hey! You stupid bastard, have you gone mad? What the hell you doing?'

Benedict glanced down at the trawler, then ignored it to give all his attention to reloading the gun. He kept going back along the deck, following Sergio to finish him off.

'You'll get us all strung up, you fool' Hugo called through the loudhailer. 'Leave him. Let's get out of here.'

Benedict kept scrambling and slipping towards *Kingfisher*'s bridge.

'I'm leaving – now! Do you hear me? You can stew in your own pot. I'm getting out.'

Benedict checked and looked down at the trawler. He shouted and pointed at the bridge. Hugo caught one word: 'Diamonds.'

'All right, friend! Do what you like – I'll see you around,' Hugo hailed, and hit the trawler's throttle wide open. The roar of the diesels and the churning of her propeller convinced Benedict.

'Hugo! Wait! Wait for me, I'm coming.' He scampered back to the ladder and started down it.

Hugo throttled back and brought *Wild Goose* in neatly under the ladder.

'Jump!' he shouted through the hailer, and obediently Benedict jumped to hit the foredeck heavily. The shotgun flew from his hands to fall into the water alongside. Benedict cast one longing glance after the gun, then crawled to his feet and limped back to the wheelhouse.

Already *Wild Goose* was plunging away into the wind, but as Benedict entered the wheelhouse Hugo turned on him with his pink albino face set in a snarl of rage.

'What the hell have you done, you bastard? You lied to me. What was that explosion?'

'Explosion – I don't know. What explosion?'

Hugo hit him a stinging open-handed blow across the cheek.

'We agreed no killing – and you put us all on the spot.' Hugo's attention was focused completely on Benedict who had backed into the furthest corner of the wheelhouse. He massaged the dark red finger marks that stained his cheek.

'You set scuttling charges in *Kingfisher* – didn't you, you dirty son of a bitch. God, I hate to think what you've done with Lance and the girl.'

Outside the storm was nearing its climax. A rain squall swept down on *Wild Goose* – sure sign that the wind must soon drop.

Automatically Hugo switched on the rotating wipers to clear the rain from the screen, as he continued to harangue Benedict.

'I saw you trying to murder the Italian. Christ! What for? He's one of us! Am I next on your list?'

'He had the diamonds,' mumbled Benedict. 'I was trying to get them from him.'

And Hugo's expression changed; he turned away from the wheel and stared at Benedict.

'You haven't got the diamonds? Is that what you're saying?' His tone was almost hurt.

'I tried – he wouldn't – '

And Hugo left the wheel and was across the wheelhouse like a white leopard. He grabbed the front of Benedict's coat, and screamed into his face.

'You left the diamonds! You stick my head in a noose – and I get nothing out of it.'

He was trembling with rage and his pale eyes bulged from their sockets.

Looking into those eyes Benedict realized his own danger. In the time it had taken him to leave *Kingfisher*'s deck and reach the wheelhouse of the trawler he had decided to let Hugo think that Sergio still had the diamonds. Squeamish as Hugo appeared to be about drowning Johnny and Tracey, despite his repeated demands for 'No Killing', Benedict knew intuitively that Hugo had no intention of splitting a million pounds' worth of diamonds with him.

Once Hugo was certain that Benedict had the stones on board, Benedict knew there was no chance that he would reach South America alive.

The crossing might take weeks, the crew of the trawler were in Hugo's pay and loyal only to him. Benedict must sleep, and they would take him in the night.

On the other hand, of course, Benedict had no intention of splitting a million pounds' worth of diamonds with Hugo Kramer. He let his voice whine as he cringed in Hugo's grip.

'I tried. Sergio had them. He wouldn't – that's why I shot him.'

Hugo drew back his hand to slap Benedict again. Benedict twisted slightly, and drove his knee into Hugo's crutch, sending him staggering back across the wheelhouse, clutching himself between the legs and whimpering with the pain.

'Right, Kramer,' Benedict spoke softly. 'That's a little lesson for you. Behave yourself, and you'll get your fifty grand on the other side of the Atlantic.'

They stared at each other. Hugo Kramer weak and pale with agony, Benedict standing tall and arrogant again.

'Treat me gently, Kramer. I'm your meal-ticket. Remember it.'

Hugo gaped at him. The positions had reversed so swiftly. He pulled himself upright and his voice was thick with agony, but humble.

'I'm sorry, Mr van der Byl, I lost my temper. It's been a hell of a – '

'Skipper! Ahead!' The warning was shouted by the coloured crewman, Hansie.

Hugo stumbled to the untended wheel, and peered out into the storm.

Wild Goose was shooting down another slope of green water, and just ahead of her bows Hugo saw one of the huge yellow buoys that *Kingfisher* had laid down and then abandoned. It was held captive in the trough of the swells by the anchor cable. The cable was drawn as tight as a rod of steel across the trawler's bows, lifted just above the surface of the water; shivering drops of water flew from it under the tension of the buoy's drag.

'Oh God!' Hugo spun the wheel and threw *Wild Goose*'s engine into reverse – but she was racing down the swell, and her speed was unchecked as the cable scraped harshly along her keel.

Then came the harsh banging and clattering of the drive shaft as the cable fouled the propeller – followed by a crack as the shaft snapped. *Wild Goose*'s engine screamed into overrev as the load was lifted from it.

Hugo shut the throttle, and there was silence in the wheelhouse. *Wild Goose* swung beam on to the seas which came boiling in over her deck. Without her propeller she was transformed from a husky little sea creature to a piece of driftwood at the mercy of each current and the whim of the wind.

Hugo's head swung slowly until he was looking down-wind to where the massive shapes of Thunderbolt and Suicide just showed through the rain squall.

'Cover your ears – tight!' Johnny Lance pressed Tracey against the bulkhead as far from the cyclone room as they could get. 'There are twenty-five pounds of plastique in there – it will blow like a volcano. He will have used short fuse, fourteen minutes. We won't have long to wait.'

Johnny set Tracey's shoulders squarely against the steel plating, and crouched over her – trying to shield her with his own body.

They stared into each other's eyes, teeth clenched, the heels of their palms jammed hard over their ears and they cowered away from the blast that must come.

The minutes passed, the longest minutes of Tracey's life. She could not have borne them without screaming hysteria except for that big hard body covering her – even with it she felt her fear mounting steadily during the molasses drip of time.

Suddenly the air lunged at her, driving the breath from her lungs. Johnny was thrown heavily against her. The blast sucked at her eardrums, and burst in her head so that bright lights flashed across her vision and she felt the steel plates heave under her shoulders.

Then her head cleared, and although her eardrums buzzed and sang, she found with a leaping relief that she was still alive.

She reached out for Johnny, but he was gone. In panic she groped, then opened her eyes. He was lurching down the long conveyor room, and when he reached the locked door at the far end he pressed his face to the peephole.

The fumes of the explosion still filled the cyclone room, a swirling bluish fog, but through them Johnny could make out the shambles that was the aftermath.

The huge cyclone had been torn from its mountings, and now sagged against the far bulkhead – crushed. It was worth only a single glance before Johnny froze into rigidity at the true horror.

The gravel pipe had been severed cleanly just below its juncture with the upper deck. It protruded for six feet, but now the force of the jet through it was flicking and whipping it about as though it were not steel but a rubber garden hose.

The jet was a solid eighteen-inch column, a pillar of brown mud and yellow gravel and sea-water that beat against the steel plates of the hull with a hollow drumming roar.

In the few seconds since the explosion the cyclone room was already half-filled with a slimy shifting porridge that rushed from wall to wall with the movement of the ship. It was like some monstrous jelly fish which each second gathered weight and strength.

Tracey reached Johnny's side and he placed his arm around her shoulders. She looked through the armoured glass and he felt her body stiffen.

At that moment the yellow monster spread over the window, obscuring it completely. Johnny felt the first straining of the steel plates under his hands. They fluttered and bulged, then began to protest aloud at the intolerable pressure. A seam started, and a fine jet of filthy water hissed from the gap and soaked icily through Johnny's jersey.

'Get back.' Johnny dragged Tracey away from the squeaking, groaning bulkhead. Back along the narrow conveyor room they stumbled, moving with difficulty for the deck beneath their feet was slanting as *Kingfisher* began to lean under the increasing weight in her belly.

Still holding Tracey, he reached the locked door and resisted the futile desire to attack it with his bare hands. Instead he forced his brain to work, tried to anticipate the sequence of events that would lead to the final destruction of *Kingfisher* – and all those aboard her.

Benedict had left the other entrance to the cyclone room wide open. Already that viscous mass of mud and water must be spreading rapidly through the lower levels of the hull, following always the avenue of least resistance – finding the weak spots and bursting through them.

If the walls of the conveyor room held against the pressure, the rest of the hull would be filled and they would be enfolded in the tentacles of that great yellow monster – a small bubble of air trapped within it and taken down with it when it returned to the depths from which it had come.

Would the bulkheads of the conveyor room hold? The answer came almost immediately in the squeal of metal against metal, and the crackle of springing rivets.

The monster had found the weak spot, the aperture through the drying furnace into the conveyor, ripping away the fragile baffles, bursting through the furnace in a cloud of steam, it gushed into the conveyor room bringing with it the sewage stench of deep-sea mud.

Kingfisher made another sluggish roll, so different from her usual spry action, and the mud came racing down the tunnel in a solid knee-high wall.

It slammed both of them back against the steel door with a shocking strength, and the feel of it was cold and loathsome as something long dead and putrefied.

Kingfisher rolled back and the mud slithered away, bunched itself against the far bulkhead then charged at them again.

Waist-deep it struck them, and tried to suck them back with the next roll.

Tracey was screaming now, nerves and muscles reaching their breaking-point. She was clinging to Johnny, coated to the waist in stinking ooze, her eyes and mouth wide open in terror as she watched the mud building up for its next assault.

Johnny groped for some hold to anchor them. They must keep on their feet to survive that next rush of mud. He found the locking handle of the door and braced himself against it, holding Tracey with all his strength.

The mud came again, silently, murderously. It burst over their heads and punched them with stunning force against the plating.

Then it sucked back once more, and left them down on their knees, anchored only by Johnny's grip on the locking handle.

Tracey was vomiting the foul mud and it filled her ears and eyes and nostrils, clogging them so that it bubbled at her breathing.

Johnny could feel her weakening in his arms, her struggles becoming more feeble as she tried to regain her feet.

His own strength was going. It needed his last reserve to drag them both upright.

The locking handle turned in his fingers, spinning open. The steel door against which he was braced fell away, so that he staggered backwards without support but still clutching Tracey.

There was just a moment to recognize the big, reassuring bulk of Sergio Caporetti beside him and feel an arm like the trunk of a pine tree steady him before the rush of mud down the conveyor room hit them and knocked all three of them down, sending them swirling and rolling end over end before its strength dissipated in the new space beyond the conveyor room door.

Johnny pulled himself up the bulkhead. He had lost Tracey. Dazed but desperate he looked for her, mumbling her name.

He found her swilling aimlessly in the waist-deep mud, floating on her face. He took a handful of muddy hair and lifted her face out, but the mud had hold of his legs, pulling him off balance as it surged back and forth.

'Sergio. Help!' he croaked. 'For God's sake, Sergio.'

And Sergio was there, lifting her like a child in his arms and wading to the ladder that led to the deck above. The mud knocked Johnny down again, and when he surfaced Sergio was climbing steadily up the ladder.

Despite the mud and water that blurred Johnny's eyesight, he could see that Sergio's wide back, from shoulders to hips, was speckled with dozens of punctures as though he had been stabbed repeatedly with a knitting needle. From each tiny wound oozed droplets of blood that spread like brown ink on the blotting-paper of his sodden jacket.

At the head of the companionway Sergio turned, still holding Tracey in his arms; he stood like a Colussus looking down at Johnny wallowing and slipping in the mud below.

'Hey, Lance – go switch off your bloody machine. She drown my ship. I sail her myself now – the right way. No bloody fancy machine.'

Johnny steadied himself against the bulkhead and called up at him:

'Sergio, what happened to Benedict van der Byl, where is he?'

'I think he go with *Wild Goose* – but first he shoot the hell out of me, not half. Fix your machine, no time for talk.'

And he was gone, still carrying Tracey.

Another rush of mud carried Johnny down the flooded passage and threw him against the door to the control room. Already his body seemed to be one aching bruise, and still the battering continued as he tried to unlock and open the control room door.

At last, using the suck of the mud to help him, he yanked it open and went in with a burst of yellow slime following him and flooding the compartment shoulder deep.

Clinging to the console of the computer he reached up and punched the master control buttons.

'Dredge Stop.'

'Dredge engines Stop.'

'Main engines manual.'

'Navigation system manual.'

'All programmes abort.'

Instantly the roar from the severed dredge pipe, which had echoed through the ship during all their strivings, dwindled as though some vast waterfall had dried. Then there was silence. Though only comparative silence, for the hull still groaned and squeaked at the heart-breaking burden it now carried and the mud slopped and thudded against the plating.

Weak and sick, Johnny clung to the console. He was shivering with cold, and every muscle in his body felt bruised and strained.

Suddenly the ship changed her motion, heaving under his feet like a harpooned whale as she swung broadside to the storm. Johnny roused himself with alarm.

The journey back through the flooded passages to the companionway was an agony of mind and body – for *Kingfisher* was now behaving in a strange and unnatural way.

The scene that awaited Johnny as he dragged himself on to the bridge chilled his soul as the icy mud had chilled his body.

Thunderbolt and Suicide lay less than a furlong off *Kingfisher*'s starboard quarter. Both islands were wreathed in sheets of spray that fumed from the surf that was breaking like cannon-fire on the cliffs.

The maniacal flute of the wind joined with the drum of the surf to produce a symphony fit for the halls of Hell, but above this devil's music Sergio Caporetti bellowed, 'We got no power on port main engine.'

Johnny turned to him. Sergio was hunched over the wheel, and Tracey lay on the deck at his feet like a discarded doll.

'The water she kill port main.' Sergio was pumping the engine telegraph. Then abandoning the effort, he looked over the side.

The reeking white cliffs were closer now, much closer – as though you could reach out a hand to them. The ship was drifting down rapidly on the wind.

Sergio spun the wheel to full port lock, trying to bring *Kingfisher*'s head round to meet the sea and the wind. She was rolling as no ship was ever meant to roll, hanging over at the limit of each swing, so that the wheelhouse windows seemed but a few feet from the crests of the green waves. She hung like that as though she meant never to come upright again. Then sluggishly, reluctantly, she swung back, speeding up as she reached the perpendicular and the great mass of mud and water in her hull shifted and slammed her over on her other side, pinning her like that for eternal seconds before she could struggle upright again for the cycle to be repeated.

Sergio held the wheel at full lock, but still *Kingfisher* wallowed down towards the cliffs of Thunderbolt and Suicide. The wind had her the way a dog carries a bone in its teeth. Under half power and with her decks awash *Kingfisher* could not break that grip.

Johnny was a helpless spectator, held awe-bound so he could not break away even to succour Tracey who was still lying on the deck. He saw everything with a supernatural clarity – from the dribbling little shot holes in Sergio's back, to the ponderous irresistible rush of the white water up the cliffs that loomed so close alongside.

'She no answer helm. She too sick.' Sergio spoke now in conversational tones which carried with surprising clarity through the uproar of the elements. 'All right then. We go the other way. We take the gap.'

For a moment Johnny did not understand, then he saw it. *Kingfisher*'s bows were coming up to the narrow opening between the two islands.

A passage less than a hundred yards wide at its narrowest point, where the vicious cross currents met head on and leapt fifty feet into the air as they collided. Here the surface was obscured by a thick froth of spindrift that heaved and humped up as though the ocean were fighting for breath under the thick cream-coloured blanket.

'No.' Johnny shook his head, staring at that hideous passage. 'We won't make it, Sergio. We won't do it.'

But already Sergio was spinning the wheel from lock to lock, and unbelievably *Kingfisher* was responding. Helped now by the wind she came around slowly, seeming to brush her bows across the white cliff of Thunderbolt, and she steadied her swing and aimed at the gap. It was then Johnny saw it for the first time.

'Christ, there's a boat dead ahead!'

The steep swells had hidden it up to that moment, but now she bobbed up on a crest. It was a tiny trawler, flying a dirty scrap of canvas as a staysail at her stubby mast, and struggling piteously in the granite jaws of Thunderbolt and Suicide.

'*Wild Goose*!' roared Sergio, and he reached for the handle of the foghorn that hung above his head.

'Now we have some fun.' And he yanked the handle. The croaking bellow of the foghorn echoed off the cliffs that were closing on either side of them.

'Kill my boys – hey? Shoot me – hey? Trick me – hey? Now I trick you – but good!' Sergio punctuated his triumphant yells with blasts on the foghorn.

'Christ, no! You can't do it!' Johnny caught urgently at the big Italian's shoulder, but Sergio struck his hand away and steered directly for the trawler as it lay full in the narrow passage.

'I give him plenty warning.' Sergio sent another blast echoing off the cliffs. 'He no give me warning when he shoot me – the bastard.'

There was a group of men on the trawler's foredeck. Johnny could see that they were manhandling an inflatable escape raft, a thick mattress of black rubber, towards the nearest side of the trawler. But now they were frozen by the bellow of *Kingfisher*'s foghorn. They stood looking up at the tall cliff of steel that bore down on them. Their faces were pale blobs in the gloom.

'Sergio. It's murder. Turn away, damn you, you can miss them. Turn away!' Again Johnny lunged across the wheelhouse and grabbed at the wheel.

Sergio swung a backhanded blow that cracked against Johnny's temple and sent him reeling back half-stunned against the storm doors.

'*Who* Captain for this bloody ship!' There was blood on Sergio's lips, the shout had torn something inside him.

Kingfisher's bows were lifting and swinging down like an executioner's axe over the trawler. They were close enough now for Johnny to recognize the men on the trawler's deck – but only one of them held his full attention.

Benedict van der Byl cowered against the trawler's rail, gripping it with both hands. His hair fluttered, soft and dark, in the wind. His eyes were big dark holes like those of a skull in the bone-white face, and his lips a pink circle of terror.

Then suddenly the trawler disappeared under *Kingfisher's* massive bows, and immediately after that came the splintering crunching sound of her timbers shattering. *Kingfisher* bore on down the passage between the cliffs without a check in her speed.

Johnny fumbled with the catch of the storm doors, and the wind tore it open. He staggered out on to the exposed wing of the bridge and reached the rail.

He stood there with the storm clawing at his clothing and looked down at the wreckage that dragged slowly along *Kingfisher's* hull, and then was left behind.

There were human heads bobbing among the wreckage, and the wash from *Kingfisher's* propeller pushed them towards the cliffs of Suicide.

A wave picked up one of the men and carried him swiftly on to the cliff, sweeping him high and then swirling back to leave the body stranded on that smooth white slope of granite.

The man was still alive, Johnny saw him clawing at the smooth rock with his bare fingers, trying to drag himself above the reach of the sea.

It was Hugo Kramer; even through the fog of spray there was no mistaking that head of pale hair and the lithe twisted body.

The next wave reached up and dragged him back over the rock, tearing the nails from his hooked fingers as he tried to find a hold.

He was swirled and flung about in the turbulence below the cliff before another wave lifted him and hurled him on to the granite. One of his legs was broken at the knee by the force of the impact and the lower part of the leg spun loosely like the blade of a windmill as the water tugged at it.

Once again Hugo was left stranded but now he made no movement. His arms were flung wide, and his leg stuck out at a grossly unnatural angle from the knee.

Then from among these mighty waves there rose up a mass of green water which dwarfed all the others.

It reared up with slow majesty and hung poised over the granite cliff before it fell on Hugo's broken body with a boom that seemed to shake the very rock.

When the giant wave drew back, the cliff was washed clean. Hugo was gone.

The same wave that destroyed him came down the passage between the cliffs and, in contrast to its treatment of Hugo Kramer, it was tender as a mother as it lifted *Kingfisher* and carried her out into the open sea beyond the reach of those cruel cliffs.

Looking back into the gap between the islands, the last trace that Johnny saw of the *Wild Goose* was the black rubber escape raft tossing and leaping high on the turmoil of broken water and creamy spindrift.

'They'll have no use for that,' he said aloud. He searched for a sight of any survivor, but there was none. They were chewed to pulp in the jaws of Thunderbolt and Suicide, and swallowed down into the cold green maw of the sea.

Johnny turned away and went back into the wheelhouse. He lifted Tracey from the deck and carried her through to Sergio's cabin.

As he laid her on the bunk he whispered to her, 'I'm glad. I'm glad you didn't see it, my darling.'

At midnight the wind still howled about the ship, hurling sheets of solid rain against the windows of the bridge. Forty minutes later the wind had veered through a hundred and eighty degrees and become a light south-easterly air. The black sky opened like a theatre curtain, and the full moonlight burst through so brightly as to pale the stars. Though the tall black swells still marched in martial ranks from the north, the gentle wind was soothing and lulling them.

'Sergio, you must rest now. I will take the con. Let Tracey dress your back.'

'You take the con!' Sergio snorted scornfully. 'I save the ship – and you sink her for me. Not bloody likely.'

'Listen, Sergio. We don't know how badly you are hurt. You are killing yourself.'

The same argument spluttered and flared intermittently during the long night hours while Sergio clung stubbornly to the helm and coaxed the labouring vessel back towards Cartridge Bay. He insisted on detouring far out to sea to avoid the islands, so that when the bright dawn broke, the land was only a low brown line on the horizon and the mountains of the interior were a distant blue.

An hour after dawn Johnny made radio contact with the very agitated operator at Cartridge Bay.

'Mr Lance, we've been trying to raise you since yesterday evening.'

'I've been busy.' Despite his fatigue Johnny grinned at his own understatement. 'Now, listen to me. We are coming into Cartridge Bay. We'll be there in a couple of hours. I want you to have a doctor, Doctor Robin Sutherland, flown up from Cape Town – also I want you to have the police standing by. I want somebody from both the Diamond police and the Robbery and Murder squad – have you got that?'

'The police are here already, Mr Lance. They are looking for Mr Benedict van der Byl. They found his car here – they have a warrant . . .' The operator's voice broke off and Johnny heard the mumble of background voices, then – 'Mr Lance, are you there? Stand by to speak to Inspector Stander of the C.I.D.'

'Negative!' Johnny cut in on his transmission. 'I'm not talking to anybody. He can wait until we get into the Bay. Just you have Doctor Sutherland ready. I've got a badly wounded man on board.'

Johnny leaned over the radio set and shut off the main switch, then he stood and made his way slowly back to the bridge. Every muscle in his body felt stiff and bruised, and he was groggy with tiredness, but he took up the argument with Sergio where they had left off.

'Now listen to me, Sergio. You must lie down. You can take us in over the bar; but now you must get an hour or two's rest.'

Still Sergio would not relinquish the wheel, but he consented to strip to the waist and let Tracey examine his back.

In the expanse of white muscle were little black holes each set in its own purple bruise. Some of the holes had sealed themselves with black clotted blood, from others fluid still oozed – clear or pink in colour – and there was a faint sweetish smell from the wounds.

Johnny and Tracey exchanged worried looks before Tracey reached into the first aid box and set to work.

'How she look, Johnny?' Sergio's jovial tone was belied by his face which was a lump of bread dough touched with greenish blue hues.

'Depends if you like your meat rare.' Johnny matched his tone, and Sergio chuckled but cut it short with a wince.

Johnny put a cheroot between Sergio's lips and held a match for him. As Sergio puffed the tip into a glow, Johnny asked casually, 'What made you change your mind?' And Sergio looked up at him quickly, guiltily, through the cloud of cheroot smoke.

'You had us cold. You could have got away with it – perhaps,' Johnny persisted quietly. 'What made you come back?'

'Listen, Johnny. Me, I've done some damned awful bloody things – but I never killed a man or a woman – ever. He said no killing. Fine, I go along. Then I hear the plastique blow. I know you two in conveyor room. I think the hell with it. Now, I climb off the wagon – but she's going too fast. I get bum full of buckshot.'

They were silent for a while. Tracey was absorbed in patching the shot-wounds with adhesive tape.

Johnny broke the silence. 'Was there a big diamond, Sergio? A big blue diamond?'

'Si.' Sergio sighed. 'Such a diamond you will never see again.'

'Benedict had it?'

'Si. Benedict had it.'

'Did he have it on him?'

'In his coat. He put it in his coat pocket.'

Tracey stepped back. 'That's all we can do for now,' she murmured and caught Johnny's eye, shaking her head slightly and frowning with worry. 'The sooner we get him to a doctor the happier I'll be.'

A little before noon Sergio took *Kingfisher* in through the entrance to Cartridge Bay, handling the mud-filled ship with all the aplomb of the master mariner, but as they approached the first turning in the channel he sagged gently to the deck and the wheel spun out of his hands.

Before Johnny could reach the helm, *Kingfisher* had yawed wearily across the channel. She had so little way on her that when she went up on the sandbank there was only a small jolt and she listed over a few degrees.

Johnny pulled the engine telegraph to 'STOP'.

'Help me, Tracey.' He stooped over Sergio and took him under the armpits. Tracey grasped his ankles. Half dragging, half carrying, they got him through to his cabin and laid him on his bunk.

'Hey, Johnny. Sorry, Johnny,' Sergio was mumbling. 'First time I put ship on bank – ever! Idiot! So close – then *wap*! Sorry, hey, Johnny.'

The motor launch left the jetty and came down the channel towards the sandbank on which *Kingfisher* lay stranded. The launch was crowded, and the whine of the outboard engine raised a storm of water fowl into a whirlwind of frightened wings.

As it drew closer Johnny recognized some of the occupants. Mike Shapiro and with him Robin Sutherland, but there were also two uniformed policemen and another person in civilian clothes who stood up in the launch as it came within hail and cupped his hands about his mouth.

'I am a police officer. I have a warrant for the arrest of Benedict – '

Mike Shapiro touched the man's arm, and spoke softly to him. The officer hesitated and glanced up at Johnny again, before nodding agreement and settling back on to his seat.

'Robin, get up here as quick as you can,' Johnny shouted down at the launch, and when Robin came over the side Johnny hustled him towards the bridge, but Mike Shapiro hurried after them.

'Johnny, I must talk to you.'

'It can wait.'

'No, it can't.' Mike Shapiro turned to Tracey. 'Won't you take care of the doctor, please? I must speak to Johnny before the police do.'

Mike led Johnny down the deck and offered him a cigarette, while the three policemen hovered at a discreet distance.

'Johnny, I have some dreadful news. I want to break it to you myself.'

Johnny visibly braced himself. 'Yes?'

'It's about Ruby – '

Johnny made his statement to the police inspector in *Kingfisher*'s guest cabin. It took two hours for him to relate the full story, and during that time one of the uniformed policemen discovered the crew locked in the paint store below decks. They were half poisoned with paint fumes but able to make their statements to the police.

The inspector kept them waiting in the next-door cabin while he finished his interrogation of Johnny.

'Two more questions for now, Mr Lance. In your opinion was the collision between the two ships accidental or deliberate?'

Johnny looked into the steel-grey eyes and lied for the first time.

'It was unavoidable.'

The inspector nodded and made a note on his pad.

'Last question. The survivors from the trawler, what were their chances?'

'In that storm they had none. There was no hope of effecting a rescue with *Kingfisher* almost disabled, and considering the condition of the surf in the passage between the islands.'

'I understand.' The inspector nodded. 'Thank you, Mr Lance. That is all for the present.'

Johnny left the cabin and went quickly to the upper deck. Tracey and Robin were still working over Sergio's bunk, but Robin looked up and came immediately to Johnny as he stood in the doorway.

'How is he, Robin?'

'He hasn't a chance,' Robin replied, keeping his voice low. 'One lung has collapsed, and there appear to be perforations of the bowel and intestine. I suspect a massive peritonitis. I can't move him without risking a secondary haemorrhage.'

'Is he conscious?'

Robin shook his head. 'He's going fast. God knows how he has lasted this long.'

Johnny moved across to the bunk and placed his arm about Tracey's shoulders. She moved closer to him and they stood looking down at Sergio.

His eyes were closed, and a dark pelt of new beard covered the lower part of his face. His breathing sawed and hissed loudly in the quiet cabin, and the fever lit bright spots of colour in his cheeks.

'You magnificent old rogue.' Johnny spoke softly, and Sergio's eyes blinked open. Quickly Johnny stooped to him.

'Sergio. Your crew – your boys are safe.'

Sergio smiled. He closed those dark gazelle eyes, then opened them again and whispered painfully, 'Johnny, you give me job when I come out of prison?'

'They won't have you in prison – you'd lower the tone of the place.'

Sergio tried to laugh. He managed one strangled chuckle, then he came up on his elbows in the bunk with his eyes bulging, his mouth gaping for breath. He coughed once, a harsh tearing sound, and the blood burst from his lips in thick black clots and a bright red spray of droplets.

He fell back on the pillows, and was dead before Robin reached his side.

Tracey was asleep in the bedroom next door. Robin had sedated her heavily enough to keep her that way for the next twelve hours.

Johnny lay naked on the narrow bunk in the second guest room of the Cartridge Bay depot, and when he switched on the bedside lamp his wrist-watch showed the time as 2.46 in the morning.

He looked down at his own body. The bruises were dark purple and hot angry red across his ribs and flanks from where the mud had battered him against rough steel plating. He wished now that he had accepted the sleeping pills Robin had offered him, for the ache of his body and the whirl of his thoughts had kept him from sleep all that night.

His mind was trapped on a nightmare roundabout, revolving endlessly the two deaths which Benedict van der Byl must answer for in the dark places to which he had surely gone.

Ruby and Sergio. Ruby and Sergio. One he had seen die, the other he could imagine in all its gruesome detail.

Johnny sat up and lit a cigarette, seeking a distraction from the tortured images with which his over-excited brain bombarded him.

He tried to concentrate on reviewing the practical steps that would be necessary to clear up the aftermath of these last disastrous days.

He had spoken that evening by radio to Larsen, and received from him a promise of complete financial support during the time it would take to clear the mud from *Kingfisher*'s hull and recover the diamonds in the conveyor tunnel, and to tide over the period of salvage and repair before the dredger was ready to begin once more harvesting the rich fields of Thunderbolt and Suicide.

A salvage team would fly in tomorrow to begin the work on *Kingfisher*. He had cabled IBM requesting engineers to check out the computer for water damage.

Six weeks, Johnny estimated, before *Kingfisher* was ready for sea.

Then his unruly imagination leapt suddenly ahead to Ruby's funeral. It was set for Tuesday next week. Johnny rolled restlessly on his bunk, trying to shut his mind against the thoughts that assaulted it – but they crowded forward in a dark host.

Ruby, Benedict, Sergio, the big blue diamond.

He sat up again, stubbed out his cigarette and reached across to switch out the bedside lamp.

He froze like that, as a new thought pressed in on him. He heard Sergio's voice in his memory.

'*Such a diamond as you will never see again.*'

Now he felt the idea come ghosting along his spine so that the hair at the nape of his neck and on his forearms prickled with excitement.

'The Red Gods!' he exclaimed, almost shouting the name. And again Sergio's voice spoke.

'*In his coat. He put it in his coat pocket.*'

Johnny swung his legs off the bunk, and reached for his clothes. He felt the pounding of his heart beneath his fingers as he buttoned his shirt. He pulled on slacks and sweater, tied the laces of his shoes and snatched up a sheepskin jacket as he ran from the room.

He was shrugging on the jacket as he entered the deserted radio room and switched on the lights. He crossed quickly to the chart table and pored over it.

He found the name on the map, and repeated it aloud.

'The Red Gods.'

North of Cartridge Bay the coast ran straight and featureless for thirty miles, then abruptly the line of it was broken by the outthrust of red rock, poking into the sea like an accuser's finger.

Johnny knew it well. It was his job to find and examine any such natural feature that might act as a barrier to the prevailing inshore currents. At such a place diamonds and other seaborne objects would be thrown ashore.

He remembered the red rock cliffs carved by wind and sea into the grotesque natural statues which gave the place its name, but more important he remembered the litter of ocean debris on the beaches beneath the cliff. Driftwood, waterlogged planking, empty bottles, plastic containers, scraps of nylon fishing-net and corks – all of it cast overboard and carried up by the current to be deposited on this promontory.

He ran his finger down the chart and held it on the dots of Thunderbolt and Suicide. He read the laconic notation over the tiny arrows that flew from the islands towards the stark outline of the Red Gods.

'Current sets South South-West. 5 knots.'

Above the chart table the depot keys hung on their little cuphooks, each labelled and numbered.

Johnny selected the two of them marked 'GARAGE' and 'LAND-ROVER'.

The moon was full and high. The night was still and without a trace of wind. Johnny swung the double doors of the garage open and switched on the parking lights of the Land-Rover. By their glow he checked out the vehicle; petrol tank full, the spare five-gallon cans in their brackets full, the can of drinking-water full. He dipped his finger into the neck of the water container and tasted it. It was clean and sweet. He lifted the passenger seat and checked the compartment beneath it. Jack and tyre spanner, first aid kit, flashlight, signal rockets and smoke flares, water bottle, canvas groundsheet, two cans of survival rations, tow-rope, tool kit, knapsack, knife and compass. The Land-Rover was equipped to meet any of the emergencies of desert travel.

Johnny climbed behind the wheel and started the engine. He drove quietly and slowly past the depot buildings, not wanting to awaken those sleeping inside, but when he hit the firm sand at the edge of the lagoon he switched on the headlights and gunned the engine.

He cut across the sand dunes at the entrance to the bay, and swung northwards on to the beach. The headlights threw solid white beams into the sea mist, and startled sea birds rose on flapping ghost wings before the rush of the Land-Rover.

The tide was out and the exposed beach was hard and shiny wet, smooth as a tarmac road. He drove fast, and the white beach crabs were blinded by the headlights and crunched crisply beneath the tyres.

The dawn came early, silhouetting the mystic shapes of the dunes against the red sky.

Once he startled a strand wolf, one of the brown hyenas which scavenged this bleak littoral. It galloped, hunch-shouldered, in hideous panic for the safety of the dunes. Even in his urgency Johnny felt a stir of revulsion for the loathsome creature.

The cold damp rush of the wind into his face refreshed Johnny. It cooled the gritty feeling of his eyes, and eased the throb of sleeplessness in his temples.

The sun burst over the horizon, and lit the Red Gods five miles ahead with all the drama of stage lighting. They glowed golden red in the dawn, a procession of huge half-human shapes that marched into the sea.

As Johnny drove towards them the light and shadow played over the cliffs and he saw a hundred-foot tall figure of Neptune stooping to dip his flowing red beard into the sea, while a monstrous hunchback with the head of a wolf pranced beside him. Ranks of Vestal Virgins in long robes of red rock jostled with the throng of weird and fantastic shapes. It was eerie and disquieting. Johnny curbed his fancy and turned his attention to the beaches at the foot of the cliffs.

What he saw started his skin tingling again, and he pressed the accelerator flat against the floor-boards, racing across the wet sand to where a white cloud of sea birds circled and dived and hopped about something that lay at the water's edge.

As he drove towards them a gull flew across the front of the Land-Rover. A long ribbon of something wet and fleshy dangled from its beak, and the gull gulped at it greedily in flight. Its crop was distended and engorged with food.

The sea-birds scattered raucously and indignantly as the Land-Rover approached, leaving a human body lying in the centre of an area of sand that was dappled by the prints of their webbed feet, and fouled with dropped feathers and excreta.

Johnny braked the Land-Rover and jumped out. He took one long look at the body, then turned quickly away and braced himself against the side of the vehicle.

His gorge rose in a hot flood of nausea, and he gagged it back.

The body was nude but for a few sodden tatters of clothing and a sea boot still laced on to one foot. The birds had attacked every inch of exposed flesh – except for the scalp. The face was unrecognizable. The nose was gone, the eye sockets were empty black holes. There were no lips to cover the grinning teeth.

Above this ruined face the shock of colourless albino hair looked like a wig placed there as an obscene and tasteless joke.

Hugo Kramer had made the long voyage from Thunderbolt and Suicide to the Red Gods.

Johnny took the canvas groundsheet from under the passenger seat of the Land-Rover. Averting his eyes from the task, he wrapped the corpse carefully, tied the whole bundle with lengths of rope cut from the tow line, then laboriously dragged it up the beach well above the high-water mark.

The thick canvas would keep off the birds, but to make doubly certain Johnny collected the driftwood and planking that was scattered thickly along the high-water line and piled it over the corpse.

Some of the planking was freshly broken and the paint on it was still bright and new. Johnny guessed this was part of the wreckage of *Wild Goose*.

He went back to the Land-Rover, and drove on towards the Red Gods which lay only a mile ahead.

The sun was well up by now, and already its heat was uncomfortable. As he drove he struggled out of the sheepskin jacket without interrupting his search of the beach ahead.

He was looking for another gathering of seagulls, but instead he saw a large black object stranded in the angle formed by the red stone cliffs.

He was fifty yards from it before he realized what it was.

He felt his stomach jar violently and then clench at the shock.

It was a black rubber inflatable life raft – and it had been dragged up the beach *above the high-water line*.

As he climbed out of the Land-Rover Johnny felt his legs trembling beneath him, as though he had just climbed a mountain. The hard knotted sensation in his chest shortened his breathing.

He went slowly towards the raft, and there was a story to read in the soft sand.

The smooth drag mark of the raft, and the two sets of footprints. One set made by bare feet; broad, stubby-toed and with flattened arches, the prints of a man who habitually went barefooted.

These tracks had been made by one of the coloured crew of *Wild Goose*, Johnny decided, dismissed them and turned his whole attention to the other set of footprints.

Shod feet, long and narrow, smooth leather soles; the imprints were sharp edged suggesting new shoes little worn, the length of the stride and the depth of prints were those of a tall heavily-built man.

Johnny realized with mild surprise that his hands were shaking now, and even his lips quivered. He was like a man in high fever; light-headed, weak and shaking. It was Benedict van der Byl. He knew it with complete and utter certainty. Benedict had survived the maelstrom of Thunderbolt and Suicide.

Johnny balled his fists, squeezing hard and he thrust out his jaw, tightening his lips. Still the hatred washed over his mind in dark hot waves.

'Thank God,' he whispered. 'Thank God. Now I can kill him myself.'

The footprints had churned the sand all about the raft. Beside them lay a thick piece of planking which had been used as a lever to rip the emergency water container and the food locker from the floor-boards of the raft.

The food locker had been ransacked and abandoned. They would be carrying the packets of iron rations in their pockets to save weight, but the water container was gone.

The two sets of prints struck out straight for the dunes. Johnny followed them at a run and lost them immediately in the shifting wind-blown sands of the first dune.

Johnny was undismayed. The dunes persisted for only a thousand yards or so, then gave way inland to the plains and salt flats of the interior.

He ran back to the Land-Rover. He had his emotions under control again. His hatred was reduced to a hard indigestible lump below his ribs, and he contemplated for a few seconds lifting the microphone of the Land-Rover's R/T set and calling Cartridge Bay.

Inspector Stander had the police helicopter parked on the landing-strip behind the depot buildings. He could be here in thirty minutes. An hour later they would have Benedict van der Byl.

Johnny dismissed the idea. Officially Benedict was dead, drowned. No one would look for him in a shallow grave in the wastes of the Namib desert.

The crewman with him would be a complication; but he could be bribed and frightened or threatened. Nothing must stand in the path of his vengeance. Nothing.

Johnny opened the Land-Rover's locker and found the knife. He went to the raft and stabbed the blade through the thick material at a dozen places. The air hissed from the holes, and the raft collapsed slowly.

Johnny bundled it into the back of the Land-Rover. He would bury it in the desert; there must be no evidence that Benedict had come ashore.

He started the engine, engaged the four-wheel drive, and followed the spoor to the foot of the dunes.

He picked his way through the valleys and across the knife-backed ridges of sand.

As he descended the last slope of the dunes he felt the oppressive silence and immensity of the land enfold him. Here, only a mile from the sea, the moderating influence of the cold Benguela current did not reach.

The heat was appalling. Johnny felt the sweat prickling from the pores of his skin and drying instantly in the lethal desiccating air.

He swung the Land-Rover parallel to the line of the dunes and crawled along at walking speed, hanging over the side of the vehicle and searching the ground. The bright specks of mica in the sand bounced the heat of the sun into his face.

He cut the spoor again where it came down off the dunes and went away on it, headed arrow straight at the far line of mountains which were already receding into the blue haze as the heat built up towards noon.

Johnny's progress was a series of rushes where the spoor ran true, broken by halts and painstaking casts on the rocky ridges and areas of broken ground. Twice he left the Land-Rover to work the spoor through difficult terrain, but across one of the flat white salt pans he covered four miles in as many minutes. The prints were strung like the beads of a necklace, cut clearly through the glistening crust of salt.

Beyond the pan they ran into a maze of black rocks, riven by gullies, and guarded by the tall misshapen monoliths.

In one of the gullies he found Hansie, the little old coloured crewman from *Wild Goose*. His skull had been battered in with the blood-caked rock that lay beside him. The blood had dried slick and shiny, and Hansie stared with dry eyeballs at the merciless sky. His expression was of mild surprise.

The story of this new tragedy was written in the sandy bottom of the gully. In an area of milling, confused prints the two men had argued. Johnny could guess that Hansie had wanted to turn back for the coast. He must have known that the road lay beyond the mountains, a hundred miles away. He wanted to abandon the attempt, try for the coast and Cartridge Bay.

The argument ended when he turned his back on Benedict, and returned on his old tracks.

There was a depression in the sand from which Benedict had picked up the rock and followed him.

Standing over Hansie, and looking down at that pathetic crushed head, Johnny realized for the first time that he was following a maniac.

Benedict van der Byl was insane. He was no longer a man, but a raging demented animal.

'I will kill him,' Johnny promised the old white woolly head at his feet. There was no need for subterfuge now.

If he caught up with Benedict and did it, no court in the world would question but that it was self-defence. Benedict had placed himself beyond the laws of man.

Johnny took the deflated rubber raft and spread it over Hansie. He anchored the edges of the rubber sheet with rocks.

He drove on into the dancing, shimmering walls of heat with a new mood on him; murderous, elated expectation. He knew that at this moment in time he was part animal also, corrupted by the savagery of the man he was hunting. He wanted payment in full from Benedict van der Byl in his own coin. Life for life, and blood for blood.

A mile farther on he found the water container. It had been flung aside violently, skidding across the sand with the force of its rejection; the water had poured from its open mouth, leaving a dried hollow in the thirsty earth.

Johnny stared at it in disbelief. Not even a maniac would condemn himself to such a horrible ending.

Johnny went across to where the five-gallon brass drum lay on its side. He picked it up and shook it, there was the sloshy sound of a pint or so of liquid in it.

'God!' he whispered, awed and feeling a twinge of pity despite himself. 'He won't last long now.'

He lifted the container to his lips and sucked a mouthful. Immediately his nostrils flared with disgust, and he spat violently, dropping the can and wiping at his lips with the back of his hand.

'Sea water!' he mumbled. He hurried to the Land-Rover and washed out his mouth with sweet water.

How the contamination had occurred he would never know. The raft might have lain for years in *Wild Goose* without its stores being checked or renewed.

From that point onwards Benedict must have known he was doomed. His despair was easy to read in the blundering footsteps. He had started running, with panic driving him. Five hundred yards further on he had fallen heavily into the bed of a dry ravine, and lain for a while before dragging himself up the bank.

Now he had lost direction. The spoor began a long curve to the northwards, running again. It came round full circle, and where it crossed itself, Benedict had sat down. The marks of his buttocks were unmistakable. He must have controlled his panic here because once more the spoor struck out with determination towards the mountains.

However, within half a mile he had tripped and fallen. Now he was staggering off course again, drifting southwards. Once more he had fallen, but here he had lost a shoe.

Johnny picked it up and read the printed gold lettering on the inner sole. 'BALLY OF SWITZERLAND, SPECIALLY MADE FOR HARRODS. That's our boy Benedict, all right. Forty-guinea black kid,' he muttered grimly, and climbed back into the Land-Rover. His excitement was climaxing now. It would be soon, very soon.

Farther on Benedict had wandered down into the bed of an ancient watercourse, and turned to follow it. His right foot was lacerated by the razor flints in the river bed, and at each pace he had left a little dab of brown crumbly blood. He was staggering like a drunkard.

Johnny zigzagged the Land-Rover through the boulders that choked the water-course. The gully deepened, and spiky cockscomb ridges of black rock hedged it in on either hand. The air in the watercourse was a heavy blanket of heat. It seared the throat, and dried the mucus in Johnny's nostrils brick hard. A small noon breeze came off the mountains, a sluggish stirring of the heavy air, that provided no relief but seemed only to heighten the bite of the sun and the suffocating oppression of the air.

Scattered along the river bed were bushes of stunted scrub. Grotesque little plants, crippled and malformed by the drought of years.

From one of the bushes ahead of the Land-Rover a monstrous black bird flapped its wings lethargically. Johnny screwed up his eyes, uncertain if it was reality or a mirage of the heat and the tortured air.

Suddenly the bird resolved itself into the jacket of a dark blue suit. It hung in the thorny branches, the breeze stirring the folds of expensive cloth.

'In his coat. He put it in his coat pocket.'

With eyes only for the jacket, recklessly he pressed down the accelerator and the Land-Rover surged forward. Johnny did not see the knee-high boulder of ironstone in his path. He hit it at twenty miles an hour, and the Land-Rover stopped dead with the squeal of tearing metal. Johnny was flung forward against the steering-wheel, the impact driving the breath from his lungs.

He was still doubled up with the pain of it, wheezing for breath, as he hobbled to the jacket and snatched it out of the bush.

He felt the heavy drag of the weighted pocket.

Then the fat canvas bag was in his hands, the contents crunched nuttily as he tore at the drawstring. Nothing else in the world felt like that.

'Such a diamond as you will never see again.'

The drawstring was knotted tightly. Johnny ran back to the Land-Rover. Franti-cally he scrabbled in the seat locker and found the knife. He cut the drawstring and dumped the contents of the bag on to the bonnet of the Land-Rover.

'Oh God! Oh sweet God!' he whispered through cracked lips. His eyesight blurred, and the big blue diamond glowed mistily, distorted by the tears that flooded his vision.

It was a full minute before he could bring himself to touch it. Then he did so reverently – as though it were a sacred relic.

Johnny Lance had worked all his life to take a stone such as this.

He held it in both hands and sank down into the scrap of shade beside the body of the Land-Rover.

It was another five minutes before the hot cloying smell of engine oil reached the conscious level of his mind.

He turned his head and saw the slowly spreading pool of it beneath the Land-Rover chassis. Quickly he rolled on to his stomach and, still clutching the diamond, crawled under the vehicle. The ironstone boulder had shattered the engine sump. The Land-Rover had bled its lifeblood into the hot sand of the river bed.

He wriggled out from under the body of the Land-Rover and leaned against the front tyre. He looked at his wrist-watch and was surprised to see it was already a few minutes after two o'clock in the afternoon.

He was surprised also at the conscious effort it required to focus his eyes on the dial of the watch. Two days and two nights without sleep, the unremitting emotional strain of those days and nights, the battering his body had taken, the long hours in the heat and the soul-corroding desolation of this lunar landscape – all these had taken their toll. He knew he was as light-headed as in the first stages of inebriation, he was beginning to act irrationally. That sudden reckless charge down the boulder-strewn river bed, which had wrecked the Land-Rover, was a symptom of his present instability.

He fondled the great diamond, touching the warm smooth surface to his lips, rubbing it softly between thumb and forefinger, changing it from hand to hand, while every fibre of his muscles and the very marrow of his bones cried out for rest.

A soft and treacherous lethargy spread through his body and reached out to numb his brain. He closed his eyes for a moment to shut out the flare, and when he opened them again with an effort the time was four o'clock. He scrambled to his feet. The shadows in the gully were longer, the breeze had dropped.

Although he moved with the stiffness of an old man, the sleep had cleared his mind and while he wolfed a packet of biscuits spread with meat paste and washed it down with a mugful of luke-warm water he made his decision.

He buried the canvas bag of rough diamonds in the sand beneath the Land-Rover, but he could not bring himself to part with the big Blue. He buttoned it securely into the back pocket of his slacks. Into the light knapsack from the seat locker he packed the two-pint water bottle, the first aid kit, a small hand-bearing compass, two of the smoke flares and the knife. He checked his pockets for his cigarette-lighter and case.

Then without another glance at the radio set on the dashboard of the Land-Rover he turned away and hobbled up the gully on the spoor of Benedict van der Byl.

Within half a mile he had walked the stiffness out of his body, and he lengthened his stride, going well now. The hatred and hunger for vengeance which had died to smouldering ash since he had found the diamonds now flared up again strongly. It gave power to his legs and sharpened his senses.

The spoor turned abruptly up the side of the gully and he lost it on the black rock of the ridge, but found it again on his first cast.

He was closing fast now. The spoor was running across the grain of the land, and Benedict was clearly weakening rapidly. He had fallen repeatedly, crawled on bloody knees over cruel gravel and rock, he had blundered into the scrub bushes and left threads of his clothing on the hooked red-tipped thorns.

Then the spoor led out of the ridges and scrub into another area of low orange-coloured sandhills and Johnny broke into a jog trot. The sun was sliding down the sky, throwing blue shades in the hollows of the dunes and the heat abated so that Johnny's sweat was able to cool him before drying.

Johnny was intent on the staggering footprints, beginning to worry now that he would find Benedict already dead. The signs were those of a man in extreme distress, and still he was driving himself on.

Johnny did not notice the other prints that angled in from the dunes and ran parallel to those of Benedict, until they closed in again and began overlaying the human prints.

Johnny stopped and went down on one knee to examine the broad dog-like pug marks.

'Hyena!' He felt the sick little flutter of revulsion in his stomach as he spoke. He glanced around quickly and saw the other set of prints out on the left.

'A pair of them! They've smelt the blood.'

Johnny began to run on the spoor now. His skin crawled with what he knew could happen when they caught up with a helpless man. The filthiest and most cowardly animals in Africa, but with jaws that could crunch to splinters the thigh bone of a full-grown buffalo, and their thick stubby fangs were coated with such a slime of bacteria from a diet of putrid carrion that their bite was as deadly as that of a black mamba.

'Let me be in time; please God, let me find him in time.'

He heard it then. From beyond the crest of the next dune. The horror of the sound stopped him in mid-stride. It was a shrill giggling gibbering cry that sobbed into silence.

Johnny stood listening panting wildly from his run.

It came again. The laughter of demons, excited, blood-crazy.

'They've got him.'

Johnny flung himself at the soft slope of sand. He reached the crest and looked down into the saucer-shaped arena formed by the crescent of the dune.

Benedict lay on his back. His white shirt was open to the waist. The blue trousers of his suit were ripped and shredded, exposing his knees. One foot was a bloody lump of sock and congealed dirt.

The pair of hyenas had trampled a path in the sand around his body. They had been circling him for hours, while greed overcame their cowardice.

One hyena sat ten feet from him, squatting obscenely with its flat snakelike head lowered between humped shoulders. Brown and shaggy, spotted with darker brown, its round ears pricked forward, its black eyes sparkling with greed and excitement as it watched its mate.

The other hyena stood with its front paws on Benedict's chest. Its head was lowered, and its jaws were locked into Benedict's face. It was leaning back, bracing its paws on his chest, tugging viciously as it sought to tear off a mouthful of flesh. Benedict's head was jerking and twitching as the hyena worried it. His legs were kicking weakly, and his hands fluttered on the sand like maimed white birds.

The flesh of his face tore. Johnny heard it distinctly in the utter silence of the desert evening. It tore with the soft sound of silk – and Johnny screamed.

Both hyenas bolted at the scream, scrambling over the far crest of the dune in horrible clownish panic, leaving Benedict lying with a bloody mask for a face. Looking down at that face Johnny knew he could not kill him now, perhaps could never have killed him. He could not revenge himself on this broken thing with its ruined face and twisted mind.

He dropped on to his knees beside him, and loosened the flap of the knapsack with clumsy fingers.

Benedict's one ear and cheek were hanging over his mouth in a thick flap of torn flesh. The teeth in the side of his jaw were exposed and the blood dribbled and spurted in fine needle jets.

Johnny tore the paper packaging off an absorbent dressing and with it pressed the flap back into place. Holding it there with the full pressure of his spread fingers. The blood soaked through the dressing, but it was slowing at the pressure.

'It's all right, Benedict. I'm here now. You'll be all right,' he whispered hoarsely as he worked. With his free hand he stripped the packaging off another dressing, and substituted it neatly for the sodden one. He maintained the pressure on the clean dressing while he lifted Benedict's head and cradled it in his lap.

'We'll just dry this bleeding up, then we'll give you a drink.' He reached into the first aid kit for a piece of cotton wool and tenderly began to clean the blood and sand from Benedict's nostrils and lips. Benedict's strangled breathing eased a little but still whistled through the black lips. His tongue was swollen, filling his mouth like a fat purple sponge.

'That's better,' Johnny muttered. Still without relaxing pressure on the compress dressing, he got the screw top off the water bottle. Holding his thumb over the opening to regulate the flow, he let a drop of water fall into the dark dry pit of a mouth.

After another ten drops he propped the water bottle in the sand, and massaged Benedict's throat gently to stimulate the swallowing reflex. The unconscious man gulped painfully.

'That's my boy,' Johnny encouraged him, and began again feeding him a drop at a time, crooning softly as he did it.

'You're going to be all right. That's it, swallow it down.'

It took him twenty minutes to administer half a pint of the warm sweet water, and by then the bleeding was negligible. Johnny reached into the kit again and selected two salt and two glucose tablets. He placed them in his own mouth and chewed them to a smooth thin paste then he bent over the mutilated face of the man he had sworn to kill and pressed his own lips against Benedict's swollen dry lips. He injected the solution of salt and glucose into Benedict's mouth, then straightened up and began again dripping the water.

When he had given Benedict another four tablets and half the contents of the water bottle, he stoppered it and returned it to the knapsack. He soaked the compress with bright yellow acriflavine solution, and bandaged it firmly into place. This was a more difficult task than he had anticipated and after a few abortive attempts he passed the bandage under the jaw and over the eyes, swathing Benedict's head completely except for the nose and mouth.

By this time the sun was on the horizon. Johnny stood up and stretched his back and shoulders as he watched the splendid gold and red death of another desert day.

He knew he was delaying his next decision. He reckoned it was five miles to where he had abandoned the Land-Rover in the gully. Five miles of hard going, a round trip of four hours – probably five in the dark. Could he leave Benedict here, get back to the vehicle, radio Cartridge Bay, and return to him?

Johnny swung round and looked up at the dunes. There was his answer. One of the hyenas was squatting on the top of a dune watching him intently. Hunger and the approach of night had made it unnaturally bold.

Johnny shouted an obscenity and made a threatening gesture towards it. The hyena jumped up and loped over the back of the ridge.

'Moon rise at eight tonight. I'll rest until then – and we'll go in the cool,' he decided and lay down on the sand beside Benedict. The lump in his back pocket prodded him, and he took the diamond out and held it in his hand.

In the darkness the hyenas began to cackle and shriek, and when the moon rose it silhouetted their evil shapes on the ridge above the saucer.

'Come on, Benedict. We're going home. There are a couple of nice policemen who want to talk to you.' Johnny lifted him into a sitting position, draped Benedict's arm over his shoulder and came up under him in a fireman's lift.

Johnny stood like that a moment, sinking ankle deep into the soft sand, dismayed at the dead weight of his burden.

'We'll rest every thousand paces,' he promised himself, and began plodding up the dune, counting softly to himself, but knowing that he would not be able to perform that lift again without a rock shelf or some support, against which to brace himself. He had to make it out of the sandhills in one go.

'— Nine hundred and ninety nine. One thousand.' He was counting in his mind only. Husbanding his strength, bowed under the weight, his shoulders and back locked in straining agony, the sand hampering each pace. 'Another five hundred. We'll go another five hundred.'

Behind him padded the two hyenas. They had gobbled the bloody dressings that Johnny had left in the saucer, and the taste of blood was driving them hysterical.

'Right. Just another five hundred.' And Johnny began the third count, and then the fourth, and the fifth.

Johnny felt the drip, drip on the back of his legs. Benedict's head-down position had restarted the bleeding, and the hyenas warbled and wailed at the smell.

'Nearly there, Benedict. Stick it out. Nearly there.'

The first cluster of moon-silver rocks floated towards them and Johnny reeled in amongst them and collapsed face forward. It was a long time before he had regained enough strength to shift Benedict's weight off his shoulders.

He readjusted Benedict's bandages, and fed him a mouthful of water which he swallowed readily. Then Johnny washed down a handful of salt and glucose tablets with two carefully rationed swallows from the water bottle. He rested for twenty minutes by his watch, then using one of the rocks as an anchor he got Benedict across his shoulder again and they went on.

Johnny rested every hour for ten minutes. At one o'clock in the morning they finished the last of the water, and at two o'clock Johnny knew beyond all possibility of doubt that he had missed the watercourse and that he was lost.

He lay against a slab of ironstone, numb with fatigue and despair, and listened to the cackling chorus of death among the rocks nearby. He tried to decide where he had gone wrong. Perhaps the watercourse curved away and he was now moving parallel to it, perhaps he had already crossed it without having recognized it. That was possible, he had heard of others stumbling blindly across a tarmac road without realizing it.

How many ridges had they climbed and descended? He could not remember. There was a place where he had stumbled into a scrub thorn and ripped his legs. Perhaps that was the watercourse.

He crawled across to Benedict.

'Brace up, bucko. We're going back.'

Johnny fell for the last time a little before dawn. When he rolled his head and squinted sideways at his wrist-watch it was light enough to read the dial. The time was five o'clock.

He closed his eyes and lay for a long time, he had given up. It had been a good try – but it hadn't worked. In an hour the sun would be up. Then it was finished.

Something was moving near him, soft and stealthy-footed. It was of no interest, he decided. He just wanted to lie here quietly, now that it was finished.

Then he heard the sniffing, the harsh sniffing of a hungry dog. He opened his eyes. The hyena was ten feet away, watching him. Its bottom jaw hung open, and the pink tongue lolled loosely from the side of its mouth. He could smell it, a stink like an animal cage at the zoo, dung and offal and rotting carrion.

Johnny tried to scream, but no sound came from his mouth. His throat was closed, and his tongue filled his mouth. He struggled on to his elbows. The hyena drew back, but without the ludicrous panic of before. Leisurely it trotted away, and then turned to face him again from a distance of twenty yards. It grinned at him, slurping the pink tongue into its mouth as it gulped saliva.

Johnny dragged himself to where Benedict lay, and looked down at him.

Slowly the blind bandaged head turned towards him, the black lips moved.

'Who's there?' A dry husky whisper. Johnny tried to answer but his voice failed him again. He hawked and chewed painfully, working a trace of moisture into his mouth. Now that Benedict was conscious Johnny's hatred flared again.

'Johnny,' he croaked. 'It's Johnny.'

'Johnny?' Benedict's hand came up and he touched the bandages over his eyes. 'What?'

Johnny reached across, lying on his side, and untied the knot at Benedict's temple. He peeled the bandages from his eyes, and Benedict blinked at him. The light of dawn was stronger now.

'Water?' Benedict asked.

Johnny shook his head.

'Please.'

'None.'

Benedict closed his eyes and then opened them, staring in terror at Johnny.

'Ruby!' Johnny whispered. 'Sergio! Hansie!'

A spasm of guilt twisted Benedict's face, and Johnny leaned closer to him to hiss a single word into his ear.

'Bastard!'

Johnny rested on his elbows, swallowing thickly, then he spoke again.

'Up!' He crawled behind Benedict and pushed and dragged him into a sitting position.

'Look.'

Twenty yards away the two hyenas sat expectantly, leering idiotically and bright-eyed with impatience.

Benedict began to tremble. He made a mewing whimpering sound. Johnny worked him slowly backwards until he had him propped against a rock.

He rested again, leaning on the rock beside Benedict.

'I'm going,' he whispered. 'You stay.'

Benedict made that mewing sound again, shaking his head weakly, staring at the two slobbering animals ahead of him.

Johnny slung the knapsack about his neck. He closed his eyes and called upon the last reserves of his strength. With a heave he got to his knees. Darkness and bright lights obscured his vision. They cleared and he heaved again and he was on his feet. His knees buckled and he grabbed at the rock to steady himself.

'Cheerio!' he whispered. 'Have fun!' And he went lurching and staggering away into the wilderness of black rock.

Behind him the mewing whimper rose to a bubbling scream.

'Johnny. Please, Johnny.'

Johnny closed his mind to that cry, and staggered on.

'Murderer!' screamed Benedict. The accusation checked Johnny. He leaned against another rock for support, and looked back.

Benedict's face was convulsed, and a thin line of bloody froth rimmed his lips. The tears were pouring unashamedly down his cheeks to soak into the blood and antiseptic stained bandages.

'Johnny. My brother. Don't leave me.'

Johnny pushed himself away from the rock. He swayed and almost fell. Then he staggered back to Benedict and slipped down into a sitting position beside him.

From the knapsack he took out the knife and laid it on his lap. Benedict was sobbing and moaning.

'Shut up. Damn you!' whispered Johnny.

The sun was well up now. It was burning directly into Johnny's face. He could feel the skin of his cheeks stretching to bursting-point. The veils of darkness kept passing over his vision, but he blinked them away. The flutter of his eyelids was the only movement he had made in the last hour.

The hyenas had closed in. They were pacing nervously back and forth in front of where Johnny and Benedict sat. Now one of them stopped and stretched its neck out, sniffing eagerly at Benedict's blood-clotted foot, creeping inch by inch closer.

Johnny stirred and the creature jumped back, bobbing its head ingratiatingly, grinning as if in apology.

The time had come to fall back on their last line of defence. Johnny hoped he had not left it too late. He was very weak. His eyes and ears were tricking him, his vision jumped and blurred and there was a humming sound in the silence as though the desert was an orchard filled with bees. He spun the cog-wheel of his cigarette lighter and the flame lit. Carefully he applied it to the fuse of the smoke flare, and it spluttered and caught.

Johnny lobbed the flare towards the hyenas, and as the clouds of pink smoke spewed out, they fled in shrieking terror.

An hour later they were back. Slinking out of the rocks, cautious again. Johnny saw them only in flashes, between the bursts of darkness in his head. The insect drone in his ears was louder, it was confusing, making it difficult for him to think clearly.

It took him ten minutes to light the second flare. His throw was so weak that the flare pitched only a few inches beyond his own feet. The pink smoke spread over them.

Johnny felt the blood humming in his ears as the swirling pink clouds engulfed him. The sulphurous bite of the smoke in his throat choked him. The sound in his ears became a drumming roar, a rushing clattering hissing bellow. Then there was a wild wind in the stillness of the desert. Miraculously the smoke cloud was ripped away by the wind.

Johnny looked up into the sky from which the great wind came. Twenty feet above him, hanging on the glistening dragon-fly wing of its rotor, was the police helicopter.

Tracey's face was framed in the cabin window of the helicopter. He saw her lips form his name before he fainted.